NIGHTINGALE

TABLE OF CONTENTS

Expansion

Kate Canterbary

CHAPTER ONE
Will

"THAT COUNTEROFFER CAN choke on my dick."

I pressed a fist to my mouth to hold back the grin forming there. Even after eight years, the shock of those words from this petite redhead hadn't worn off.

If it hadn't happened yet, it wasn't going to.

"No, I understand you're not going back to the agent with that as the only response, Tom." Shannon pulled her bag onto her lap, diving through the contents as she continued speaking to her chief of staff. "If that's how they want to play, we'll take our ball and go home. We don't need this property nearly as much as they need to unload it. Are they under the impression there's a shortage of 1880s brownstones in the Back Bay? Because there isn't. I could buy up every available property and keep us busy for the next decade. I don't need this one. If they can't recognize a fair offer when one comes their way, I don't have the time to dick around with them."

My wife didn't relax too often.

I pointed at the parking garage ahead. "Wrap it up, peanut. You're going to lose him in a minute."

She batted my hand away. "Ignore the counter. We don't entertain that kind of douche waffling. Okay? Good. Call me when they lose their shit and ask to backtrack to the original offer."

She ended the call as I pulled up to the garage's automatic gate. I waved our access badge at the keypad before glancing back at her. When the gate opened, I held out my hand. "The phone, Shannon."

"I'm not handing over anything until we touch down on the island. I need the entire morning to work," she replied. "I have two more purchase and sale agreements to revise for Sam, several million dollars to move, and a delicate situation with one of Matt's properties to look after."

"These fucking guys." I headed toward an empty parking spot. "Matt doesn't need a babysitter and Sam's problems can be pushed down to your legal assistants. Or Tom. Put these people to work, Shannon, and hand over the phone."

"First of all, no, and second, how would you like me to delegate these requests of yours without my phone?"

Getting my wife to unwind usually required brute force. It didn't come naturally to her. Not without putting up a good fight. If I wanted her to chill the fuck out—which I absolutely did—I had to fight that fight and play a serious game of keep away with all the devices that kept her on her bullshit.

"I'd like your brothers to recognize that you're leaving the country for two weeks. I'd also like them to realize they've known about this for approximately four months. That should have been fair warning to them that it was time they sort their issues without your help."

I shifted into Park while my wife glared at me. That didn't bother me. I knew her glares. I understood her glares. Hell, I *liked* her glares. I loved that she got out of bed every morning with this kind of firepower locked and loaded.

"I expected to work on the flight." She gestured toward the small terminal in front of us and the pair of private jets on the tarmac. A small mountain of lingering snow glinted back from the edge of the runway. Such was March in New England. "Is there a reason I can't do that?"

I blinked at the runway. This was the first time in five years that we were vacationing without the kids. There'd been long weekends here and there but nothing more than that. Even our honeymoon had been nothing more than a weekend away in Montauk. It was also the first time since that Montauk trip that my wife wasn't pregnant or nursing a baby.

We had fourteen nights on a private Caribbean island ahead of us and I wasn't about to give up a single second of this vacation for anything.

"That's what I thought," she said in response to my silence. "So, I'm going to—"

"The phone, Shannon." I plucked it from her hand. "Just because they need you doesn't mean they're entitled to you."

She watched while I powered down her phone and tucked it into my pocket. With a chilly stare, she said, "I'm the only one who can move millions of dollars."

The best thing about my wife—the thing very closely related to her complete inability to relax—was that nothing stopped her. Nothing stood in her way.

Not even common sense.

"Let's negotiate," I said.

She grinned like I was inviting myself to my own funeral and it was cute. Almost cute enough to make me forget that I knew enough about her work to know Tom could tee up the money and her brother Patrick could sign off on the transaction.

"Is this a hostage situation?" she asked.

I dragged a gaze over her torso, along the line of her legs. I wanted to pull down her turtleneck sweater and suck on her skin just to remind her that, as fun as this argument was, it was also futile. "Do you want to play a kidnapping game? I do have a private jet waiting for me." I glanced at the back seat. "I'm sure I have a zip tie around here somewhere."

She tapped her finger against her lips as she murmured to herself. "I don't really want to be tied up and tossed in the luggage compartment. I get the impression I'd be cold and dirty by the time we land in Mobile to pick up Jordan's mom and her boyfriend, and that just seems like too much to explain. She's so excited about Jordan and April finally getting married this weekend. We should let her have that without involving her in our little games."

I shrugged. My business partner's mother had seen stranger things. I was sure of it. Aside from that, I didn't play games that left my wife cold or dirty in ways she didn't want to be. And she knew that.

"I was thinking more along the lines of a steady stream of mimosas while I empty my inbox. I figure I'll be finished before I reach the bottom of the champagne bottle." She fussed with her ponytail long enough to distract me from the task at hand. "Champagne makes me quite pleasant but I'm hearing this is still a problem for you."

Champagne drunk Shannon was an undeniable favorite of mine. She was putty in my hands when she started in with the giggles and hiccups. I'd asked her to marry me when she was champagne drunk.

"I keep the phone," I said. "You keep the laptop *until*"—I held up a hand when she turned those emerald green eyes on me—"until we touch down in Mobile. Then, you're done for the next two weeks."

She responded with an impatient jerk of her shoulders. "If there's a disaster, I'm—"

"There will not be a disaster."

"*If there is*," she said pointedly, "I'm logging in."

"I'll allow for the possibility of disasters if you acknowledge they are unlikely to occur."

She reached for her purse, set it on her lap. Sawed her teeth over her bottom lip. "Fine."

I felt the shift between us like a change in the wind. We were finished negotiating, finished sparring. I'd used all the brute force she'd tolerate. The walls were down, the armor disintegrating. All that remained was the way she bit that lip.

"You know, peanut, they're going to be fine with my parents. The girls are going to swindle them for everything they're worth and we're going to come home to find three little warlords running the place, but they're going to be fine."

She nodded, saying, "I know" with just enough of a wobble for me to know she was working very hard at keeping herself from crying.

"My parents will call us every day," I said.

"I know." She looked out her window as if I couldn't see her blinking away tears in the reflection. "But Amalia's teeth are still coming in and Abby's been having such a hard time with speech therapy and—"

"And they are going to be all right," I said. "I'm going to miss those little terrorists too. We haven't been away from them in forever and I don't even know how to sleep without tiny people between us, but I know they're in capable hands with my parents."

She dabbed her eyes with her sleeve. "It sounded like such a good idea to go to this wedding and stay on the island after but—"

"It *is* a good idea. That hasn't changed."

"I know but—"

"Shannon." I dropped my hand to the back of her neck. She wasn't ready to look away from the window but that didn't matter. She was allowed to have the space she wanted, even if she didn't need that space from me. "Our babies are going to have the time of their lives. They have a Navy Admiral and a combat nurse waiting on them hand and foot. They have your sister and her doctor husband never more than twenty minutes away. They have all your brothers, all your sisters-in-law a phone call away. You trust all of those people, right?"

"Of course I do," she snapped, her words sharp and watery all at the same time.

I circled my thumb along the tight cords of her neck. "Then trust yourself, peanut. Trust that you are an incredible mother and you've done all the right things for our babies. Trust that they will be safe and cared for—and extremely spoiled—while I spend the next two weeks caring for and spoiling you. Neither of which I've done in a long time because there's always a child or two attached to you, not to mention needy-ass brothers blowing up your phone every five minutes."

"I don't need you to do any of that."

"Believe me, I know. You don't need a damn thing. But *I* need it. I need to get you away from everything so I can have you all to myself."

She was silent for several moments. I went on rubbing her skin while quiet breaths shuddered out of her. Then, "I think I asked for a steady stream of mimosas and there are no champagne flutes in my hands right now."

I tipped my chin toward the tarmac. "Let's go."

CHAPTER TWO

Shannon

"GOOD MORNING, MRS. Halsted. Welcome aboard. I'll take that coat for you," the flight attendant said as I stepped onto the plane.

Behind me, Will said, "My wife needs some champagne with a splash of orange juice before takeoff."

"Of course, Mr. Halsted. Right away. And anything for you?" she asked.

Will steered me toward two pairs of seats situated on either side of a shiny mahogany table. "All I need is for you to keep my wife's glass full for the next three hours."

"Right away," she repeated before marching toward the back of the cabin.

I shot him a smirk. "Eager to fulfill orders, are we?"

He dropped into the spot across the table from me, his broad shoulders spanning the full width of the luxurious seat. Dressed in dark jeans, a gray t-shirt, and a half-zip pullover, he held up his hands and let them fall to his lap. "My wife wants champagne, my wife gets champagne. Can't penalize me for getting the job done on time."

There was something about the golden scruff covering the line of his jaw that made me smile. It reminded me of our blonde babies, not a single one of them born with even a shimmer of red in their hair. And that reminded me of the way he held them to his chest, their heads tucked just under his chin and their little fingers always fisted around his shirt. As if he'd ever let them go.

They'd be fine with Bill and Judy. They'd be fine. I knew that. I believed it as thoroughly as I believed anything. But that didn't stop the pangs of worry. All the years spent looking after my siblings, all the time I'd taken up the role of stand-in mother had prepared me not at all for the real deal. I had three little pieces of my heart walking around outside my body now. *Everything* was different. Everything.

Except for Will.

There were moments when I thought fatherhood had changed him or maybe the domesticity of working primarily from a home office or even living outside of Boston—and it was possible those shifts had stretched him, filled him out a bit.

But he was the same man he'd always been.

He was exactly as pushy and rude and steady as he'd been when I met him the night before Matt and Lauren's wedding. The same man who'd dismissed the orgasm he gave me as insufficient and then broke the bed trying to do better. The same man who knew all of my secrets and kept them under lock and key for me. The same man who saw straight through me and liked that chaos enough to stay.

And that was the thing about my husband that made my heart beat in my throat. He'd seen me at my worst and never looked away. I couldn't scare him off, couldn't overwhelm him, couldn't even intimidate him. He knew me. He saw me. He understood me. And he chose me.

I pulled out my laptop while Will watched. I really needed to move some money around this morning. Actually, I should've done this yesterday but one of

Riley's projects received a stop work order from the city and I lost control of the day trying to right that ship. Patrick was able to approve payroll expenses and sign off on the purchases we had lined up, but he'd also collapse like a cheap tent if I asked him to manage something outside his usual scope of work. Tom could handle most of it though he had a million other things on his plate before he and Wes departed for the wedding tomorrow afternoon.

Once we were in the air, Will leaned forward and asked, "What would they do without you?"

"Don't start."

"I'm just wondering," he went on, "how your brothers would function if you didn't take care of everything for them."

"We know how they'd function. We've seen it play out every time we have a baby. They survive well enough the first month, they start dropping by more frequently in the second month, and the office more or less migrates into our dining room in the third and fourth months." I glanced at him over my laptop screen. "Until you scare them off, that is."

"I've been scaring them off for years and I'm not about to stop," he replied, looking quite pleased with himself. "That's why they lost their shit when you finally told them about me. They knew they were living on borrowed time."

I scoffed at that. "You're giving yourself a fair bit of credit, don't you think?" Before he could respond, I continued. "And they didn't *lose their shit*. I don't even think I told you what happened that day. It was just"—I glanced out the window as I thought back to that Monday morning meeting—"it was *a lot*. As are most big conversations around that table."

He folded his arms over his chest. "Tell me now. I want to hear it."

The flight attendant stopped by with a fresh mimosa for me and coffee for Will. Once we were alone, I said, "There's nothing you need to hear."

"But I love your ridiculous meeting stories," he said. "Everyone talking over each other. Yogurt controversies. The breakfast burrito travails. The way you spend half the time handling family shit and deciding where we're all going for a summer holiday. I love getting texts from you at eight in the morning like 'Is Chatham good for August? I need to know ASAP.' Makes my fucking day. I live for all the meeting updates you share with me."

I rolled my eyes. My husband did not live for these updates. He did, however, enjoy complaining about my brothers. "There was nothing remarkable about it. I just told them you'd moved into my place with me and we'd been hanging out for a couple of years."

It was physically impossible to conjure a more smug grin than the one on his face right now. "And how'd they take that?"

I took a sip of my mimosa as I thought back to that dark December morning. The top floor of the brownstone we'd converted into the Walsh Associates office had terrible lighting. It was dark in there on the brightest days and it was an honest to god cave come winter. Gathering there at seven thirty in the morning and getting work done was a challenge without copious amounts of coffee.

On that day, I'd decided it was time to tell my brothers everything. For a number of very valid (to me) reasons, I'd chosen to keep my relationship with Will private. It hadn't been a secret in any shameful sense but in the way that I needed something I didn't have to share with—or justify to—anyone else. At that time, it had been necessary to take what I needed without anyone else telling me what *they* needed from me.

I'd also run out of time for keeping that kind of secret to myself. My brother Riley had known from the start because he couldn't help but walk in on people at the most indelicate times. Will's sister Lauren—who was my brother Matt's wife—had figured it all out. And we'd passed the point of needing the secrecy. We'd realized we didn't have to escape from the world to be who we wanted to be anymore.

But my brothers didn't respond to change with much grace. To be fair, grace wasn't a strength of theirs.

"*I have a quick update I'd like to share with the group,*" I said, closing my laptop and stacking my notebook on top of it. I clasped my hands around my coffee cup as I waited for everyone's attention.

"*Please tell me you're not canceling Christmas,*" Matt said.

"*Let's not worry about Christmas,*" Sam said.

"*What's happening?*" Riley asked.

"*If we could shut up for more than fifteen consecutive seconds, we'd find out,*" Patrick barked. He said this but it didn't stop him from giving me slightly panicked glances. Patrick and I usually communicated via instant messenger during meetings and I always alerted him when I was about to drop a bomb. He hadn't received any such warning today.

"*This is a personal update,*" I started, "*and not one that is subject to your commentary, although I doubt you'll heed that request.*"

"*Oh my god,*" Riley murmured. "*Something terrible is happening.*"

"*Nothing terrible is happening,*" Matt replied. Then, to me, he asked, "*Is something terrible happening? Are you all right?*"

"*I'm fine,*" I said. "*And not to be an asshole or anything but everyone needs to shut up.*"

"*That's what I said,*" Patrick muttered.

I glanced around the table at my four brothers and Andy Asani, the junior architect and only person in the world Patrick liked. She gave me an encouraging smile that suggested she knew where I was going with all this and she was on my side.

"*I am in a relationship,*" I said, ready to continue with more information but the boys were too busy shouting across the table.

"*I knew something was up!*" Matt shouted.

"*You could've said something. Oh my fucking god, Shannon. Why do I have to find out this way?*" Sam said.

Riley crossed his arms over his chest. "*I deserve a prize for not saying a fucking thing this whole time.*"

Matt glared at him. "*You knew? He knew? How did he know? I didn't even know! I mean, I knew something was going on but it was just suspicion and come to find out, Riley's known since—since when, Shannon?*"

Patrick shook his head. "*Some warning would've been nice.*"

Andy held up her hands. "*None of this is necessary, you know. Shannon's allowed to have a private life.*"

"*Of course she's allowed a life,*" Sam shot back. "*But we share everything.*"

"*No, we don't,*" Riley snapped. "*Not even close.*"

"*Then—I mean—what the fuck does that mean?*" Sam replied. "*We sit here every Monday morning and go through all of our work and personal shit and—*"

"*Just shut up, Sam,*" Riley said. "*You can be wrong for once in your life. And don't make me remind you that you keep more secrets than anyone. Unless you're willing to disclose all of them to us right now.*"

"I think that's an exaggeration," Sam said.

"I think it's in your best interest to be quiet," Riley responded. "There are things you don't want to share with this table. I'd suggest you stop pushing the issue."

"Really would've preferred some warning," Patrick said with a heaving sigh.

"We should pause," Andy said. "If we're not able to embrace and support Shannon, we should pause this conversation and come back when we can."

Matt folded his arms on the table. "Who? Who is it?"

I met his steady gaze. Matt's wife's brothers were not his biggest fan. There was no real animosity between them but Will and Wes didn't think anyone in the world was good enough for their little sister. And while Matt let most of that roll off his back, I knew this would chafe him just a bit.

"Will Halsted moved in with me recently. We've been together since the wedding," I said to him. "On and off. Mostly on."

"Is there anyone who didn't hookup at my wedding?" Matt asked.

Riley raised his hand. "I did not."

"Seems false," Patrick muttered.

"And yet it's completely true," Riley said. "The most action I got was a broken nose and a bottle of tequila I didn't even get to drink. Interestingly enough, there are other people who hooked up at that wedding and no one gives them any shit. Curious."

Sam held up a finger. "We'll explore all of that in a minute." To me, he asked, "Lauren's brother? The Navy SEAL guy? Is that who you've been visiting recently? All these trips you've been taking?"

Patrick leaned toward me. "Can you tell me which one is Will? He and his brother look a lot alike and I can't keep up with those kinds of details."

"The one who looks like Chris Hemsworth," Andy said.

"Which one is he?" Patrick asked.

"I'll explain it to you later," she said.

"Are you moving to California?" Sam asked, suddenly pushing to his feet. "Fucking hell, that's the announcement. Isn't it? You're moving to California."

Matt joined him in standing. "You're not moving. Patrick, tell her she can't move to California."

"Matt, my friend, you should stop talking," Andy said. "Try listening."

Patrick ran both hands through his hair. "You need to warn me before you do this sort of thing, Shannon."

Riley leaned back in his chair, his arms crossed over his chest. "Isn't Will stationed out of Virginia? Why are we even talking about California?"

"You can't move. What do you expect us to do here? You want Tom to take over? None of us can manage money," Sam shouted.

"If anyone knows that, it's me," Patrick said.

"This is a family business," Matt said. "You can't just leave. You're one of the most important pieces of this place. We can't do this without you. We literally do not know how. I can build anything you want but I can't tell you the first thing about permits or zoning or—fuck me—taxes. We need you, Shannon, and I'm not trying to be a dickhead here, but you can't just leave us."

"I don't want to agree with him," Riley said, gesturing toward Matt, "but I kind of do agree with him. I'd rather you not leave us."

"Of all the things to pull out of nowhere," Sam said. "I can't believe you're doing this."

And there it was, the maximum amount of bullshit I'd tolerate in a given meeting. "All right. No more talking from any of you. The two of you"—I pointed to Matt and

Sam—"*sit your asses down and close your mouths. You've said enough.*" I pointed to Riley. "*You. Stop being cheeky. I know what you're doing. Stop.*" I shifted to face Patrick. "*You do not require written notice fourteen days before I say something you've vaguely known for quite some time. You'll be fine. I promise.*" I glanced at Andy. "*Thank you for being rational.*" I clasped my hands on top of my notebook. "*Here's what's going to happen. I'm going to address some of the noise you children just threw in my direction. You're going to listen without interrupting. Once I'm finished, you'll accept that I do not owe you or anyone else an explanation for my choices. Understood?*"

"*Are we allowed to speak or do you just want us to nod?*" Riley asked.

Ignoring him, I said, "*Yes, I did travel to meet Will on several occasions. We went to San Diego last month—*"

"*Fucking knew it,*" Sam said.

"*You will be quiet or you will leave,*" I said to him. When he only blinked in response, I continued. "*Yes, Will was stationed in Virginia. His most recent Navy contract has ended and he will not be returning to the SEAL Teams. No, we are not moving to California. I wouldn't just pick up and walk out on this place since we finally have it under control. I've put too much of my life into saving this business to leave it and hope you don't run it into the ground within ninety days.*"

"*Well, that's a relief,*" Matt muttered.

"*Will knows my life is here. That's why he's moved in with me. He's still sorting out his life after the military and getting treatment for an injury he sustained a few months ago. That's as much as I know.*" I glanced around the table. "*It's worth noting that I've stood by while you guys have gone through…everything you've gone through over the years. Whether it's finding your people*"—I gestured toward Patrick and Matt—"*or hitting the bottom and climbing back up*"—I gestured toward Sam—"*or just fucking up on the regular*"—a nod to Riley—"*I've been right here for you. Sure, I've probably given you a hard time about it and I've probably kicked your asses along the way, but I've been here for you. I've helped you, whether you asked for it or not, and I've been on your side. I've disagreed with all of you at one point or another and I've still been on your side. Remember that, okay? Remember that I'm here for all of you and it would be really cool if you'd do the same for me.*"

I tucked my notebook and computer under my arm, stood, and returned to my office.

"You just…left?" Will asked.

"Fuck yes, I left," I said.

He held up his palm and I met it with a soft high-five. "You're such a badass."

"Yeah, I know." I shot him a grin as I reached for my drink. I wasn't keeping track of how many times this glass had been refilled but I knew it was more than a few. "Which is why I don't understand how you get bent out of shape about me dealing with these things all the time. I can handle it. Quite well, I might add."

Will gestured to the flight attendant when I set my empty glass down on the table. She swapped it out for a fresh glass in the blink of an eye. My husband was hell-bent on getting me drunk this morning.

Not that I was complaining.

"I've never once doubted you," he said. "Not once."

"Then why do we have to tussle over me working?" I asked with a wave toward my laptop. The screen was dark and I'd accomplished little more than initiating the financial transactions. Those purchase and sale agreements would have to wait until I sobered up. I knew those contracts like the back of my hand but I didn't take that kind of risk. Not when millions of dollars were involved. "I'm good at this shit. Let me be good at it."

"You're great at this shit," he said. "We tussle because they ask too much of you, too often. You clear the decks for them when they could just easily clear their own decks."

"Think of it this way," I said, reaching for my drink. "They're incredibly competent when it comes to the work of restoration, renovation, and sustainable design. They are not competent when it comes to finance, compliance, and a bunch of other important things like scheduling and time tracking. Instead of putting all my energy into making them semi-capable in those areas, I just let them focus on the things they do well."

"You're adorable when your cheeks get pink like that," he said.

"You're changing the subject."

"I am," he agreed. "I don't want to talk about your brothers anymore."

"Then what do you want to talk about?"

He pressed his palm to the lid of my laptop, closing it. "I want to talk about the next two weeks. I haven't escaped with you in a long time."

"What are we going to do without the kids and our families and work?"

"Nothing," he replied with a laugh. "We're going to do nothing. Beach, pool, bed, bar. That's it. We're going to sleep late and I'm going to surf and you're going to wear that huge fucking beach hat and we'll pretend we have no responsibilities in the world. And I'm going to get you naked and keep you naked for more than fifteen minutes at a time because there will be no children screaming for our attention on this island."

I looped a finger around the chain at my neck, dragged it back and forth. The necklace had been a gift from Will after Amalia arrived. A trio of diamonds for our trio of girls. I'd joked about needing a replacement when our next baby arrived. That was thirteen months ago. "Did Jordan buy the island out for the wedding or did he buy the island?"

Will gave a weary shake of his head. "That's what you're focusing on? I have a lot more work to do here if you're more interested in these details than anything I just said."

"You don't know," I said.

He nodded. "Yeah, I have no idea what he did. I just know the island is heavily guarded and completely private."

"I had no idea when I married you that you offered this many perks," I said. "Private jet, private island, private security force. Lucky me."

"Trust me," he said. "I'm the one who lucked out here."

CHAPTER THREE
Will

"IT USED TO be that we barely made it inside the hotel room before you had your hand in my pants," Shannon called as she breezed into the villa, the long skirt of her dress swirling a second behind her.

"You're not wearing any pants," I said, though it didn't seem like she'd heard me. She was busy wandering through the spacious rooms, the sandals she'd changed into shortly before landing thwacking against the tile floors.

"Semantics," she said. "Remember the time we went to Montauk and barely managed to close the door behind us?"

I headed toward the windows facing the water. This island didn't offer much in the way of waves worth surfing but I didn't see that as a limitation. Any day spent in the water was a good day. "Yeah, I never told Jordan about that," I called to Shannon. "Let's not mention it to him, okay? He doesn't need to know we had sex on the floor. He'd never let me forget it."

She appeared beside me, her gauzy white sundress swishing around her legs. I loved that dress. She always wore it in June or July, when summer had finally settled in. It reminded me of late nights in the backyard with our girls running wild in bare feet and swimsuits, their faces stained red and orange from popsicles, and Shannon nestled on my lap near the fire pit. That dress reminded me of the best things.

"Are you trying to forget it?" she asked, nudging me with her elbow.

"I couldn't if I tried," I said. "And I don't have my hand in your pants because we're spending the afternoon out there." I pointed to the lap pool right outside and the nearby lounge chair that could comfortably accommodate an orgy. "Get yourself into one of those cute little swimsuits and I'll keep my hand busy before we have to show up for Jordan and April's dinner event tonight."

She pointed at the pool. "You're going to swim for an hour or two."

"Only after you fall asleep."

"I'm not going to fall asleep," she argued, as if she wasn't still feeling the champagne.

"Prove me wrong, peanut. I love that shit."

After changing into swim shorts, I waited on the patio for my wife. She'd made noises about wanting to organize her clothes and I knew tipsy Shannon well enough to know she'd handle that task within five or ten minutes.

I checked out the pool and followed the brick path that led to the beach. The sand was fine and white, the tide low and the surf gentle. This place was perfect. I knew April and Jordan hadn't invited too many people for the festivities so I wasn't surprised to find the beach mostly empty. Owning one of the most successful private security firms on the planet meant keeping your circle of friends close and your protection details closer.

The happy couple was getting married in two days and not a moment too soon after nearly four years of Jordan waiting for the right moment to propose. Thank god they hadn't needed that long to plan the wedding.

I headed back to the patio, surprised when I found it empty. Since ten minutes had already passed—plus another ten minutes for whatever else she wanted to do—I went looking for her. It wasn't a huge surprise when I found her asleep on the bed, her red hair fanned out across the white pillowcases and several swimsuits clutched to her chest like she'd planned on sitting for a second but passed out instead.

The reason I'd never stop getting after Shannon about her work and her end-lessly needy brothers was that she had no perception of her limits. Back before we were married, before we had kids, she'd work the craziest hours. Up at the crack of dawn, busy all day, parked in her office until nine, ten, eleven at night. And she'd get up the next day and do it all over again. She'd forget to eat, forget to sleep, forget to breathe. All in the pursuit of saving the family business—and also saving her family.

That was why we'd run away together, why we'd escape from the worlds we lived in, and those were the only moments I ever saw her slow down. And the woman I met when she slowed down was one of my favorite sides of Shannon. She was the same fierce woman, of course, but it was there that she let me know her, let me see her when she wasn't trying to save the world.

Her entire identity was tangled up with saving the world but I knew the woman underneath all that and there was never a time when I didn't want us to claw our way back to those moments. And I believed she wanted it too, even if she kicked and screamed the entire time.

Even today, with the business thriving and her siblings living content, comfortable lives, she didn't recognize what she'd accomplished. She didn't see that she wasn't required to keep saving them and I wasn't sure she'd ever see it. That was the problem with living so many years in survival mode—and the reason I put myself between her and that never-ending urge to save everything and everyone.

"All right, peanut," I whispered as I pried the swimsuits from her grip. I straightened out the summer white dress and drew a light blanket up to her shoulders. I bent down, kissed the constellation of freckles streaking across the ball of her shoulder. "Sleep now. We have all the time in the world."

✧ ✧ ✧

IT WAS LATE when we walked back to the villa, the moon high overhead and waves lapping quietly along the shore. "We go to a lot of weddings," I said, my arm around Shannon's shoulders.

"We do," she agreed. "Any favorites over the years?"

"Ours," I said.

"We got married at the town clerk's office," she said with a laugh.

"We did, and aside from the fact we pulled off the greatest trick either of our families had ever seen, that weekend belonged entirely to us. It wasn't about anyone but me and you. We did it our way and I wouldn't change a damn thing about it."

"Yeah," she said after a moment. "You're right about that."

I led her into the villa, my hand on the curve of her waist and my fingers itching to free her from this dress. This one was pink, a color she rarely wore because she believed it clashed with her hair, and it made me a little stupid with the way it dipped low between her breasts and hugged her hips just enough to remind me of her curves. Hell, it made me a lot stupid. "Have I told you that you look beautiful tonight?"

"Once or twice."

"Have I told you this dress"—I ran that hand over the curve of her ass—"is complete fire and I couldn't take my eyes off you all night?"

"You didn't mention that, no."

"Now that I have, I hope you don't mind that I intend to rip it off you immediately."

"I'll allow it," she replied, "as long as you don't destroy it. I'd like to wear it again. No actual ripping, please."

I steered her into the bedroom, inching up the dress as we walked. I had it up and over her head as I backed her up against the bed. That left her in a tiny pair of panties, a strapless bra, and heels that brought her up to the height of my shoulders. I motioned for her to turn around. "You know what I want."

She turned, but not before tossing a sharp glance at me over her shoulder. "Always so arrogant."

The words weren't halfway out of her mouth when I brought my palm down on her ass. It was a light slap though her answering moan as I slipped my hand between her legs was deep and rich, a noise that'd been trapped inside her for far too long.

"Should I put that smart mouth of yours to work?" I edged her feet apart to widen her stance and give me more room to work. She groaned when my fingers ducked inside her panties, and then again when I traced her seam, and again when I circled her clit. "Or would you prefer I continue? It's your choice, peanut."

"You talk such a big game, commando. It's so cute. Precious, really."

"Watch yourself," I warned. "I'll have you tied to that headboard before you can pretend like your pussy isn't clenching and crying for me right now."

She dropped her head back against my chest, reaching blindly for my belt. When she found it, she did her best to open the latch and pull it free but I batted her hand away when she went for the button and zipper. I'd handle it from here.

"You're actually quite adorable," she said as I stepped out of my shorts and yanked the linen shirt over my head. "You're so sweet with your—"

I brought both hands to the back of her panties, and in one rough jerk, tore them right in half. They dropped to the floor while a stunned breath shuddered out of her.

It was worth noting that ripping underwear was difficult. Elastic didn't tear. If I didn't know what I was doing, I'd leave her with fabric burns—and that was not the kind of foreplay we enjoyed. But I knew these panties because she always wore them with dresses like this, and I knew they were delicate enough to rip without hurting her.

"You were saying?" I leaned in, pressing my lips to her neck and pushing my cock right up against her ass.

"What the hell was that?" she snapped, wiggling her backside just enough to make me black out for a second.

When I regained consciousness, I pushed two fingers inside her while teasing her clit. "I was expediting this portion of the events."

"I—you—*what?*"

"Are you trying to say something, sweetheart? I can't understand you." I bit my way up her shoulder with a laugh. "Use your words, wife."

A sigh rattled out of her as she kicked off her heels. "There are moments when you are an egotistical bastard."

I flipped open her bra, tossed it over my shoulder once it was free. "Get on the bed, peanut."

I stepped back while I waited for her to comply with my request. It gave me a second to stare at her body—which was amazing—and stroke my cock—which was interested in moving matters forward. But it also gave me a second to remember we were in no rush. For once in five years, we wouldn't be interrupted by a crying baby, play-screaming kids, or any issue associated with our children. We didn't have my parents clamoring around the house or our phones buzzing at all hours. And I didn't have to be especially careful because she wasn't pregnant or nursing anymore.

That…that was a different issue.

When Shannon kicked back the blankets and settled against the pillows, she shot a bored glance at my shaft, asking, "Am I supposed to be impressed by that?"

"You just love testing my patience, don't you?" I climbed onto the bed, crawling up to meet her.

"Ah, yes. You and your fragile patience. Tell me more about that."

She watched me, that indifferent expression still pulling at her lips. I fucking loved it. I just loved it. I loved the way she pushed and pushed and pushed until I had her cornered, had her pinned, and I could whisper the words she'd never admit to needing: *there's nothing you could ever say or do that would push me away.*

I spread her legs, held them wide until she twined them around my waist. "But that's just it. I don't have any patience," I said, stroking myself along her seam. "Not when it comes to you."

Her back bowed, she asked, "Why not?"

It would've been nice to slow this down. To tease her for a few more minutes. Maybe get on my belly and lick her clit until she kicked me in the head. And maybe I'd do that tomorrow night or any other night but I didn't have the patience for it right now. All I could do was consume her, consume every last inch of her. I hadn't realized how much I'd needed to escape with her—and only her—until this precise moment.

I pushed into her with a lazy thrust, one that belied all the urgency in my body. "Because it's you and me, Shannon. It's always been me and you against the world and there will never be a time when I don't need all of you. Never a time when you won't belong to me."

"Don't say nice things to me when you're trying to rip me in half with your cock. It's rude," she said.

"Be a good girl for me and stop talking."

"I've never been a good girl for anyone," she replied. "Not about to start with you."

I leaned down, swiped my tongue over her nipple. "I can't even believe how much I love you. This is fucking insane. You say these things and I just want to"— the headboard knocked against the wall with a dull thump—"I just want to drive myself so deep inside you that you can't remember a time when you weren't mine."

Shannon parted her lips to speak but nothing more than a rumbling sigh came out. I pumped into her, all the way in and then all the way out, and seized that moment to flip her on her stomach. I delivered another slap to her ass, one hard enough to startle a light squeal out of her.

"What the fuck was that?" she said into the mattress.

I hooked an arm around her waist as I leaned over her, my lips on her neck. "The way you beg for more is so fucking pretty."

"This bitch doesn't beg," she said, running her hand up my thigh and around to squeeze my ass. She squirmed against me, her backside rocking hard against my cock.

Mmhmm. Not begging at all.

"What are you waiting for?" she asked.

I nipped at her skin. "Nothing," I said, holding her tight before pushing inside her again.

This position was good for her. It hit every spot she needed and it always left her soft and sated in the best ways. I shifted a hand between her shoulder blades, the other to her hip, and punctuated each of her whispered pleas for *more, yes, that, yesyesyes, Will* with long, dragging thrusts that I felt in every limb of my body.

Everything was hot, overwhelmingly hot, and the exquisite clench of her body had me seeing stars. But more than all of that, more than any amount of bone-melting pleasure, was the nagging throb of rightness that came from being *this close* with my wife. Nothing in the world compared to the way we could be together, the people we allowed ourselves to be when no one else was watching and the only thing that mattered was loving each other all the way through.

"Will, I'm—"

Her walls gripped me hard and that was a good start. Not enough, but a good start. "No, you're not. I'm not letting you off with any weak little orgasms," I said.

"Would you just shut—*ohh*," she gasped as another series of spasms moved through her. That one was a little better. Stronger, a few pulses longer. We were on the right track. "Fuck, fuck, *fuck*. Will."

"Shannon," I panted, forcing her deeper into the mattress. The headboard sounded more like a fog horn at this point. Thank god we were in a villa and didn't have anyone on the other side of the wall. "Let me make this good for you. *Let me.*"

I watched as she bit the pillow and I knew how this was going to end.

I gathered up her hair, looped it around my palm. My hips were moving faster now, operating without much involvement from me, and I was teetering closer to the edge than I wanted.

"You're causing me a lot of problems right now, wife," I said.

She moaned into the pillow.

"I'm trying to fuck you the way you deserve but your body feels like heaven and your ass is so cute I want to bite it," I said, resting my free hand on the delicious curve of her backside. I swiped my thumb between her cheeks, enough of a tease to make her feel as crazy as I did. "Give me a little more, pretty girl. Get those fingers on your clit. Let me watch you. I want to see those fingers moving while my cock is inside you. Give it to me."

She nodded, her eyes wide and fixed on mine as she brought her hand between her legs. Her fingers brushed either side of my cock and that set off a growl rumbling up from my chest. I snapped my eyes shut because I didn't have the strength to hold on much longer, I just didn't have it in me, and I listened for the sound of the ocean to distract me from blowing.

Shannon's hand stilled, pressing hard against her clit. The time it took me to register that change was like the heavy silence before an explosion. She groaned into the pillow, a muffled *fuck* coming through the fabric, and then a blast of heat and wet and pulsing spasms left me kissing and sucking and biting all over her shoulders, her neck, anywhere I could find to press the proof that we did this, we made this happen into her skin while my body pumped everything I had to give into her.

I was halfway to blacking out again but I wrapped my arms around Shannon, rolled her to the other side of the bed, and held her while she panted and quivered. We stayed there for several minutes, our chests heaving and shivering as the aftershocks moved through us.

Eventually, I tucked her hair over her shoulder and kissed her forehead. "I've been wondering about something."

"It's not like you to wonder in silence," she replied.

"Yeah." She was right about that. We didn't beat around bushes. I didn't see how anyone could manage that with a woman like Shannon. "Am I trying to get you pregnant on this vacation?"

All of our babies had been surprises. We'd never planned them. Despite that history behind us, Amalia was about thirteen months old and still didn't have a sibling on the way.

She paused for a long moment. Then, "I don't know."

"Do you want another baby?"

She glanced up at me. "Do you?"

"I want whatever you want. I love our kids. I'd love another if that's what you want. I'd want for nothing if we stopped with these three."

Running a fingertip along the surgical scar on my shoulder, she said, "From the minute the test turns positive to the minute they put that baby on my chest for the first time, I am aware that my mother died while pregnant."

"I know."

At some point in the third trimester, Shannon always took me by the hand and led me into her home office. She showed me the drawer where she kept all of our financial documents, all of her online account passwords, all the paperwork that went with the house. Then, she opened the closet and pointed out a box. She'd say, *If anything ever happens to me, this is for you and the girls.*

Those moments killed me. I didn't let her see it but they absolutely killed me. From those points forward, I never let her out of my sight. If I had to step away, I made sure my mother was nearby to look after her.

Those moments twisted so deep in my gut that, back when Shannon was pregnant with Annabelle, I called Patrick up one night to rail at him about her workload and demand he hire more help for her because she was obviously stressed to troubling levels. He explained their mother had died at the same point in her pregnancy that Shannon was dragging me into her office.

I remembered sitting up awake that night, watching her while she slept. I remembered convincing myself nothing like that would happen to us.

I kissed her forehead again. "I know," I repeated, tightening my hold on her. "I don't want you walking around with that kind of worry on your shoulders."

"Every time Erin loses another baby, I feel like it's unfair that it's been so easy for us. I feel like I shouldn't want one more."

"But you do," I said.

"Maybe? I'm not thirty-five anymore," she said with a wry laugh. "And it scares me. I think about my mom and how I'm older than she was when she died."

The overwhelming urge to put my fist through a wall came over me. "Shannon, sweetheart, it hurts me to hear you thinking about that."

"If we have another," she said, "that one will be our last."

"If that's what I'm agreeing to, you have to agree to tell me when you're thinking about your mother. No more of this keeping it to yourself. If it crosses your mind, it comes out of your mouth. Do you understand me?"

She bobbed her head against my chest.

"No, peanut, no bullshitting me. I am serious. I will come on your tits until I can get my sac snipped if you don't *promise* to stop entertaining this shit alone."

"I promise," she snapped, "though it's been months and nothing's happened. Maybe we have all the kids we're meant to have."

"If that's the case, we'll have our hands full with these three," I said.

She nuzzled deeper into my chest. "I love you, you know."

I slapped her ass. "I love you too."

"Let's not talk about getting pregnant anymore," she said. "We're very busy escaping from the real world right now."

I rolled her to her back and kissed my way from her neck to her navel. Settled between her legs, I said, "This is what I've been saying all day."

"And now we finally agree," she replied.

"That's enough talking out of you." I swiped my tongue over her clit. "Hold onto that headboard. I have work to do."

EPILOGUE
Shannon

Approximately ten months later

ADELINE LAUREN HALSTED, the last of my babies, was born just in time for Halloween.

✧　✧　✧

Thank you so much for reading *Expansion*. You can read more about the Walsh family starting with Matt and Lauren in *Underneath It All*. Read it now. katecanterbary.com/v2books/underneath-it-all

Famine's Homecoming

Laura Thalassa

ANA DA SILVA

Vancouver Island, British Columbia, Canada

October, Year 27 of the Horsemen

M Y EYES MUST be deceiving me.

I stand near the grill where Sara is cooking, my back to her and Victor's massive house. My eyes are glued to the far edge of the property, where several riders are ambling in on horseback. My breath catches when I first notice War.

They've come back.

I can feel hope blossoming in my chest, but I don't want to believe it—not right away. The world has been a mess for far too long. It feels too impossible to believe that a few determined people might be able to change that.

But then I notice a pair of people on horseback who I don't recognize. Could this be Lazarus and Death?

If they're riding in here, next to War, and no one is killing each other, then perhaps—

Fuck, we might all actually be okay.

Next to me, Sara shouts something about pussies and winning, but I don't care because—

Famine.

He's finally back.

My feet are moving, and then I'm sprinting towards Famine, nearly tripping over my own feet in the process.

The Reaper swings a leg over his saddle, and then he's running towards me.

I crash into him, and he swings me in his arms, my skirt swishing around us. I crush him to me, my arms wrapped tightly around his neck, my face nestled against his. I breathe him in, letting his hair tickle my face. I can hear him laughing, even as I fight back my tears.

"I *missed* you." I say it with more emotion than I intend. It's been a *long* few months. A long few years, actually, if I'm being honest.

"Not as much as I missed you, my flower." He whispers in my ear, smoothing a hand over my hair. "I'm still not sure I like humans," he admits. "They're mostly annoying—though maybe that's just my brothers."

I laugh softly against him. "Be nice. They're family."

"If you insist." He turns his head and presses a kiss to my cheek. "Let me see you," he says, pulling away a little so that he can take me in.

Our eyes meet, and I hear his ragged exhale. "Fuck, I missed your face."

I reach a hand up and cup his cheek, my thumb stroking his skin. "You're mortal." It's half a question, half a statement.

He hesitates, then gives me a sharp nod.

"I'm sorry." I know it's a good thing—it's something Famine himself wanted. But my horseman had told me long ago that it was an uncomfortable, claustrophobic experience for him to exist as a human. Before he had this form, he'd been this expansive thing that was connected to the earth and the sky.

How much worse must it be for him now that his vast powers are gone?

"Do not apologize to me, Ana," he says. "I would do it all again in an instant to have this with you."

I swallow and try to accept that. My eyes dip to the T-shirt and jeans he wears. It's such a small detail, and yet he looks so utterly different without his armor and black attire.

"Is your armor gone too?" I ask.

He gives a nod.

"And your scythe and scales?"

"It's all fucking gone," he says, reeling me back into him. "It doesn't matter. I get to live and die alongside you, and that's all I ever wanted."

THERE'S A BED shortage.

Don't get me wrong, this is a good problem to have—but it's still a problem.

Victor and Sara have a big house, but there's a small army of us. There was Sara, Miriam, and Miriam's mother, sister, and brother-in-law, who journeyed overseas to be with her. Plus, there are all the kids. So many damn kids. We have a freaking army of them.

"We can set something up in the living room," Sara is saying. At least, I'm pretty sure that's what she said. I've been picking up on English, but I still can't always follow the conversation.

The entire group of us sit around the large dining table, our plates littered with the remnants of dinner.

Famine says something back to Sara in English that causes her to cough and Pestilence to shake his head. Lazarus's eyes have widened and her cheeks flush a little.

"Can you translate that?" I ask.

The Reaper glances at me with a smirk. "I told them that unless they want to see what sort of kinks you and I are into, we'll be needing some privacy."

I try not to laugh. "You can tell them that I'm not shy," I add, just to further rile the group up.

It's not a lie. Hazards of being a former sex worker.

He raises his eyebrow in challenge, then turns to the group. Just as Famine's opening his mouth, I place a hand on his chest.

"We will find another place to sleep," I say in halting English. I point in the vague direction of the front door. There's an abandoned house down the road, and I've had my eye on it for some time.

Before anyone can respond to that, Famine scrapes back his chair and stands.

"Well, this was a nice reunion," he says.

Bending down, he scoops me out of my seat and slings me over his shoulder.

I swallow my yelp and instead slap at his back.

"What are you doing?" I demand as the Reaper stalks out of the living room, leaving our dishes and patchwork family behind.

"Getting us out of a tedious conversation," he says. "I like the sound of this house you spoke of."

"Goodnight, asshole!" War calls out in Portuguese.

"Night," Famine replies, waving to the horseman with his middle finger.

I can hear murmured conversation. Doesn't matter the language barrier; most of us know what the middle finger stands for.

Famine swipes a lantern sitting on a narrow side table in the entry hall.

"They probably need that," I say.

"Flower, do I strike you as the type of person to care?" he says, opening the front door.

He carries me outside, kicking the door shut behind us.

"I really would have assumed that after saving the world, you'd get better with other people," I say.

He slaps my ass, causing me to jerk in his arms. "Not on your life."

Famine carries me for several more meters before I whack his back again. "Do you even know where you're going?"

"Does it matter, Ana? I have you in my arms. I could go anywhere."

A soft, warm feeling spreads through me at his words, and I have the oddest urge to cry.

My abrasive horseman. I've missed him so much.

"Right now it *does* matter." I struggle against his hold until, reluctantly, Famine puts me down.

I grab his hand. "Come on. There's an abandoned house nearby that we can stay at."

Famine comes to a dead halt. "Last time you led me to an abandoned house, it practically ate me."

I remember the one. It seemed to house an entire ecosystem within its decaying walls.

"Shut up. You'll love this one."

✧   ✧   ✧

FAMINE STARES UP at the structure, a frown on his face.

I was wrong. He doesn't love it.

Shit.

The house looks like your typical fancy cabin except for one distinct difference—it was built around several massive evergreen trees. It makes the house look slightly strange—every so often part of the structure is distorted to make room for a mini courtyard that houses a tree.

"What do you think?" I finally ask.

The Reaper frowns. "Is this a temporary house ... or a permanent one?"

I hesitate.

If there was one thing the last year gave me, it was time to think. There was nothing left for me back in Brazil. Not in any real sense. My family and friends were long gone.

But here—here there was family and the promise of community. Miriam and Ana and Lazarus too—they all knew what it was like to love a horseman. Like me, they had lost nearly everything. It made us all outcasts and unlikely friends. And the horsemen themselves were brothers.

Perhaps we didn't have to part ways.

"I was thinking ... we could stay here," I say softly.

Famine turns to me, the swiped lantern rattling a little with the motion.

"You would want that?" he asks. "Even with the language barrier?"

"I'm learning," I say. After a moment, I add, "Brazil was my home, but it's just a place. And I like your strange family. They're funny and kind."

The Reaper stares at me for a second or two longer, then turns his attention back to the cabin. "You were right, Ana," he says, beginning to nod. "I love it."

He does?

Before I can respond, the horseman sets down the lantern and grabs me again, swinging me over his shoulder.

"Will you stop that?" I say.

"Never," he says, picking the lantern up once more and marching us up to the house's front entrance.

Using a boot, he kicks out at the door. Wood splinters ... but the door remains firmly shut.

"The fuck?" Famine mutters.

"Awww, is someone not as strong as they once were?" I say, unapologetically baiting him.

"I wasn't trying that time," he insists.

Famine kicks the door again. And again. It takes him four tries before the wood rips free from its lock holding it in place and the door swings open.

"You're fixing that," I tell him.

In response, he slaps my ass again.

"I'm taking that as a *yes*!" I say.

Once the Reaper has carried me inside, he sets me down. Famine gazes at the vast entry hall and common room. The lantern's soft light bathes everything in a dim, flickering light, and it makes the shadows dance.

The two-story house is cavernous, the few remaining pieces of furniture covered by drop cloths. This isn't the first time I've been in the house—I've jimmied one of the back windows open and slipped inside before—but now that I'm showing it to Famine, I'm taking it all in as though for the first time.

My heart beats fast. I want him to like it because I do. It's strange and unconventional, and it makes room for the wildness of the forest around us. It seemed as though it were made for Famine himself.

The Reaper wanders into the kitchen, and I follow him like a shadow, my gaze returning again and again to his form. It's been hours since he returned, and I still can't manage to pry my eyes off of him for long.

"No rodent nests? No mold?" he says, staring up at the walls. "I'm almost disappointed, Ana."

"Keep saying that, and that dick of yours is going to end up not getting the welcome party it's been craving," I respond, leaning my hip against the kitchen island.

Famine's eyes heat. "You and I both know that's an empty threat," he says, taking a step towards me. "Setting aside the fact that I *know* you want me right now as much as I want you, you and I are both aware you like all the rude shit I say."

I tilt my head, my curly hair shifting. "I like your *mouth*." I correct him. "What comes out of it is another matter altogether."

"Another matter ...?" the Reaper repeats, looking scandalized. He fully steps into my space. "Take it back," he demands. That sharp, almost predatory edge has entered his voice. It doesn't matter that he's relinquished his task; there's a part of me that will always be put on edge by this side of him. Unfortunately, it's the kinky, fucked-up side of him—and me. So ...

"No."

"No?" He raises a brow.

Ever so casually, the horseman sets his lantern down on the island. Then, in one swift motion, Famine grabs me around the waist and lifts me onto the counter.

He steps into my space, pressing himself in between my thighs. "Take it back," he repeats, running his hands up my outer legs, "*or I'll make you.*"

"You don't scare me, Reaper," I taunt. "Your powers are all gone."

Famine's hands slip higher and higher as a cruel smile curves on his lips. My linen skirt bunches around his arms as they move across the tops of my thighs, then inwards. Famine pauses only for a moment when he gets to my panties. Then with a savage rip, he tears my underwear away.

"Hey!" I jerk.

But then Famine has already pushed away my skirt and spread my thighs apart. He spends a minute staring at my pussy.

"Have I missed the sight of you," he says directly to my vagina. Famine isn't a butt guy or a breast guy. His tastes are far more twisted and erotic.

Before I can come up with some tart remark, he cups my pussy, the brush of his skin against my sensitive flesh making me hiss out a breath.

Famine removes his hand and leans in. His mouth meets my core, and I gasp when his lips press an intimate kiss to my clit.

This situation is not exactly how I imagined our first evening going, but I can't—

I nearly yelp as his tongue delves into me.

"Dear God, Famine," I say, my hands going to his hair. I can't decide if I want to push him away or pin him to the spot.

The horseman's mouth moves to my clit, and he nips it.

Jesus!

I cry out, the burst of sensation so intense it's almost uncomfortable. He sucks on the sensitive bundle of nerves, prolonging the exquisite agony.

"Tell me again, flower, how you like my mouth best," he demands.

"Oh, I definitely love it best like this."

"Do you?" he murmurs against my skin, and I hear the warning in his voice.

Still, it doesn't prepare for when his mouth returns to my clit. He sucks it again, but this time he doesn't let up, even as I writhe around him.

"Stop," I plead with him. "You've made your point."

The Reaper pulls away a little, his eyes flashing in the dim light. "Have I?" he says. "Because I don't think I have. Take back your words and I just might let you ride out your orgasm on my face." As he speaks, he runs a finger over my thumb, circling it and causing my hips to jerk.

"You ... jerk," I breathe, looking down at him. "You know I love your stupid mouth and all the ridiculous things that come out of it." I wrap my legs around my horseman. "But right now I don't want your mouth. I want *you* inside *me*—now."

For all the games the two of us play, we've been apart for far too long, and it shows. I can't keep up this ruse any longer, and by the shine in Famine's eyes, neither can he.

Leaving my legs wrapped around him, Famine pulls me off the counter, grabs the nearby lantern, and leads us through the abandoned house.

I think Famine is going to take me back to the living room, but he passes it by, heading up the central staircase instead.

We haven't explored these rooms together, so it's sheer dumb luck that Famine manages to find the master suite.

Most of the walls are fitted with huge glass panes that, during the day, probably showcase the Douglas fir trees that encircle the house. Whoever last lived here left the furniture in this room nearly untouched.

There's a neatly made bed, two bedside tables, and a basket holding a moth-eaten throw blanket. All of it looks like a time capsule from some bygone era. There still appear to be electric table lamps.

The Reaper walks over to one of the side tables and sets the lantern down, then carries me to the foot of the bed. Before I can protest, he tosses me onto the ancient mattress. A plume of dust kicks up, causing my eyes to water. I wave my hand, trying to dispel some of it.

Famine, too, looks affected by the dust, grimacing a little. "Mortal bodies are so goddamned sensitive," he says.

With that, I sneeze.

The Reaper hesitates. "We *could* do this outside ..."

"I am not interested in freezing my tits off," I say. This far north, even an evening in the fall is uncomfortably chilly—at least for someone like me, who's used to Brazil's heat.

"Flower, I would *never* let your tits freeze off. Maybe a few toes, but not—"

I lift a sandal-clad foot and push him back. "Enough of the lies, Famine," I say softly, giving him a heated look. "You and I both know you'd let your dick freeze off before any of my toes got cold."

He catches my ankle, and inspects my toes. "Fair enough." He nips at one, then kisses my ankle. Famine sets my leg back down so that he can gather my skirt in his hands and—

Riiiip.

"Famine!" I gasp. "I didn't bring any extra clothes!" All the rest of my things are back at Sara and Pestilence's place.

"Is that right?" the Reaper says, hooking his hands into the collar of my shirt.

I narrow my gaze at him. "Don't you *dare*."

Riiiip.

He shreds my shirt in half.

"Goddamnit, Famine!"

"Poor, sweet Ana, laid bare and now at my mercy. Since you don't have any other clothes, I guess you're just going to have to stay here, naked, until you've won me over enough to get the rest of your—"

I snatch his T-shirt and—

Riiiip.

It tears down the middle, and I flash a petty little grin.

Beneath the material, the Reaper's markings glow a soft green. My taunting response dies in my throat as I stare at his chest.

"Your tattoos stayed," I say instead, awed by the sight of them. I should've known they would; I've seen War's own glyphs glittering on his knuckles. Still, the sight of them makes my throat swell with emotion.

At least this one thing wasn't taken from him.

The Reaper's expression softens. "You're happy about that?"

I make an agreeable sound at the back of my throat, sitting up so that I might touch his glyphs—and all the rest of him.

"One of the many things I love about you, Ana," Famine says, pushing me back down against the mattress, "is that you have never wanted me to be normal."

"Normal is overrated," I say smoothly.

Although, to be fair, *abnormal* can be isolating and lonely, as the both of us know.

Famine shrugs off the tatters of his shirt. "I liked this shirt, I'll have you know."

"Awwww," I pout, "I feel *so* bad for you."

The Reaper shakes his head, a devilish, amused look on his face.

He reaches for the top button of his jeans.

Jeans! It hits me all over again that he now wears human clothes. It's strange and a little sad and oddly thrilling, all at once. I'm an emotional mess.

The Reaper shucks them off, then returns to me. Sliding an arm under my waist, the horseman drags me up the bed. He is still eye-crossingly strong, but I swear I can sense the effort it took him to move me.

Mortal.

It really hits me then, with all of its beautiful, messy implications. Gray hairs, wrinkles, sickness—even, eventually, *death*.

I cup Famine's face and take him in. He's still obscenely—almost inhuman-ly—beautiful, but this is a face that will now age alongside my own.

"You will die one day," I whisper. Threaded through that confession is all the fear that comes with the prospect.

"I thought we were fucking, Ana," he says, "not talking about this depressing-ass subject."

I give him a tight smile, but my eyes are watering. I will the tears away, but instead, a couple leak out.

"*Fuck*," he breathes, then his thumbs go to the corners of my eyes, wiping away my tears. "Don't cry, flower. It's going to be okay." He kisses away the last traces of water from my skin. "I promise, sweet thing, it will be."

I wrap my arms around his neck, and pull him to me, burying my face into his shoulder.

"I almost lost you," I admit, "and now I have to deal with the fact that I *will* lose you one day." My voice breaks, and all of my stress, all of my fear and anxiety over the last year just pours forth. It's been hard, these months away from him. I've had to live with the reality that each day could bring about humankind's annihilation, and that I might die without ever holding my horseman again.

Famine presses me tightly to him, rolling us a bit so that he can better cradle my body. He shushes me, smoothing down my hair and rubbing my back.

The Reaper tilts his head and leans down so that he can kiss my collarbone.

"Don't forget that I will lose you, too, one day," he says. "It's an unthinkable agony, Ana." He exhales, then meets my eyes. "We're both fucked, aren't we?"

"Completely," I agree.

Famine's hand slips down to one of my breasts, and he cups the mound. "But on the bright side, now I get to play with these tits for at least a few more decades."

Despite myself, a laugh slips out. "Shut up," I say softly, pushing his shoulder lightly.

"Only if you put something in my mouth," he replies smoothly. "I prefer pussies, but tits work too."

I laugh again, my hold loosening on him.

I assume the Reaper's joking until he leans down and lightly sucks on my nipple.

My breath leaves me all at once. I want to tell him that I'm not finished dis-cussing heavy things, but my body has forgotten what the horseman's touch feels like and it's overruling my brain.

The Reaper smiles against my skin, then gives my flesh a nip. The sensation causes me to arch against him, and he makes a low, delicious noise.

Famine moves his attention to my other breast, treating it to the same ministrations. I thread my fingers through his hair, my breath growing ragged.

His toffee-colored hair tickles my skin as he moves his attention down, down, down my body, trailing kisses as he goes. I tense, knowing what's coming.

"Famine, you don't have to do this again," I breathe, my core already aching to have him inside me.

"Do I ever do anything I don't want to, Ana?" he says. The horseman presses a kiss to my pelvic bone. "I just want to say hello one more time to my favorite flower ..." His mouth moves lower, skimming across my seam.

I still haven't gotten used to him going down on me, to his getting pleasure purely from giving it to me. It's times like this, when he wants to bring me to orgasm over and over without his own release that I fight a war within myself. I know he does it on purpose too; Famine is determined to reprogram my mind to link sex to receiving pleasure, not giving it.

Famine slides his hands under my thighs, spreading them in the process.

I feel his hot breath against my core, and then the long, slow swipe of his tongue as he tastes me for the second time tonight.

I gasp, my hips jerking forward.

"Hold still," he commands again, iron in his voice. I grasp at the sheet beneath me, twisting fistfuls of it in my hair. I'm so used to him following a threat like this with his plants that I obey out of habit.

I make soft, pleading noises as Famine kisses and sucks on my outer lips, and then my inner ones, working himself closer and closer to my core. The entire time, I try to stay still, though I cannot seem to help the jerk of my hips every time he touches a pressure point.

Without any warning, he delves his tongue into my core.

I cry out, the sensation, overwhelming. And yet I ache, wanting his cock instead of his tongue.

"*Famine*," I moan, as he sucks and nibbles, making his way to my clit. He draws the bud into his mouth, rolling his tongue over it.

The Reaper glances up at me, those unnerving green eyes of his sharp with intent. Still teasing my clit, Famine slips two fingers into me, and he makes a beckoning motion.

My orgasm rips through me suddenly and unexpectedly, and then I'm crying out, my body twisting to get away from his intense touch.

Famine holds me in his viselike grip, forcing me to ride out every wave of my climax.

It's only when I go boneless that he finally withdraws his mouth and fingers. But then his hand is back, pressing against my throbbing clit once more. He begins to stroke it over and over.

I grab his wrist. "Too much," I breathe.

"No," he says simply.

I begin to scoot back, away from him, but the Reaper moves up my body and catches my mouth with his, settling his body heavily over mine and preventing me from escape.

As he's kissing me, I feel the hard brush of his cock. I try to reach for it, but he won't even let me do that.

Famine shifts his hips and settles the broad tip of it against my entrance.

My arms come around his back and my fingers dig into his skin. I'm practically shaking with anticipation. I've missed being connected to him so damn much.

Right when I think the Reaper is about to push into me, Famine pauses.

Cursing under his breath, he pulls away from me.

"What are you doing?" I all but cry out.

Famine leans his forehead against my sternum, his hand leaving my clit so that he can wrap both his arms around my waist.

"I'm mortal," he says, as though that explains *anything*. He gives a rueful laugh.

"Wasn't that the goal?" I ask, confused.

The Reaper pushes himself back up to his forearms so that he can look me directly in the eyes. "I can get you pregnant now."

My eyes widen with understanding. Among Famine's former powers was the ability to control his own fertility.

But now it's gone.

My heart beats like mad at the repercussions of that, and I let myself imagine—not for the first time—the possibility of having a child with Famine. They'd be devious little shits, considering who Famine and I are. The thought has me biting back a smile.

The Reaper's brows come together as he stares down at me. "What was that?" he demands.

"What was what?" I ask.

The horseman catches my jaw in his hand, studying my features in the dim light. "Your face just did something funny, and I want to know why."

I hold his gaze for several long seconds. Then take a deep breath. "I've been reconsidering my stance on having kids."

For a moment, the Reaper doesn't seem to breathe—he doesn't move at all.

"Are you serious?" he finally says.

I bite my lower lip, feeling oddly exposed, having this conversation with him. "Yeah?" I say. "Do *you* want kids?"

Famine leans back on his arms a little. "You know I do," he says, his voice raw.

"Then fuck me away," I say, already trying to claw him back up to me.

Still, he hesitates. "Don't tempt me if you're not sure, flower. Because if you are, I'm *never* leaving this pussy."

"You won't leave my pussy alone either way," I say, calling his bluff.

He smiles, then leans down and kisses my mouth, and I can still feel his grin against my lips.

"True," he admits. After a pause, he says, "You're sure?" All his usual posturing is gone.

I kiss him roughly. "*Yes*," I say, faking exasperation.

My answer is rewarded with a punishing kiss. Famine settles himself against me once more and angles himself at my entrance. Then, with a brutal shove, he thrusts inside.

I cry out at the sensation of being filled up all at once. My back arches off the bed, and I grip the Reaper tighter, my core clenching around him.

He groans into my ear. "My God, Ana, you feel so fucking divine."

Famine withdraws almost all the way out, then plunges forward again, clearly relishing the way we fit together.

I gasp at the sensation, every nerve ending set on edge.

Even with all the foreplay on his end, Famine's cock is still uncomfortably large. But with every thrust my body loosens, making room for him.

"I've fantasized about fucking you every night since I left," he breathes, his strokes coming faster.

I moan in response, already too consumed by the feel of him to form a coherent response. The truth is that I missed him more than I've missed anything in my life.

The Reaper looks down at me, and there's something in his expression that reminds me of the man I first found, muddy and mutilated. I remember how he cried in front of me, and the raw look he gave me when he realized I was helping him.

He's looking at me now like he looked at me then—as though I'm his redemption.

All at once he withdraws. I cry out at the aching emptiness.

Famine gives a low laugh, all signs of his momentary vulnerability now gone.

"No need to protest, flower," he says, grabbing my hips. "I am nowhere *near* finished with you." With that, he flips me so that my ass is bared for him.

He runs a hand over it, and then smacks it.

I cry out, jerking forward.

"What the—" Before I can finish, he slams himself back into me.

The noise I make as I jerk forward doesn't sound human. I forgot what sex with this horseman was like—savage, twisted, and always a little kinky.

Famine pumps into me with brutal force, until I'm writhing beneath him, my nails digging into the sheets. Our flesh is making wet, slapping noises every time it comes together, and with every pounding thrust, the Reaper draws me closer and closer to climax.

He leans over me, cupping my jaw with one hand, his other hand closing around a breast.

"Such a soft, accommodating flower," he says, praising me. "Now." His voice hardens, his breath fanning out against the skin of my cheek as he continuing thrusting into me. "*Come for me.*"

Such a high-handed, demanding bastar—

The Reaper pinches my nipple just as he drives into me.

It's too much all at once.

"*Famine!*" I cry out as my orgasm explodes through me, darkening my vision.

The Reaper groans as my core clenches around him, and then I can feel him coming too, his thrusts growing deep and erratic, each one stretching out my own climax longer and longer.

Eventually, my orgasm ebbs away, and the horseman's own movements slow until, almost reluctantly, Famine slips out of me.

The two of us collapse on that dusty mattress. The Reaper draws me to him, our legs tangling together. I lay my head on the Reaper's chest, where I can hear his ragged breathing. It causes the corners of my mouth to curl. He gets winded now; what a completely mundane, mortal thing. There's a strange anticipation I feel at the thought of discovering each little change in him. And yet—

"Say something to me in Angelic," I say softly, reaching out to trace one of his glyphs.

He doesn't question my demand.

"*Rinfajato uva, uwa uje durugafawiva vip.*

"You are beautiful," he translates, "and I am blessed."

I smile and bury my face in his skin. "I love you too," I say.

He kisses the top of my head, and the action moves me just enough to catch a whiff of something I smelled earlier. Only now is it registering.

I wrinkle my nose. "You stink like a human."

The room is quiet for a long moment. Then Famine lets out a loud, booming laugh.

"I hate to break it to you, flower," he says, "but for the rest of our mortal lives, you'll probably have to lower your standards. I now am in the unfortunate habit of eating and sweating and"—I see him shudder in the dim light—"*shitting*. What an ungodly activity shitting is."

It's now my turn to laugh. "How undignified that must be for you."

"I have been humbled before God," he agrees.

We settle into silence, our bodies cooling as we lie there together. I almost let us drift off that way. But there's one last thing I need to ask. It's the question that's lingered even after Lazarus and the horsemen regaled us with the grand tale of how they ended the apocalypse.

I draw in a deep breath. "So it's truly over?" I ask.

The thought is still nearly incomprehensible. My world has always been on the brink of total collapse. It's hard to wrap my mind around the possibility of anything else.

Famine shifts, gathering me closer to him. "It really is, flower," he says, his voice already heavy with sleep. He kisses my temple. "Humanity has been redeemed."

✧   ✧   ✧

Thank you for reading Famine's Homecoming! For more from author Laura Thalassa, visit her website.
www.laurathalassa.com

QUEENSIDE

SKYE WARREN

CHAPTER ONE

Avery

ANCIENT GREEKS LOVED mirrors. It's so tempting to think of the past in terms of statues and Coliseums and fights to the death, but people in ancient times were like us. Mirrors are a prime example. They made them from polished metal long before they began to use glass.

We've been getting ready for important engagements and checking ourselves out in the mirror for just about forever. We've been presenting a brave face forever.

I'm part of a long-standing tradition when I take my place in front of the full-length mirror In the master bedroom to assess myself. I'm wearing a white button-down shirt, a plaid pencil skirt, and sensible but stylish flats. It's a look that appears classic and effortless, even though an embarrassing amount of thought went into this outfit.

It's a new chapter in my professional life. An important one.

"You should have just worn the bustier," comes the voice over the phone. My friend Harper is on speaker phone. She sent over an outfit that included a leather bustier, a PVC pipe skirt, and stilettos. It was her idea of a joke. Or maybe she actually would wear it as some kind of feminist political statement. Either way, I'm not that ballsy.

I don't want to stand out. At least here in my new job as an associate professor at Tanglewood University, I want to fit in.

"Oh, she'll wear the bustier," comes the voice from the door.

Gabriel stands there in white shirt sleeves and black slacks leaning against the door. The glint in his golden eyes is a promise that tonight we will be using Harper's gift. A blush heats my cheeks. It doesn't matter how many times he's taken me or the things we've tried under cover of night. It still makes me flush when he looks at me that way. Hungry. Feral.

"I have to go," I tell Harper.

"Okay, break a leg," she says, before hanging up the phone.

I turn sideways so that Gabriel can see my outfit. "Is this good?"

His lips quirk, but the smile doesn't reach his eyes. "You look beautiful."

"Beautiful," I say.

"Sexy," he says.

I scrunch my nose. "Sexy?"

He starts walking toward me. "Like a hot librarian."

That makes me laugh. I guess I can accept hot librarian.

"It's the plaid, isn't it?"

"It's everything." He taps the clip that holds my hair up into a bun. "And I approve. Not that you need my approval. You're going to do great, Avery."

Butterflies flutter in my stomach. I'm more nervous than I expected, but this is more than just a job. It's my first foray into working.

After having two kids, I didn't think I would start work anytime soon. I envisioned sending them off to preschool, but even during nap time, I worked on my papers. I've been published in a few academic papers and even quoted in a few books, but my last paper made quite a stir in the academic community which led to Tanglewood University offering me this position.

"I just want it to go well," I tell him. "For me and for us. If I can make a career here, if this works out long-term, then I'll be able to be a professor without having to move somewhere."

Shadows flash through his golden eyes. "I told you, I can go anywhere. You're my home."

Warmth squeezes my heart. He has said that, but the fact is Tanglewood is his home. It's mine, too. I don't want to have to move, but I do want a career. I do want to be a professor, which means that Tanglewood University is my only shot.

I approach him and put my hands on his chest. He feels tense. Is it only because I'm tense, because I'm nervous, or is there something else?

"It's okay that I'm doing this, right?" I ask. We already have a nanny who comes in and helps us. She's great with Helen and Archie. Which would already be enough, but Gabriel also decided to work from home on the days that I'm gone. He's overprotective, but I can't blame him.

Not after the way he was raised.

"Of course," he says. "You deserve this. Don't feel guilty for even a second."

I push up on my toes until our mouths are inches apart. "Then what's wrong?"

He sighs. "I'm a possessive bastard."

"And that's a problem how?"

He hesitates and then finally, reluctantly, he answers, "This is a part of you, and a part of your life, that I can never touch. What if you like it too much? What if it takes you from me?"

My eyes widen. "Why can't you touch this part of my life?"

A harsh laugh. "I'm not a college graduate. I don't have a Ph.D. or a master's or a bachelor's. I don't even have my goddamn high school diploma. Maybe you'll meet some professor and realize you could do better."

Tears sting my eyes, but I force them back. He would only see it as pity, when in reality it's love.

"There is no one better," I tell him, before turning his neck down, before showing him with a kiss, with my teeth and tongue and lips, what my words alone can't prove.

CHAPTER TWO

SUNLIGHT DAPPLES THE pebbled walkway. A few students lounge in the grass, but the campus is pretty empty. Parking was a breeze. The semester hasn't started yet. We're in that liminal space between summer and fall, but the college still breathes with its own energy.

Gothic buildings rise out of neatly trimmed lawns and little brass plaques with notes about each one's history. The trees and the stonework are what appear on the brochures to entice students to come here. It's a good, solid public college with good, solid statistics. They aren't making waves in the academic community about feminism in ancient Greece the way my old advisor did. Smith College has a long-established pedigree, comparatively.

That's my alma mater, and at one point, I imagined working there. Now I think I might actually do more good here. These bright minds deserve a rigorous education as much as a student at Smith. Tuition at Tanglewood is only a fraction of the cost of a private college. This is arguably where it's more relevant, where it will do more good.

Then there's the practical side.

This is the only major university in a hundred-mile radius. With two small children at home, I can't afford a long commute. And I don't want to uproot my entire family.

Which makes this the opportunity. Once in a lifetime.

A faded bronze plaque announces this building as *Classics Studies.*

The doors swing shut behind me, and I take my first few steps across the old wood floor. It's been polished and cleaned so many times that the slats are buried beneath a thick coating. I can't help but think of all the other people who walked here before me, inhaling the scent of carpet cleaner and polished hardwood and knowledge.

A sign up above the door points my way to the offices. I'm not expecting much. Not even with the buzz that my latest paper received in the academic community. I'm still an associate professor. I'm still the new girl. But there are desks up there. And one of them is mine.

Mine. It's a surreal feeling. A first-day-of-school feeling, only I'm on the other side now.

I go through the open door with my head held high. A woman in a blue knit sweater smiles at me from behind the secretary's desk.

"You must be Avery Miller," she says, rising from her seat. "Professor Weller said you'd be in this morning. Welcome to the Classics department."

She leads me down the hall to an office on the left.

"Professor," she says. "Ms. Miller's here for her first day."

My new boss is standing by the window, a book in his hands. He's tall. Slender. Handsome in a princely kind of way. He closes the book and strides across to me. "Avery," he says. "It's lovely to meet you. Let me show you around, and then we can get to work."

The secretary disappears, and the professor leads me through the department's space. He motions to a door on the right, a look of anticipation on his soft features. "That's the room reserved for breastfeeding. Or pumping. Whatever you need to do in there."

"Oh," I say. "Thank you."

"You're welcome. Personally. I mean that." He shakes his head. "Not all of the departments have dedicated space. I insisted. It was a bit of a crusade. You wouldn't imagine the amount of emails and meetings. I spearheaded the effort. For the women. And the children."

"Well, that's—that's good. Thank you."

He gives me a brilliant, vaguely patronizing smile, as if he had the room made just for me, even though the sign is already cracked. "Too many department heads live in the Middle Ages. Here's the copy room. The machine can bind and collate, and—"

I follow him through a lightning-round tour of the floor, ignoring the sensation that something is off. I'm glad for the reserved room, obviously. But his description of himself as the hero makes me uncomfortable. I keep trying to ignore that his gaze flicked down to my breasts, snug and well covered, when he brought up breastfeeding.

No, the glance was probably just instinctive–not even sexual. Of course it's a good thing that he spearheaded the effort. He deserves praise for that. I'm used to Gabriel. He came by his knowledge of the world a different way. He thinks of women as his equal, but he also feels it's his duty to protect the more vulnerable around him. Not with emails and meetings, though.

With money. With power. And if necessary, with his fists.

We head back to Weller's office, and I catch my breath. Books are neatly arranged on the shelves. File cabinets. The big desk in the center.

Off to the side, on a much smaller desk, is something I recognize.

"This is you." The professor gestures at the desk, a sly pleasure in his expression.

"My paper." I pick up the stapled sheets. My academic work, on my new desk. *The Buried Contributions of Female Philosophers in Ancient Greece.* "You printed it out."

"You've made waves," he says, though it doesn't sound altogether like a compliment when he says it. Not everyone appreciated my observations. But he couldn't have minded, not if I got hired in his department. Right?

I brush the cool, thin pages with my fingertips. I've read words here a million times. My heart warms anyway. These are the words that got me this job. All the hours I spent on this argument meant something to the people at Tanglewood University, and in this department.

Yes. Having this printed and waiting on my desk is a good welcome.

These sheets of paper represent so much of me. They're more than my life's work. They're about recognition. Recognition for all the women who've gone before me, who've had children and built a professional career–far before society ever officially allowed it.

That wasn't the controversial part.

I covered the usual mentions. Themistoclea, who taught Pythagoreas. Leontion, who was a student of Epicurus. Even in validation of them we must relate them to men.

It was more than that, though.

Most scholars have dismissed things like child rearing, bedtime stories, and gossip as unimportant. Because most scholars are men. Women know that these things are at the heart of society. Ours and in Ancient Rome. My paper made the point that ignoring these foundational moral beliefs is a short-sighted view. And worse, that it's an inaccurate view.

That had some old professors up in arms. I didn't do it to spark controversy. I want to fit in here, but I couldn't pretend that the status quo was right.

"I'm grateful that you–" I begin, but at that moment Weller steps in close.

Too close.

His hand meets the side of my waist and slides down a couple of inches. My body freezes at the contact. He's hovering over my shoulder, as if he's looking down at the paper, too. He's got his hand on my hip. It wouldn't be out of place if we were on a date in some high-brow restaurant waiting for our table. It's like a blaring red STOP sign in this small office.

"Please take your hand off me." My tone is flat, but I don't know how else to be. Why would he think it was okay to touch me this way?

"You should be grateful for the attention." Every word out of his mouth is condescending. "A mother of two. Not exactly a supermodel anymore. I could have hired anyone for this position. I hired you. And you need to stay on my good side if you want to stay in the department."

Shock steals my breath for precious moments. "This is inappropriate."

"Is it? Then you'd better not tell anyone. Because if you do, your name will forever be associated with scandal. It's always worse for the women."

He taps the paper on the desk.

And I realize they weren't there as a welcome. He put them here as a threat. *The Buried Contributions of Female Philosophers in Ancient Greece.* It might as well read *The Buried Contributions of an Associate Professor in Tanglewood University.*

My stomach sinks. "You're bluffing."

"Am I? The head of the History college is my cousin's wife. And contrary to the laudable feminist ideals that are trending now, she believes in the old way. That 'the male is by nature superior and the female inferior, the male ruler and the female subject.'"

"Aristotle," I say, my voice hollow.

Men have been sexist bastards for a long time. Long before Professor Weller.

And they learned how to protect themselves. *It's always worse for the women,* he said. And he's right about that. If this got out, I would be the Monica Lewinsky of the academic world.

Humiliation stings my eyes. There's nowhere for this conversation to go. Nothing for me to do here. I turn on my heel and leave, rushing past the secretary and out into the fresh air. My hands shake while I dig my keys out of my purse and get behind the wheel. I'm going to be getting home early, but it's where I need to be.

Gabriel comes out at the sound of the door closing behind me, concern in his golden eyes. "Was the first day supposed to be this short?"

It feels wrong not to tell him everything, but it's my fight, not his. More than that, he's a caveman. He'd probably punch Weller...or worse. He could end up in jail.

Our children need their father.

I shake my head. "I'm not sure it's right for me."

He comes to me and leans down to kiss me like we've been apart for days instead of an hour. "What's wrong?"

"I'd rather not remember how that went." I lean into his warmth. "Make me forget."

He hesitates. And I understand it. He wants to help me. He wants me to fix my problems, but he can't do that now. This is one I'll have to face alone. Tomorrow. For now I let him pull me into his arms. I let him kiss me until I'm dizzy and breathless. I let him make love to me on top of our comforter, too hurried to climb beneath the sheets, panting and mindless in our bliss.

CHAPTER THREE

NORMALLY I IDENTIFY with the scholars of ancient times. With the pacifists and the thinkers. That's what I am at my heart, a philosopher like the women I wrote about. Except today I identify more with the warriors. That's how it feels, like I'm riding a chariot into the quiet building. Like I'm a Spartan going out to die for a greater glory.

Okay, that might be a little dramatic. But it still feels like a big deal for me to walk these halls so fresh after my humiliation. It hasn't even been twenty-four hours.

My heels click on the sidewalk with determination.

At the door of the department building, I check my phone, tucked into the pocket of my slacks.

I'm ready.

The secretary's eyes go wide as I storm through the door and sweep past her desk. "Mrs. Miller," she calls after me, her voice urgent. I don't turn around. "Mrs. Miller, if you could—"

I'm not stopping for her. I head straight for Weller's office door and push it open like it's mine. Not his. And it shouldn't be his. He doesn't deserve to be the department head.

He scrambles out of his chair as I come in. Surprise crosses his beautiful, ascetic features before he schools it into an expression of disapproval. I imagine he's practiced that in the mirror.

"The conversation yesterday was inappropriate and wrong. You shouldn't have touched me. Or threatened my job."

"A threat?" He laughs. "I'm trying to help you."

"And sleeping with you will help me."

He gives me a patient smile. "Avery," he says. "We got off on the wrong foot. I'm not your enemy here. I'm the one who insisted on hiring you. And I'm willing to forgive your tantrum, but you'll need to keep me happy if you're going to have any chance of success here."

"Keep you happy?"

"We'll be working together closely if you're capable of understanding your role. That role is not to make a fuss. It's to do what I tell you to do. I'm your boss."

"So when you touched me yesterday, that was just you...explaining my role to me."

"What else would it have been?"

Gabriel tried to get me to talk after we made love, but I refused. Instead he held me. He held me for long hours while I feigned sleep. It occurred to me over those hours that I can't have been the first subordinate he's tried this on. Other professors. Other university staff. And maybe even students. "Some people might call it sexual harassment. An abuse of power."

"And some people might say you make up stories for attention." His eyes flash. "Did you come here to argue with me or did you come here to beg for your job back?"

"Neither." I take my phone out of my pocket and hold it up so he can see that I've been recording us. I'm still recording us. "If this university wants to brand me with the scarlet letter, that's on them. But if I let you hurt other women, that's on me."

He glares at my phone with narrowed eyes and a bright red face. "You bitch."

"I have safety. I have security. I have the privilege to throw my career away, if that's what it takes. Other women don't. Other professors might not, either. And the students who you take advantage of. They might not be in a position to speak out, but I am."

I push the red button in the center of the screen. It stops the recording and saves it in several places on my phone so it can't be easily deleted.

And then I turn my back on him and walk out.

The president of the university has an office just across the courtyard. That's my next stop.

✧   ✧   ✧

SIX HOURS LATER I'm bathing my children, feeling almost back to normal. I'm still a little shaky inside, but with the help of glitter bubble bath, the children don't notice. Helen uses bath paints to draw on the white tile, making fanciful swirls. Archie throws the white foam into the air, exclaiming. It's an ordinary evening. As ordinary as a bright green blade of grass. Or the sunlight on a warm day. Ordinary perfection.

Gabriel appears with two warm towels, fresh from the dryer—one with a pink castle and the other with a blue puppy. We tell them stories and sing them songs.

And when their blinks are coming slow, when their heart rates calm, we turn out the light and step outside the room. In the shadowed hallway, Gabriel pulls me close. He runs his fingers through my hair. "Why didn't you tell me?" he asks.

It's painful to hear the question. I can hear in his voice how much he wanted to be by my side. How it hurt him that I faced it alone. How much he wants to be with me for everything. That's why we're together. Both of us know what we have in the other person.

"I had to do this myself. I had to stand up for myself and for every other woman he's screwed over. And I wanted him to hear it from me, not from anyone else."

A thoughtful silence. "What happens now?"

I sigh, nestling closer in his arms. "The university is still going to launch an inquiry. That's how things work there. Committees and meetings. Confidential emails. I don't know what will happen with my job. And frankly, I don't care."

"You don't care?" He arches an eyebrow, doubting that I'd be over it so quickly. Two days ago, I might have thought the same thing.

It was a big deal, getting the job at Tanglewood University. I thought it would be the ideal solution for us. We'd be able to keep our home, and I'd be able to grow in my academic career.

I still want those things, just not at the price the professor demanded.

Not at the price of my self respect.

And besides, I've already made a different argument.

To myself and to the academic world.

The things we do at home, with our families, make a difference. It's easy to think of relationships and storytelling as non-essential work. At least, less essential than being a professor.

But it's not true. What mothers and wives do at home matters. It's essential. Someday, centuries from now, historians will look back at our lives the way I looked back at ancient Greece.

I'll keep doing this work, whether I teach at Tanglewood University or not, because I believe in it. I know that I have contributions to make, that I have more buried contributions to uncover. Whether I write about them in renowned academic journals or whether I post about it on Instagram, my message is the same. It's about the breadth of the human experience. About the unsung heroes. It's not all wars and politics.

Sometimes, it's about the strength of a single family.

Gabriel places a single kiss on my forehead.

I close my eyes and breathe him in. "Whatever they decide, I already have what's most important to me. This. You, me, and the bedtime stories we tell our children."

✧ ✧ ✧

Thank you for reading QUEENSIDE! Gabriel and Avery feature in my book THE PAWN, which is available for free from wherever you get books…

DOWNLOAD The Pawn now >
www.skyewarren.com/books/the-pawn

"Wickedly brilliant, dark and addictive!"

– Jodi Ellen Malpas, #1 New York Times bestselling author

A Little Surprise

Katee Robert

PERSEPHONE

"**Y**OU SEEM DISTRACTED."

I jolt and then curse myself for letting my mind wander. I don't see my sisters as often as I used to, aside from the Sunday dinners our mother holds. This brunch is different, though. It's just us for once. So much has changed in such a short time. I've married Hades and effectively become queen of the lower city, though Hades would hate to be called a king. Psyche married Eros, which still bothers me, but she seems happy and that's all I ask.

Callisto? I shake my head. Callisto is Hera, and I don't know that Olympus will survive her marriage to Zeus. I don't understand what motivated her to make that choice, but Mother is practically dancing with joy over finally achieving her aim of having one of her daughters married to the leader of Olympus.

"Persephone?"

I shake my head. "Sorry. Just having a moment."

"You seem distracted the last couple days." Eurydice smiles, but it doesn't quite reach her dark eyes. She's been spending more and more time with me in the lower city and, while I am so happy to have her, I worry. Her breakup with Orpheus hit her hard and she hasn't bounced back the way I'd hoped. I'm not sure how to help her beyond giving her time.

"I've got a lot on my mind." It's nothing more than the truth…if not the full truth.

Her smile falls away and she tugs at the floral print wrap that she's fastened her curls back with. She's been trying out different styles in the last couple months, spending weeks in menswear and then switching to cute little dresses and heels and now landing somewhere more eclectic. Today, she's wearing shorts with more holes than fabric, heels, and a loose white shirt that looks like it belongs in a historical romance cover.

Callisto swirls her whiskey almost violently before sipping it. Trust her to drink *whiskey* at brunch. "You've been quieter than normal." She crosses one long leg over the other. She's gone through a style transformation since her marriage, though her clothing today is so purely Calypso, it makes me smile. Tailored pants, sky-high heels, and a pale lace top that's very chic but borderline indecent. I'm sure Zeus just *loves* that last bit. Obeying the letter of his desire for Callisto to dress more professionally, if not the spirit of it. "What's going on?"

Guilt flares, even though I have nothing to feel guilty for. "Maybe I just like hearing what you've all been up to."

"Mmhmm." Psyche twists a strand of long dark hair around her fingers. Her floral dress almost matches Eurydice's head wrap. "Now give us the real reason."

I've never been able to keep secrets from my sisters.

But this isn't a secret, because it's not official yet. It's a suspicion sprouting in my chest, making me both giddy and terrified. I want to keep it to myself just a little while longer. Maybe that's selfish, but I think I can be forgiven for it.

I finish my orange juice and set the empty glass on the table. "I'm not ready to talk about it, but when I am, I promise I'll share."

They give me three identical looks of sisterly suspicion. It's Eurydice who breaks the growing silence. "You aren't divorcing Hades, are you?"

"What?" That startles a laugh out of me. "No. Absolutely not. This is nothing bad. I promise."

Callisto flicks her dark hair over her shoulder. "If he *did* step out of line, don't bother with divorce. Hades was a myth for thirty years. That title would go back to being a myth if he were to disappear."

I roll my eyes, even though part of me is afraid she's perfectly serious. "Please stop threatening my husband, Callisto. No disappearing people."

"You know how Mother likes her pigs."

I do. I'm nearly certain she's *disappeared* people by feeding them to said pigs, although I have no desire to actually confirm that. Some things, it's best a daughter doesn't know about her mother. "Again, Hades and I are doing wonderfully and I would appreciate it if you stopped acting like you're going to make me a widow."

"*Fine.*" Her lips curve in a sharp smile. "Even if threats are my favorite hobby, I'll just turn them to *my* husband instead."

The thought of my sister threatening our current Zeus fills me with no little alarm, but I know better than to argue with *that*. I glance at my phone. "I've got to go. Should we pick another time now or touch base later?"

Psyche scrolls through her phone. "I've got to go through my schedule, but I'll send some options this evening if that works."

There was a time when we all lived in my mother's house and didn't have to backflip through four increasingly packed schedules to make time for each other. I'm so happy with my life now, but there are elements that are incredibly bittersweet. This certainly qualifies.

I glance at Eurydice. "Are you staying on this side of the river tonight?"

"No, but I'm stopping by Mother's place for a bit this afternoon." She sits back in her chair and gives a tense smile. "Charon is picking me up later."

I bet he is. I still haven't figured out if my youngest sister is aware of his obvious interest in her, but I'm trying very hard to resist the urge to meddle. Charon doesn't need my help, after all. Neither does my sister, though I'm still not sure if she's actually oblivious or if she just needs more time to mend her broken heart. "I'll see you at dinner, then."

"I don't know if I'll be back before then, so don't wait up."

I raise my brows, but Eurydice is an adult and can do what she wants. She hardly has a curfew, and our house is large enough that she basically has a wing to herself. Still...I worry. "Sure. Call if you need anything."

Psyche manages to drag her attention from her phone. "I'll be down at Juliette's later this week to take a look at the new line she's developing. I'll text you and, if you're free, I'll swing by for a drink."

"Sounds good." I don't tell her that if my suspicions are correct, I won't be drinking in the foreseeable future.

The trip back over the River Styx to the lower city passes in a blur. Without my sisters' presences to hold back my thoughts, the not-knowing presses close enough that I have a hard time drawing breath. I have to take a test. I know I do. But once I do, then I'll *know*, and once I know, I'll have to deal with the emotions involved, no matter what the test says.

It's not logical to have waited days after I suspected the truth, but there's nothing logical about what my emotions are doing right now. I keep swinging wildly between fear and joy and every messy feeling in between.

I have every intention of sneaking up to the room I share with Hades to put myself out of my misery of this in-between stage, but I barely make it through the doors when the dogs announce my presence to anyone within hearing distance.

They've grown alarmingly in the last eight months, shooting right past mid-sized and into massive. Hades thinks there must be some mastiff mixed into their bloodlines, because they're each easily over a hundred pounds.

I hold up my hands. "Yes, I'm home. Hush."

Cerberus, the little asshole, immediately sits and points his nose to the sky. He howls loud enough to make my hair stand on end. Scylla and Charybdis immediately follow suit, filling the entryway with the song of their people.

"Traitors," I mutter.

I don't hear Hades approaching, but the dogs somehow do. They stop howling and give happy yips, turning into a black river as they rush to circle him, shoving their big heads into his hands as he tries to make his way down the hall to me.

My husband looks good. He's always looked good, of course, but something has relaxed in him since the events that brought us together. He doesn't hold himself so tensely, and he smiles so readily.

He's smiling now as he finally manages to extract himself from the dogs. "You're home early."

"Am I?" I'm all false innocence.

Hades raises a brow and pulls me into his arms. "Yes, little siren, you are. Last time you went to brunch with your sisters, Charon practically had to pour you and Eurydice into the car to bring you home." His smile widens, his expression relaxed. "You had some outlandish suggestions on what I should do to you, and then you passed out on the couch before I could get some coffee and crackers to sober you up."

I run my hands up his chest to loop around his neck. "If I remember correctly, you did several *outlandish* things to me the next day after we finished work."

"What can I say? My wife is both brilliant and devious." He presses a quick kiss to my lips. "In all seriousness, is everything okay?"

I almost don't tell him. If I have complicated feelings about possibly being pregnant, Hades is sure to have even more. My father might be distant both physically and emotionally, and my mother might be a loving monster, but I had a happy childhood and have mostly healthy relationships with my sisters and mother now.

Hades grew up an orphan. Or at least believing himself to be an orphan. Finding out his father is alive, that he thought Hades was lost along with his mother... There's no recovering those thirty-odd years they lost together, but they're tentatively figuring out how they might have places in each other's lives.

Hades says he wants to be a father, but that's all theory right now. If I'm pregnant, that shoves us from theory right into reality. I don't know how he'll feel.

"Persephone." He catches my chin lightly, his brows drawing together. "What's wrong?"

I might be able to omit to my sisters—barely—but I can't do it to my husband. I draw in a shuddering breath. "I think I might be pregnant."

He freezes. "What?" He's so still, I'm not sure if he's breathing or not.

Nerves flare to life inside me. This is why I wanted to be sure before I brought this to him, but it's too late for that now. "My period is almost two weeks late. I didn't notice sooner because things have been hectic with all the Olympus scheming going on. It might be nothing, though, but I didn't want to say anything if I wasn't sure and I'm not sure." I'm babbling but I can't seem to stop. "I bought tests and then I chickened out on taking them and… Please say something because you're freaking me out."

He shakes himself as if waking from a dream. "You have the tests here?"

"Yes, upstairs."

Another of those shakes and he focuses back on me. The frown is gone, but I'd rather he was glaring at me instead of his expression falling into smooth lines. Retreating. He's retreating from me and I don't know how to stop it. I suck in a harsh breath. "Hades, please."

"Give me a moment."

I want to keep talking until he's here with me, but I press my lips together and wait. We'd discussed this being a possibility when I took my IUD out a few months ago. I'd sort of planned to start a new form of birth control, but never got around to it. We've been using condoms, except it turns out that we both really get off on the *I shouldn't* element of having unprotected sex, and so we got a little lax at times with actually using those condoms.

We'd talked about the risk after the first time, had both agreed that now probably wasn't the time to have a baby with so much upheaval in Olympus politics…but the next time we were in bed together, somehow our heated make-out session turned into his bare cock pressing against my entrance and me lifting my hips and…

And here we are.

Hades opens his eyes. He looks calmer now, more in control. "I love you, little siren. We knew this might be an outcome of our playing fast and loose for the last few months. Let's find out for sure one way or another."

He takes my hand and snaps a command at the dogs. They instantly stop circling us and race off toward the room that's become theirs. We head upstairs. My heart is beating too hard. In our bathroom, I pull out the three boxes of pregnancy tests that I bought and smuggled in here a few days ago.

That seems to snap him out of his shell shock more than anything else. He eyes them. "How many tests did you think you'd need?"

"There are so many different brands. I didn't know if one was more accurate than the other and…" I shrug, but I can't quite manage a smile. "I panicked."

"You should have come to me." He pulls me into his arms again and hugs me close. "You shouldn't have been scared and alone in this, Persephone. You're *not* alone. Whatever the test says, and whatever you decide, we're in this together."

Whatever I decide.

I close my eyes and hug him tightly. Of course he wouldn't take a positive test as an inevitable outcome. We'd agreed, after all, that now isn't a great time for a baby.

Except…

I don't know if I care that everything isn't lined up perfectly. I don't know if things will *ever* line up perfectly.

"What about what you want?"

He presses a kiss to my temple. "You know I want a family with you. I won't pretend I'm not scared shitless at the thought of being a father, but I have the utmost faith that together we can figure it out." Another squeeze and he takes a step back. "But I don't want my feelings on this to pressure you before you're ready."

Gods, I love this man.

I grab a box at random. "Well, let's find out if all these dramatics are for no reason or if we need to figure it out for real."

In the end, it takes exactly two minutes for the little plus sign to appear on the test. We look at it and then each other. I feel like I'm in a free fall. "Hades." I swallow hard. "Hades, I'm pregnant."

"That's what the test indicates," he says hoarsely.

I try to think rationally, to weigh the pros and cons and everything, but suddenly I don't give a fuck about any of them. Now that there's no wondering and no gray area. No running scenarios or telling myself that I'm being dramatic and emotional for no reason.

I'm pregnant.

I lick my lips, wondering why my eyes are burning. "I… I want to have a baby with you, Hades. *This* baby. I don't care if the time isn't perfect. I don't know if there *will* be a perfect time. If you—"

"Yes." He hauls me into his arms and off my feet. "*Yes*, little siren."

I kiss him. Or he kisses me. I'm not entirely certain. It doesn't matter, not when we're ripping each other's clothes off as we back out of the bathroom to the bed.

I'll never get tired of the way Hades kisses me. It's so much more intense now that we know exactly what the future holds. He palms my breasts. I hadn't noticed how they seem more sensitive than normal, but the feeling of his mouth on me bows my back and draws a cry from my lips.

He starts to kiss his way down my stomach, but I'm too impatient. "No, I don't want to wait." I dig my hands into his hair and tug. He follows my lead, surging up to reclaim my mouth. I arch against him. This is both like and not like how we've played on the edge for months. Naked and writhing against each other. Letting the kiss rile us up.

His cock catches my entrance and, this time, there's no hesitation, no careful teasing to allow one or both of us to stop it before we go too far. Hades surges into me, sheathing himself to the hilt.

He doesn't give me a chance to sink into it, though. He shifts back and slides down next to me, arranging me half on my side. He grabs one thigh and spreads me wide. In this position, he has full access to my body as he sinks back into me again. I am entirely wrapped up in him. There's no place I'd rather be.

He kisses me as he strokes my clit. Slowing us down and winding my pleasure higher with each movement. He kisses me again, cupping my jaw even as he fucks me slowly. I don't want this ever to end, this perfect moment of desire and understanding and joy.

My body has other ideas. It always does when in Hades's clever hands. He strokes deep and the penetration with his fingers on my clit send me spiraling. I sob against his lips as I orgasm.

"I love you, Persephone." He doesn't pick up his pace, barely letting me catch my breath before his fingers are at my clit again. Softer this time, aware of just how sensitive I am, but no less unrelenting. "I would have no other as my wife." His breath catches. "As the… As the mother of my child. It was only ever going to be you."

We don't stop for a very long time. He takes me in every position. And when he finally comes, he goes down on me until he's recovered enough to take me again.

It's well past midnight when we finally collapse in a sweaty tangle of limbs. Hades tugs me close and presses a careful hand to my stomach. "I suppose we should buy some baby books."

I give a hoarse laugh. "I'm sure my mother will have more than a few bits of advice once we tell her."

"Yes." His breath ghosts against my temple. "Would it be horribly selfish to ask to keep this just between us for a little while?"

"Not at all. I like the idea of keeping this just for us." I shift onto my side to face him and throw a leg over his hips. He runs his hand over to my lower back and urges me closer yet. Despite everything, his cock stirs against me. My laugh goes a little reckless. "Again, husband?"

Hades kisses me and presses me onto my back. "I hear that new parents don't have much time or energy for this sort of thing." He palms my breasts and lavishes kisses on them. This time, he ignores me when I tug his hair. His dark eyes go wicked. "We should get in all we can before that happens."

"We have like...nine months."

"You're right." He flicks one nipple with his tongue. "Not nearly enough time."

"Hades!"

He lifts his head, expression going serious. "This might be just for us right now, little siren, but it's going to make waves in Olympus when we announce the news. You carry the next Hades. More, a new Hades will be born before a new Zeus. It's bound to get..." He sighs. "Messy. I'm going to be an overprotective asshole for the duration, and I apologize in advance."

"This Zeus isn't like the last one," I whisper. He seems to want stability, but will he be threatened by a new heir to the title Hades? Poseidon doesn't have any permanent relationship at this point. Zeus just married my sister, but I'd bet everything I have that Callisto isn't going to have a child with him until she absolutely has to. Hades is the first of this generation's legacy titles to have an heir.

"No, he's not." He searches my face. "And I am not my father. I will allow *nothing* to hurt you, Persephone. I'll burn all of Olympus to the ground and salt the earth before I let you come to harm. You...or our child."

That prickling in my eyes is back. This whole pregnancy is going to be so fraught for him—for both of us. I'm going to have to be careful not to tread on old wounds even as I establish my own boundaries. "I will not consent to being locked away in this house for the next nine months." I catch a strange look in his eyes and push forward. "Or eighteen years. Or at all."

He tenses. "Persephone..."

"I mean it, Hades. I love you and I respect that this is going to be a challenge for you, but we are not your parents and I am not defenseless. I promise not to take undo risks or recklessly do things to upset you, but you will not put me in a cage for my so-called safety. I won't allow it."

He considers me for a long moment. "You will allow me to negotiate."

"How are you going to—*oh*." He presses two fingers into me, easily finding the spot that makes me go boneless and needy. "That's not playing fair."

"All's fair in love and war, little siren." He goes back to my breasts even as he continues to fuck me with his fingers. "Let's talk about timelines."

"You can't..." I can't think straight with him touching me like that and he knows it. "Gods, Hades, that feels good. Don't stop."

He kisses his way up my throat and nips my earlobe. "No matter what we negotiate or decide, I will keep you safe. I swear it."

I dig my fingers into his hair and tug him over until I can speak against his lips. "I'm always safe with you." I set my teeth against his bottom lip. "Now, make me come again, husband."

✧ ✧ ✧

Thank you so much for reading my story A Little Surprise! If you'd like to see all of Hades and Persephone's story, be sure to check out Neon Gods!

ORDER NEON GODS NOW>
www.kateerobert.com/neon-gods

AVEKE

TIJAN

CHAPTER ONE

Ava

H E WAS HERE. Again.

This was, what? The fourth time this week. Eight, sharp. The last four evenings in a row. And he came in, took the stool at the far end, and sat. Just, sat. His head folded over. He took a breath before he lifted, and a wall came back over him, like he needed one second before readying to slip on the mask that the rest of the world saw. Then he tipped his head back, his eyes went to the television right above him, and as Brandon gave him a beer for the night, he'd sip and watch his best bud play soccer on the television. And like tonight, if it wasn't his best friend's team playing, we'd switch it to another game. Score if it was someone we knew playing, because around these parts, that wasn't that uncommon, but not tonight.

There was a hockey game, but not the team he liked to watch.

Brandon wasn't working tonight since I told him twenty minutes ago that I'd close for him. Brandon had a woman and he was happy, so he was starting to let me close most nights for him. So tonight I moved down the bar, met his eyes briefly before he saw me reach for a tall glass and pour his favorite beer from the tap.

He was tired. I caught the wariness before he switched. A wall came down, and then he reanimated to the cocky jerk that most people took Zeke Allen for being. Wealthy. Preppy. (If that was still a descriptor for someone our age. We're in our twenties, so I suppose instead of preppy, we could use the word "blessed" to describe him.) He didn't seem like he aged.

Muscular. Big broad shoulders. He was built like a bodybuilder. Dark blond hair.

A very big square jawline, but it was so prominent, that it alone could get so many women in bed with him. I'd seen him in action many a night, and he never had to work hard. He tended to buy them a drink, ask them how they were, and within a few minutes (always depending on how long Allen wanted to chat or not) they'd head out.

Zeke was gorgeous when we were in high school, not that he and I attended the same school. With our neighboring towns, one could say I was on one side of the tracks and he was on the other. The privileged. He went to a private school, which seemed to get more private and exclusive as the years passed. I was from Roussou. It used to be a good place, thriving, and then it took a turn and not many seemed as privileged there anymore. I think it was doing better these last few years, due to some local businesses that brought in a bunch of people, but still...it was hurting.

I finished his pour and took the remote for the television. Placing both before him, I gave him a nod. "Think Kansas City Mustangs are playing tonight."

He grunted, took a sip, and picked up his remote. "Thanks, Ava. Thinking I'd like to watch The Javalina tonight."

He was already changing the channel before I turned to fill another order.

I knew Zeke would sip his beer and want another in twenty minutes. Then a third on the hour. He'd stay almost to closing, stopping long before he'd need to drive to sober up. For a guy whose reputation was known to be a bully and an obnoxious jackass, he wasn't like that anymore.

Eyeing him from the corner of my eye, I'd like to ask what happened to change his ways. One day.

CHAPTER TWO

Ava

"**A**VA, WHY ARE you single?"

We were on beer number four of the night. He started at eight. He was on this round a little after one in the morning. We closed at two, but if Zeke needed extra time, I wouldn't kick him out. He could stay while I closed up. I had no problem with that.

I grunted, sliding his beer over to him. We were on the late-night sports highlights, and the place was going strong. It didn't bother me. I was the only one behind the bar, but I had a system down, so it was fine. Brandon was particular about who was behind here, and I'd been working at Manny's in various departments since I was sixteen, so I was trusted.

I grinned. "Why? You volunteering?"

He grinned back, a chuckle before lifting his beer. "Just seems weird. You were with that Roy guy for a while and then…" His eyes grew distant and his head cocked to the side. He was thinking, trying to remember my love life, but he wouldn't remember because while he went to a D1 school, I stayed home and attended the local community college.

I knocked my knuckles on the counter in front of him. "Don't think too hard, Allen. I'm single because I want to be." I moved down the counter. Three women were eyeing him all night, and they were on their fourth round of shots. The one who'd been paying all night waved more money toward me, so I started reaching for three more shot glasses.

"No. Wait." She leaned over, saying loudly, and I got a good whiff of her perfume mixed with booze as she breathed on me. "We want a shot with him too. Four shots."

I didn't move, but I looked at Zeke from the corner of my eye.

This had happened before. Many times, and Zeke was always a good sport about it, but for some reason, I was hesitating. That wasn't good for business or my job, so I grabbed the Patron, what they'd been drinking all night. "You want them poured here or by him?"

She hesitated too, and I saw some self-consciousness set in. Her two other friends were ignoring us, almost gawking at Zeke. She bit down on her lip and leaned over again. "You know him?"

I nodded.

"What do you think?"

I opened my mouth, but halted on what I was going to say because the truth was, Zeke would've already grabbed one of them if he was interested. The girls were not being subtle, and he knew the game. He was a master at playing it.

"How about I pour yours here and take his to him? He can wave you down to say thanks?"

Her smile was wide and quick. "That sounds great!"

I did as I said, and ignored the other two girls' grumbling as I took the shot to Zeke. I placed it a little away from him and bent down, pretending like I needed to grab something under the counter. "Giving you a heads-up. That shot there is for you, paid for by those three girls. Yellow halters." (Every single one was wearing yellow.) "And they're hoping you'll wave them down to thank them for the shot."

He barely reacted, taking the shot, flashing them a smile in thanks, and he tipped his head back for the shot. He mouthed it, then followed with his emptied water, and as he set that glass down, I saw that it magically grew a little bit more water than what had been in there.

I looked up, caught him watching me, and he gave me a wink.

My pulse jumped, and I almost dropped my washcloth because fuck, my stomach got some tingles.

I looked down, surprised, because I hadn't had this reaction to someone in a long time. I was almost dumbfounded, not knowing how to proceed. It'd been that long.

"You're Zeke Allen, right?" One of the girls came over.

His gaze stayed on me for a moment before turning to her. "I am." He gave her a once-over before smirking. "Please tell me I didn't fuck your older sister, or mother."

She gasped.

I started laughing.

There was the old Zeke I remembered.

For a second, I almost missed the jackass.

He slid off his stool and threw a bunch of bills onto the counter. Ignoring the girl, he lifted his chin up toward me. "You're too hot to be single, Ava." He knocked his knuckles on the counter before heading out.

"What a dick!" The one girl was scowling in his direction. Her two friends joined, and the second one (not the one who paid for all the drinks. She had stayed back the whole time.) huffed at me, her hand finding her hip. "You don't have to laugh at Laughlin. I thought we were in the whole *women empowering and lifting each other up* era?"

I fought against rolling my eyes. "Sweetie, I wasn't laughing at your girl. I was laughing at Allen, because for him, *that* was tame." I began moving backward, going back down the bar. "Also, Laughlin is a cool name."

The girl eased up, her head straightening. "Thank you."

A guy had moved in behind the girl who paid for everything, and as I filled his order, I couldn't help myself. I asked under my breath to her, "They going to pay you back for tonight?"

She jerked upright, stiffening. "I don't know what you're talking about."

I stepped back, eyeing her. "Right." I gave her a soft, but sad smile. "Here's some female empowering two cents: if you gotta pay for them, they're friends with your cash, not you."

She flicked her eyes up, just as the others called her name. "Whatever." She stalked off after.

I don't know why, but I watched her go.

Maybe I saw a bit of me in her. Sadly, it wasn't the part that had friends. It was the part that felt like a schmuck. That was me back then, and still was.

I lied to Zeke. I wasn't single because I wanted to be.

I was single because no one that I wanted, wanted me back.

CHAPTER THREE

Ava

THE HOUSE WAS lit up when I got home, but that wasn't uncommon.
I walked through, turning off everything. Grandmum's oxygen machine was buzzing in the background, but I still went in and made sure everything was working properly. She was settled in her bed, folded up like a ball, and turned to the side. She was so tiny, but that was a family trait. All the women were petite. All of us had blonde hair too. Grandmum's was white by now. Mom's was dark blonde, and I was a mix between with honey-light blonde hair. I saw a tip of Grandmum's hair sticking outside of the blanket, but she was fully covered up by the blanket. I stood in the doorway, watching out of habit to make sure her chest rose. Once I saw the steady rhythm of her deep sleep, I turned her light off too.

It was her habit to leave it on. She once told me she kept it on because she never knew when Grandpap was coming home and the habit stuck. She couldn't sleep unless the light was on. Growing older, learning more, I was more figuring she kept it on in case he tried to sneak in after they separated. He never gave her a divorce. That was one thing he held over her head, and how my grandmum grew up, she didn't fight him. She was just happy he never brought his shotgun to finish her off.

Women shouldn't have to live like that, but some did. Grandmum did.

I left her room and checked on my mom next.

She'd taken to the same habit as Grandmum. Her light was on, and she was sleeping in almost the same position as her mama. The main difference, her wheelchair was positioned next to her bed and she didn't have an oxygen machine. Instead, though, she had a fan propped up for noise.

I turned her light off and moved through the living room. That light too.

Doors were locked. I checked them two more times before I headed upstairs.

None of the lights were on up here, but neither my mom nor Grandmum came up here. It was the reason it was mine. I got the whole floor, but I only used the large bedroom on the end.

I cleaned up and got ready for bed.

Once I settled in, my window was open because temps were fine at night, I rolled to my side. But I faced the door and the one window I had propped open. That was it. I couldn't handle sleeping with noise. If someone broke in, it was up to me to protect everyone. That was my role in the family.

I took a deep breath, feeling sleep starting to spread through me, but right before I drifted off, I flashed back to Zeke.

"You're too hot to be single, Ava."

I drifted off with a grin on my face.

I didn't believe him, but it felt nice to hear.

CHAPTER FOUR
Ava

THE SMELL OF bacon and coffee woke me, and my stomach grumbled, waking me even further.

I knew my mom could cook just fine. She was a wizard in her wheelchair, but I still hurried getting up for the day. I didn't shower last night because I didn't want to wake anyone up. Both needed their sleep, so I hurried with a shower this morning.

I grabbed my phone, pulling it from the charger and stuffing it into my back pocket before I went downstairs.

The sounds of the grease sizzling filled the room, along with the coffee machine brewing.

I was already smiling before I got to the kitchen because my mom didn't need to cook for me. She and Grandmum liked to sleep in. Not me. Or I didn't think I did. I never had, to be honest. Sleep was a privilege for me because I worked so much, so her doing this was for me.

They also weren't big breakfast eaters, though Grandmum would nibble on some dates when she woke.

But once I hit the doorway, I saw the brochure laid out on the table and my heart sank. I lost my appetite.

This wasn't going to be one of those happy mornings.

I looked over.

My mom was watching me, sitting back down in her chair. Metal tongs were in her hand, and she'd unlocked her wheelchair so she could see me better.

Tiny, but toned arms. Her hair was clipped back with tiny barrettes, framing her face from ear to ear. They were rainbow colored. She had on mesh shorts.

She swallowed, her eyes flaring from grief before she said what I never wanted to hear from her.

"We need to talk about Grandmum."

CHAPTER FIVE
Zeke

WE WERE ON the golf course when instead of lining up his shot, my buddy burst out laughing.

I frowned. "Dude."

He was almost falling over, but turned to me, raising his nine iron behind him. "Zeke! That is fucking hilarious. Look!"

Brian was almost falling over from his laughter.

Jesus. What the fuck.

I got out of the golf cart and moved so I could see whatever this was. When I got there, holy...*fuck*. But I wasn't laughing. Ava was walking across the green, but not in a way where it was obvious she was on a mission or had a destination in mind. No. She was going this way, then that way, and going in a circle. She was walking backward. She was all over the place, and she was drinking from a bottle of vodka at the same time.

I drew in a breath as Brian kept laughing. "You know who that is? That's that Ava chick. You know, the one who worked everywhere." His laughter went up a notch. "We'd go to the pizzeria. Ava. We'd go to Manny's. Ava. We'd go to Nooma's. Ava. It became a joke, remember? We'd drink if she popped up somewhere. She was at the gas station too. Damn. Girl got around."

One day I'd tell Brian how close he was to getting his face punched. Or how close he was to waking up in a hospital bed. I didn't trust myself right now.

He sighed, his laughter finally fucking subsiding. "I doubt she works here. She's as wasted as I was on my twenty-first birthday."

"Brian." Finally I could speak, through gritted teeth.

"Yeah?" He swung my way.

"*Shut the* fuck *up.*"

"Wha—she's not in our social circle. What are you doing?"

Ignoring him, I started down the hill, carrying my own alcohol in hand.

"Zeke!"

I raised a middle finger in the air and yelled over my shoulder, "Take care of my shit."

"What are you doing?"

I raised my middle finger higher.

By the time I got to her, he was gone with the cart.

Ava had no idea I was there. Her head was down except when she'd tip it back for a drink, and she was moving in a way—I saw the headphones. She was dancing, listening to whatever as I saw her pull her phone out of her pocket and skip to the next song.

It was a lively one because she began jumping around, her head going the opposite direction. Her arms were doing…something.

I wouldn't call this dancing. It was more like flailing around with a baseline of rhythm.

I watched her for two complete songs before her eyes opened. Seeing me, she startled, gasping, and a screech came out of her at the same time.

I smiled and held up a hand. I mouthed, "Hi."

"What?! I can't hear you!"

I nodded, pointing to her headphones.

Understanding dawned and she started laughing, pulling off the headphones. "Hi. Sorry. I forgot I had them on." Her music was blaring out of them. She didn't move to stop or pause the song. She was frowning at me, half-squinting. "Zeke? What are you doing here?"

I cocked my head to the side. The glaze was minimal. She wasn't slurring. She was speaking like she was sober, and without the electrocuted dancing, she now looked sober too.

I was somewhat impressed.

"Right." I motioned around us. "We're on a golf course, where I do the normal douchey thing and golf a few times a week, and your question is as if I'm the one out of place."

At my words, she jerked her head around, sweeping in the entirety of the Fallen Crest golf course. Her eyes were almost bulging when she focused back on me. She spoke in a shocked whisper, "What am I doing here?"

I was nodding, but I edged closer and reached out, taking away the vodka from her hand. She didn't notice. Then I almost started laughing. She'd barely drunk any. Maybe two shots' worth. "Are you drunk or not? I'm having a hard time telling."

"I think I'm drunk."

"You barely touched this."

Her gaze snapped to the bottle as I raised it, and she looked confused. Her eyebrows came together before she held her hands up, both of them, and gasped. "I didn't even feel you take that."

She *was* drunk.

She raised her gaze back to me, her hands still up in the air. "I parked at Manny's, grabbed a bottle, and just started walking. I wasn't paying attention. Dancing, drinking." Her voice dropped low again. "I've never drunk before."

Whoa.

My head went back an inch. "Never?"

Her eyes still wide, she shook her head at the same time. "Never. I accidentally went to a party once because my boyfriend was the local Uber. He went to pick someone up and I had to go to the bathroom. He thought I went in to stay and join the party."

I—I had no words. I was quite aware that most of my life, if there was a night I didn't party, *that* was the oddity.

"Oh my God. You're looking at me like I'm a freak." Her face flooded with color, and she closed her eyes. She was still holding her hands up.

"Okay." I didn't know what was going on here, but I moved in, took both her hands, and lowered them for her. She opened her eyes, and there was no reaction that she knew I did that. "Have you eaten today?"

She shook her head.

"You want to eat?"

"Um." She started chewing on her bottom lip, her eyebrows still pulled together. Then she stopped. Her face cleared. She blinked. "No. I need to keep drinking." She grabbed my beer and took a long drag. I was waiting for the sputtering, thinking she didn't realize she reached for the wrong bottle, but nothing came. She kept drinking.

I got fixated on how her throat was working, chugging that down.

She was taking long and slow drags, and she kept going.

It clicked she just chugged a third of my beer and I had a thirty-two-ouncer with me today before I grabbed it back. "Stop."

She reached for it, stepping with my arm.

I moved, turning and using my body to check her. "No."

"But—"

I raised the beer so she could see it clearly. "That wasn't yours."

Her mouth opened. She was going to argue, but she stopped. A gasping sound came next before she slumped, her forehead falling to my arm. It was raised right in front of her. She moaned. "Oh, no. I'm so sorry. I'm a mess."

If two shots of vodka already had her wasted, that beer was going to finish her off.

I glanced back to the country club, but she'd be a mess there. I didn't think Ava would want people seeing her like this.

Taking her arm, I began to walk to the parking lot.

"Wha—where are we going?"

"You need some food."

She started to put on the brakes.

Nope. I wasn't having this.

And I wasn't questioning myself why I was doing any of this as I let her go, put both caps on the alcohol, and stuffed them into my pockets. I had large pockets. Then I turned, bent down, and picked her up. She was slung over my shoulders.

"Wha—Zeke! Put me down!"

I kept going. "You need food, Ava, or you are going to regret that beer. Trust me."

She got quiet. Being slung over my shoulder probably wasn't the best idea either, but I didn't want to waste time fighting with her.

She tried to raise herself up, so maybe she was thinking the same thing. "How do you know?"

"Huh?"

"How do you know I need food?"

Right. She never drank before.

"Of the two of us, I'm thinking we should go with my knowledge of drinking."

"Oh." She got quiet. "That's a good idea."

So, food it was.

CHAPTER SIX

Ava

S O THIS WAS what being drunk felt like. Huh.

I was sitting in Zeke's kitchen, in a chair, by the table, in the corner, in his kitchen—I already said that—and whoa. Wowee. I moved my head upside down, or as much as I could, and the kitchen looked amazing this way too. We should all look at the world this way.

Wait.

I twisted around, laying my head down with my feet up and oh yeah. This was so much better.

We could walk on the ceilings. The shelves could be benches. It made so much sense now.

"What the fuck are you doing?"

"Huh?" I swung my head around and WHOA! Zeke was like a god. Standing. Defying gravity. Staring down at me.

This was amazing.

I was having a spiritual event.

"You're going to get sick if you don't sit upright."

I started to tell him that would defeat the whole point, but I felt a rush of nausea coming on and he *was* a god. He totally knew what was going to happen before it happened.

Then I let go and fell. I crumbled to the floor, and oomph. That hurt.

Hands touched under my arm and I was being lifted up. I moved, not thinking, just reacting, and when I blinked, I was holding on to Zeke like a monkey. Legs around his waist. Arms around his shoulders and he was holding me in place with a hand under my ass.

I almost wiggled because that felt kinda good.

I'd not done anything with a guy in so long. It was embarrassing. Made me feel pathetic at times, but then I remembered why and oh yeah. That was real-world shit. I didn't want to deal with real-world shit.

"Hey." Zeke's voice was all soft. He was watching me, his head angled back so he could see me better, and the concern in his gaze was undoing me. He frowned a little. "Why were you drinking today, Ava?"

I didn't want to look in those eyes anymore.

I turned, my throat closing up. I blinked away a few tears, but dammit. One got free, sliding down my face.

Zeke walked us over to a counter. He shifted, putting me there, but he didn't move back. Reaching up, he cupped the side of my face with such tenderness.

Still undoing. A second tear got out.

He wiped both away with his thumb, but he was still holding my face. "Talk to me. I've known you for a long time, but never seen you like this."

He was right. I worked. I was strong.

I never broke, ever.

Not when my grandfather was finally arrested and we were safe.

Not when my father left us.

Not when my mom lost her legs.

But today—I was losing everything.

"My grandmum is going on hospice."

I felt Zeke tense, and I closed my eyes, waiting for him to pull away.

I didn't really know Zeke. It was a weird budship that started with us because he was just as lonely as me. Him, who had the world at his feet. He could go anywhere in Fallen Crest and people wanted to talk to him, be seen with him, but he began changing.

I knew he was fierce about some of his friends, one of his best friends, but that best friend was in Europe. Was that it? He was missing that friend?

"You changed when your best friend came to town."

He stiffened again, but a surprised chuckle left him. "What? Topic change there."

I relaxed a little. This felt safer to talk about. "You both were gods at your school. I watched. I saw everything. You were such an asshole, but then Blaise came to town and a different side of you came out." I was back to whispering, confessing, "I liked seeing that, though you terrified me."

"I did?"

He didn't sound surprised.

I nodded. "You were a bully, Zeke."

He frowned, his body still tense, but now going rigid. "I know." His tone was rueful. "That changed, but I never should've been what I was."

"Was it your best friend that changed you? What happened?"

His eyebrows went up, and he was almost talking to himself. "Man. I... Yeah. Blaise coming back helped because he stood up to me, put me in my place, and I was a jackass. I needed that, but it was other stuff too." He laughed a little. "My dad caught me taking something I shouldn't have, and well, he kicked my ass. Not physically, but he took everything away. Like house staff, my car, money. Everything. I had to take care of the house and it's not a big event. It was normal what he did, gave me structure, but I needed it. He humbled me a lot, but I realized he actually loved me. Like real love, where he gave a fuck if I was growing up to be a future white-collar criminal or not."

"Really?"

He nodded. "Nothing super traumatizing or anything. I just got some love that was missing. My dad stepped up. Blaise was back in my life. And I made a conscious choice to look for good guys to be like. I didn't want to be lazy. I wanted to be a better person and yeah. Fast-forward a few years and I guess here I am." He grew more focused. "What about you?"

I tensed. "What do you mean?"

"What happened to you? You were always quiet, hardworking, but you weren't jaded. I saw you too."

A zing went through me. He had?

I thought about all the hard times, and I shook my head. There was no beginning and the end... I couldn't go there. "Life. That's all."

"Life?"

I nodded. Pain sliced me, and I felt a knife being shoved into my throat. "My mom told me today that when Grandmum goes into hospice, she's going with her. She's going into a facility, said it was time."

"What about Grandmum?"

"It's time, Aves. We had a talk and she wants to do a hospice bed in the nursing home. There's a room there they can use for her."

"When did you decide all of this?"

"I had a meeting with them."

"No. No, Mom. We can take care of her here. I'll get time off—"

"Ave." She wheeled her chair closer and stopped, folding her hands in her lap. "You have taken care of us most of your life, and, honey, you're too young for this. I'm going to move into my own place."

"What?!"

"It's not that bad. It's a new program. It's set up where I'll have my own place, and I've got some friends there already."

"You're not old. You're not—you're normal except for the chair. What are you thinking?"

"I'm thinking we need to sell the house to handle some of the extra bills, and I'm thinking that I want you to live life where you're not taking care of me anymore. You can help, but it's not like I'm dying anytime soon. It's not what it sounds like. It's my own place, but I got people close to help if I need it. I don't want you to worry about me."

"You're my mother. That's my job. That's not going to stop if you move somewhere else."

"See. Right there. That's why I need to make this move. You know I've got some other health concerns. They ain't going away."

Grandmum was dying. My mom was moving. We needed to sell the house.

I was losing everything I knew.

CHAPTER SEVEN
Zeke

JESUS. I WAS stunned.

Ava told me what was going on, and pieces were fitting together of why she worked so much. How she must've felt in high school, and I was such the opposite that I was getting another humbling kick in the ass. Right up the ass.

Fuck.

I couldn't comprehend any of this.

"You're fucking amazing."

Ava gave me a weird look. We'd moved to the living room. The conversation continued as I brought in a pizza and she was looking tired. I was thinking some of the alcohol was soaking up those carbs. She wouldn't be so sick, but she was also feeling what she'd been hoping to avoid.

"What?" She laughed, but I saw the confusion too.

I leaned forward, scooting to the edge of my couch. "You're amazing, Ava."

She quieted, her eyes widening, and she seemed to slink into the loveseat, like she wanted to disappear.

I shook my head. "I was such a jackass in high school." I leaned back, my eyes still on her. "My mom's an alcoholic."

"I didn't know that." She said that so quietly. Small.

I snorted. "It's not a big deal, at least to me. To each their own, I figure. She thinks it's her getting by, but she's just wallowing. She doesn't want to change, but not a big issue for me. Alcy or not, she's a good mom to me. She just likes her wine, and then she goes in her room and cries." Though, thinking on it, I winced. "I mean, I don't like that she's that sad, but that's for her to fix. Anyways, sharing that because I've always known I didn't need to take care of my parents. And I've always known that there'd be assets for me. I never worried about any of that, and you, I don't know the breakdown of health insurance or whatever and you've not talked about the males in your life or even if there were or are any, but you're fucking amazing, Ava. You're looking at me like you've got no clue why I'm saying that to you, and that makes you even more amazing."

All the sex. The booze. The literal stupid shit we did in high school. The drugs. Then college. Joining a fraternity.

And she was here. Working. Caring for her mom, her grandmother.

I'd been living life, but I'd not been appreciating it while I did it, and her, she hadn't been living, but she would've appreciated every second of it if she had.

Fuck.

Fuck!

She was there, here, under my nose, and I never saw her.

"Why'd that jackass let you go?"

"Jackass?" She was back to whispering.

"Your boyfriend in high school."

She shrugged. "Just grew apart. He's got a new fiancée now."

I shook my head, only looking at her now. "He's a dumbshit jackass, then."

Her lips twitched, the faintest smile, and damn, but that sight made my heart race.

CHAPTER EIGHT

Ava

TIME WENT TOO fast, and too slow all at the same time.

After that day with Zeke, we packed up Grandmum and moved her to the nursing home. I worked full-time at Manny's, but I also worked full-time at a horse stable outside of Fallen Crest. It was new, and the main point was to offer boarding and equine therapy. It had started recently becoming a place for rescue horses as well. I liked the balance between the two jobs. One was pouring drinks or serving people food, and the other was helping with the horses. I did most of the office work, but there were times I snuck out to the barn and spent time with the horses. There was a magical calmness to them that was addictive once you picked up how to feel it. I was in good standing with both jobs, so they let me scale back time so I could be with Grandmum.

My mom and a few of her friends were packing up the house, and she took me to the place where she was going to move into.

She was right, as much as I hated to admit it. It was a one-floor apartment in a house, and it was all hers. The whole place was wheelchair-accessible, and I met some of the housemates on the other floors. Next to the building was a health clinic, so they had nurses there and they had a system if any assistance was needed for off-hours.

It was a good setup for her.

I was just arriving to Manny's, the first night in a long time where I left Grandmum's bed.

I didn't want to go, and I wasn't scheduled, but I couldn't stay there. I couldn't sit there, watching her go, knowing my mom was leaving too (in her way) and it got too much for me. Work was my escape. It was my constant. In a way, work was my home, and once I stepped inside Manny's, I felt like a part of me could breathe.

I didn't know how to "just be." I needed movement. I needed busy.

I needed the chaos of Manny's, but as soon as I stepped inside, Brandon was frowning at me. He gave a nod to Derek, our other bartender, before slipping away and heading my way. "Your grandma?"

I shook my head. "I need to work. I'm not scheduled, but do you need the help? I just… I need to not think right now."

He was studying me and frowning at the same time, but then he gave a shrug. A kind smile was next. "I'll never turn you away, Ava. You're family now. I hope you know that."

I choked up, my throat swelling, but I shoved that down and nodded. My head fell down. "Thank you." I moved past him, stowing my purse under the bar in the locked drawer, and after that, it was work mode only.

CHAPTER NINE

Ava

I FELT HIS presence before I saw him, and I only needed to look up once he slid onto his stool.

His eyes were on me, narrowed a little. "Hey."

We hadn't talked since that day, which was a bittersweet moment for me. The first time I got drunk. A friend helped me out, and we talked the entire rest of the day. He made food for me, showed me his beautiful home, one that had me wishing for my "once upon moment" before he gave me a ride home and then saw where I lived.

I was proud of our house. It wasn't much. A bit run-down with peeling paint, a few cracks in the sidewalk, a few rotting porch posts, but it was my home. It would always be my home. Of that, I was very sure. Everything else, not so much, but I'd never have another home like that.

So yeah, when Zeke dropped me off, a part of me could've shriveled up in embarrassment.

That was the younger me. This different me stood proud and I brought him in, showed him around, and we sat and talked even longer in my living room.

I must've fallen asleep because when I woke up, I was in my room and he was gone.

That'd been six days ago.

"Hey." I poured his usual drink.

"How are things?" The way he said it, it could've been casual, but I was starting to know Zeke. He wasn't intending it as casual. He wanted to know.

I shrugged, my throat choking up. "It's going." I started to move away.

He stopped me, putting his hand over mine on the counter. "Ava—"

"I know." I slid my hand out from his. "I don't want to talk about it."

Just then, a presence interrupted us. A female slid onto the stool next to Zeke's and she did it with zest. It was an abrupt and almost coarse sensation, cutting into our moment. "Don't want to talk about what?"

I stepped back, physically and everything else pulling away.

Kit Carlson. She went to school with Zeke. She was in his social group, and she was watching me as she was taking off her jacket with narrowed eyes.

She asked, "What's going on?" She indicated me with a slight head nod. "Ava, right?"

I nodded. I didn't speak. That'd always been my role back in the day, and I was easily stepping back into it. Kit came around, but not that often. After college, she remained local, but I knew she married some big CEO type of guy. I wasn't surprised.

She frowned. "Zeke?"

He was half-turned away, but at her last question, his shoulders drew up, and as they fell, the old Zeke shield was back in place.

He looked back, a half-smirk/half-grin was in place. His eyes lit up, looking mischievous but also dark at the same time, and he nudged her shoulder with his. "Nothing, Carlson. Or am I supposed to be calling you Hughes now?"

She snorted, easing back, and the narrowed eyes relaxed. "You can save that name for a different kind of hangout." Her smile was sly and seductive, and my stomach turned over.

They were sleeping together.

Or they had.

And she was married.

"What would you like to drink?" My voice came out clipped.

Zeke stilled.

She didn't. She threw her hair back and extended her hand, her nails freshly manicured and sparkling pink. "A rosé, and don't let the glass get empty."

Right. It would be one of those nights.

I poured her drink and remained at the opposite end of the bar for the rest of the night, giving Derek her instructions. I felt Zeke's gaze on me, but I heard her laugh, so I knew she was loving Derek's attention. He was a flirt. Wealthy socialites like her were his forte.

I tried not to focus on them, her with Zeke. I did. I really tried, but a few times I glimpsed over and saw how her hand was on Zeke's arm, or his leg, or how their shoulders were touching each other. She rested her head on his arm at one point, half-draped all over him.

My stomach kept churning until I couldn't handle it anymore, and why I was so pissed—I didn't know.

Whatever.

Zeke always slept around. He had a shitty reputation back then, and why would that change now? Even if he'd been kind to me a few times?

Who was I really? Nobody.

I stayed till closing, though Brandon told me I could leave. I didn't.

Derek went home. Brandon headed out. I insisted on doing the cleanup.

I had no clue when Zeke left or if he went with Kit. I went into the back, and they were gone by the time I came back out, but now, when it was almost three because I'd been dawdling, I heard a toilet flush in the back.

The door opened.

Footsteps sounded. Someone was coming down the hallway.

A shiver went down my spine. I thought everyone was gone, and I moved back, I'd already turned the lights off, and flattened myself against the wall. I could dart out the side door and run if I needed, but then the figure showed and I let loose my breath.

It was Zeke.

"I thought you left."

He made his way to me, through and around the tables with their chairs turned upside down. His head cocked to the side. "I was hiding."

A snort left me, one that was a little too relieved if I was being honest with myself. I leaned back against the wall, content to let him keep making his way to me. "Hiding from who?"

He stopped just in front of me, and I could see his eyes from the parking lot light shining through the window. They were clear and very focused on me. He was sober. "You know who I was hiding from."

Kit.

"You and she are none of my business."

He took a step closer, still watching me. So intense. "Maybe I want us to be, maybe for one night?"

My stomach knotted up again. What was he doing?

I swallowed tightly. "I don't know why you'd say that—"

"I don't fuck married women."

My eyes closed. He went right there, straight to the point. I opened them again. "Did you used to?"

"I used to fuck Kit, yes, but not when she was married. I can be called a lot of things, but I'm not a cheater and I'm not disloyal. I like Kit's husband."

"She's a cheater."

"Again. That's not me."

"Are you going to tell her husband she cheats?"

Gah. Why was I involving myself? All my life, I was "less than." I was the working class. I never had money, probably never would. I'll work till I die, but until a week ago, I thought I'd always have my family beside me. I knew different now, and I was breaking.

Right now. Right here.

I was looking at something I wanted, maybe if it was just for a night? Could I?

Did I dare?

I wanted to, so badly.

Zeke sidled closer, his eyes almost glittering from how fierce they were looking at me. "Kit and her husband have an agreement. They both know what they're getting out of their arrangement."

My mouth dried up. "Are those the sort of agreements you like?"

"No." Even closer. I could almost feel him. A slight twitch of an arm and we'd be touching. He added, "Again, a lot of words can be used to describe me, but I'm loyal. Once I care about someone, I lock on and I don't let that person go. It's a fault of mine."

What were we both doing here?

My head was swimming. I was confused.

"How's your grandmother?"

Those words undid me. All the fight left me, almost fleeing in its retreat, and I folded. I began to slump down, but Zeke caught me. He moved in, his arms holding me upright, and his leg pushed against mine.

"She's dying."

"I know. I'm sorry. I should ask, how are *you* doing?"

I shook my head, a tear sliding down my face. "I'm here when I should be there. What does that tell you?"

He took a deep breath and moved in more fully.

His arms went around me and he stood there, holding me. It took me a second to realize he was hugging me.

A sob broke free, and I reached for him, grabbing on to his jacket.

"Why are you being kind to me?"

He angled his head back, searching my face. A new softness came over him and he shifted so he could run a hand over my cheek, wiping my tear away. "Because whether you like it or not, I'm locked on."

That undid me all over again, and I reached for him, just needing him.

I was giving in.

I leaned forward and my lips touched his. A soft graze because did I really want to do this? But it felt so good. *He* felt so good.

I groaned, a carnal need exploding in me, and I had to have more.

Had to.

I needed it like air.

He reached up, cradling my face as he pulled his head back, searching me. He saw something there that made him groan, and his mouth was on mine. He wasn't soft. He was hard, and I wanted that.

Mouth to mouth. I tried to devour him as he was trying to devour me.

Pleasure coursed through my body, filling me up.

I was scrambling, trying to push up his body because I was blind to anything but him.

An ache was deep inside of me as we kissed.

His tongue slid inside, claiming me. I let him. I was claiming him back.

God. Please.

This. So much of this. More.

Ignoring his jacket and shirt, I reached for his jeans and undid the button.

He stilled, his mouth leaving mine, but his head bent next to mine and I felt his breath on my neck.

I kept working, undoing his zipper and I reached inside, finding him already hard and straining against my touch.

He groaned as I wrapped my hand around him and began stroking him. "Fuck, that feels good."

I was beyond words. My head rested on his shoulder as I kept working him. He held me until he stifled a curse, and then he batted my hand away.

I cried out, protesting.

He shifted again, this time he yanked my jeans down, stepping on them to push them the rest of the way. Once they were clear, I was being lifted higher for him.

My legs wound around him.

Then he was there, his cock at my entrance and he surged inside.

We both paused at the feel.

I moaned as he cursed under his breath. "Goddammit." His hand flexed, one cupping my ass and the other bracing us against the wall. "I can't go soft. I can't— tell me that's okay. Jesus, Ava. Tell me that's okay."

"It's okay." I gasped just as he began to move inside of me.

He went hard, surging in, sliding out, and sheathing right back inside of me. *Fuck.*

It was hard and intense. There was nothing smooth about this sex, but I loved it. Wave after wave of pleasure was crashing down on me.

He held me up and I wrapped my legs as tight around his waist as I could, and he pounded me.

I saw stars when I came.

CHAPTER TEN

Ava

THE NEXT MORNING, my phone rang and it was the call.

Come to the nursing home because Grandmum was going. I rolled over in Zeke's bed, dressed, and didn't say a word. When I came out of the bathroom, he was dressed as well and waiting for me.

To this day, I don't know how he knew, but he knew.

He drove me to the nursing home.

He was there. That was the best way to put it. He was, just, there.

I went into the room and sat, holding Grandmum's hand and my mom's. I had no idea how long we sat there, but it felt like time stopped. There was a vacuum around us. It was only us, only what we were going through, and that was all that mattered. The other world kept going, but I ceased paying attention to it.

Me. Mom. Grandmum.

Until Grandmum went.

Zeke drove me places. He brought me food. He was in the background, always. He wasn't always there, but he was mostly there.

My mom noticed him, but she never asked, and he never made a fuss to be introduced.

Grandmum already had everything planned ahead of time, so the funeral was small. A few neighbors came. Some of my mom's friends. But Grandmum kept to herself. She had no siblings, and my mom didn't either, like me.

Zeke didn't go to the funeral. He asked if I wanted him there, but I didn't. I just wanted it small. I wanted to hold my mom's hand the whole time, so that's what I did.

It was a week after when Mom's move was final.

A month later when the house was sold.

I had people who checked on me. My bosses from Manny's. My bosses from the horse stable. My colleagues from both places. Roy even called. There were still others, some people who thought kindly of me from high school. Two of my community college classmates. Flowers and food were sent, but now I was in my apartment and it was the first night.

My first night being alone.

I couldn't handle it.

CHAPTER ELEVEN
Zeke

Ava: Wanna come over?

"Dude." Blaise sat down in the chair next to me, spying my phone. "Who's that? You got a new girl?"

I shot him a grin, but responded to Ava first.

Me: What's up?

I was very aware of my best friend watching me while I was waiting for her response. He didn't get back that often. His schedule playing for one of Hungary's football clubs didn't give him a lot of time in the off-season. But he was here and I got to hang out with him, so we were making the most of it. A night at the house, drinking, playing FIFA, and planning on doing whatever. I loved my boy. Any time spent with him was good for my bro-soul.

But this was Ava.

Ava: Nothing. It's cool. I'll see you at Manny's later. I have a shift tomor-

row.

I frowned because Ava didn't call or text. She didn't ask me to come over, and I was the dumbshit for not putting that together till now.

Pushing up from the chair, I hit dial on my phone and went into the other room.

Her dial tone sounded before it went to voicemail.

"It's Zeke. Tell me what's going on. Call me back, please."

"Holy fuck." Blaise was in the doorway to the living room, his thirty-two-ouncer in hand. His eyes were big. "I have never heard you talk to anyone like that, with that tone of voice. Who the fuck are you and what have you done to my maniac best friend?"

I shot him a grin, but I knew it was distracted and I hit redial.

It went straight to voicemail.

Something was wrong. I felt it in my gut.

"Can you do me a favor?"

Blaise took a step backward. "Now I'm even more alarmed. You look concerned, and I swear, the last time I saw this look on your face was when you thought I was going to do something to land both of us in prison."

I grunted.

My best friend was smart and had hawk-like observation. He'd already deduced someone on the phone was important to me and he'd know within one phone call who it was. But that could blow me up or Ava up, and I didn't know if she wanted that. We had sex once. The next morning, her life shattered and well... Why the fuck was I still standing here?

"I gotta go."

"About time you make that decision."

I ignored him, looking for my wallet and keys. We'd just started drinking, so I was still good to drive. "That was...uh—" Where were my keys?

I heard them jangling as Blaise held them up in the air. He dropped his act, getting all serious. "I know who that was. I know what's been happening in her life, and yeah, you dumbfuck, get your ass over there." He tossed them my way and I caught them, but I half-glared at him.

I said, "Don't say anything—" I started for the door.

"Zeke."

I turned back.

He said, a somewhat sad smile on his face, "People care about her."

I reached for the doorknob and my hand squeezed it tight. "She doesn't think anyone cares about her."

"Then you've got your work cut out for you."

Damn. I loved him for a reason. "Thanks, man." I never told him about Ava, but he knew somehow.

He took a long drag of his beer. "Go. No. Wait. Hold up."

"What?" I half-snarled.

He smirked, laughing. "People care about you too, dumbshit."

I snorted. "Love you, man."

"Love you too."

I was gone after that.

Chapter Twelve

Ava

I WAS IN the bath when I heard an abrupt knocking, then shouting, then a crash, then a stampede as someone was running in my apartment. I started to stand up just as they arrived at the bathroom. The door flung open and Zeke was there, his eyes wild and panicked.

We both stopped in shock, but I remembered I was standing up, in my bath, and I was naked. Yes, we had sex, but that was in the throes of hotness. Me in the bath, not so much hotness happening here.

I dropped back down, thankful for going crazy with the bubbles, and scowled at him. "What are you doing here?"

He was scanning the room, raking a hand through his hair. He didn't answer right away.

"What are you looking for?"

"Booze. A razor. I don't know." Not seeing any, his eyes jerked back to me. The wildness had not dissipated. "Are you okay?"

"Yes! I'm in the bathtub." I was seething, embarrassed, and happy he came over. How messed up was I? "What are you doing here?"

He stepped inside, moving to sit on the closed toilet. He leaned forward, but he wasn't watching me. I could relax a little, moving farther back. He said, "You never text me or call. I didn't think about that."

I bit down on my bottom lip. Why was my heart skipping a little here? "That's fine. I was…" Terrified. Feeling crazy. "Bored."

His eyes shot to mine, and narrowed. "You're lying."

I looked away.

"Look." I could hear him shifting so he could see me more fully. "Blaise is in town. That's the only reason I didn't race over here. I don't get to see him that often anymore, but I should've just come over right away. You sent that one text and I was already here. If that makes sense?"

It had me feeling a certain way. A good way.

I didn't tell him that, though. I moved the water around a little. "I didn't mean to interrupt your bromance time with Blaise Devroe. I know how much you love him."

I risked a look and saw the slight grin on his face. His eyes were almost firmly trained on where my breasts were located under the water. I sank a little lower, and his gaze jumped back to my face. His grin just widened. "He told me to get my ass over here."

I almost hiccupped. "What?"

"Huh?" His gaze went back to my boobs.

"Zeke!"

"Yeah?" His gaze never moved.

"Your best friend knows about you and me?" And also, what did he know? Thinking on it, what *was* there even *to* know?

"I guess. Look." He stood, taking out his phone, his wallet, and his keys. He put them all on the bathroom counter. His shoes and socks were next.

"What are you doing?"

"That's a big tub." His pants came off.

"Zeke!"

His shirt, and whooooooaaaaa… Zeke worked out. Zeke worked out a lot. He was fully muscled and his stomach was all sorts of hard. I had not fully appreciated his physique during the one time we had sex or the hugs or even the cuddling we did that night. My mouth was salivating because I was all sorts of appreciating it now.

He was in the tub in the next second, and I half-shrieked, scooting back as far as I could. It was a big tub, but not that big. Before I could move anymore, he reached over, took hold of my waist, and I was lifted in the air, and then he maneuvered us so I was between his legs, my back to his chest, and I could sink down in the water.

Oooooh.

This was… This was amazing, and relaxing, and then his hand began moving over my leg and I was burning up from a whole different reason. "Zeke!"

He chuckled right behind my ear, and even that, with his baritone, sent sensations through me. I didn't know how to handle this, any of this.

"This is way better." He moved again, and I felt him press a kiss to the back of my neck. He began lifting water over me, moving it around, and as he kept kissing my neck, as I let him keep kissing my neck, he began to wash me at the same time.

If my grandmum were alive and if my mom were still living with me in the house, and this had happened, I would've considered this day heaven. And at the reminders of all the changes in my life, I tensed.

Zeke lifted his head. "What's wrong?"

I sighed, settling back into him. "I wanted you to come over because this is my first night here. I've never not lived with someone—"

His arm muscles bulged, on both arms. He asked, cutting in roughly, "Do you like it?"

"What?"

"Do you like living alone?"

"I haven't experienced it. I can't answer that."

"Move in with me."

"What?!" I jerked forward and twisted so I could see him.

As I was learning, Zeke just took care of the problem.

He lifted me up, in all my naked gloriousness, and flipped me around so as I came back down, I was fully straddling him. We both paused at the feeling of him against me, but then I leaned back. "I just moved in here."

He shrugged, his gaze skirting from my mouth to my arm. He began tracing circles on my sides. "You don't like living alone. I didn't know that was the issue." His gaze moved to my eyes. He was somber, almost earnest. "I have that huge house. You could take an entire floor if you want. The basement is renovated to be its own living space. You could have that or the second floor. I don't care. I don't really like living alone either."

I didn't say anything for a moment. "Are you serious?"

He nodded. "Yeah. I'm always around people or usually. High school, I was always partying. College, I was either at the frat house or I was with Blaise or his brother's group. I bought this house a year ago, and I get it. It sucks living alone. Move in. You can be my roommate."

"You are serious."

A second nod, and his mouth moved into a serious line. "Sex or not, you'd be the perfect roommate. And I mean that. If we're not having sex, that's cool."

"I just moved in. I paid for the first month and I signed a lease."

He leaned back, a cocky smirk appearing. "I know a lawyer. He'll break your lease before he's even had breakfast."

I didn't know who he was talking about, but I was surprised, but not at the same time. I let out a short laugh.

"What?"

I shook my head. "You're flashy to me. You live in the fast lane, and me, I'm a tortoise in the slow lane. Sometimes I forget what your life is like when you're with me."

"Ava."

He sounded so serious.

"What?" I asked.

"You're so clueless about how many people care about you. I don't know if I should find it adorable or concerning. I think it's both for me."

I tensed, but shook my head. He was being his crazy self right now.

"How about it?" His hand went to the back of my neck, and as he pulled my head toward his, his hand slid up into my hair. He cupped the back of my head. "Wanna be my roommate?"

My breath caught and held in my chest. That was nuts. Me in Zeke's huge mansion? "You bought that place?"

He nodded, leaning even farther. "Yep. With my own money. No inheritance, nothing from my folks. I think it drove my dad crazy, but made him hella proud at the same time. My house is almost as big as theirs."

"What do you do for a job? We've actually never had this conversation."

"I do stocks. I'm a math genius, but no one knows that, and I'm really good at stocks."

I remembered his place. He must've been.

He was grinning again, eyeing my mouth. "How about it? Roommate?"

I groaned, but I must've made the decision because the resistance was gone.

I'd lived my life a certain way for so long. Living with Zeke, no matter what came, was going to be something so different, I was thinking I was desperate for that change.

"This is so insane."

"But?" He looked up, his eyes were dancing. "We can even give my house a name. Aveke. Ava and Zeke together. How about it?"

"But." Oh God. I just moved in. "You have to help me move my stuff."

"I'll get some movers." And as soon as he said those words, his mouth was on mine.

It didn't move away for a long time, a really, really long time.

✧ ✧ ✧

MY EYES OPENED. 3:33 a.m. Zeke had fallen asleep next to me.

I had absolutely no idea what we were doing. Sex? Roommates? Were we dating? I hadn't a clue, but I smiled and my chest felt lighter, and for the first time in a while, I felt the first stirrings of being okay.

I'd have to see, though.

Until then, I curled up next to Zeke and he reached for me in his sleep. He tucked me into his side.

Yes. I could start to like this a whole lot. I'd worry later if this was either going to shatter me or heal me.

I was going to believe in the latter.

For right now, that was more than good enough for me.

✧   ✧   ✧

I hope you enjoyed Zeke and Ava's short story! This will be turned into a long novella.

For more stories, like Blaise's in Rich Prick, go to www.tijansbooks.com.

A Summer in Paris

Jennifer Probst

I'VE CHANGED MY mind. I'm not going."

Allegra paced back and forth, chewing on her thumbnail and hoping her mother wouldn't challenge her. Yes, it had been her dream to travel overseas and learn to cook. Yes, she'd be crazy to cancel her spot to learn under some of the most talented chefs in Paris for the summer. Yes, she was just getting cold feet and giving in to doubt regarding her abilities, her future, and her choices.

Yes to all of it.

She still wasn't going.

Her mother studied her expression as if trying to gauge the proper tactic to employ the best results. Allegra refused to let her see too much. They'd gotten close over the past few years, but she also knew her mother would play hardball when forced. No way would her Mom allow her to walk away from a dream she'd been working hard for. Somehow, Allegra had to convince her it was better to delay.

"Why don't you want to go?"

It was early evening and Mom was having another client crisis that needed attention. Allegra had shot out her statement while her mother walked into her office, hoping work distracted her, but Mom spun back around and slid onto the dining stool, propping her fingers together as if she was ready for an all night discussion.

Great. She'd underestimated Mom again. In the old days, her mother would have never been able to pull herself away from a big account. After their trip to Italy three years ago, everything changed and now all that attention was razored in on her only daughter.

Was it wrong to wish just this once she'd be able to fly under the radar?

Allegra let out a sigh and said the only excuse possible. "Just because."

Mom shook her head. "That answer worked once when you were four. Try again."

Allegra groaned. "I think it's too much for me right now. I mean, did you see how many students signed up for this? The competition is insane—and some classmates aren't even talking to me anymore because they're pissed I got in and they didn't."

"That's how the world runs sometimes, sweetheart. It's not pretty, but it also shows quickly who your real friends are."

"I think senior year would be better for me. I'll be closer to graduation and can explore opportunities where I can get a job right away."

"Fair enough, but there's no guarantee you'll get picked next year." Her mom's tone was gentle but firm. "This is your time, Allegra. It's one summer and won't interfere with your studies. This is what you've been working so hard for. Don't let it pass you by." A shadow flickered over her face. "Life is too short. I think we all learned that fact in Italy, didn't we?"

Yes. That magical summer had changed her life. She'd fallen in love, discovered a passion for cooking as her career, and gotten closer to her grandmother and mom. After that awful cancer scare with Nonni, Allegra was stunned to watch her regain her health and begin going on travel tours on her own, and with her friend, Milton.

Allegra shook her head at her mother's words. "I need more time," she said stubbornly. "I don't think I'm ready."

Her mother's face softened. "You're scared. But you're ready."

Allegra stopped pacing as the words hit through the hard shell she'd tried to build. Hating the inner anxiety and doubts even after she'd been able to meet every challenge at the Culinary Institute, she allowed herself to tell the truth. "If I go to Paris, and fail, I'll disappoint everyone."

The smile that wreathed her mother's face surprised her. "No. If you go to Paris and fail, you will learn valuable lessons. Then you will pick yourself up off the ground, tilt your chin high, and try again. Don't ever expect to succeed at everything you try or you'll be disappointed. Do you think I built a successful company without a shitload of errors and humiliations? Do you think I don't look back and wince? But guess what? I'm also proud of those errors because of my success. It wasn't easy. And if you go to Paris, it won't be easy either. But you can do it."

"You said shit."

Her mother laughed and Allegra laughed with her. Her chest didn't feel as tight anymore, even though she still wasn't sure. But dumping on her Mom made her feel better. "I'll think about it."

"Good." She wrinkled her brow. "Okay to order pizza tonight? I'm fried."

"I never get sick of pizza even though Naples ruined me forever."

A dreamy expression crossed her mom's face. "Do you think Enzo can smuggle them on the plane home for us? Kind of like Uber Eats International?"

Allegra grinned. "Great idea, Mom. I think you need to start a new business. When is he coming home?"

"End of the week."

Mom had fallen in love with their Italian tour guide, Enzo, during the trip. For the first time in her life, work became less important and her focus changed. Enzo eventually left Italy to settle in New York and they'd finally gotten engaged. He traveled back and forth to see his family but this past week Mom had too much stuff going on to get away.

Allegra was excited to watch her mother not only gain happiness on a personal level, but actual calm. Less like a dizzy hamster spinning on a wheel. And she loved the way they looked at one another. Like a secret handshake, their gazes could meet across the room and there was a spark that made Allegra long to experience it for herself. Once, she had, but it wasn't meant to be. The past two relationships she'd been involved with had fallen short, but as Mom reminded her, she was too young to really want to settle when she had a burgeoning career in front of her.

Still, she always wondered if anyone would ever compare with Ian.

The thought of her first lover and dear friend made her heart ache, but she pushed the feeling aside. They hadn't spoken in a while. The man she'd met on her trip decided to enter the priesthood and was focused on his own journey. Allegra knew his commitment to God and serving others was needed in the world, but selfishly, she wished he still belonged to her.

With a sigh, Allegra trudged into her room, slipped on her AirPods, and cranked up some music to drown out her thoughts.

✧   ✧   ✧

CHEF ARDOIN SHOOK his head so hard, Allegra wondered if his hat would fall off. But no, the tall head piece that both intimidated and made her starstruck didn't budge. "No, no, you need to whisk faster as you pour. Why isn't your pan hot? How do you expect to create a flavorful sauce if you can't even prep correctly?"

Allegra tamped down her embarrassment and fought off the flush threatening to flame her cheeks. She felt her fellow students staring—some in sympathy and a few in glee. Everyone took their turn under the chef's private tutelage, which was both a curse and a blessing. Was she wrong to think her spot in the hot seat was meaner than most?

She risked a quick glance at his hard profile, his thin nose a sharp blade on his face. Steely gray eyes stared back at her, but that gaze also held years of experience and time spent exactly where she was beginning. There was no place in the kitchen for weakness. It was a good reminder.

"Sorry, Chef," she said, easing the heat up on the flame. Her fingers cramped a bit as she mixed the liquid faster, quickly tasting and adding a few more seasonings under his hard stare.

The lesson was long, grueling and left her in doubt of her talent. By the time the students were released from the famous Le Cordon Bleu and headed back to the apartments, Allegra was tired of pretending not to care. Yes, it was the start of summer and she'd only been in class two weeks, but she was homesick and heartsick.

She was also beginning to regret coming to Paris.

"Don't worry," Evelyn said, patting her shoulder. "He treats everyone the same. You're not special."

Allegra gave her new friend a weak smile. "Oh, I know. I think I'm just having a hard time adjusting. I'm sure it will be fine."

Evelyn had family in Paris and many of the other CIA students were well traveled. The past two weekends they'd all split up and Allegra was left alone. She'd walked the streets, grabbed a croissant at a pâtisserie, and tried to enjoy her solitude, but ended up back in her bed, snuggled under the covers.

Ugh, she hated being a loser. She was finally living her dream and figured she'd be endlessly happy from now on. But she was beginning to discover some hard growing pains and a strange loneliness, even when surrounded by people.

"Hey, we're going for drinks. Come with us?"

Allegra craved a safe place to lick her wounds, but forced herself to accept the invite. "Sure. I'm in."

The night turned out fun, but she felt a bit outside the group and wished some of her other friends at the Culinary had been able to join her in Paris. They kept telling her how lucky she was, which she knew. She only wished she believed in her talent like the teachers who'd chosen her.

They walked home, a few of the students tipsy. Her phone beeped. She slid it from her pocket, expecting to see a text from her mom, but the words made her stop short.

How are you? It's been too long. Enjoying your summer?

Ian.

Fingers trembling, she shot off a reply with no hesitation. *Was wondering where you've been! Summer has been different. Guess where I am?*

Italy with your Mom and Enzo?

No. Paris. At Le Cordon Bleu for cooking school.

She waited for the three dots but they didn't come. They reached their apartment but she stayed outside, staring at her screen, heart beating fast.

The phone rang and she quickly picked up.

"Hello?"

"I can't believe you're in Paris!" His voice was warm and familiar, like a soft blanket wrapped around her in a tight hug. "I knew you'd get picked to go. Didn't I tell you?"

She laughed, her spirits already lightening. "Yeah, you did."

"Tell me everything. How is it? Are the chefs mean like I imagine?"

"Chef Ardoin is definitely scary but also a good teacher. We're working on sauces, which isn't my best talent."

"Then you'll get better and close the gap." A pause settled over the line, filled with emotion. "I've missed hearing your voice, Allegra. There's been a lot going on here. I'm working with another priest to help more refugees. We're raising money to build homes where they can be safe."

Grief and pride mixed within. Ian was making a difference in the world day by day, dedicating his life to both religion and humanitarian purposes. Emotion choked her throat. "That's amazing, Ian. Times are so hard lately, with too much bad going on in the world. Do you ever get worried evil will eventually overrun everything?"

She wondered about that sometimes. Sitting in the dark, watching the news, realizing she was helpless to fight so much.

"Never," he said simply. "All it takes is one good person to make a difference."

Allegra gave a soft sigh. "Then I'll try and believe that, too."

"Good. Tell me about your cooking. What have you been making?"

They talked for a long time. She confessed her doubts and loneliness. He told her of his frustration sometimes with the way the church worked, and the struggle to trust the process. The night closed around her. The stars twinkled. The moon glowed. They shared stories and caught up and when the conversation finally ended, there was a feeling of peace inside of her she realized she'd missed. Ian soothed that part of her heart.

Maybe he always would.

"You better get to sleep. You need all your focus for Chef Ardoin tomorrow."

A smile curved her lips. "Yeah, I need to toughen up."

"No, Allegra. You just need to believe in yourself like I do. You need to trust you are exactly where you should be for a reason."

The words touched her. Grateful tears stung her eyes. "Thanks. It's almost a full moon."

"I know. That's why I called. I looked up and felt you needed me."

She choked out a laugh. "Stop being so sweet and getting me mushy."

"Sorry. Go kick some cooking ass and show them all what you can do. How long will you be in Paris?"

"Till mid August."

"Then I'll come and visit you. If you promise to cook for me."

"I'll always cook for you, Ian. And yes, come visit."

"Good night."

"'Night."

She took a deep breath and tilted her head up. The moon was ripe and glowing with an inner radiance that seemed to sink deep inside of her.

Allegra went to bed with a smile on her face.
And knew she was exactly where she should be.

✧   ✧   ✧

I hope you enjoyed this short bonus story from *Our Italian Summer*! If you'd like to read the book and experience Allegra's extraordinary journey through Italy, go here: Our Italian Summer (jenniferprobst.com).

Daddy's Little One Night Stand

Honey Meyer

CHAPTER ONE

T HE MODERN WORLD didn't have a ton of use for men who were good at killing. Legal use, anyway. That was one shitty thing about leaving the Navy. He'd been good at that, took pride in serving his country and being there for his teammates. He'd known his place, worked hard, honed his body and his mind until he was almost a machine. Out here in the civilian world? That was a whole different story.

Sometimes Knox thought he shouldn't have left. He could've been a lifer—stayed in until they forced him to take a desk job or he got killed. But he liked to do things on his own terms and ETSing when it was his call instead of an ugly surprise seemed like a better option.

Didn't make trying to fit in any easier, not even after three years out. He'd bounced from place to place, job to job looking for…someplace, something that felt as good to him as active duty had. Hadn't found it yet, but he'd keep looking. Tomorrow. Nah, make that Monday.

Tonight, he was enjoying a night out with some of his buddies from the service. They'd all finally finished their tours, most of them had found something to do, and they'd come up to Anchorage to celebrate one of their own's marriage.

Wasn't a surprise that Gavin had found a girl he wanted to settle down with. No, Gavin Bayard was as loyal and true as the day was long, even up here during Alaskan summers. And Gwennie was a woman worth settling down for—the curvy blonde was as sweet and soft as a cream puff. He knew she was tough, too, though. Had to be if you were a pediatric oncology nurse.

Jesus, he'd rather be taking heavy enemy fire than take care of sick kids all day. Severed limbs and blown-out skulls of grown-ass men he could deal with. Kindergartners with cancer he could not. Well, Gavin would take care of her. That's what Gavin was good at.

And him? He had other skills, some of which he planned to make good use of tonight.

Their band of brothers and Gwennie were spending the evening at Covert, the best fetish club in Anchorage. A damn sight nicer than most of the ones he'd been to in his travels, Knox was pretty pleased to be a member here. Gladly paid his dues even though he was currently doing a stint at a cannery on Kodiak Island. Then again, he'd kept his apartment in Anchorage too. Not a hardship when the cannery was covering room and board and he was receiving some real fat paychecks from pulling a shit ton of overtime.

The work was boring as fuck but easy as hell compared to life in the Navy so he'd do it for a while until he got sick of the smell. Then he'd find something else to do. Maybe even give in to Taj and let his buddy hire him to work at his upscale security firm. For now he'd rather be working the slime table at the cannery than babysitting Hollywood brats or making sure some billionaire didn't step in dog shit. How Taj had the patience for that bull hockey, he didn't know.

Even though Knox didn't mind the noise and the hustle and the long hours of his current gig, it was nice to be able to take a couple days off here and there and have someplace to crash when he was coming to one of his favorite places on earth. Especially now that Gavin and Gwennie were in town. They'd moved up here a few months ago.

Their group had commandeered a few tables in the central room of the club, sipping on a beer or pop and shooting the shit while more people arrived. Like the membership of most kink clubs he'd been to, the frequent flyers of Covert tended to be night owls.

He didn't mind the wait. It was good to catch up with his buddies. The six of them had been through hell and back, completing missions under conditions most people couldn't imagine. And unlike their fallen comrades, they'd lived to tell the tales. Looking around the tables, Knox knew he was looking at more than friends; he was looking at family.

✧   ✧   ✧

LUJHA FULLER SHIVERED as she shrugged off her coat in the anteroom of Covert. They did a good job of keeping the rest of the club warm but it was always unpleasant to come in from the frigid outdoors and still be kind of chilly. Especially since she was usually wearing something skimpy underneath her calf-length coat. Like she was tonight.

She had learned well enough to wear snow boots and bring her heels with her though. Only made that mistake once. Fucking Alaska. Why had she come here again?

Oh right, to get away from that abusive shitstain of a now-ex-husband and her parents who'd told her to suck it up. Well, she wouldn't. If she was going to get hit, it was going to be on her terms, and it would be done by a man who could get her off afterward.

Not like that limp-dicked fuckwad Aaron. It wasn't so much the limp dick that had been the problem. He could've tried some Viagra for god's sake. Or a toy. Heaven knew it didn't take a factory-direct cock to get a person off. There were myriad other ways he could've gone about pleasuring her. His hands, or Christ, his mouth. But he'd only used his mouth to tell her she was fat and stupid and ugly and a fucking embarrassment and that's why he couldn't get hard. Then he'd use those hands to hit her for it. And the one time she'd suggested using a dildo to help her climax he'd backhanded her so hard he'd chipped her tooth.

Did she want to live with that for the next fifty years? She did not. And even though she watched true crime shows religiously, she didn't think she could get away with murder. So blowing out of town after she had her college degree in hand it had been. Like, a real degree. A BS in accounting. The one she'd painstakingly earned in secret after realizing Aaron was a fucking monster and no one was going to save her but herself.

And now she was here, toeing off her snow boots to replace with her platform Mary Janes that looked so much cuter with her ass-skimming plaid jumper and white thigh highs and her Peter Pan collared school girl shirt, the placket of which was being strained by her tits. They looked phenomenal in this push-up bra if she did say so herself. And she fucking well would since that was another thing Aaron had beaten her for. Wasn't her fault people couldn't keep their eyes off her cleavage.

She checked in with Tryce at the desk, and after putting her bag in her locker, headed to the main room to see who was here, what was going on. More often than not she made plans with someone to scene or meet up but she hadn't been sure she'd make it tonight so her dance card was empty. Hopefully there would be a familiar face or an intriguing stranger she could monopolize for the night.

There were already sounds of people enjoying themselves coming from the long hallway that ran from the central space to the back of the building. Private-ish rooms that could be booked in advance, she probably wouldn't be playing in any of those tonight. But maybe in one of the two bigger rooms that flanked that hallway.

Or possibly tonight would be the night that she would meet her dream daddy and he'd bring her upstairs where there were a couple of small classrooms, a principal's office, a locker room, a few nurseries, one larger med-fet room with curtains that could be drawn around the exam tables, and one smaller exam room. Lujha would take any one of those, please and thank you. More likely she'd end up cuffed to a Saint Andrew's cross or strapped to a spanking bench down here. Still good.

Not quite what her little heart desired most of all, but she would take it and be grateful. Thankful for pleasure, freely and joyfully given, happy with the bruises that would bloom overnight on parts of her body that she'd consented to being hit.

There were a few familiar faces in the main lounge, although no one she was particularly excited to see. No one who she ached to play with again or who she'd been eyeing since she'd joined the club about three months before.

And then… Yeah, then. There was a group of six men lounging around a few tables they'd pushed together. One of the men had a woman perched on his lap and the picture made her green with envy. The blonde was clearly a little—the frilly dress and lace-cuffed ankle socks plus the pigtails and the adorable barrettes in her hair said so—and the man whose thick thighs she was gracing obviously adored her.

Lujha wanted that for herself so badly that watching them was painful, like looking directly into the sun. The other men in the group weren't helping matters any. She could tell from a glance they were all current or former military—growing up near an Army base would make a girl a good judge of these things. While they weren't all her type, there was something compelling about the group of them.

Especially the one who'd just caught her staring. Dammit.

CHAPTER TWO

*H*ERE COMES TROUBLE.

That's what he'd thought the second the stacked brunette had sashayed into the room in a school girl getup that made him want to bite his fist. The lust coupled with a bone-deep, oh-shit sensation only intensified when he saw how she was looking at Gavin and Gwennie. Yep, that girl was looking for a daddy.

While Knox would be happy to take her over his knee and spank that generous ass of hers, he didn't think that was all she was looking for. Nah, that girl looked like she could get spanked any day of the week and twice on Sundays. What she looked like she yearned for was to be *loved*, and that was not a thing he did.

"See something you like?"

"Shut up, Taj."

"What? I'm not supposed to say anything when you're practically drooling over that woman like she's fucking filet mignon?"

"Look, if you'd been eating, breathing, and dreaming about salmon for three months you'd be salivating over some grade A beef too, alright?"

Taj snorted. Asshole.

"So are you going to go get her or what?"

"First of all, it's not that easy."

"For a dreamboat like you? Sure is. Next, motherfucker."

Why was he friends with this jackwagon again? There was the whole saved-each-other's-bacon-more-times-than-he-could-count thing, and oh yeah, Taj was one of the smartest people he knew even if the guy looked like he spent all his time pumping iron and downing raw eggs and protein shakes. Who did he think he was, a cross between Bobby fucking Fischer and goddamn Mr. Olympia?

For all that Taj was an annoying douche canoe, he wasn't wrong about it being relatively easy for Knox to pick up women. He wasn't going to be Sexiest Man Alive like Dane Henley or anything, but he did alright for himself. Dropping that he'd been a SEAL never hurt either. Got him a thank-you-for-your-service blow job more often than you'd think.

But that's what was giving him pause. Some women would get on their knees because they liked a man in uniform, or invite him between their thighs because he took good care of himself and they probably figured he could blow their backs out. They were right. He was a damn good lay, especially for the ladies who enjoyed a solid pounding. This girl though?

"Second, look at her. She's going all gaga over Gavin and Gwennie. If that's what she's after, I'm not her guy."

"So maybe she's looking for Mr. Right," Taj mused, thick arms crossed over his chest. "Doesn't mean she wouldn't settle for a Mr. Right Now tonight."

Huh. It was annoying when Hovick had a point, and part of what made him so throat-punch-worthy was that he often did.

"So why don't *you* shoot your shot?" he asked his obnoxious friend. "You're an ugly bastard but put a paper bag over your head and I'm sure she won't mind."

He wasn't sure ugly was the word, but Taj had a certain effect on women. The majority of them found the massive guy intimidating if not downright terrifying—he couldn't blame them because the dude was six-six and looked like he could bench press a bus. But the rest wanted to climb the rough-hewn guy like a tree. Whatever floats their boats.

"Nah," Taj said, tipping his chair back. "After she gave us all the once over, she's been eyeing you when hearts aren't beating out of her eyes looking at the happy couple."

Knox could argue but why? Especially when the brunette's gaze did wander back to him and pink washed over her cheeks when she noticed him looking back.

Fine then. He'd give it a shot, and if she wasn't down to fuck or play or both then he'd come back and chill with the guys and Gwennie some more. And if she was? So much the better.

✧   ✧   ✧

SON OF A bitch.

If someone had put those six guys in a line-up and asked which of them she wanted to bring to her bed it would be the one who was walking toward her. Too good-looking by half, and judging by the smirk on his face and the strut in his step, he knew it too.

Light brown hair, bright blue eyes, a dusting of scruff that accentuated his jaw, and clothes that were snug enough to show off how he bulged in all the right places? Yeah, he was a womanizer. Playboy. Skirt chaser. Casanova. Whatever you wanted to call a guy who was looking to carve a few more notches into his bedpost.

Good news for him then, because Lujha wanted to be carved.

Yes, for sure she wanted a daddy. A real one. One who would cuddle and coddle her, call her precious and dote on her. One who would brush her hair and look after her, put her to bed when she was sleepy, and wanted more than anything for her to be her best self.

And yes, fine, fine, perhaps he would also take a hairbrush to her backside if she misbehaved and would do filthy things to her that she'd really enjoy but claim she didn't. Maybe he'd plug her ass and clamp her nipples and lap at her pussy until she begged him to stop and he wouldn't. Not until he'd tongue-fucked her to an orgasm so intense she'd be hoarse the next day from screaming his praises.

Or whatever. Not like she'd thought about this much. Or at all. Definitely hadn't fantasized about any or all of that while she'd rubbed one out laying beside her truly reprehensible husband who'd only begun to show his true colors once they'd tied the knot.

This guy? Would never come near her to ask for her number, never mind offer a ring. Nah, all he wanted was to fuck around and find out what exactly she had under this pervy outfit she had on, and that was great.

Someday her daddy would come and that would be a wonderful day. Until then? She'd get railed by fuckboys until she couldn't walk straight. Hopefully this soldier, sailor, airman, marine, whatever the hell he was, would not only have a dagger behind all that swagger but would also know a quirt from a tawse and she'd be able to indulge her masochistic streak before he rearranged her internal organs. She'd be pretty mad if he was all muscle and no hustle but there was a wolfish look in his eyes that hinted at a beast behind those baby blues. Perfect.

"Evening," he said as he rocked on up, not even bothering to pretend he wasn't looking her up and down.

That was fine. She gave him the same assessing once over before responding.

"What branch?"

He blinked and she was a little surprised it didn't take more to stun him. But the haze cleared quickly.

"That obvious, huh?"

"Half of you are still sporting high-and-tights, so yeah."

He gave her a half-cocked smile that made her stomach flip and said he appreciated her savvy.

"Navy," he confirmed, and held out a hand. "Chief Petty Officer Knox Truett at your service."

Already had better manners than Aaron. Bigger, warmer hands too. If the strength in his grip weakened her knees, what would happen when that broad palm made contact with her ass as he spanked her? What about when he thrust those thick fingers inside her pussy?

Worth finding out.

"You can call me Lulu. Want to play?"

CHAPTER THREE

S O MAYBE HE'D been wrong about this woman. Lulu. Or maybe Taj was right
and she wanted a man like Gavin in the long run but she'd settle for a man like
him for a sprint.

Why did that maybe bother him a little? He should be relieved, so he fixed his
smile he could tell had faltered for a split-second.

"I sure do like the look of you," he told her, and that was god's honest truth.
"Let's have a seat and we can figure out if we have more in common than an itch to
scratch. Can I get you a drink first?"

"No. You sure your friends won't mind you abandoning them to play twenty
questions with me?"

"Those guys? They're rooting for me to play a lot more than twenty questions."

They found an empty table and Lulu didn't even let him pull out her chair.
Okay. He was capable of charming the pants off women but it kinda seemed like
that wouldn't be necessary tonight.

Once they'd sat down, she folded her hands on the table and looked more like
a lawyer negotiating a contract than a little girl longing for a daddy.

"Are you a member here?" Before he could answer, she seemed to remember
something, and added, "I know they train you boys to have nice manners but I
swear to god if you call me 'ma'am' I'll kick your shin and these shoes have heavy
soles so it'll hurt."

Yeah, little miss Lulu wasn't anything like he'd been expecting.

"I am, but I haven't been here much in the past few months. Been working
down in Kodiak. You?"

"Mm-hmm, but only for a few months now. No wonder I haven't run into
you before. Pretty sure I'd remember that."

"I definitely would."

He tried and failed not to look at her chest when he said that but Lulu didn't
seem to mind. At least she didn't frown or kick him under the table. No, she was all
brisk but flirty business as she went through things that were on and off the table,
safewords, hard limits. He definitely didn't have to worry he was seducing an
innocent. This girl knew what was up.

He ticked off his own limits, went over safer sex practices, and they exchanged
cell phones to review each others' latest STI results. He didn't mean to pry but she
must've known he'd see her name on the EMR screen. Lujha. Her name was Lujha
Fuller and according to her records she was twenty-eight. Made him feel a little
dirty knowing he had almost a decade on her but not necessarily in a bad way. Not
like anyone was going to mistake him for her father or anything. He didn't know if
he could handle that.

"So are you ready now or do you need to tell your friends you'll be busy for a
bit?"

If he had his way, he'd tell his buddies he'd see them tomorrow morning at the
church but he couldn't quite get a read on Lulu. She'd defied his expectations and
now he felt a little off balance. It's not that he minded her pragmatic approach—
hell, he was glad she wasn't looking to him for romance or devotion because he
didn't have any of that to give—but...

Eh, he was probably overthinking. Or maybe being some kind of arrogant and sexist prick, assuming she'd have some kind of feelings toward him other than wanting to get in his pants. He should knock that off.

"I'll let them know. You could meet them if you wanted to."

"I don't," Lulu said with a shrug. "I'm going to grab a couple waters and wipe down that corner bench. Don't take too long, sailor."

And off the fuck she went, tiny plaid skirt just barely covering her backside. Alright then.

✧   ✧   ✧

SHE APPRECIATED THAT Knox didn't take all damn night checking in with his friends. Appreciated even more that when he came back to the spanking bench she'd claimed, he was toting a black duffel bag. Aka toy bag, aka domly bag of fun.

Did tops ever get those mixed up like people did with the practically identical black and navy blue suitcases everyone had at airport baggage claims? It would be really awkward to go home with someone else's sex toys. Eh, not her sex toys, not her problem. All of hers were tucked safely inside her nightstand. The ones that would fit anyway. The rest were in a bottom drawer where they would stay until it was their turn in the rotation.

"So, shall we?"

She could tell Knox didn't know quite what to make of her, although he seemed to like her just fine. Amused, bemused, confused, didn't matter to her as long as she got her ass beat and an orgasm out of the deal. If this man kinked half as good as he looked, he'd feature in her fantasies for weeks if not months. Maybe even be a regular play partner if she got lucky, although maybe he was headed back down to Kodiak. Or somewhere else entirely.

She'd found Alaska to be full of wanderers, nomads, people who were looking for a place where they belonged. Sometimes Anchorage was a base camp of sorts on their way out to the bush, sometimes it was a pit stop to another place entirely. Sometimes it was like the Hotel California and people who'd meant to leave long ago died here. Lujha hadn't figured out what it would be for her yet.

"We shall," he agreed.

She expected him to pat the lower level of the bench, tell her to kneel on the padded vinyl and bend over. Rest her chest and arms on the upper platform. But the man confounded her by sitting on the lower bench himself and circling a hand around her wrist. Tugging her closer until the fronts of her thighs pressed up against the side of one of his.

Lujha didn't think of herself as petite by any means—she was five-six and had sturdy peasant thighs—but Knox made her feel small somehow. It was just that he looked like he did squats with a moose on his back. That's what she told herself anyway when her breath caught. It had nothing to do with the way he was looking at her, the intensity of his attention.

Why was he putting her over his knee? Did he not understand how spanking benches worked for fuck's sake? She'd chosen this piece of furniture so she wouldn't have to be this close to him and now he was fucking up her shit. How dare. But there was also no way she was going to stop him.

No, she let him guide her until she was draped over his lap and his massive hands were rubbing her lower back and upper thighs.

"We haven't played together before so I'll check in more than usual. Feedback's welcome but don't get mouthy, you understand?"

He swatted her gently just under the hem of her skirt to emphasize his point and she had to bite back a moan. Had to bite her tongue even harder on the "Daddy" that wanted to escape her mouth. But she managed the "Yes, sir" they'd agreed on.

Knox didn't waste any time after that. Flipped up her skirt, started covering her butt cheeks with firm, measured spanks. Efficient and methodical in a way she adored, Lujha could feel herself getting wet already and her skin wasn't even stinging.

After a few minutes of the same treatment with a steady increase in the harshness of the blows, he rubbed her cheeks.

"How you doing, Lulu? Scale of one to ten."

"Two, sir."

Two on her pain scale anyway. She couldn't quite describe the rest of the effect he was having on her. Probably because it didn't make any fucking sense. He'd been spanking her for like five seconds, why should that mean anything? Chief Petty Officer Truett wasn't special.

"Good girl."

She always liked it when people told her she was a good girl. Uh-huh. She was probably just imagining that it made her want to purr and spread her legs more than usual. It wasn't that he murmured those words at some magical pitch that resonated with the tuning fork of her arousal.

Jesus, Lujha, calm down.

Maybe she was ovulating. There was no other explanation for the excessive horniness coursing through her.

"Sounds like you should ask me to take your panties down, little girl. You said you wanted to be at a seven or eight and I don't see that happening without me spanking your bare bottom."

People had said things a million times filthier than that to her and she'd rolled her eyes. Maybe yawned. This fucking guy had her *whimpering*. The nerve.

"Come on, now. Ask."

Humiliation was a hard limit for her. She'd had enough of that to last three lifetimes from Aaron. She knew what her ex-husband had done wasn't the same as the erotic, playful, and above all consensual way kinksters poked at those tender spots, but she didn't think she'd be able to touch that particular kink with a whaling harpoon.

But Knox's coaxing insistence didn't feel like the scalding singe of humiliation that would leave her scarred. More like the coiling, sultry heat of embarrassment that flushed her face and also sent blood sluicing through her veins to make her breasts and her pelvis feel swollen and tight. Sensitive, alive.

She couldn't hold her hips still as she squeezed her eyes shut tight and fairly begged, "Please, sir."

"Please what?" he pressed.

Ugh, why couldn't he just hit her? Hard? But the truth was that this delicious agony was better, even as she rubbed her flaming face against her shoulder.

"Please take my panties down, sir."

The wicked man slipped a few fingers under her waistband and dragged the backs of his knuckles between the fabric and her flesh. Made her want to crawl out of her skin. In a good way. The best way. Was that a thing? Had to be a thing, but maybe Knox had invented it. She'd never experienced it before.

"For what?"

The bleat of protest she let out was pathetic and not a little mortifying. She should have felt flayed alive when Knox chuckled in response, the low sound vibrating through his body and into hers. Instead she felt like even the softest glance of a finger over her clit would make her come. She wanted that. And if she could just do what he asked, Knox would give it to her. Not leave her wanting like Aaron always had. Earning this man's approval was so simple, and in return he'd give her pleasure.

"So you can spank my bare bottom, sir."

Lujha could've cried with relief when he stripped her underwear down to her thighs and started to spank her in earnest.

CHAPTER FOUR

KNOX PLAYED WITH partners who he'd enjoyed before. He might even go so far as to say many. But none of them, not a single living soul, had ever made him feel as powerful, as duty-bound, and Jesus Christ, as impassioned as Lujha Fuller.

It didn't make any sense. He'd just met her, barely touched her, and yet it felt crucial that he hold her softly in his big, callused hands. How was it possible to feel so in control but also so fucking out of it at once?

He'd started spanking her again, his hand ringing with the force of every blow as he peppered her backside, flesh against flesh, turning her fair skin pink and then red. Deliberate still because he wouldn't really hurt her but it took every ounce of concentration he had. And he had a lot of it. Sometimes it had felt like the entire world had depended on him being able to keep a level head when any reasonable person would have descended into panic.

He could understand now why panic had looked so damn good. It was easier.

And the *sounds* this woman was making. Fuck, they penetrated his brain in some way he couldn't explain and it felt like even though there must be a hundred people in the club, they were the only two. His world had shrunk to a pinprick but that pinprick was blinding him. Like he'd been crawling through the dark, a creature in a cave, and the first finger of dawn had curled over the horizon.

It made no fucking sense that his brain was getting scrambled over a woman. But whether it made sense or not, he felt like his world had turned upside down almost from the moment he'd tipped Lulu over his lap. What the hell?

He tried to distract himself by concentrating on what he was doing. Giving her the most painstaking, meticulous thrashing she'd ever received. But that only made it worse.

His voice was hoarse when he demanded, "One to ten, where are you?"

Like this was the first time he'd gotten hard over spanking a woman instead of somewhere in the thousandths.

She mewled in response and he hauled her closer against him, brought his hand down hard and sharp once on each perfect cheek.

"Tell. Me."

"Seven, sir. Please."

She sounded like she was in far more pain than a seven and he knew how she felt. All his nerves were on fire, everything in him that had felt dormant was alive.

It suddenly seemed very, very important that he hear his name fall from her lips.

"Please what?"

"I...I..."

"You what, little girl?"

Lujha mewled again, buried her face in her arm and he hated that he couldn't see her. Drove him straight out of his head.

"I need you."

They'd negotiated sex before. It had sounded very casual then, bordering on clinical when she'd been sitting across the table from him. It didn't feel that way now, even with his dick straining behind the zipper of his jeans.

How did it feel just as intense to slide a single finger through Lujha's slick, wet, heat as it had to penetrate other lovers with his cock? *How?* But here he was, gritting his teeth to keep from embarrassing himself as he slipped two fingers into her pussy. She pressed back to take more and he gave it to her, thrusting hard with his whole arm while her whimpers rose in pitch and urgency.

"That's it, Lulu. Come on. Give this to me. Say my name when you do. Come for me, little girl."

He could feel her grinding her mound against his thigh, and then there was that precious sensation he'd been waiting for; the telltale squeeze of her internal muscles hard around his fingers that said she'd obeyed, that he'd gotten her there.

Her sharp, startled cry seemed to last forever as he waited and then—

"Yes. Oh, god, sir. I'm coming. Yes. Please, yes. Knox."

✧   ✧   ✧

WHOA.

Lujha was still draped over Knox's lap, boneless and spent except for the occasional near-painful pulse of an aftershock. Now that was what she'd call an orgasm. It would be pretty damn difficult for her to settle for anyone else until the memory of this had faded. If it ever did.

Given the other scenes she'd done—some of which had lasted hours, involved a plethora of implements, and on rare occasion more than one top—a hand-spanking should've been amateur hour. Junior varsity, Triple-A ball, whatever you wanted to call it.

She didn't know what the fuck to call what had just happened but there was nothing, not a single thing, that had been second rate in that...experience.

She was drunk on it. A little dizzy as he shifted her prone form to cradle her in his lap. With her head lolling on his shoulder, she could inhale the scent of him. After all that, he had the nerve to smell good. He was probably the devil. A devil that was tugging a blanket over her and holding her close.

"Lulu?"

"Mmm?"

"Y'okay?"

"Mmm."

His chuckle was less wicked but more smug. Apparently he spoke girl grunt. Luckily he didn't seem to expect much more from her. Was this like a regular thing for him? Did he always make women feel this way? She didn't want to think too much about what the answer might be.

Lujha resented the slow creep of her senses returning. It felt too much like reality encroaching on a really nice dream. But the solid, warm, and muscular body underneath her was definitely real. Knox was real and enough of her brain cells had started firing again that she was embarrassed.

That wasn't supposed to happen. Yeah she'd wanted to get her ass beat and wring a climax out of the experience but she'd never intended for *that* to happen. Fucking life changing. She'd been so cool, almost arrogant, and now she felt concussed.

What the hell was Knox thinking? Had he felt the same or was he glancing at his black, military grade watch every five seconds waiting for her to recover her senses and get the hell off his lap?

She tried to sit up completely but he stopped her, arms like steel bands tightening over the blanket he'd covered her with.

"Not so fast. Where do you think you're going?"

"Up?"

"No."

His casually imperious attitude should've bothered her. Didn't. Instead Lujha sunk into his hold and sighed. And was a curious mix of elated and completely at peace when he told her, "The only place you're going is home with me, little girl."

✦   ✦   ✦

Thank you so much for reading my story "Daddy's Little One Night Stand"! You can read the rest of Knox and Lujha's story in *Daddy's Little Second Chance*, the first book in the Frontier Daddies series. Find out more about *Daddy's Little Second Chance* and my other books by signing up for my newsletter.
http://readerlinks.com/l/2373983

Old Money

Amelia Wilde

MASON

IN REAL ESTATE, and in life, there's something to be said for letting go.
Of old ideas, for instance. Old obsessions. Society places a premium on
keeping a tight grip on everything until your hands give out. It's not a way to live.
Your bones can't take that kind of pressure indefinitely. And when you open your
palms, you might find you were holding on to nothing.

The old me would have finished the Cornerstone Development at any cost. I
was halfway there after it burned. I had teams of people working around the clock
on demolition so I could follow through. If it weren't for her, I wouldn't have
stopped to ask why I was doing it.

It was a mindless pursuit of money.

More than that, it was an escape from my ever-present guilt.

A pre-existing plan can be a good reason, but it wasn't. Not this time. A rebuilt
Cornerstone would only have been a monument to the sunk cost fallacy. I owned it
in the first place because Charlotte's father hadn't been able to let go. Not just of
the building, but of his own guilt.

It cost him his life, in the end.

A luxury development isn't worth a life cut short. All the money I could wring
out of the completed development wouldn't have made Charlotte happy. I took her
to the empty site shortly before our wedding.

"If you could build anything here, what would you build?" I asked her. "A
factory to produce your clothes? A design studio? An art school?

She shielded her eyes with her hand and looked over an empty property. A
blank slate.

It's not blank anymore.

Charlotte sits next to me in the car, a notebook on her lap, a pencil flying over
it. She always has something to design. Ideas for her next collection. Possibilities for
celebrity commissions. No one can get enough of her.

They'll never get as much as they want. I'm too much of a selfish bastard for
that.

These notes look a little different. More words. Fewer sketches.

"Let us out here, Scott."

Charlotte startles. "That drive took no time at all."

"We can go around the block again, sweet thing."

She shakes her head and tucks her notebook into her purse. "No, I'm excited
to see this."

I get out first and help her out of the car. Charlotte sighs, a big, bright smile
on her face. "It should always be summer."

"Summer's almost over."

"It should always be this nice, then."

"We could move. I'd take you anywhere."

She laughs. "And leave your family here? I don't think so."

Scott's let us out a couple of blocks before the former Cornerstone site, but I can hear it. Music floats to us on the breeze. Kids shout, their voices catching on the corners of nearby buildings. She didn't want a factory or a design studio or an art school.

Charlotte's eyebrows lift as we walk. "It sounds like lots of people are here."

"I told you they'd come."

It's impossible not to follow the music. Charlotte walks a little faster as we go down the block. I was here with her, once. The night of the fire. Walking the other direction as fast as my fucked-up knee could carry me, covered in soot and ash, Charlotte pale and afraid. Today couldn't be more different. Clear blue skies. A wedding ring on her finger. The only thing that hurts is a mild anxiety that this project won't have turned out the way she dreamed.

We cross the street, turn the corner, and Charlotte gasps. "Oh, wow."

It feels like stumbling across a jewel, if that jewel was made from green grass and trees and the wind moving through.

The original plans for the Cornerstone Development are a thing of the past. My revised plans, too. Now the entire site is a public park, a joyful, natural place for the community.

Charlotte slips her hand into mine, her fingertips going to her necklace. Once upon a time, it was my mother's. A gift from my father. Now Charlotte wears it to match her engagement ring and her wedding band. Touching the sapphire like this is an old habit. She does it when she's lost in thought, or surprised, or nervous.

She might be all three.

I tuck her hand into my elbow. "Take a walk with me."

One more street to cross, and we're there. The sidewalk at the edge of the park winds in gentle curves, leading toward shady trees. Leaves rustle near a brand-new playground. The music is from a local band. They've set up shop in a small performance space in the center. All the sidewalks lead there eventually.

"Mason, look at the balloon guy."

Charlotte points to a man making balloon animals. His red shirt stands out against a backdrop of sunflowers in a wide planter. He magics the animals out of the balloons while simultaneously telling the children a story that involves all the animals, one after the other. The kids love him. They all want to stand the closest. Somehow, none of them get impatient for the balloons. They're wrapped up in the story, too.

My wife bites her lip. I can tell she wants to get closer, but she's too sweet for that.

If we went over there now, someone would recognize us. The scandal of our sex contract was a flash in the pan compared to the ongoing tussles between politicians and celebrities and socialites, but our faces were all over the Internet. Charlotte doesn't want the park's opening day to be about that, or about us. The developer I hired for the park wanted to name it after her. Or at the very least, hold an opening ceremony. Charlotte holding a giant pair of scissors to cut a big ribbon while cameras flash, probably. She refused. It's about the community, she said.

It is about her, though. This is all for her.

We keep strolling down the sidewalk, past a fountain where littler kids are splashing chubby hands in the water, parents leaning down to keep them from tumbling in. Dappled light from the trees brushes over Charlotte's face. She keeps her hand in mine.

"What do you think, sweet thing?"

I pose this question to Charlotte as casually as I can. It's total bullshit. If this park isn't everything she dreamed, I'll raze it to the ground and start over. I don't care what it costs. Her happiness is worth everything I have and then some.

It's the one thing I won't be letting go of. Not even if our lives burn down around us.

Charlotte's watching a tall man walk along the sidewalk with his baby daughter in his arms. The child's a year old, maybe. A year and a half. She's got round cheeks and curls that match her dad's hair. Bronze, I think, but the sun brings out notes of gold. The two of them are…bright. Almost shining. The baby watches where he points right up until the moment she rubs her eyes with both hands and tucks her cheek into his shoulder.

If he keeps walking in that direction, he'll find a building tucked on the opposite side of the park. There are restrooms and nursing stations and a place for indoor activities on rainy days. A fish pond and an in-ground xylophone that you play by jumping on. I've personally tested it. When it's not so busy, I'll bring Charlotte here so she can feel the bells in the soles of her feet.

I glance down at her for her answer and find her wiping tears from her cheeks.

The sight of her crying stops my heart. "Tell me what it is, and I'll fix it, Charlotte. Anything."

She steps closer, folding herself into my side. "There's nothing to fix. Really. This is better than what I imagined." A small, heartbreaking shrug. "I miss my dad. I wish…you know. I wish things had gone another way for him. Wish that he could see this. But it's perfect, Mason. Look at all the kids. And that baby was really cute."

The longing in Charlotte's voice makes me want to find the nearest private space, push up her dress, and fuck her until she's pregnant. Until I'm the one walking here with my daughter. Until all three of us are here.

This train of thought is interrupted by a sound I've come to know very well.

The click of a camera shutter.

I turn my head at the same moment the reporter comes into view, still taking photos.

Fuck.

We're not anonymous anymore.

"Mrs. Hill," he says, his voice carrying. He's coming in fast, almost at a jog. "Mrs. Hill. Can you comment on your involvement with the Cornerstone Park project? Was it included as part of your agreement with—"

What the fuck does this guy think he's doing?

I step in front of Charlotte and put my fist into his shirt collar. "Don't talk to her."

"Hey, man. Mr. Hill. Easy." He's worried for his camera. A professional like him probably dropped several thousand dollars on it. He should be more worried about his face. I back him up several steps and deposit him on the ground. "I just had a few questions."

"We didn't agree to an interview. Get any closer to my wife, and you'll be filing this story from jail if you're lucky and a hospital bed if you're not."

The asshole puts his hands up, but I can see from the glint in his eyes that he's not going to walk away so easily. "It's a public place."

"Mason," Charlotte says.

The press wasn't supposed to be here yet. I wanted to give her a chance to see the park without someone harassing her about the contract or the scandal. It's always Charlotte. Never me. It's fucking infuriating. I've done a lot of work on my ruined knee, but it throbs.

Charlotte's hand on my arm brings me back to earth. She stays by my side as she smiles at that prick with his camera. "What's your name?"

He stands and brushes himself off. "Elliot Rayne."

His tone was aggressive when he hurled those questions. And hostile when he argued with me. Now that he's faced with Charlotte's grace, he looks sheepish. She has that effect on people. She brings out the best in people.

"I work for the Lower East Herald. We're a community paper. We cover things like an elderly man getting kicked out of his apartment for rent hikes. Or bikes for kids programs." He ducks his head. "Or park openings. When I say you guys here, I figured I could make it a national story."

I respect ambition, but not when it involves my wife. "No comment."

She gives me a small smile. "Actually, I would like to make a statement."

"Excellent." The camera comes up into his hands.

"One photo," says Charlotte, gently. "Then you'll need to take notes."

I arrange my face into a less murderous expression and lean into Charlotte. God damn it, it's going to be a good photo. The lighting here is soft. Great. "Are you sure about this?" I mutter.

"Yes," she says, sounding quietly, perfectly confident.

Elliot Rayne snaps a photo and then flashes a notepad.

"I consulted on the design for the park with my husband," she says. "We wanted it to be a place where families could spend time together."

He scribbles down her words. "This site was originally dedicated to luxury condos. Did you pivot to green space because buyers pulled out after your contract went public?"

I'm going to kill him.

Charlotte loops her arm through mine and holds me back. How is she still smiling? How is she still so beautiful, and so sweet?

"When I was a girl, I used to sit by my dad's desk and color while he worked. He was an involved businessman, so that was how we spent a lot of our time together. But my favorite days were when he would finish his calls and take me to a small park near our house."

The reporter's writing slows. "Your father passed away this year, didn't he?"

At least he doesn't bring up the way her father died—by his own hand. I'm sure someone who recognized us on sight would know the details.

She nods, her expression one of both deep sorrow and irrepressible serenity. "Yes. So he'll never see this park, or the families enjoying their time here. I'd like to think that if I asked him to choose between luxury condos and a day at the park with me, he'd choose the park. I ran out of time with my dad. The best I can do is give that to other families."

"Do you plan to bring your own family here? When you have kids?"

"Of course. It should be warm enough for a walk in the stroller." She puts a hand against her flat stomach. "By that time, anyway."

The reporter laughs. "Great. Thanks. I'll get out of your way."

He jogs past us, giving me a wide berth.

"I'm sorry, sweet thing." Fuck these people and their cameras and their questions. I turn Charlotte toward me, away from the rest of the park, and smooth her hair back from her face. Her hands go to my waist. Easy. Comfortable. "That was bullshit. I know it's not the easiest day." She's looking up at me, her eyes sparkling. The corners of her mouth are lifted. Almost a smile. "We can go, if you want to. If that motherfucker—"

Wait.

My mind replays the reporter's questions. Charlotte's answers. Her hand on her stomach.

"Warm enough for a stroller?"

"Yeah." She rubs her hand up and down my waist. "It's warm enough here in the summer for new babies to be outside, I think. I mean—blankets are probably a good idea, but I think it'll be fine."

I take her face in my hands. "Did you tell that man a joke? Charlotte. Was it a joke?"

She wrinkles her nose, beaming now. "I found out an hour before we were supposed to leave. I spent the ride trying to figure out how to tell you. I was maybe going to read a speech, but I'm not that good at speeches. Anyway, I'm pregnant."

I lift her straight off her feet and into my arms. She shouldn't be standing on the ground. Not even brand-new concrete. I kiss her, and she tastes like sunshine and tears. She tastes like letting go. She tastes like holding on.

"It's yours," Charlotte adds.

I start walking down the path. Any direction. I need my driver, and the car, and a place to be alone with her.

"You're funny," I tell her. "You're very funny, Ms. Van Kempt. I can't believe how much I love you."

"That's convenient," she says. "Because I'm absolutely head over heels for you."

"A baby," I say, disbelieving. And so goddamn proud. A baby. Mine. Hers. My heart feels like it's going to beat straight out of my chest. I thought a fire had ended my life, but no. No. This is living. I whirl her around in the sun. Her body and mine, around and around, in a park full of flowers and families and a long-awaited happiness.

✧   ✧   ✧

Thank you for reading OLD MONEY!

Want more of Mason and Charlotte? Read NET WORTH now >
awilderomance.com

Sultry and stunning, Net Worth is the perfect revenge romance.

—New York Times bestselling author Skye Warren

It Started in Paris

Meredith Wild & Chelle Bliss

CHAPTER ONE
Hayden

PARIS IS A twisted kind of salve for a broken heart. Busy streets. Prideful and unapologetic people. A violent and decadent history. For my part, love is decidedly not in the air, which I'm glad for, because I'd likely choke and die on it.

Romance hits me in odd places, though. In the intimacy of a poorly lit café. On the stone benches that line a maison courtyard. In Montmartre, where I spend most of my time walking the streets, avoiding tourists, and contemplating the city from the highest points. Something about seeing all of Paris at once gives me solace.

I'd arrived content to spend a week with Martin, my childhood best friend turned artist expat. Impulsive and giving zero fucks about anything that didn't feed his addiction for the pleasures of life, he was the perfect host for a pit stop on a trip designed to forget the past.

Only four months have passed since I discovered my beautiful fiancée bent over our Upper East Side balcony. Night had fallen, but even the loud city streets couldn't drown out her vow to come *so fucking hard* for Colin, my younger brother and the worst human being I've ever known. Of course he was too busy getting her there to notice that I'd arrived, or that my heart was being beaten to death with every animal thrust into my future wife. My future ex-fiancée.

"You're thinking of her again, aren't you?" Martin eyes me, smug knowing in his eyes. With a scarf flung around his neck, quietly assessing me through round, dark-rimmed glasses, he looks as Parisian as anyone else who's been implanted here through good fortune.

I avoid his gaze, feigning interest in the passersby in front of our regular midafternoon haunt, Café Resto.

"I'm not thinking of her," I lie.

Martin's laugh is dry. "I'm an artist. It's my occupation to notice the intricacies of life and people that others can't or won't. Your face... It does this twitchy wrinkle thing when you think of her. It's very unattractive."

"I'll try to be easier on the eyes. If only for your sake."

"Try it for your sake. You need companionship, and you'll never get it looking like that."

It's my turn to laugh. "I don't need companionship. Do you have *any* idea—"

"What you've been through? Sure I do, Hayden. We've discussed it *ad nauseum*. Natasha was immature, impressionable, and let's face it, probably somewhere deep inside she was unhappy too."

"Colin coerced her," I say, hating my own flesh and blood as much as the woman I'll never see again.

"She allowed herself to be coerced. *C'est la vie*. It doesn't mean you have to hate her for the rest of your life. It means you need to move on and find someone who lights a fire in you again."

"Says the terminal bachelor."

He shrugs and withdraws a delicate tin of expensive cigarettes from the interior pocket of his blazer. Lighting one, he follows my gaze onto the street.

For a few minutes, my challenge seems to linger like the smoke from his cigarette in the still air.

"I'm too in love with my life to reassign all my affections to one person," he finally says.

"So if you fall in love with a woman, you have to fall out of love with Paris."

He rolls his eyes.

I'm just happy we're no longer talking about Natasha and me. Because Martin may be absolutely right, even if his words strike a paralyzing kind of fear in me. Companionship had been the death of my soul. A thick black fog that was far from lifting. How could I ever seek it out again?

"All right, then. You've given me no other choice. I'm taking matters into my own hands." Martin leans in over the small café table, eyeing me keenly again. "I'm setting you up with someone. She's astonishing. If you don't fall head over heels in love with her, I'll... I'll..."

I lift an eyebrow. "You'll what?"

"I'll give up macarons for a month."

"You will not."

"I will. Two maybe. I'll appreciate them so much more after a solid absence. Now, if you only fall into bed with her, and you *don't* fall head over heels in love with her, then *you* have to give up macarons for a month."

"You make no sense at all."

"It'll all make sense when you meet her. I've been trying to fall in love with her forever. And if you don't, then you're truly hopeless and you don't deserve to eat another macaron in your life."

"By that measure, neither do you."

He shrugs again. "But I'm not you, Hayden. We both know that."

I'm silent a moment. Intrigue lights up little fires around my fear, singeing the edges of my resolve. Martin is passionate and excitable on any given day, but I can see a difference in him when he speaks about this mysterious heart-thieving woman.

"What's the catch? She must have a fatal flaw."

He pinches his brows together but says nothing for a moment. "She's a little reclusive. Eccentric maybe. But"—he looks up with a grin curving his lips—"like I said, she's... Well, you'll see."

"What's her name?"

His smile broadens.

"Her name is Chloe."

✧   ✧   ✧

Chloe

IT'S BEEN THREE weeks since I've gone out and done anything remotely social. Martin has a way of luring me out. Mainly because he's one of the few people who understands me. Our one-night stand ages ago turned into an odd kind of friendship. That's not always how it goes. A bottle of wine turns into two. A chance meeting turns into sheet-clawing sex. But not everyone wants to stay in my world after that.

I sling my purse strap across my torso and check my reflection in the big mirror in the entryway. I twirl my long black hair into a makeshift knot at the base of my neck and pull on a jacket over my sweater dress. It's short enough to show a few inches of leg before my thigh-high suede boots cover the rest. I always try to look good for Martin. Not because I want to fall into bed with him again, but who knows. One bottle of wine could turn into two.

I hike several blocks toward the restaurant we always meet at. It's dark and moody, and the food is rich. Wrapped in its shadows, I can almost feel as if I haven't left home at all.

I find Martin at a table in the back. He smiles when I approach. Rising, he glides his arms around my waist and kisses me. His lips linger on mine like he's savoring me...or trying to. He's not always so forward. The intimate touch wakes dormant nerves that haven't felt human contact in weeks, bringing warmth to my cheeks.

"How are you?"

His voice, absent of any lusty notes, distracts me from assessing the way my body suddenly feels. I take the seat beside him when he slides over in the booth, making room for me.

"Same as always."

He looks me over with something like wonder in his eyes. "I half expected to meet you here twenty years from now to find that you haven't aged a day. You're as consistent as anyone I've ever met."

The waiter arrives with a bottle of our usual red, pouring a taste for Martin to sample first. He nods a silent approval, and soon our glasses are full and we're alone again.

"And what about you? What's your passion this week?"

His lips curve into a secretive smile. "Matchmaking, I think."

"That doesn't sound like you at all."

"I know, but I do have a beating heart, and I worry for my friends who don't belong in this life of ephemeral infatuation and soulless fucking."

I laugh. "Who are these unlucky friends of yours?"

He lifts his gaze. "Oh, here he is."

He is a tall drink of water. I see hints of American roots in his innocent blue eyes, golden skin, and sandy-blond hair. His white shirt peeks out from under his black peacoat, and his jeans mold attractively over well-built thighs.

"Hayden!" Martin waves him closer. "Come meet my beloved Chloe."

Our eyes lock as he approaches. My next intake of breath gets lodged somewhere along the way. I should get out more, because something about the intensity of his stare—the sadness and pain and longing in it—makes the impact of Martin's kiss feel almost brotherly compared to what I'm feeling now.

He lingers beside the table a moment. "You're Chloe."

The matter-of-fact way he says it renders me speechless. Like nothing else can be said. His gaze falls to the place where Martin's hand rests on my thigh. Martin must notice because I feel his thumb disappear under the edge of my boot and gently stroke the skin underneath.

"Chloe, this is Hayden. If I believed in best friends, I would give him the title. In any case, he's one of the best people I know."

Martin's comment seems to break the tractor beam between me and his friend.

Hayden sits across from me and offers a tight smile to Martin. "I'm touched. Truly."

He shrugs out of his jacket and starts studying the menu.

Meanwhile, I study him. The fine reddish stubble along his strong jaw. His hands, strong but elegant. I wonder what they might feel like teasing my skin if Martin weren't here. Suddenly I'm a little furious with Martin for awakening my senses so boldly and so quickly, because I can't stay ahead of the thoughts this beautiful stranger is inspiring.

I draw one leg over the other. Martin's touch slips away, but when I glance over my shoulder at him, his eyes are glimmering with humor. What is he thinking?

Before I can riddle out his expressions, he pushes his sleeve up and looks at his watch. "Oh, hell. I just remembered I have to be somewhere."

I frown. "What? Where?"

He shrugs. "A thing at a place. Sorry, love." He gives me a peck on the cheek before tossing a few bills onto the table. "Hayden, you can offer Chloe some pleasant company, right?" He winks at me. "Until next time."

Hayden's lips are tight. He seems frozen in the absence of his friend. After a moment, he takes Martin's abandoned wineglass and lifts it to his lips.

His throat bobs when he swallows. When he licks the ruby traces of it away, the tiny movement holds my attention far more than it should. Especially when he catches me staring at him, reigniting that breath-robbing tractor beam between us.

"Where are you from?" he asks.

I open my lips and scramble to figure out how to speak again. "Montana."

He raises his eyebrows and takes another drink.

"How about you?"

"New York. Born and raised and recently sworn off."

"Why?"

He shakes his head slightly. "Martin set this up, you know."

I blink twice.

Martin set us up?

I laugh. It's loud and unexpected and marks the second I put it all together. Matchmaking. Of course.

My revelation melts into a quiet hum of understanding.

"How long have you known him?" Hayden asks.

"Almost a year. But we don't meet often."

"He says you're reclusive."

I pause. A knot of concern takes up residence beside my unabashed attraction toward this man. "What else does he say about me?"

"That you're astonishing."

He says it like he owns the sentiment.

Heat blooms across my skin. My instinct is to rip away my scarf and fan myself with the menu. Men have poured their adorations over me before. Some are foul, others are tender.

Nothing beats the steady look in Hayden's eyes or our proximity or the certainty that I'd do almost anything to hear him say that again.

CHAPTER TWO
Hayden

C HLOE CALLS THE waiter over and orders a second bottle of wine.
I watch her as they speak, trying to unravel her while she isn't looking. She doesn't seem to be shy.

The waiter says something too quickly for me to translate, and Chloe tips her head back, laughing as she reaches out and touches his arm.

She glances in my direction, blushing as our eyes lock, and the quaint café suddenly feels smaller and warmer than a few moments ago.

Martin was right about Chloe, but he downplayed her beauty. There's an elegance about her. An air of ease, as if she could belong anywhere, but she's too exquisite to blend in. Her ivory skin and dark hair make her blue eyes more striking as she stares across the table at me.

"Where were we?" Chloe asks as soon as we're alone again.

The conversation has been easy, flowing from one topic to another without faltering. I can't remember the last time I've spoken to a woman for this long besides Natasha, but she only wanted to talk about herself.

"You were telling me about your childhood back in the States."

"Right." She traces the base of the empty wineglass sitting in front of her. "After my mother passed away, my aunt took custody of me. She decided to homeschool me, so my days were quiet. I never really seemed to fit in with girls my own age. I was never sure if it was me, if I was different somehow, or if it was just because I was an only child." She pauses. "I'm still not sure, I suppose."

Her story sounds impossibly lonely. I imagine a young Chloe, a soft-spoken wisp of a child with the same riveting blue-eyed gaze that seems to peer right into one's soul, feeling so alone in the world because of her unfortunate loss.

Until recent events, I'd always thought I was lucky for having a brother, a built-in friend and life-long companion. When I was younger, I could never imagine him not being in my life, sharing the good times and the bad until our dying breath.

But that was before...

"How about you?" she asks, drawing my attention back to the present and away from the torrid memories which seem to haunt me every time I close my eyes.

"My parents are alive, still together, and back in New York," I tell her, hoping the clipped way I say the words doesn't hint at the chasm of pain that exists beneath them.

Chloe leans forward and pushes her wineglass to the side. Her black hair unravels from its loosened knot and spills over her shoulders along her breasts, accentuating her cleavage. "Any siblings?"

For a moment, I think about telling her I'm an only child too. I no longer think of Colin as a brother after his betrayal, but no matter how badly I want to deny his existence, I can't.

"I have one brother." I pause as the waiter sets down the new bottle of red and refills our glasses before disappearing again.

"And?" She tilts her head and holds my stare across the table like she knows I'm leaving something out.

"We had a falling out. *C'est la vie.*" I repeat the words Martin spoke earlier, letting them roll off my tongue easily.

I don't miss the sadness that flashes behind her eyes.

"I'm sorry."

"Don't be. I'm not. What brought you to Paris?" I try to change the subject, having devoted enough thought to my brother to last a lifetime.

"At some point along the way, I decided I wanted to be an artist." She laughs softly. "I was young and pretty naïve. I fell in love with Paris in movies and books when I was a child. I knew as soon as I was old enough, I'd come here to live."

I ease back into my chair, picturing Chloe sitting near the top of the steps in front of the Sacré-Cœur Basilica, with her sketchpad in her lap as she draws the endless city landscape.

"*Are* you an artist?"

"I endeavor to live a creative life." She averts her eyes and tucks her hair behind her ear. "How about you?"

"Why did I come to Paris?"

She nods, holding my gaze intently again, as if she's been hoping to find out the answer since the moment she laid eyes on me.

"I needed to get away from New York for a little while, and I wanted to see Martin." I leave out my heartbreak, opting for an easier topic. One we have in common.

"Martin has spoken about you a few times, but I only know stories from your childhood. Tell me about Hayden the man."

I laugh. "There's not much to tell."

She studies me as she turns the stem of the wineglass between her fingertips. "Are you an artist too?"

"Definitely not. I never had the skill. That's Martin's wheelhouse. And yours, it seems. He spent hours trying to teach me how to draw when we were younger. Eventually, and thankfully, he finally gave up on me."

She gifts me with a sweet smile that makes me want to tell her more, even if that means dancing around the minefields Natasha left in my life.

"I was working toward my doctorate in psychiatry at NYU. I decided to take a break. Reevaluate things."

Her smile softens. "So you like to get into people's heads?"

I shrug. "Human behavior can be as devastating as it is fascinating. I love my work, but the mind can be a scary place. Dig deep enough, and you might not always like what you find."

She looks down, then to the side at another couple settling at a nearby table. Her thoughts seem far away.

I try to figure out how to shift gears when she turns her attention back to me, her gaze thoughtful.

"Is that your passion, then?"

I do a gut check on how I feel about the life I left behind and wince a little. "Not really."

"Then you haven't answered my question." She pauses, taking a small sip of wine. "Who is Hayden the man?"

Six months ago I would've said I was a man deeply in love with both my fiancée and my work, but now I find very little pleasure in anything that fills my life. I came to Europe to escape, thinking I could leave behind the memories, but they followed me. Haunting me at every turn.

"Maybe I came to Paris to find the answer to that very question."

I pause for a moment, wondering if I'm coming off as completely insane.

Who can be such a stranger to themselves? Who rambles aimlessly for four months without a plan? A purpose? Even as I internally berate myself for devoting so much time to a soul-searching quest that's returned little to no results, the lack of judgment in Chloe's careful gaze quiets the voice inside me. Where I expect hesitation from her, or more probing questions, in the silence I can sense her quiet acceptance along with something else…something like understanding—like maybe she's not a stranger to the same quest.

"Have you found what you were looking for?" she asks softly, almost hopefully.

I nod as the small flicker of lust I thought I'd never feel again reignites. For as long as I've been in Paris, I've felt nothing close to this. But there's something about Chloe that draws me in. Makes me want to get closer to her and let her get closer to me.

"I think I have."

✧ ✧ ✧

Chloe

I LICK THE last drops of wine from my lips, savoring the tangy sweetness.

Hayden's sharp gaze dips to my mouth. "I feel like walking. Would you care to join me?"

I uncross my legs, hoping in vain that it might quench the ache between them caused by the handsome man across from me. Except the shift sends a rush of blood to the place that's already aching for a man's touch.

Hayden's touch…

I delay my reply, take in a steady breath, and consider a second, unspoken proposal. One where we walk directly to my apartment, or his, and explore each other's bodies until the sun rises. Still, I can't remember the last time I went for a walk without a destination. To wander the streets of Paris at night for nothing more than pleasure is too romantic a proposition to refuse. When Martin abruptly left us, I was worried that the entire evening would be a waste, but I realize now I was very wrong.

"I'd love to."

He stands and puts on his coat, a simple motion that I could watch on repeat a dozen more times. He adjusts his collar, which stretches the fabric of his shirt tightly across his torso for a moment, giving me the briefest outline of his chest muscles. The way his jeans hug his thighs and thick, long legs as he reaches for his wallet makes the dull ache turn into a full-on throb. The material is practically molded to his body and leaves very little to the imagination.

"Do you have a favorite spot in the city?" He holds out his hand to me like a true gentleman.

His hand is softer than I expect as I slide my palm into his, rise to my feet, and peer into his eyes. "The Basilica at night. When the lights of the city twinkle like a million stars in the sky, it's absolutely breathtaking."

Hayden smiles and closes his fingers around mine. "Show me."

My heart flutters with excitement as he holds my hand, guiding me toward the door. I expect him to release his grip as we wind our way through the tight streets, but he doesn't. The intimate contact is tender and sweet. And genuine, without pretense, a rare quality I suspect is sewn into the fiber of Hayden's being and very few other men who walk this earth. I can see a mirror of desire in his stolen glances, but I don't get the feeling that this stroll is part of a master plan to seduce me.

"Here," I say as we approach the railing in front of the Basilica, overlooking the city. "Look."

Hayden releases my hand as we move toward the edge, and it takes everything in me not to whine. I immediately miss the feel of his skin against mine and the warmth of his touch.

"It's beautiful," he says.

I follow his gaze, momentarily mesmerized by the horizon of glittering lights.

"I could look at this view for a lifetime, and it wouldn't be long enough to enjoy it," I say with no small amount of wonder.

Wispy gray clouds stretch across the darkened sky like thick brushstrokes. Dozens of tourists line the fence, snapping selfies and chatting in different languages. But when Hayden moves behind me, his body heat licking at my back, I forget everyone else.

"They say Paris is a city of many pleasures," he says with his mouth close to my ear.

I shiver at the deepness of his voice and wrap my fingers around the cold metal railing, stopping myself from reaching for him.

I turn my head, just enough to see his eyes. Our mouths practically touch. He's watching me, no longer bothering with the view.

"It is." My voice is husky and full of need. There's nothing I can do to hide the attraction I have for this man I just met.

"Sometimes I think I've been denying myself the best of them."

My lips part, and my next breath is hard to take in. "Why? Why deny your-self?"

He drops his hand to my hip. His fingers press into my skin, gently but with unmistakable strength. I think he's going to say something, answer the invitation I've just given him. I search his eyes, waiting for his words. But none come, as the air around us crackles with possibilities.

I turn in his arms, waiting for his kiss, wanting his touch more than anything. I don't have to wait long for him to give me what I want...his lips.

At first, he holds back, kissing me softly, like I'm breakable...or maybe he thinks I'm the one who's unsure. I place my hands on his stomach, feeling the firm ripples of muscle underneath the fabric of his shirt.

He kisses me harder as I slide my fingers around his sides, closing the space between us and making my desire for his touch and kiss very clear.

The crowd around us seems to melt away as his kiss becomes firmer and more demanding. When his tongue breaks through my lips, touching my own, the dull ache I felt earlier becomes exquisite torture. I yield to him, kissing him like my next breath depends on our connection.

The sweetness of the wine on his warm tongue mixed with the cool air sends goose bumps across my skin. I can barely breathe with the way his hands grip my hips and his tongue sweeps inside my mouth, savoring me. He lets out a tiny moan, and I practically go weak at the knees.

If he weren't holding me so tightly, I might collapse into a puddle at his feet.

"Hayden," I whisper like I'm begging.

For more of his touch.

For this kiss to turn into more.

For him to sate this new hunger he's inspired.

CHAPTER THREE
Hayden

M Y NAME ON her lips, all needy and breathy, is like a tiny orgasm over every inch of my skin, transforming my long-forgotten knot of resentment into a white-hot ball of lust. The heated embrace and all it inspires is so potent that I have to break our kiss to catch a breath.

Laughter erupts close by, reminding me we're not alone. But I'm too lost in Chloe's eyes, twinkling now like the sea of lights beyond, to look away. Breathtaking... She's utterly breathtaking. The small pause from our ravenous kissing sobers me a little. Reluctantly I loosen the grip that's probably too bold to have on a woman I've just met.

I exhale unsteadily. "I'm sorry."

Little lines form between her brows. Even her frown is sexy. "Sorry?"

"I didn't mean to come on so strong. I thought the walk would distract me."

"From what?"

I lick my lips and fixate on hers, still wet and red from our kiss. I should slow this down. I should rationalize that chasing this unexpected rush of passion with a total stranger might not be the healthiest choice, for her or for me. But she is warm and soft and smells like exotic perfume that I'm too eager to get all over my sheets so I can relive how her body felt under me long after she's gone home.

I can feel her heartbeat against my chest as she leans forward, closing up the tiniest space I made there seconds ago.

"Hayden," she whispers. "Tell me what you need a distraction from." She slides her hands from my back to my ribs, gliding them slowly south until they're settled low on my tightened abdominals.

She's perilously close to my dick, which, long neglected, has announced its approval of this woman and her proximity by straining painfully against my zipper.

I ignore the instinct to draw her hard against me and let that single wordless gesture answer her question. The way she's looking at me, like she's already been taken under by the same desire, makes me wonder why I'm holding back at all.

Besides, this is Paris. For the first time since I set foot in this city, I'm feeling like Hayden the man. Hayden the lover who hasn't completely forgotten all the ways to give a woman more pleasure than she can handle.

My blood surges. My skin prickles as I let myself imagine how divine it'll feel to sink into her... To feel her come.

I brush the backs of my fingertips across her cheek—the barest touch—nothing compared to the things I want to do to her. She closes her eyes and leans into the caress like a kitten.

"Chloe... You're too beautiful for any man to not want to take home and spend hours worshiping."

She flutters her eyes open, new heat shimmering in their depths.

"I know this sounds completely shallow," I say. "And I admit that it's really premature to even tell you this, but I haven't been able to stop thinking about that very thing since I first saw you. I'm so fucking attracted to you, I have no idea how to slow down and do this right."

"It's not shallow if it's honest, Hayden. And it's not premature if it's what I want too, is it?"

I drag my thumb along her lower lip like I already have the right to touch her however I please.

Her hands glide a centimeter lower, and I'm ready to black out from restraint—restraint I can no longer maintain.

I take her hand and pull her away from the view. "Come on. Let's go."

✧   ✧   ✧

WE ONLY MAKE it two blocks from the Basilica on our journey to find a cab before Chloe pulls me through the arched doorway of the Hôtel Montmartre Mon Amour. A fitting name, I realize through the haze of my desire and the whir of Chloe's fluent exchange with the gentleman at the front desk who is securing us a room.

"You want to stay here?" I ask, whipping out my credit card when I recognize numbers are being discussed.

Chloe beams up at me. The spontaneity of her choice seems to charge the air between us, adding another layer to this totally unexpected evening.

"I've always wanted to stay here. Never had a reason, so this is perfect," she says.

I lift an eyebrow and let my gaze travel over the lobby and its loud art and decor. The walls are painted red and covered with enormous photographic stills of black-and-white cinema stars. I have no idea why, and I don't have time to ask, because as soon as I scribble my signature on the receipt and we have a key in hand, Chloe is beelining to the little elevator that will take us to our room.

It's barely big enough for two, which should freak me out the way too many of the city's old claustrophobic lifts do, but the minute the doors close, Chloe's fingers are in my hair, pulling me down into a hungry kiss.

"Touch me," she gasps. "Please. Everywhere. I need your hands on me."

I happily oblige, losing myself in the hot rhythm of our mouths while I roam my hands greedily over her subtle curves.

I memorize the way her narrow waist slopes to a firm and ample ass. When I reach the hem of her dress, I drag my hands up the back of her stockinged thighs. My God, I can't wait to get her naked.

I start to question how far I'm willing to go in this elevator when I notice she's trembling.

Our mouths break apart as a desperate whimper leaves her lips. I blink, giving myself a full second to recognize she's shaking from sheer pleasure. Nothing else.

And just as I begin to marvel at the reality that I've never affected a woman so quickly and so easily, the elevator stops and the doors open.

We rush to find the room, which isn't hard because the hotel floors are small. We tumble into the room, which is as oddly decorated as the lobby, with a bright purple leather couch lining one wall. I entertain a brief fantasy of fucking her there, but the bed is easier and closer.

We fall onto it, tugging at each other's clothes until we're nearly naked. I'm feasting on her breasts, enjoying more of her gasps as I nibble on her raspberry-colored tips, working every inch of her with my mouth or my hands until she's trembling again.

If I didn't think it was impossible, I'd worry about making her come from my touch alone. She pushes at my chest, unlatching me from my systematic and promised worship of her flesh.

"Condom. Boots. I need you naked." The string of simple commands makes absolute sense to me, as if our physical interactions have replaced our ability to formulate full thoughts and sentences. But this new, rude language is all I need to act.

I push to my feet and drop the condom from my wallet onto the bed. Three seconds later, I'm stripped. I reach for her foot and tug her boot off. Then the other.

She sinks her teeth into her bottom lip as I take the band of her stockings and slowly drag them down, revealing more pale, silky flesh that I need time acquainting with. Her mound is perfectly bare. I don't think—hell, I can't think. I answer the magnetic pull, spread her legs around my shoulders, and bring my mouth toward her perfect, glistening pussy

"No." She pushes on my shoulders firmly enough to halt my approach.

I look up. "No?"

"If you put your mouth on me there, I'll explode."

I grin. "Isn't that the point?"

She shakes her head and coaxes me up her body. I let her, begrudgingly.

"Yes, but I want to explode while you fuck me, Hayden."

I settle my pelvis against hers and swallow hard, forcing myself to ignore how her words incite the beast in me who wants to do nothing else *but* fuck. Because Hayden the man who hasn't been with a woman in four months is becoming rapidly reduced to operating on instincts alone.

But I have to keep my head.

I have to stay tuned in to the fascinating, exquisite creature under me so I can make this as incredible for her as I already know it's going to be for me.

I cover her body with mine and kiss her slowly, from her lips to her jaw to the elegant column of her neck.

"You're shaking, Chloe," I whisper against her ear.

"I'm sorry… I just want you so much."

I lift my head to meet her eyes, my own wide and bewildered at her ill-timed apology. "My God, why are you sorry? Do you have any idea how intoxicating it is to affect someone this way?"

She licks her lips nervously. Her cheeks are flushed as she seems to search my gaze. "Being with you…is like sensory overload. In a good way, of course. You feel…" She closes her eyes a moment, and when they open, there's something so innocent and honest about the way she looks up at me. "Hayden…you feel amazing. Every time you touch me, it's like a blanket that's warm from sunshine. And somehow, when you look at me the way you do, it feels the same way."

I'm still piecing together all the things she's said. Things she's embarrassed of now, I'm guessing from the flash of worry behind her eyes and the slightest ease of her body's vibrations. I don't waste a second bringing our mouths together and kissing her so deeply and so thoroughly that I'm not satisfied I've done it right until her body is reacting to me again.

I break away and reach for the condom, acutely aware of my own sensitivities. "Let's turn that sunshine into an inferno, shall we?"

✧   ✧   ✧

Chloe

I HOLD MY breath as Hayden eases into me, filling me by slow and gentle drives. He's so careful with me. He touches me with such measured passion, a part of me wishes I could tear away his restraint and feel him really let go. Except he's too perfect right now. He's a dream...a fantasy I didn't think could ever exist in the real world.

His lips part when he looks between us and skims his palm from my hip up to my rib cage like I'm the most precious thing he's ever seen. Every touch is electric. And the way he feels once he reaches the deepest part of me...I finally release the breath I've been holding, with a satisfying moan at the exquisite fullness.

He sweeps his lips over mine, kissing me almost reverently. "You're incredible," he whispers.

Our gazes find each other. I don't know why, but those two words stun me. He doesn't even know me. He doesn't know anything about me, but from the look in his eyes, I know he fully believes his words.

I try not to think about what he'd say if he knew me better, because he never will. Instead, I fold my legs around his narrow hips, tangle my hands into his golden hair, and urge him into a rhythm that's like his kisses. Deep and thorough. A perfect blend of carnal possession and adoration that I can't imagine I could ever grow tired of.

I suck in a breath and fight the fierce urge to climax. I could have come the second our bodies joined. But I don't want this to end. Not so soon. Every minute that passes is a test of willpower I have none of. Not after weeks of choosing the solitude of my life and my paintings over the complicated world outside my apartment.

Hayden's world...

When the rhythm changes, and his hungry grasps over my flesh become less gentle, my control slips. I dig my fingernails into his sides and tense against the overwhelming rush.

I can't hold it back anymore. It feels too good. *He* feels too good. Pure male perfection, from the small sounds of pleasure he makes against my ear to his now savage thrusts. I've admired his strength all night, but to know it is divine. To feel the weight of him pinning me to the mattress, the force of his hips joining us in this race to completion, is more than enough to push me over.

"Yes, yes. Oh, God, yes..." I hiss out the last word until it morphs into something else. A sharp intake of breath. An explosion of feeling. I cry out loudly when the orgasm takes hold of me fully, almost violently. I close my eyes and revel in the moment where I'm almost completely outside myself yet somehow able to appreciate how he's gone deeper, taken more of me, a claiming that draws out a second wave of all-consuming pleasure.

I hang on to the euphoria, wishing it could go on and on forever. But gradually, the sweet tension releases, and my eyes open to Hayden's gorgeous face. His jaw is tense, every carved plane pinched with restraint.

I bring my fingers up to caress over his tight muscles, wanting him to follow me down. "Tell me what you need, Hayden. I'll do anything you want."

And I will.

Everything about this man makes me want to fling open every door of my body and let him do and take as he pleases. The possibilities alone stoke a new flame in my belly. I'm ready to climb with him once more when he speaks.

"Just you. Just this." His voice breaks with his rough movements.

Then he closes his eyes, and he thrusts so deeply, I'm momentarily robbed of breath. He holds himself there, touching my womb, flinching deep inside me, only one word slipping softly from his lips.

My name.

Chapter Four

Hayden

I DRIFTED TO sleep with Chloe nestled in my arms, euphoria thick in my veins. When I wake, the room is dark, I blink a few times until the bedside clock comes into focus. It's nearly three a.m. Before I can turn, I somehow already know she's gone. I skim my palm across the bed to find the sheets rumpled and cold.

I fall back onto the pillow.

"Fuck," I mutter.

My eyes adjust to the dark, and the oddities of the room's decor and my whirlwind night come back slowly, along with an odd sense of loss. I barely know her, but her perfume lingers in the air, reminding me of the way her body felt, warm and soft against my side.

Was I foolish to think that we'd at least have the morning together? Hell, it's been a matter of hours, and I'm already longing for her again like a damn teenage boy.

I rise with a frustrated groan, switch on the light, and search for my clothes. I dress, distracted by the unmistakable reality that I've been ditched by my beautiful, enigmatic one-night stand. Then a folded piece of hotel stationary on the desk catches my eye. I open it, revealing a couple of handwritten lines.

Thank you for a night I'll never forget. Sorry I couldn't stay. —Chloe

My brain is still foggy from sleep, my thoughts jagged with the abrupt slap of rejection I awoke to. I brush my thumb over her neat script, hope tugging at me as I reread her words.

Chloe.

I don't even know her last name. I know almost nothing about her, except that I can make her shake and scream my name. That and the indisputable truth that I want to see her again.

✧   ✧   ✧

"MY, OH MY. You are looking rather *renewed*, if I do say so myself." Martin shrugs out of his coat and lays it casually over one of my kitchen chairs.

I haven't slept since I left the hotel in Montmartre in the wee hours of the morning. I doubt I look refreshed.

"Coffee?" I offer flatly.

"Of course."

I pour us two cups of strong, black brew and join him at the table. Neither of us drinks. Martin's grin is smug and irritating. I'm doing my best to burn a hole through him with the intensity of my stare, as if somehow I can force the information I need out of him.

"Who is she?"

Martin brings his mug to his lips, delaying his answer.

I hate him for it.

"You set us up. I think it's only fair that you elaborate on why."

He smirks. "I thought you'd be an interesting fit. Was I right?"

I work my jaw.

"You slept with her. Wow. A good fit indeed." His expression breaks into a full smile. "I had no idea I'd be such a gifted matchmaker. I may have to try this more often."

"Do I look satisfied?"

He cocks his head. "A little? Let me guess. Our elusive Chloe disappeared in the middle of the night."

I clench my jaw tight enough that I worry for the integrity of my molars. "Of course you'd know her MO."

Martin frowns. "Calm down, Hayden. I see the murder in your eyes already. It was only once, and it was a long time ago. Now we flirt and talk about art, and I adore her in a way that has nothing to do with getting her into bed."

"Then how did you know she'd leave?"

He sighs... The first signs of resignation showing in his softened expression. "I know this is going to be hard to understand—especially for you, Hayden—but try not to take it personally. Chloe is her own person. She's different. You can't hold her to normal standards."

"I can't?"

"Not if you have any chance of seeing her again."

Something about the finality of those words gives me pause. Of course I want to see her again. I'm desperate to, in fact, and Martin's the key to making it happen. But what am I getting into? This woman has me this twisted up, and it's been less than twenty-four hours.

I drum my fingertips on the table, my doubts gradually eaten up by the fact that I'd do nearly anything to feel her in my arms again, to have another chance to bring her into my life for a little longer.

"Fine," I say quietly. "She's different. Tell me why. Explain."

He shakes his head slightly. "You're the shrink. I thought you'd have her figured out in no time."

A dry laugh escapes me. "Maybe if I had more time. But now I have no idea where she is."

Martin eyes me a moment before retrieving his cigarette tin and trapping one between his lips. I feel some of my hope slip away.

"Who knows? Maybe she doesn't even want to see me again," I mutter.

Martin shakes his head, but I don't know what it means this time.

"Do me a favor," he says. "Please don't fuck this up. I like Chloe."

"Of course you do. You've slept with her." Bringing it up again is shallow, but I can't help myself. I'm feeling a little too raw about it all.

He pulls his cigarette free and leans across the table toward me, his eyes narrow. "That has absolutely nothing to do with it. You may be convinced I don't care about anything, but I care about her. I take pride in keeping the very best people in my circle of acquaintances. She's among them."

"So am I."

"You're basically family. That's different."

"Thanks."

He sighs and lights his cigarette, even though I've told him a hundred times he can't smoke in my rental.

"So," he finally says, blowing smoke out the side of his mouth.

"So what?"

He half smirks. "So aren't you going to ask me for her address?"

✧ ✧ ✧

Chloe

I FUMBLE THROUGH my drawers, half my brain committed to the task of finding something to wear, the other half lost in snapshots of memory from last night. I wander to the living room and park myself in front of the painting I've been agonizing over for too long. Unfortunately I have no fresh inspiration now.

The guilt I feel for leaving Hayden without a real goodbye has been nagging me all day. Men don't normally care—at least I figure they don't. But I feel like Hayden would. Something about his sweetness, the way he danced around his past like something or someone was still hurting him tells me that his heart is bigger or softer than most. The awe in his eyes when he made love to me is something that I may not ever forget.

I try to ignore the guilt and the desire and the sparks of affection as I mix color on the palette beside me. I dab my brush through the paint and dot it along the bottom edge of the painting I'm at risk of overworking. I should be happy with it already, but I'm on edge and distracted, a poor judge of where the work stands.

All I can see is Hayden hovering over me, looking down at me like I'm the most beautiful creature he's ever seen. He's not like anyone I've ever met. Most of the men I've been with, they covet, they hunt, they fuck, and they forget. And usually I'm okay with that because it's what I've always come to expect. It's why I've refused to commit to any of them. But somehow I've convinced myself that Hayden is some kind of real-life Prince Charming, with glittering blue eyes and the body of a god and a touch that made me feel cherished.

Then there's a short but loud knock on my door. I wipe my hands off hastily, rise, and walk to the front door. I lift onto my toes to look out the peephole.

"Hayden?"

He's standing with his hands in his pockets, scowling at the ground. Then he lifts his head, his expression suddenly hopeful.

I slap my hand to my mouth because he definitely heard me. I look down at myself. I'm a mess.

"Chloe? Are you there?"

I don't give myself time to think. I unbolt the door and open it. He looks me up and down.

"How did you find out where I lived?"

He looks down a moment before meeting my gaze again. "Martin."

"Right. Of course."

I hear voices from the apartment across the hall and usher Hayden inside.

"Can I get you something to drink? Wine? Coffee?"

He shakes his head, his gaze still fixed on me.

"I'm sorry. I was working. If I'd known you were coming by, I would have changed."

He frowns. "You're perfect."

I laugh nervously. "Hardly."

He takes a few steps closer, and my heart rate jacks up. He reaches for me, touches my cheek, and slowly trails his fingertips down my neck, my chest, and then gently twisting his hand into the loose fabric of my T-shirt.

"I took a risk coming here," he says. "I wasn't sure you wanted to see me again."

I know guilt must be written all over my face when the flash of lust in his eyes changes into something else—something tentative. His touch falls away.

I swallow, not sure how to delicately explain that most of my interactions with men have been brief, and it has a lot to do with me.

"The truth is, I haven't stopped thinking about you since I woke up this morning." The admission falls off my lips. It's not a lie. Something about Hayden makes me want to tell him the truth every chance I can. That and I'm on fire being this close to him again. I draw in a fortifying breath. "I wasn't sure if you wanted to see me again either. Everything happened really fast. I figured it'd be easier that way."

His brows furrow. "You figured wrong."

I reach out and follow the line down the front of his button-down shirt. "Well, you found me."

"Thank God. Because we didn't finish what we started."

CHAPTER FIVE

Hayden

HER EYES WIDEN and her cheeks turn an adorable shade of pink. I feel like a madman raking her in. I can't think straight. I came here to talk, but the second I stepped through the door, all I could think of was getting inside her again, reliving last night's ecstasy and more. Now that I know she wanted to see me again too, I've lost my grip on the original plan entirely.

"Not nearly." I slide my hand around her back, pulling her flush against me the way I've been dying to.

The way she fits in my arms, her palms resting gently on my chest, where my heart's started to race, feels alarmingly good, like somehow she belongs here. As right as it feels, it's not enough to satisfy this new craving, this Chloe-shaped obsession that's consumed me since I first set eyes on her.

I can't let myself think about the last time I wanted a woman this badly. I'm not sure I ever have. All I know is that I have to have her—all of her. I let my hands roam. She shivers in my arms as I palm her ass.

"I didn't get to taste you." My voice is a low rasp.

She stares up at me with parted lips and shallow breathing. "I..."

"Will you let me this time?"

My mouth is so close to hers, I can feel her warm breath skid across my face as she nods. "But...I need you to know something."

I take a step forward, moving her closer to the wall behind her. "Tell me." I make the command gently, hoping it's quick and we can get back to the carnal fantasies I'm too eager to turn into reality.

I can't help myself. I need to taste. Consume. Then I want to bury myself in her and lose control again.

She sucks in a breath as soon as her back touches the cold, hard plaster. I kneel down, gazing up at her as she peers down at me. Her chest heaves, infecting me with the deep satisfaction of knowing how I affect her. I can't wait to feel her come apart with my mouth on her.

I bite my lip to stifle a grown as I glide my hands over her silky skin. I find the edge of her tiny shorts before slowly inching them down her legs.

"Hayden… I've never…" She closes her eyes, opens them again. "I don't date. I don't do relationships. With men, with women. It's too complicated. Most importantly, it affects my work."

My eyes are locked on to hers. My heart is beating too loudly to ignore as I play back her words.

Why should I care? This is sex. Lust. Temporary. I don't even live here.

Why do I care?

Because it's Chloe, and she's completely bewitched me. And I can't walk away right now. Not in an hour. Not tomorrow. I want more.

I shake my head. "Chloe, if you want me to leave, I will. Before I do, you should know that I've been in Paris for months, and I've never felt anything like this. I've seen beautiful, breathtaking things and met interesting people, and nothing or no one has been as breathtaking and fascinating to me as you." I touch her cheek, hoping I can change her mind. "Sometimes I have mixed feelings about Martin's impulses, but I think he probably wanted us to meet for a reason, don't you?"

She nods after a moment. "I think he had his reasons, yes."

"And you trust Martin, right?"

She grins a little. "Yes."

"Then let's give our eccentric friend a little credit and see where this goes. We don't have to call it a relationship, per se. We can just call it Chloe and Hayden."

She sighs softly, like she's about to come up with another reason to say good-bye to me forever, so I do the only thing I can think of to stop her. I cup my hand at her nape and pull her to me, kissing her deeply and passionately, pouring my silent plea into her mind like my unending desire for her body.

I've never been one to chase a woman, but I'm ready to fucking sprint to keep Chloe this way. Close and soft and wrapped all around me.

She moans a little when we separate. I feel like I'm cheating, putting that lusty look in her eyes in the middle of her objections, but I don't care.

"Do you want me to stay?" I ask her.

She lifts her head slowly, and her eyes lock on mine. "Of course," she says, giving me hope and warming my soul.

"In Paris?"

She blinks, like she's catching on to the deeper meaning. The promise that I'm offering her. The promise to stay…

"Everyone should stay in Paris as long as possible," she utters softly. "It's the only place I've ever lived where it seems all things are possible."

"But do *you* want me to stay?" I repeat, needing to hear the words to make my decision. "I've been everywhere I've wanted to be. I've seen every landmark I wanted to see. The only thing I haven't done that I want to do"—I take a deep breath, knowing what I'm about to say is too soon but needs to be said—"is spend more time with you."

Her eyes brighten for a moment and then darken like a veil has been carefully placed over her emotions. "My work is everything to me, Hayden. If I can't paint, if I can't create, I don't know if there will be anything left of me. It's happened once, and I can't let it happen again."

I study her devastatingly beautiful features. "You're worried that this…relationship with me…would get in the way of that?"

She gives me a weak smile as she pulls her hands free from my body. "You can't stay here forever."

But I keep her with me, pressing her hands against my chest, loving the warmth of her palms through my shirt. "Forever is a myth, Chloe. All we have is today. This hour. This minute. This second. It could all end in a split second and become nothing more than the past. If I had to pick where to spend my final moments, I'd want to be right here with you."

She bows her head, breathing deep and heavy, as she soaks in my words. "And when you leave…" Her voice trails off as she lifts her eyes to mine. "You'll leave only devastation in your wake."

I inch closer, lifting my hand and placing my finger under her chin so she can't look anywhere except at me. "And if I were to walk out your door right now…and never come back…" My thumb grazes the soft skin of her chin as I try to memorize every plane and dip of her face. "How would you feel?"

She shakes her head slowly, eyes glistening. "Devastated."

I nod, knowing I'd be right there with her. Forever wondering *what if?* What if Chloe from Paris had been the one to show me how to love again?

"Hayden, have you ever had your heart broken?"

I tense my jaw. "I have, and I swore I'd never let it happen again."

"I did too. And this is how I make sure it never happens again."

"There's something about you, Chloe. Something that draws me to you. Maybe whatever this is will fade as fast as it's burning. Spend some time with me, maybe just a week, and once we've both had our fill and the fire fades, I'll go."

Her eyes widen. "A week?"

Leaning forward, I brush my lips against the ball of her cheek, inhaling the sweetness of her skin. "Maybe after days, or months, of nothing but pure uninhibited pleasure, we'll get each other out of our systems."

I know I'm lying. Not just to her but to myself. I've never felt this way about anyone. Not even Natasha. Sure, I was attracted to her, but I didn't crave her. I didn't think about her nonstop. Her body didn't fill my fantasies, calling to me like a beacon in a storm.

Chloe does that to me.

Only Chloe.

She blinks slowly, like she's trying to focus on my words, letting them penetrate her lust-filled gaze. "What about my work? I need to paint."

I nod, running my thumb across her jaw line. "Then paint. And when you're not painting, be with me. When you need inspiration, we'll go find some. And if you need space, I'll go bother Martin. But I want you in my life."

Her mouth opens and closes as she stares at me.

"Say something," I tell her, searching her eyes for a hint of what she's feeling.

She swallows roughly and sweeps her tongue across her bottom lip.

"Yes, Hayden," she rasps. "That sounds amazing. Perfect, actually."

Then my mouth is on hers, pushing her backward and covering her body with my own.

For the first time in months, I'm happy. And nothing has ever been more important than making Chloe happy too.

✧   ✧   ✧

Thank you for reading! Be sure to check out *Misadventures of a City Girl* by Chelle and Meredith.
www.waterhousepress.com/collection/book/misadventures-of-a-city-girl

DOING IT RIGHT PREQUEL

HARLOE RAE

This is a short introduction to Mason Braxter and Presley Drake from Doing It Right—a second chance, small town romantic comedy. Enjoy!

THEN (EIGHT YEARS AGO)

Mason

OAK TREES HAVE abrasive bark with a tendency to shred my skin. I'm getting a personal reminder while climbing the trunk of one that's rooted mere feet from Presley's window. This sneaky maneuver is a damn cliché, but I'm all about seeing my girl after dark.

Another scrape lashes at me, but I barely flinch. A shallow flesh wound won't deter me. There's plenty of damage already reaped. My focus is set on a specific goal, and I refuse to be defeated.

With a final shuffled scoot from my ass, I'm close enough to knock. I tap against the paned glass with a bent knuckle. My exhausted limbs tremble the branch beneath me. What a fucking sight I'd make crashing to the ground. Coach would probably bench me from our opening game as punishment for thinking with my dick. A scoff spouts from my smirking mouth. Only if he wants us to lose.

I pump my fist when Presley's lamp flickers on. The tree doesn't appreciate my cocky celebration, attempting to buck me off for that slight movement. My thighs scream in protest while I flex to regain a stable position. Practice ended at seven, but I stayed behind for three more hours. My right arm is the consistency of slush. Gunner and Miles even quit on me by nine. So much for my support system. I was left launching the ball at an empty target downfield.

It doesn't help that I'm sweating my balls off while straddling this gnarled branch. The summer heat hasn't loosened its hold, even as the stars and moon shine bright. I wipe at the moisture clinging to my brow. That quick shower I rushed through seems like a wasted effort.

Presley's shadowed silhouette appears beyond the sheer curtains. In just a tank top and cotton shorts, her curves are on full display for me to devour. My balance wavers while I wait for her to grant me entry. I'm almost dizzy from a single glance. Maybe I should've had a power bar on the drive over. Too late now. With an upward tug, she removes the barrier between us.

"Ten?" Her soft voice is heavy with sleep. "What's wrong?"

The aches and pains disappear into sizzling lust at the sound of her voice. Not to mention the nickname she has for me. I'm so fucking gone for this girl.

My smile is sluggish and dopey as I stare at her. "Just needed to see you."

Presley's blue eyes dart to the side. "But it's almost eleven o'clock."

"Is that too late?"

"I dunno," she murmurs.

"You gonna send me away, Peppy Girl?" I trap the air in my lungs while waiting for her verdict. It was a risk showing up after she didn't answer my texts. I should've guessed she'd already gone to bed. That doesn't mean I'm ready to raise a white flag and retreat.

"No," she breathes a beat before my chest pinches from the strain. With a flick of her slender wrist, she beckons me forward. "Come in."

I release a loud exhale while clamoring over the sill. "You won't regret this."

"Never do." She peeks at me from under her lowered lashes.

My vision adjusts quickly in the dim lighting. Her room is shrouded in darkness, but I can see more than she probably notices. Pebbled nipples poke through the thin fabric of her shirt. I gulp at the fast-acting arousal clogging my bloodstream. This must be some sort of record. My throat is sandpaper, the rasp making me choke.

No teenage boy in the history of getting a glimpse at tits could look away. It's a feat I don't want to attempt. Guilt plagues the feverish desire surging through my veins. I respect her enough to not openly leer for longer than a full minute.

Heat pools in my groin and I avert my gaze. If I keep staring, I'm bound to pop an impressive boner. Presley won't let me stay if that happens. That's my assumption anyway.

"What's wrong?" She repeats her concern with more force.

The deep furrow carved between her brows alerts me that she won't accept a flimsy excuse. I'd expect nothing less from my daily dose of sunshine. She loves me with the same fierce passion that I devote to her. The truth is that she's my solace and relief and soothing comfort wrapped in one irresistible package. It feels like I need her more than my next breath. Another freaking cliché. Just consider me a lovesick sap when it comes to Presley Drake.

"Nothing's the matter," I insist. "Just tired. Stayed at the field longer than usual."

Her lush lips twist into a tempting pout. "You push yourself too hard."

The twinge cramping my muscles agrees with her. "For good reason."

Presley scoffs. "That's what you always say. Why do you insist on testing your limits? You're gonna hurt yourself."

"I have to be the best."

"You already are." She smiles, but the expression lacks her typical sparkle.

"That's cute, Pep." On instinct, I narrow the distance separating us. A burst of wildflowers, summer sunshine, and reckless abandon infiltrates my senses. That last wispy tendril is my bad influence on her. She's only naughty with me, and that drives me absolutely crazy.

Flames flicker in those bottomless blue depths as she appraises my not-so-subtle shift in stance. "Will you ever be satisfied?"

There's no question when it comes to her. I have been since day one. But with myself? "I have a long way to go."

She blinks in rapid succession, that fire getting smothered with each flutter. "At what cost?"

Now I reach for her hand, lacing our fingers in a complicated tangle of soft and rough. "I'm building a future for us."

Presley lowers her gaze to our clasped palms and gives me a gentle squeeze. "We're only sixteen."

"And I only have limited years to play ball. The better I am, the longer we can live on my salary." That's if I'm lucky enough to get chosen in the draft. This is everything I've been training for since the Tiny Mites.

"I'm capable of contributing," she says with a crooked grin.

"And you will." I lower my forehead to touch hers. "But I need to do everything I can to provide for us."

"Why?"

"That's my dream, Pep." I've only been repeating it every other day since we met in seventh grade.

Her smooth thumb rubs along my chafed knuckles. "I have dreams too."

I tug until she collides flush against my chest. "Do those include me?"

She snuggles into my hold, sincerity shining from her unwavering focus. "Always. You're my Ten. It doesn't get better than you."

"Good." I breathe a thick sigh. "I just wanna take care of you. Will you let me?"

A stubborn notch juts her chin. "What if I wanna take care of you?"

"We can take care of each other," I offer in compromise.

"Okay," she relents. "But I'm scared you're going too far. What if you get injured?"

"Don't think like that," I plead. "I've got it under control."

"Do you?" She squints in the yellowish glow from the single lamp.

"We don't have to talk about this right now." These precious moments alone shouldn't be wasted on misplaced worry. Seductive possibilities tease me while I hug her closer.

Presley loops her arms around me in return. "That's what I said earlier."

"Should've listened," I murmur while stooping to brush her lips with mine. "Don't wanna fight with you."

"Me either," she exhales across my mouth.

"Just let me hold you for a bit, okay?"

She pauses, wheels appearing to spin. "In bed?"

"If you're willing." I refuse to take more than she offers.

Already nodding, she guides our huddled form toward her rumpled sheets. "Very much so."

When she confesses those whispered words, another burst of feverish longing rips at me. She drops on the mattress with an airy bounce and scoots over to make room for me. I'm most likely frothing at the mouth from the mere thought of joining her. Presley lies down, her midnight hair cradled by a fluffy pillow. My actions are clumsy while I rush to fill the gap she created.

Her body clings to mine within seconds. Those ample tits are squished against my solid pecs, the contrast leaving me reeling. I try to fill my brain with pictures of kittens and ice baths and my dad's hairy feet, but she's just too damn sexy.

We're aligned so close that our noses brush. The coy expression she flashes at me is a thinly veiled craving for a late-night snack. I'm in a load of trouble for being near her without taking the edge off first. That doesn't mean I expose the war waging on my control. Quite the opposite as I offer the signature smirk that she goes breathless over.

Presley traces the shape of my dimples. "These are mine."

I'm quick to agree with a jerky nod, our foreheads bumping. "They only appear for you."

"Darn skippy, champ. No one else gets my special grin." She winks while dancing her fingers along my flexing arm.

"Never," I vow.

"Kiss me," she breathes across my jaw.

Our lips crash in the following thump from my heart. The organ beats solely for her, especially when she parts her mouth with a muffled sigh. I'm quick to swipe my tongue out to glide along hers. She's all too eager to return my enthusiasm with a slippery stroke of her own. That fluid motion has been practiced over the years. We don't fumble as the desire notches higher.

Each mewl is a hushed promise. Young we might be, but commitment thrums between us. Age is just a number. Presley often tells me her soul recognizes mine, and the warmth spreading through me is proof. Each brush of bare skin is a hot jab stoking my hunger. Forget sweet nothings. These tender, speechless sentiments mean everything.

I drift a palm along her side, fingers itching to dip under the flimsy material. From personal experience, I'm all too aware how silky her skin feels under my calloused palms. I settle for spearing my fingers into her hair. Presley tilts into my touch, fisting my shirt in the process.

This position grants me full access to her front and does wicked things to me. There's no doubt she can feel exactly how hard I am. Another minute of this and I'll be humping her leg that's wedged between mine. I haven't pushed her for more, and I won't. Not until she's ready. With a slight shift, I attempt to gain an inch of distance between her hips and mine.

Raging adolescent hormones perfume the air. We've never rounded second base, always pausing before impulsive lust could sink its claws in. That reminder has me pumping the brakes. A failed attempt as she toys with the hem of my faded tee. That tease only serves to drive my need higher. If we push more boundaries, I'll be tempted to roll her underneath me and grind us together until I bust in my boxers. The idea pumps molten lava into my veins.

It's pointless to deny my desperation for her. There's a steel pipe tenting my shorts in the effort to reach her. I'm nearly blind with lust, more than ready to let my primal horniness rule the roost. But she's not making a demand for more. I maintain my wits to read her cues, even as the lust grows into a billowing cloud.

Besides, I can't screw around in her parents' house. That would be the ultimate betrayal of their trust. Sneaking in through the window is bad enough. This mental battle is crushing my already frazzled resolve into minced meat. Then Presley goes and wiggles her hips, nudging my very aroused dick in the process. She gasps and breaks from my lips, wide eyes flinging to mine.

The haze ebbs ever so slightly as I struggle to regain some semblance of composure. "I can't help it, Pep. You make me want more."

She gnaws on her bottom lip that's swollen from my kiss. "You do the same to me."

"We have forever to do this."

"But let's not wait that long." The plea is heavy in her words, threatening to feed the beast in my gut.

"We won't. You'll always be my girl." I very much need a distraction. "That's why I'm building a future for us."

"It shouldn't hurt you this much. Please don't go to such extremes anymore." She squeezes my biceps and I wince.

"The pain will fade. I need to make sure the scouts find me."

She lifts a palm to cup my cheek. "How could they miss you?"

"We live in a tiny town, Pep. Meadow Creek is barely a dot on the map."

Presley huffs, the disbelief hot on my skin. "But our team is good."

"Well, yeah. Our division is shit, though. There are far better out there. Those that actually make it to state."

Her eyes narrow on mine. "What're you saying?"

"Nothing," I blurt.

"It sounds like you wanna be on those teams instead."

I grab her hand, thread our fingers, and pepper her skin with kisses. "Just a pinch of envy. Those guys have an advantage."

She studies my rapt focus on her inner wrist. "You could move."

My lips still in their assault. "As if that's ever gonna happen."

"Why not?"

It's my turn to scrutinize her with a squint. "My parents aren't going to uproot their lives to put me in a different school."

"You could open enroll to one not that far," she murmurs.

I recoil in an exaggerated manner. "Careful, Pep. I'm beginning to think you're trying to get rid of me."

Her scoff is hollow. "Don't be silly."

I skate a palm along her side. "That's right, I'm not going anywhere. We're just getting started."

She hums and cuddles against me. "Uh-huh."

"I'm gonna marry you someday, Presley Blake."

Blue depths the color of paradise settle on me. "Yeah?"

"If you'll have me."

Her mouth twitches with a slanted grin. "Should be the other way around."

"Your jokes are killer tonight," I tease.

"I'm not kidding."

I hike my brows at the crisp retort. "So, you don't trust me? Or believe how much I love you?"

Presley's gaze skitters away. "It's not that."

"Then what?"

"I dunno."

With a thumb on her chin, I tug until she's looking at me again. "Tell me what you're afraid of."

"Maybe you'll find someone else. You just said there are far better out there." She wrinkles her nose.

The mere suggestion of another girl definitely smells putrid. "On a very different topic. It's not possible where you're concerned. I already have the best."

Her smile is pleased. "You're suave, Ten. Throwing out those swoony lines to reassure me."

"That's because you're meant to be mine." Now that the chomping lust is fading, a drowsy layer settles over me. It feels good to relax with her in my arms.

"We can't fall asleep," she reminds.

I'm already nodding, more than aware how this situation ends. Soon enough I'll be alone wrapped in cold sheets. My fist will be keeping my dick company while I replay her wriggling against me. That thought leaves me frigid and itchy to maintain this comfort.

Instead, I let my eyes slide shut with the image of Presley dressed in a white gown sending me off into blissful unawareness.

✧   ✧   ✧

I hope you enjoyed this prequel for Doing It Right. What happens to Mason and Presley?

Find out in the full story—available now!
harloe-rae.blog

LAST SECOND CHANCE
PROLOGUE

ROBIN COVINGTON

"**W**E'RE SO PLEASED that you and Ms. Cain chose our chapel for the wedding, Mr. Woodward."

I nodded at the wedding chapel manager, George Button, easing on my suit jacket as the on-site staff scurried around the space getting organized for our last-minute request to get married. It wasn't chaos, these folks were professionals and a couple rolling in at two o'clock in the morning was business as usual.

Actually, they reminded me of the team on game day. All that practice paid off when we hit the field on Sunday. It might look like chaos and anarchy but it was choreography—a precision design. And when we did it right, we won.

And we won all the damn time.

The chapel, with its warm wood walls and backlit stained-glass windows, wasn't one of the neon-bright ones on the other part of the strip. One of the oldest wedding chapels, it had a solidity and character that made you feel like the vows you took here meant something. And I wanted that for us. This might be happening at two in the morning and two weeks after our second-first date but this wasn't a joke. What Dinah and I had was real and this step was inevitable. I knew it. She knew it.

"I'm a *huge* Red Wolf fan, Mr. Woodward," Mr. Button continued, bent over the table as he prepared the paperwork for the wedding. He was wearing a wedding band, the gold scuffed from daily wear—completely different from the brand-new platinum pair I had sitting in a box in my pocket. Mr. Button glanced up from where he was sorting the stack of papers and marking others with "sign here" sticky flags. He flung his arms out wide, papers whipping around and multi-colored tabs shimmying back and forth. "Huge fan. You guys were my team even *before* you started winning."

I grinned at his enthusiasm. "Reds" fans were absolutely incredible. You can't forget the people who stood by you when the years were lean. Three Super Bowl championships later and our fans were rabid—in the best way. My whole life I'd loved playing football but nothing beat a game under the lights of the Red Wolf stadium with the fans yelling so loudly that the ground shook under your feet. Unbelievable.

"Man, I appreciate that. The next time you're in Rogue City, pop me an email and I'll have some tickets for you at the gate."

I straightened my collar and adjusted the cuffs on my shirt again, anxious to get this ceremony started.

Where was Dinah? How long did it take to put on a veil and some lipstick?

What was it they said in that movie where the heroine had an orgasm in the diner? Something about wanting your life to start immediately when you knew that you had the person you wanted to spend it with?

I knew.

And I wanted to get my life started now.

The double doors at the back of the chapel opened and the wedding planner poked her head into the opening. She made some complicated hand gestures and Mr. Button snapped into action as if his spine was directly connected to the flick of her wrist.

"Are you ready to score a touchdown?" Mr. Button teased, his grin contagious even if his metaphor was pretty fucking cheesy.

And I was having the best night of my life so I grinned back at the man and let him manhandle me into position at the bottom of the steps of the altar. The sound system speakers crackled and the "Wedding March" filled the small space, bouncing off the wood-paneled walls and spilling down the aisle as the doors opened and my heart fucking stuttered to a stop in my chest.

Dinah stood at the end of the long run of carpet, her white dress silky, skimming the floor and hugging her curves. Her black hair was loose around her shoulders and down her back, just the way I loved it. She carried deep red roses and the color perfectly matched the lipstick that covered her sexy-as-fuck mouth.

I knew I was supposed to wait for her to come to me but that wasn't going to happen. It took five long strides to get to her. I grabbed her and took her mouth, groaning into the kiss when she swept inside my mouth with her tongue. It was hot and needy and when we broke apart we both laughed.

Dinah reached up and rubbed the pad of her thumb across my bottom lip. "You know, red is really your color."

"Not as good as it looks on you." I pulled back and raked my eyes over her body. "You look amazing, baby. I love you."

"I love you, too." She pressed a soft kiss against my lips, her breath warm against my cheek as she moved deeper into my embrace. Dinah trembled a little, her body echoing all the thoughts pinging around in my head. And then she gave them a voice, "They'll say we're crazy. Two weeks isn't long enough to know."

Yeah, that's what they would say. But they were the same assholes who said that my moving to Rogue City to play for the Reds was a career-ending mistake on my part and that we'd never be a championship team. They were the same people who said that Dinah Cain would never fill an arena with fans singing her own songs back to her.

What the fuck did "they" know? Nothing. Not what mattered.

I tightened my hold on her, pressing a kiss to her temple before looking down at her, making sure I had eye contact. I needed her to see what was happening here. I needed her to see that being anywhere else was futile. Not when our gravity had us linked together with no way of breaking the connection. But I needed her to see that it wasn't compulsion that had me here with her—this was where I wanted to be. Nowhere else. Never again.

"But *we* know, baby," I said, ready to let her go back down the aisle if that was what she wanted but praying to all the gods that she wouldn't ask me to do it.

Dinah examined my face, her gaze pulling me apart and dissecting me like one of her songs. I hovered between victory and defeat for a few seconds before her expression changed, calmed and her eyes locked with mine. What I saw in them almost brought me to my knees—whether it would be to send up a prayer of thanks or to worship her was to be determined. Both were entirely possible and entirely viable.

"*We* know," she answered and turned in my grip as she turned to face the altar and slipped her hand in mine.

We took that first step together and I never doubted it for one second.
She was the most amazing woman in the world.
I loved her.
And she was mine.

✧ ✧ ✧

Two years later
Rogue City Red Wolves Stadium Press Room

DINAH CAIN WAS still the most amazing woman in the world.

But I didn't love her and she wasn't mine.

And nobody knew it except the two of us.

I guess that wasn't technically true. The people who needed to know the truth were in on it. The inner circle included our managers, senior publicity reps, and the world's most discreet divorce attorneys.

My team didn't even know that my marriage was over. We were getting geared up for pre-season training with a new quarterback and everyone questioning our ability to make another run for a championship. We didn't need the distraction that my personal shit would bring.

The press didn't know my marriage was over.

And they couldn't find out until it was done.

Which was going to be a son-of-bitch play to execute because I had to pretend that everything was fine for the next three weeks.

In public. As co-chairs of a high-profile charity event.

I looked over at Dinah, watching as she huddled with her PR Team doing the last-minute prep before the press conference kicked off. Her hair was shorter but still spilling over her shoulders in silky black waves. The pink was gone, a change from the last photo I'd seen of her on social media, replaced with streaks of red and gold. The realization that I didn't know she'd changed her hair color pinched, sharp, and metallic, deep inside me but I pushed it down. Ignored it. Just like I had done for the last twelve months every time it became clear to me that when it came to facts about my wife—I was the last one to know.

And I hated it.

Dinah paused and looked over at me and all the sounds in the room faded to a jumble of noise and nothing. The last two years and about a million miles of harsh words, unanswered phone calls, and texts, stolen weekends that ended in more distance and resentment than reconnection pulsed between us. She swallowed hard, her whole body actively pushing down the memories that I know shuttled through her mind because they were the same ones that kept me awake at night.

The good ones.

The best ones.

The ones we tried to forget as we moved toward the goal of ending us.

I turned away, breaking the contact before I gave up the secret that I held closest to my soul. The one that I didn't even let myself acknowledge too often.

The secret that I still loved my wife.

And I had one last chance to get her back.

✧ ✧ ✧

ARE YOU READY TO READ THE REST OF DINAH AND KING'S STORY?
Preorder it Here!
Releases May 9, 2022!!!!
robincovingtonromance.com/last-second-chance

MENACE HAS A BEAUTIFUL FACE

JENIKA SNOW

AMARA

"YOU'RE GROWLING AGAIN, Nikolai." I didn't bother looking over at my husband, but I could feel his gaze on me, felt the vibrations of the animalistic sounds he made.

"I'm about to ruin someone's fucking vacation if the piece of shit doesn't stop looking at you."

I lifted my hand and curled my finger around the edge of my sunglasses, pulling them down the bridge of my nose, looking at him over the rim.

Nikolai was sitting on the lounge chair by the resort pool, his body turned toward me, his elbows braced on his thighs, and his big, hard and muscular tattooed chest and arms on full display.

I felt a shiver move through me at how sexy he was, that dangerous aura that surrounded him, that violence that poured from him. People kept a wide berth when we were walking by, and rightfully so. Nikolai was definitely a force to be reckoned with.

"Honey, you're doing that psycho thing again." I couldn't help but smile at the way he glowered at me. "I'm sure he's just looking around. People-watching. I'm sure he's not staring at me given the fact he's probably with his wife or girlfriend."

My husband, heir to the Desolation, NY Russian Mafia, who I'd been arranged to marry by my Cosa Nostra father, was definitely not someone you wanted to mess with.

He was deadly, coldhearted and ruthless... and he was so overprotective I wouldn't put it past him to kill the man in question simply for looking in my direction.

Maybe talking him into taking a belated honeymoon in a public resort wasn't the best idea.

When I'd healed from the gunshot wound inflicted after the drama of finding out my father had been sleeping with Francesca since she was fifteen, the daughter of one of his Italian Mafia associates, I'd broached the subject with Nikolai about finally going away.

Of course I wanted a honeymoon, the real reason I wanted away from Desolation, NY and everything that had to do with my Cosa Nostra side and Nikolai's Bratva side, was because I wanted to act like things were... normal. Even if only for a short time. Another reason I'd been adamant about going to a public resort.

I loved spending time alone with Nikolai, but being around others—at least for this vacation—who had no idea the dangerous and volatile things that happened right under their noses made me feel like my life was just like theirs. Uncomplicated.

And surprisingly Nikolai had agreed to go away on the condition he picked the resort. And of course the one he'd picked was so lavish and exclusive I was pretty sure I'd already seen a handful of celebrities and governmental officials in just the last three days we'd been here.

Nikolai's brow was pulled down low as he looked at something—someone—across the pool. Then he started growling again.

"I should have forbidden you to wear that bikini."

I laughed softly. "And you know how that would have gone." He cut his gaze over to me. Although his face was a mask of hard indifference, I saw the way his eyes softened and his nostrils flared. "You know you can't say no to me."

He made a low sound deep in his throat, and faster than I could anticipate, he reached out and curled his hand around my throat and pulled me forward. My husband loved his hand necklaces, and I grew wet instantly from them.

His mouth was pressed to mine but he wasn't kissing me. "I may bend to you—only to you—my sweet girl, but we both know who you belong to."

I was breathing so hard, my pussy wet. I clenched my thighs together to stem off the arousal, but all that did was pinch my clit between my lips and pull a needy moan out of me.

His grin came on slow and I felt it abasing my lips. "That's my good girl. Your tight little cunt is getting all wet for me, isn't it?" My breath hitched. "You like being my little whore, baby, isn't that right?"

That needy sound came for me again. I should have been offended at what he just said, but he and I both knew I was so ready for him right now.

For a second he just stared into my eyes and let his mouth gently press to mine, and then he groaned and ran his tongue over my lips, licking, sucking the flesh into his mouth before letting it go with a wet pop.

"Mmm, I want to fuck you here, right now, right in front of everyone so they know I'm the only man who gets to look at you, touch you, and fuck your tight cunt."

My eyes fluttered, threatening to close. I saw Nikolai pull back slightly, a smirk on his mouth as he glanced over my shoulder. Then all heat and desire left him like the snap of a finger. A wall closed down over his expression, his eyes became dead and hard and dangerous.

"That fucker is dead." I opened my mouth to placate him again, but I knew it would be fruitless. Nikolai was already in a war zone of jealousy and possessiveness, so there was no reasoning with him.

He rose before I could stop him and strode away, all menace and rage clouding around him.

I stood and grabbed my towel, wrapping it around my body as I followed Nikolai, knowing I was about to stop my husband from murdering yet another man for me.

Nikolai was a beast with long legs and rage fueling him, so of course I wasn't fast enough to reach him before he was nose to nose with the "threat," a man six inches shorter than him and at least a hundred pounds lighter.

The guy wore swimming trunks that had pineapples plastered across the material, one of them embarrassingly placed right over his crotch. His arms and chest were so pale that he already had red splotches over his skin from being in the sun for too long.

He had to tip his head back to look at my husband, and although it was very clear he was scared shitless by a six-and-a-half-foot-tall tattooed man flaring his nostrils and breathing heavily as if he were seconds away from committing homicide in front of a lot of witnesses.

He also looked like he was about to piss his pants, and rightly so.

"I'll ask you again, which isn't something I give anyone, so count yourself fucking lucky."

I heard Nikolai groan, his Russian accent even thicker from his anger. People had stopped what they were doing to watch, and in some instances gawk, and I could see the bartender was two seconds away from calling security.

Another low growl came from Nikolai and I saw a few people looking around. I even heard someone murmuring if a wild animal had gotten loose. I covered my mouth to stifle my laugh, because even though I was pretty sure Nikolai wouldn't actually kill the man right now, I wasn't so confident he wouldn't throw some punches enough that the poor guy landed in the hospital.

"Niko," I said softly. I adopted the nickname shortly after I'd gotten shot, mainly to tease him, but after I'd said it, I saw the way his gaze had softened, and there weren't a lot of things that could soften the heart of a man like Nikolai Petrov.

So it just kind of stuck, and I wasn't ashamed enough to admit that if I really wanted to get my way, buttering him up with sweet words, promises of letting him bring me to orgasm, and throwing in the nickname certainly was in my arsenal that I used.

I saw his jaw clench but he didn't move, didn't look away from the other man. I placed my hand on his tattooed forearm, feeling his skin warm beneath my palm, the muscles flex.

"Niko, why don't we go upstairs? I'm sure this man was just looking for his girlfriend and happened to glance my way." Another flex of Nikolai's jaw, and another low rumble that came from deep within his chest. I could feel the tension surrounding him like electricity crackling in the air.

"No he fucking wasn't," he finally gritted out. "I'm pretty sure I saw this asshole eye-fucking you all the way across the courtyard."

The man finally had the intelligence to take a step back, and I tightened my hold marginally on Nikolai's forearm. Although realistically it wouldn't have kept him from going after what he wanted, but he didn't move, so I knew he wasn't too far gone in his anger not to at least listen to me and see reason.

"Look at me." I kept my voice soft, low. One heavy exhale. Two. And on the third his nostrils flared and he turned to look at me. I could tell by his expression that not resorting to violence was hard for him to do, so I gave my big, bad Russian mobster a soft smile and lifted my free hand up to cup his jaw. He'd shaved this morning but he already had a light sprinkling of scruff along his cheeks.

"How about we just go back to the room." I stepped closer, pressing my body against his, my breasts to his chest. I knew he could feel how hard my nipples were. God, even though we were surrounded by spectators, I felt a flush move through me. He was just so hard where I was soft. He was big where I was small. I was so dainty compared to Nikolai.

I was just a little doll. *His little doll.*

And although I could tell I had his attention, I knew Nikolai was still very aware of the man who'd inadvertently pissed him off and still stood a few feet to the side. So we were all standing on very thin ice, so to speak.

"He's not worth the trouble that it'll cause kicking his ass. Besides, I don't want our honeymoon to be cut short because they called security and kicked us out."

Nikolai made a noncommittal noise deep within his throat and lowered his gaze to my mouth. "Making sure he can't see will do wonders for making me feel better, *printsessa*," he said in a rough voice. "You don't want to watch as I slowly drain the life out of his body with my bare hands?"

I glanced over at the man. I could see his eyes were wide and his pulse was beating rapidly at the base of his throat. He was also pleading with his eyes to keep my "bodyguard" in check so he didn't die today.

I would have laughed if he didn't look so terrified. And if I didn't know how deadly Nikolai really was.

I glanced back at my husband and slowly licked my lips, enticing him with that one move. And I knew it did the trick when he groaned softly.

"I can think of other things that I'd like you to do with your hands."

And that's all it took for the situation to be diffused and Nikolai to reach down, grip my waist in his big hands, and throw me over his shoulder. Then brought his big palm down on my ass, giving the cheek an audible smack, which caused a collective gasp of shock from the patrons.

I giggled at how scandalous they probably thought all this was, when in reality this was pretty mild caveman actions for my Russian Mafia husband.

He stalked away from the bar, across the courtyard, into the hotel, and up to our room. He growled out, "I'm going to paint this gorgeous ass red for wearing this bathing suit in front of everyone and making me so jealous, baby girl."

I didn't remind him he was jealous about everything that concerned me, or that my pussy was already wet at the idea of him bending me over his lap and spanking my bare ass.

He knew by the husky sound he made what he did to me, especially as I squirmed against him.

And God was I looking forward to all the deliciously dirty things Nikolai had planned.

NIKOLAI

I SLOWLY, SILENTLY, shut the hotel room door behind me and watched as Amara's pupils dilated and her breathing increased. Her hard, tight little nipples pressed through the white material of the minuscule triangle top.

Her bathing suit had equal parts red-hot need, and searing jealousy waging war inside of me.

I fucking loved that it barely covered her, the white a contrast to her olive skin tone and pitch-black hair. But in the same breath, the fact any fucker saw all that golden skin made me want to kill something... or someone ten times over. Hell, I thought I'd done a pretty good job of controlling and restraining myself from first-degree murder a hundred different times since we'd arrived at the resort.

"You know I like when you act all afraid of me, *kukolka.*" I moved a step forward, going for my trunks and pushing them down, freeing my already thick, hard cock. I only stopped long enough to kick the shorts aside, grip my cock, then I was moving toward Amara again.

I lowered my gaze to her breasts, my shaft jerking in my hand. I ran my palm over my cock, smearing pre-cum over the crown and down the length. My muscles clenched at how fucking good that felt.

"Look at you in that tiny fucking bathing suit." I looked down her flat belly, over her flared hips, along her long, tanned legs, and made my way back up so I was looking at her pussy. "I bet the material that cups that bare pussy is soaked, isn't it?" I took one more step toward her, then smirked when she moved one back, the floor-to-ceiling window of our honeymoon penthouse suite at the resort stopping her escape.

She didn't answer, but I didn't miss the sound of arousal that came from her slightly parted lips.

"Take it off," I said in a calm voice. "Take the bikini off and show me what's mine." I was jerking off in slow, steadied movements now. "You wanted to wear that in public and I didn't go apeshit over it—"

She snorted in the daintiest way that had my dick fucking aching. I cocked an eyebrow at her.

"I didn't kill anyone, so that's me not going apeshit, darling." She slowly licked her lips and I watched the act, my dick jerking in my hand, pre-cum a steady flow out the slit at the tip. "But then the bastards were looking at my girl and I'm feeling extra possessive and territorial right now, *malishka.*"

I gave her a second to comply, and when she didn't get to it fast enough, I lowered my head and took a step closer.

"That's five to start, sweetheart."

"F-five?" Although she stuttered, I could hear the pleasure in her voice, and smelled how wet her cunt was.

"Five times I'm going to bring my palm down on that plump, perfect ass because you wore that fucking minuscule bikini." I tightened my fist around my cock and pointed the tip at her as I moved my palm toward the tip.

She glanced down just as I squeezed out a drop of pre-cum.

"But I'm gonna add a few more in there because you're not being my good girl and listening right now."

She reached up and undid the string around her neck, then undid the one behind her back. The top fluttered to the ground and her perfect fucking tits were on display. Her nipples were a dusky rose, tightened by the chill in the air and her arousal.

"All of it," I gritted out, my balls tight to my body as I kept lazily stroking myself.

When she did as I wanted and stood there naked, I took a long moment to just look my fill of her. All creamy, olive flesh, and a bare pussy that had my mouth watering. I was so fucking rock hard staring at that feminine slit, knowing how tight she was, how sweet she tasted.

"See how much better it is when you listen to me like a good girl?" She moaned softly and I saw her clench her thighs together.

I made her "suffer" for a long minute, just pleasuring myself as she stood there completely naked, bare to me. I could see a flush rising along her chest and creeping up her neck. She was embarrassed that I watched her, appraising her like she was a piece of artwork at a museum.

I smirked because I knew that also turned her on. I knew the embarrassment, the mortification of when I called her those degrading names made her pussy drenched.

"Turn around." She dragged her tongue along her bottom lip before listening to me, her hands now flat on the glass, her head straight ahead.

I looked out the window from our penthouse, the ocean cresting in the horizon, the resort's lavish property stretched out below.

We were high up, nearly touching the clouds. I picked this resort because it was exclusive, high-end, and would afford us the privacy I not only needed, but wanted with Amara.

My girl wanted a tropical vacation, so I gave it to her, even though I would have much rather taken her to Russia, stayed in a cabin in the middle of the woods with a winter storm raging all around us just so she had to use me for warmth.

My cock kicked up at the very thought. But then again… looking at her like this, the sunlight streaming through the glass from the front, shadowing the long line of her back, the flare of her hips, and the plump perfection of her ass, was worth sharing her with society.

It was enough to make me groan and move closer.

I used my foot to kick her feet apart, curled my free hand around her hip, and popped her ass out more. Then I leaned back and looked at her pussy, all open and primed for me.

She was soaked, her hairless pussy freshly waxed, her lips glistening and pink, swollen from the blood flow of arousal.

"Look at how red your pussy is, baby."

Her thighs were glossy and I slid the hand not currently wrapped around my aching cock between her legs to stroke her slit. She trembled from that light touch, rested her forehead against the class and moaned long and low.

"I'm going to make it even redder."

"Niko—"

I cut off her words as I brought my hand down against her cunt, slapping the tender flesh until she yelped and rose on her toes.

"Good God," she breathed out, and just as I saw her turn her head to look at me, maybe outraged by her desire for more, I brought my hand down on her cunt again.

She arched her back, closed her eyes, and moaned out long and loud. I'd since let go of my dick, and the motion of me spanking her pussy had the fucker bobbing between us, the tip pressed to her thigh, my pre-cum smearing all over her flesh like a brand.

I spanked her cunt a handful more times… until the tears started sliding down her cheeks and she murmured incoherently. Only then did I start tweaking her clit, pulling the bundle of engorged nerves between my thumb and forefinger until she once again rose on her toes and pleaded for me to let her come.

I leaned in close so my mouth was right by her ear, and my hand cupped between her thighs. I didn't add pressure, but I could feel how soaked my palm was, my girl so unbelievably wet that when I finally did slide my dick into her tight heat, it would make the most filthy sound imaginable. "Not yet, *krasavitsa*. You still owe me your punishment."

She made a soft mewling noise of disappointment and I grinned before gently biting down on her earlobe. I had her in my arms and was seated in the leather chair beside the window a second later.

After adjusting her so her belly was flat against my thighs, I smoothed my hand down the length of her spine and over the curve of her peachy ass.

"You're going to be my good girl, Amara, and count them down, aren't you?" She whispered her compliance and I moved the long fall of her dark hair over one shoulder so I could see her face.

I cursed at how gorgeous she was, and kept murmuring in Russian that I'd kill anyone who even thought about her. She was mine. Only mine.

"Are you ready?" She nodded and looked up at me with glossed-over eyes and blown pupils. "It wouldn't have mattered if she was ready. I was doing whatever the fuck I wanted regardless and she'd thank me afterward with a soaked pussy.

I slowly ran my palm over her ass. Back and forth, building the anticipation before I struck.

"You like being my little whore, don't you?" She closed her eyes and bit her lip before nodding. I hummed in approval. "Yeah you do. My dirty little whore."

She moaned, and just as her voice tapered off, I lifted my hand and brought my palm down on her left cheek.

The crack of my flesh against hers was loud in the hotel room, and Amara bowed her back, her voice rising as she gasped out. "Count them off, baby."

I smoothed my palm over her cheek again and again, giving her a second to obey me.

"One," she moaned and I cracked her ass again. "Keep going or I'm gonna make it harder, hurt more." She was crying now, her pussy so wet that every time I smacked her ass, she clenched her thighs together, her wetness dripping onto my lap.

I spanked her three more times, rubbing her cheeks between each blow, warming the skin, soothing the sting away. My cock was a hard rod between us, digging against her belly so that every time she squirmed, it gave me the most delicious fucking friction.

On the fifth crack of my hand against her ass, I was done playing around. The sound of her crying, begging me to make her come was my undoing. I unleashed the beast inside of me, the primal animal that was about to fuck his woman until she couldn't walk straight.

I was up and out of the chair a second later, lifted her into my arms, and strode to the bed. I unceremoniously dropped her on the mattress, adjusted her so her belly was flat with the bed, her legs hanging off the edge, her ass raised in the air.

She moaned and spread her legs impossibly wider, showing me her drenched cunt, causing a growl to be pulled from the center of my chest.

I leaned down and sank my teeth into her right ass cheek, licked the flesh before doing the same thing to the left side. I did the same to her hip bone, before licking my way along the center of her spine, and pushing the hair off her back. And then I bit the side of her throat.

She was thrusting her ass back against me, grinding her pussy on my cock, getting the length juicy from her arousal.

I moved back down and got on my haunches, spread her cheeks apart, and feasted on her pussy. I licked and sucked, my face wet from her juices, her moans filling my ears. I sucked her clit into my mouth in hard pulls that elicited jerky movements from her. Her body trembled, her orgasm right at the surface. I could feel it, sense it surrounding us.

I stood, straightened and reached between us to grab my cock, notched the head at the entrance, and one hard thrust, I pushed all my dick into her tight cunt.

The sound that came out of me was rough, a harsh bark of noise as my balls pressed against her pussy, my groin flush with her bottom.

I broke away and curled one hand around her hair, yanking her head back so her throat was bare.

Her eyes were closed, her mouth parted before she begged, "Fuck me."

I grabbed her hip with my other hand and snarled as I pulled out and slammed back in. Over and over I did this, my thrusting hard and rough. I knew I'd leave bruises on her body tomorrow, marks of my brand, of my ownership.

"Oh God, Niko," she cried and I pulled out only to slam back in harder.

"I know, baby. *Fuck*, I know." I looked down at where we were connected and slid my hand to her cheeks to spread them so I was able to watch myself slide in and out of her pink pussy. "Say it, be a good girl for me and say what I want to hear."

Her breath hitched when I thrust my hips forward, burying myself deep in her.

"I'm only yours. Your good girl. The only woman who will ever make you feel good."

I hummed in approval and spanked her ass, watched the flesh jiggle, then positioned my hands back and her hips and fucked the hell out of her.

"You're doing so good," I growled. "Taking all my cock even though I'm big and I know it hurts this little pussy."

I felt her pussy clamp down on me and groaned at how good that felt.

"I can't fucking wait to knock you up, Amara." I bared my teeth, feeling beads of sweat lining my brow. "To get you big with my baby. To know I'm the reason you're like that…" I couldn't finish my sentence, the very thought of getting Amara knocked up causing my cock to thicken impossibly further, my primal desire to breed her making me crazed.

I was throwing my hips back and forth so hard and fast the only thing keeping her stable were my hands on her waist. "If you thought I was possessive of you before, wait until I get you pregnant."

She cried out as she came for me and I followed right behind, slamming into her once, twice, three times, then stilling and pumping all my cum into her, so much that I felt it slip out from where we were connected.

When I was spent, my balls drained, her cunt full of my seed, I collapsed over her, my hands on either side of her body, caging her in as we both caught our breath. I could feel the contractions of her orgasm around my cock and rested my forehead on her shoulder as I groaned.

With a bite to the side of her neck, and one more rough sound leaving me, I straightened and pulled out. But I made sure to watch as I pulled my dick out of the tight fit of her pussy and saw my cum start to slip out and trail down her inner thigh.

"You should see yourself right now, baby girl. So fucking dirty that my dick is about to get hard again." I gave her ass a light smack and collapsed on the bed beside her, instantly pulling her in close and placing my hand right over the small bullet scar on her side.

She curled against me, her warm breath fanning over my chest as I drew circles along the raised flesh.

"Did you mean what you said?" she said softly.

"Yeah, I did. You're my dirty girl, but I'm totally fucking into that." I buried my face in the crook of her throat and inhaled, groaning at how sweet she smelled. I ran my tongue over the sweat that lined the spot where her shoulder and neck met.

"I meant about a baby." Her voice was whisper-thin and I lifted my head to glance at her face.

She was looking away, her teeth pulling at her bottom lip. I gently gripped her chin between my thumb and forefinger and turned her head in my direction. For a second I just stared into her blue eyes, getting lost in them.

She'd never know she was my sanctuary, my peace in an inner war-torn detestation I dealt with in the black, charred parts of my soul.

"I don't fucking deserve it. I don't deserve you for that matter, but I'm so damn selfish when it comes to you. I refuse to ever let you go." I leaned in and kissed her lips, and murmured, "I want you to have my babies. In fact, I might have gotten you pregnant now. It's not like you're on birth control and fuck not taking you raw."

Her breath hitched at my vulgar words. I sobered.

"I want it all with you, *printsessa*. Everything." I let those words sink in. Her smile was slow but brilliant, and when she used her body to push me onto my back, I let her have this one moment of control. "To know you'll carry my child one day…" I slipped my hand down to curl it around her throat and leaned in to kiss her. "I'm ready for it all when you are," I murmured against her lips.

She made the sweetest sound and I pulled her on top of me. I rested back on the mattress and stared at Amara. Fuck, she was beautiful above me, gorgeous as she straddled my waist.

Her hair was a wild black mass from getting good and fucked, her lips were red and swollen from my kisses, and bite marks covered her tender flesh from my teeth.

"Maybe I am already pregnant." She looked down at my already hard cock. "Think you have round two in you just in case I'm not?"

I ground and lifted my hips, digging my erection against her pussy. "I walk around with a perpetual hard-on because I'm always thinking of you."

I growled when she pressed her cunt down and ground it against my cock.

"Go on, Amara. Be a good girl and fuck me like you mean it."

And God damn did she do just that.

✧   ✧   ✧

Thank you for reading *Menace Has A Beautiful Face*! Want to read more of Amara and Nikolai? Check out *Reckless Heir*, available now.
jenikasnow.com/books/reckless-heir

NEVER TOO LATE

K.A. LINDE

CHAPTER ONE

I'D NEVER WANTED anything in my life like I'd wanted him.

That was just fact.

Always had been.

Always would be.

It could be that love, that sick desperation, had come out of a time when I was too stupid to know better. To know to guard my heart and not put it out on display. To not give it away completely.

When I was too young and naive to think that by loving someone so completely, loving them to madness, would make them stay. Would make it work.

It didn't.

It never had.

I should have seen it for what it was. I should have known that those baby blues, the strong jaw, the sweet, delectable lips were too good to be true. Couple that with the fact that his family had more money than God, and the Holdens were a force to be reckoned with. A small-town nobody like me had no chance of surviving him.

My heart certainly hadn't.

And ever since he'd left with no word, I knew I hadn't weathered the storm. I'd just clung to the post, hanging on for dear life, as my life swept out from under me, as all rational thought fled in the wake of my need for him and I irrevocably surrendered a piece of my heart. My whole heart.

At the time, I'd drowned in a myriad of questions. Drowned in the not knowing. It was amazing how much someone could sink deeper and deeper just to find out the answer to a question. I had so many. *Why did he leave? Why didn't he tell me? What could have possibly happened that wrenched us apart?*

But still, those weren't the ones that kept me awake at night. They made me hate him, even as I never stopped loving him. But it was one question—one simple question—that always flooded my mind.

Do you love me?

I hadn't asked it then because I couldn't survive the answer.

And it was so easy, so damn easy, to just believe that love was there ... that love was enough. To not have to ask to find out if the love was even true. And on other days, it was impossible—heart-wrenching, world-shifting. back-breaking—to just not fucking know.

It didn't matter how many times I told myself that he loved me. The way he stroked my hair as I fell asleep in his arms, the way he wrapped an arm around my waist when we were together claiming me in his own way, the way he would look at me ... as if *he* was the one drowning in *me*. But doubt always crept back in.

I hadn't seen him coming.

And I hadn't guessed he would leave either.

I closed my eyes against the pain that thought brought on. No matter how many years were put between us, it still made my chest ache and my stomach cramp to remember the night he left.

Rob Holden had stolen my heart six years ago with just a smile. And he'd rent the still-beating mass from my body a short year later.

I hadn't seen one glimpse of him since then.

Not one dark brown lock of hair.

Not one toothy grin.

Not one piercing stare.

Until today.

CHAPTER TWO

"**F**UCK."

It was the only logical thing I could say when I saw him. There never was much logic around Holden. Not one goddamn day of it. There was only a hazy euphoria, coupled with a gut-wrenching ache.

He shouldn't be here.

Not in Charleston at Becky's, a tiny diner on the outside of town, where I'd worked to help pay for college.

Where we'd first met.

He'd been at Duke Law and driven into town for the weekend to see his family. He stopped at Becky's on a whim since it boasted the best pie in the tri-county area, and he found me.

He was almost too handsome in khakis and a button-up with the sleeves rolled to his elbows. The way the rich kids always wore their clothes—effortlessly. His hair fell forward over his eyes as he sank into a booth in my section and ordered apple pie. Our eyes met, and the rest was history.

We spent the next year in a clandestine mess of a love affair. Driving the four and a half hours between Durham and Charleston as often as either of us could manage it. We never made plans for the future. I was at College of Charleston, hoping to make it through my marketing degree, and we both knew that he was going places while I was stuck here.

It hadn't mattered to me—who he was, how much money he had, what his degree was in. I only wanted him.

Until one day, he'd left without so much as a good-bye.

I'd looked him up online and found that he'd graduated top of his class and gotten a job at a fancy firm in New York City. I saw the tall blonde model he was dating in the society papers. I'd been played. It was as simple as that. Except it had been anything but simple.

And now he was here.

In that same damn booth where we'd first met.

It had been six years since I'd first seen him walk into Becky's. Five years since he'd walked away without a word. And though everything felt exactly the same between us the moment that I saw him, I wasn't the same girl I'd been then.

I'd graduated with my marketing degree. First-generation college student on both sides of my family. I joined a marketing firm in Charlotte right out of college, but I hated the drudgery of it all. I wanted more. So, against everyone's wishes, I opened my own firm, taking my top two clients with me, and my star lifted.

Everything had changed. And nothing had.

Though I had significantly more money than before, Becky's was still home.

"You want me to talk to him?" Beth asked from the counter.

It was her booth. She could probably handle Rob Holden. But no … this one belonged to me.

I shook my head. "I've got this."

He was seated with his back to me. He hadn't even looked up when he first walked in. Just strode straight to *our* booth.

With a lump in my throat, I walked across the diner. "Hello, Holden."

Holden's body tensed. He knew the sound of my voice as well as he knew every inch of my body. He'd mapped it out with his hands and tongue and cock.

He turned slowly, as if in a dream. The lines blurry, ready to shift to another scene. He was dressed even nicer than he had been that first time we met. Living in the big city meant fancy suits and fancy haircuts and a fancy fucking car and probably a fancy fucking girlfriend who wouldn't deign to show her face in this sort of joint.

"Ever," he said as he caught sight of me.

Thank fuck I was still in the slim, dark trousers and white blouse I'd worn to work. I had my own office now with a dozen people underneath me. And still when he looked at me, I was reduced to nothing.

His eyes crawled down my body, as if he could barely comprehend what he saw. The woman I'd grown into.

"It's good to see you."

"Is it?" I snapped back.

His bright blue eyes roamed the diner. He seemed to place where he was, tracked his way across the white-and-black tiled floor, across the red booths and jukebox, and then back to me. As if it wasn't calculated, as if he hadn't already known.

"You still working here?"

I barked out a laugh. "Do I look like I work at Becky's?"

"No," he admitted.

"Are you honestly going to stand there and act like this wasn't on purpose? That you didn't come sit in this booth for a reason?"

He arched an eyebrow at me. Always calm, always cool. "I didn't know you'd be here."

"But you hoped I would," I said baldly.

He smirked, and I was transported back in time. Back to when that smile was the only fucking thing that mattered in my orbit.

"What if I said yes?"

I sucked in a breath. Because I hadn't planned for any of this. I had no fucking clue what to do from here. Did I sit down and order pie? We'd eaten our weights' worth in homemade apple pie that year together.

But now? Now, we weren't those people. And I didn't want to stain my diner with new memories of him. Not after how he'd hurt me.

"Never mind," I ground out with a shake of my head.

"Sit down, Ever."

"No," I spat instantly.

"Why not?" His smile was sincere, and I hated him for its sincerity.

"Because you left," I croaked. "You left, and you left me here."

"Ever …"

Holden rested a hand on my sleeve. Everything narrowed to that one touch. To the feel of him taking control of me, as he had so many times before. Because he knew as well as I did that I'd never had anyone like him. And one touch, one look in those blue eyes, told me that he could give me all of that again.

For a price. And the price was my heart.

"No," I whispered, pulling away. "You can't do that."

"What if I told you I missed you? What if I told you I came here on purpose?"

My heart throbbed in my chest, beating a sharp staccato. "It doesn't change the past."

"Nothing can change the past."

"You live in New York."

"I'm here now."

"What are you really doing here anyway?" I couldn't help but ask.

"My brother's promotion to CEO."

"Nolan is taking over for your father?" I asked in surprise.

I hadn't heard that. Not that I had my ear to the ground for his family. But Holden Holdings was the largest company in Charleston. They were gradually expanding to own the entire coastline, buying up small businesses and converting them into their conglomerate.

"He is. Will you have a seat?"

I shot him an incredulous look. But he just gestured to the booth, and finally, I plopped down across from him. It was hard not to look at his hands, drumming on the table in front of us. I knew exactly what he could do with them.

I jerked my eyes back to his face. But that wasn't much better.

If it was possible, he'd gotten even more attractive. More refined. Or maybe it was my imagination that had colored him in a haze, and now, he was drawn before me in perfect clarity.

Here he finally was. The man with the answers to all of my questions. And I could barely look at him.

"I'm sitting."

He laughed as the words left my mouth. "As insolent as ever."

A shiver ran down my spine. I'd heard those words uttered in the dark of night. The sweet feel of him taking control of my *insolent* little mouth.

"Don't," I whispered.

His hand slid across the table. It folded over mine. I should jerk away. I should yell at him for the audacity. But sparks erupted at the mere brush of his hand. My stomach catapulted up my throat. Everything went so still.

"I wanted to see you," he said, his voice earnest.

I could see the truth in his eyes. Even if it made no sense to me. He was the one who had left. He was the one who had hurt me.

"Why?" I gasped out.

"To see how you're doing."

"Don't you think you forfeited that right when you left?"

He shook his head. "Are you with someone?"

I scoffed. "Are you?"

"No," he said quickly. Then, after a pause, he added, "Not anymore."

A thrill went down my spine. The idea of him with someone else made me physically ill. But knowing that he could be mine ... again ... it was impossible. I knew it, even as the traitorous thought flitted across my brain. Rob Holden could never be mine again.

But fuck, it had been so long since anyone had handled me properly.

"Tell me what you're thinking."

"Good."

"Good?" he inquired.

"I'm glad you're not with anyone else."

He smirked, leaning forward and turning my hand palm up. He drew figure eights on my wrist, and I had to suppress a shiver. I shouldn't let him touch me.

"Are you now? Why is that?"

I didn't want to do this. I'd been reeled in the first time. That had been his fault, but if I was reeled in a second time … that would be my own damn fault.

I withdrew my hand and balled my hands into fists in my lap. "Just tell me why you left."

"You know why."

But I didn't. I still had no clue. One minute, we had been on a yacht, sipping champagne and enjoying the holiday with his family in Charleston. The next, he was gone. All of his stuff was out of my apartment, as if he'd never been there at all. My roommate had been baffled. If it hadn't been for her shock, I would have sworn Holden was a beautifully sculpted dream.

"I can't do this again. You left. I should know by now that you always choose yourself first."

He laughed, sharp and sardonic. "That's rich, coming from you."

"I have no fucking clue what that means."

"I'm sure," he said with an edge to his voice.

I rose to my feet. "I'm not playing this game with you again, Holden. I can't do it. I can't survive you a second time."

I crossed my arms over my chest and left Holden alone in our booth. It was the hardest thing I'd ever done. Made impossible by the fact that he followed me. Grabbed my arm in the parking lot of the neon-lit diner and pleaded for me to wait.

"Ever, don't go."

"What do you want from me?" I asked, closing my eyes and fighting to regain the one scrap of courage I had left in his presence. Because if he asked for more, I knew what my answer would be.

"I just want to talk."

I shook my head. "I'm leaving."

"What if I asked you to stay?"

"Why are you doing this to me?" I got out.

He swung me around until I was nearly against his chest. His hand came to my chin and gently forced my face upward to look into his. "Because I still think about you. I dream about you. I've tried to stay away," he said as if the words physically pained him. "I've tried everything. I came here tonight, hoping for just a glimpse of you. But in person …" He ran a hand back through his dark hair. "In person, you're a vision. A goddess. A celestial. I don't give a fuck about our past. I don't care how it started or how it ended. But I just fucking need you."

My body listed toward him at those words. The ones I'd longed to hear for so, so long. The ones I'd never quite given up hoping for.

"Hate me all you like. Vilify me if you want." His arm slid around my waist until I was pressed against him. I could smell the expensive cologne he wore and the hint of spearmint on his breath. A million nights of lust-induced happiness flashed through my mind. "But give me one night. Give *yourself* this."

"One night?" I mirrored. "And then?"

"And then I go back to New York."

Could I give myself over to his commanding hands and demanding cock and cruel, all-too-knowing mind?

It wasn't even a question.

I closed my eyes and sighed. "One night."

CHAPTER THREE

THE PROBLEM WITH men was either they wanted to fuck me hard with no connection or they wanted a connection and they fucked like pussies.

And my masochist self lay somewhere squarely in the middle.

I wanted him to love me and fuck me like he hated me.

I wanted him to need me as much as I craved the humiliation.

I needed love and pain and desire and anger and desperation and truth, all rolled into one package.

And I'd never found that package again after Rob Holden walked out the door.

I'd gone to BDSM clubs, thinking kink would satisfy me, but Doms didn't love me how I wanted them to love me. I wasn't submissive enough. I was too bratty. And the ones that wanted me bratty didn't satisfy me in other ways.

I'd gone on blind dates with men that my friends had insisted I'd fall for. And one of the guys, I did, but my vibrator had ended up getting more use than his cock. At least I could ride *myself* as hard as I needed.

So, as I parked on the street in front of my Victorian townhouse in downtown Charleston, it was with anticipation I hadn't felt in years. I should have said no. I'd tried to talk myself out of doing this the entire drive into the city. But I wanted him with a desperation that made me wet with desire before we even reached my door. I knew exactly what he could do, and I was willing to have my heart broken a second time to live for just one more night.

"Nice place," Holden said as we came up to the front door.

"Thanks. I bought it two years ago. I'm kind of obsessed," I admitted with giddy excitement.

His eyes darkened at my words, but I had no idea why he'd care where I lived. It was a far cry from the shithole apartment we'd fucked in hundreds of times.

I pushed open the front door and let him inside.

"I can see why," he said softly at the first glimpse of my house.

After paying back all of my student loan debt, I'd invested heavily in property. I'd learned long ago that passive income was the way to go, and if I had the means, I was going to buy up as much as I could. I'd even bought my parents a new house in our hometown. They'd refused anything fancy, but I'd wanted them out of the double-wide I'd grown up in.

But my Victorian was my baby. One of my closest friends worked as an interior designer, and we'd carefully sculpted the entire house to the dream I'd always wanted. Perfectly modern but cozy. A place I could keep forever.

The door slammed shut behind Holden, and I shivered. That solid reminder that he was here.

"Do you want a drink?" I asked to give myself something to do.

"Do you need liquid courage?"

"Well, I never thought I'd see you again. So yeah, maybe." I headed into the kitchen, running my shaking hands along the quartz countertop. "Wine or whiskey?"

He smirked. "Whiskey."

"Of course."

I grabbed the good stuff. If any night was the night for it, it was tonight. I poured us each a knuckle's worth and carried the glasses back to him.

His eyes still surveyed the room, as if he was assessing its worth. How much all of this must have cost me.

"Holden," I murmured.

His eyes skated back to mine, and then he took the glass in hand. He lifted it in cheers. "To money and how it buys happiness."

I winced at the words. A mockery of everything I had. I hated him then. Everything I'd worked so hard for so easily made into a fucking joke. But Holden downed the whiskey like a shot, not even grimacing as it burned down his throat.

"Aren't you going to drink yours?" he asked.

"I'm remembering how much of an asshole you can be."

"That's why you fell in love with me."

"No, it isn't," I snapped back.

"Don't lie to yourself." He took my untouched glass of whiskey and set both on the coffee table. "As if you could ever end up with someone *nice*."

He said the word *nice* like a weapon. Wielded it as deftly as a sword. Nice was a curse. Nice guys didn't tie you to a bed and feast on your pussy, refusing to let you come for what felt like days. But nice guys didn't leave with no word and shatter your heart either.

"Why are you here?" I forced out one more time. "You don't have to do this. You don't have to hurt me."

His hand came to my throat, circling it with ease. His hands … those powerful hands. So capable, unparalleled. "Oh but, Ever, you want me to hurt you."

I could have sobbed at those words. The truth in them. The throbbing in my core from him manhandling me. And he knew it. He fucking knew it.

"Is your cunt wet for me?"

"Yes," I whispered, barely a breath.

"On your knees."

And I could do nothing but comply.

The polished hardwood floor I'd spent a fortune refinishing dug into my knees as they hit the ground. He kept his hand on my throat the whole time, as if guiding me to my place before him.

"Take out my cock."

I didn't need to be told what to do, but we both knew I liked it. I dropped my gaze to look at his pants, but he squeezed tighter.

"Eyes on me."

I clenched my legs together as desire pooled deep inside of me like I hadn't known in years. I met his steely stare and reached blindly forward until I found the waist of his pants. I popped the button and dragged the zipper to the base. Then, I deftly reached into his boxer briefs and removed his straining cock.

I wanted to look at it. I wanted that desperately. But I couldn't break his gaze.

His other hand came to his cock, and he stroked it a few times. The soft thwacking sound of skin against skin. Then, the head of his cock was against my lips. He hit me with it once, twice, three times. Pre-come dripped onto my lips, salty and tangy. And oh, I wanted to lick it off.

He smirked at me, watching my sweet torment. And the truth was, this turned him on as much as me. He needed my pain as much as I needed his torture.

"You remember how I like my cock sucked?"

I nodded.

"I won't go easy on you," he growled low in warning.

"Please don't," I whispered.

The plea barely left my mouth. His nostrils flared as desire shot through his too-blue irises.

"Open your mouth."

And I did.

He released my throat and thrust his cock into my mouth with enough force that I nearly gagged on him. I barely held it back as he pushed himself deep in my mouth. And he wasn't even all the way in. At the height of our relationship, I'd only just learned to deep-throat him. It had been too long since then, and as much as I willed my throat to relax, it wouldn't listen.

Tears came to my eyes, and I looked up at him as he guided himself out of my mouth and thrust back in. There was determination on his face. As if all he wanted was to conquer my insolent mouth. It had never worked, but each time, it felt as if I were getting closer. I'd let him try as much as he wanted.

Despite the tears and the ache in my jaw and the annoying gag reflex, I wanted him to use my mouth as his plaything. I wanted all of it. And he knew it as well as I did.

"Fuck, I've thought about this mouth," he gasped as he thrust in again. "I've dreamed of the way you let me fuck it."

So had I.

My fingers dug into his sides, but all I wanted was to sneak a finger into my underwear. Just the barest graze of my clit, and I'd explode in a minute. I was so turned on that my entire body was tender and sensitive.

I moved one hand to my hip, then my thigh, then closer. I got one beautiful touch against my clit before he noticed what I was doing.

"Are you touching yourself?" he snarled.

I could say nothing with his huge cock stuffed down my throat. But it wasn't really a question.

Slowly, so slowly, he withdrew his pulsing cock. He'd been so near to coming. I could taste him in the back of my throat. I groaned in protest.

"You don't come unless I tell you."

His thick hand was around his cock now. Pumping it fiercely as he held the back of my head. I could see how close he was. The veins in his cock pulsing as he grew larger in his hand.

"I'm going to come," he ground out.

"Yes," I gasped.

And then thick ropes of come shot out onto my face and down my chest, over my white blouse. The taste of him was on my lips and the feel of him all over my body. I'd never look at this shirt, now covered with his seed, the same again.

"There," he grunted as he finished. He looked down at the come staining my shirt and coating my skin. And he smiled. "Perfection."

CHAPTER FOUR

I'D FORGOTTEN WHAT it was like to be cared for until Holden followed me into the bathroom. He gently removed my shirt and tossed it into the bathtub. Then took a washcloth and cleaned my face and chest. He was gentle but commanding. Never a sense that he wasn't in control. In fact, I completely relaxed into him as he made sure I was okay before proceeding.

"I think I'll have that whiskey now," I said on a breathy laugh.

He dragged the washcloth across my shoulder one more time and then dropped it in the tub. "I thought you'd be begging me to let you come."

And I couldn't lie and say I didn't want that. I stood in my bra and trousers, and it was the only reason he didn't know that my thong was nothing but a useless accessary at this point. Or how close I'd come to orgasming.

"Will you?" I asked, lifting my chin to meet his gaze.

"Perhaps."

I shot him a smirk back. "My room is upstairs. We could—"

"We'll get there," he said instantly.

But first, he unsnapped the button on my trousers and drew them down my legs. I trembled slightly at his touch as he dragged his hands back up my thighs. He skipped over the thong and unclasped my bra, letting my impressive rack fall out of place. He eyed them like he was writing a memo about them for a court case.

He drew a finger over one erect nipple and then the other. "We will come back to you later."

I moaned in need, but he was already moving his hands down to my thong. He took the material and slowly removed them. Then, he brought them to his nose and inhaled.

"How wet are you?"

I whimpered as he pressed the material to my nose and let me smell my own arousal. "Holden, please."

"Please what?"

I wasn't above begging. "Fuck me. Just fuck me."

"That's not what you want."

He was wrong. I wanted it desperately. But he was also right. I wanted him to take his time. I wanted him to make me come undone. And most of all ... I didn't want the night to end.

He leaned back casually against the counter and surveyed my naked body. I had more muscle on me than I'd had the last time he saw me naked. I was a regular at the gym down the street, which had made me hard where I used to be soft. Lean where I used to be curvy. Hours at the gym had been a substitute type of torment.

"You're beautiful, Ever."

My cheeks flushed at the compliment. He had always been liberal with them in our relationship. But every single one was pointed, weighted. As if he had carefully thought through the implications of each word and how they'd fall upon my skin. Today was no different.

He took my hand and drew me out of the downstairs bathroom. He bypassed the stairs that led up to my bedroom and walked me to the high-backed white chair, which was my first new purchase I'd ever made for the house. He walked me back to it.

"Here?" I teased, sinking down onto the armrest.

He lifted me effortlessly and turned me sharply in the other direction. A second later, my face was in the cushion, stomach braced over the armrest, ass in the air. A gasp escaped my lips at the swift motion.

"Here," he confirmed.

I could tell that I was on perfect display. Every inch of me bare to him.

He toed my feet apart. "Wider."

I fought to comply, but I clearly wasn't quick enough because he roughly spread my legs until I had to dig my hands into the chair to hold myself up.

"That's better. Are you comfortable?"

"No," I growled softly.

He chuckled. "Oh, that mouth of yours. I forgot how much I enjoyed it."

"And here you'd think I wouldn't have anything left to say after you stuffed it full of your cock."

"I think you'll have a lot to say here in a minute."

His hand came down hard on my ass, and I bit back a cry.

But then he was gone. I lifted my head to see what he was doing, but he wagged a finger in my direction. So, I humphed and dropped back down. I heard a door open in the kitchen. And a few seconds later, he returned.

"What are you—"

"Shh," he purred, running a comforting hand down my spine.

I wanted to tell him where he could go stuff his silence, but I didn't get the chance. Suddenly, his fingers were running up the inside of my thigh, ever higher. He trailed gently over my waiting pussy before moving to the other thigh. I made a sound of objection, but he just placed a kiss on my ass cheek.

Then, I felt exactly what he had gotten out of the kitchen. Ice moved up my thigh, running the same trajectory as his hand. I shouted in surprise and bucked against him, but he was already there, keeping my chest down. When he reached the apex of my thighs, he teased the ice slowly over my clit. I gasped in torturous pleasure. The heat and cold all mingling together until my brain was fuzzy with confusion and need.

As he moved the ice to the other thigh, he brought his mouth to my clit.

"Oh," I moaned as the warmth from his mouth traced away the cold from the ice.

It was a blazing Charleston summer night. Even in the house, I couldn't ever quite escape the heat. But here, for the first time all summer, I was cooling down. And heating up, all at the same time.

The ice teased down to my ankles, the backs of my knees, then up to my hips, and along my back. All while his tongue circled and licked and sucked on my clit until I felt everything in me coalescing to this uncontrollable place. But he'd told me not to come. He'd told me to wait.

So, I dissolved into incoherent pants. "Please, Holden, please. Oh God, let me come," I whimpered. "I just … oh fuck. Now?"

"Not yet," he said, withdrawing from my clit as an orgasm teetered at the brink.

I sagged forward in despair as my own wetness threatened to drip down my thighs. I was so close. And the ice play was only heightening everything. He lifted me halfway to fondle my nipple with the ice in his hand.

"I can't," I told him. "I need to come."

"You can wait, and you will," he encouraged. His voice was syrupy sweet. "I haven't finished my perusal." He popped the last of the ice into my mouth. "Suck on that and think about me."

I did as directed as he lowered himself to the floor behind me. One hand slid up and down my pussy lips. I could hear the squelching sound of my own arousal as he swirled his fingers through my wetness. Then, without notice, he plunged two fingers deep inside of me.

I bucked against him and moaned again. I wasn't going to be able to hold out. I had been close when I'd gone down on him. How did he expect me to not come when he was inside of me?

Then, his mouth descended at the same time, and I saw stars. I clenched my inner muscles, trying so hard not to come. I couldn't even think straight as I yelled at my lower half not to give in. But fuck, I couldn't stop.

"Oh fuck," I screamed as my orgasm hit me in the face like a two-by-four.

I spasmed around his fingers and chomped down on the ice in my mouth. My cries were loud and incoherent as the best orgasm of the last five years crashed over me.

"Tsk-tsk," Holden said. "I didn't tell you to come."

"I know. But you … you just feel too good. You're too good."

I looked up in a sex daze to see him smirking triumphantly. He looked beyond pleased, as if he'd known all along that I wouldn't be able to stop. He'd wanted me to come anyway.

"I haven't come like that in five years," I said as my body sank toward the floor.

"Well then, it won't be the last now, will it?"

He lifted me off the ground and tossed me over his shoulder. I was still in my sex daze, so I barely made a sound as he carried me up the stairs. I directed him to the last door at the end of the hall. He deposited me onto the king-size bed in my bedroom.

I had imagined Rob Holden in this room more times than I cared to admit. But watching him undress before me, seeing him in all of his naked glory, was better than I ever could have imagined. He'd broadened in the time since I'd last known him. His abs were a solid eight-pack with that tasty V leading exactly where I wanted him. My orgasm had clearly affected him, as his cock was now erect again.

He grabbed my ankle and jerked sharply, pulling me flat on the mattress. "The first time will be fast. I've wanted to sink into that cunt for far too long."

"And the second time?" I asked with open lust on my face.

"The second and third and every time after that will be as torturous as you like it, Ever."

I shivered. "Good."

"You have restraints?"

I bit my lip and nodded. "Of course."

"You've used them since me?"

"Of course," I bit out.

"And you didn't come?"

"I came sometimes. It just wasn't the same. Are you picturing me with someone else?"

His hands balled into fists. "I am now."

"Does it kill you inside, like it kills me to think of you with someone else?"

"Yes," he admitted. That one word a breath of tense emotion. The ache in his eyes. The knuckles of his clenched fists turning white.

"Make me forget," I begged. "Make me forget anyone but you."

CHAPTER FIVE

H OLDEN FOUND THE restraints. He flipped me onto my stomach and took his time in fastening my hands together in front of me and tying them to the board at the head of my bed.

"How is that?"

I shifted my hands back and forth until my wrists almost slipped out.

"Tighter," I said with a taunting smirk.

He arched an eyebrow and tightened the bonds until I gasped. They didn't cut off circulation, but there was no way I was wiggling out of them either

He gave them one more experimental tug and then said, "Better."

Holden ran a hand down my spine as he came around behind me. He lifted me to my knees, keeping my face planted in the mattress and my arms stretched long. It was uncomfortable, but I liked it. I always had. I wanted things to hurt a little more, to stretch past the point of comfort, to make me lean into the pain, knowing he was the cause and the only way to get relief.

"Are you comfortable?" he teased, running his hands up my ass.

"No," I repeated.

He slapped my ass cheek hard, and I rocked forward into my shoulders.

"Fuck, you look good like this."

"All tied up?"

"Mine," he said so softly that I almost missed it.

Then, he was at my entrance, and all thought fled my mind. I squirmed backward, wanting him inside of me already, but he just slapped my ass again.

A murmured, "Yes," escaped my lips.

He did it again and again until my ass stung, and then there was the barest brush of his hand against my skin as he massaged the tender flesh.

"Are you going to come when I tell you this time?"

I bit my lip hard to keep back the *no*. Because somehow, just from him tying me up and spanking me, I was already horny as hell again. It should have been like this with anyone, but it wasn't. Holden and I had something special. A wild abandon, a desperate need, a haunting, determined love. And maybe he'd never told me before, but I felt it all the same. That connection should have been stretched too thin to snapping with the years between us. Instead, it had rebounded and doubled down. One touch from him was an electric energy pulsing through me.

"Ever?" he growled.

"Tell me when I can come," I acquiesced to get him the fuck inside of me.

"You're going to be bad, aren't you?"

A finger slipped inside my pussy, and I couldn't bite back my moan.

"Yes," I admitted.

"Will you be better behaved if I get this out of your system?"

He withdrew his finger and pressed the head of his cock inside. I grabbed the ropes holding me into place. It took everything in me not to push back to get more of him.

"No," I said honestly.

He chuckled low, and the sound settled deep in my belly. "Fuck, I missed you."

It was the last thing he said before he swiftly thrust forward into me. I gasped in shock at the sheer size of him. He felt fucking amazing. Better than my faded memories of him. After he'd left, I used to use my fingers to make myself come, thinking of him plowing into me. But over the years, it hadn't been as clear. Just the want of him was still as potent as ever.

His hand came down on my neck, pushing my head harder into the mattress. The other came to my hip as he reared back and slammed into me again. It started slow but savage. As if he was punishing me for the years apart. Ripping me open so I could never forget what he felt like again.

And it didn't matter that it was his own goddamn fault that we hadn't been doing this every day for the last five years. I took the punishment like I deserved it.

There was no other way for me to function.

Just his cock slipping through my wet folds and then slamming back in harder and harder than the time before. My shoulders burned with the effort of holding my position. My head smashed into the comforter, and I was barely able to get air. But my pussy sang a symphony.

And then I felt something wet against my ass.

I jerked my head to the side. The bastard had found the lube with the restraints. It slipped along my skin as he used his free hand to massage across my sore ass and then added a dribble more for my asshole.

"What ..." I managed to get out.

Then, his thumb was at my back entrance, and I stiffened in anticipation. Which was the wrong move. I needed to be relaxed. But I could hardly relax with him pounding into me like a tyrant with one finger poised over the pucker of my asshole.

"You've never said no to anal," he told me as his thumb pressed inward.

My eyes slammed shut, and I couldn't bite back my moan. I was so full. Completely full already. He released my head, so he could grasp my hip and pick up his rhythm. His cock was buried inside of me. His balls slapped hard against my clit as he rocked into me. All while that thumb rained sweet torture on my ass.

I couldn't have stopped the orgasm if I tried.

It was a runaway train, bursting off of the tracks and sliding into a deep ravine. It started in my core and exploded through my entire body. I was rigid, back arched, screaming out his name, until I had no more words and everything was nonsensical.

"Fucking hell," he groaned.

I could feel him straining to keep up the rhythm as my pussy sucked him for all its worth. My orgasm was catastrophic. Even Rob Holden wasn't immune to that sort of pressure.

He jackhammered inside of me as I came down from the swift orgasm. Then he came with a vengeance, emptying himself deep inside of me.

It was a full minute later, when there was nothing left between us but heavy breathing, that he finally withdrew. He left me there, all tied up and exhausted, while he went to the bathroom.

He returned with a washcloth, and after cleaning up the liberal lube he had used, he gently untied me.

I collapsed to the side in a state of delirium. His smile was the most beautiful thing that I'd ever seen. He scooped me up in his arms like I was a rag doll and deposited me into the waiting shower. He must have turned it on already because the water was boiling. He soaped me up, using the cucumber bath wash I favored, and insisted on checking the welts on my ass.

I made some half-coherent statement that they weren't that bad. But when I got out of the shower and toweled off, I realized how wrong I had been. They were worse than I'd thought. It only made me smile.

A sore bottom meant a good day. A very good day.

CHAPTER SIX

I TUGGED ON a pair of cheeky underwear and a tiny white tank top that did nothing to contain my breasts. His mouth was open with need when he saw my nipples peeking through the material.

"Round two?" he asked, grasping me around the waist and drawing me up to him.

"Are you ready? You've already orgasmed twice," I reminded him.

"I'm insatiable," he said, nibbling on my earlobe.

"I want this forever," I said dreamily as I rubbed my chest against him.

He stiffened at the words and then released me. "None of your other beaus have satisfied you?"

"Would I be here right now with you if they had?"

He frowned and looked away. His face had gone inscrutable again.

"What?"

"Then why did you do this, Ever?"

"Do what?" I looked at him in confusion. "I didn't do anything. You're the one who left."

He dropped his arms from me. All playfulness evaporated in an instant.

"What?" I demanded. "This is *your* fault."

He snorted. "Nice try. As you sit here among these riches."

I blinked at him. "What the fuck are you talking about?"

"You know exactly what I'm talking about."

"Enlighten me."

"There's no point. I don't want to hear your lies."

"I *never* lied to you," I snarled. "You were the one who left in the middle of the fucking night. You took everything and said not a word. If it wasn't for my roommate, I would have thought you were a fucking dream."

"You still cashed the check," he spat.

I reared back in alarm. "What check?"

"The one my father offered you to get rid of you."

I opened and closed my mouth.

"See? You can't even deny it." He pushed away from me. His hands went into his hair, and he looked ready to punch his fist through my wall. "You took the money, just like all the others."

"I didn't take any money from your father," I said, my voice straining as the pieces came together for me.

"Then explain this house." He gestured around at the Victorian I now lived in.

But I didn't back down from the question. I just tilted my chin and said, "I own a multimillion-dollar marketing firm."

It was his turn to go speechless.

I nodded as I watched everything come together in his mind too.

"I graduated with my degree. I started my own business. I'm my own boss. And, yeah, I *own* this place, and I didn't need your fucking father to pay for it. How could you ever think that of me?"

"He said that you—"

"Of course he fucking said that!" I shouted. "And he did offer," I said with a sigh. "We were on that yacht. He cornered me and offered to pay for my schooling, to set me up with a nice place, and to keep me *comfortable*. You see, I knew I was the wrong girl for you in every way that didn't matter. Your daddy? He wanted someone high class. Someone like the girls you dated after me. But I refused his money then, and I certainly don't need it now. I told him to go fuck himself."

"You never told me," he said, his voice going hollow with grief.

"I didn't want you to carry that with you. It was my shame alone."

His head fell into his hands. "My two girlfriends before you took that deal."

"That's not my fault, Holden." I held my hands wide. Finally, the entire truth was between us. And we were more naked, barer than we ever had been before each other. "You didn't even have the decency to confront me."

"Fuck," he growled. "Fuck him."

"Did he ever stop trying to ruin your relationships?"

"No."

"The only one who can stop him now is you." I crossed my arms over my chest and sighed. "You should probably go."

"Ever ..."

"You thought the worst of me. How do you expect me to move past that? You believed that I had chosen some stupid money over you. I was madly, desperately, hopelessly in love with you." Tears came to my eyes, and I pushed against his chest. "You were my everything. Not because of the money or your name. Just because of *you*."

"Was?"

"What?"

"You're not still in love with me?" he asked, his voice hoarse.

A tear slid down my cheek. "Were you *ever* in love with me?" The question spilled out before I could stop it.

I'd loved him. I told him I loved him. And even then, he never said the words. I'd never asked. Never let myself ask.

And when he'd left, I'd assumed that he'd played me the whole time. My love was red hot and real. Oh-so real. His was false. It'd had to be. That year couldn't have been as perfect as my memory made it seem. Because no man who loved me could leave me like that.

"More than anything." He took my hand in his. "I loved you then. I've loved you every day since." He kissed my fingers. "I love you still."

The words rang over me like truth. I wanted to hate him for admitting to his feelings now. Now, when it was too late for us to figure out all our shit. With years apart and the pain of being without him.

"Then ... why? How? How could you leave?"

"I was a fool."

He dropped to his knees before me. The man always in command, always in charge, always dominant fell to his knees like a submissive. And in his eyes, I saw blatant regret. I saw that the years had not been as kind to him as I had assumed. The pretty pictures in the society papers were the highlight reel. Not reality.

Reality was the man lowered before me. Doing what he never ever would have done five years ago. His pride would never have allowed it.

"I don't deserve your forgiveness, Ever," he said, bringing my fingers to his lips again. "I left. I didn't give you a chance to explain. I believed the lies my father had said. But I have regretted that decision every day for the last five years. It was why I came to that diner. Why I sought you out when I was told that I should leave you behind."

"That doesn't make up for the five years where I had no idea why you'd left," I said, my voice cracking.

"It doesn't, but I will spend a lifetime making it up to you."

"How?" I asked, unable to believe the words.

"I'll start by bringing you to my brother's party tomorrow."

My eyebrows shot up. "But won't your father be there?"

"Precisely."

"I don't—"

"And then I'll take a job in Charleston. My siblings have wanted me closer, but I couldn't come back, knowing you were here." He rose from his knees and brought his hands up to cup my jaw. I looked up into those big blue eyes and saw how much he wanted this. "Please, Ever."

"It's too late," I choked out.

"It's never too late. I messed up. You have every right to believe the worst of me and tell me to go fuck myself. I'd understand if that's your decision. I'll walk out that door. But I'll come back the next day and the next and the next after that because we're meant to be together. You know that."

And though my heart hurt so much from everything that had happened, I didn't have it in me to deny him. I wanted it to be true too much to say no. Maybe it wasn't too late. Maybe it would never be too late for Rob Holden.

"Okay," I whispered. "Okay, the party and then … and then we'll see what happens."

He pulled me hard against him. "You won't regret this."

"It's not forever."

"Oh, but it is," he said. He smirked as he drew my mouth against his. "Forever and ever."

✧　✧　✧

Thanks for reading about the wonderful Holden and Ever in this short, *Never Too Late*. Though it's a complete standalone, it exists within my Coastal Chronicles world, which I'm planning to expand to include Nolan Holden and the rest of the Holden family next year! If you want to read more about the angsty world filled with rich boys and smart girls and lots of second chances, start with *Hold the Forevers*.

www.kalinde.com/books/hold-the-forevers

Bonus Epilogue from Boyfriend Bargain

Ilsa Madden-Mills

This epilogue takes place between the last chapter of *Boyfriend Bargain* and the epilogue originally included. If you don't want to be spoiled, make sure you read *Boyfriend Bargain* before this bonus epilogue.

CHAPTER ONE
Zach

STAND IN front of my locker at the Predators' arena wrestling with my tie for the fourth time. My heart races.

Suit from the tailor: check.

No game, practice, workout, or travel tonight: check.

Sugar taking the night off: check.

All I need is the ring,

"Looking good out there, Z," says our first line center Mikah. "Keep that up and you'll be pushing me for ice time."

He slaps me on the back, a lopsided smile on his craggy face. With a dark beard and a head full of frizzy hair, he's a veteran on the team. When I joined the Preds, I expected there to be rivalry between us since I'm the sparkly new guy, but he's encouraged me all the way.

He grins at me, probably reading the fear on my face. "Ah, you've got the shits, yes, Z?"

I smirk. It was *one* time before a game. "Fuck off. Just tell me you have it."

"Course I do. Mikhail always comes through." He thumps his chest.

A month ago, when I mentioned I was looking for a ring, he sat me down and told me to avoid the jewelry stores, even the ones that cater to the country music stars. He knew a wholesaler who dealt in conflict-free, nearly perfect stones.

We met with his friend in a swanky office building downtown. I brought my own appraiser to review the rocks. I picked out a doozy.

But now, the ring is late. It was supposed to take a month, and it's been two.

It must be tonight, if it isn't now, it will be two weeks before we have a night to ourselves.

I stare at his hand waiting to get my first glimpse of the little box when—

"Nam nuzhno obsudit," says one of our defensemen, Andi. He's fresh out of the shower and dressed in gym clothes, his face grave. I nod at him, but all his focus is on Mikah.

"Konechno, konechno, davayte sdelayem eto," says Mikah as he puts an arm around him. Mikah appears to be comforting him, but I don't speak Russian. All I know are the curse words.

"Mikah, the ring?" I ask, hating to intrude on this moment, but...

"Oh, sorry. Good luck, friend." He winks and tosses me the small box.

I catch it as the two hockey players disappear into Coach's office.

I slowly open it and my heart picks up. The setting is platinum with a four-carat round-cut diamond in the center. I tilt the ring back and forth, mesmerized. It's just a ring, an expensive one for sure, but it's also the promise of permanence between Sugar and me, a pact that we'll always be there for each other.

My phone buzzes. I close the box and answer. "Hey, babe, I was just thinking about you."

"Sweet! Same. Are you on your way? I was going to start cooking." Her voice sounds harried and I smile. She isn't the best cook, but you didn't hear that from me.

"Leaving now. Be home in twenty."

"Okay, pot is boiling. Come and get it! Love ya."

"Love you."

✧   ✧   ✧

As I DRIVE through the downtown Nashville streets, I run through my spiel. She can't possibly say no—although she has before. The first time was while we were fucking in the shower—amazing sex—so that one doesn't really counts.

The last year has been hard but good. She started law school at Belmont while most of my time was taken up by hockey. Plus, I'm still doing therapy three times a week for my anxiety issues.

I've always been high strung and anxious but managed to keep it under control—until last year, my senior year at Hawthorne University. With the pressure of trying to win a national championship for my team, things imploded. Even after I passed out during a game, I pushed it aside and moved on. But trauma and grief aren't easy to battle alone. My mom died of cancer and my high school girlfriend was killed in a car wreck. I'd never dealt with it. Late in the season, I was forced to face it and get help.

DING. There's a text from my coach.

U still in the facility? Need you.

I groan as I pull my Escalade into a gas station and park. My fingers fly over the phone. **I got plans—I'm nearly home.**

Call me ASAP911.

Shit. I hit dial.

CHAPTER TWO

Sugar

THE POT ON the stove is boiling as I taste the homemade sauce again. I keep thinking it will get better but it doesn't. It's too sweet. Oh well, Z will hardly notice. He eats everything.

I shift the lingerie I have on under my sweatpants. It's a skimpy lace teddy that pulls up as a thong in back and barely covers my nipples in the front.

Really sexy.

Really expensive.

Really itchy.

Over that, I'm wearing gray joggers and a black Hawthorne Lions sweatshirt. I spent an hour on my makeup and hair. It looks like I went somewhere earlier and needed to be dolled up, but now I'm home and wearing good ole loungewear. The best part, my messy bun can be let down by pulling out just one pencil strategically placed to allow my blond hair to fall down over one shoulder.

I'm ready for our night with no interruptions.

It's not like we don't have sex, there's plenty of that. It's about time. Between him training and traveling on the road and me in class and studying every night, it's crazy. We haven't had a good seduction night in forever. We'll have dinner, a bottle of wine, kiss nice and slow...

Then, BAM, sexy lingerie hidden is revealed.

I finish setting the table for two in front of our penthouse window when Z's face pops up on the ESPN channel on the TV in the den.

I grab the remote and rewind just as the elevator opens and he stalks in wearing a mouthwatering gray suit.

I smile broadly. "Hey, you! I was just about to watch an ESPN story about you? I didn't know they did one."

"Go ahead and hit play. I wanna see this."

He tugs me to him and we kiss. A nice hello, nothing overtly passionate...yet.

I hit play.

The anchorman starts, "Some interesting geo-political drama is playing out in Nashville tonight where two of the Predators' starting skaters may not be playing this week. For more we go to Ashley Fuentes in Nashville."

The image changes to a reporter standing in front of the arena.

"This evening two of Nashville's best players, Russian center Mikhail Sokolov and Ukrainian defenseman Andriy Kovalenko, held a press conference where they stated that they're sitting out tomorrow's game as a form of protest over Russia's invasion of Ukraine. Both men read prepared statements in Ukrainian, Russian, then English moments ago.

"Sokolov, an all-star and extremely popular player in Russia, started off by condemning the invasion of his homeland and announcing support for the anti-war protests going on in Moscow. Kovalenko urged the UN to condemn this act of aggression and personally called on Vladimir Putin to withdraw troops from Ukraine."

Z takes my hand and clenches it. Issues like this, especially when he knows people involved, affect him deeply.

The reporter continues as she glances up at the camera. "Both men commented on the personal friendship they share and reinforced that they are united in their opinions on the violence. Sokolov was asked if he was concerned about facing repercussions in his home country. He answered that he could not sit by and do nothing. As a side note, we should point out that the Predators are the most watched NHL team on Russian TV because of Sokolov's popularity. Kovalenko was asked if he had family still in Ukraine. He became visibly emotional as he detailed that his father took his younger sister to the Polish border yesterday, but he went back home to help defend the country."

I gasp. "That's awful. How old is his dad?"

Z grimaces. "In his fifties."

We look back at the TV as the reporter speaks to the anchor. "Roger, this press conference was emotional. It ended with these two friends standing and embracing. Hopefully that image can get attention and help end this senseless conflict. Live from Nashville, this is Ashley Fuentes for ESPN."

The image switches back to the anchor with an image of Z over his shoulder, the one I saw earlier.

"On the sports side of this story, this opens the door for rookie Zach Morgan to make his first start tomorrow against Vegas. He's impressive on the third line and I'm sure lots of Nashville fans will be eager to see how he does. Good luck, Preds."

They move on to another story and I turn off the TV.

"You're starting tomorrow?"

"I found out when I called Coach. Apparently, the press conference started after I left."

"Have you talked to Mikhail or Andi?"

He nods. "I texted with them. I offered to sit out with them, but they want to carry this themselves. Andi said that it's not about me, the Preds, or the NHL. It's just to get their point across to their home countries."

"I hate what they're going through. It must be hard for them to live here and see everything on the news." I exhale.

"They feel helpless. We're meeting tomorrow as a team to see if we can start a fund for the refugees."

I hug him. "That's a great idea. Are you nervous about starting?"

He gives me a searching look. "I feel for them, yeah, but I'm tense about other things too."

"You wanna talk?"

"Not yet."

"How about a dinner made by your girlfriend?"

"Perfect." He gives me a slow kiss that deepens as our tongues twine together. His hand runs down my back and curves over my ass, then he gives it a playful squeeze.

I wonder if he can tell there's a thong there.

"You're wearing sexy undies," he murmurs.

"Hmmm."

Not yet, tiger. Keep the pencil in your hair. Slow seduction tonight.

I playfully push him away.

"I'll put on the pasta. Bread and sauce are ready. Nice suit, by the way. When did you get it? Why are you wearing it?"

He shrugs as we go in the kitchen. "I picked it out a few weeks ago. A tailor came to the arena and measured me. It was delivered today, so I thought I'd try it out. You like?"

He spins to give me the full effect. Then moves his head to shake his blond "hockey hair," which is shoulder length and wavy. I like very much.

"I was going for a more relaxed look tonight." I grimace.

He smiles. "You look beautiful, and it, um, smells great in here."

He pats his jacket pocket, then pulls out his phone and car keys, placing them on the counter.

"Did you lose something?"

He shakes his head. "Nah. I'll change while we wait for the pasta."

"When you get back, open the wine," I call as he disappears into the hallway.

I drop the angel hair pasta into the boiling water and swirl it around. I don't see him sneaking back in the kitchen.

A few minutes later, he comes out wearing jogging pants with a drawstring in the front and a tight Predators workout t-shirt. Much more relaxed, sexy as hell.

He picks up one of the wine bottles and examines the label. I bought four, all of his favorites. "You pick," I tell him as I stir the pasta. "By the way, I talked to Eric today, mostly about this week's rose ceremony on *The Bachelor*, but there was something weird in his voice." Eric is Z's best friend who's still at Hawthorne and plays hockey for the Lions.

"He didn't seem as perky as he usually does," I add. "Maybe call him? His father is at it again, pressuring him not to play. There may be a girl problem, too. You know Eric, always acting like he's fine, but he needs a chat."

"A girl problem? Huh. He usually moves on without too much drama."

"He didn't give me details, but when I asked about how his love life was going, there was definitely a change in his tone."

"I'll give him a call." He walks up behind me and hands me a glass of wine. "Later. To us," he says as we clink glasses.

"Yes." We both drink staring into each other's eyes.

Now on to stage two of this seduction...

CHAPTER THREE

Zack

WE SIT DOWN and eat. She tells me about her classes and two of her professors that may be in a secret relationship. I talk about practice and our plans to see my dad over the holidays.

Every few minutes, my eyes wander to the kitchen cabinet where I slipped the ring earlier. I put it up when she checked on the pasta.

After everything going on with the team, I'd decided not to ask her. But now, I'm second-guessing my second-guessing. *Maybe that's a third guess.* Sure, I don't have the fancy suit on anymore, but she saw me in it, so that counts. I smirk.

I just can't imagine having another night as nice as this just between us. It's everything I enjoy, us ignoring the world for a small amount of time as we focus on each other. It's the little things that mean the most. Her grin when she dances around the den to country music, her laugh when I can't figure out how to fix the dripping faucet in the guest bath and have to call a plumber, the moment she kisses me each morning.

"Shall we move this party to the couch?" She raises an eyebrow.

"Sure. More wine?"

She responds with a grin. "Of course."

I follow her into the kitchen as we remove our dishes from the table.

Before she turns around, I reach over to where I hid the ring, then drop down to one knee. My mind races through my speech. The problem is, I don't see the cat.

Long John Silver is clearly coming out to say, *Hey, owner, pet me,* but my knee lands on his tail.

"Raaaaar," he yells as I move back up, but then crash sideways into a cabinet. The box sails through the air and plops on the floor. Somewhere.

She flips around and sees me lying on the floor doing an awkward James Brown split.

The cat gives me a *go to hell* look.

She winces. "Are you okay?"

"Sure, sure. Just, um, spot of water on the floor, nothing to worry about, nothing to see." I stand up and straighten, unease crawling over me. My gaze darts around the floor, my chest exhaling when I see it. "Wait, turn around, I need to, um, fix something."

She gives me a quizzical look but turns. I grab the box from under a bar chair.

I get back onto one knee and open the box and clear my throat.

"Turn around," I murmur.

She does, her eyes big as she takes me in. "Z…what…"

I inhale a deep breath. "Sugar, I have felt truly alone most of my life until you. You understand me. You accept my flaws. I love you. More than hockey. More than penthouses or fancy cars and definitely more than Long John Silver. Shit, this is bad and not what I planned but my brain just crapped out and now I'm winging it. Sugar, be my wife. Be mine forever, babe."

Tears mist her eyes. "Oh, Z. I love you so much." She chews on her lip. "Um, it's empty."

"What?" I frown.

"The box."

I twist it around, cursing as I crawl on the floor. I shout when I see it next to the cat food bowl. "Damn it, hold on." I place the ring in the box and scoot back into position in front of her.

Another deep breath. "Sugar, I have felt truly alone most of my life until you. Shit, I already said that part." I pause, trying to recall the next line. Dammit. *Dammit.*

She gets on her knees in front of me, her fingers carding through my hair. She kisses me, her lips soft. "The answer is the same, Z. We need to wait for things to settle. We just graduated college. Planning a wedding would be nuts. I love you. You love me. We are deliriously happy. I don't want the extra stress on us. I know you're my man and I don't need a ring or a piece of paper to prove it."

"It was worth a shot." I sigh. She isn't ready. I'm not either truthfully, but I'm afraid of losing her.

"I love the ring, by the way, so don't lose it, 'kay?"

I pull her closer. "Should I have done a hot air balloon?"

She giggles. "Please, no. I'm terrified of those."

"At a hockey game on the jumbotron?"

"Whatever you do, I will love it."

"Yep. Don't worry, I'll make it great." I cup her face and kiss her deeply, leisurely. We have time. And she's not going anywhere.

My proposal comes together a few years later on a ski trip. This time I do it right. No fancy suit, just me and her and our family in front of a roaring fireplace at Christmas.

She said yes.

✧　✧　✧

Our Story

Melanie Moreland

LUCAS, AGE 6

"**M**OMMA?"

"Yes, Lucas?"

"I don't wanna do this."

She knelt down in front of me, smiling. Wrapping her arms around me, she let me bury my face in her hair. I smelled it. I liked how my momma's hair smelled. It was pretty—like her.

"Tell me why."

"Because."

"Because is not a reason, Lucas Michael Allen. It's just a word."

"People will be looking. I don't like people looking."

"But I need you to do this."

"Why?"

"Because Zoey is scared to walk down the aisle alone. I need you to be big and strong, hold her hand, and walk with her. It would make Auntie Lisa so happy."

I frowned. I liked Auntie Lisa. She made good cookies. She wasn't my real auntie—she was my momma's best friend, but my momma said it was the same thing. And Zoey was pretty nice—for a girl. She had brown hair, and her eyes were blue like mine. She wore jeans and shirts and let me play in her tree house, which was really cool. She never cried if she got dirty, and she had great comics. I didn't like the idea of her being scared. So maybe if it made Auntie Lisa happy and Zoey not be scared, I could do this.

But the looking…it always made me nervous. People pointed and whispered, and I didn't like that.

"Lucas."

I looked up at my momma.

"Today is a special day for Auntie Lisa. She found her hero, and today, Zoey gets a new daddy. Everyone is going to be looking at them, not you. I promise."

My eyes widened.

Uncle Derek was a hero? Did he have a cape?

I must have said that out loud, because Momma laughed and tweaked my nose. "You can ask him after the ceremony."

She held out her hand. "You look so handsome, Lucas. Just like your daddy. Can you do this for me?"

"Will Daddy be proud?"

"He'll burst his buttons!"

I grinned. I wanted to see that.

"Okay, Momma. I'll walk with Zoey."

"That's my boy."

✦   ✦   ✦

I GAPED AT the little girl across the room.

That wasn't Zoey.

This girl was wearing a frilly dress, and her shoes had bows on them. Her hair was long and hung down her back. I didn't know Zoey had that much hair. Her face was clean too. I bet her momma made her scrub behind her ears like mine did. It tickled.

Zoey grinned at me, and my eyes widened.

"Zoey—your teeth are gone!"

She giggled. "I fell off a sthwing and knocked 'em out. But look!" She leaned close, poking at her gums. "New ones are comin'!"

I squinted and saw the little white lines on her gums. I nodded—they looked just like mine when my teeth came out. But mine came out because they were loose, not because I fell off a swing. Zoey was always falling. That was probably why they wanted me to walk with her today. I could hold her up.

Auntie Lisa came over, clapping her hands. "Look how cute you are, Lucas!"

I puffed out my chest, shaking my head at her. "Boys aren't cute," I clarified. "My momma said I was handsome."

She and Momma looked at each other and laughed. "Handsome, then. Isn't Zoey pretty? You two will be the perfect couple!"

I had no idea what a couple was, but I looked at Zoey again. She looked different from how she usually looked, but Auntie Lisa was right. "Yes," I said seriously. "Zoey is very pretty today."

They started talking, and I moved closer to Zoey. "I'll hold your hand, Zoey. You not have to be scared."

Her eyes were wide. "I have to toss petals. I need both hands."

I looked down in disgust at the pillow Auntie Lisa had given me—it had frilly stuff on it. "I have to hold this because it has the rings on it." I frowned, not sure what to do. Then I smiled. "We can both hold the basket, and I'll put my hand on top of yours, like this," I explained, showing her.

She smiled widely, showing the big gap in her mouth. It made me smile back. "Thanks, Lucas."

There was something I wanted to ask, and I knew if I asked Zoey, she wouldn't laugh. Looking around, I leaned down so I could whisper. "Zoey, does Uncle Derek have a cape?"

❖   ❖   ❖

DESPITE WHAT MOMMA said, people looked. But I remembered my promise, and instead of looking back, I looked at the basket between us and concentrated on my hand covering Zoey's and making sure she didn't trip going down the aisle. The petals she kept throwing were very slippery.

It was boring standing to the side with Daddy, but his hand felt nice on my shoulder. Twice, I saw Zoey wobble a little. The second time she did it, I rolled my eyes. She'd told me her shoes hurt her feet. She should just take them off—why wear them if they hurt? I tried to get her to look at me, but she was too busy squirming and playing with the leftover flowers in her basket.

Finally, while all the grown-ups moved and went to a table to do something important, Zoey lifted her foot, shaking it. I knew that was what was bothering her.

I shook my head and called over to her. "Take your shoes off, Zoey."

I heard people chuckle, but I ignored them. Zoey shook her head, and I sighed. She was so stubborn. I went over and stood beside her. "Take them off so your feet don't hurt."

"I can't—I don't think you're allowed to at church."

I groaned. She was so silly. "Of course you can," I assured her. "Look, I will too."

I kicked mine off and wiggled my toes. "That feels better."

Zoey hesitated, then I helped her pull off her shoes, watching her wiggle her toes too. "Yeah," she agreed with a nod. "Better."

People were laughing, and I glared at them. Grabbing her hand, I tugged her down the aisle, ignoring my momma's voice telling me to stay.

Nobody was laughing at Zoey and me.

✧　✧　✧

LATER, AFTER SUPPER, I sat in the corner, feeling grumpy. Momma had scolded me for dragging Zoey down the aisle and taking off my shoes, even when I told her it was for Zoey. Daddy laughed and told Momma to calm down because I was only looking after my girl. I had no idea what that meant, but Momma stopped shaking her finger at me, and Auntie Lisa said it was the "sweetest thing ever."

I shook my head. It was just shoes.

I was tired and I wanted to go home, but all the grown-ups were dancing. Supper was weird, with lots of foods I'd never seen before, and I didn't like it. Momma said there'd be cake, but I hadn't seen it yet. That just made me grumpier.

Zoey slid into the seat next to me and smiled, showing off the wide gap in her teeth. "Hi."

"Hi."

"What's wrong?"

I turned away. "Nothing."

Her voice sounded funny when she spoke again. "Are you mad at me, Lucas?"

"No."

Stupid girl.

"I have a surprise."

"I don't want no surprises."

"You'll like it."

I hesitated. I was grumpy, but I really did like surprises. "What is it?"

"You have to come to another table to get it."

"I like it here." Nobody could see me here. Nobody was laughing.

"It's a good surprise."

"Fine," I huffed. I knew Zoey wouldn't stop until she showed me. And she wasn't really stupid. I was just feeling mad.

She tugged my hand, and I followed her across the room, ignoring the people looking at us. We got to another table, where Uncle Derek was waiting, a big grin on his face.

"There's my favorite guy!"

I rolled my eyes at him, but he shook his head and lowered down so he was my height. "You *are* my favorite guy, Lucas. And what you did today? You deserve a reward."

"What did I do?"

"You helped Zoey. You saw she was hurting, and you put her first and took care of her."

"I got in trouble, and people laughed."

He ruffled my hair. "Nah, kiddo. You're not in trouble. Sometimes people laugh because you make them happy, not because they're making fun of you."

"Really?"

"Yup. You added a great memory to this special day—one I'll never forget. And that deserves a treat." He stood up and indicated the table. My eyes widened at what was there.

A cheese pizza, two chocolate milks, and two pieces of cake.

I looked up at him. "For us?"

"Yep. I ordered it in special for you and my Zoey. Dinner was too grown-up for you. Now, you two sit and eat, and when you're done, I'm gonna dance with my new daughter."

He walked away, and I grinned at Zoey. "I know you've never seen it, but I think he does have a cape."

✧   ✧   ✧

"Lucas?"

"Hmmm?" I asked, concentrating on making sure I got every last crumb of cake off my plate. It was good cake, with lots of thick, chocolate frosting. I glanced over at Zoey's plate, wondering if she was going to finish hers. There was lots left on there.

"Will you dance with me?"

I gaped at her. "I don't *dance*, Zoey. I'm six."

"Everybody dances."

I shook my head. "Not me."

"Please?"

I groaned.

"Please, Lucas?"

"People will look," I mumbled.

"I'll hold your hand and it won't matter—like at the church." Then, as added incentive, she slid her plate my way. "You can have the rest of my cake."

I was tempted because it was really good cake. "And your chocolate milk?"

"Yes."

"Okay."

She jumped up and held out her hand. Nervously, I looked around. Everyone seemed to be busy dancing or talking, so maybe they wouldn't notice us.

I took her hand, and we walked over to the dance floor.

My momma and daddy were there, and he grinned down at me. "Taking a turn, Lucas?"

"Zoey wants to," I grumbled. "I don't really wanna. And I don't know how."

He hunched down. "Trust me, son. You're going to do a lot of things in life you don't want to do because of a pair of pretty blue eyes." He looked at my momma. "Isn't that right, Sylvie, my love?"

She swatted his head. "Carson! Stop teasing him."

Laughing, he stood up and shook his head. "Just watch me, Lucas."

He put his hands on Momma's waist, and she wrapped her arms around his neck. He waited until Zoey and I mimicked them, and then he started moving his feet. I did the same thing, wondering how long I had to do this for—after all, there was cake waiting for me.

Zoey put her head on my shoulder, and I was about to pull away until I saw

Momma had done the same thing to Daddy. He had his cheek pressed to her head, and with a sigh, I did the same thing, just like he told me. I shuffled my feet, trying not to step on Zoey's toes. I didn't think she'd like that.

Dancing seemed kinda boring to me.

Although I had to admit, I did like how nice it felt to have Zoey's head on my shoulder. Her hair smelled like bubble gum. I liked it.

Not that I would ever tell anyone that.

Ever.

AGE 16

M Y HANDS TIGHTENED into fists so hard, they ached.

"Say it again, asshole." I straightened my stance. "I dare you."

Jim Mitchell glared up at me from the ground, blood dripping down from his nose, pooling in the dirt in front of him.

"You broke my fucking nose," he whined.

"Touch or disrespect her again, and a broken nose will be the least of your worries," I sneered at him.

I glanced over at Zoey, who was sitting on the grass. Her friend Naomi was beside her with her arm wrapped around her shoulder. Tears ran down Zoey's face as she cradled her arm close to her chest. My own chest ached the way it always did when something was wrong with Zoey. I needed to make it better.

Mitchell stumbled to his feet, wiping at his face. "Pussy-whipped," he muttered.

I grabbed his arm, wrenching him close. "At least I'm getting some," I hissed into his ear. "My dick knows what something other than my hand feels like." Then I pushed him away. "You've been warned, Mitchell."

He lurched away, and with a sigh, I turned toward Zoey. I needed to take her to the nurse, and then I would walk myself to the principal's office. It would be better than waiting for the inevitable announcement to come over the intercom.

"Lucas Allen—report to the principal's office immediately."

I'd been through this enough times; I knew the drill. This wasn't the first altercation I'd had with Jim Mitchell—and I was certain it wouldn't be the last.

Sitting down, I gently tugged at Zoey's arm. "Let me see, Petals."

As always, my pet name for her made her smile. I started calling her that after Lisa and Derek's wedding in reference to the petals she had scattered as we walked up the aisle. She claimed to hate it at first, but that quickly changed. I rarely used it unless we were alone, but I knew it made her smile. I liked her happy. I hated it when she cried.

"Tell me what happened."

She shrugged. "I tripped."

"Zoey," I growled.

Naomi spoke up. "Mitchell was in her face, Lucas. Being a pig—as usual. She tried to get around him, and he grabbed at her."

Anger started bubbling in my chest again. "What did he say this time?"

Zoey gazed up at me, worry shining from the blue pools of warmth. "He was just being Jim."

"Zoey…"

"You have to stop this, Lucas. You can't protect me every minute of every day. You're going to be in trouble again because of me!"

"Best reason to be in trouble." I felt along her arm, frowning when she winced. The skin was grazed, her hand bloody, and bruises were already blooming on her forearm. "Okay. To the nurse's office."

I helped her up, wrapping my arm around her. I liked her tucked into my side. Slowly, we walked toward the nurse's office. "You okay?" I asked in a low voice.

She nodded but stayed quiet.

Mrs. Andrews saw us walk in and pointed to the back room. "You know where to go, Zoey."

I helped her onto the table, the paper covering crackling as she sat down. I hunched down so I could see her face. "Hey, don't be mad at me, Petals."

She looked up, her face sad. "You must get so tired of having me around, Lucas. I only cause you trouble."

I stared at her in disbelief. "Zoey, you don't cause anything. Mitchell is a typical bully—you're the smallest one around, so he picks on you. That's on him, not you." I slipped my fingers under her chin and dropped a quick kiss on her mouth. "I'm never tired of having you around—ever."

I couldn't remember my life without Zoey. She was always there. First as a little kid, growing up with me. Summers of shared popsicles and giggles, sandy beaches, fires, and marshmallows.

Our first day of school together, when her small hand slipped into mine and I held it tight, feeling better because she was beside me.

The first class outing, sitting beside each other on the bus as we visited a local farmer, and I held her hand again when she slipped in the mud. She cried because her jeans got dirty, so I purposely fell too, to make mine match. I hated to see her cry.

The first vacation our families took together. Both of us with wide eyes of wonder as we walked into Disneyland, once again, our hands clasped tight as we tried to take it all in.

I had shared all my firsts with her.

Every first day of school. School dances and outings. Every Easter, Thanksgiving, and Christmas. First snows, first dreams…first kiss.

✧　✧　✧

IT HAPPENED SO naturally, walking home from a dance. We went as a group—we always did, but tonight had been different. Zoey looked different—she felt different when we danced. When I heard Al say how hot Zoey was, I looked at her, really looked at her, and I was shocked.

She had grown up right before my eyes, and until that very second, I had never noticed. Her dark hair was long and wavy, hanging halfway down her back. She had a way of brushing it over her shoulder that was sexy. Her eyes were blue—so clear they resembled a cloudless summer day. Her lips were full, and I suddenly wanted to kiss them. She was tiny, not much over five feet, and I felt like a giant next to her. Her breasts were small but perfect, the dress she was wearing showing off their roundness. I found myself wondering what it would be like to touch them. Touch her. Right then, it hit me.

She was more than my best friend. She was my other half.

I spent the rest of the night in purgatory, suddenly seeing every other guy as my competition, even my friends. I wondered how to tell her. How she would react.

What if she rejected me?

I was glad when the dance was over and we said goodnight to our friends. She didn't seem upset that I didn't want to go for burgers at the late-night diner. When I said I wanted to go home, she simply nodded.

I paused at the entrance to the park. "Let's go for a swing." Zoey loved it when I pushed her on the swing.

Her smile was warm and happy as she let me tug her into the dark, deserted area. She settled on the wide leather seat, and I leaned down, hands on her hips, my mouth near her ear. "You ready, Petals?"

Her reply came in a breathy voice I'd never heard before. "Yes, Lucas. I'm ready."

I pushed her, smiling at her delighted giggles. I stood back, leaning against the cold metal and watching her soar, secretly admiring how the actions caused her skirt to lift and bunch, showing me her shapely legs. As she slowed, I stood in front of her, my legs spread wide, her between them. We stared at each other, both still. Her breathing picked up, and I lowered my head to her level. Our gazes held, mine begging her with a silent question. She nodded almost imperceptibly, and then our lips touched. Pressed together softly and parted. Again. Then again. Each time a little harder, holding a little longer. When she sighed, her breath hot against my mouth, I bravely touched my tongue to her bottom lip, and then I was inside. It was brief, fumbling, wet, and awkward.

It was perfect.

Ten minutes later, we were both pros, our tongues sliding and gliding together, our breath mingling, and I knew no matter what else happened in my life, it would be with her by my side.

I dropped my head to her shoulder, panting. "Be my girlfriend, Zoey. I want everyone to know you're mine."

She giggled softly, her breath a warm puff of air against my neck. "I think most of them think so already."

I lifted my head. "What about you? Is that what you think?"

"It's what I hoped," she whispered, her eyes glimmering in the dim light.

I kissed her again. No fumbling, no awkwardness. As with everything else in my life, when Zoey was part of it, it became easier…better. School, crowds, dances…kissing.

Leaning over her, I worked the snaps on my leather cuff and wrapped it around her wrist. My dad had given it to me when I was twelve. It was too big then and rather small now—I had a new one at home, but for some reason, I kept wearing this one, waiting for the right time to take it off. The time was perfect. I had to use the last snap, and although it was still loose, it looked right sitting on her wrist. I lifted her arm and kissed the thin skin of her inside wrist, the tiny blue veins pulsating with life under the pale covering. The cuff would protect that life—just like I protected her.

"It's official for everyone, then. Now they can see we're together. My girl."

"Lucas Allen's girl," she murmured. "I like that."

"I like it too."

✧   ✧   ✧

ZOEY'S VOICE BROUGHT me out of my memories.

"What did you say to Jim?"

I pursed my lips. "Nothing."

"Fibber."

I huffed a sigh. She always knew. Quietly, I repeated what I'd said to him, feeling my ears turn red. Zoey looked at me, shocked. Using her good hand, she slapped my chest. "But we're not...we've never..."

"I know. I just wanted to piss him off."

She rolled her eyes. Pressing my lips to her ear, I chuckled. "It's not like we haven't done...a few things, Zoey." I grinned against her warm skin. "Lots of things."

She blushed and looked away. "You're a jackass."

"*Your* jackass."

Her lips twitched.

"Now, tell me what he said to you," I demanded.

"No."

I lifted her chin. "Why not?"

"You'll go find him and beat him senseless."

"Well, it won't take much to make that idiot senseless. One more good punch should do it."

"Lucas."

Now I had to know. "Tell me, Zoey. Right now."

She whispered his words, and I grasped the paper on the exam table, tearing it into shreds. "I'll kill him."

She cupped my face, wincing as she held my cheeks in her hands. "No. You won't do anything. Promise me."

Her blue eyes were wide with fear. "I need you with me, Lucas. Please."

I could deny her nothing. I never could. "Okay."

Her warm mouth covered mine, and I felt my entire body relax into her. She always did that for me—calmed me and centered my focus. I pulled her tight, kissing her back, needing her taste in my mouth and her scent in my lungs.

Remembering where we were, I drew back, keeping my arms around her. I held her close, burying my nose in her long hair and breathing her in.

"Am I forgiven?"

"Yes."

I kissed her again—soft and sweet the way she liked—and stepped back as I heard the door opening. "Good."

Mrs. Andrews bustled in, her tongue clicking away. "What have you done this time, dear?"

"She was pushed, Mrs. Andrews. I don't think it's broken, but it's badly sprained. There are some contusions along with cuts that need to be cleaned and dressed. Some Tylenol would help with the pain as well. I think she needs to go home and rest, too."

Zoey rolled her eyes, and Mrs. Andrews snorted.

"Thank you, Dr. Allen," she said with a smirk. "I'll take it from here."

I opened my mouth to protest, when the intercom crackled to life.

"Lucas Allen—report to the principal's office immediately."

I groaned, and Mrs. Andrews shook her head. "They need that on a continuous recording."

"I'm not that bad," I protested.

"He was defending me," Zoey spoke up.

"Mitchell again?" she asked.

We both nodded.

"That boy. He needs to be taught some manners—although not necessarily with your fists, Lucas. Go take your punishment. I'll look after your girl, and you can pick her up."

"I don't know if they'll let me go home with her."

She picked up my hand, holding it high. "Zoey isn't the only one needing some mending. I think you cracked a knuckle. I'll bandage it up when you get back."

Given how much it was aching, that news didn't surprise me. Zoey's injuries were far more important, though. I'd worry about myself later.

I dropped a kiss on Zoey's head. "Back soon."

"Let's hope so. Drummond might toss you in detention and throw away the key."

I winked at her. "You can spring me later."

She shoved me. "Go."

"Miss me?"

She smiled. "I already do."

❖   ❖   ❖

I SWALLOWED HEAVILY when I walked into Mr. Drummond's office. It was pretty full. My parents, Jim's parents, the douchebag himself—his nose a flaming red, bordering on purple—and Zoey's mother were all in attendance.

This was new.

The joys of living in a small town. They were all so…close. I hadn't expected to see them all together…all *here*.

At least they hadn't called in the big guns, I thought. At least Derek—

The door opened, and Derek Fraser walked in, looking every inch the criminal lawyer he was. Dressed in a black suit, he was scary, towering over everyone in the room. There was none of his usual friendly greeting to me, asking how his favorite guy was. In fact, he didn't look at me. Instead, there was only a stony glare cast around the room as he walked to Lisa, then he folded his arms over his chest.

"Let's get on with this. I'm a busy man."

Oh shit.

They were all staring at me, and I felt a shiver run up my neck. I still hated being looked at, and with Zoey stuck in the nurse's office, I couldn't hold her hand and be calm.

I sucked in a deep breath, trying to act nonchalant. "Hey. What's the occasion?"

"I had to call your parents here, Lucas. What happened today has gone beyond a playground scuffle."

I held back my laughter. *Playground scuffle?*

We hadn't had a playground scuffle since we were nine. I looked over at Jim, glaring. I'd beaten his ass then too.

"You broke Mr. Mitchell's nose, son."

I shrugged. "I sorta figured that when I felt his bones give."

"Lucas!" my mother admonished while my father glared at me, and Derek groaned.

Mr. Mitchell started shouting. "We're going to sue! I want him suspended! In fact, I want him expelled! I don't want him anywhere near my son—he's a bully with a temper!"

I gaped at him. Did he know his son at all? He was the biggest loudmouth ass around and loved to pick on everyone smaller than him.

"*I'm* a bully? *I'm a bully?*" I yelled.

Derek stepped forward, his hand on my chest. "Calm, Lucas."

I grabbed my phone, shoving it toward Derek. "He pushed her, Derek. Look at her arm! I was only defending her."

His finger stroked over the screen of my phone, looking at the pictures I'd taken of Zoey's arm. His frown deepened, and I could hear a low growl building in his chest.

"I'm not a bully," I insisted. "He was talking smack to her and making her uncomfortable, and when she tried to ignore him and move past, he shoved her. I saw it!"

Now everyone was looking at Jim.

"Is this true, Jim?" Principal Drummond asked.

His face turned almost as red as his nose. "She tripped." His voice dropped. "Bitch is always tripping."

It was only Derek holding me back that stopped him from having a black eye to match his bloody nose. Lisa gasped, and even his parents looked shocked.

"Don't you dare refer to my daughter as a bitch," Derek ordered, his voice filled with fury.

"That's nothing compared to what else he says," I muttered.

"Like what?" Derek demanded.

I saw Jim's eyes widen and his head shake frantically. I crossed my arms and leaned back.

"What did he say to Zoey this morning, Lucas?"

I drew in a deep breath and repeated what I'd finally gotten Zoey to tell me. "He told her he planned on her sucking him off, then he wanted her to ride his dick like a pogo stick."

Chaos broke out. Parents were yelling; Dad was now holding Derek—who was hollering the whole time about having Jim tossed in jail and throwing away the key—back from a cowering Jim Mitchell. The wimp was hiding behind his mother, looking terrified and making me want to laugh at his immature actions. He wasn't such a bully when someone bigger was around. The principal was looking rather pale. I stepped toward the door. Obviously, my work was done.

I looked at Principal Drummond. "I'm gonna go get Zoey from the nurse's office and take her home now."

He waved me away.

I flipped off Mitchell before I slipped out the door.

AGE 18

THE ROOM WAS dark, the only light from the streetlamp outside. Zoey's mouth was hot and wet as she kissed up and down my neck.

"Petals, baby...we need to stop."

"No, Lucas. Not this time."

I drew back, panting, desperately trying not to thrust my aching cock against her leg. "We said we'd wait."

"We *have* waited, Lucas. We've waited over a year—we're both eighteen. I want to give you this for your birthday. I want to give you me."

I groaned as she stroked my stomach with her fingers, slipping them under the waistband of my sweats, slowly running them from side to side.

"Please, Lucas."

"I don't have…"

"I'm on the pill."

"Since when?"

She leaned up, running her tongue along my jaw. "Since the first time you used your fingers to make me come." Her teeth nipped my skin. "I knew I wanted you inside me instead," she murmured, her voice sounding shy.

What she was doing to my cock didn't feel shy, and I hissed as she wrapped her fingers around my shaft. She was so good with her hands. And her mouth. We'd basically done everything except the final act—trusting and learning as our touches grew bolder and our boundaries stretched.

All firsts for both of us, and all done together.

Our lips fused together again, tongues sliding and caressing. Her hand continued to work me, sliding up and down in long, slow strokes, sending ripples of pleasure down my spine.

I wanted this. I wanted her.

"Your parents…" I protested feebly, already knowing the answer.

"Won't be back until tomorrow. We have all night and morning. Please, Lucas, make me yours—totally yours."

I couldn't deny her or myself anymore.

Piece by piece, the thin fabric that separated us was discarded. For the first time, we were completely bare with each other. I marveled at her skin, how soft and smooth it was under my fingers. How sweet it tasted under my tongue. My muscles clenched and my spine shuddered as she explored my chest, running her hands over my legs and thighs, once again holding me in her hands.

She gazed down at me in wonder. "You are so beautiful," she whispered.

I scoffed. "I'm not beautiful, Zoey."

"You are to me. I love your body. How you feel under my fingers. Your handsome face. How you look at me."

I smiled at her. I was a decent-enough-looking guy. I worked out with my friends and kept in shape. I kept my light brown hair short, and I was lucky enough never to have been plagued with acne. I was over six feet tall, and I thought my eyebrows were too thick, my nose too big, and my mouth too wide, but Zoey always disagreed with me. She said my eyebrows set off my deep blue eyes and my nose was the exact right size. As for my mouth, she loved everything about it. How it kissed her. Smiled at her. Licked her.

She saw only good.

I cupped her face. "I love looking at you, Zoey. And I love how much you love me." I pulled her back to my mouth and kissed her until she was breathless and needy. Until all I could see, feel, and taste was her. We explored each other leisurely, knowing we had all night. Knowing we were finally going to have another first—the way it was meant to be—with each other.

When we were both ready, when every doubt that lingered had been erased, I hovered over her, our gazes locked, the intensity of the moment thick in the air.

"This is just the start, Petals. You know that, right?"

"I know," she whispered.

"I'm going to marry you one day, Zoey."

Her smile was wide. "I know."

AGE 26

THE CHURCH WAS quiet this time of day. I knew the pastor was in the back somewhere, and soon, the sanctuary would be filled with voices and busy hands as they decorated the altar and pews. Memories washed over me as I looked up the aisle.

Holding Zoey's hand, the basket clasped beneath our fingers, making sure she didn't trip—something that hadn't changed to this day.

Watching her squirm in discomfort and hating the fact that she might be in pain—being too young to understand how I was feeling.

I remembered the look of embarrassment on my mother's face as I kicked off my shoes and helped Zoey tug hers off before leading her back down the aisle to escape the muffled laughter.

A smile pulled at my face.

So many things had changed over the years, and yet so little was different.

Zoey more often wore dresses now instead of jeans, although her shoes were usually flats—and regularly ended up kicked off under the table or discarded by the sofa. Mine generally followed suit.

She remained clumsy, and I still held her hand, scanning the area we were walking for hidden obstacles only her feet could find. I held her up physically—she held me up in every other way.

She made me want to look after her that day, and the feeling had never changed.

We had been together through everything. No matter the obstacle, we'd over-come it. Even when I left to go to medical school, we had persevered and loved each other through the lonely months, using every means at our disposal. We used air miles for flights, FaceTime, Zoom—anything and everything to stay close and in touch. I flew so often I knew most of the airline staff by name.

Goodbyes were hell; hellos were sweeter than nectar. We pushed through it. Together.

We'd grown up together, fallen in love, and learned together, ignoring the whispers that said we'd grow apart—that people don't fall in love at the age of six and stay that way.

Today, we'd prove them wrong. Today, I'd marry my Petals, my Zoey.

I made it through medical school and returned home to start my residency, just as we planned. Nothing would keep us apart again.

I recalled the day I'd told Zoey I had been accepted to medical school in a different province.

She hugged me hard, congratulating me. But I saw the sadness and worry in her eyes.

I tilted up her chin. "What?"

"You'll be in Ontario, and I'll be here in Alberta. What about us?"

I shook my head. "Nothing changes, except some distance, Petals. I'll come home every chance I get. You can come and see me. It's only for medical school. I'll apply for residency closer to home. But they have the courses I want to specialize in at McMaster."

"We'll be apart for three years."

"We talked about this. You'll get started using your early childhood education degree. You're going to make an awesome teacher, Petals. We're going to work hard for the next few years, and then our life together can start. We'll get married. I'll get through

residency, you'll teach, we'll be together. Once I'm a doctor, we can start our own family."

She nodded, looking unsure. *"What—what if you meet someone else?"*

I kissed the end of her nose. *"Now you're being ridiculous. Why would I want someone else? I have you. My girl. My best friend. My lover and confidante. You are everything I want. Everything I need."* I laughed softly. *"Zoey, I'm going there to learn to be a doctor. For our future. Not to look for a new girlfriend. I'm going to do what I have to do, then I'm coming home to you and we're going to get married. Understand? You are it for me. We clear?"*

She smiled, still sad, but not worried.

"Crystal."

A voice broke through my musings. "Lucas."

I smiled as I turned to our wedding planner. "Isa. How are you?"

"I'm great. Is everything okay?"

I nodded. "Just having a few moments of peace before the day. It all started here, you know."

She grinned widely. "Zoey told me—friends from childhood. It's an amazing story." She chuckled. "She mentioned the shoes as well."

"I've never lived that down."

"In all my years as a wedding planner, I haven't run into that one yet."

"Well, we have no kids in the wedding party—chronologically, anyway. I can't vouch for the maturity level of Cary and Ralph at times. Lydia and Naomi are pretty safe bets."

"No altar shenanigans, then?"

I winked at her. "I can't guarantee what's gonna happen when I get to kiss Zoey."

Laying her hand on my arm, she laughed. "Keep it PG, Lucas. You have an audience."

"Don't remind me." I still hated people looking at me. It was better when Zoey was beside me, but I hated being the center of attention.

She patted my arm and winked. "Your girl will be there. Just focus on her."

"I will."

I was actually feeling quite relaxed. Neither Zoey nor I were big on the huge, lavish wedding thing. We'd opted instead for an intimate ceremony and dinner afterward, followed, of course, by dancing. I was much more amenable to holding my girl and swaying with her on the dance floor these days.

Zoey was, as with how she handled everything else in her life, calm, warm, and gracious. I had heard horror stories of bridezillas, but my girl was the exact opposite, and the whole process had been easy. Isa had commented more than once how she wished all her clients were like us. We wanted everything low-key, and she had done it to perfection.

I reached into my pocket and pulled out a small box. "Can you, ah, give that to Zoey for me?"

"I will."

"It's her something blue."

"I'm sure she'll love it."

I looked down the empty aisle and drew in a deep breath. "See you soon."

She nodded. "Soon."

✧ ✧ ✧

CANDLES FLICKERED ALL around, the glow casting soft light across the church. I shifted nervously, meeting my father's eyes. He winked and straightened his shoulders, silently telling me it was okay and to be strong. I stood a little taller so he knew I'd gotten the message. Beside him, my mother was already crying, dabbing at her eyes with a lace hankie. Time had been kind to them both, and they still projected love—for each other and for those around them. They adored Zoey, and from the day I'd come home and told them she was now my girlfriend, they had been nothing but supportive, helping us in any way they could.

Across the aisle were Lisa and Derek. He still referred to me as his favorite guy, and Lisa's cookies were as tasty as ever.

Sitting with Derek and asking him if it was okay to be more than friends with Zoey had been the most nerve-racking moment of my life. No matter how much he liked me, Zoey was his daughter—he'd adopted her right away, and she became Zoey Fraser—and he took his role as her father very seriously.

"You gonna treat her right?"

"Yes, sir."

"I don't want her pressured, Lucas." He looked at me knowingly.

My eyes widened when his meaning sank in. "Never, sir." *The words burst out of me before I could stop them.* "I think I love her, Uncle Derek. I know I'm young, but I've loved her since the day you married Auntie Lisa. I can't imagine my life without her."

He leaned back, stroking his chin, and then grinned. "Took you long enough."

"I know."

"Be good to her."

"I will."

"Good. I've retired my cape, but I'll bring it out if I have to."

Because, yes, as it turned out, Derek did have a cape—a red one. He let me try it on once, swearing me to secrecy. A true sign I was, indeed, his favorite guy.

Lisa smiled at me, and I returned her affectionate gesture easily. She was still my mother's best friend, one of my strongest allies and a constant source of needed input when it came to her daughter. She had dealt with our good times, our rare but ferocious arguments, and she'd been the one I'd gone to when I was worried about leaving Zoey behind when I went to medical school. She had sat me down and told me how integral I was to Zoey's life.

"If there are two people in this world meant to be together, it's my daughter and you, Lucas. She's as worried as you are." She took my hand. *"I know this will be a difficult time for you, but it will make you stronger as a couple. Enjoy the time. I want her to enjoy it as well. You can't cut yourself off from life because you're apart. But know all your experiences will be part of the journey you have going forward with each other."*

By the time she'd listed all our shared experiences and the love she knew her daughter had for me, I'd realized how silly I was being.

I blinked as Cary nudged me in the ribs, and I realized the music was playing. I smiled at my best friend, who had been part of my life almost as long as Zoey. Ralph had joined our little circle when we were in high school, after moving here to Calgary. We'd all remained close, and I was thrilled to have them stand up with me.

Lydia drifted down the aisle, resplendent in her red dress, her rich brown hair in an upsweep that added inches to her already impressive height. She winked at Ralph as she slipped by, patting my arm as she smiled. Naomi followed her, the red of her dress showing off her ebony skin and black hair well. Cary beamed at his wife, and she giggled as she did a quick step to the right and dropped a kiss on his smiling mouth. I winked at her, loving her free spirit. She was Zoey's best friend, but she was a loyal, fierce comrade to us all.

The music changed, swelled, and Zoey appeared in the doorway. Her delicate beauty made my breath catch in my throat. Her gown floated around her like a cloud, her dark hair swept off her face, showing her elegant neck. The earrings I had left for her earlier glittered in her ears. A small bouquet of roses and lilies was in her hand, matching the ones in my lapel.

She walked the aisle alone, explaining she wanted this final journey to me just to be hers. Our eyes locked and held, at times her beauty obscured by the tears that filled my vision. She was mine. From today forward, nothing would separate us. Everything we'd worked for, every sacrifice we'd made, was worth today.

Derek met her at the front, kissing her cheek and clasping our hands together. Our eyes spoke of love and never wavered. Tears glistened in her eyes and mine as words of commitment and vows we would both cherish were exchanged. I spoke of my life with her and how she filled my every thought. Her voice quavered as she spoke of marrying her best friend—her hero—and I couldn't resist leaning closer to wipe away the lone tear that slipped down her cheek as she spoke, nuzzling the soft skin until the pastor cleared his throat.

When I was able to take her in my arms and seal our union with a kiss, it was one of love, passion, and promises. Promises for a future together.

Because that was how we were meant to be—together.

After the paperwork was signed, making it official, the pastor introduced us as Mr. and Mrs. Allen. I grinned down at her, tucked into my side, and lifted her hand, bringing it to my lips for a lingering kiss.

Then it happened. Ralph, Cary, Lydia, and Naomi, in one synchronized move, kicked off their shoes and paired off, walking down the aisle as they laughed. My mother gasped into her hankie and then began to giggle as my father shook his head and grinned. Lisa burst into laughter, and Derek let out one of his deep guffaws.

Looking down at the pile of heels and dress shoes, I started to chuckle. With a cheeky wink, Zoey sent her shoes flying past me, her height shrinking a good four inches. She quirked her eyebrow in challenge, and with a grin, I toed off my dress shoes, then bent over, lifting Zoey into my arms and striding down the aisle, amid much applause. Even Isa was laughing in the corner. As with everything with Zoey, it was perfect.

I kissed my wife.

"I love you, Petals. I love my life with you."

She snuggled her head into my chest.

"Always, Lucas."

I liked that word.

It was a good place to start.

✧   ✧   ✧

Thank you so much for reading! I loved introducing readers to Lucas and Zoey, and plan on expanding this story in the near future. Make sure to subscribe to my newsletter to get notification when more of Our Story – https://bit.ly/MMorelandNewsletter

PROFESSOR PLATONIC

LUCY LENNOX

CHAPTER ONE
Jack

I STARED AT my email while the blood drained from my face to my toes.

To: Jack Wilde

We regret to inform you your application for participation on the Raintree Arctic Ecology and Evolution research expedition was not successful.

There was more to it than that. Probably. Bullshit explanations about how many qualified candidates had applied and how tough the competition had been. How hard it was selecting only one recipient for the honor.

And I understood it all. Of course I did. Graduate students from around the world had applied to go on the groundbreaking expedition. They couldn't take everyone.

But I was devastated. Not getting the research fellowship meant having to go home to Dallas and listen to my mother complain about my "denial of real-life responsibilities" and my father ask me yet again when I was going to "stop fussing with that environmental nonsense and get a real job."

"You look like you're gonna hurl, dude," my cousin Hallie said before popping a potato chip in her mouth. She was visiting Houston for the weekend to see a friend's art show and had stopped by my apartment to drop off a suit my mom had bought me. An interview suit. "What's up?"

"I didn't get a spot on the research expedition this summer," I said, feeling numb. "Everyone I talked to said they thought I was already considered part of the team. My application was supposed to be a formality."

She settled into the hand-me-down sofa my roommate had left behind when he'd moved out. If I didn't find another roommate soon, I was going to have to give up the lease and find a cheaper room to rent next semester. It was either that or ask my parents for help, which would occur precisely when hell froze over.

"What do you think happened?" Hallie asked. "I thought you were already working with the people leading the expedition?"

"I was. I *am*." Not only had I helped craft the grant proposal that was funding the expedition, but I'd also helped originate some of the research planned for the expedition. I was one of Dr. Raintree's favorite grad students.

It didn't make any sense.

The only person who hadn't seemed all that convinced had been my evolutionary biology professor.

My stomach dropped. *Professor Henry.* The only person in my academic community who still treated me with cold indifference had been responsible for one of the two most important recommendations on my application.

If I hadn't been chosen for the expedition, it had to have been something Professor Henry wrote.

My fingernails bit into my palms. "That fucking bastard," I hissed under my breath.

Hallie's eyes widened. "Who?"

"My evolutionary biology professor. He was supposed to write me a recommendation for the program, but the man hates me. He won't even make eye contact with me and acts like every time I ask him a question, I'm wasting his time. I'm sure this is on him."

"Why would he hate you? You're smart as hell and the hardest worker in the whole family."

I loved my cousin's loyalty. She was a fierce defender of the people she loved. I shot her a smile. "Thanks, Hallie. But it doesn't matter. It's done. I can't argue with their decision without doing further damage to my reputation. And these are the researchers and professors who can hopefully help me get a job after I finish my degree, not to mention some of them will be on my thesis committee. I'm sure it'll be fine. I just..." I sighed.

I was so fucking tired. I'd worked my ass off lately, holding down a full-time job as a lab technician while also pursuing a graduate degree. Because Barrington University wasn't cheap, I'd worked hard to try and get my degree completed as quickly as I could so I would rack up the least amount of debt possible.

In case my parents were right and I couldn't make a go of this as a career.

I shrugged. "I was already feeling sorry for myself after taking my evolutionary biology final this morning. Even though I thought I did well, the professor's probably going to screw me on the grade."

"Okay," Hallie said, rolling the chip bag closed with a loud crinkle and sitting up. "You know what you need? Hug therapy."

My family was a little strange.

"You sound like your hippie sister-in-law," I muttered. One of my Wilde cousins had married a woman named Nectarine who did yoga and believed in all kinds of woo-woo shit.

"I read an article about this last week, and I'm dying for someone to try it. Remember when you and I were at Doc and Grandpa's anniversary trip and everyone was all, 'Oh, gee, look at my soul mate who wants to sex me up and then spoon me adorably all night,' and you and I were like, 'Ew, how about just the spoon part?'"

I stared at her, trying to figure out what the hell she was trying to say. I did recall having said that, but I'd been lying through my teeth. I'd wanted the sex too; I'd just wanted the comfort more.

She sighed. "So the article I read mentioned there's an app that's like a dating app but also has other things like a classified section for getting help doing stuff around the house and whatever. Shit like that."

"You mean Heart2Heart?"

She pointed at me. "Yes, that's it. Well, they have this platonic section where you can seriously just say you want someone to hold hands or spoon with. This article talked about... wait. *Dude.* I sent you the article! You didn't read it?"

She didn't wait for me to answer before waving her hand in the air like it didn't matter. "Anyway, I sent it to you because it was about the evolutionary need for human touch and how it's become a biologic imperative for... I don't know. Some brainiac bullshit about neural circuitry. The point is. You need some."

I blinked at her. "I need some."

I needed some all right, but I needed the kind of human touch with a dick involved. And hard fucking. I needed angry sex to work out my frustration over this expedition rejection. That was what I *wanted*, at least. But I wasn't going to pursue it.

I was taking a break from sex with strangers after a particularly bad experience with a guy who was too annoying and rough. The experience hadn't turned dangerous, but it had been just close enough to remind me it *could* have. And I didn't need that kind of stress right now on top of everything else.

"It would be nice to have someone to snuggle with," I admitted. "I can't think of the last person I slept with where there was spooning involved."

Hallie sighed. "Yeah. Same. You haven't really dated anyone since Lowell, have you?"

I glared at her. "I've just been rejected from the most important career opportunity of my life, and you have to bring up Lowell? Do you hate me?"

She stretched her leg across the sofa to nudge my hip with her foot. "Sorry, Jack. He was an ass. Probably still is. Besides, he probably wasn't any good at cuddling to begin with. The man was about as comforting as a bag of sticks and rocks."

Hallie wasn't wrong. My ex was not only stiff and oddly formal, but he was also all elbows and knees. And way more interested in marine microplastics and their effect on food webs than me. Which was fine. Ocean pollutants were, indeed, a serious issue. But so was my need for affection.

"Great, now I've slipped from disappointed to morose," I muttered. "Maybe I need alcohol."

Hallie leaned forward and grabbed my laptop. "No. You need a big bear of a guy to snuggle the shit out of you tonight. I'm going to hook you up."

I ignored her as she began typing because my mind was suddenly diverted by the mention of a big bear of a guy.

Professor Henry was a big bear of a guy. I'd spent the first two weeks of my first semester daydreaming about him naked. Unlike many of my previous science professors, Professor Henry was fairly young. I'd have been surprised if he was even close to forty yet.

He was tall and broad, thick with muscles, and broody as fuck. His thick, wavy hair always seemed to be windblown and matched the dark beard he wore. Which, of course, perfected the lumberjack look he had to have been going for with his typical "jeans and flannel shirt" ensemble.

But he was a hateful asshole. Obviously. After those first two weeks of ignorant bliss, I'd learned he had it out for me. He called on everyone except for me. He returned my assignments with harsh notes of criticisms and warnings to do better.

And he'd even avoided me during his office hours.

That had stung like a bitch.

I'd run into Yi Shao coming out of Professor Henry's office, beaming as if she'd been privy to the answers for the upcoming exam. But when I'd knocked on the doorframe to ask him a quick question, he'd gruffly explained he was already late for a departmental meeting and would have to answer my question via email instead.

His answer had been short and unhelpful. He'd reminded me that the most successful graduate students were the ones who knew how to seek the answers they needed without expecting them to be handed to them on a silver platter.

Professor Henry's admonishment had intimidated me and caused me to second-guess my relationship with every other professor in the program.

And now here I was, facing another rejection at his hands.

I felt my confidence crumbling. Normally, I had a positive outlook and was pretty good at overcoming challenges like this, but tonight... tonight I really was tempted to crawl into the comforting arms of a stranger and accept whatever affectionate touch I could get.

I glanced up to see Hallie's eyebrows lifted in question and her fingers poised on the keyboard. *Will you let me do this for you?*

I blew out a breath and nodded.

Why the hell not? One night in a stranger's arms for platonic snuggling. If I didn't stop to think about how pathetic it sounded, it might turn out to be a nice change from the alcohol-induced pity party I'd already planned.

After a semester of feeling like I was the most unlikable human on earth—thanks in part to Professor Henry—I could use a night where someone at least pretended to care about me.

CHAPTER TWO

River

STARED AT the message from my mother.

Mom: *Therapeutic touch. I've decided you need some. Check out this link your father found.*

While I contemplated whether or not to entertain another one of her zany ideas, a kid in line behind me at the grocery store bumped into me, and my thumb slipped. The child's mom apologized, but I waved her off. When I looked back at my phone, the link had loaded.

My sister would say that was fate telling me to look at the link. My brother would say that was nothing but an obnoxious kid fucking with my life.

Since I was an academic who craved information of all kinds, I couldn't help but read the information on the screen.

I've had a very bad day and could really use a hug. Male ISO male for platonic but affectionate sleepover. No sex or commitments. I don't want to talk about it, just hold me all night and tell me it's going to be okay.

Something about the listing made my heart squeeze. I had uncomfortably similar feelings. And the guy who'd posted it sounded so melancholy, I wanted to do exactly as he'd said and pull him into my arms to tell him everything would be okay.

But since I was also a realist who'd heard way too many horror stories of dating apps gone awry, I was for sure not going to pursue it.

I also knew better than to engage with my mom about this, so I ignored her message and paid for my groceries before hopping in my Jeep to head home. Even though I had a handful of undergrad exams left to grade, I had a four-day weekend to get them done. After the disappointing workweek I'd had, I was in desperate need of at least one night off from the demands of my job.

My phone rang halfway home, and I sighed. I considered ignoring her call, but then guilt took over.

"Hi, Mom," I said instead.

"I just feel so awful about what's happening in your department." Typical Mom. No segue. She just dove right in and cut to the heart of the matter with a knife.

"It's not my department anymore," I corrected. "Today was my last day."

"No, I know. And you can be sure your father and I will be thrilled to have you closer to home, but I still can't believe that professor has the nerve to keep working there after the scandal he caused."

"Thankfully, no one knows about it yet," I reminded her. I didn't want to think about the drama in my department at work. I was grateful I'd been recruited away from Barrington before the scandal had come to light, and I especially looked forward to moving back to the Northeast. Texas had never been my favorite place to live, and I missed my family and friends.

Mom's voice had a dreamy quality. "My son… a Yale professor." She sighed, and I could hear the smile in her voice. "Just imagine the bragging I can do at bridge night."

I barked out a laugh as I pulled into the driveway of my rental house. "Bridge night" was the name she and her colleagues used when they got together once a month to discuss civil engineering's intersection with architecture. Telling her fellow Cornell professors that her son was taking a position at Yale was like waving a red flag in front of a particularly snotty—albeit incredibly well-educated—bull.

"Go for it. Now that the semester is over, I give you permission to brag as much as you want. Thanks for keeping it quiet up to now. I didn't want to jinx anything."

"I understand. Now all that's left is to pack up your stuff and start the long drive."

She made it sound so easy, but she probably also assumed that I didn't have four years of crap accumulated everywhere, including my lab at work. The idea of having to go through it all in the next two weeks was exhausting.

… just hold me all night and tell me it's going to be okay.

The guy who'd posted on that app had voiced my own feelings. Part of me wanted nothing more than to curl up with someone tonight and hide from my obligations and the work ahead. But I wasn't sure I was capable of holding someone all night without wanting to kiss them and touch them sexually.

Could I do it?

"River, honey?"

I snapped back to the conversation with my mom. "Yeah." I turned off the ignition and grabbed my phone and messenger bag. "Sorry. I just got home."

"Well then, I'll let you go. But I just wanted to say congratulations. We're very proud of you."

I heard my dad's voice in the background but couldn't make out what he was saying.

Mom laughed. "Dad says if you're too close-minded—by which he means boring and repressed—to consider therapeutic touch, you could always get a massage. I'm sure there are plenty of places in Houston. Just don't go to one of those 'happily ever after' ones."

I snorted. "I think you mean 'happy ending,' and don't worry." I didn't tell her that the app she'd sent me also offered plenty of "happy endings" for free. I didn't need to pay to have someone stroke me off.

After finishing the call and unlocking the back door, I went about my usual routine of watering my houseplants, checking the mail, and spending way too long reading over a flier for commemorative gold coins.

Which was when I realized that, holy shit, I actually *was* boring and repressed.

And I *still* couldn't get that Heart2Heart post out of my mind.

I didn't want someone to stroke me off. What I wanted was for someone to give a shit about me. Reassure me that I wasn't making a big mistake by leaving my current research project and my students to move across the country to a university where tenure wouldn't be guaranteed.

I pulled up the post again and stared at it.

I've had a very bad day and could really use a hug.

This nameless, faceless stranger had managed to put my feelings into words. And he had the balls to ask for help which was something my father, as a psychologist, had worked very hard to instill in me.

My thumb hovered over the Reply button.

And then I clicked it.

CHAPTER THREE

Jack

MY HANDS WERE shaking. I wondered idly if I was more nervous about the expense of a hotel room than about meeting up with a stranger, but I had to admit it was most likely the hotel room thing.

I'd hooked up with strangers from an app before, so that wasn't quite as nerve-racking. But then again, it was always a little worrisome when I hadn't seen a photo of the guy to make sure he wasn't a fellow student. Or worse, a professor.

My stomach flipped over. What were the chances it would be one of my professors? Zero. Completely zero chance. First of all, two of my professors were women. Second, one of them was pushing retirement age and seemed happily married to his wife of a million years.

Thirdly, the only other professor remaining in the list of possibilities was Professor Henry. And he was definitely not the kind of guy who would respond to a post on an app. He was sure as hell not someone who would respond to a request for *comfort*.

I felt myself relax. The thought of Professor Henry offering a student a hug was laughable. I wasn't sure his body even relaxed enough for a hug, and I sure as hell knew his demeanor was about as friendly and comforting as a crocodile having a very bad day.

I bit back a laugh imagining how Professor Henry would react to seeing me on the other side of the door. When the stranger had responded to my post, he'd written, "I've had a bad day, too, and didn't know how much I needed a hug until I saw your post."

That was definitely not written by any of my science professors. But if it had been, Professor Henry would take one look at me, sniff judgmentally, and turn on his heel without a word.

Asshole.

Just thinking of him made my blood boil. The more I thought about it, the clearer it became that he'd had it out for me all semester. I had to remind myself there were kind people out there in the world who supported students. People like Dr. Malley, who'd contacted me from Royce University to inquire about whether or not I'd consider a transfer to help work on her research on the evolution of infectious diseases in the local black-capped chickadee population. Or Professor Jin from Dalhousie, who'd emailed me about an expedition in Nova Scotia the following semester that still had room for another research student.

After getting the rejection from Raintree, I realized I needed to take some time to consider where I wanted to go next. Maybe I didn't want to stay here at Barrington if Professor Henry was going to be such an obstacle to my academic success.

The firm knock on the door made me jump. At least I didn't need to think about my academic career right now. Right now, I only needed to accept a hug and physical affection from a random stranger.

I took a deep breath and opened the door.

When my brain inadvertently put Professor Henry's face on the poor stranger from Heart2Heart, I blinked rapidly to try and clear it away.

It didn't work.

"Mr. Wilde," he said in his familiar deep voice. The voice that reached down into my belly and made me want to *crawl*.

I couldn't breathe. This wasn't right. This couldn't be happening. I blinked several times more, silently begging my brain to fix this horrifying malfunction.

When I tried sucking in a breath, I made a wheezing sound and knew without a shadow of a doubt I was suffocating.

"Sorry," I gasped, letting go of the door to move back into the room. *Air.* I needed air. I wasn't getting any air. Maybe the window…

"What's…? Fuck… Jack? Jack!" His firm grip around my elbow startled me and caused my toe to catch on the carpet. I pitched sideways, but Professor Henry's arms came around me to keep me from falling face-first onto the bed.

I couldn't catch my breath, and the fear I was actually going to suffocate made it exponentially worse. Still, part of me still felt like this had to be a dream because I couldn't conceive of a world where Professor Henry *called me by my first name.*

"Can't… br… br…"

He moved me to the foot of the bed and sat me down before squatting down between my knees and taking my face in his big, warm hands. "Look at me."

I blinked again. *Please let this be a horrible mistake. Please tell me this isn't happening.* Just when I thought I'd reached the lowest possible level of mortification, I learned I had further to fall.

"Jack," he barked. "Listen to me right now, and do as I say. You are okay. It's okay. Look right here at the space between my eyes. See this? There's a little freckly spot right there. My sister says it's the shape of a tennis racquet."

I couldn't help but do what he asked. His voice had always been deep and in charge. When he spoke, people listened, and it was no different with me.

I focused on the tennis racquet.

"Breathe slowly," he said, lowering his voice and slowing it down. My eyes widened in surprise at the gentle tone, but I was too panicked to say anything.

His thumbs brushed over my cheekbones. "Shhh. Slow it down… that's it… in… out… You're okay. You're okay."

I felt hot tears of embarrassment fill my eyes and spill over before I could blink them away. "S-s-sorry," I whispered, still trying to breathe. "Y-you d-don't h-have…"

"Shhh. Don't try to talk. I'm here. I'm not going anywhere." He hesitated for a minute before flashing me an easy smile, something I'd never, ever seen on his face before. It was like the sun coming out from behind a dark rain cloud.

The damned thing lit up the entire room and made my heart throw itself against my ribs.

"Besides," he continued. "If I'm not mistaken, you owe me a hug."

I squeezed my eyes closed in mortification and felt more tears spill out. This was the absolute worst moment of my life.

And it was happening in front of Professor Henry.

How would I ever recover from this?

CHAPTER FOUR

River

WHEN THE DOOR opened, revealing Jack Wilde on the other side, my heart had done a funny little dance of confusion. First, I couldn't help but think how incredibly inappropriate it would be for me to engage in any physical touch with a student, but then I'd reminded myself he was no longer my student.

I'd already turned in all of my grades for graduate students. The only remaining grades outstanding were for a few students in a low-level undergraduate course.

After I'd successfully reminded myself the fraternization rule didn't apply here, I felt indescribably giddy.

I was going to get to hold Jack Wilde in my arms all night long.

If he would let me.

This was too good to be true. I'd had an inappropriate crush on this particular grad student since three days before the semester started when I'd seen him jogging on a treadmill at the gym while trying to hold back a bad case of the giggles at something on his phone.

He hadn't succeeded.

I'd watched him nearly stumble off the equipment while snorting with laughter. Every time he'd tried to get control of himself, he'd look back at the phone and start laughing again.

He was magnetic. I couldn't keep my eyes off him. Even now, I wanted to drink in every facet of his beautiful face.

But he was panicking. And I couldn't blame him.

I'd spent the entire semester terrified of stepping out of line, of being caught staring, or worse, getting hard in front of the damned class because he was just that sexy.

His eyes were bright blue green, and his sandy-brown hair was slightly overgrown and always looked messy, like he'd rolled out of bed after being well fucked all night. He was quick to smile and even quicker to make a new friend and put others at ease.

He was the holy trifecta of funny, sweet, and smart.

I wanted him more than I'd ever wanted anyone, including the celebrity crushes I'd had as a preteen.

But Jack Wilde was off-limits.

Or he had been. Now he simply hated me.

I'd done everything I could to avoid him. It had been neither professional nor pretty. I'd avoided eye contact in class. I'd resisted calling on him for fear I would be seen playing favorites. And I'd written the shitty recommendation that had cost him his dream placement on the Raintree expedition.

No wonder the very sight of me had made him choke.

I moved up onto the bed next to him and put my arm around him, pulling him into my chest. How did I explain all of this? How did I even begin to apologize?

His voice was muffled at first until I realized I was holding him too tightly. "What?" I asked.

"I was trying to focus on the tennis racquet."

"I'm sorry," I said, meaning it more genuinely than anything I'd ever said to another human being. "I... I need to explain."

Jack's breathing was finally slowing down, and the fact he could make a complete sentence was a very good sign.

"It's fine," he said. "I'm feeling better anyway."

He tried to pull out of my embrace, but I tightened my arms without thinking. "Don't."

Jack lifted his face to me. His eyes were red-rimmed but still bright and beautiful. The tip of his nose was pink from being pressed against my shirt. "I'm okay," he said again. As if that was the only reason I was holding him.

"I'm not," I admitted softly.

Jack studied me for a minute before snuggling into my chest again and returning the hug. We stayed like that for a long time, holding each other without a word of explanation or understanding.

Except... except I did understand. I understood why he needed this. Why he needed comfort.

One of his professors had screwed him over by denying him a spot on the research expedition he'd so desperately wanted.

I pulled away from him and moved to squat in front of him again so I could see his face. He looked surprised and confused but didn't say anything. I wondered if he was scared or hurt or angry.

Without thinking, I took both of his hands in mine, which only seemed to make his shock more intense. His eyes were almost comically wide.

"I need to tell you something," I said, scraping my teeth over my lip. "And I couldn't tell you before now because I was your professor, and also the university was trying hard to keep it under wraps."

Jack blinked, his inky lashes still wet from tears. "What... what is it?"

"It's about your research," I began.

Jack's nostrils widened, and his lips pursed. "Oh."

"No, wait," I said quickly, trying to think. *Just spit it out, asshole.* "It's not what you think."

"Really? Because I think you fucked me over by sabotaging my application."

He could see the truth on my face because he yanked his hands out of mine.

"Jack," I said. "I did. But let me explain."

He pushed me until I rocked back on my heels and hit the ground on my ass. Clearly, he wanted to get away from me. Instead of following him over to the large window, I rested against the dresser and waited.

"Go on," he said after a minute. He didn't turn to face me. Instead, he looked out the window as if the Houston skyline had something interesting to offer.

"Raintree is part of a fraudulent research grant scheme."

He turned to face me. His expression was fiercely defiant. "What? No way."

I balled my hands into fists to keep from going over there to hold him again. I wanted to touch him so fucking badly. Instead, I focused on giving him the explanation he deserved.

"It's true. Dr. Raintree has been pocketing the bulk of the grant money. He gets his grad students to help apply for research grants, the grant money comes to him, and then he half-asses the research and pockets most of the money. He's had two expeditions in the past five years get canceled for bad weather, and the money hasn't been returned or used for other research."

Jack stared at me in disbelief as his brain worked through what I was saying. He was a smart guy. I knew he'd have done his research on the Raintree expeditions, and he'd know about the canceled trips.

"How do you know about this?" he asked.

I sighed and dropped my chin to my chest. "I've been watching him for the past four years. I finally couldn't stand it anymore, and I said something to the dean. If... no, *when* word gets out, it's going to put all of us in a bad light. The university wanted time to mitigate the fallout."

"You turned him in?" he asked.

I nodded cautiously. I couldn't decide if he thought I was a terrible human being for ratting out a colleague or a decent one for trying to protect the students and the program.

He reached up to run his fingers through his hair and yank on the ends. I could tell the information was taking time to process. "So... what does this mean for the department? Is Dr. Raintree leaving? And what about the students in the middle of research?"

"I don't know. That'll be up to the dean."

My fingers itched to touch him. Now that I was here, now that I knew he wanted—no, *needed*—touch, I couldn't stop imagining my hands on him.

"Come here," I said.

Jack's eyes widened. "W-why?"

"I want to hold you."

My heart thundered even though I tried my best to project a calm, controlled demeanor.

"Why?" he asked in a slightly higher-pitched voice.

Instead of answering him, I pinned him with a look—one I hoped held all the longing and frustration I'd been repressing for an entire semester.

Jack's chest rose and fell before he whispered, "You can't mean it."

"I do. I wanted to hold someone tonight. It's been a hell of a week. A hell of a *semester*. My colleagues turned their backs on me when they learned what I'd done. I had to find another job. I felt so isolated and alone, I was willing to take comfort with a stranger. But now that I know *you* were the one who wrote that post... I want it even more."

Emotion flashed through his eyes. Surprise, and if I wasn't mistaken, heat. My chest tightened.

"Please," I added softly.

CHAPTER FIVE

Jack

THIS WAS TOO good to be true.

I moved toward him slowly, waiting for him to laugh and admit it was all a setup of some kind. But then I saw the sincerity in his eyes. His chest heaved up and down, revealing maybe he wasn't quite as calm and collected as he appeared to be about this.

"Isn't this fraternization?" I asked weakly.

"I already turned in your grade. I'm no longer your professor."

It was true. I'd checked my grades before heading to the hotel and hadn't really been surprised at the strong showing in my evolutionary biology class. In being a total hard-ass to me all semester, it turned out Dr. Henry had managed to thoroughly prepare me for the final.

I'd aced it.

And now my hard-ass professor was summoning me to... his lap? For hugs? What was happening right now?

"I thought you hated me," I blurted.

His eyes darkened, which made my skin prickle. "That's the opposite of how I feel about you, Jack."

When he said my name, my stomach swooped and left me light-headed. It was amazing how much longing and *want* he could pack into that single syllable.

"W-why?" I hated how unsure and vulnerable I sounded right then, but I *felt* unsure and vulnerable. I'd never been good at hiding my true feelings.

Professor Henry sighed and looked down at the hands he held clasped in his lap. "Because you're beautiful and smart. You're funny and warm." He looked up at me. "You're exactly the kind of man I've always dreamed about being with."

My breathing sped up again, enough to make me wonder if another panic attack would come on. "You're messing with me," I said, stopping in my tracks before getting too close.

"Does it look like I'm messing with you?" His eyes stayed on mine with an intensity that filled the room, and I had to shake my head.

"I don't want to pressure you or do anything you don't want. So tell me... do you want me to leave?"

No. Definitely not. No. No, please.

"I don't know," I admitted, lying through my teeth.

His body language stayed relaxed, but his expression didn't. It was almost like he wanted me to listen, to understand.

"I saw you before the semester started," he said, surprising me. "You were at the gym, laughing at something on your phone. I couldn't stop staring at you."

My heart ticked wildly in my neck. I didn't know what to say, so I stayed quiet.

"You were sexy as fuck. Sweating from your run and wearing these little running shorts that revealed your long, muscled legs and your tight ass. I almost got hard right there in the student fitness center."

I hoped to god my breathing didn't sound as erratic as it felt.

He continued. "But it was your laugh that really got me. You couldn't stop. And your joy lit up the space around you. Everyone who heard you got a smile on their face. That night when I went home, I decided that if I saw you again, I was going to ask you to spend the afternoon with me... or the evening... or, fuck, forever, if you'd have let me. But you never came back to the gym—"

"I tripped over one of those electric scooters people leave all over campus," I whispered. "Tweaked my ankle."

"When I saw you walk into my classroom a few days later, my heart leapt out of my chest. There you were, *finally*, only..."

"Only, I was your student," I finished for him.

He nodded. "And I was your professor."

The puzzle pieces clicked together. His avoidance of me, the lack of eye contact, his short answers to my questions. It made sense, or... it would have, if not for the fact he was way out of my league.

"*Fuck*. But that wasn't fair," I said, feeling anger bubble up. "You should have said something. I thought you hated me. I thought I couldn't do anything right. I thought... I thought I wasn't cut out for this field!"

Professor Henry surged to his feet, grabbing me by the shoulders and leaning down to meet my eyes. "You *are*," he said with a clenched jaw. "You're one of the brightest students in the entire program, and if I made you doubt that for a single second, I'm even sorrier than I can express."

Hearing him apologize lifted a heavy burden I didn't realize I'd been carrying. I respected him as a scholar, and his approval carried weight with me. If he believed I had something to contribute to the study of evolutionary biology, then maybe I could stop second-guessing myself all the time.

Maybe I could stop listening to my parents' opinions.

"Professor—"

"I'm *not* your professor anymore," he growled. "Call me River."

River. Even thinking of him that way felt incredibly intimate.

Perfectly intimate.

"River," I said slowly, testing the syllables.

He exhaled softly.

"I wish you'd told me."

"About Raintree or about my attraction to you?"

There was the slightest hint of a smile at the corner of his mouth, and I wanted to explore it with the tip of my tongue. I was nearly giddy with the idea that I might actually get to.

I swallowed. "Both?"

"And what would you have done if I'd told you?" He moved his hands down my arms until he could weave our fingers together. My breathing hitched.

"Uh..." I couldn't think with him this close, with saliva filling my mouth and blood filling my dick.

River's eyes flicked between mine as if trying to read me. One of us moved closer.

I breathed in, catching the scent of him. Aftershave that smelled fresh and masculine. I wanted to press my nose to his neck and get more of it.

"I don't know," I admitted.

"I couldn't tell you about Raintree. All I could do was try and make sure you weren't one of the students he left hanging in the wind. I was under a legal agreement not to disclose anything—" He sucked in a breath. "You're driving me crazy," he added under his breath.

I leaned forward until my forehead was on his collarbone. He'd come here to give me comfort, so I was going to take it.

"Why didn't you tell me you wanted me?" I asked his shirt.

His arms came around me and pulled me closer. I exhaled and felt my entire body give in and relax against him.

"I didn't want you to drop the class," he admitted, nuzzling his cheek against my head. "Seeing you was the brightest spot in my week, and I couldn't give it up."

I tilted my head up until my nose brushed the skin of his neck. God, he smelled so fucking good. "I wanted you too," I admitted before letting my lips brush his neck too.

"Jack," he breathed. "I came here—" His voice cracked. "I came here to give you platonic comfort."

I reached up to grab the sides of his face with my hands and meet his eyes with mine.

"I don't want comfort anymore."

CHAPTER SIX

River

JACK WAS IN my arms, hot and willing, sending me every signal he wanted me as much as I wanted him. How was this possible?

"Are you sure?" I croaked. My vaunted self-control was practically nonexistent.

Without saying anything, Jack lunged up on his toes and kissed me hard on the lips. I grabbed the back of his head to hold him there as I took advantage of the situation.

His mouth was perfect, soft and warm, open and eager. He kissed like he'd been as starved for it as I was. Even though he was shorter and smaller than me, his body was solid and strong. His physical confidence made me grin against his mouth. Now that he knew how I felt about him, he seemed much less timid.

Braver. *Determined.*

I pulled myself away from him long enough to meet his eyes. "Wait, stop," I said, setting him away from me. "I promised it would be platonic. If we're changing the rules, I need you to be sure…"

His grin was adorable and teasing. "Did I seem unsure to you when I had my tongue down your throat?" His lips were red and full, slick from our kisses, as if I'd needed visual proof.

I brushed his hair back from his face and pressed a small kiss to the apple of his cheek. "You're so fucking sexy. I can't believe you're here with me."

"Me?" he squeaked. "You're, like, Barrington's most desirable professor. Why in the world would you settle for an ecology geek like me when you could have anyone you wanted?"

"I'm an ecology geek who finds other ecology geeks incredibly attractive." I moved my mouth closer to his ear and lowered my voice. "And you forget I've seen you in your running shorts."

Jack shuddered and let out a little breathy sound. I continued teasing his face and neck with small kisses while I told him just how sexy I found him. While I spoke, his ears turned red, and his breathing sped up. He was responsive as hell, which turned me on even more and made me handsier than ever.

"Want to touch you everywhere," I admitted. My voice sounded husky and rough, which matched the animalistic feelings I was having toward him. It was getting harder and harder to hold back when part of me wanted to push him down on the bed and fuck him. *Hard.*

"Please," he breathed. "Please touch me. Want your hands—" He sucked in another shaky breath. "Everywhere."

I pulled off his shirt before dropping to my knees. When I looked up to check his expression—to make sure he was still okay with what I was doing—he looked at me with dazed eyes, a stubble-reddened chin, and glossy lips.

"Fuck, you're sexy," I said. "You're killing me. Let me suck you off."

Jack's mouth was slightly open, but all he did was nod. I reached for the button of his jeans and flicked it open before yanking down the zipper and reaching inside the dark red cotton to pull out his hard cock. It was fucking perfect. Hard and smooth with a deep pink head.

I leaned over to taste it, running the flat of my tongue down the front of his shaft before pulling the tip into my mouth and sucking.

"Oh fuck," he cried, reaching for my hair with his hands. He grasped my head and held it as if he was afraid I was going to pull off.

I wasn't going anywhere.

I bobbed my head up and down slowly, wrapping my tongue around him while I worked his pants and underwear down to his ankles.

My cock throbbed, and my balls felt heavy. Having Jack's dick in my mouth and his scent in my nose was an unexpected gift. I'd come here hoping to find a kind stranger to share a nice hug with, and now I was miraculously having sex with the man I'd been crushing on for months.

When I met his eyes again, my heart jumped. He was so fucking beautiful and sexy.

I pulled off to ask him what I could do to make him feel good. His grin was adorable. "Uh, that was feeling pretty damned good, to be honest. More of that would be—*gnffff.*"

I swallowed him down and reached for his sac, rolling his nuts in my hand and pressing a finger behind them. Jack's fingers tightened in my hair as he let out the most amazing sounds. I wanted more of them. I wanted to see him come completely unraveled because of me.

My mouth stayed on his hard, wet cock while I did my best to remove his clothes. Jack mumbled incoherent things, which made me smile around his shaft. He was so fucking sweet, I wanted to take care of him. To hold him. For more than just one night.

I couldn't believe my luck, that I was here with him like this.

His body was gorgeous. Lithe and fit, healthy and strong. He smelled like soap, and I realized he was the kind of guy who would have made sure to shower out of consideration for whoever was coming to be with him tonight.

Thank *fuck* that was me.

I pulled off him and met his eyes. "Get on the bed, sweetheart."

Jack's eyes widened at the unexpected endearment, but he did as I said. I watched his bare ass as he crawled across the large bed to lie on the pillows.

I waited for him to meet my eyes again, and then I took my time undressing.

CHAPTER SEVEN

Jack

I F I DIED right here and now, I could honestly say I'd lived a full and complete life.

Watching Professor Henry... *River*... take his clothes off for me was some kind of glitch in the space-time matrix that I was not going to squander.

Even if all I ever got of him was this one night, I was going to enjoy the ever-loving fuck out of it.

His shoulders were wide, and his chest was covered in dark hair. A slight layer of padding covered his abs, and it was bisected by a dark trail leading from his chest to his groin.

I wanted to lick his happy trail.

He was every fantasy I'd ever jacked off to. Big, broad, masculine. In charge.

When he pulled off his pants, the bulge in his boxer briefs revealed more than I expected and everything I'd ever fantasized about. My ass clenched in anticipation.

"Fucking hell," I said without realizing I'd spoken out loud.

River's lips widened in a grin. "Yeah? Like what you see?"

I bit my bottom lip and nodded. "I'm going to kill my cousin for suggesting a platonic sleepover. This is so much fucking better."

The sound of his deep laughter filled the room and made the last remnants of my nerves fall away. River Henry was here, he was willing, and he wanted me. Badly.

It was all I needed.

I reached down to stroke myself. "You're taking too long."

His eyes darkened. "What do you want, Jack?"

"I want you to fuck me," I admitted breathlessly. "And I want to feel your hands and mouth all over me."

He stalked toward me, his eyes so intense I felt dizzy from being their target. "You have no idea how many times I've fantasized about being inside you," he said in a low growl.

My breath came faster. "Please."

Instead of joining me at the top of the bed, where I was sprawled in a puddle on the pillows, he started at the bottom. And licked his way up the inside of one of my legs.

The sound of my desperate panting filled the room. "Please," I said again. There was no other feeling left. Want. Desperate hope. "Please," I whimpered again.

He nosed my balls before licking my shaft again. When his hands grasped the back of my knees and bent them up, I clenched again.

And then his tongue landed on my hole.

My vision whited out. His mouth was aggressive and possessive. His tongue, lips, and teeth—and that fucking *beard*—owned my ass while I lay there babbling nonsense and clutching the sheets in my fists.

"F-fucking f-fuck me," I begged at one point, and his face reappeared in my vision. His hair was wildly messy, and his lips were red and wet.

"I want you so much I'm afraid I'm going to come before getting inside you," he admitted. "Condom?"

"Hm? Hm? Whuh?" It took me a minute to understand what he was asking. I shook my head frantically. "On PrEP. You?"

He nodded. "Same. You good bare? You sure?"

I nodded too and felt my heart thunder even harder. Professor River Henry was going to bareback me. I was going to feel his bare cock inside me. It wasn't something I'd done with anyone else, despite being on PrEP. Lowell had been a stickler for tidiness and hygiene, and I'd never fully trusted hookups enough to try it.

But I trusted River. And I wanted this too badly to stop.

"Lube," I gasped. "I have some in my backpack."

Before I finished saying the words, River was across the room, rifling through my bag.

"Toiletry kit," I said, reaching down to stroke my aching cock. "I was worried I might get too turned on and have to rub one out in private," I added with a breathy laugh.

River came back over with a knowing smirk. "And did you? Did you get so turned on by your platonic stranger you couldn't keep from getting hard around him?"

His thick dick bobbed heavily in front of him, and I couldn't look away.

"I'm not the only one."

"No. You're definitely not." He crawled on the bed again and kissed the tip of my dick before moving up to kiss the center of my chest and then my mouth. His heavy weight pressed me into the mattress and gave me a taste of what it would feel like to be held down by his larger, stronger body.

I had to bite back another plea.

Soon, I'd forgotten everything but River Henry and his commanding kiss. When his knee nudged my legs apart and his slick fingers began working my hole, I sucked in a breath and almost choked.

The deep rumble of his laugh vibrated through his chest into mine, and it made everything inside of me melt into a puddle of want.

River Henry owned me. And he could keep me as long as he wanted. I was his. I would do anything to feel his fat fingers teasing my hole and his rough chest hair abrading my tender nipples. To see the heat in his eyes and hear him say my name.

"Breathe," he murmured as he moved between my legs and pressed his tip against my entrance. "Push out... that's it... breathe... good... *oh god*. Fuck. Jack, *fuck*."

His dick was enormous. My ass burned in the stretch, but when he finally bottomed out, I panted through it, comforted and encouraged by a constant stream of words spoken hot against my neck.

I groaned as the pain turned into hesitant pleasure, and I suddenly realized how fucking good it was going to be. With every pulse of his hips, his cockhead brushed against my gland and lit me up inside.

I arched my head back and groaned again, which seemed to rile him up.

River's teeth grazed my neck, and I felt the bulge of his biceps behind my legs as he held them bent to the sides. When he began to move faster, in and out, I cried out and begged him to go harder, faster, *more*.

His own noises of pleasure filled the room, filled my stomach, filled my heart, as he made my body his. He took all of me, filling me up and making me want as much of him as he'd give me.

"River!" I screamed as I felt my climax barreling down. I didn't want it to end, but I wanted to feel this, feel complete release in his arms and underneath him.

"That's it. Come for me. Show me how much you want this. I'll be right there with you, Jack. Fucking hell. Your body. I can't…"

The release hit me full force, contracting my muscles and sending my brain flying. I was only vaguely aware of River shouting my name, his hot, damp skin against mine, the thick, delicious burn of his cock inside me, and the scent of our spunk between us.

It was the single hottest moment of my life.

CHAPTER EIGHT

River

I WANTED TO laugh. I wanted to sing. I wanted to shout my incredulity from the rooftops.

Jack Wilde lay a sweaty heap underneath me. His stomach was coated in jizz, and he had a goofy grin on his face. It shouldn't have been life-changing… but I knew it was. The single night that would change the course of my life forever.

I was going to fall in love with this man.

I knew it the way I'd known I was gay the summer I turned fourteen and saw a Nike ad on television. I knew it the way I'd known that I was meant to study biology. It was simply one of the truths of my life.

"Why are you staring at me like that?" Jack asked, suddenly looking self-conscious.

"I want more than this," I blurted with no finesse whatsoever.

His eyes flashed with pain and disappointment. He tried to roll away from me as my words hit my ears, and I realized how they'd sounded.

"Stop," I said. "I mean, wait. Stop. Please listen."

I could see Jack turtling up. He was going into insecure self-preservation mode, the same kind of emotion that had undoubtedly caused his panic attack earlier.

I brushed the sweaty hair back from his face. "Jack… I want more *with you*. I want you. But I want… I want more than one night. I want this to be the beginning of something."

The change that came over his face was breathtaking. "Really?"

I leaned in and pressed a kiss to the edge of his mouth before moving it to his cheek, his eyelid, his temple, and his forehead. "I've wanted you for a long time. I never knew you'd be interested in me too. And I…"

For some reason, my brain chose this moment to remind me of all the obstacles. I was moving back east. He was a Texas boy through and through. He—

Jack grabbed my face and forced me to meet his eyes. "Now you listen," he said. "I want that too. So whatever just made your face fall… you need to tell me right now. If you've changed your mind that fast, I need to know."

He was adorable in his newfound confidence. I wanted to see more of it.

"I didn't change my mind. But I'm moving to Connecticut. To take a job at Yale."

His face lit up. "You got a teaching position at Yale? That's incredible!"

I realized we had a lot to talk about, and I hadn't even cleaned him up yet. I rolled off him and pulled him up, throwing him over my shoulder to carry him to the shower.

He yelped and then laughed—the same pure, joyful laughter I'd heard that first day at the gym. The best sound ever.

Once I stood him up under the hot spray and joined him in a full-body hug, I exhaled.

This was everything I'd ever wanted. Comfort. Excitement. *Home.*

"I want you in every way," I admitted softly against his ear.

He pulled back and met my eye. He looked a little unsure again. "Dr. Malley at Royce University has been trying to get me to transfer to join her research team. Isn't that close to Yale?" He bit his lip. I could tell he was worried I was going to scoff at the implication of him moving with me.

But I felt the opposite. My heart soared. I leaned closer and held him extra tight. My throat felt like there was a giant knot in it. "That would be incredible," I managed to say "Would you... would you consider it? The program there is well respected. More even than Barrington's. So even if you changed your mind about... about me..."

Jack pinched my ass, shocking me into a yelp. I pulled back and stared at him in surprise.

"I know this is fast," Jack said. "But I am ready for a change. I need to get some distance from my parents and from Texas. And if the Dr. Raintree scandal is going to break, the department here is going to take time to recover."

"So you'll come?"

"I mean... I'll need to find a roommate and an affordable place to live..." He flashed me a cheeky smile. "Know anyone in the area who might also be looking for a place?"

I grabbed him up and spun him around, kissing the hell out of him and eventually running soapy hands all over his body.

After drying each other off, we moved back to the bed and slid under the covers, talking nonstop about how much we'd hidden from each other all semester, how we'd each had secret crushes on each other, and how we planned to tackle a big move together while being careful to respect each other's boundaries.

"Okay, but..." Jack grinned at me. "I'm not sure I want to have *that* many boundaries with you."

"Same," I said with a laugh. "But I want to make sure you're happy. Always."

He snuggled closer and wrapped his arms and legs around me until we were tangled together in a delicious ball. After a few minutes, his sleepy voice made its way to my ears.

"Okay, but we can't ever tell anyone how we really met. It's way too embarrassing."

I pressed a kiss to his hair and bit back a laugh. "Not even my parents? The proponents of healing touch?"

He shook his head, releasing a faint smell of hotel shampoo into the air. "No. Because if they know, then my family will find out and tease us forever. The Wilde clan does not let things go."

Two weeks later, I realized he was right when I met most of his extended Wilde family, the gorgeous pack of cousins and their equally beautiful husbands. I was shocked by the sheer number of gay men in the Wilde family. But not at all surprised that Jack Wilde was the sweetest and sexiest of them all.

And he'd been right. As soon as they found out how we met, they never did let us live it down.

But two months later, I became one of those Wilde husbands when we spontaneously decided to get married during a trip to Las Vegas with some of his cousins. I'd never forget the moment Jack Wilde became Jack Henry.

And two years later, when I checked the mail, watered the plants, and dropped a kiss on my husband's forehead, I realized it was a damn good thing that Wildes never let anything go.

> To: Dr. Jack Henry and Dr. River Henry
>
> *We are pleased to inform you your application for sponsorship of the Henry Arctic Ecology and Evolution research expedition has been approved.*

I let out a whoop that had my husband running down the hall.

"You did it, Dr. Henry," I said proudly.

"*We* did it," he replied.

And we spent the rest of the night practicing touch therapy… in a decidedly nonplatonic manner.

✧   ✧   ✧

Want to read more about Jack's sexy cousins?

Go here to enjoy the bingeable Forever Wilde series!
www.lucylennox.com/books/facing-west

Royal Elite Bonus Epilogue

Rina Kent

AIDEN

N OISE.
Too much fucking noise.

If there's anything I hate, it's the presence of people in my space. And not just people—but many of them. Like a fucking army that's thirsting for blood—most possibly mine.

The situation isn't even funny anymore, or tolerable, or anything in between.

I trudge to the grand hall of our second home in London. Our house in Oxford is an architectural masterpiece that my talented wife has spent a lot of time and effort to annex with the plot of land we bought back then. But the London house? Her level of obsession in creating this thing doesn't even compare to her passion for the first one.

She's matured as an architect since we finished our studies in Oxford and has put every ounce of energy and expertise into building this mansion.

And yes, it was annoying as fuck to have to share her time with damn rocks and painters and the arsehole contractors who thought it was an acceptable idea to steal her from me. I might have tortured them for that—I was patient and waited for them to finish their contracts with Elsa first, though.

Something she eventually found out about, shook her head, and whispered, "You'll never change, Aiden. Not that I want you to."

The first part of that sentence is a given and doesn't really matter, but the second part? It's exactly why this fucking woman gets everything she asks for. I'm beginning to think it's a tactic that little minx has come up with to tear through my walls.

Not that she ever needed any force. Ever since we were kids, Elsa has been the only one who can penetrate each of my fortresses with no effort whatsoever.

Still, I hate that I have to share her time with our fucker friends who pretended they didn't see the text I sent in our group chat, which basically said "get the fuck out of my house."

Half ignored me, but my cousin went ahead and replied.

Levi: *You're so cute when you're grumpy.*

Cole: *Aiden and the word cute don't share the same continent, planet, or solar system. Did you perhaps mean "grotesque," Levi?*

Aiden: *The only grotesque thing will be your balls hanging at the top of my office door, Nash.*

Cole: *Charming, as usual, King.*

Charming these little fuckers is the last thing I want to do.

We're thirty-four now, my cousin is thirty-five, and I still can't figure out the exact moment where I completely fucked up and invited these parasites into my life.

Probably when I accepted the invitation to play with them when we were children. Oh, who am I kidding? Even with that, I would've canceled the friendship subscription sooner or later, but the trial period somehow extended to a lifetime one.

The main reason for that unfortunate event is that my Elsa is big on friendships and gatherings and the whole bloody social circus. Sometimes, I fucking loathe that she needs anyone other than me. Probably because she and our kids are the only ones who matter to me.

Okay, and maybe my family—for genetic reasons.

I glare at Cole from across the garden. He's sitting on the armrest of a chair, one arm around the shoulder of his wife, Silver, and the other holding his youngest daughter, Ariella, on his lap. She's just three years old, about four years younger than her older sister, Ava, but she has an uncanny resemblance to her father. They share the same dark hair, facial structure, and maybe even the character. She only takes after Silver with her blue eyes.

Where Ava is growing up to be more and more like her mother, Ariella is a clone of her father.

Because one Cole isn't enough, so now, I have to deal with two of them.

Bloody perfect.

"Leave," I mouth at him.

The bastard just smirks and mouths back, "How about a no?"

Then he whispers something in Silver's ear for which she blushes before throwing her head back laughing. Ariella, aka Cole's clone, uses the chance to slip out of her father's hold and hobble like a drunk to the other kids in the garden.

They're the ones who are bringing the whole fucking house down with their noise. The leader of the unholy orchestra is none other than Ronan. Now, I would love to print a picture of a clown and paste it on his back just for pure spite, but the last time I did that, his wife, Teal, made me lose a deal, also for pure spite.

So I'll do it when I don't have to battle against that woman for business.

"You're supposed to be my sister-in-law, Teal," I told her in front of Elsa, trying to put her in her place for her deed.

She merely flipped her hair, grabbed her son Remington's hand, and said in her toneless voice, "And you're supposed to be my brother-in-law, Aiden, so how about you think of that before you bother my husband again? You do that and I might consider not crushing you next time."

And that attitude of hers isn't exclusive to me alone. Cole gets his share of her venom, too, since he's the number one wanker toward Ronan. My only consolation about the whole Teal thing.

Though to my and Cole's defense, Ronan is seriously the best comic relief to ever exist. Even now, he's making Xander chase the kids with him.

It's a rare cloudless day in London. The sun shines on the vast garden and the pool where all of the action is happening.

Ava, who's almost seven years old, and Remi, who's nine, scream their heads off as they scatter in different directions. Glyndon, Levi's youngest daughter at ten, and Cecily, a year older, missed the memo about running away. Glyn just sits on the grass to study some red flowers, then puts them in her shiny brown hair with blonde streaks while Cecily crashes directly into her father's legs.

Xander bends over from laughing. "You're supposed to run the other way, Cecy."

"But I don't wanna run away from Daddy."

"That's my little girl." He grins, throws her over his shoulder, and takes off after Brandon.

But his twin brother, Landon, puts his leg out and he trips and falls on his face.

Bran, although eleven years old, bursts out crying, so his mother, Astrid, goes to him and holds him in her arms. Landon, however, doesn't even stop and keeps running all the way to the back of the garden. But his feet come to a halt when he finds his father, Levi, right in front of him, his arms crossed and his brows knitted.

Lan grins. "I did it, Dad. I won!"

"By tripping your brother?"

"Well, he's a weakling."

"Landon!" Levi scolds. "What did I say about calling your siblings names?"

"But he is."

"No games for you for a week."

"But that's not fair. I should be awarded for winning, not punished."

"You're being punished for hurting your brother and calling him names."

While getting involved in these affairs sits between the discomfort of having my wisdom teeth removed and actually hosting this party, I still walk up to them.

Upon seeing me, Landon's expression lights up and he steps behind my leg.

"Come here, Landon," Levi calls in his stern parental voice, but the kid just hides further, so he sighs. "Stop shielding him, Aiden."

I pat my nephew's head. "Don't be jealous that Lan likes me better."

"I didn't do anything wrong, Uncle," Lan whispers from behind me. "I only won."

"Landon!" Levi's voice rises, and even though the kid stiffens, he stares at his father dead in the eye.

Well, fuck.

That's the same look I used to give my own father when I was his age.

I turn to Lan and get on my haunches to face him. His attention immediately slides to me and he watches me with big blue eyes that resemble the fucking Arctic Ocean.

"Good job on winning, Lan."

I can feel Levi getting worked up, but he thankfully keeps his lips shut.

"Thanks, Uncle! Can I get a new game?"

"No."

His expression falls. "But why not? I won and should have a reward."

"That's true, but you also hurt your brother in the process, so your reward was taken away as a form of punishment for your actions."

"It's not my fault he's a weakling."

"No, but you're his older brother and you should take care of him."

He huffs. "Only by ten minutes."

"It still counts. Bran and Glyn are under your protection and you shouldn't hurt them. It's exactly like how I was under your father's protection when we were young."

I wasn't, and Levi was a busybody who thought it was his mission to hurt anyone who hurt me or even caused me discomfort, because he's loyal like that. And while I didn't need protection, I'll never forget the way he brought me candy and gave up his favorite chessboard for me when I lost my mother.

"Really?" Landon looks between me and Levi, whose expression softens.

"Yeah, really," his father says. "You're the strongest of your siblings, and as the strongest, it's your mission to protect them."

"I'm really the strongest, Dad?"

Levi sighs. "You are."

"Okay!" Landon grins. "I won't take the award this time, but I'm not giving up my games either."

Then he runs to Astrid and Brandon, seeming to make an effort to apologize to his brother.

"He's..." Levi trails off and sighs.

"Different." I rise to my full height and face the scene with my cousin. "He's just different, Levi. Not an alien or a parasite, so stop looking at him like one."

"He's my fucking son. I don't look at him that way."

"But you wish he was a neurotypical species that could be easily subdued."

"Not really. You aren't neurotypical and neither am I. But I hate it when he hurts Bran and Glyn to get what he wants. I know it's how he's wired, but Astrid and I are worried about him."

"He's going to be fine. Just stop punishing him for things he doesn't understand. At least, not before you lay it out for him."

"I know, I know." He shakes his head, then picks up Glyn from the grass, and she giggles uncontrollably as she jams a few of the flowers she's plucked into her father's hair.

A small hand pulls on my trousers, followed by a low, "Daddy?"

I stare down to find a little man dressed in a brown hoodie and white trousers staring up at me with big dark blue eyes. He holds up a living worm the size of my finger to show it off. "Look what I found."

I narrow my eyes at the squirming ugly thing in his hand and cool my expression. "What a...beautiful worm. Where did you find that, Creighton?"

My youngest son, seven years old and an oddball of a human being, grins, displaying his missing teeth. "I know, right? It was crawling away so fast, but Eli helped me catch it. He was so quick and blocked it when it had no way out! It was so fun."

"I'm sure it was," I say with feigned excitement. That brat Eli only keeps teaching him bad habits.

Don't get me wrong. I'm glad he at least gets along with his brother, unlike Landon and Co., but this isn't the type of influence we endorse in our house.

Or, more likely, not the type of influence Elsa likes. She pretends she's fine with Eli's changes and Creigh following in his steps, but she often talks to me about what we can do as parents to raise them better.

I'm a firm believer in not shackling kids or trying to mute their energy. But I have to remember that Elsa is wired differently from me and sees our children as a possible threat to society.

On the contrary, our kids will own fucking society. Those who allow themselves to be used shall and will be used.

If not by us, then by others. So why should we let them reap the benefits?

Of course, I don't tell her this or her heart condition will get worse. Something I avoid with everything in me, including by having a vasectomy right after Eli's birth because she almost died during the process.

Including by adopting Creighton because his story broke her heart. The day I agreed to raise a child that wasn't my own, a fact no one—me included—believed would be possible, Elsa cried the longest I've ever seen her. But they were happy tears, thankful tears.

Love tears.

She said it was the best gift I'd given her, after Eli. She always wanted a second child and became depressed when we were told by the doctors that she'd be putting her life in danger if she gave birth again. So Creigh is our little miracle. One with a bloody past, but our miracle all the same.

I pick him up in my arms and spend a minute watching him squish the struggling thing. "Hey, Creigh, that worm wants to go, so how about you let it?"

"Nooo, Eli said we can see what's inside it. He went to borrow a knife from Mummy. Said to keep an eye on it for him."

"It looks ugly on the inside, though."

"But Eli said we won't know until we see for ourselves."

"Okay."

"*Really?*"

"Sure. I'll go with you."

"Yay. Thanks, Daddy!"

"There's something you need to know beforehand, though."

His eyes widen and his lips part. "What...what is it?"

"If you or Eli cut it open, your mummy will be upset and will cry for a whole night, like when you guys killed her goldfish."

He purses his lips. "We...we didn't do that. The neighbor's cat did."

"You threw it to the neighbor's cat, Creigh."

"No..."

"You and Eli can lie to your mummy, but not to me, Creigh, remember?"

He bows his head. "I'm sorry."

"Does that mean you won't upset your mummy again?"

He throws the worm away and it pauses on the grass as if not believing it's finally free before it crawls at full speed.

"Good boy."

"Do you forgive me, Daddy?"

"If you don't do this type of thing again."

"Kay!" He slaps a noisy kiss on my cheek. "Love you."

"Love you, too, punk." I put Creighton to his feet, ruffle his hair. "Now, go play with the others."

He shoots off at full speed and tackles Remi to the ground, and they cackle with laughter. But then they squeal when Ronan grabs them both from behind.

I do one last sweep of the scene. Cole is trying to catch an elusive Arielle. Teal, Silver, Kimberly, and Astrid are sitting around the garden table enjoying their cocktails and chatting amongst each other.

The children are either running or being dramatic for unknown reasons. After I make sure Creigh is still playing with Ronan, I go inside the house.

I find Eli sneaking out, his footsteps almost inaudible.

Sometimes, I can't believe he's twelve years old now. It feels as if I held his newborn body only yesterday. I was losing my shit about Elsa's difficult childbirth, and I honestly don't know if I could've had any affection toward him if something had happened to her.

But the moment she smiled through her tears and held him to her chest, I knew that I would love him as unconditionally as I love her.

I knew that I would protect my family with my life.

Eli has my dark hair, my grey eyes, my straight nose, my slightly mean mouth, and the shape of my ears. He's my version of Cole's Arielle. But sometimes, he reminds me of my father.

Of the aloof coldness, the heartless actions, and the limitless possibilities. But Jonathan says he's a carbon copy of me, and I guess I still haven't come around to accepting that.

Eli pauses near the patio to stare at the scene outside. Or, more specifically, at Ava, who's playing tug-of-war with Landon, Cecily, and Brandon. She and Brandon are losing, all thanks to Landon's efforts.

"It's okay if we lose, Ava," Bran tells her soothingly. He's an angel, my nephew, and reminds me so much of Mum, which means he'll probably be a sad fucking person.

"No, I don't want to lose. Help me, Bran!"

"Okay, okay."

"Give up already," Lan calls from the other side, his eyes gleaming.

Eli glares at him, then at Brandon, then at Ava. Only Cecily—who's merely half interested in the game—seems invisible to him.

Creigh and Remi join the tug-of-war. My youngest son takes Ava and Brandon's side and Remi helps Lan and Cecily.

Eli starts to march out, but I grab him by the collar of his shirt. "Going somewhere?"

He freezes at my dark tone that's entirely different from the way I addressed Creigh or even Lan earlier.

Eli is different.

Way too different.

"Hi, Dad." He feigns a smile. "Mom is feeling unwell. You should probably go check up on her."

"Try again."

"I mean it. I swear."

"Are you telling me if I reach under your shirt, I won't find a knife you stole?"

His face goes blank.

"Give it."

"I don't know what you're talking about."

"You have until the count of three to hand it over or I'll take away your access to the library."

"You're being unreasonable, Dad. I have to study for my exams."

"Then you'll fail these particular exams. And guess who'll look at you with disappointment? That's right. Your mum."

He purses his lips. Brat thinks he's the only one who gets to use affection from Elsa as a weapon. I taught him that.

"Three...two...one."

Eli retrieves the wrapped kitchen knife from his shirt and hands it to me, huffing. "That little snitch Creigh."

"He didn't snitch. I told you that you can hide from the world, but not from me, Eli." I grab his face, my thumb and index finger squeezing his cheek. "I made you. I am you."

He smiles. "Don't worry, Dad. One day, when you're old and weak, I will win."

"We'll see about that. In the meantime, this is between you and me. If you get your mum or your brother involved, I won't forgive you."

"I don't want to win against Mum and Creigh. I only want to win against you."

"I won't make it easy."

"Even better." He grins. "Also, when are we going to meet Uncle Asher's son again?"

When we went on a family trip to the States a few months ago, Eli connected with my acquaintance's youngest son, Killian. He's about Creighton's age, but he has a similar personality to Eli, if not worse.

Ever since then, Eli has formed a connection with him—or as much of a connection as he can form with someone outside his immediate circle.

I doubt the only reason he wants to meet Killian Carson again is so he can win against him in a game of wits.

Which is why it's imperative to keep the two separate. Asher and his wife, Reina, are already at their wit's end about the nature of their second son. Their eldest, Gareth, is like the two of them, but Killian resembles the worst nightmare from their past. A fact that they're unable to accept, even as he shows the signs.

In short, Eli and Killian shouldn't meet for the foreseeable future.

"Let's make that a never," I tell him.

Eli simply shrugs, then stalks in the direction of the game. With one push to the losing team's side, he brings Landon, Cecily, and Remi crashing to the ground. Then just because he's a punk, he pushes hard to bring Ava, Creigh, and Bran to the ground, too.

Then he merely gives a blank sideways look to Ava and trudges to Levi, pretending he didn't just ruin their game.

"Did we create a monster?" Slender arms wrap around my waist from behind and I close my eyes for a brief moment to inhale my wife's scent, get drowned in her warmth, and feel her heartbeat against my back.

The rhythm is slower than usual today, exhausted, probably unwell, as that brat Eli told me. I know he cares about his mother and even his brother. It's me who he's constantly out to outsmart.

Most likely a mirror of my relationship with my own father.

I grab her hand that's at my waist and spin around to face my Elsa. Her blonde hair falls to her back, shiny, perfect, and angel-like.

Sometimes I look at my wife, the mother of my children, and wonder how on earth I was blessed with this woman.

How on earth I got so lucky to be able to call her mine, to be able to hold her every night, fuck her senseless until I can't get enough, and then sleep with my head cocooned where her heart beats.

I have to make sure she's all right, that the blood pumping in her heart doesn't suddenly decide to stop.

That possibility is my worst nightmare.

I refuse to imagine my life without her. Because unlike what everyone thinks, Elsa hasn't only shaped the man I've become today, given me the children I never thought I needed, but she's also forged her existence deep within my soul.

She's not only a part of my life. She *is* my life. And breathing without her holds zero fucking importance.

"We did not create a monster. That little brat just needs more knocking down." I place my hand on where her heart beats and she grabs my wrist in an attempt to push me away.

"I'm fine, Aiden, and don't talk about knocking down our son so casually."

"Let me take care of him." I push my hand farther, until she's almost unable to resist.

"Eli is my son, too. I can't just let you be the only one who takes care of him…

And stop feeling me up like a creep."

"You just found out that I'm a creep? I thought it was a known fact. Now, you quit trying to hide your suffering from me. Your heartbeat is irregular."

"It's fine. It's that I worked a bit too hard today."

"Which wouldn't be the case if you hadn't hosted this gathering. Be right back. I'll go kick everyone else out and then take care of you, sweetheart."

She grabs my hands in her smaller, hotter ones, her shoulders shaking with laughter. "Would you stop trying to kick everyone out whenever they show up here?"

"Not if they cause you discomfort."

"You kick them out even when I'm comfortable, and seriously, I'm really fine. I just need to maybe lie down in your arms for a bit?" Not waiting for my reply, she lunges into my embrace, her hands wrapping around my waist.

I sigh, returning her hug. Having her in my arms is the best feeling in the world. "You're not getting away with hiding your illness with a mere hug."

"How about if I suck you off in the shower later?"

"Not when you're not well, sweetheart."

She releases a breath against my chest. "You've become a bore lately." Then she places her chin on my chest, and her electric blue eyes clash with mine. "I still love you, though."

"Is that so?"

"Yeah, I kind of don't have a choice. I thought maybe I'd get over you with time, but things have gotten worse, not better. It's been fifteen years and I still love you like that hormonal teenager. The thought of living without you gives me heartache, irregular palpitations, and the worst of attacks."

An unnatural shine gathers in her lids and I lower my head and lick those tears like I did that first time fifteen years ago. My wife shudders in my hold, her lashes fluttering closed as I take my time to drink her tears for myself.

My cock hardens in my trousers, and it's useless to communicate with the sucker that it's not the time for this. "You never will. I'm here to stay, sweetheart."

"Promise?"

"Promise."

She relaxes in my hold, then her eyes widen when she rubs her stomach against my groin. "Aiden! Are you hard?"

"Fantastic deduction skills, Sherlock."

She laughs, a mischievous look spreading in her eyes. "Are you sure you don't want that BJ after all?"

"Absolutely not." I gather her in my arms. "But I'll test the waters, and if you're really fine, you're mine for dinner."

My wife's arms wrap around me and she can't stop smiling. I love that I'm the one behind her happiness. The one who can put a smile on her face whenever and wherever.

"What about everyone else?" she whispers in a sultry voice.

"Everyone else can go fuck themselves." And then I carry my beautiful miracle upstairs.

✧　✧　✧

Levi: *Have any of you seen Aiden?*

Xander: *This is literally his house. He must be somewhere.*

Cole: *He probably disappeared with his wife in one of the rooms as if he's still in school.*

Ronan: *Can someone tell me why we're texting while we're in the same fucking house?*

Cole: *To leave evidence for Aiden to read when he finishes his fuck fest. When you find this, call me so we can talk about better impulse control.*

Xander: *Says the one who's constantly thinking of ways to impregnate his wife again. What type of Levi drug are you on?*

Levi: *You fuck off. Jealous much?*

Xander: *I'm perfectly happy with one offspring. Isn't that right, Ron?*

Ronan: *Remi is an army on his own. Besides, I don't want to share Teal too much.*

Xander: *Exactly. Not like these two going all out on a breeding kink and shit.*

Levi: *Stay mad, Knight.*

Cole: *Should we send Eli to interrupt Aiden?*

Levi: *I would rather not traumatize my nephew, thank you very much.*

Cole: *He obviously needs some traumatizing since he hurt my Ava earlier. No one stops me when I finally break that little shit's legs.*

Xander: *You do realize that you're threatening a kid with violence, right?*

Cole: *As if you wouldn't do the same if Cecily was the one hurt.*

Xander: *I'd shake the fuck out of him, but I wouldn't hit a kid.*

Cole: *Call me subhuman, then, because I definitely would. And that brat isn't a kid. He's like a younger version of Aiden.*

Levi: *Who's oddly interested in your daughter. Seems you and Aiden are unfortunately connected for life.*

Ronan: *My condolences, Cole.*

Xander: *I can't wait to see how this one will play out.*

❖   ❖   ❖

Thank you for reading this bonus epilogue. If you haven't checked out Rina Kent's world, you can jump in with my latest standalone, Empire of Hate. www.rinakent.com

She's the One

Helena Hunting

NOLAN

"HEADS UP, STEVIE'S friends are coming to the game tonight, so you need to be on your best behavior." Shippy, my older brother, who also happens to be an NHL player, is standing in the doorway to my bedroom, his hands on his hips. His expression is pinched and disparaging, which is typical. The only time Bishop doesn't look angry is when his girlfriend, Stevie, is around.

Regardless, I take the opportunity to needle him. "I haven't even done anything yet, and you're already giving me your disapproving-dad look."

His eyes narrow further. "That's because I know you. And I also know that you'll flirt with anything with boobs and a pulse. You cannot hook up with Stevie's friends." Stevie currently lives in the apartment next door, but Shippy, whose actual name is Bishop, spends pretty much every single night at her place. Which means I get this apartment all to myself more often than not.

I give him a thumbs-up. "Got it. I can't hook up with Stevie's friends." But that doesn't mean I can't flirt with them.

"I mean it, Nolan, do not ask for anyone's number. Treat Jules and Pattie like they're family, not like they're potential notches on your bedpost."

"Can I treat them like distant relatives of a step-aunt or something? You know, so only related by marriage?" I'm just pulling his chain.

He purses his lips. "Do not make me regret this, Nolan."

"Dude, it's been months since I've picked anyone up at a game, why would I start with Stevie's friends?" I tug a long-sleeved shirt from a hanger and add, "I'll be on my best behavior."

"That's what I'm worried about," Shippy grumbles. "I gotta roll out, Stevie says she's heading to the arena in an hour and she'll stop by and pick you up on the way."

"Cool, cool. Thanks, bro. See you at the arena. Have a good game, eh."

He nods, drums on the doorjamb like he's thinking about saying something else, but then turns and heads down the hall, leaving me to finish getting ready without him nagging me. In Shippy's defense, I used to use the fact that my brother is an NHL player as a way to pick up women. The worst part is that it actually works. Although, none of them was bound for relationship status. It was mostly just one night of fun and done. It was a pretty hollow existence, so I stopped.

Fifty minutes later Stevie texts to let me know she's ready to roll, so I grab my coat and meet her in the foyer. Her hair is a pale shade of green and she's sporting a green jersey with Shippy's name and number on the back.

"Ready to watch Seattle win some hockey?" Stevie asks.

"Sure am." I grab the apartment keys from the table and make a move to step into the hall, but Stevie stops me.

"You got your insulin with you?"

I pat my breast pocket. "Right here. We're all set."

"Cool, cool." Stevie steps back, giving me room to step into the foyer and close the door behind me.

I'm a type one diabetic and Stevie has had the misfortune of driving me to urgent care in the past when I wasn't taking care of myself the way I should. For a while I was living like every day was my last, until I realized it was putting stress on my brother and our relationship. He's my best friend, and we're tight. After a come-to-Jesus talk with Stevie, I realized if I kept it up, I was heading down a bad path. The kind that could put me in an early grave. So I started taking better care of myself.

"Thanks for driving tonight. I'm sorry I can't be the DD, but in a couple of months I'll have my license back and then you can rely on me for transportation, rather than the other way around." Again, my lack of license has to do with my previous mismanagement of my condition. Now I'm extra careful about everything.

Stevie pushes the button for the elevator. "Eh, I don't mind. I have early clients tomorrow morning, so getting stupid drunk at a hockey game isn't a great idea. Besides, we're stopping to pick up my friends Pattie and Jules on the way." I've heard about Pattie and Jules, but I've never met them before. They're Stevie's co-workers at the off-campus physical therapy clinic she works at.

The doors slide open and I hold out a hand, motioning for Stevie to go ahead of me before I follow her inside. "Yeah, Shippy gave me a warning and told me to treat them like family and not a potential hookup."

Stevie laughs. "Sounds like Shippy."

I shrug. "I have a pretty long track record that would indicate his worries are valid. I told him I'd be on my best behavior."

She smirks knowingly. "I'm sure he found that reassuring."

"Not really."

Stevie flips her long hair over her shoulder. "Pattie and Jules are big girls. They can make up their own mind about you."

"Is that you giving me permission to turn on my Winslow charm?"

That gets me another laugh. "I think that's always turned on full blast for you, isn't it?"

"Someone has to balance out Shippy's surly." My brother has a huge heart, but he doesn't present as the friendliest guy in the world. The first time he met Stevie he called her face a boner killer and accused her of being his teammate's mistress. They got off to a bad start, until Shippy realized his error—that she was not a mistress, she was his teammate's younger sister, and then he went and fell in love with her. And by some miracle, she fell in love with him, too.

We reach the parking garage and I hold open Stevie's door before I take my spot in the passenger seat. Twenty minutes later we pull up in front of a two-story house a few blocks away from the local college.

As soon as the SUV rolls to a stop, the front door opens and two women step out onto the front porch. I unbuckle my seat belt, and hop out of the vehicle so I can open the door for them.

The one in front is tall and lean, her long hair is pulled up in a ponytail. Her head is down and she's busy checking the contents of her purse. The second woman is hidden behind her, and she's a good head shorter. It isn't until the first woman is about ten feet from the SUV that she looks up from her phone and notices me. She hesitates a step, causing the woman behind her to stumble into her with an oof.

"What the heck, Jules?" The woman behind her, who by logical deduction is Pattie, steps to the right, bringing her into view.

And suddenly Shippy's warning not to flirt seems like a task I'm doomed to fail.

Because Pattie is exactly my type.

"Oh! Hey." Her eyes flare when her gaze finds me.

She's petite, maybe only reaching the top of Jules' shoulder, and athletic. She has a heart-shaped face, framed by a pixie cut that complements the softness of her face and her delicate features. Her dark hair matches her chocolate eyes. One side of her mouth quirks up in a smile, popping a dimple in her cheek.

I'm such a goner. I fucking love dimples.

She steps around Jules and extends a hand. "You must be Shippy's brother, Nolan, right?"

I mirror her smile and envelop her hand in mine. The oddest sensation accompanies the contact. Like I've been shot through with a current, not of electricity, but a wave of calm. I've never been a believer in love at first sight, lust sure, but not love. However, in this moment, I feel a strange sense of rightness. Like I've just found the one thing I didn't realize I've been missing. It's fucking weird. Also, I'm pretty sure I've been standing here, holding her hand and staring at her for several very long seconds. I clear my throat. "Yeah. That's me. And you must be Pattie, I've heard so much about you. It's great to finally meet you." Shippy's going to be so pissed at me, because there's no way I can *not* flirt with this woman.

She bites the edge of her lip and her grin widens. "You too."

We're still shaking hands.

"You and Shippy look a lot alike," she adds.

"He's a lot buffer than me and also a lot less personable." I wink and let go of her hand, not because I want to, but because we're past the point of it being socially acceptable.

Her gaze moves over me on a slow, assessing sweep. "Buff is overrated. I like lean."

I like you.

"Well, I am definitely that. Can't put on weight to save my life. And believe me, I've tried." I pat my flat stomach. Where my brother has a six-pack, I have the idea of one. Shippy is all hard lines and muscles and I'm the less defined, less athletic version. I'm more mini-putt and bike rides than hockey and violence.

The sound of a door closing startles both of us, and I realize that Jules has taken the front seat, putting me and Pattie in the back together.

Stevie glances over her shoulder, eyes sliding my way. I shrug. She smirks and shakes her head, like she's unsurprised by this development.

I'm introduced to Jules, but I spend most of the drive chatting with Pattie. I'd like to say I try not to flirt with her, but she's flirting with me, and not flirting back would be considered rude. At least that's going to be the story I'm going with when Shippy invariably calls me out later.

I learn that Pattie and Jules live with their cousins and they bought the house together as an investment property. I also learn that her favorite color is blue, she loves pizza and cuts things like cherry tomatoes and grapes in half before she eats them so they don't pop in her mouth.

Stevie pulls into a spot and we put the conversation on hold as we climb out of the SUV. As usual, I get stopped by security because I'm carrying my insulin, so it takes us a couple extra minutes. I used to leave my stuff at home so I wouldn't have to deal with the embarrassment that sometimes comes with security asking why I'm carrying needles with me. But I've gotten over that, and as soon as I show them my medical alert bracelet, I'm good to go.

Once we're past security I offer to grab drinks for everyone while they find our seats.

"I can come with you," Pattie offers.

"Sure, that'd be great." I exchange a look with Stevie, who gives me an arched brow, but doesn't comment otherwise.

Jules and Stevie make their way through the crowd toward the hall leading to our section and Pattie and I join the throng of people waiting in line for drinks and snacks.

It's loud in here, voices echoing in the cavernous space, so Pattie stands close enough that our arms brush and I bend so I can hear her better. "I can't believe we haven't met before now. Do you come to a lot of Bishop's games?"

"Whenever my schedule allows it. I probably come to about half of his home games."

"It's great that you're so close, and supportive. Jules and I try to go to my cousins' football games as often as we can, too. College football isn't the same as having a brother who plays for the NHL, but I can sort of understand what it's like for you and Stevie."

"I think college ball breeds some pretty rabid fans, much like professional hockey."

"Oh it totally does! I've had girls at my clinic ask if I can introduce them to my cousins."

"This doesn't surprise me at all."

The line is slow moving, so we bond over the perks and pitfalls of having sports-famous family members. Eventually we make it to the front of the line, order drinks, argue over who's paying—I tell her she can get the next round—then weave through the crowd to our section. I motion for Pattie to go ahead of me, and I follow her down the aisle to our seats. We're in the middle, right at center ice, about ten rows up from the ice.

I take my seat beside Pattie and we pass the drinks down the line, settling in as the players take the ice for warm up. I spot Shippy by the net, with Kingston, the team goalie. The wives and girlfriends of the players have a box they often use, and I've been up there a few times this season. But with Pattie and Jules here tonight, we're taking advantage of the ticketed seats.

Jules nudges Pattie, who leans in so she can hear Jules better. "What? Where?" Pattie scans the rows in front of us. "Oh, fuck my life."

"What's wrong?" I follow her gaze, scanning the area, but there are lots of people making their way down to their seats, so it's hard to say what or who has gotten her attention.

Pattie gives me a tight-lipped smile. "Nothing. It's nothing."

I arch a brow. "It's obviously something."

She sighs. "See that guy wearing the blue baseball cap." She inclines her head slightly and her eyes slide to the right.

Four rows down, a big dude and a woman with long blond hair make their way to the pair of empty seats almost directly below us. "Yup. I see him."

"I went out with him."

"How long ago?" Does that mean she's on the rebound?

"A couple of months."

The woman takes her seat and the guy hands her their drinks, then glances in our direction.

"Fuck a duck." Pattie slides down in her seat.

When his gaze catches on her, his eyebrows shoot up. His gaze slides my way, and he makes a face that tells me maybe the end of whatever they had wasn't entirely amicable.

I lean in close, eyes on the ex, who is now shrugging out of his jacket and taking his sweet time settling in his seat, which means he's blocking the view for everyone. It's only warmups, but still. "Is he a dickbag?" I think I already know the answer to that question.

"Sure is," Pattie mutters.

"Want me to act like your date?"

She turns to look at me, maybe to see if I'm serious. It means her face is only inches from mine. There are gold flecks in her eyes, and she has a fine smattering of freckles across the bridge of her nose, like a small constellation of stars scattered there. "You would do that?"

"If you want me to, yeah."

She glances toward the dude, who has finally managed to get his ass in his seat. He's now nuzzling the blonde's neck, but he keeps looking back here. It's embarrassingly juvenile. And weird.

Her gaze returns to me. "Okay. Yeah. That would be awesome."

"Is it cool if I put my arm around you, then?"

She bites her lips together and nods. "Yes. Super one hundred percent okay."

"Okay. I'm coming in for an extended side-hug." I stretch my arm across the back of her seat and let my hand dangle near her shoulder. She fits perfectly.

Pattie leans into me a little and murmurs, "I hope this isn't awkward for you."

"What's awkward is the way that guy keeps trying to eat that woman's hair," I reply. "It seriously looks like he's channeling his inner squirrel."

Pattie snickers. "It really does, doesn't it?"

"Okay. I need you to tell me the story about this guy. Were you doing someone a favor? Was it a blind date setup that went awry?"

"I met him on a dating app."

"Ahh. It's one of those exes. Tell me more."

She blows out a breath. "It's really not all that exciting."

"Still wanna hear it." I tip my chin down and she tips hers up.

Our noses are almost touching again.

"You don't really," she whispers.

"Why? Is it embarrassing? Have you met my brother? Did you see it when he announced, falsely to the world, that Stevie was pregnant with sextuplets?" He did it in a bid to save his best friend's girlfriend from being mobbed by the media, so his heart was in the right place, but Shippy has the tact of a rabid porcupine on a good day.

Pattie's eyes grow wide. "Oh my God, that's been fodder for months!"

"I know. I've been keeping up with the hockey blogs and people are still wondering what happened even after Shippy tweeted that he only said it to make a point."

"Which was what, exactly?"

"That people love drama."

"Mmm. Well, he's not wrong about that, other people's drama is always entertaining, and he sure got a lot of attention for the whole sextuplets thing."

"That he did. Back to the ex. I need to know more."

"He's not like an *ex*, ex. I didn't go out with him long enough for him to break my heart or anything."

"Well, that's good to know. But what if he comes over here and decides to try to talk to you? Don't you think it would be helpful, as your date, to have a bit of background on him?" I'm trying to figure out how that dude ended up with Pattie, who looks like an adorable pixie he could put in his pocket, when his new flavor seems to be a Barbie doll.

She rolls her eyes. "Fine." She grabs her plastic cup of white wine and takes a hefty gulp.

"Damn, this must be one hell of a story."

"It's probably pretty typical of online dating." She takes another gulp. "So he's not my usual type."

"What's your usual type?" She mentioned liking lean, and that dude definitely fits more into the I-pump-a-lot-of-iron category.

She lifts a shoulder. "Non-athletes. I work with athletes every day, so when I date, I generally go for the opposite. Anyway, he seemed like maybe he had some depth. Based on his profile it seemed as though he wasn't only concerned with a zero-carbs diet and the gym, which I'm not knocking, since I basically spend all day, every day working with people in a gym setting. Also, it said he was an avid reader, another thing I can appreciate."

"I feel like there's a but coming." I arch a brow.

"I assumed avid reader meant books, with some variety."

I nod knowingly. "You know what they say about assumptions."

"They make an ass out of you and me. To be fair, he was an avid reader of *Men's Health Magazine*. And also *Sports Illustrated*. So much so that he has a temperature-controlled room where he keeps all of his special-edition magazines."

"Did you happen to see this collection firsthand?"

"No. Thankfully I just got to see a picture of it."

I'm relieved to hear that. "How many dates did you go on?"

She pulls the scarf she's wearing over the bottom half of her face and mumbles something.

I grin at her discomfort. "I'm sorry. I didn't catch that."

She mumbles it again, still from behind her scarf.

I tug it down. "One more time."

She mouths the word *four*.

Her cheeks flush further. Which means I have a million more questions. "That seems like maybe it was three too many chances."

"Well, here's the thing. Our first couple of dates it was tough to have a conversation."

"You need to explain that."

"Like we would end up in loud places where it was difficult to talk. Like on our first date we played laser tag, which is super fun, but isn't great for conversation. Also, it was with a group of people. And the next date we went biking, which again, is fun, but apparently he's super competitive about it, because I spent the entire time out of breath, and again, it was with a group."

"I see a pattern emerging."

"Right? So date number four happens. He picks me up and we go to this nice restaurant. Just the two of us. They have an amazing menu and what does he order? Steak and salad, no baked potato."

"Ah, the carb evader. Did he order vodka soda with a slice of lemon, too?"

"Just soda water, no vodka. At first I thought maybe he was being responsible because he was driving, but really it was just about keeping the calories down."

"Please tell me you ordered the loaded baked potato in retaliation."

"Oh you know I did, with bacon and extra sour cream. I also ordered a Coke *and* a glass of wine."

"Ah, so you have a defiant streak. I highly approve. Did he look at you with judgment and horror?" I ask.

"It's like you were there." Pattie leans in, dropping her voice slightly. "But here's where it gets interesting. All through dinner he keeps asking me questions. He wants to know all about my job, how I ended up working there, did I love it. It seemed like he was hanging on my every word. So here I am, thinking this guy is genuinely interested in me and my job. At the end of the date he asked if I wanted to come back to his place and at this point I'm thinking maybe there's more to this guy than I originally thought. Sure he's a little obsessed with clean eating and working out, but maybe I'd misjudged him?"

"So you went home with him?" I have the strange, irrational urge to punch him in the face.

Pattie shakes her head, and the relief I feel is instantaneous. "I had to work the next morning, and I still had this feeling like something was off. And I was right to feel that way, because when he dropped me off, he asked if there were openings at my clinic for personal trainers, and did he think I could put in a good word for him."

I can only imagine what my expression must be right now. "I did not see that coming."

"Neither did I until it happened, and then everything sort of clicked into place." She shrugs. "I work at a really great clinic, so I get it, but it was a tacky move."

"It's a very high level of tacky. I feel a lot more prepared should he feel the need to talk to you."

I feel a sharp poke on the back of my hand and glance up to find Stevie giving me her cringey face while also tipping her head toward the ice.

I follow her gaze and notice Shippy in the middle of the rink, doing some kind of warmup, his annoyed gaze fixed on me.

Pattie looks from Stevie to Shippy—who is glaring daggers at me—to me.

I raise my hand in a wave, to which Shippy gives me the "I have my eyes on you" gesture. Pointing to both his eyeballs and then toward me. Of course, we're in the middle of the arena, so people start looking around, trying to figure out who has his attention.

"Oh fuck." Stevie pulls her hood up and slouches down in her chair. If her hair wasn't mint green, she might be slightly more successful in getting less attention. "Thanks a lot, Nolan!"

"What's going on?" Pattie asks.

"Uh, well . . . my brother may have given me strict orders not to flirt with you or Jules." Lying seems pointless, especially since Shippy has the social graces of a hangry toddler and will most definitely call me out in front of Pattie when we're at the bar after the game.

Her nose scrunches up. It's pretty damn adorable. "Why would he do that?"

This is the part I don't want to be overly forthcoming about. I'm not sure there's a great way to phrase my taking advantage of my brother's fame in the past. So I go with the version of the truth that's less damning. "Because I'm a naturally flirty person, and he's in love with Stevie, and for some strange reason, she's also in love with him and he's worried that I might somehow compromise that."

She still seems confused, bless her and her adorable scrunched nose. "By flirting with me?"

"I think he's probably looking further down the line. Say should you respond well to my flirtatious advances, and let's say we actually end up going on a date, but for some unknown reason it doesn't work out, because, say for instance, I too have a room full of old *Sports Illustrated* magazines. I don't in case you were wondering. Or, another worse possibility is that I'm a terrible sloppy kisser. Anyway, Shippy is concerned that I'll create tension and conflict for him. And as nice as he is to look at, and as successful as he might be, I think he feels pretty fortunate that Stevie tolerates him on a daily basis and he doesn't want that to change."

Pattie taps her lip. "But what if you aren't a terrible kisser? What if, by setting these parameters, he dooms us both to a lifetime of wondering and what-ifs?"

"That would be tragic. And Shippy would probably feel bad."

"But nowhere near as bad as we would." She motions between us.

"Probably not, no."

"Besides, you're just doing this to help make it less awkward to have my not-really ex, eating his new girlfriend's neck while also looking back at us every few minutes to make sure we're witnessing it." Her eyes dart to the side and back to me.

I don't spare the ex a glance, because I know she's right, that's exactly what he's doing. It's bizarre.

"I mean, I'm altruistic, but I'd be lying if I said I wasn't happy to have my arm around you, while also getting to know you."

Pattie bites her bottom lip. "I'll admit I didn't have to think too hard about your offer to help a girl out."

We both smile.

And then the buzzer goes off, signaling the start of the game.

For the next hour we watch the action on the ice. Pattie is an exuberant hockey fan, cheering on the team whenever they have control of the puck. My arm starts falling asleep about halfway through, but there's no way I'm going to move it. Not unless Pattie asks me to.

At the end of the first period, the girls go to the bathroom and I hit the men's room so I can relieve myself and also give myself another shot of insulin. The lineup for the women's bathroom is stupid, so I offer to get into line for another round of drinks, since that line is equally long. And of course, because fate seems to be in a mood today, I end up in the line beside the douche ex's new girlfriend.

She's wearing enough perfume to choke out an entire department store. She's also tall, leggy, and outfitted head to toe in fitness gear. Her jacket boasts the name of a local gym. I'm one thousand percent sure this guy has a dating theme and it has less to do with the women and more to do with their job connections.

A minute later douche-hole comes out of the bathroom and uses her butt to dry his hand. If I had Pattie's cell number, I would text her and tell her not to meet me in the line like she said she was going to. But I don't. I do, however, have Stevie's, so I fire off a text in hopes that she will issue the warning for me.

But the moment I press send, Pattie appears at my side.

Her gaze shifts from me to her ex-ish douche-hole to the right of us and she mutters, "Seriously? Why can't I catch a break?"

Her frustration is understandable. I want to wipe that look off her face, and I also want to help Pattie reclaim the power-balance and reverse the awkwardness in douche-hole's direction.

"I have an idea, but it involves a public display of affection, our lips getting to know each other, and you finding out if I'm a sloppy kisser or not." I give her a slightly cringey, questioning smile. This could either go really well, or get very awkward in a hurry.

She bites her bottom lip and her eyes drop to my mouth. "I'm in."

Pattie steps closer and wraps one warm hand around the back of my neck.

I slip my arm around her waist and I drop my head as she pushes up on her toes to meet me.

I mean for it to be an innocent peck. Just a quick brush of my lips over hers. But instead of either of us pulling away, we both part our lips. Her mouth tastes like mint. Mine probably tastes like diet soda. We tip our heads, tongues stroking out, once, twice, a third time. She makes a surprised, contented sound and loops her arms around my neck, and I wrap my arms around her waist.

I stop hearing the noise of the people around us. All of a sudden it's just me and Pattie, and nothing matters but this kiss. It's tentative and sweet with the promise of more. Something wild and hot lurking just below the surface, waiting to be set free.

"Dude, get a room," a voice says from beside us.

I'd like to say the heckler is the reason we stop kissing, but it isn't. We ignore him for several more sweeps of tongue, until there's a simultaneous buzzing from below both of our waists. Mine is coming from my front pocket, hers is coming from her purse. We reluctantly part lips and bodies.

Neither of us reaches for our phone, but we do shimmy forward in line since there's now a significant gap between us and the people in front of us. And I think the three people who were behind us are now in front of us.

Pattie and I make eye contact, and have a very extensive silent conversation in two seconds before our gazes drop to each other's lips again.

"You are definitely not a sloppy kisser," Pattie says.

"I'm super glad to hear that, and I'm also very glad my thinly veiled excuse to kiss you worked."

"It was pretty transparent." Her tongue peeks out to wet her bottom lip.

"I know. But it seems to have worked in my favor. After the game would you be interested in going for coffee? We can get to know each other better?"

"I'd like that. Maybe we can let our lips get better acquainted, too."

"Sounds perfect."

Pattie grins and that dimple pops in her cheek.

I lean in and press a kiss to the divot.

It feels like this is exactly where I'm supposed to be, and Pattie is exactly the person I'm supposed to be with.

✦   ✦   ✦

Thank you so much for reading She's The One. For more stories featuring these characters, you can check out my All in Series. You can read Stevie and Bishop's origin story in A Favor for a Favor.

helenahunting.com/books/a-favor-for-a-favor

There is No Hole
in Kindness

L.B. Dunbar

"**M** ISS, ARE YOU alright?"
Perfect. Just perfect.

This is the last thing I expected to happen today.

After leaving the small-town bakery with only minutes to spare before it closed, a torrential downpour began while I stood on the stoop. Balancing my tote and a paper bag containing one of the best-looking baby Bundt cakes, I snapped open my umbrella and risked the deluge.

Only stepping onto the sidewalk, a gust of wind caught between the buildings and jacked my umbrella. The rickety thing snapped backward to look like an art deco buttercup flower, offering no protection from the cold, pelting rain which rode the wind and came at me sideways. In an effort to right my worthless umbrella, I spun on my heels in hopes the direction of the gale would snap the thing into its proper position. In my efforts to twist, the wind took me as well, forcing me backward when the umbrella momentarily expanded. As I tried to hold my balance, the heel of my overly priced stilettos slipped into a grate in the sidewalk. Stuck by the ridiculous physics of a thin heel wedging into an even slimmer iron slat, my ankle gave way and I collapsed onto my ass.

Where the broad and slightly rebellious-looking baker has just asked me if I'm okay.

For a moment, I sit in the puddle, allowing the chilly rain to pour over me, plastering my hair to my face and further drenching my already soaked dress.

This is what I get for wanting to celebrate.

For wishing for something more in my life. For wishing for something I never thought I'd have.

I almost laugh until the concern in the dark eyes of the large man standing over me has me swallowing instead. His jeans are saturated at his ankles, above a pair of solid biker boots. His white T-shirt plasters against his body, making it opaque, accentuating the dark hairs on his chest and the solid muscles of his upper arms. He's thicker in the midsection but not fat. Firm, actually. A paw of a hand extends toward me and slowly I lift mine to accept his help.

My umbrella is nowhere in sight. The bag containing my Bundt cake sits amid a shallow puddle on the sidewalk. My foot has slipped out of my shoe. My lacking pride is the only thing present. I've never been so embarrassed. And my backside uncomfortably aches.

"Let's get inside, yeah?" He yells over the torrent of rain, swiping at his face to clear it. His eyes are kind. His voice rough. A sprinkling of silver peppers among the darkness of scruff on his jaw.

I nod and accept his assistance, as he holds my hand and gathers up the remains of a wasting paper bag. Once we enter the cool breeze of the bakery, I shiver. Teeth chatter. Tailbone throbs. I'm off-balance wearing only one shoe.

He tosses the waterlogged container on the counter and turns to face me. The thickness of his hand is a comfort as he pushes back my hair. The heat of his skin is surprising under the blast of air-conditioning.

"We should probably get you out of those clothes." The depth of his voice has my body humming in a new way, but I still choke around my next word.

"What?"

"Got a change of clothes in that bag?" He nods at my tote which surprisingly remained looped over my arm, but water drips through the seams. I'm certain everything inside the leather is soaked. Why do bag companies make totes without closures? And why did I own something that couldn't protect my belongings?

Oh right, it matched my now-ruined shoes.

"No." My teeth continue to chatter.

"Only speak one word at a time?" His rugged tenor doesn't match the hitch to one corner of his lips, suggesting a smile is hard won from him. Still, the expression is doing strange things to my lower belly.

Or maybe that's something else inside me.

Don't be ridiculous. I only took a test this morning. Surely, I can't feel anything yet. I don't even know anything definitive, although I'd read home-tests are ninety-nine percent correct.

"I-I'm sorry. I ruined the cake." Hopefully, he can't decipher between welling tears and water on my face as I'm on the verge of crying over a baby Bundt cake. Then again, maybe it's simply my emotions which have been pinging all over the place since this morning.

"No worries." He pauses, stepping back to size me up while tipping his head. His hand still holds mine or maybe mine is clinging to his. I don't want to let go. His palm is so warm. His fingers strong. "I have a T-shirt that might fit you more like a dress, but it'd be warmer than what you are wearing."

At thirty-nine, everything in me should send off warning bells. I don't know him. I'm not from this town. No one knows I made this stop. But while his dark eyes could be interpreted as dangerous, the heat in them glides over me like a coat of protection.

I nod, blindly following him to the back of the bakery, limping on my one heel.

When we step inside the office, he finally releases my hand. Rummaging through some boxes, he pulls out a large T-shirt with Curmudgeon Baker on the back. He scowls at the shirt before handing it over to me.

"It's going to be loose on you, but it will be dry. I'll step out while you change, but if you hand me your things, I'll toss them in the dryer."

I weakly smile. "It's dry clean only." A tumble in a dryer would ruin the material of my dress, if it isn't already destroyed.

His eyes roam my soaked outfit, pausing for a second before turning his head to the side. Without a word, he slips around me and softly closes the door. Once he leaves, I glance down at my dress to find it suctioned to my body. My nipples are protruding sharp peaks suggesting how cold I am, or is it something else? The way he was looking at me. The heat in his gaze. I shiver again.

Shaking my head, I dismiss crazy thoughts. He wasn't looking at me in any way other than a drowned rat. With shaky fingers and chilled limbs, I work to remove my dress. Deciding my bra and underwear will only cause discomfort under the dryness of a fresh shirt, I remove them as well. I run my hand over my backside, confirming the length of the oversized T-shirt covers my backside. Every attempt to bend forward forces me to catch my breath and wince at the pain in my tailbone.

Glancing around the office, it's an accountant's nightmare. Papers stand in stacks on the floor. A box full of receipts. The desktop covered in haphazard piles. But the thing that attracts my gaze the most is a large zipper sweatshirt draped over the back of the desk chair. Taking a liberty, I swipe up the soft cotton and wrap myself in another layer for warmth. The collar smells like vanilla and oil which is a strange combination yet surprisingly refreshing. I smile to myself as I inhale what I assume is the scent of the curmudgeon baker himself.

A soft knock comes to the door, but it opens before I answer. "I figured you might want these. I don't have shoes that would fit you." That crook to his lips happens again. He's making a joke. His feet must be four sizes bigger than mine, and he's holding out a pair of socks. "Or you can keep hobbling on one foot."

When he looks up at me, the heat in his eyes flares. His gaze lowers from my face to the sweatshirt dangling too long on my arms and the T-shirt that hits above my knees.

"Thank you." My voice is still unsteady but I'm not certain it's the cold making my throat rumble.

He nods once and drags his gaze away, staring off to the side once again. He's freshly dressed in a dry pair of jeans and a light gray Henley shirt. His close-cropped hair is damp. A towel hangs over his shoulder.

"I hope you don't mind." I shrug and smooth a hand down an edge of the open zipper-sweatshirt.

He shakes his head, and I take the socks from him, wincing as I bend forward to slip them on.

"Are you hurt?"

"Besides my pride?" I joke. "My backside is killing me."

At the mention of my ass, he chokes, and I glance up to find him swiping his thick fingers around his mouth, stroking at the bristly hairs on his chin. He looks more like a biker than a baker but he's the man who filled my cake order.

"Are you the curmudgeon baker?" I ask, righting myself and wincing again as pain shoots up my spine.

"A joke from my family," he mocks.

"But are you the owner of Sylver Fox Bakery?" I tip my head. He's solid brawn, and I can't imagine his hefty fingers delicately decorating baby Bundt cakes, but the judgement is unfair.

"Yeah." His gaze lowers for the floor and the corner of his mouth tips up again. Pride fills his voice but his cheeks pinken the slightest bit.

"What? Only answer one word at a time?" I tease.

His head pops up and those dark eyes dance with mischief. He stares at my saturated hair. "I brought you this." Dragging the towel off his shoulder, he hands it to me.

"Thanks," I mutter again, swiping it over my face and inhaling a stronger scent of vanilla and laundry detergent. I rub the material over my hair and finger-comb the long locks as best I can.

"How about some coffee?" He tips his head toward the storefront, and I follow wearing his socks. While we walk, I twist my hair around itself forming a messy bun for a temporary fix.

Gingerly, I sit on a hard-surfaced booth bench, trying to balance on one cheek. He rounds the counter, pours two mugs of coffee and comes to the table.

His head tilts. "I'll be right back."

When he returns, he holds a bed pillow in his hand. "For your ass."

I laugh as he takes a seat across from me. "I'm Aria, by the way."

"Nice to meet you, Aria." He lifts his mug, watching me over the rim. In typical conversation this is where he should tell me his name, but he doesn't offer, and I don't ask.

As silence grows, I glance around the bakery. Display cases line one side while booths line the opposite wall. The floor is giant black and white square tiles while subway tiles on the wall give the place an old-world-bakery feel. Or maybe it's new world as the stark white and clean lines has made a resurgence. With the hum of the air conditioner no longer buzzing, music can be heard.

"Imagine" by the Beatles fills the space.

"Beatles fan?" I hitch a brow, glancing at him over the rim of my mug. He shrugs, casual coolness across from me, watching me drink my coffee. One arm rests against the back of the booth; the other hand cups his mug. Silence has never been so comforting, but I can't keep quiet for long. I glance up at a quote on the wall.

There is NO HOLE in Kindness.

The capitalized Os are shaped like donuts.

"Strange quote." I turn back at him.

"This location used to be a donut shop." He pauses as if that explains everything.

"Donuts have holes."

He shrugs again. "Bundt cakes do as well." He tips his head to read the quote himself. "It was here when I bought the place. Figured it brought the previous owners thirty-two years of business luck. I left it on the wall."

Taking a second glance, a faint outline surrounds the quote, as if fresh paint didn't match the original color.

"Maybe it's a metaphor. Like kindness is cyclical."

He shrugs again and scoffs while lifting his mug. "Maybe it was a nicer way of saying don't be an asshole."

"Maybe." I glance back at the quote and then at him. "Got any other quotes for good luck?"

His lip quirks up on one side and he tips his chin. "What do you need luck for?" Those dark eyes of his scan my face and drop to my chest.

Why do I need luck? I should already feel like the luckiest woman in the world. But my eyes instantly well. Damn my emotions.

"I'm pregnant," I whisper, saying the words aloud for the first time.

His arm along the back of the booth slips to the seat. His hand on the handle of his mug flattens on the tabletop. His entire demeanor shifts, and that hint of dangerous becomes more apparent. He leans forward.

"Husband must be happy." His rugged tone which once sounded kind is now edgier.

"No husband." I swallow around the truth, keeping my gaze aimed at the table which continues to blur.

"Boyfriend, then?" His voice croaks on the word.

I shake my head. How do I explain to a stranger that there isn't a husband or a boyfriend? Not even a baby daddy. The father of my child is number 04359. A sperm donor.

"Shit." The gruffness filters into my ear.

Suddenly, I'm hefted out of the booth and wrapped in thick arms. My head is pressed to his chest where the rapid rhythm of his heart is a balmy song. Thrown off guard at first, my arms are trapped between us but, slowly, I loosen them and circle his waist. Tears slip down my nose.

I don't know why I'm crying. This is what I wanted. This is what I paid for.

But I'm still scared . . . and his simple questions remind me I'm doing this alone.

"Want me to kill the bastard? I know people." The tenor in his question tells me he isn't joking but there's no one to harm.

I shake my head against his solid pecs, anxiously giggling despite the flow of tears. "I'm good."

His hand glides down my back, pausing just above my ass. His other cups my head, holding me in place against him. I close my eyes, inhaling the vanilla scent of him. We stand like this for long enough, I don't want to move, but slowly the awkwardness of hugging a stranger settles in.

I pull back while his hand at the base of my spine keeps me close to his body. His eyes search mine and I wish I could read his thoughts. I wish I could tell this stranger all of mine.

But wishing is what got me where I am.

Pregnant and thirty-nine.

"I was here to buy a Bundt cake. A little celebration of sorts." The explanation sounds even odder than telling him I'm pregnant. While some might celebrate with champagne, I can't. A *baby* Bundt cake felt appropriate for a future birth. In roughly nine months, I'll have a true birth date to remember.

And I'll be celebrating alone.

He huffs above me, swiping back at hair coming loose from my makeshift bun. Stepping away from me, the reality of standing in borrowed socks and a stolen sweatshirt hits me. He must think I'm a nut.

As he walks away from me, I shamelessly check out his backside, rounded and firm in tight-fitting jeans. He rounds the counter once more but quickly returns to where I stand with a baby Bundt cake on a small plate and two forks in hand. He nudges me to take my seat and he slides into the booth across from me again.

Placing the plate between us, he holds up a fork and nods for me to do the same.

"To babies and Bundt cakes." His tone rings slightly sad. He taps my fork like we are clinking glasses of champagne and then he presses the plate in my direction, suggesting I take the first bite.

The moist lemon cake perfectly balanced with a rich buttercream frosting melts in my mouth. I moan as I close my eyes, not even exaggerating the orgasm on my tongue at the texture and flavor.

When I open my lids, his eyes smolder back at me, and the strangest fantasy fills my head.

He's the father of my baby and he's so excited by this news he wants to take me on this table to commemorate the good news.

Horror strikes my face, and my eyes widen at my imagination. My fantasy would only complicate things.

Softly, he chuckles, pulls the plate closer to him and fills his fork. Watching him, he sucks at the utensil, taking his time to savor the experience within his mouth. A place on me that has no business beating, thumps strong and fierce. Slowly, he removes the tines, taking his time to release the fork, now clean of cake. My mouth dries, wondering at the mystery of his tongue. Wondering what his lips might feel like clamping on to parts of me. How firmly does he suck? How roughly does he kiss?

My body heats but shivers return with a carnal need to answer questions about him.

I still don't even know his name.

However, we share this piece of cake, and silence between us fills with another Beatles song. I fight back my lust and come to a decision.

A simple act of kindness might be more seductive than spreading me on this table.

No holes *is* a metaphor. Kindness goes around and around in quiet gestures, like fresh socks, a warm sweatshirt, a celebratory piece of cake, and a secretive smile.

And one day, I hope to repay the curmudgeon baker for his generosity in a grand way.

✧   ✧   ✧

Thank you for reading my contribution to this anthology.

If you enjoy small-town, grumpy silver foxes, you might also enjoy Silver Brewer. lbdunbar.com/library/silver-foxes-of-blue-ridge/silver-brewer

THE DANCE

KANDI STEINER

A LETTER FROM THE AUTHOR

Poetry was my first introduction to writing. It started in third grade, where I mostly wrote poems about boys, and now that I'm in my thirties? Well... not much has changed. I love love, and love to explore all the emotions we feel as human beings through the written word. I write poetry when it strikes me, when a moment is so powerful it demands to be captured somehow. Sometimes it's early in the morning with my coffee in hand, and other times it's late at night when I'm in a crowd full of strangers. I hope you'll enjoy these five unpublished poems that I've written over the last few years.

XOXO,
Kandi

WHEN YOU'VE FOUND your person, you simply just know. I can't tell you how you will feel, exactly, but you will know. Maybe they'll make you feel the way you did when you were a child, in the safety of your mother's home the night before Christmas. Maybe they'll feel like a song, one you've always known, one that always makes you dance. Maybe you won't be able to place it at all—whatever *it* is—but you'll just look at them and see it. "This is what forever looks like," you'll say to yourself. "This is where my search ends."

m y p e r s o n
Kandi Steiner

I think this is it.
How scary that moment is,
when it hits you,
when you know that
what could have been forever
is actually just for now,
and very soon,
for not,
and perhaps one day,
forgotten.
f o r g o t t e n
Kandi Steiner

I loved the way his tongue danced

along my inner thigh,
like a ballerina on stage,
tiptoeing that delicate line.
Spin and twirl, ballerina,
in that tasty skirt of pink.
Remember your performance isn't over
until the crowd is on its feet.
t h e d a n c e
Kandi Steiner

What hurts most of all is one day
you will find her
the woman you said I could never be.
And you will stare into her eyes
and tell her about all the women
all the stepping stones
on that rocky path
that led to her.
And I'll still be here
where you passed me along the way
wishing the road ended here
with me
instead.
d i f f e r e n t p a t h s
Kandi Steiner

I believe in sun kissed cheeks.
I believe in nights that blend into mornings,
in talking about anything other than the weather,
in loving so hard that the only way out is to break and rebuild again.
I believe in crying when life is beautiful
and when it's ugly, too.
I believe in making choices,
and not wondering whether they are right or wrong,
but whether which path they might lead me down next.
I believe in new chapters
and in re-reading old ones when my heart tells me to.
I believe in a love that died when you said goodbye,
and in the love I found after you were gone.
I believe in getting lost in the mountains
and paving new roads
and talking to strangers.
And I believe that having different beliefs is what makes us all so beautiful,

so uniquely human,
small and grand at once.
h u m a n
Kandi Steiner

✧   ✧   ✧

MORE FROM KANDI STEINER

A Love Letter to Whiskey
(AN AMAZON TOP 10 BESTSELLER)

An angsty, emotional romance between two lovers fighting the curse of bad timing.
kandisteiner.com/books/a-love-letter-to-whiskey

Always and Forever

Dylan Allen

MORE

Addie

I DON'T BOTHER to put on gloves to wash the plates. My nails are a lost cause. I hold my hands out in front of me and grimace at the state of them.

When I was working at the firm, I didn't go more than 10 days without a visit to a nail salon. These days, my nails are the last thing on my mind.

When the baby was born, Simon and I agreed that it didn't make sense for me to keep working when we had absolutely no need for the income.

I loved my job at the Foundation, but it was nearly as intense and demanding as the firm had been. To my great surprise, I found that raising my children was the hardest, most thankless, and most rewarding labor of love imaginable.

But after eighteen months of being entirely focused on them, I feel lost. While I was visiting my parents, I caught a glimpse of myself in the mirror and for a split second I didn't recognize the woman staring back at me. She looked nothing like the Addie I knew. The leggings and oversized t-shirt that had become her uniform were a fry cry from the closet full of expensively tailored clothes made of beautiful clothes that made me feel and look like a million dollars.

The mirror revealed more than my altered physical appearance, I could see the lack of luster in my eyes.

I love being a mom, but I really miss being a lawyer, a lover, and a bestie.

I want to try and be her again. I just hope Simon understands.

His quiet footfalls alert me to my husband's presence a few seconds before he puts a hand on the counter on both sides of my body and cages me there. "Gotcha."

"I'm not going anywhere, babe – you don't have to hold me hostage."

A chuckle rumbles low in his chest and I step back so I can feel the vibration of it. "Recent history says otherwise. You left me for an entire month, and it felt like three lifetimes."

My heart swells and my relief is so potent, I can taste it.

My desire to find myself again wasn't the only revelation I had in Houston. Since we became parents, I feel less like his wife and more like the mother of his children.

He hasn't tried to touch me since I got back from visiting my parents. In all honesty, he hadn't tried to touch me much before that. I was afraid it was because my body has changed. But in that mirror I realized that it was because *I* have. I came home hoping we'd find a way to reconnect.

I was worried for nothing. He seemed to be waiting for me to reach out, too.

"Well, I'm here now and I'm not going anywhere."

"Damn straight." He grips my jaw with one hand, tips my head up, and brings his lips down on mine. My eyes close as he lays a wet, hot possessive kiss on me that makes my knees buckle. The sippy cup in my hand slips out of my grasp and lands with a splash and hot, soapy water splashes all over me. I break our kiss and turn back to the sink. "One sec,"

Simon puts a hand on my shoulder. "Just leave it, Addie."

I shake my head, "I'm almost done. Go relax, I'll join you soon."

He nuzzles my neck with nose. "You smell fucking amazing."

I roll my head back onto his shoulder. "That's it."

His phone rings, loud and shrill, and the moment is gone. He answers it. "Hey, Reece – yeah, no it's fine." He gives me an apologetic smile and rushes down the hall to office. Reece Carras is one of his firm's biggest clients and he lives in Los Angeles, where it was only two o'clock in the afternoon.

I was so ready to forget everything but my husband and how much my body needed his, but I also understand that his work is demanding and didn't resent it at all.

Disappointed by the interruption, but undeterred, I find my silver lining and get to work cleaning the plates.

I'm nearly finished when, one after the other, the kids wake up. I hear their simultaneous cries and rush to get them before they wake Henry up. They're both congested and miserable.

The cold they'd been battling since we got back from visiting my parents has miraculously spared Simon and me. Their fevers were gone, but stuffy noses made sleep fitful. I took them down to our room where my humidifier was already set up.

I get them both settled, press a kiss to each of their cheeks. I close the door without so much as a click and lean against the door and refocus my thoughts on the evening I planned.

I hurry back to the kitchen, eager to finish clearing the plates and cleaning so that we can pick up where we left off as soon as he's done with his call.

I submerge my hands back into the sink full of hot soapy water and grab the sponge and get back to work. We have a dishwasher, but I used our wedding china tonight and it has to be hand washed.

Tonight was going to be a new beginning for us, I hoped.

After the kids went down the first time, I showered, washed my hair, shaved, put on the grapefruit scented body lotion he loves, let my hair air dry and didn't put on a bra.

He looked at me like I was his favorite meal served up on a platter, and I wanted him to feast until he was full. But first, I wanted to flirt and build some anticipation.

I batted my eyes at him, trailed lingering kisses on his jaw as I cooked us dinner, I could feel that old rhythm returning. It had been a long time since we'd had a night like this. He seemed a little unsure of himself at first, but by the time we'd finished dessert, we were both a little tipsy from the bottle of Pinot we shared over dinner. And that kiss before his phone rang…whew.

After three years of marriage, and with three children all under the age of five care of, I love how his kisses still make me burn.

"Did I hear the kids?" Simon asks as he comes back down the hall. He comes to stand behind me, this time, his clever hands knead my shoulders and I groan in pleasure as tension seeps out of me.

"Yeah, they woke up crying. I put them in our bed and they fell asleep in minutes."

"You've got to stop doing that, Addie." He grumbles in my ear, real irritation in his voice.

I know he doesn't like them sleeping with us. He's afraid it will become a habit. But he's not the one waking up with them. "It's the only way I'll get any sleep." I shift a little so our bodies are no longer touching. Just *talking* about them being sick exhausts me.

"I know, I just miss you." He comes to stand beside me at the sink, grabs a dish towel, and starts wiping the things I've already washed. My heart melts just watching him.

"And you've spent all night giving me that look…" he shoots me a scowl.

I smile, eyes wide with feigned ignorance. "What look?"

He scoffs, not buying my act. "The one that always means you're thinking about all the ways I can make you come." He steps behind me again and his big hand glides across my stomach. His caress is rough, his hand not lingering, but moving up to cup my breast and squeezing hard enough to make me whimper.

"Oh, *that* look." I tip my hips backwards and roll them.

"But now the kids are in our bed."

"Since when have we needed a bed?"

"We don't. But I happen to like having room to work."

"You're not the only one," I say and nudge him with my hip.

He snorts and casts me a sidelong glance full of skepticism he usually reserves for weather forecasts and campaign promises.

Ouch.

"You don't…believe me?" I ask, but only rhetorically because that look said it all. I just don't understand how he could think I'm any less eager for intimacy with him than he is with me.

"All I know is you guys have been back from Houston for a whole week, and I'm still rubbing one out in the shower every morning, because I can't get my wife alone long enough to fuck her."

I hear the complaint and the frustration in his voice, but I'm so relieved that he wants me just as much as he always has, I can't help but smile.

He's…so sexy.

Fuck these dishes. They can wait. But I don't think I can. I rinse the soap off my hands and wipe my hands and lean my hip on the counter, turning so I watch him work. "You've been rubbing one out in the shower?" I ask.

He follow my lead and drops the dishtowel and the tiny plastic plate he was drying and turns so we're face to face. "Every morning."

I give him a once over and thank my lucky stars this walking wet dream is all mine. His body is honed by all of the miles he runs every week and tonight, he's dressed in a pair of low slung blue jeans that hug his slim hips and long, muscular thighs and a plain black t-shirt that clings to his broad chest and strains against his deliciously sculpted biceps.

"Every fucking morning," he repeats, his voice dropping an octave as he palms the straining bulge of his hard dick. "Sometimes more than once."

My eyes follow the movement of his hands as he strokes his length through his jeans. His eyes are hooded and full of so much need that I clench my thighs as I feel my body respond to his invitation. "Tell me what you imagine while you're in the shower and you've got your soapy hands on that big, delicious cock? God, I can just imagine it," I pant. My breaths are coming faster, my nipples pucker and pussy is already wet when I lean back on the counter and watch him.

"Yes." I say back, my eyes trained on his hand, my mouth watering with anticipation.

"You want to watch?" He unsnaps his jeans, pulls down the zipper and slides his hand inside.

He shoves his jeans and boxers down around his hips. His cock, in all its thick long glory, springs free. He grabs it and gives it one long, slow stroke. His eyes close and his head tips back exposing the strong column of his neck.

"Addie, I think about your pussy, about eating it, sucking your hard little clit into my mouth, fucking your tight pussy with my tongue until your thighs tremble around my head and you're screaming my name."

A sheen of sweat break out over my entire body as I watch him stroke himself, eyes flutter but I don't dare close them and miss a second of this fantasy. "Tell me more."

His chest heaves as he picks up the speed of his strokes. "I remember how your cunt clenches my fingers find your g-spot, how you get so wild and tell me how much you need my dick inside of you."

His eyes open suddenly and he levels his gaze on me. His dark brown eyes are like molten chocolate.

"And I think about sucking your nipples when I squeeze inside your tight pussy. And fucking you so hard that you can't stop coming."

I groan and reach for the button of my own jeans without taking my eyes from his.

"And then, when I'm coming, Addie, I imagine your hot, soft, slick with my kisses mouth on my neck, those little claws of yours raking down my back and the way your body milks mine for everything it's got when I come inside of you."

My hands slip into my jeans, I'm not wearing any panties and my fingers glide easily over the slick, sensitive skin of my pussy until they're on my clit, rubbing in tight, small circles. With my free hand, I pinch my hard, aching nipple through my tank top and a whimper tears from my throat.

My eyes drift closed for less than a second before Simon growls, "Oh fuck no." Confused, I open them but the question on my tongue dies. The determination and lust burning in his narrowed eyes tells me everything I need to know. He wants me fiercely. More than he ever has. Leaking breasts and all. He takes one long step and brings our bodies flush.

"What?"

"You're not going to get yourself off while I stand here and watch."

He pushes my hand aside and lifts me up so my ass is on the counter. And his hands, those magical hands I've missed, are on me. His fingers move in a coordinated effort. He rubs my clit with his thumb while two of his fingers plunge inside me starts to finger-fuck me. His head comes down and his other hand moves up my shoulder to yank my tank top down; and then, his mouth is on my breast. He flicks my nipple with his tongue before he captures the whole thing. I use one hand to keep my balance and the other to his head to hold him in place. I wrap my legs around his thighs.

His fingers leave my body and his hands come up to pull my jeans all the way down to my shins and then in one firm tug he yanks them all the way off. He pushes my legs back so they are hanging from the counter I'm perched on. And then he walks over the fridge.

I sit forward confused, the action bringing my legs together. "What are you doing?"

He looks over his shoulder at me and frowns. "No, baby. Leave them open." He pulls out a can of whipped cream. He turns and stalks toward me. His eyes fixed on the space between my legs. When he reaches me, he drops to his knees bringing his face level with my pelvis.

Without looking up at my face, he commands, "Hold yourself open for me, Addie."

My hands move quickly to obey, exposing my throbbing clit, letting him see me completely.

He takes the can of whipped cream, points it at his target and presses the dispenser.

I yelp as the cold cream hits my heated skin. But before I can make another sound, his hot mouth covers me as he licks the cream, his tongue dipping inside me before it moves up. And then my clit is in his mouth, pulling in that gentle, but constant rhythm that gets me to orgasm in seconds.

He stands up as soon as I start to come and grabs his cock a lines it up with my entrance. With a few sure strokes, he's inside me. And it is fucking *bliss*.

His strong hands lift me off the counter and walks us through the living room, sits down on the couch so I'm straddling him.

"Do your work, baby. Let me watch you." He says gruffly as he pushes my hair out of my face.

God, I love this man. There isn't anything I could deny him. I rise and fall onto what I know is the most magical dick in the world while he leans back, watching me. His eyes roam my face, my neck, my shoulders. And that I feel the heat of his eyes as surely as I would if he had touched me.

He pulls my tank top over my head, cups my breast with one hand and plays with my nipple, while his other hand comes to my lips. He puts his thumb inside my mouth and I suck it. After a few seconds, he snakes that hand around my waist and his fingers part the crack of my ass. His thumb pushes past the tight ring of muscle and I bear down to make his ingress easier.

And with his cock in my pussy and his thumb in my ass, I find my orgasm; blistering and verging on the level of bliss that is almost unbearable, for the second time that night. Simon grabs my hips and thrusts up hard and fast as I lean forward on his chest. And when he comes, he bites my shoulder as his hand tangles in my hair and he holds me to him.

When we've caught our breath, he starts to pepper kisses on my shoulder.

"I've missed you, Addie. I'm so glad you're home. Next time I'll find a way to come with you and the kids."

I just snuggle deeper into him, so glad to be in the arms of this man who allowed me to lose myself in love without the fear of losing myself.

"I love you, Simon." I mumble as I feel myself start to drift off.

"To infinity and beyond, Addie." He sounds sleepy, too.

"Mommeeeeeeee!" Comes the loud, demanding call of my son from our bedroom, and just as I start to respond, he shouts "Daddeeeeee!"

Simon and I look at each other and smile as we disengage.

"Want to run away?" I ask him as he walks to the hallway that leads to our bedroom to check on our children.

"Not a chance." He responds instantly, giving me quick smile over his shoulder as he disappears into the dark of the hallway.

And just like that, I fall in love all over again.

ENOUGH

Simon

I LOVE OUR life, our kids, my work, the bloom in my wife's cheeks. For the first year she was home, Addie was in her element. She glowed, even when she was exhausted.

So when her light dimmed a couple months ago, I knew she was something much worse than exhausted.

She was bored. When she said she was going to see her family, I thought the change of scenery would do her some good.

Her trip was meant to be a one week visit.

Her parents held something they called "cousin camp" at their house in Houston and all their grandchildren came and stayed with them for the week.

For the first time in years, she had the entire *days* to herself.

She saw friends, went for runs, enjoyed bath time – and extended her trip four times before she finally came home.

And it was a kick in the gut to see that bloom back on her cheeks after time apart from me.

I was a husk of myself while they were gone. The first few days, I enjoyed having a lie in, The quiet nearly drove me crazy. and the bed was cold without her. They came back and the kids were sick and work was insane – but so was I. When she asked me to come home early that night because we had to talk, I thought she was going to tell me she was leaving me.

But halfway through dinner, I realized I'd gotten the wrong end of the stick. And even those interruptions couldn't stop us from finding each other again.

I woke up feeling like I'm back in the game. My woman is happy and all is right in my world again.

"It's a beautiful morning," I sing to my reflection as I knot my tie. "Simon, we need to talk." Addie calls from the bathroom.

My mood shifts. Those are not the words I wanted to hear from her this morning. "Why do you sound like you're about to give me bad news?"

She walks into my dressing room and stands behind me so our eyes meet in the mirror. Her expression is grave and her lips are pursed.

"You know you never need to be afraid to say *anything* to me," I remind her in a gentle but reproachful voice.

"I want to go back to work," she says—gently, but unyielding. "I have a list of vetted nannies and some creche's. A few very close to your office. I need more." She wasn't asking my opinion, knew she didn't need my permission, she was just informing me.

I'm not surprised that she wants to go back to work, but it hurts that she was worried about telling me. There's something else I feel but I get my arms around it.

I smile at her. "Of course. That's great. Do you have prospects lined up?"

"Yes…" She frowns at me like my answer is confusing.

"You expected me to protest?" I ask, not sure if I'm amused or offended.

"No, but I did expect pushback."

"Why?" I demand.

She shrugs, and folds her arms across her chest the way she does when she's feeling defensive. "Because you love it that I'm home and taking care of our kids myself."

I look at her askance. "I loved it because I thought *you* loved it."

"I do. But I'm fading...I know they should be enough. But, I have so much I want to do."

I turn to face her and cup her cheeks. "Then go do it. Don't feel guilty for needing something that's just for you. I do. I'm not worried that the kids won't know I love them because I went to work everyday. I go to work so I can be the best me for them."

"Are you sure they'll be okay?"

"Yes. Because we're their parents and we'll make sure they're okay. Do what's best for you. Because that is what will be best for all of us."

"Oh Simon," she sighs. "I know you want me to be happy, but you deserve to have what you want, too."

"What I want, I already have." I drop a kiss on her lips before she can respond and then stride out of the dressing room and grab my phone and call my assistant.

"Good morning, Simon," Marsha answers sounding more chipper than normal.

"Morning, I'm glad you're in a good mood because I need you to be very charming for me today."

✧   ✧   ✧

"SO, YOU'RE JUST up and going to Greece?" My brother, Kyle, is pacing my bedroom holding my six month old daughter in his arms while I pack.

"Yup. For a whole week."

A week ago, when Addie asked if I wanted to run away, I said no and I meant it. But after our conversation about her going back to work, I realized that we *both* need to get away. Alone.

Her sister is taking the kids for the week. She can't come for them until tomorrow morning. So, Kyle is staying with them tonight. Nothing was going to keep us from making this flight today.

Addie didn't utter a word of protest when I surprised her with the tickets yesterday. She's the light of my life, I've been so basking in it that I hadn't given her a chance to recharge...and bask too. If anyone deserves she does.

She's worked hard to forgive her parents and to forgive herself and she's an amazing mother who is excellent at nurturing other human beings. At letting me and everyone else around her just be themselves.

My children are so comfortable in their skin and it's because she affirms every single part of them, quirks, anxieties, their triumphs and she does the same for me. So today, is all about refilling her cup and giving her a day to be apologetically herself.

Including in the bedroom.

When we worked together and sleeping together, we had to hide it at the office. but unable to keep our hands off each other in the office – she'd stuff my handkerchief into her mouth to muffle the sound.

I'm going to start by eating her pussy until she screams loud enough to leave her throat raw in the morning. When she's wet and and loose and ready, I'm going to fuck her until she tells me she's full.

My phone buzzes with a text. It's from her. It's picture of her holding a dozen shopping bags.

The message reads, *"I am so ready for this."*
She ran out to get waxed and to buy some new bathing suits.
I write back. *"You still have to pack. Get your sweet ass home."*
"Wild horses couldn't keep me away. Love you."
"Love you more."

✦ ✦ ✦

Thank you for reading Always and Forever. If you want more from author Dylan Allen, visit her website.
www.dylanallenbooks.com

THE PERFECT DISTRACTION

PIPER RAYNE

CHAPTER ONE
Killian

I STAND IN front of the door to Happy Daze Tavern and push my hand through my dark hair.

I swapped out the bustling city of San Francisco for Climax Cove, a small town in Oregon, for one reason and one reason only—my six-year-old daughter, Caprice. I enjoy a big city and all its amenities but I'm a single father now and something about raising my daughter in a city didn't sit well in my gut—like a meal that isn't digesting well. And I'm a guy who always listens to my gut. In my entire thirty-three years as a lawyer, I've rarely gone against my gut, and when I have, I've always been sorry.

So, when a lawyer here in Climax Cove was retiring and looking for someone to take over his practice, I decided to visit. Since I liked what I saw, I decided to move us up here. Sure, I'm not going to be making money hand over fist like I did at the big firm in San Francisco, but I also won't be billing sixty-hour workweeks and relying on a nanny to raise my daughter.

Caprice has been through more than any six-year-old should. The peace of a place like this, while I anticipate it might make me a little stir crazy, will be good for Caprice. It's not about me anyway.

Hence why I open the door to Happy Daze Tavern and step inside.

My eyes take a moment to adjust to the dim lighting inside, but when they do, I spot a group of men near the back sitting in a sort of haphazard circle of chairs.

"Can I help you?" I look to my left to find a guy standing there, maybe a decade older, with coppery-colored hair and an easygoing smile.

"Yeah, I'm here for..." I trail off, feeling ridiculous for the words that are about to come out of my mouth.

The guy at the bar flips the towel over his shoulder. "Let me guess—the Single Dads Club meeting?" He raises an eyebrow.

"Yeah. Is that it in the back?" I nod toward the group of men, some older and some younger than I am.

"Sure is." He studies me for a second, then sticks his hand out over the bar. "You must be new here. I'm Dane. I own this place." He motions with his pointer finger to our surroundings.

"Hey." I step up to the bar and shake his hand. "Killian Roberts. Nice to meet you. I took over the law practice down the street."

"Oh right. I heard about that. Not much news that doesn't make the rounds through here. Welcome to Climax Cove."

"Thanks." I take a quick glance over at the meeting that looks like it's just about to get started.

"They're a great group of guys," Dane says. "I used to be a member of the club myself until I found my girl. How old is your son or daughter? Or is it plural?"

I sit on the nearest barstool. "Daughter. Caprice. She's six."

Dane nods. "Her mom?"

I sigh, not really wanting to get into it. "Died about nine months ago."

"I'm sorry to hear that." He frowns but doesn't ask for any more details. "Well, can I get you something to drink before I throw you to the wolves?" His eyes alight with mischief, and I get the distinct impression that this guy and trouble used to be best friends.

"Sure, how about a beer."

"I get the feeling you might need something stronger. How about some Rock Hard Whiskey?"

I chuckle. "That sounds good, thanks."

He begins making the drink and a sliver of light casts over the bar when the door to the outside opens. I turn to look over my shoulder and see a guy I'd put at about Dane's age come through the door wearing jeans and a flannel shirt, gray sprinkled throughout his beard. He saunters over to the bar and braces his hands on the edge.

"Charlie wanted me to stop in here and make sure you guys were still good for dinner out this Saturday night."

Dane turns and looks at the guy over his shoulder. "Did you check with the boss?"

"I was just across the street, and she wasn't at the bakery. Sydney said she had to run out to deliver something to Mr. Fitzgerald as a favor."

Dane scoffs, pouring the whiskey over the ice in the glass. "I think Mr. Fitzgerald just likes checking out my wife's ass." He looks at me over his shoulder. "Mr. Fitzgerald is eighty and the town pervert."

I laugh as Dane slides the glass over to me. "Thanks." I raise it and take a sip.

"Garrett, this is Killian. New in town. He's taking over the law practice and popped in for the club meeting. Has a six-year-old daughter."

Garrett chuckles good-naturedly and shakes his head. "Good luck to you, my friend. Brace yourself for the teenage years."

I cringe. "So I heard." I push up off the stool. "Well, it was good meeting you both."

Garrett nods and Dane points at me. "When you're done at the meeting, pop across the street to my wife's bakery, Mad Batter. Grab something to bring home to your daughter. Tell Ava I sent you and I'll get bonus points in the bedroom tonight." He winks.

I smile at him. Maybe small-town living will grow on me. Everyone's already been so welcoming to my daughter and me.

I nod. "Thanks, I will."

With my drink in hand, I head over to the group of guys I'm hoping I can form a friendship with and will help me navigate life as a single dad.

CHAPTER TWO

Sydney

I GLANCE AT the clock for the thousandth time this shift. Twenty minutes until closing, thank God. Since I guess no one wants baked goods today, the day has passed by slowly.

It's not that I mind working at Ava's bakery—quite the opposite—I'm thankful to her for giving me a job when I couldn't find one in my field after I graduated college last spring, but at twenty-two I'd hoped to be doing more by now.

I've lived in this small town my whole life and I thought I'd be living in a big city somewhere making my mark on the world. Instead, after graduation, I found that there were zero job prospects and ended back in Climax Cove, working at my stepmom's friend's bakery.

And as if that wasn't enough, I broke up with my boyfriend last month after finally realizing that the guy was a lying, deadbeat loser. I've tried to keep my chin up, but it's been hard. Life is just not going the way I pictured it. My friends Chloe and Sasha keep telling me I need to move on, forget the jerk all together, and believe me, I want to. It's not that I'm pining away for him or anything, it's just that I live in a small town, and I've known every guy in this town since they were picking their noses.

I'd love a little fun and adventure but instead I'm stuck here serving cupcakes and cookies day after day.

Until the bell over the door goes off.

I say a small prayer hoping it's not my dad again. He was just in here looking for Ava and of course the conversation turned to what I was going to do with my life. Which always pisses me off because my dad should know it's not like I'm not trying to find a job in my field.

I come out from the back of the bakery, fake smile in place to help whoever is there and stop when my eyes meet with a pair of eyes that resemble the color of spring grass on the mountains that surround this town.

A man stands there. A man I've never seen because if I had, I'd definitely remember him. He's older than me by close to a decade, dark hair, and a trace of a five o'clock shadow. His snug-fitting Henley makes it clear he works out. His jeans aren't the kind most of the men in town wear—worn and looking like they've had them for years. No, his are different, designer if I guessed and it's clear this isn't your typical small-town guy.

"Can I help you?" I ask, stepping up to the counter.

His eyes take me in, roaming from my face down to my waist where his view is cut off by the counter. My nipples pebble in my bra, and I'd put money on the fact that he notices because his tongue darts out of his mouth licking the bottom lip, and he clears his throat.

"Is Ava around?" His voice is deep and rough, not the cultured voice I'd expected by looking at him. Something about that juxtaposition makes the apex of my thighs tingle.

"She won't be back today. Can I help you with something?" Though I didn't mean it to, my voice sounds a little breathy, like an invitation.

He shifts in place. "Uh, yeah." He clears his throat and swallows hard. "Dane said I should stop by and grab something to bring home. Said whatever I pick won't disappoint."

"Oh, does your wife have a sweet tooth?" I glance down at his left hand. No wedding ring or tan line.

"I'm not married."

"Girlfriend?" I arch an eyebrow.

I'm being completely transparent, but I don't care. Not even a little. This man walking in here is the most exciting thing to happen to me all year. I'm not going to waste the opportunity the universe granted me.

He shakes his head.

Interesting.

Then I remember what day it is. A day I'll always remember.

"Were you just at the Single Dads Club meeting?" I lean forward and rest my chin in my palm and don't miss the way his gaze strays down the V-neck of my T-shirt.

"Yeah." He clears his throat again and pushes his fingers through his thick hair.

I wonder what it would feel like to run my own fingers through his hair. If I'm lucky, I'll find out.

"Anything here you feel like tasting?" The words hang out there for a moment before I straighten up. "In the display... I can give you a sample if you want to try before you buy."

Again, his tongue slides out and licks his bottom lip. "How about you pack up some of those cookies that say Eat Me?"

I'm not sure if he meant for it to sound like an invitation or not, but I accept.

I've always believed that life is short, and to take happiness where you can find it. Plus, they say the best way to get over someone is to get under someone and this man will do just fine.

"I'm Sydney, by the way." I reach out over the counter and he gives my hand an extra squeeze before letting go.

"Killian. Good to meet you."

I grab one of the pink boxes with the Mad Batter Bakery company logo on top and use the tongs to place his cookies inside. "New in town?"

The color in his face deepens and the shyness is endearing as hell. "That obvious?"

I shrug as I set the tongs down and close the box, handing it over to him. "It's hard not to notice someone new in town." I walk over to the other end of the counter to ring him up and he follows.

"I'm taking over the law practice down the street." He gestures in that direction with the hand not holding the box.

A lawyer. Didn't expect that. In fact, I didn't know lawyers could be so hot.

After he pays, he stares at me for a moment.

It's now or never. He's about to walk out of here, and though it's not like I'll never see him again—this is a small town—it won't take long for the rest of the single women in town to sink their claws into him.

"What are you doing right now?" I blurt out, not sounding near as nonchalant as I'd hoped.

He stills and his hands tighten on the cardboard box, indenting it on the top. "I was going to go home and give these to my daughter." He raises the box of cookies.

"Any chance you might want to grab a drink across the street? I'm off in"—I glance at the clock—"five minutes."

His face goes blank for a moment and my own heats. God, maybe I misread the signals. Maybe he's not into me at all.

"Never mind," I stammer. "I was just—"

He steps closer to the counter. "I want to. I do, it's just... I'm old enough to be your father."

I huff out a laugh. "Not quite. I'm twenty-two and I'm guessing you're what... early thirties?" He nods. "You'd have to have been having sex before you hit puberty to be my dad, Killian."

The corners of his lips tip up. "I'm still eleven years older than you."

"Is this reverse ageism at play?"

He chuckles, some of the tension leaving his body. "You know what I mean."

"It's just a drink. Not a lifetime commitment."

He thinks about that for a moment and then nods. "Yeah, okay. Let me tell the babysitter. I booked her until later tonight because I didn't know how long that Single Dads Club meeting was going to be."

"All right. I'll meet you over there. Order me a rye and ginger." I wink.

"Will do, Sydney." Something about the way he says my name hits me in the center of the chest, but I brush off the feeling. "See you in a few."

He turns and disappears out the door but not before I get a chance to check out his ass which I'm happy to report is fantastic.

CHAPTER THREE

Killian

TWO HOURS FLY by.

It's obvious Sydney must spend time at Happy Daze because we arrived right when Dane was leaving for the night. He said hello to her by name and studied us for a few seconds which I could have chalked up to being a small town and everyone knows everyone, but he gave her a look like I often give Caprice when she pretends she's going to stick her tongue out to me.

I mean, they can't be an item. Dane said his wife, Ava, owned the bakery. It probably is that Climax Cove is a small town and everyone knows everyone and their business. Something I hadn't considered when I'd agreed to have a drink with her. Not to mention there's clearly an age difference between us.

After we'd had a couple of drinks, she asked if I could drive her home. Apparently, she'd walked to work for the exercise this morning. I'd stuck to beer so that driving wouldn't be an issue, so what was I going to say—no?

Besides, I enjoy her company and she's the first female besides Caprice that's made me laugh in a long damn time. I don't want the night to end, so I agree, trying to wring out every last drop of time with her.

She directs me to her place which is housed in a small complex on the edge of town. My guess, based on the size of the place, was there are only six apartments or so in the building. I pull my Range Rover into a spot facing the building and look at the path leading to the entrance. It's lined with hedges and isn't very well lit because the large trees on the grass to either side hang in front of the two light poles framing the pathway.

"I'll walk you to your door." I unclick my seat belt and remove the keys from the ignition.

"You don't have to do that. It's fine."

I look over at her. "I realize I'm not in the city anymore, but I'm not letting the woman I spent my night with walk down a dark path by herself, and I'm certainly not leaving until I know you're safe inside your apartment."

A small smile graces her plump lips and she nods, pushing open the passenger door.

We walk side by side down the path, not saying a word but every so often our fingers brush against the others and the odd, now foreign to me, sensation like being plugged into an electrical socket hits me. I know without a doubt that if I ever take this woman to bed, once will never be enough.

I shake my head, trying to clear the thought from my mind as we come up to the main entrance of the building.

"What?" Sydney asks, her head tilted to the side.

"Nothing." I can't think about taking this woman to bed. I've just landed in town, I have responsibilities, and not to mention, she is *way* younger than me.

Still, I can't deny the pull I've had to her all evening. From the moment I saw her really.

"Thanks for some good conversation tonight." Her voice is soft and breathy.

"Thanks for the invitation. It was nice to be out of the house for once." She stares up at me expectantly and I push a hand through my hair, not knowing what to do.

Our gazes hold and she takes a step forward, pushing her hand into my hair. Her fingers follow the same path mine did moments before.

I freeze. "What are you doing?" I wheeze out. When her chest is close enough to brush mine, it takes everything in me not to let myself reach out and wrap my arms around her, dragging her closer. I fist my hands at my sides instead.

"Earlier today, I was wondering what it would feel like to run my hands through your hair."

Blood rushes between my legs and my dick hardens. "Sydney…" Words lodge in my throat. Logic tells me to push her away, that nothing should happen between us. But my heated blood thrums through my veins and whispers that she's of age and we are two consenting adults, what's the harm?

"Yes, Killian?"

"You should use your keys to go inside."

Her gaze holds mine. "Am I going in alone?"

"I shouldn't," I answer truthfully, but my voice is raspy and lacks any real conviction. "My daughter is at home and I'm not in a place to put any energy into a relationship right now. We just moved here and—"

She puts her finger over my mouth, cutting me off. "I'm not looking for a list of excuses, Killian, and I'm not looking for a commitment. I'm looking for someone to get lost in tonight. I'm looking for an orgasm."

My cock painfully presses against the seam of my jeans. I consider my options—leave and go sit in an empty house by myself for a few hours since Caprice is already in bed or stay and have sex with one of the most beautiful, enticing women I'd ever met.

Maybe it's weakness or maybe it's something far simpler. Maybe's it's that I haven't been laid in such a long time and I'm horny as fuck, but my answer surprises even me.

"How does two orgasms sound?" I reach out and palm the back of her neck, dragging her forward.

"Perfect," she says and wraps her arms around my neck.

I bring my lips down to hers and she immediately opens for me, moaning low in her throat when our tongues touch for the first time. I squeeze the back of her neck with my hand and deepen the kiss, groaning when she pushes her ample breasts into my hard chest.

One of her hands escapes my neck and starts snaking down my chest toward my groin and I pull away.

"Inside. Now."

She doesn't balk at my authoritative tone. No, I think she likes it because her eyes dance and she grins, biting down on her bottom lip with her teeth. Turning from me, she fishes her keys from her bag and unlocks the door, leading me inside.

I follow behind her as she takes the stairs to the second floor and leads me to the apartment at the end of the hall. She fusses with the lock for a minute and I come up behind her, gripping her hips and bringing my lips to where her collarbone meets her neck. She tilts her head to give me better access and her hair slides away, revealing more skin.

Everything about this woman is primed to drive a man insane. From her big doe eyes and her luscious curves to her sarcastic wit and the scent of her skin. It's like she's been developed in a lab with the sole purpose of making me lose my mind. Because that is exactly what I'm doing by being here but fuck it.

In for a penny, in for a pound. I'm here and I'm going to make the most of our night together.

Finally, she manages to unlock the door and I follow her inside. I take a brief look around, seeing pretty much what I expected to—the apartment of a woman in her early twenties. Lots of pictures of her and her friends, mismatched furniture and lots of shoes by the front door.

I don't bother looking long because my gaze is immediately drawn back to Sydney when she unbuttons her pants.

"You don't waste time, do you?" I take a step closer to her.

"I've been imagining this for hours. And I'm kind of impatient." She pulls her shirt up over her head to reveal a lacy black bra.

There is no way I can keep my lips and my hands off her any longer, so I take over for her, kissing her while I work to unclasp her bra and drag the straps down her arms until the lace cups reveal her pebbled nipples.

Holding the weight of her breast in my palm, I brush over one nipple with my finger before lowering my head and tracing the outline with my tongue. Her hand fists in my hair and I repeat the act on her other breast, then work to shimmy her pants down. She toes out of her shoes and helps me to get them down the last bit.

I stand back at my full height and take Sydney in. She's gorgeous beyond belief, and it's all I can do not to bend her over the couch and drive into her. But I'd promised her two orgasms.

While one hand cups the back of her neck, I slide the other one down the front of her black lace underwear to find her soaked.

"This all for me?" I arch an eyebrow and she nods, biting into that damn bottom lip of hers again.

My finger coasts over her already swollen clit, and she jolts at my touch. I use the hand at the back of her neck to keep her looking at me while I do it again. Her eyes drift closed for a moment until I roughly say, "Look at me. Watch me while I make you come."

Sydney's eyes snap open, and she does as I ask. I can tell it's a struggle for her to keep them open when I push a finger inside her, and then another. When I use my heel to apply pressure to her clit, again her eyelids slide closed for a second, but pop back open a second later as though she remembered my directive.

I drag my fingers in and out of her, fucking her until I think her knees might give out. Her forehead is creased and has a thin sheen of sweat by the time she explodes around my fingers, and I have to move the hand at her neck to her waist to keep her from collapsing to the ground.

"That's one," I say with a cocky smirk.

She looks at me with sated lust and I know if I allowed myself, I'd drown in those eyes.

Chapter Four
Sydney

AFTER THE WORLD'S most mind-bending orgasm, I lead Killian to my bedroom, thankful that I tidied up before work today.

I sit on the bed and look at him for a moment. His deep green eyes are hooded with lust, and an erection strains the confines of his designer jeans. Even though I just came harder than I ever have before, I'm desperate for him to be inside of me.

I reach up and begin to undo his jeans. "It seems unfair that I'm basically naked and you're still fully clothed."

His fingers thread through my hair on the side of my head and he watches as I pull the zipper down, his grip tightening when I rub a hand over his thick length.

Before he lets me shimmy his pants down, he reaches for his wallet in his back pocket and removes a condom wrapper from inside and tosses it casually onto the bed. I'm immediately turned on from how confident and sure he is, as though there isn't even a question that he'll be using it.

I mean, I'm practically naked and undressing him, but still. This man exudes power and strength and it makes me want him all the more.

He pulls his Henley over his head while I work to shimmy his pants down past his knees, and when I look up to grab the waistband of his boxers, I notice his bare upper half.

Guys my age have nothing on this man. He is fit as fuck, and his broad chest and muscled abs cause my mouth to hang open. I want to run my tongue over all the dips and curves of his chest and explore each one in detail.

But it's clear from the expression on his face that Killian is as eager as I am to be inside me.

"You going to finish the job?" He nods down to where my hands are still wrapped around the elastic of his boxer briefs.

"It's just... you're so hot." I feel every bit his junior when the words leave my mouth, but his answering chuckle takes off some of the sting of my embarrassment.

"Coming from the hottest woman I've ever seen, I'll take that as a compliment."

His compliment warms my chest, but I push aside the feeling. I cannot afford to get sentimental about this. This is a hookup, plain and simple.

I draw my gaze from his and watch his erection spring free when I pull his boxer briefs down. His hard length sways back and forth, and I'm near giddy at the fact that soon that girth will be between my legs.

I've had a number of sexual experiences in my twenty-two years, but none with a man of his size. I'm not scared though. I'm so wet for him I don't doubt that the feel of him moving inside of me will be enjoyable.

"I want you inside me," I tell him.

"What the lady wants, the lady gets." He bends and reaches for the condom wrapper, ripping it open while I make my way up the mattress.

I lie on my back waiting for him, and once he pulls the condom down his length, he makes his way closer to me.

"Oh, this gives us all kinds of possibilities," he says.

My forehead wrinkles for a moment, unsure what he's talking about, but he's looking beyond me to the wall and then I realize he's talking about the mirror.

Last month I found a large mirror at the thrift store and mounted it on the wall behind my bed to look like a headboard. I haven't yet been with anyone sexually in my bedroom since, and I'm just realizing that not only did it look like a cool décor piece, but it also makes having sex in my bed a lot more interesting.

"I can't be the only one to enjoy the view." Killian places his large hands on my waist and flips me over so I'm facedown on the mattress. Then he uses those same hands to tug my ass up and his erection brushes against my ass cheek. I practically purr.

When I push up on my hands and raise my head to look straight in front of me, my insides clench. Killian is in the mirror behind me, meeting my gaze. He glances down at my ass in front of him and appears torn on whether he wants to watch me in the mirror or in person.

"Please, Killian." I'm not above begging. I am desperate to feel this man push into me.

With one hand on my waist, he grips the base of his cock and rubs the head through my slick folds. A groan escapes me and my hands fist the comforter. Then he lines himself up with my entrance and slowly pushes in.

All the air leaves my lungs in a rush as I stretch to fit around him. Inch by inch he makes progress, pushing in and then letting me get comfortable and then pulling out and pushing in a little further.

Once he's all the way seated inside, he holds himself there. I don't think I've ever felt this full. This desperate for movement.

"You okay?" he asks.

I nod, meeting his gaze in the mirror in front of me. When our eyes lock, he pulls out and slides back in slowly. The muscles in his chest and the little of his abdomen I can see flex with the effort. Again, he withdraws slowly but this time he slams back into me and a sound leaves me. He does it again.

Before long I'm a writhing mess and he has his hands in my hair, holding it in a makeshift ponytail to anchor himself while he picks up the pace. He gravitates between watching us in the mirror and where we're joined but I keep my eyes on our reflection in the mirror the entire time.

His face is intense and brutal looking. My tits sway back and forth every time he pummels into me and my core tightens around him in preparation for an earthquake of an orgasm. Killian must feel it too because he leans forward and brings his hand around in front to apply pressure to my clit.

With just a few circles of his fingers, I detonate and explode into a million pieces, like stardust. I buck a few times as the orgasm takes over every cell in my body.

"Fuck you're beautiful when you come."

I have no energy to respond, I'm so spent. I can only watch as he uses one hand to apply pressure to my back so that I go down completely onto my front on the mattress. I angle my hips up and his hands are on either side of my shoulders as he continues fucking me.

This position hits me differently inside, and before I know it, I'm coming all over again while he lets out a near roar, stilling inside me and jerking a few times. His face is slackened when I look in the mirror, and I watch him pull out of me and roll over on his side.

He places a possessive hand on my ass cheek while he lies on his back, me on my front, both of us trying to catch our breath.

"That was three," I murmur.

His head turns to the side, forehead creased.

"Three orgasms you gave me."

He chuckles and rolls my way, placing a chaste kiss on the back of my shoulder. "I couldn't help myself." Then he rolls back the other way and stands from the bed. "I'm going to go take care of this condom."

I don't say anything but instead just lie there enjoying the peaceful, sated feeling for as long as possible. The truth is that in my head, I'm already bummed that there will be no repeat of what we just did.

He comes back in the room, and when he doesn't join me, I roll over onto my back and see him standing just inside the door. He looks uncomfortable and pushes a hand through his dark hair. "I'm sorry to do this, but I have to go." He glances at the expensive watch on his wrist. "My babysitter is only there for another twenty minutes."

If I'm honest, I'm a little hurt even though I shouldn't be. I mean, this was a hookup only. I made that clear. So what if he has to leave so soon?

"Sure, yeah, of course." I try to keep my voice more casual.

He makes his way over to the bed and leans down with one knee on the mattress. "I'd prefer to stay here all night, get to know what you taste like, watch you come around my cock again, but I can't."

Killian looks guilty as he leans in and gives me a slow kiss. When we part I thread my fingers through his hair briefly. "It's fine. Really."

He presses his lips together and nods. I watch as he gets dressed, and I grab the robe off the back of the chair in front of my desk, slipping it on. Then I walk him to my apartment door where we both stand there awkwardly for a moment.

Finally, I say, "Well, guess I'll see you around town."

Something flashes across his face but it's so fast I can't be sure what it was.

"Yeah, thanks for a fun night," he says and leans in, placing a chaste kiss on my cheek.

When he turns and leaves, I force myself to close the door rather than watch him walk down the hall. The click of the lock sliding into place feels so final that I rub at my chest on the way back to my bedroom.

There's no reason to feel melancholy about how my night went. I was blessed with a third orgasm, so why do I feel as though I'm missing out on something more?

CHAPTER FIVE

Sydney

THE FOLLOWING WEEKEND, I'm back working a shift at the bakery on my own, daydreaming about where I was a week ago—in bed with Killian.

I haven't seen him since he left my apartment, and if I'm being honest, I'd hoped that I'd have run into him by now. It's surprising I haven't. Climax Cove is a small town to begin with and add on that he works down the street.

But I can't fault him for not reaching out. I made my intentions clear that I was only looking for a good time, not a "happy ever after" and that's still the case. It's just… I find myself thinking about him a lot. More than I have any other hookup I've ever had. Remembering the way his dark hair felt through my fingers. Not even just physically, but our time at the bar as well. The way his green eyes sparkled from my innate sarcasm, or how he really listened to me when I talked about something.

I stand behind the counter, daydreaming about Killian and what it might be like to be with him again when my dad walks into Mad Batter.

Screech.

Kill libido.

"Hey, Dad. You picking something up for the boys?"

It would surprise me. He usually tries to keep both my half brothers away from sugar because at nine and five, they are prone to be hyperactive after any treat.

"You alone?"

Uh-oh. That line between his brows on the bridge of his nose is deep which usually means a parental lecture of some kind. I love my dad, and we have a good relationship, but he was the only parent for most of my life, until he married my stepmom, Charlie, almost a decade ago. And he's overprotective to a fault. Something that still grates on me today.

He scratches at his beard and that secures it—lecture commence.

"It's just me here. Ava usually takes today off unless there's a large order to go out at the beginning of next week."

He nods, lips pressed into a thin line. "I heard something… something I don't like hearing about my daughter." He raises an eyebrow and stares at me as if I'm physic and might know what the hell he's talking about.

"Are you going to tell me what you heard or am I just supposed to guess?" I cross my arms, already annoyed that he's still in my business at twenty-two.

He roughly shoves his hands in his jeans pockets and blows out a breath. "Heard you and that new lawyer in town might've… spent some time together."

Gross. My dad knows I hooked up with Killian? I guess I shouldn't be surprised, small-town gossip being what it is. I should be surprised it took an entire week. Still, even if this isn't exactly the conversation I want to be having with my dad, there's no way I'm going to back down and let him think that if he pushes me around, I'll come to heel.

"I think what you mean is that we slept together. How did you hear about that?"

His eyes widen for a moment as though he's surprised I'm being so forthright with the information, but he recovers quickly. "Someone saw you two making out in front of your building and then the two of you went inside. Doesn't take much to get tongues wagging. Word of it got back to Charlie who mentioned it to me when she asked if you had a new boyfriend and should we invite him to dinner."

Seems my stepmom and I will be having a little chat about information my dad does and doesn't need to know.

I shrug. "It's not a big deal."

"Not a big deal?" He pulls his hands from his pockets and takes a step toward the counter. "Syd, the guy hasn't even been in town for a week and you're sleeping with him? Not to mention he's practically old enough to be your father."

I roll my eyes. "God, you sound just like him."

Apparently, that's not the right thing to say because my dad's hands fist at his sides and the skin that's not covered by his beard gets red. "Sydney…"

"You're one to talk. I mean, you got my mom pregnant right out of high school and then you ended up marrying your best friend's little sister. You're not exactly a paragon of virtue, Dad."

He lets his head drop forward and pinches the bridge of his nose, something he's done many times before when he's trying to gather the patience to deal with me.

"We're not talking about me—"

"No, we're talking about me and I'm a grown adult now, Dad. I'm not some teenager who needs you to vet every guy I'm interested in."

His head whips up, and he narrows his eyes. "So, you like this man? You two are an item? He wants a relationship with you? Because he's a single father, Syd, with a young daughter from what I hear. A relationship with him isn't something you can take lightly."

I know he's right. I did. I never saw my dad with anyone the entire time I was growing up until he and Charlie got together when I was twelve. I don't know if he ever slept with anyone else or if he just kept anyone he saw away from me, but I can't imagine I would've been happy having women rotate in and out of my house.

"Well, you can relax, there's nothing going on between us. It was a hookup, that's all."

My dad cringes. "Christ, you're going to send me to an early grave, I swear."

I still. I hate when he says things like that and he knows it. I'd never known my mother and my dad is the only biological parent I have left. He must see from my expression that his words affect me because he motions for me to come out from around the counter.

I do, and as soon as I'm clear of the counter, he steps over to me and surrounds me in one of his big bear hugs. My dad is a big man, and whenever he hugs me like this, it makes me feel small, loved, and protected. He's the only man who's ever made me feel so safe.

Sinking into the hug, I squeeze him a bit when he says, "I'm sorry. I shouldn't have said that. I just worry about you, kid." He pulls away but keeps his hands on my shoulders. "You've always been so headstrong. I should've given up trying to tame you years ago, huh?"

We both chuckle.

"I know you're an adult now, Syd. I do, but no dad wants to hear rumors about his daughter circulating around town. I can't help but worry that you're going to get hurt or get in over your head."

I frown. "I'm not going to live my life for other people, Dad. You know that. But I am sorry you had to hear about me hooking up with some guy. You can relax though. We're not dating, there's nothing between us. We had an agreement before we… you know." I spare him the details.

A slight cringe crosses his face again and his hands drop. "I know you're probably hurting after you ended it with that douchebag last month, but you deserve only the best, okay?"

I nod. "Do you want any treats for the boys or did you really just come in here to warn me off the new big bad wolf in town?"

He rolls his eyes and chuckles. "Suppose I might as well grab something since I'm here. Charlie won't be pleased but I'll make it up to her tonight." He winks.

"Gross, Dad."

He laughs. "Payback, kid."

I shake my head. "Touché."

After I pack up my dad's order and he pays, he invites me to his place for dinner the following night, and I agree.

The afternoon goes by quickly as the store ends up being busy. It's close to closing time when I'm in the back making sure everything is ready for me to lock up when the bell dings.

I come out to serve the customer and stop when I see Killian there.

"Hey," he says, walking up to the counter.

He's in another Henley, a dark green that matches his eyes and in a different pair of jeans. More relaxed and worn than the ones he wore last weekend.

"Hey." I turn up the wattage on my smile and my nonchalance, but the truth is my heart is beating a fast rhythm in my chest. My memory didn't do justice to how good looking he is, or the power and authority that seems to radiate off of him. "Here to grab something for your daughter again?"

He looks a little sheepish for some reason. "I promised her I'll bring home some cookies after every meeting I go to."

"Okay, what can I get you?"

While I play "confident at casual sex" when we are together, the truth is I'm not exactly an expert. I don't know how to act in this situation. It seems like we're pretending it never happened, so I just go along with the act.

Killian gives me his order and I ring him through, sliding the box toward him across the counter.

"Thanks." He hesitates before he speaks again. "These aren't the only reason I came in here today." He lifts the box in the air.

My heart rate picks up to a sprinting pace from a slow jog. "Oh?"

He clears this throat. "I know we said it was just going to be a casual thing last weekend, but I'm wondering if you'd like to do something together."

My forehead creases. "Are you asking if I want to hook up with you again?"

He sets the box down and shakes his head. "I'm messing this up. No, I'm not asking that."

"So, you don't want to sleep with me again…" I ask slowly.

"No, I do… Fuck." He pushes his hand through that dark hair of his, and my hands ache to feel the silky strands again.

"I'm confused."

"I'm trying to ask if you'd like to go on a date with me. A real one. Not just a drink across the street at the local bar. But I get it if you don't want to. I know you said you weren't looking for a relationship or anything. And I have Caprice and…"

Something warms in my chest, and I resist the urge to rub my palm over the spot.

I'm shocked. Truly shocked. I mean, if he asked me to hook up again after my shift, I wouldn't be and truth is I probably would have said yes. But him asking me on a real date? I did not expect that. At all.

"Feel free to tell me no. I just couldn't stop thinking about you all week. And not just sleeping with you, although the image of you in that mirrored headboard of yours while I fucked you from behind is forever a core memory of mine now, but I enjoyed our conversation and I realized I want to get to know you better."

The way this man is so open about his feelings is foreign to me. I've spent most of my life trying to contain mine under lock and key.

It's on the tip of my tongue to say yes and then I remember what my dad said about dating him—he has a young daughter, he's in a different place in his life. He has his shit together and I most certainly do not.

But I do want to get to know him better. I've thought about him all week, too. One date doesn't mean we're going to get serious. Maybe we'll figure out we don't have much in common besides the way our bodies seem to fit perfectly together.

I know that's a lie the moment the thought flicks through my head.

There's a tightness in my chest and I realize what it is—fear. Fear that things could go right with this guy and then what will that mean, and fear that things could go very wrong.

But what's life without a little risk, right?

So, I straighten my back and look over at him. "I'd love to go on a date with you."

Let the adventure begin.

✧   ✧   ✧

Thank you so much for reading our story, The Perfect Distraction. If you want to dive deeper into the Single Dads Club world you can read Garrett, Dane and Marcus' story here.

piperrayne.com/single-dads-club

'Beard In Hiding' Extra Scene

Penny Reid

Dear Readers: This scene takes place after Diane and Repo's "the end." I'd originally planned to include it as an epilogue, but ultimately decided against the idea for . . . reasons. I hope you enjoy a quick peek into their travels and adventures. <3 Penny

✧   ✧   ✧

Many moons later

IT TOOK SOME time spent in the mirror, giving myself and my breasts several pep talks, warm hugs, and firm talking-tos, but—eventually—I left the safety of our cabin for the beach. Head held high, hands on my hips, I marched determinedly toward the water. Despite my fears, I didn't encounter a single soul on my way to the lounge chairs I'd watched Jason set up earlier from the safety of the cabin's balcony.

Apparently, we were well and truly alone.

See now, I wasn't against out-of-doors nudity. I was just against *my* out-of-doors nudity. Well, I supposed I had been against it, until today. But these travels with Jason while we'd been on the run from the law had broadened my horizons. I'd done all sorts of things I'd never considered proper, many of which had made me blush, and all of which I'd ultimately enjoyed.

"I will enjoy the look on his face, that's for sure," I muttered to myself, spotting the top of Jason's salt and pepper head where he reclined in the lounge chair.

I never thought I'd be interested visiting in a topless beach. But here I was, strutting around bare-chested as a jaybird—except of my sunhat and sunglasses—and loving every minute of it. Can you imagine? At my age?

Of course, we were the only two on the beach since it was our private beach for the next three weeks, but still. I felt very brave.

Jason was very brave as a rule, yet I didn't consider his presence on this beach particularly brave. He wore no shirt, but he was also a man with loose morals—very much a man with very loose morals—and thus likely hadn't needed to engage in any mirror pep talks before donning his swim trunks and meandering over to this white, sandy beach.

But, honest to God, may He have mercy on my lusty soul, I would not have Jason any other way.

A fissure of unease and excitement made my belly twist, and I modified my marching step to a tip-toed sneak. I didn't want Jason to know I was coming. He'd told me I could wear my bathing suit since we'd be alone, that there was no need to go topless if I wished to remain covered.

What I *wished* was to surprise the hell out of him.

The gently crashing waves of blue masked my sandy steps, the twisting in my belly becoming a lovely hum as I drew even with his lounger. Next to his sat mine, unoccupied. Some six or so inches separated the chairs.

Peering at Jason's bare chest, I loved that my beautiful man wore nothing but low slung swim trunks. All that delectable skin, sinew, and muscle glistening beneath the sun. My mouth watered as I covertly ogled him from behind my sunglasses.

I wonder if he needs more sunscreen. I decided I'd offer to apply it.

Giving our surroundings one more cursory scan, I lifted my chin higher, reset my hands on my hips, and glanced down at my breasts.

Hmm.

Sucking in a breath, I arched my back, lifted my chin higher, reset my hands on my hips, and said pertly, "Excuse me."

Jason opened one eye. He then immediately opened the other and both widened as they moved over my body. He looked hungry. I grinned.

"Is this seat taken?" I lifted one hand to from my hip and gestured to the lounge chair next to his with a very blasé movement. He'd placed both of our towels on it.

"Be my guest." His voice was a rumble and his mouth curved with a whisper of a smile.

I noted that his gaze never strayed from my nipples, and his eyes seemed both pleased and excited.

Well. That's the kind of reception a lady likes to see.

"Thank you," I said haughtily, hiding a grin. Walking around Jason, I was just about to sit down on the lounger when he grabbed the empty chair and pulled it flush against his.

"Sit," he said, patting the surface in what looked like an absent-minded movement, his stare still fastened unabashedly to my breasts. He licked his lips.

Making a soft *hurrumph* sound, I swung my hips and gave him the backside of my thong bikini bottoms just before I plunked down on the towel. I'd barely stretched my legs out in front of me before Jason had turned on his side, grabbed my hip, leaned over my body, and fastened his mouth to my nipple.

"Ah!" My body betrayed me, my back arching reflexively as his tongue swirled and tested. "Wait—Jason, wait a minute."

He didn't wait. In fact, the hand at my hip slid around to my mostly naked bottom, rubbed it possessively, and then gave it a hard smack. I moaned, a spark of electric longing running down and between my legs, twisting in my belly.

I'd discovered so many interesting things about myself during our travels. For one thing, I loved to camp. I never thought I'd be the outdoorsy type, but it turns out I was.

Additionally, I loved spicy food. Really, really spicy food. Our trip to Nepal had opened my eyes to the different types of cuisine I'd been missing while sequestered in my tiny Tennessee town. I had no idea goat and spicy gravy tasted so delicious.

Also, I loved to be spanked. I'm not talking about repeated smacks, over and over. But one, well-timed, firm wallop to the backside instantly flipped my sexy switch.

It had all started when we visited an adult toy shop and I purchased a book on sexual positions and female pleasure. Obviously, since most of my mature life had been spent cowering under a cloak of shame, I was now curious about what else I'd been missing. Jason made everything so easy. I felt comfortable asking him to try new things, positions and such, and he never made me feel silly or stupid.

I really shouldn't have been surprised that Jason smacking my buttocks drove me crazy. Everything he did, every single thing we'd tried thus far seemed to turn me on. But right now, I didn't want to be turned on. Not yet.

I wanted to play first.

"Jason," I said his name on a sigh, my fingers pushing into his hair to soothe him. "Wait a minute. Slow down."

I'd also learned quite a lot about my sexy travel companion over the last few months. For one thing, he'd been very reluctant to spank me at first, but with gentle and persistent coaxing, he'd finally relented. Also, Jason loved it when I played with his hair. It instantly relaxed him. *Usually.*

Still feasting on my breast, his stroked my backside one more time before trailing his hand around to the front of my bikini.

I grabbed his wrist, panting. "Hold on. I want to play—"

He twisted his wrist, skillfully catching hold of my hand and bringing both his fingers and mine into the waistband of my bikini bottoms. I gasped, more than ready.

"Play with yourself," he scraped out, touching my body just briefly. He then leaned away, removing his fingers and folding them behind his head. Eyes blazing a trail from my legs to my lips, he said, "I'll watch."

Narrowing my eyes at his posture, I wanted to pout. This kind of playing hadn't been what I had in mind. I'd wanted to play with *him*, not have him watch as I toyed with myself.

Well now, Diane. You're an out-of-the-box thinker. Maybe you could do both?

Smirking to myself, I nodded. He wanted to watch? Well then, I'd give him one hell of a show.

Removing the hand he'd placed in my bikini bottoms, I hooked both my thumbs around the waist band and slipped them off. His eyes flared even as he frowned.

"What are you doing?"

"Playing," I said sweetly.

Laying flat on the lounge chair, I bent my knees and brought the backs of my ankles to my bottom. I then let my legs fall open and I trailed my fingertips up my stomach to my breasts. They must've taken my pep-talk seriously, because they felt amazing in my hands, heavy and sensitive. I squeezed, pinching my nipples between a thumb and forefinger, tilting my hips and moaning.

"Fuck, Diane." He moved as though to reach for me.

I caught his hand and winked at him. "Ah-ah-ah. Not your turn to play yet."

Jaw tight, he withdrew, but didn't return his hands behind his head. Instead he kept them clenched in fists on his stomach. That made me want to laugh. But I didn't.

Instead, I returned the task at hand. Namely, giving myself pleasure. You better believe I was an expert at self-pleasuring, what with that year spent engaging in little else, when I'd been determined to unlock the secrets of my body, secrets my upbringing and my ex-husband had labeled shameful.

But none of that mattered now. The waves crashing in the distance, the sun soaking me above, the light breeze tickling my skin, and my man's hungry eyes on my glorious body—that's what mattered.

Palming my breasts again, I closed my eyes and gave myself over to the sensations, the smell of suntan lotion, the salty taste of the sea air, the heat within me. Moaning, I walked my fingers down my body, tilted my hips again, and slid my middle finger home.

I heard a rustling sound and I cracked an eye open just in time to see Jason's swim trunks be tossed to the side. And I opened my mouth just as he reached for me, his expression broking no argument this time, though—sorely—I was tempted to argue. I was tempted to make him wait, draw it out, make him desperate.

But I wanted him too much, and so I let him turn me onto my stomach and climb over me from behind, his knee spreading my thighs wide, his hand coming to brace himself above my body as he bent and whispered in my ear, "You are a fucking tease, woman."

"I am?" I tried to sound innocent even as I lifted my bottom in the air. "How on earth will you punish me?"

A low chuckle rumbled out of him, the sound cut off as he pushed inside, becoming a growly grown. He found his rhythm and reached around my body, his fingers lightly circling my clit, playing with me like I'd barely had the chance to play with myself.

"You're so wet," he said, voice low and dark as he pumped into my body. "Have you been thinking about me? Hmm? Thinking about this?"

I nodded, my movements jerky. I was having trouble holding myself up on the lounger, his forceful thrusts knocking me off balance. I loved it. I loved how aggressive he was sometimes, just as much as I loved how soft and slow he was at other times. I loved how he simply wanted to go down on me and asked for nothing in return, and how his eyes always filled with wonder whenever I went down on him.

I also loved how he held me after—each and every time—and how those moments were just as sensual and fulfilling as what we were doing now.

"I want you riding me, gorgeous. I want your tits in my mouth." He gave me a quick and hardy smack on the fleshy part of my ass, making my sex clench and a moan erupt from my mouth.

My limbs were shaking as he pulled out and rearranged us—him beneath, me on top—lifting me with strong, capable arms and bringing me down to receive him. Jason's head pressed back as I took all of him, a gasp catching in my throat. His half-lidded stare blazed over my body. He lifted his torso as he lifted my breast, sucking it into his mouth and tonguing it roughly.

I cried out, losing my rhythm as he repeated the action with my other breast, using the pad of his thumb to give the new wet nipple less than gentle strokes, just how I liked, causing the first electric shivers of my orgasm to race down my spine.

"I like this view." His voice was gruff, his lips and teeth and tongue assailing my skin, making me tense with desire. "I want this view every damn day for the rest of my damn life."

My labored breathing meant I couldn't respond. I was so close. So close. I just needed—

Jason reached between us and pressed his thumb against my clit, then tapped it, then circled it, and then repeated the series of touches until I cried out, my body locking, my nails digging into the flesh of his broad shoulders.

"That's right, gorgeous. Come for me. You know I love how your greedy pussy comes on my cock."

He didn't stop. He just kept stroking and rubbing my clit as my body tensed over and over, paralyzed with pleasure. And he took control, thrusting upward with brutal, fast strokes, forcing me to hold on and take it, take all of him. I came and I came, my head whipping back, my throat hoarse and raw as the last of my cries was lost to the crashing blue waves in the distance.

He must've reached his pinnacle as well—though I wasn't mentally present for it—because he captured my lips with a voracious kiss, a sweet something he always did after his own climax, like he needed to be closer, like he wanted to merge our bodies into one, never to be separated.

Spearing my fingers into his hair, I fisted and tugged the strands, returning his avaricious kisses with my own, hoping he felt the thundering beat of my heart and knew it was for him. It was all for him.

Goodness, how I loved and adored this man. Yes, I loved and adored the pleasure he brought me, and the journeys he took me on, and how me kept me safe and took care of me.

But, honestly, all of that was secondary to the wonder of himself. His wicked intelligence, his creative, fascinating take on topics I used to think were boring and cumbersome. He made every day an adventure, whether we sat inside and read books or made passionate love on a topless beach.

How on earth had I gotten so lucky?

And what on earth would I do without him?

Hopefully, I'd never have to find out.

✧   ✧   ✧

Penny Reid is the *New York Times*, *Wall Street Journal*, and *USA Today* bestselling author of the Winston Brothers and Knitting in the City series. She used to spend her days writing federal grant proposals as a biomedical researcher, but now she writes kissing books. Penny is an obsessive knitter and manages the #OwnVoices-focused mentorship incubator / publishing imprint, Smartypants Romance. She lives in Seattle Washington with her husband, three kids, and dog named Hazel.

Come find me –
Website: http://pennyreid.ninja

The Whitney

Alta Hensley & Livia Grant

CHAPTER ONE
Dex Cohen

I 'LL HAVE YOUR car brought around to the front portico, Mr. Cohen. We'll have your belongings loaded up for you as soon as you're ready to leave. Welcome back to The Whitney."

"Thanks, Terrence. I appreciate your help, and it's good to be back. The hotel looks as good as ever."

I pull a fifty out of the pocket of my jeans and hand it to the head bellman. His broad grin does little to bolster my sour mood.

After the heavy door to our suite slams closed, I beeline it to the wet bar. I have a four-hour drive ahead of me, but that doesn't stop me from pouring myself a shot of bourbon.

"You plan on picking up a DUI today?" My father's booming voice fills the room from the doorway.

I throw back the shot, enjoying the slow burn as it goes down to my empty stomach before he can stop me.

"I'm twenty-one now. It's legal," I counter rather lamely.

I half expect him to give me shit, so his request of, "Pour me one," catches me off guard.

Not one to look a gift horse in the mouth, I take the opportunity to pour two more shots before turning and meeting the old man near the couches.

Taking his shot, he waves his other hand toward the open chair. "Have a seat."

We've done nothing but argue for the last two weeks, so I'm not really in the mood to go another round.

"I need to get on the road before rush hour."

"Sit." It's an order. No one, including me, ignores an order from Hans Cohen.

After taking my seat, my father raises his glass. His "Salute," is followed by a fast downing of the high-end liquor.

I follow suit, more than happy to get in another shot before I head back to college where cheap beer will be my daily beverage. It's just one of the top-ten reasons why I tried to get out of returning to campus this fall. I learned all the damn place had to offer. I belong in NYC, next to my father, living at The Whitney, and learning the only business I care about from him.

He doesn't agree.

We sit in silence long enough I start to wonder if the old man is losing it. I'm about to push back to my feet when he picks up a previously unseen folder from the cushion next to him and tosses it across the coffee table to me.

I pick it up, slowly opening the folder. Inside is a stack of paperwork with a single photo of a pimply-looking kid on top. He looks vaguely familiar, but I can't place him.

Glancing up at my father, I silently wait for him to explain. I don't have to wait long.

"You know Sebastian Rossi?"

It's a stupid question. The man is only one of the most notorious art thieves across multiple continents. He's damn near royalty in my father's world having *acquired* multiple pieces previously thought to be theft-proof for his exclusive clients. For the right price, he is said to be able to deliver almost any piece of art. That he's never been convicted makes him a legend in my father's circles.

Since NYC has no shortage of high-end pieces for his acquisition, he's been my father's guest at The Whitney more times than I can count.

"What's this kid have to do with him?"

"I know you don't want to return to Harvard for your senior year. You've made it clear to me that you think spending another year there is a waste of time, but like I told you when we chose your school, there's a lot more at stake than grades and graduation. Not only are you gaining the education to take our financial enterprise to a whole new level, more importantly, you've done well making dozens of connections with some of the most influential families in the country."

He pauses as a small kernel of satisfaction sparks in me. My father is a hard man, and his little speech is as close to a compliment that I've gotten from him in a long time.

I don't have much time to enjoy the feeling as he continues on. "This year, I'd like you to shift some of your focus to this young man."

I glance back down at the kid's picture, a feeling of dread growing. I'm not a fucking babysitter.

"Who is he?" I ask again.

"He's Sebastian's illegitimate son and technically the heir to his extensive estate. As you know, the Rossi family is practically European royalty. Sebastian's extra-curricular activities aside, he is the head of his extended family now that his grandfather died, and while he has three daughters with his lovely wife, and many nieces and nephews who will fight to carve up the legitimate side of the family wealth, he is hoping to mold this young man into a worthy heir for his more lucrative acquisitions business."

Trying to read between the lines, I still have no clue what my father is asking me to do.

"And what does this have to do with me?" I ask.

"His name is Atlas Giannopoulos. His mother is part of a wealthy Greek shipbuilding family. Her father was less than happy when she turned up unwed and pregnant at seventeen. She got sent off to London and has raised Atlas there, trying to keep him sheltered from getting sucked into either the Rossi or Giannopoulos family dramas, and for the most part, she's succeeded.

"Sebastian has provided for them financially over the years, but he made paying for the kid's college education contingent on him studying in the States, away from his mother, in hopes of molding him into a proper Rossi, if you get my drift."

So, he really is asking me to fucking babysit.

"And let me guess. He's going to be a freshman at Harvard this fall." I don't pose it as a question. I don't need to.

"I know this is a heavy ask, but you need to look at this as an excellent opportunity to solidify not only my relationship with one of our best clients, but more importantly, for you to build your own partnership with not just one but two very powerful families. Sebastian came to me to specifically ask for our help. You've obviously done something right because you're on his radar and he chose Harvard for his son, not because of the school's reputation, but because you will be there."

Conflicting emotions war inside me. The idea of having a fucking freshman on my coattails all year makes me dread returning to campus even more than I did an hour ago. Still, that Sebastian Rossi has specifically asked for my help and is trusting me to mold his son's education helps that earlier kernel of happiness grow into real pride.

A reluctant sigh escapes as I ask, "And what is it exactly Sebastian would like me to do with the kid?"

My father's gaze pins me as he answers. "Turn him into a man. Apparently, his mother has coddled him. Sebastian needs to know if the kid has what it's gonna take to inherit the darker side of his business or if he needs to start making alternate plans."

My old man doesn't realize it, but he's just paid me another compliment. He has ridden my ass so hard all summer, I've become resentful because he's still treating me like a fucking kid. Clearly, if he's asking me to turn the Rossi kid into a man, he's indirectly saying I'm now a man in his eyes.

I mull the request over before I poke for more answers. "Anything more specific? Does this kid even know I exist or am I supposed to be pulling his strings from behind the curtain?"

"I'll let you ask those questions of Sebastian in person. I gave him your contact info. He's arriving in Boston tomorrow and will be in touch."

My pulse escalates. I've had dinner with the man many times over the years with my father, but he's paying me yet another compliment by trusting me to meet with Rossi alone.

Before I can ask any more questions, my father adds, "Not only is this an opportunity for you to build on our business relationships, but I transferred the fifty grand Rossi offered for your help into your personal account this morning. It sounds like it's just a down payment for your assistance. Depending on how the year goes, there could be more coming your way at the end of the year."

I know how lucky I am. Money has never been something I've been short of. Still, as a twenty-one-year-old, I won't turn down an extra 50K in my personal account. It will help me upgrade from cheap beer to high-end bourbon for my senior year.

Funny. I'm suddenly much less apathetic about the coming semester.

CHAPTER TWO
Dex Cohen

IT'S LATE. I needed to be on the road hours ago, but the little talk with my father was too important to cut short. Glancing at my watch, I curse, knowing rush hour traffic is easily going to add an hour to my trip back to my off-campus condo in Cambridge, just outside Boston.

I rush out of the elevator as soon as it hits the ground floor of The Whitney. My friends at school give me shit for living in a hotel but, honestly, I wouldn't have it any other way. It's all I've ever known, and glancing around at the opulent lobby, a wave of homesickness hits and I haven't even left yet.

One more year and then I can stay home at The Whitney for good. I've put in three years already. If it were up to me, I'd drop out and just stay in the city to work full-time alongside my father in our family business. But despite turning twenty-one over the summer, my father reminds me often that staying home or going back isn't up to me, and this morning's revelations about my added goals for the year only make it more important for me to return to Harvard.

"There you are! I was afraid you'd left without saying goodbye."

The feminine squeal belongs to Sara, one of the many front desk receptionists at The Whitney. Little does she know, I had absolutely planned on leaving without seeing her again.

I feel her grabbing my forearm, pulling me to a stop in the middle of the grand lobby. I made the mistake of fucking her once at the beginning of summer break and she hounds me for repeat performances every chance she gets. While not the biggest problem in the world, I prefer to do the hunting when it comes to sexual encounters.

"Hi, Sara. I don't really have time for long goodbyes today. I should have been on the road a couple hours ago."

"But I thought you said you were going to come down to say goodbye last night when I got off shift," she pouts.

I hate clingy women. The only thing that has kept Sara in my good graces is she's never tried to bring emotions or commitment into the equation. She's only interested in being my fuck buddy... and there's a part of me that respects her for that.

"Yeah, well, I was busy packing my shit to leave today." I try to pull my arm free again, but she's determined.

"Well, lucky for you, I just went on my lunch break. How about you let me send you off with a smile on your face?"

This little partnership of ours has more than run its course, but regardless, I am a healthy twenty-one-year-old man. While I have no problems finding women to fuck when I'm in the mood, finding partners who don't have an ultimate goal of getting a ring on their fucking finger is starting to get a bit harder.

I glance at my watch. It's already too late to get out of the city before the Friday afternoon exodus north. Why the hell not.

I grab her hand, pulling her into motion toward the elevator, nodding at the bellman we pass on the way there, a grin on his face as he knows exactly what we're up to.

Only when I push the button to the tenth floor does she finally complain. "Why are we going to ten? Why don't you ever take me to your suite?"

Hell, if I'm going to tell her, it's because she works for the Belov side of The Whitney and my suite is in the Cohen part of the hotel. We may do business under the same roof, but our clients and employees do not co-mingle. Ever.

"We only have time for a quickie, that's why. Do you want to do this or not?" I ask, ready to walk away if she bitches anymore.

"Fine." She pouts as the doors open to the tenth floor. I know every detail about what happens under the roof of The Whitney and that's how I know the housekeeping team is long gone from this floor, leaving the large supply closet locked and closed. When we get to the door at the end of the hall, I take out my master key and open the electronic lock with a quick swipe.

The houseman had left the lights on and, for a brief second, I worry someone is still working on the floor, but the shelves are fully restocked with linen, towels, and cleaning supplies. All personnel should be gone until the turndown team comes back in a few hours. The lingering smell of a cigarette hangs in the air, no doubt from one of the employees smoking on their break.

Wasting no time, I throw my backpack to the floor and grab Sara by her biceps, pushing her to her knees in front of me. The grin on her face reminds me how much the little whore loves rough treatment, just another reason I haven't kicked her to the curb already.

My fingers are on my belt, unbuckling it and yanking my jeans and boxer briefs down in a fast motion. My cock is already expanding, looking forward to the unexpected treat Sara's mouth is about to provide.

Like the greedy little slut she is, she lunges forward just as I thrust my hips, filling her throat with my growing erection in the first plunge. My low groan of pleasure is involuntary as Sara puts her tongue to good use on the underside of my shaft.

Carnal pleasure pushes all other thoughts out of my brain. My hips move in a fast rhythm as I chase my growing orgasm. If I wasn't such a dick, I'd slow down and try to reciprocate some of the pleasure, but I never said I wasn't an asshole. And anyway, I've played this game with Sara often enough to know that she's already got her hand up her skirt, flicking that little clit of hers so she's ready to explode herself by the time I shoot my wad down her throat.

Several minutes pass where the only sounds filling the room are the slapping, gagging, slurping, and groaning brought on by the blowjob in action.

Close to my climax, I've closed my eyes, but the unmistakable sound of something falling on the other side of the rack of linen has my eyes flying open. Are we not alone?

Sara must have heard it too because she's trying to pull her face away from my body. But I'm too close to coming, and I realize I don't really give a shit if one of the housekeepers sees us in action. Every one of them knows who I am and the power I hold here at The Whitney. It would be career suicide for them to complain.

A few long seconds pass without any more noises. I've almost convinced myself I was hearing phantom sounds when a flicker of movement catches my attention from behind the rack of clean linen.

I smile. Knowing we have an audience only enhances my pleasure as Sara continues deepthroating my shaft. The rhythmic gagging along with her regular gasps for air push my desire higher.

It isn't until I see the jet-black head of hair in the opening that I start to worry about who our spectator might be. My suspicions are confirmed when none other than Katja Belov, only daughter to the man in business with my father, pops up higher, clearly trying to get a closer look at the sexual favor already in progress.

Fuck. I pause my thrusts, my cock still shoved down Sara's throat.

Katja is just like family. She's too innocent and naïve to have a front-row seat to a blowjob. Hell, she's the closest thing I'll ever have to an annoying baby sister, as well as an angel in my life.

We should abort. I know it, but I'm so damn close to shooting off I hesitate, giving Sara the chance to gasp for a few breaths.

I keep my eyes trained on Katja's location until she pops up again. This time our eyes meet in a heated gaze from across the room. Eyes wide, her cheeks are pink with embarrassment, betraying just how innocent she really is. My brain shouts to put my dick back in my pants, but it's no surprise to find that my brain is not in charge… my dick is, and right now, it's throbbing with the need to come.

I'm just starting to pull my hard-on out of Sara's mouth when Katja sticks that pink little tongue of hers out to wet her lips unconsciously. Even with a few feet separating us, I see her eyes glazing over with a soft sexuality that in that moment feels like my kryptonite.

Seconds later, I see her panic at being seen by me, erasing the beautiful submission I saw seconds before—and I hate it.

When she glances away, eyeing up the door as if she's going to run, I grind out one word.

"Eyes."

Perhaps Sara is looking up at me from her knees, but I'll never know because Katja has obeyed my order. It's easy to forget that I'm supposed to feel brotherly toward her since she's broadcasting nothing but raw sexuality through those big green eyes of hers.

Our gaze is intense. When she tries to glance away, I shake my head, silently warning her to stay still.

It's a fascinating feeling to have one woman sucking my dick while making love with another woman in my head, but I don't even try to deny that's what I'm doing. I've always known Katja was going to be a beautiful woman one day, I just didn't know that day was today.

I know I only have a few minutes before she'll bolt from the room, so I decide to see how far I can push my luck.

"Touch yourself," I order, gazing directly into Katja's eyes.

They widen as she realizes I'm talking to her. It's tempting to reach out and yank the linens from the shelf between us. I don't want anything hiding her from me, but I also know she'll run if I take away her cover. Regardless, I know she's following my orders when that pretty mouth of hers forms a perfect O and her eyes flutter, glazing over with a beautiful wave of innocent bliss.

Just knowing her fingers are touching herself—and at my demand—has ropes of cum shooting down Sara's throat in seconds. The sound of her gulping me down almost covers the quiet whimper coming from behind the linen as I enjoy watching Katja close her eyes while she clearly enjoys her own orgasm.

Time stands still for a few long seconds as all three of us recover from our exertions. I'm watching Katja's face as Sara demands from her knees, "Okay, it's my turn."

Her voice ruins the moment and I'm stuck there watching as Katja emerges from her sexual haze and bolts for the door. It's stupid, but I want to call after her for some reason. To explain to her that Sara means nothing to me, but then I realize how stupid that sounds. Katja's just someone I've grown up with. I shouldn't have feelings—especially sexual—for her either.

But as I make my excuses and ditch out, like an asshole, without reciprocating in any way, I know it's a lie. I do care about Katja, like a brother should, except the feelings barraging me as I finally start my long drive to Boston don't feel very brotherly.

It's a good thing it will be a few months before I see her again. Maybe by the time I return to The Whitney, I'll get my head screwed on straight again.

Or maybe not...

✧   ✧   ✧

Are you ready to walk through the doors of THE WHITNEY?

I'm the villain in this story... and there is no happily ever after.

Her family's empire is an illusion, a fairy tale built on deception and treachery.
Now the princess of Manhattan royalty has made a fatal mistake.
She betrayed me.
She will regret the day she turned me into her enemy.

Dex and Katja's story begins with DEVIL'S CONTRACT.
altahensley.com

Trauma

Julia Kent

"HOW DO YOU recover from trauma?" I asked, the question more rhetorical than direct.

But it made him tense. Of course it would.

We were naked in bed, sweaty and slick after making love, my rumpled hair stretched across his chest as Tyler frowned at me, the tuck of his chin brushing stubble against my shoulder.

"Huh?"

"You look like your nickname, Frown."

"Not my fault I have resting bitch face, Maggie."

Wrapped in his arms, I was safe. *We* were safe. The question, though, was anything but, and I knew it. That didn't make me stop myself from asking it, though. Some questions had a mind of their own.

Some words had to come out.

My fingertips traced a line along the maze of one of his tattoos. It stretched from wrist to shoulder, a beautiful, colorful mandala, with twists and turns, geometry bleeding into art and coming back to sharp lines, a visual feast.

So complex. So shocking. It reflected Tyler's heart.

He didn't answer me. The man was an economy of words in human form. All I got was a short sigh, almost a huff. I licked my lips and inhaled deeply, enjoying our earthy scent. Soft cotton sheets the color of a faded lemon twisted around our legs, the late-September heat wave reminding me why New England was so fickle in the fall.

Give it another week and we would need down jackets. Gloves. Wool hats.

And air as sharp as knives would cut through our lungs like, well...

Like trauma.

"How do you recover from trauma," he muttered, the words coming out as a pensive commentary, less question and more koan.

"Wrong time?" I ventured, wondering if asking that kind of question after making love was smart. We were two broken people, but had found a way to unbreak ourselves in bed. Nude, scared, unflinching and willing to take the chance, we'd used vulnerable sex as a way to claw ourselves back from the half-dead into a more secure spot in the world, in each other's arms, clinging like we would lose gravity if we let go.

Sometimes, catching Tyler after great sex was the only time a portal to his emotions cracked open enough to get him to talk.

Sometimes. Not always. The man was an enigma, after all.

"Thinking," he said as his arms bulged, flexing, then loosening, as if his body had its own idea about how to answer me.

We'd been together for two years, and at this point I had learned to live with the single-word answers. Tyler didn't think in words. They weren't his first language.

Music was.

Sex came in at a close second.

His arms tightened around me. "You okay?" he asked.

No. I'm worried.

"I'm fine," I said, the words finally no longer a lie. "Just because I'm over the worst of it doesn't mean there isn't residue."

That got me a slight huff of laughter.

"No shit."

Colors along his skin ranged from red to yellow, orange with touches of green in the beautiful rainbow-like tapestry of his arm. It hurt to get that tattoo, I knew. But there was so much beauty in the hurt he'd endured.

Just like trauma.

Unlike abuse, though, he'd *chosen* the tattoo. Selected the design. Made the decision to push through the pain to find the pleasure.

Choice *mattered*.

Tyler hadn't chosen to have a fuckwad for a father. Hadn't chosen to have his loving, if ineffective, mother die of cancer when he was eleven. Hadn't chosen when he was thirteen for one of his father's drug-dealing associates to—

No.

I wasn't going to let that invade my mind right now. Trauma had a way of re-traumatizing you if you thought about it too much. It was self-validating, desperate for attention, because it feared being forgotten more than anything else.

If you didn't think of the trauma, was it real? That was the central issue with it. Trauma was both victim and mindfuck, both survivor and tormenter, because it couldn't stop inserting its own memory into you at the worst of all times, because even trauma didn't believe the abuse had happened.

Poor trauma. Until you made friends with it, held it, tended to its wounds and listened to it, trauma would be a feral animal trapped deep inside you, shoving its way into your mind.

You had to constantly think about it to keep it alive, to make sure it wasn't swept under the rug. But thinking about it *hurt*.

Balance was what we needed. How do you find balance when all you know is pain?

Tyler was my balance. I was his. That was a start.

"I think," he said, his words vibrating against my ear, where I rested my cheek along his neck, "that when we go through bad things, the bad thing becomes part of us. And then we make everything worse trying to make it *not* be part of us. It just is. Makes us who we are."

"What do you do when you have two different pieces inside you fighting, one of them trying to accept it and move on and one of them still shattered and in denial?"

"That describes my life, Maggie."

"Not anymore," I corrected him, stroking his arm with a broad touch. His fingers found my bright electric-blue hair. I felt a smile change the contour of his face against my cheek. For a guy whose nickname was Frown, I sure could make him smile more than he should.

Which made me feel like a goddess.

"You heal," he whispered. "You heal as much as you can, and then you get damn lucky and find someone like you."

As I tipped my head up to give him a kiss, I heard shrieks outside my window. Not the kind you worry about.

Screams of joy from undergrads partying on this otherwise quiet Saturday night.

I worked as a residence hall director, and Tyler was here with me at this small college in the suburbs of Boston, spending the night. He was used to noise, and so was I. You work at the university for long enough in this field and you know instinctively what to tune into and what to tune out.

Those were happy undergrads. Years ago, I was one of them.

Until...

His eyes caught mine, transformed into a black hole, the kind you want to draw you in, where you wish you could disappear and explore, leaving everything you know behind.

"I want to crawl inside you, Maggie. I want to find every piece of trauma in you, collect it in my arms, stuff it in my pockets, grab a bag and fill it with everything that hurt you, and then haul it out of you, set it into a big pile and burn that motherfucker to ashes."

My throat tightened, tears forming a sheen on my eyes that surprised me.

I knew enough from professional classes and trainings that Tyler and I had done something called trauma bonding. It wasn't technically true, because we hadn't experienced the actual traumas at the same time or with each other, but the technicalities didn't matter.

Trauma bonding *fit.*

Our relationship had forged its identity through sharing each other's trauma in conversations and confessions. Tyler really, truly had healed me by making love to me for the first time since I had been gang-raped as an undergrad so many years ago, and I provided him with an unconditional love that he'd never experienced in his abusive, dysfunctional home.

I had crossed thirty-one and he was six years behind me, our music career surprisingly, pleasantly successful, though still small. Yet underneath it all we were two wounded people.

Broken people.

Broken didn't mean destroyed, though. You could break something and make it whole again. It would always have cracks, but as Leonard Cohen said—that's where the light comes in.

Tyler and I were each other's light.

Maybe the damage wasn't raw and weeping, but the scars were there. Scar tissue stands out. It's tight. It itches. It makes sure you know it's present, even when the scars are on the inside.

Or *especially* when the scars are on the inside.

"Something happen to make you talk about this?" he pressed.

"Nothing specific. Thinking about life," I whispered, kissing him, the act one of simple faith that he wouldn't reject me. Faith that he wouldn't hurt me.

Faith that the freedom to kiss him was always there.

Faith like that *sustains.*

He kissed me back with an urgency I didn't expect, heat burrowing up inside me, all of my bare skin against his begging for an answer to a question that he had just unleashed.

A question without words.

"You," he said as his knee parted my legs and his hand moved to touch me until I gasped with pleasure. "You have me now," he said, eyes narrowing, combing over my face as if he were memorizing me. "And I have you now, Maggie." His throat spasmed, and he shook his head slowly, eyes still on mine.

Tyler's intensity was heavy. It was a privilege to have the weight of it in the air between us. No one else got to see that his intensity existed.

Only me.

Only *me*.

Do you know what an honor that was?

"No one's ever going to hurt either of us again. As long as we keep being together."

"And talking our way through," I whispered back.

He looked away and rolled his eyes. In a rare show of language-based emotion, he used a fake voice to parrot me. "And as long as we keep talking about it and processing it, it loses its power."

His words were ones I'd used a thousand times.

"It's true."

"I know. Hate that it's true. Hate that I suck at talking, and that's the best way to heal. Hate that my limitation is strongest in the place inside me where I'm weakest. Not a good fit, Maggie. Not a good fit. I wish I could be as eloquent as you."

"Me?"

"You know how to connect your heart to your mind to your mouth and use all three together to get better. I don't."

That was the most I heard Tyler say to me in ages, our naked bodies rubbing away the tension that never really left. When he was all out of his limited inventory of words, he used touch to tell me how he felt. And yet touch was incendiary for us both, a tool used by malevolent forces in our separate lives to control us. Hurt us. Use us.

Turn us into objects.

Touch, though, was a way to reclaim our personhood. When we were together in bed, we set the rules.

We saw each other's humanity.

We connected with *love*.

Love is the biggest *fuck you* to people who try to unfairly control others.

And that *fuck you* is an act of faith, too.

"You see me," I whispered, not knowing where the words came from. "You really see me."

"I see you because you let me see you, Maggie. And I'm grateful for it. Grateful that you chose me. I don't know what kind of man I'd be without you, but I know that because I *am* with you, I'm a much better one. You don't just make me want to be a better man for you. You make me want to be a better man for *me*."

Emotion thickened his words. "I don't know how to be in this world. I know how to hold a bass. I know how to let a song come out of my head through my fingers. I know how to get dressed and eat and go about my day. I know how to talk to people when there's nothing but screaming behind my eyes the entire time. I can barely stand it, but I can do it now. It's not like that all the time anymore. It used to be."

His erection pressed against my leg. Having sex right now felt like a shortcut. We needed to talk more than we needed to thrust and moan and lose ourselves in ecstasy.

It would be easy. We could go somewhere else in our bodies, push our skin and nerves with wet and wild lust to the far reaches of their capacities, sending waves of endorphins through us to ground each cell, to give a new vibration so we could shiver our way to exhaustion in an uncertain world.

Tyler's words, though, were more rare than sex, more healing than endorphins. We needed to heal.

Healing was an act of love.

An act of belief.

An act of *will*.

But more than that—it was an act of defiance.

Laughter poured into the air like honey, the group outside so casual, so free, goofy and silly. They knew nothing of our pain. Their freedom had nothing to do with our oppression. So why did I hate them in a flashpoint of emotion?

"I hate that," Tyler said, as if reading my mind.

"What?"

"*That.*"

As if on cue, someone outside laughed hard, a boisterous and free sound that made Tyler sigh.

"Exactly that," he said. "I don't know what it's like to laugh like that, Maggie. I used to get really angry at people who could. Hatred's still there, but it's way less. Now I just appreciate that they can. I'm glad it's out there somewhere in the world. Maybe someday I'll touch it again. I think I had that, you know, when I was little. Real little. Before things went bad with my mom and dad. Before Dad started dealing and doing drugs. Before Mom got cancer. Before she died. When me and Johnny were best friends, before he turned into a meth head who stole everything from me."

He never talked about his younger brother, Johnny.

Ever.

A long, grainy sigh came out of him, full of all the repressed emotions he'd spent years covering up. In his family of origin, once his mom died, it was lethal to show emotion.

Literally.

So different from my own upbringing. My mom and dad were happily married. Dad was a lawyer, Mom a software engineer. We grew up in a nice suburb of St. Louis, and my sister, Lena, was now a lawyer, too.

Guilt permeated every cell of my body, every string in my soul's harp when I thought of how different our childhoods had been.

And yet here we were, both scarred, both searching. If damage were a person, it would be a loner. We were two loners who sensed each other, finding common ground in something no two people should ever share, but often do:

Being violated.

He cleared his throat and continued. "Those years before weren't great, but they were good enough, you know? Good enough to remember what it was like to be a kid who could just laugh like that. Sometimes I think that's what the screaming inside me is. It's just that little kid trying to get out so he can laugh."

"I want to hear you laugh," I confessed, as if I were transgressive. As if I were asking for something forbidden.

"Jesus, listen to me," he groused. "Lying in bed with this luscious, gorgeous woman, and all I can do is talk about how fucked up I am."

"I want to hear you laugh," I insisted, driven by the thought, the need, the impulse to watch Tyler being free. Unchained. Unraveled by laughter, so joyful, so unlike any other version of him I'd had the privilege to know.

"What're you doin'?" He grunted as I took my fingers and ran them softly up his ribs. He twitched. "Cut it out, Maggie!"

"I want to hear you laugh."

I went for it. Using just the right amount of pressure where his ribs met his armpits, I tickled him until he started gasping and making something close to a giggle sound.

It occurred to me then that I had never heard Tyler giggle. I'd heard him chuckle. I'd heard him laugh in surprise. I'd certainly heard him moan and groan and grunt in sexual pleasure.

But never, not once in two years of being together, had I heard the man giggle. Now I had a new goal.

"Maggie!" he said, trying to grab my wrists, but I was too quick. "Cut it out!"

"I want to hear you laugh."

"Maggie." His voice carried a tone of low warning.

"What're you going to do to me? I'm naked in your bed, Tyler, and I'm tickling you. You can't threaten me."

"Oh, yeah?"

I found myself flat on my back in under a second, Tyler's hand hovering right over my armpit.

"You wouldn't!"

Moonlight glinted off of his eyes. They twinkled, his mouth turned up in a smile. Oh, that smile. I'd unlocked some piece of him only I could see.

That made me a goddess, for real.

And then he tickled me until I giggled so hard I nearly peed.

His eyes flared with desire, the perpetual frown on his rugged face turning to marvel.

"Maggie, your tits look fantastic when you laugh. They just bounce, up and down, and up and down, and up and down," he said as I gasped and moaned from the sheer torture of what he was doing to me. So much stronger than I could ever hope to be, Tyler had me fully pinned down and at his mercy. There was nothing I could do. The tables had been turned.

"Please," I gasped. "Stop."

He did.

"Thank you for acknowledging that consent is a thing."

"Says the woman who just tickled me without *my* consent."

I had to think about that one for a minute. "You're right. I'm sorry. I never should've done that."

"It's okay," he said, pulling me back into his arms, though now my skin was so sensitive and my lungs felt like I had gone for a brisk jog. "I know why you did it," he said.

"Because I love you."

"No matter how many times you say it, that never gets old."

"I really do want to see you laugh, like the little boy inside you," I murmured against his chest.

"Me too, Maggie. Me too."

"You will."

"A long time ago, I didn't think I would." He kissed my temple. "Being with you makes me see it's possible."

"I didn't think I'd ever have sex again," I whispered. "Because of you, I did. I *do*. And it's joyful. Good. Everything I want it to be. Not just because it's good sex.

Because it's good sex with *you*, Tyler. When you make love to me, you literally *make* love. You create love. You infuse it in my body. I invite you in and ask you to go through every part of me and make love *in* it."

"That's the nicest fucking thing anyone's ever said to me."

He kissed me then, whole and full, his tongue parting my lips, his hands roaming everywhere, grabbing my ass, sliding up my hip, cupping my breast, touching and finding, tracing and owning.

Lost in the kiss, I heard laughter outside again, on the campus common, a place where students should be free. Wild abandon belonged there.

My anger dissipated. Good for them.

I was happy they were happy.

It felt good to cheer on someone else's joy.

Tyler's mouth spread against mine in a smile. "I love you so much, Maggie. What did I ever do to deserve you?"

"You deserve everything good in life, Tyler. And if I'm good, then welcome to good."

"You're more than good. You're great. You're *perfect*."

"Let's be great together," I whispered as I reached down to grasp his greatness. "Perfect together."

He inhaled sharply. "That whole *make love* thing?" he asked. "That thing you said I do in your body?"

"Yeah?" I squeezed gently, stroking up until I heard him hiss again.

"How about you show me how you do that? Make love *in* me, Maggie."

"You, uh, want me to use a strap-on?"

"No." The word sounded strangled.

And then he laughed.

It was a tinny sound, injured and a bit painful to hear, but it was a laugh.

"More!" I cried out, clapping.

"I think if I have enough love in me, the laughter comes next."

"I think you may be right."

"The pain's never going away," he said slowly. "When I was a kid, I thought it would. It doesn't. It's always there. Like a scar."

I laughed through my nose, a sad sound that made him tenderly stroke my cheek. "We talk about scars a lot, don't we? Scars are roadmaps. They're history books. They're diaries on your skin."

"Like tattoos. Except I chose the tat. Didn't choose the rest. God, if I could go back in time, I'd choose anything but what life gave me."

"I was just thinking the same thing," I confessed. "How you choose pain when you get a tat."

"The pain is nothing. Marking myself is how I tell all the people with control over me that they lost."

"I never want to mark you, Frown." I used his nickname on purpose and got a big smile instead.

"Too late. You did. Your love is everywhere on me, Maggie. *Everywhere*."

"That's the nicest thing anyone has ever said it me, Tyler."

He held me close.

"Good. *Good*, Maggie. Because you're the best thing life has ever given me."

"I try."

"You succeed."

"You're making me horny, Tyler. Quiet achievement with brooding loners is my love language."

A tiny chuckle came out of him. Another success.

"See? Perfect, Maggie. We can find our way through the trauma because you're so perfect."

"No," I said before kissing him. "We make our way through the trauma because we refuse to let it beat us."

"I love you more than ever because you believe that, Maggie."

"Then love me a lot, Tyler. Love me more than you ever imagined possible."

"I'll die trying."

"Die trying while we make love."

"*That*, I can do."

And so we did.

✧ ✧ ✧

Thank you so much for reading *Trauma*. If you'd like to learn more about Maggie and Frown, check out their book, *Random Acts of LA.*, a full standalone in the Random series by New York Times bestselling author Julia Kent. jkentauthor.com/books/the-random-series/random-acts-of-la

Slava Ukraini!

UNSTOPPABLE

BRITTNEY SAHIN

CHAPTER ONE

Washington, D.C. – *May 2023*

EMILY DROWSILY TURNED her head and snuggled her cheek against the cool pillowcase. She slowly opened her eyes to the early morning sunlight filtering in through the partially open wooden blinds. As soon as spring had arrived, Emily made a habit of leaving the blinds open a crack when she realized the sun was ahead of her alarm clock by a good ten minutes. Ten glorious minutes during which she and her handsome husband often enjoyed a hot morning quickie before they woke the kids.

So the strange aching sensation still lingering in her gut was worrisome. It had grabbed hold of her last night as she cleared the dinner table, right after Liam received orders he and Bravo Team would be spinning up today.

"Do you ever think about that day?" she whispered, unsure if he was awake, even though they were usually on the same pre-alarm-schedule.

"Which day?" Liam's voice was naturally husky and deep, but his morning voice inspired a whole new level of fill-me-up-buttercup and bang . . .

Fill me up, buttercup? What-the-what?

Emily blinked and redirected her attention to her husband. His short dark blond hair was messy in a sexy way, and his lids were still shut, hiding his ocean-blue eyes. "Hmm. Right. We've had quite a few of those kinds of days, haven't we?" She forced a smile, hoping it would hide her worry lines so he didn't see them when he did open his eyes.

Was she always nervous right before Liam operated? Absolutely. Emily had good reason to worry—he was a Navy SEAL. Add to that, he was an "off-the-books" elite operator. As Bravo Four, Liam, and the rest of Bravo Team, technically didn't exist. They answered only to the President and were sent on missions that were not only considered extremely dangerous, but almost impossible as well. Though one of those missions led to them adopting their daughter, Elaina, a few years ago and . . .

"I'm talking about the day you made me promise to—"

"Find love again if I bite the dust?"

"Not funny," she scolded, slapping the back of her hand against his broad naked chest. Eyes still closed, he snatched her wrist like a cobra striking its prey . . . such a hotshot. An easy smirk cut across his lips as he angled his head and finally parted his lids, then brought her palm to his mouth and pressed a soft kiss there, his tongue darting out to teasingly touch her skin.

"Why, my love, are you thinking about that day? You find some other charming Aussie-slash-American you want to trade me in for?"

Damn that sexy wink of yours. He might have been one of the world's best snipers, but he'd also nearly died on her once. Screw that promise—she'd never move on from him. Never. *But no, nothing will happen to you. It can't. But . . . shit.*

Liam frowned and slowly lowered her hand as she rolled to her side. "What's wrong?" His tone inched deeper into more serious territory this time.

"I have a bad feeling about something. I—I don't know why." She abruptly shifted upright and snatched the covers to her chest as she rested her back against the headboard.

Liam followed suit, then turned a little and reached for her legs beneath the covers to drape them across his body, situating her to face him. Well, this conversation had yet to "down, boy" his morning wood. He was hard as a rock beneath her legs.

"So, no before-I-spin-up sex, huh?" He cocked his head and palmed her cheek, smoothing his thumb in small circles there.

"I mean . . ." She wanted to. But her stomach was killing her.

A sharp line cut between his brows as worry grabbed hold of him now. "Fuck, babe. What's going on?" He paused for a second, analyzing her like he was outside the wire, downrange and searching for tangos in his line of sight.

Focused. Intense.

And while he was acting nervous at the moment, she knew her man wouldn't have anything but a steady hand and mind when on an op.

"I'll be back next week, whether the op is complete or not. You know I wouldn't miss Elaina's doctor appointment. And no fucking way some bad guy is gonna keep me from being there for our family. Okay?"

"You promise?" Maybe he was right. It was Elaina's appointment she was panicking about, and she was misplacing her worries, focusing on his impending mission because that was familiar. That was a "normal" fear she knew how to navigate. Worrying about the results of her daughter's MRI . . . no, not so much.

"She's going to be okay. If anyone would know if something is wrong, it'd be Elaina, right?" Liam captured both her cheeks between his big palms this time and tears filled her eyes.

Their 12-year-old daughter's biological parents were super geniuses, and hell, Elaina was even smarter than them. But Liam and Emily had quickly learned Elaina was gifted in other ways. She somehow just knew things. Saw things before they happened.

"These headaches though." Emily closed her eyes, her stomach banding uncomfortably tight. "What if that's why . . ." She couldn't finish that line of thought.

"The doctor just wants to rule everything out. She'll be fine. She's our Elaina. Unstoppable. Like me." Emily heard the smile in his voice, so she opened her eyes to verify it was there. Adorable and a little crooked. Her Chris Hemsworth look-alike hubby always knew how to calm her racing heart whenever her lawyer-brain took over and she began overthinking.

"Mommy! Mommy!"

Before Emily had a chance to say more, their almost two-year-old son, Jackson, flung open their bedroom door.

"Hey, sweet pea." She quickly erased the tears and shifted her legs free from her husband's lap when she spied Elaina out in the hall hovering near the door.

Jackson threw himself onto the bed, nearly tackling Liam, who played along and let himself be pinned down.

"I tried to stop him in case you two were getting in some of your early morning, um, cardio, but he beat me to your room," Elaina said, hanging back in the doorway.

Liam froze and pivoted his focus to Emily, his eyes wide.

Morning cardio, huh? Well, that's great. My daughter knows we have morning sex. Splendid.

Liam's cheeks stained red with embarrassment before Jackson began squeezing his face, smushing his mouth to make "kissy lips" as he liked to call them.

Chills scattered across Emily's arms as she got out of bed. "How are you feeling today? Any headache? Up for school today?"

Elaina had been missing school on and off since the severe headaches had begun about two weeks ago.

"I'm okay." Elaina shifted around Emily to peer at Liam lifting Jackson up and flying him through the air like he was Superman.

Well, Liam looked like Thor, the God of Thunder, so maybe Jackson was Thor, Junior. Liam's teammate, A.J. from Echo Team, even had a miniature Thor hammer made with Jackson's initials on it as a birthday gift last year.

"Good, good. But if anything changes at school, go to the nurse. Have her call me."

"You have court today."

"I don't care." Emily tucked Elaina's dark hair behind one ear, revealing one of her diamond studs. Elaina had bought them with the check her biological dad had sent her for her birthday in January. Elaina's mother had been killed years ago, but her father had chosen not to raise Elaina, which was his loss. Emily and Liam's gain.

Speaking of a check, that reminded her . . .

"Babe, can you do me a favor on your way out today?" Emily massaged the knot of tension at the back of her neck and turned to eye her husband now standing in only his boxers by the bed with Jackson clinging to his back, legs wrapped around his muscular abdomen.

"The check." Liam snapped his fingers. "Right. Yeah, I can deposit it on the way."

"The scanner thingy still isn't working on the app, and it's kind of a big check to leave sitting around." The most recent check Elaina's biological father had sent. This one had been for Easter, and she kept forgetting to deposit it into Elaina's account.

"Scanner thingy?" Liam laughed, and that sexy laugh of his had her regretting they didn't have time for a pre-spin-up quickie.

As if on cue, the alarm on her phone sounded. Liam shut it off and hoisted Jackson up and onto his shoulders. Super dad. "Let's get you kids fed and dressed, shall we?" He set a quick kiss to Emily's cheek as he walked past her but halted in his tracks when Elaina shifted before him and slapped a hand to her forehead. "Elaina, sweetheart?" He quickly set Jackson down, then braced both her arms, but Elaina immediately jerked back as if he'd literally shocked her, so he let her go.

Jackson rushed to Emily's side, obviously sensing something was wrong, so she lifted him into her arms. "Your head?"

Elaina held both palms in the air, breathing hard as she stared at Liam. Her lips parted but . . . nothing came out. "Pancakes," she whispered, slowly looking Emily's way as if she'd just made the hardest decision of her life. "How about pancakes for breakfast?" And then she abruptly turned and left.

"What just happened?" Liam turned to Emily, gripping the back of his neck, a puzzled look crossing his face. "Now I'm worried. Maybe I shouldn't go. Tell the President I—"

"You have to go." Elaina reappeared in the doorway, eyes dead set on Liam. "Well, to the bank. You need to go there. The one with the glass walls. It has lots of glass. Um, it's the one near the White House." She nodded. "Yeah, that's the one where you should deposit the check. I like that one." And then their daughter was gone again.

Emily blinked as her squirmy son began to slip from her arms.

Liam stroked his jaw, eyes contemplative. "Well, fu . . ." He let go of the curse at the realization that their son was still there. "I guess I'm needed at the bank today."

CHAPTER TWO

"THEY'RE TALKING ABOUT making a movie out of my life." Knox tossed a hand in the air from behind the wheel of his new GMC Yukon Denali. "Well, about my pops. But by association . . ."

Liam smirked, tucking away his worries from this morning to focus on Bravo Five who'd picked him up from the house a few minutes ago. Liam needed to give him a heads-up about Elaina's mention of the bank before they arrived there.

"Is that legal? Can they make a movie about your family while your dad is still in office?" Hell if Liam knew. But Knox's dad was the President of the United States and shouldn't he be entitled to some privacy? Or well, maybe that meant the opposite? He wasn't sure, but he wasn't thinking all that straight right now.

Liam had hated leaving Emily this morning, knowing she was a mess about Elaina's appointment, especially after Elaina's random bank comment, which of course, wasn't actually random at all.

"I'm not sure to be honest, but so help me, they better cast a good actor to play me." Knox lightly laughed and turned on the radio.

"We all know who will get the role of your old man." Liam shifted in his seat to better look at his buddy while they were stopped at a red light. "You think we can meet him?"

"Ha. You mean, if they hire my dad's doppelganger to play him? Denzel? That'd be about the only good thing to come from a movie about my family, I suppose."

Liam grunted at the thought of the actor who would most likely be cast to play the role of his "character." That was, if he made it to the big screen. He was one of Knox's best friends, so maybe. "Just don't let them hire *my* doppelganger. Don't need my wife fawning all over that man."

"Nah, brother, he's got nothing on you."

"Yeah, yeah. Sure." Liam set his fisted hands on his jean-covered thighs, trying to rally his thoughts. Would he be able to operate while worried about Elaina? Would he miss a shot? Get one of his brothers killed? *Shit.* "Eva's family," Liam blurted a moment later when the thought struck him. "If a movie is going to happen regardless, why not go to someone we can trust? You know, control the narrative."

Their team leader, Luke Scott, was married to a screenplay writer whose family was basically Hollywood royalty, and they directed and produced many of the major movies on the big screen.

"Good point. I'll mention something to my dad. And well, ask Luke to talk to Eva." Knox turned down the radio and quickly glanced at Liam. "You think Charlie Team is ready to operate without their training wheels?" he asked, quickly changing the subject. Charlie Team was a relatively new addition, established when it was clear that Bravo and Echo Teams were no longer enough to handle all the bad shit swirling around out there in the world. Plus, the new team would also be able to step in and give the others a break. "I sure hope Luke and Jessica can let go of their type A personalities long enough to allow the newbies off the bench and in the game."

Jessica, a former CIA officer, had been the driving force behind the creation of the off-the-books teams back in 2013. She and her brother, Luke Scott, who also served as Bravo One, had assembled the best of the best when it came to men and women who knew the intricacies of stealth operations. "Charlie Team is pretty green. I don't know if they should roll out without one or two of us on an op anytime soon."

"They were all Tier One guys before we poached them to our side. Maybe they can hang with the big boys. Or, even on their own without us."

"Glad you're confident because I may need one of them to swap places with me today. I don't think I ought to spin up." There was no choice really. His head would be elsewhere and that endangered the lives of his teammates.

Knox let up off the gas pedal for a moment. "What's wrong? Need me to turn around?"

Liam swiped both palms through his hair and shook his head. "Elaina's head-aches are getting worse. She's got an MRI appointment next week, and Emily is nervous. *But* no, we can't turn around."

"Shit, man, I'm sorry. You know she'll be okay though. No other option." Knox jerked a thumb over his shoulder. "So, why am I not turning around?"

Liam caught Knox's brown eyes for a beat. "Because Elaina said I need to go to the bank today. And she insisted it be this particular branch."

Knox's brows slanted inward. "That's pretty specific, even for her."

"Yeah, she doesn't normally, well, see things that aren't clearly connected to us in such detail. I'm not sure what to make of it. But she said I had to go before we spin up." Liam thought back to Elaina's words this morning and the desperate look on her face. "There are metal detectors at this bank, so we'll be rolling in unarmed."

"I can't see Elaina placing you in harm's way without good reason. I guess I should let my dad know we'll be running late?" Knox grabbed his phone from his pocket and tossed it to Liam. "Can you send him a text? Just say we're in heavy traffic."

Liam scrolled through his phone and found his dad listed as "Pops" and then sent him the message.

"We're here," Knox announced, pulling into a parking space in front of the bank a few minutes later. Damn, Liam hated walking into an unknown situation armed with only a check in his back pocket from Elaina's biological father rather than his rifle. Or at the very least, a knife.

"Why don't you stay out here?" Liam suggested. "Elaina didn't say you needed to come. Just me." What if something went sideways and he placed Knox in danger? No, he couldn't take that risk.

Knox scoffed. "Since when do we ride solo? Last time one of us went alone into something . . ."

Right. Nothing good ever came from solo ops. He was right. But that didn't make *this* decision the right call.

"We're headed into a bank, so I'm guessing we're going to be dealing with a robbery," Knox went on as though it'd be a walk in the park. "That's the only thing

I can think of, and I'm pretty sure you and I can handle some bank robbers. Even unarmed."

"It's your decision, man. But I don't need your parents or especially your wife kicking my ass if you get a scratch on that handsome face of yours." Liam winked, trying to dispel the shit feeling in his gut that had been there since Emily had cried that morning.

"It's okay. Both my left and right sides are equally camera ready. I can turn a cheek if needed." Knox grinned, flashing his white teeth, then they hopped out of the SUV as if it were a regular Monday. "Head on a swivel, brother."

Yeah, the last thing he wanted was for Emily to actually have to make good on the promise of marrying someone else if he bit the dust.

"This is definitely the place," Liam said, glancing at the walls of reflective glass after they'd passed through security. All that glass would be a nightmare for a sniper on overwatch if they needed an extraction.

"Looks okay so far. Do we hang around until some bad shit happens?" Knox asked in a low voice as they approached one of the lines to deposit the check.

"I guess so." This was the first time Elaina had ever sent him on an assignment based on her visions. Normally she only issued vague warnings or predicted if one of the teammates would be having a baby.

"Twelve innocents in my view here. Two kids. I don't like this," Knox added. "Maybe I pull the fire alarm and get them out of here before—"

"Too late," Liam said, as he caught sight of an armed man raising a weapon. One shot shattered the wall of glass at his right and caused the place to erupt in terrified screams.

"Six," Knox said under his breath, confirming Liam's nightmare. "Six armed tangos and pretty sure one is packing explosives."

"Everyone on the ground!" The masked man who'd just barked out the order had to be the leader of this pack of fuckers, and Liam wanted nothing more than to defy him and engage in a face-off. Instead, he gritted his teeth and took a knee but stopped when he saw that Knox remained standing. "You got a problem following orders?" the man growled out as he slowly approached Knox.

These assholes had to know a silent alarm had been tripped, and help would be on the way as they quickly fanned out, secured the entrances, tied up the two guards, and forced everyone facedown on the ground.

This was a hostage situation, one these guys had anticipated while they robbed the bank.

"You're going to let all of these people go," Knox stated in a matter-of-fact tone. "You only need me."

"What are you doing?" Liam hissed, looking up at his best friend.

"Him too. He needs to go." Knox tipped his head, angling it toward Liam, who huffed out a breath and stood up again despite the M4 aimed his way.

"Damnit, I know what you're doing, and hell no," Liam said under his breath as the armed man came closer. The whimpers of fear died down and silence surrounded them as everyone pinned their eyes on Knox in anticipation. There was a good chance a few people also recognized him. "Elaina wants me here," Liam reminded him.

"Who the fuck are you and what makes you so damn special?" The mask covered all but the man's dark eyes that held more than a hint of crazy. Liam wasn't so sure the guy would even believe the truth when Knox revealed it. His best friend wasn't accompanied by Secret Service or an entourage of security, as per his request.

Knox wasn't a typical President's son.

Knox lifted his chin, his jaw tightening as he held his arms out to the side. "Just getting my ID for you," he said as he slowly reached around to his back pocket, retrieved his wallet and casually tossed it at the robber's feet. No fear in Bravo Five. Typical. "I'm the son of the President of the United States. I'm Charlie Bennett." He paused to let the information sink in. "So, like I said, you only need me."

CHAPTER THREE

E MILY STARED AT the vending machine in the hallway at the attorney general's office where she worked. *Oreos? Probably not the best nine a.m. snack but . . .*

She inserted the money, then closed her eyes and waited for the Oreos to fall free from the metal clip. Elaina and Liam loved Oreos. They'd spin the tops and predict which side the cream would wind up on, and now, well, she wanted to cry again.

Her hands went to the glass as she tried not to have a total meltdown for everyone to see.

Don't worry, love. Everything will be okay, Liam had whispered in her ear before kissing her goodbye that morning.

No, not goodbye. Never "goodbye." Goodbyes felt permanent. It was always a "See you soon" kiss.

Emily opened her eyes, and her stomach dropped when she caught sight of a familiar face in the glass behind her. "Owen." She spun around to face one of Liam's teammates. Bravo Two. Second in command to Luke Scott. A former pilot before becoming a SEAL.

"The bank?" she asked, knowing that if any recognition flashed in Owen's eyes, then that was why he was at her office right now.

Owen nodded, but his gaze quickly shifted and Emily followed his focus to her admin exiting her office, her face pale. "Emily, it's all over the news. The President's son has been taken hostage at the bank right down the street."

Emily's knees went weak and Owen was at her nine o'clock within a second, assisting her to remain upright. She shouldn't have been surprised given Elaina's words that morning though.

"President Bennett's son negotiated with the robbers to release all hostages except for him and his friend," her admin went on. "Why doesn't he have Secret Service . . . and oh God, don't tell me his friend is your—"

"Liam," Emily confirmed.

"Come on, my team is outside the bank already. Luke sent me to get you," Owen said near her ear to keep from being overheard. "We need to go."

Did that mean Bravo Team planned to intervene? But how? They worked in the shadows. Never visible to the public eye. They wouldn't be sent into a bank with cameras all over them.

Emily snatched her phone from her office and they hurried out of the building.

"We need to go by foot. Traffic is at a standstill because of the hostage situation," Owen explained while on the move.

Before she could make sense of how fast everything was happening, her phone began ringing. "It's Elaina's school." She kept up her pace with Owen and answered, "This is Mrs. Evans."

"Hi, Mrs. Evans, we're calling to let you know that Elaina walked out of her first period class this morning. Quite abruptly and with no explanation. We tried to stop her, but she took off out of the building, and our security guard lost track of her."

Emily halted on the sidewalk and ended the call without a response. Elaina's school was only two blocks away, so she most likely had hightailed it on foot from school to the bank.

Owen pivoted at the realization she'd stopped in her tracks. "Elaina took off from school." She closed her eyes, trying to think, ignoring the surrounding foot traffic. "She has to be on the way to the bank. She knew Liam needed to be there this morning, but I don't know why she'd go," Emily quickly told him, opening her eyes, and Owen reached for her elbow.

"Only our guys would wind up in the middle of a bank robbery on their way to spin up," Owen grumbled, encouraging her to move again.

"I asked him to deposit a check, and Elaina insisted he go to that bank. She somehow knew he was needed, but there's no way Elaina would place Liam in danger if she thought something would happen to him." Although, Elaina's visions weren't always very clear, so she wasn't sure what to think. But like hell would she let Elaina blame herself if anything were to go wrong.

No, everything will be fine.

"Let's just say these bank robbers fucked with the wrong people," Owen bit out, his deep tone ringing clear despite the sounds of the city surrounding them.

The bank down the street was hard to miss with the flashing lights and media vans scattered everywhere.

Owen grabbed hold of her hand, and as he guided her through the crowd, she searched for Elaina. Her hair was down today, right?

"Have you seen Elaina?" Emily rushed out as soon as she spotted Luke's sister, Jessica, standing next to the open door of a black van. Jessica nodded and tipped her head toward the interior.

"She just got here. Pretty shaken up," Jessica said as Owen let go of Emily so she could climb inside the van.

Tears filled her eyes at the sight of her frightened daughter, and the fact that her husband was currently being held hostage inside a bank not even a hundred feet away. But Liam had been in much worse situations and he always pulled through.

Elaina had her feet up on the seat and her arms wrapped around them.

"Sweetheart." Emily scooted next to her and pulled her into her arms. "It was dangerous taking off from school like that."

Elaina lifted her chin and swept her dark hair away from her face to peer at Emily. "I had to come. I realized while in class that I—I needed to be here." She lifted her hand and pressed it to her forehead as if another headache was stirring. "I couldn't tell Dad. I'm sorry," she sputtered. "I couldn't tell him anything else because if I did, he would've died."

"Wait, what?" Emily whispered, her body tensing.

"He had to come though, or a girl and her mom would've died. But if I told Dad those details, for some reason that would have changed something . . . and *he'd* die instead." Elaina swiped a tear from beneath her eye. "I don't know how to explain it, but I could see multiple outcomes."

Oh my God. Elaina had never had such specific visions before, and she wasn't quite sure what to make of it. "Well, you didn't tell him specifics, so does that mean Liam will be okay?"

"I think so." She nodded. "But I didn't know Uncle Knox was with him. I didn't see that. I don't know why, so . . ."

Emily did her best to hide her fears, hating that she was sitting outside the bank helpless. "It's okay. Everything will be okay. They're unstoppable. You know that."

"Hey."

Emily turned to see Luke outside the open door. "The President can't negotiate," he began in a low voice. "It'd set a dangerous precedent, and Knox would have known that. *But* he is going to let us join SWAT and go in and extract our guys. We'll be masked and suited up. No one will know it's us. There's no way we're letting anyone else take point on this."

Before Emily had a chance to respond, Elaina suddenly sat taller and announced, "Tell everyone to back up from the bank." She held her forehead and groaned. "The left side. Now," she rushed out. "Now!" she damn near screamed.

Luke didn't hesitate. He knew Elaina was special, that she possessed unexplainable abilities. But this was off-the-charts "special" compared to what they'd all been privy to before now.

"It's . . ." Elaina's voice trailed off when a blast erupted nearby, rocking the van and prompting Emily to hold on to her daughter until the van settled.

"I guess they don't need us after all," Owen said a minute or two later, though Emily wasn't really sure how much time had passed since the blast, but . . .

"What?" Emily peered out of the open door to see Owen smiling.

A smile? Her heart leaped.

Elaina bolted out of the van before anyone could stop her, and Emily quickly followed her, praying Owen's smile meant Liam and Knox were out of the bank.

"Be careful," Owen called out after them, but all Emily could focus on was the sight of Liam and Knox.

They were advancing down the front steps of the bank, hands in the air.

Blocked by the wall of police officers, Elaina jumped up and down, hands in the air, waving to Liam to try and get his attention. "Dad!" she cried. Smoke from the explosion still hung in the air, and Emily doubted Liam could hear her over the noise of emergency vehicles and news crews.

"Liam," Emily couldn't help but call out, and she stood behind Elaina, wrapping her arms around her as they both impatiently waited for the police to let Liam and Knox come their way.

"Elaina. Emily." Liam pulled them both into his arms the second he was able to get to them. "I'm okay," he said into Emily's ear, a reminder of their conversation in bed that morning.

"What in the hell happened?" Asher, Bravo Three and Jessica's husband, appeared a few seconds later as Knox joined them, dismissing Secret Service and other officers clamoring for his attention. Questions and medical help weren't important to either Liam or Knox at the moment. But they both appeared to be uninjured aside from a few scrapes.

"There were only six guys. We managed to overtake them, but one of them had explosives on him and, well, you can see how that went," Knox said while searching the crowd, probably looking for his wife, Adriana, who had surely been notified. Hell, Knox's wife was Secret Service.

Liam dropped to a knee before Elaina. "You saved some people today, so it seems."

"But I could've gotten you and Uncle Knox killed," Elaina said, her tone solemn. "I'm sorry I couldn't tell you more, but if I did . . ." She let her words trail off.

"You two just had to go and be heroes, huh?" Asher teased, trying to lighten the mood.

The crowd of officers and agents kept pushing closer, but Bravo Team kept them at bay, allowing Liam a moment with his daughter.

"Yeah, yeah," Knox said. "Six to two. Easy odds once civilians were out of there."

"Well," Asher responded as Knox's wife finally reached them and flung herself into her husband's arms. "Well, I was planning on doing some Spiderman shit and scaling that building to help ya out," Asher added after Knox finished making out with his wife.

"Spiderman?" Elaina's soft laugh was music to Emily's ears and it placed a smile on Liam's face as he rose to his full height. "Aquaman, sure. You're way too muscular to be Spiderman, Uncle Asher."

Liam pulled Emily to his side, and the world around them, and all the insanity seemed to fade away in that moment. "I guess we know who will play him in your movie," he said to Knox, and despite the small cut above his eye, he casually winked.

Emily wasn't sure what that was all about, but the fact these two men just took down six bank robbers and were outside joking right now, proved one thing.

They really were unstoppable, weren't they? And maybe she didn't have anything to worry about.

Elaina's headaches though . . . "We're not out of the woods yet."

Liam must've managed to overhear her, because he tightened his grip and kissed the top of her head.

"I'll get us out of anything," he responded, and she lifted her chin to set eyes on her husband. "You can trust me. I'll protect our family." He nodded. "And I'm not going on the op today. I'm right where I'm needed the most."

CHAPTER FOUR

"**M**OM, I'M FIIIINE." Elaina winked at Emily, copying Liam's signature move, from across the dinner table. "My MRI results are perfect. Blood work is great. Doctor can't find anything wrong with me."

Of course Emily was relieved her results were clean. But her daughter was still in pain, and that was hell.

Liam reached for Emily's hand and squeezed it. "She's okay."

"But the headaches are—"

"Because of my visions," Elaina interrupted Emily and stood from the table and helped Jackson out of his seat. "My visions are more intense. More specific. And they hurt my head." She shrugged as if it were no big deal. "I'm working through this in my own way. My body will adjust to the changes. When I was younger and my mom was putting me through those, um, tests . . . I got the headaches too."

What? This was news to Emily.

"They went away once my body got used to them." Elaina circled the table and patted Emily on the shoulder, acting like the parent right now. And well, she was wise beyond her years, that was for sure.

"What can we do to help?" Emily asked softly as she stood, carried her plate to the sink, and scooped Jackson into her arms.

"Nothing." Elaina offered her a reassuring nod. "I don't know why I see what I see. I don't understand it. But maybe it's not so bad? Two innocent people didn't die in that bank that day because of my head, right?"

"That's a burden. Too big of a burden for you to carry," Liam said while pushing away from the table. "You need to be a twelve-year-old."

"I can be both." Elaina's smile was infectious, but Emily was still struggling to wrap her head around everything. "Let me give Jackson his bath. You two haven't gotten your cardio in for a while since you were stressed about me."

"Elaina," Liam rasped, his cheeks going red.

"What? I saw a video that said cardio is good for the heart." Another wink from their wise-beyond-her-years daughter as she carried a squirming Jackson out of the room.

Liam scratched his jaw, eyeing Emily for a moment. "She's one of a kind, huh? Just like her mother." He reached out and settled his hands on Emily's waist and brought his mouth near hers.

"More like her dad," she whispered right before Liam set her on fire with a searing kiss.

His hand traveled to her ass, and he squeezed tight, which had him swallowing her murmur with his mouth. "How about that cardio? Good for the heart and all."

With the news about Elaina, and Bravo Team back home from their operation as of this morning, Liam lost five years in age from his face. And it had been forever since they'd made love, so maybe . . .

"If it's good for the heart, who am I to deny my husband?"

Liam grabbed hold of her hand and guided her to their bedroom. His firm grip somehow soothed her. Calmed her mind. But the mere thought of sex with her husband had her heart racing.

Once alone in their room with the door locked, Liam quickly discarded his clothes and helped Emily peel hers free.

"I'll never get tired of this," Emily said around a hard swallow, her gaze cutting over her husband's toned, muscular body. He stood a few feet away, stroking his cock from root to tip while studying her.

"You better not. And don't trade me in for my doppelganger if there's ever a movie."

"What is this movie talk?" she asked with a laugh before he released his hard length and hoisted her into his arms only to toss her onto their bed.

Liam climbed on top of her and braced himself over her. The man was an expert at exciting positions. Great with angles.

But she loved nothing more than for him to be on top. Looking right into her eyes. And filling her deep.

"Knox says they want to make a movie about his family." He positioned himself onto his forearms and placed his tip at her soaked center.

"Oh really?" She lifted her brows and teased her tongue between her lips. "So, um, you thinking Chris Hemsworth is going to play you in this movie?"

"Don't even think about it," he returned with a growl and lightly nipped her lip. "You're mine. I don't share."

"I mean, he's basically your twin, so . . ."

"Ohhh," he responded with a low but dark laugh. "You want that kind of cardio-sex, do you? Because, woman, you talk about me sharing you, and your ass is gonna wind up red, I promise you that."

"Mmm." She tucked her lip between her teeth and gave him her best seductive stare. "You're irreplaceable. I thought I made myself clear. And you're never leaving me."

"Good answer," he rasped.

"The only answer," she whispered before her husband plunged deep inside her and her hips bucked to join him. "*But* . . . I wouldn't be opposed to that kind of cardio-sex."

✧   ✧   ✧

Interested in learning more about Liam and Emily?

Their book is *Finding Her Chance, A Stealth Ops Novel.*
brittneysahin.com/finding-her-chance

A Feather in the Flames

Brenda Rothert

CY AIR HITS my face as I slip out a side door of an abandoned office building, my breath clouding the air.

I zip up my coat and pull its hood up over my head. It's windy today. If my hair wasn't pulled back in a ponytail, it would be whipping around in the breeze, making it hard to see.

Not that there's much of a view. The small Ukrainian city we're in has been torn apart by war, its buildings mostly blown-up shells. Everything is gray and vacant here. If the eerie silence had a color, it would be a nondescript, bleary shade of gray.

As soon as I sit down on the concrete stairs next to another volunteer nurse, Cassia, she takes a pack of cigarettes out and passes me one, following it with her lighter.

I use my hand to block out the wind as I light it, then fill my lungs with the smoke that will provide me a few seconds of relaxation. Wordlessly, I pass back the lighter.

We don't talk when we're on breaks out here. It's not like nursing back home in Indianapolis, where we'd spend break time talking about plans for our days off, the fucking nerve of our charge nurse or who was going to make a Starbucks run. No words were exchanged the first time either when Cassia passed me, a non-smoker, one of her unfiltered cigarettes after we lost a pregnant woman to gunshot wounds two months ago.

Here, we just soak in the silence. The few blessed moments when we're not in motion, trying to do everything we can to save dying and seriously injured patients without most of the supplies we need. There are no best safety practices here. No policies about how many people must sign off on medications. This week, there aren't even any antibiotics.

What we have usually isn't enough to save the people who are brought in with their eyes full of suffering. We can feed them and warm them with the thick wool blankets we have an endless supply of. Some weeks, we can give them medicine to ease their transition. Though we don't speak their language, we can hold their hands and give them the comfort of not dying alone.

Cassia leans her side against mine, and I rest my head on hers. She lives in Toronto when she's not volunteering for Healing Hands; we probably never would have met if not for this experience. Our bond is unbreakable, though. We don't have to talk about what we've seen in our four months here. It's imprinted somewhere deep down inside us, in a place words can't reach.

I'm halfway done with my cigarette when the side door is pushed open.

"Jen, I need you."

He's gone as quickly as he came. It was Pierre Dalton, one of the volunteer doctors here. He's a steady presence, giving his all for at least sixteen hours every day. I stub out my cigarette, deposit it in an empty can and stand up.

Time to get back to work.

✧   ✧   ✧

I WASH UP and put on a clean mask, ready to assist, but Pierre shakes his head when I walk into the room. A young man lies lifelessly on a makeshift exam table, blood puddled on the floor beside him.

"I'll get a body bag," I say.

Growing up Catholic in Midwestern America, I was taught to fear hell. It was billed as a fiery place for sinners who didn't seek redemption. But after 138 days here, I know hell exists on many planes, and it's not the fire that makes it almost unendurable, but rather the endlessness of it. Here, there are flames that lick and scorch but never consume.

By the time I bring the body bag into the room that was formerly an office, local volunteers are there, ready to take over.

People here take care of their own, as much as they possibly can. Every day, people risk their lives bringing the wounded here for help. Their bravery is like a flower defying all odds and springing up through a crack in concrete. They're outmatched and the odds are against them, but they refuse to stop blooming.

"I'm rounding on my patients," I tell the volunteer nurse in charge, Diana.

"Will you check on my patient in Bed 14? I need to go do patient intakes."

"Of course."

Each of us has a small cubby where we keep our things; in this building's past life, these little cubes probably held outgoing mail, but now they hold canteens, balled-up sweaters, and cell phones. I take my stethoscope from my cubby and wrap it around my neck, stretching my arms as I walk to the first room of patients.

Patient 816 is asleep; I leave him in peace and go to the next one.

Sometimes we know our patients' names, and other times we don't. To keep things clear, we assign them numbers. It's impersonal, but efficient.

I take vital signs on a few patients and bring water to all of them. When I reach the bed of patient 849, it's empty, other than an intricately folded swan sitting on top of a gray wool blanket.

The people who brought patient 849 in after he was injured in an explosion told us his name was Anatoly. He lost his hearing in one ear and was wounded by shrapnel, but he was luckier than many. He'll survive, but I haven't seen him speak a word to anyone in the two weeks he's been here.

Anatoly spends his free time folding paper into intricate origami designs; the ledge beneath the window near his bed is lined with birds, flowers, and other shapes. He's a bear of a man—well over six feet tall, with broad shoulders, light brown curly hair, and a short, matching beard. Every time his dark, intense eyes meet mine, I wonder what he's thinking. I like watching him use his massive, calloused hands to do such precise work.

In this place where joy can feel impossible to find, his swan doesn't need to be real to be beautiful. It reminds me that somewhere in the world, there are graceful swans swimming in peaceful waters.

I hear movement behind me and turn to see Patient 831 walking from the bathroom back to his bed. He's a middle-aged man with stitched-up wounds on his backside. Even if I spoke his language, there's no way I could convince him to wear clothes. When I try to put them on him, he pushes my hands away. Clothes must hurt his wounds, but I can't even convince him to wear a robe. Patient 831 is and will continue to be naked, and it no longer fazes anyone here.

From another room, a male voice yells Ukrainian words we hear often here. I don't know exactly what they translate to, but I think it's close to "help me."

My spine stiffens and I rush over to put my clipboard down. I've picked up enough Ukrainian in my time here to get me by, and from the frantic sounds of the voices now filtering into the intake area, we're going to need all hands on deck.

I quickly wash up and get clean gloves on, then walk to the intake area where we assess patients.

My pulse pounds when I take in the scene. There's so much blood. Women are pressing their hands to wounds, patching them with anything available, scarves and strips of fabric, trying their best to calm the people they brought in.

A woman is slumped in a chair nearby, a circle of blood at her feet. I go to her and search beneath her coat, trying to find the source of the bleeding. Her hand finds mine and our eyes meet. I can feel the life draining out of her as her grasp loosens. I say the words I've repeated so many times.

"It's okay. I'm here."

Her hand goes slack in mine just as someone tugs on the side of my scrub pants. When I turn, there's a boy looking up at me, his brown eyes round and solemn.

As he leads me to a man who is doubled over on the floor, he says a Ukrainian word that I think means "father."

I assess him quickly, the other volunteers doing the same around me. There's usually no system here. We choose patients in order of greatest need and do our best to help them.

This man doesn't have any obvious wounds. He's very thin, and from the loose skin on his face and neck, I wonder if he's in pain due to malnourishment. We regularly see men struggling with it, because they've given the precious little food they could be eating to their families.

I smile at the boy and cup his cheek in my hand, hoping to reassure him that I'll help his father. Between the two of us, we get his father up from the floor and help him walk to one of the large rooms of waiting beds. As we slide him into a bed, he tries to resist, but he doesn't have much strength to do so.

The boy follows his father into the bed, curling up beside him and putting his arm around his chest. I use my hands to mimic drinking something and putting something in my mouth to the boy, and then I point across the room.

When I return with bottled water and granola bars, the boy gazes at the food, longing and uncertainty swirling in his eyes. I pass him a bottle of water and he sits up, unscrews the cap and immediately puts it to his father's lips.

"Just a little," I say gently. "And then wait"—I point at the watch on my hand—"and he can have a little more."

When I put four granola bars on the bed, the boy tears one open and holds it in front of his father's mouth. My heart breaks and warms at the same time. Yes, there's evil in the world, but there are also people like this boy, who doesn't even look ten years old but is putting his father's needs above his own.

His father doesn't seem to have the energy to bite the granola bar, so I get him some crackers instead. I use my hands to show the boy that I'll feed his father the crackers while he feeds himself a granola bar. He looks from the bars on the bed and then back at me, hesitating.

"It's okay," I tell him.

Still, he looks wary. I try again, but he doesn't move.

Anatoly approaches then, towering over me as he stands beside me and passes the boy a perfectly folded origami leaf. He says something to him in Ukrainian, and

I just look on in stunned silence.

The man who didn't utter a single word as shrapnel was dug out of his skin is talking for the first time since being brought in two weeks ago. Whatever he says works, because the boy picks up the granola bar and tears it open, and then immediately eats another one and drinks the water.

I set tiny pieces of crackers in his father's mouth, and he swallows them, murmuring his thanks in his native tongue.

When I look for Anatoly, he's not standing beside me anymore. Patients are being brought into the room, and it's getting loud. He often leaves the room when it gets loud, and I figure that's what he did until I see him at the bedside of a patient who lost a leg a month ago, Viktor.

Somehow, Pierre managed to amputate his leg, which was badly infected when we came in. Given his limited supplies, it was nothing short of a miracle it was successful.

Anatoly bends down and puts his arm around Viktor's waist, and Viktor wraps his arm around Anatoly's shoulders. At the hospital I work for in Indianapolis, I'd run over there and tell them we need to wait for the physical therapists. Viktor is cringing, clearly in pain.

Here, though, there are no luxuries. The more Viktor can get out of bed, the better off he'll be.

Anatoly gets him standing on his good foot, encouraging him to try to hop.

It's hard, though, for a man who has lost so much strength while lying in bed. Viktor looks back at the bed over his shoulder, murmuring something, but Anatoly shakes his head.

Viktor is clinging to Anatoly and looks like he's on the verge of tears, but a few inches at a time, he keeps going.

✧ ✧ ✧

"IT'S MY MOM'S birthday," Cassia says a few hours later.

It's evening, which usually means things get quieter here. We're taking inventory of supplies, waiting for Valeria, the Ukrainian woman who comes here once a week and takes us to her home, one at a time, for showers.

"Happy birthday to her," I say. "How old is she?"

"Sixty. My aunt will cook dinner for the whole family, and she always bakes Mom a three-layer cake. Vanilla with vanilla frosting. That's her favorite."

Cassia is missing home. I am, too. I miss dinners with friends and listening to music while driving. There were so many little things I took for granted. As quickly as the sense of nostalgia sets in, though, it disappears.

I'm where I'm supposed to be. Even on the hardest days, I know that.

"I've never been so excited about a shower," Cassia says, grinning.

"I'm right there with you."

The water pressure isn't the greatest at Valeria's home, but at least the water is hot. That weekly full-body and hair lathering is almost a spiritual experience. I've had dried blood in my hair for three days now. After my shower tonight, the week will reset.

Doing inventory is nothing if not predictably frustrating. We have an abundance of some supplies, like blankets, bandages, and painkillers, and a desperate need for other things, like antibiotics and sterilizing solutions.

Pierre is the veteran in the group, and he sometimes reminds us that food, water, and painkillers are the most critical supplies. Locals always make sure we have enough food for everyone, though fresh food is a scarcity. We have clean, safe water, and usually, we have electricity. It scares me to imagine what life here would be like without those essentials.

Of all the unknowns, the one that haunts me most is whether we've seen the worst of this war yet. Is there a plane of hell we can't even fathom yet to come?

✧   ✧   ✧

AFTER FINISHING INVENTORY, I go to my storage cubby to get my coat, which hangs on a hook beneath the cube. I'm first up for a shower this week, and I want to be ready as soon as Valeria arrives.

There's something unfamiliar in my cubby, but I can't make it out in the darkness. We don't use electricity for lights after dark, because that could make us a target for bombers.

I take out my cell phone and shine its light on the object. It looks like a feather. I pick it up and inspect it closer, and I see that it's not a real feather, but an origami one. The folds are perfect, creating a symmetrical work of art.

Anatoly.

Tears spring to my eyes. This thoughtful gesture couldn't have come at a better time. My birthday is in three days, though I don't plan to tell anyone here about it. Given what people here are enduring, making it another year is gift enough.

I move the feather into the back of my cubby to keep it safe. Beautiful things have to be protected.

✧   ✧   ✧

A FEW HOURS later, I return from Valeria's home clean and full of home-cooked food. She always makes the same meal—varenky, which tastes like dumplings filled with cabbage and onions, and a cornmeal stew called banush.

A few university students who were displaced when their homes were destroyed are living with Valeria and her family, and one of them, Isak, speaks fluent English. He always translates for the volunteers and Valeria, and tonight he caught me up on what they were hearing about the war.

None of it was good. Tonight everyone was particularly somber, and Isak told me he was trying to get Valeria and her family to relocate to a safer part of the country. They refused.

When I walk into the small room Pierre is alone in, he's sitting behind a desk, his chin resting on his steepled hands.

"Your turn for dinner at Valeria's," I tell him, taking my coat off.

"They bombed everything," he says blankly. "It's all gone."

"What's gone?"

When he names the nearest city to us, my heart races. I sit down, feeling dizzy.

"But Valeria was just there earlier today," I say, unable to process what Pierre told me. "Her sister lives there with her husband and—"

Pierre shakes his head. "It's gone, Jen. Even the hospital."

"Oh my God."

The heaviness of it all makes it hard to breathe. Even hospitals aren't safe. I don't bother asking Pierre what he thinks this means for us.

We'll have more patients. Likely very soon. More volunteers came to Ukraine a week ago, and they've been trying to get to us, but it hasn't been safe.

They'll make it here. Or they won't. We'll have enough to feed everyone here. Or we won't. There are more unknowns than knowns.

"You might want to think about evacuating," Pierre says softly.

I shake my head, adamant.

"How old are you?"

"Twenty-nine." I smile sadly. "But I feel a lot older."

"I'm fifty-two. But you've still got so many years in front of you. So many people to care for. And you can't do that if—"

He shakes his head and looks away.

"It's not safe out there, either," I remind him. "And this is where I want to be. I know we can't save everyone, but …"

Silence hangs between us, thick and full of foreboding.

"I love you like we're family, but you look exhausted," Pierre says, lightening the moment.

"You don't look so great yourself."

He sighs heavily. "Go get some sleep. You're going to need it."

My limbs are heavy with fatigue, but I already know I won't be able to sleep. We moved our operation into this building nearly two months ago, because the war was getting close to the place we were working out of. We're going to have to move again.

How, though? How will we move all of our patients when the roads have been destroyed and bombs are being dropped day and night?

The flames of this hellish war are creeping close. I can feel the heat. There's a certainty that eventually, the fire will consume all of us.

On my walk to the oversized supply closet where I set up my sleeping cot, I see a figure standing next to a window, outlined in moonlight. Stopping, I take him in.

It's Anatoly. He stands straight, his wide shoulders square as he stares into the darkness. Part of me knows I should tiptoe past him and crawl into my cot for a few hours of sleep. Things are going to get bad sooner rather than later.

I'm drawn to him, though. I approach him, and he turns when I'm a few feet behind him. For a few seconds, I look up at his face in silence.

He's beautiful. Not just because he's tall, strong, and classically handsome. His soulful dark eyes tell me something words never could.

Anatoly isn't scared. In some ways, he's already lost his life to this war. I don't know if he was completely alone before hell came to his doorstep, but he is now. Many of our patients have a frantic need to leave and look for loved ones, but he never did.

"Thank you for the feather," I say softly.

His Adam's apple bobs as he swallows, and he slowly reaches out and brushes his fingers over my cheek and then down to my jawline. A shiver tingles down the length of my spine as he cups my face in his massive hand.

Tears well as I lean into his touch. With his calloused palm, he's showing me the only tenderness and affection I've felt since arriving here.

I cover his hand with my much smaller one, unwilling to lose the connection between us. This calm before the storm soothes my soul, reminding me how much moments like this are worth fighting for.

With a single step, I close the gap between us and lean against Anatoly, resting my weight on his chest and my cheek in the crook of his neck. He drops his hand from my cheek and wraps both arms around me, holding me tightly.

It feels blissful to close my eyes and cry into his shirt. I let my anger and fear spill out, and he never loosens his hold on me. After a minute, I pull back slightly and look up at him.

His dark gaze holds me captive. I've given myself over to whatever fate has in store for me here. My days may be numbered, but I'll spend every one of them helping patients who need me. In this moment, though, I decide to give myself over to what feels good and right. To something that will remind me how beautiful humanity can be.

I put my hands on Anatoly's bearded cheeks and get on my tiptoes, stretching up to press my lips to his. He meets me halfway, bending to kiss me.

It's soft and tentative at first, a sweet first meeting of our mouths. Soon, though, our kiss grows deeper, and we press our bodies together, his arms wrapped tightly around my waist and my hand cupping the back of his neck.

When I pull away from him and take his hand in mine, he knits his brows together in confusion. I wish I knew the words I wanted to tell him in Ukrainian. Instead, I bring his hand to my breast and press my hand over his, and his eyes widen.

Soon though, his expression shifts from confused to hungry and knowing. He gently squeezes my breast and I release a soft exhale.

I take his hand again, leading him toward the supply closet I sleep in. He follows, and soon I find myself sneaking into the closet with him, my heart racing with anticipation as I close the door behind us.

My only lights in the closet are my cell phone and a candle. I use my cellphone for light to strike a match and light the candle. Anatoly stands behind the door, his gaze following my every move.

His eyes never leave me as I kick off my shoes and socks, pull my clean scrub shirt up over my head and then untie my pants and push them down. I'm about to unclasp my bra when an explosion sounds in the distance, making my hands freeze.

It wasn't close enough that we need to flee the building, but it confirms what everyone here already knows—soon, the war will be upon us.

Anatoly takes his shirt off and drops it to the ground. In the dim light, I see the shrapnel wounds still healing on his shoulder, and the dark, light brown hair on his chest that trails off above his abs.

I remove my bra and slide my panties to the floor, Anatoly's gaze washing over every inch of me as he pushes down his pants and underwear and I see that he wants me as much as I want him.

He comes closer, shadows dancing over the lines of his face in the candlelight. The cold brings on goose bumps and a slight shiver, and he takes the blanket from my cot and wraps it around my shoulders.

It's been a long time since anyone has cared for my comfort. I'm a caregiver and being on the receiving end makes my heart swell with gratitude.

I put my arms around his shoulders, using the blanket to surround us both. His body is warm and hard against mine, but his mouth is soft and sweet as he kisses my lips, my neck, and my chest.

My breath is uneven. I close my eyes, not thinking about anything but how good his mouth and hands feel on my skin.

Another explosion sounds. Was that one closer?

I put it out of my mind, gently pressing my palms to Anatoly's chest to show him I want him to lie down on the cot. He does, and I admire his masculine lines for just a moment before climbing on top of him, bringing the blanket with me.

His hands find my hips, one palm sliding up my back and then back down as I ease myself onto his length. He gasps at the sensation as I take as much of him as I can, then move my hips back and take a little more.

Our bodies move together, both speaking a language that transcends words. Anatoly wraps his arms around my back and pulls me close, his hips doing the work while we're chest to chest, his breath warm against my lips.

If this is my last day in this world, this is how I want to spend it. Sharing myself with this man who has also felt the flames of this war. Loving him in a way more powerful than any weapon.

Minute by minute, we close out the world around us. We're both breathing hard as we chase our release. Every movement is ecstasy; I could swear we were both made for these few perfect moments.

I shatter into a million beautiful pieces, feeling nothing but bliss for a few seconds I wish could last forever. He's right behind me, his whole body tightening as he groans deeply with his release, holding me close.

I keep my cheek on his chest, my tears trailing onto his neck. He caresses my hair. Slowly, our breathing returns to normal.

There's a loud booming sound outside. I jump, and Anatoly smooths his palm over my back.

Are the explosions from the enemy, closing the distance between us? Or is it the Ukrainians, flighting back with everything they have and destroying enemy tanks?

Part of me wishes we knew. Part of me doesn't.

Anatoly stretches a long arm over to a supply shelf, where he grabs a piece of paper. I slide out from beneath his other arm, curling at his side as his hands work the paper the way he wants it, folding, inspecting, and then folding more.

The slice of heaven we found in this darkened closet can't last. If we're going to move to a new location, which is likely, I need to get to work. But I can't bring myself to go just yet.

Watching Anatoly's fingers mold a sheet of paper into a work of art is mesmerizing. I could lie here with him like this for a thousand nights and never tire of it. Somehow, though, I know tonight is the only night we're going to get.

He finishes, having transformed the paper into a figure, and he passes it to me. I hold it closer to the candle so I can see what it is.

An angel, its two intricately folded wings stretching out in perfect symmetry on either side.

I smile at Anatoly, my angel in this hour of darkness. He's given me not just comfort, but hope. When I looked at that piece of paper a few minutes ago, I hadn't seen an angel, but he had.

Maybe there are more unseen angels out there.

✧ ✧ ✧

Thank you so much for reading my story A Feather in the Flames. For more on my books, please visit my website.

www.brendarothert.com

HOMECOMING

REBECCA YARROS

CHAPTER ONE

Braxton

MY EARS POPPED as my truck gained altitude on the road from Gunnison to Legacy, Colorado. I'd been driving for two straight days, leaving my old job as a structure firefighter to get home and resurrect our town's iconic hotshot crew.

I wasn't thinking about my jaw-clenching anger that my little sister had put herself in danger and signed up too, forcing my hand to join her, to protect her.

I wasn't even thinking about the fact that the crew was the reason our Mom had died eleven years ago in the wildfire that had consumed our little town.

Nope, I was going twenty over the speed limit on a winding mountain road because my lifelong best friend, Summer, had called earlier, hell-bent on a little revenge on her ex in the form of a one-night stand. Guess I didn't have to be the Man of Honor anymore, since she'd called off the wedding.

It shouldn't have bothered me. Summer was twenty-four years old, just like me. She was fully capable of making her own choices. It was her body, yada yada.

But hearing those words sent my brain into a tailspin, and my right foot had hit the gas.

That had been hours ago. She'd probably changed her mind. She was probably curled up on the couch in her yoga pants, binge-watching *The West Wing* for the fourteen-billionth time. She was probably cursing out her piece of shit ex-fiancé and the woman he'd decided to cheat on her with.

Probably.

But the possibility that she wasn't, that she was actually going to follow through with her plan and take a stranger home had me taking the curve a little too fast on way too little sleep.

"It's none of your business," I muttered to myself, but it didn't help. There was a gnawing, blistering ache in the middle of my chest that said otherwise.

I'd done my damndest to ignore the feelings that had grown over the last couple of years and shoved them completely aside the second she'd shown me her engagement ring. But she wasn't engaged anymore. She wasn't even dating anyone. And I wasn't about to stand aside and watch her move on without at least throwing my hat in the ring and telling Summer how I felt.

Because in the last few years, I'd fallen for my best friend.

And that was worth a potential speeding ticket.

CHAPTER TWO

Summer

BRAXTON: YOU CHANGED your mind right? You can't be serious about this.

I read the text message from my best friend and typed a quick response back as another shot of tequila appeared on the bartop in front of me.

Summer: Dead serious.

I'd filled him in on my plan earlier tonight while he'd been on the road, finally making his way home after six years of being gone from our tiny mountain town.

Braxton: Where are you?

Summer: Wicked.

Wicked, our town's local bar was the perfect place, and tonight was a perfect time for my first one-night stand. Because that's what you did when you found out your fiancé had been screwing around on you for months, right? You went out and got trashed. You celebrated dodging a freaking bullet. You got revenge in the form of orgasms. Yep, I wanted *all* of that.

It had been three weeks. I'd cried my tears, forfeited my deposits on at least four different vendors, and deleted the asshole off every social media account I had. Now I was two shots of tequila in and ready for my revenge sex, ready to feel something besides anger and...relief.

If I'd found out a month from now, I would have been married to Dan. A shudder of disgust rolled down my spine. Married. Forever. To a guy who couldn't keep it in his pants and never really cared if I got off as long as he did. Maybe I hadn't dodged a bullet as much as I'd avoided a nuke.

"What about him?" My friend, Sage asked, pointing at a trio of guys playing pool. This place was packed. Sure, it was Friday night, but it didn't hurt that all the hotshot firefighters were coming back into town—Braxton included—now that the new crew had been approved. In fact, at least one of the guys lining up to hit the cue ball was on the Legacy crew.

"Pretty sure that's River Maldonado," Penny said from my other side. "And he has a girlfriend. She's super nice."

"Ok, then what about that one?" Sage nodded toward the end of the bar.

"Charlie Pright?" Penny laughed. "She'd be better off with Dan."

That was the problem with small towns. Everyone knew...well, everyone.

The door opened, welcoming in an icy blast of snow-filled April air, and we all glanced over our shoulders to look.

No. Freaking. Way. My stomach clenched and the pounding of my heart drowned out the heavy beat streaming from the corner jukebox.

Braxton was here.

Braxton, who was supposed to be crossing the Colorado border *tomorrow*.

Braxton...who was...*holy shit*. Brax was really freaking *hot*. When had that happened? It had only been a few years since we'd seen each other in person, and FaceTime didn't do him justice, not anymore. Somehow, the line of his jaw had hardened, his frame had filled out in a way that had my jaw slackening, and the intensity in those brown eyes hit me like a third shot of tequila—straight in my stomach—as he scanned the crowded bar.

Our eyes locked.

"Oh my Lord," Penny whispered, "is that—"

"Braxton!" I called out, jumping off my barstool and immediately slipping through the crowd that separated us.

He grinned and started toward me.

We met in the middle.

I squealed, my smile uncontrollable as he picked me up into a bear hug. Uncaring that people stared, my reflexes took over and I wrapped my legs around his waist like we were teenagers again, goofing around in the halls of our high school.

My arms squeezed tight around him and I buried my face in his neck.

Home. He always smelled like home, and safety, and the kind of trust that was built when you'd known someone your entire life.

"You're home!" I mumbled, content to hold on as long as he'd let me.

"I'm home," he replied, his arms contracting, like he was in no hurry to put me down, either.

"Brax!" A deep voice boomed over the noise and we both looked up to see River waving from the pool tables.

Braxton gave him a nod and lowered me to the ground.

"When did your hair get so long?" Braxton asked, his smile bright as he freed the auburn strands from the zipper of his open coat and tucking them behind my ear.

"When did yours get so short?"

We both laughed and he pulled me into another hug, my head fitting under his chin like it always had. "God, I missed you, Summer."

"She's missed you, too," Sage said, appearing at our side. "I mean, not that we mind being her second-best girls, but we're both aware that you're always going to hold that top spot."

"Hey, Sage, Penny." Brax let me go to hug them both.

"I thought you were coming in tomorrow?" I asked.

"I was making great time, and drove even faster once you said you were on a mission to fuck away Dan's mem—"

"Braxton Rose!" I hissed, covering his mouth with my hand. I'd almost forgotten the mouth on him, the way he said exactly what he was thinking. He'd never cared what other people thought about him, which had always been one of his best qualities—and he had a ton of them.

More than one head turned our direction and heat crept up my neck, no doubt flushing my cheeks. Just because I had a goal in mind didn't mean I wanted the rest of the town to know about it.

"Ymmmhnnuccmmbb," he mumbled against my palm.

"Don't you dare say that again." I gave him a glare and lifted my hand.

"You can't be serious, Sum," he repeated. Penny and Sage made themselves scarce.

"What if I am?" My brows rose. "I'm a full-grown woman, and as you can see," I flashed him my bare left hand, "I'm free to do whatever I want."

His jaw flexed once, twice, and those deep brown eyes of his bore right through me, like he was peeling back the layers of bullshit I'd caked on over the last few years to examine what remained beneath. "You forget that I know you, Summer Jones. If you take some stranger home with you tonight, you'll regret it as soon as the sun rises. And we both know I'll be the one doing my best to put you back together, so why don't we both save ourselves the trouble and *not*."

The truth of his words stung and killed off what was left of the buzz I'd been working on. "You don't *know* that," I argued. "Maybe I've changed while you were off fighting fires. Maybe I've had a slew of one-night stands. Maybe I've taken so many strangers home that…that…" My mind betrayed me and went blank.

So. Freaking. Frustrating.

"That what?" He urged, raising a single dark brow in challenge as the song changed in the background.

"Give me a second and I'll think of something!" I may as well have stamped my foot on the floor.

He laughed, and I would have stormed out, or done something equally dramatic if the deep, rumbling sound hadn't soothed the part of me that had missed him more than anything. "Summer, you've dated three guys, all of whom were various shades of awful. If you'd gone through a Tinder stage, I would have known about it."

"Like you?"

"Like me," he agreed. "Now, we have three choices. One: we can hang out at the bar and catch up. Two: you can come with me so I can check into a hotel and we can talk somewhere quieter." He made a face. "Plus, I desperately need a shower. You can even continue to lecture me about how wrong I am."

A smile tugged at my lips. "And option three?"

He winced. "You can continue your mission, if that's what you really want." It was the sheer exhaustion in his face that moved me. He looked like he was ready to drop on the spot.

And honestly, spending the evening catching up with Braxton just sounded like a way better time than picking through the Friday night regulars in the name of vengeance.

"Fine. Let's go." I smiled, my chest going all gooey with how much I'd missed him. Phone calls and FaceTime were great, but it wasn't the same as being around him. "But you're staying at my place. Not the hotel."

"Purse and coat." Sage thrust the objects toward me.

"You don't mind?" I asked her, slipping my arms into my jacket.

"Like it's even a question." She scoffed. "You were gone the second he walked in. Go catch up. We can commence operation one-night stand tomorrow night." She winked and then disappeared back into the crowd.

Braxton grinned like he'd won a prize, and my stomach tightened, awareness sizzling through me in an all-new way.

"Looks like I'm all yours for the night."

"Looks like it."

CHAPTER THREE

Braxton

KILLED THE shower and stepped out onto the turquoise bath mat, wrapping the gray towel around my waist that Summer had left out for me.

Shit, I'd forgotten my clothes in the living room.

"Have everything you need?" Summer called out from down the hall of her apartment.

"Almost," I answered, drying off enough that I wouldn't track water through the place, then opened the bathroom door. Knotting the towel, my feet padded across the hardwood floor as I walked toward the living room.

The hallway opened up at the dining area, and there was Summer, lounged out on the couch in the living room, a giant bowl of popcorn cradled in her lap. She'd changed out of her bar clothes and the jeans that had made my mouth water, into a soft pair of leggings that were going to make it hard to think, and the worn, zip-up hoodie with the CU Buffalo logo that I'd bought her for Christmas our sophomore year in college.

"I forgot clothes," I muttered, reaching over the back of an armchair to dig through the backpack I'd brought in. I grabbed my gray sweatpants and a clean, white t-shirt before I noticed that she was silent.

Silent and gaping slightly, her lips parted as her gaze tracked a bead of water down my chest.

"Summer?" I asked, a corner of my mouth tilting into a smirk.

Her gaze jerked to meet mine and she snapped her mouth shut.

Caught you.

"Clothes. Right. Yeah, you should put those on." She blinked quickly, then whipped her attention back to the television. "Is there a movie you want to watch?"

"Lady's choice. Be right back." It took a matter of minutes to change into the clean clothes and hang my towel up. Everything at Summer's had its place, and she kept it there. She'd always been that way. I noticed the gaping holes in her gallery wall, where pictures had obviously been hung, on my way back to the living room and shook my head. Dan had been such a fucking moron.

Who the hell had someone like Summer and *cheated* on her? She was everything a guy could want—smart, kind, beautiful, and funny as hell with a contagious laugh. She was also loyal to the people she loved, all of which were the reasons she'd been my best friend since we were practically babies.

My hands itched with the impulse to punch Dan into the next century for what he'd done to her, but he was long gone. The smartest thing he'd ever done was pick up and move to Wyoming with his mistress.

"That's better," I said, stuffing my dirty clothes into my bag.

"I said I'd wash them for you," Summer lectured.

"Letting me crash in your guest bedroom is more than enough. You're not doing my laundry." I sank down onto the opposite end of her dark leather couch, noting that she was still on the browsing screen for *Netflix*.

"Your new place isn't exactly ready." She shrugged.

"I did come in a day early." I reached for the glass of iced tea she'd poured me earlier and took a drink.

"You did." She nodded, tugging her lower lip between a row of even, white teeth. She glanced toward me, then looked away quickly.

"Spit it out."

"You were planning on staying in Kansas tonight," she whispered. "You were supposed to stop driving *hours* ago."

"I was," I agreed, drinking in the sight of her. Damn it, why hadn't I wised up to my feelings when we'd been in college? Why had it taken this long to figure out why I always craved more time with her? My stomach tensed as I fought back the nerves that threatened to make me screw this all up.

I had to be careful. I could survive if she didn't feel the same way about me. It would hurt, but eventually I'd be ok. But the threat of losing her as my best friend had my heart beating erratically.

"You didn't have to drive the rest of the way for me. I hope you know I'm more than capable of having a one-night stand," she said, tilting her chin up. "And I appreciate that you're worried, but I can separate feelings from sex. I promise. I'm not going to fall for the next guy I happen to let into my bed." Her green eyes flashed with challenge.

God, I hoped she was wrong about that.

I hope she wants me the same way I want her.

Eventually. Sure, driving in and dumping my heart on her door had seemed like a great plan, but if she needed time then I was going to have to give it to her. Besides, I was home to stay, so there wasn't any rush, right?

"It's not like you haven't had your fair share of flings, and you've come out unscathed." She arched an eyebrow at me.

"Fucking someone else isn't going to help you hurt less." I leaned forward, pulling her bare foot into my lap. "And it's Dan's loss." I rubbed the arch of her foot and she relaxed, her cheek resting on the back of the couch. "He was a fucking idiot to cheat on you."

"Repeatedly cheat. I know of at least two women. He used to freak when I'd go out with the girls. He'd get all controlling and ruin my night." She sighed hard. "And man, did he hate you. He despised every second we spent on the phone. And honestly, the joke's on her, because that man couldn't find my clit if I drew him a freaking map."

I nearly spit out my tea.

"And there's this horrible sense of...relief." She raked her hands through her hair. "Like a part of me had always known that he was wrong for me, but I pushed through anyway. Do you know how many red flags I ignored? I almost made the worst mistake of my life, but instead, I'm free." A smile lit up her face.

"You're free," I agreed. *And gorgeous.*

She slid her foot free from my hands and sat forward on her knees. "And there's nothing wrong with wanting to *finally* get some good sex, right?"

"Right." Was it getting hot in here? I shifted on the couch. Fuck, I could picture it right now, watching her neck arch as she came. What kind of sounds did she make? Did she whimper or scream?

"Because when it comes down to it, sex is just a physical need. I can use a guy just as easily as he could use me. Just for sex."

"Just for sex," I repeated, white-knuckling my glass as her cheeks flushed.

"Exactly." She nodded. "Just two people using each other to get what they need. And *man*," her head rolled back. "I have *needed* for freaking years! You can't fault me for being out there looking for someone who can give as good as he gets."

"I don't fault you for anything," I clarified, frustration climbing up my throat. *I'm just being a jealous asshole.* When I had exactly zero right to be. She wasn't mine.

"Great, then as my best friend, help find me someone to use," she said, like it was the best idea she'd ever had.

Fuck. That.

"Use me." It was out of my mouth before I could stop myself.

Her green eyes flew wide.

What the hell, in for a penny, right?

"Use me," I repeated. "You want to get off? I'll give that to you. I'll give you whatever you want. No strings. No pressure. No small-town gossip for you to face in the morning. I will flip you onto your back and make you come as many times as you can take it, and trust me, I know how to find your clit. You can take whatever you want from me. Just...use *me.*"

Her lips parted as she stared at me with an expression I couldn't read.

Was that interest? Revulsion? Shock? Had I just fucked up our entire friendship? My heart pounded and my stomach lurched at the possibility.

I had to take it back. Shit, was that something I *could* take back?

"You know what? Forget I said anything." I jumped to my feet and pretty much fled to the kitchen, but there was no escaping the kind of idiocy I'd just displayed. I put my glass by the sink and let my head hang as I gripped the cool granite of the counters, counting in my head to try and steady my breathing.

I was at thirty-five when I heard her footsteps behind me.

"Braxton."

"Just forget it."

"Turn around." Her touch on my back sent jolts of electricity through my body.

I did as she asked, and we stood there, our eyes locked as the tension grew between us, quickly reaching a breaking point.

Then she kissed me and I unraveled.

CHAPTER FOUR

Summer

I THOUGHT KISSING him might be awkward, but it wasn't. His lips were soft as I feathered my mouth over his.

Use me. That's what he'd offered, shocking me to my toes for all of a minute or two before heat had rushed over me, and now here I was, kissing my best friend.

"It could get awkward," I whispered.

"Only if we let it." He speared a hand through my hair, parted my lips with his tongue, and took control of the kiss.

Holy shit, he was good at this.

As good as I'd always imagined he would be, and I'd caught myself daydreaming about it a time or two...or a thousand.

My arms wound around his neck, and he gripped my ass and spun, lifting me to the counter as he took my mouth with teasing licks and deeper, sensuous strokes of his tongue. Our mouths came together again and again, each kiss better than the last as we explored and tasted. He sucked my tongue into his mouth and I moaned.

I parted my thighs and he stepped between them, pulling me flush against his hips. My breath caught at the feel of him. "You want me," I whispered.

"What's not to want?" He kissed my jaw, then my neck, sending shivers down my spine. "You're beautiful, Summer."

My head fell back and he caught it, his lips ghosting over mine.

"Tell me what *you* want. I'll do anything you ask."

My eyes popped open. How the hell could I tell him what I wanted when I didn't even know? It was like I'd strolled into a brunch buffet at the country club and couldn't begin to guess where to start. I only knew I was starving. "You," I finally answered. "I want you."

His pupils flared as I dragged my tongue over my lower lip.

"Where do you want my hands?" he asked, sliding one up over the curve of my waist and brushing his thumb just beneath my breast. "Where do you like to be touched?"

"Everywhere." I took his hand and lifted it to cup my breast. "I trust you."

His fingers flexed slightly and his breath stuttered just before he took my mouth again, the kiss deepening. I felt it in every nerve, tingling my fingers and coiling warmth between my thighs. Urgency drove my fingers into his hair and had my hips rocking against his as he kissed the breath right out of me.

My hoodie hit the floor and my shirt followed. I had no inhibitions, no shyness. This was Braxton. It wasn't like he hadn't seen me in a bikini before.

"Tell me if I do something you don't like," he said between kisses as he made his way down my chest, pausing to kiss the swell of each breast.

I had the feeling that there wasn't much I wouldn't like when it came to him.

He kissed down and down, his lips passing my belly button and skimming the waistband of my pants. His eyes met mine in question as he hooked his fingers into the elastic.

I nodded and arched my hips to help him get my pants off. They landed near my hoodie. Or somewhere. Whatever. I was too busy kissing him again to notice.

This was complete and utter madness, and yet I couldn't bring myself to stop, to slow it down. He touched me and I burned, flames of need licking up my thighs as his hands stroked my bare skin.

"So smooth," he said against my lips. "So soft." His fingers trailed higher, grazing the line of my purple thong and brushing over my center. "So wet."

"Touch me." I sent up a prayer of thanks to the underwear gods that I hadn't chosen the plain white cotton earlier.

Our eyes locked, our breaths panted against each other's lips as he slipped his fingers under the purple satin. Then we both groaned.

He hadn't been lying earlier. He knew exactly how to find my clit. He stroked, pinched, and teased me until my hips rocked on their own, seeking friction. Then he smiled against my mouth and kissed me again, ending it with a delicious nip of my lower lip as he dropped to his knees. His mouth hovered over the juncture of my thighs.

"Brax?" I barely recognized the breathy mess that was my own voice as I looked down at him.

"I want to fuck you with my tongue." He arched his eyebrow, just like he always did when he was about to challenge me, push me out of my comfort zone.

His...*yes.*

"Yeah, I'm okay with that." I nodded and lifted my ass.

He grinned and tugged my thong down my thighs, letting it fall to the floor beside him. Then he pushed my thighs apart, baring me completely to him, and yanked me to the edge of the counter. "Hold on to something," he ordered.

My hands fumbled, one grabbing the counter, and the other bracing on the cabinet behind me as he settled his mouth over me.

"Oh my *God,*" I cried out.

He swirled his tongue around my clit, then lashed at it with quick, deft strokes before dipping down and spearing into my entrance.

Sensation after sensation rocketed through me, each one adding to the coiling tension building in my stomach. Each thrust of his tongue made me moan, each flick of his fingers over my clit had me keening.

"You taste so fucking good." The vibrations from his words made my thighs clench and the look on his face—complete and total focus driven by lust—nearly sent me over the edge. Then he switched, stroking my clit with his tongue and thrusting one, then two fingers inside me, curling them at just the right spot.

"Braxton." I let go of the counter and grasped his head as my body strained, reaching for that sweet breaking point I knew had to be coming.

"Let go. I've got you." He worked me with his mouth and fingers until my muscles trembled. Then he took me over, and I came.

Stars. Lights. Whatever, it was all heaven. Waves of bliss rolled over me, suspending me in unimaginable pleasure. My hips bucked against his mouth as he eased me down with that magical freaking tongue. I would have slid right off that counter into a puddle of contentment if he hadn't caught me.

We were both struggling for breath as he stood and rested his forehead against mine.

"That was absolutely incredible." I brushed my lips over his.

"Thought it might take the edge off." He grinned, then kissed me hard. I could taste both of us in that kiss and it only made me ache for more.

"There are condoms in my nightstand," I said, locking my ankles around his waist.

An unmistakable flare of heat raced through his eyes. "You're sure?"

"More than sure." I nodded just in case the words weren't enough. "You. Me. Bed. Now."

"Yeah, I'm okay with that," he repeated my earlier words with a smile, then kissed me as he lifted me by my ass, carrying me through my apartment. "Fuck, Summer, I want you."

We fell in a tumble to my bed, and I yanked at every article of clothing that my fingers came in contact with. His shirt? Gone. His pants? See ya later.

He unclasped my bra with an expertise that I appreciated, and we were finally, gloriously naked.

I pushed him to his back and then openly ogled my best friend. "Good God, Braxton, have you been living at the gym?" Every line of him was cut to perfection, the muscles of his abs rippling as he laughed in response.

"There's not much else to do between calls."

"You're freaking perfect." My fingers trailed along the dips and hollows of his body and I swallowed when I reached the hard length of him. Then my eyes popped wide.

"We don't have to," he said, reaching for my hand.

"Uh, yeah. We absolutely *do*." I lunged for the side of the bed, yanked open the nightstand drawer, and ripped the box of condoms open. A quick rip and the foil packet was open. My gaze jerked toward his. "Can I?"

"Abso-fucking-lutely." Raw hunger was etched in every line of his face, sending another jolt of need through my veins. He hissed through his teeth as I rolled the condom on and I raised my eyes toward his. "This is going to be so damned good, isn't it?"

"It already is." I nodded and straddled his hips.

He took himself in hand and nudged against my slick entrance, then grasped my hips as our eyes locked.

My heart thundered. I sank down slowly, my body stretching to accommodate him with a delicious burn as I sank down inch by inch, until I had him to the hilt.

He groaned and I answered with one of my own.

"So. Damned. Good," I whispered as I rose up and sank back down.

Those were the last words spoken as our bodies took over. I rode him with abandon, swirling my hips with every rise and slamming back down onto him with every fall. He met me with each thrust, pulling my hips into his.

Each stroke was better than the last. It was like we'd been making love for years instead of minutes. Our bodies communicated wordlessly, each giving and taking. Our hands explored, our mouths kissed, our breaths mingled in shorter and shorter pants.

He kept my rhythm, letting me take the lead, and only minutes later, I felt my body quicken again, that spiraling pleasure reaching for me once more. My hips rocked frantically against his as my whole body began to shake.

Then his fingers were on me, stroking me higher, until I let go, shattering into nothingness as I called out his name in surrender.

I'd barely managed to suck in a breath when he flipped us over and rose over me.

"Summer." He looked at me with an emotion I was scared to name, cradling my head and taking my mouth in a consuming kiss as he pounded into me, hard and strong, keeping me on the high as he drove on toward his own peak.

He shuddered, rippling over me before falling to my side, tugging me with him so we faced each other, our hearts racing and breathing scattered.

"That. Was. Incredible," he said between breaths, brushing a kiss over my mouth.

"Agreed." It was all I could manage as my mind and body barely clung to consciousness.

Silence stretched between us, but it wasn't awkward. It was perfect. Slowly, the sweat cooled on our skin and our heartbeats steadied.

This moment could go any way. Back to friendship. Into awkwardness. Onward to something…more. Something that was only ours. Something I hadn't realized I desperately wanted until this exact moment.

He was Braxton, how could I not want him?

"What now?" I dared to ask.

He cupped the side of my face and smiled. "Usually I'd ask you for your number."

"You already have my number, smartass." I kissed his chin.

"In that case, what do you say to round two?" He tilted my face towards his and I fell into his dark brown eyes. "And maybe a first date? No pressure on either. It's whatever you want."

My heart lit up like a Christmas tree. "Yes to both."

He grinned. "Yes to both."

"Oh, and one more thing." I ran my fingers through his hair and his brows knit slightly.

"What is that?" He stroked my cheek with his thumb.

"Welcome home, Brax."

✧   ✧   ✧

Thank you so much for reading my story Homecoming! You can read more in my small town, hotshot firefighting Legacy world starting with Point of Origin, available now.

ORDER POINT OF ORIGIN >
www.rebeccayarros.com/books/point-of-origin-a-legacy-novella

ASHER BLACK: A BONUS SCENE AS TOLD BY ASHER

PARKER S. HUNTINGTON

Author's Note: This is a scene from *Asher Black* told in Asher's POV—the scene in which Asher finds Lucy at Wilton University, showing up in her class. The original scene is written in Lucy's POV.

Asher Black

LUCY JUMPED IN her seat, whipping her head to face me. I set my paper down, folded it back into a tight roll, and tipped a brow at her. Shock rounded her green-hazels. A sharp breath wheezed out of her.

She looked seconds from keeling over, which would be unfortunate, considering I had plenty of questions to ask her, the first one being—what the fuck?

"Oh, God," she whispered, and if I had to guess, I'd venture she had no clue she'd spoken out loud. "Is he here to kill me?"

"Still debating it," I offered, spinning the custom titanium lighter Vincent had gifted me on my eighteenth birthday between two fingers.

He'd engraved his favorite proverb on it.

Senza tentazioni, senza onore.

Where there is no temptation, there is no glory.

Life Tip #1: You can run from the law, but you can't run from temptation.

For the record, my score sheet looked like this:

Temptations resisted: zero.

Arrests: also zero.

Lucy groaned. Her two tiny fists gripped each side of her seat's armrests. She curled herself forward, resting her head atop her knees before peeking up at me from below. "Will you give me one wish first?"

"No."

"Good." She nodded. "I don't need a wish." But then she straightened, reached for her opposite wrist, and pinched the sensitive skin there. Blinked slow. Pinched again.

You're still awake, Miss Ives. Perhaps not for long.

"I'm awake, aren't I?"

I didn't dignify that with a response, instead reclining on the seat, pulling out my phone, and checking today's trading for Black Enterprise. +3.96%. Bet René was choking on his Rémy Martin right about now.

Lucy adjusted her strap, fingering it to the point where it should've fallen apart by now with her aggressive fidgeting. She wore a tiny top. Nearly see-through. Peppered with caramel-colored splash stains. Probably not intentional, but could be, New York fashion being as odd as it was.

It showed about as much skin as the slinky dress she'd worn the night she'd called the cops at Rogue. Yet, for someone who had a habit of dressing minimally, she seemed uncomfortable with all the skin showing. Or maybe it was my presence that unhinged her.

Either way, her shoulders sloped forward as if she could hide within herself, and she continued to mumble sentence after sentence. Horror etched on her face. Spitting them out rapid-fire style like she moonlit as a rapper.

I slanted my head to the side, listening. Trying to make out what I could.

It sounded something like this...

If there is one thing the gazillion mob movies and books I consumed during my post-Hallway Incident research have taught me, it's that he's here to take care of me.

Take care, as in code for—kill me.

Hide my body six feet under a construction site, where they'll build a low-income housing complex over me and won't find my corpse until fifty years later when some rich billionaire asshole buys the complex, evicts the poor, knocks it to the ground, and builds a hoity-toity apartment tower over it.

Oh, and Shawn Spencer will come to solve my murder case, so at least they'll figure out who killed me, and it'll be funny—

I tuned out her rambling when she pivoted to discussing the merits of movies over television. Her lips continued to move, though, so fast she seemed borderline mid-seizure. Like she'd either keel over from exhaustion or talking-induced oxygen deprivation.

I didn't need to kill her. If she had any sense of shame, her embarrassment would do the job for me. Maybe that was why the rest of her classmates offered us a wide berth. We sat in one of those massive lecture halls. A three-hundred seater. The type of giant auditorium that could comfortably house a few football teams. Or the cast of *Sister Wives*.

I soaked in my surroundings. No one close enough to eavesdrop. No one in the first two rows at all, in fact. But a few of her classmates had their attention pinned on us. The ones closest to us. Not even trying to hide it.

I met someone's stare until he lowered his eyes.

Good boy.

Figured I had a few more minutes before people realized who I was and the fanfare started.

Beside me, Lucy heaved in a breath mid-word. She'd gotten winded. I recognized the incoming panic attack. Her chest surged. Up. Down. She opened her mouth to say something, but nothing came out.

Until it finally did.

"How can you be so brazen?"

"Occupational hazard," I offered. "I have a nasty habit of toying with my prey."

She took a few minutes to collect herself. The little hand on the clock ticked past the bolded two. The professor was late. Something that rarely happened during my time at Wilton eight years ago.

When she'd calmed enough to speak again, Lucy pulled her shoulders back and decided, "You're not here to kill me."

I cocked a brow, not replying. Knowing her, she'd continue talking without provocation.

And she did.

"You'd be dumb to." It came out matter-of-fact. With so much strength behind it, it amused me. I enjoyed her nerve. I wanted to be the one to break it. She continued, words rushing out of her, "Coming into my class and sitting next to me, in front of witnesses, is too messy. You're not here to kill me."

Truthfully, I remained undecided. Death was too finite for revenge. I preferred extortion, but anything a broke college student had to offer didn't appeal to me.

Unless…

Well, it required trust.

I'd come up with a plan. Out there, even for me. One birthed from what Owen had declared at the country club. I needed good press, and I needed it now. This—giving Lucy free reign to show me who she was—would either convince me or lure me away.

I didn't answer her.

Instead, I scrolled through the stock indexes of my competitors. The only company with a green arrow was Prescott Hotels, but they'd yet to build a presence in the city, which made me less inclined to butt heads with its owner. The notorious Nash Prescott.

I pocketed my phone and glanced at my watch. Nine-sixteen now. Her class ended at ten.

Punctuality. An undervalued trait. In my opinion, if you don't respect your own commitments, you don't respect yourself. And me? Well, I don't respect people who don't respect themselves.

Lucy's hyperventilation had gotten louder. More obvious. Figured I should stop her, because she did have a point—witnesses.

I leaned closer to her, voice low. "Calm down."

She didn't.

If anything, her panic worsened.

"Calm the fuck down," I said, not bothering to hide my irritation. So far, she'd reached oh-for-six on reasons to loop her into my plans. "You're drawing attention to us, and you don't want to do that."

Another shaky breath.

"W-why shouldn't I?" She swallowed thickly, and I'd put money on the fact that it had taken all of her courage to ask me that. To not flee my proximity. "Give me one r-reason why I shouldn't scream."

The expression I sent her way silenced her.

Eviscerated her hope.

I could see the light drain from her eyes.

And it became more obvious by the second that she was not the right fit for my needs. I'd give her another few hours to prove her worth, but it seemed as likely as a plastic-free Vestry-Street housewife.

"Don't even think about it." I ran a finger down her armrest, just grazing her forearm. "I tracked you here. I can track you anywhere, except next time, I won't be so nice."

"This is nice?"

I flashed her my best smile. "Very."

You're breathing, aren't you?

My eyes dipped to her chest, catching the ragged inhales.

Well, barely...

She sank her teeth into her lower lip. "You're following me out of class after this. Aren't you?"

I nodded. That much was obvious. I needed something from her, and playing with your meal before eating it was just bad manners.

But it was also fun.

"How rich are you?"

I didn't answer.

"Rich enough to track me?" she followed up.

"I don't need money to track you."

"Right."

She looked anywhere but me.

I gave her thirty seconds of panic before I tossed the *Scoop* newspaper on her lap. The one with my face plastered on the cover. "Fix it."

She unfolded the paper with stricken fingers and read straight from the body, "*We have the latest scoop on all things Asher Black. Last time we uncovered his illicit boat ride. This time, it's a 9-1-1 call to his club.*"

Her hazels cut to me. I kept my face neutral, gesturing her to continue with a subtle tip of my chin.

Clearing her throat (amateur time-buying technique, by the way), she continued to read, "*Sources say the caller reported an unidentified man for harassing a clubgoer with a gun. Raise your hand if you think it was Asher Black!* Wow," Lucy spit out, her disgust evident, "you really can't exist without these vultures writing about you, can you?"

Her words surprised me. Tilted all my expectations for one startling second. Of all the things to say, that was the one I'd least expected. For starters, she held the bulk of responsibility for what had happened. But I hadn't expected outrage. Or pity. Was that what that was? Hard to know. I didn't have much experience with the emotion.

I began to answer but stopped, feeling the moment people realized I was here. The air shifted. Whispers of my name drifted down to us, courtesy of the stadium-style seating. Something like excitement followed. Buzz. It reached the first row in fast waves.

A few people stood. From the corner of my eye, I saw a group of girls walk down the aisle steps, heading toward the front row. It was almost full now. One of the girls parted from the group, tucking a strand of hair behind her ear. She sent me a suggestive smile.

I didn't glance her way.

I was still staring at Lucy, something like a frown on my lips. Of all the people who would've called the cops on me, I didn't understand why it ended up being her. Didn't understand what I'd done to her.

Revenge?

A false 9-1-1 call was risky and excessive. And given the opportunity, I would've made up for the lost orgasm with a bonus one. (A steal, if you asked me. Two-for-one deals were rare in the Black empire.)

"I don't know how to fix this, but fine. It's a reasonable request, given that I did call the cops on a consensual encounter and obviously inconvenienced you to the point where you felt the need to stalk me...I mean, *track* me down. So, I'll fix this. Somehow." Lucy swallowed and gave me a nod, but her words sounded more like a pep talk to herself. She whispered, so low I needed to tilt my body toward her to hear, "I won't scream. I won't run. I'll stay here like a good little girl, and you won't hurt me. Deal?"

And then she turned away before I could reply.

It almost made me laugh.

Almost.

That girl took a seat next to Lucy. The one blinking her lashes so fast, she resembled a porn star faking an orgasm. She eyed me curiously, not even bothering to conceal her interest. Lucy, however, seemed relieved for the distraction. And annoyed.

She sighed, crossing her arms. "Why are you sitting next to me, Nelly? You're one of Minka's lackeys. You don't even like me."

I shifted, studying Lucy.

Interesting.

Figured she had bite, but I enjoyed seeing it in action.

Nelly's jaw dropped. Which told me all I needed to know. Lucy didn't make a habit of talking back. Guess I was the only one with the privilege of being on the receiving end of her sass. Lucky me.

"It's Nella," the girl said. Stiff. Her eyes shifted to me. "And I was going to ask Asher if you were bothering him."

Lucy held in a snort. I could see it in her rigid shoulders. The way they jerked up at the words. And I'd known Nella-Nelly-Whatever for point-two seconds, and even I knew she was full of shit.

I'd approached Lucy. Not the other way around. Nella-Nelly-Whatever knew that, too, because I'd caught her eyes tracking me as soon as I'd entered the classroom.

"Bull." Lucy dragged out the word. "You saw me sitting here in the splash zone. With no other seats in the other rows." She jerked her thumb toward me. "Also, doubt you're on a first-name basis with him."

Splash zone?

Fuck.

Goddamn Rolland.

Lucy continued, barreling forward with her words, "You probably even thought it was funny. Then, you saw him," she nodded in my direction without looking at me, "sit down and thought you would come over here all demure and innocent to get into his pants." She inhaled and paused, breaking the roll she was on. Excitement sparked in her hazel eyes, which I'd realized by now meant she was about to do something that would piss me off. "Well, you're welcome to take my seat and try."

Of course, she'd take the opportunity to switch seats.

Right after promising me she wouldn't escape.

Little liar.

A few things happened at once.

First, Nella's eyes widened. Probably wasn't the direction she thought Lucy was headed. I'd thought she was two seconds from embarrassing her.

Second, Lucy snatched her bag and moved to leave. She was halfway out of her seat when the third thing happened.

My palm wrapped around her waist, pulling her back into her chair. She opened her mouth, probably to protest, but I shifted my arm so it hung loosely around her shoulders, my fingers casually dipping into the side of her slinky camisole.

She wasn't wearing a bra.

We both knew it.

I could feel her rapid heartbeat against my fingertips.

A light sheen of sweat coated the area of her neck brushing my arm.

Even the quickening of her breaths was audible.

She was my prey. A meek little animal for me to toy with before going in for the kill.

I leaned into her ear and whispered, "You didn't think it would be that easy, did you?"

She amused me. Well, her fear did. This was the same woman who'd tested me in the alley outside of Rogue. The same woman who'd called the cops after I left her hanging. Yeah, I needed something from her, but I'd be damned if I didn't toy with her before asking.

She tried to shrug me off her shoulders, but I only tightened my grip. My fingers dug into the side of her breast, memories of that night flashing through me. Of my hands and mouth on hers.

Nella-Nelly-Whatever huffed, crossing her arms, eyeing the way I tightened my arm around Lucy's shoulder with her lip twisted at the bow.

I glanced at the clock.

Only a few minutes had passed.

Damn.

Rolland was about twenty minutes late, which wasn't off-brand for him. As a business student, I'd never actually taken his class, but he'd garnered an impressive reputation as someone you didn't want to be within ten feet of.

And he didn't even have to kill anyone to gain it.

Tenure. The death of accountability.

No one was fazed when Rolland came in, looking disheveled and wearing his coat inside out. Doctor Ferdinand Rolland taught quantum mechanics and always existed in his own world. His inability to arrive to class on time and make eye contact with his students overshadowed his sheer brilliance.

He'd already started his lecture on Heisenberg's Uncertainty Principle, and he hadn't even reached the front of the class. The lecture room microphone remained at the podium, unattached to his shirt.

The only people who could hear him sat in this row—me, Lucy, Nella-Nelly-Whatever, and the harem of mafia bunnies that had migrated down here.

And in a grand act of karmic justice, Doctor Rolland opened his mouth and spit flew onto Nella's cheek.

Life Tip #2: Karma's never met a bitch she didn't want to slap.

✧   ✧   ✧

Thank you for reading this scene from *Asher Black* in Asher's POV! If you haven't checked out my latest release, read ***DARLING VENOM*** now. www.parkershuntington.com

Dear Delaney

Kelsey Clayton

DELANEY

M Y GRANDMOTHER USED to tell me, "*Stay young, Delaney. Getting old is a bitch.*" I can still remember the way she frowned at every wrinkle and stuck her nose up at everyone who tried to tell her that all parts of life are beautiful. She was a sweet woman, though secretly miserable inside, and she stayed that way until her passing when I was sixteen.

Over the years, I wondered why she was never able to just enjoy the things around her. It wasn't until my wedding day, when I walked down the aisle to Knox, that the pieces fell into place.

She was lonely.

My grandfather was an incredible man, or at least that's what I've heard. He passed away when my mom was young—a tragic car accident with a drunk driver gave him no chance at survival. No matter how many people surrounded my grandmother with love and affection, she was always missing the other half of her.

Her best friend.

Her forever soulmate.

I feel her pain as I sit in my rocking chair, clutching the diamond necklace Knox bought me for our first wedding anniversary and staring at the flowers on the table that have long since withered.

I can't throw them away.

I can't rid myself of one of the only things I have left of him.

When my health started to decline, he did what he always would: he tried to take on the world and be my own personal superhero. It took a year of arguments and an instance when I almost set our house on fire before he agreed to put me in a facility. But he still came to visit. Every day, he would sit with me from sunup to sundown, never letting me miss him for a single second.

And then one day he didn't arrive.

I think I knew it in my heart. Opening my eyes that morning, I could feel something was horribly different. And when Malakai and Hudson came in with fresh tears wiped from their eyes, my worst fear was confirmed.

They said there was nothing we could have done. No way to know it was going to happen. Just a massive heart attack that took him in a millisecond.

He probably didn't feel an ounce of pain.

But he didn't have to. The pain is mine. For me to live with the unfillable void that he left behind. It's unforgiving and takes no mercy, just like him.

A knock at the door grabs my attention, and I quickly wipe away the single tear that managed to escape as Hudson steps into the room.

"Hey, Mom," she says softly.

I give her the best smile I can manage, seeing her father's crystal blue eyes staring back at me. "Hi, sweetheart. How are you?"

She shrugs. "It's not getting any easier, but I didn't think it would."

"Well, it's only been a few weeks. How are the kids?"

"They're okay. Handling it as well as I expected. They miss him, though."

The corner of my mouth twitches, but before I can say anything, Malakai walks in holding an old, black shoebox. The tattoos that brighten his skin bring me right back to when he was seventeen and begging me to let his dad give him his first tattoo. And the grin he gave me when I finally relented is one that I'll never forget.

"It's my favorite old lady!" he jokes.

I roll my eyes playfully. "And it's my favorite delinquent."

Raising kids always comes with challenges; raising twins even more so. But Kai always managed to put Knox's antics to shame. It's a miracle that any of us made it through, and that he's still alive—though he's still the same sarcastic ass he's always been.

"What's that?" I ask and nod at the box.

He smiles as he passes it to me, and I rest it on my lap.

"If this is another prank, I'm changing my will so Hudson gets everything."

Both my kids chuckle, but Kai shakes his head. "We found it while cleaning out the house. It was tucked away behind some old coats in the guest room closet."

My brows furrow as my frail hands slowly lift the lid to find unopened letters, addressed to me, in Knox's handwriting. There's no postage on them, showing he never actually attempted to give them to me, and all of them have been reopened after being sealed shut.

Seeing his handwriting makes my heart ache, but I'm desperate to have anything I can from him. I start from the back of the pile and pull out the first envelope.

Delaney,

Fuck.

What the actual fuck am I doing?

I should be staying as far away from you as possible. God knows I'm only going to ruin you. I'm a train wreck. Entirely fucked in the head. A whole goddamn carnival's worth of red flags. And yet, I'm lying awake every night, letting thoughts of you plague my mind.

Do you know what you're doing to me?

Do you have even the slightest indication?

Fucking hell, Bambi. I hate how gone for you I am already. And I hate knowing what a bad idea this is. And I really hate knowing that I don't have a damn say in the matter.

You've fucked all my rules from the start.

No chance you're going to stop now.

Knox

A wet laugh bubbles out of me, remembering how hard he tried to push me away. He never stood a chance. We were meant for each other from the start.

Passing the letter over to Hudson, I take out the next one.

Laney,

I'm sitting here watching you sleep, like some kind of sick fuck.

And now, looking at those words staring me back in the face, makes me realize how screwed I really am. You really should run for the damn hills, you know that?

The shit Trayland pulled tonight was pussy behavior, but seeing you on the sidelines, wearing my jersey—yeah, I'd jump someone for you, too.
Knox

Carter Trayland. Now that's a name I haven't thought of in a while. From what I remember, he and Jace London took the corporate world by storm, becoming everything we always knew they would be. Tye was really close with Tessa for a while, running Safe and Sound together and making a difference for kids who needed it. It wasn't until their daughter grew up and had kids of her own that they moved across the country to be closer to her. And no one could blame them for it.

Knox did eventually get his revenge on Carter for attacking him that night. Although, he did it in the most Knox way possible. And Tye was in on it.

For weeks, they left little clues and breadcrumbs that made Carter believe something was going on. A sock under the bed. A sweatshirt Tye wore that she insisted was Carter's. A couple late nights she spent unaccounted for.

And when Carter thought his worst fear was coming true, that he was losing yet another woman to Knox Vaughn, the promise to get payback was fulfilled.

I chuckle to myself as I remember the look on Carter's face as he banged on my door, ready to take out an unmatched wrath on Knox, only to find his closest friends all drinking wine while the kids played in the living room.

Delayed retribution.

Bambi,
It's been a long time since I enjoyed my birthday. But like you do with everything else in my life, you flipped that around without me having a damn say in the matter. It's like you always know exactly what I need, and right now, I fucking need you.
If any other girl uttered the words you did tonight, I would've run for the hills. But something about you, and the way the words slipped off your tongue...fuck. I want to hear them on a constant replay for the rest of my damn life.
I love you, Delaney. I may not be able to say that out loud right now, but goddamn am I in love with you. You make me want to try harder. To be the best version of myself. To be someone deserving of you.
I fucking love you, Bambi.
My Bambi.
Knox

His words bring a pink tint to my cheeks. I knew it. Long before he said it, I knew. I could see it in his eyes. Feel it in the way he held me close, even when he was sleeping. He may not have said it, but I didn't need him to.

I knew.

Delaney,
I've come to the realization that you're never going to get these letters. They'll stay tucked away in a safe place, like all the memories we have together—bittersweet things to torture myself when I'm feeling extra self-sabotaging.
Fuck, do you have any idea how much this is breaking me? I wish you were

here. So much of me wants to pull you back into my arms and tell you everything, but I know exactly what you would do. Because you're strong, and when you want something, you don't let anything stand in your way. And I can't let you take this on. It's too dangerous. Too risky.

But God, Bambi. Please don't think this is easy for me. It's not. Pushing you away was the hardest thing I've ever done. And the pain that lingers in your absence is a merciless one.

I just miss you.

Knox

"You and Dad split up at one point?" Hudson asks, now resigned to reading over my shoulder because I'm taking too long.

I nod. "For a couple months when we first got together. It was one of the most painful points of my life."

I don't need to add the unspoken *until now* that rests on my tongue. The two of them both know that living in a world where he no longer exists has been anything but easy on me.

"If you missed each other so much, why weren't you just together?"

"Because your father was a stubborn man who insisted he knew best and would set himself on fire if he thought it meant keeping me safe."

Delaney,

I wish you'd let me go. Not because I don't love you with every fucking fiber of my being, but because every time you grab at me, I'm tempted to let you. Tonight, seeing you at Zayn's party, I felt like I could finally breathe and was painfully suffocating all at the same time. Having you that close to me and yet not being able to wrap my arms around you...it was the worst kind of torture.

If you only knew I was doing this to keep you safe, maybe then you'd understand. But you're never going to know, and I'm never going to get over you.

Knox

A smile pulls at my lips when I remember that party. I was so determined. No one was going to get in my way, not even Tessa and the way she begged me not to go. Seeing him again brought a whole new wave of pain, but I would have drowned repeatedly if it meant getting to spend a single second in his presence.

"Damn, Mom," Kai jokes. "You must have been a badass if you had Dad this fucked up."

I chuckle and say nothing as I move onto the next letter.

Callahan,

Forgive me for not writing your first name. I tried. It's just too painful.

If what I saw today was any indication, you've officially moved on. I can't say I didn't expect it. A gorgeous girl like you had no business being with a teenage dirtbag like me. However, it may have been a little easier to see if it was anyone other than Trayland.

Scratch that.

Not even then.

Despite all the hatred I feel for him, I hope he makes you happy. You deserve everything good in the world, and if he's the one who can give it to you, if he can make you smile the way you did with me, then so be it.

In the meantime, I'll be here—loving you the best way I know how.

Vaughn

"Wait," Hudson balks. "You and Mr. Trayland? Really?"

Kai rips the letter out of my hands as I roll my eyes. "No way. And Dad didn't kill him?"

"Oh, trust me. He wanted to."

The day Carter asked me to prom, Knox had a look on his face that was absolutely homicidal. If it wasn't for Zayn taking the brunt of his anger, he probably would've done some serious damage. Carter was strong, but nothing could come close to Knox on a "Delaney Warpath," as Tessa always called it.

I notice the next letter is a skip in time, but I'm not upset about it. Reliving the time I nearly lost him, while knowing what it feels like now to be forced to live without him, is not something I'm interested in.

Delaney,

It's been a while since I've written one of these. Not that you would know. You haven't the slightest clue about this box of unspoken words.

I thought about giving them to you once or twice. I pictured watching as your eyes moved quickly across each page, desperate to read all the things I couldn't say out loud at the time. You have always jumped at any opportunity to get a peek inside my brain.

I wish I could get a look inside yours.

Twenty years to life if I'm convicted.

I've never been one to admit fear, but the thought of having to spend the rest of my life away from you is enough to send a chill down my spine.

I think if they send me away, I'm going to give you these letters. You'll need to know how serious I am when I tell you to go be happy. I don't want you to let me hold you back. Just like I said to you in The Underground—I want you to go be the greatness you were always destined to be.

I love you,

Knox

Reading becomes more difficult as my eyes start to water.

I never told him, but that was the second scariest time of my life, only being topped by the two weeks he spent in a coma. Not knowing if he was going to be ripped away from me, thrown into a prison he didn't deserve to be in—I don't think I slept for weeks.

"Dad almost went to jail?" Hudson shrieks.

I hold the letter to my chest. "Okay, there are some things about your father you just don't need to know."

Kai crosses his arms over his chest. "He told me the story."

"He did?" my daughter and I ask in unison, me surprised, her indignant.

He nods. "When I got into all those fights in high school. I think it was supposed to be a lecture, but he just ended up sounding like a legend."

I blink back at him, slowly shaking my head. "You really are just like him. God help us all."

Hudson laughs at her brother's expense while he smiles proudly, and I grab the next letter from the box.

Bambi,

What are you doing to me?

If someone told me last year that I'd be following the valedictorian of HGP (which I still think should stand for Hoes, Gays, and Prostitots) across the country, I would've laughed in their face. I never thought I would be that guy. And yet, remembering the look in your eyes as you asked me to come with you, I know without a doubt—I'd follow you anywhere.

Knox

I remember how anxious I was leading up to asking him that. North Haven was always Knox's *safe* haven. A place he never intended on leaving. It was everything he's ever known. Hell, it's one of the reasons we ended up moving back here once I graduated.

This place will always be home.

Soon to be Mrs. Delaney Vaughn,

I'm not a fucking hallmark card, Bambi. We both know that. But today was the closest I've ever come to feeling like one.

Proposing to you was always a when, never an if, but no matter how much I mentally prepared for it, nothing matched what I felt when I got down on one knee.

For someone who has literally had their life on the line more times than socially acceptable, I should've been a lot less nervous staring up at you—not that saying no was an option. I wasn't kidding when I said you'd wake up in Vegas with a ring on your finger.

I still think you're out of your damn mind for wanting to spend the rest of your life with me, but I'm so grateful, because a life without you isn't one worth living.

Yours forever,

Knox

"Why is it so hard for me to picture Dad nervous?" Hudson questions.

Kai laughs. "You didn't see the way he looked when he found out you were seeing Van."

"Homicidal and nervous are not the same thing," she corrects him.

I can't help but chuckle. I can still picture the look on Grayson's face when Knox pushed him against a wall and told him that if Pretty Boy Jr. hurt his little girl, it would be Gray that paid for it. Decades of being best friends didn't matter when it came to Hudson. And by the way Grayson swallowed harshly, he knew it was no idle threat.

"All right." Kai straightens up. "Let's go, Huds. We still have a lot to get done."

She groans softly but doesn't argue as she gives me a hug and presses a kiss to my snow-colored hair. "Sav will be here tomorrow morning for brunch. She told me to tell you she's bringing mimosas. Just be careful."

The corners of my mouth raise. "Please. Grayson has been switching out the champagne with sparkling water since she broke her hip while drunk three years ago."

"I was referring to the trouble you get into together."

She's got me there.

Kai hugs me and the two of them head out while I go back to reading the letters.

Mrs. Vaughn,

I don't think I'll ever get tired of the way that sounds.

You're lying next to me, sound asleep, and I can't stop looking at the ring on my finger. Although, it's so much less of a claim on me than your initial that's permanently inked on my skin. Not to mention the proposal that's etched into my chest. But anything that ties me to you is more than okay with me.

I can't believe I get to grow old with you.

To spend the rest of my days by your side.

Yeah, I could live with that.

I love you,

Knox

P.S. – I hope you know divorce is never an option. It's against my religion.

An involuntary bark of laughter shoots out as I read the last line. Knox and religion went together like nuns and dildos. But he would have used anything as an excuse to keep me with him. While he always thought I was too good for him, he knew in his heart that we belonged together.

And so did I.

It's why I fought so hard for it.

I read through the next few letters with a heavy heart, missing him more now than I did the day I lost him.

Laney,

Three weeks late. Two pink lines.

The reality that I'm going to be a dad still hasn't set in all the way. Probably because it's overrun by the reality that I'm going to have to share you. You and I both know I'm a selfish son of a bitch when it comes to you, and I failed sharing in kindergarten. But the thought of a miniature you running around doesn't sound so bad.

She'll have my eyes and your innocence, and she'll have me wrapped around her finger the same way you do.

And I'll get to watch you look at someone else the same way you look at me.

I'm going to be everything both our fathers weren't.

A little family of my own.

I love you and our baby,

Knox

Delaney,

Like everything else in your life, you just had to be an overachiever with this, too, didn't you?

Twins. Two babies. Double the diapers, and bottles, and vomit. Don't tell them about how I damn near fainted in the doctor's office. They need to think I'm tough. To them, I'm Dad. That's basically Superman in kid language.

Fucking twins.

Only you, Bambi. Only you.

I love you, our babies, and your overachieving uterus,

Knox

Bambi,

Tonight, we became parents.

You have always been the most important person in my life since the moment you wrecking-balled your way into it, but tonight, it was like my entire world shifted. Seven years together. Married for one. And somehow, you managed to become even more to me tonight.

I guess kids bind you together in ways no amount of promises can.

The admiration I felt as I watched you give birth to our children was unlike anything I've ever known before. You're absolutely incredible, you know that? Seeing you with Malakai and Hudson, my life is complete.

And for the sake of being a total sap, thank you for making me the happiest man alive.

I'm so in love with you,

Knox

Learning how to be parents was the first time I ever saw Knox's confidence falter. From the moment he laid eyes on them, he loved our kids with everything he had, and I think that's why he was so afraid.

Afraid he'd screw them up.

Afraid he'd let them down.

Afraid he'd be anything less than they deserve.

I knew exactly what he was feeling, because I felt it too, but he was the most incredible father. He was not a patient person and yet managed to have all the patience in the world for them. Well, at least until he had to teach Hudson how to drive. After the one time he tried, he refused to ever be in a car with her again.

"She's going to kill us all," he used to say.

Although he said that a lot, about both Hudson *and* Kai.

Especially Kai.

I read each letter, hanging on every word, until I find one that has me laughing through my tears.

Delaney,

Whoever said having kids is a good idea needs a fucking psychiatric evaluation. I know, I know. He's our son, and we love him. Yeah, got it. But holy fucking shit.

Was I this bad?

I have to apologize to my mother.

Fuck, I have to apologize to your *mother.*

It's like one minute he's all right, and the next, I'm afraid he's going to intentionally light the goddamn house on fire. He gets that from you, you know. Maybe not you specifically, but that's classic CBP behavior. Definitely something he got from your side of the family.

At least there's hope for Hudson. Daddy's little princess. She'll never do anything wrong.

Okay, stop laughing at me now.

Let me live in my fantasy world.

I love you, and our perfect daughter, and our son's psychopathic ass,

Knox

P.S – If I ever go missing, I hope they know to investigate him.

No one could deny that Kai was a handful. And no one really expected anything otherwise. After all, he's Knox Vaughn's son. He was bound to cause mischief.

He still does.

All of the kids have been very close, and they were throughout growing up. But the trouble they got into rivaled all else. Some things even we couldn't protect them from. They had to fight their own battles, no matter how much we wanted to take on their burdens for them.

THE DAY TURNS to night as I read letters from all different occasions.

Our anniversaries.

The kids' high school graduation.

The day we renewed our vows.

Each one pulls more of a reaction out of me than the last.

Tears flow freely from my eyes as I get down to the last two letters, feeling like I'm losing him all over again, but this time knowing it.

Delaney,

Today, I heard the words that I've dreaded all my life.

"I'm sorry, Mr. Vaughn. Your wife's condition is terminal."

They said there is nothing they can do.

That the best thing we can do is make the most of the time we have left.

You held my hand as my heart broke, and I held you as you cried.

I hope you know that you changed my life. I was just some stupid kid, going nowhere in life. The only thing I cared about was where the next party was going to be.

You should've run for the hills that first night, and something in those doe eyes of yours wanted to. Don't even try to deny it, Bambi.

But you stayed.

You gave me something to fight for.

Something to want.

Something to need.

And if it wasn't for you, I don't know what ditch I would've ended up in, but I definitely wouldn't be where I am now.

Everything I am, I owe to you.
Forever grateful and forever in love,
Knox

Throughout all the years we spent together, that night was when we clung to each other the tightest. He really did hold me while I cried—running his fingers through my hair and whispering words of affirmation in my ear. He wiped away my tears and then his own, and he kissed me the same way he always did.

Nothing could ever change the way he felt about me.

The way we felt about each other.

I swat at the stream of tears as I grab the last letter from the box.

Bambi,

This house is too quiet without you.

Your lingering scent and the pictures of us through the years that hang on the walls, they're not enough. I need you here—tracing my tattoos with your finger and complaining how loud the TV is.

I know. It's safest for you there. And you know your safety has always been my number one priority, but that doesn't make it any easier. Being away from you has been and always will be my worst nightmare.

I spent the night opening each one of the letters I've written you and reading them back over. It was bittersweet to relive everything we've been through, and there's no denying we had one extraordinary life together. I just wish it never had to end.

I think that if you go before me, I'll be right behind you.

And I know what you'd say.

"Don't be stupid. The kids need you."

But the truth is, I was just never meant to live a life without you.

I love you always,

Knox

I hold the letter to my chest as sobs wrack through my body. The pain of missing him is unlike anything I've ever felt before. It's harsh and unrelenting as it rips me apart from the inside out. And I can't judge him for thinking those things, because I know. I feel it, too. I've held on for the kids, but I feel every ounce of his longing.

I grab a piece of stationary and a pen from the table, trying my best not to let my tears drip onto the paper as I start the letter.

My Dearest Malakai and Hudson,

Please take these letters and use them to experience the love story I had the incredible fortune of living through. Let yourself feel every word and know how strongly your father and I felt for each other. Our story is one that not even the greatest of fairy tales can rival, because it was ours, and it was real.

I can only wish for you to have the same with your significant others.

I love you both from the bottom of my heart,

Mom

Leaving the paper on the table, I carefully put back every one of Knox's letters before climbing into bed. My cheeks are soaked with the tears that won't stop coming. I lie back and clutch my necklace tightly in my hand as I close my eyes—finally allowing myself to let go.

"I was never meant to live a life without you, either."

Peace.

That's the only way to describe it.

A warm, bright light shines over everything, casting a glow over the striking colors. There's no pain. No fear. Just the feeling of love and belonging.

My gaze travels over the flower-filled meadow until it lands on him.

All the years of aging have gone, leaving him looking the same way he did when we got married—the time he called the happiest in his life.

I blink and he's in front of me, smiling softly as he puts his hand out.

"Hey, Bambi."

Everything feels right again as I throw myself into his arms. We laugh together the way we used to. He picks me up and spins me around before pulling away to put a hand on my cheek.

"I've missed you," I tell him.

His grin widens. "I was always right there."

He pulls me in and covers my lips with his own. The kiss is everything I needed. In that instant, I feel it. The love we have for each other is one for the ages, and I've never known anything more—we were always meant to be together, in life and after.

He kisses me one last time and pulls away, lacing his fingers with mine as he starts to pull me along.

"Where are we going?" I ask with a chuckle.

He turns around and smirks at me, and the words he uses are ones I know all too well.

"Do you trust me?"

✧   ✧   ✧

Thank you for reading DEAR DELANEY! Want more from author Kelsey Clayton? Visit her website.

www.kelseyclayton.com

SEALing His Future

Susan Stoker

Two of the most popular of Susan Stoker's characters meet on a Navy SEAL mission…and one finds out the truth about the woman he thought loved him and was waiting for him to return home safe and sound.

Baker – 37 years old

BAKER RAWLINGS WAS tired.
Exhausted.

The last two months had been hell. Of course, when he'd joined the Navy SEALs, he hadn't expected the missions to be sunshine and roses, but for some reason, he hadn't expected every single one to be a nonstop, adrenaline-filled, terror-inducing, this-might-be-my-last-moment-on-earth mission either.

This latest had started out all right. They'd been sent overseas to rescue three prisoners of war. Their intel was solid, and Baker's team was working with another group of SEALs he respected. Their leader was a man named Tex. He was young, but had one of the deepest needs to help others that Baker had ever seen.

The night before everything went to shit, Baker and Tex had gotten a few moments to talk about something other than the battle plan and how they were going to get the three men who'd been taken captive out alive.

They'd spoken about their families, what their first meal would be when they got home from the mission, and whether they had anyone waiting for them back home.

Tex had admitted he didn't have anyone special. Baker had found himself opening up to the young man, telling him about Tabitha.

"I thought she was it for me," Baker said. "That she was the love of my life. But almost as soon as she moved in with me, she changed. Became withdrawn. She seems irritated when I'm home, and just as pissed off when I get orders for a mission. Nothing I do seems to satisfy her."

"So you're breaking up with her when you get back?" Tex asked.

Baker shrugged.

"Look, man. I know I'm younger than you and don't have as much life experience as you, but why are you settling for a woman who doesn't even sound like she likes you all that much?"

Baker shrugged.

"When I get married, it's going to be for good. I'm going to find a woman who loves me exactly how I am, warts and all. She's going to be strong enough to stand on her own two feet when I can't be with her, but still willing to lean on me when shit gets tough. I don't care what she looks like, how much she weighs, or if she already has ten kids when we meet. I just want someone who loves me for me."

Baker snorted and rolled his eyes. "Good luck with that."

"I'm serious," Tex said quietly. "I'd rather be single for the rest of my life than settle for someone who merely tolerates me."

"You gonna make the SEALs a career?" Baker asked. He might think the kid was a little naïve, but he couldn't help but like him all the same.

"Maybe. I'd love to be able to do something with computers. I'm pretty good with them, if I do say so myself. I'd like to use my skills to help the Navy. Find missing people, track down the enemy, use what I know to help soldiers and special forces teams on missions. That kind of thing."

Baker couldn't help but be impressed.

"What about you? You've been doing this SEAL thing for a while now, huh?" Tex asked.

Baker chuckled. "Yeah. I'm a lifer. Not sure what I'll do when I get out. But that time is comin'. Been at this for what seems like all of my adult life."

"Where do you want to go when you're out?" Tex asked.

"Hawaii," Baker said without hesitation. "I want to learn how to surf. Enjoy the warm weather. Eat Hawaiian food."

"Not to mention check out the hot chicks in bikinis," Tex teased.

"Exactly," Baker joked.

Tex stared at him for a long moment before saying, "It's not my place, and we don't even really know each other, but if I've learned anything in my short time as a SEAL, it's to trust my instincts. And if yours are telling you that something's up with the woman who's back at your house, you need to move on."

Baker nodded. "Yeah." He'd pretty much already decided to have a long talk with Tabitha when he got home. Being a SEAL was who he was. If she'd moved in with him hoping he'd quit the military and hang out at home with her, doing a nine-to-five job, she'd seriously misread the situation. He'd loved her once. And that love had slowly but surely died. It was time for them both to move on.

He hadn't had time to talk to Tex much after that. As team leader, he needed to go over the upcoming mission with his own team. Then they'd had to get some rest before heading out early in the morning to rescue their countrymen.

But as with just about every single mission, nothing had gone right. They'd rescued the POWs, but not before their captors had done their best to take everyone out. Baker's team had sustained several injuries, but thankfully nothing critical.

His new friend Tex, however, had unfortunately stepped in the wrong place at the wrong time and triggered an IED. He was currently being flown to Germany in order to attempt to save at least part of his leg that had been blown to bits...and hopefully his life.

Making friends was a difficult thing in the military. Not only was the government constantly making their soldiers and sailors change duty stations, the risk of losing someone to an explosive, mortar fire, or a stray bullet was extremely high...especially as a SEAL. Baker hadn't met many people he'd had an immediate connection with, but he'd enjoyed spending time with Tex and thought he was uncannily mature for his age. He sent a short prayer into the world for the young man to make it through the many surgeries he'd be undergoing.

Now, it was a relief to finally be heading stateside, although Baker had to deal with Tabitha when he got home. He wanted to hope that things would be different when he got there. That she'd be overjoyed to see him, would sit on the couch and simply hold him while he decompressed. But the chances of that happening were slim to none.

In the last email he'd received from Tabitha, she'd bitched about the lawn work needing to be done, she didn't have enough money to repair her car, and that, when she'd agreed to move in, she hadn't realized she'd be basically living alone.

Sighing, Baker rested his head on the back of his seat on the military plane. He had earphones on, but they weren't plugged in; they were just to keep anyone from attempting to have a long conversation with him. He liked most of the men on his team, but he needed some space.

He thought about the conversation he'd had with Tex once again. How sure the other man had been when he'd talked about finding a woman who loved him exactly how he was. That would be harder with a prosthesis. But he had a feeling if anyone could find someone to love him exactly as is, it would be Tex.

The flight home was long, and Baker should have slept, but as usual, his mind wouldn't shut down. His time as a SEAL was coming to an end in a few years. He hadn't thought much about what he'd do when he got out...but Tex had inadvertently given him an idea.

Baker also had an affinity for computers. What if he did as Tex suggested? Used his abilities to track down intel? To help the Navy and other governmental agencies get information on men like those they'd just taken out, men who'd taken American soldiers captive?

For the first time in a long time, excitement swam in Baker's veins. He was good at making people trust him. He wanted to combine that with his computer acumen to continue to serve his country, while not having to put himself in the direct line of fire.

But first he needed to deal with Tabitha.

Baker sighed.

The plane touched down, and while he hadn't exactly expected Tabitha to be at the airport to greet him—especially since when the SEALs returned home from a mission, there weren't any big parades or special parties thrown in their honor—he was disappointed nonetheless. Inevitably, there were always a few wives and children waiting. Word would get out, and those who could, always came to meet their loved ones. But not Tabitha.

Baker greeted his team's spouses and made sure everyone was good to go—and that they'd be at the after-action review of the mission the next afternoon—before heading to his vehicle. He threw his rucksack in the backseat before climbing behind the wheel.

It was drizzling, which didn't help his mood. The more he thought about moving to Hawaii once he retired, the more he looked forward to it. Sunshine, cool breezes, and surfing. He needed that more than he'd realized.

Baker pulled into the driveway of his small condo and took a deep breath. The last thing he wanted to do was fight with Tabitha, but he had a feeling what he wanted and what he was going to get were two completely different things.

He hefted his bag over his shoulder and headed up the walk. The condo was quiet and dark. After unlocking the door, Baker walked in and called out, "Tabitha?"

He flicked on the light in the foyer...and winced as he looked around.

Baker wasn't a man who needed a lot of stuff. He didn't especially like clutter, but ever since Tabitha had moved in, his condo had become a dumping ground for all her crap. When he was home, he could keep most of it contained, but in the two months he'd been gone, she'd either been on a ton of shopping sprees, or she'd completely disregarded his need for everything to be in its place.

There were shopping bags all over the couch and table, and clothes were strewn everywhere. Her shoes littered the floor in several places. Baker could just see the counter in the kitchen, and it looked as if there were dirty dishes on every available surface. If she'd done even one load of laundry or dishes in the two months he'd been gone, Baker would be surprised.

The exhaustion that sat heavy on his shoulders pressed down even harder. He wouldn't be able to sleep until at least some of the crap everywhere was cleaned up.

"Tabby!" he bellowed, too angry to walk up the stairs to the bedroom to wake her.

But only silence greeted him.

His head pounding, Baker dropped his rucksack and sighed. He should be worried about where his girlfriend could be, but at the moment, all he could think about was where to start cleaning up the mess she'd left him.

And Tex. He hoped the SEAL was all right. He had no idea if he had family who would head to Germany to sit by his side as he healed. Losing his leg would certainly end his SEAL career, which was a blow to the Navy for sure. Baker had a feeling the man would've risen in the ranks extremely fast.

Just when he was about to head into the kitchen to see the full extent of the damage, and calculate how long it would take him to clean before he could get a shower and some sleep, a knock sounded at the door behind him, making Baker jump.

Laughing a little at himself, he turned and opened it. He blinked in surprise at the police officer standing there.

"Are you Baker Rawlings?" the man asked.

Panic set in. Had something happened to his parents while he'd been deployed? Had Tabitha been in an accident? "Yes," he told the man. "What's wrong? Is it Tabby? Is she okay? Has one of my teammates been injured?"

"No one's been hurt. Can I come in?" the officer asked.

Baker was confused. If no one was hurt, why was the man here? Knowing he wouldn't get any answers until he heard what the officer had to say, Baker backed up and gestured for the man to enter.

"I'd offer you a seat, but as you can see, the place is a mess. I just got home from a mission and I haven't even had a shower yet," Baker said a little grumpily.

"I'm sorry, I won't take much of your time. I'm Detective Prince. We've been conducting an undercover assignment after receiving a tip. I'm sorry to be the one to tell you this…but Tabitha Grundel has been arrested for conspiracy to commit murder."

Baker blinked. "*Murder?* Who did she want to kill?"

"You."

Baker could only stare at the man. "What?"

"Again, I'm sorry to be the one to break this to you, especially right when you got home. But since getting that tip, we've been following Miss Grundel and her boyfriend. We've had them under constant surveillance. We have hours of phone and text conversations between the two of them and a third person, the one who was actually going to do the deed. The plan was to make it look like a home robbery. Tabitha would have unlocked the back door to your condo to let the third man enter, and when you came downstairs to investigate, he would've shot you. She was then going to call the police and claim someone broke in."

Baker's head was spinning. All he could do was repeat, "*What?*"

"It seems the plan was to collect your life insurance from the Navy and sell all your belongings, then move to California."

"She has a boyfriend?" Baker knew he sounded completely off-kilter, but he couldn't help it. He needed to think—but right now, it was nearly impossible.

"Yes."

"And he was going to break into my house?"

"Well, not him. But the person they hired to kill you, yes. And technically he wouldn't have had to break in, since Tabitha was going to leave the door open for him."

"Let me guess…she was going to break the window to make it look like that's how he'd gained entry?"

"Yes."

Baker shook his head. He'd known all along Tabby wasn't the smartest person in the world, but she was kind and upbeat, at least in the beginning. She was also beautiful, and pretty decent in bed. Baker was ashamed that he'd let such superficial attributes keep him from seeing the real, apparently *devious* woman underneath.

Then something else the officer said sank in. "Wait—my life insurance?"

"Yes. Apparently she thought that since she was living with you, it would be awarded to her…she mentioned something about being a common-law wife in her texts and conversations with her boyfriend."

"Virginia isn't a common-law state," Baker told the officer, something the man was obviously well aware of.

"You know that, and I know that, but apparently Tabitha and her boyfriend didn't."

Baker rubbed his forehead. His headache had morphed into a full-blown migraine. He should be more upset upon learning his girlfriend had not only been cheating on him, but had plotted to kill him for money that wouldn't ever be hers. Instead, a large part of him was relieved.

He wouldn't have to break up with her. Wouldn't have to deal with telling her that she needed to move out.

"What now?" he asked wearily.

The officer looked sympathetic. "We'd like to have you come down to the station and answer some questions. Give us some background, tell us what you can about Tabitha."

The last thing Baker wanted to do was tell anyone what an idiot he'd been when it came to his now ex-girlfriend. Admit that he'd kept her around longer than he should've simply because it was easier than dealing with her temper and the inevitable outburst that would come with him breaking things off.

"Will the charges stick?" he asked.

"Yes," Detective Prince said firmly. "We waited until we had all the evidence we needed before arresting her. All three who were involved will see jail time."

Whatever she got wouldn't be enough for Baker, but as of this moment, he didn't care. The moment the detective told him she'd been arrested for conspiring to kill him, he'd already washed his hands of her. She'd have to deal with the consequence of her actions. "I have a meeting on the base I can't get out of tomorrow afternoon. Can I come in the day after tomorrow?"

"Yes, that would be fine. For what it's worth…I'm sorry. This is a pretty crummy thing to come home to after being deployed."

The officer wasn't wrong about that. "Thanks."

"Thank you for your service. I understand you're a Navy SEAL?"

Baker nodded.

"Right. I probably don't need to say this, but…watch your back," Detective Prince said.

Baker straightened. "Do I need to worry about any other players being involved in her plot?" he asked.

"No. But desperate people do desperate things, and Tabitha Grundel was pretty desperate when she was being led away in cuffs. There's no telling what she might do behind bars. Who she might try to contract to finish what she started."

"You *did* tell her that even if I'm dead, she's not getting a penny of my life insurance, right?" Baker asked. "I'm assuming in your reconnaissance and research, you found that my parents are my beneficiaries?"

The officer nodded. "Yes, we did discovered that, and we informed Miss Grundel. But she refused to believe it. She told us that you said you'd take care of her if anything happened to you while you were on a mission."

"Yeah, I would've. My teammates would've made sure she had a place to live and that my final expenses were paid. I didn't mean I was making her my beneficiary," Baker said with a shake of his head.

"Yeah, well, she obviously interpreted that differently," Detective Prince said with a shrug. "Anyway, if you have any questions before we meet, here's my card."

Baker took the business card with a nod. He closed the door behind the man and stared at the wood for a long moment. Then he turned to face the mess that was his house.

Making a split-second decision, Baker headed for the stairs.

Fuck it. He'd clean up later. And by clean up, he meant throw every single one of Tabitha's belongings into the fucking dumpster.

He made a mental note to talk to his commander tomorrow about transferring to a different base. Maybe across the country, to California. He wanted to check on Tex and make sure he made it through surgery…and look at real estate in Hawaii.

After a long, hot shower, Baker lay on his bed and stared at the ceiling. He was beyond tired, but his mind wouldn't shut down. He thought about what Tex had said, about the kind of woman he was looking for.

"I'm going to find a woman who loves me exactly how I am, warts and all. She's going to be strong enough to stand on her own two feet when I can't be with her, but still willing to lean on me when shit gets tough. I don't care what she looks like, how much she weighs, or if she already has ten kids when we meet. I just want someone who loves me for me."

Baker wanted that. The problem was, he wasn't sure she existed. He was almost forty, and if he hadn't found his other half by now, he was afraid he never would. All his life, he'd felt as if she was out there…somewhere. But finding her had turned out to be more difficult than he'd ever expected.

He'd once thought Tabitha was that woman, the other half of his soul, but even before he'd asked her to move in, he realized she wasn't. Rather than be lonely, he'd continued to date her anyway.

No more. Baker was done with casual dating. It didn't matter if he never had sex again; he wouldn't settle for another half-assed relationship. He'd rather be celibate and alone the rest of his life than be tied to someone he wasn't madly and passionately in love with.

He wanted someone who made him laugh. Who didn't mind his protective personality. Who could stand at his side and be proud of him, and who was strong enough to withstand anything life might throw their way. He wanted someone selfless and friendly, who would be happy to see him again whether they were apart two hours or two months.

In return, she'd get all of him. Everything that he was. His devotion, his loyalty, and he'd do whatever it took to protect her from the shit life had a way of throwing at people. If she was out there, she'd be the most important person in his life, and he'd make sure she knew that with every fiber of her being.

Baker sighed.

He was being maudlin. He wasn't sure such a woman existed. At least not for him.

He had a few more years of service in the Navy to go, but then he was retiring, moving to Hawaii and becoming a beach bum. He would see about using his skills to continue to serve his country. He'd stay busy and single…and that would have to be enough.

Just as he drifted off to asleep, he had a hazy vision of a woman with brown hair, wrinkles around her eyes, and a laugh that made everyone around them turn and stare. She was petite, with more pain in her gaze than any one person should have to bear.

And when she turned to look at him, she whispered, "Be patient, Baker. Our time will come."

◇   ◇   ◇

If you've read any of my stories, you've met Tex and know he didn't let losing his leg hold him back. He's been an anchor for so many of my Heroes and heroines. I loved connecting Tex with BAKER. If you want to know more about the mysterious Baker, you can start with Finding Elodie, which is the first book in my SEAL Team Hawaii Series. His story will come…

Read on!

EVERY PIECE OF YOU

TERRI E. LAINE

TUGBOAT

I NEVER THOUGHT I would be back in Mason Creek except to visit. Yet here I was, bags unpacked with the rest of my possessions in storage until I figured things out. They said home was where the heart was, which was one of the many reasons I found myself in my childhood home with my parents.

After a failed marriage and I wasn't yet thirty, I fled the city for the hills, or rather the mountains of Montana.

My best friend still lived in the area. So there was that.

"Madeleine, breakfast is ready."

That was a familiar phrase. Though I didn't think I'd ever hear Mom saying it again after I'd said I do. But I had no one to blame for that but myself. Benji had been handsome and rich, but there had been a ton of red flags. He was looking for a "don't ask, don't tell" kind of wife and that was never me.

When I found out that marriage to him didn't mean we were in an exclusive relationship, I left, to his great surprise. He thought since he could provide, I should be a quiet mouse at home and a showpiece when we were in public. How young and naïve I'd been.

Truth was, my heart had always been here, even though it had been broken to the point of no repair. That had left me vulnerable for any man like Benji to take advantage.

"Madeleine." I looked up to find Mom standing in my doorway. "Did you hear me call?" she asked.

"Sorry," I said and glanced back out my window. "I'll be down in a minute."

"Okay. If you're not hungry, I can put it away for now."

I mustered up a smile. "Thanks. I'm coming though."

She nodded and disappeared back down the stairs. I looked back through my window. The one that led to the boy next door. Though it hadn't been that boy I'd fallen for. Just another boy who'd been there often enough, we'd more than noticed each other.

After breakfast with my folks, I drove the short distance to town to meet my best friend.

"Maddy," she said when I got out of my car after snagging a parking spot near the square.

"Kinsey," I shouted in response and hugged her fiercely.

"You look good," she said after we peeled apart.

I gave her the same once-over she'd given me. "You look great as well. Family life is treating you well."

Her smile dimmed some. "Why don't we grab some coffee? I'm not sure Java Jitters was here before you left, but it's the best."

"Pony Up was," I teased.

"Too bad we weren't old enough to drink then."

"But we did when I came back that Christmas before I graduated college."

"Oh, yeah. You brought Benji with you."

I blew out air, not sure why I brought the bastard's name up in the first place. "Maybe we should get coffee first."

We walked in and the atmosphere was buzzing. The place had more of a cozy coffee bar feel than you'd find in a bigger city. "Wow, this is nice."

"Yeah. Jessie owns it."

I wasn't sure I knew her. "She was a grade ahead of us. Anyway, she's cool. She and the new doc in town hooked up and they are due to have their firstborn soon."

That was the thing about small towns, everyone knew everyone's business.

As we waited to place our order, she filed me in on stuff she hadn't shared during our many phone conversations. Then again, this last year, I mostly called her to complain about my failing marriage.

"Mr. Hawkins, the owner of Pony Up, was murdered."

My eyes popped wide. "Really? Here in Mason Creek?"

"Yeah. Anyway, Emma runs the place now." I knew who Emma was. She'd been in high school with us, though a few years younger. There were rumors that one of the hottest guys in school had a thing for her. "She married Aiden."

"No way," I said in surprise. He'd been that hot guy.

"She's pregnant too. It seems like everyone is around here." She paused when the line moved, but it still wasn't our turn. "And Nate is back."

"Nate Bowmen?" I asked.

"One and the same. He's still super hot. Every single woman in town has her eyes on him. Maybe you should give him a go."

I shook my head. "Not interested. I just finalized my divorce. I'm not ready for anything just yet."

Kinsey knew me better than that. "You're thinking about him."

That him being the boy I dated in high school. The one that had been in the window across from mine at least once a week. The same one I thought I'd marry one day.

"I always think about him," I admitted.

"He's still in Mountainside. He comes to town from time to time. I see him with his cousin at some of the barn dances. He's not the same."

I gave her a look. "You still go to those things."

"I'm married, not dead. And what else is there to do? Besides, better to get the gossip firsthand. And you know there is no hiding who's with who at those things. Speaking of which, there's one tonight and you're going with."

"Am not," I said.

"Are too. You owe me."

I couldn't argue because it was our turn to order. Once we had our coffees, we found a small table up front near the windows.

Kinsey dived right in, switching topics like me going with her tonight was a done deal. "What are you going to do now that you're back?"

I shrugged. "Find a job, I guess."

"A job?"

"Remember, I signed a prenup," I said.

"I thought he didn't make you."

"He claimed he didn't care. But his family did. I did it anyway. I wanted his parents to know I wasn't in it for the money."

Her mouth fell open. "You got nothing?"

I shrugged. "Almost. But there was a cheating clause." I paused to let that sink in. "Benji added that in good faith to me. Either he didn't care or maybe he married me for love, too. I don't know. But when the lawyer came with the final paperwork for me to sign, he gave me a check."

She widened her eyes and leaned in. "How much?"

I leaned in too. People in this town had big ears and even bigger mouths. "Enough so I can buy a house and, if I'm careful, I might never have to work," I said. I wouldn't tell her the amount in the open like this in case we were overheard.

"Then why are you looking for a job?"

It was a valid question, and I sat back. "Idle hands and all that. I'd get bored sitting around."

"You can apply at the firm in town."

My degree was in accounting and I had my CPA in Chicago, but not here. Plus, I hadn't worked a day since I'd gotten married. Passing the CPA exam was for me. Benji, however, didn't want his wife to work ever. I shook my head. "I'm not certified here in Montana. Besides, I'm not looking for gray hairs, just something to pass the time."

She pointed at a hiring sign with a mischievous grin. "You should apply here."

I thought about it and said, "I should. Now tell me about your life."

We talked for at least an hour. She was cryptic about what was going on in her life. She spent more time filling me in on the status of every person in our high school graduating class until we finally left the coffee shop. She had to go home, and I did the same.

CHAPTER TWO

SOMEHOW, I'D LET Kinsey talk me into going to the barnyard dance. Standing in my bedroom several hours later, I felt a little nostalgic and giddy over going to the dance tonight as I checked myself out in the mirror.

I'd chosen a yellow dress. One I'd bought on sale on a whim the day I filed for divorce. It had been summer then, but I hadn't worn it until now. I put on some cowboy boots and slipped into my shearling-lined jean jacket I had since high school. I'd left it home because my ex-husband thought it was too country for our city life. But it still fit. I smiled at the little *fuck you* aimed at Benji.

When the doorbell rang, I'd just finished dabbing on lip gloss. I pushed at my brown hair streaked with fading highlights. My ex thought my hair was too mousy and insisted on expensive salon visits. Every time I went, I'd felt like I was losing another piece of myself as he changed me into the woman he thought I should be, rather than loving who I was.

One more look in the mirror solidified that I'd either let all the old highlights grow out or I'd go to Serenity, the salon in town, and chop off my hair to shoulder length, something my ex would have hated.

"Madeline, Kinsey's here," Mom called from downstairs.

"I'm coming." After one last look, I left my room.

Before I left, I kissed my dad on the cheek.

"Be home at a decent hour," he said. "I know you're an adult, but your mom will worry."

I grinned at him. "Love you too, Dad."

Mom shooed us out the door, and we got into Kinsey's SUV.

"This is different," I teased, giving her ride a once-over.

"Stop. Mack wanted me to get a minivan. That wasn't happening."

Mack was her husband. The one she hadn't spoken much of during our coffee outing. Though she didn't say it, I had the feeling things weren't so great.

"Is he coming tonight?" I asked.

She shrugged. "Who knows and don't ask."

Kinsey was like that. She wasn't a talker about herself, but a damn good listener. She'd tell me all when she was ready. I didn't push.

Once we arrived at the farm that was hosting tonight's dance, Kinsey had to make a spot as vehicles were everywhere and not in an orderly fashion.

"Are you ready for this? He might be here tonight," she sing-songed.

I wasn't sure I was ready for anything but admitted to myself I'd worn this dress, hoping I might see him.

"Come on. Let's get a beer before they run out," she said, taking my hand as I'd frozen in place.

The first thing I saw inside were all the familiar faces. Some had left and moved back like I had. I was stopped and chatted with a few girls I knew while Kinsey went to get us beers. I promised to have lunch with the pair before they left and caught up with their husbands.

While waiting on Kinsey, I surveyed the room and there he was. Barnes. The boy I'd fallen in love with was now a man. His sexy smirk was gone, but his face was filled with a smile so warm I shivered from the heat of it. Only a second later, my heart sank. It wasn't hard to see he only had eyes for the gorgeous woman in his arms as they danced.

"Oh boy," Kinsey said, handing me a beer. She spotted what I had. "I don't know her. She's not local."

I turned away. "It doesn't matter." I threw up my empty hand in frustration. "How could I expect he would wait for me? I'm the one that left and got married."

"Only because his mom cockblocked you guys."

That was true, but there was so much more. "She blames me for the accident."

"You weren't even there," Kinsey protested.

"He was there because of me."

Just then, a group of rowdy guys entered. Kinsey's husband, Mack, among them. She rolled her eyes and turned in the other direction. "There's Nate Bowmen," she said. "You should go over there."

"I told you. He's hot, sure. But I'm not interested." He wasn't Barnes. If I were to ever give my heart to another person, it would only be to him.

"Oh look," Kinsey said, sounding excited about potential drama. We watched as Nate cut in between Barnes and the woman he'd been dancing with. "See, you had nothing to worry about."

Maybe she thought so, but I watched as the pain of rejection covered Barnes's face. He'd liked that girl. But even I could see the sparks between Nate and Barnes's former dance partner.

"Maybe we should go," I said and drank down my beer.

I hoped since her wayward husband came in and she made no attempt to speak to him, she'd want to go, too. That wasn't the case.

"Oh, no you don't. We've been here for like five seconds," she said.

I groaned. "I'm going to get another beer," I said as a slow song filled my ears.

A guy slid into my vacant spot and started chatting up my friend who didn't seem to mind his company. There was definitely a story there.

I stood in a short line at the makeshift bar when a cute guy came over. "Don't I know you?"

"Steve," I said, as recognition set it. "It's been a while."

"Maddy Phillips. You are a sight for sore eyes. Care to dance?"

I glanced at my empty hands. I'd discarded my cup in the bin before I got in line. "I'm really in need of a beer, but maybe later."

He nodded and walked off. Why had I done that? Steve had been a nice guy in high school. I was really shocked he didn't have a ring on his finger. I'd have to ask Kinsey about him. He'd been a grade ahead of me and not mentioned when Kinsey had given me the update earlier.

Truthfully, I'd said no to the dance because I didn't want to have that awkwardness of our first one being to a love song as the DJ had played a few in a row so far. Though the real reason was my heart was and had always belonged to Barnes.

I'd thought I'd loved my husband, but my lack of care outside of the normal *I can't believe he lied and cheated on me* hadn't been sadness. In fact, I'd been relieved. But I'd been too late in returning home. Barnes had eyes for another.

When I got back to the spot I'd occupied with Kinsey, I found her gone. I searched the room and spotted her near the wall, speaking to her husband. Neither looked happy.

As I glanced around to decide what to do, I ended up locking eyes with Barnes. The woman that had been dancing with him two or three songs ago was speaking in his ear. Then I could have sworn she shoved him in my direction.

My breath caught and there was no finding air as it was locked down with anticipation. I focused on his face. Every angle I had memorized long ago. He was just as handsome as he had been, and even more. The scruff on his face was a sexy bonus.

"Um…" he stammered as I felt a little faint, having not breathed until that moment. "Would you dance with me?"

I nodded, unable to speak, and held my hand out. He took it. My fingers tingled at each point where our skin connected. As he led me into the dance area, my belly did flip-flops.

LeAnn Rimes, "How Do I Live," came on and the lyrics were like pieces of my heart vocalized. His hand on the small of my back nearly brought me to tears. I'd dreamed about reconnecting with him a thousand times. Even though he didn't remember me, I leaned my head on his chest as I fought back a sob.

When the song ended, I made the mistake of looking up. There was nothing there, not even a hint of recognition.

"Thanks for the dance," I said and stepped away. I gave myself props for not running away. I walked a little briskly but didn't run.

When I found a darkened stall, I stepped inside and let out the sob I'd been holding. Kinsey must have watched the whole thing, because she found me a minute or so later.

"He didn't remember you." It was a statement, not a question.

"No, but I made the mistake of hoping," I sobbed.

Barnes had been Mountainside's, a neighboring town, starting quarterback. I'd been one of Mason Creek's cheerleaders. Our romance was not widely known. I would have been the biggest traitor in school if it had. It hadn't been easy keeping our relationship out of either of our towns' gossips' mouths. But we had done it until senior prom. I'd brought him to mine, and he'd brought me to his. By then, it didn't matter what anyone thought. We planned to go to college together. He'd been recruited to one of my top school choices I'd gotten accepted to. Our future was planned.

"It doesn't matter. Get out there and get to know him now," she urged.

"And what, keep our history a secret?"

She shrugged. "Maybe tonight and see where it goes."

I exhaled. It wasn't like I'd given him a real chance. Maybe he might remember. Maybe I could jog his memory. I took a leap of faith and let her lead me out of the stall.

"Maddy."

I glanced up to see Barnes.

CHAPTER THREE

K INSEY GAVE ME a smile and walked off, leaving us alone.

"Your name is Maddy, right?" I hated the uncertainty in his eyes.

I choked back a sob and nodded. "My memory isn't what it used to be. But I know you, don't I?"

"I hope so. I remember you."

We'd slowly been closing the distance, but he stopped.

"That guy is gone."

There was so much finality in his words, tears spilled from my eyes. I steepled my hands and practically covered my mouth, hoping to stop myself from crying.

"I'm not the same guy you remember, Maddy." He spoke slowly and measured.

The memory hit me all at once. Barnes had gone to the store outside of Billings that long-ago day and slipped on a patch of ice. In a freak accident, he'd fallen hard enough to cause a brain bleed. They were able to stop it and save his life, but he'd been in a coma for a while. When he woke up, he didn't remember very much of the past and had to relearn to do the most basic things like speak and walk. His mother blamed me and didn't allow me to visit him in the hospital or even when he finally came home. Evenutally, I left for college, having never spoken to him again since the accident.

"I know," I said, as I'd heard rumors he changed.

The cocky guy with jokes and huge smiles for everyone, especially me, was gone.

"Everyone thinks I'm slow. Truth is, words come slower to me, as do my memories. But I'm not as dumb as they think I am."

"But you let them think that," I said because I heard that rumor and no one ever said he'd balked at what people are saying.

"It's just easier to let people think what they want." He paused. "Some things I never forgot." My heart stopped beating in my chest. "I never forgot you."

I breathed out pain. "Your mom wouldn't let me see you."

"I know."

"You didn't reach out?" I said, a little harsher than I meant to.

"I wasn't the same. I couldn't hold you back from going to college, especially after Mom said you got rid of it."

My jaw dropped. "What? I didn't."

"You had the baby?"

The reason he'd been out the day of the accident was because I'd thought I was pregnant. Barnes being the guy he was had volunteered to drive to Billings and get me a test. We couldn't buy one in town unless we wanted everyone to know.

In answer to his question, I shook my head. "I don't know if my period would have come or if it was all the stress and worry, but I got it two weeks later."

"Oh." Then we just stared at each other, until he finally said, "I heard you got married."

"It was a mistake," I said in a rush. "I never got over you. Are you married?" I asked quickly, so he didn't feel the need to respond to my admission of feelings.

"No."

"I saw the woman you were dancing with," I said, and hated how jealous I sounded.

He smiled, and that was the smile I remembered. "That's Avery. We work together. She and Nate Bowmen have a thing."

"Oh," I said.

"She's nice. She sees me not as the broken, failed quarterback, but as a person. I like her, but not as much as I like you."

"Oh," I said again, feeling my cheeks fill with heat. "You like me?"

"Maddy, I've always loved you. I did then and I still do now."

Though years passed, my feelings hadn't changed. Maybe because I never had the chance to resolve them. "Me too."

Then, as if we were magnets, I was in his arms. His lips were on mine. It wasn't the same fiery kisses of the past, but a slow mingling of mouths as if he was testing the waters.

When we pulled apart, he said, "I haven't kissed anyone since you."

That shocked me. He was as handsome as ever. Any woman would be lucky to have him. Their loss, my gain. "I haven't kissed anyone like this since you."

We just stared at each other for another second.

"I've changed," he said as if to give me a final out.

"So have I." I wasn't the same girl from high school.

"Most people call me Tugboat now."

"Am I most people?"

His head slowly moved side to side. "You were never most people. But we should take things slow and see."

"We should," I admitted, but neither of us moved.

Still in his arms, I craned my neck to look up into his warm brown eyes.

"My truck is out there." Damn, if there wasn't a hint of that smirk of his.

I grinned. "You should show me."

And boy did he. If people assumed because he wasn't the smooth talker he'd been, that he was less; they were so wrong. Even out of practice, being with him was better than anyone I'd ever been with.

Though we'd taken that leap, we still had miles to go. We needed to get to know our older selves. There were no guarantees things would work out. Especially since his mother hated me. But I was excited about the future for the first time in years.

❖   ❖   ❖

Thank you so much for reading my story, Every Piece of You! You can read more of my contributions in Mason Creek world with Perfect Bastard (Tugboat/Barnes is in this one) and Perfect Night. ORDER PERFECT BASTARD NOW > www.terrielaine.com

If Only They Saw the World Like You...

A.L. Jackson

EDEN

"**H**APPY BIRTHDAY, KITTEN."

The scrape of the gruff, deep voice nudged me from sleep and sent a rush of warmth sweeping over my skin. My eyes blinked open to find him hovering over me from the side of the bed. His dark gaze smoldered in a seductive welcome. The man was so unbearably gorgeous that looking at him made both my pulse speed with anticipation and peace go vibrating through my veins.

"It's already starting out that way if I wake up to you right there."

I yelped then giggled when he was on me in a flash, rolling me from where I was on my side to my back. The man pinned me by the wrists, a wicked smirk kissing the edge of his mouth.

Love spun. This deep, overcoming feeling that promised all was right.

That every hardship that had brought us to this place had been worth it.

I reached out and touched his striking face, running my fingertips down his chin until I was touching the tattoo of the baby owl with the skull's face that was imprinted on his throat.

This man so different then me, my opposite, my perfect match.

"Strike the *happy* birthday. I'm pretty sure it's going to be the best birthday ever," I whispered.

Trent scoffed the sweetest sound that still somehow felt intimidating, and he nibbled at the tips of my fingers as I moved to trace them over his lips. "Best ever? It hasn't even started yet, baby. You have no idea what you're in for."

Excitement raced. A flashflood of energy the poured from him and into me. "Oh really? And what is this best birthday going to entail?"

A grin coasted over his lips. The man was all rough, hard edges, covered in ink, but it was him who covered my soul.

Held me like an embrace.

Gave me the greatest joy.

"How about you get that sweet ass out of bed and get dressed so I can show you."

He leaned down and pecked a soft kiss to my lips that felt like a tease.

A moan got free because with Trent Lawson, it was never enough.

He chuckled against my mouth. It tickled my senses and twisted my stomach in want. "Ah, someone is eager."

"Always."

He dipped in and whispered in my ear, "Don't worry, Kitten, I have plenty of fun planned for you."

It was straight seduction.

My heart pounded.

"But first things first." He sat back, taking me by the hand and helping me out of bed. I sent him a soft smile, one filled with all the love I held for him, for his son who'd become mine, for our daughter that we'd get to meet in four months, for this life we'd been given—one I'd never dared to dream.

But he'd become that—A dream. A reality. My heart's reason.

He groaned a needy sound, and he wrapped himself around me from behind and pressed his face to the side of my neck. "Hurry, baby, before I change my mind and keep you tied to this bed all day."

Light laughter rippled out, and I spun back to look at him. "You say that as if I would mind. I need nothing, Trent, nothing but you and this family."

"That's why I'm gonna give you the whole fuckin' world."

✧   ✧   ✧

FORTY-FIVE MINUTES LATER, Trent was pulling into the parking lot of the private school where I taught both kindergarten and ballet classes. A school my father owned and loved as much as I did.

I glanced at my husband, a teasing smile pulling to my face. "What, you're going to make me work on my birthday?"

Not that I would mind.

I loved my job.

Loved the children.

Loved that I got to share in some small part of their lives.

Trent reached over and grabbed my hand. He brought my knuckles to his lips and murmured, "Nah, Kitten. No work for you today...just a surprise."

"And am I going to like this surprise?" Mischief coated my voice.

Trent grinned, all kinds of sly and making my heart race.

I loved when he looked at me that way. It was always a promise that he was going to devour me later.

"I think you just might."

The parking lot was empty, and he pulled into a spot in the front. He was out and around my side in a flash, opening my door and helping me out.

"Come here."

Trent threaded our fingers together and started up the sidewalk. But rather than leading me to the main building, he pulled me around the side and trudged us through the playground to the vacant lot at the very back. It'd once been intended for more classrooms, but the funds had run out, so it was used at times for our outdoor festivals in the warmer summer months.

A frown pulled to my face as a confused giggle slipped free. "What are we doing out here?"

My attention jumped around, looking for an indication. A present or maybe a picnic breakfast to share beneath the gorgeous spring sky that covered Redemption Hills, the small city where we lived.

He squeezed my hand before he released me and spun around, lifting his arms out to the sides. "What do you think?" He almost shouted it, his own excitement riding out.

"Of the vacant lot?"

"Yup."

I laughed. "I think my husband has lost it."

He moved back for me, every step he took on his motorcycle boots slow. Purposed. He reached out, wrapping me in the strength of this muscled arms, his voice gravel. "Nah, baby, I haven't lost it...I've found it. Found it in you. Joy. Purpose. Direction. All the things I'd never fuckin' thought I'd have."

I sank against him, inhaling deep as I relished the feel of the hard lines of his body pressed against me.

His voice turned to a rumble. "And I hope in some small way this expresses what I see in you."

"What is that?" The words were a wisp of confusion.

"You're standing in the future spot of Eden's Adventurers."

Surprise locked the air in my lungs.

"What do you mean?" My hands fisted in his shirt, and I edged back so I could read his expression.

In it was a hope that gleamed through his menacing demeanor. "Construction starts Monday. A free preschool for parents trying to get on their feet. Hope is to also be able to supply formula and diapers. Food for those who need it. A safe place that supports this community."

My spirit thrashed.

He'd remembered. He'd remembered the night when we'd first gotten together when I'd told him about that secret dream. That I hoped for a safe place for the children of this community. There were so many who came to our school in need...with needs bigger than we'd been able to supply, even though my father and the entire team did the best they could.

For that reason, the school barely ran at a profit.

Everything extra given.

But there was still a huge void that needed to be filled.

"I don't understand...how?"

"Logan and Jud helped me pull it together. Building is fully paid for, and it's funded for the first three years."

Moisture blurred my eyes, and I rapidly blinked as my pulse spiked. As my chest filled. As emotion overflowed.

My throat thickened, and I couldn't speak.

"It's in your name because it represents the person you are."

Tears fell in fat streaks down my cheeks.

Trent angled down and spread his palm over the side of my face, his thumb tracing the angle of my cheek as he murmured, "If only people saw the world the way you do, Eden Lawson. Not as a place to be taken, but a place to be contributed to. If they saw we were put here to love and care for other people, for the land, rather than to conquer it? If people loved like you? There'd be a whole lot less pain and suffering in this world. That's why this place will bear your name. Because of that type of love. Because it's the type of hope it will represent."

"Trent."

"Kitten. I mean it, baby. I mean it."

"And you mean everything to me," I choked out, overwhelmed.

"That's a good thing because you are that world to me. You're the one who taught me to cherish it. Life. That it matters."

TRENT

IT WAS CRAZY when you met someone who changed your entire perspective. When you found someone who made you a better person simply from being in their space. One who made you want to be better, do better, because they showed you in the end, it was really what mattered.

Never in a million years could I have imagined finding my redemption in a girl like Eden, and there would never be a day in my life that I took that for granted.

I peeked at my girl where she sat in the passenger seat of my car, face so pretty, spirit so good, her eyes taking me in like there was a chance she could see me the same as I saw her.

She'd fucked with my head from the moment I'd met her.

Twisted me up and forced me to look inside myself.

"What?" Her teeth raked her bottom lip and a bit of that blush crept to her cheeks.

My dick stirred at the sight.

I came to a stop in front of the valet at the hotel where we were spending the night, our son, Gage, at his uncle Logan's for a sleepover.

Truth be told, I wanted my girl alone.

Naked under me and screaming my name.

We'd spent the day at the lake. Hiking and exploring and loving, then had eaten dinner at this awesome restaurant that overlooked the lake.

But tonight, I'd have even a better view.

"Just lookin' at you."

That redness flared. "Is that so?"

A groan rumbled in my chest, and I leaned over the console and dragged my index finger down the length of her throat. "About to get a closer one, too."

A giggle slipped free. One of needy anticipation.

Energy swirled. A bond. A connection. Perfection.

We got held there, staring at each other, and she yelped when her door whipped open. "Miss."

All kinds of shy, she giggled, glancing once at me before she climbed out just as I was doing the same. I passed off my key and grabbed the tag, then I all but hauled my wife for the bay of elevators inside the expansive lobby.

Eden's laughter billowed, her breaths short when I tugged her into the elevator, gasping when I pressed her against a mirrored wall so I could take her by the hips and smash my mouth to hers.

She giggled under it, this joy seeping free. "Someone's anxious."

"Been dyin' to get in this body all damned day."

I buried my face in her neck, kissing a path over her quivering pulse point.

Her giggle turned into a moan. "Trent."

"Just wait, Kitten."

"I don't want to wait." The words were the rasp of a breath.

Shit.

She was gonna do me in.

The elevator door swept open to the top floor, and I had her swept up and in my arms and striding for our room. I kept hold of her while I touched the key to the reader, and Eden was laughing all over again as I carried her through the threshold.

Not quite wedding style since she was upright and I had hold of her ass, kneading as we went.

She grinned down at me though it was fire that flashed.

Sparks in the air.

Short-circuiting all thought except for the one that I was going to get lost in her.

"Little Temptress." I grunted it as I carried her through the living room and directly to the bed in the attached room.

Another giggle lifted from her when I tossed her to the middle of the bed.

I stood at the bottom of it so I could appreciate the delicious sight for a second.

Girl laying in the middle, blonde hair all around, her sweet body writhing in anticipation, covered in this modest floral dress that came down to her knees. Girl still looked like a fucking pinup.

Lush and ripe and every fucking fantasy I'd ever had.

"Not right it's your birthday and I'm about to unwrap the best gift one could be given."

Her chest arched, and she let go of a needy sound. "No, Trent, you're wrong, I'm pretty sure you're about to give it to me."

My cock ached, and that attraction that was never going to dim bounced from the walls, growing brighter with each pass.

"That so?"

Her tongue swept her bottom lip, and she barely managed a nod of her head. "Yes."

Came out a plea.

I reached out and unbuckled her sandals, pulled them from her feet, and ran my hands up the outside of her legs, all the way up until they slipped beneath the fabric of her dress and I was cupping both sides of her gorgeous ass.

I crawled onto my knees on the bed as I went, winding my shoulders up between her thighs so I could take hold of her underwear and drag them down her legs.

I dove right in, spreading her so I could lap up her pussy, every bit of her throbbing and desperate for me.

Eden gasped. "Trent."

I answered by sucking at her clit and slipping three fingers in real deep. Thrust them twice and my girl was already winding up.

One more time and a good hard lick and she was coming apart.

Blunt nails sank into my shoulders while her entire being quaked. My name a chant on her tongue.

Loved it.

Loved her coming on my fingers.

Loved her shouting my name.

Loved her taking up all the space in my soul.

"Trent." She mumbled it that time as she was coming down, and I edged back onto my knees so I could look at my girl all hot and flushed, body twitching with the afterglow.

"Yeah, baby?"

I had every intention of winding her right back up.

That gaze met mine. So intense. So real. Shined so bright with everything I never thought I'd get to feel.

"Love me," she whispered.

"I'm going to be lovin' you for the rest of my life."

I peeled her out of that dress. My heart stuttered all over again at the sight of her completely bare, the little bump where our daughter grew curving my wife's body in the most profound kind of bliss.

"You are the best thing I've ever seen."

I meant it.

Inside and out.

Body and soul.

Her hips jutted from the mattress. "You are the picture of my life."

I edged back and pulled my tee over my head, kicked out of my boots, and wound out of my jeans, grinning at my girl who watched me with this awe as I did.

"You break my heart a little bit every time I look at you." It was praise. This girl so real as she took every inch of my body in.

My cock was stone, head fat and throbbing with the need to drive home.

Her fingertips traced over the thunder of a heart that belonged to her. "I love you, Trent Lawson."

"With all I have, Kitten."

"Then have me."

A grin curled at my mouth, the mouth that dove in and plundered hers, our tongues a tangle of devotion. Eden whimpered, and her nails raked down my stomach until she fisted me in her sweet, precious hand.

She gave me one good stroke before she was poising me at her center.

I took her whole. Thrust deep and right. Girl gripped me tight, walls of her pussy clutching my dick.

Sparks of bliss shivered over my flesh.

Every touch.

Every time.

"Fuck. So good, Eden. You have any idea, baby, what it feels like being in you?"

She whimpered. "More."

I propped myself up on my hands so I could watch down on her as I owned her sweet body. Tonight, I took it slow. Gazing down on her beautiful face as I drove deep.

My muscles flexed and bowed.

Her breaths came shorter as the promise of ecstasy flushed her skin.

My pace increased, the snap of my hips coming quicker and quicker with each drive of my body. Could feel it rising, the way pleasure sparked and danced along my cells.

Eden rasped, her fingers at my chest, like she could find her way inside.

She was already there.

Already there.

I angled so I could slip my hand between us. I rolled my thumb over her engorged clit. She whimpered, held on tighter, while I stroked and drove faster.

Eden ruptured. Her entire body coming off the bed, a song of rapture whispering from her tongue.

My fingers sank into her hip, taking a handful as I thrust fast and deep.

Pleasure slammed me from all sides, and I called out her name.

I came and came, the satisfaction of having this girl like nothing else.

"Why do you feel so good?" Her thoughts almost mirrored mine.

How, every time?

I laughed a low, possessive sound and sank down so I could kiss her. "Because you were meant for me."

Eden sighed, then she sent me a sweet, sloppy grin as she touched my face. "You know each birthday you're going to have to top the last, don't you?" It was purely a tease.

A grin pulled to my mouth. "Don't worry, Kitten, we're gonna have so much fun..."

✧   ✧   ✧

Thank you for reading *If Only They Saw the World Like You...* If you enjoyed this peek into Trent & Eden's life, you can read their full story in Give Me a Reason, Book One in the Redemption Hills series >
www.aljacksonauthor.com/give-me-a-reason

Hard Score

Rachel Van Dyken

JAGGER

M Y GRANDMA KEEPS calling from Ukraine—she terrifies me more when she smiles than when she glares. My mom always said that when Grandma was smiling, she was plotting some sort of punishment, but when she glared, it was because she was proud.

I grew up overseas, then moved to the States for soccer, fell in love with my agent's sister, and the rest is history.

Except for it kind of isn't since Grandma wants to know if I've given Willow her ring yet.

And who the hell taught that woman how to text anyway?

My phone buzzes again, perfect, a meme of the Godfather.

I sigh and put my phone back in my pocket.

I've been dreaming about this proposal for the last year, but Willow's wild, like the wind during a hurricane. She's all over the place and now one of *the* best sports agents at Matt's firm.

So far, she's made ten grown men cry—saw one of them leave the house wiping his eyes, thought it was good news, and I was all like good for you bro, got picked up for one of the big teams?

And while he did, she had berated him for staying up late drinking and said a whole bunch of unrepeatable things that had me wincing as he listed them.

"Well, um, hang in there." I patted him on the shoulder and lifted my hand away when he shot me a glare.

"Can't you tame her?" He jerked away.

I rolled up my sleeves. "And that's your problem. You think girls need taming when maybe you just need to not be a dick."

I shoved past him.

And was actually happy when I saw him get benched.

I check my Rolex, then roll my hands through my long dirty blond hair. My jaw clenches.

Is she even coming?

I'm at my penthouse in downtown Seattle, overlooking the water, freezing my ass off, waiting on the open balcony with wine, dinner, and some sort of cheese tray that Matt promised would make her do that little bounce thing where she claps and eats then claps.

Kind of like a seal, but a really fucking cute one.

The sound of the door opening and closing has my heart going into overdrive, and of course, my phone buzzes again.

"Be right there!" Willow calls.

I can already hear the sound of her designer heels flying against our hardwood floors and imagine the vision of her undoing her bra like she does every day, tossing it wherever's convenient.

She's a terror to live with, but I know in my soul if I lived on my own and didn't trip over her heels bruising my body—my soul would be the one bruised, and that would be so much worse.

So I risk life, limb, and sanity for her.

The soft pad of her feet against the floor brings a smile to my face. I don't even need to turn around before I feel her arms wrap around my middle, her cheek resting against my back, most likely getting a bit of makeup on my jacket—not that I care, let her rub her face wherever the hell she wants, and I do mean wherever.

"Good day?" I ask. She squeezes tighter.

"Mmmm. Long day."

"Ah, success must be difficult."

She pinches my side, resting her chin on my back. "Yeah okay, world's best goalie, tell me again your sob story about how hard life is while standing in your million-dollar penthouse. I can wait for your brain to stumble around a bit to come up with a good excuse. These things sometimes take time."

"Words?"

"You trying to win arguments." She teases.

God, I love her.

I turn around and pull her against me. "You like it when I lose."

She blushes slightly. "Because then you owe me orgasms."

"Which is why our chalkboard in the kitchen bothers the shit out of your brother."

"He flips it around every single time."

"Until I told him not to touch the chalk."

She bursts out laughing, her dark hair framing her face so perfectly I have to touch it just briefly before leaning down and pressing a kiss to that smart mouth. Her lipstick's off, half her makeup's probably on my back, and I just want to throw her over my shoulder and take her into our bedroom.

She looks down at the wine and small spread. "What's the occasion?"

"Saw myself in the mirror, thought I should celebrate."

She rolls her eyes. "Was it the dick or the face? I can't decide?"

"Both." I laugh. "Now…" Oh man, I'm cracking, suddenly shaking. I take a step back.

Her pretty brown eyes rake over me before she smiles and winks. "It's okay, just take a deep breath."

I frown. "I don't know what you—"

"—Grandma got tired of you not answering her texts, starting in on Matt, then me, and since I know she used to be a spy, I'm kind of in the mood to answer when she calls and all that." She smiles. "Ask me so I can see it."

"We still talking about my dick?" I try to deflect.

"Jag." Willow crosses her arms. "Don't ruin this perfect moment with your mouth"—her eyebrows raise—"or maybe ruin it with your mouth again and again later?"

"Dirty girl." I'm again reminded why I love her because she gets me. Even though the surprise is ruined, I slowly get down on one knee and reach into my pocket, pulling out my grandma's old ring, the one my grandpa gave her so many years ago, the one she kept on her hand for over fifty years, until a few weeks ago.

It's a Victorian era rose cut diamond set on a simple yellow gold band, with smaller diamonds twisting along the sides.

It's beautiful.

Meant for a queen.

Willow gasps and stares down at it. She's no longer smiling or joking; she has tears pooling in her eyes.

"Willow I—" Why the hell is this so hard? "I love you so much, and I want to spend the rest of my life with—" I sigh. "Fuck it." I stand.

Her eyes widen.

"I'm not that guy, the romantic one who says all the right pretty little things. Maybe it's just how I was raised, but I can't do it this way. But I will tell you this. I fucking hate tripping over your heels every night when I'm going to the kitchen, yet I would miss it like hell if they weren't there. And finding your bras everywhere makes me so horny when you're gone. I think you do it on purpose."

A tear slides down her cheek.

"You're a mess, a total mess, but in all the best ways. I respect you, love you. And want to spend the rest of my life being your best friend, only the one who grumbles every day about how bad your singing is in the shower and telling you yet again to use the toothpaste like a human, not a rabid animal." I hold out the ring again. "Will you marry me?"

"It's quicker." She sniffs. "The whole toothpaste usage."

"It's savage."

"And I do leave my lingerie around, so you go to work hard, then play hard, then come back and play even harder"—she moves closer to me—"with me."

"I always play hard—and rough." I grab her left hand and lift the ring to her finger. "Is that a yes?"

Willow slides it onto her finger and nods her head. "I would never say no to you."

"And yet you do, all the time." I kiss her on the nose.

She laughs, then lifts her mouth to mine; our lips meet briefly before she says, "Because it's so much fun pissing you off…"

I grunt because I know she likes to stir shit, and I wouldn't want it any other way. I crush my mouth to hers. I taste the wine I was drinking earlier on her tongue. Her kisses always destroy me because they're rarely soft; they fight for the dominance I want that she never gives; our kisses are like a war I'll never win. I'll never stop trying though.

Her hands go to my ass while mine go directly to her breasts, spreading my fingertips across her bare nipples, feeling them through her simple black silk tank, still sadly half-tucked into her pants.

I pull away. "Hungry?"

She backs up and lifts her arms over her head.

"What? Are you stretching or?"

"Take it off." She teases. "We can eat after."

"After…" I play dumb even though I'm already moving toward her and lifting that shirt right off her body and tossing it forgotten on the ground.

She's perfect.

This moment was our perfect moment, even in its chaos and mild arguing. I see my life reflected in her eyes.

And know it's right.

WILLOW

THE WAY HE looks at me makes me want to burn all my clothes in a giant bonfire and dance around it naked until he catches me. His gaze always burns with this insatiable hunger that drives me wild.

He makes me want to run only so I can be caught over and over again.

Once my shirt is off, his eyes blink slowly. He licks his full lips, and all I can think is, damn, that's why every single clothing company wants this guy modeling for them.

Perfect body.

Massive, yet lean.

Gorgeous, cheeky smile. Sharp jawline and an intensity nobody I've ever known has both on the soccer field and when he's looking at me, kissing me, fucking me.

He reaches for me after my shirt lands on the floor, but I get to him first. I waste no time in grabbing the collar of his white shirt and jerking it open. I think I hear buttons hit some of the food or maybe a wine glass.

"Hello there," I say to his gorgeous abs as I lower to my knees and start un-buckling his belt. He's already hard, pressing against his zipper in his own version of hello.

I smirk and whisper. "Soon…"

Jagger curses, wiping a hand down his face.

With a dark laugh, I finally get his belt undone and unbutton his trousers, the sound of the zipper going down is so erotic chills run down my spine. I'm still in my pants, but I'm completely topless. The slight wind has my body chilled, but I don't really care as I get up and pull him by the pants back into the house.

I slam his body against the now closed glass door and start kissing down his neck as he attempts to kick off his pants and undo mine.

After a few failed attempts, we're both completely naked. He flips me around, lifting me up with both hands and pressing my bare ass against the glass.

I laugh between wine-infused kisses. "Our poor neighbors."

Jagger laughs with me. "Hey, it's a free show. They should thank us."

I lightly slap his shoulder. "They have kids!"

"It's sex education, babe!" He laughs harder and doesn't even give me a warn-ing as he thrusts into me.

I've been ready since I kicked off my shoes. He goes in deep. "Jag," I moan, raking my hands down his back. "That's almost too much."

"Is my fiancée complaining about my giant dick?"

"God, you're such an ass." I hook my ankles around him, pulling him in deeper as he moves, pinning me against the glass.

His teeth nip at my jaw. Heated kisses trail up until our mouths are fused. I hold onto his shoulders as he lifts me higher.

"Need to taste those tits." He sucks on each nipple like he missed dessert.

I'm a panting mess when his mouth returns to mine.

I'm so close.

It's been a hellish day, and I just wanted to come home to him.

To my Jagger.

"Get there." He slams me harder against the glass.

I let out a shriek that could wake the dead and collapse against him; his hips pump harder until he lets out a gruff yell.

He's still inside me when I kiss him again.

A hard knock sounds at the door, followed by another.

"Think they'll go away?" he asks.

I shake my head slowly and start laughing so hard tears stream down my cheeks. "Yeah, probably not."

"I know you're in there!" My brother's yell sounds violent, which amuses me more as I slowly slide down the glass door to my feet.

We quickly put on enough clothes to be decent while the knocking continues.

Jagger winks at me as we walk toward the door and finally open it.

Standing there is my brother, his wife Parker, and their newborn, Maggy.

Matt looks exhausted, then again, newborn.

Parker just looks as amused as I do; then again, she is my best friend.

"Sup, bro?" I ask.

"Sup? Bro? Are you fucking kidding me?" Matt yells. He yells often. He is an agent. And new dad. Brother. Poor guy needs a vacation. "I saw ass!"

"Whose?" Jagger frowns.

"YOU!" Matt jabs his finger against Jagger's chest. "I told you! No more sex! You'll wake the other neighbors, end up on the news, fuck you're going to end up on the news again, and your grandma's going to call me and threaten my life again and that of my firstborn and—"

"—Bro…" Jagger shakes his head. "That's her way of saying congratulations!"

Matt looks ready to punch my fiancé, so I eye Parker and hold up my hand. "LOOK! We're official!"

"THE RING!" Parker shoves past Matt and tackle hugs me while the guys continue staring at each other. "We need to celebrate!"

"We have wine!" Jagger announces, his smirk present as my brother curses under his breath.

"Fine." Matt exchanges arms with the infant. "But I want two free nights of babysitting since I had to see my sister's ass. Whose idea was it to become neighbors anyway?"

"Ours!" Parker and I say in unison while Matt grumbles the entire way into the apartment.

Matt gets a bit more relaxed when offered a glass of wine while I change real quick and take the baby for a bit, sitting with Parker in the kitchen.

"He's stressed," I say.

She shrugs. "He's protective, big difference."

I smile over at her, then back at the guys arguing about another deal Jagger doesn't want to take that Matt's convincing him he should.

"They're such dicks though, I mean really." I snuggle her baby closer, my niece.

Parker flicks her long dark ponytail and rolls her eyes. "Duh, that's why they need us."

"Cheers to that." I clink my glass against hers.

She's not drinking anything but water.

I stare at her, then look down.

She shakes her head. "Shhhhh, Irish twins just might kill him."

I bark out a laugh. "Can I video his reaction?"

"We'll go viral so fast." She laughs. "And yeah, I was already going to ask you to."

"Poor bastard." I laugh. And then stare down at my niece with her bald little head. She's sleeping, dreaming, it seems.

One day I'll have a baby too.

All because my brother fell in love with his soccer star.

❖   ❖   ❖

To read more of this world, check out The Red Card Series by Rachel Van Dyken
rachelvandykenauthor.com/all-books#red-card

I Wanna Be Yours

Xio Axelrod

THE THING ABOUT grief, or at least as I've understood it to this point, is that it's caused by loss. The sudden absence of something vital that leaves space inside you, a hole that wasn't there before. But what if—and hear me out—what if there had only ever been the hole? What if there had only ever been emptiness? Absence?

If, say, the void was all you'd ever known, and the thing that was supposed to have been there, believed to have been a part of you, had never been, could you grieve? Would you feel the loss of the theoretical?

How can I mourn a father who never really thought of me as his son?

My head hurts.

I pull my phone out of my jacket pocket and open Spotify, searching for something that will mitigate this mood I'm in. Or at least give it a decent soundtrack.

"Cut Me" by Moses Sumney catches my eye. I start the track, about to look for a follow-up, but realize *grae* is the perfect album for this moment. I'm lost in these morose thoughts, and I need something to anchor me.

"Hey."

The warmth in that one syllable chases away the creeping cold that has settled into my bones. I turn to find Johnny looking at me with sympathetic eyes. From anyone else, that look would grate. *Has* grated over the last few days. People are weird enough about death. They become unbearable when they know *you* have issues with the deceased. Only Johnny has given me space when I needed it.

"Hey yourself." I open my arms, and Johnny pulls me in, enveloping me completely. I hum with a relief that surprises me. He's only been out for a few hours, but I sag into the embrace. "Did everything go alright with the rental return?"

I feel him nod. "It's all set. How about you? How are you holding up?"

Shrugging, I loosen my grip on him and lean back. "M'fine." I try to reassure him, though I can't seem to meet his eyes. Ugh, I feel so emo.

A finger under my chin lifts my face, and Johnny ducks his head until I finally look at him.

"Oh, babe." He frowns and tries to pull me into another hug, but I wave him off and head towards the kitchen. "What can I do?" he calls after me.

"It's nothing a nice cuppa won't fix. You want one?"

"Sure," he says, following me. Johnny stops at the counter, but I know he's watching every move I make, looking for ways he can swoop in and save the day.

"I'm okay. Really." My voice is artificially cheery, even to me. I set about making a pot of tea, my movements careful.

"At the risk of pissing you off, you're not okay. And that's understandable," Johnny adds as I turn to glare at him. "You're allowed to feel however you feel, Frankie."

I set everything down and turn, leaning against the sink as I face him. "That's the thing, though. I don't know what I'm supposed to be feeling, what to do, who to…" Dropping my head into my hands, I groan. "I'm angry."

"That's valid."

"And I'm hurt. It's like… It's like I've been robbed." When Johnny doesn't respond, I look up. "You have something to say. Say it. It seems we're opening this can of worms."

His hesitation makes my heart swell. This man. He's so worried he'll hurt me. It's written all over his gorgeous face.

"Go on," I say, sounding a bit more like myself. "Gran always says holding in your words will make them turn to stone in your chest. Then the weight of them will pull you under 'til you drown."

"That's…quite a visual." His smile barely lifts the corners of his mouth. He folds his hands on the counter. "I think you're not giving yourself enough grace."

"Grace?"

He hums. "There's no manual for grief, especially in situations like this. You barely knew your dad."

"Yeah, well…" I turn back to the tea. "I gave up trying."

"You're not the one that gave up, Frankie."

That stings, and fresh tears prickle my eyes. "Why am I crying for a feckless twat who never wanted me? Fuck."

"You're sad for what could have been." Johnny steps around the island and comes to my side. After checking the amount of tea in the strainer, he fills the pot with hot water from our dispenser and sets it aside to steep. "Come on."

Taking my hand, Johnny leads me to our breakfast nook. I love this space. It's so cozy. A cushioned bench sits inside the enormous bay window that overlooks the Japanese maple in the garden. The seat is wide and comfortable enough to sleep on, as I've discovered on many an afternoon.

The nook was one of the things that sold me on this house, despite its other shortcomings. I'd been dead set on a finished basement until I'd seen this little slice of heaven and imagined all the mornings that Johnny and I could spend here.

Johnny lowers himself, leaning against the wall before pulling me down to sit between his legs. I love being surrounded by him. His warmth and his strength.

I lean my head back and watch the rain trail down the glass. "You're a good man."

"I'm just a man, babe. As are you."

"Nah, we're different. You always look for the good in people. In everything, really."

"You don't?"

Shaking my head, I can't help but laugh a little. "I'm too much of a cynic." Maybe that's why my own father wanted nothing to do with me.

Johnny runs a hand over my hair. I can't imagine what a mess it is now, but he doesn't comment.

"You're a little cynical, I admit."

Now I really laugh. "Only a little?"

"A true cynic wouldn't grieve as you do right now." He shifts behind me until his chin is on my shoulder, his words in my ear. "You have a huge heart and a forgiving one. You left the door open for him. You are a bona fide giver of second chances."

"And a third, and a fourth," I reply bitterly.

"Yeah, you are," he agrees. "You're being sarcastic, but I'm living proof of how big your heart is."

I sit up and turn to look at him. "What are you talking about?"

Searching my face, Johnny pushes a curl out of my eyes. There's a day's worth of scruff on his jaw, scruff that probably matches my own. He's still wearing his dress shirt but has shucked the jacket and tie. I look down at myself and realize I'm still in the suit I wore to the funeral. The discomfort is somehow comforting.

"I love you," Johnny says, and my gaze snaps to his. Those whisky-colored eyes of his swimming in emotion.

"I love you, too," I say, choking up. God, I'm a wreck.

He smiles. "I know. And it's a fucking miracle."

"What? Why?" I sit cross-legged, which isn't the most comfortable position in these slacks. "You're bloody brilliant."

"I'm lucky you think so, but how many times did I let you down before I finally got my shit together?"

"That's totally different." I take his hands in mine. "You had been through a lot. You only needed time."

"I guess we both did," he says, and I nod. He squeezes my fingers. "And that's not something your dad ever gave you, even though you kept a ton of it reserved for him."

"It's not like I was sitting around waiting." The lie comes easily now. I've been telling it to myself since I was a schoolboy.

Johnny presses his lips together.

"I wasn't," I protest weakly, trying to pull my hands back.

Johnny grabs them tighter. "Regardless, he's the one who missed out. Not you. Him. He missed out on loving you. You are amazing. You're..." He takes a big, shaky breath, and now I'm wondering if *I* should be the one consoling *him*.

"What's going on with you, babe? I know I've been self-absorbed more than usual lately. Did something happen?"

Oh, God. His expression is so sad. My heart is breaking. He blinks away the obvious tears that have formed in his eyes, and he shakes his head as if to clear it. "No, nothing."

Uh, yeah. I'm totally not letting that go. "Talk to me."

"I..." He closes his eyes and swallows hard. "I'll be right back."

Before I can respond, Johnny shoots up and out of the kitchen. I hear him pound up the stairs, and I'm left sitting here. Bewildered.

Moses isn't cutting it anymore. I need something else. I'm scrolling through my Spotify library when I hear Johnny returning. I throw on the new Bloc Party and toss my phone on the table.

My boyfriend comes to a halt on the other side and is just...standing there. He looks like he's going to be sick. I start to rise, but he holds up a hand. The other is shoved into his pocket, his arm rigid like he's afraid to let go of whatever's in there.

"Johnny?"

"The first time I saw you," he begins, "I thought... Well, I couldn't. I couldn't think. I could barely breathe."

"What? Why?"

"I don't know," he says, exhaling with a laugh. "I mean, I know *now*, but I didn't then."

I recognize the look in Johnny's eyes. I've seen it often in the time we've been together. It's possessive, a little fierce, and a tiny bit scary in the best way.

"Oh." It's all I can say.

"Yeah." He runs a hand through his thick, auburn hair. "At that moment, I knew I wanted to know everything about you. Everything. But you, well… You made it clear early on that you weren't interested in talking to me."

I grimace. "Have I apologized for that?"

"Repeatedly." His smile is soft, and we hold one another's gazes for a moment.

Nothing makes me forget the world like John Burton. Not whisky, not music, not sex. He's all of that and more, rolled into one being. "Thank you for going to the funeral with me."

He looks as if I've insulted him. "Where else would I be, Frankie?"

Straightening his shoulders, John moves to his full height. I didn't even realize he'd been slumping until now. There's a determined set to his jaw. He nods sharply.

"As I was saying, I wanted to know you. And yeah, I had a lot going on. Still do."

"But you're not alone anymore."

The smile that breaks out across his face is blinding. I'll never get used to it. "No, I'm not alone anymore."

John moves to sit next to me, removing his hand from his pocket as he does. He places his fist on the table, and there's something in it. Something he's holding on to for dear life.

"What's that?"

His hand flexes around the object. "I'll get to that."

"Okay," I say, but my gaze is fixed on his fist as if I can summon X-ray vision and see what's inside.

Johnny chuckles. "Frankie."

"Yeah?" When he doesn't reply, I finally rip my gaze away and meet his eyes. At his amused grin, I roll my own. "You know I'm not good with waiting."

"Oh, I disagree. I think you're very good at waiting when you think it's something worth waiting for."

"Maybe."

"Definitely. You waited for me. For us."

I had. And I'd do it again, over and over, to have what Johnny and I have together. It's something I never thought would happen for me. "You are worth anything. Everything."

"So are you, Frankie."

I want to make a joke, blow off the sentiment because my dad—the man who helped to bring me into the world—hadn't thought so. He's left this world, left me behind, without anything of him to hold on to. Whatever part of me that loved him, or wanted to love him, hates him now.

A warm, softly calloused finger glides over my brow. I didn't even realize I'd closed my eyes. Blinking, I look at Johnny. My Johnny, who takes my hand in his and places something small and hard into my palm.

When I look down, my brain short-circuits. "What…?"

Johnny closes his hand over mine, obscuring the thing from view.

"I don't believe in soulmates or anything like that," he says. "But I do think two people can fit together so tightly, so *rightly*, that few others could do the same for them. When you met me, I was barely alive. I worked, I slept, I ate, and I worried. The worry was the only constant in my life, Frankie. It was the only thing I knew. What if someone recognizes me? What if I don't make enough money to help Lexi and her grandma? What if this is all there is to my life? Forever?"

"Nah, you would have figured things out," I say, hating the memory of his haunted eyes.

"Maybe, but who knows how long it would have taken me if I hadn't met you?"

The thing in my palm presses into my skin. It's hard and soft, small and square. My heartbeat trips over itself. "Johnny…"

He smiles. "Anyone who chooses not to have you in their life is a fucking fool, Frankie. A fucking fool. It's as simple as that. Your dad, your exes, old friends, whoever it is or was that let you walk out of their lives. Fools, all."

"Or they're the smart ones." *They know how shite I am at all this.*

"Well, maybe I'm not very smart because I want you in my life," Johnny says, exhaling a long-held breath. "I need you with me. Always."

He uncovers my hand and sits back, holding my gaze. Waiting.

I'm afraid to look down, and I say so.

"You don't have to if you don't want to, but just know that I love you. I think I'll always love you. And I am grateful for you. You are worthy, though I know you struggle to accept that. You're a good partner, a good friend, a good colleague, and even a good son when you're allowed to be one." He gives me a slight shrug. "This is probably the worst proposal in history, and my timing is more than questionable, but you're the best man I know, Franklin Llewellyn, and I couldn't stand another second of you doubting that."

By now, tears are streaming down my face, and I can feel how splotchy I probably look. "*Jesus*," I say, exhaling. Finally, I look down at the tiny velvet box. My hand is shaking. Fuck, *I'm* shaking. "Fuck me."

"Anytime you want."

I bark out a laugh because, holy shit! "Are you seriously asking me to marry you?"

Johnny's expression sobers. "I had planned to talk to you about it the night we got the news about…"

"The reservation at Sampan."

He nods. "I wanted to go back to the restaurant where we had our first date. I thought we'd talk about what we wanted for the future. And if we were on the same page, I was gonna… I don't know…"

"Slip a ring on my finger right then and there?"

He grins, sheepish. "Something like that. Have you ever thought about it?"

"No, to be honest. But," I quickly add before the light in Johnny's eyes can dim. "I don't have anything against the idea, despite the whole heteronormative narrative that surrounds it."

"Well, there's that." Johnny rubs the back of his neck, his cheeks turning red. "If you hate it—"

"I just said I don't have anything against it, in theory. In practice, the only person on the planet I'd ever even *consider* tying the knot with is you."

"Yeah?"

"Who else?"

"Didn't you and Garrett…?"

Ugh. I really don't want to talk about my ex in a moment like this, but I guess it's only fair. "I thought Garrett and I were long-term, but marriage wasn't on the table."

"I see."

I fiddle with the box in my hand. "Can I open it?"

"Oh! Of course, sorry." Johnny scrubs his face with his hands. "And there's no obligation or anything, just… Yeah."

Christ, he's freaking adorable. And I am the luckiest arsehole on the planet.

The rings, there are two, are thick bands of white metal. I pull out the smaller one—because I have average hands compared to Johnny's paws—and examine it. Tiny musical notes encircle the band. They're antiqued in black against the silver. Looking closer, I can see the faintest lines of a staff.

"It's the Arctic Monkeys," he says. "*I Wanna Be Yours.*"

"Oh, fuck. Really?" I look over the notes again, and the song pops into my head. "When did you get these?"

"Remember when we went to Vermont?"

It's my turn to stare at Johnny. My heart s pounding in my chest, and fire is racing through my veins. "John. That was two years ago. You've had these for two years?"

He pulls his bottom lip into his mouth, wetting it, and I'm momentarily distracted by how much I want to kiss him right now.

"Like I said, when I first met you, I wanted to know everything. Who you were, what you liked, where you saw yourself going. I wanted to know what you looked like first thing in the morning and how long it took you to fall asleep at night. I wanted to know what you'd look like falling apart under my hands or my mouth. I wanted to see you angry, or drunk, or giddy. I wanted you, Frankie. I just wanted you. I want you."

I set the box on the table and launch myself at him, claiming his mouth in an attempt to drink down all of his incredible words. I'm delirious with desire for this man, and I want to give him every damn thing. I bury a hand in his thick hair.

Johnny pushes my jacket off my shoulders, then his arms band around me as I straddle his lap. The ring is still clutched in my hand, the metal warm against my palm as I plunder his mouth.

Johnny breaks the kiss and we come up for air, both panting like we're running from the law.

"I fucking love you," I say, rocking my erection against his. "Never thought it was possible to love someone as much as I love you."

His gaze is locked on my mouth, his hands are like iron bands on my thighs. He's trembling, or I am. I can't tell. Johnny dips his head and licks a stripe along my collar, his breathing heavy against my neck.

"Wait," I manage to croak, panting and throbbing and generally coming undone in more ways than one. "Hang on."

Johnny sits back, and I pat his chest. I open my hand. The ring is still there, along with a ring-shaped impression on my skin. We both stare down at it.

"You don't have to."

"Wait," I repeat, trying to catch my breath. I locate my phone and open the Spotify app, navigating to my Arctic Monkeys library. When "I Wanna Be Yours" spills from the speaker on the counter, I toss the phone aside and turn back to Johnny, who is quietly observing me.

"You sure about this?"

He nods. "Never been surer. But if it's not something you want, I can live with that. We don't need—"

"Shhh." I kiss him. Quickly, because otherwise… "I want this with you. Because we can make it whatever we want."

"Yes. We can." His smile is hopeful. "We can be whatever you want us to be, as long as I have you."

"You do."

"That's all I need."

"Then, I do."

"Oh," he says, breathing hard. "Oh, Frankie." This kiss is softer, gentler, but no less intense. I feel it in my marrow. When it ends, Johnny takes the ring from me and slips it on my finger. It's gorgeous and fits perfectly. God, he knows me so well.

"Hang on, don't you want a ceremony or something?"

"We don't have to if you don't want to, but these are engagement rings."

"Wait, really?" Excited, I reach for the box and snag the other band. "I get to put a ring on it, too?"

"Damn right." His fits perfectly, too, and we spend a moment admiring them.

Johnny slips his fingers between mine, the rings sliding together with a tiny *ping.* "I'm sorry about your dad."

I shrug. "Thanks."

"I mean, I'm sorry he didn't take the opportunity to know you."

"His loss." I sound flippant, but the sadness remains. I suppose it will always be a part of me, but I know I'm not alone anymore. That I'll never be alone again if Johnny and I have our way.

I kiss my fiancé. Jesus, that sounds weird, even in my head. "I need to get out of this get-up."

Johnny's expression turns positively wolfish. "I think I can help with that."

"Oh, you fucking better," I say, nipping at his bottom lip. "Upstairs?"

"What's wrong with right here?" Johnny pushes my hips until I stand and guides me to sit on the breakfast table.

"What are you—?" I don't have time to finish before Johnny deftly unbuckles my trousers, pops the button, and draws the zipper down. I can only moan when he circles my cock with his long, thick fingers. "*Fuck.*"

"Patience," he says before lowering his head to tease me with that wicked tongue.

"Patience from the guy who has me propped up on the kitchen table?" I'm incapable of words or thought after that. Johnny has me in his mouth, and I'm his. His.

And he's mine.

✧   ✧   ✧

Read the beginning of Frankie and Johnny's love story in the Frankie and Johnny Duet: When Frankie Meets Johnny (Book 1) and Frankie and Johnny: Let the Music Play (Book 2). **Start reading here >**
xioaxelrod.com/when-frankie-meets-johnny-2

LOVE LETTERS

JAY CROWNOVER

LOVE LETTERS
Devlin

WE ALL HAVE a memory, a moment, a situation that seems like it should be nothing more than a throwaway memory. One we look back on and realize it was actually a significant, life-changing handful of seconds that shaped the rest of our lives. The moments might be big or small, but they all shared the same thing; they were moments that slipped away unappreciated and uncelebrated. They were moments not given their proper praise and attention until the long-reaching impact from those significant seconds was reached.

My moment came towards the end of 5th grade. I was in class learning about the different classifications of animals. I was particularly interested in reptiles and all the creepy-crawlies. I thought it was funny that the girls squealed and made noises when talking about snakes and spiders. I minded my own business, head in my book, when a meticulously folded piece of paper hit my desk. At first, I thought it was one of my friends messing around, trying to get me in trouble. I was going to brush it off onto the floor and forget about it. I had no desire to spend recess inside. I loathed being cooped up all day and tied to a desk. Recess was the only part of school I enjoyed.

It took a second for me to realize the note wasn't just a crumpled piece of trash thrown by one of my boys. It was perfectly folded into the shape of a heart, and my name was written in scrolling, girly handwriting across the front of it. There was even a tiny heart above the "I" in *Devlin*.

Wide-eyed and curious, I looked around the room, trying to spot the culprit who had dropped the note on my desk. Everyone else had their heads buried in their books, and those that didn't were whispering to their neighbors and keeping a close eye on the teacher to avoid getting in trouble for talking during reading time. Absolutely no one was paying any attention to me. That wasn't anything new. I wasn't the class clown. I wasn't an easygoing kid who adults and other children flocked to. I wasn't the sports star who was picked first for every team. I wasn't the super genius who had all the right answers for every question.

Nope, I was the quiet kid who kept his head down and minded his own business. I was the kid who tried to blend in and disappear, because I'd learned early on in my house that any kind of attention was bad attention. If I became part of the scenery, I didn't get dragged into the fights between my mom and dad. If I disappeared, I couldn't be used as a weapon for one to hurt the other. If I was furniture, neither one bothered to pit me against the other. So, I was silent, and I was still, which was part of the reason sitting at a desk all day was torture. It wasn't normal for a boy my age to be as quiet and composed as I was all the time. When recess came I was like an animal let loose from its cage.

At the moment, my calm was gone, as my head swiveled every which way trying to find the pair of eyes eagerly waiting to watch me open the prettily folded paper. My gaze skipped over all of the boys in my class and narrowed on any and all of the girls that were even slightly looking in my direction. I didn't think much about girls beyond the fact that I thought some were nice, and some were not so nice. I liked their hair, how long and shiny it usually was and they all smelled a lot better than most of my boys. I thought Ashley in the front of the class had a nice smile, and I really liked the way Holly who sat by the windows always seemed to have a little bounce in her step when she walked, but neither of them were looking at me. I was surprised that I was a little disappointed.

Carefully, I started to unfold the heart. I pulled the paper flaps apart like they would tear and the whole thing would disintegrate. I smoothed it flat on my desk and made a little cage with my book and my arms so that no one could read it. I didn't know what was written on the pages but I was very protective of those words. They were mine, written for me and I didn't want to share them with anyone else.

The scrolling, flowy, obviously female handwriting filled the page with a simple question. It was the note we all dreaded getting caught passing and having the teacher read aloud in class.

I like you. Do you like me?
Circle Yes or No

I balked for a second because I was suddenly sure this note wasn't meant for me. I didn't chase girls. I didn't bring them valentines or sweets. I didn't tell them they were pretty and offer to walk with them to the bus. I avoided them and they avoided me, so how could one of them like me? None of them even knew me.

I flipped the note over to make sure it was indeed my name on the front. There it was with that little heart drawn over the I. It was meant for me and I had no idea what to do with it.

"Well, do you?" I jerked in my seat and turned a furious shade of red as my book fell over and clattered onto the floor. I reached for it at the same time a much smaller hand tipped with black-painted nails and encircled in ten different rings did.

My gaze met one that was a sparklingly blue surrounded by heavy black eyeliner. Most of the girls in our class weren't allowed to wear makeup yet, but Ani wasn't most girls. She seemed far older than Holly with the skipping steps and Ashley with the nice smile. She seemed fierce and edgy with her dark makeup, punk rock wardrobe, and unabashed willingness to confront people and things. I did everything in my power to fade away, and Ani didn't even have to try to stand out. She was the equivalent of a flaming red dress worn to a funeral. I didn't know what to do with someone like her, so I avoided her and typically pretended she didn't exist.

I tugged the book free and put it back on my desk careful to cover the note. "Do I what?" I sounded sulky and petulant but I couldn't help it. She took me by surprise and she was looking right at me, unflinchingly and unafraid.

"Do you like me, Devlin? Because I like you." Those blue eyes blinked innocently at me as I continued to gape at her in shock. I put a hand on the note like it would trap the words there on the paper where I could ignore them, and pretend like they didn't have a person attached to them forever.

"I don't like anyone like that, Ani." How could I when all I knew of boy-girl stuff was anger, resentment, and ugliness. I hoped I never liked anyone the way my mother and father liked each other. I would never want to be that cruel and hateful towards anyone, especially someone that liked me.

One of her dark eyebrows arched up and her midnight hair slipped over her shoulder as she swiveled in her seat to stare directly at me. I wasn't used to being the center of anyone's attention. It made me flush and I nervously played with the edges of the paper she left on my desk.

"Are you just trying to be nice, Devlin? You can tell me if you like someone else." Her bottom lip stuck out in a little pout and I couldn't look away from it.

"I'm not trying to be anything, Ani. I don't like-like anyone and I don't think you really like me. You don't even know me." No one did because I wouldn't let them.

Her pout turned into a grin that flashed lots of white teeth and a dimple in her cheek. Her smile wasn't as nice as Ashley's, but there was something about it that made me like it more.

"But I like what I do know about you. Isn't that enough?" Her words tumbled around in my head because maybe it should be enough. I thought about my parents and how my mom hated and yelled at my dad every time he had to travel for work. How she screamed that she never signed on to be a single parent. And I remembered my dad screaming back at her that when he married her, he expected to come home to a 10 every night, not a 2. He was gone and she filled the void with food and other unhealthy habits. Some would say she let herself go. My parents hated what they didn't know about each other, and that overshadowed what they originally liked about each other.

I gave my head a firm shake and deftly picked up my pencil to circle that carefully drawn NO. I saw Ani look away as I did it, but the message was clear...I don't like you the way you like me...even if maybe, possibly, probably I wish I did.

TEXT

Ani

CITING BAD INFLUENCES and my unbreakable penchant for getting into trouble, my parents pulled me out of public school right smack-dab in the middle of 7th grade. They paid a small fortune for me to go to a private, Catholic school that was a pain in the ass. I knew my parents simply had my best interests at heart. But they took my unending rebellion as me acting out and breaking the rules to spite them. I viewed it as me being the person I was always going to be. Well, the person I was going to be once I wasn't the sick girl anymore. I wanted to live my life to the fullest and experience everything there was to experience without fear holding me back and worry holding me down.

I wasn't born one of those happy, bouncing babies. Nope, when I came out I wasn't breathing. I was upside down and blue. There was a whole laundry list of things that were wrong with me and my parents thought they were going to have to bury me instead of getting to take me home to the nursery they painstakingly decorated. It was touch and go for the first six months, but eventually my innate stubbornness and fight won out. I beat the odds and my parents took home a happy, mostly healthy baby girl...until I wasn't.

I was five when I remember not feeling so well. I didn't want to eat, I had no energy and even the smallest tasks seemed to take Herculean effort. My mom knew there was something wrong immediately even though nothing on the outside had changed. I had vague recollections of getting all kinds of poked and prodded, of sitting through test after test. But what I remember most is my parents crying. My mom collapsing in my dad's arms as he struggled to keep her up off the floor. They threw a lot of big words around that I was too little to understand, leukemia, radiation, prognosis, remission…I didn't get what the words meant but I knew I was sick, really sick, and that it was making both my mom and dad cry.

I couldn't go to school anymore. My whole family practically moved into my hospital room, which was no fun for my older brother who was just starting to come into his own as Mr. Popular at his high school. The stuff they gave me that was supposed to make me feel better, made me feel 100 times worse. My hair fell out. My face changed and everyone wore themselves out trying to convince me it would all be better soon. Soon wasn't soon enough.

It took two years for me to be declared cancer-free. Two long, agonizing years that put everyone I loved through the wringer. I was so tired of being sick and of watching the way my sickness took its toll on my family. I wanted to be anything other than the girl with cancer. I wanted to be anyone who wasn't the girl who almost died, more than once. I wanted to live every minute of the life I had left to the fullest and experience everything that I had missed while I was stuck in a hospital bed.

My parents called me reckless and foolish. They wanted to wrap me up in bubble wrap and put me on a shelf where nothing could break me. I refused to live that way. I refused to hide from anything or waste a second regretting anything.

My attitude led to a fair amount of trouble. It also led to my first ever heartbreak.

Devlin James thought I didn't know him, so I couldn't like him. I was convinced that I did.

I knew all about the way he never spoke unless he was spoken to.

I watched the way he watched everyone else like they were going to attack, so he had to be ready to defend himself.

I listened to his quiet words and deliberate way of speaking.

He played rough and hard with his friends at recess, like that was the only time he could let loose and be free. Like he was let off a leash that was too tight for a few precious minutes each day. With his golden hair and tawny eyes, he was pretty. However, it was his sullen, brooding demeanor that I couldn't stop thinking about. He was no typical little boy, and considering I was no typical little girl, I thought he was made just for me.

Fearlessly, I asked him if he liked me. With heart-shattering honesty, he told me no. I believed him, because I could see it in his face that he was telling the truth. He didn't like anyone and he was okay with that. I tucked my heartbroken tail between my legs and told myself nothing ventured, nothing gained. I'd survived worse than an honest rejection from a boy I had a crush on, so the pain would pass.

And it did, but slowly because I still sat right in front of him in class for the rest of the year, and instead of hiding behind his books or goofing off with his friends like he used to, he would stare at me until I caught him. He would guiltily look away, like he was doing something wrong and that hurt my heart.

We had different teachers in 6th grade, so I hardly saw him and that helped ease the sting even more. By 7th grade, I found myself entranced with music and the kids that liked skateboards and loud punk rock music. I decided I liked boys with blue mohawks instead of boys with floppy golden hair and sad brown eyes. Those boys with the wild, colorful hair were the ones that got me in trouble. I skipped class, missed curfew, got caught smoking, and was busted for wearing things to school that weren't appropriate. Private school became my own little prison and all I could do was daydream about boys with wild ways and sad eyes.

I never forgot about Devlin. I stopped thinking about him all the time. He creeped in when I thought about things I missed, when I pondered on things I couldn't have. Occasionally, I compared him to the boys that I chased with crazy hair and no conformity. I wondered what it was about his silence and his stillness that had drawn me to him in the first place. I felt like I was a river raging and churning, trying to cut my way through life with brute force. Devlin was the opposite. He was like a boulder in the middle of the torrent. Unmovable and unaffected by the crashing waters around him. He stood sentinel and stoic while the flow was forced to split and separate around him.

I got detention one day after school. A common enough occurrence since there were so many rules to remember on any given day, and I could only keep up with half at my best. My mom couldn't come get me because my brother had a soccer game. She ordered me to walk the few blocks between the schools so that we could all ride home together. He still got to go to public school, not only because he made good choices but also because the boy hadn't been sick a day in his life. I was convinced my parents actually believed having me in a Catholic school would somehow ward off the bad health juju I'd been born with.

I didn't particularly care for sports, but I did like to cheer my brother on whenever I got the chance. If anything happened to me in the future, I wanted him to know I was his number 1 cheerleader, his biggest fan. He had been mine when I needed it most, so the least I could do was throw a little rah rah his way.

I cut through a couple of alleys that my mom would have a heart attack if she knew that's what I was doing and stopped by my favorite convenience store to grab a slushie. I recognized a couple of the kids standing outside smoking. I gave a wave that was ignored and scowled that I was so easily dismissed without the proper accessories to mark me as one of them. It made me wonder if all those wild boys I chased after only pretended to be tough and cool with their hair and their clothes. They were wearing a costume, and if you didn't wear the same one, they had no time or place for you.

Still stinging at the blatant dismissal, I didn't notice the quiet boy with sad eyes until I plowed right into him. Cherry slushy went all over both of us. It covered the front of my pristine white uniform shirt and splashed, staining his perfectly white sneakers. The icy mess trickled sticky and sloppy off my arms, but I couldn't move because Devlin James, the boy that checked NO, was standing in front of me, with his golden hair and dark eyes. They looked so much sadder. Devlin had sprouted up a few inches, so I had to crane my neck back to look at him, and when I did, I forgot everything and everyone. His silence always said so much, and in the quiet that echoed between us, as we both stood frozen and covered in syrup, it told me he was just as floored to see me as I was to see him.

It was just me and him, him and me. We stared at each other silently until I couldn't take it anymore. I dropped the now empty Slushy cup and leapt forward so I could hug him. He was holding a football, so I couldn't get as close as I wanted, but he did lower one arm and give me an awkward side-hug back. It made me tingle all over.

"Long time no see." My words rushed out on an excited breath.

He nodded, dark eyes skimming over my hated outfit and lingering where the slushy stain was spreading across the start of what I was sure was going to be an impressive rack. I deserved at least that after everything I'd already been through.

"I heard you changed schools." Devlin sounded completely uninterested in the reasons why, so I didn't give them to him.

"I did. Private school, obviously. How have you been?" I wasn't really expecting an answer, so I was floored when he gave me one.

"I've been okay. My folks just got divorced. It was pretty ugly." He blinked at me like he was surprised he answered as well. He tossed the football to his other hand and shifted his weight from foot to foot. "How have you been?"

I shrugged and cringed as icy wetness found its way down the front of my shirt. "Good. I'm always good. Any day I wake up and nothing is wrong with me is a good day, but that's a long story."

Devlin looked at me and then looked at his cellphone clearly checking the time. He sighed and tossed the ball back into the air. "I kinda do want to hear it but I don't have time. I've got practice in ten minutes."

I grinned at him and pulled out my own phone and handed it over to him. "Put your number in there and I'll text you." He took the phone with a lifted eyebrow and twitching lips. "So you're a jock now?" He'd never been a joiner when I crushed on him with all my young infatuation.

"I'm not a jock. I didn't like being at home after school and playing sports was the only thing I could think of that keeps me busy. It's not so bad at home anymore and I'm actually pretty good with this thing, so I'll stick with it until it isn't fun anymore."

I took the phone and saved his information. He didn't need to see that I saved it with a heart-eye emoji next to it. That would send him running.

"Sorry about your shoes." They were now a rosy pink color but that somehow worked on him.

He shook his hair, golden strands falling into his eyes. "Don't worry about it. It was cool bumping into you, Ani."

I couldn't hold back the smile that split my face. "Same, Devlin. I'll text you." I held up the phone and wiggled it indicating that I really would reach out to him. I missed the way being around him shut out all the noise that was constantly telling me to go-go-go. I didn't feel like I was cramming hours into minutes when I was near him. Time seemed to slow and moments seemed to stretch.

He nodded and his gaze got serious. "Ani." He paused and took a breath. "No more 'do you like me, yes or no' notes, okay? If you text me, it has to be as my friend and nothing more."

Ouch. That stung a little and it was a little presumptuous on his part. "I go to a new school, and there are lots of different boys in my life now, Dev. I'm not still hung up on you. Don't worry."

He sighed with obvious relief. "I mean I do like you, just not like that."

I gave a laugh that was dry and had no humor in it. "Right, you don't like anyone like that. I remember."

He flushed and shuffled his feet which made me gulp. "Actually, there's this girl in my class…" I held up a hand to cut him off.

"I get it. We're friends. I can do that. I told you I liked you, Dev. That didn't change just because you didn't like me back. I'll be in touch." I stepped around him but took a second to put a hand on his shoulder which brought his eyes down to mine. "You take care, okay?" I wasn't sure why I was compelled to tell him that when it made me roll my eyes every time someone said it to me. But I had a gut feeling Devlin James was in desperate need of care.

I walked away fully intending to text him in the next couple of days but life happens; other things got in the way, my heart still hurt a little, and I wholeheartedly launched a campaign to persuade my parents into letting me get back to public school. Devlin got put on the back burner.

It was two weeks later when I realized I had his number and hadn't used it. I told him I could be his friend, even if that wasn't the role I wanted to play in his life. I felt obligated to keep my word. I was the water raging and he slowed me down and redirected my flow. I needed that in my life in whatever capacity I could get it.

Lying upside down on my bed with my feet on the wall and my phone dangling over my face, I sent out the first of a million texts we would eventually send back and forth to each other.

– Sorry I was so slow reaching out. I'm trying to convince my parents to let me come back to public school for high school, and that's taken a lot of groveling and begging. I think I'm starting to wear them down though.

The last part was a total lie. They weren't budging, so I was going to have to enlist the big guns, my brother. I knew if we tag-teamed them, there was no way they could keep saying no.

There wasn't a reply for a long time, and when my phone finally pinged, I almost rolled off my bed in the excitement to see if it was from Devlin. I sighed like a romantic comedy heroine when I saw his name and my heart twisted when I saw his response.

– That would be cool. I got used to looking for you in the halls. You were always smiling.

I was never smiling. But whenever I caught him looking at me, I couldn't help but flash some teeth.

– We'll see how it goes. Wish me luck.

– Why did they take you out of school in the first place?

I knew it was coming. He said he wanted my story and I intended to give it to him. It felt like I was always giving this boy words that were ripped right out of my heart.

– I was sick when I was younger. Really sick.

– ?????

– I had leukemia.

– Like cancer?

– Not like cancer...actual cancer. I wasn't given very good odds of making it through since I was born with a lot of health problems. But I beat it and I'm here today. I'm trying to live life to the fullest but my parents worry about every little thing I do.

– Like what?

– Well, the reason they pulled me out of the public high school was because I got busted smoking.

– I would be pissed about that too. Smoking is gross. :(

– Yeah, but everyone tries it at least once. I want to be a normal kid and make the same kind of mistakes every other normal kid gets to make. My parents don't want me to ever be at any kind of risk. They are overprotective.

– Sounds like they have a reason to be.

– Whose side are you on?

I scowled at my phone and swung my legs back and forth over the edge of the bed. This wasn't how I anticipated the conversation going.

– I'm on the side that wants you to be around for as long as possible. You're lucky your parents actually give a shit about you. You could have parents that don't even know where you are half the time. Better to be over-loved than under-loved.

Something told me he was speaking from personal experience, and that made my insides ache. I was going to ask him about it when he told me he had to go because he had homework to do. I offered an easy goodbye and was shocked the next night when he was the one who reached out to me first.

It wasn't anything as deep as our first conversation but on and on it went. Every night, sometimes right after school, and sometimes way later than either of us should be up, we texted. Back and forth we went, learning all the things there was to know about each other. Sharing our lives through text message. I even grinned and toughed it out with a congratulations text when he mentioned the girl that he liked had finally returned some interest.

I was a good friend and so was he. I would never tell him that now that I knew him, well, as much of him as he would let me know, I liked him even more now than I originally did.

FB MESSAGE / TWITTER / INSTAGRAM
…sliding into those DMs ☺

Devlin

"**W**HAT ARE YOU doing?"
   The sharply asked question was the first indication I was in trouble. The second was the way the girl that was leaning heavily into my side suddenly stiffened and pulled her body away from mine. She spent the last hour trying to get close to me; she was all practiced come-hither looks, the perfectly planned toss of her hair, fake interest in all things football. I let it work because she was cute and because I was all about no effort. If she liked me because I wasn't hard to look at and could throw a football, then I wouldn't feel bad about not bothering to remember her name or what she looked like after we hooked up. I'd learned pretty quickly once I'd started noticing girls noticing me, that I wasn't really cut out to be anyone's boyfriend.

When you were saddled with that title, it meant there were questions asked. Questions about why no one was ever at my house to look after me. Questions about why neither of my parents were ever at any of my football games. Questions about why I never had anyone to look out for me or care about where I was or who I was with. I didn't want to answer those questions. And I didn't want to fight with a girl that was supposed to be mine, about the girl who was really the most important person in my life. Girlfriends thought they could pressure me to spend less time with Ani. They thought they could pout and ply me with their considerable charms in order to distract me from the blue-eyed, black-haired devil that I would drop everything for without question. At first, I foolishly thought they were jealous because Ani was so pretty and fun to be around, but no matter how many assurances I gave anyone that she and I were nothing more than friends, the jealousy never went away. It took more girlfriends, and Ani losing several boyfriends, for me to realize that they weren't jealous...they were desperately trying to figure out why Ani was the only person I let in.

I might share my body and my time with someone else, but Ani was the only person I ever let inside my heart. I didn't necessarily open the door for her, but in her typical hurried, chaotic way, she had shoved herself in and made herself comfortable. There was no shaking her loose, so I didn't bother trying, even if it meant I wasn't going to get laid.

I tapped on the screen of my phone to close the private message I was responding to. Ani was supposed to meet me at this party. I told her parents I would keep an eye on her if they agreed to let her come, but the night before she was busted sneaking out of the house to meet the older boy she was currently seeing, the one who neither her parents nor I approved of. Now she was grounded...like she usually was...and as a result, she was blowing up my phone for updates on who was hooking up with who. Her parents never let her switch schools, so she lived vicariously through all the messages, posts, and pictures I put up for her throughout the school year. Making her feel included and missed was the least I could do after everything she had done for me.

It started with those middle-of-the night texts. Having her words to keep me company in the dark was the first I could remember not feeling alone in my house while my dad ran off to remarry, and as my mom started dating for revenge. Ani's words made me laugh and they offered comfort when I finally confided in her how much I hated being by myself all the time. Sure I had friends...and girls...but when I went home at the end of the night, it was just me and the quiet. It drove me insane and made me feel restless and trapped.

Ani set me free.

She invited me over for dinner one night. At first, I declined. We were friends and boy/girl friends didn't need to take the step of meeting the parents. I only did that for girls I was dating and really wanting to sleep with. Ani was smart though, and the next time I texted her complaining about being sick of eating cold pizza, she showed up on my doorstep with her older brother and an armful of leftovers from her mother. I hadn't had a home-cooked meal in longer than I could remember and it was so good that I wanted to cry. Also, having company instead of eating alone over the sink, hit some part of me that I didn't know was fragile and tender. I didn't turn her down the next time she invited me over, and her parents, her kind, loving parents wasted no time in pouring some of that extra love they had all over me. It was the first time in my life I felt like I could breathe easy.

I looked at the irritated girl who had been nibbling on my neck a second ago and lifted an eyebrow. She was cute, but even the promise of her mouth doing dirty things to various parts of my anatomy didn't dull the disappointment that flooded me when Ani told me she was on lockdown. Nothing was very much fun when she wasn't a part of it.

I sighed and slid away from my current admirer, rising to my feet and wobbling a little bit as the beer I'd been guzzling from a red Solo cup hit my system. I wasn't feeling the girl and I was no longer feeling the party. I rubbed a hand over my face and gave my head a little shake to see if I could break up some of the fuzz that was making my brain feel like cotton.

"I've gotta go." I didn't tell the girl that I was messaging Ani, or that I was liking her tweets about being a prisoner in her own home. I didn't tell her I was stalking Instagram because I wanted to see that familiar face with its aqua eyes and frame of jet-black hair. All my life I stayed in one place, locked in a pattern of retreat and hiding so that the people I loved couldn't hurt me or use me to hurt each other. Ani roared into my life and forced me to move. She pushed and pulled, she dragged me to a place that was better, and right now, with my head foggy and my heart sluggishly thumping, I felt like I needed her more than ever. I knew it was the booze and melancholy over the fact that we were both going to be graduating soon. But I couldn't stop my feet from finding their way towards her house.

It made everything inside of me hurt when I thought about the fact that we were going to colleges on opposite sides of the country. I couldn't fathom how hard that goodbye was going to be. She was the only reason I ever felt like I belonged anywhere and all of that was going to go away.

It took well over an hour for me to haul myself across town to her house. I had a car but I was in no condition to drive and the last thing I needed was a DUI or an accident to endanger the very high-profile scholarship I'd signed to play football for a prominent California college. I didn't always make the best decisions, but my inherent sense of self-preservation never failed to kick in when I needed it.

Ani's house was dark but the porch light was on. Her brother had left for college a few years ago, and when he went, he left behind his battered old pick-up truck for her to use. The monster was sitting silent and imposing in the driveway indicating that she hadn't climbed out the window and put the thing in neutral making an escape. Everyone knew there was no keeping Ani from what Ani wanted to do, but occasionally, she would surrender the keys and play nice with her parents to keep them from worrying themselves sick over her. She would not be tamed, but her wild heart knew how to take care of those that let it run free.

I slid around the side of the house and made my way around to the backyard. Both Ani and her brother had bedrooms that were off the basement of the house. A privilege that Ani almost got taken away every single time she missed curfew or disappeared in the middle of the night. I doubted her parents would actually ever move her, considering the revolving door of friends she had coming in out of the place. They knew that she left the sliding glass door unlocked so I could come and go as I pleased. I'd spent more nights crashed out on the sectional in the big TV room than I did in my own bed as the years progressed. As long as I wasn't in Ani's room, her big-hearted parents never blinked an eye.

One night, after a particularly painful loss on the football field, I'd passed out curled up next to Ani's small frame, her hands in my hair as she assured me everything would be fine. I didn't like to lose and took a lot of pride in being good at what I did on the field. Her words soothed jagged edges and her touch calmed the things inside of me that always felt like they were thrashing around, fighting against ropes and chains that held them.

As innocent as the situation was, her father had some stern and unforgettable words for me when he found us wrapped around each other the next morning. I understood, because I cared about his girl just as deeply as he did. I would never do anything to hurt her and I hated that sometimes, when she thought I wasn't listening or paying attention, she would remind me how callously I rejected her when we were kids. She'd done so much for me, I wanted desperately to go back in time and check yes on that little note she left on my desk.

The door rolled open with a whisper of sound. Ani was sitting on the couch where most of my favorite memories were made. Her head whipped around as I stumbled across the space between us and collapsed in a heap next to her once I threw myself over the back of the couch. Her blue eyes widened and her mouth dropped open in a little "O" of surprise as I plopped my head on her lap and let the warmth of her skin sink into my face as I closed my eyes and rubbed my cheek against her thigh.

Her dark hair slithered across her shoulders and tickled my forehead as she leaned over me so the tips of her fingers could trace the curve of my eyebrows and the arch of my nose.

"Bad night, hotshot?" Her tone was laced with humor but there was worry underneath it. She knew I wasn't the type to show up on her doorstep wasted and depressed. I didn't let those parts of me touch her. I typed the words out, gave them to her silently, but I never brought them to her. After everything she had suffered through and survived, I felt stupid being sad and angry just because my parents didn't give a shit about me. Usually when there was a party, it was one of the few nights I didn't seek her out for comfort and kindness. I wasn't beyond letting a warm body and soft hands make me feel like I was something special, like I was someone wanted. I wasn't above letting my dick lead me around, but tonight it was another part of me calling the shots. My heart.

"It wasn't any fun without you there." I sighed and peeled my eyes open to look up at her. "It made me realize that pretty soon you aren't going to be anywhere anymore."

Her fingers feathered through my hair and the edges of her rings were cool against my forehead.

"I'm always going to be there, Dev. I just won't be in the same state." Her voice was quiet as well and I realized leaving was going to be as hard for her as it was for me. She forced me to move. I forced her to slow down. We were the constant in each other's lives.

"Was the guy worth it?" I never thought they were. She was always chasing after some loser that never appreciated how great she was. All she wanted was someone that could show her a good time, someone that never tried to clip her wings and hold her down. She went through boys fast enough that she had a reputation, but I knew that it was a reputation she didn't really deserve. She was looking for something that she hadn't found yet, and the boys that filtered in and out of her days were nothing more than stepping-stones on that journey. She never kept her feet planted on any one of them for very long.

"They never are." Her voice got wistful and quiet. "I was scrolling through Instagram before you showed up. He posted a bunch of pictures of him and some girl at a party, so clearly. No loss there." Her thumb traced the edge of my jaw and the gentle touch had me leaning into her even more. "I, however, was sad I was going to miss seeing you tonight, so I'm glad you stopped by. Even if you smell like a brewery and can barely keep your eyes open."

She was always happy to see me. She was the only person that was. She took me whatever way I came.

"The walk over cleared my head up a little. I wasn't having fun. I was sitting on a couch with some girl's tongue in my ear while I was stalking you on Messenger. I realized I would rather be where you are than anywhere else." Her breath hitched a little at my words and her too-blue eyes widened. It was something I thought often but that wasn't the kind of honesty I gave to anyone. I hated how vulnerable it made me. I knew firsthand that it was the people that were the closest to you that had the power to hurt you the most and I never wanted to let anyone have that kind of power again. The thing was, I trusted Ani not to hurt me and I knew that I would never do anything to hurt her.

Her lips quirked up a little bit and she lowered her head so that all of her dark hair fell in rivers of darkness around us and suddenly all the fuzz and cloudiness that filled my head evaporated. She was, without a doubt, the most important person in my life, with that little smile, those blue eyes, and that curtain of midnight hair that surrounded us...suddenly, she was the center of everything. I felt like an idiot for ever having tried to fill that space up with someone that wasn't her.

"Do you like me, Dev?" It was the question that started it all, the one I answered wrong.

I reached a hand up so that it slid along the side of her neck, under her hair. Her pulse thumped against my palm and her breathing hitched. Anticipation throbbed, like a living thing between us, as she leaned over me even more, shutting anything that was before her out. There was only this girl and this chance to answer that question right since she was giving me a second chance.

"What if I more than like you, Ani?" She was the reason I knew that love didn't have to hurt. She was the one that showed me you could care about someone without them using your feelings for them against you. She was the reason I knew love didn't have to be a trap; it could be something that finally set you free.

I didn't think a kiss upside down and off-center from the way she was leaning over me would be the kiss that defined what kisses should be. It was a kiss that was about so much more than using another person to forget about yourself and the things in life you couldn't change and control. This wasn't about chasing fleeting pleasure to avoid permanent pain. All this was about was the way this girl's lips felt against mine. It was about the way she made everything feel like it was a possibility. It was about the way her touch, her taste, settled deep into my bones and became a fundamental part of all my best memories.

It was a kiss that rushed and raged, just like she did. It was a kiss that went unchecked and unstoppable, just like she was. It was a kiss that churned and spiraled into a vortex of things that were so important and imperative, just like this girl had always managed to be in my life.

The kiss didn't stay a kiss for long. Hands moved across shaking skin, and our positions changed so that she was the one trapped underneath me. Eyes locked and breath mingled as we shifted wordless from one kind of important to another. Her hair tangled around my hands and her legs anxiously moved against mine. Our bodies told secrets that neither one of us dared to voice aloud. Pulses jumped, clothes seemed to magically disappear, as we let ourselves fall from one kind of way of being everything to one another into another kind of consuming, intense, uncontrollable way of being together. In all honestly, I liked this one a whole lot more.

After the fall and rise, after the calm and the collection, we lay there in the dark, her hair a midnight blanket around us. We were quiet, contemplating the way we had to say goodbye to our old friendship while welcoming in the complication of our new relationship without losing any of the things that kept us tied so tightly together in the first place. Her fingertips lightly danced over the damp center of my chest, circling around the spot where my heart seemed to be telling her all the words I couldn't get my lips to say.

"I more than like you too, Devlin. I always have." She liked me when I didn't like myself and that was how I knew I would love her when I didn't know how to do that either.

EMAIL

Ani

To: Ani-Mal21@universitymail.com
Subject: Miss you

Haven't heard from you in a while. Just wanted to check in. Practice has been brutal as we gear up for the bowl game and that hit I took in the last game did more damage than I thought to my shoulder. I keep missing your calls, but I hope you know every voicemail you leave, I listen to at least 1000 times. Every selfie you send, I stare at until my eyes cross, and every time I have to say goodbye when we get off of FaceTime makes my heart feel like it's going to explode. I miss you. I miss us. I hope those art classes you were so excited about are going well. I got the picture you painted for me and I hung it on the wall. I reserved tickets for you and the family for the game next week...you still haven't told me if you're coming or not. We haven't seen each other since my birthday, Ani. I'm dying here.

Call me.
Text me.
Tweet me.
Facebook me.
Hell, send me a carrier pigeon so that I know this sucks for you as badly as it sucks for me.
I love you, Wild One.

– Dev.

I stared at the words until they blurred as tears filled my eyes. I missed him and I missed us just as much but time and distance had a potent way of opening one's eyes to the reality of a situation.

All I'd ever wanted was Devlin. I got him, but only for a short handful of minutes. We hooked up and stayed hooked through graduation and the summer before college. We battled through distance and uncertainty during the first three years of school. We logged endless frequent-flier miles, round trips on buses, breakdowns in shitty cars, just to see each other as often as we could. We worked our way through jealousy and homesickness. We fought through doubt and despair. We shouldered through all of it with eyes firmly on the prize of being together at the end of all the sacrifice and soldiering on.

But now the future was here. There were no more wistful daydreams, no more candy-colored visions of a perfect ever after. We were two people moving in opposite directions and I didn't know how to turn the tides. My river decided it flowed in the direction of New York. Early on in college, I'd found my niche. The throb and thump of the big city called to my restless soul. I loved my crappy, cramped apartment. I loved that I could get takeout at 3 a.m. I loved the quirky, vintage shops on every corner. And most of all, I loved the art. There was expression and exploration everywhere I looked. I wanted a part of that. I settled on an art major, got heavily into illustration and graphic design and through chance, and a night with too many tequila shots, stumbled my way into a tattoo parlor. It was art that was alive. It was a form of expression that a human could take with them beyond the grave. It was armor they could wear to define who they always wanted to be. I got a sword tattooed along the entire length of my forearm because I wasn't the sick girl anymore, I was the girl that conquered life. I was the girl that fought and won.

I mentioned the new passion to Dev in passing but his schedule for both school and training was all over the place. I rarely knew what city he was going to be in without having to look on ESPN GameDay. He was supportive, because he always was, but he had given no indication that he had plans to move to New York or even somewhere on the East Coast. He was going to get drafted, everyone knew it. And he was going to have to go where the team that picked him up first was located. I was proud of him, but I had no intentions of following him. I *still* wanted Dev, but I also wanted a life and a career I could be proud of. I wasn't the girl who was going to look pretty and cheer on her guy...I mean I was going to do both those things...but I was going to do other, more important things as well.

Wiping the tears away, I hit the reply button and sank my teeth into my lower lip. I'd been avoiding talking to him face-to-face for the last month because I'd been offered an apprenticeship in a tattoo shop that was world-renowned for the caliber of artists it produced. I couldn't turn the opportunity down. I couldn't say no, and that meant I wasn't going to be at the bowl game, which was the last one of Dev's career. They said he was going to win the Heisman. I didn't even know what that was.

> To: DevilshlyHandsome@collegemail.com (I picked that email addy out and refused to let him change it.)
> Subject: These are the hardest words I've ever had to write
>
> I miss you too, Dev. You have no idea how much. I listen to your messages, I stare at your Instagram, I love the way you look in your uniform. I stalk Skype to see when you're on so we can talk, my heart flips over when I see you sent me a Snapchat. I love you, Dev. It's the one thing in my life I was always really good at. I loved you and I never screwed it up or did anything reckless and heavy-handed to break it apart.
> I still love you, but I also love me. I love who I am here.
> I love this city.
> I love the opportunities I have here.
> I love my life here.
> I know we've never talked about what comes next, but next for me whatever it is, has to be here, Dev. You'll go where the game takes you and I know you would always come back to me but I've only had bits and pieces of you for the last years and I'm tired of sharing you with the rest of the world. I will never ask you to change your life and your plans for me, because I know how hard you've worked to obtain everything you've accomplished.
> I hope you love me enough to grant me the same courtesy. I want to love you forever, but I don't know how to do that when forever keeps us

apart from one another.

I'm taking an internship in the city. It starts the week of your big game. Mom and Dad will be there to watch you, and my brother is flying in with his wife and son...but I'm not going to be there this time, Dev.

I'm not going to be there for any of the rest of the games.

I know this is a conversation we should have face-to-face, but I can barely see the keyboard through my tears. I know it's the right thing, and we've always been better at giving each other words we can hold on to rather than ones that are forgotten when the other person is done talking.

You will always be the person I love more than anyone else. I have always more than liked you.

Love always,
– Ani

I read and read the letter no less than a hundred times and with shaking fingers hit send. I shut the laptop down and threw myself across my bed, clutching a pillow and sobbing uncontrollably. I heard my phone start to light up, email notifications, calls, text messages...all the ways we stayed connected blasting at me. He was trying to reach me every way he could think of and I ignored them all.

I was changing courses. I was breaking new ground. I was water falling over a cliff into the unknown below and I selfishly couldn't wait for the crash.

WORDS THAT LAST FOREVER
Devlin

4 years later

S HE BROKE MY heart through email.

She took away everything with words that were never spoken and I couldn't say I blamed her. I remembered the look on her face when I told her I couldn't like her the way she wanted me to when we were nothing more than kids. I didn't know it at the time, but I was breaking her heart. I wanted to take my actions back because I now knew how badly it hurt.

I tried to get her to reconsider. I begged, I pleaded, I promised things that weren't mine to promise. I was angry at her, but more than that, I was angry that deep down I knew she was right. Our paths were dividing, forking off into separate directions, and as much as either one of us might want to fight the current, there was no pushing the river. It naturally flowed the way it was destined to.

The first year I was drafted, I was too busy to suffer from a broken heart. Plus, my body was abused so badly between games and endless training and practices that every other part of me hurt twice as much as the ache in my chest. She sent me a birthday card and one on Christmas. She dropped an email in my inbox saying she was watching me play, and she would send a text here and there mentioning that she saw me go down on the field and asking if I was okay. We shifted from something more to something less, but I couldn't live my life without her in it, so I took the friendship she offered and returned it. I sent her flowers when she finished her apprenticeship, and I begrudgingly sent her a congratulations email when she told me she was engaged. I hated the idea of her moving on, but we were a lifetime and a whole country apart from one another, so all I wanted was for her to be happy.

I went back to killing time with girls who were nothing more than a distraction. My parents pretended to get along for the press and for propriety but none of their machinations over the years had changed. Now, they each thought I was the family bank, and half the time I was willing to hand over the cash just to get them to go away and leave me alone. I wasn't bringing anyone else into that, and even though I knew she had someone else and a life that didn't have room for me in it, my heart was still locked on Ani. It only beat a proper rhythm when she was the one dictating the tune it should play.

I lived my life as fully as I could. I played hard, on and off the field. I got better at my sport but ended up feeling more alone than I ever had in my life. Ani sent an email telling me that her fiancé had cheated on her with another artist that worked in the shop with them. She called off the wedding and was branching out to open her own shop. They were words that sounded sad. They were words that made me realize nothing was destined and I alone had the power to decide what direction I wanted to go. Rivers were dammed up all the time to create lakes and reservoirs. They didn't always have to run the direction nature wanted them to take.

My team made it to the playoffs. We almost won the Super Bowl. My contract was up and I was a free agent. It took a lot of bartering, more meetings than I'd ever sat through in my life, and multiple agents and lawyers to make the trade happen, but happen it did. I wasn't going to New York, but Philly was close. I figured if I could at least get my foot in the door with Ani, we could make it work with that minimal distance between us, and if she sent me on my way, then there was enough space between the two cities that I wouldn't have to be reminded of my rash decision every single day.

The trade was big news. My face was all over the TV and on every sports magazine that one could think of. Ani sent a text asking if it was true that I was coming to Philly. I told her it was and asked her if she wanted to get together once I was settled in with the new team in my new city. She didn't reply back for a long time, so I instantly regretted letting my reckless heart do my thinking for me.

She eventually got back to me, and when she did, the message practically jumped off my phone with her excitement. There were so many heart emojis and exclamation marks I could barely make out the words that were scattered between them. It made me smile. I missed her exuberance and her wild enthusiasm for everything. I missed her.

It took a few months to get myself moved and it took a couple more to find my groove and my footing with the new team. Throughout that time, the messages from Ani came more frequently and she even started sprinkling in a late-night phone call here and there. The sound of her voice brought back every good memory I had. It also reminded me of sweaty nights spent wrapped around each other in the dark. Sex was always fun, but with Ani, it was something more. It was something that mattered. It was something that filled up holes I had in my soul.

I didn't tell her I was coming to see her. I didn't want her to worry about me on top of getting her new shop up and running. She invited me to the grand opening, and while I wanted to go, I had an away game and couldn't swing it. She was disappointed, but she told me she understood. Our entire relationship from start to finish was based on words we shared. Words written and exchanged when we couldn't say the ones that were needed most. I was an expert at reading into what was hiding behind those words she sent. I was close, but still so far away and she was wondering if it had been a good idea to let me sneak back in that door to her life. I was going to have to show her she was it for me, that compromise and cooperation were small prices to pay if it meant she and I ended up together.

When I pushed into the door of her shop, I felt like I was walking into Ani's heart and soul. The place was bright, vivid, wild, and warm. Everywhere I looked my eyes landed on something that was interesting and reminded me of the girl I'd loved since before I knew what love was. My lips quirked a little when I caught sight of my college jersey framed and hung on the wall, my signature scrawled across the back of it and next to my name a heart with D+A in the center. I'd given it to her when I left for college and I had no words to describe how happy I was she'd held on to it all this time.

The guy behind the desk had a tattoo on the side of his face and gauges in his ears that looked like Frisbees. His eyes widened as recognition hit him, and he pointed a tattooed finger at me. "Hey, I know you, aren't you..." He trailed off as I nodded and reached back to stick my hands in my pockets.

"I am. Is Ani here? We're friends." There was a quiet murmuring throughout the shop as the other artists and customers gave me curious looks and as some tried to work up the courage to come and talk to me. Luckily, there was a squeal from somewhere towards the back of the shop, and the next thing I knew, I was hit by a tiny blue-eyed tornado. Her limbs wrapped around me as her feet left the ground. I held her close with a hand on her ass so I didn't drop her. She smelled like all the best parts of the past and she felt like the only future I wanted. Her black hair now had a bright red streak in the front of it and she had a little jewel that glittered above her lip, but she was still my Ani. She looked better than I could have imagined, and she was obviously happy to see me.

Her lips touched my cheek and the featherlight caress made my entire body tighten. I set her back on her feet and bent down so I could touch my lips to her forehead. We had one hell of an audience but I'd lived most of my life in the spotlight lately, so it was nothing new. I brushed my fingers against her cheek and watched as she blinked back tears.

"I missed you." My voice broke because I wasn't used to having to actually say the words that she needed to hear.

Her fingers wrapped around my wrist and her lashes lowered. "Missed you to, Dev. I had no idea you were coming."

I let my lips twitch into a smile. "I want a tattoo and I knew you would murder me if I let anyone else mark me permanently."

Her eyes widened and her breath hitched. "You want a tattoo?"

Most of the guys on my team were inked from head to toe but it had never been something I was into. Or rather, I never ran across anything I liked enough or that mattered enough to have it on my skin forever.

I nodded and stepped away from her so I could once again reach my hand in my pocket. Suddenly nervous, I had to clear my throat as my fingers touched the fragile paper that I hauled with me everywhere I went. Parts of it were torn and tattered, but when I held it out to her, the heart over my name was still visible and I knew that she recognized it right away. Her fingers shook as she put her fingers to her mouth as her lips quivered.

"I know what this is." Her fingers were light on the paper and her eyes asked me a million questions.

I shrugged. "I didn't check the right box back then."

She tugged on my arm, dragging me past whispering clients and wide-eyed looks from her staff. The buzz of tattoo machines was almost enough to drown out the thunder of my heart and the rush of blood between my ears…almost.

She pulled me into her office and shut the door. She leaned back against it, the note she wrote me all those years ago caught in her fingers. "You want me to tattoo my note on you, Dev? You want to go back in time?"

I shook my head. "I want to start over, Ani. I want to check YES. I want you to know that I've liked you since the beginning and that I'm willing to do the work in order to make you like me back. I've been with you, and I've been without you…with is so much better."

She gulped and put a hand to her heart. "This is crazy. I haven't seen you in years."

I took a few steps closer to her and then kept going until I could cup her soft cheek in the cradle of my hand. "You told me once that you were always going to be there, even if you weren't in the same state. It's true. You've always been there, Ani."

She bit her lip again, but her eyes stayed locked on mine. "Our lives are so different, Dev. We're so different."

I grinned at her and lowered my head so my lips could lightly touch hers. It was like no time had passed at all. I was right back to where she was the center of everything, where she made it easier to breathe. She was freedom. She was the path I took to being the person I was always supposed to be.

"Those differences don't matter now and they didn't matter before. What matters is that I like you, Ani…I more than like you and I never stopped." My eyebrows arched up questioningly and I could see heat move into her face where I was still holding her. "Do you like me? Check yes or no."

I hoped that she made the right choice. I shouldn't have worried…she always made the right choice.

The paper dropped to the floor between us as her arms lifted up and wrapped around my neck. She rose up on her tiptoes so that all my favorite parts of her pressed temptingly against all the hard parts of me.

"I check yes, Dev, but I never just liked you…it's always been love."

Her lips crushed mine and our hearts beat in time. I promised myself that when the time came to ask her to marry me, I would hand her a ring and a note.

Ani, will you marry me: check yes or no… I knew what the answer would be. She checked YES!

✧   ✧   ✧

Thank you for reading LOVE LETTERS. Want more from author Jay Crownover? Visit her website.
www.jaycrownover.com

THE REMATCH

SIENNA SNOW

CHAPTER ONE
Danika

"**F**INALLY FINISHED," I said as I released a yawn and pushed back from the scope in my lab at the Dayal-King Gallery.

Later tonight, I'd hand over the appraisal of a two-million-dollar sculpture to one of New York's most avid collectors. She planned to auction it for five times the base value but needed my sign-off to place the item for sale.

I rarely accepted last minute jobs, but this client happened to be someone I worked with regularly in my main business. A business where individuals, organizations, government agencies, and such hired me to provide discreet cybersecurity investigations—i.e., hacking.

I was doing this as a favor to her. And because she'd doubled my standard fee, I couldn't turn down the offer.

Plus, I loved my dual jobs—art appraiser and underground hacker. Who would ever believe the sweet, nerdy, art-loving Danika Dayal-King was anything but what she projected to the world?

Well, there was one person who'd always known the truth.

Nikhil King.

I lifted my gaze from the ancient marble piece, leaning back in my chair. I licked my lips and envisioned the gorgeous man so dangerous that anyone who crossed him regretted it. A man with an empire so vast, those in both legitimate and questionable aspects of society came to him for assistance. A man with midnight eyes, golden skin, and a face designed to tempt a woman to do every wicked thing imaginable.

Hell, I'd done those things and went back for more, every fucking day.

Once upon a time, he'd represented the forbidden fruit, the one thing I could never touch. Now, he was my safe place, my anchor in a world that would destroy me if it knew my secrets.

He protected me, and I protected him.

At that moment, my cell phone rang on the table next to me.

Reaching over, I answered without a glance at the display, "Hello."

"Are you up for a game of poker?" a deep voice that reminded me of sex dipped in chocolate asked.

My heartbeat accelerated, and a shiver slid down my spine. Of course, the very man my thoughts had drifted to only moments earlier would call me.

Pushing down my libido, I posed my own question. "What's the buy-in?"

"The usual."

"Meaning?"

"I work in favors. You of all people know this best." The humor in his words had me smiling.

I could never forget that was how we started.

Three years ago, I'd gone to him with a bargain, and he'd turned the tables.

To exact my revenge on my uncle, Ashok Shah, I would become his.

Body, mind, and soul.

The best damn decision I'd ever made.

"And what favor will I owe you?"

He hummed, sending a pulse of liquid heat straight to my core. "I believe we never finished that long-ago game. Let's revisit it. Depending on the outcome of the match, the favor is carte blanche."

My breath grew shallow, knowing how the night would end, no matter who won. "You're willing to risk anything I want in a favor?"

"You'll have to agree to the game." The rasp of his voice grew deeper. "Just know, if I win, you can't say no."

His words had my heart skipping a beat. Whatever he wanted, it was big. Well, I could be just as exacting.

"Then the same goes for me."

"Why do I get the feeling you plan to extract a favor of high value?"

"Because you are very suspicious. Do we have a deal, Mr. King?"

"You have yourself a deal."

"Location?"

"It's a need-to-know type of establishment. I'm sure you have the resources to find it, Little Rabbit."

I narrowed my eyes. Nik knew damn well I wouldn't have to utilize my skills to find the club. He deliberately used my hacker name to annoy me and remind me he held all my secrets.

From the time we were children in our poverty-stricken neighborhood, he'd known where my interests had lain. Time and distance hadn't changed that. I could find out anything and everything I wanted.

Although it still annoyed the hell out of me that until that game three years ago, I hadn't known the very club where we would meet tonight belonged to him and his brothers. I researched everything and anything about the businesses I associated with, and I'd somehow missed the tiny loophole they'd used to hide their tracks. It would nag me forever.

Oh well, I'd get over it.

Eventually.

"Is that how we're playing it?" I rose from my seat and took the sculpture, set it inside its container, and closed the lid.

"Yes. My house, my rules."

Rules he was well aware that I loved to break. My take on it was that since he expected the best security infrastructure for his properties, it was my job to learn all the ways to bypass his systems. This way, he would know any weaknesses.

"Time?"

"Nine o'clock."

I glanced down at my watch, seeing it was close to seven. It looked as if I'd have to send Rich, my security lead, to make the drop for the art piece.

"Not giving a lady much time to get ready."

"I'm sure you can manage it. You can wear jeans and a T-shirt. Just be there."

"Hill."

"Yes, Danika."

"I'm going to win."

"We'll see. Although, one thing is definite."

"And what is that?"

"I'm not the one who's going to end the night begging." He hung up.

I braced my hands on the table, exhaling. The man was fucking potent, even through the phone. Never had anyone affected me the way he did.

Now we'd revisit that very game that had set the motions of sending me down the rabbit hole that was life with Nikhil King. A game we never finished because our need to fuck had gotten in the way of besting each other at the table.

Well, now that I was thinking about it...we'd never gotten around to the fucking part, either, due to a potential raid on Nik's club.

Tonight, I'd be ready.

Back then, he'd had the advantage. He'd set the rules, held all the high cards. This time I wouldn't let my hormones cloud my concentration. He liked to play dirty. So could I.

Chapter Two

Nik

"ALL CLEAR, SIR," my driver and bodyguard, Lake, said as he pulled into the alleyway leading to the entrance of the Library, a little past eight thirty in the evening. "The team secured the area prior to our arrival."

"Thank you." I scanned my phone, reading through the names of all the players at the tables tonight.

As usual, the underground poker club I ran with my brothers overflowed with patrons. Everyone, from the Manhattan elite to those who ran the streets of the underworld, played at our tables. The one thing most of them had in common was that they or someone they knew owed me or mine a favor. And then there were those who I called "the others," who were allowed admission because they were useful in various aspects of my family business.

Finishing off the last of my whiskey, I set the tumbler in the holder, stepped out of the car, and made my way toward the back doors. The scent of coffee and baked goods wafted through the air from the twenty-four-hour bookshop, cafe, and bakery that sat above the club. It provided the perfect cover for our operation.

Only those with the proper order at the counter acquired the correct numeric password for the security doors leading into the club. And even after punching in the codes, the patrons went through a rigorous screening. We had a few hard-and-fast rules.

The house took its cut in cash, no exceptions. No electronics of any kind. And no weapons.

Rarely had anyone broken our rules. The cost to them wasn't worth the infraction.

Well, there was one person in particular who broke the latter two of our rules given the slightest opportunity.

The floor manager, Amir, approached me the second I stepped inside. "We have everything set up the way you requested."

"Good. Has her security called in to give you her ETA?"

"Their ETA was an hour ago. She is at her usual table." His response had me shaking my head.

The woman could never follow directions.

I moved into the hallway leading to the gaming room, pausing at a side corner that gave me a clear view of the VIP section without anyone noticing me.

The goddess with amber eyes and sun-kissed golden skin sat at a table positioned directly in the middle of the room.

My body stirred at the sight of her—utter perfection.

She wore a strapless deep blue gown that gave her the aura of a queen. Her exposed shoulders and upper back allowed a partial glimpse of all the ink on her body. Sanskrit words hiding her biggest secret adorned the column of her spine, and the stylized body tattoo of a tiger ran the length of her shoulder down to her thigh.

Once upon a time, she hid her light to fit into a world that wasn't hers. Now she could own a room with a look. Today, the only mold she needed to fit was her own.

The one thing that hadn't changed about her was her love of jewelry. And from the look of the necklace and bracelets she wore, she planned to make me work for every inch of ground in our upcoming battle. However, the rings on her finger would remain exactly where they sat.

She laughed at something a local politician said to her and then pushed her bet into the pile at the center of the table.

The play lasted another fifteen minutes, and as expected, she won the round.

Now to see if her luck held out.

In the next moment, her gaze lifted to mine. Undisguised heat filled her amber irises, making me very glad my suit jacket covered my body's reaction to her. A knowing smile touched her full lips a second before she licked them and scanned me from head to toes and back up again.

I stepped out of the shadows and strolled in her direction while continuing to hold her stare. A light flush crept over her cheeks, and her breath grew unsteady as I neared. Never had a woman looked at me the way she did, wanted me the way she did, or battled with me the way she did.

Damn, she was beyond beautiful. And she was all mine, especially tonight.

When I was barely a few feet away from her, she stood, tilting her head up to meet my eyes. I towered over her by at least a foot, but it never took away from the regality of her presence.

I offered her my hand. "Ready for our game?"

"Absolutely." She slid her palm across mine, and that familiar spark whenever we touched shot through every nerve of my body.

I closed my fingers around her delicate ones and then led her out of the room. There was no doubt in my mind the patrons of tonight's club activities studied the interplay between Danika and me with engrossed curiosity. Our interactions had drawn interest from the very first time she had approached me at the bar of this club with her proposition.

We remained quiet as we moved through the main gaming hall and the social area. After passing one of the security checkpoints I kept in place, we entered a dimly lit passageway. When we reached the far wall, I set my hand on a metal plate. A moment later, a panel opened to reveal the office. We stepped inside.

Once I closed the door, I said, "Before we start our match, I need to do something."

Danika turned to face me and lifted her chin. "What is that?"

"This." Cupping her throat and jaw, I brought my mouth down to hers.

She fucking tasted incredible, like elderberries and smooth whiskey mixed with her natural essence. She pressed her body against mine, setting her palms against my chest.

Her immediate surrender into my touch felt like a victory even before we started. This woman belonged to me.

She knew it. I knew it. Hell, every-fucking-body in New York knew it.

The need for her had me wanting to forget about my plans so we could just spend the night fucking.

No. I had more control than the boy she'd met in that shit neighborhood long ago. Every time with her was a seduction.

I increased the pressure on her neck while sliding my tongue along hers in a dance meant to drive her insane, to make her crave, to distract her.

This was the game before we even reached for a card.

She fisted the front of my shirt, releasing a desire-filled whimper.

I pulled back with a bite to her bottom lip meant to leave a sting, not to hurt. It was a reminder of the predator she was tangling with tonight.

"Concede, and we can go directly to how our first night here would have ended if we hadn't been interrupted," I said as I stared down into Danika's dark, hypnotizing amber gaze.

Her pupils dilated further, and the flush on her cheeks deepened, giving her a youthful glow. This woman was seduction and innocence wrapped in a package of deadly intelligence.

As if trying to calm her body, she blew out a breath and then pursed her lips before responding with, "*You* concede."

"Do I look like a man who ever steps away from a challenge?" I lifted a brow.

This woman would never yield to a man who wouldn't meet her head-on in any encounter.

"Then I guess we will play." She shifted around me and strolled to the poker table.

I almost laughed when she noticed the arrangement on the table and shot me an "Are you serious?" glare over her shoulder.

When I'd arranged for this night, I'd given my staff specific game setup instructions. First, I wanted a clear table, no poker chips. Second, they were to prepare two stacks of cards, shuffled, evenly divided, and positioned so the players would face each other. And third, a tray large enough to hold Danika's favorite drinks and anything of value we discarded during play was set strategically on one side of the table, close enough to reach without interfering with my long-term plans.

We weren't playing poker tonight but the same game we never finished on that long-ago evening three years ago.

War.

A children's card game.

A game we'd first played on the steps of a corner shop in our old neighborhood. I'd gone by a different name then, ran with a different crowd, did things I couldn't say I was proud of doing. Our lives weren't easier back then, just simpler.

Danika's uncle hadn't separated us yet, and Arin, my adoptive father, hadn't taken my brothers and me under his wing. We were just two teens, completely into each other, killing time together.

I stepped up behind Danika, bringing my thoughts back to the present and the goddess shaking her head as she studied the table.

The heat of her petite body created a heady sensation that always seemed to ground me. This tiny woman, who barely came to my shoulder, was one of the most solid presences I'd ever had in my life.

Danika glanced over her shoulder. "What are the rules for play?"

"The same as last time. This isn't the game of speed we grew up with, but our adult version."

"Yes." A wicked smile touched her full lips. "Strip war."

I glided my fingers up her arms, over her shoulders, and along the exposed ink going down the column of her spine.

Only a select few could decipher the meaning of the Sanskrit words written down her back.

Beware of the Little Rabbit.

She was the ultimate meaning behind those words, tiny but mighty. Her hacker side could destroy companies, family fortunes, and God knew what else with the stroke of a few keys.

A low hum escaped her lips as she closed her eyes and leaned into my touch.

"We flip at the same time. The high card keeps their clothes, and the low card discards an item." I leaned down and kissed the juncture where her neck and shoulder met. "You can still concede."

She laughed, stepping away from me. "Not a chance. Let's play, Mr. King."

"After you, Little Rabbit."

CHAPTER THREE

Danika

I SLID INTO my seat at the table and waited for Nik to approach. He took his time strolling toward me. I knew what he was doing—making me wait, building my awareness of him.

"Want a drink?" Nik asked as he came into view and gestured to the tray ready with my favorite cocktail.

"No, I'd rather get straight to the game."

"Have it your way." Nik took the seat next to me, brushing his knee against mine on purpose. "Ready?"

He set one hand over his stack and his other on my knee. My core clenched, and I couldn't hide the goose bumps that prickled my skin.

His lips tugged up at the corner, seeing my reaction.

"Don't try to distract me."

"I wouldn't dare." He glided his palm higher. "Draw."

We flipped. Nik's nine of spades beat my four of hearts.

"Take off your dress."

"I don't think so. Your deciding what comes off wasn't part of the rules." I reached up and unfastened an earring and then set it on the drink tray.

He narrowed his gaze. "Then let's amend the rules."

"Not a chance."

"Have it your way."

We both reached for our stacks again and turned over our cards.

Nik won a second time.

As I readied to unlatch my other earring, Nik pushed my hands away. "I'll do it."

"That's not part of the rules."

"There weren't any rules saying I couldn't be the one to take it off you."

I saw the challenge in his expression and decided to let him have his way, tilting my head to the side. "Go ahead."

He glided his fingers up my neck and then leaned down to trail his tongue along the same path. I shivered, wanting more of his touch.

"You aren't playing fair." My voice grew husky, and my nipples beaded, rubbing against the fabric of my dress.

"The game is called war for a reason."

"I will get you back."

"Be my guest."

We played in the same way for the next twenty minutes. Both of us touched and teased and lost as much as we won.

"Now, all you have left is that dress."

"And my underwear," I corrected as I stood and turned for Nik to unfasten the last piece of my multistranded necklace and then added, "Whereas you only have those boxers."

Nik let his body rub mine as he reached around me for a card.

God, he smelled good. His intoxicating scent played havoc on my senses, and my burning desire for him heightened.

We both flipped our cards.

Damn.

"What were you saying?"

He turned me to face him, but instead of reaching for the side zipper of my dress, he cupped my face and ran his thumb over my lips.

"Do you have any idea what you do to me?"

I covered his hand with mine.

This man with a reputation for his ruthlessness, for his cold calculation, softened for me. But then again, he'd always been Hill to me. The boy with shattered dreams who I'd left behind and somehow fate brought back to me, albeit through a bargain.

"Let's finish this game."

He unzipped my dress, letting it pool at my feet, and then grasped my waist and set me on the table. He separated my thighs and stepped between them. His cock strained in his boxers, creating a tent in the material and making me lick my lips.

His dark, penetrating gaze studied me in a way that made it seem as if he could see into the depths of my soul.

Maybe he could.

He slid his fingers into my hair, fisting it and drawing my face toward his.

When all that separated us was a fraction of a centimeter, he said, "Draw your card."

The undisguised arousal in his voice intensified the throbbing deep in my core.

The way he held me kept me from moving too far, but I managed to reach behind me. Then, just to draw out the play, I took my time to let my fingertips graze the stack of cards.

"You're about to lose."

He smirked and pressed his nearly naked and very aroused body against the soaked material of my underwear. "Is there a loser in this game? Either way, I'm going to bury myself in your beautiful pussy."

My breath grew shallow, and it took all of my strength not to whimper.

"Go on," he encouraged. "I want to end this so that I can fuck you."

I drew my card, setting it on the table. Neither of us looked down, only staring into the other's eyes.

God. This man made me crave him, like a woman starved for days.

"Hill," I whispered.

"Yes, Danika."

"Kiss me."

His gaze shifted for a brief second to my lips, pupils dilating and making his eyes go completely midnight.

"What about the game?"

"W—we can try again in another few years."

"And the favors?"

I gripped his broad shoulders. "How about an even exchange?"

"Are you willing to commit without hearing the details? Making a deal with the devil is dangerous."

"I can face any challenge you throw my way. Besides"—I paused for a brief moment—"my original deal tied me to you for life."

"That it did." He closed the distance between us, sealing our mouths together. Finally.

Nik's intoxicating taste exploded over my senses, whiskey with a hint of orange mixed with his essence. His kiss consumed me, forcing every nerve in my body to fire to life and my core to flood with desire.

The pressure on my neck intensified, as did the desire coursing through my veins. I ached for him like nothing I'd ever experienced before.

He exuded raw, masculine power—confidence, strength, control.

My need for him ratcheted higher, and I wrapped my legs around his waist, trying to grind my aching clit against his boxer-covered cock.

He cupped my breast, squeezing the puckered tip of my nipple in a tight hold. Breaking our kiss, he tilted my head to the side and trailed his lips down my jaw and to the juncture where my shoulder and neck met.

I gasped the moment his teeth grazed the wicked, sensitive spot only he'd ever known about, and my fingers dug into the muscles of his arms.

I needed more, so much more.

"Hill, please."

"I know, baby." He pushed me back until I was lying flat on the table. "Grab the edge of the table above you. I want to hear you scream my name before I slide into you."

Goose bumps prickled my skin, and my heartbeat accelerated. My upper body arched as I followed his directions.

"You're a fucking goddess." He trailed his fingers down my throat, between my breasts, over my abdomen, and to the lace edge of my underwear.

I gasped when his warm breath skimmed under my navel, and the curve of his lips told me he found it amusing to surprise me.

He gripped the sides of my thong as he lowered to his knees, sliding the material down my hips and then disposing of them on the floor.

He lifted my thighs over his shoulders, and a low hum vibrated from his lips. "I love the smell of your arousal."

He jerked me forward, pulling me flush against his mouth. His tongue speared through my slick folds and circled my clitoral nub.

My body bowed at the onslaught of delicious sensation, and without thought, I released my grasp on the table and threaded my fingers into his hair.

"Danika."

The use of my name sent a shiver coursing through me. It was a command. I closed my eyes, and as ordered, I returned my hands over my head.

He continued to feast on me, flicking, teasing, laving. My pussy contracted, first in tiny spasms and then hard clenches. A sheen of sweat broke out over my skin as I writhed on the table, and my orgasm neared.

The second he thrust his tongue deep into my vaginal canal, I erupted.

"Hill," I cried out, my mind filling with exhilaration and unending pleasure.

I'd barely come down when he wiped his mouth on the inside of my thigh and rose to his feet.

The lust and hunger etched over his face reignited the barely quenched arousal pulsing in my core.

He offered me his hand and tugged me toward him the moment I slid my palm across his. Our mouths fused in a dance we'd shared more times than I could remember. The taste of my essence was a heady presence between us.

I pushed his boxers down, freeing his beautiful, thick, hard cock, and murmured, "I will shoot anyone who dares to disturb us this time."

"I'm fine with that. I'll even help you clean up the mess." He bit my bottom lip, giving it a slight sting.

"Now, Hill." I slid my arms over his shoulders and gazed into his mesmerizing onyx eyes.

He glided his fingers up my spine before taking hold of the back of my neck and tilting my head up.

"Are you sure you don't want to know what I expect from you?" The intensity of his gaze had my heart skipping a beat.

"Maybe you should be the one asking me that question."

"You're mine, Danika. My entire empire is at your disposal."

Before I could respond, he aligned his thick cock and drove in to the hilt.

We both cried out.

I savored the fullness of him inside me. It was an addictive feeling I'd never stop wanting, needing.

He slid out and thrust back in. His movements were slow, measured, meant to push my need higher and higher. It was torture and ecstasy all blended into one, especially the way he pulled me into each roll of his hips and pump of his cock.

This man knew how to work my body. The muscles of my soaked core flexed and flooded with desire, and I needed more, so much more.

"Harder. Fuck me harder."

His fingers dug into my hips, and a feral light touched his dark eyes. "As you command."

My nails dug into his shoulders as his pace shifted to something hard and untamed. We moaned and gasped, the sounds of sex filling the room. I threaded my fingers into his hair, drawing his lips to mine. My pussy quickened and then clamped down, flooding his length with my desire.

"Hill. Oh, God. Hill."

I threw my head back as my body convulsed around him, and moments later, he followed me with his own release.

CHAPTER FOUR
Nik

I HELD DANIKA'S satiated body against mine. My cock was semi-hard and still pulsing inside her from the last of my orgasm.

"You're fucking beautiful."

Danika smiled and said, "You're not so bad yourself, Mr. King."

Freeing myself from her body, I lifted her into my arms and carried her to a nearby sofa. I positioned her against me and then draped a blanket over her. Immediately, she nuzzled into my side.

I shook my head.

I kept a fucking blanket in my office for her.

This woman owned me in a way no one else would ever know. Men like me weren't allowed to have weaknesses. But then again, most men in my situation could never dream of having a woman of Danika's caliber in their lives.

She saw the man behind the mask. She couldn't have cared less about the money or the empire I wielded. Hell, she'd seen me as worthy even when I wore a beaten-up hoody and ran with my local gang as a teenager. Even back then, I'd known she was out of my league, a girl too intelligent for the neighborhood we lived in but too poor to leave it. That was until her uncle had snatched her away.

Now all these years later, after fate brought us back together, I knew there was more out of life. Hopefully, she'd agree to my request.

No matter what I'd said, she'd always have a choice with me.

"I can hear you thinking. Spill it."

"It's about my request."

"So we're calling our deal a request now?" The undisguised humor in her voice had me grinning down at her.

"Something like that."

She rose to a sitting position and faced me, her deep amber gaze searching mine. "Why are you hesitating?"

"Because what I want requires complete cooperation from you."

She studied me, and then her mouth curved at one corner, in the same way she tended to do after solving one of her hacker projects.

"I already said yes."

"You don't even know what I want."

She shifted to straddle my thighs, her naked breasts pressed to my chest and her slick pussy firmly seated along the length of my now-reviving cock.

"It's the same thing I want."

I fisted her hair and drew her face close to mine. "And what would that be?"

"The next generation of Kings."

We held each other's gazes, the emotions of everything we'd endured over the last few years between us. Danika's uncle no longer posed a threat to her or anyone we claimed as part of the King family. She was essentially free of her past.

But dangers would always remain a regular part of our lives. We ran our world on the fringes of society. Yet, even knowing this, a family with Danika was what I wanted.

I broke the silence and asked, "Are you sure?"

"Absolutely."

"Then I guess there is only one thing left to say."
"And what is that?"
"You have yourself a deal, Mrs. King."

✦   ✦   ✦

Thank you so much for reading The Rematch. You can read Danika and Nik's story from the beginning in Dangerous King by Sienna Snow.
siennasnow.com/dangerous-king

TWISTED BONUS SCENE

ANA HUANG

ALEX

"WHO'S FEATURED IN the exhibition again? I couldn't find any details online." Curiosity filled Ava's voice as the town car wound its way through central London toward the Clarke Gallery.

I'd needed an excuse to fly us to London for the weekend, and a "special photography exhibit" seemed as good a one as any, considering Ava herself was a photographer.

"It wouldn't be a surprise if I told you, would it?" I teased. "You'll find out soon enough." I wrapped an arm around her waist and drew her closer, trying to ignore the velvet box burning a hole in my pocket.

For six months, it'd sat in the back of my drawer, taunting me. Daring me to ask the most important question of my life.

If I didn't need the damn thing because an archaic tradition had brainwashed society into thinking a diamond equaled love, I would've already chucked it in the Potomac for its insolence.

"True," Ava acknowledged with a small yawn. "But still. I'm dying of curiosity." She snuggled closer into my side and buried her face in my shoulder. I dropped a kiss on top of her head while the streets of London whizzed by outside the window.

Ava and I had visited the city at least half a dozen times together—sometimes for business, other times for pleasure. Both her job as a travel magazine photographer and my role as CEO of an international real estate development empire took us on the road often, but we tried to meet up abroad when we could.

I wasn't a sentimental person, but I had to admit, London held a special place in my heart. It was where we'd reconciled after our breakup almost three years ago and where we lived while Ava finished her post-graduate photography fellowship. For that reason alone, it took the top spot on my preferred-destinations list.

Ava released a second, bigger yawn.

"Tired?" I rubbed her arm. She was all softness and warmth to my hard, icy edges, and the sensation of her silky skin loosened some of the anxiety building in my chest.

She'll say yes. Probably. Maybe.

"A little," she murmured. "But I'll be okay. I'm excited for the exhibit."

"Hmmm." Concern shredded the edges of my already-frayed nerves.

Had I fucked up the timing?

We'd landed in London last night and slept in that morning.

Correction: Ava slept in while I worked. My sleep had improved over the years, but insomnia still haunted me more often than not, and I rarely slept more than a few hours at a time.

But that was me. Ava had had a long week at work, and then I made her fly straight to another continent. I should've given her more time to adjust to the jet lag. She'd taken two weeks off from work so we could travel to France and Spain after London—our engagement celebration, *if* she said yes—so it wasn't like we were in a huge rush.

I should've waited until tomorrow.

My free hand tightened around my knee. I rarely made strategic mistakes. Then again, I rarely felt as unsettled as I did in that moment, so it was a day of firsts all around.

I hated it.

Our chauffeured town car pulled up in front of the gallery. It was located on a quiet side street, and the interior lights blazed in the windows, bathing the modern white facade in a golden glow.

I was Alex Volkov. I didn't get nervous.

But I'd be damned if my stomach didn't twist into a thousand knots as we walked up the steps toward the glass-fronted entrance.

After months of planning, the moment was almost here, and I felt like a damn schoolboy working up the courage to ask his crush out for the first time.

Did other people experience these things on a regular basis? The racing pulse, the hammering heart, the uncertainty and fucking *humanity* of it all? If so, no wonder a majority were insufferable. Their emotions short-circuited their common sense, and now, I was one of those insufferable idiots.

Whoever invented feelings deserved to be shot.

"Are you okay?" Ava slid a glance in my direction. Concern etched tiny grooves in her brow. "You look pale. I hope it's not the sushi we had at dinner."

Great. Just how I wanted to look before I proposed. Like I was dying from food poisoning.

"I'm fine." I forced a smile. It felt as unnatural as the anxiety eating away at my stomach. "It's the lighting."

Judging by her skeptical expression, the excuse sounded as believable to her as it did to me, which was not at all, but in true Ava fashion, she didn't press the issue. Instead, she gave my hand a small squeeze and rubbed her thumb over the top.

Some of the tension released from my shoulders, and I squeezed her hand back.

No one could ground me quite like she could, even when she was the source of my nerves.

The front desk assistant greeted us with a knowing smile when we entered. "Good evening, Mr. Volkov, Ms. Chen. The exhibition is right this way." She gestured to her left, playing her role perfectly. "Enjoy."

Ava smiled. "Thank you."

The gallery staff had spent the day setting up the space with Fiona, the proposal planner I'd hired. Until six months ago, I hadn't even known proposal planning was a job, but Fiona was supposed to be the best of the best.

She better be, considering how much she charged. Just because I could afford her didn't mean I liked wasting money on incompetence.

Perhaps that was why I'd micromanaged the entire process, from choosing the exact roses Ava liked to tasting all the desserts until we settled on a cake that cost more than flour and sugar should ever cost.

"Are we the only people here? It's strangely quiet." A hint of suspicion leaked into Ava's voice and ratcheted my pulse up another notch.

"It's a private exhibition. Invite only." I placed a hand on the small of her back and guided her down the marble hall.

Technically, I wasn't lying. It was private to us, and I did the inviting.

"Why am I not surprised? You're such a snob." Ava nudged my side. "It wouldn't hurt you to mingle with the so-called plebeians once in a while."

"That's where you're wrong. It would hurt me immensely. Mostly my patience, but also my faith in humanity."

"You don't have much faith in humanity."

"Then we better not destroy the little bit I have. Don't you think?"

My mouth tugged up at her laugh. Even when filled with exasperation, it was the most beautiful sound I'd ever heard.

I rubbed an absentminded thumb over her silk-clad back.

I'd told Ava the exhibition was a black-tie event. I didn't care whether she was dressed up for the proposal or not, but she would never forgive me if I sprung a ring on her while she looked anything but her best.

"Make sure her nails are done before you pop the question." Josh, Ava's brother and my best friend, kicked his feet up on my coffee table. "Or she'll murder you."

"Explain to me how you, of all people, know that." Josh and his girlfriend Jules, who coincidentally happened to be Ava's best friend, had no plans to get married anytime soon. They were too busy working, traveling, and annoying the hell out of me.

"Easy." Josh flashed a quick grin and popped a chip in his mouth. "Unlike you, I know what women want."

Sometimes, I regretted mending our friendship. He was a pain in my ass half the time, though I had to admit he was probably right about the nails. He grew up with Ava, after all.

But all thoughts of Josh dissipated when Ava and I rounded the corner and entered the exhibition space. The roar of blood in my ears nearly drowned out her soft gasp at the sight before us.

The entire space had been stripped of its usual furnishings. Instead, a two-person table sat in the center, set with candles, champagne, and an elegant display of blue roses that matched the petals strewn artfully across the hardwood floors. Strings of tiny lights stretched across the walls and served as twinkling holders for the Polaroid prints of pictures Ava had taken over the years. There were dozens of other details Fiona had painstakingly arranged, but I was too busy examining Ava's face for any hint into her thoughts to notice.

"What...I..." Her mouth opened and closed in an adorable imitation of a goldfish.

"Welcome to the Clarke Gallery's special exhibition, featuring Ava Chen." Another smile touched the corners of my mouth at Ava's stunned expression.

The proposal planner was worth every fucking penny.

"Alex..." Ava walked over to the Polaroids and skimmed her fingers over one of the photos I'd selected.

I could've delegated the task to my assistant, but I wanted to make sure the picks were perfect, so I'd spent weeks poring through all the pictures Ava had taken of us over the years. Fortunately, she'd organized them all into neatly labeled folders on her computer. Unfortunately, there were thousands of them, which was why it took me so damn long to go through them.

In the end, I'd narrowed them down to a few of my favorites—a picture of us apple picking in Vermont, which had somehow become an annual tradition despite my protests; an up-close shot of our hands intertwined on the center console during a road trip to New York; a selfie of us kissing at the Tidal Basin with flowering cherry blossoms in the background. I despised cherry blossom season in D.C. and the hordes of tourists that accompanied it, but Ava insisted on seeing the trees in person every year, so there we were.

"Yes, Sunshine?" Despite the hot rush of apprehension in my blood, I couldn't help teasing her a little.

Ava turned to face me again. "What is all this?" A hint of breathlessness punctuated her words.

"Like I said, it's a photography exhibit. And a confession."

She didn't take her eyes off mine as I closed the distance between us. "A confession," she repeated.

"Mmhmm." I stopped in front of her, so close her soft floral scent filled my lungs and clouded my thoughts. So close I could count each lash framing her beautiful dark eyes and measure her heartbeats with each shallow rise and fall of her chest. "I brought you here under false pretenses."

"I can see that. What are your true intentions, Volkov?" Despite her mock stern tone, her eyes glinted with laughter and a dozen shades of emotion.

"Some of them are too depraved to utter this early in the night, Sunshine." Amusement softened my face at the blush staining her cheeks. "But there is one thing in particular that I…" I swallowed hard, trying to form the right words in the right order. "That I can no longer keep to myself."

All traces of levity evaporated, leaving the air as thick and heavy as molasses.

Ava stilled. Her breaths rushed out faster while a bead of sweat trickled down my spine.

I'd negotiated multimillion-dollar deals and faced off against some of the world's richest and most powerful people without breaking a sweat, but there was something about the woman standing before me that destroyed all my defenses.

At the end of the day, everyone except Ava was irrelevant.

"When I first met you, you were Josh's sister. Nothing more, nothing less." At the time, I'd been so bent on revenge I couldn't see anything else. It took me seven years before I finally realized I'd been chasing after the wrong thing all along. "I didn't understand your optimism. I didn't trust your kindness. And I could not, for the life of me, understand your fascination with cameras."

Cameras were useless to me unless they were used to capture incriminating evidence against my enemies, of which I had plenty. My hyperthymesia had rendered photographs obsolete in my world.

That was, until Ava swept in and turned that world upside down.

"But now I understand."

"Understand what?" Her whisper settled in my chest like a warm weight.

"Understand why you want to capture every moment like it's the most beautiful one you've ever experienced. Why you cherish every photo like you're afraid the memory will slip through your fingers. And the reason I understand those things is because…" Another hard swallow disrupted my speech. I'd planned to keep it short and simple. I wasn't the best at saying nice things, and the fewer words I used, the less likely I was to fuck them up. Still, getting through it was a struggle given how clammy my palms were and how fast my heart was galloping.

"That's how I feel about you. I want to experience everything with you, Ava. From the smallest, most mundane moments to the biggest, most life-altering events. I didn't think I was capable of a fraction of the emotions I've felt since I met you, and they've made me a better person than I ever thought I could be. You turned my life from something I was living to something worth living for, and while we've created many memories together over the years, I'm hoping we could create more in the future with you not as my girlfriend…but as my wife."

I knelt on one knee and retrieved the ring box from my pocket. I blamed the small shake in my hand on the icy draft gusting from the air-conditioning vent.

"Ava…" I opened the box to reveal a custom-cut diamond Delamonte ring. She clapped a hand over her mouth, muffling her gasp. "Will you marry me?"

Silence rang through the candlelit space in the wake of my question.

She stared down at me, her eyes wide and bright with unshed tears. She was so still she could've passed for a hyperrealistic statue.

A minute passed without any answer, followed by another.

Another bead of sweat snaked down my back. I was dimly aware of the photographer I'd hired to capture the moment from a hidden spot by the doorway. She was probably wondering what the hell was going on, but she was the least of my worries.

What if Ava *didn't* want to marry me?

We'd been dating for almost three years and living together for almost as long. We had small fights now and then, but our relationship had been mostly smooth sailing since we got back together.

But what if I'd misjudged everything? Ava loved me. I knew that. But did she love me enough to spend the rest of her life with me?

Dread trickled through my veins and solidified into stone. I was two seconds away from crumbling into smithereens when she finally nodded.

A tentative balloon of hope inflated in my chest.

"Is that a yes?" I asked cautiously.

A half laugh, half sob bled through the hand covering her mouth. "Yes, you idiot." Her muffled voice was thick with tears. "Of course I'll marry you!"

It took a second for her words to register. Once they did, my trapped breath finally escaped my lungs in a rush of relief.

"Good." I tried to contain the emotion in my own voice as I slid the ring on her finger. The six-carat diamond blazed like a fallen star, but most importantly, it fit perfectly. I'd known it would, considering I customized it to Ava's measurements, but the sight of her wearing it caused a suspicious burn behind my eyes.

Plus, Josh would be relieved to hear her nails looked perfect.

I stood and cleared my throat. "Otherwise, the flight home would've been quite awkward," I added, trying, and failing, to regain my composure.

Yes.

She said yes.

*She said **yes!***

A grin blossomed on my mouth as the import of what just happened hit me, and I swept Ava into my arms and off her feet.

Fuck composure. That could wait for another night when I *hadn't* just gotten engaged.

Her surprised laugh bounced off the exposed brick walls and warmed my skin.

"Figures that would be the first thing you say to me after you propose." She looped her arms around my neck and rested her forehead against mine. Her voice still shook with emotion, but I heard a hint of her usual sass as well. "What am I going to do with you?"

I kissed away the tears dampening her cheeks before I gently brushed my mouth over hers. "Drive me crazy for the rest of our days, I presume."

"Sounds about right." Ava's smile blinded me more than any diamond could. "But you love it."

"I love you," I corrected.

Her smile faded into something more tender. "I've figured out your secret,

Volkov. You can be pretty sweet when you want to be."

"Don't tell anyone, or my reputation will be shot." I brushed my lips over hers again. "It'll be our secret, *Mrs. Volkov.*"

"Don't rob me of my fiancée phase. I'm not your wife yet." She laughed again when I gave her hair a gentle yank.

"Maybe not, but you've always been mine." I pressed my mouth against hers in a proper kiss. Softly at first, then harder until her soft moan filled my ears and her fingers threaded through my hair. "I love you," I whispered.

"I love you too."

Her murmured reply melted any lingering tension in my muscles. It wasn't the first time we'd said those words to each other, but it was our first time saying them as an engaged couple.

If someone told me five years ago I would be engaged—to Josh's sister, no less—and *happy* about it, I would've dismissed them as delusional and banned them from all my properties. Now, I couldn't imagine anything that would make me happier than seeing her walk down the aisle toward me.

Ava and I were the unlikeliest of couples. She was the bright sun to my cold moon, the optimist to my cynic, the rose to my thorn.

But if there was one thing she'd taught me, it was that sometimes, the most unexpected things in life were the most beautiful.

✧   ✧   ✧

Want more of Alex and Ava? Their full story is available now in Twisted Love.
anahuang.com

Thank you so much for reading!

HACKER IN LOVE

LAUREN ROWE

CHAPTER ONE
Hannah

"HI, HANNAH BANANA Montana Milliken!" Kat Morgan says, answering my call. She's my co-worker turned bestie who's been MIA from our office in Seattle over the past week while "working for a client" in Las Vegas. At least, that's what our boss thinks. In reality, Kat's been living her best life in Sin City with some young billionaire playboy mogul she met—a guy who had no problem hiring her for a fake account, so she could come play with him, without consequence to her job.

And what have I been doing back at the office, while Kat's been playing with her rich playboy in Vegas? Picking up the slack on her actual accounts. But I'm not pissed about it. In fact, It's something I've been thrilled to do for her, given how many favors Kat has done for me since we started working together a few years ago. The chances are low I'll never get to bang a billionaire in this lifetime, after all. So, I've been thoroughly excited to live vicariously through my blonde bombshell of a bestie this past week.

"Sorry to bother you again," I say to Kat on speaker phone, my elbows on my desk. "I need some more input on the barbeque account." I tell Kat the latest issue that's arisen and, not surprisingly, she brilliantly suggests a perfect solution. When that topic is done, however, I take the phone off speaker, look around my cubicle area to make sure our boss isn't somewhere nearby, and ask if Kat's still having as much fun with her billionaire playboy as she was having a few days ago, when we last spoke.

"Yeah, I am, as a matter of fact," Kat says, and by the weirdly professional tone in her voice, it's clear to me the guy must be within eavesdropping distance.

"He's there and able to overhear our conversation?" I venture. Because if there's one thing I know about my carefree, vivacious work-bestie, it's that she absolutely revels in spilling the tea about her ever-exciting dating life.

"Actually, yeah, he *is*."

"Gah. I'm *dying* to know the latest!" I whisper-shout, making sure our boss won't overhear me, if she happens to be nearby.

"*Gah*," she whisper-shouts back excitedly, letting me know whatever tea she's holding back is piping hot.

"Okay, girl. If it's going *worse* with him than the last time we spoke, say 'no.' If it's going every bit as good, then say 'maybe.' And if by some miracle the man has taken things to the next level and is blowing your mind and wildest expectations in ways you've never experienced before, then give me a resounding 'yesssss.'"

"*Yessss*," Kat says, without hesitation, surprising me. From what she said about the guy last time we spoke, I didn't think it was even possible for things to get any better.

"Holy shit, Kat! But you already told me he's a five-alarm fire!"

"*More*."

I shake my head. *Oh, to be Kat Morgan, just for a day.* "Does he have a friend?"

I tease. But it's a joke, obviously. I mean, yes, I'd love to be set up with a quality guy. Dating apps are my version of hell. But I'm well aware Kat's suave billionaire wouldn't have a friend who'd be a fit for someone like me—a bespectacled, sarcastic girl-next-door type with an office job and exactly zero trust funds. Surely, billionaire playboy birds of a feather flock together. Which means any friend of Kat's billionaire would only want to get set up with a glamorous spitfire like Kat—a gorgeous supermodel type who effortlessly brings every hot guy she meets to their knees. Because that's how the world works, right?

Apparently, not—because this time, much to my surprise, Kat replies to my usual joke with, "Funny you should ask that, Banana. He *does*. And he's the coolest guy you'll ever meet. Actually, he's a *fucking genius*."

"What? Oh my gosh!"

With a giggle, Kat calls out to someone on her end of the line. "Henn!" she shouts, "My adorable and funny friend, Hannah Millikin, wants very much to say hello to youuu!"

I inhale sharply, feeling flabbergasted by this unexpected turn of events. I've made that same stupid joke several times to Kat, whenever she's regaling me with yet another amazing story about some hot escapade—"*Does he have a friend?*"—and she's never once replied with anything but a cute little giggle.

"To *me*?" a male voice replies on Kat's end of the line, and there's no missing the genuine surprise in his tone.

I press my phone into my ear, eager to hear whatever Kat is going to say to the guy . . . But, suddenly, I hear absolutely nothing. Not even ambient noise. Which means clever Kat must have muted the call to keep me from hearing her conversation. Damn! What the heck is she saying to convince the guy to chat with me? Oh, God. I hope she's not trying too hard to convince the poor guy, because I certainly wouldn't want to—

"Hello, Hannah Millikin," a male voice says into my ear. "I'm Peter Hennessey, but everyone just calls me Henn."

Butterflies. That's my body's immediate and involuntary reaction to the sound of this man's sweet, earnest voice. He doesn't sound like a smooth playboy by any stretch, the way I bet Kat's billionaire would, but that suits me perfectly. Is Henn the billionaire's driver or lawyer, perhaps? Or is he also a billionaire, like Kat's latest fling, but a nerdy kind who's maybe a bit on the shy side?

"Hi, Henn!" I blurt, much more loudly than intended. "I'm sorry if Kat's coerced you into talking to me!"

Henn chuckles, probably taken aback by my energetic tone. "No, no, I'm glad to talk to you."

Oh my gosh. Is it possible to swoon over nothing but a man's earnest, sweet voice? Because that's exactly what's happening to me right now. "Oh, that's great to hear," I manage to say, even though my entire body feels like it's blushing along with my cheeks. "I'm glad to talk to you, too. I hope you take whatever Kat said to get us together with a grain of salt, though. I'm sure she made it sound like I *demanded* to talk to you, but what I actually said was, 'Does he have a friend?'"

Henn chuckles. "Yeah, she did kinda make it sound like your idea, actually."

"I knew it! I bet Kat's telling both of us different things to push us together, like the twins in *The Parent Trap*." *What am I doing? I'm babbling the stupidest shit ever! Pull yourself together, Hannah!*

"She's a sneaky one, for sure," Henn says. And I'd swear from his tone, he's smiling from ear-to-ear on his end of the line.

"She sure is."

Butterflies. They're once again ravaging me. Not because of the content of our silly little exchange—which, let's face it, isn't one for the record books in terms of substance. But because, just this fast, Henn's genuine sweetness is coming through to me, loud and clear.

"So, what are you doing in Vegas?" I ask.

"Um, you know . . . just working."

"What do you do?"

"I'm a computer specialist—a freelance programmer."

Interesting. Given that Henn is friends with Kat's mogul billionaire, I have to imagine the "freelance programming" Henn performs is at an extremely high level.

"Where do you live?" I ask, trying to keep the conversation going, now that it's clear Henn isn't going to say anything more.

"Um, L.A., New York, Toronto, Denver. I go wherever the job takes me, and I can work from anywhere, so I travel a lot. But I mostly live in L.A. in a crappy-ass apartment."

Yet again, I'm intrigued. Do billionaires have friends who live in "crappy-ass apartments"? That's news to me. Sounds like my initial hunch was correct and Henn works for the billionaire, in some capacity. I genuinely don't care if Henn is rich or poor, of course—I'm simply trying to get a better sense of the guy. Why is he friends with a billionaire, yet he lives in a crappy-ass apartment?

"Where do you live?" Henn asks, marking the first time he's the one filling an awkward silence between us.

"Seattle."

"Oh, yeah, duh," Henn says. "Kat just said she works with you."

"Yeah, we work for the same PR firm. Do you ever get up to Seattle?"

"Yeah, sure, I get up there sometimes—I love it there. Good salmon."

Oh, God, my heart is thundering and my skin is hot. I've never felt this kind of reaction to nothing but a voice before! I realize we're not saying anything particularly notable. And yet, the sound of his voice is drawing me in like crazy. Henn seems sweet and awkward. Not even close to a womanizer. Plus, he's a computer geek? Oh my God! *He's exactly my type!* "Yeah, we have the best salmon in the Pacific Northwest," I say lamely. And when he doesn't say something in reply to that, I clear my throat, feeling flustered, and proceed to say the stupidest thing ever: "*I love salmon.*" It's a true statement, yes, but such a basic, stupid thing to say, I can't help rolling my eyes at myself.

"Me, too!" Henn replies enthusiastically, like I've just said something endlessly fascinating. But that's all the man says. Is he so tight-lipped because he's super shy . . . or because he's now dying to get off the call with this lame-ass woman he was tricked into talking to in the first place?

Well, shit. I decide to shoot my shot now, sight unseen, figuring I'd rather get rejected now than hang up and wonder if I was imagining our mutual chemistry.

My heart is thumping. I've never made the first move with a guy, ever. But something tells me I'll regret it, if I don't do it now. I clear my throat. "Well, I know some great places for salmon in Seattle. Next time you're here for work or whatever, let me know and I'll take you to a place where we can feast on salmon to our stomachs' delight."

Our stomachs' delight? What was I thinking? What twenty-five-year-old talks like that? Is it any wonder I keep getting ghosted on dating apps, when I constantly turn into an eighty-year-old when messaging with someone I'm interested in?

"*Indubitably,*" Henn says, sounding not the least bit put off by my weird word choice.

"Awesome," I say on an exhale, feeling relieved and excited. "I hope we'll get to enjoy that salmon feast, one day soon."

"Yeah, I hope so, too." He pauses. "Thanks."

"No, thank *you.*"

What are we doing? But before I can think of something else to say to alleviate this awkward moment, the sound of my boss's voice in the next cubicle sends my heart hurtling into my mouth.

"Well, I'd better go," I say abruptly. "I'm at work."

"Oh, okay, bye," Henn says. "It was great to talk to you."

"To you, too. Bye, Henn."

"Bye now," he whispers, with so much longing in his voice, goosebumps erupt across my skin.

"Bye now," I whisper back.

There's a muffled sound on Henn's end of the line, before Kat's voice returns in my ear.

"Hey, girl. Isn't he the cutest?"

"Hold on." I listen to my boss's nearby conversation for a moment, and when I feel confident she's not going anywhere for now, I gleefully return to Kat. "He's *adorable!*" I whisper-shout. "So sweet and nerdy and awkward—exactly my type!"

"I know, right?"

"Can I see him?"

"Sure, I'll send you a picture."

My phone beeps a moment later, and when I look down, little hearts overtake my pupils. For one thing, Henn is precisely my physical type—a nerdy, goateed hipster with dark hair and a delightful combination of sweetness and snark in his eyes. But even more important than any of that, Henn's dark eyes exude unmistakable kindness. Gentleness. *Intelligence.* All of which, at least for me, make him drop-dead gorgeous.

"He's so cute!" I gasp out, barely containing myself. "A smoke show!"

Kat giggles. "*And* word on the street is he's a *phenomenal* kisser, too."

I pause and tilt my head. Well, that's an unexpected, intriguing comment. Is Kat friends with Henn's ex? How on earth would she have that kind of inside intel?

"Word on *what* street?" I ask.

"I'll tell you later," Kat whispers. "Gotta go."

"Okay. Tell me later. And, please, tell Henn I think he's handsome, okay?"

"I will."

"No, wait, don't tell him that. I don't want to come off as too eager."

"You won't. He'll be thrilled."

"Has he seen my photo?"

"Hannah?" Shit. It's my boss, Janice, standing at the entrance to my little cubicle. When our eyes meet, she touches her watch with a steely smile, signaling it's time for our daily ten o'clock meeting.

"Gotta go," I whisper to Kat.

"Okay, bye, Banana. Thanks again."

Shoot. I so badly wanted to hear Kat's reply about whether Henn has seen my photo, and now I'll have to wait until after my meeting to text Kat and find out! Oh well. I gather my laptop and notebook and head into the meeting, trying my damnedest not to think about Henn and his adorably awkward, earnest voice—a sweet voice that somehow made my skin tingle and my heart race, before I'd ever seen his handsome face.

CHAPTER TWO
Hannah

"OKAY, MAGGIE," MY boss says to my fellow account manager, after we've sat down for yet another daily meeting. "Why don't you start today's presentations with a run-down of the Foster account?"

It's been over twenty-four hours since yesterday's phone call with Kat and then Henn, and I keep finding myself wondering if Henn and I will one day enjoy a salmon feast in Seattle, like we talked about. I still haven't heard back from Kat about Henn's reaction to my photo, if she showed it to him at all. Which is fine, of course. There's no rush on that. And, hey, if it turns out Henn isn't attracted to me the way I am to him, that's okay, because you can't win them all, and there are plenty of fish in the sea. Maybe not plenty of fish who are exactly my type, the way Henn is. But, still, I refuse to let myself get too excited—

Buzz.

My phone on the conference room table vibrates with an incoming text . . . and when I look down, it's from Kat:

URGENT! Code RED! Call me ASAP, Bananaaaaaaaaa!

"Excuse me," I blurt, rising from my seat.

"Everything okay?" my boss asks, as my co-worker stops talking mid-sentence.

"Uh, yeah. It's fine." I hold up my phone. "Just a time-sensitive personal matter I need to handle. Sorry. I'll come right back."

I rush out of the conference room, my stomach twisting, and race into an empty room next door.

"Banana!" Kat shrieks in greeting.

"Is everything okay?" I ask, nervously pressing my phone against my ear.

"Everything is amazing! I showed Henn your photo and he went apeshit gaga crazy over you!"

"No."

"Yes! So we all think it'd be fun to go on a double date."

"When?"

"Tonight—in Vegas!"

"*What*? How? But I've got work."

"Yeah, you've got work *in Vegas!*"

"Huh?"

Kat giggles. "Josh wants to 'hire' you for the same 'PR campaign' I'm 'working on' out here, so you won't have any problems dropping everything and flying out here right away! He already has your flight picked out for three o'clock today!"

"*Today?*" I echo lamely, too overwhelmed to think clearly. This kind of thing never happens to me. Am I dreaming?

"All you have to do is say yes and Josh will pay for everything," Kat says. "Your hotel room, food, flight, entertainment. Say yes, Hannah!"

My heart is exploding. "*Yes!*"

Kat squeals. "Josh said he's going to treat all of us to a 'world-class dinner' tonight—and then pay for a girls' trip for you and me for the next few days, too, since both Josh and Henn unfortunately have to leave Vegas first thing tomorrow morning."

While I express extreme enthusiasm and gratitude, Kat gives me the flight information and instructs me to get my ass home to pack a bag. "Make sure you pack a swimsuit and some sexy, sparkly dresses," she insists. "Josh said he wants you and me to paint Sin City red, on his dime, for as long as we want to stay. Spa appointments, fine dining, shows . . . Whatever our little hearts desire, Josh said wants us to have it, and do it, in grand style."

Whoa. Of course, I push back, simply because it's too generous an offer. I tell Kat I'm beyond thrilled, but that Josh's offer is too much to accept. But when Kat says Josh simply won't take no for an answer, I excitedly send my boss a text, telling her situation, as Kat continues to talk about how much Josh loves showing people a good time.

"That's Josh Faraday for you," Kat insists.

The tone of Kat's voice is like nothing I've heard from her before. She must *really* like this guy.

"You really like Josh, huh?" I ask.

Kat sighs like a Disney princess. "I do. Too much, I'm afraid."

"Is there such a thing?"

"There is when the guy you're falling for has made it clear he doesn't want a relationship."

"Oh. But you're irresistible, Kat. I'm sure—"

"No, not this time. But it's okay. I'll enjoy the ride, as long as it lasts. Now, go pack, honey. I'm sure I'll talk your ear off about Josh when you get here."

As Kat finishes talking, a text lands on my phone. It's my boss, Janice, telling me I'm cleared to go to Las Vegas for the new account, and to keep her posted.

"Janice just gave me the green light to come to Vegas!" I shout, making Kat cheer. "I'll head home and pack now."

"Fab."

"Please, thank Josh profusely for me, until I can get there to do it myself, okay?"

"Will do. But trust me, I've been 'thanking him profusely' every night since we've been in Vegas, and he keeps saying he's getting much more than his money's worth."

Laughing, I head out of my cubicle, wave to my boss as I pass the conference room, and make my way out the front door of our office.

"I'd bet my next paycheck you're wrong about Josh," I say. "He's gonna fall for you, Kat. Everyone always does."

Kat audibly shrugs. "I hope you're right. Either way, it's vitally important I don't fall for him. I'm never the one who falls first, and I refuse to start now!"

"He'll fall first."

"We'll see. I'm doing my best to make it happen."

"I'm sure you are."

"Have you left the office yet?"

"I'm driving home, as we speak."

"Good girl."

"Hey, what did you mean yesterday when you said 'word on the street' about

Henn is that he's a good kisser? Who gave you that piece of spicy intel?"

Kat snorts. "I gave it to myself when I kissed Henn the other night."

"What?"

"It's okay. It was right in front of Josh—at his suggestion."

"*What?*"

Kat laughs at my reaction. "It's not as scandalous as it sounds. It was actually very innocent and funny. Josh and I were giving dating advice to Henn, and Josh was going on and on about how important it is to be a good kisser, if you want to 'bag a babe—to be able to 'curl a woman's toes' with that very first kiss, if you want to hook the fish on your line. And much to our surprise, Henn said something like, 'Well, no worries on that front. I might be hopeless at approaching women in the first place, and terrible at maintaining a conversation at first, when I'm still nervous, but if I miraculously get to the part where I get to kiss someone, I've got no doubt I'm a *fantastic* kisser.'"

My cheeks burst into flames. "*Wow.*"

"Well, Josh thought that was a mighty big statement," Kat continues. "So he demanded prove it. At first, he wanted to hear about Henn's technique. But when Henn said he couldn't describe it, Josh suggested Henn kiss *me*, so *I* could verify if Henn could back up his big talk."

"Holy shit, Kat."

"Did I mention we were drinking? So, anyway, I said that was fine with me, that I'd be happy to judge Henn's kissing technique, and Henn wound up giving me a tender little smooch, right on the spot, that damn-near curled my toes."

"No way."

"Yep! If I'd had romantic feelings for him, I swear I would have felt that sucker right where it counts. He had fantastic technique, just like he said. Ten out of ten."

"Did he kiss you with tongue?"

"Yeah, a little bit. The perfect amount, actually."

"And Josh was fine watching him kiss you?"

Kat snorts. "I think Josh got a little jealous, in the end, which was good to see. At least, I hope he did. But the kiss was pretty innocent, honestly. And Henn is Josh's best friend since college. They're like brothers. As twisted as it sounds, I think Josh was genuinely trying to help Henn up his game with women, when he suggested the kiss. Henn is super shy and tongue-twisted when it comes to women, especially ones he's attracted to, and we both really want him to find love with someone."

Butterflies release into my stomach at the thought that someone might possibly be me. "I'm glad to hear Henn is tongue-tied with people he likes. He was so cute on the phone yesterday, but I definitely felt like I was doing the heavy lifting in terms of keeping the conversation going. I couldn't tell if he was actually interested in me or just going through the motions because you'd forced him to get on the phone."

"Henn was one hundred percent interested. And that was *before* he saw your photo. Once he saw your face, I swear, the top of that boy's head practically popped off. He looked like a cartoon character whose tongue unrolled onto the floor."

I giggle. "Oh my gosh, Kat!"

"Henn will probably be a bit shy when you meet him tonight. But give him a chance, okay? Once he gets comfortable, he turns into the cutest, funniest guy, ever."

"I'll let him take as long as he needs to get comfortable. Thank you for setting us up."

"You know how much I love matchmaking! Oh, hey, are you wearing your glasses today?"

"Yeah. But I'll switch into my contacts when I get home, so when Henn sees me for the first time—"

"No, no, don't do that. The reason I asked is Henn mentioned he has a *thing* for cute brunettes with glasses." Kat snorts. "You might even call it that boy's *kink*." Kat giggles at my gasping reaction, and then adds, "In fact, if you really want to get Henn's motor running tonight, I'd suggest you wear those cat-eyed glasses of yours—the ones with the thick, black frames."

"But I only wear those thick ones when I'm at home. They make me look like a retro nerd librarian."

"Exactly. If you wear those beauties, along with a top that shows off even the slightest bit of cleavage, I guarantee Peter Hennessey will fall head over heels in love with you the moment he sees you."

I snicker. "Well, that sounds wonderful. But honestly, these days, I'd settle for Henn falling head over heels in *lust* with me at first sight. It's been so damned long, Kat."

She giggles. "*Hannah Milliken*. You little minx."

I bite back a smile, imagining myself having wild, uninhibited sex with Henn tonight. "Tell me the truth. Do you think me having sex with a guy on a first date takes you out of the running to become his girlfriend? I wouldn't want to ruin my chances with Henn, long-term. But I'm also in the mood to, you know, go with the flow and do whatever feels right in the moment."

"Well, first of all, I can tell you with certainty that Henn isn't the kind of guy to judge a woman for being comfortable with her sexuality. And speaking generally, if a guy doesn't think you're girlfriend material because you want to have sex with him on the first date, then he's a caveman misogynist asshole who isn't boyfriend material, anyway. So, good riddance."

"Good point."

"In fact, I'd even go so far as to say you *should* sleep with a guy you're attracted to on the first date, if only to figure out if he's worthy of you."

"What?" I say, laughing.

"If you fuck him and he asks you out again, then he's a keeper. Best way to find out."

"I never thought about it like that. Probably because I've never slept with anyone on the first date."

"Well, I have. Lots and lots of times. And trust me, I've never once regretted it. Not even when the sex was shitty, because that's helped me kick the guy to the curb, that much faster."

"God, I'd give anything to have your confidence."

"So, have it. All you have to do is decide, Banana. It's as simple as that."

I smile. I know Kat's being sincere, but I have to believe it's a lot easier to have Kat Morgan's swagger when you look like a goddamned supermodel and have the sparkle of a thousand-watt light bulb. "Thanks. I'll do my best."

"Be yourself, though. Always be yourself. Although, for tonight's purposes, make sure you're the version of yourself who wears those nerdy glasses, a push-up bra, and a *really* low-cut blouse."

I giggle. "Roger."

"Rabbit."

"Okay, I'm home. I'll see you soon!"

"Woohoo! I'll pick you up at the airport, so text me when you've landed! Can't wait to watch the sparks fly between you and Henn tonight!"

CHAPTER THREE

Henn

"I SHOULD CHANGE into my black shirt, shouldn't I?" I say to Josh. My best friend has been sitting on a leather couch in the penthouse suite he's booked for Kat and Hannah, calmly drinking a Scotch while waiting for the girls to arrive from the airport, while I've been pacing the expansive space, my eyes bugging out and my heart thumping.

"No, that blue one looks great," Josh replies. "Calm down, Henny. You look like a million bucks." He winks. "Hannah's not gonna be able to resist from tackling you."

"Thanks again for flying her out here," I say. "Let me pay you back."

"Hell no. This is on me. We've got lots to celebrate. By the way, that thing I said the other day about you needing to 'dick it up' with women to have more success with them?" He shakes his head. "Don't do that with Hannah. That was terrible advice. Just be yourself, okay?"

"I don't think I have a choice in the matter, to be honest."

The sound of female laughter wafting through the suite's closed front door attracts our attention, and two seconds later, Kat and Hannah appear, both of them giggling and practically glowing with excitement.

Bam.

At the sight of Hannah, I feel like I've been struck by a thunderbolt. She's even cuter in person than in all the photos I've devoured of her. And yes, that's *photos*, plural, since I've now scoured the internet for every photo I could find of one Hannah Milliken of Seattle—all of which only made me even more attracted to her and excited to meet her. Not to mention, more certain I don't want to fuck up this golden opportunity by "dicking it up" with her, as Josh suggested the other day, or, even worse, acting like too big a dork and scaring her off.

As Kat and Hannah come to a stop in the middle of the suite, Hannah releases her rolling suitcase and Kat gestures to her adorable friend. "Henny, this is my beloved Hannah Banana Montana Milliken."

Oh, no. As I walk toward the pair, the very thing I've been fearing might happen, the one thing I've told myself must not happen under any circumstances, begins happening. Namely, I can physically feel my brain beginning to scramble. My mouth turning dry and my tongue turning and twisting inside my mouth. Oh, God, no.

"Hi, Henn," Hannah says brightly. "I'm so happy to meet you."

"Hab-be bleet choo. *Schmamazing.*" Oh, God, no. It's worst-case scenario!

Hannah smiles, her blue eyes sparkling behind her sexy black-framed glasses. "Thank you. You look pretty amazing yourself."

She understood that gibberish? Well, that's it. Put a fork in me, I'm done. She's perfect.

"I'm Josh," Josh says, appearing at my side and extending his hand. "Glad you could make it, Hannah."

Hannah thanks Josh for his generosity and everyone else launches into a bit of conversation while I stand by, trying to find my voice.

"Josh got a reservation at some fancy restaurant that's apparently impossible to get into!" Kat gushes to Hannah, batting her eyelashes at Josh. "Tell Hannah that thing you told me, Josh. You know, about the chef."

Josh talks a bit about the chef at his chosen restaurant, and then launches into a little anecdote about the last time he went there and Hannah agrees the place sounds amazing.

Josh looks at me, obviously discerning if I'm ready to talk yet. And when I subtly shake my head, he returns to the women and says, "After dinner, I thought we could gamble for a bit, if you ladies are game, and then I thought maybe we'd go dancing at this club our buddy Reed co-owns."

"Oh, I *love* dancing!" Hannah gushes, sounding genuinely thrilled. She looks at me. "Do you like dancing, Henn?"

Fuck.

This is it.

Tongue, don't fail me now.

I swallow hard, take a deep breath, say a little prayer my tongue has finally untwisted enough for me to answer her coherently, and say, "Yeah, I love dancing."

"Me too!" Hannah says, like she didn't just say that a second ago. Like we've just discovered something surprising we have in common.

"Yeah, me, too!" I say, even though I just said it a second ago, and I can't help noticing Josh and Kat looking at each other with big grins on their faces. I clear my throat. "I maybe like dancing a bit too much. I get pretty enthusiastic on the dance floor."

"There's no such thing as being too enthusiastic on a dance floor," Hannah declares. "The more energy, the better!"

Josh snorts. "I'd reserve judgment on that, Hannah. God love him, Henn tends to take the phrase 'let the music *move* you' to new levels. It's one of my favorite things about him, to be clear. Our entire friend group lives to get this boy drunk and watch him let him loose on a dance floor."

"Guilty as charged," I say. "So, I won't take offense if you pretend you don't know me when I really get going."

Hannah's face is a vision of pure kindness. "Henn, you could literally never embarrass me. I also *live* to let loose on a dance floor. In my opinion, dancing like a fool is a whole lot cheaper than therapy."

My heart is thumping in my throat. This girl just keeps getting better and better. "I couldn't agree more. As far as I'm concerned, if at least half the 'cool kids' on any given dance floor don't think there's something seriously—maybe even medically—wrong with me, then I'm not doing it right."

Hannah giggles. "Words to live by, sir! In all seriousness, though, I think dancing is a great way to remind yourself not to give a fuck what people think, you know? I'm a people-pleaser by nature, so it's always a good thing for me to try to remember."

My heart is pounding like a jackhammer. My smile is hurting my cheeks. "Indubitably," I say, incapable of taking my eyes of her baby blues. She's literally the cutest girl I've ever seen in my life, and this connection I'm feeling with her, just this fast, is unlike anything I've experienced in my life.

"*I knew it*," Kat whispers softly, but enthusiastically, to Josh. And when I peel my eyes off Hannah's beaming smile to glance at her, our resident matchmaker is grinning at Josh like the cat who swallowed the canary.

Josh smirks. "Okay, Madame Matchmaker. It's time to cool your jets and let these two intelligent people figure it out for themselves now. You've done your part."

Kat stifles a squeal. "Obvioiusly, I'll step back now. My job here is done."

Josh chuckles. "Yeah, 'cause you're so *chill* when going after something you want, right? So *zen* about letting things be what they're gonna be?"

Rolling her eyes, Kat grabs Hannah's arm. "So, are you ready, as you are now, to head out for some pre-dinner drinks, or do you need to change or freshen up or something?"

Hannah looks down at herself. "Can I just throw on a dress and freshen my makeup? It'll take me two minutes."

"I think you look amazing, as you are," I say, blushing as I say it. "But, of course, do whatever you need do. Take your time."

"Two minutes!" Hannah shouts, her face matching my blush. With that, she grabs her rolling suitcase and scurries toward the bedroom.

"I'll freshen up my makeup, too," Kat announces. But before she turns to walk away, she shoots me a little wink.

"She's the female you," Josh says, when both women are gone.

I smile. "Is that why I think she's so cool?"

Josh laughs. "Indubitably."

"She's really pretty. And so nice. Did you see the way she translated my gibber-ish? The girl speaks fluent Henn!"

He chuckles. "You're already a goner, aren't you?"

I purse my lips, pondering the question. "I'll put it this way: I'm not sure if I'm a goner yet. I need more information to be able to say that. But I've definitely never felt this kind of instant chemistry before and I'm excited to see where that might lead."

Josh rolls his eyes. "Such a bullshitter. You're a goner."

"What about you?" I ask. "Are *you* a goner?"

Josh shrugs. "I'm not prepared to say that yet. All I know is I've never felt this kind of instant chemistry before with anyone. And I'm . . . open to seeing where that might lead."

"You're such a bullshitter."

"No. I swear it's the truth."

I shrug. "Well, hey, that's a helluva lot more than I've heard you say in a very long while. So, it's not nothing."

"It's definitely not nothing."

"We're ready!" Kat bellows, re-entering the room with Hannah. And when I see Hannah, and the little blue dress she's wearing that shows off her cleavage and makes her blue eyes even bluer, my heart physically stops. *Oh my God.* Before the girls get close enough to overhear me, I nudge Josh's arm, lean in and whisper to him, "Okay, yeah, if I wasn't before, then I'm now, officially, a goner."

Chapter Four

Henn

"GO HENNY! GO Henny!" Hannah chants, as I boogie down the corridor next to her like my life depends on it. We're headed toward the suite she'll be sharing with Kat for the next few nights, but, apparently, at least a portion of our souls are still on that dance floor.

"Take it away, Bananaaaaa!" I shout, flinging my arms toward the length of the hallway—and to my absolute thrill, my girl doesn't hold back, but, instead, begins shimmying and bopping like a stick of dynamite that just got lit. "Go Banana, go Banana!" I chant, goading her on even more, and the giggle that erupts from her sends butterflies into my belly.

"That's it, right?" Hannah asks, motioning to an upcoming room.

"That's it."

When we parted ways with Josh and Kat in the lobby, they were headed to Josh's suite for the night. Which means, if it seems like Hannah's giving me a green light, I could get a goodnight kiss from her—and maybe even get invited inside for a make-out session.

After coming to a stop in front of her door, we stand mere inches apart, smiling at each other. Does she want me to kiss her now? I think so, but—

Without warning, Hannah throws her arms around my neck and presses her lips to mine. So, of course, I wrap my arms around her, open her lips with mine, and slide my tongue to hers. In response, she runs her fingers through the back of my hair and returns my kiss with unexpected passion, letting me know she's every bit as into me as I'm into her. And that's when all hell breaks loose inside me. She tastes incredible. Smells like heaven. And as her tongue swirls with mine, it feels like I was born to kiss her. Like I've been waiting my whole life for this kiss. It feels like destiny.

As our kiss intensifies, I back her against the door of her hotel suite and rest my palms on her hips, feeling drugged by the insane chemistry coursing between us. Indeed, the chemical reaction between my body and Hannah's is taking my breath away. I read somewhere that the dopamine hit released during an amazing kiss can activate the brain like a hit of heroin or cocaine. And I've always thought, "Well, that's got to be a bit of an exaggeration." But now, kissing Hannah, I know those researchers were exactly right—because this kiss feels like a blissfully narcotic rush.

"Oh my God, Henn," Hannah breathes, fisting the back of my hair and grinding herself into the straining bulge lodged between her thighs. "Kat said you're a fantastic kisser, but nothing could have prepared me for . . . *this*."

"Best kiss of my life," I admit, my chest rising and falling sharply with hers.

"I've never done this on a first date," she says, biting her lower lip. "But that kiss . . ." She visibly shudders with arousal. "Do you want to come inside and . . .?" She does a little shimmy, apparently intending to nonverbally finish her sentence.

"Hell yeah, I do," I reply, even though I'm not positive what that little shimmy means. Either way, though, whether she's inviting me inside to make out some more or have sex with her, I'm in.

"Oh. In case it wasn't clear, *this* . . ." Hannah shimmies again. "Was me inviting you to come inside to have *sex* with me."

"*Hallelujah.*"

Laughing, Hannah fumbles around in her little purse for her key card, while I shift my weight excitedly and thank my lucky stars for my best friend's foresight. On any other night, I wouldn't have condoms with me right now, simply because I'm not the type of guy who constantly needs to carry them around, just in case. But thanks to Josh, and him insisting on slipping me a couple at the club, I have *two*.

"Aha!" Hannah says, finding her key. She unlocks the door and I open it wide for her, letting her pass first, and when we're both inside and the door is closed, we immediately lurch at each other like feral animals. After kissing our way into the bedroom, stripping off clothes as we go, Hannah gets rid of her bra and panties—woohoo!—so I follow suit, practically tripping over myself as I rip off my underwear.

And that's it. We're now standing mere inches apart, at the foot of the bed, in nothing but our birthday suits, looking at each other in lustful awe.

"You're fucking gorgeous," I whisper. "Talk about turning my floppy disk rock *hard.*"

Hannah giggles. "You turn my floppy disk pretty damned hard, too."

We crawl onto the bed and resume kissing, with both of us moaning and shuddering excitedly. This woman is everything I've ever fantasized about. No, she's even better than I've fantasized, simply because I didn't know a girl like Hannah was even *possible.*

My cock hard and straining and my breathing ragged, I begin devouring her beautiful breasts, which prompts Hannah to begin stroking my hard dick in a way that's surely going to end things much more quickly than I'd like.

"Let me make you come before you do any of that," I say, touching her hand to stop her movement. "I'm way too wound up. I won't even make it to the main event if you keep doing that to me."

Hannah bites her lip and removes her hand.

"Lean back and relax," I insist. "I'm going to make you feel fucking incredible."

"It sometimes takes me a while to get there . . ."

"That's okay. Take as long as you need. I've got all the time in the world."

Her nostrils flaring with excitement, Hannah lies back as instructed, at which point I return to ravenously licking and sucking her nipples and breasts, only this time, adding the additional stimulation of stroking and caressing between her legs. After a while, when she's moaning and quaking at my touch, I press my finger to her clit, and begin massaging it in circles. And when it's abundantly clear I'm getting awfully close to penetrating her firewall, I widen her legs, crawl between them, and begin devouring her swollen tip and lips with my mouth, while fingering her G-spot. And that's it. Within minutes, it's this combination of stimulation that finally makes her eyes roll back into her head. *Duly noted for future reference.*

"Oh, God," she blurts. "I'm close. So close. Don't stop."

I moan my enthusiastic reply, since I've currently got a mouth full of pussy. But I have to imagine she's getting the drift of my meaning: *I won't stop till you come, baby.*

She begins gyrating and moaning like crazy. Gripping my hair and ears. And when I sense she's on the bitter cusp, I add another finger inside her, and my thumb in her ass, and that's all she needs to come undone. With an arch of her back and a loud wail that can only be described as rapturous, Hannah widens her legs, arches her back, and shrieks as her most sensitive flesh ripples beneath my tongue, lips, and fingers.

"Oh, God, Hannah, I have to get inside you," I grit out, feeling like I'm being physically electrocuted with arousal, yearning, and need. My breathing loud and my body quaking, I grab a condom from my wallet—thank God—crawl over Hannah, bring her arms above her head, and sink myself deep inside her, provoking guttural groans from both of us as my body fills hers.

"Yes," Hannah purrs as her body molds to mine. "Yes, yes, yes."

"You feel so fucking good," I murmur, barely able to speak. I pick up the pace of my thrusts, not because I consciously want to do that, but because I literally can't slow down. Because I'm in a frenzy of arousal now, swept away by the pleasure I'm feeling with this incredible girl. Just this fast, I'm imagining myself fucking only this girl and nobody else, ever again. And the thought is only spurring me on, even more.

I cup Hannah's breasts as I continue fucking her, and then squeeze her nipples, while Hannah grips my ass and tilts her pelvis to receive my cock as deeply as she can.

We're both absolutely losing it, spiraling higher and higher together, until, suddenly, Hannah digs her nails into my ass, arches her back, and comes with me deep inside her.

I've never felt a woman's orgasm from the inside out before. And all I can say is this sensation—the way her body is sending ripples of pleasure careening across my cock—is literally the closest thing to pure ecstasy I've ever felt.

I growl with my release, as Hannah grips my hair and shudders, before both of us lie still together, breathing hard.

"Well, that was barely tolerable," Hannah says, breathing hard. And, of course, I laugh.

I roll off her and begin taking care of the condom. "Yeah, I suppose if I've got nothing more interesting to do, I might as well do *that* with you. I suppose."

As I head to the bathroom to throw the condom away, Hannah is giggling behind me, cooing about how amazing that was.

"Yeah, it was supernatural," I admit, returning to the bed. "Like, I sincerely didn't know sex could feel *that* good."

"Same," she says, stretching to her full length and purring again. "You want to spend the night here with me?"

"Hell yeah, I do."

"What time does your flight leave?"

"Nine."

She juts her lower lip. "I wish you could stay."

"So do I. More than anything. Unfortunately, I've got a big job I have to do this week." I run my finger along her breast. "I'll be free next week, though. I could come to Seattle and we could have that 'salmon feast' you promised me."

"I'd love that."

"Cool."

"Cool."

Sighing happily, she lays her cheek on my chest, and I hold her for a long moment in silence, my head spinning with crazy thoughts. Is it weird that I can totally imagine myself down on bended knee before this girl one day? Is it crazy that I can already imagine myself spending sleepless nights with her, trying to calm our cranky newborn? Jesus Christ, I can totally imagine myself sitting next to her on a porch, both of us with gray hair, like we're in an ad for blood pressure medication. God help me, I can easily imagine *all* of it, as surely as if I'm seeing memories already lived, rather than mere possibilities. It's never happened to me before. Not even close. And I can't deny it, I'm fucking excited.

"What exactly do you do for a living, Henn?" Hannah asks after a bit, filling the silence. "I know you said you're a freelance computer programmer, but what does that mean?"

"I'm a freelance white-hat hacker."

"*Oh.*"

"Clients, some of them big ones, hire me to try to break through their cybersecurity, through any means necessary, and then fix whatever vulnerabilities I might find."

"To keep them safe from the baddies?"

"Exactly."

"So, you're one of the good guys?"

"Always." I wink.

"Do you ever do anything illegal with your superpower?"

I pause. "Technically, yes. But always for the greater good. Never for personal gain."

She processes that. "So, you're a vigilante, then? Sometimes?"

"Yeah, sometimes. But only when I agree with the cause." I watch her carefully, my stomach twisting and clenching. "Do you have a problem with any of that?"

"You don't steal from people?"

"Never. My core business is traditional, white-hat hacking. Finding vulnerabilities and fixing them. And yeah, I dabble on the side, occasionally, when the spirit moves me to right a wrong."

She smiles. "I think that's cool, honestly."

I exhale from the depths of my soul. "Cool."

"You've been working in Vegas this week?"

"Yeah."

"Were you doing a white-hat, traditional job, or righting a wrong?"

"It was righting a wrong. A really big one. Saving the world, you might even say."

"Oh wow. That's sexy."

"It was, if I do say so myself."

"Your life is so exciting."

"Sometimes. To be clear, though, nothing I'll ever do for work will hold a candle to what we just did, in terms of pure excitement."

She giggles. "I'm glad the feeling was mutual."

"Me, too. Thank God."

Hannah strokes my arm. "I had so much fun with you tonight, Henn."

"I had so much fun with you, too, Hannah," I reply, because that's what any sane, normal man would say in this situation. *I had fun with you, too.* If I were being completely honest with her, however, I'm sure I'd say, "Yeah, I had the best night of my entire fucking life tonight, Hannah." Or, at least, "I can't wait to see what happens next."

Hannah yawns, so I pull her to me and tell her to get some sleep, and she snuggles into me like being in my arms is the most natural thing in the world. Soon, her body slackens and her breathing becomes rhythmic. But as Hannah falls asleep in my arms, I'm wide awake, buzzing with thoughts and images of this perfect night. I think about the easy, fun conversation we had during our three-hour dinner, and how we made each other laugh so many times, we both almost hyperventilated a couple times. I think about the way Hannah and I danced at that swanky club like lunatics—part of the time, like we were two gorillas, literally, with both of us pretending to "groom" each other's "fur." And I realize I was the weirdest, craziest, most authentic version of myself with Hannah tonight—the precise version of myself I am with my family and best friends. Has that ever happened before with a woman I'm interested in, romantically? I truly don't think so.

A buzzing sound on the ground next to the bed pulls me from my thoughts—and I suddenly realize my phone is still in my pants.

Curious, I carefully unravel myself from Hannah and grab my pants. And when I pull my phone out of the pocket, I've got a text from Josh:

> **Josh:** All good with Hannah? Kat wanted me to make sure you got her safely to the suite.
>
> **Henn:** Don't use Kat as an excuse to text me. We both know what you really want to know is did I wind up using those condoms you slipped me at Reed's club?
>
> **Josh:** LOL. Well, did you?
>
> **Henn:** None of your business. (BUT I OWE YOU SO FUCKING BIG, FARADAY!)
>
> **Josh:** Awesome! Glad it's going well.

I look at Hannah on the bed for a long moment, admiring her beautiful face in the moonlight, and, once again, find myself imagining a future with this woman.

> **Henn:** It's going better than well, dude. Don't tell Kat I said this, so she doesn't tell Hannah and scare her off, but I'd bet anything I met my future wife tonight.

✧　✧　✧

Thank you for supporting the people of Ukraine! Henn and Hannah do not currently have their own book from their POV, but they've been beloved side characters in many of my books for a while now, including the trilogy where they first meet: *The Josh & Kat Trilogy*, which you can start reading now! www.laurenrowebooks.com/josh-kat-trilogy

Morning Coffee...and Stuff with Hook and John

Gina L. Maxwell

"COME ON, ALREADY. Stop fucking around and just *give it to me*." Unfortunately for me, the coffee pot doesn't give a damn what I tell it. It goes right on hissing and gurgling until finally the black liquid streams into the carafe at what feels like an unusually slow pace just to spite me. Glaring at it doesn't work but I don't budge from my spot at the counter, desperate for the caffeine today. If I could mainline the stuff without killing myself, I would.

Last night wasn't one of my better ones. I couldn't sleep for shit, so I spent a few hours reading and surfing the internet in the living room before switching to a punishing workout. Anything to keep myself from waking up the sleeping giant in my bed for some carnal fun. Not that I think he wouldn't be totally on board, but there's no reason for both of us to be sleep-deprived.

Somewhere around 5 a.m. I managed to exhaust every muscle in my body. I hopped in the shower for a quick suds-and-rinse, but was hit with the memory of finger-fucking John under the spray of hot water until he came so hard he nearly collapsed. With that pornographic highlight reel in my mind, I took the extra time to rub one out, rewriting the details so that he came with my cock buried deep in his tight ass—a fantasy I'll eventually make a reality, but not for a while yet. I'm good at playing the long game, and I like keeping Darling on the edge.

Afterward, I threw on my black track pants and made a beeline to the kitchen for some coffee. The coffee that's taking for-fucking-ever to brew.

Finally, the last few drops fall into the pot. Not wasting any time, I pour myself a cup and risk third-degree burns with my first sip. Releasing a satisfied breath, I head to the small kitchen table, slip on my black-framed glasses, and open my weathered copy of *The Count of Monte Cristo* as I caffeinate. Within minutes, my body relaxes, and my mind is sufficiently distracted.

Until my bedroom door opens and the sleeping giant emerges, rumpled and groggy and too goddamn sexy to ignore.

Clad only in a pair of tight boxer briefs, Darling yawns and absently scratches his chest as he crosses to the kitchen. I allow myself a brief glance then force my eyes back to the worn pages of my book. I can feel my heartbeat pulsing in my cock, but as far as he knows, I barely notice his presence. I like to make him work for my attention. And no matter how much it frustrates him, I know he gets off on it twice as much.

"Morning," he says, his voice sandpaper-rough like the rugged scruff on his jaw.

"You figure that out because the sun is rising or because a bluebird sang to you from the windowsill?" Yeah, occasionally I like to compare him to a Disney princess. It amuses me. But it's his own fault for being so damn chipper all the time.

John skips the coffee and starts to gather the ingredients for his gross shake as he tosses a wry grin over his shoulder. "Actually, it was your sunny disposition that gave it away."

Without looking at him, I take a drink of coffee and flip him off with the hand holding the book. He chuckles and goes about his morning routine. "So what's on today's agenda?"

"Same shit, different day, Darling."

"Did somebody wake up on the wrong side of the bed this morning?"

Turning a page, I mutter, "I'd have to have slept first."

At that, he faces me. "Shit, man, sorry. I didn't hear you get out of bed."

I can practically feel his frown, which irritates me. My insomnia isn't his issue to worry about. "If I'd wanted you to hear me, you would've."

"Still…" John moves to stand next me but doesn't say anything else. He's waiting for me to acknowledge him. To give him more or converse with him like a normal person. But I'm nowhere near normal, and neither is this arrangement we've put ourselves in.

Swallowing a sigh, I finally look up, maintaining a bored expression. "What?"

Concern swirls in his amber gaze, making my chest tighten. "You have dark circles," he says softly and sweeps his thumb across the thin skin beneath my eye. The tenderness he offers so easily has me warring between leaning into his touch and running for the goddamn hills, neither of which is an option.

Snatching his wrist, I hold his hand away from my face. "I don't need you to coddle me."

"It's not coddling, Hook, it's called caring, and I *want* to care for you."

"Yeah, well, I want someone to blow me while I enjoy my morning coffee, but we don't always get what we want, do we?"

"All you have to do is ask, you know."

I quirk an eyebrow at him even as all the blood in my body rushes to my groin. "I'm Captain of the Neverland Pirates. I don't ask. I give orders."

"Then you shouldn't have a problem getting what you want if you have a willing body to follow them," he says, his voice husky as his erection begins to stretch the cotton of his underwear not even a foot from my face.

Slowly, I turn sideways on my chair and lean back against the wall with my legs spread. Even though he's the one standing, I'm still very much in the power position. I'm relaxed and sure of myself. He's tense and waiting for my command. I can keep us locked in this limbo as long as I want. His own alpha tendencies might eventually get him to break rank and make the first move despite the consequences. Then again, he enjoys my punishments almost as much as I enjoy doling them out, so there's not much of a deterrence there.

I rake my eyes over his hard body and his even harder dick. Part of me wants to stop this game, pull him out, and jerk him with a finger in his ass until he begs me to let him come all over the table. But he started us on *this* path, so I'm going to make us finish it.

"And are *you* a willing body, Darling?"

"You know goddamn well I am."

I pretend to ponder his response as I tuck my thumbs into my waistband and pull my track pants down to mid-thigh. "Not good enough. Let's try that again." Grabbing my thick length, I give it a couple of slow tugs, squeezing at the head to release a clear drop of pre-cum.

John's chest heaves with shallow breaths, his gaze glued to what my hand is doing as he rasps, "Fucking hell."

"I wanna know if your body's willing, Darling. Answer me properly."

Golden pools snap up to meet my icy blue ones. He licks his lips. "Yes, Captain."

"Good," I say, releasing myself to pick up my book and mug. "Then get on your knees."

John doesn't hesitate, simply drops like a devout Catholic in church. But after yanking off my pants, instead of praying to God, he starts worshiping my cock.

He sucks me down to the back of his throat. I almost groan with pleasure but manage to hold it in. He'll get no sounds from me. I don't even watch him. I stare at the pages of my book and pretend like the words aren't swimming in front of my eyes. Occasionally I drink my coffee. Not that I can taste it anymore with every cell in my body preoccupied by the glorious things John is doing with his mouth.

I can feel him getting frustrated with every second I don't give him a reaction and it makes me grin behind my book when I lift it to turn the page. As I lower it again, I fix my expression as though nothing is out of the ordinary. As though a half-naked god of a man isn't on his knees, sucking my cock like it's his last meal and lighting my nerves on fire In the process.

John must've taken the page-turn as a personal affront because he growls and ups his game with a slow, deliberate lick from testicles to tip in one, long swipe. When he tongues the pre-cum from my slit, my hips jerk, but I grit my teeth and lock it down.

"Fuck, you taste good. Wanna lick every inch of you."

"No one's stopping you, Darling."

"*You* will."

Setting the book down, I issue the challenge with an arch of my brow.

His full lips curve into a sly grin. "Say when," he says, like he's about to top off my coffee, not devour my cock. Which he does, all the way to the root, then sucks on me like a goddamn Dyson as he pulls back and starts all over again.

Fire ignites in my belly and licks up my spine, going higher and higher every time he swallows around the head of my dick between pumps from his mouth and the light graze of his teeth. Beads of sweat pop out on my forehead and my hands curl into fists, but I hold my ground and don't move, don't drive my hips up and fuck his face like I want. I'm in total control. I'm positive I can ride this out long after he eventually begs for my cum down his throat.

Popping off my dick, he makes good on his promise. His tongue explores my shaft like he's making a mental map of every inch, cataloging the path of every vein. Then he travels lower, giving the same attention to my balls, licking and sucking each one into his mouth until they're as tight as stones.

Fuck me. I'm starting to be *less* positive that I can ride this out like I thought.

Releasing a slow exhale, I make the mistake of closing my eyes—just for a few seconds—and that's all it takes for John to change the game.

He hooks one of my legs over his shoulder and shoves against the inner thigh of my other one, opening me wide. My eyes snap open but before I can ask him what he's doing, he locks that golden gaze of his on me and arrests the words in my brain. Then he runs his tongue down my shaft, lower over the seam of my balls...and lower still.

"Darling," I grind out, half warning, half pleading.

"All you have to do is say when," he whispers.

He's issuing a challenge. A damn big one. Either I let him continue and some-how keep what's left of my stoic appearance, or I call him off and prove that I'm anything *but* unaffected and lose.

The thing of it is, he knows he has the upper hand. He might not know that I haven't allowed anyone else to explore me the way he plans, but he knows I haven't allowed *him* to do it, which means he's pushing boundaries, hoping I crack. But he severely underestimates how badly I hate losing.

I focus on taking even breaths as John pulls my hips to the edge of the chair, wedges his broad shoulders between my legs, then dips his head to place a wet, open-mouthed kiss on the sensitive flesh behind my testicles. He changes the angle of his head and does it again, searing me with his lips and the heat in his eyes. It's fucking filthy yet oddly tender, reverent yet claiming, and it twists me up in ways I didn't expect.

John moves his head lower. My ribs and nostrils expand with the heavy breaths I take while watching him. I know what's coming—I can see it in the mischievous glint in his eyes—yet I'm still not prepared for how *fucking good* it feels when he laps my hole with the flat of his tongue like I'm a goddamned ice cream cone.

"Jesus fuck!" I shout, throwing my head back as lightning tears through my body.

He groans. "Mmm, more."

Then he makes a feast of me. He jacks my cock roughly while his mouth devours everything else. Infinite sensations consume me from the suction of his lips, the glide of his tongue, the grazes of teeth. I feel like I'm drowning and being reborn, all from a fucking blow job. I want more. I *need* more. I won't fuck him yet, though. It's not time. Not nearly.

But I'm done letting him have the reins.

Grabbing his head with both hands, I lift his face to look up at me and give him my best pirate smile. The one that spells trouble for whoever it's on. "Fucking *when.*"

In a flash, I push him down flat on his back on the kitchen floor, his wrists pinned above his head. I smash my mouth on his and delve inside, plundering. Staking my claim with every lick, every scrape, every bite. *Mine, mine, all fucking mine.*

Angling his hips up, he rubs our dicks together. The friction of cotton and the delicious pressure drags a growl from my chest to mingle with Johnathan's keening moan.

"Fuck me," he rasps. "I need you to fuck me."

"Oh, I intend to," I say, my evil grin hovering above his lips. "Just not the way you think."

Keeping his wrists shackled in one hand, I move up his body to straddle his rib cage before spitting in the center of his chest to provide lubrication. Then I stare into his eyes as I start grinding my steel-hard cock against his spit-slick skin. My movements are slow and measured, and my body is angled up so he can get a good look.

"Oh fuck," he croaks. "Why is that so hot?"

With my free hand, I grip his jaw tightly, my thumb and fingers denting his stubbled cheeks. "Because it turns you on when I debase you for my own pleasure."

I don't like the flash of conflict I see in his eyes. Either we put an end to that shit right now or this entire scene stops. Dipping down, I speak directly into his ear. "Don't overthink it. Your instincts are different with me, but that doesn't make them wrong. Trust them. Trust *me,*" I whisper then nip at his earlobe. "Do you trust me, Johnathan?"

"Always, Captain." His voice is steady and sure.

"Good boy." I rise back up, repositioning his hands on either side of his head so I can straighten my arms and give him a show. "Now watch as I fuck myself on this hard body you insist on showcasing every chance you get."

His "*Fuck yes*" is like a starting pistol going off in my head.

Unleashing my usual control, I pin my cock between us and thrust against him like I'm finally pounding into his tight ass, getting faster and rougher with every stroke. Our eyes lock, his back arches, and my sweat drops off to mix with his. I clench my jaw with the effort it takes to hold my climax at bay, but then he furrows his brow while *his* jaw drops open on a soundless cry, and I know he's coming in his fucking briefs.

That does me in. My balls draw up tight and the fire swirling at the base of my spine shoots up through my dick. I stripe John's neck with so much cum it looks like a collar and short leash. I don't hate the way it looks.

Mine.

As soon as I'm sure I can move without collapsing, I sit back and snag the hand towel from the counter. Fighting the urge to rub the white evidence into his skin, I start to clean him up but stop when he smiles up at me. "What?"

"You said 'when' so I wo—"

I slap my hand over his mouth and glare at him. "Finish that sentence and I won't touch you for a week. Got it?" He nods and I go back to swiping the towel over his neck and chest, but he gets that dopey grin on his face again. Sighing, I ask against my better judgment. "What now, Darling?"

"You're taking care of me."

Rolling my eyes, I wad up the towel and toss it behind me, making a mental note to grab it for laundry later. "I was making sure I didn't have to clean my floor when you get up."

John pushes up, palms the back of my head with one large paw, and brings me in for a searing kiss. When the shock wears off, I retaliate and bite his lower lip hard enough I'm surprised I didn't draw blood. His smile tells me he's too happy with himself to care.

"Sure you were. Don't worry, though, I won't tell the guys and ruin your rep," he says, laughing.

I answer by palming his face and pushing him back down as I stand and head to my bedroom.

"Damn, Hook. I hate it when you leave, but I love to watch you walk away."

I shake my head. "Flattery won't get you very far with me, Darling."

"Then what will?"

Pausing in the doorway, I look back to where he's propped against the table, grinning like a cat with a belly full of cream. This would be so much easier if I didn't find him so damn charming. I should tell him that nothing he does will work. I *should* tell him that. But that's not what comes out of my mouth.

"Sucking cock like that sure as fuck won't hurt your chances."

He bites his lip as he thinks about his answer, and I find myself holding my breath until he finally says, "Then consider me at your disposal."

"You agreeing to follow my orders, Johnathan?"

"I am, Captain," he says with a serious nod. "Always."

✧   ✧   ✧

Thank you so much for reading my bonus scene featuring my all-time favorite couple, Hook and John! If you want to experience their seriously epic, angsty love story from the very beginning, read both of the LOST BOYS NOVELS, available now.

ginalmaxwell.com/series/lost-boys

PAPER RING

C. HALLMAN & J.L. BECK

CHAPTER ONE

Gwen

JUST WHEN I thought this night couldn't get any worse, red and blue lights flash in my rearview mirror. *Fuck!*

I glance down at the speedometer. 79 mph. *Fuck, again.* I'm pretty sure the speed limit is 65 here.

Unreasonable fear creeps up my spine. Yes, I'm speeding, but that's it. It's not a big deal. People speed all the time. I'm gonna get a ticket and go on with my night. Nothing to worry about. At least, that's what I keep telling myself as I pull onto the side of the highway.

We're just outside of town, and it's a cloudy night. The area is completely dark without any illumination from the sky or the city, making the cruiser's headlights behind me seem even brighter.

I put my car in park and squint my eyes, watching the black silhouette of the police officer get out of his car and walk toward me.

My heart is racing, and my fingers tremble as I reach for the button to let my window down.

Why am I so nervous?

"Good evening, ma'am," the cop greets as soon as he is close enough to peer down at my face. With one hand on his gun holster, he grips a flashlight in the other, searching the inside of my car like I'm hiding a drug dealer in here.

"I'm sorry I was speeding," I blurt out after cursing Gia in my head for making me do this again. "My roommate called and asked me to pick her up from this guy's house, and I was just trying to get there as fast as I could. I know that's not an excuse. I should definitely drive the speed limit, especially at night. I know that, but—"

"Is that why you're in your pajamas?" The cop interrupts my rambling, shining his flashlight directly on my chest.

I lower my head and stare at my bare legs, covered only by a pair of thin plaid shorts. The white tank top I'm wearing is not much better, considering there is no bra beneath it. My cheeks turn hot, and I'm sure they redden to match my embarrassment.

I let my long, uncombed hair fall into my face, hiding my shame with an auburn curtain. "Um, yes. I was asleep when she called. I didn't really think clearly."

"That happens." The cop smiles. "Sounds like you were just being a good friend." He lowers the flashlight, letting me get a better look at him for the first time. He appears to be in his early forties, judging by the gray in his hair and the frown lines on his forehead.

"I'm sorry again."

"No worries. I'm just gonna have to check your license and registration, and you'll be on your way to pick up your friend."

"Of course!" I turn to reach for my purse, which I usually have on the passenger's seat. Today, there is only my phone. "Shit. I must have forgotten my purse while I was rushing out, but I have my registration here somewhere... I think."

Flipping on my interior lights, I start rummaging through the glove box. There are fast-food receipts, unopened mail, random flyers, and take-out menus, but nothing that looks like a registration.

"Let's start with your name and birthday, okay?"

"Gwendoline Anne Baker. I actually turned eighteen yesterday." Not sure why I mentioned that part. It's not like he cares.

"Well, happy belated birthday," he says flatly while scribbling something down on a notepad.

"Um, thanks. What exactly does a registration look like?" I ask like a complete dumbass. The officer raises one eyebrow at me, as if he's wondering if I'm joking.

"Who is this car registered to?"

"Me, I think? Or maybe my... husband." I murmur that last part. Even after two years of being married, I'm still not used to saying it. Mostly because I haven't seen my so-called husband our entire marriage. I don't even know why he gave me this car, and right now, I don't know why I've been driving it for two years without once questioning who it's registered to.

He was right... I am a naïve child.

My nerves are already on edge, but the cop manages to kick them up a notch when he starts walking around the car and saying something I can't make out into his radio.

I give up my search for this stupid registration and keep my eyes on the police officer, who is coming back to the driver's side now. I'm about to apologize for a third time when he suddenly reaches for the handle of my door and pulls it open.

"Get the fuck out of the car, with your hands where I can see them!" His voice blasts into my ear like I'm in the front row of a concert.

I flinch away from him, shocked and freaking out by what is happening. The cop's gun is pointing straight at me. My hands come up automatically to protect my face, as if my fingers could stop a bullet.

"Get out!" he orders again, less patience in his tone.

"Okay!" I yell back, making sure he can hear me over the loud, erratic beating of my own heart.

My whole body is shaking, and it has nothing to do with the temperature and everything to do with the man holding a gun against my head while screaming at me. "Turn around!"

I spin around so quickly I slide out of one of my flip-flops and almost fall to the ground.

"Hands behind your back," he orders, and again, I do what he says without thought. A moment later, he grabs my wrists roughly, pulling my arms back uncomfortably while he secures handcuffs on me.

Tears well in my eyes as the cool metal presses against my skin. The cop twists me around towards his cruiser, never even letting me put my other flip-flop back on. He sets me in the back seat of his cruiser, letting my legs dangle out the side.

"Do you have any idea what kind of shit you're in? Stealing a car?" He shakes his head. "You look like such a nice girl. Why do stuff like this? Do you even know who you stole from?"

"I didn't steal this car. It's mine."

"So, it's your car, but it's registered to someone else?"

"I told you, it might be in my husband's name."

"You can cut the shit, okay. There is no way out of this. Just sit tight until backup gets here. I'll have a female officer come and take you in." He gives me one last disapproving look before walking to the back of the car to lean against the corner.

I guess all I can do now is wait.

CHAPTER TWO

I SPEND THE next ten minutes trying not to cry. I don't even know why the tears keep rolling down my cheeks. I'm not scared anymore. I'm more angry than anything. Angry with Gia for making me pick her up in the middle of the night. Angry with Emmett for giving me this car and definitely angry with myself for being so naïve and stupid.

The headlights of an approaching vehicle have me looking up into the road. This must be the female police officer. The vehicle slows down and pulls up behind us. I watch as the door opens and a large figure heads toward us.

It doesn't take me but a moment to realize that this person is not another cop. It's the one individual I wouldn't have expected to see tonight... or ever again, for that matter.

Emmett Carter. My husband.

He walks past the cop without glancing at him, his eyes trained on me the entire time until the moment he stops in front of my feet. His gaze moves up and down my body as if to scan every inch of me.

"Mr. Carter." The officer clears his throat and stands a little straighter beside us. "I called—" That's all he gets out before Emmett slams his fist against his jaw, making his head snap to the side. His eyes roll back, and his body goes down.

My gasp is masked by the thump of him hitting the ground at full force. His head bounces off the pavement like a basketball, making me yelp out for him.

"Why did you tell him your name was Baker?" That's the first thing out of the mouth of the man who married me two years ago, just to dump me the same day.

"What else was I supposed to tell him?" I'm surprised by how even my voice is at this point.

"Your real last name."

"I wasn't sure if you wanted anyone to know. I figured you might be ashamed." I actually have no idea if he would be. I have no idea what he wants since he's never shared a fucking thing with me.

He ignores my comment completely and counters with another question instead. "What the fuck are you wearing? Your top is basically see-through. I can see your tits, and looking at the length of your shorts, I bet I can see your ass if you stand up."

My mouth pops open, and I suck in a sharp breath, feeling like I just got slapped. How dare he criticize my outfit. As if he has any right?

"What do you care?" He's never cared about me before. "You don't get to tell me what to do! If I want to walk around naked, I fucking will!" Two years ago, I would have never spoken to him like this. My parents taught me better. From a young age, they trained me to be a perfect wife to a man like Emmett. Taught me everything there was to know about pleasing and obeying a powerful man. Talking back was definitely not on that list.

I'm not that girl anymore. Two years of hating him, of being angry and hurt, are all coming to fruition at this very moment.

The cop groans again, but I can't make myself glance over. It's like Emmett is holding me under some kind of spell. I can't look away from his scowling face. His strong, clean-shaven jaw is twitching like he is trying not to grind his teeth too hard. And his brows are pinched together just as tightly as his lips are pressed shut. But what really draws me in are the stormy blue eyes now holding me hostage.

I should probably apologize, for both making him come out here tonight and the way I just spoke to him. Yet, I force my own lips shut and swallow back the apology sitting on my tongue. I don't owe him anything.

He moves so quickly that I don't have the time to even try to get away before his hands grab my upper arms, and he pulls me from the car. With only one flip-flop and my hands still cuffed behind my back, I'm so unsteady on my legs that I have no choice but to fall against his firm chest.

Turning my head away, I try to twist my body away from him, which only makes him dig his fingers deeper into my arms. I wince in pain, jerking from his touch. He suddenly lets go, and for a second, I think I'm going to fall back against the car. Emmett grabs me once more. This time, around my hip. Then he lifts me up and throws me over his shoulder so roughly it knocks the wind out of me.

"Wait!" I croak after I catch my breath. "My friend. I need to pick her up."

"I already sent someone to get Gia," Emmett says casually while carrying me back to his car.

"What? How do you know my friend's name… or where she is?"

"Forget about her; you have yourself to worry about now." His voice is low and gravelly, promising pain and whatever else he has planned for tonight.

His threat hangs heavy in the air as he lowers me to my feet, just to shove me into the back of another car. I almost hit my forehead on the door, but Emmett pulls me back just in time, sitting me up before sliding in next to me.

Someone else is sitting in the driver's seat. Like Emmett, he is wearing a dark suit, his hair is cut neat, and his shoulders are broad and muscular.

"Sir?" he asks.

"Home," Emmett growls out the order.

The driver pulls onto the highway, and I awkwardly try to sit sideways with my hands still cuffed together behind my back. I turn away from Emmett, looking out the window into the black night.

"Lean back," Emmett orders, grabbing my shoulder. If it wasn't for his hand pulling me toward him, I wouldn't think I even heard him right.

"What are you…?" The words get lodged in my throat when the side of my head meets his warm thigh. Suddenly, my mouth goes dry. What the hell is he doing? His fingers wrap firmly around my throat, not tight enough to restrict my breathing but tight enough to have me worried.

I'm facing him now, trying to look anywhere besides his crotch, which is only a few inches away. Squeezing my eyes shut, I concentrate on calming my breathing and not passing out. Closing them helps only a little because I can still feel his hands on me. Still smell his spicy cologne and hear his heavy breathing.

Fuck, he must be angry. Who knows what I interrupted him doing tonight? My thoughts are running rampant with scenarios of how his night started and how mine is going to end.

My mind comes up with many outcomes… and none of them are good.

CHAPTER THREE

STARTLE AWAKE, disoriented and panicked because I don't know where I am.

"Relax." Emmett's gravelly voice vibrates through me, and I'm catapulted back into reality.

I'm still lying across the back seat of his car, cuffed, half-naked, and with my head propped up on his legs. His hand is still on my neck, but it's cradling the side now, his thumb softly stroking my jawline.

For a moment, I wonder if I actually fell asleep or if he choked me out without me realizing it. I wouldn't put it past him.

"We're almost there."

"Where are you taking me?"

"Home." I know right away he's lying. If he were taking me back to my apartment, we would have been there already.

"This is not the way to my place."

"Your new home," he explains calmly.

"Why are you moving me? I like my apartment, and I love my roommate." His fingers tighten slightly around my neck at the word love. It happened so quickly I'm not sure that it happened at all.

"You are my wife; you should live with me. I'll have your things moved in the morning."

The fact that I'm in a vulnerable position at the moment, one where he could easily snap my neck, apparently doesn't help me control my anger, and I lash out. "Now! Now, you want me? After two years of ignoring me, you suddenly changed your mind and find me worthy of living with you?"

The bastard has the audacity to smile. He fucking smiles like this is all a joke. Like my entire life is nothing but a joke to him.

The car comes to a stop, and the driver steps out as soon as the vehicle is in park. The interior light flickers on, blinding me for a second. I force my eyes open, wanting to at least see coming whatever he has planned.

The front door closes, and the back door opens a moment later. Instead of getting out, Emmett stays seated. "I don't want anyone to see her. Make sure all the men are gone."

"Of course. I'll take care of it," the driver confirms before stepping away.

"How am I supposed to live here if no one is allowed to see me? You can't keep me a secret forever, you know."

"Everyone who works for me knows about you."

"Sure they do." I don't believe a word he says. "Then why can't they see me?"

"Because if one of my men sees you in this outfit, I will use my favorite carving knife to cut his eyeballs out and feed them to the sharks."

Sharks? I don't know why that's my first thought after that monster of a sentence. Probably my sleep-deprived brain's fault. I try not to read too much into what he just said, mostly because the last time I let myself believe he actually liked me, he dumped me.

The driver didn't close the door, making it easy to hear his approach. "All clear."

Emmett wastes no time. Grabbing me under my arms, he pulls me out of the car with him. My feet barely touch the graveled driveway when I'm lifted up in the air again and thrown over his shoulder.

Too tired to fight him, I just let my head hang low as he walks me into his house and up the stairs. With each step he takes, my body bounces against his shoulder.

"If you don't put me down, I'm gonna throw up," I warn, not joking one bit.

My stomach churns as he throws me down onto a soft bed. I fly off the mattress slightly, landing on my front with my face shoved into the blanket... a blanket that smells like him. Oh, god. I'm in his bed.

Turning my head to the side, I blink my eyes open and scan the room. "Take the cuffs off, please. My arms hurt."

"I should leave them on tonight as your punishment."

"My punishment?"

"For leaving the house like that."

My mouth opens to counter with a witty remark, but whatever I was thinking evaporates into air when Emmett's hand lands on the back of my calf. Slowly, he runs the rough pad of his thumb along the inside of my leg, and up my thigh until he's almost touching my shorts.

I don't move. I don't even breathe. Too stunned to do anything. Emmett has never touched me like this. Actually, no one has ever touched me like this.

His fingers run over my skin, leaving a tingling hot path behind that feels so intense I worry it will leave a permanent mark. Even worse, I want it to. I want him to mark me, so I can hold on to the moment forever, so I never forget what this feels like.

His hand inches up painfully slow. His thumb is now brushing against my shorts, sending a shiver down my spine.

Suddenly, he pulls away, leaving my skin cold and wanting more. I don't even realize I'm making a disapproving sound until Emmett chuckles. *Asshole.*

Turning my face, I bury it into the soft comforter, thankful that I don't have any makeup on. He might have seen my puffy eyes from my angry tears, but at least I don't have black streaks running down my cheeks.

With my face hidden, I listen to Emmett move around the room. He opens, then closes a door, maybe the walk-in closet. Then he gets something from a drawer near the bed. The sound of clothes being taken off has my stomach in knots.

Does he think I'm going to sleep with him?

The bed dips with Emmett's weight as he climbs onto it. "Wait! What are you doing?" I wiggle away from him, but he quickly places his hand between my shoulder blades and holds me down.

"Relax," he says. As if that was so easy. His hand moves to my wrists, where he does something to the handcuffs. The metal bites into my skin, causing me to hiss out in pain. Then, suddenly, the right cuff pops open, and my wrist is free.

Emmett rubs the part where the metal was pinching my skin before placing my arm by my side. My shoulder is stiff, making the movement feel both painful and relieving. A moment later, my other wrist is free, and Emmett gives it the same treatment.

"You've had a long night, so I'm going to let you go to sleep now, but tomorrow, I'm going to strip you bare and fuck you senseless."

"The hell you will!" I sit up, all exhaustion forgotten in a heartbeat. "You can't just say shit like that after not talking to me for two years!" I spin around to face him, realizing he is not wearing anything besides a pair of boxers.

"You are my wife. Why shouldn't I fuck you?"

"Because I don't want you."

"Are you sure about that? I remember you throwing yourself at me at—"

I don't let him finish. "I wanted you two years ago! I was ready then."

"No, you were not. You were a child, molded into the image of a perfect wife by your parents. You were groomed for so long you didn't even know how to be normal. I didn't want a brainwashed wife. Not then, and not now."

"Then what do you want?"

"A queen."

CHAPTER FOUR

A *QUEEN?* WHAT the hell is that supposed to mean? That's the big question running through my mind as I sit on Emmett's king-sized bed while he waits for me to respond.

Problem is, I don't know what to say. His bare torso is not helping to keep my thoughts organized at all. For being in his late thirties, his body is remarkably toned. My eyes are drawn to the intricate tattoos painted across his taut skin. The artist must have drawn on him directly; the artwork is moving so perfectly with the shape of his physique.

There is a large skull on the center of his chest with a snake swirling around it and coming out of one of the eye sockets. Around it are wilted roses that are so detailed and realistic-looking that I want to run my fingers over them just to see what it feels like.

Emmett clears his throat and folds his arms over his chest.

Shit, what was the question again?

"I'm tired," I rasp out, flustered. "I want to go to sleep now." I get up from the bed to stand on my wobbly legs. "Where is the guest room?"

"You are sleeping here… with me… in *our* bed." I open my mouth to protest, but he is faster. "Trust me, it's not worth fighting about. You are not going to win. So save your energy and get comfortable."

"Fine!" I yell, throwing my hands up. "But I'm not sharing a blanket with you." I climb back into the bed and lie down on the edge farthest away from him.

This is probably the most childish thing I have done, but I couldn't care less. The truth is, it's not worth the fight. He is right about that. I know I'm not going to get past him, but I don't have to make it easy on him either. Just because he's decided he wants me now doesn't mean I still do.

Emmett sprawls out on his side of the bed, pulls the comforter up to his chest, and flips off the light. "Suit yourself, but this is the only one I have, I'm afraid."

Sure it is. I roll my eyes in the dark. He lives in a fucking mansion with only one blanket.

Turning onto my side, I curl up, pulling my legs to my chest in an effort to stay warm. It's not particularly cold in here, but lying still, on top of being exhausted, makes it difficult to get comfortable.

At least I won't have to worry about falling asleep, which I'm not planning on doing. I need to stay up, so I can leave before he wakes up.

For a long time, I remain in this position, forcing myself to breathe evenly to make it sound like I'm asleep. As time passes, it gets harder and harder to stay still and not shiver.

Did he turn up the air conditioner on purpose?

With a deep sigh, Emmett moves around beside me. He is not touching me anywhere, but I know he must be closer now from the way the mattress has dipped slightly. My own body wants to get closer, seeking out the warmth he would provide.

Just thinking about it has me shivering a little more. Exhaustion has made me weak, and I turn my body toward him out of instinct.

He is closer than I thought because I only move a few inches, and I'm close enough to feel his body heat.

I shouldn't, but I can't help myself. Moving the last couple of inches, I find myself pressed against his side. The heat of his body resonates through me, and I bite back a sigh.

Now that I'm warming up a little, my courage starts to build, and the exhaustion fades a bit. No matter what, I can't fall asleep here. I have to escape, find a way out.

The minutes tick by at a snail's pace, but Emmett's breathing finally evens out enough that I'm certain he is asleep. I have no idea where I'll go once I'm out of this room, but I'll figure that out later.

I shift against the silk sheets, like I'm rolling over in my sleep. My heart hammers against my ribs, the fear mounting deep in my gut.

What if he wakes up? What if I can't escape the room? The questions compile, and before I let myself wallow in the fear of what-ifs, I scoot closer to the edge of the bed.

I'm teetering, a breath of an inch away, when I finally do it. I roll out of bed and onto my feet, the mattress dipping ever so slightly as my weight shifts off it.

Once on my feet, I pause for a moment, my breath escaping me like I've run a mile. Emmett remains sleeping, his eyes closed; his gorgeous features appear almost serene.

Like a mouse trying to escape a mousetrap, I back away slowly, my steps small and quiet. Every few seconds, I look over my shoulder to check if he is still sleeping. By the time I make it to the door, the bed seems like it's a million miles away.

Air escapes my lungs as I take the brass knob into my hand and twist it. It's so quiet you could hear a pin drop. Peering over my shoulder one last time, I see Emmett sitting up in the bed, and the invisible rope around my neck tightens.

"Did you really think escaping me would be that easy?"

His voice sends a shiver down my spine, and instead of doing the sensible thing, I do the only thing that makes sense in my mind: I run.

I've barely made it over the threshold when I hear his heavy footfalls behind me. Each step forces me to move faster, my muscles burning as my fight-or-flight instincts kick in.

One step, two steps... I can do this. I panic at the last moment, trying to decide which way to turn in the dark hallway, giving me a poor sense of direction. It's that indecision that gets me caught.

The air swooshes out of my lungs as a thick, muscled arm wraps around my middle. A scream rips from my throat, and I'm hauled backward against what could be considered a wall of steel.

His hard muscles press against my backside as he lifts me up and carries me back to where I ran from. "There is no escaping me, Gwen. No fighting this. You're my wife, and it's time I made good on that transaction."

Every word rumbles out of his chest and into me as I struggle against his grasp, my legs flailing and my fists forced to my sides.

The bedroom gets closer, and the window to escape disappears. Once we step back into the room, he releases me and slams the door; the sound echoes through the space, rattling my insides.

Chest rising, he growls, "Strip."

I lift my chin, wanting to defy him, all while knowing I'll end up doing it anyway.

"And what if I don't want to…" I'm not sure how I get the words past my lips without sounding weak, but somehow, I manage.

Emmett lurches forward, his fingers grasping the front of my shirt, and he pulls the fabric tightly. The cotton rips at my shoulder from the force, and cool air kisses my skin.

This man might be my husband, but he's not the same man who showed disinterest in me two years ago.

"Take off your clothes, or I'll take them off for you, and believe me"—his hot breath fans against my cheeks—"you don't want me to be the one to do it. I'm not in the mood for pleasantries. I want you naked, my willing wife, and your pussy ready for me to use."

CHAPTER FIVE

A TREMBLE WORKS its way down my spine. Does he have to be so vulgar? I swallow my fear, refusing to show him how terrified he truly makes me.

"Let me do it," I say, trying my best to keep my voice sounding strong. He merely nods and steps back. I can tell the effort it takes for him to allow me to do this myself. He says he's not patient, but he's clearly trying for me. I slowly pull the shirt off and over my head.

My nipples harden the moment the cold air kisses my skin, but I pretend that I'm not affected by the temperature or him. I look up and toss the shirt onto the floor at his feet. Emmett licks his lips. His gaze darkens, burning a path across my skin as he follows the movement of my fingers when I shove them into the waistband of my shorts.

"Has my wife let another man touch her before?" His tone is icy cold, and I sink my teeth into my bottom lip as I push down my pajama shorts.

I could lie and tell him *yes*, or I could tell him the truth. "Yes, more than once." The lie rolls off my tongue fluidly. "I've been on many dates."

Emmett tips his head back and barks out a laugh that's dark and sinister. "I'm going to give you the opportunity to change your answer since I already know you're lying." My mouth goes dry, but I somehow hold myself together.

"I'm not a virgin. If that's what you are asking," I quip.

Taking a step forward, he reaches out, and his knuckles gently caress the underside of my breast.

"You're a shit liar, and I know it because I've watched you every fucking day. I made certain that no one else touched what was mine."

Whatever my response might have been gets lodged in my throat when his knuckle brushes against my nipple. A gasp parts my lips at the onslaught of sensations that ripple through me from that one simple touch. I don't want to react, but how can I not?

His hand brushes against my chin, and he gently lifts it, forcing my eyes to meet his.

"I'm going to fuck you, my wife, and when your virgin pussy comes around my cock, the blood of your purity coating the skin, we'll both know that you were lying."

"And you'll discover I wasn't," I fire back, using the last of my strength. Like a man starved of air and life, he pounces on me, his lips find mine like a beacon of light, and he devours me from the inside out.

I can't protest or speak. All I can do is drown inside him. He makes quick work of his clothing, tossing the articles onto the floor as he guides us back toward the bed.

I should at least attempt to get away again, but the truth is, I don't want to run. I've wanted Emmett since before I became his wife.

Dipping his head, he kisses me with a tenderness I don't expect. His tongue presses against the seam of my lips, begging for entrance, and I open for him, letting him massage my tongue with his own. I've never French kissed anyone before, but the sparks of pleasure kissing brings makes me feel as though I've been missing out.

Emmett's hands are everywhere, in my hair, trailing along my body, and clawing at my panties. His body blankets mine once we're on the bed, and this sense of protection and security washes over me.

He breaks the kiss and sinks his fingers into the waistband of my panties. He's completely naked now, his straining cock between us.

"You make me so fucking hard, so fucking crazy. Two years I've waited for you. Every day that I've had to stay away has been torture, but you're here now, and I'm going to make you mine. Officially. Forever."

"What do you mean you've waited two years? As in... you didn't sleep with anyone else?"

"Would you be jealous if I had?" The bastard smirks.

"No," I lie again, my mother's lessons coming through. She always told me I should look the other way at my husband's cheating. Men of power can have any woman they want; all you have to do is satisfy him enough to stay married.

"We really need to work on your honesty, but that's going to have to wait," he chides and rips my panties down my legs. Without the protection of my underwear, I'm vulnerable.

Emmett eases my thighs apart and stares at my pussy.

"Nothing but a thin strip of hair..." he says, but I get the feeling he's talking more to himself. My mother always told me I needed to be ready for a man, whenever, and that no man wanted a woman who wasn't groomed.

His fingers dip between my legs, and I draw in a ragged breath when he spreads my pussy lips and moves his head between my thighs.

"What are you doing?" I croak. I know what he's doing, but I can't seem to imagine he would want to do it with me.

"I'm tasting my wife's virgin cunt," he growls against my folds without even looking up. Then he's on me; his mouth suctions against my clit while his tongue flicks the tiny bundle of nerves.

It takes everything inside me not to scream. The pleasure is unlike anything I've ever felt before.

With each lap of his tongue, I grow wetter, my arousal mounting while the impending orgasm claws at my insides.

"Oh... god..." I squeak, my muscles tightening.

"Come on my fucking tongue." His voice rumbles against my folds, and his fingers sink into my skin, holding me in place, with no possibility of escape. The pleasure builds and builds like a storm, and I'm blinded by it.

But right at the height, seconds before I'm about to catapult over the cliff's edge, he pulls away.

"Don't stop!" I beg, looking up at him through my lashes.

He smirks, the bastard actually smirks, and then he does something I never expected. He slaps my pussy. At first, I'm shocked. The slight sting of pain is jarring, but then he does it again, and I find myself gasping, the air getting caught in my lungs.

"You like me slapping your pussy, don't you?" All I can do is nod as he delivers another slap, this one right over my clit.

"Do it again," I beg, wanting the release that I know is coming.

Emmett leans forward, his nose brushes mine, and I can taste the desire he has for me in the air.

"You come when I say you come. Your pleasure is mine, Gwen. Your pain is mine. You're mine, and nothing, not even time, will fucking change that."

I feel his fingers at my entrance. I'm sopping wet now, ready to come at any second. He enters me slowly, and I know he can feel what I feel. A smile graces his lips.

"So tight and ready for my cock. Like you could make me believe that another man had you? Not when I sink a finger inside you and can feel how tight you are."

"I've been with others," I continue the charade.

"We'll see..." He grins and starts to pump his thick finger inside me while keeping pressure against my clit. "Come for me, liar... gush on my fingers."

The stimulation is enough to push me over the edge, my muscles quake, and I clench around his finger, abiding by his demand as I ride the wave of euphoria.

I'm trembling when I come back down. He's added a second finger, and a slight sting of pain fills my center as he stretches me.

He fucks me with his hand for a few more moments before pulling his hand away, bringing fingers to his mouth, and licking them clean of my arousal. The image is so erotic I find it hard to divert my eyes, but when he moves up the bed, his body covering mine, and I feel the brush of his cock on the inside of my thigh, I manage to direct my attention elsewhere.

He is huge, the head thick while his length's veiny and long. Fear tingles low in my belly. Perhaps I made a mistake by lying to him.

"Ready to eat your words, wife," he says a moment before his lips press against mine. He swallows my response with his kiss, and I fall deeper into the pleasure.

I'm vaguely aware of his cock pressing against my entrance, but I'm so caught up in his kiss, in the way he's touching me, hiking my thigh up over his hip, and holding me in place, that I don't register it's happening until he's slid all the way inside of me.

I gasp against his mouth. The pain clashes with the pleasure I felt previously, and it's like I'm being pulled apart. The burning in my core intensifies, and I want to tell him to stop, but I grit my teeth and stare deep into his eyes, feeling the tears welling there.

"You're a liar, wife, but that's okay. You're my little liar," he snarls and then sets a grueling pace, slamming into me at a punishing pace. The pain is searing, and I gasp every time he thrusts forward, but there is pleasure beneath the pain, and as his grunts and the slapping of flesh fill the air, another orgasm builds.

Beads of sweat slide down the side of Emmett's face. "Fuck, your pussy is so tight I don't know how much longer I'm going to last. I'm going to blow right inside your cunt, but first, you're going to come. You're going to strangle my cock with this virgin pussy."

"I don't know if I can," I whimper.

"You can, and you will," Emmett growls.

He slows his pace and snakes a hand between our bodies. He finds my clit and starts rubbing circles against it, igniting a fire deep in my abdomen that I've never felt before. Suddenly, I realize he was right. The pleasure builds and builds, and he starts to move a little faster.

My muscles tremble, and I bite my lip to stifle the scream that's threatening to escape.

"Come, come now!" Emmett orders, and like an obedient wife, I do. I explode, my entire core tightens, and my eyes drift closed as I pulsate around his cock.

"Oh, shit, fuuuuck..." he snarls, and then he's fucking me, his hands holding me in place with a bruising force. I'm so lost in him I have no idea what is up or down. I simply hold on to him, letting him drown in me like I drowned in him moments ago.

Then I feel it; he explodes. His warm cum fills me in spurts, coating my insides while he slows, his eyes squeezed shut and the muscles in his neck tight. He continues to come, so much so that I can feel the sticky liquid dripping out of me.

Sagging against me, he buries his face in the crook of my neck. We're both panting and sweating, and I know that he knows I was lying now. Still, I wait for him to rub it in my face.

Instead, he lifts his head, his gaze collides with mine, and he whispers, "You're mine now, forever and always, wife."

✧ ✧ ✧

Thank You so much for reading Paper Ring!

For more J.L. Beck & C. Hallman books check out our website. www.bleedingheartromance.com

Protected

Rebecca Zanetti

CHAPTER ONE

J ANIE KAYRS-KYLLWOOD SAT straight up in the bed, her heart hammering against her rib cage. She gasped and sucked in air, trying to breathe. Her mate stretched his arm across her and flipped on the bedside lamp.

"Nightmare, Janie Belle?" Zane asked lazily, his surreal green eyes sleepy.

"Vision." She shoved her light brown hair away from her face. "Two-pronged. Somebody is making a move against Garrett and Hope at the same time. We're being attacked." Garrett was her younger brother and Hope her daughter, and fear nearly froze her in place.

When Zane wanted to move fast, he did. In a second he was out of the bed, tossing her jeans over his shoulder to land on the comforter, his phone already to his ear as he barked in orders. The male sounded like the head of the demon nation, which he was, going from sleep to battle-ready in less than a human heartbeat.

Which his was not. He was half demon and half vampire, with the demon part pulling dominance.

Janie was human. Well, immortal human since she'd mated Zane. She scrambled to pull on her jeans and a blue sweater, bumping her hip on the dresser in the small room. They'd rented the cabin for a weekend getaway up in the mountains for some snowy fun, and she was too far from the center of the camp. Too far from her five-year-old daughter, and way too far from her adult brother, who was somewhere in Oregon. Or Washington State. She didn't know.

She yanked on socks and her tennis shoes before running into the quaint living room, where Zane was pulling on boots. "What's happening?"

Zane turned, his dark hair falling over his forehead. "Phone just went dead."

Janie paused. "Dead? Our phones can't go dead." There wasn't even a storm going on outside right now. They were in a safe camp with the rest of the family coming the next night. Right now, it was just the two of them and her parents with her daughter across the camp—way too far away. "What's happening?"

Zane stood outlined from the dawn light peeking through the blinds, his body strong and solid muscle. At six and a half feet, he should look gangly, but he was all brutal strength. Even the harsh angles of his face looked dangerous, and right now, he appeared deadly. "I don't know. When did you start having visions again?"

She lifted a shoulder. After having given birth five years ago, her visions had waned. "I don't know. Lately they've been coming back a little. Nothing strong but glimpses into the future that I can't decipher yet." She'd never been able to control the visions, and they often led to contradictory options, so it was a little terrifying to know they were returning. If only she could somehow force the images of the future into her brain that she needed to know about. "Please tell me you spoke with Hope before the phone died?"

"No. But she's having a sleepover at the other end of camp with your parents, and I'm sure she's still there. It's too early to go anywhere." Zane's voice remained level and calm, but tension rolled off him faster than an oncoming storm. "I'm so pissed I can't teleport any longer." The ability for all demons to do so had ended with an abnormality that had something to do with string theory and the p-brane, and hopefully would return someday.

"We still have the snowmobile." Janie took in a deep breath and secured her now light brown hair in a band. She'd been playing with different hair colors lately, and her new highlights matched her daughter's, because Hope had spent plenty of time in the sun during their last vacation.

Janie hustled to grab her coat off the hook by the door. If anybody could keep her baby safe, it was her parents. Her adoptive father, Talen Kayrs, was arguably the most dangerous vampire on the planet, and Cara had spent decades learning to fight, although she immortal humans only retained mere human strength. "I wouldn't have had the vision if there wasn't danger coming." She couldn't point to a factual basis for that claim, but she knew it with her very being. "We have to get to her and somehow warn Garrett." Why weren't they running out the door? "Zane?"

He dug into a pack and tossed her a green gun. "I don't know. I sense something. Someone. Shoot anybody who comes through that door."

"Absolutely not. I'm coming with you." She moved for the door just as the front window exploded.

✧   ✧   ✧

ZANE KYLLWOOD LEAPT for his mate, taking her petite form down to the ground and protecting her from the flying glass. Was that a grenade? In one smooth move, he had her up and covered by his body as he carried her into the bedroom and kicked the door shut with his boot. The entire camp was under attack? "Stay down." He placed her between the closet and bed so she could shoot toward the door or the window.

Then he went out the window, his senses settling into the intensity of battle. All questions of who was attacking or why, not to mention how, went right out of existence.

There was only right here and right now and destroying whoever had just threatened his mate and might be going after his child.

His boots hit the snow and sunk a foot, but he was already moving around the side of the cabin to the front, his gaze searching the tree line. He couldn't see them, but he could sense them. Maybe smell them. Burnt hamburger and whiskey. Seriously? He scanned the heavily snow-covered pine trees, zeroing in on the scent.

Two men. Human. What the hell?

He scratched the shadow of his whiskers, noting the sun rising over the mountain and sparkling on the snow. He could go straight at them, even though there was wide-open land between them. If humans were attacking him, it was just a mistake. A deadly one, but not one leading to war. They probably had no clue who he was or that he was the leader of the demon nation.

One thing he'd learned from watching the humans was that when a leader of a superpower was weak, the world burned. When the leader of the *most* powerful nation blinked, enemies struck with no conscious across the globe.

Zane Kyllwood had never blinked.

He'd keep his family and his people protected regardless of the cost. So he ducked his head and barreled across the snowy landscape straight at the trees. Gunfire erupted and bullets slammed into his shoulder. Human bullets? He shoved the irritating metal out with his mind and reached the duo, tackling them both into a massive pine tree. Guns dropped and the first guy grunted in pain while the other passed out cold.

Zane stood and brushed snow off his shirt, staring down at them.

The unconscious man was around thirty with a thin wool coat over jeans, and his nose bled through the snow. The other guy was a little older with deep lines extending from his eyes. He just wore a flannel and it appeared Zane's assault had broken both his right arm and his clavicle.

Zane frowned. Killing humans wasn't his thing, and they couldn't hurt him. But they had attacked his cabin with Janie inside. A grenade wouldn't kill her, but she could've been injured. "Talk."

"Ug." The guy spit blood and then wiped off his mouth, leaving a trail down his ice-crusted beard.

"Try again." Zane cocked his head.

The guy's eyes were bloodshot and his body shook. "We needed the money. Were hired to throw a grenade through the window."

Was he tweaking? Zane leaned forward. "What are you on?"

"Everything." The guy smiled and blood slid along his teeth.

This wasn't making sense. Unless…Zane turned in time to barely miss a sword slicing through his neck. The blade glanced off his shoulder and pain burst through his arm. He ducked his head and charged the attacker, catching him mid-center and plowing them both into another ancient tree. With two immortal bodies hitting it, the tree cracked in the middle, shooting a schism up to the highest boughs. With a furious roar, the tree split in two and fell, destroying other trees on the way down. It hit the ground with a resounding boom.

Zane backflipped to his feet just as three enemy immortal soldiers bounded out of the trees. The Kurjans had learned to mask their scents?

Damn.

CHAPTER TWO

JANIE JUMPED AS the ground shook from what sounded like a forest blowing apart. Grasping the gun, she moved for the window and eased herself into the chilly morning. Her breath fogged the air as she shoved through thick snow to the snowmobile and jumped on. She could hear fighting in the trees, and she could sense the enemy close.

While born human, she'd inherited some of Zane's gifts when mating him, and she knew when the Kurjans were near. The Kurjans were the enemies of all vampires and demons—by their choice. Her mate was one of the most powerful fighters in the immortal world, but their child was in danger, and she didn't have time to wait behind and just shoot people infiltrating the cabin.

She didn't have the patience for it.

If somebody came after her family, she just couldn't wait for rescue. For years she'd trained to fight—her entire life actually. As a human, even a mated one, she'd never have immortal strength or speed.

But she had a snowmobile.

She ignited the machine and swiftly turned it toward the trees, following a clear path across the snowy ground left by Zane. Zipping between two spruce trees, she quickly took in the scene.

Zane grappled with two Kurjan soldiers as a third stayed to the side, weapon pointed at the melee. It was a green gun, like hers, that shot lasers that turned into bullets that harmed immortals. Terror coated down her throat. For centuries the Kurjans had been unable to venture into the sunlight with their pale translucent skin. Their scientists had been hard at work to create an antibody to the sun for them and had recently succeeded.

Their skin was pale and their hair either black, tipped with red, or red, tipped with black. These all had black hair with bloodred tips.

She turned the Polaris again and shot forward, straight at the soldier with the gun. He pivoted and tried to fire, but she plowed into him, tossing him up into a tree like he was a beach ball. He fell back down to the ground hard, still firing, and landed on his face. She flipped around and ran him over, the snowmobile making a nice jump as she did so.

"Damn it, Belle," Zane bellowed, throwing one of the Kurjans so far he almost hit the damaged front porch of the cabin.

Janie slid off the machine, gun out and firing at the prone Kurjan on the ground. The immortal's body jerked with each bullet and his blood ran the icy ground red. Finally, he lapsed into unconsciousness.

The guy wouldn't die, but he'd be out for a while. She paused and sank to her knees in the snow.

Zane cracked the neck of the other soldier and then stood, facing her as the body dropped.

Her heart caught and seized. Sometimes she forgot. He was her mate and she loved him with everything she'd ever be, but even so, sometimes she forgot the raw beauty of the sheer deadliness in every line of his immortal body. He stood in the snow after having battled immortals and humans, a thin line of blood sliding down the side of his angled face. His eyes blazed an unreal green fire, and power cascaded along his steel-cut muscled form.

"I told you to stay inside the cabin," he ground out, his voice low and garbled. Blood dotted his shoulder but he'd probably already healed the wound.

"We have to get to Hope." She shook herself out of the stupor and kicked through snow to the machine, not surprised when Zane beat her there.

He plucked her in front of him as he sat. "We'll talk about disobedience and danger after."

"Humph," she said, grabbing the handlebars as he opened the throttle. She felt better after having run over the enemy a couple of times, but she needed to see her daughter. Yet she knew, deep in her soul, that her father would never have let anything happen to Hope. Even so, she couldn't help but breathe in relief as they drove up to Talen's cabin to see him standing over three prone Kurjan soldiers, all unconscious and bleeding in the snow.

"We were attacked," Talen said, sounding bemused. He was as tall and broad as Zane with thick dark hair and a jaw made of pure stone. While hundreds of years old, he looked thirty. Until one stared into his eyes. The years of war were stamped hard there. He kicked one of the Kurjans with his boot, watching the body flop. Then his golden eyes rose to check out Zane and Janie. "You two okay?"

"Yes." Janie jumped off the sled and rushed for her father, hugging him. "Is Hope all right?"

"Of course." Talen tilted his head to study the bodies on the ground. One stirred, and he kicked him in the jaw, ending the stirring. He looked at Zane. "Attacked." He sounded more bewildered than angry. "They're not very good. It wasn't even a good fight." Now he sounded regretful.

Zane nodded. "Let's take them away from the cabin and have a little discussion. Our phones were knocked out, and that's problematic. The Kurjans apparently have a new electronic weapon." He pushed off the snowmobile. "Belle? Stay inside this time." His voice was mild but a thread of pure menace flowed through it.

Considering the discussion with the attackers would probably include torture, maybe, she didn't argue. Instead, she rushed inside the cabin where her mother was sitting with Hope at the table, both eating cereal that looked like it had extra marshmallows in it. "Hi." She reached her daughter and gathered her in a hug. "I missed you."

Hope absently patted her arm, chewing happily on the sweets. Her sun kissed hair was already tied in braids and her blue eyes danced with the happiness found in too much sugar. "Hi, Mama. Talen gots in a fight." She sighed and wiped milk off her lips. "It was too short for him, though." She sadly shook her head.

Janie sank into a chair at the table and looked at her mom, who still appeared to be around twenty-five or so. They had the same hair color and blue eyes, so most people upon meeting them figured they were sisters at this point. Being immortal definitely had its advantages. "Any word from my brother?"

"No. Why?" Cara asked, concern for her son bright in her eyes. "Is Garrett in trouble again?"

"I don't know. I had a vision of danger coming for him as well as Hope." But there wasn't any time limit to the vision, was there? "It might not be immediate?"

Cara poured another mug of coffee from the pot on the table. "I'll try to get ahold of him when the comms come back on."

Janie gratefully took the warm drink. "It's so weird seeing Kurjans in the sun."

Cara winced and then reached for her coffee mug. "Right?"

Hope kicked her little feet beneath the table, wearing her favorite unicorn T-shirt and jeans. "The ones outside didn't come to hurt us. I donna know why they came." She smiled, showing yellow marshmallow in her teeth. "They don't want us to know they want more war yet."

Janie's stomach went cold as Cara stiffened. "How do you know that, baby?"

Hope shrugged.

Janie reached for her daughter's small hand. Hope was the only female in the world with vampire blood in her, considering vampires genetically only made males until Hope had been born. She was a miracle perhaps made by science or perhaps by fate. Either way, she had gifts Janie very much feared she hid. "Did you have a vision?"

"Maybe." Hope chewed thoughtfully, her eyes looking much older than a five-year-old's ever should. "Visions or dreams are the same, right, Mama? I dunno. I want the Kurjans to wanna be friends. Don't you?" She returned to her cereal bowl.

Friends? Could one become friends with their mortal enemy? It'd be nice, but not all people wanted the same things in life. Janie would love peace. The Kurjans didn't see peace as an interest, and without the same goals, how could they reach a peaceful existence, especially when the Kurjans just wanted more power? It was a mistake to assume that everyone would fight for the same things.

The sound of a helicopter split the silence outside.

Cara sighed. "I guess we're done camping and snowmobiling here."

CHAPTER THREE

B ACK AT DEMON headquarters in northern Idaho, just down the lake from the vampire headquarters, Zane waited until Janie had finished talking to her brother via a video conference. When she vacated her chair, he sat down and waited until she'd left the room. "If your sister thinks you're in danger, you probably are," he murmured.

Garrett was a solid form of strength, even through the camera. His sizzling gray eyes remained somber. "I can handle any danger. Just take care of my sister."

Zane lifted one dark eyebrow. "It's time for you to come home, G. Whatever secret mission you're on has to end. Now."

"No." Garrett grinned, for a second looking like that smartass kid Zane had once known. "Now get busy and get me a nephew, would you?" He clicked off without another word.

Zane rolled his eyes and wandered through the secure home to the bedroom, where he found Janie unpacking from their interrupted weekend. "Your brother wants a nephew." Was it possible they'd ever have another girl? Hope was a miracle and those probably came along only once in a lifetime, if ever.

Janie partially turned, her pretty face still looking stressed. "Hope is only five. He knows immortals take forever to procreate. It's shocking we have so many little ones running around right now. I think there's something to that old adage that any population grows after a war." She rubbed at a bruise on her wrist that must've happened when she'd driven a snowmobile into a Kurjan.

Yeah, that had been hot. Zane wanted to be irritated that she had plowed right into danger, but her ferocious heart was one of the reasons he loved her. Besides, the danger level had been rather low, and he'd known that the second he'd stepped into the wind. "So. Visions again?"

She bit her lip. "Maybe. I was hoping that since I had a vision, Hope would stop having them, but I doubt that's how it works." She removed her earrings. "Not that I'm positive she's having visions. Could be just dreams or that she knows things. Is psychic."

Zane wrapped an arm around Janie's waist, pivoted, and tossed her on the bed. "Something to worry about another day."

His mate's eyes sparkled as she landed softly and bounced. "Same with Garrett?"

"Your visions rarely have a time line. That kid could be in danger in a century." Not that Garrett was still a kid, but to Zane, maybe he always would be. Who knew? "The Kurjans did knock out our comms, which I think was the real reason for the attack. It was a test run." Which was why he'd dropped the captured soldiers outside of a Kurjan encampment all tied up and in the sun. Their new defense against the sun didn't last for too long, so they probably would've had a blistered sunburn by the time they were picked up. He couldn't bring himself to kill an inexperienced scouting team. Plus, he'd implanted trackers in their heels and recorders in their earlobes while they'd been out.

Janie slowly unbuttoned her shirt. "I'm surprised you let them all live."

He kept his face calm. "I let them live so I could gather information." She didn't need to know about the show of force his nation would take the next day to deter any future attacks by small Kurjan bands. He learned a long time ago that the enemy stood down when faced with a viable threat, and he'd also learned to always strike back with more force than the enemy had shown. It was the only way to keep his people and allies safe. "Now. About that son?"

"You immortals are so odd to have kids through centuries. Most of you, anyway. Can you imagine having a sibling hundreds of years younger than you?"

"It'll probably happen," he agreed, standing tall by the bed. "If my mother would take a break from robbing banks, I'm sure she'd like another few sons." He yanked his shirt over his head to toss onto the floor. "Are you worried about new visions?" He was.

"No. I've had them most of my life. But it'd be nice to be able to control them."

He sighed. While he wasn't angry with her, if she was having visions and if the Kurjans were doing test runs with new technology, danger was coming for them. Again. "We do need to talk about obeying orders in the field."

Her eye roll did nothing to ease his mind.

✧ ✧ ✧

JANIE LOVED PUSHING him. Zane wanted so badly to be modern and kind, while every instinct in his immortal body roared for him to control and protect. The war between his mind and his heart, in so many different areas, was what made Zane Kyllwood an excellent leader for the demon nation. It also made him the perfect mate for her. "I don't know how to obey."

"I'm aware." His jeans hit the floor as he moved forward, all male animal and muscle. "Take off your shirt."

All the fear, all the emotion of the morning pooled into one hot flare of desire. No matter how long she lived, she'd feel this for him. She narrowed her eyes even as flutters danced through her abdomen. "You want it off, you take it off."

He smiled like a panther finding prey in the brush. "My pleasure." Faster than she could track, he reached and yanked her shirt over her head. One snap and her bra flicked open. She removed it, scooting further up the bed, her gaze on the warrior still smiling at her. A killer smile, full of lust and something else. Something that would always be just for her.

His briefs hit the floor and, fully aroused, he put one knee on the bed, reaching for the button of her jeans. With one hand he unzipped and slid them down her legs, pushing her onto her back. His head dropped and sharp teeth teased sensitive skin as he tugged her cotton panties down to her ankles where she kicked them off.

She groaned as he nipped at an ankle before moving back up. Desire whispered along her skin and love filled her heart. She'd loved him since the first time she'd looked into the heated eyes now above hers.

"Ah, my Janie Belle. When are you going to learn?" A rough shadow ran along his jaw. His full lips quirked as he settled his bulk against her skin, the shadows ever present in his eyes lightening for this moment.

She reached up and ran her hands through the thick black hair he'd allowed to grow to his collar. "Never."

His lips twitched and one hand grabbed her ass to tug into his hardness. "I could handle anything in this life but losing either you or Hope. That matters." His eyes lost all amusement. "You gave yourself to me. You're mine to love and protect, no matter what." He shook his head, slowly entering her, inch by swollen inch.

About halfway in, he paused, dropping his forehead to hers. "You're perfect."

She lifted her head, brushing his lips with hers. Need, hot and full, pulsed where they met and she wrapped her legs around his hips. "Safety is an illusion, Zane. You know that as well as I." Although she believed in her very soul that he'd protect their little family to the death. Maybe beyond.

"True." His green eyes flared with a light nowhere near describable with the human language. "I would greatly appreciate it if you kept yourself out of danger, although you're a true menace on a snowmobile." He thrust hard, fully embedding himself in her.

Janie cried out, feeling him through her body, through her heart, possibly to her soul. Her tumultuous soul with its power and future destiny, whatever that might be. Immorality drew out fate, didn't it? Was it possible to have many destinies or fates to fulfill? She often thought so, and so long as Zane was by her side, she could handle them all.

Zane gripped her hips with both hands, one with a faded mating mark on his palm. "Do we understand each other?"

She grinned, even as desire warred with caution throughout her. "I seriously doubt that."

"You will," Zane said in an agreeable tone that gave her pause. He pulled back and slid slowly back in again. Several times.

Love and heat consumed her from the inside out. "Zane," she breathed, tracing his ribs one at a time down to the hollow of his back. Her thighs clutched him harder, urging him to go faster. "Go faster."

He chuckled against her collarbone, nipping a path to the soft spot where her neck met shoulder. He bit down, his mouth enclosing the space in heat while desire quickly replaced the sharp flash of pain. Nibbling up her jaw, moving too slowly inside her, he brushed her lips with a kiss. Then he descended and went deeper.

His tongue took hers, his mouth engulfed hers, his body heated hers.

"I love you." The words escaped from somewhere deep she couldn't fathom, from somewhere reality couldn't reach. There was only the two of them there. Forever.

He stilled, a warm flush cascading through his body as it covered her. His head lifted and the heat in his expression warmed that place so far from reality. "I have no doubt your love has saved us both through the years and will continue to do so. You're all mine, Belle."

A soldier with the heart of a poet. Janie smiled. Hers. Forever. "I'll protect you."

Almost all the way out of her, he slammed home with a grunt. "That's my job, baby." He increased his speed and the strength of his thrusts, and she urged him on, digging her feet into his butt. Sharp light filled her head and behind her eyelids as the orgasm rippled through her. She cried out his name.

He followed her into bliss, his fangs slicing into her shoulder in a mark as old as time.

She mumbled and was asleep before he moved. His chuckle followed her into a deep sleep where dreams left her alone until the morning and another vision struck.

This time, she turned over in the bed to see Zane on his side, watching her.

His gaze was alert in his rugged face. "I felt it. You had a vision."

She didn't question how in tune they were to each other. "Yeah."

"Do I need to get up?" He stretched lazily but the intensity didn't abate.

"No." She pressed her hand over his heart. "The vision is cloudy, but I saw both of our brothers in danger from their mates. Or in danger from the *threat* around their mates." She couldn't get it straight. "Sam and Garrett are together, riding motorcycles with the Grizzly MC, with women riding behind them."

Zane played idly with her hair. "When?"

"I don't know. There's fire chasing Sam and something invisible and sinister chasing Garrett." Why couldn't she see more?

Zane sighed. "Sounds about right." He rolled her onto her back and covered her. "Since there's no time line, we'll call them later. For now, let's get busy giving them both a nephew."

"Or niece," Janie said, tunneling her fingers through his thick hair.

Anything was possible.

✧   ✧   ✧

Thank you for reading this short story from the Dark Protector series and for donating to Ukraine! Learn more about the Dark Protector series and Garrett's upcoming book in June, called Garrett's Destiny.

rebeccazanetti.com/book_genre/dark-paranormal

Rescue Me

Samantha Chase

CHAPTER ONE

LAUREL BAY'S ANNUAL Spring Fling block party was known for the three F's: food, fun, and festivities. But this year they were going to have to add a fourth F.

Fighting.

Ivy Davis sat on the front steps of Donovan's Pub and shook her head. "I expect this sort of thing on St. Patrick's Day, but not during the Fling."

Beside her, her best friend, Ryleigh Donovan, said, "This is why we can't have nice things."

In front of them was a massive brawl with about a dozen people hurling insults and throwing punches. There was no way of knowing what specifically started it, but it wouldn't be long before the onlookers were going to end up getting drawn into the melee.

Ivy got on her tiptoes and tried to see if any cops were coming their way to try to break it up, but so far, all she saw were people just like her and Ryleigh helplessly watching. "Should we call the cops?"

Looking over her shoulder toward the pub, Ryleigh said, "I'm sure my dad already did."

Ivy followed her friend's gaze. "If all the wild arm gestures are anything to go by, then yeah. He's on the phone with them now." Turning back to the crowd, she heard glass break and said a silent prayer that someone was coming to break this up before anybody got hurt.

"You know what sucks about this?"

"The list is endless."

"First, there's a good chance you're going to get called into work," Ryleigh told her. "You know someone's going to get hurt, and you're gonna go and help out until the squad gets here..."

"Well, I am a paramedic..."

"I know, and it's awesome, but I would hate for you to get dragged into this mess on the first night of your vacation."

It had been a long time since Ivy had taken any time off and she desperately needed a break. Unfortunately, her friend was right. If anyone got hurt here tonight, she was going to jump in and do what she could until an ambulance arrived.

"This sort of thing is going to ruin a great tradition," Ryleigh went on with a weary sigh. "You just know if the city even plans another Spring Fling, there are going to be so many rules and restrictions put in place that it won't even resemble how awesome it's been for like...ever." She paused. "All because of these jerks."

"You know two of your brothers are part of those jerks, right?"

"Figures." They both fell into silence for a moment. "I expect it from Patrick and Jamie. They're both ridiculously easy to get riled up. I just hate how they sucked Connor into it."

For a second, Ivy was certain she misunderstood. But just to be sure...

"Connor? As in…"

"Connor Easton." Turning, she gave Ivy a weak smile. "Sorry. I guess I should have mentioned that earlier, huh?"

Connor Easton was Ivy's first boyfriend, first love, first…everything. He was a year older than her and they had dated through her last three years of high school. She'd had a crush on him long before that, but it wasn't until they were both in high school that Connor had suddenly noticed her. They always said they would start planning their future once she had graduated. Ivy had been confident he would propose to her as soon as she tossed her cap in the air.

But…he didn't.

A week after graduation, her entire world got turned upside down. She thought they were going to finally talk about their plans now that they were both done with school. Only…Connor had plans that didn't include her.

Granted, enlisting in the Marines was an honorable thing to do and she was proud of him for it. But when he showed up at her house that last day and told her they were through and he didn't want any distractions moving forward, he had pretty much destroyed her. He'd walked away as if he didn't have a care in the world and it left her feeling as if the last three years had all been a lie.

"Ivy? Are you okay?"

"What? Oh, um…yeah. Sure." She shrugged even as she scanned the crowd with new eyes. Connor was in there somewhere and…

"I really did mean to tell you he was home, but I didn't want to ruin our day. This is our tradition—hanging out at the Fling and eating our way around the block." Grasping Ivy's shoulders, she gave her a slight shake. "Just yell at me and tell me I'm a terrible friend and get it over with."

Frowning, Ivy knew she could say that and probably should, but…dammit, she was too concerned about what she was going to do when she saw Connor again after almost seven years. Before she could even give it some serious thought, a shot rang out and people took off running in all directions.

Ivy and Ryleigh jumped to their feet in a panic.

"Holy crap! Do you think…?"

It was total chaos for several moments before they spotted Patrick and Jamie Donovan.

But no sign of Connor.

"You two idiots!" Ryleigh cried. "What the hell was that all about?"

Ivy wasn't interested in why the fight happened. No doubt it was over something stupid. The only thing she was concerned with was catching a glimpse of the boy who had once been her entire world.

Not a boy anymore, she reminded herself. Connor was a man now.

And it was ridiculous how much she wanted to see him.

The brothers were laughing, and for some reason, it made Ivy snap.

"Where is Connor?" she yelled, and all joking immediately stopped.

"Uh…"

"He was right beside me a minute ago," Jamie said as he turned to look around. "Oh, shit!" He took off running and Ivy followed.

Across the street was a small park, and it took her less than a minute to realize someone was lying on the ground.

Connor.

Her heart kicked hard in her chest as she stopped at his side and instantly dropped to her knees beside him to assess his injuries. There was blood all over the right side of his face and she forced herself to go into paramedic mode. "Ry? Call 9-1-1!"

"I'm on it!"

She checked his pulse and looked for outward signs of where the blood was coming from.

"Connor?" she asked. "Connor, can you hear me?"

He groaned.

Ivy gently felt around his head and noticed the bleeding was coming from a gash above his right eye. There was a lump on the back of his head and she wondered if it happened when he fell. Other than that, there didn't seem to be other wounds.

"Connor," she said firmly, hoping to get him to open his eyes so she could look at them and see if his pupils were dilated. In the meantime, she took in his appearance as she checked his pulse. His sandy-brown hair was cropped much shorter than she'd ever seen it and his body was all broad and muscled. The boy she remembered was gone, and yeah...he was a grown man now. "Can you tell me what happened?"

After another groan that sounded more like a growl, he slowly opened his eyes.

"Oh, shit," he moaned as he opened his crystal blue eyes. "Am I dead?"

Ivy was too stunned for a moment to answer, but Jamie chimed in. "No way, dude. Why would you think you were dead?"

"Because my head feels like it's about to explode and I'm looking at an angel," he said.

Jamie laughed. "Not an angel, dummy. It's just Ivy."

She wanted to kick him for putting it like that, but...maybe later.

There wasn't time to say anything because the ambulance arrived and the paramedics ran toward them. Ivy stepped aside and gave his stats to Devin Lawson, her supervisor.

"Thanks, Ivy," he said as he examined Connor. "We've got it from here."

"Um...sure," she murmured, but then she caught the look of utter panic on Connor's face and was immediately back at his side. He reached for her hand and held it so tightly that she wanted to grimace. "Do you want me to go with you?"

He nodded.

"Okay, then." Looking up at Devin, she said, "Prepare for an extra passenger."

CHAPTER TWO

I VY WAS SITTING up front with the driver while Connor had to answer dozens of questions from the big paramedic who was treating him.

"You look familiar," Connor commented.

"Devin Lawson," he replied with a grin. "You and I played football together in high school. Welcome home, man. I heard you just got back."

"Yeah." With a mirthless laugh, he said, "Not the greatest reception."

Nodding, Devin agreed. "I hear ya." Pausing, he checked the wound on Connor's head. "The good news is this gash should just need some stitches. It's not too deep. The bump on the back of your head is probably going to give you a bitch of a headache for a few days. They'll want to do X-rays for it, though."

"I figured."

The drive to the hospital was short, and Connor was aware of Ivy following behind them and staying just off to the side while he was admitted. Within minutes he was in a triage room, and after a nurse confirmed all of his information, she left, and it was finally just the two of them.

She looked hesitant and scared and just as beautiful as he remembered. This wasn't how he imagined seeing her again would be.

Hell, he wasn't even sure if he ever would see her again. Especially not after his last deployment...

"You should sit," he told her, and it was crazy how gravelly his voice sounded. "We could be here a while."

Pulling a chair closer to the bed, she sat. "Head injuries usually take top priority. I'm sure someone will be back here any minute to whisk you off for a CT scan. Then, depending on what they find, they'll determine whether they need to admit you or if it's safe for you to go home." She paused. "Are you staying with your folks?"

"No, uh...they're currently at their place down in Florida and don't know I'm home." Looking back, Connor knew it had seemed like a good idea at the time—not telling them he was coming home, but now he wasn't so sure. "I'm staying with Jamie until they get back."

Her big green eyes went wide. "Oh." Then she paused. "Then I guess we should call Jamie?"

"Why? He already knows I'm here."

"Well, yeah, but...he'll need to come and get you at some point. I just thought..."

Unable to help himself, Connor reached out and took one of her hands in his. "Hey," he said softly. "It's okay. Once we know something, I'll call him. For all we know, he and Patrick and Ryleigh followed us here and are out in the waiting room."

Glancing over her shoulder, she said, "Maybe..."

He knew she was itching to go out there and see for herself, but he wasn't willing to let her go yet. When he gently squeezed her hand, she faced him. "Ivy...I..."

"Okay, Mr. Easton!" an overly cheery nurse said as she walked in. "Time to take you for some pictures!" She moved around the room and made sure he was secure in the bed before releasing the brakes on it. Then she turned to Ivy. "I promise to have him back to you just as quick as we can!"

He repeated her name, but she took a step back and gave him a weak smile. "I'm going to give Ryleigh a call and let her know what's going on."

"You're going to be here when I get back though, right?"

She nodded, but the nurse had them on the move and all he could do was settle in for the ride.

✧　✧　✧

A LITTLE OVER an hour later, he was back with Ivy and being prepped for stitches.

So not the way I envisioned this night going...

He still had a ton of questions he wanted to ask Ivy, but she was chatting with the physician and nurse who were working on him as if they were old friends. It was ridiculous to feel like an outsider—especially in this situation—and yet...he did.

Closing his eyes, Connor forced himself to relax. Getting stitches wasn't anything new, but right now, his anxiety was starting to get the better of him and he just wanted everyone to leave so he could have five minutes alone with Ivy.

"I thought you were off this week, Ivy," the physician said casually as he began stitching Connor's head.

"Yeah, wasn't this supposed to be the start of your long-awaited vacation?" the nurse added.

Even with his eyes closed, he knew Ivy was probably blushing.

"Um...yeah," she said quietly. "But are we ever really off the clock?" Then she laughed, but he knew it was from nerves. "I wasn't going out of town or anything. It was just a staycation."

"I can't believe you turned down going on a cruise," her nurse friend commented. "I love those things. All-you-can-eat buffets, tropical locations, and you know there are always a ton of hot guys on board. If someone invited me to go..."

"It's not really my thing," Ivy told her. "What I wanted most was to just be able to sleep in and relax and have nothing to do. I've got books I want to read, some recipes I want to try, and zero responsibilities. It's going to be glorious."

"And over way too soon. Mark my words."

It took another ten minutes for them to be done. "Just relax for a little while, Mr. Easton. I'll be back in once we have the results from your CT scan."

"Thanks, Doc," Connor said and didn't let out an easy breath until he and Ivy were alone again. Then he didn't hesitate before trying to get some answers. "So you're a nurse now?"

Pulling up her chair again, Ivy sat and fidgeted slightly with her hair. "A paramedic, actually."

"Really? Wow! Good for you!" Then he paused. "I thought you were going to go to school for nursing."

"That's how it started, but then I had the opportunity to work with some paramedics over in Magnolia Sound and I sort of got hooked. Apparently I do well in high-stress situations." With a small laugh, she shrugged. "I do love it, but I was starting to feel a little burned out lately and opted to take some time off."

"And didn't want to go on a cruise." He smiled at her. "You never did like being on the water." That was something he definitely remembered. They'd gone out on a friend's boat one time to go fishing, and she'd gotten so sick, they'd never gone again.

"And I still don't." Smiling back at him, he watched as she started to relax.

She wore her blonde hair shorter than she used to, but her face was still as perfect as ever. He wanted to tell her that but didn't think she'd appreciate it.

At least not yet.

"So, are you home on leave?"

"No. I'm done. I was discharged a few days ago." He didn't want to talk about why. She would find out soon enough.

All Ivy did was nod and Connor had to wonder if maybe this wasn't such a great idea. Perhaps he should have just had Jamie come with him because the awkward pauses were...well, awkward. In his mind, he envisioned him and Ivy talking easily like they always did. There had never been a lull in conversation or a time when one of them didn't have something to say. But right now, it felt like neither of them had anything to discuss.

Forcing himself to sit up slightly, he frowned when Ivy immediately jumped to her feet to help him. She placed some pillows behind him since the bed wasn't controlled by a remote. "I can adjust this from back here if you want to sit up more," she suggested, and he had no choice but to nod.

"Thanks."

As soon as she was seated again, Connor figured he had literally nothing to lose by simply saying what was on his mind.

"I didn't tell anyone other than Jamie that I was coming home because there were things I needed to do," he began as he studied his hands instead of her. If he looked at her now, he might not get through this. "I knew if I told my folks or reached out to any friends or family, people would want to see me and make demands on my time and...I wasn't ready for that yet." Pausing, he let out a long breath.

"Connor, you don't owe me..."

He didn't let her finish

"There's something you should know. Something I never told anyone." He paused again because this was the moment where an already shitty situation could get even worse. "I never planned on enlisting in the military, Ivy. My plans were the ones you and I made together. We were going to go to the same college and..." His words died off, but he forced himself to look at her. "I came home one day and my parents sat me down and told me they had lost everything—their savings, their retirement, my college fund..."

"How...I mean, I don't understand."

Join the club...

"Their financial advisor took off with everything. He wiped out the accounts of dozens of clients and disappeared," he explained. "They weren't even sure how they were going to live and provide for their kids, let alone put one of them through college. I needed to do something to ease some of their burdens, so..."

"So you joined the Marines," she finished for him.

Nodding, he murmured, "Exactly."

"Why didn't you explain any of this to me?"

"At the time, I was honoring their wishes. They were mortified and freaking out and...it was awful. I hated leaving them, but I hated leaving you more." He wanted to reach for her hand but didn't because she was sitting stiffly with her arms folded. "You have to know that I was ashamed too. Once they got their lives back together, I told myself I'd write to you to explain, but...I got deployed. And when I got back, it felt like so much time had passed and I didn't want to disrupt your life."

He was about to say more when Ivy stood and walked out.

CHAPTER THREE

IVY STORMED OUT the front doors of the hospital as her heart beat madly in her chest.

Seven years ago, Connor Easton had turned her world upside down, and here he was doing it again. It was one thing to hate him for being a selfish jerk, but how could she continue to hate him when he'd done something so utterly selfless to help his family?

He could have told me...

She paced along the sidewalk with every kind of pent-up frustration. People walked by and looked at her like she was crazy, but she didn't care. Hell, maybe she was crazy because the longer she paced, the more she realized it wouldn't have changed anything even if he had told her the truth all those years ago.

Other than her heart being broken due to rejection, it would have been broken because he was gone.

Tomato-tomahto...

So, where did that leave her now? Did this really change anything? The past was the past, and maybe Connor was just here to finally clear his conscience and then he was going to move on.

"Probably should have asked before storming out," she mumbled. Her phone vibrated in her pocket, and when she looked at the screen, she saw a text from Ryleigh.

Ryleigh: Hey! Any updates?

Ivy: Still waiting on CT results but he seems fine

Ryleigh: Whew! You doing okay?

Ugh...am I?

It was too complicated to get into in a text message, so she did the only thing she could.

She lied.

Ivy: I'm fine. We're just chatting and waiting for the doctor to come back in

Ryleigh: I'm glad you're there with him. Let me know when he gets the results. Jamie didn't want to bother him and I told him I'd keep him informed

Ivy: Will do

It would have been easy to stay outside and stew on Connor's revelation, but she didn't believe in running away from her problems. Plus, she truly was concerned about his health. So she'd go back inside and wait for the results with him and—no doubt—finish talking about the past so they could move on.

There was a part of her that knew it wouldn't entirely be possible. She'd dated a lot of guys over the years, but none of them ever made her feel the way Connor had. And if she were truly honest with herself, she'd admit that just the sight of him tonight brought all those feelings back.

She'd moved on because she didn't have a choice.

But maybe she had one now...

Feeling a little more in control of her emotions, Ivy walked back into the hospital and back to his triage room, where she found him lying in bed with his eyes closed. Her first instinct was to go over, hold his hand, and rake her hand through his hair to comfort him. Unfortunately, she wasn't sure that was the right thing to do. Instead, she went and sat back down in the chair she had vacated only minutes ago.

"I wasn't sure you would come back," he said quietly, his eyes still closed.

"I wasn't sure either," she admitted. Letting out a long breath, she figured she'd say what was on her mind and then they could finally move on. "Connor, you pretty much destroyed me when you left."

He nodded. "I know."

"And it took me a long time to get over it. To get over you. It was the hardest thing I've ever done, and while I understand why you did it, it doesn't change anything. I'm sorry you felt like you didn't have any options or that you didn't think you could share with me what you were going through, but...I appreciate you finally telling me the truth. I think that's the closure I needed, so...thank you."

Now he did open his eyes and he looked furious.

"You think I did this for closure?"

"Um..."

Slowly, he pushed himself up until he was sitting up straight. "This wasn't about closure, Ivy. I wanted to come back and see you to make things right."

"O-kay...but that would mean..."

"Look," he interrupted. "I know I have no right to ask anything of you. It's been a lot of years and there are obviously a lot of hurt feelings, but...I want a chance to make it up to you."

"Connor..."

But he wasn't through. "If things hadn't happened the way they did, you and I both know we'd be married now and have a family of our own."

It was true, but it didn't make it any easier to hear him say the words out loud.

"I want another chance, Ivy," he said firmly. "I know I don't have any right to ask and I have no idea what is even going on in your life right now, but I want you to know that I'd really like to make things up to you. To make things right."

Holy. Crap.

Swallowing hard, Ivy tried to figure out how to even respond to him.

Did she want another chance? Could she possibly go there with him again? She'd barely survived him walking away once; there was no way she'd be able to do that again.

On top of that, she had a good life right now—a good job and...and...

Yeah, I've got nothing...

Basically she had a job she loved, her family and her friends, but she wasn't living. It was something she had planned on thinking about during her staycation. A couple of weeks to just sort of relax and look at her life and see what she wanted to do from here.

You and I both know we'd be married now and have a family of our own...

It had always been what she wanted more than anything—to be a nurse and to be Connor Easton's wife. And for the two of them to have babies. Oh, how she longed to have a baby of her own. A few of her friends had gotten married and were starting their families, and Ivy had figured she'd get her baby fix by being the fun aunt.

But what Connor was offering was everything she'd thought she lost.

Or wouldn't have.

He was watching her with a serious gaze and no doubt trying to figure out what she was thinking.

"I...I don't know what to say." She forced the words out to buy herself some time. "That's a lot to ask after all this time. I'm not sure I can give you an answer just yet."

He sighed as he lay back against the pillows. "It's okay, Ivy. I'll wait. Hell, I'll wait as long as it takes."

"Connor...you have to know..."

The door opened as the doctor who had stitched him up came walking in. "Good news, Mr. Easton. Your scans are clear."

"Oh, um…"

"You have a mild concussion, so you'll need to rest and take it easy for the next several days. And if you continue to experience any pressure in your head, headache, confusion, dizziness, nausea, vomiting, slurred speech, amnesia, or fatigue, then you need to come back and see us, okay?"

He nodded.

"I'll get your discharge papers ready and the nurse will be in with them shortly. Take care of yourself."

Ivy pulled out her phone and was about to text Ryleigh when Connor spoke.

"What are you doing?"

"I'm letting Ryleigh know what's going on, and…you know…we'll need rides," she explained. "We'll need to let Jamie know that he needs to keep an eye on you and not let you sleep for too long. I'll go over the instructions with him to make sure he understands."

Connor reached out to stop her. "Can you just hold off on that for a minute?"

"Uh…sure."

Shifting on the bed, Connor sat up again and carefully swung his legs over the side.

"You probably shouldn't be doing that yet…"

But he wasn't listening. Ivy moved in close in case he didn't fully have his balance. Head injuries were tricky and the last thing he needed was to fall again.

Once he was steady on his feet, he took several steps away from her and she noticed he was limping. "Did you hurt your leg in the fight?"

"No." After he was on the other side of the room, he turned and faced her. "There's one more thing I need you to know." He paused. "Something you need to see." Another pause. "I'm not showing you this for sympathy. This is just because you deserve honesty."

It didn't take a genius to see where this was going.

He'd been in the military. He'd been deployed. He was discharged sooner than he should have been.

"Connor…"

Slowly, he reached down and raised the pant leg on his left side. His gaze never left hers. "Helicopter crash. I blew out my knee and I've got burns up my entire leg to my hip," he said as if she couldn't see them. "This happened three months ago. I'm going to have to have another surgery or two, and I'll probably have a limp for the rest of my life, but…I'm alive." He shook his head. "Not everyone on that flight is."

"Oh, Connor…" She fought the urge to go over and hug him, but knew he didn't want her to feel pity.

She was angry at how he was stupid enough to get in the middle of a neighborhood brawl when he was in this condition.

Something she'd bring up at another time.

"I know this may sound forward, but…" he said, interrupting her thoughts.

She knew what he was going to ask.

She just knew it.

But she said yes anyway.

CHAPTER FOUR

I DIDN'T SURVIVE three deployments to be taken down by a stupid street fight in my hometown.

He hated how weak he felt and how out of breath he was by the time they got to Ivy's second-story apartment, but he would gladly climb another ten flights of stairs if it meant being alone with her.

It was after one in the morning, and he knew he wouldn't mind a couple of hours of sleep, but considering he was the one to ask to go home with her, Connor figured he owed it to her to at least stay awake.

"Can I get you something to drink?" Ivy asked once he sat down on the couch. "Or something to eat?"

"I'm good." He paused and looked around at her place. It was a pretty-decent-sized two-bedroom apartment, but what he noticed more than anything was how she had put her personal stamp on the place. She had always favored more of a beachy decor, but there were tons of framed pictures of her friends and family scattered around, as well as a bookcase filled with a crazy number of books. Ivy always loved to read and she preferred paperbacks to e-books. And if there was a hardcover edition, she'd take that over everything.

She sat down at the other end of the sofa and yawned. "Sorry. Long day."

And that's when he realized he should have called Jamie and let him take him home. It was late, both he and Ivy were tired, and nothing was going to get settled tonight. It was purely selfish of him to even ask her to let him go home with her.

"Yeah, I uh…I probably should have just let Jamie come and get me. Sorry."

But she shook her head. "I know it's not late for him, and I'm sure everyone's still hanging out at the Spring Fling—or at least having drinks at Donovan's. Which means he shouldn't be driving anyway. Although…I could have taken you to his place."

"That's what I was thinking."

"I still could," she offered around another yawn.

"Ivy, I can tell you're exhausted, and to be honest, I am too. If you don't mind me crashing on your couch, we can talk more in the morning."

"That sounds good."

She rose and walked out of the room and Connor couldn't help but feel disappointed. He had hoped she'd at least think about the sleeping arrangements before agreeing so quickly to him sleeping on the couch. It was a decent size and he knew he'd be fine, but knowing Ivy was sleeping in the next room was going to guarantee that he wasn't going to get much sleep tonight.

Well…that and the concussion…

When she walked back into the room a few minutes later, she had a couple of pillows and a blanket in her hands but she didn't put them down.

If anything, she was hugging them tightly against her.

"Uh…Ivy?"

"Hmm?"

Connor started to rise to take them from her, but her words stopped him.

"I'm being ridiculous, right? I mean…you're injured. I'm going to have to wake you up a few times during the night to make sure you're okay."

"Um…"

"We're not strangers," she went on, more to herself than anything, "and it's silly to pretend we are. Obviously nothing's going to happen because you have a concussion and stitches and…"

Yeah, no need to let her keep going and hammering the point home on how he wasn't able to do all the things he'd really like to be doing with her…

He walked over to her and took the blanket from her hands. "Even if I wasn't all banged up, there is no way I'd even suggest doing more than sleeping tonight. It's been a long time and…" He shrugged. "I just wouldn't ask that of you."

"Oh."

Was it his imagination or did she sound disappointed?

Or was it wishful thinking on his part?

Probably wishful thinking.

"So…?"

"Right." Shaking her head as if to clear it, Ivy led the way down the hall to her bedroom. And just like the rest of her home, the space was exactly how he imagined it would be—a queen-sized bed with all-white bedding, light furniture, and a crystal chandelier. It was very feminine, and if it were any other woman, Connor knew he'd feel awkward as hell even walking into the room. But this was Ivy and he was just happy to be there.

She excused herself and went into the bathroom and he took the opportunity to strip down to his boxers so she wouldn't have to see all his scars and slid into bed.

And then paused.

Did she sleep on the right side? The left? The middle?

"Well…shit." Deciding the safest bet was to sit in the middle and let her tell him which side to move to. There was a TV mounted on the wall in front of the bed and he wondered what she currently liked to watch. Looking over at her nightstand, he saw a stack of books and was about to reach over to see what she was reading when she walked back in.

And that's when he seriously cursed the fact that he was injured be-cause…damn.

She wasn't wearing anything particularly sexy. If anything, it was rather plain. But the blue cotton hit her mid-thigh and had thin little straps, and all Connor could think of was peeling them off her shoulders and…

"I usually sleep on the right side," she said, interrupting his thoughts. Connor moved over as Ivy slid beneath the sheets beside him. She gave him a nervous smile. "I'm going to try to wake you up a few times to make sure nothing's gotten worse with your head."

"I'm sure I'm fine."

"This isn't up for discussion. Head injuries are serious, Connor."

He knew that, so he didn't even try to argue.

"Try to get some sleep while you can," she said as she reached over and turned out the light.

And that's when things got awkward.

He could feel the heat coming off of her body, smell her perfume, hear her breathe…it was like sensory overload and he wasn't sure what to do about it. Ideally, he would have been on the right side of the bed so he could lie on his right side and face away from her. The left side of his body was still a mess and it was painful to lie on it. If he turned onto his side and faced her…

"Connor?"

"Hmm?"

"Are you okay?"

"Yeah, how come?"

"You're just being very still. Are you in pain?"

As much as he hated to bring it up, he knew he wouldn't get any sleep if he didn't.

"With my injuries on my left side, I tend to sleep on my right side. But I felt if I turned on my side and faced you that it might be weird and make you uncomfortable."

"Oh. I guess that makes sense." She went quiet for a moment. "Do you want to switch sides?"

What he wanted was to haul her into his arms and not have this be so difficult.

"No," he said. "If you're okay with me facing you, then…"

She laughed softly. "It's fine, Connor. Go to sleep."

Carefully, he rolled onto his side and finally let himself relax. He was almost asleep when he felt Ivy move closer.

Connor held his breath and waited to see what she would do next, and before he knew it, she was practically pressed up against him from head to toe. He whispered her name and felt her warm breath on his neck. He slowly maneuvered so his arms went around her, and she hummed sleepily.

For years he'd slept alone—sometimes on a lumpy cot, sometimes on the ground, and sometimes in places that were too dangerous for him to truly rest. But this right here? This was the most perfect thing to happen to him since leaving Laurel Bay. No one would ever know how much he longed to come home and have his old life back. So maybe for tonight he could pretend; pretend the last seven years never happened, that this was his and Ivy's bed, and this was the life they had planned.

And then, for the first time in far too long, Connor relaxed and fell into a deep sleep.

CHAPTER FIVE

"CONNOR? CONNOR, YOU need to wake up and tell me what day it is?" Ivy whispered a few hours later. But as much as she wanted him to wake up, she was kind of relieved he was still asleep and maybe didn't know how she had practically wrapped herself around him in her sleep.

Like a damn boa constrictor.

"Connor? Come on, what day is it?"

His arms slowly wound around her and pulled her in close. "What do I get if I answer correctly?"

She had to fight the urge to laugh. "You'll get to go back to sleep."

"Mmm…not good enough."

And because she was half asleep and a little delirious herself, she decided to play along. "What do you want?"

"That's a loaded question," he said gruffly.

He was all warm skin and hard muscles, and Ivy had a feeling she'd give him whatever he wanted. "Tell me," she quietly prompted.

"A kiss. Just one kiss."

It wasn't the worst idea, she thought.

Licking her lips, she nodded. "Okay. One kiss. What day is it?"

Connor pulled her even closer and she could feel every inch of him.

Every. Hard. Inch.

"Saturday," he growled as he slowly rolled her beneath him and covered her lips with his.

Ivy didn't even have to think about it; she simply wrapped her arms around him and kissed him back. It was the kind of kiss that started slow and sweet but then just went deeper and deeper until it became almost carnal.

One leg came up and wrapped around his hip and then the other, and she didn't even care how needy she was being. This was Connor; being with him like this was as natural as breathing to her. It didn't matter how many years had passed; everything about this moment was comfortable and familiar and sexy as hell.

Raking her hands up into his hair, she wanted to tug on it, but it was too short. So her nails scraped along his scalp until he hissed in pain and pulled back.

Dammit.

Too late she remembered the bump on his head and now the moment was gone.

"Connor, I'm sorry. I wasn't thinking. I..."

He rolled off of her and slowly pulled her into his arms just as they had been a few moments ago. "Shh...it's okay," he said sleepily. "Go to sleep."

And so she did.

✧   ✧   ✧

THEY REPEATED THAT same scenario two more times—minus scratching his injured head—before finally getting up in the morning. Ivy worried about it possibly being weird now that the sun was up, but...it wasn't.

They worked together to make breakfast, and while they ate, he told her all about his time in the military. Her heart ached when he told her about his deployments and the accident on his final one that left him scarred.

"Do you know when you'll have to have more surgeries?" she asked.

"I told the doctors I wanted to come home and just take some time where I wasn't in rehab. After a while, it was starting to mess with my head and I felt myself slipping into a depression. I knew coming home would help get me back on track."

"Then why didn't you tell your family?"

Reaching across the table, he took her hand in his. "I told you, seeing you was my top priority." His thumb gently caressed her wrist. "It was important for me to talk to you, and then—depending on how that went—I'd be able to figure everything else out."

She laughed nervously. "That's a lot of pressure on me."

"It wasn't meant to be." He paused. "The way I ended things with us was my biggest regret. Every time I got deployed, I prayed I'd get to come home so I could make things right." Then he shook his head. "I should have prayed to come home in better shape."

"Connor..."

He waved her off. "I don't want to go there. I want to hear about you," he said as he smiled. "Tell me what it's like to be a paramedic."

Slowly, she pulled her hand from his and rose to get herself a second cup of coffee. "I'll be honest. I never realized how busy our little town was until I started training. Now I feel like we are a bit of a hotbed of accidents and injuries!" Looking at the kitchen table, she frowned. "Why don't we go sit on the couch? It's much more comfortable."

Connor agreed, but they sat down at opposite ends. Ivy told him about college and the courses she took and all the training she went through both in Laurel Bay and a short stint over in Magnolia Sound. Before she knew it, it was lunchtime.

"I had planned on shopping for groceries today," she told him, "so I don't have a lot here. But we could just order something to be delivered if you'd like."

"Whatever works for you," he said, but when Ivy stood to get her phone, he stopped her. "Listen, I don't want to be presumptuous here. I know last night there were extenuating circumstances and that's the only reason why you agreed to let me come home with you."

She wasn't sure exactly how to respond, so she waited him out.

"But...I'd really like a shower and clean clothes, and if it's okay with you, I'd like to ask Jamie to bring my stuff over."

"Oh, um..."

He moved a little closer. "I hadn't even unpacked at his place. It's just a couple of pieces of luggage and maybe...you know...I could stay here with you instead."

It was crazy how much she wanted to say yes, and rather than overthink it, she simply went with her heart and nodded. "I'd like that."

Leaning in, he kissed her softly before pulling back and smiling. "Okay, you order lunch and I'll call Jamie and let's see where the rest of the day takes us."

An hour later, they were sitting around her kitchen table with Jamie, Patrick, and Ryleigh Donovan—who not only brought Connor's luggage over but lunch too. Ivy wanted to be disappointed that their friends were horning in on what was supposed to be a time for her and Connor to get reacquainted, but they were all laughing and having such a good time that it was hard to be mad.

"What about Liam?" Connor asked. "He's still got another couple of years to go, right? I know he enlisted the year before me, but..."

"He just re-upped," Ryleigh said. "I think he's coming home for a short stay in the fall, but...who knows if it will really happen."

"What's the occasion? Or is it just a scheduled leave before he deploys?"

"Arianna's college graduation," Patrick replied. "Well...graduation party. She'll graduate in May, but she's got an internship in San Francisco for the summer."

"Mom and Dad really wanted to have a party for her right after the ceremony, but Ari was pretty adamant about wanting Liam home to celebrate with us," Ryleigh explained.

"Personally, I think we'll end up having a small party in May and the big one when Liam's home, so...more excuses to celebrate," Jamie said with a big grin. "So, what are you two up to for the rest of the day?" Then he winked and nudged Connor. "Bet you're wishing we'd all leave, huh?"

Connor chuckled as he shook his head. "It's good to see you still haven't grown up."

"Dude, growing up is highly overrated."

"Don't waste your time, Con," Patrick chimed in. "We've all been waiting for him to grow up. It's just not happening."

They all laughed, and Ivy looked over at Ryleigh and read the question in her eyes. With a slight nod toward the bedrooms, she stood. "You guys keep talking about all the ways Jamie needs to grow up. Ryleigh and I are going to have a little chat of our own in the other room."

Connor grinned at her. "I'm not even going to pretend I don't know you're talking about me."

Ryleigh patted him on the shoulder. "Awesome. Thanks."

Once they were alone in Ivy's guest room—which doubled as her home office—Ryleigh shut the door and gave her a knowing grin. "So...you took him home and now he's staying with you." Her smile grew. "You two move fast!"

"Okay, okay...I know it looks like that, but..."

"Ivy, come on! He asked Jamie to bring all his luggage here! It's pretty much everything he owns, and it's all sitting in the corner of your living room!"

Sighing, she sat down on the bed. "Is it wrong that I'm okay with this? I mean...shouldn't I be pushing him away a little or at least making him work for it a little bit?"

Sitting beside her, Ryleigh sighed. "If the two of you had met up at the Fling last night in a normal way, I think you would have. But it was wild and dramatic and...haven't the two of you been apart long enough?"

While Ivy knew she had a point, it still felt weird how...it didn't feel weird.

"Is this the right thing, though?" she quietly asked. "He left me and I was devastated and..."

"Did the two of you talk about it?"

Nodding, she said, "We did, and I know it was a hard decision for him to make back then, but...does that mean it's okay to just pick up where we left off?"

For a moment, Ryleigh didn't say anything. But when she did, she didn't hold back. "Ivy, you and I have been friends since the third grade, so I think I know you pretty well. You, my friend, have been miserable ever since Connor left. You date, but no one has ever made you forget about him." She squeezed Ivy's hand. "I know you've slept with other guys, but...it's like you felt guilty about it. Obviously you never got over him, and you've been given a second chance. Don't question it and don't make it more complicated than it has to be. Just...let yourself be happy."

"It just sounds too easy..."

"That's because it is." Standing, Ryleigh walked to the door. "Now I'm going to go and drag my brothers out of here, and I don't want to hear from you for a week. Do you understand what I'm saying to you?"

Unable to help herself, she laughed.

"Now go get your man!"

CHAPTER SIX

A S MUCH AS Connor enjoyed spending time reconnecting with his friends, it was Ivy he wanted to be with.

Alone.

He wished they could crawl back into bed to finish what they started multiple times the night before, but right now, he knew it wasn't possible. His head was pounding and the rest of him felt like hammered shit, so...

Definitely no sexy time.

Yet.

As if reading his mind, Ivy walked over with a bottle of ibuprofen and a bottle of water. "You looked like you were in pain."

All he could do was nod. There were so many things he wanted them to talk about, but...not right now. He swallowed a couple of pills and drank down half the bottle of water before he relaxed against the sofa cushions with a sigh. She was right there beside him, and just having her close helped him relax.

"How about this," she began quietly. "We just sit and maybe watch a movie or something with the sound on low."

"That sounds good."

There was no discussion about what to watch. Ivy simply put something on for background noise. As much as it pained him, Connor felt his eyes getting heavy and knew he would fall asleep.

And he did.

The next time he opened his eyes, the apartment was a little darker and he knew several hours must have passed. They were both more reclined on the couch and Ivy was curled up against him, snoring softly.

It was the most content he'd been in years.

Seven, to be exact.

There wasn't a doubt in his mind that this was what he wanted. Ivy. The future they should have started years ago. And while he realized it wasn't going to be as easy as simply saying he wanted a second chance, Connor knew he'd do whatever it took to prove to her he was in this for the long haul.

Shifting slightly, he aligned their bodies and softly kissed her lips in an attempt to wake her up. She instantly responded, and before he knew it, they were a tangle of arms and legs and Ivy was beneath him. His body was screaming for release—to strip them both bare and claim her again and again and again.

Unfortunately, the ibuprofen had worn off and his head was back to pounding. He mentally cursed as he slowly broke the kiss.

"You are beyond tempting," he said, placing one last kiss on her lips. "But..." Rolling off of her, Connor sat up and carefully raked a hand through his hair.

Without a word, Ivy handed him the pain relievers and the water. "I can't believe we fell asleep." She stood and stretched. "I feel like all we've done is sleep, wake up, eat, go back to sleep, and now..." Glancing over at him, she laughed softly. "It's almost dinnertime."

Yeah, only sleeping and eating probably isn't the best way to work through our past...

Ivy walked to the kitchen and he heard her sigh loudly. He slowly got to his feet and followed. "What's up?"

"Still didn't buy groceries."

Connor rested his hands on her shoulders. "Tell you what, let's get some Chinese food and then we can really sit and talk about...well...everything. Then tomorrow we'll go shopping together."

"That works."

After that, they settled into their own little world of domestic bliss. There was no other way for him to describe it. Dinner arrived and they sat and talked for hours about everything that happened after he left. Ivy cried, and Connor held her and cried with her. There wasn't anything he could do to change the past, but he was damn sure going to do everything he could to make their future everything they had once dreamed it would be.

Hell, he'd make it better.

When they went to bed that night, Ivy kept up the routine of waking him up every couple of hours, but he was beginning to suspect she was enjoying their reward system of kissing each other senseless.

And so was he.

The following day they went out and grocery shopped, and he learned that Ivy loved to cook, still had a serious sweet tooth, and was a bit obsessive about the quality of her produce. They ran into mutual friends and spent so much time talking with people that it took almost three hours to get back home.

Home.

Connor really liked the sound of that.

They made sandwiches for lunch and talked about their families. Ivy had two younger sisters who were both currently in college. He told her about how both his younger brother and sister were doing the same.

"So things got better for your folks after…?" she asked without really looking at him.

He nodded. "It took years. I sent money home, my dad took on a second job, and my mom took on every kind of job she could. She was a virtual assistant before it was really a thing. At one point, she had four different clients and I still don't know how she kept track of it all, but…she was the real hero in all of this."

"She was always amazing."

"That she is. Anyway, about three years ago, the financial guy was found and prosecuted. And while they didn't get all their money back, they did get about half of it. But over the years, they simply rebuilt." He shrugged. "They bought a vacation place down in Florida with my aunt and uncle, and that's where they are now."

"When will they be back?"

"In two weeks."

"Are you going to wait until then to surprise them?"

He chuckled. "That was the plan, but we saw so many people in town today, I'm not sure they'll all keep my secret."

"That's true. One of the curses of living in a small town. Everyone knows your business."

When they finished eating, something occurred to him. "I didn't have a headache today."

"That's a good sign," she confirmed with a smile. "The lump on the back of your head is practically gone. I noticed it this morning."

Yeah, she had been incredibly gentle every time she touched his head after that first night, but now he was hoping it meant they wouldn't have to be quite so cautious.

But he opted to keep that thought to himself until they went to bed later.

Outside, the sky turned dark and gray, and it wasn't until the first rumble of thunder that either of them realized the weather had changed. He remembered how much Ivy used to love a good storm. She used to say it was the perfect weather for snuggling under the blankets and watching a good movie.

Or making love.

At the flash of lightning, she turned and faced him, and Connor instantly knew she was thinking the same thing as they moved toward one another.

They were barely touching, but when Ivy looked up at him, he saw it all in her eyes. "Connor, I…"

"Yeah," he growled. "Me too."

In the next instant, he hauled her into his arms. The kiss was instantly untamed and borderline frantic. His need for her was more intense than he'd ever felt before—maybe it was because it had been so long since he'd had sex, or maybe it was because it was Ivy…

It was Ivy.

It was always Ivy.

They may have been young when he left—barely even adults—but that hadn't changed anything. He knew he loved her then, just like he knew he loved her now. Getting to know her now that they were older only made him love her more.

"Connor," she panted breathlessly. "The bedroom…please…"

There was no need for her to ask him twice.

Lifting her up into his arms, he strode down the hall to her room and placed her on the bed. He stripped out of his shirt as he kicked off his shoes and watched as Ivy pulled her own shirt up and over her head before tossing it to the floor. They were both naked in the blink of an eye, and as much as he would have preferred to slowly peel the clothes from her body, there would be time for that later.

They had an entire lifetime ahead of them.

Covering her body with his, Connor smiled down at her. "You are so beautiful, Ivy. I've missed you."

Her eyes shone bright with tears as she nodded. "I've missed you too."

Slowly she wrapped herself around him, pulling him close, and he knew they were done talking for now. Right now, he wanted to touch all her smooth, silky skin. Then he was going to taste every inch of her.

And he was going to love her forever.

CHAPTER SEVEN

FOR THE REST of the week, they stayed in their own little world.

Sort of.

Their friends did give them a few days to themselves, but then the invitations to go out to eat or go for drinks at Donovan's Pub started coming in, and as much as Ivy wanted to keep them in their bubble a little longer, it was a good thing for them to go out too.

This was going to be their lives.

Together.

It was super-fast and a little crazy, but…she'd been in love with Connor for far too long to waste any more time. He was back and he was hers.

And she'd never been happier.

Ivy had one more week off from work and she planned to spend every minute of it with Connor. For his part, he was happy to take another week before he really needed to get serious about finding a job and then deciding on when to have his next surgery. She hated it for him, but was relieved that she'd get to be there for him this time.

It was Sunday night and they had opted to go out to dinner, just the two of them. Ivy had agonized over what to wear since it had been ages since she'd gone out on a formal date. Connor looked incredibly handsome in his charcoal-gray suit, and she was glad she'd gone with the strapless burgundy dress. They totally complemented each other.

The steakhouse he took her to was one of her favorites. It was someplace they used to joke about when they were younger because they never could afford to go. So being able to go there for dinner together was kind of a big deal.

They had made reservations and were seated almost immediately. There was a small candle in the middle of the table and the whole atmosphere was very romantic. Connor ordered their wine, and once it was served, he raised his glass.

"This is something I used to dream of," he began somberly. "A fancy date night with my favorite girl. There were times when I thought it would never happen, and I hate how it took seven years for it to come to fruition."

"Me too. But I'm glad we're here."

"Here's to us and our future." He touched his glass to hers and it made her smile before taking a sip.

They ordered their meals and sat in companionable silence for a moment before Connor reached across the table for her hand. "I have something for you."

"Oh?"

He nodded. "Before everything happened back then, I had bought you something for your graduation that I never got to give you."

There was no way he could have possibly held on to a gift for all this time, could he?

She watched him pull something out of his suit jacket pocket with his free hand.

A ring box.

"If you remember, I worked for Coleman Construction over in Magnolia that last year and then washed dishes at Donovan's at night."

"You worked a lot," she said quietly.

"At the time, I was working toward something." He placed the small box down on the table between them and opened it. It was a simple gold band with a tiny solitaire diamond in the middle. "And for all those hours, I still couldn't afford much." He paused. "Ivy, this ring doesn't mean now what it meant then. Back then, this was all I had to offer. It was meant to symbolize how much I loved you and wanted to marry you."

Now she was mildly confused.

"And…now?" she nervously asked.

"Now it's a promise for something more," he told her. "I know it's too soon to ask you to marry me—even though we both know I'm going to. We need a little more time and I'm okay with that. But this ring is a promise to you that I will be asking." He gave her a boyish grin as he released her hand and took the ring from the box. "And I hope you'll say yes when the time is right."

Tears stung her eyes as she nodded. "Is it wrong that I want to say yes right now? That it doesn't matter how soon it is?"

"Ivy…this ring is…it's…"

"Perfect," she finished for him. "It's perfect and all I could ever want. You're all I ever wanted. I don't need another ring, Connor. That's not what it's about."

He slid the ring on her finger and sighed. "I know it's not, but you deserve something better. Something more." He squeezed her hand. "I want to give you the world because that's how much you mean to me."

"I can't believe you held on to this all these years…"

He shrugged. "It was all I had left of us and it was small enough that I could keep it with me always." Pausing, he leaned in and kissed her hand. "I never forgot you. Forgot us. Thank you for rescuing me that night in the park and for giving me a second chance."

Ivy felt the tears rolling down her cheeks. "We rescued each other. I felt lost and unsure of what I really wanted to do with my life, and then there you were. I love you, Connor. Always."

"I love you too."

The meal was great, the conversation flowed, but more than anything, it was the perfect night because it was the first big step toward their future.

✧   ✧   ✧

Thank you for reading Rescue Me! Want more from author Samantha Chase? Sign up for her mailing list and get exclusive content and chances to win members-only prizes!

www.chasing-romance.com/newsletter

A Beaumont Family Christmas Epilogue

Heidi McLaughlin

CHAPTER ONE

Rush

T HE POWDERED SNOW flies in front of me and ends up coating my goggles. People around me cuss. I ignore them. I don't understand how people can complain about the snow spray while on the mountain. If they don't like it, why in the hell are they here? I turn and face the hill and spot my best friend, Boomer, coming toward me. When he's within a few feet, he does the same thing. I raise my hand in a high five. "You just wasted that dude."

Boomer lifts his goggles. "Did you see the bowling pins? Who the hell stops on the slope? That shit is dangerous."

"It's vacation," I point out. "Lots of noobs out there right now."

"Yeah, well, they need to stick to the bunny hill or some shit. Leave the real stuff to the professionals."

Boomer's angry. I get it. It's hard when you're a professional and people who aren't as good as you get in your way. Their lack of knowledge on the slopes could cause an accident, and the last thing either of us needs is to get injured. We have goals, and those goals include five rings, our flag flying, and our national anthem playing when we win gold. Thankfully, we don't compete in the same disciplines because I'd hate to go up against my best friend.

"Come on, man," I say as I pat his back. "Let's grab some lunch." I raise my goggles and reach down to release my bindings. Boomer and I carry our boards toward the lodge, and once we're inside, we shuck off our jackets. The lodge is pretty warm, and we don't want to overheat. We're taken to a table near the large hearth and told our server will be with us shortly.

"Rush, look." He nods toward the table next to us, and thankfully I'm sitting at the perfect angle to follow his gaze.

Her eyes meet mine, she smiles, and it's like I'm soaring through the air, free-falling without a care in the world. I can't take my eyes off the girl, even when her friend leans in and says something. We continue to look at each other, and I do my best to memorize what I can. All I can see of her hair is what hangs down her back. She has it in a braid—typical skiing fashion—and she wears a tuque that matches the jacket hanging on her chair behind her. I tilt my head, and in response, she bites her lower lip, looks down, and then back at me.

Shit.

"Rush?"

I can hear Boomer, but his voice is fuzzy like he's underwater.

My chair jostles, and I glance at my friend. "What?"

He hands me a napkin. "Wipe your drool."

My eyes go to the dark cloth in front of me and then back to Boomer's. "What are you talking about?"

Boomer laughs and nods toward the table. "You're staring like a kid at the ski swap."

"Am not," I say but look back at the table. She's still looking, but so is the guy at her table. I frown and pick up the menu.

"Do you know who that is?"

I shake my head. "No, why should I?"

Boomer leans closer. "If I'm not mistaken, that's Eden Davis, that surfer girl I follow on Instagram."

I give Boomer a look, letting him know I have no idea who he's talking about. He rolls his eyes and pulls his phone out and presses a bunch of buttons, and then shows me his phone. I watch the video playing and am wholly impressed by what I see.

"There's no way they're the same person."

"Totally same. I'm telling you, that is Eden Davis, and she's like *legit* legit when it comes to surfing." Boomer is so excited that I can't help but laugh. I hold my menu up and look at this Eden again and find not only her but her friend staring. The girl next to her is cute as well but looks younger. I'm thankful they can't see me smiling because then Eden may figure out that I'm attracted to her.

The waiter comes, and we place our order. I do everything to avoid looking at the table across from ours. The paper from my straw is now in tiny little pieces, and I have turned Boomer's into a snake. I've folded and refolded my napkin, trying to turn it into a boat or sailor hat, but to no avail. I'm interested in what's happening at the other table, curious to know what they're talking about, and I want to ask her if she is this Eden person that Boomer seems obsessed with. Yet, I can't or won't. I'm not the type of guy who is forward with girls, at least not since winning the Snowboarding World Championship in the half-pipe. Since then, the female population finds me. If it's not on the internet, it's at school. Right now, the only place I feel safe is on the mountain.

Our food arrives, and it's a welcome distraction from the tension in the air. Every so often, I can't help but look at the other table, hoping she's still sitting there and also wishing they'd leave. Boomer clears his throat, and I glance at him. He's holding his phone up for me to see. "What?"

"She just posted that she's here. It's definitely her."

"You're obsessed," I tell him.

His mouth drops open, and he says, "Yeah."

"Why?"

He shrugs. "I guess it's the water aspect. She shreds those waves. And this one time, she posted a video of a shark behind her. It's fucking crazy."

"All I hear coming out of your mouth is how snow is safer."

Boomer laughs. "For us, yes."

"Maybe she'll teach you to surf."

"It's not me she's interested in."

With zero hesitation, I glance toward the other table, and sure as shit, she's watching me. Maybe she watched the championship and is trying to figure out if I'm the same guy who won. She's not on her phone, at least not at the moment, unlike Boomer, who hasn't put his down.

"You should talk to her."

My head moves side to side, slowly. "I'm not interested."

"Yes, you are. And I'm not saying you need to hook up and declare your love for one another. Just talk. She seems like a kick-ass chick, and honestly, you could use some fun in your life."

"I have to train. Unfortunately, the powers that be don't care if I won Worlds. I still have to try out for the Olympic team."

"So does she, in a sense. According to her website, she's heading to Australia soon for some big surfing competition, and everything I look up says she's going to win."

"How come surfing isn't an Olympic sport?"

Boomer shrugs. "Why are you asking me?"

I go back to my food and try to forget my surroundings. Stowe is my preferred mountain when I want to remain anonymous, and it's the only place that I purposely stay away from the half-pipe. As much as I love flipping in the air, the pipe here is a free for all, and there are too many people trying their own tricks. It's a recipe for disaster. Besides, if someone knew I was there, they'd all flock to that side of the mountain, and I wouldn't get any time on my board.

The three people across from us finally stand, grab their jackets and head out the door. Eden leads, and our eyes lock on each other's. It's then that I see her stunning blue eyes that look just like the ocean. She smiles, does the head tilt thing again, and it's like all is right in my world. It's like I can see for miles and miles, and there isn't anything in my way. My heart pounds, and I watch her walk out of the restaurant. When I turn back around, Boomer is laughing.

"Shut up."

His eyes move to space in front of my plate. A piece of paper sits there, and I reach for it. Inside, she's written her name and phone number.

"What's her name?" Boomer asks. I feel like I should make up something to get him off his high horse, but her name falls from my lips before I can stop them.

"Eden Davis."

"I knew it," he says as he pumps his arms in the air. "I told you."

I nod and study the paper. It's like I'm trying to memorize a number I'll never use, but I can't take my focus off her handwriting. It's small and dainty, and she connects her letters in a way I've never seen. It's different from what mine or my sister's looks like.

"She's not from here," I state.

"No, she lives in California," Boomer says.

"No, what I mean is, she writes like she's from another country." I show him the piece of paper, and he nods. "I'm trying to place who writes like this. I've seen it before, on the circuit."

"Why are you deciphering her handwriting?"

I shrug. "I'm just taken aback by it, I guess."

"Go talk to her."

"No," I say to him. "First of all, I wouldn't know what to say. I'm not some charmer or some guy who is quick on his feet; and second, I'm on school break, and I'm assuming she is as well. Just by what you've said shows me that neither of us has time."

"For what, a friendship? A relationship?" Boomer tosses his napkin onto the table. "You know you can be friends with someone and not be in a relationship. From what I see, you have a connection, and that is something you should explore, and you're both busy, so at best, you have someone to chat with when you're in your bunk at night. It's not a crime to get to know someone of the opposite sex. Your coach isn't going to make you run laps because you're talking to a girl."

"My dad will."

Boomer waves my statement away. "Rush, you're on vacation. Live a little. Your dad is thousands of miles away. He can't stop you from chatting with someone, especially someone like Eden Davis. She's a knockout and seems to have eyes for you."

He pushes his chair out and stands. "I'll meet you outside." Boomer leaves me there, still staring at the paper with her name and number on it. I slip it into the side pocket of my snow pants and make sure I've secured the button. While I don't plan to call her, I don't want to throw her number away.

When I get outside, I find Boomer chatting with the trio. He looks over his shoulder at me and has the biggest shit-eating grin I've ever seen on his face—bigger than when he won Worlds in slopestyle.

I have two choices. Grab my board and head toward the lifts, or go over there and introduce myself. The first option is obvious. Snowboarding makes me happy. The second option makes my palms sweat and my knees weak.

"Shit," I mutter as I make my way toward the group. Again, as soon as my eyes meet Eden's, my entire body feels like it's vibrating, the same way it feels when I'm about to drop into the half-pipe and go for the win.

"Hey, man," Boomer says as he puts his arm around me. "This is Rush Fennimore, and this is Eden Davis, Paige Westbury, and Mack Ashton."

"Nice to meet you." We shake hands, but either me or Eden make sure we're the last ones to do so. The moment her hand is in mine, I feel a zap of energy and enlightenment. I hold her hand longer than customary and watch her, looking to see if she feels the same spark between us. I'm probably imagining all of this.

CHAPTER TWO
Eden

MY DAD AND uncles write about love at first sight, falling in love, or reconnecting with someone from your past. And my mum, she's a die-hard romance reader and watcher. If she doesn't have a book in her hand, reading about some long-lost love, she's binging some new romance show on one of the channels. In fact, every room in our house has boxes of tissues at the ready because my mum is sure to cry at the drop of a hat.

I finally know what they mean when a guy walks into the restaurant with messy hair and red cheeks from being outside. His snow pants and jacket are white, but his gloves are red, and I heard avid skiers do this in case of an avalanche or they go off trail. The brighter colors are easier to find, so the fact that his suit is white—just like snow—doesn't make sense. I watch him and his friend meander the tables and rejoice when they're shown to the one next to us.

Despite Paige gabbing away in my ear, I'm fixated on this boy. Or do I refer to him as a man? Part of me hopes he's my age because if he's much older, my father will have a heart attack. Although, it's funny to watch Jimmy Davis squirm. He's having a hard time coming to terms with the fact that I'm no longer a child, even though I'll always be his Little One. He thinks I should stay twelve or thirteen or that boys should know better than to talk to me. My dad lost his ever-loving mind when I showed interest in . . . *what was his name?* For the life of me, I can't remember, but he was ten years older and promised to show me the way of the world. Thankfully, I know my worth and told him to take a hike. Of course, the distance between here and Australia probably played a part in us going our separate ways.

The hostess blocks my line of sight for a moment. I lean over to look past her, unable to take my eyes off the guy who has all my attention. Our food comes, and I barely mutter a thank you as our waiter puts the plate down in front of me.

"Get a grip," Paige nags. "It's like you've never been out in public before."

"He looks familiar," I tell her quietly.

"He looks like Quinn, which is why you're so fascinated with him," she retorts. Paige is right. If Quinn wasn't part of my family, I'd have eyes for him. I guess I sort of do and hate Nola for being in his life. Ever since he started dating her, Quinn has spent less time with me. I know nothing will ever happen with us, but he's still my crush.

Paige jabs her elbow into my side and snickers. "They're staring, and one of them has their phone out. Do you think they know who we are?"

Who we are? Paige wants to be famous, and I suppose, according to Page 6, she is. They've dubbed her the Rockstar Princess, and anytime she's away from home, she seems to make the papers. I know my Aunt Josie hates it, but Paige loves every second of it. She reads all the comments on her Instagram and eats up the attention, but unless you're a die-hard Betty Paige follower, no one knows who she is, and deep down, I think she hates that.

"No, I don't think so. It's not like we wear shirts saying who we are or who our parents are."

Mack coughs. "You do."

I roll my eyes. "Obviously, when I'm surfing, but I'm not now. It's not like I have a beacon on my jacket saying, 'I'm Eden Davis.'"

"Surfer Girl," he corrects. I hate that nickname and wish it never stuck. It's Quinn's fault. He started calling me this when I was younger, and it somehow made it to the media. Now everyone refers to me as Surfer Girl.

The cutie from the other table looks up, and our eyes meet. "Wow. I finally get it."

"Get what?" Paige asks.

"What my mum says about how she feels when my dad is around."

"You don't even know this guy," Mack points out. "He could be a stalker."

I glance at Mack and frown. "He's not Ted Bundy or Jack the Ripper."

"No, especially since they're dead. But he could be someone."

I roll my eyes at him. "You just don't believe in love at first sight." Truthfully, neither did I until this guy walked in.

"Yes, he does," Paige says. Without looking at her or Mack, I know they're holding hands. This is the only time they can be themselves and not have adults standing between them. I'm seventeen, and my favorite hobby is eavesdropping on adult conversations. I know for a fact that my aunt is concerned Paige and Mack are going to take things too far, and they're going to become teenage parents. I talk to Paige about the birds and the bees and tell her she can talk to me anytime. She also has Peyton and Elle, although the answer might vary depending on who she goes to. Peyton is Paige's sister-in-law and would likely tell her to abstain from sexual contact.

In contrast, Elle gives it to you straight. No sugarcoating. None of this you-have-to-wait-until-you're-married crap. When I went to Elle, she handed me a banana and a condom and taught me how to put it on, and said, "If he can't, you do it for him, or you leave." She also talked about being in love and all that, but has the give-no-fucks vibe when it comes to societal rules. What really gets me is that my Uncle Liam has welcomed Mack into his home because he has some family shit going on. I guess he's not that worried.

"You should stop staring," Paige whispers. "You look wicked creepy."

She's right. I try eating, but now I'm self-conscious and afraid I'm going to drip ketchup on my shirt or leave ranch dip on the corner of my mouth. He won't stop looking at me. Even when he has the menu covering his face, I can see his eyes peering out over the top. I suppose if I stop looking, he will too, but he doesn't, and neither can I.

I cut into my burger, using my knife and fork. Mack laughs because he doesn't get it. He doesn't know what it's like to live with my dad, who abhors eating with his fingers.

"They're going to think you're from another planet."

"Technically, I am."

"You're being a bit dramatic," Paige says. "You're from the United States, and you have dual citizenship. England isn't a planet. It's a country."

"I'm aware." Sometimes the age difference between us is clear, like now. I'm not some twit who doesn't know the difference between a country and a planet, but Paige sometimes doesn't understand sarcasm or humor, and it shows.

I continue to eat but do so without taking my eyes off the guy across from me. He's going to think I'm a stalker or have a staring problem. I supposed if he were to ask me what my problem is, I could lie and tell him it's a rare disease with no real name yet. Plausible, if he's gullible.

"Is this how you flirt?" Paige asks.

"I don't know. Is it? Is there a proper way to flirt?" Am I doing it wrong? Am I not sending the subliminal messages through my pheromones?

"You should give him your number," Mack says. "We're here until after Christmas, might as well hang out with people our age." I think Mack wants me to find someone, so I'm not the third wheel when it comes to him and Paige. Given a chance, they'll go off into the woods and do precisely what their parents are afraid of.

At the other table, the guy shows the cutie something on his phone. They're talking in hushed tones, and I'm unable to make out what they're saying. Of course, if everyone in the restaurant could stop talking, I'd appreciate it. I want to *hear* what he's saying to his friend.

"You should post a video or a picture and tag Stowe," Mack suggests.

"Why?"

"Because I'm pretty sure that his buddy is scrolling, and it might pop up for him."

I like Mack's idea and do as he suggests. My stomach growls as I load an image of me on my snowboard and type out, *Frozen water has nothing on this girl.* Once it's posted, I go back to eating, knowing I'll need something in my stomach if we plan to get a few more runs in. I'm thankful snowboarding has come easily to me. It would be rather embarrassing to still be on the bunny hill, learning.

We finish eating, and when the bill comes, I ask the waiter for a piece of scratch paper.

"What are you doing?" Paige asks.

"I'm going to give him my number—Mack's right. We're here until after Christmas, and maybe he wants to hang out. Hell, maybe his mom is the biggest *4225 West* fan, and he wants to bring her to our lodge to have a dance party or something."

Paige laughs so hard she snorts. "Can you imagine? Oh gosh, the drama. I sort of hope it happens."

She's right. The women would throw a fit. They're all nice on the outside but get near their men, and the claws come out. My mum is quiet, reserved. Touch my dad, and suddenly my mum has fangs and nails that are pointy daggers.

I write my name and number on the paper and fold it. After I have my coat on, I take a step toward the table where the cutie sits, watching me. I expect Mack and Paige to walk on the other side, but they're right behind me in solidarity. I love my family.

I set the paper on the table as I pass by, but he doesn't see it because he's watching me. I try not to panic, but my heart races ten times faster than normal. I don't want to turn around and pick it back up, but I'm tempted.

When we get outside, I walk as fast as I can away from the door. I bend and place my hands on my knees. "I can't believe I did that, and he didn't even see it."

"What do you mean?" Mack asks.

"He watched me the whole time, never looked at my hand or anything."

"His friend saw," Mack tells me. "I'm sure he will tell him."

"Okay, that's good, right? Holy crap, I can't believe I did that."

Paige puts her hand on the side of my shoulder. "Calm down. You'll give yourself a panic attack."

She's right. I nod and take a couple of steps toward our equipment when I spot the cutie's friend coming out of the restaurant. "Holy crap on a cracker." In an instant, Paige and Mack are next to me, and Mack's leading the conversation telling this guy who we are, and introductions are made. I want to ask him about his friend, but I don't have the courage to do so.

"I told my friend in there who you are. That video of the shark behind you is freaking awesome. Were you scared?"

I laugh and shake my head. "Not until someone showed me the video. I honestly had no idea he was there. Then, I freaked out. It's weird because I'm never worried, but at that moment, it's like my life flashed before my eyes."

"Her mother tried to make her stop surfing," Paige tells Boomer.

"No way, you can't quit. You're Surfer Girl."

I want to roll my eyes, but I refrain. I don't want Boomer to think I'm a snob. "Surfing's in my blood," I tell him. "I'll never quit."

"My buddy and I were just saying how surfing needs to be an Olympic sport."

"It is an Olympic sport," Mack points out.

Boomer's face deadpans. "It is?"

I nod. "It was new this year."

"Well shit," he says as he runs his hand over his beanie. "Damn, I'm sorry. I think I was probably training all summer and forgot to pay attention. Did you compete?"

I shake my head. "No, I'm not sure I'm interested. Some people think surfing is a hobby and should be treated as such. I'm not sure where the classification between hobby and sport falls, but people have strong opinions about it, and some feel surfing is boring."

"Those people have never had a shark chase them," Boomer says.

"There is that." I glance toward the door and find his friend walking toward us. Boomer didn't give us his name, which almost had me asking, but I held off. Our eyes meet, and I can't fight the grin spreading across my face.

"Hey, man," Boomer says as he puts his arm around the cutie. "This is Rush Fennimore, and this is Eden Davis, Paige Westbury, and Mack Ashton."

Rush Fennimore.

Eden Fennimore.

I clear my head and watch as he shakes Mack's hand and then Paige's. When he reaches for mine, I give it to him eagerly. Our gazes meet, and his caramel brown eyes instantly transfix me.

"Hi," I say in a sickly-sweet voice. "I'm Eden."

"It's a pleasure to meet you," he says. "I'm Rush."

Rush. That's what I feel when he holds my hand, a rush of . . . everything. Everything my dad and uncles have put into a song, or my mum has said about one of her favorite books—the rush of emotion, ecstasy, and longing. For the first time in my life, I long to touch someone in ways I've only read about or seen on television.

CHAPTER THREE

Rush

OUR CONVERSATION STALLS and the five of us linger. No one knows what to do or how to proceed. I can't seem to take my eyes off Eden, nor can she look away from me.

"Do you guys want to go sit in the lodge?" The words are out of my mouth before I realize what I've said. I know I had thoughts of talking to Eden more and could picture us sitting around the fire, but I hadn't meant to suggest it. I can sense Boomer staring at me, and I refuse to look at him.

Eden smiles brightly and nods. "Yeah, that would be great. I'd totally invite you back to our house, but my parents are there, along with my aunts and uncles, and no one needs their noses butting in our business."

I motion for them to follow me, and after we pick up all our gear, we make our way toward the main lodge. It's not really set up for people our age to hang out. When my father and I come here, he sits by the hearth with his legs crossed and sips on scotch or bourbon. It's very posh, but whatever. It's the only place I can think of where we can chat which isn't outdoors, where it's freezing.

We leave our boards outside and make our way in. Thankfully, no one is sitting by the fire. Eden sits on the couch, choosing a corner. I take the chair directly opposite her. I want to be able to see her while we're talking, and if I sit next to her, I'm afraid I might try to hold her hand or something.

"Good afternoon, Ms. Davis and Ms. Westbury. What can I get you and your guests?"

Eden turns red, but Paige looks at all of us. "What would you like? You can order anything."

"Um . . ." I don't know what to say and look to Boomer for help. He shakes his head.

Mack speaks up and orders something to drink, so I do the same, as do the girls and Boomer. As soon as the waitress leaves, Boomer leans forward and says, "What was that?"

"What?" Paige asks.

Boomer points. "How come the waitress knows who you are?"

Eden looks at Paige, and it's like they're having a secret conversation. Eden seems very uncomfortable, and I don't understand why. She clears her throat. "Our dads are famous," she says, but it's so quiet I can barely hear her.

"Wait, what?" Boomer asks. He's on the edge of his seat like the girls are dangling a chocolate chip cookie in front of his face.

"Paige's dad is Liam Page, the lead singer of 4225 West. And Eden's dad is Jimmy Davis, the bassist and piano player."

I watch embarrassment wash over Eden's face, and it confuses me. So, what if her dad is in a band or famous? I've never heard of the group, so what do I care?

"Wait, so your name is Paige Page?" Boomer asks. I stifle a laugh.

Paige rolls her eyes. "No, my dad uses Page as a stage name. But I am named after my great-grandparents. My last name is Westbury."

"Stage names are confusing," I say to no one in particular, and then I look at Paige and Eden. "I don't know your dads' band, so I don't think it matters."

Eden nods. "Some people use us to get to them. It's annoying."

"Still doesn't explain why the waitress came up to you," Boomer says.

"Because the staff knows we're here and we're to be taken care of," Eden says.

"Ah, gotcha," Boomer says, but I think he is still confused. I sort of get it. People come up to me and ask for photos or an autograph, but I've never had the hotel staff treat me differently. I watch Eden and Paige for a moment and wonder if they live under scrutiny. Are they free to do whatever they want, or do their parents monitor them because of the media? Now, I have questions but don't want to come off as some nosey guy who is only interested in them because of their fathers.

Eden clears her throat, and I glance at her, meeting her gaze. Jesus, she's beautiful and doesn't strike me as someone with a famous dad. Although, I'm not sure I've ever met anyone uber-famous, and I suppose all of that will change after I win the gold medal at next year's Olympics. I've seen what winning has done to Shaun White—and I'm not gonna lie—I want that kind of lifestyle. No more worrying about much of anything except landing the craziest jumps ever.

"What do you do?" Eden asks. "As in, do you go to school? Work? I feel like you know everything about me already, but I don't know much about you."

Boomer slaps me on the shoulder and laughs. "Rush here is going to bring home the gold in the half-pipe."

"Is that so?" Eden looks at me when she asks, not at Boomer. She wants to hear about me, from me, not him.

I nod. "God willing, of course. But . . . huh . . ." I'm suddenly nervous to tell her about myself. So far, I think Eden's a cool chick, and I want to hang out a bit more, but I bet she hangs with a lot of people way cooler than me.

Nah, I'm pretty freaking cool.

"I go to a private school, not far from here," I tell her. "It's a school dedicated to skiing and snowboarding. I'm on the snowboarding team, and this summer, after I graduate, I will start training for the Olympics."

"That's pretty awesome," Mack says.

"What's awesome is that he's only been competing for a year and is already one of the top boarders in the country."

Eden watches me, and I'm reasonably certain I'm blushing. "What's your event, again?"

"Half-pipe," I tell her.

"I'd like to see you perform," she says. "I feel like it's only fair since you have watched my videos." Eden laughs while I shake my head.

"Hey," a voice says from next to me. I turn, and my mouth drops open.

"Hi, what are you doing here?" Eden asks.

"Wait, you know him?" I point to Quinn Freaking James.

She nods, and Paige giggles. "He's our cousin," Paige says as if we're supposed to know this.

"Okay, now I'm officially jealous," Boomer adds. "This whole time, I'm thinking it's no big deal that your dad is in a band, but Sinful Distraction is my favorite band, and *holy shit*!" Boomer's voice squeaks at the end, and our three companions laugh.

Quinn looks from Boomer and me to the girls. "You cool here?"

"Yes," Eden says. "Rush was just telling us how he's going to win the gold in the half-pipe, and I'm trying to convince him to show us his tricks."

"No shit?" Quinn states.

"Uh . . ." I can't find the words and feel like I'm becoming the biggest fanboy in the history of fanboys.

"Let's head out there." Quinn motions toward the doors. Mack, Paige, and Eden all stand.

"It's not safe," I tell them.

"What do you mean?" Mack asks.

"There are too many people. A lot of novices, and it's not safe."

Eden looks at Quinn and raises her eyebrows. "I'll take care of that. I'll meet you out there." He leaves, and Eden stares at me, waiting for me to stand.

"What's he going to do?"

Eden sighs, and her face creases. "He's going to clear the pipe so you can board."

"What? How?"

"Well, he's going to go to the concierge and tell them that he wants to use the pipe, in private, and they're going to shut it down for him."

"Holy shit," Boomer mutters. "He can do that?"

"And so much more," Eden says. "Come on. I want to watch you. Maybe I can learn a thing or two."

The five of us head outside and grab our gear. When we get to the lift, we pair off and unfortunately leave Boomer to ride up the mountain by himself. He could've sat with Eden and me, but thankfully he took a social cue and realized I wanted to spend a bit of time alone with her.

Once we're on the chair, I find the nerve to say, "I hope you don't think—"

"That you're hanging with us because of who our family members are?" she interrupts me to ask. "I don't, and neither will Paige."

"And Mack?"

Eden looks behind her. "Our family is different. We're super close, very tight-knit, and do a lot of stuff together. But it's complicated. Like, none of us are actually related. My dad joined Liam's band eons ago, and he met my mum through my mum's best-friend Josie, who is Liam's wife. Quinn's sister Peyton is married to Paige's brother, Noah. Quinn's dad is the drummer for 4225 West. However, Peyton is the daughter—well, one of them because they're twins—of Katelyn and Mason. Mason died a long time ago, and Harrison adopted the twins, and to really confuse you, Mack is Noah's step-brother. Mack's dad raised Noah for a bit. It's truly complicated."

I hold my hand up. "This sounds like a soap opera."

Eden laughs. "It sort of is, but they're all super cool people, and we're a family. Like, if I need anything and I'm not comfortable going to my parents, I can go to my aunts, and they'll help me. Or go to Quinn or his girlfriend."

"That must be nice. It's just my sister and me."

"What happened to your parents?"

I shake my head. "Oh, no, nothing. They're around. I'm just saying I don't have a big family or a ton of cousins. Both my parents are only children. We occasionally see my parents' aunts and uncles, but it's nothing like you've described."

"My family can also be overwhelming," she tells me. "I didn't want to come on this trip, but Aunt Josie wanted us all here. I'd rather be in Hawaii, surfing."

"I'm sorry."

Eden looks at me. "Don't be. I think I might like the snow now."

Right now would be an opportune time to reach for her hand, but big bulky gloves prevent us from doing so. Instead, I lean into her, pressing my shoulder into hers and ducking my head a bit lower. "I really hope I don't embarrass myself."

"You won't."

"I love your confidence in me."

The lift arrives at the top. I reach for her forearm and help her off. She thanks me, and we step aside to wait for the others. Once everyone is off, we trek toward the half-pipe, which I'm surprised to see is empty.

"Wow, he's got some power," Boomer says. He straps up, fastens his helmet, and drops down.

"He's been waiting to do this all day."

"He's not doing any tricks, though," Paige points out. "Isn't that the whole point of this?"

"This isn't his element. Right now, he's checking for bad spots, so I know what to avoid when I go down."

"That's a good friend," Eden says. "Maybe I need a friend to fly a drone or something over where I surf so I'm not racing a shark to shore."

Everyone laughs, including Eden.

"Don't tempt your dad," a voice from behind says, and I recognize it instantly. "Rush, right?" Quinn sticks his gloved hand out to shake mine. "Quinn James. I'm Eden's—"

"I already tried to explain it," Eden interjects. "He called us a soap opera."

"*How Beaumont Turns* or something like that," Paige says with a snicker.

"Don't give your mom and aunts anything to think about," Quinn says and then claps his hands. "I'm excited to see what you can do, Rush. This is one of my favorite Olympic sports."

Nervous doesn't begin to describe how I feel. I nod, pull out my earbuds, and turn on my playlist. "I'll be back," I say as I wink at Paige. I have never wanted to impress someone more than I do right now.

Once strapped in, I move toward the front and lean back to keep my board stationary. I look at the pipe, imagine my routine and how I will land every trick and drop in. "Here goes everything," I say as I glide toward my first flip.

CHAPTER FOUR
Eden

RUSH COMPLETES A couple of runs. Each one is better than the last. He's pumped up, and his enthusiasm matches mine when I'm about to head into the water. After a bit, a small group forms, and the people around us chat about how Rush will win gold and how he's at the top of the rankings when it comes to his element. I make a mental note to look him up online when I'm back at the house later. I want to know more about him, but it's clear that he doesn't like to talk about himself, which I get.

"You're incredible," I tell him when he's finally back to the top of the half-pipe. "You look like you're having a blast out there."

"I am. You know, it's probably a lot like surfing. Do you wanna try?"

"No, she doesn't," Quinn says. I glare at him, but he ignores me. "Think about it, Eden. Do you know how to do a flip?"

I shake my head slowly, not only hating that he's right but also speaking for me. I should've been able to make this decision by myself. Granted, I probably would've made the wrong decision because I want to impress Rush.

"Yeah, that makes sense. I probably shouldn't have asked," Rush says. His face lights up, "There's a wave pool at the lodge. Do you want to go there and show me what you can do on a surfboard?"

"Wait, what?" There's an indoor wave pool, and no one thought to tell me? I could've brought my board. I could've spent my time in a warm place instead of on this mountain.

But then you wouldn't have met Rush.

Boomer sets his hand on Rush's shoulder and shakes his head. "They closed it down about three weeks ago."

"What?" I say again. "So, there are no waves?"

"Sadly, no. It would've been gnarly to see you in real life, though." Boomer holds up the hang loose sign, and I roll my eyes.

"I don't speak like that," I tell him. "Not even when I'm on the circuit."

"But that's half the fun," he says, looking dejected. Boomer walks away, looking like a sad puppy dog. I study Rush and swear I see a hint of sadness on his face. Did he want to spend more time with me or just see me in action? I like the idea of both.

"Is there a place we can go and hang out?" I ask him. "Our place will be too crowded, and we won't be left alone, especially once they find out you're an Olympic hopeful. Plus, my dad can be a bit crazy"

"Crazy?"

I nod. "I'm his only child, and he thinks all men are just like he used to be before he met my mum. And I've never brought anyone home before."

"How old are you?" he asks.

"Seventeen. You?"

"Eighteen," he says as he looks around. "We can go back to the bunkhouse if you want. It's like a college dorm, with a sitting room and stuff."

"Okay, give me a minute." I look over at Quinn, who is now chatting with a resort employee. I go to him and ask to speak with him for a minute. "Can you do me a favor?"

"Are you going to try and kill yourself?"

"No, but I like Rush and want to get to know him better."

"Okay," he says, dragging his word out longer than it needs to be. "What does that mean?"

I roll my eyes at him, and he smirks. "Well, what I'm asking is that if I leave with him and you go back to the house, can you not say anything to any of the adults, and can you take Paige and Mack with you or entertain them somehow?"

"What are you guys going to do?"

"Nothing but talk. I like him, and with everyone around, it's hard to get to know someone."

"How old is he?"

"My age, and he goes to some snowboarding academy where he trains all day. He's staying here on the mountain in some dorm thingy."

Quinn looks over my head and then back at me. "A 'dorm thingy?'"

I shrug.

"Share your location with me, and I'll make sure Paige and Mack don't say anything."

"Mack would never," I remind Quinn. I love Paige, but I don't know if she'd keep this a secret from Peyton and Elle. Peyton would tell Noah. Noah would slip, and my dad would find out. Damn family. I share my location with Quinn and then put my phone back into my coat pocket. "Thank you."

"You're welcome, and don't be late for dinner."

"I won't." I hug him and then make my way back to Rush. "Okay, I can go now."

"Is he your babysitter or something?" I look at Rush oddly, and his already red cheeks turn crimson. "Sorry, that was rude."

"I get it, but my dad is like most other dads—protective. If they all go back without me, I'm screwed, and the National Guard is looking for me. Quinn's going to occupy them for a bit."

Rush glances around and then pulls his phone out. "I'm going to text Boomer and tell him to go chill for a bit. Unfortunately, he'll think we are doing something scandalous."

"Will he post that online?"

"Oh, hell no. He respects everyone's privacy. But if I don't tell him to scram, he'll come with us."

"Got it."

After Rush sends the text, he puts his phone back. "Ready?" he asks as he holds out his hand. "The fastest way down is through the pipe."

"I don't know." Now that Rush finished his show for us, the patrol person has opened it up to other snowboarders. The pipe is busy.

"You know how to stop, right?"

I nod. "I'm okay, once I get down there. It's the getting down there part that has me a bit freaked out." I point to the slope that leads into the pipe.

"Follow me."

I do as he suggests, and when we get to the scary part, he talks me through how to get down. "It's sort of like crawling," he says as he stands in front of me on his board. Every time I adjust, he adjusts. I think he's there to catch me if I fall. Finally, when we reach the bottom, it's smooth sailing. Rush doesn't board ahead of me or tell me to hurry up, and at one point, he reaches for my hand when the slope becomes bumpy.

"Okay, that was fun. Much better than the hills the instructor has us on."

"Wanna go again?" he asks as he motions toward the lifts.

I shake my head. I'm not sure how to tell him I'd rather go to his room and talk, and thankfully he reads my mind. After we release our bindings, Rush takes my board and carries it with his. I feel like if I tell him I can carry it, he'll agree but not hand it back. We walk until we come to a brick building. He sets our boards against the wall with other boards and skis and then holds the door open for me.

"You can take your boots off here, just don't step in a puddle."

There are piles of boots in an alcove, spread about. "How do you know what pair belongs to who? They all look the same."

"I take mine to my room." He picks up our boots and takes my hand. We head up two flights of stairs, down the hall and around the corner, stopping in front of a door marked 215. Rush tries to maneuver the bulky boots under his arm and unzip his pocket simultaneously. He fumbles until I take the boots from him.

"I can help." I take the boots from him. Rush hesitates for a couple of seconds, but finally lets me take them.

He chuckles, and I think it's cute that he wants to do it all by himself. He opens the door and waits for me to enter. "It's not much, but it's cheap, and a lot of kids from the nearby high schools and colleges stay here. Most of us are on ski teams, though."

The door slams, and I jump slightly. "This is nice."

"It's not," he says, laughing. "It's a concrete box with two beds. We have to bring our own sheets and blankets. I bring my sleeping bag because it's easy to carry."

"How far is your school from here?" I set the boots down and walk to the window. The view is of the trees. I turn and look at him and see that he's taken his coat off, so I do the same. When he starts to unzip his pants, I turn away.

"I'm wearing pants underneath."

"Oh, right. Me too." I undo my ski pants. Once they're off, I fold and set them on the nightstand. I have never been in a room with a boy, and I'm not really sure what we're supposed to be doing. My heart is pounding. It's thumping so loudly I swear Rush can hear it. He steps closer. Close enough to touch me, and when his fingers touch my hair, I let out a small gasp.

"Do you have a boyfriend, Eden?" he asks quietly.

I shake my head quickly and meet his gaze, which is a huge mistake. He licks his lips, and his eyes roam from my eyes to my lips and back. "Do you have a girlfriend?"

He shakes his head slowly. "No." We're quiet and assessing each other. I take a chance that maybe he'd like it if I touch him and place my hands on his chest. I can feel his pecs through his shirt and imagine he's probably very toned from all the training he does.

"Have you ever been kissed?"

Back and forth, my head goes. I'm embarrassed and look down at the gap between us. Rush's finger caresses my cheek until he gets to my chin, and then he gently pulls my head up. He looks at me intensely, longingly. I want to say something. I think about telling him that while my dad tours the world, I'm sheltered because my parents are afraid something will happen to me. But I can't say anything because once I open my mouth to tell him I'm inexperienced, he presses his lips to mine and catches me off guard.

I stagger back a bit, glance at him, and touch my lips with my fingers. It takes a couple of seconds for my mind to register what happened, and once it does, nothing stops me. I step toward Rush, removing any space between us, and kiss him. I don't have the foggiest idea of what I'm doing, but he does, and *oh my God* . . . when his tongue touches mine, every part of my body feels like it's on fire. And even though we're as close as we can get—without taking this to levels I'm not ready for—it's not close enough. I want to feel his skin against mine and slip my hand under his shirt. He moans, and all I can think about is what it would feel like if he touched me.

Rush moves us to the bed, falling on top of the mattress. It's graceful, and we never stop kissing. But then, his lips are no longer on my mouth but around my ear, and he's tugging on my earlobe. It's then that I realize I am no longer in charge of my body. It has a mind of its own. My hips move toward his, and he returns the gesture. Rush leans back on his knees and tugs the collar of his shirt over his head, exposing his abs one at a time.

Holy shit. What am I doing?

Rush puts his hands down on either side of me and looks into my eyes. "We won't do anything you don't want to do."

"What if I want it all?"

His eyes are dark as he seeks the truth from me.

"Up until now, you've never kissed anyone."

"Up until now, I've never felt like kissing anyone."

Until I met you.

Rush smiles. "I'm happy I'm your first."

Be my first for everything.

He rests his head on his hand and sets his other one on my stomach. "When Boomer told me who you were, none of it mattered because I thought you were the most beautiful girl I had ever seen and way out of my league. But you stayed to talk to me, and now you're here."

"I've never looked at anyone the way I saw you today. It was like my whole world shifted and became clearer."

"Mine too."

"But . . ."

"How'd you know there was a 'but' coming?" he asks.

"Because we have this thing called distance hanging between us. You live here, and I live in Malibu."

He nods. "But I'm done with school soon and will have some time before training starts. Maybe I can come to visit, and you can teach me how to surf."

I sit up and pull my shirt off.

"What are you doing?" Rush asks.

"If you're coming to Malibu, you're going to see me in my swimsuit." I point out. Rush smiles as his fingertips ghost along my skin.

"What do you want to do, Eden?" he asks as he places a kiss between my breasts.

I don't know how I manage to speak, but when I do, all I can say is, "Everything."

✧   ✧   ✧

I hope you loved being back with the Next Generation Beaumont crew and getting to know Eden and Rush (he's a cutie). Do you need to catch up on the gang? New stories coming this year!

heidimclaughlin.com/all-books/tbs-the-next-generation

Zodiac Academy: The Shimmering Springs

Caroline Peckham & Susanne Valenti

CHAPTER ONE

Seth

I RAISED MY wolfy nose towards the full blood moon and howled, the answering call of my pack sending a rush of power slamming through my veins. I'd beaten Maurice down this very morning, the pack politics still a little rocky since I'd arrived at the academy and asserted my dominance. I'd had so many fights this week that if I hadn't been taught healing before I'd come here, I'd have been covered in cuts and bruises just like the rest of the freshmen were.

Most of them were trailing around campus being feasted on by Vampires and Sirens, beat on by Minotaurs and pissed off Dragon Shifters too. Well, one pissed off Dragon Shifter in particular considering there weren't a lot of those. Darius was taking a sadistic kind of joy in playing predator just like me and the rest of the Heirs were since we'd started at Zodiac. It was a new hunting ground, and the pecking order wasn't established yet, so we were having one helluva time establishing it.

The older years were testing us, trying to find out if we really were made from the strongest flesh and blood in the kingdom, and fuck did it feel good to unleash the power that had been brimming in my veins ever since our early Awakening.

I'd been pack leader over my siblings for years and no one had posed me a challenge in so long that it felt incredible to be able to let loose at last. On day one, I'd walked right up to the top of Aer Tower, stormed into the Aer Captain's room and kicked him in the balls. He'd shifted into a Griffin and tried to peck my eyes out with his giant beak, and I'd blasted him with every scrap of air power in my veins, sending him smashing through a window and then I'd beat up his little buddies one at a time too when they'd postured at me.

It was funny how arrogant some of the Fae in this place were, even though I was the Heir of one of the most powerful Fae in the land, they still fancied their chances. But I was an unstoppable force, a hellhound with a thirst for all the souls I desired. My mom always said every goal in life should revolve around power. Every win, every fight, every fuck, it all had to elevate my rank in this world. So I made it my mission in life to succeed in every way possible. I wanted to be the best alongside my friends, the four of us like stars right here on earth, deciding the fates of our kind. We were kings among cattle and I was ready to rule.

That very same day I'd taken my position as Aer Captain, Caleb had fought with the Medusa girl who ruled Terra House. Apparently she'd fallen to her knees and sucked him off right there and then, though maybe that was just my imagination running riot. I mean, that seemed like the natural thing to do after you got beat by a powerful leviathan like Cal. Or me.

It was what my new pack had been doing for me all week. Every time I beat a new challenger, they either fell into line and started begging for my cock, or they came back another day for a second or third beat down. I enjoyed both equally. Sex and fighting were the same kind of thrill, chasing a high while you sweated your way through the match. Someone was always forced to submit. And that someone was never me, because even if I was beat, I'd come back. Time and again. I'd claw my way back from the brink of death just to prove I couldn't be beat. It was in my blood, a fountain of power was bursting through my chest and I wanted everyone to drink from it so they knew the taste of a true winner.

Darius had claimed Ignis House in a ferocious battle with the Cerberus who had been ruling over it which had left the guy in three pieces in the Uranus Infirmary. I'd been there for that one, howling in encouragement as the two beasts collided on the lawn outside their house. I'd even gotten splattered with some of the blood from the hind leg Darius had severed when he'd tossed it aside. It had been epic. Well worth the detention he'd gotten for excessive use of Order skills. Besides, legs could just pop right back on and work right as rain after several days in the infirmary, lengthy magical healing and a whole lot of agony, so what was the problem?

I'd seen Max's fight too when he'd lured the Pegasus girl to the Orb and used the full strength of his Siren gifts to make her give out every dark and dirty secret she kept until she handed him her captaincy with tears running down her face. All of it was as public as we could make it. Our parents had encouraged us to make a splash, to hit the headlines, make the Fae here understand that we hadn't been bluffing when we'd told The Celestial Times of our immense strength.

Sometimes it was cruel, and sometimes I enjoyed it when it was. The darkness in me had grown since I'd gained my power, I knew how easily I could be corrupted by it. But when I was alone with the other Heirs, away from the pressures of the world and the call of ultimate, unending power, I found myself again. The guy who cracked jokes, who loved those boys deeper than I even knew my heart could go, and who wanted nothing more than to stay in that bubble for as long as I could. Ruling this world seemed so damn appealing so long as they were always at my side. It was us against the world, ruling from the top, because anything less was complete failure. It was what I'd been born for, what I was made to do, and I was sure I'd have crumbled under all of the demands upon my soul if it weren't for the fact that my best friends in the whole fucking world shared that burden too. We wore our armour on the outside, so thick and impenetrable that no one could get through it but us. But within it, we had our own circle of safety, comfort, freedom. It was a tiny space built just for us, but so long as it existed, I could face everything else. I could be the monster the world needed me to be, the ruthless creature who was revered and applauded and who everyone placed their faith in.

I barked to my pack in goodbye, veering off the path and darting away from them into the undergrowth to a chorus of mournful howls as I abandoned them, heading towards the three Fae who I needed to be with tonight.

This week had ben exhilarating, but it was exhausting too, and I needed to shed the war paint this evening and just *be*.

I soon made it to King's Hollow, our little sanctuary in The Wailing Wood that we'd claimed for ourselves the very first day we'd arrived here. There hadn't been many Fae powerful enough to unlock the secret of it attending the academy since our parents' time, so the place had practically been calling our names to be used for our own secret paradise.

I shifted back into my Fae form and pressed my hand to the trunk, the tree letting me inside as the magic washed over me. It had only ever meant to be for the most powerful of Fae here, and since we'd claimed it for our own, we'd strength-ened the wards around it so only we could gain access. Though sometimes

Professor Orion showed up here to hang out with Darius, promptly disappearing whenever me or any of the Heirs appeared. I knew Darius had been friends with him for years, but the dude had issues, and since he'd shot a peach into my mouth during sex ed the other day and nearly choked me to death on it for talking too loudly about my sexual experiences, I couldn't say I was much of a fan of him.

I shoved the door open at the top of the stairs, practically panting with how excited I was to see everyone and as I spotted Cal on the couch, I ran at him, diving on top of him and licking his face.

"By the sun, put your fucking cock away," he demanded, though he laughed as I continued to lick his rough cheek and nuzzle him.

I whipped around at the creak of a floorboard behind me, finding Darius trying to tiptoe away from me and I leapt on him next, wrapping my arms and legs around him as he cursed and I howled my joy at seeing him.

"Clothes," Max said firmly, pulling me off of Darius and shoving a pair of sweatpants into my hand, a wave of willingness washing from him into me.

I pulled them on, pouncing on Max next, making sure he got a big lick too. They loved my licks. Even when they grimaced and pushed me off, they never tried that hard to stop me. I guessed I was just irresistibly adorable or something. Magnetic, my mom called me.

"What are we gonna do tonight?" I asked as I released him, throwing myself down on the couch as Caleb flicked a finger and cast a vine to grab me a beer and plant it in my hand. I opened the bottle with my teeth, taking a long swig to quench my thirst from the run I'd been on with my pack. "Shall we watch some more of that Pegasus porn we found online? Two horns, one cup."

"Nah, I wanna party." Caleb downed his beer and I watched his throat work as he swallowed every drop.

"I wanna fuck with some other freshmen later," Darius said darkly, a smirk curling his lips as a little smoke filtered between them. He was a savage bastard, and he always got the wicked in me burning a little hotter. I was pretty sure we were a bad influence on each other, but not even the stars could tear us apart now if they wanted to. We were brothers forged and made, and there wasn't a force in Solaria who could crack the foundations we'd built for ourselves. Our paths were set. The Solarian throne was our fate and there were no roadblocks in our way to stop us from claiming it.

"Have you got anyone in particular in mind?" Max asked, excitement trickling into the room from him and making my own keenness heighten.

"A couple of nutcase royalists have been studying prophesies in the library, trying to find clues to our downfall and the rise of the old bloodlines," Darius said and we all sniggered at that.

Yeah, the chances of the Vegas rising up from the dead and returning for their throne was as likely as the peace sign making a solid comeback.

"Is Grus involved?" Max asked, his voice deepening a bit.

"She's always involved in that shit," Caleb said. "I think she's cracked in the head."

Darius shrugged. "I don't even give a shit about their insane endeavours, but a little birdy told me they're having a party tonight and guess what they called it?"

"What?" I bounced up and down excitedly.

"The Anti-Heir Hoo-Ha," Darius deadpanned. "And according to my source, they're planning some big, *hilarious* stunt to try and humiliate us."

Caleb's finger knotted in my shirt and he yanked me closer, making me look to him and realise his fangs had extended. He was fucking hungry and that made me kinda hungry too.

"Tell me more," he urged of Darius and I was pretty sure he hadn't even realised he had hold of me. Angry little Vampire. I loved when he got murderous. It made me want to howl to the damn moon.

"Alright, sit down." Darius walked away, grabbing another beer and sending a lick of frost out across the glass.

I dragged Caleb back onto the couch and Max smirked as he dropped into his favourite seat.

Darius had an air of danger about him tonight that had my skin prickling all over. I could always sense my friends' moods, whether they wanted my snuggles, needed my snuggles, or if it was simply not snuggle time. But the mood which always got me the most riled up was this one, the animals in us peering from our eyes and the atmosphere crackling with tension. The stars were turning our way, amused by what chaos we were going to cause tonight, and we never disappointed them.

Darius dropped into the wingback by the fireplace and the flames roared at his back, his Element taking charge of them and sending heat blazing through the space. He was left in shadow, silhouetted by the blaze at his back and for a second, he had a look of his father about him, his eyes narrowed and the slant of his mouth twisted by cruelty. A whimper left my throat and I leaned into Caleb, not liking the feel of Lionel Acrux here in our sacred space. Darius was rarely soft with anyone, but if he was, it was with us. And that was the truth of my friend, not the one moulded by his father's hands. I liked to play with power as much as the rest of the Heirs, but I didn't want to be carbon copies of our parents. I wanted to still be *us* when we took our seats on the Council, but sometimes it scared me how easily I could become a fierce and heartless creature. Where did the games stop, and the brutality begin? It all seemed to slip together so easily, especially now that we were in a place where we were encouraged daily to embrace our inner Fae, to crush our lessers, to rise like we were born to rise.

I shoved my worries down into the place in my chest which I never looked at, locking them away and straightening my spine as I faced the darkness in my friend with the darkness in me. I'd worn it like a cape at first, easily unclasped and folded away whenever I needed, but more and more it felt like a second skin, binding to my flesh never to let go. Between these four walls, I could still peel it off, but it was all too easy not to. The problem with darkness was that it tasted like rapture and freedom. And fuck did I want to be free.

"They'll be down at The Shimmering Springs," Darius explained. "Grus is trying to recruit for some sad little society that'll actively oppose us."

Max barked a laugh, swiping his thumb over his beer and making the liquid sail out of it right into his mouth with a touch of his water magic. "That girl irritates the hell out of me. I can't believe Orion put her on the Pitball team. Do you know what she said to me in Cardinal Magic yesterday? That I couldn't even diddle a dandelion if it bloomed beneath my fiddlestick and told me where to put it. What the fuck does that even mean?" Max scrubbed his knuckles over his chin.

"Yeah, she's nutso, man," I agreed.

"I could diddle a dandelion," Max muttered, clearly still caught up on what Grus had said to him as he frowned moodily at his beer.

"Just ignore her," Cal said, shrugging and slinging his arm over the back of the seat behind me, spreading his legs wide, looking like he gave no shits in the world.

His approach was always the chillest road he could take. He was less inclined to be an active prick unless the opportunity was right under his nose, then he couldn't resist. Though I swear he liked watching it more than doing it, his twisty little smile always following me whenever I picked out a freshman to play with.

"Oh, like it's so easy," Max tossed at him. "She's everywhere and she's willing to go against us single handedly too. I cast a silencing bubble around her in Water Elemental class so I couldn't hear her speech on the 'Depravity of the Charlatan Council' but she just started miming it to me instead!" Max's right eye was getting twitchy and I could see this girl was really getting to him.

"Don't worry, brother," I said, smiling at him brightly. "We'll crush her to-night and she won't bother you anymore."

Max offered me a half smile in thanks, though I could see his thoughts were still whirling about Grus. Fucking royalists. They were basically a cult at this point, just a few lonely larrys still clinging to the old ideals and pretending things could ever go back to the way they'd been. It was sick if you asked me. The Savage King had bent our kingdom over and fucked it in the ass without consent. Grus had to be cuckoo if she wanted that kind of leadership reinstated, though whenever that argument was tossed at these whackos, they always argued that the king's failings didn't dismiss the good he'd done in his earlier years, or the good the royals had done centuries before him. But what they forgot to take into account was that the Celestial Council were the solution to allowing failings like that to ever happen again. The Savage King had lost his mind and taken it out on Solaria, but if that happened to one member of the Council, then there were three others in place to keep them in check and overthrow them if necessary. It was a balance, a much better way of protecting the people of Solaria than allowing one royal on the throne to decide everything no matter what mood they happened to be in. I may have been a power hungry fuck, but I did take my future seriously. And when I sat on the Council at the sides of my brothers, I knew we'd do the right thing by Solaria because the four of us were bound by duty and had been trained to rule well our entire lives. There was no one better than us to lead our kingdom to greatness, and I believed that from the bottom of my soul. Because if it wasn't true, my entire life was null and void and I might as well just throw myself into the giant volcano in Beruvia and be done with it.

Darius told us some more about the plans he'd heard for Grus's party and I started to relax as we sank a few beers and our conversation turned to light-hearted stories from our childhood instead. I could feel the blackness in my chest giving way to rays of sunlight as I cracked laughs and bounced up and down on the couch.

"Do you remember that time we decided to run away?" Caleb said with a wide ass grin on his face.

"Oh my stars, we were like ten weren't we?" Max said, leaning forward in his seat as his eyes gleamed with the memory.

"It was right after that meeting with our parents where they impressed the 'importance of being an Heir' on us," I said, putting on a deep voice for those words as I mimicked Lionel.

Darius carved a hand down his face. "Fuck, I'd forgotten about that. I took a bunch of Father's gold in my backpack."

"We were gonna hitchhike our way to the Polar Capital," I said, a laugh tumbling from my throat.

"Yeah, only because we couldn't get our hands on any stardust. Even Lionel didn't leave that lying around," Caleb said as he chuckled and sipped more of his beer. "Do you remember that stupid blue flat cap you wore to try and 'blend in'?" Caleb nudged me and I pursed my lips.

"I still stand by that hat. Who's gonna expect an Heir to be wearing a flat cap?" I insisted and Max roared a laugh.

"You looked like such a dickhead," Max said through his laugh.

"You can talk. You turned up in that big trench coat that belonged to your dad," I threw back at him and Max's laugh stuttered out in his throat.

"It had like fifty magical pockets which I could hide shit in," he defended himself as Darius and Caleb shared a look, grinning stupidly.

"It was four times too big for you," Caleb said and I laughed, loving that we were mocking Max now instead of me.

"It trailed along the ground," Darius snorted and smoke poured from his lips as he lost it and Max gave up trying to pretend it had been a good idea, laughing along with us.

"My dad lost his shit when he caught up to us," Darius huffed and a grim memory crossed his eyes, making my stomach knot. "It was still worth it." He sipped his beer, his smile hitching back in place as he swallowed but there was something forced about it now.

"My mom made all of my siblings fight me for dominance again that week," I sighed. "And she wouldn't heal me between any of the fights, but she healed all of them."

"You still won though." Caleb smirked at me and my chest puffed up as I nodded in agreement to that, clinking my beer to his. His mom had just told him to 'take some time to reflect on the future he wanted' which he'd done by sitting himself down beside a window while it was raining before deciding he wanted to be an Heir after all, and that was that.

I leaned against him as peace washed over me, not sure if I even wanted to go out to fuck up Grus's party anymore. I just wanted to stay here, surrounded by my best friends where I didn't have to pretend to be anyone or anything. But if Grus was trying to make some stance against us, I knew the Fae in me wouldn't let it stand. We had to squash it before it gained legs like we did with any opposition we faced.

Another hour slid by and Darius finally got to his feet, the rest of us rising too as the energy between us changed. Our smiles started to slip and I felt a venomous beast awakening from slumber within us, wetting its lips for blood.

I felt the darkness coiling up around me and hugging my skin, and I embraced it, letting it sink within my bones and enjoying the rush it gave me. "It's game time." I bounced from foot to foot and Caleb rolled his shoulders, yawning widely and revealing his fangs.

"That blood moon making you hungry, bro?" I asked and Caleb's eyes flashed onto my throat, the Devil in his gaze. It was a well-known fact that blood moons made Vampires all kinds of hungry and that red beauty in the sky tonight was clearly having an effect on him. The moon really could be a dirty girl when she wanted to be, and I liked her style.

"The hunt is calling," he said, releasing a heavy breath and I realised the restraint he was holding onto tonight. But he wouldn't attack any of us. He could get blood anywhere he wanted and he knew we'd offer out our blood to him too willingly if he needed it. Although...I didn't hate the idea of him trying to claim it from me in a more thrilling way.

"I'll tell you what..." I said, swaggering closer to him as I offered both my wrists out to him, making his eyes dart between each of them like he was trying to decide between two mouth-watering desserts. "You can have a bite of me—"

Cal stepped forward and I danced away, throwing up an air shield to stop him advancing.

"*If,*" I continued, and he licked his lips, staring at me with an intensity that made my heart race. "You beat me to The Shimmering Springs without your Vampire speed." I wiggled my eyebrows temptingly and Caleb smirked.

"Done," he agreed and I shoved my way past Max, flying out the door and throwing up an air shield behind me. Caleb slammed into it with a curse, and I felt him tear through the magic with a flesh of fire at my back as he followed me down the stairs. But I was already out the door, howling to the deep red moon in the sky and racing off into the trees in the direction of The Shimmering Springs.

"Go on Cal!" Max called after us as footfalls pounded close behind me. "Munch on his neck!"

"Traitor!" I called back and Darius and Max's laughter made me grin as I pushed myself on.

I threw up air shields left and right, hearing Cal colliding with them with growls of anger and my laughter rang through the air as I chanced a look behind me at him. Mistake. I smashed into a wall of earth that Caleb cast and staggered backwards, my ass hitting the ground as I lost my footing and my head spun from the impact.

Caleb tore past me with a whoop and I growled, shoving myself up and taking chase, the two of us breaking out of the woods and hitting the rocky terrain of Ignis Territory. Cal was fast even without his Vampire gifts, but I was one determined motherfucker and I gritted my jaw and sprinted after him. I whipped his legs out from beneath him with air and he went flying up over my head as I took the lead again, trying to hold on to him as he dangled like a fish out of water, but he severed my power with a slash of a vine, the next strike of it slapping right over my ass.

I howled like a new born pup, stumbling to my knees and clutching my ass, finding my sweatpants ripped open across it and my skin stinging from the strike.

Caleb raced past me again, laughing his head off and I healed the sting in my flesh as I shoved myself up and hurried to catch him. He started ripping holes into the earth at my feet and I leapt over them again and again, panting heavily as I used my own earth magic to close some of the bigger ones which I couldn't jump.

"You spank my ass, Cal, I'll spank yours back!" I called after him, casting a paddle in my hand, my eyes locking on my peachy target tucked in his jeans. That ass was *mine.*

The springs came into view up ahead and I cast air beneath my feet, whizzing forward at a tremendous speed as I let the storm gather and propel me toward Cal's back.

I was as fast as a goose racing south for winter, as silent as a gnat caught in an updraft, and I collided with Cal so hard it knocked us both to the ground, our limbs tangling and our heads cracking together as we rolled across the earth.

Caleb softened it with his magic, making us bounce further until finally I was on top of him, him face down and me shoving his head into the mud. I yanked his pants down and spanked his ass with the paddle, victory making me grin ear to ear and Caleb threw an elbow back which smashed into my face and sent me flying onto my back.

I went down like a sack of shit, panting and laughing as I let the paddle dissolve in my hand and Caleb yanked his pants back over his ass.

"Motherfucker," he growled at me, his fangs out and laughter bubbling in his throat.

A massive foot stamped down on his back and he was flattened to the ground as Darius walked casually over him and Max nearly kicked me in the dick as he trampled me too.

"You both lose," Darius said as he and Max stepped officially into the rocky area which sloped down to the springs.

"Na-ar," I growled, getting to my feet. But Caleb was already up, running forward to make it onto the rocks before me then he wheeled around to face me, his eyes alight with his win.

"Blood," he demanded and I rolled my eyes, stalking towards him and shoving my wrist against his lips hard enough to make his head jerk backwards.

"You're a sore loser," he taunted, grabbing my arm and taking his time to decide exactly where his bite was going to go as he examined my veins.

He drove his fangs into me and I growled wolfishly through the pain, the alpha in me rearing up and demanding I fight him off. But he was the only Vampire in the world I could pull back my instincts for to allow him to feed from me. It didn't feel like he was taking from me, it felt like offering power to an extension of my soul. And the deeper he drank, the more my heart pounded, allowing more blood to pump between his lips as the groan that left him made a smile twitch up the corner of my lips.

Satisfying my pack members was in my nature, and I pushed my fingers into his hair just before he tugged his fangs free of my skin. My fingers tightened a little and I moved into him, nuzzling his cheek in a way that his kind didn't usually accept from anyone. But everything about me and the Heirs defied all the laws of Fae. Each of our needs were unique and often contradictory to each other's but somehow, we found an equilibrium between us, and so long as all of us were getting our needs met, it worked.

Caleb needed to feed just like I needed to touch. We were polar opposites, but here we were, each balancing one end of a scale like the Libra constellation embodied. That made a lot of sense to me seeing as my rising sign was Libra.

"Better?" I asked him and he nodded, his eyes reflecting that big red moon for a second and making him look more Nymph than Fae.

"And you?" he asked and I nodded, releasing him, though my fingers were always tingling for more. Because every time I spent too long without the warmth of another Fae close, I remembered the Forging my parents had put me through when I was a cub, leaving me on a mountain alone to defend myself for a full week. So now, whenever I was away from my brothers too long, I remembered that chill, I could feel it frosting my bones, fear swelling in me, begging me to find them once more, to reassure myself my kin were near.

"I'm always good when you're close, Cal," I said, giving him a sideways smile as we started walking after Max and Darius, the sound of music reaching us from the springs. My pants were still slit open over my ass, but I was kinda enjoying the breeze dancing across my butt cheeks. "Don't ever disappear on me."

"I won't," Cal swore, and those words gilded my heart in iron, strengthening it until it was an impenetrable thing that no one could get inside. No one but him and my boys.

CHAPTER TWO
Caleb

THE THUMPING OF music which sounded almost tribal drew us further into the embrace of The Shimmering Springs, clouds of steam rising up from the pools of heated water and sweeping around us to obscure our vision and hide our approach.

"The royal bloodline must not be forgotten!" Geraldine's voice called out loudly, echoing off of the rocks under the influence of an amplifying spell. "Nor the intended purpose of the Celestial Council – to serve like the underdogs they are!"

A noise followed her which held a few cheers, several drunken whoops and a whole host of booing.

I licked my lips, my heart pumping at the upcoming challenge and the taste of Seth's blood dancing across my tongue.

Since the moment I'd Emerged as a Vampire, I'd been offered up blood from almost every and any Fae I wanted, and I had spent the last few years sampling endless varieties of my favourite drink that there was, but nothing compared to the way the other Heirs tasted.

Nothing.

And with the blood moon hanging low, fat and red in the sky overhead, my desire for more and more of it was only growing.

Mom had called me earlier, reminding me that the bloodlust would run hot through my veins all night tonight no matter how often I fed, and I knew I was going to need a whole lot more than that taste to satisfy me before the sun rose, but it was a damn good start.

"Do not fall prey to the allure of those four dazzling dingbats who showboat around our most prestigious of academies as though they were born to sit their unworthy behinds upon the throne of our fallen king and his poor, murdered children! Remember that they are but dogs without a master, running loose among a field of sheep, slathering at the jaws for a taste of power which was never rightfully theirs!"

"And whose should it be then, Grus?" Max cried out as he stepped around a corner between two bubbling pools and the rest of us followed him into the open area where she was conducting her little speech.

Geraldine twirled to face us from her position standing on a tree stump which I had to assume she'd crafted using her earth magic, and the explosion of turquoise taffeta which she had wrapped around her body whipped around from the movement as she raised her chin and looked down on us.

"Oh-ho!" she cried. "Speak of the slanderous salamanders and they shall cometh!"

The crowd of students who were gathered around her all stiffened as they took in our arrival, the thirty or so of them shifting where they stood or sat around the rocky area, most of them in bathing suits and looking like they'd been here enjoying the springs rather than showing up specifically for this gathering of the Geraldine gang.

I looked at the poster which Geraldine had stuck to a rock behind her, the words on it bringing a snort of amusement to my lips.

Join the Maintainers Of Idealist Sovereign Traditions – get your M.O.I.S.T. badge today!

There was a space at the bottom of her poster for people to add their names if they wanted to join her moist club. She had precisely one sign up and that was herself, the big brown M.O.I.S.T. badge pinned proudly over the chest of her impressive dress and a bucket more of them sat waiting beside her in hopes of someone claiming one.

"Who are you calling a salamander, Grus?" Max barked, sauntering towards her and tugging his shirt off to reveal the navy scales which were crawling across his skin.

Seth nudged me with an excited grin and I smiled back, both of us waiting to see which emotion he'd use to bring her to heel first.

"Take a moment to ponder upon your reflection, you great trout," she said dismissively. "Then your question shall answer itself."

Fear crept along my spine as Max flexed his fingers and I gave in to the chill of it for a moment before tightening my mental shields and blocking him out.

The crowd recoiled as they felt the press of his gifts and the four of us stalked forward slowly, the air crackling with tension as everyone waited to see what would happen next, and the feeling of fear grew stronger and stronger.

Darius reached out to shut off the music, taking a bottle from the table of drinks which had been gathered for this little party and knocking the cap off before taking a long drink from it.

His eyes brightened as he swallowed and he grinned widely just as one of the girls from his House stepped forward and touched a hand to his arm.

"Umm, Darius? I just thought you should know that bottle has Footloose Faraday in it," she said, biting her lip in a way which was definitely an attempt at seduction as she twisted a lock of red hair around her finger. She was pretty hot, but either Darius wasn't in the mood to get laid or just wasn't into her because he barely even spared her a glance, his focus on Max who was still facing off against Grus who was scowling at him as she fought off the effects of his Siren gifts.

"Thanks, Marge," Darius said dismissively, shaking her off and offering the bottle to me. "I noticed."

I shrugged as I accepted it, deciding I was up for letting my inhibitions drop and taking a long drink of the magical beverage for myself, the heat of it tingling all the way down to the pit of my stomach as I swallowed.

Seth snatched it from my hand before I was even done, the Wolfish look on his face making me laugh even as I cursed him out and the drink sloshed down my chest, soaking through my shirt.

"You're looking a little tense there, Grus," Max growled as he stalked closer to her but I had to say, I couldn't see it. She had her chin raised high, that same haughty look on her face which she always got when she laid her eyes on any of us as she just stared him down and challenged him to do his worst.

"I do not fear the mind games of a petulant patty cake playing at being a ruler," she sneered. "No tricks of your fancy fins will send me a-splutter, you cantankerous crustation."

Max gritted his jaw as he stepped closer to her and the people at the front of the crowd cowered away, one of them shrieking in terror and tearing off between the rock pools as the overflow of Max's gifts got too much for him to handle.

Seth sank the last of the Footloose Faraday, his eyes flashing silver with his inner Wolf as he tossed the bottle aside, smashing it against a rock and making another student scream loudly before the noise turned into a startled whinny as she lost control and shifted into her Pegasus form, her bikini exploding and the elastic snapping out to slap Max in the eye.

He cried out as he lost his hold on his gift and my gut plummeted as unrestrained terror poured from him and slammed into every single person surrounding us without aim.

Seth howled as he was damn near trampled by a fleeing Griffin and Darius barked a laugh as he ducked beneath the claws of a Manticore as it took off into the sky, a half shredded pair of swimming trunks hanging from one of its furry ass cheeks.

I shot away from the carnage and sobbing students, bolstering my mental shields as the wall of terror crashed over everyone and the sight of them all running got the bloodlust in me pumping to new heights.

I sped between the bodies, my fangs snapping out and the desire to take chase consuming me while a little voice in the back of my head purred why not?

The voice was about three parts the magical drink and four parts my own animal instincts, and before I could stop myself I was shooting towards the girl who still stood above the chaos in a swathe of turquoise taffeta while she yelled out for people to grab a M.O.I.S.T. badge before they left.

Geraldine shrieked as I collided with her but before she could do a thing to fight me off, I had her pressed against the rocky side of one of the pools and my fangs were sinking deep into the flesh of her throat.

I groaned at the taste of her blood as it rolled over my tongue, my fists locking in the gauzy fabric which covered her body as I took a deep drink from her and felt the rush of the blood moon's influence pouring down on me.

Damn she was powerful, her blood a mix of flavours which reminded me of that confusing sensation of listening to three different songs while they were all playing at once.

"Remove your fangs from my gizzard you curly haired Lothario or I shall be forced to defend myself!" Geraldine cried, her hands slapping against my shoulders with considerably more vigour than my prey could normally manage once under the influence of my venom.

I snarled at her as I drank deeper, the bloodlust making my muscles tense as I took what I needed, swallowing greedily and ignoring her protests.

There was a rustle of taffeta like a snake striking through the long grass and her knee collided with my dick so suddenly that I jerked back with a curse, releasing her from my bite and wheezing as I cupped my junk.

"By the fucking stars," I hissed a moment before a fist slammed into my jaw and I was knocked on my ass by Max as he bared his teeth at me.

"Back off, asshole, this is my fight," he warned, his eyes flashing with a challenge which I wasn't going to give in to.

I healed my balls with a surge of magic and shot to my feet, a smile cracking across my face as I faced off against my brother and prepared for the fight he was offering.

But before we could get into it, a flash of movement caught my attention from my left and my eyes widened in alarm a second before Geraldine hurled a huge glob of stinking, dripping mud right at us.

I shot away with my Vampire speed half a beat before the strike could land but Max wasn't so lucky, catching the entire heap in the face as he whipped around at the threat and ended up coated from head to foot in it.

"Take that you pumped up pufferfish!" Geraldine cried. "I shall be forever

M.O.I.S.T. and you won't ever stop me!"

She ripped her dress off while everyone who still remained stared at her in shock, and I caught sight of her huge tits about two seconds before she shifted into her enormous Cerberus form and took off with a bark of laughter which echoed all around the rocks which surrounded us, the bag of M.O.I.S.T. badges and her dress each clamped in the jaws of one of her three heads.

I fell about laughing, gripping my side as I leaned back against the edge of the rock pool and Max roared a challenge which made the air around us vibrate with his emotions. A mixture of anger, lust and amusement pushed into me and I opened myself to it, enjoying the sensation of his power as it chased away my own feelings for a few minutes and gave me a crazy kind of rush.

We had a whole army of fan girls and guys lurking in on us now, made up of the people who had managed to stay through the terror overflow or had shown up as the news of our appearance spread over campus like it always did. There was a whole host of them batting their eyes, flexing muscles and trying to do everything and anything they could to draw the attention of one of the Heirs who would one day rule this entire kingdom.

I'd been born and bred for this and had had an idea of what it would be like for us when we emerged into the world properly after our Awakening, but the reality of what we had here wasn't something any of us could have prepared ourselves for.

In the years since our early Awakening, the four of us had been privately educated away from everyone else. We'd been given every fundamental lesson that would be taught throughout our freshman year and beyond, and we had been given extra lessons in all things combat to ensure that we would be able to take this place by storm once we arrived. And we'd done that and then some. We just hadn't been fully prepared for what it would be like to be thrust into this place, away from the shielding of our parents and among Fae we didn't know. It was overwhelming, the constant attention, girls and guys throwing themselves at us all the time, wanting to be our friends or more, anything at all really, just wanting to attach themselves to us in any way they could.

And we were making the most of it at every given opportunity.

I couldn't even walk into a room without a line of Fae forming to offer me their blood. And it would have been fucking rude to refuse.

Seth's pack had shown up and were lingering nearby, trying to get close to him as they did most of the time, watching him, waiting for his attention to fall their way. He smirked as his gaze ran over them, giving them a heated look which made me certain that he was thinking with his cock as he considered each of them in turn.

"I'm going to teach that royalist nut job a lesson," Max growled, water magic flooding from his hands as he directed it at himself and scrubbed the mud away in a fit of rage.

There were a bunch of Fae trying their hardest not to laugh but I didn't bother hiding my amusement as I laughed loudly, shooting aside as he sprayed water my way in annoyance and coming to a halt sitting on a ledge beside Seth where I promptly dropped my arm around his shoulders as he laughed too.

"You want help on your hunt, brother?" I asked as Max finished cleaning himself and turned to follow after Geraldine.

"No," he replied in a fierce growl.

"Send us a pic if she manages to cover you in shit again though, yeah?" Seth called after him as he took off and he flipped us off over his shoulder before disappearing down the rocky path Geraldine had taken.

"Well, that was too easy," Darius sighed as he moved to join us, another drink in his hand which the redhead had given him, and she trailed closer to us with a hopeful look on her face as she eye fucked him so graphically that I had to look away from her porno gaze. "I was hoping for a real fight tonight."

"Blood moon got you hungry too?" I teased, grinning at him as I eyed the pulse in his neck.

"When am I not hungry for a fight?" he tossed back, glancing away from us hopefully like he thought a decent opponent might present themselves.

But instead of anyone stepping forward, his challenging look was only met with bent heads and submission all around and he sighed in disappointment.

"I'll kick your ass if you're hungry for a fight?" I offered, flashing my fangs at him as he looked back to me again, his pupils shifting into the reptilian slits of his Dragon form.

"Come run with us, Alpha," a girl pleaded before Darius could accept my challenge and we looked around at Seth as his packmates all started bouncing at the idea of that, howls escaping their lips which echoed all across the springs and set my skin prickling.

Seth tipped his head back to look up at the moon and I watched the way his features lit up at the idea, though he glanced our way hesitantly like he was torn between running with his kind or staying with us.

"How about we all go for a run?" I suggested. "One loop around the grounds then back here for a fight and a party and whatever the hell else takes our fancy."

"Will you actually run with us this time?" Seth asked, narrowing his eyes on me suspiciously. "Because the last time you came running with my pack you just shot off to get laid and left me out there in the dark."

I sniggered because that was an accurate assessment then held my hand out to him. "I swear that I won't sneak off to get laid this time," I promised and Seth smiled widely before slapping his hand into mine and a clap of magic rang between our palms as the deal was struck.

Seth turned to howl at his pack and they all cheered, whooping loudly and stripping their clothes off in a rush as they prepared to shift.

Darius stripped down too, tossing his drink to the redhead who looked like she was in danger of drooling all over the floor. He turned his back on her before dropping his pants and shifting so suddenly that several Fae screamed.

It wasn't every day you got to see a ten ton Dragon appear in front of you after all and Darius was one beautiful golden beastie when he was in his shifted form.

He took off with a beat of his powerful wings and a roar loud enough to make the rocks vibrate all around us. Seth shifted next, leaping forward and landing on four huge, white paws in his Wolf form and he howled loudly as his entire pack shifted at his back, the lot of them taking off down the rocky path which led towards Fire Territory to the east of The Shimmering Springs.

I glanced at the redhead as she gawped after them, her mouth hanging open in awe and I slipped closer to her as my fangs prickled.

"Hey Marge?" I asked, making her snap around to look at me.

"It's err, actually Marguerite," she corrected and I nodded like I gave a fuck about that.

"Right. Yeah. I was thinking you could give me a drink?"

She blinked at me then nodded, whipping around towards the drinks table like

I'd been after a fucking waiter and I sighed as I shot after her, snatching her wrist into my grasp and biting down before she'd even managed to look back at me again. The moon was making me damn insatiable tonight and I growled as I drank from her, the bland taste of her blood not even coming close to satisfying what I needed. By the stars, it was boring. It tasted as dull as lukewarm puddle water.

"Oh, sorry," she gasped. "I didn't realise you meant—"

I cut her off by releasing her, shoving her arm back at her and resisting the urge to wipe my mouth clean on the back of my hand. My gaze moved to the path that Seth had taken, the memory of his intoxicating blood sliding down my throat circling in my mind, and I growled as I prepared to go after what I was really hungering for.

"Will you tell Darius about me feeding you?" Marge called as I stalked away from her. "So he knows how willing I am to do whatever I can to support all of the Heirs."

"Right, yeah," I agreed dismissively, forgetting what I'd agreed to before she'd even finished talking and as she started going on about me putting in a good word for her in her mission to suck my best friend's cock, I shot away. She was welcome to pledge her allegiance to Darius's dick if she wanted to. He had a whole gaggle of girls who had already done so though, so I wasn't going to waste my time promising to steer him towards her in particular. Who knew, he might be tempted her way if she put enough effort in, but that shit had nothing to do with me.

I shot away from her boring blood and desperate words, racing after the howling Wolf pack at top speed as the night air tousled my curls and the exhilaration of my pace made my heart riot.

I cupped my hands around my mouth and howled to the blood moon, Seth's answering howl coming from up ahead before setting off the entire pack.

I sped between the furry bodies of the Wolves, laughing as the mixture of booze and adrenaline got my heart pumping to a wild tune, making my way to Seth so that I could run at his side.

Darius roared as he swept back and forth above us and we all howled to him as we raced across campus in a tide of beasts with the entire world at our feet.

Seth nudged his big Wolfy snout against me as we ran together and my heart soared with a pure kind of happiness which I only ever felt in the company of my best friends.

We ran like that for over an hour and when we finally closed in on The Shimmering Springs again, I shot ahead of them, stripping my clothes off as I went and grabbing a bottle of vodka before racing towards the biggest heated pool right in the heart of the springs.

Just before my butt naked self could dive into the water, a blur of motion forced me to skid to a halt and my fangs snapped out as I came face to face with Lance Orion in his professor bullshit suit as he snarled right back at me with his fangs out too.

"Fifty points from Terra for showing your cock to a teacher, Altair," he snapped, his nose wrinkling as he glared at me and I glared right back.

"And what do you lose for *being* a cock to your future ruler?" I replied scathingly as I lifted the bottle of vodka to my lips and drank a big enough dose of it to make my head spin. It was petulant and kinda pointless but the rivalry between us always did bring out the entitled prick in me.

"You and I both know that I have nothing left to lose which is why I'm also considering murdering you for nothing but the pure thrill of it," he deadpanned.

A roar interrupted us and Darius plummeted from the sky, shifting at the last second and landing on two feet in the space between us.

"Lance," he greeted and I noticed that he wasn't docked house points for having his fucking cock out.

"Darius," Orion replied, shooting me a narrow eyed look before going on. "I have a lead on some of those things you wanted to come and help me deal with."

"Really?" Darius asked, his eyes brightening with a violent look which made my muscles tense.

"What happened to our fight?" I asked him as he moved to find the clothes he'd discarded earlier, clearly planning on ditching us for his special buddy. Orion looked all kinds of smug about that too and I shot him a death glare in reply.

"I just got a better offer," Darius replied, tugging his jeans up and kicking on his shoes, not bothering to hunt down his shirt as he turned to leave with Orion. "I'll kick your ass in the morning."

I opened my mouth to call after them but the sound of my name drew my attention to the water and I turned to find a group of four girls giggling and waving at me, all of them very much naked and the invitation they were offering up clear.

A growl rolled down the back of my throat and I tipped my head back to look up at the moon where it now hung full and fat right in the centre of the sky, the pull of its power the strongest it would be all night and my blood pumping hot and fast in my veins as the need to feed consumed me.

I shot into the water in a blur, making the girls squeal as they found me among them in less than a heartbeat and I grinned at the closest one as she reached for me.

"You look hungry," she said, biting down on her bottom lip, the red colour of the moonlight making her dark skin gleam with its glow, and the need of my kind rising desperately within me.

I nodded once, grabbing her in the next moment and driving my teeth into her throat, making her moan loudly as our naked bodies were crushed together.

Her blood swam over my tongue and I drew it in with an ache in my chest which wasn't in any way satisfied by the low buzz of power she held in her veins.

Her friends moved in to surround me, their bodies pressing against mine from all sides, the skim of hard nipples and roaming fingers dancing across my flesh and awakening other needs in me, but it wasn't enough.

I tugged my fangs free of the girl's neck, turning and grabbing the wrist of the one on her left, sinking my fangs in deep and growling as I tasted even less power in her veins which made my heart pound all the harder with the need for more.

A hand wrapped around my cock which was making some poor effort at getting hard, but the unsatisfying blood was a serious turn off no matter how many girls there were surrounding me. I tugged my fangs free again, even the sight of their blood mixing with the bubbling water nowhere near enough to raise my interest in them.

I swear I could hear the moon whispering in my ears, urging me to take more, find what I ached for. I spun around so fast that the girls shrieked, though the one I found myself facing didn't back away, instead tilting her head in offering and sweeping her brunette curls aside to give me clearer access.

I bit her harder than I meant to, though the loud moan she released said she liked that and her hand found my dick beneath the water once more, pumping it hopefully as I swallowed her blood down in greedy gulps only to be disappointed once more.

"Fuck," I cursed as I tugged my teeth out of her flesh and knocked her hand aside. "I need more than this."

I turned to look at the last girl who was rubbing her hands over her tits and leaning back against the rocky edge of the pool, her thighs parted in offering as she waited for me with a need in her eyes which was kinda tempting.

But before I could give her any more of my attention, a huge splash sounded the Wolf pack arriving, all thirty of them diving into the pool in their Werewolf forms and shifting beneath the surface, causing the rest of the partiers to scream in alarm.

Seth surfaced right in front of me, water washing down his cut abs as he flicked his long brown hair back like he was performing in some kind of fans only video and making me swallow thickly as I looked at him.

His dark eyes met mine as he clawed his fingers through his hair to tame it away from his face, the feral look on his face letting me know that the Wolf in him was still very much present beneath the pull of that beautiful fucking moon.

"Hey, Cal," he said, his voice a rough caress around my name which drew my lips up and revealed my fangs to him. "Are you still thirsty?" he asked in surprise though his eyes lit with the thrill of that fact.

"The beast in me won't be easily tamed tonight," I replied, my heart thumping harder as he closed in on me, and I couldn't help but stare at the pulse points across his exposed body where his blood pumped hot and fast after the excitement of his run.

"Well, I bet I can help with that," he said, shifting towards me and making me lick my lips as my attention fixed on a throbbing vein which tracked through the V at the base of his abs right before the water lapped around his waist to conceal it.

He stopped before me, his eyes running down my body and making me smile as he didn't bother to hide his appreciation.

"Damn, are you sure you aren't at least a little bit gay, Cal?" he teased. "Because you look real good all wet and thirsty."

I took a long drink from my bottle of vodka and shrugged. "Your tits aren't big enough for me," I said as I offered him the bottle for his own drink, though as I looked to his chest to make my point, I couldn't say I hated the sculpted lines of his pecs all the same.

Seth's fingers brushed against mine as he took the bottle from me and I forced myself to hold still even as my gaze zeroed in on his neck and my fangs practically throbbed with the need to bite him. To get what I'd been craving and the moon was demanding.

Seth finished the bottle off then tossed it to one of his packmates as he swam past us, not even reacting as the guy cursed when the bottle smacked him on the head and drew blood.

I didn't spare the blood any attention either, my restraint snapping as I lunged at him, taking hold of his jaw in one hand and driving my teeth towards his throat so fast that Seth sucked in a surprised breath. But the asshole had clearly been expecting it before I struck anyway and I cursed as my fangs slammed against a solid air shield which he'd placed a hairsbreadth from his skin, making me jerk back again with a snarl.

"Woah, calm down big boy," Seth laughed as earth magic flared in my palms and vines curled their way up my arms as I prepared to fight him to claim the drink I needed.

"Give me a taste, Seth," I hissed, my head spinning with the need in my flesh as I felt the gaze of the moon pressing down on me even more forcefully.

"You look like you need to get laid, brother," he laughed, waving a hand at the group of girls who were still trying to win my attention back, but I'd practically forgotten they were even there.

"They can't give me what I need," I snarled, baring my teeth at him in a challenge which I was really fucking close to forcing upon him, and his gaze roamed over me as he seemed to take in how close I was to the edge.

"Yeah...I see that. Come on then, I got you."

Seth took my hand and I frowned at him as he tugged me after him but gave in, my desire for his blood too powerful to resist and my attention fixed on his throat while his grip on my fingers felt akin to the only thing tethering me in place right now.

He barked a command at his pack to move aside for us, tugging me across the pool before striding beneath a waterfall of heated spring water and drawing me into the secluded cavern behind it.

Seth released me as we made it into the dark space, the shimmering pool there making the cave wall glisten with a multitude of tiny rainbows which danced across his wet skin too, making him appear like some kind of ethereal creature brought to me by the moon herself.

He grinned at me as he took a seat in the water, tilting his head to one side and eyeing me with interest.

"You're still shielding," I said in a low voice, my control hanging on a knife's edge as I let my fangs sink into my bottom lip and offered them some small reprieve.

Seth's grin widened at being caught out and he shrugged, not bothering to deny it.

"I kinda like seeing the beast in you, Cal. I'm thinking of riling it up a little more just so that I can find out how dark you get when the worst of you is baited."

His words set a fire in me and I took a step forward, but before I could close the distance between us, a girl stepped through the waterfall at my back and drew my attention to her.

"I thought Alice could help us liven up this party," Seth explained, crooking a finger at her and she offered me a sultry smile as she passed me by, her hand skimming down my arm before she moved to sit in Seth's lap, kissing him passionately while I just stood there and watched them.

Seth opened his eyes as he continued to kiss her, that silver shine to them again as he looked at me, the challenge there clear.

"You want me to play Wolf?" I asked, looking at the beautiful girl in his lap and finding that idea almost as appealing as the thought of his blood caressing my tongue.

"Yeah," Seth agreed, breaking their kiss and giving me his Wolf's grin while she began to move her mouth down his neck, moaning softly.

He beckoned me closer with one finger just like he'd done for Alice and I snorted at the idea of me submitting to him, but moved nearer all the same.

"Fine," I agreed, my cock hardening as I closed in on them and moved to take a seat beside him, my leg brushing against his and my skin heating at the contact. "But you'd better know what you're asking for by bringing another Alpha into your pack."

I held his eye as I reached for Alice, taking hold of her thigh and drawing it over my leg so that she was half straddling both of us and Seth's arm pressed to mine.

She turned her head, capturing my mouth in place of his and sinking her tongue between my lips.

I growled as I deepened the kiss, Seth's hand brushing the back of my neck and his fingers pushing into my curls as he leaned in too.

His jaw brushed against mine and I growled, part in warning, part in lust as Alice turned to meet his kiss once more, leaving me to move my mouth down the side of her neck instead.

My heart pumped harder as the call of her blood drew me in and my fangs grazed against her flesh, making her gasp as her hips rocked with need.

"Tip your head, Alice," Seth growled. "Give him what he wants, and we'll give you what you want in return."

Alice nodded, her head rolling back as she exposed herself for me and I let my gaze roam down to the peaks of her nipples as Seth's large hand moved to tug on one, his heated gaze meeting mine as Alice dropped her hand beneath the water and began to pump his cock in her fist.

I groaned at the sight of his pupils dilating, my pulse thundering and fangs aching, forcing me to lunge forward and bite her with a deep growl.

Alice moaned as I began to feed and I sighed, her blood so much more potent than the others I'd fed from since arriving at this party and getting a whole lot closer to satisfying the need the moon had awoken in me.

I moved my hand between her legs, my fingers scoring a line up Seth's thigh in the process and making him groan as he looked between me and Alice, enjoying the show.

Alice moaned loudly as I sank two fingers inside her, more of her blood rolling down my throat as I began to pump them in and out, loving the way her blood pulsed between my lips the more worked up she got.

Her hand wrapped around my dick and I groaned, fucking her with my hand and drinking more of her blood while the pounding in my head settled just a little.

But the more I drank, the clearer it became that it still wasn't enough, a growl escaping me as frustration filled me and my muscles tightened with a need that wasn't going to be sated.

"Come on, Alice, you can do better than that," Seth snarled, and my heart leapt as his hand moved onto my thigh, the touch of his skin against mine making the animal in me rear its head and my cock jerked in Alice's grip.

Seth's hand joined mine, his fingers caressing the back of my hand before pushing inside her too, making her moan loudly as he found a rhythm with me as she cried out between us, her pussy tightening around us as she began to come.

"Fuck," Alice gasped. "Oh fuck, by the stars, Alpha!"

I drove my fingers into her with a desperate kind of need, her blood pulsing faster as she reached her peak, teasing me with the promise of what I so desperately needed while she cried out and her pussy clamped around mine and Seth's fingers.

Her orgasm sent a rush of blood between my lips and I snarled furiously as the release I needed was denied, knocking her hand away from my cock and pulling my teeth from her throat in frustration.

Seth tugged his fingers out of her, pulling my hand away too and barking a command at her to work harder as his fingers knotted in my hair and he jerked me around to look at him.

"Tell me you want me, Cal and I'm all yours," he said, his eyes flashing with a cocky kind of power and I snarled as I bared my bloodstained fangs at him.

"Fuck you," I snapped, clawing a hand through my curls as I tried to rein in the bloodlust which was threatening to take control of me.

Seth whimpered wolfishly as I closed my eyes and suddenly the water was shifting around me, his body moving towards mine and knocking Alice off of us as I felt him drop the air shield from his skin.

I lunged for him without even opening my eyes, a snarl rolling from my throat as my fangs sank deep into his flesh and I groaned loudly as the rush of his blood finally caressed my tongue.

"By the stars," Seth moaned as I pushed him back against the rock wall, my cock driving against his thigh and the lust ignited by the pure power laced within his blood making me grind my hips against him without thought.

Seth's hand pushed into the back of my hair, fisting tight as he drew me closer and his other hand moved down my arm, digging into my bicep as I gripped his waist and the muscle flexed tight.

I lost myself in the taste of him, the feel of his body bowing to mine and the purity of his power flowing into me through his blood as I swallowed greedily, the power of the moon making my fucking head spin.

I drank until I was intoxicated by him, and his head fell back while he panted through the bloodlust, the rush just as intense for him as it was for me.

His thumb brushed against the side of my cock and I groaned headily, drawing my teeth out of him and turning my head toward his without thought.

Seth's mouth met mine as he turned to me too, my heart leaping with the alien feeling of his stubble raking against mine. The deep sound of the growl which rolled up the back of his throat made a shiver track down my spine.

His lips parted for me and I sank my tongue between them, groaning deeply as he met the stroke of it with one of his own, his thumb tracing up the side of my dick once more and making me lose my fucking head with the mixture of lust and blood drunkenness.

Seth drew me closer, the kiss deepening as my brain slowly caught up to what we were doing, where this was going and how much I found myself wanting to keep it going.

I ground my hips against him, feeling the press of his cock against my leg in reply to the firm thrust of mine against his, and I found myself considering something I'd never once given thought to before.

I drew back a little, looking into his eyes and reading the same lust there that I was sure he could see in mine.

"Seth?" I panted, a question and an offer in that word as his thumb traced a path up the length of my cock once more as I began to shift my hand from his waist towards his.

"Yes," he said, the need in him clear and I bit my lip as I drank it in, wanting this to go further, so much fucking further.

Alice was gone and I had no idea when she'd left but I found myself glad that she wasn't here. I didn't know if this was the moon or his blood, some combination of both or something far more powerful, but I did know that I didn't want to leave this cave until I found out.

I leaned in, my mouth on his and he licked his bottom lip, clearly wanting more too—

"Don't mind me!"

I jerked back in alarm at the sound of Professor Washer's voice behind me, spinning and finding him emerging from the water on the far side of the cave, his Siren scales coating his skin and a smile on his lips which was all kinds of false embarrassment.

"I just need a little gulp of air before I slip back down into the moist depths of this hole. You two know all about that, I'm sure."

He slipped back under the water just as Seth yelled a curse and threw a blast of air magic at his head. I swiped a hand down my face as the madness of the moon's power faded from my limbs and disgust over our gross lurking professor sank into its place.

"Shit," I said, breathing a laugh as I exchanged an awkward look with my best friend. "The moon is all kinds of fucked up tonight."

"Err, yeah," he agreed. "I'm even hornier than usual which is saying something."

I barked a laugh, glancing away. "Me too. And the bloodlust has me all kinds of fucked up. I doubt I'll even remember half of this night come morning."

"What happens beneath the blood moon stays beneath the blood moon," Seth offered with a grin and I nodded.

"Yeah, sounds about right."

An awkward silence hung between us for several seconds and I glanced back over to the place where Washer had disappeared.

"I'm feeling the sudden desire to get the fuck out of here," I said.

"Agreed." Seth followed me as I led the way out of the cave again and we found the pool beyond it empty too, the partiers having moved on or fucked off back to bed for the night.

I glanced up at the moon, finding it lowering in the sky with clouds slipping over it to hide it from view, the most potent of its magic dampened now and letting me think a little clearer.

"See you for breakfast?" I asked, glancing back at Seth and finding him looking up at the moon too.

The corner of his mouth hooked up and he nodded. "Yeah. Breakfast."

I turned away from him and shot across campus towards my House and my bed, leaving the blood moon at my back and shaking my head at the madness it had woken in me tonight. Then again, every night since I'd started at Zodiac Academy had ended in one insane story or another, so I was going to just put it down to another drunken night of insanity and leave it at that. Seth was my best friend and I wasn't attracted to guys anyway.

It was all just a little moon madness, and I knew we'd go right back to normal tomorrow. This wasn't going to change shit between us. We were bros, so screw the moon for fucking with us. Not even she could damage the bond between me and Seth, nothing could. Not the moon, the sun or every star in the heavens. We were the best of fucking friends, and that was how it would always stay.

✧   ✧   ✧

Thank you for reading our short story featuring two characters from our Zodiac Academy series and supporting Ukraine in the process! If you'd like to read more about them then you can check out book one here. Hugs and snugs, from Caroline and Susanne xx

carolinepeckham.com/creeping-shadow-book-trailer

Royal Oath

T.K. Leigh

CHAPTER ONE

H OME.
 It's a word that usually conjures fond memories.

Memories of love. Of laughter. Of belonging.

Coming home after a long time away is often a time of celebration. Moms hug their daughters, telling them how much they missed them. Fathers embrace their sons, asking how they're getting on in the world. Siblings make jabs, sometimes tease each other about a new love interest. But through it all, one thing endures.

Their love for each other remains true.

That's not what it's like for me.

There are no warm greetings.

There are no hugs from my mother saying how much she's missed me.

There's no love.

There hasn't been for years now.

Instead, the second I step out of my chauffeured vehicle and stare up at the imposing walls of Lamberside Palace in the European Nation of Belmont, I'm met with nothing but stiff formality.

Custom.

Tradition.

After all, there's no room for love in a monarchy.

Or so I've been told throughout my life.

"Your Highness," a man in a dark suit greets me with a bow, as is expected of him.

"Good afternoon, Oliver." I offer one of the palace butlers a cordial smile.

"How were your travels?"

"Uneventful. It's a short flight from Paris."

"Lovely to hear. The Queen Mother has requested to see you upon your arrival." He does a once-over of my attire. "Would you like to take a moment to…freshen up?"

I've been around this life long enough to know that's his polite way of suggesting I change into something more in line with the royal dress code.

The skinny jeans, white off-the-shoulder billowy top, and wedge sandals revealing my brightly painted toes certainly aren't appropriate attire.

Especially the wedge sandals.

My grandmother hates them.

But I'm not going to cave in to her archaic requirements.

Not yet anyway.

"That's not necessary. My grandmother's time is valuable. We can go there directly."

Oliver arches a brow, silently questioning if I'm certain. When I don't respond, only holding my head higher, he nods, extending his arm toward the entrance.

As I cross the threshold into the lobby of the palace's residential wing, a weight settles on my chest.

Or perhaps a noose wraps around my neck.

To everyone on the outside, I live a fairy-tale life. I have the best clothes. Designer handbags. Expensive shoes. Not to mention, a vault containing priceless jewels dating back centuries.

But it's all a façade. A show we put on to keep the public entertained. To stay relevant in a world that finds the concept of royalty less and less relevant with every passing day.

Nothing about this is real.

It makes me long to feel something that *is* real, even if it's fleeting.

"Is my father in residence?" I ask as Oliver leads me through the familiar corridors, everything maintained with the precision and care of a museum. Considering the palace is over five hundred years old, I suppose it *is* a museum.

"He's in London through next week. I can schedule an audience with him upon his return if you'd like."

I force a smile, doing my best to act as if the idea of having to go through my father's private secretary in order to see him isn't a big deal. Considering my father's been king for fifteen years, I should be used to it at this point.

But I still miss the time when he was simply my dad with no intention of ever ascending to the throne.

It's amazing how quickly your life can change. One minute, we were living a peaceful existence in the country, my father's only claim to fame being the fact his father happened to be king.

The next, his older brother, and first in line to the crown, perished alongside his entire family in an avalanche during a skiing holiday. My uncle, aunt, and cousins may have died on that mountain.

But a part of me died there, too.

My childhood died.

My freedom died.

My independence died.

"That won't be necessary. I'll just see him at some point, I suppose."

"Of course, ma'am."

Nearing the door to my grandmother's study, Oliver slows to a stop and gently knocks.

As if alerted to our approach seconds beforehand, it immediately swings open. My grandmother's private secretary, Lieutenant Colonel Williams, greets me with the same stoicism I've come to expect from all members of the palace staff.

Particularly from our private secretaries, who are all former military.

"Your Highness." He bows. "This way, please." He allows me to enter the sitting area, then leads me across the room, stopping outside a set of ornate double doors.

I smooth a hand down my hair, taming my long blonde waves as best I can. At least I didn't put on too much makeup this morning. I've never been one to wear an inordinate amount in the first place, preferring just a bit of liner around my green eyes and gloss on my lips.

After knocking, Lieutenant Colonel Williams opens the doors and steps over the threshold.

"Her Highness Princess Esme," he announces, then moves to the side.

As he does, my grandmother turns her cold eyes on me, lips downturned, her displeasure with my appearance obvious.

"Your Majesty," I greet with a curtsey, even though it's not required. The obligation to do so died when my grandfather passed away. Now it's merely a gesture of respect for her years of service to the monarch. Service that she continues to this day as one of my father's top advisors.

"Have a seat, Esme." She gestures to the chair opposite the desk.

I do as I'm told and sit, crossing my feet at the ankles, angling my legs down. It's about as comfortable as sitting with a stick shoved up my ass, but it's protocol.

"How are you settling back in?"

"I've only just arrived. Haven't even been to my private quarters. But it appears everything around here is exactly as it was when I left for university. Nearly four years ago."

"Do I sense a hint of annoyance in your tone?"

"Merely an observation."

"You may find it…dull that nothing's changed much in the past four years. Our customs and traditions are important. They're what make us…us. Without them, our monarchy would be nothing. Do you understand?"

"Yes, ma'am."

"Good." Her voice brightening, she attempts something resembling a smile, but it looks foreign on her face. "Now that you're finished with university, it's time to start thinking of your duty to the crown."

I nod. "I've been giving that some thought. There are a number of causes I believe—"

"And that means getting married."

I snap my mouth closed, uncertain I heard her correctly. "Excuse me?"

She huffs out an annoyed breath. "It's pardon, Esme. How many bad habits have you picked up while away? Have those friends of yours undone all of your etiquette training? You don't *excuse* yourself. You *pardon* yourself."

"Okay. Then *pardon* me," I say somewhat dramatically. "But I thought I heard you mention something about me getting married."

"I did."

I blink, lips parting, but no words come, rendered utterly speechless by the turn this conversation has taken.

"I've arranged for you to meet a variety of suitable matches over the next few weeks. All young men from important families, a union which would be mutually beneficial to both parties. Of course, I'd like to announce an engagement by the end of the summer. Then a spring wedding. I do think that's the best time of year for a wedding. Don't you?"

She doesn't look up from her notepad, prattling on as if she didn't just pull the proverbial rug out from beneath me. As if we're discussing which place settings to use at the next state dinner. Not the fact she wants me to get married, and to someone on a list of eligible people she's pre-selected for me.

"Tomorrow night, I'm hosting a gala for several visiting dignitaries. Maximus Wells will be in attendance. He's a fine match for you. His father is running for president over in the States. So I—"

"I'm sorry, but what fresh hell have I walked into?" I blurt out, finally finding my voice. "Have I just stepped out of the twenty-first century and onto the set of some regency romance where I'm to paraded around a room full of horny men, and then the powers that be get to decide who I'm to marry? You do realize how bloody absurd this sounds. Right? Tell me you haven't lost your goddamn mind."

Pinning me with a glare that would have most people running for cover, she forms her lips into a tight line, squaring her shoulders.

"I'll ignore your rather...colorful language for the time being, as it appears some etiquette refreshers are in order. But I assure you, this is no 'fresh hell,' as you put it," she says, using air quotes. "This is your reality, Esme. You're the Princess Royal. Second in line to the crown. As such, you have a duty to marry, and marry well. Lord forbid anything happens to Gabriel. In that case, you'd be next in line to the crown, which is why it's so important you have a...masculine presence supporting you."

Every feminist bone in my body is on the verge of rioting, ready to burn bras and dismantle the patriarchal system that's still alive and well, even in the twenty-first century.

"Now I trust you haven't been sexually active?" She lowers her glasses over her eyes, pen in hand, ready to jot down my response.

"Excuse me?"

She glares at me, but doesn't correct me.

For once.

"It's important to know."

"I..." I shake my head, still in disbelief over this conversation. Then I avert my gaze. "No."

"And your monthly cycle? It's regular? No issues?"

"Why does that matter? Is there, like, an application to date me I don't know about?"

She heaves a frustrated sigh, removing her glasses. "It's imperative we're aware of any potential reproductive problems beforehand. Regardless, I'll schedule an appointment with the palace physician so he can do a thorough check. Make sure everything's in working order."

"Working order?" With every word she speaks, I feel less like a person and more like a piece of property. "Are you shitting me right now?"

"Esme! This behavior is incredibly unbecoming of a woman with your breeding and status. I'd caution against using language like that tomorrow. Otherwise I'm not sure how you'll be received."

Unable to stand listening to another second of this, I jump to my feet, my words spilling from me before I can stop them. "I'm not one of your goddamn horses that you can parade around and put out to stud. I'm a bloody human being. And I'd appreciate it if I'm treated as such."

Not even stopping to curtsey, I storm out of her study, needing to get as far away from her and her ridiculous plan as possible. I'm so mad I can barely see two feet in front of me. All I know is that I've been back less than an hour and I wish I never came back.

Wish I escaped while I still had the chance.

Wrapping my arms around my stomach, I keep my head lowered, not looking where I'm going until it's too late and I run into something incredibly hard and firm, the force of my impact causing me to nearly lose my balance.

I teeter on my feet, but before I fall, a pair of hands dart out and grab my hips, keeping me upright.

CHAPTER TWO

I WHIP MY head up, inhaling a sharp breath when a pair of familiar eyes stare back at me.

That's all it takes for thousands of butterflies to flap their relentless wings in my stomach. It's as if no time has passed since the last time I stared into these eyes.

Since I felt his lips against mine.

Since I succumbed to his kiss in the hours before he left for basic training.

I should look away. Should increase my distance. Should step out of his hold.

But something's always drawn me to Creed Lawson, even though nothing can ever come of this attraction. Not only because he's my brother's best friend. But because in three short years, he'll be sworn in as one of the elite few tasked with protecting the lives of the royal family.

An honor to many.

And a legacy for Creed.

After all, a member of the Lawson family has been a part of the royal guard from the inception of this monarchy over five hundred years ago.

His family's legacy to protect is as steeped in tradition as my family's legacy to rule. To govern.

Once Creed swears that oath to protect us above all else, any romantic notions I've foolishly held on to will go up in flames. It will no longer merely be a bad idea because of his close relationship with my older brother.

It will be forbidden.

It hasn't stopped me from thinking about him over the years, though.

And as my eyes skate over his frame, it's evident the years have been good to Creed Lawson.

Very good.

I've always found him attractive, even as a lanky teenager. But he's no longer the lanky teenager he was when he left for boot camp.

His once lean physique has been replaced by broad shoulders, defined biceps, and a sculpted chest I can make out through the gray t-shirt that clings to him like it's made for his body and his alone.

"Creed," I exhale, but his name is all I can muster, my mind going to places it shouldn't.

He parts his lips, about to say something, but before he has a chance, my name echoes from elsewhere.

Creed jumps away from me just as my brother wraps me in his arms, giving me exactly what I've needed since arriving here. I return his hug with more enthusiasm than normal, squeezing him as if he's the only thing keeping me grounded.

In a way, he is.

It was a promise we made all those years ago when our lives were irrevocably changed. When we were ripped from our normal lives and thrust into the spotlight as the new Crown Prince and Princess Royal. No matter what life throws at us, we'll always have each other's backs.

And after my conversation with my grandmother, I need his support more than anything.

"I'm so bloody happy to see you, Anders," I choke out, using the name I've called him all his life, instead of his given name of Gabriel. My father's name is

Gabriel. My brother is Anderson... Anders. My grandmother may loathe the idea of anyone calling the future monarch anything so informal as a truncated version of his middle name, but I don't care.

He was Anders before all this.

And Anders he'll remain.

"Hey." He pulls back, meeting my eyes, his concerned gaze tracing over my face. "Are you okay?"

I force a smile, not wanting the first time I'm seeing my brother in months to be polluted with my grandmother's ridiculous plans for my future.

"It's just so good to see you." I wrap my arms around him again. "To see a friendly face."

He rests a gentle hand on my back as he hugs me to him. "I know how you feel. I'm thrilled to have you back, too." He gives me one last squeeze before dropping his hold on me. "I have big plans for us this summer. Lots of sailing and drinking on the boat. And you can tell me all about life in Paris."

The picture he paints is exactly what I'd hoped my summer would look like. Spending time with my brother and friends. Doing anything and everything we want without a care for what anyone has to say.

I fear those days will soon be gone.

"Sounds perfect." I squeeze his hand. Then I glance at Creed. "And what brings you to Lamberside?" I ask him.

"I'm based out of Montrose now," he explains, referring to the capital city of our small nation.

"He just finished his special ops training," Anders adds. "So he's now officially special forces and is based out of here for the summer."

"And after that?" I press, partly because it's the polite thing to do.

Partly because the idea of Creed being nearby for the foreseeable future excites me.

"Depends where I'll be stationed," Anders explains.

I dart my eyes toward him, expression wide. "What are you talking about?"

He shrugs, shoving his hands into the pockets of his cargo pants. Couple them with the t-shirt and the faint scent of gunpowder, I get the feeling they just spent the past few hours at the shooting range.

"Duty to the crown. Now that I've graduated Harvard, I have to do my military service. I start boot camp at the end of the summer. After that, Creed will follow me to wherever I'm stationed. A trial run for when he's sworn in to the guard."

"Seems a lot's going to change at the end of the summer."

Anders tilts his head, furrowing his brow. "What do you mean?"

I open my mouth, on the verge of telling him about my conversation with our grandmother. But compared to serving in the military, especially when our country is currently involved in the conflict in the Middle East, my duty to the crown doesn't seem so severe. At least my life won't be on the line.

Just my happiness.

"Nothing," I assure him finally. "You'll be going away. As will Creed. So I guess that means we'll need to make sure this is a summer we'll never forget."

He slings his arm around me, pulling me along the corridors. "And we're starting now. Drinks?"

I exhale a long breath. "Most definitely."

CHAPTER THREE

"**S**O THEY WANT you to get engaged by the end of the summer?" Harriet whisper-shouts after I inform her and Marius about the unnerving conversation I had with my grandmother yesterday.

"Shhh." I hush her, glancing around to make sure no one's eavesdropping in on our discussion.

Hundreds of people mill about the Great Hall of Lamberside Palace, the who's who of Belmont society present for a gala thrown in honor of whatever dignitaries are visiting at the moment.

I have a feeling my summer will be one gala after another as my grandmother attempts to match me with a man she deems a suitable husband.

"That appears to be the plan." I swallow down another large gulp of champagne. "Apparently she has suitors lined up for me to meet all summer. Like I'm a mare she's trying to breed. I guess I should be happy she's bringing the potential studs to me instead of sending me to them, as is typically the case with horses." I shake my head, taking another sip of champagne to push down the bile rising in my throat. "It's like a reverse harem gone very wrong."

My friends stare at me for a beat, then burst out laughing, a brief break in decorum. "Reverse harem?" Marius says through his laughter.

At least Harriet and Marius both hold titles and are typically invited to these things. If it weren't for them, I'd hate everything about tonight. They keep me grounded. Remind me there's life outside the palace walls.

"That's what it feels like. Minus the sex." I roll my eyes. "God forbid I have sex before marriage."

My friends whip their wide eyes to me, mouths agape, staring at me as if I just revealed the location of Jimmy Hoffa's body.

"What do you mean, Ezzie?" Marius leans toward me, his voice no louder than a whisper. "You've had sex. Yeah?"

I pinch my lips together. My silence is the only answer they need.

"Seriously?" Harriet shoots back. "You spent the past four years in Paris. You can't tell me the opportunity didn't present itself there. The French invented casual sex. And in my experience, multiple orgasms."

"It's not so easy for me. My guards kept any guys I was remotely interested in as far away from me as possible. Apparently, they're not only tasked with guarding the royal heir, but also the royal hymen."

Harriet and Marius gawk at me once more before breaking into another fit of laughter. I can practically feel the daggers my grandmother's shooting at me, since we're definitely drawing attention to ourselves. But I haven't seen my friends in too long now. I need their support in what I can only imagine will be a difficult summer.

Need some sort of normalcy.

"The royal hymen," Harriet repeats, holding her stomach.

"That settles it," Marius announces.

"What?" I ask.

"It's time to get you laid, princess."

"I'm not sure sex will solve this little dilemma."

"She's right about that." Harriet forms her lips into a tight line. "But do you really want your first time to be with someone your grandmother chooses for you? They dictate everything else about your life, from the way you dress to the way you hold your spoon. Don't give them this, too. You may not have control over much. But you can control this."

"So...what? Am I just supposed to go up to someone and ask them to fuck me?"

"Your Highness!" Marius covers his heart with his hand, feigning shock. "Such language!"

"I hear much worse coming out of that mouth on a regular basis, Mari."

"True." He winks. "And I don't think you can just go up to anyone. It needs to be someone you trust. Someone who won't go to the bloody pappos with the story."

I scan Marius' frame, everything about his physique impressive, thanks to his Norwegian roots. "How about you? I trust you."

"Me?" His eyes widen, spine stiffening.

"Why not?"

"Don't get me wrong," he continues quickly. "I'm bloody flattered. Any other time, I'd haul your beautiful ass into the nearest dark corner to have my wicked way with you." He grins lasciviously, always the flirt. "But I'm not meant to be your first, darling. That's too important to waste on someone you don't have feelings for. At least not like that."

"Then who do you suggest? Hate to break it to you, but the list of people I can trust is quite short. Apart from Anderson, you're the only member of the opposite sex on it."

"Don't forget Creed," Marius reminds me.

All it takes is hearing his name for my skin to flush, those butterflies in my stomach taking flight once more.

"C-Creed?"

"You can try to deny it all you want..." Marius gives me a knowing look. "But I've seen how you keep stealing glances his way. He does look rather dashing in his military dress." He waggles his brows. "And the way he's been eye-fucking you... Well, I think it's time the two of you stopped torturing yourselves and just...bang it out." He thrust his hips, punctuating his words.

"He's Anderson's best mate," I argue.

If Marius managed to pick up on the tension between Creed and me, who else has?

I didn't think anyone would notice. Thought whatever I once felt toward him would disappear with the passing of years.

Thought I'd forget about the way his mouth moved against mine when he declared he couldn't leave for boot camp without at least knowing how my lips tasted.

Did he remember the kiss like I did?

Or has it been lost in the crowd of all the other kisses he's enjoyed since then?

"I honestly don't see why it can't just be you."

"I'm truly flattered." Marius runs his hands down my arms. "And like I said, any other time..."

"I know. Dark corner. Wicked things."

"I don't want to steal this from you. And you and Creed... There's something there. Has been for years. You'd have to be blind not to see it." He glances at Harriet. "Am I right, Harri?"

She nods in agreement.

"So what?" I laugh nervously. "I'm just supposed to walk up to him and ask him to sleep with me so I'm no longer a virgin? There's no way he'll go for that. He's too...noble."

"If that's the case, it's not because he hasn't thought about it. If I were a betting man, and I am, I'd go all in and wager he's thinking about it right now." He winks. "But in the event he *is* too noble..." He shrugs. "Consider me your plan B."

It's ridiculous I'm even having this conversation. I don't know many normal people who would discuss propositioning their brother's best friend to deflower them.

But as I learned years ago... I'm not a normal person.

Not anymore.

On a long sigh, I shift my attention away from my friends, scanning the room. As if knowing exactly where to look, my eyes immediately go to Creed. When his gaze locks with mine, a shiver trickles down my spine, a warmth settling low in my belly. The way he admires me reignites something inside me. Something I didn't think I'd feel again.

Even surrounded by hordes of women fawning over how amazing he looks in his uniform, he still makes me feel like he only sees me.

"You see, darling..." Marius continues, leaning toward my ear. "This is exactly what you deserve for your first time. This feeling you're experiencing right now. Times a hundred."

"A thousand, even," Harriet adds.

"You won't have that with me."

At the sadness in his tone, I face Marius, about to apologize, but he cuts me off.

"It's okay. I get it. I'm chuffed to be your plan B. It's an honor I take quite seriously," he says with mock solemnity. "And should I be called upon to serve, I will deflower the fuck out of you."

I can't help but laugh, my heart expanding.

This is one of the things I love about Marius. We've been friends most of my life. And as we matured and grew into the young adults we now are, his attraction to me also grew.

But being the amazing friend he's always been, he's never pushed it. Refuses to sacrifice our friendship.

More importantly, he refuses to allow me to sacrifice my happiness.

"Well then..." Pushing out a long exhale, I grab a glass of champagne from a passing server. "If I'm to do this, I'm going to need more to drink." I lift my glass toward them, then bring it to my lips, downing almost all of the effervescent liquid in one gulp.

"That's my girl."

CHAPTER FOUR

I CAN DO *this*, I tell myself as I make my way across the room, offering cordial smiles to people I don't recognize.

I do my best to play the part I've been trained to play, but the more I'm sucked into polite conversation, the more I second-guess whether this is a good idea.

So what if I've never had sex? Maybe I'm blowing this entire situation out of proportion.

My grandparents had an arranged marriage. As did my uncle and aunt. I may not remember them well, but from what I do recall, they seemed happy. If they could find happiness in a partner chosen for them, perhaps I can, too.

"Esme, darling," a voice calls out, pulling me out of my thoughts.

I look up, meeting my grandmother's saccharine smile that's no more real than some of the boob jobs I've seen here tonight.

Cognizant of the fact her greeting is more of a summons, I plaster the same smile on my face and walk toward where she stands amongst a circle of men in tuxedos and women in formal gowns.

"Your Majesty," I say with a small curtsey.

She turns to the handful of people. "May I present my granddaughter, Princess Esme." As she goes around the circle, each individual bows or curtseys. I try to remember each name she recites, but my thoughts are consumed by Creed. Whether I can really ask him to sleep with me. To take my virginity.

"And this is Maximus Wells, Jr.," my grandmother says, introducing the last individual in the circle.

Unlike the others who bowed or curtsied, he grabs my hand without me offering it. I expect my grandmother to chastise him, inform him of the proper rules as she's prone to do whenever someone breaks decorum, regardless of who they are.

But she doesn't.

Instead, she looks on as he raises my hand to his mouth and feathers a kiss against it.

Another gross disregard for the rules.

"Pleasure to meet you." His lips curve into a smile that causes my stomach to churn.

I'm more than aware of who Max Wells is. The son of an American tech mogul who's currently running for president. Even as I've watched him campaign for his father on television, he gave me a bad feeling.

In person, those feelings are multiplied. His dirty-blond hair boasts far too much product than necessary. His fair complexion makes me question if he's been exposed to any vitamin D lately. But what truly unnerves me is his smile. Most other people probably think him a handsome man from a family akin to American royalty. A true catch, especially for someone who *is* royalty.

But there's something off about him. I feel it in the way he grips my hand almost possessively. See it in the glint in his eyes. Smell it in the air.

"Likewise," I say somewhat coolly. When I yank my hand from his, I feel the burn of my grandmother's glare on my skin. "If you'll excuse me…" I smile, about to take my leave when my grandmother wraps her hand around my forearm, keeping me locked in place.

"Mr. Wells will be spending a bit of time in our beautiful country this summer. He's entered the regatta next weekend."

"Is that right?" I reply politely.

"It is." He leers at me, raking his gaze over me in a way that makes me feel as if I'm nothing more than a prize pig he's selecting for slaughter. "I thought perhaps you'd do me the honor of accompanying me on my boat."

I manage to free myself from my grandmother's grip. "Thank you for the invitation, but I must decline. I've already agreed to join my brother on his boat. As is the custom in our family." I look around the circle, gritting a smile. "Enjoy your evening."

Before my grandmother can attempt to stop me, I spin on my heels, my feet not carrying me nearly fast enough from the room and onto the terrace.

Once outside, I suck in a deep breath, desperate for some air when it feels like life is suffocating me the longer I remain in this place.

I head to the railing and lean against it, looking up at the moon shining brightly in the darkened sky. A gentle breeze blows around me, wrapping me in a brief moment of peace.

"Rough night?"

I stiffen, darting my eyes toward a darkened corner as Creed steps out from the shadows.

"You could say that," I answer, running my clammy hands along my gown.

This is the first time I've been alone with him in five years. Since that kiss.

"What are you doing out here?"

"Just…thinking. After five years in the military, including the last year spent in the jungle for special teams testing, I forgot how things can be around here."

"Me, too. Minus the whole military thing, of course."

"Naturally."

A silence passes between us as I stare at him, attempting to find the courage to get through this conversation. If I had any doubts about whether I should do this, my recent encounter with Max Wells only serves to solidify how necessary it truly is.

But how do I even go about asking this of him? Knowing Creed as I do, the direct approach is probably best.

"I'm a virgin," I blurt out.

He blinks, his shock at the turn in conversation obvious. "Umm…"

"And I don't want to be anymore. This is probably going to come off as a…strange request. You'll think I'm crazy for even asking this of you. And maybe I am. But I was hoping you'd…" I wave my hand around, avoiding his stare. "Help me take care of that."

"I'm sorry." He coughs, clearly taken aback. "Are you asking me to…sleep with you?"

"I know how it must sound." I laugh under my breath. "Now that I hear it out loud, it sounds absurd. But my grandmother is hell-bent on announcing an engagement by the end of the summer. For me," I clarify, my words coming fast as I attempt to explain my reasoning behind this proposition. "And this guy who seems to be her top choice—"

"Is it Max Wells?" His jaw twitches, nostrils flaring.

I nod subtly. "I don't get a say about much that goes on in my life. I've made my peace with that. I can try to resist all I want, but I know from experience that if my grandmother wants to announce an engagement by the end of the summer, she will be announcing an engagement." I draw in a shaky breath. "I don't want to give them this, too," I manage to say through the lump building in my throat. "I want to be the one to decide who gets to be my first."

"And you're choosing me?" he asks in a soft voice.

"I am."

"You're my best mate's little sister." He runs a hand through his dark hair. "And the Princess Royal." He leans toward me, his proximity causing a shiver to roll through me. "I'm to be royal guard in a few years' time."

I tilt my head back, meeting his eyes, barely a breath separating us. "But you're not yet."

He hesitates, neither pushing forward nor pulling back. As he licks his lips, his eyes float to my mouth, his breaths coming quicker, pupils dilating.

He can try to hide it. Try to ignore it. But some forces are too powerful to fight forever.

And this thing between us is one of the most powerful things I've ever experienced.

My lips ghosting against his, I murmur, "There's nothing saying we can't. Not right now."

His Adam's apple bobs up and down in a hard swallow, every muscle in his body growing rigid. He flexes his hands, desperate to reach out and yank my body against his, but at the same time, knowing he should walk away. This is the delicate dance we've mastered. Torn between our hearts and heads.

"Except my conscience." He steps back, purposefully not looking at me, as if that will take the sting off his rejection.

"But your conscience will allow some stranger I have no history with to sleep with me after my grandmother all but whores me out to the highest bidder," I snip out.

"Don't put it that way. Please."

"It's the truth."

"Esme…" He shakes his head, pinching the bridge of his nose. Then he brings his gaze back to mine. "I… I can't."

I squeeze my eyes shut, swallowing back the tears wanting to fall. I refuse to cry. Not over this.

I didn't cry when I was told I had to leave the only home I knew to live in this damn prison.

I didn't cry when I learned my mother was sick and may soon lose the control of her limbs.

I didn't cry when I walked into her bedroom to discover her unconscious body.

This life has dealt me harsh blow after harsh blow, and I've taken them all in stride.

I'm not going to let it break me over this.

My head held high, I spin from Creed, hurrying toward the grand staircase leading to the famous Lamberside gardens.

"I'm sorry," he calls after me.

I whirl around to face him. "Don't, Creed. Just…" I form my hand into a fist, pushing down everything I want to say but won't. It won't change things. "Just don't. I don't need your pity. Don't need your apologies. I don't… I don't need you."

He parts his lips. Something in the way he peers at me makes me think he's about to reveal some earth-shattering truth. But as expected, he lowers his head and turns, disappearing back into the gala where I'm sure he'll find some other girl to go home with.

One his conscience doesn't forbid him from pursuing.

CHAPTER FIVE

WITHOUT A SINGLE care for the verbal lashing my grandmother will surely unleash on me tomorrow for disappearing from the gala and behaving so rudely toward one of our guests, I continue down the stairs and make my way toward the gardens, the focal point being a maze of high hedges.

During my younger years, I often came out here whenever life within the palace walls became too much. Surrounded by beautiful blossoms and fresh air reminded me of my life before. I spent hours exploring these mazes, to the point where I'm probably one of the few people who can find my way from one end to the other with little trouble.

It's been a few years since I've navigated through these hedges, but it's like riding a bike. The flowers may have changed. There may be a few more marble busts or benches along the way. This place still offers me the escape I desperately crave right now.

As I approach a wall made up entirely of wild orchids, I pause, drawing in the familiar aroma, recalling running through orchid fields as a child. It was my mother who requested this wall be put in the garden. She claimed it was an homage to where she grew up.

In reality, I think she wanted to give us somewhere to go that would remind us of our life before. Even if only in scent.

Sometimes that's all it takes to provide you the comfort you need.

"So this is where you've disappeared to."

Whirling around, my heart ricochets into my chest as Max saunters up to me, leering at me the same way he did mere minutes ago.

For once I wish I'd adhered to my grandmother's rules and wore something slightly more conservative. Instead, I insisted on choosing my own gown, a gold dress that clung to my body with a deep V at my chest and an even deeper one at my back.

"Just wanted a bit of fresh air." I force a smile, pushing down the nerves growing more pronounced with each step he takes toward me.

"Is that all?" He arches a brow.

"Yes. Now that I have, if you'll excuse me…" I attempt to sidestep him, but he wraps his hand around my bicep in a harsh grip.

"We need to have a little chat."

"About what?" I struggle to wiggle away, which causes him to tighten his hold even more.

"About the way you embarrassed me in front of a handful of diplomats and ambassadors. Are you trying to make them laugh at me? At my father?"

"Looks like you do a pretty good job of that yourself," I shoot back. "You don't appear to need my help in that area."

He glares at me, nostrils flaring, eyes wild, making me question if perhaps he's on something.

Based on what I know of him, he most likely is. His affinity for prescription drugs is well known.

Suddenly, he reels back, landing a hard blow to my face. The force of it knocks me to the ground. I bring my hand to my cheek, blinking through the initial shock.

"Not so high and mighty now, are you? Your grandmother assured me you'd be agreeable to this little arrangement. And that's what I expect. Absolute cooperation."

I rub my face as he advances toward me. When I see him loosen his belt, panic shoots through me. I attempt to stand, but before I can, he's on top of me, pinning me with his hips. Kicking at him, I reach for his face, clawing my nails into his skin, which only pisses him off even more. He draws his arm back, about to slap me again. This time, I'm prepared, and quickly roll to my side before he can land a blow, a move I learned in my self-defense training. The sudden motion unbalances him, allowing me a moment to make my escape.

I shoot to my feet and run as fast as I can in my heels. But it's no match for his speed and he manages to catch up to me in a few seconds. With a viselike grip on my arm, he pins it behind me, then slams my head into one of the hedges.

"No one embarrasses me like you did and gets away with it."

"You must have small-dick syndrome," I bite out, refusing to play the helpless victim. "Perhaps a side effect of all the drugs. Is that why you have to force yourself on women? Because you know the second you drop your pants, they'll just laugh at how small it is? Call you wee man? Or maybe millimeter monster? Tinkie winkie? Pinky pants? Baby mushroom?"

With each slang term I throw, his irritation grows, his hold on my arm tightening, becoming more and more painful. But I don't relent. It's not in my nature.

"No. That's not it. I know. Itsy bitsy teeny weeny tiny balls beside a peeny!"

"Enough!" he growls, twisting my arm with such force I'm confident he's on the verge of dislocating my shoulder. "I'll show you just how wrong you are."

Using his body to trap me in place, he moves his hand down my frame. For the first time, I regret being so rash. My behavior went against everything I learned during my defense classes. Being a high-profile target, I'm required to go through routine training on how to react when in any type of hostage situation.

Not antagonizing my captor is rule number one.

Then again, I've never been one to adhere to the rules.

When he clamps his teeth onto my neck, I release a howl, attempting to buck him off me. I don't expect it to work. It *shouldn't* work. Not without help.

To my surprise, it *does* work.

One minute, his hand is sliding beneath the slit of my dress, body crushing mine. The next, I'm free, his weight no longer pressing against me. At the sound of a fist hitting flesh, I turn around.

"What the bloody hell do you think you're doing?" Creed pins him to the opposite hedge, a fury unlike anything I've ever seen vibrating from him.

"J-just having a bit of fun," Max replies shakily. "She asked me to do that. Likes it rough. It's harmless. Really."

"Harmless?" Creed repeats, tightening his grip on him, every inch of his body shaking as he attempts to reel in the anger wanting to be unleashed. "It didn't look bloody harmless to me."

When heavy footsteps sound, Creed snaps his gaze toward his left, three members of the royal guard coming to an abrupt stop.

Including Mitchell, my own personal guard.

Grabbing Max by the bicep, Creed drags him toward Mitchell, his rage only seeming to increase. "Where were you?"

It doesn't matter that Mitchell has seniority over Creed. I have a feeling that will change tomorrow. And Mitchell probably knows it, too, which is why he answers Creed as if he's subordinate to him, instead of the other way around.

"I didn't notice Her Highness leave the gala."

"It's your bloody job to know where she is at all times, regardless of who's flirting with you." He pushes Max at him. "Get this asshole out of here and make sure he doesn't come within a mile of Her Highness ever again. You got it?"

"Of course." Mitchell looks my direction as the other members of the royal guard restrain Max's wrists behind his back. "My sincerest apologies, Your Highness." He bows, then follows the other guards out of the garden.

Not wasting a second, Creed rushes toward me and holds me at arm's length, his concerned eyes raking over every inch of me. "Are you okay?"

"I'm fine." I blow out a laugh, but even that can't hide the anxiety still filling me over what nearly just happened. "You should have seen the other guy."

"You certainly did a number on him." He flashes me a smile before his expression falters. "He didn't..." He trails off, his voice catching.

I touch my hand to his chest. "No. He didn't."

Relief rolls off him in waves as he pulls me into his chest, holding me close for several long moments. "Thank God." He exhales a long breath, kissing the top of my head. "Thank God."

I melt into him, basking in the feel of his arms around me for this brief moment in time, neither of us caring about anyone seeing us like this. That doesn't matter right now. In a few minutes, it will, but for now, I'm going to enjoy the warmth of his embrace, since I know it's fleeting.

Placing another kiss on my head, he pulls back, forcing my eyes to his. "Let's go get those cuts cleaned up."

CHAPTER SIX

"**O**UCH!" I WINCE when Creed dabs ointment on yet another one of the scratches on my face as we sit on my bed, a first-aid kit between us.

"Hold still and it won't hurt as much. It's just a few cuts. Stop being so dramatic." He playfully rolls his eyes, then returns to playing doctor.

Truthfully, they're not that bad. Some scrapes. A bit of bruising around my eye and cheek where Max knocked me to the ground, as well as marks on my arm and neck. But that's it.

As Creed's reminded me several times, it could have been a lot worse.

Had he not shown up when he did, it nearly *was* a lot worse.

"So..." He clears his throat. "Itsy bitsy teeny weeny tiny balls beside a peeny?"

I shrug. "He deserved it."

"I'm not denying that, but you go through hostage training for a reason." He narrows his gaze, giving me a look of reproach. "So you know how to handle yourself in these situations."

"I *did* handle myself. Don't forget one of the things they teach in those defense classes."

"What's that?" He removes a tiny bandage from its packaging, then smooths it over my temple.

"Reading your enemy. Finding their weakness and exploiting it." I shrug. "That's what I did. Max's ego is bigger than all of Europe. Hell, probably all of Asia and Africa, to boot. To him, impugning his masculinity is the worst kind of offense." I flash a smile, but it does nothing to diminish the concern in Creed's gaze.

"He could have seriously hurt you, Esme." He peers down at me, emotion filling his eyes. It's a rare moment of vulnerability for a man who's not in the habit of displaying his feelings. At least not so overtly.

I wrap my hand around his wrist as he continues to smooth the bandage on my face. "I'm fine."

He nods, but doesn't drop his hold on me. Instead, he moves his hand to my cheek, cupping it, his thumb ghosting against my lips. A shiver ripples through me, my pulse increasing with every inch he erases between us, an invisible tether pulling us together.

It was this tether that pulled him into my room the night before he left for basic training.

And it's this tether that keeps pulling us back together, despite all the complications.

"Creed," I whimper, his breath dancing on my mouth, so close yet still just out of reach.

I can taste how much he wants this. How much he wants me.

Why should we deprive ourselves simply because, years down the road, we'll have no choice but to walk away?

Why can't we give in to this temptation now, even if for just one night?

Taking control of my own destiny, I hook my arms around his shoulders and tug him toward me, pressing my lips to his. He doesn't move right away, torn between doing what his conscience tells him is the noble thing and giving in to his desires.

"Please," I beg against him. "It doesn't have to mean anything."

He pulls back, but only slightly. Framing my face in his hands, he focuses his intense stare on me, not allowing me to escape him.

"Haven't you realized by now, Esme?"

"What?" I exhale breathily.

"With you, it will *always* mean something." His lips slowly descend toward mine, the heat of his breath causing my core to clench. "It will always mean everything."

His mouth covers mine, coaxing my lips to part. When his tongue slides against mine, I moan, that first taste after five years exactly what I imagine coming home is supposed to feel like.

But no matter how deep he kisses me, how enthralling the warmth of his hands on my skin is, I fear it will never be enough. I'll always want more.

I'll always want it all.

Deepening the kiss, he gently lowers my back to my bed, his lips never leaving mine as he crawls on top of me. When he circles his hips against me, I moan, a need unlike anything I've ever experienced consuming me.

He trails kisses from my mouth, across my jawline, before running his tongue along my neck, teasing and torturing. Pulsing against him, I scrape my nails up and down his back, savoring in his muscles. In his strength. In his protectiveness.

"Creed," I moan, struggling to reel in all the sensations filling me. From his tongue tracing slow circles. To his teeth nipping my skin. To his arousal hitting me in the spot I'm desperate to feel all of him.

Cupping his cheeks, I bring his eyes to mine. "Take me."

He pauses, not moving for several long moments, that same uncertainty from earlier returning. I swallow hard, bracing myself for his rejection yet again.

But it never comes.

Instead, he crushes his lips to mine, his kiss hitting me in places I didn't even know existed. If this is how my body responds to just his kiss, I can't even begin to fathom how it'll feel when he does other things.

"I hate the idea of hurting you," he says earnestly.

"I'd rather it be you than someone else. Plus, they say after the initial ache, it gets better."

He slowly shakes his head. "That's not what I'm talking about."

A lump forms in my throat at the sincerity in his gaze. "It'll be okay. I'll be okay."

He studies me for a beat, then sighs, freeing himself from the web of arms and legs I have wrapped around him. Not taking his eyes off me, he gradually unbuttons his shirt.

When I first saw Creed yesterday, it was clear the military has been good to him. As he drops his shirt to the floor, I can confirm without a doubt it was more than good.

It was incredible.

Superb.

Stupendous.

Extending his hand toward me, he arches a brow in invitation. When I place mine in his, he helps me to my feet.

"May I?" He glances at my gown.

Nodding, I turn around, my heart thrashing in my chest with every second that passes as I wait for him to lower the zipper on the side of my dress. Once he does, he pushes the spaghetti straps down my arms, the material falling to the floor, leaving me in just a pair of panties.

His arm loops around my stomach, pulling me against him, his front to my back. He caresses my torso, his thumb brushing against the swell of my breasts.

"You are so damn beautiful, Esme." He pushes my hair to one side, dropping soft kisses to my shoulder.

"You don't have to romance me." I laugh nervously. "I'm kind of a sure bet, so—"

He spins me around, his lips covering mine before I can utter another syllable. These aren't the first of Creed's kisses I've been treated to. But he no longer kisses as an unsure eighteen-year-old. He kisses me like the determined, confident twenty-three-year-old he's become.

"Yes, I do. If this is the only night I get with you, I need to do it right. Because I've thought about this for a long time."

"You have?"

He nods as he pushes his pants down his legs and steps out of them. "A *very* long time."

A hand on my hip, he guides me back to the bed and lowers me onto it, settling between my thighs. When he brings his arousal up to my center, his tip teasing my opening, I whimper. The newness of it all creates a mixture of excitement and fear within.

"We don't have to. If you're having second thoughts—"

I grab the back of his head, pulling his mouth toward me. "Do it."

He locks eyes with mine, simply remaining a breath inside me. It makes me hungry for more, regardless of any pain I'll endure.

I'll gladly suffer through it if it means I can keep feeling the way Creed makes me feel.

He lowers his lips to mine. "Forgive me."

Before I can respond, he thrusts into me, our cries carrying through the palace hallways.

But we don't care.

Not now that we finally made it to this place. This time. This connection.

Despite how fleeting it is.

CHAPTER SEVEN

SUNLIGHT SKATES ACROSS my face, stirring me from sleep. I blink my eyes open, my bedroom slowly coming into focus. When I notice my gown has disappeared from the floor and Creed's clothes have been collected and draped over the reading chair in the corner, I shoot up, panic rushing through me.

Sure, Creed informed his father, the commissioner of the royal guard and my father's chief protection officer, that he'd be staying in my quarters last night to give me peace of mind. His father probably assumed he'd be keeping watch on the couch in the drawing room just off my bedroom. Not spending the night in my bed after having sex with me.

Three times.

"Relax..." Creed groans, snaking an arm around my torso and pulling me flush with him. "I picked everything up," he explains, as if able to read my thoughts. "Force of habit. Leaving your clothes on the floor like that would earn you some serious PT in the military."

"Pretty sure you put in enough PT last night."

"And it was the best PT of my life," he croons, peppering kisses along my shoulder blades.

I exhale, melting into him, wishing I could stay like this all day.

Maybe longer.

"How do you feel?"

"A little sore," I answer honestly. "But it was worth it."

"No regrets?"

I turn around, meeting his eyes and running my fingers through his hair.

As nerve-racking as the idea of losing my virginity was at first, Creed was amazing through it all. After that initial thrust, he took his time. Constantly checked in with me to make sure I was okay.

And after a while, any dull ache was replaced with a burning need that multiplied until my cries of pain turned into those of ecstasy.

"No regrets," I assure him.

He brings his lips to mine, treating me to a sweet kiss that makes me want to have him once more.

But it's only a matter of time until someone invades the bubble we cocooned ourselves in last night.

"I should probably shower. And you shouldn't be in here when they bring me my breakfast."

"I know." He smiles sadly.

I touch my mouth to his, savoring in one last kiss. "Thank you for a night I'll never forget."

He sighs into me, but before he can deepen the exchange, I pull away and stand, covering my body with my robe.

He slides out of bed behind me, a stiff silence settling between us as he yanks on his pants. I pass him a half-hearted smile, then head into the en suite bathroom.

"What if I don't want last night to be the only time?" his voice rings out just as I'm about to close the door.

I stiffen, momentarily frozen in place. Then I meet his eyes. "What do you mean?"

"I know it's complicated. But I've wanted this a long time. A lot longer than you probably think. I just…" He rushes toward me, grabbing my hands in his. "I don't want last night to be the only time I ever get to feel that." He loops an arm around me, pulling my body flush with his, threading his other hand in my hair.

"I know we can't be together like a normal couple. You're a princess. And my legacy is to soon be one of the select few chosen to guard the royal family. To guard you." He smiles sadly, his Adam's apple bobbing up and down in a hard swallow.

"But until then… Until tradition and custom dictates we have no choice but to pretend we mean nothing to each other, I'd like it if you might find some room in your heart for me."

I lift my tearstained eyes to his. "Even if it ends in utter heartbreak?"

He brings a hand to my cheek. "I'd rather fly knowing I'll eventually have to come down from the clouds than to never feel the wind on my face in the first place. Wouldn't you?"

I shake my head, wanting to tell him this is a horrible idea. That there's no way this can end well. That our hearts will surely be a casualty of this war.

But I can't find the words, my heart overpowering my head.

"Okay."

His eyes widen in momentary disbelief. "Okay?"

I nod. "Okay."

He crushes his lips back to mine, his kiss sending my heart soaring to the clouds.

I may not have much say over anything in my life.

May one day be forced to marry a man I'll never love.

But right now, right here, I can make my own choice.

I can choose Creed.

And that's exactly what I plan to do until I have no choice but to walk away.

✧   ✧   ✧

Thank you for reading *Royal Oath* and supporting this incredible cause. Creed and Esme's story isn't over yet. There's much more to come with these two in 2023. But while you wait, be sure to learn where readers first met both Creed and Esme – Royal Games, a standalone road trip romance with a royal twist.
www.tkleighauthor.com/dating-games-series

Smolder

Aly Martinez

CHAPTER ONE
Ivy

H IS RICH BROWN eyes, stained the color of whiskey, danced on the backs of my lids as I rubbed circles over my clit. My breath hitched when I imagined his lips descending upon mine, gentle and ruthless as only *he* could be. I didn't like to even think his name, much less say it—no matter how many times it clung to the tip of my tongue. It was held securely in place by nothing more than my fears.

Fears he could extinguish with a single touch.

The very same fears he bred with his every breath.

Opening my legs wider, I kicked the blanket off, exposing my bare sex to the camera mounted on the ceiling across the room. It had been installed along with several others throughout my house years earlier. I'd never seen the person he'd had install them, but on the rare nights when I'd felt like picking a fight, I had ripped them down. They were replaced the next day, sometimes that very same night as I slept *alone* in my bed.

If I'd have asked him to take them down, they would have been removed immediately. No questions asked.

But I was nowhere near ready to sever that connection.

I had no idea who he'd hired to sit on the other side of those cameras. In my mind, fogged with raw desire, it was him. *Always him.* I could almost see the taut muscles at his shoulders straining against the confines of a button-down as he leaned forward to get a better view of my wetness. His long cock thickening down the leg of his slacks, and his maddening tongue snaking out to dampen his suddenly dry lips.

He liked to watch.

And I loved giving him a show.

We'd been playing this game for years—tortuous, brilliant, excruciating, blissful years.

I moaned, my stomach tightening as my impending orgasm blazed a chill over my skin. My mouth fell open and my head wrenched to the side, resting comfortably against the goose-down pillows he'd bought me. I'd never asked for those pillows. I'd simply Googled them one day, and less than twenty-four hours later, they'd appeared on my bed while I had been at the grocery store. They were divine, much like everything else in the three-thousand-square-foot house I owned outright without ever having paid a penny for it. That was if you didn't count the cost of all the tears, heartbreak, and eternal longing for a man who had claimed my soul.

The same man I couldn't be with.

Or live without.

My back arched off the mattress as my all-too-soft fingers drew me closer to the edge. His rough and callused hands would have been better. But he never would have been satisfied with just finger-fucking me into oblivion.

His hot, needy mouth would have sucked and licked at one breast while he split his attention by massaging the other with his firm palm. His tongue would have rolled over my nipple, his teeth scraping violently, causing a tidal wave of pleasure and pain. It was a combination that might as well have defined him as a man. My mind called forth a barrage of memories from the nights we'd been together.

Five years.

My push.

His pull.

His unwillingness to give me the one thing that would allow us to be together.

My unwillingness to accept him for the man I'd always known he was.

I loved him. Utterly, completely, permanently. But I'd come from a family on the wrong side of the law. I'd sworn to myself that as soon as I could escape that life I'd never look back.

But that was before I'd met *him*.

Before he'd saved my life.

Before he'd killed my brother—and then my father.

I'd shed not the first tear for either of them as they were lowered into the ground. I wore the physical and emotional scars of years of abuse at their hands, but standing at a funeral *he* had funded for no other reason than to give me closure, I sobbed while staring into the deep, brown eyes of the gentle savage I could never keep.

He loved me. Fiercely. But he also respected my choices, even when they destroyed him.

After their funeral, he'd driven me to my new house, fucked me sweet and slow, and then walked out of my life just the way I'd asked him to.

The only times he ever came back was when I called him. Not on the phone. I didn't need his number. But if I said his name, no matter how softly, he was there in a matter of hours.

I hated that he was only three syllables away. Like an alcoholic with a bottle stashed under the sink, I could never quit, knowing he was within my reach.

He didn't harass me or crowd me.

I was the one who whispered his name like a prayer.

I was the one calling for him, desperate and needy.

I was the one who cried his name even in my sleep.

And I was the one who always asked him to leave and never come back.

Too many times, he'd smiled—injured and angry—then kissed me before disappearing again.

Until next time. And there was always a next time.

The orgasm I was about to give myself was a sad substitute to any that he had given me.

One word. That was all it would have taken to bring him back. To feel his long, thick cock driving into me as his body claimed me as his own. But it would change nothing.

He had been the crown prince of Miami's underworld when my brother had first sold me to his family. I was twenty-one, broken, filthy, and penniless. But my dark knight had never treated me as anything other than a queen.

I was no prisoner in that house. I was free to come and go as I pleased. I'd even gone on a date or two over the years. He'd never said the first word to me about them. But when I'd inevitably realize that they would never be him, I'd whisper his name and he'd come for me, his arms open, ready to pick up the pieces.

By all definitions, I had an amazing life. I had a job as a vet tech that I didn't need because in our five years together, I'd never paid a bill. I drove a Lexus, which was magically upgraded every six months. Christmas, Valentine's Day, and my birthday were always celebrated with jewels and lavish trips to exotic locations. A few times, I'd gone on those vacations alone. The others, I'd whispered his name on my way to the airport. Less than an hour later, he'd been sitting beside me on his private jet, bags packed, champagne poured, a devilish glint twinkling in his eyes as he tucked me into his side. No questions asked. Just love, struggle, and a passion for each other that could never be extinguished.

As the years passed, his power in the family business grew. Now, he was the king of the largest drug ring in the country.

I'd begged him more times than I could count to leave the life of crime behind and run away with me. He had more than enough money. Hell, I had more than enough that he'd given me stashed away to support us for years. But while I never doubted that he loved me, I just couldn't make him choose me.

So there we were—in love and at a stalemate.

I panted, finding a rhythm at my clit, the pressure building almost painfully.

"Come for me, *mi alma*," he would have whispered in his thick Spanish accent. "Show me how much you love what I do to this sweet pussy."

"Oh, God, baby," I whispered into the empty room, my skin catching fire as my climax peaked. All at once, I shattered, the wave of my release stealing every thought, feeling, and emotion I possessed.

For that all-too-brief moment of ecstasy, it took everything I had not to call out for him.

It had been two months since I'd seen him last—the longest we'd ever gone.

Two months that I'd been strong.

Two months that I'd been miserable.

Two months that would boil down to nothing if I said his name, because when he showed up minutes or hours later, there was not one doubt that I would welcome him into my home, my bed, my body, and thus my heart all over again.

Tears welled in my eyes as my release ravaged me. I didn't want to spend my life in fear, wondering if the man I loved would come home at night or be shot down in the streets. I didn't want to spend my days looking over my shoulder, waiting for the police to lock my husband away. I didn't want to be alone again when, ultimately, I lost him.

I didn't want to love him at all.

I'd spent five years trying to resist.

Five years failing.

Five years smoldering in the ashes of his all-consuming fire.

Maybe it was time to stop.

Maybe it was time to accept the inevitable.

Maybe it was time to—

My bedroom window exploded. A scream tore from my throat as three men flooded into my room. One of them grabbed my arm, snatching me naked from the bed, my leg painfully twisting behind me. Consumed with terror and confusion, I fought, clawing at their hands and faces while reaching for the gun he kept stashed in my nightstand. It was a worthless effort. They easily overpowered me. Shards of glass crunched and sliced my stomach as they dragged me out the window, and my hands poured blood as I clung to the jagged edge, desperate to stay in that house.

Five years.

Maybe I was right to be afraid of his life of crime.

But right then, he was the only man who could save me.

"Mateo!" I yelled at the top of my lungs before I was finally torn free.

CHAPTER TWO

Mateo

GRITTING MY TEETH, I threw the stack of black-and-white surveillance photos on the coffee table. "And you think he took this Whitney girl to Miami?"

Leo James, owner of Guardian Protection Agency and a man I didn't quite consider a friend as much as a man I didn't want to kill, shook his head. "I honestly don't know, but I think there is a strong possibility he's trying to find *you*."

I leaned back in the leather recliner in the large living room at Guardian Protection headquarters and gave him my attention. "Me? I do realize that Jonah Sheehan is a fool, but now, you are telling me he is suicidal as well?"

Leo mirrored my position, his wide shoulders squaring as he pointedly rested his palms on his thighs. Both of our guns had been ceremonially placed on the coffee table as soon as I'd arrived. It was something of a mutual show of respect. "Look," he started gruffly. "I know you've had Mira under your protection for years, but I don't think Jonah knew about that when he broke into her apartment, put a gun to her head, and then kidnapped her roommate. My guess is he found out soon after, shit himself, then decided to return Whitney to you *personally* before you have the chance to have him decapitated. Little did the dumb fuck know, you were already here in Chicago and not at home in Miami."

I grinned at the compliment, but the mention of Mira's name made my lips fall.

Mira Benton—now York, thanks to finally breaking free of her worthless ex—was in serious trouble. That poor woman had been left in the crosshairs of every lowlife in the city when her ex went away to prison. She didn't deserve the garbage he'd led to her doorstep. Years earlier, when I'd visited Chicago to do business with her piece-of-shit husband, she'd served me drinks and then stood on the other side of the bar, talking about anything and everything for hours. Her wide smile would never falter, her presence so warm that it could thaw even the coldest heart. She was a little naïve for my taste, but for a brief moment in time, she'd ignited a rare spark inside me.

That was until I'd realized that spark was only because she reminded me of my Ivy—the one woman I wanted more than anything in the world but could never have—at least not permanently.

For months, I'd considered pursuing Mira to see if that spark could grow. It didn't matter that she was married. I could have had her. But it *did* matter that when Ivy called my name, I would stop at nothing to get back to her—even if that meant trampling Mira's heart in the process. I couldn't stomach the idea of dragging Mira into that life. I was no saint, and the list of women who had learned that lesson the hard way was long and well-used. But Mira was different.

Just not different enough to make me forget about Ivy. After five years on my knees, bloody and raw, waiting for her to change her mind, I was starting to think that maybe no one would be enough to make me forget about that woman.

As the youngest son in the legendary Rodriguez crime family, I'd had manipu-lation and control bred into me. My father believed that love was a farce for the weak and women were a commodity that could be bought and traded as freely as heroin or cocaine. One of my earliest memories was of the moans and screams coming from my father's bedroom as I sat on the counter in the kitchen, making dinner with my mother, tears sparkling in her eyes almost as brightly as the diamonds on her wedding band.

That was the way our family worked. My older brothers, Miguel and Dom, bought into it wholeheartedly. Fresh pussy became a secondary currency our men could use to pay for product. Those women... The louder they screamed, the more frightened they were, the more desperate they were to escape, the more they were worth.

But not for me.

Because no matter how long I lived, I could never forget my mother's eyes—dark, hollow, and shattered. Much like they were the day I'd found her dead in the bathtub, blood pooling all around her. And exactly like Ivy's eyes had been the day her brother had hauled her into my home as payment for over ten thousand dollars of product he'd lost in a needle at his vein. I didn't wait for that asshole to tell me her name before I'd put a bullet in his brain.

Then, in the very next heartbeat, I'd fallen in love, when she tried with shaking hands to comb down her long, dark hair, tears filling her eyes as she whispered a tragic, "Thank you."

My Ivy. So strong. So scared. So mine.

I didn't know why I'd fallen in love with that woman as hard and fast as I had, but I also didn't understand why the earth spun or why air was required for survival. They were just facts I accepted.

There was nothing I wouldn't do for Ivy Wright—including letting her go.

Over.

And over.

And over again.

I knew what she wanted, but getting out of the business was the one thing I couldn't give her. I was a wanted man. Cops, competing families, and jaded associates wanted my head on a stake. But power only responded to power. Running would have done nothing but show them the target my family name had painted on my back the day I'd taken my first breath on this earth.

Retiring to a dreadful ranch in Montana the way she'd begged me so desper-ately the last time I'd seen her was not an option.

But neither was living without her.

My chest ached, and I forced my thoughts from Ivy, trying to once again focus on Leo James. "Chicago is a big city. Just because you haven't found Jonah doesn't mean he's not here. My men will find him, and then I'll return Whitney to Mira." I stood and straightened my navy-blue suit coat, buttoning it before retrieving my gun from the table. "You have assured me that this Jeremy Lark man of yours is a good fit for her. I expect that you will call me immediately should that ever change. I do not have feelings for her the way Lark believes, but she is a friend and I do care for her—a great deal. Her safety is of my utmost concern."

Leo gave me a curt nod and rose to his feet. "Just so you know, the last time my guy got a signal off Jonah's cell phone, it was hitting a tower somewhere in Bumfuck, South Carolina. He's on the move, Mateo. And I know I don't have to remind you of this, but if we're going to get Whitney back alive, time is of the essence."

"No. You do *not* have to remind me of that at all. I'll let you know—" That was all I got out before the front door to Guardian Protection Agency flung open with a loud crack.

I spun, gun held high. Leo turned just as fast, snagging his weapon off the table on his way around.

My pulse slowed as the massive figure of my most trusted man, Jorge, came storming into the room. My relief was premature, because pure terror showed on his face.

"What is it?" I snapped.

He flicked his gaze to Leo for only the briefest of seconds before transferring his terror to me—tenfold.

"Ivy," he stated, setting my world on fire.

The blood in my veins roared louder than a hurricane as he shoved a phone into my face. It was a video of her bedroom. I watched as three men busted through the window.

Touching her.

Bruising her.

Scaring her.

Sealing their fate as dead men.

Indescribable pressure mounted in my chest when her terrified eyes turned to the camera above her bed. But it was her guttural scream that carved every single letter of my name into my soul with a jagged blade as it passed through her lips.

And then she was gone, dragged away, leaving nothing more than her blood staining the broken shards of her window.

"Son of a bitch!" Leo boomed from behind me. "That was Jonah. Was that your woman?"

She wasn't my *woman*.

She was my entire fucking life.

A knife hit me in the sternum, twisting as visceral rage erupted at the core of my soul. It was a place so deep, so hidden, so barren, that nothing but my love for Ivy existed within it. And because of that, it was the most brutal and vicious place of all.

Ignoring Leo, I barked at Jorge, "How long ago?"

"Five minutes. Javier is tailing the car. She's in the trunk, so he can't get eyes on her. What do you want us to do?"

Rip them apart limb by limb before peeling the flesh from their body inch by inch.

The shadow of death was painfully cold as it grew within me. "First opportunity Javier gets, tell him to move. And if it doesn't require him to put a bullet between their eyes, I want every one of those assholes alive."

He nodded and started away.

Fisting the front of his suit, I snatched him toward me. Low and malevolent, I rumbled, "I will gut anyone who so much as scratches her. This does not exclude my own men. Tell him to play it safe. She walks away from this unharmed or Javier doesn't walk away at all. Understood?"

His eyes flared, but he jerked his chin. "Yes, sir."

I released him with a shove. "Go. I'm right behind you."

Leo was quick to step around me as Jorge rushed out the door. "Mateo, wait."

Bumping him with my shoulder, I attempted to push past him. "I don't have time—"

He stopped me with a firm hand in the center of my chest. "What do you need from us?"

Curiously, I looked him right in the eye. Okay. Maybe Leo James was a man I *would* consider a friend.

"For the sake of your men, stay out of it. Graves are going to be filling fast tonight. I'll let you know when I have Whitney." With that, I marched out of Guardian Protection, not bothering with the elevator, instead, jogging the three flights down to the garage.

My driver was there waiting for me, door open, eyes wide. "I've called for your plane."

I nodded, sliding into the back of the black Escalade.

For the first time since I'd laid eyes on Ivy all those years earlier, I had no idea where she was.

According to the video, she was somewhere with those pricks, bleeding, broken, and scared.

And as we drove to my private plane, the memory of her screaming my name fucking shredded me because, for the first time in those same five years since she'd entered my life, I hadn't been there for her.

CHAPTER THREE

Ivy

"**Y**OU'RE A DEAD man!" I yelled as they carted me, kicking and screaming, to an old, gray sedan idling in my driveway. "He's going to rip your—" My head snapped to the side when a backhand hit my cheek.

"Shut the fuck up."

It was safe to say I did *not* shut up. Silence had never been my strong suit. "Mateo won't let you end this day with a pulse."

The man's eyes danced with humor as he let out a loud laugh. "Maybe. But that's why we have you." His rancid breath oozed across my skin as he got in my face. "He makes one fucking move on me, he'll be recovering your body." He made a show of looking over my naked body. "I'm going to assume he likes you with two legs and a head. So I'll take my chances."

I blinked at him. Clearly, this idiot did not know Mateo. His assumption was correct; Mateo was quite fond of my legs and my head. But he would find a way to knock the earth out of orbit before he'd ever allow this jackass to get away with kidnapping me.

I'd been scared out of my mind as they'd dragged me from my bedroom. But now, I was starting to feel sorry for these fools. Well, sorry in that "you deserve a slit in your throat immediately rather than torture for three days first" kind of way. I had a feeling Mateo was going to lean toward the latter when he saw the marks on my stomach.

But feeling sorry for these men who had just unknowingly signed their own death certificates did not make me any less pissed.

I'd been enjoying my evening pining over Mateo when they'd broken through my fucking window and dragged me naked from the warmth of my bed, causing me to bleed all the way down my driveway.

I mean, really, who did that?

For the last few years, I'd lived a quiet life under Mateo's care. But this cracked-out bag of bones and his douchebag friends were amateurs compared to the bastards who'd raised me.

I shouldn't have done it.

I should have waited.

I'd said Mateo's name.

He'd come for me, and when he did, he'd make them pay far more than I ever could.

Instead of being patient—another thing that was not my strong suit—I threw everything I had into a headbutt. I aimed for his crooked nose, but I wasn't tall enough and caught him in his yellow, rotting teeth.

Pain exploded at my eyebrow, but it was totally worth it as he spit his front tooth out. Blood dripped down his chin as he brought his hand up to his mouth. "You little cunt."

My scalp screamed as he fisted the top of my hair, yanking me off-balance and dragging me behind him the last few steps to the car. I stumbled with bare feet on the gravel of my driveway, the rocks bruising my soles. In the next second, I was hurled by my hair into the trunk of the car.

I wasn't alone. I landed on another woman, our bodies colliding painfully in the cramped space. She was wearing nothing but a bra and panties, and I was able to make out her brown hair and a black eye before the lid slammed closed, plunging us into darkness.

My anger began to ebb, pure panic icing my veins as the car started to move. It was slow at first, navigating out of my gated property. Then they sped up as they took the turn onto the highway. I tried to concentrate, imagining the roads I drove nearly every day, but with my head still swirling from the chaos, I couldn't tell if they'd taken the ramp to go north or south.

It scared the hell out of me. I was in the car and couldn't figure out where we were headed, how would Mateo ever know?

When the old car's vibrations were loud enough to ensure we wouldn't be heard, I moved as far away from the girl as the confined space would allow, squeezing my naked body into a ball in front of her. "Are you okay?"

"No," she croaked.

"What's your name, sweetheart?"

"Whitney Sloan."

"Okay, Whitney." The cuts on my stomach revolted as I turned to face her. "Are you hurt?"

"I don't know."

We were so close that I could feel her body shaking with quiet sobs.

"Listen, it's going to be okay."

"It's not," she squeaked. "You don't understand. They aren't going to let us out of here. They've had me in this trunk for days. I'm only allowed out at night to use the bathroom. I don't even know where we are anymore."

My stomach wrenched as I thought of how she'd survived the last few days. I wasn't a particularly claustrophobic person, but the anxiety of being locked in that trunk was already starting to creep over my skin.

"We're in Miami," I told her.

"Oh, God. I'm from Chicago."

Chicago?

What. The. Hell.

"Do you know who these guys are?" I asked while patting around for the emergency latch. The car was older, but not ancient. It should have had a way to open the trunk from the inside. It wasn't going to help us much while we were on a highway, but we might be able to catch someone's attention or make a break for it the first time we stopped.

"No," she answered. "I just woke up and they were in my bedroom. They put a gun to my head and dragged me out of my house. I'd never seen any of them before."

"Same with me. But they seem to know my man," I replied, continuing my search. Peeling the carpet back, I found the brake lights. They felt bolted in, with no way to push them like I'd seen on TV, but the wires had already been disconnected.

"There's no way out," she said, her voice quivering. "They broke the release handle after I tried to jump out the first time."

"The first time?"

"I've tried everything." She was quiet for a minute, only the sound of our labored breaths and the road passing beneath us filling the trunk. "I... I just...want to go home."

I couldn't blame her. I'd been in that trunk only a matter of minutes and I was desperate to get out. A few days? No. It wouldn't come to that. He'd come for me. I didn't know how he'd find me. But he'd come. It was what Mateo did.

"There *is* a way out. Just take a deep breath and try to relax. My man, he's... Well, he's something of a..." God, how did I even describe an anomaly like Mateo Rodriguez? The majority of the world viewed him as a vicious criminal with no respect for life or law.

But that wasn't the true Mateo.

The man I knew had saved my life more times than I could count and not just in the damsel-in-distress way like my current predicament. My Mateo had saved me on a very basic human level, proving to me over and over that I was not only worthy of love but that I deserved to choose how I wanted to receive it. He had taken a troubled and confused young woman and showed her that the term *good man* wasn't an oxymoron.

I hated that I couldn't make him give up his life of crime.

I also hated that I had to ask him to give it up at all.

And most of all, I hated that I was too damn stubborn to love him for the man he was the way he had always loved me: blindly and without question.

But there was no mistaking it, Mateo was very much my...

"Savior," I told her. "He'll come for us. I swear."

Her shoulders shook, but she said nothing else as the two of us—strangers only minutes earlier—clung to each other.

I had faith. Mateo had never let me down in the past.

Though, as tears welled in my eyes, I had to consider the possibility that there was a first time for everything.

✧   ✧   ✧

AT SOME POINT, Whitney dozed off. She wasn't much of a talker. When the car had stopped and we'd heard the voices of the men moving around outside us, she had all but crawled on top of me. She was terrified, and I couldn't blame her. The paralyzing fear was starting to set in for me too.

It had to be worse for her though. Someone snatching me from my bed wasn't all that mind-boggling. Ballsy and a blatant declaration of war? Absolutely. But with my ties to Mateo, no matter how thin I tried to keep them, I was probably on the radar of every criminal in Florida—and apparently Chicago too. But, from what I'd been able to gather about Whitney, she had no ties to crime whatsoever.

At that same stop, while Whitney had tried to cling to me for safety, I'd screamed myself hoarse. It had been hours and there was no sign of Mateo. The what-ifs had become my greatest enemy.

What if these guys had somehow managed to cut the cameras and he didn't even know I was missing yet? What if he had seen them take me but he was too far behind us to track us down? He was a powerful man with powerful connections, but it wasn't like he was a superhero Through all the doubts and anxiety, the one thing I never questioned was whether he cared enough to come after me at all.

It had been two months since I'd seen him last. We'd had a huge fight after I'd not-so-subtly suggested he retire to a ranch in Montana. He'd stormed out of my house, and I'd been too damn stubborn to whisper his name again, despite the fact that all I truly wanted was for him to rush back through my door, crawl in bed with me, and never leave.

I'd told myself this was going to be the time I finally let him go. We'd been doing the back-and-forth thing for far too long. My heart couldn't handle it anymore.

In truth, losing him was what I couldn't handle.

When I'd opened my legs earlier that night, knowing he'd be watching on the other side of the camera, I prayed that he'd finally break his rules.

For once, I wanted him to whisper my name.

He loved me, but we lived in different worlds that occasionally crossed orbits.

However, no matter how bad it got between us, whether it be two months or ten decades since we last saw each other, Mateo would never turn his back on me. This included rescuing me from the trunk of a car headed God only knew where after I'd been kidnapped by God only knew who.

The problem was never whether he'd *try* to find me.

As the hours passed, the question that soured my stomach was whether he could.

And as I felt the car once again slow to a stop, I sucked in a sharp breath, closed my eyes, and screamed his name with everything I had left.

Then Whitney and I both screamed as the sound of a gun exploded outside the car.

Chapter Four

Mateo

THERE IS SOMETHING truly beautiful about vengeance, especially when issued to such a deserving soul. As I watched Jonah collapse to the ground with a hole in the back of his head in the filthy parking lot of a Tennessee rest stop, I thought it was the most beautiful of all.

Ideally, I would have enjoyed more time to play. Every minute of the last ten hours had been spent plotting how I would peel the flesh from his worthless bones.

But not at Ivy's expense.

As expected, dead-man Jonah had been on the quickest route back to Chicago, highways the majority of the way. The fool had never even noticed my man on his tail. They'd stopped in the middle of nowhere in Georgia once for gas, and Javier had reported hearing Ivy yelling for help. A thousand rusty daggers had slayed me when I'd ordered him to stand down; but with only one of my men against Jonah and his other two guarding the car, it was not a calculated risk I could afford to take. Not with Ivy's life hanging in the balance.

So, with bile churning in my stomach, muscles straining in my neck, and an all-consuming rage devouring me, I'd flown to Tennessee with the hopes of joining the hunt.

The flight had been agony, but the minute that piece-of-shit sedan had come in to my sights, the rest of the world had disappeared. I couldn't see her, but I fell into her gravity all the same.

And when I got out of my car and heard her screaming my name, that gravity became flammable, detonating and engulfing me into a fiery conflagration.

My bullet ended Jonah just seconds after his gaze had met mine. The shock and subsequent fear on his face fed the darkest parts of my soul. I wasn't an animal. I didn't *enjoy* ending a man's life. Unless he deserved it.

With memories of Ivy screaming my name as she was dragged from her bedroom running rampant through my brain, I didn't think that anyone had ever deserved it more than Jonah Sheehan. I flat out relished in the high of watching his body fall to the ground, piss darkening the front of his jeans.

My vision tunneled as I stormed over to the car, vaguely aware of Jorge taking care of the other two men. They would share Jonah's fate after I got some answers. That could wait though.

"Open this," I growled at Javier.

It wasn't often that I was scared. Not of the men who wanted me dead. Not of the authorities who wanted to lock me away. But as I waited for Javier to lean into the car and pop the latch, I'd never been more terrified in my life.

I knew she was in there. We'd had eyes on the car for the last ten hours. But no one had actually seen her since that vehicle had left her driveway.

I'd heard her voice, so I knew she was breathing, but I had no idea what condition she was in. And just the thought leveled me.

The trunk sprang free with a click and then everything else went silent.

I'd vowed to myself the day I'd first laid eyes on her that the fear was over for her. I'd promised that I'd take care of her, sworn that my lifestyle would never touch her.

But there she was, blinking up at me, naked, covered in blood, and huddled with another woman like they were nothing more than cattle headed to market.

All because of me.

"Oh, God, Mateo," she choked out, her voice cracking in a way that I felt every jagged edge slice across my skin.

"Ivy," I whispered, full of apology. "I'm here, *mi alma*. I'm here."

I bent to lift her out, but before I had the chance, she scrambled to her knees and launched herself into my arms. She linked her arms around my neck, and her legs dangled off the ground as she clung to me. Her soft body, flush with my front, calmed me physically until my racing mind had a chance to follow suit.

"I…didn't know if you'd be able to find me," she whispered, pressing her face into my neck, her wet tears burning my skin like acid.

"You said my name, Ivy. Death wouldn't have been enough to keep me from finding you." I set her on her feet, releasing her only long enough to remove my button-down and transfer it to her. As she slid her arms in, I got a good look at the gash above her eye. My blood caught fire all over again.

Movement over her shoulder drew my attention. It was the girl who had been in the trunk with her. She'd pushed up onto her knees—matted hair, a black eye, bruises and dirt covering her exposed body. I recognized her from the photos Leo had shown me only hours earlier. She was Mira's friend—the one Guardian was so frantically searching for.

"Whitney," I said quietly so as not to spook her.

Her wide, desolate eyes flicked to mine, her chin quivering as she asked, "You…you know who I am?"

I nodded, drawing Ivy into my front. "I'm a friend of Mira's. You're safe now."

She started sobbing immediately, her shoulders rounding forward as she leaned out of the trunk, dry-heaving.

"It's okay," I assured her, running a hand up Ivy's back. "Nothing will touch either of you again. You have my word." I wasted a moment of my life giving Jonah one last glance. I would have much preferred to leave him to be eaten by the vultures, but someone had to clean this fucking mess up before the cops got involved.

"Javier. Take care of this." I turned with Ivy in my arms, calling, "Jorge." He was throwing the last of Jonah's men—bound and gagged—into the trunk of one of our vehicles.

He slammed the top at least a dozen times, no doubt breaking a few of their bones, before giving me his attention. "Yes, sir?"

I jerked my chin to the young woman and ordered, "Get her out of there and cover her up."

He didn't delay in starting on the top button of his white button-down. Blood and dirt covered the fabric, but it would at least cover her. And more, it would ensure I didn't have to stare at her fucking bruises as we flew back to Chicago, reminding me what could have happened to Ivy had I not gotten there in time.

With an arm at the backs of her knees, I scooped Ivy off the ground and headed to our SUV.

Nothing else mattered until I got her somewhere safe.

CHAPTER FIVE

Ivy

"HOW ARE YOU, my love?" His hand was locked on my thigh as I stared out the window of the different, yet identical, black SUV that had met us on the tarmac just outside of Chicago.

"Okay," I replied.

He used his fingers under my chin to tip my head back. His eyes were gentle as he whispered, "If you're going to lie, say it to my face. Now, I'll ask again. How *are* you, my love?"

He always had been able to read me; there was no point in faking it. My stomach churned as I gave him what he'd asked of me. "Not good."

He dipped, brushing his nose with mine, and swept a kiss across my lips. It was so sweet that it was almost painful. "I'll make it better. I swear on my life, Ivy. I'll make it better."

There was nothing Mateo couldn't fix.

But this time was different.

It was strange and I couldn't pinpoint it.

Hell, I couldn't even figure out what part of my emotional spectrum it was coming from.

But something inside me was...*wrong.*

The last twenty-four hours of my life had been crazy, but this was more than just shock.

I'd held it together for most of my time in the trunk of Jonah's car, but with one glance at Mateo, I'd lost the fight.

It wasn't rational.

Whitney and I were safe.

I should have been relieved. But I couldn't stop the crash of the adrenaline now that it was finally over.

I'd cried in Mateo's arms during the entire drive to his plane. Through it all, he'd held me tight, peppering kisses anywhere his lips could reach and whispering reassurances that he'd never let anything happen to me again. The only time his attention was not one hundred percent focused on me was when he'd occasionally ask Whitney if she needed anything.

She'd given him the address of where he could find some dog named Bitsy, but besides that, she just sulked in the corner, her legs tucked to her chest, a steady waterfall of tears flowing down her cheeks. The wall she'd constructed around herself was so tall that it was a miracle we could see her at all.

When we'd arrived at Mateo's private plane, I wasn't surprised to see that there were not one, but two doctors waiting for us. Whitney had refused to be checked out, and as much as I knew Mateo wanted to argue with her, he was more concerned with making sure I was okay.

From what I'd been able to see, none of my cuts were too deep, though there was no convincing Mateo of this. He'd kneeled beside me, holding my hand and kissing the back of it as the doctor cleaned my wounds. I'd said every cuss word in existence when he cleaned the gash at my eye, but luckily, despite the constant threats, Mateo had not thrown the good doctor from the plane for hurting me.

After that, I'd spent the rest of the flight with my head in his lap, his fingers constantly sifting through my hair as he carried on whispered conversations with Jorge.

It was calm and comfortable, which I so desperately needed after all the chaos. But that was when I first noticed that something didn't feel right. The easy stuff had always been the part Mateo and I excelled at. There were no drugs or violence or kidnapping on that plane. During that flight to Chicago, we were just two people very much in love, living in the moment.

We'd done that for five years.

And given the way my heart had exploded the minute he'd opened that trunk, I knew I'd do it for fifty more.

But maybe that was why I was struggling.

At night, when I closed my eyes, it was more than the easy moments that I dreamed of.

I wanted a life with Mateo. The kind with diamond rings, white dresses, picket fences, and whiskey-eyed boys who looked just like their father.

Without a doubt, he'd have married me on the spot if I'd told him that was what I wanted. For me, he would have put a rock the size of the moon on my finger and followed that immediately with an over-the-top wedding, a grand mansion, and a baby in my belly.

But in my dreams, Mateo wanted all of that too. Fiercely.

The reality was, in all our years together, Mateo had never once asked me to be with him. He knew I hated the crime. That it terrified me. And even with the knowledge that I loved him with my whole heart and my entire soul, he'd never—not once—asked me to dig deep, search my heart, and let go of my fears *for him*.

Every fight we'd had was because I wanted more from *him*.

Where was the fight because he wanted more from *me?*

It had been two months since I'd last said his name, and it had taken being kidnapped before he'd felt the need to show up again. Honestly, that hurt more than anything Jonah had done to me.

By the time we arrived at his mansion in Chicago, the trauma of the day had fallen to the wayside. A healthy dose of anger replaced it.

It wasn't fair for me to be mad at him. He had, after all, rescued me from the clutches of a madman. But then again, there would have been no reason to save me at all if it weren't for his lifestyle. People didn't want me dead. I wasn't the one who had enemies all across the country. So, as happy as I'd been to see him, I wasn't sure he deserved credit for something he had caused.

As I jumped out of the SUV the minute it was in park, I was starting to think that maybe two months wasn't enough separation.

"Ivy," he called, climbing out after me.

I didn't know where I was going, but that didn't slow me down. I raced up the steps and flung the front door open. As to be expected, the place was gorgeous—clean and crisp, decorated in muted grays. It wasn't quite a wealthy man's bachelor pad like his penthouse in Miami, but it still had a definite masculine vibe. This pissed me off more. Because someone—more than likely a woman—had decorated that house for him.

And I hadn't even known he owned it until he'd told me on the plane.

Mateo knew *everything* about me. From the pillows I liked right down to what time I brushed my teeth at night. He had the ability to watch me twenty-four seven, something I'd never minded before because it was Mateo and I'd liked knowing he was close in one way or another.

But he was only close to me.

I'd never been close to him.

I darted toward the staircase, taking them two at a time. I needed to find a bedroom and lock the door before the tears came back. It didn't matter that he'd seen me cry a million times before. These tears were about him. And I didn't want him watching like this was just another day in my life.

The upstairs was huge. At least six doors lined one hallway before splitting off to the left. I cut into the first room I came to, shut the door, and locked it.

The bedroom was large, a king-size bed the focus, with a sitting chair in the corner and a TV mounted on the wall.

Simple, but well decorated.

Better than the plush comforter that called to my weary bones was the attached bathroom. I stripped off the button-down shirt, which still managed to smell like Mateo even though I'd been in it for hours, and headed straight for the open-stall stone shower, ready to wash away more than just the day.

While standing under the stream of hot water, I started weeding through the last twenty-four hours in my head. Everything was a jumbled mess. All the conflicting emotions made it virtually impossible to dissect anything. I was so focused on trying to make heads or tails of my anger and frustration that I never even heard him come in.

"Shit!" I screamed as I caught sight of him in my peripheral vision.

"It's just me," he purred.

"Christ, Mateo. Don't sneak up on me like that."

"I wasn't sneaking. I assumed you were waiting for me." He slid under the water behind me, naked as the day was long—and it was Mateo, so it should be noted that his *day* was *really long*.

He was a beautiful man—his body a landscape of hard planes and tight abs. I knew all too well the miracles his mouth could create when he dropped to his knees or the orgasms that he could draw from my core with little more than his soapy hands at my nipples.

But as he wrapped his arms around me, his forearms crossing over my breasts as he dipped low to kiss the curve of my neck, it wasn't sexual. He often held me like that. Tight and secure. And I often loved it. Even right then when I told myself I wasn't supposed to.

"Why would you assume I was waiting for you?" I spun to face him.

He didn't as much let me go as he allowed me to turn in his arms. It was as though he were physically unable to release me.

Yeah.

Okay.

I loved that too.

Dammit.

I didn't tell him any of this and carried on with the weird hurt-frustrated-angry attitude combination I was sporting. "I locked the door and everything. That's the international signal for 'don't get naked and climb in the shower with me.'"

His head snapped back, his whole beautiful face pinching with genuine confusion. "You locked the door because of me?"

"Well, Jorge has never climbed in the shower with me, so..."

His face got hard. "That ever changes, I better be the first to know, Ivy."

I rolled my eyes as I attempted to push out of his grasp.

He didn't let me go, and a shiver went down my spine when his lips came close to my ear. "I was just checking on you, *mi alma*."

Mi alma. My soul. He'd called me that for years, and I'd always believed it. But this time, it felt wrong as it tumbled from his perfect lips.

"Why do you call me that?" I snapped.

His dark brows furrowed. "*Mi alma?*"

"Yeah."

He shifted his gaze around the shower as if the answer were printed on the walls. "It means—"

"I know what it means, Mateo. I guess I just don't understand why you call *me* that?"

He blinked, the water dripping off the ends of his lashes. "I think that's pretty self-explanatory."

I laughed without humor. "Is it? Because it's been two damn months since I saw you last. That doesn't sound like I'm your soul. That sounds like I'm an option."

He stared at me, pure awe twinkling in his eyes. "An option." He took a step forward, crowding me. "A fucking *option?*"

Pushing up onto my toes, I got right in his face and replied, "That's what I said."

His large hand found my hip, giving me a firm squeeze before shifting me back and pinning me against the cool wall, a thrill shooting through me. "I put a bullet in a man's head today. And tomorrow, I will put a bullet in two more as soon as I get the answers to how they found you. After that, I will slit the throat of any man who knew about this, enabled this, or so much as breathed your name in conversation. And that is not because you are an *option* to me. That is because if something had happened to you, they would have been burying me beside you." He rested his hand on the curve of my jaw and stroked his thumb across my lips. "You are the one thing in my life that is not optional, Ivy. You are a part of me. The only part that matters."

I shook my head. "It doesn't feel that way."

He moved in, his hands going to either side of my head, and his hips hit mine, caging me while still offering me the illusion of space. "Then I have failed you in more ways than just allowing someone to put those marks on your stomach."

Holding his dark stare, I told him an absolute truth. "The marks you've left inside me are far deeper." It wasn't often a man as strong and stoic as Mateo appeared wounded. But I'd thrown my dagger, and judging by the look on his face, it had landed right in his heart.

He pushed off the wall, making that illusion of space a reality—and not just because of his physical proximity. He was still standing in that shower, but he'd left me all the same.

For a moment, panic hit my stomach as I wondered if I'd pushed him too far.

But the truth was never wrong, and I'd been holding it in for way too long.

I took a step toward him, and he mirrored it with one away. "Why do I have to say your name?" Another step. "Why don't you ever come to me?" Another step. "Why aren't you sneaking into my house because you can't stay away?"

By this point, he'd backed out of the shower, standing naked in the middle of the bathroom, confusion etched in his beautiful face. I didn't bother turning the water off as I followed him out.

Standing just inches away, I dealt my final blow. "If you love me the way you say you do, if I am truly part of your soul, why aren't you fighting for us?"

It was as though I'd pulled the pin on a grenade.

I knew that Mateo could be a dangerous man, but his malevolence had never been aimed at me. Until now.

His voice was low and ominous as he snarled, "I have been burning at the stake for five fucking years for you. And you want to know why I'm not *fighting for us?*"

A chill that had nothing to do with cool air against my wet body pebbled my skin as his arm hooked around my waist. It wasn't gentle and the bruises on my stomach objected as our bodies collided, but I didn't move an inch.

"How many times did you tell me to leave you alone?" he rumbled. "How many fucking times have you told me that you can't be with me because I make a living doing something that you deem unsavory? How many fucking times have I paused my entire life when you call my name just to spend one fucking hour at your side? Don't you dare stand there and tell me I'm not fighting for us. I have been fighting an unwinnable war for five fucking years because I would rather die on that battlefield than live a life without you."

My breath hitched. "Mateo, I—"

He was getting angrier by the second, his arm around me tightening with every word spoken. "I have tried to honor your wishes. I stayed away because that is what you have asked of me. But now you want me to fight for us? Am I hearing this correctly?"

I didn't know if he was hearing it correctly. Because deep down, I didn't have the first clue what I wanted him to do at all. I just wanted to be with him.

I wanted to stop the games.

I wanted to fall asleep in his arms—every night.

I wanted to come home from work and find him sitting on the couch, waiting for me.

I wanted to bicker about money.

I wanted to plan vacations we'd never take.

I wanted a normal life with a normal man.

But I hadn't fallen in love with a normal man.

"Answer me, Ivy," he demanded.

My mind was still spinning, playing out the worst-case scenarios of being with a man like him. But it was my heart that had its say when I opened my mouth and replied, "Yes, I want you to fight."

I was up off my feet in the next second, dangling in his arms as he carried me to the bed. He deposited me on the mattress, sideways across the bed, immediately following me down and crashing his mouth over mine.

I moaned and he swallowed it like a man on the brink of starvation. When his cock thickened between my legs, I spread myself wide, begging for more.

He ignored my plea and instead tore his mouth away. "This is your home now. Miami isn't safe anymore. I will never recover from hearing you yell my name as those bastards dragged you out the window. But I swear on my life I will make sure that you do. I have men here who can watch you."

I writhed beneath him. "You've been watching me for forever."

He slid a hand down my side, his thumb tracing the curve of my breast before moving inward. I let out a cry when he found my clit with such ease it was though it had been calling to him.

"Yes," he said, "but now, when you decide to taunt me by playing with this pussy, I'll be here to help."

I froze when a thought struck me. "You're going to live here with me?"

The side of his mouth hiked. "*Mi alma*, what kind of husband makes his wife live alone? Besides, if I turn over the men in Miami to Jorge, he's not going to want me hovering."

My eyes flashed wide and then just as quickly filled with tears. "You're turning over the men to Jorge?"

He sucked in a deep breath. "I cannot change the life I lead, Ivy. I have too many enemies at this point to ever be able to walk away. This is who I am. This is who I will always be. But if you can accept that, I can absolutely slow down. It won't be a ranch in Montana. But I can keep you safe here in Chicago. I can keep both of us safe here."

My whole body shuddered as I fought back a sob, fearful that I was getting my hopes up for nothing. "What does slowing down look like to you?"

"I have no idea. But if you are willing to meet me halfway, we can make it look like whatever we want."

God, my heart was already so full, and then he made it overflow.

"I'd like for it to include at least one child, but if you don't feel comfortable bringing them into this—"

"I want, like, a lot of kids," I blurted out.

His laugh, so rich and masculine, warmed my already heated body. "So we'll have, like, a lot of kids." He'd repeated my statement in the most unlike Mateo way possible, thus making me smile.

"Really?"

"Ivy, if you want something, I want to be the man to give it to you. That is all I have ever wanted."

"Then I should probably tell you I don't want an engagement ring the size of the moon."

He nipped at my bottom lip. "I'm sorry. That is not a promise I can make."

I half cried, half laughed as I looped my arms around his neck. "I've been so scared for so long."

He pressed a lingering kiss to my mouth. "I'm sure what those assholes did to you yesterday did not help, but I swear—"

"Actually? I think it might have."

His body turned to stone on top of me, so I guided a hand up to his face.

"Something broke inside me in that trunk, Mateo. I saw Whitney, just a normal girl who lived a simple life, no ties to any kind of crime, but she'd still somehow ended up in that trunk with me, scared out of her mind. The difference between us was that she was convinced there was no way out and I knew, with every fiber of my being, that you'd come for me."

"Always, Ivy," he breathed, turning his face into my touch to kiss my palm. "Always."

He bent down and sealed his promise with a deep and commanding kiss. Our tongues tangled, the intensity rising with every stroke. I let out a loud gasp when his hand slipped between my legs. Again, he found my clit, circling it before he filled me with two fingers and curled them at the ends in the way he knew I loved.

I arched off the bed, screwing my eyes shut as he began a delicious rhythm of thrusts and circles. "Oh, God, yes. Mateo."

"We're going to do this," he said, more of an order than a question.

"Yes," I panted.

"You're going to let me in. You're going to marry me. You're going to give me children. And you're going to trust me to take care of all of you, because you know I would claw my way from a grave before I ever allowed anything to happen to you." His fingers became almost as urgent as his words. "Say it. Tell me you know that. Tell me you know that I will always protect you."

Sitting up as much as his body would allow, I reached between us, guiding his thick cock to my opening. "I know. And that's why I'm not scared anymore."

The pure relief in his eyes mingled with ecstasy as he sank inside me.

That night, everything changed between Mateo and me. Yet, in a strange way, nothing changed at all.

He made love to me, slow and reverent.

Then he fucked me hard and fast in the shower.

He took me from behind, his teeth at my shoulder while we were cooking dinner together in the kitchen.

And that night, before we fell asleep, I coaxed him into abandon with my mouth.

But one very important thing changed that night and for all the days to come.

The night that I'd been kidnapped was the last time I'd ever had to call Mateo's name.

From that day on, Mateo was the one calling for me.

Each and every time.

Ivy.

Ivy.

Ivy.

Mi alma.

And eventually… *Mi mujer.*

My wife.

✧   ✧   ✧

Didn't get enough of Mateo and the men from Guardian Protection Agency? You can read more about my sexy, alpha bodyguards and the women who stole their hearts in the Guardian Protection Series. Available now.

alymartinez.com/singe

THE BLESSINGS OF
ETHAN BLACKSTONE

RAINE MILLER

Somerset
March

I HAVEN'T CRAVED a cigarette in months. Honestly, I figured I was finished with that horseshit ages ago.

More the fool, me.

My naïve optimism is currently in the process of having the ever-loving shit kicked out of it. By the biggest fucking horse on the planet. A horse who is mean and doesn't give two fucks about my optimism. I'm pretty sure he has no plans to cease with the beatdown on my sorry arse, either.

A bead of sweat rolls down my back, fueling the urge to ditch my jacket. The irony isn't lost on me since it's barely spring and a surprise snowstorm just rolled through in the night. Plus, the heating allowance for the ministry building I'm trapped in at the moment? Nonexistent. The annoying itch inside my collar makes me wish I could tear off my tie and toss it in the bin by the door. No, wait, I might need that bin for being sick in a minute.

Considering what I'm about to do, yeah, I'm a shivering wreck of nerves. Ergo the desperate craving for a smoke. Even though I kicked my bad habit nearly a year ago, that memo went missing inside my dreadfully fucked-up head. Along with all of my common sense. Why the hell did I ever agree to this?

Because helping them helps you.

I focus on my breathing and go through the motions of what I've been taught since I started at the Combat Stress Centre. The image of the Keep Calm poster in Gavin's office comes to mind. For some reason that simple old poster has always helped. But most of all I remember who'll be waiting for me at home when this is over.

My girls. My girls. My girls are waiting for me.

Repetition also helps me for some godforsaken reason, so I do that too.

Who in the hell am I fooling? I can't do this. No, not *can't*—I don't *want* to do this right now. I remember Gavin's technique of giving yourself a choice rather than ultimatums. The ultimatums are fucking useless when dealing with your inner fears. Either you want to face them, or you don't. It's that simple. I can get up and leave right this minute if I choose. Nobody is holding me here.

But my arse is still stuck to the chair for some reason. Gavin suggested I come to an open meeting in Somerset to see if I found it useful. I should have asked him a bit more about what an "open meeting" entailed before I agreed to come to the fuckin' thing. Once I found out it was the kind of meeting where everyone sits in a circle and shares whatever they feel like sharing within the group? Uh…thank you kindly, but fuck no.

Sharing shit with strangers is not my thing. Not even close. But how I might know it's not my thing is a goddamn mystery because I've never done it. Gavin said hearing other soldiers talk about their experience might be a way for me to help me sort out my own bloody demons. And that's what gave me pause to even consider showing up here today. I'll admit I'm curious to hear what others have to say about their combat stress. Are they as fucked up as me? Not that I wish for them to be, but maybe it helps to know I'm not the only one who thinks peeling off my own skin would be a preferable alternative to suffering through another hellish round of flashbacks and nightmares.

I count seven of us sitting here in this dreary room with no heat. All men. I'd guess a range within ten years of my age, both older and younger. As I study each of them, I know that not one of these blokes is at ease. Everyone looks pretty much the same, all sporting a slightly different variation of *get-me-the-hell-outta-here-as-soon-as-humanly-possible* expressions carved into their faces. No explanation needed. I know where they're coming from because I'm right there with them: up to my neck in a shit-pile of *I don't want to share the horrible things that happened to me with a bunch of strangers.* Most of it is stuff that I can't even bear to remember on a good day anyway. Burying the horror away is one solution, although not a permanent one. That shit will come back to find you when you least expect it to.

I'd fucking love a double shot of Van Gogh right now. Times two.

It's a lonely club, and every man in this room is a member. A club we didn't voluntarily join. One we were initiated into without warning or consent. And from what I could tell, it was a club where membership was permanent. Once you were in, you didn't get to leave. Ever. The club will end up becoming a part of you, or it'll kill you. I chose the first option, obviously, but now at least, I can understand how some soldiers come to choose the second. I was lucky. Brynne had been there to help me find my way back. I never forget how lost I would be without her. She'd brought me back to life. More importantly, she'd made me *want* to live my life.

The massive bloke across from me interrupts my scattered thoughts. And I do mean massive. The arms on him are fucking huge, along with the rest of him. Impossible to miss all those muscles underneath just a thin, black t-shirt. He's not wearing a coat, and since I *know* this room could be renamed Antarctica, he's either oblivious to cold, or he's got the sweats like me. "I'll go first. My name is Flynn Mansfield, British Army, 4th Armoured Brigade, Operation Herrick, Afghanistan." His face gives away nothing, neither pleasantness nor unpleasantness, only the worn look of a someone who's seen far more than anyone ever should. "You don't have to speak today if you don't want. Just listen if it suits you. Everyone is different, and what works for one, might not for another. But what I've learned is talking about my PTSD does help me. Every time I recall something and share it, even if it's a small thing, the worst of the memories hold less power over me. I feel less burdened, even if just for a bit."

My ears perk right up at his little introductory speech.

I'd be lying if I didn't admit I'm fucking relieved this guy just gave me permission to keep my trap closed and be a listener. Not at all what I expected to happen today, but for the first time I'm rather glad I showed up. I *can* do this. Once again, Gavin was right. I need to give my head-peeper a lot more credit, and I will the next time I see him, but right now I'm more interested in hearing what Flynn Mansfield has to say. He seems relaxed to be talking to us, so the least I can do is give him the respect to listen to what he's sharing.

"I was part of a team responsible for training the Afghans in all aspects of policing. The task sounds straightforward enough, but you all know that nothing is straightforward in the military. What's most frustrating is how the public can never understand the primal day-to-day business of fighting an insurgency where every step taken had the potential to change lives forever. Over there, I could take tea and shake hands with someone in the morning, only to find him shooting at me in the afternoon. This was a constant reality with the Afghan army. They were so infiltrated with Taliban you never knew if the next casualty would come from the allies you were training and arming with weapons. I had to learn not to get too emotionally close to the mates I was fighting alongside because I might have to repatriate their body in the days ahead. These are not emotions that affect many people who are watching events unfold on camera 6,000km away..."

Listening to Mansfield does help. Seems counterintuitive that something as simple as listening to another person share their reason for being in this room today should help me, but it does. He talks about the things he wishes he could forget but never will. He shares those experiences he can only hope will someday find a permanent home somewhere inside the psyche of his past. A place where those traumas will learn to reside without tormenting his soul.

That's what I hope for. The hope that I can simply live with the memories in a quiet way that respects the experience for what it was but doesn't give license for it to define the reality of my life now. I just want to make peace with my past.

Or to have my past make peace with me.

I'll take it either way.

As Mansfield finishes what he wanted to share, the group gets quiet again. He looks over, his dark eyes homing in on me, a silent invitation given without any expectation or demand. Respectful.

Instead of looking away and avoiding the call, I give him a nod of respect and find that maybe *I do* want to share after all.

I raise my hand to let them know I'll go next.

"Please," he says, gesturing to me with an open palm.

"I'm Ethan. Ethan Blackstone. British Army, SAS, Captain, Afghanistan. I'm thirty-three years old and work in private security. I was taken captive by the Taliban and held for twenty-two days. By some miracle of godly grace, I made it out of there with my head still attached and my body intact. I'm a very lucky bastard. I know that, and I guess that's what's hardest for me to reconcile. Yes, I have PTSD, and a shit ton of survivor's guilt as I was the only one of my team to make it out alive, but for me, my struggles didn't start until I had something to lose.

"I lived day to day, sometimes from one smoke to the next before my reckoning came. When I first returned home, I know I was still in shock and closed off. My father and sister aren't the prying kind, and I appreciated that they didn't, but I knew I wasn't fooling anyone. They could clearly see how the war had changed me. They didn't bring it up, and neither did I. I didn't even have many nightmares beyond my first few days after rescue. It was like I was able to bury the experience as if it never happened. Denial made daily life seem so much easier. For a time. I got my shit together and started my company. Life sort of fell into a routine of work and not much else. Even though I still felt empty and closed off emotionally, I pretended well. I fought to rationalize the flashbacks and the nightmares, but just as my struggles began when I finally had something to lose, they were also my way out of the darkness. Something worth living for. That would be my family. I have a wife and a daughter, and everything I do now...is for them..."

✧   ✧   ✧

THE SWEET SMELL of baking bread met me the minute I opened the door and stepped inside. Destination kitchen. Brynne knows it was my first group meeting up here, so I imagine she'll be anxious to hear how it went. She's nothing but supportive and I try my very best to be the same with her. Before I left for the meeting, Brynne and Marie were busy making the beautifully decorated Ukrainian Easter bread or *paska*—a family tradition handed down from Marie's Ukrainian grandmother—and from the delicious smell hitting my nose, I'd wager the both of them were still at it. She'd explained they were to make three loaves: one to honor nature, another to honor the dead, and a third to honor those on earth. A beautiful sentiment and tradition to pass along to our daughter.

Our first Easter spent here in the country, and it was shaping up nicely. Last year the house had been too upended with renovations to consider trying to forge out some comfortable space for gatherings when it was in such a state of disorganization. Especially with a newborn Laurel in this house as had been the case last Easter. But a year's time had changed things. My wife definitely was *not pregnant* this year. And Stonewell Court had been beautifully refurbished where she stood high along the Somerset coast. The old place was now as solid as the rock foundation underneath her fine architectural bones, much to my relief, and looked the part of Neo-Gothic Georgian manor house she'd been built to be. That last part was knowledge that came to me courtesy of Brynne, who knew all of the art and architecture shit related to the house that I could appreciate but probably never understand very well. I'm a security expert, and happily leave all the artistic pursuits to her. She is the art and architecture authority after all.

I'd never regretted my impulsive decision to buy Stonewell for us after we'd discovered it on a walk when I'd brought Brynne to Somerset to meet my sister and her family for the first time. The estate agency sign had called to me right away. I grinned remembering the "other" surprise we discovered that weekend. Yeah, lots and lots of changes for us since that day in July when we wandered up the drive to check out the old house behind the iron gates.

Changes that had given me the kind of life I never believed I'd ever have.

But *I did* have it.

By some holy plan completely out of the bounds of my control or direction, I'd been blessed with a precious life.

And I knew nothing but gratefulness at the knowledge of that fact.

In the past year, Brynne had spent a lot of time and effort on turning this house into a home for our family. And she had done it beautifully. As evidenced by the masses of flowers arranged in vases and pots set around the place. It truly looked like spring had sprung around here...or was about to as soon as this surprise spring snow faded away. Brynne sourced from the local fields as well as the gardens at Stonewell, of which she'd gotten busy digging in the dirt about as soon as the ink was dry on the deed. She said it was a kind of therapy for her, working in the garden amongst the flowers. A place to bury the demons of her past down deep into the good clean earth where maybe something wonderful might come from her efforts. I understood. I had my own demons to deal with...and my own ways of doing so.

Loving her was my best therapy. Loving her and being loved by her was one hundred percent saving my life. I knew that was my truth without a single shred of a doubt.

I stopped at the great room and admired the arrangement of purple flowers— still her most favorite color—placed in front of the cathedral window that went floor to ceiling and looked out over the park grounds and the circular drive leading up to the front steps. Mother Nature had dropped a surprise snowfall down on West England last night, and even though it would make the roads a bitch to navigate, the snow created a pretty picture when you were looking at it from inside a heated building. I didn't have to worry about guests traveling in to see us with poor road conditions either, because my dad and Marie had made it up here from London the day before the storm. I can't help thinking about the safety aspects of most every situation. It's just how my brain works. I know for damn sure Brynne and Laurel won't be in a car alone on these roads until the snow has completely gone.

Keeping my girls safe is my mission in life.

I'd just put the snow chains on her Rover myself in preparation for the drive over to Hannah and Freddy's for dinner in a few hours. I could have had our caretaker, Robbie, do it, but I like getting my hands dirty and knowing a job is absolutely done right. It's a short drive anyway over to Hallborough. When the weather's nice we walk back and forth between houses all the time. Zara's here almost every day and already quite the expert babysitter with Laurel. She loves her little cousin fiercely and it's apparent Laurel, at just a year old, adores Zara. Watching and learning at her every move, soaking up all of her child wisdom. I'm probably royally screwed in about fifteen years from now when my baby girl's a teenager. Shuddering at that horrifying idea, I look out the window instead.

The snow has made everything look pristine and quite like a scene from a Dickens' novel here in the country as opposed to London. The country life was something I'd not anticipated I could fit into so easily, but we'd both found we loved being in Somerset as much as possible. Knowing we would be here for a good ten more days was a pleasant thought. BSI execs take a holiday every quarter, which we fully deserved for the work we did. I know Neil and Elaina were happy to get up to their place in Scotland for a nice long stay. Any events scheduled for this time were handled by other capable employees who would see Blackstone Security ran smooth until Neil and I were back to London.

I could see my dad and Sir outside tramping about in the thin layer of snow. Sir was in love with his rag bone and could retrieve it for hours if he could find someone up for it. The scene I was witnessing looked like he was putting Dad to the test right now, but both seemed to be enjoying themselves which was the point after all.

Having my dad here with Marie was another blessing I realized. I'd always wondered how it had been for him to be single for all those years after Mum died. I imagine he'd just focused on Hannah and me since we were so young, and then it became routine to be alone because he was just doing what he had to do to get through each day without her.

Meeting Marie had changed everything for my father.

And how well did I understand that bit of news.

Crystal clear understanding because it had been like that for me with Brynne. One look at her and I was driven to know her, to have her attentions on me. And what a lucky bastard I'd been that she became mine in the end. A supremely lucky one is all I know.

Now I could be happy my dad was similarly blessed with a woman who loved him. Technically Marie was my stepmother but it didn't feel that way really. I have one mother and I am totally content with the knowledge that somehow she's aware of me from wherever she is in the vast universe. I know Marie understands my feelings about my mum and doesn't presume to take her place in any way, but just be a part of our family as Dad's wife. Just another reason why she is so perfect. That, and the way she loves Brynne and has always supported her. She's also the best, most loving gran to Laurel. The way I saw it, we could all only benefit from having Marie in our lives, and I was happy they were here to spend Easter with us in the country this year. Maybe we were starting a new tradition to celebrate in Somerset for holidays instead of London.

Brynne and I had watched the snow falling last night right here in front of the window on the sheepskin rug. We'd done some other things too, after Dad and Marie had gone to bed and we were alone with just the drifting snowflakes reflecting off the lights out front through the window.

I closed my eyes and remembered us in this room last night. How she looked and felt in my arms and spread out on that sheepskin rug. *So fuckin' good.*

It would be nearly impossible for me to forget the sight of my beautiful girl's eyes on me as I made love to her in front of the fireplace, and I relished the chance to show her how much I loved and needed her as often as possible.

Everything was so good with her—a baby and the past year hadn't changed that, either. If anything, we were stronger than before. My sessions with Dr. Wilson at the Combat Stress Centre in London were helping me to accept my past and to put it in its place without destroying my present. One day at a time was the best advice he gave me, and also not allowing a past event to hold more power over me than any other. The good should be given just as much influence as the bad. All were a part of the makeup of my psyche, and I was learning to put that ideology into practice with my doctor's help and the steadfast support of Brynne. Besides, the good parts of my life now were so good, they helped to override all of the bad shit from my past.

Brynne still amazed me at how wise she was when it came to facing fears. It was like she was made for me in all my fucked-upness, and no other woman on earth could have been more perfect to help me find my way back into the land of the living. I was convinced that nobody could have done what she did in transforming the hopeless life of Ethan Blackstone.

Only Brynne.

Again, I have to wonder at what kind of divine intervention occurred in leading me to finding her.

Looking up at the little angel statue sitting up high on a shelf—a Christmas gift from my sister—I give the angel a wink, bringing up the image of our mum from memory. I wonder if she knows we named Laurel after her. I hope so.

I turn to leave the great room and head toward the source of the wonderful baking smells.

I can hear them long before I get there. Brynne and Marie are laughing at something, and I discover what it is when I get to the doorway and lurk without announcing myself. They're decorating Easter eggs while the bread bakes. Specifically, *pysanka*—the intricately designed Ukrainian Easter eggs. Brynne did them last year and explained the tradition to me like this: *pysanka* are given to friends and loved ones to represent the gift of life, and are usually decorated to match the personality of the receiver.

My little Laurel is on Marie's lap watching her mummy put lines of dots in shapes and swirly designs on the colored eggs with a stylus dipped in dye. Such a little beauty she is already. Just like her mother…

"I think Daddy will like this one," Brynne says to Laurel. "This egg looks like the colors of Simba's fishy stripes," she says amid more laughing.

"Da da da da da," Laurel babbles while gumming two fingers.

"You are saying 'Daddy,' aren't you, little one?" Brynne asks her.

"I think she is," Marie says while smoothing over the curls on her little head. "She reminds me of you and Tom when you were this age, Brynne."

"That makes me happy to know. She is definitely a daddy's girl like I was," Brynne says softly, and I imagine she is remembering her own father.

Laurel's blue eyes find me in the doorway and widen. "Da-Da!" she shouts, bouncing on Marie's lap in my direction.

"Ah, the jig is up when she spies her daddy," Brynne says with a wink at me. "And I think that is confirmation right there that she is definitely saying 'Daddy,' don't you agree?"

I give Brynne a kiss. "I say yes, of course," I answer as I hold my arms out to take Laurel from Marie. I think my heart just stretched a little bit more at hearing my baby girl say "Daddy" for the first time. She pats my face and continues to say, Da-da-da-dee-dee, over and over, seemingly very pleased with herself. She has to be the most brilliant one-year-old child ever born, right?

Emotions sweep over me in a way I have never experienced, and I can feel the weight of eyes on me—watching. Laurel, bless her sweet baby heart, breaks the spell by bouncing and reaching out toward the window, giving me the distraction I need to keep from shedding sappy tears in the middle of my kitchen in front of Brynne and Marie.

I knew exactly what she wanted, too.

"You want to see if Mr. Squirrel is out on the wall stealing the poor birds' food again?"

I receive an affirmative grunt and kicks to my abdomen—her efforts to get my arse moving.

"Oh, let's take her outside, Ethan, I want to take pictures of the two of you in the snow before it's all gone, and she can watch Mr. Squirrel pilfer bird seed at the same time."

"I can't say no to that offer, baby. Let's do it."

After bundling Laurel into a snowsuit and mittens, we head outside together and experience snow for the first time all together. The thieving red squirrel is there as expected, dashing back and forth along the stone wall delighting Laurel to no end, which is the only reason he is allowed to be around. Sir would have endless entertainment chasing him off if he was here with us right now.

I don't think I could be any happier than I am already, but Brynne has something to say about that. She is watching me and analyzing where my head is at most likely. She knows me better than anyone else and realizes how emotional I got when Laurel called me "Daddy" in the house a few minutes ago.

She weaves her arm through mine and snuggles up close into my side as we watch Laurel shriek every time Mr. Squirrel streaks across the wall in a panicked dash with his stolen loot. "I was gonna wait to give you this news but I think now is the perfect time to tell you something, Mr. Blackstone."

My heart stutters a little at her words. I hope the bloody thing serves me well for a lot of years to come, because it sure takes a regular thrashing since Brynne came into my life. "What news is that, Mrs. Blackstone?"

She looks up at me with a smile, her beautiful eyes sparking greenish-brown, and touches my cheek. "You are an amazing father, and I love you."

"You never cease to amaze me, baby, and you are a perfect mother."

She nods thoughtfully, never taking her eyes off mine. "So…it's a really good thing, then, we're such outstanding parents because in the fall we'll have a new baby Blackstone wanting some attention."

I don't know exactly what I said or did at that point except I remained standing because Laurel was in my arms. There was some kissing and maybe a happy tear or two might have slipped from my eye, but all that mattered to me was that I was in the here and now. With Brynne and our children.

I had survived other things in order to make it here to this place in my very wonderful life.

My very blessed and wonderful life.

✧　✧　✧

This has been a small peek into the next book of *The Blackstone Affair* series— **The Blessings of Ethan Blackstone**. Yes, it is coming, and I can't wait for you to fall in love with this wonderful man all over again.

Taken by Moonlight

Pepper Winters

"**D**O YOU MIND crying quieter? You're ruining the serenity."

My head whipped up as I swiped at the soaking lakes of tears on my cheeks. "Who—who said that?" Narrowing my eyes, I glared at the beach. My vision wobbled with wetness and the moonlight only cast a meagre silver glow. Gentle waves crashed on the white-sand shore, palm trees swayed in the softest tropical breeze, and night insects continued buzzing and chirping even though my ears strained to hear past them for signs of whoever dared be so rude.

Swallowing back my tears, I balled my hands and stood.

Sand stuck to my gold-threaded sarong that I'd bought especially for this trip. I'd stupidly agreed to let Lawrence take me shopping (spending my money no less), listening with hope that he'd booked us a stay on this island because he'd finally learned that marriage should not include his fists or temper.

I used to be gullible.

I'd been born into decadence and been sequestered away from pretty much everything, and stupidly believed my parents had my best interests at heart when they arranged a marriage between myself and Lawrence.

I didn't have to go through with it. After all, we weren't in the dark ages anymore, but he'd been nice. I'd fallen for his ruse and by the time our honeymoon came around, I finally understood what a terrible mistake I'd made.

And now, I'm crying pathetically on a beach while the bruises from my darling husband are covered in waterproof concealer, yelling at a total stranger.

"I know you're out there. You can't tell me to cry quieter and then go silent."

The waves crashed, insects buzzed, and finally, a voice that sounded as if it'd been formed from midnight and velvet said, "I think I preferred your crying. Your voice is even more annoying."

"That's it." I stomped down the sand, looking every which way, my copper tangles kissing my shoulders. "I'm done with men being assholes. If you want to insult me, do it to my face."

"Why? So you can scream some more?"

I squinted into the darkness, my tears well and truly gone. Whatever pity I'd felt for myself burned into rage. "If you don't like my voice, perhaps you'll like my fists better."

A dark chuckle licked across the sand.

I trembled with fury. "Come out. Unless you're a spineless fool who can only mock women from the shadows."

A shuffle sounded, followed by the softest grunt as if whoever he was had stood. The hish-hish of sand on feet hit my ears just before a tall, muscular man appeared from the darkness. The moon did its best to illuminate him but failed.

His skin was almost as dark as the night, gleaming with the glow from the white sand. His eyes were just as black—a raptor stare that made me feel as if I'd been hunted and caught. His hair was short, cropped close to his head and so thick it looked as if he wore a cap of darkness.

He was the exact opposite of Lawrence with his dirty-blond hair and muddy-brown eyes.

He smiled, his teeth blindingly white and perfect in the night. It wasn't a smile that I was used to seeing: spoiled with the uppity balance between scorn and politeness. His smile screamed danger. It fit on his handsome predator face with canines a bit too long and lips a bit too full. His eyebrows came down, shadowing his dark eyes, his entire body tight with lethal grace as he stepped closer toward me.

"You were saying?" he asked softly, so softly it sounded like a menacing purr. "You want to hit me because I told you to quit your sniffling?" His head tilted to the side, his eyes raking over me. "I suggest, if you *are* going to try and hit me, that you pick a wise spot. And make it hurt enough to make me second-guess paying you back." He closed the distance until his scent fed up my nose, citirus and ocean with the faintest hint of metal. "Because if you don't, then you'll wish you never spoke so boldly."

My heart fluttered with warning. A warning I didn't entirely know what to do with. I hated him at first sight yet there was something...something I didn't like tugging against my tummy as if the threat he represented was the biggest aphrodisiac.

I backed up a step without thinking.

His wolfish smile widened. "Wise decision."

That pissed me off.

It made all the pain Lawrence had given me, all the tears I'd cried, and all the mess I was in swell into a fireball in my chest.

I bared my teeth.

I balled my hands.

And threw myself at this new nightmare.

He grunted as my palm struck his cheek. My hand stung and the slap of my skin against his echoed over the ocean, sounding loud enough to wake all the other sleeping married couples who were here for marriage therapy. The villas were spaced far enough apart not to hear others' arguments or makeup sex.

The resort called Rapture could not be faulted in any way.

But him.

This asshole ruined my one moment of solitude.

I didn't even care I'd slapped a total stranger all because of a quip. A quip I should've just walked away from.

His hand came up to cup his cheek just as my knee swooped up to kick him where all men ought to be kicked.

His arm shot downward, somehow snatching my knee before it connected and digging his fingers into the sensitive joint. "Not how I saw tonight going," he growled.

With a twist that seemed inhuman with strength, he tossed me to the side.

I went tumbling.

The sand wasn't as soft as it looked as I landed flat on my back. Sand stuck to my bare shoulders where my black bikini exposed so much skin. Air exploded out of my lungs. I struggled to catch a breath.

With a savage curse, the man stepped over me until I lay between his spread legs. His stare locked with mine, his monster-dark eyes menacing. "You actually struck me." He dropped to his knees, trapping my waist between his thighs. "I told you payback would hurt."

"Stop. What are you—" I dug my hands into the sand, trying to scramble backward.

He merely bent forward, stabbed one fist into the beach by my ear and pressed the other like a collar around my throat.

I froze.

His forehead furrowed into harsh lines as his skin gleamed with moonlight. "Definitely wasn't expecting you to have the balls, but to be honest, perhaps that spirit will keep you alive longer."

Wait, what?

I clawed at his wrist as his fingers tightened around my neck. His touch zinged through me, making my blood hiss. "Let go of me!"

"Quiet. You'll wake the other sleeping couples."

"HELP!" I screamed, bending my head back and yelling at the golden lanterns twinkling in the tropical foliage where other villas hid. "HEL—"

His other hand clamped over my mouth, imbedding sand into my cheeks. "I said..." He bent closer, his eyes glinting with no mercy. "*Quiet.*"

I thrashed beneath him, bucking my hips and squirming in every direction. The bows on my bikini loosened and my top shifted warningly.

I stiffened.

No way did I want this asshole seeing my bare breasts. Who the hell knew what else he'd do?

He took my sudden stillness as obedience and slowly lifted his hand from around my mouth. "Stay quiet and I'll treat you kindly. Scream and I'll treat you cruelly. Run and..." He smiled, running his tongue over his pearly white teeth. "...you'll wish you never stepped foot on this island."

My mouth went dry as he cocked his head, the sinew and muscle in his neck stark against the moonlight. "Do you hear me, little heiress? Or do I have to repeat myself?"

I went cold. "You know...who I am?"

He grinned. "I know every wife currently on this godforsaken shore."

"Why?" *Keep him talking. The longer he talks, the more chance you have of getting away.*

"Why?" He reclined onto his heels, his body still towering over mine. "Because I'm in the market."

"For a wife?"

"For a payday."

"I...I don't understand."

But I did.

I'd read enough articles online about pirates in Asia. Pirates who ran ashore and stole women right off their lounger, their husbands knocked out and left to wake up to an empty ring finger and no wife.

Admittedly, the articles had been a few years ago and pirates didn't seem to be a thing anymore, but I'd still read them. Still feared them. Ever since Lawrence bought the tickets to Rapture and told me, in a suspiciously cagey way, about a virtual reality experience called Euphoria that promised couples the best sex of their lives, I'd been wary.

And sex with him? As if that was supposed to entice me to go when I'd been locking my door for the past year to avoid his fists.

But then he'd mentioned that along with sex, the island offered world-class therapy to heal broken marriages. He'd taken my hand and blinked his boring brown eyes and actually *apologised* for what he'd done to me and begged for a chance to do better.

Pity for him, my gullibility had faded the moment I married him.

He only wanted to get me out here, on an island in the middle of some warm sea, to do his best into conning me to stay.

Another year and my inheritance would kick in. Another year and he'd claim it all. Claim my inheritance that was a thousand times bigger than his. An inheritance that was the sole reason my life had been so sheltered right from birth.

Actually, sheltered didn't quite cover my abysmal childhood. Perhaps imprisoned would've been a better term for the amount of life skills and travel I'd been allowed to do.

I hadn't even been allowed to go to a friend's house unless they'd been vetted by my father's head of security and a guard drove me there and straight home.

"Your mind is racing a million thoughts a minute," the guy murmured. "What the hell could you be thinking about so intently when I have you between my legs?" To prove his point, he squeezed my waist with his thighs, deliberately shifting off his heels so he sat on my hips instead.

His weight sent my pulse skyrocketing again, sending mixed signals to my head.

Forcing my voice to stay steady, I snipped, "I'm thinking how much trouble you're going to be in when they catch you."

"Trouble for what?" he asked, genuine curiosity in his husky tone. "I've done nothing wrong."

I scoffed and shoved at his thighs, cursing the way my fingertips tingled. "You're sitting on me."

"So?"

"You don't have my permission."

"I'm not the type of man to ask."

"Oh, I'm aware. Believe me." I stopped touching his legs, balling my fingers into tight fists and lying prone on the sand. "You're just like every other asshole in the world."

His eyebrows formed a severe line. "As if you'd know? You're everything that's wrong with the world at the moment." His face formed into a sneer that should've made him look ugly but had the unfortunate ability of making him even more roguishly arrogant. "A rich little white girl, crying at midnight on some exclusive beach, all because her rich white husband didn't buy her the diamond necklace she wanted."

Pure anger blazed through my chest. I didn't even care he pinned me to the sand anymore. I was done being stereotyped and ridiculed. I knew how everyone looked at me. I daren't show my true sadness because no one believed I had anything to be sad about. I hid my true feelings from everyone.

Everyone.

But not anymore, you bastard.

Slapping my hands on his thighs, I burrowed my hands up his shorts so I could sink my nails into his bare flesh. The shorts he wore were as dark as his skin, silky and slightly damp as if he'd been swimming before harassing me. The t-shirt he wore was also slightly damp, smelling like the salt of the ocean with a faint whiff of seaweed.

He sucked in a breath as I did my best to draw blood with my nails.

But he didn't hit me or retaliate, he just sat there with his raptor stare and threats.

"You don't know me," I hissed. "You will *never* know me. Go ahead and judge me all you want, but I don't care what you think. I don't care what anyone thinks anymore. I'm done. Do you hear me?"

He finally flinched as something slippery coated my fingertips.

Ripping my hands from his legs, he held up my fingers, twisting them for the moonlight to catch the black crimson of his blood. A savage smile came to his sickeningly handsome face. "You are just full of surprises." Letting my hands go, he cupped my cheek, sending another scatter of sparks throughout my body. "Who the fuck are you and why am I getting hard?"

My eyes instantly dropped to his shorts.

He wasn't lying.

The silky material had started to tent.

My heart switched its gallop for crazed palpitations instead. "Let *go* of me." I slapped his legs as I squirmed. "I mean it. Let me go or I'll—"

"You'll what?" He grabbed my chin, holding me still. "Keep doing things like this and I can practically promise you, you'll be cheating on your husband tonight." In a sinuous move, he unfolded his legs until he lay over me, his body between my thighs, keeping me spread. The hardness in his shorts lined up perfectly with my open sarong, pressing against the tiny scrap of black bikini.

I didn't just stiffen.

I turned to marble.

Holding my chin, he ran his finger over my bottom lip at the same time his hips pulsed against me.

His eyes flared at the contact, the blackness of his stare contracting with what looked like wicked lust. My palpitations skittered into smoke, making it hard to breathe.

Looking down the length of my body, he licked his lips, staring at where we were joined below. For the longest moment, he didn't say a word but then he whispered black as midnight, "Fuck, you really shouldn't have let me do this."

I grabbed his hips, wanting to draw his blood again. I went to push but instead I clung hard, slicing my nails into his flesh. "I didn't *let* you do anything."

"No?" His eyes hooded, his voice turning thick with something that sent my entire body liquefying. "You're pulling me into you." He groaned as his hips pulsed again. "You're giving me pain which I should probably tell you, turns me the fuck on."

Instantly, I removed my hands, glaring at his blood beneath my nails. "Get off."

"Christ no."

I shivered as he rocked against me, sending my body flashing with hot and cold, fear and sickening awareness.

"Not until I know who you are and why I can't seem to stop thinking about what you'd do if I ripped off your bikini and buried myself inside you."

"I'd kill you."

"You could try."

"I'd scream."

He chuckled, rocking again with a guttural groan. "Believe me, you'd be screaming if I fucked you."

"You'd be dead."

"I'd like to see you try. I really, really would." He licked his lips again, his tongue shockingly wet and pink against his dusky dark skin. "I can't promise I'd last long if you fought me. I can barely restrain myself now."

"You're a bastard."

"That is true but you're a spoiled little bitch who deserves it, so...I can live with it."

I opened my mouth to scream.

He clamped a hand over my lips. The lust in his gaze twining with danger. "I wouldn't do that if I were you. Not when I'm this hard and really fucking struggling to remember what I came here to do."

I tried to bite his hand.

He just chuckled as if my fighting for my virtue was foreplay. "I wasn't expecting you, spoiled little heiress. I was not expecting you at all." He bent his head, nuzzling my nose with his. "Who the fuck are you, Bellamy Whitaker?"

My name on his lips was the bucket of ice water I needed.

My hands flew to his shoulders, and I shoved him back with strength I didn't know I had.

He reared upward, his hips pressing harder against mine for balance.

Bloody freaking hell—

Why did he have to press in that *exact* spot?

I hid my tremble.

He didn't.

His head hung low as a visible shiver shot down his spine. "Jesus. Christ." His hips circled, pressing so hard I became intimately aware of his shape and size without even having seen him.

He was bigger than my husband was, that was for damn sure.

He was far more dangerous than my fist-happy husband, that was also fact.

Yet for some idiotic reason, the panic I usually felt when Lawrence found me in the giant mansion we co-habited or cornered me in the shared bathroom before I could scurry to my bedroom and a locked door didn't flare.

Lawrence had done a fine job on educating my fear response until I flinched at the barest of breaths from him. I'd learned not to fight when he wanted me and did everything he asked when he stripped me and bent me over the nearest piece of furniture.

If I didn't, his hits were far less full of passion and far more painful with violence.

Yet it didn't explain why I wasn't sobbing with terror.

Why I wasn't fighting with everything I had.

See, this was why my father wouldn't let me out. Why I wasn't allowed around boys. Why I was imprisoned in my room with stuffed unicorns and pretty tulle until I turned the spinster age of twenty.

I was broken.

Some shattered part of me was actually getting off on some stranger dry humping me on the beach.

The man bowed his head, his mouth hovering over mine. "Your mind is whirring again. You thinking what I'm thinking?"

"Doubt it," I hissed. "I'm thinking how nice it would be to skewer you in the heart with one of those beach umbrellas."

He sighed as if disappointed in me all while his mouth skated super soft over mine. "Liar." His tongue licked my bottom lip, sending a bolt of electricity right between my legs. "You're thinking why you're wet. Why you're not pushing me away. Why you're allowing a total bastard to dry hump you until he's so fucking close to coming in his shorts."

I tried to speak but couldn't.

I squeaked some denial instead.

"Tell you what, Bellamy," he murmured, his breath skating over my mouth with the faintest scent of citrus. "Scream. I'll let you scream, right now. Scream until the whole fucking island can hear you. Do that and my initial plan for you will continue." He licked me again, the tip of his tongue entering my mouth until I squirmed in the sand for an entirely different reason. "That plan you ask? I'll tell you. I've come for a payday. I know that will make you think I'm here to snatch and sell you and, in my line of work, I'll never say never to peddling flesh, but…in my current line of business, I'm only interested in your money."

"I have no money," I gasped against his tongue.

He sighed again, his body pressing mine deeper into the sand. His hips rolled, dragging his hardness along my clit until my legs tried to scissor closed. "Let's not lie to one another. I told you. I know who you are. You're a Silverwood. Or at least, you were until you married into the Whittaker family. I've done my research. Your fortune doesn't kick in for another year, yet you live on a very ample allowance that is more than enough to satisfy me. Your wedding rings are also worth stealing. So you see, little heiress, my only task tonight was to take you aboard my ship, complete a few wire transfers, relieve you of your marital goods, and then drop you off so your dear loving husband doesn't suffer a heart attack at your loss."

I stiffened at the mention of being used for my money—just like everyone did—only to be returned to the one man I wanted nothing to do with.

"And if I don't scream?"

His head wrenched up, his dark eyes blazing with hunger. He studied me for a bit too long. He looked past who I was to who I wished to be.

I wished to be brave, bold…free.

My heart pounded and his hips continued to press against me until we both panted indecently.

I hated that a total stranger—a thief no less—had made me wetter than my husband ever had. The only man apart from Lawrence to ever put his hands on me and he'd done it without my permission. And, horribly, taught me just how messed up I was because I liked it.

Slowly, he lowered back down again, his nose to my nose, our eyes still linked. "Don't scream and…" He swallowed hard. "Fuck, I won't be responsible for what I do."

"What exactly will you do?" I taunted. "Fuck me?"

"Eventually."

"Eventually?" My eyebrows shot up. "The sun will rise in an hour or two. Do you plan on keeping me spread eagle on the beach while other married couples come out to discuss their problems? Or perhaps you'll invite my husband to watch you defile his wife."

His jaw clenched and his eyes that were as black as the sky seemed to turn blacker still.

His mouth suddenly slammed against mine.

I gasped.

He groaned.

His tongue dove past my lips.

He didn't just kiss me, he set me on fire with a lightning storm. His tongue lashed against mine, hungry and possessive, claiming me as if he'd always had me.

I fought back.

I met his invasion with a swift shove of my own tongue, flinching when I dipped into his mouth.

That was not my intention.

I'd just meant to stop him, not kiss him back.

His tongue speared back into my mouth, hot and demanding.

I met him again, tangling with him, fighting, struggling.

His chest rumbled with a primal growl and whatever kiss he gave me splintered into war.

Grabbing my cheeks with both his hands, he held me still as he plundered my mouth. He bruised my lips. He bit my tongue. He was everywhere and everything. A rocking, thrusting, licking, biting storm that swept me away until I lost all sense of who I was.

What the hell am I doing?

He dragged me out of my thoughts and deep into my body.

A body that'd been tormented, ignored, and bruised. A body that suddenly woke up in a blaze of awareness, drunk on the spirals of need this total stranger caused.

I let him kiss me.

He devoured me.

And for the first time in my life, I knew what it felt like to be wanted.

The kiss evolved past just lips and became our entire bodies instead. I couldn't fight instinct, all while my mind blared with horror. I was a slave to sensation as my hips rocked up on their own accord just as his thrust down. We both flinched. Both grunted. Both attacked each other with raw indescribable desire.

One of his hands fell away from my cheek and cupped my breast.

Cupped was a mild word.

Snatched was better.

I arched my back at the lacerating lightning he sent to my core. Hs shoved aside my loose bikini and fisted my flesh, pinching my nipple, making me cry into his mouth.

Nothing had ever felt so good, so wrong, so deliciously bad.

This man was a self-admitted criminal. He deserved to be arrested and caged for what he'd done without my consent but...not once did he give me pain. Not once did he make me fear. Not once did he make me beg for him to stop.

Oh, God—

He dipped his head and sucked my nipple into his mouth, pulling hard, trying to eat me alive instead of kiss me.

I snatched handfuls of his hair, jerking him as my body fought for something.

Something...

Bright and tight and blinding.

Oh, God, don't, don't—

As if he could hear my thoughts, his hips lost the pretence that he wasn't a scrap of material away from fucking me and drove against me. His erection rubbed on my clit; the silkiness of his swimming shorts slid perfectly along the slipperiness of my bikini.

I didn't stand a chance.

His fist remained on my breast all while his mouth came back up my body, biting and licking until he found my lips.

He fell on me with a savage curse, his kiss depraved and dark.

He wasn't quiet like he'd told me to be. He grunted with each rock, his breath hot against my cheek as if he couldn't stop. His back hunched and his hand slid from my breast to between my legs.

My eyes flared; I tried to say no.

I moaned as he shoved aside my bikini bottoms and sank two fingers deep, deep inside me.

I bowed in his hold.

Shock made me scream.

His mouth silenced me all while his fingers took from me something I hadn't given.

His thumb pressed on my clit; his hips continued rocking against his own hand as his fingers pulsed against that magical spot inside.

And the bright, tight, blinding wrongness exploded.

My core rippled outward, an orgasm barrelling down my legs to my toes. My entire body went stiff as I clenched with wave after wave of pleasure. Pleasure that I'd never felt before. Pleasure that turned me boneless and mindless because I'd never felt that with Lawrence, never felt that with my own hand, never even known something like that was possible.

A throaty roar spilled from him as he let go and followed me. His entire body shuddered with waves that seemed almost painful as he jerked between my legs. His kiss mimicked his release, his tongue thrusting in time with his trembles, his skin sweaty as he finally pulled away.

Panting hard, he looked down at me as if he didn't understand how this had happened. For a blistering moment, he was maskless and the hunger swirling in his stare made my heart skip a beat because what'd just happened hadn't sated him, it'd just made him want more.

Slowly, without speaking, he withdrew his fingers from me and placed my bikini back into position. With grace that reminded me of night creatures who hunted innocent stupid things like me, he stood.

Brazenly, he grabbed his spent erection still tucked in his shorts and shifted it, a grimace on his face. He didn't offer me a hand to help me up. He didn't leer at my bare breasts or treat me like a belonging like Lawrence did.

He merely crossed his arms, spread his legs, and growled, "I steal things because it pleases me. I've made a fortune stealing from others who have bigger fortunes and I never apologise for being what I am."

Holding out his hand, his fingers still glistening from my release, he snapped, "Your wedding rings. Give them to me."

I scrambled upright, shaking my head. Wobbling on my feet, I retied my top with shaking fingers. "You can't have my rings."

"I'm taking them. With or without your consent."

"Just like you took me?"

He nodded; his jaw tight. "You're lucky I managed to keep at least some self-restraint." He raked a hand over his sweaty face. "Even now I'm not sure if I can stop myself from throwing you against that palm tree and fucking you anyway." His eyes blazed black. "So, I'll tell you again. Give me your wedding rings and the rest—the kind donation you were going to make to my crew—forget it. Consider me well paid."

I crossed my arms, my skin prickling. "You just called me a whore."

"It's better than calling you what I really think."

"Oh, please, tell me what you really think. It's not like you've spared me from anything up till now."

He bared his teeth. "Easy. I think you're easy. Not only are you a spoiled little white girl but you're also a cheater. How many other men have you been with without your devoted husband knowing? This was probably a little fantasy to you. Let the bad pirate finger-fuck you in the moonlight."

And just like that.

I reached my limit.

Ripping my wedding rings off—the cushion-cut diamond flanked with two champagne brilliants that'd cost fifty-two thousand dollars and the heavy gold band that'd shackled me to Lawrence—I threw them at him.

They glittered briefly as they bounced off his chest and vanished in the sand.

"What the fuck!" He looked at the ground. "Why would you do that?" He bent, doing his best to see the expensive jewellery in the lacklustre moonlight.

He was at the perfect height for my foot to connect with his jaw.

I kicked him.

And...immediately wished I hadn't.

He stumbled backward with a shocked groan, his hand cupping his face. For a split second, he smouldered with rage that sent fear scattering down my spine. I knew that look. That look always ended in pain.

But then a dark grin broke out over his face; his white teeth stained red from where he'd bitten his tongue. "Fuck me...who would've thought I'd find something priceless?"

I crossed my arms, my finger feeling empty without my rings but also blessedly right. Those rings were toxic. Not wearing them granted me some freedom from Lawrence even though the eyes of the law said I was still his.

Stepping into me, scattering sand and not caring he buried my rings, he grabbed me by the cheeks. "I said I'd fuck you eventually. I meant it. I was going to take you aboard, keep you hostage, play with you, fight with you, fuck you..." His voice thickened. "I want you, Bellamy. Fuck I'll even admit that I want you more than money at this point and that has never happened to me before...but...I was prepared to walk away. I was doing such a good job at consoling myself with the taste of you on my fingers. You're a married fucking woman. I don't dally with other men's property—unless it will make me rich." He flashed a wolfish smile that stole my breath. "But you...you keep doing things that make dark things inside me take notice." His fingers feathered through my hair. "You really shouldn't have done that."

I rocked backward, trying to get away. "Let me go."

"Not going to happen." He shook his head. "I told you I like pain, yet you kicked me anyway. You were so close to being free. So fucking close to saying goodbye to me and keeping me as your dirty little secret. You would never have seen me again."

He ran his thumb over my bottom lip, his velvety voice putting me in a trance. "But now, it's your husband who will never see you again."

I choked on a breath. "What—"

"I'm stealing you." He announced it as if it were a deal struck with no negotiation. Taking my hand, he dragged me toward the waterline. "I'm stealing you, not for money or for ransom. I have no intention of letting anyone know I have you." He looked over his shoulder with his raptor stare. "No one will know where you are because then no one will make me give you back."

I dug my heels into the sand. "You can't just *steal* me."

"Watch me." He kept dragging me toward the ocean.

"Stop." I tried to scratch his hand as I looked back at the glittering villas in the palm trees. Lawrence was asleep in one of those, snoring in the finest cotton, dreaming up new ways to torment me. We were due to try Euphoria for the first time tomorrow. To enter a simulation where any fantasy could come real and we'd drink an elixir that would ensure both of us were willing and wanting, ensuring that sex would be out of this world—according to the brochure.

Sex had the power to make or break a couple.

Sex had the power to completely change a person.

I should know.

It'd just happened, and I hadn't even had sex with this man.

One tiny (okay huge) orgasm and I no longer knew who I was meant to be.

This was happening too fast, too crazy, too much.

Panic rose. "Let me go."

The man slammed to a stop and spun to face me. With his teeth clenched, he fumbled with the knot at my hip, loosening my sarong and throwing it into the air where it swirled to the sand.

"Hey!"

"You don't want that on while swimming." He resumed yanking me toward the ocean. "I don't want you drowning. That would not make me happy. I hope you can swim, Bellamy. My ship is too big to come to shore and a speedboat is too noisy."

"I'm not swimming anywhere."

"Unfortunately, yes you are. I've made up my mind. I want you. Therefore, I'm stealing you."

"If you don't let me go, I'll scream. The island has guards, they'll—"

"Fuck." He slammed to another halt and pinched the bridge of his nose as if trying to keep his temper. He opened his mouth to speak but closed it again as if he couldn't get his thoughts in order.

I knew the feeling. I felt as if my world was upside down and back to front and I couldn't explain why the thought of not seeing this man again upset me more than the thought of divorcing Lawrence, but at the same time, sanity insisted that I stop him because what sane person would *ever* admit she actually liked what he'd done. Liked that he seemed to be as drawn to me as I was to him. Liked that he'd shown me a tiny sliver of what intensity and being wanted felt like after living such a painful disappointment in my sheltered, sad little life.

Dropping his hand from his nose, he looked at where he held me, twining his fingers with mine, sending another wash of electricity through my blood.

He exhaled hard enough for me to hear before he looked into my eyes and growled, "My name is Rayvn. I've pirated these seas for over a decade, and I've amassed more wealth than I'll ever be able to spend. No one can catch me. No one can touch me. I have everything I've ever fucking wanted…until now." His black eyes glowed with starlight. "One chance, little heiress. I'll give you one last chance." Stepping into me, he wrapped his fingers around my throat.

It ought to feel intimidating and dangerous but somehow it felt worshipping and full of want. "Scream and I'll let you go. I can't promise I won't track you down and I can't promise I won't steal you another night, but I will promise that you can return to your husband and cry into his arms at the thought of a monster capturing you. I'll give you the night to get used to the idea. I'll let you cry until you truly understand that when I see what I want, nothing stops me from taking it." His fingers tightened, choking me. "Nothing. And I want you. So fucking much."

Dropping his hand, he glanced at his palm as if a part of me had imprinted on him. He didn't look up as he murmured, "But don't scream. If you walk into that ocean with me and let me have you in every way I want, then I'll bring you back. Eventually. I'll let you go. Eventually. I vow on my ethics as a pirate that I will take you, fuck you, sail the seas with you, and treat you like a sadistic queen. In return, you will see the world. You won't have to give me a penny because I'll take my fortune from your flesh. And...*eventually*, you'll be free."

His head came up, his eyes locking on to mine.

Ever so slowly, his hand lashed around my wrist, and he tugged me none so gently toward the ocean. "You have as long as it takes to step foot in the water to decide. After that...it's over."

My heart pounded in my ears.

My legs were wooden as I jerked and tripped behind him, unable to catch a proper breath.

He promised travel, after I'd been imprisoned.

He offered passion, after I'd been beaten.

He offered life, after I'd been dead for so long.

The sea came closer.

The sea was almost at my toes.

The sea embraced my feet with wet welcome.

He looked back and waited.

He gave me three thundering heartbeats to scream.

I held his stare.

I cursed myself for being so stupid.

I didn't scream.

His lips pursed and a dark kind of madness lit his face. "Wise choice." He pulled me deeper.

I didn't scream as he dragged me into the gentle waves.

I didn't scream as the shore dropped away and he pulled me swimming beside him.

I didn't scream.

And if I'd known what he'd do to me—alone on his ship, trapped and forgotten by all those who knew me, I should have.

I should've screamed.

Loudly.

✦   ✦   ✦

If you enjoyed reading this chapter called Taken by Moonlight from a new Dark Romance coming soon, please add The Thief and The Heiress to your Goodreads so you'll know when it releases!

THE LAST WARD WEDDING

KARLA SORENSEN

T HE TEXTS WEREN'T the thing that alerted me that something was wrong. Not even the missed calls. It was when I arrived home, and she didn't greet me. The wedding was forty-eight hours away, being held in the backyard of the house that all the girls had grown up in, and she was nowhere to be found.

"Where is she?"

They all looked up at me, varying degrees of exhaustion on their faces. Molly sighed, flopping back on the couch. "I lost track of her about an hour ago. She said something about ribbons and mints, and ..." Her voice trailed off. "I honestly don't know. I think she's losing it."

Lia tied off a small delicate white mesh baggie filled with ... I wasn't quite sure, but there was a mountain of them on the family room floor.

Wearily, I ran a hand down my face and sighed. My sisters snickered. The only one who remained quiet, watching me with a tiny smile on her face, was the one set to walk down the aisle in two days' time.

"She say anything?" I asked Claire.

Claire shook her head. "Not to us, but we could see it in her face."

I raised my eyebrows. "What?"

Isabel tossed another baggie onto the pile. "The impending mental break-down."

Molly laughed.

"That bad?" I asked.

Claire winced. "Maybe a little?"

Lia nodded. "A lot. She had the crazy eyes right before she bolted. Kinda like she got last week when she couldn't get the balloon arch just right."

"I *told* her to hire that out," Isabel said. "Those things are a giant pain in the ass."

I sank onto the couch next to Molly, curling my arm around her when she shifted to lay her head on my shoulder. "How many more of these you guys have to do?"

Lia checked her watch. "We're almost done. Which is good because I have to get home to tuck the little man into bed."

"I need to tuck myself into bed," Molly said around a yawn. I kissed the top of her head, and she smiled against my shoulder, running a hand over the twenty-two-week baby bump underneath her black shirt.

My wife was hiding somewhere in our house, wedding-meltdown in full effect, and I knew I'd find her eventually. But I didn't often get a quiet moment with my four sisters. For years now, we'd been slowly adding significant others into the mix. Boyfriends became fiancés as months passed. All but one had become husbands.

Lia was the first to bring a baby into our crazy mix, and damn if that kid didn't steal a giant chunk of my heart that I didn't realize was still up for grabs. Molly got married first. Then Isabel. She and Aiden had two girls and Paige wasn't sure she could handle all the happiness they brought her.

Lia and Jude got married next, a wedding that featured a few international athletes that even had me a little starstruck. Perks of my sister marrying a former British footballer.

And that left Claire. The quiet one who probably caused me the most sleepless nights. Not because she was trouble, or because she broke the rules, but because she didn't. There was so much worry in watching a heart like hers grow into adulthood, because I never wanted her to lose the sweet, soft side of her that made her so special.

To everyone's complete surprise, the man who captured that heart was big and tattooed and had an edge to him that hid what a giant fucking sap he was for my sweet, soft sister who was so good at knowing what everyone needed.

They took their time, and in true Claire and Bauer style, they'd asked Paige and me to hold a small backyard wedding the same day he slid a delicate antique ring onto her finger.

For a few minutes, I watched my sisters talk and laugh, trying to remember what it had been like years and years ago, when it was just the five of us against the world.

Isabel nudged me with her foot, and I blinked out the memory. "What's that face?" she asked.

I sighed. "Memories. Wasn't that long ago we were sitting in this room arguing about who got the pick the movie to watch. Or whose turn it was to get the good seat on the couch."

Lia grinned. "Remember when Isabel dumped a bowl of popcorn over my head because she hated my choice of movie?"

"You made us watch *The Princess Diaries* for six weeks straight, Lia."

"I was finding popcorn in the couch for the same amount of time," I muttered.

Molly laughed. "Don't you miss it?"

I closed my eyes at the sound of their laughter, these four bright, funny, caring women who'd been my entire world for as long as I could remember. They were starting families of their own, and nights like this, they were few and far between. I didn't ever want to forget what a gift they were.

I missed the popcorn throwing.

The screaming matches.

The stickers I couldn't ever quite clean off the walls.

The way they'd mess up a bathroom beyond any human comprehension.

The long talks we'd have—through their tears—about mean friends and bullies and boys they liked. How they taught me that loving someone that much meant you had to watch them suffer things that you couldn't fix.

And even though the years had brought us so many new people to love, my own wife and son included, there was something almost holy about those early days when we carved out a path for our family. "Yeah, kid. I miss it."

My throat must've sounded tight, because she lifted her head and popped a kiss on my cheek. "Don't cry."

"I'm not," I said gruffly.

I was.

Claire watched the exchange as Lia tied up the last bag and pronounced their labors complete.

Lia helped Molly up off the couch, laughing as her sister groaned at the ache in her back. Isabel joined them, laying a hand on Molly's gently rounded stomach. And from the floor, I saw Claire's gaze linger on her sisters, a melancholy expression stealing over her pretty face.

I stretched my leg out and tapped the side of her thigh with my foot. She blinked away from the scene in front of us, advice being given about easing pregnancy back pain from the two sisters who'd already done it.

I tilted my head so she'd join me on the couch, and she did with a widening smile.

"You ready?" I asked quietly.

She let out a slow breath. "Yeah."

"No nerves?" I pressed my shoulder against hers. "Because if you want to slip out the back, I can take Bauer."

Her face turned to mine with a disbelieving list of her dark eyebrow. "Can you?"

For just a moment, I thought about the reality of fighting a professional snowboarder a couple decades younger than me. I glanced down at her. "Maybe."

She laughed. "No nerves," she said. "I would've married him ten times by now."

"I know." I sighed again. "I should go look for Paige."

My sister nodded slowly. "Yeah, you probably should."

"What happened?"

Claire glanced over at her sisters while they packed up their stuff in the kitchen. The dining room table was covered in wedding paraphernalia, as was my office, and the family room. "She was working on the head table centerpiece with Molly," she said quietly. "And Lia and I started laughing because one of the leaf stems looked like a snake."

"Okay," I said slowly. Paige had been working herself to the bone to make sure Claire's wedding was perfect, but nothing about it had made her break down yet. Seemed unlikely that my wife—one of the strongest women I'd ever met—would be undone by a single centerpiece.

"Then Isabel brought up that one time we put a snake in your shower, right after you guys got married." She grinned, and I caught a glimpse of the little hellion she used to be, right alongside Lia. "Remember that?"

I exhaled a laugh. "Yeah. I remember. I'm pretty sure the neighbors heard Paige scream when she found that one."

Claire's face smoothed out in a thoughtful facial expression. "Something about my wedding—it being the last one of the four of us—it's triggering something for Paige. A sense of loss she didn't have with the others, I think."

"Have I mentioned how helpful it is that you're a counselor?"

"For kids," she said on a laugh. "But yes, you have."

I smoothed my hands along the tops of my thighs. "Tell me what to do, Counselor Claire?"

"Just … give her a hug and tell her it will be okay. She's allowed to feel what she's feeling and she shouldn't beat herself up over it. Life transitions don't always trigger the emotions we expect them to, and my educated guess is that Paige is feeling a little embarrassed that she's struggling with it."

I turned to the side and studied her face. "You're going to be a great mom, you know that? I may have to call you for advice more often."

Claire, to my surprise, teared up, sliding her hand over mine. "Where do you think I learned how to be a great parent?"

I blew out a slow breath and tried to blink back the burning sensation pressing at the back of my eyes. "You four made it easy," I said in a gruff voice.

She flung her arms around my shoulders and I heard a quiet sniff. Wrapping my arms around my little sister, I glanced over at the kitchen to see the other three watching us with soft smiles and bright, glassy eyes. I cleared my throat, because any longer and the whole house would be a giant weeping mess and I still had a redheaded wife to track down.

Claire wiped at her face as she stood. "Love you, big brother."

I ruffled the top of her dark hair, like I used to when she was younger. "Love you too."

With their stuff collected, and our collective emotions under control I stood at the front door and watched my four younger sisters walk out to their cars lining the street in front of the house. As they drove off, I felt just a little pinch of that loss that Claire mentioned.

The house was silent when I closed the door. With the four girls and their growing families often over for meals, and our son, Emmett, tiptoeing into the teenage years, a quiet house was something Paige and I didn't experience very often.

I called her name and listened for a response, frowning slightly when I didn't get one. My office was empty, as was our home gym. She wasn't in the backyard, already set up for the intimate ceremony that would take place on Friday evening. There were fairy lights strung from the house, anchored in the center of the massive tree in our backyard, swooping in a graceful arch over the place where Claire and Bauer would say their vows. I'd caught Paige staring at it the last few days, making sure everything was exactly the way it should be.

As I climbed the stairs, I called her name again, but heard nothing. Our son, Emmett, was at a friend's house, so I gave a cursory look into his bedroom, but she wasn't there either. When I reached our bedroom, and found it dark and quiet, I felt my first tug of worry. It wasn't like Paige to hide from me when she was upset. In the decade plus that we'd been married, I knew every facet of my wife's personality.

Her anger when someone she loved was mistreated, which is what made her the very best mother in the entire world. Her humor, when the situation demanded it. Her ability to look at every situation from a perspective so uniquely Paige that no one else could quite master her advice-giving for the girls and Emmett. Not even me.

But emotions like this, the kind that would have her hiding her face, I wasn't sure when I'd ever seen it. As I stood in the hallway, I glanced at the door to the room that used to be the twins'. And I heard a small, pitiful little sniffling sound.

My mouth curved in a wry grin as I pushed the door open. It was set up as a makeshift office/guest room. When Lia let little Gabriel sleep over, we had a Pack 'n Play in the corner next to the wall, and a small stack of bins with the kids toys she'd started buying in the couple years since he'd been born. The closet door was open, and her legs were stretched out on the floor, protruding from the dark space.

I tugged my Wolves hat off and ran a hand over my hair. "Care for some company?" I asked quietly.

One of her feet slid backwards, followed by the other, until only the tips of her pink and white sneakers were visible. "Sure."

When I edged around the foot of the bed, I finally saw my wife's face, and even after so many years, it never failed to make my heart race. The most beautiful woman in the world, with the biggest heart, and she was mine.

Her arms were wrapped around her shins, chin resting on her knees, and her big blue eyes were red-rimmed from whatever big feelings she'd let out in that little closet. "I don't know if there's room for you, though. You're really big."

"Thanks," I said dryly.

Paige's lips curved up in a smile.

"Stay there," I told her, when she went to move. I slid to the ground, bracing my back against the side of the bed and stretched my legs out, motioning for her to give me her feet. Paige stretched her long legs out, and I carefully removed her sneakers, setting them next to me on the floor. When I dug my thumbs in the arches of her feet, she groaned. "Why you hiding in here, wife?"

She didn't answer. "Did the girls leave?"

I nodded, keeping my attention on her feet while I gave her the same massage I used to when she was pregnant with Emmett. After working on the balls of her feet, and the arches, I smoothed my hands around the fine bones in her ankles, moving to the other foot.

"I didn't mean to hide from everyone."

My eyes glanced up to hers. They were clearer now. "Wanna talk about it?"

She let out a tremulous breath. "It's the last one, you know? The last wedding. When the twins started talking about that fucking snake, and the pranks they played on me when I first moved in ..." Her voice trailed off. "And then all I could think about was how fast time went. They were so little when I met them, and now they're all married and having babies and they're so smart and kind and amazing and they're gonna be too busy to see us anymore and Emmett is basically an adult, and he's going to leave us soon, too—"

My chuckle broke into her tirade, and when she narrowed her eyes dangerously, I did it right back. "Emmett just turned twelve, Paige. We've got a few years before he abandons us."

"I suppose," she answered quietly. "And I know they won't get too busy to see us. They're still here all the time. But ... they were my first babies, you know? I love them so much that sometimes I don't know whether to cry or laugh or puke."

"Puke?" I asked with a smile.

Paige nodded. "If someone I didn't know said that, I'd probably want to gag. How obnoxious, right?"

Her voice wobbled, and I watched helplessly while a tear spilled down her cheek.

"I know what you mean. Claire made me cry downstairs too."

Paige emitted a watery laugh. "Did she?"

I nodded. "I told her she was going to be a great mom someday, and she told me that she learned to be a great parent from me."

My wife shifted out of the closet, and when she settled herself onto my lap, I slid my arms up her back. Her red hair tangled in my fingers and she cupped my face in her cool hands. "You are the best fucking dad in the entire world, Logan Ward," she whispered. "It's so hot, I can't even stand it."

I laughed.

She leaned forward and pressed a butterfly-soft kiss on my lips. The top, and then the bottom. I closed my eyes and breathed her in.

Paige wrapped her arms around my neck and tucked herself against my body. Where I held her tightly, her rib cage expanded on a deep breath.

"Feeling better?" I asked.

She nodded. "Yeah. I just needed you, I think."

I smoothed my hand in soothing circles on her back, let the peace of the moment settle like a warm blanket. Then she told me about what they'd worked on. What was left to do. How beautiful Claire would look in her dress—I'd heard the phrase "garden princess" about seventeen times since she bought the thing and I still wasn't sure what that meant, but apparently it was good. Something with "deep Vs" and "romantic lace sleeves," and every time they described it to me, I nodded dutifully even though most wedding dresses looked alike for me.

All I knew was that every penny spent on those dresses, those four weddings, was damn near the proudest I'd ever been to shell out a shit-ton of money for a single-day event in my life. I would give them anything I had, a thousand times over.

"I think I'm gonna sleep for a week when this wedding is over," she said, nuzzling her face into my neck and breathing deeply.

The thought of a bed and Paige and a stretch of uninterrupted days, it had me closing my eyes. Some guys wanted a beach vacation. Maybe mountains to hike, or big, historic cities to see. I just wanted rest. And her. That's how it had always been with us though. It didn't matter where we went, what life morphed into, as long as we had each other.

"Think Emmett can fend for himself if I joined you?"

Her fingers played with the collar of my shirt. "Sure. He's resourceful."

"Can you imagine what he'd feed himself for an entire week on his own?"

She laughed. "Cheese quesadillas and waffles."

My hands pushed up underneath the hem of her shirt so I could feel her skin underneath my fingers. Paige was so soft. She kissed the edge of my jaw, and I breathed in the sweet scent of her shampoo.

We sat like that for a few quiet minutes, and when she pulled back, her lips were curved in a mischievous smile.

"What?" I asked.

She touched her thumb to the middle of my mouth, and I pressed a kiss to it. "We're alone," she said.

"We are."

Her eyes traced over my face. "Like, really actually alone. All night."

Heat licked down my spine, because that almost never happened. The way my hands had been moving on her back changed. No longer soothing, I pressed harder along the curve of her spine, down below her hips and up the side of her waist where I could feel the weight of her breasts. "We are," I repeated. "What do you want to do about it, wife?"

She bit her lip, curling her hands into the hem of her shirt and tugging it over her head. Her fiery tangle of hair settled over her shoulders, and I leaned forward to press a kiss to the top curve of her breasts where the simple black satin of her bra pushed them higher.

Her fingers dragged over the plane of my chest, curling over my shoulders and biceps.

"I'd like to start right here," she said matter-of-factly.

I hummed, tugging a bra cup down and sucking one of her nipples into my mouth with a hard pull of my cheeks. She gasped, clutching the back of my head.

"Then where," I said against her skin, licking a path to the other side of her chest. Her hand was between us, frantically shoving at the waistband of my gym shorts. "Tell me what you want."

"Oh," she moaned, curling her hand around me while I scrambled to push my hands into the openings of her shorts. "I—Oh shit, like I can think when you"— she gasped when I curled my fingers—"when you do that."

When my fingers found her ready and waiting, I swore under my breath.

Maybe it wasn't the most romantic way to woo my wife, shoving the bare minimum of our clothes out of the way so we could do it on the guest room floor, but even after all those years, Paige still had the power to turn me into an impatient, greedy brute.

The day before, she woke me by sliding her hand underneath the blankets, and we managed to sneak a quiet round in, me moving slow and steady between her legs while Emmett slept. But this ... this was a gift we hardly ever got.

Alone.

All night.

No young ears or grandkids sleeping down the hall.

Were my hands shaking? Maybe a little.

And we started ... right there ... just like that. My shorts hardly pushed past my ass, hers shoved to the side with my greedy hands, and my wife rode me until my eyes rolled back in my head. With my hands wrapped tight onto her writhing hips, she clenched around me with a crying moan.

Paige slumped against me, laughing breathlessly. She moved her hips in a slow circle, and I hissed out a slow breath. When I did, she raised her head, eyes wide in her face.

"You didn't ..." Her voice trailed off.

Surging forward, I took her mouth in a ravenous kiss, sucking her tongue into my mouth and pushing my hands under the hem of her shorts so I could feel the warm flesh of her ass.

She laughed at my bruising grip.

"We're moving to the shower," I told her.

"Oh?" She dropped her head back, and I licked up the side of her neck.

"Yeah. I love how your hair looks when it's wet," I whispered. "It's easier to grab on to when it falls down your back."

She swore.

"Then bathroom counter." I sucked on her earlobe. "Because the height is perfect and I never, ever get to anymore."

She whimpered.

"Then," I whispered into her ear, "we're going to bed. And I'm going to finish our night with my head between your thighs, because it's my favorite place in the world."

When I pulled back, Paige's expression was dazed, delirious.

She gripped my face and took my mouth in a helpless, passionate kiss. Our tongues tangled wet and sloppy, and I bit her bottom lip.

"All of them?" she moaned. "It sounds *delightful*."

With my thumb and forefinger, I took her chin and made sure she was looking straight at me. "All of them. Because I'm not done with you yet, Paige Ward," I growled against her mouth.

She curled a hand around the back of my neck, resting her forehead to mine. "You better not *ever* be done with me," she said.

"Never," I vowed. "Not for as long as I live."

✧   ✧   ✧

If you like steamy marriage-of-convenience stories about grumpy football players, four mischievous younger sisters, and a feisty former model who barrels into their life, you should check out Logan and Paige's story—*The Marriage Effect*! www.karlasorensen.com

THE NIGHT WE MET

SUSANNAH NIX

"TANNER, CHECK IT out." My older and much larger brother Ryan prodded me in the ribs with a massive elbow. "I think your soul mate's sitting over there."

Reluctantly, I dragged my attention away from the book I was reading. "What are you yammering about?"

We were at the Rusty Spoke, the local ice house where our younger brother Wyatt's cover band was playing tonight. I hadn't much wanted to come out tonight, but Ryan had guilt-tripped me into it by pointing out that I hadn't been to one of Wyatt's shows in a while.

I'd arrived early and alone, camping out by myself at an empty picnic table toward the back of the patio where I could read my book while I waited for Wyatt and his friends to take the stage. Ryan had shown up an hour later with some of his buddies from the firehouse where he worked. I was at a particularly good part of my book, so after exchanging greetings I'd gone back to reading and left them to their work talk.

"Your soul mate," Ryan said with a grin. "I found her for you."

I looked in the direction he was pointing, still not understanding what he was talking about. The outdoor bar had gotten a lot more crowded since I'd arrived. Most of the tables had filled up and groups of people were standing all around us and along the fences enclosing the Rusty Spoke's patio. I wasn't sure who I was supposed to be looking at among all the drinkers who'd come out tonight.

Then I saw her.

A blonde woman who appeared to be close to my own age was sitting two tables over with a book in front of her. As soon as I spotted her, I knew that was who Ryan had been talking about. The Rusty Spoke wasn't exactly a popular reading spot, so it was funny there was someone else here tonight who'd brought a book to a noisy bar.

I'd never seen her before, which was fairly unusual in a town the size of ours. I wasn't the most outgoing person, but half the faces here tonight were at least somewhat familiar to me. Not hers, though. I felt certain I'd remember if I'd seen her before.

And yet...something about her felt so *familiar*. The moment my gaze landed on her, I had an inexplicable sense of recognition. My breath actually left my body as my diaphragm relaxed like I'd just spotted someone I'd been looking for.

"She's cute," Ryan said, leaning over to speak in my ear. "Maybe you should go talk to her."

Her face was turned down, half of it hidden behind a spill of hair the color of sunshine, but I had the impression she was more than just cute. If she pushed her hair back to reveal more of her face, I felt certain I'd see she was beautiful.

Nevertheless, I shook my head. "When a woman's reading a book in public like that, the last thing she wants is some stranger taking it as an invitation to hit on her."

Everything about her posture, her absolute focus and the way she was curled over her book with her hands tucked into her lap and her arms tight at her sides, holding herself so still she almost looked like a sculpture, told me she preferred to be left alone to read in peace. We were kindred spirits that way. The knowledge made me want to meet her, to talk to her, to *know* her, even more. But it was also what prevented me from doing it.

Ryan arched a thick red eyebrow at me. "I'm not suggesting you hit on her. I'm suggesting you talk to her. Seems like you two might have a lot in common."

"Intruding on her solitude to start up an unsolicited conversation in a bar is functionally equivalent to hitting on her. She won't thank me for it." Having said that, I turned my attention back to my own book.

"Chicken," Ryan muttered, gifting me with another elbow jab and a few taunting chicken noises. Without looking up, I showed him my middle finger, and he laughed before turning back to his friends.

I attempted to keep my eyes and my focus on my book, but now that I'd noticed the woman, I found it difficult to concentrate. Despite my formerly intense interest in the story, my eyes kept sliding away from the page and over to her table.

The more I looked at her, the more my curiosity grew. It had been a long time since I'd met anyone interesting and new. Longer still since I'd met anyone I felt like I had anything in common with.

She appeared to be alone. The space next to her on the bench was empty, and the other people at her table were ignoring her as much as she was ignoring them.

Was she a student trying to catch up on her assigned reading while she waited for her friends? Or was she someone like me who preferred the company of a good book to socializing? If that was the case, what had brought her to the Rusty Spoke tonight? And then of course there was the most pressing question of all: What was she reading?

As I ignored my book in favor of contemplating these questions and more, the group of people standing behind her broke out into uproarious laughter. A guy in a plaid shirt jostled a guy next to him in a Cowboys jersey, inadvertently causing him to slosh his beer all over the woman and her book.

I jumped to my feet, shoving my own book under my arm as I grabbed the napkin dispenser off my table. By the time I made it over to the woman, the two guys responsible for the spilled beer had just finished offering a sheepish apology.

"It's okay," the woman told them, flicking beer off her bare arm. "Don't worry about it." Her expression was tight, but her voice was soft—more resigned than annoyed.

"Here." I set the napkin dispenser on the table beside her. "Did it get on your book?"

She looked up at me in surprise, and something happened when our eyes met. Something I'd read about in a thousand books but never experienced before. Time seemed to stop for a second. All the people and noise around us faded away to static as I got my first good look at the woman's face. I felt my heart stutter and lurch, almost as if it was rearranging itself inside my chest.

Looking into her face was like taking a breath of fresh, sweet-smelling air. She was definitely beautiful. I'd been right about that. Her eyes were wide and silvery gray, framed by thick brown lashes. A scatter of delicate freckles dusted the tip of her nose and the tops of her cheekbones. Her full pink lips, slightly glossy and parted, were the kind that could make you lose your train of thought.

Finding myself momentarily tongue-tied, I pulled out a handful of napkins and held them out to her.

"Thank you." Her lips curved in a shy smile as she accepted them and wiped off her beer-drenched arm and shoulder.

The people who'd dumped beer on her had already sidled away, leaving the two of us effectively alone among the crowd of people on the patio. When she dabbed the napkins inside the low-cut collar of her shirt, I averted my eyes from the tempting sight of her damp cleavage.

While I was looking elsewhere, I caught my brother Ryan watching us. He flashed a big grin and gave me a thumbs-up. Smug bastard. He was going to enjoy giving me shit about this for quite some time, I had no doubt. Rolling my eyes, I pulled out another handful of napkins and blotted at the beer that had fallen onto the pages of her book. Fortunately, it was only a few small splashes, not enough to cause any real damage.

"Here, I can do that." When she took the napkins from me, her fingers brushed against mine.

She stilled at the contact, seeming startled by it. A blush colored her cheeks as I withdrew my hand, and I wondered if she'd felt the same shock of electric heat I had. My fingers were still tingling where she'd touched me, so much that I curled them into my palm, rubbing my thumb over the misbehaving nerve endings.

"Lucky thing it didn't get too wet," I observed as she finished drying off her book.

"Right? It's a library book, too." Her lips pursed as she finished drying off the table. "I'd hate to face the wrath of Mrs. Urbanczyk after bringing back a water-damaged library book stinking of beer."

"That's the downside of bringing a book to a bar, I guess. You never know when beer's going to spontaneously rain down from above."

"Thank goodness you were so quick with those napkins. Thanks again for the help." She looked up at me with a brilliant, sunny smile and my heart did that stutter-stop thing again.

Of their own volition, my lips pulled into an answering smile. "I can't sit idly by when there's a book in distress."

She took in the book tucked under my arm, and her smile grew. "I'm Lucy, by the way. There's room if you want to sit down."

"I'm Tanner," I said as I squeezed onto the bench beside her. There wasn't all that much room, and my hip bumped against hers as I settled into place.

Lucy shifted toward the end of the bench a little, but we were still sitting close enough that I could feel her leg brushing against mine under the table. "Tanner King, right?"

I felt my smile fade. My family was well known on account of owning the ice cream factory that was our town's single largest employer. People tended to treat me differently because my father was rich and wielded a lot of influence around here. They wrongly assumed that meant I had money and power that made me worth sucking up to.

Although I'd grown up in privilege and owed my job at the family company to nepotism, that was as much as my influence had gotten me. There were no company shares or trust funds in my name, I made the same salary as my middle-management peers, and I was about the last person my father was likely to take advice from. Once people found that out, they often lost interest in me.

"You're Wyatt's brother," Lucy went on before I could reply. "He and my brother Matt are in the same band."

I blinked in surprise at the coincidence. "Is that why you're sitting here by yourself reading a book? You came to see your brother's band play tonight?"

She directed an amused glance at the book I'd set on the table. "Like minds, I guess."

I couldn't help smiling again. "I guess so."

"I was a year behind you in school. That's how I knew who you were."

I stared at her in wonder, unable to believe she'd been so close to me for most of my life and I'd never noticed her before. "Why don't I remember you, Lucy?"

She looked away with a shrug. "It's not like we had any classes together. I wasn't in many extracurriculars, and I didn't really go to football games or parties or anything like that. I was pretty much your standard wallflower."

"Me too." I couldn't get over how beautiful she was. Those expressive lips of hers were impossible to look away from. "I've never been very social, to tell the truth."

Her gaze returned to mine with another one of those shy smiles. "I remember seeing you around, but our paths never crossed enough for us to meet."

"That's too bad," I said, and her cheeks turned that lovely shade of pink again. "It's funny, I noticed you while I was sitting over there reading my book and wanted to come over here and ask what you were reading but didn't think I should intrude. If it hadn't been for that bozo spilling his beer, I'd have missed out on meeting you tonight too."

"Then I guess I'm grateful he spilled his beer on me."

I felt my neck heat and reached up to rub my chest, which was doing funny things again. "It's a shame we couldn't have figured out a way to meet without you having to wear stale beer the rest of the night."

"It's not so bad." Her mouth quirked as she brought her wrist to her nose. "It's sad to say, but I've smelled worse perfumes."

"So what are you reading? If you don't mind my asking."

She flipped the cover of her book up so I could see it.

"*Shadow and Bone*. Are you enjoying it?"

"So far. Have you read it?"

I nodded. "Wait'll you get to *Six of Crows*."

"What about you? What are you reading?" Before I could answer, she reached out and turned my book over. "*Mexican Gothic*. I've heard a lot about that one. Is it good?"

"It's riveting, creepy, and weird. I haven't been able to put it down."

"Should I let you get back to your reading, then?"

I shook my head, no longer quite as interested in untangling the mystery that had previously kept me enthralled. "It'll keep. The nice thing about books is they're always willing to wait for you."

"You sure?" Lucy's smile was teasing. "Far be it from me to keep anyone from a good book."

"Considering I've been waiting my whole life for us to meet, I'd much rather talk to you."

As I watched her cheeks flush pink, I had the strangest feeling that what I'd said was actually true. I had been waiting my whole life to meet Lucy. And now that I had, nothing would ever be the same.

✧   ✧   ✧

Thank you so much for reading my story, "The Night We Met." You can read more about Tanner and Lucy in my steamy, small town King Family series starting with *My Cone and Only*, available now. ORDER MY CONE AND ONLY NOW www.susannahnix.com/mcao.html

THE PROCEDURE

KATIE ASHLEY

CHAPTER ONE

"YOU'RE GOING TO do what to my balls?!" Aidan Fitzgerald bellowed.

In the chair next to him, his wife of three years and mother to his three-year-old son, Noah, and two-year-old daughter, Caroline, rolled her green eyes. "Stop being so dramatic."

Aidan jerked his gaze from the doctor over to her. "Excuse me? Did you even hear what he's saying? He's talking about puncturing my balls, babe."

While he had happily volunteered to schedule a vasectomy consultation, Aidan hadn't been prepared for the graphic details that the procedure entailed. For most of his life, he'd heard about men getting 'snipped.' Of course, he had no idea what that snip actually entailed. Had he known, he might not have been so quick to volunteer his balls to the slaughter.

Crossing her arms over her chest, Emma countered, "It's barely a pinch. Might I remind you I pushed two watermelons out of a hole the size of a lemon, and one of those times wasn't medicated?"

While the doctor chuckled, Aidan was undeterred. "And might I remind you that it's a very sensitive area not just to me, but to all men?"

Emma leaned forward in her chair. "Keep cheapening my labor experiences, and you won't need a vasectomy anymore." Cocking her brows at him, she added, "We won't be having sex ever again!"

Now it was both the doctor and Aidan chuckling. It was moments like these when Emma's fiery personality matched her auburn hair that he remembered why he fell in love with her. It had been at his company's Christmas party when he'd first witnessed the fire. Back then, he was well-known for his womanizing ways. At thirty-two, he wasn't looking for a relationship that lasted longer than the night.

At the party when he saw Emma, she was a vision—a red-haired temptress in a green dress that hugged her ample curves and showed off her fabulous rack. It was lust at first sight, and he wanted nothing more than to take Emma home with him. At first, she seemed interested, but after her work friends gave her the lowdown on the type of man Aidan was, Emma let him know in no uncertain terms that he was the last man she would *ever* sleep with.

After her declaration, it seemed all was done between them. But then fate intervened in the most unexpected way. One night as he was leaving work, Aidan had heard a man and woman arguing in the building lobby. While he might've been a cad, he still wouldn't allow a woman to be harmed in any way in his presence. When he'd rushed forward to tell the man to leave her the hell alone, he had been shocked to find the woman was Emma.

Mortified at Aidan's presence, Emma had sprinted away to the safety of the women's bathroom. While he had been ready to rearrange the dude's face, he quickly learned the guy wasn't trying to get fresh or do harm to Emma—he was her best friend, Connor. With his adrenaline pumping, Connor let it slip what the fight was about: Emma wanted a baby, and she wanted Connor to father it. It was problematic not only because Connor was gay, but more importantly, because his partner, Jeff, was refusing to allow him to be the donor.

After Connor had left, Aidan had waited around to check on Emma. When he offered to buy her a drink, she accepted. Somewhere between her first and second margarita, Aidan had seen a way to fulfill his fantasy of getting Emma in his bed.

It was a little proposition for the two of them to both get something they wanted. He offered to be her sperm donor but with a catch. They would do the physical deed rather than him going solo in a plastic cup at a clinic.

Regardless of how she had originally felt about him, Emma decided to take him up on his offer. What occurred next were many hot and sexy baby-making sessions. While the end goal was a baby, neither one of them expected to fall for the other, but that's exactly what happened after Noah had been conceived. Instead of immediately riding off into the sunset, their growing love underwent a couple of roadblocks.

But in spite of the trials that threatened to derail them, their love won out. In the end, it turned out the thing that brought them together—baby-making—was something they did exceptionally well. The search for a permanent birth control measure was how they had come to end up in a doctor's office.

Knowing he was in deep shit, Aidan held up his hands in defeat. "You're right. I'm a total ass. There's nothing to compare to what you've been through bringing our children into the world."

Her murderous expression immediately softened. "Thank you."

He leaned across his chair to kiss her. With a wink, he said, "You and your vagina are truly heroic."

As her face turned crimson, Emma shrieked in annoyance before shoving Aidan away. "Can we please finish the consultation?"

"Yes, my apologies, Dr. Warren. Please continue."

Dr. Warren smiled. "Mr. Fitzgerald, while I can understand your apprehension, I can personally attest to the benefits of the keyhole method."

"You've had this done yourself?"

With a nod, Dr. Warren replied, "Five years ago."

"And everything is okay?" Aidan gestured to his crotch. "You know, down there?"

"Yes, Mr. Fitzgerald. Everything is fully operational just as it was before. My wife would also sing the procedure's praises."

After exhaling a relieved breath, Aidan eased back in his chair. "Excuse me for freaking out, Doc, but it's not quite what I had in mind when someone said a 'no scalpel vasectomy.'"

Once he heard about the two incisions some of his work colleagues had experienced, Aidan was all about any approach that didn't involve something sharp near his balls. Somehow, he had imagined a laser searing the tubes that carried semen. It wasn't until he'd sat down for his consultation and the mention of 'locking forceps with a sharp tip' totally freaked him out.

"I can understand how the verbiage might have been overwhelming. However, the keyhole procedure is less invasive and doesn't even require stitches. All in all, the total time from prep and anesthesia is only fifteen to twenty minutes."

"So, I'll be totally knocked out for it?" Aidan questioned.

"Yes," Dr. Warren replied.

"Works for me."

"Other benefits include fifty percent less pain, less chance for infection, and a quicker return to sexual activity."

Emma snorted. "I'm sure you just sold him on the procedure with the mention of being ready for sex quicker."

Aidan laughed. "You know me too well, babe."

With a chuckle, Dr. Warren replied, "He wouldn't be the only one."

Rubbing his hands together, Aidan said, "You've totally sold me. Can we do it today?"

"While I appreciate your enthusiasm, we'll need to book a pre-op appointment."

Aidan bobbed his head. "Let's do it."

"Well, there is just one drawback I should mention."

Aidan felt his mood momentarily shift. "Fabulous. What is it?"

"This procedure does require you to use a back-up method of birth control for the first fifteen to twenty ejaculations or roughly about twelve weeks."

"That won't be necessary," Aidan replied. Reaching over Emma's chair, he placed his hand on her bump. "With Emma four months pregnant with our third child, we felt now would be the perfect time."

Nodding, Dr. Warren replied, "Good planning." Turning his attention to Emma, he asked, "When are you due?"

"June 12."

"That will give you more than enough time to ensure there is no sperm left in the vas deferens."

"The what?" Aidan asked to which Emma rolled her eyes.

"Were you not paying attention?" she demanded.

"After hearing about puncturing my balls, I kinda tuned out," Aidan admitted.

"The vas deferens are the tubes that carry semen," Emma replied.

"Gotcha."

Rising from his chair, Dr. Warren said, "I'll go get the referral on the computer, and then the two of you can discuss a good date."

Once he left the room, Emma took out her phone. As she opened the calendar app, she asked, "Do you want to take the first date they have available?"

Aidan nodded. "I don't want it hanging over my head for a long time."

Cocking her brows at him, Emma asked with a grin, "Less time for you to chicken out?"

He scowled at her. "I won't chicken out. You seem to forget I was ready to have a vasectomy after you got pregnant with Caroline."

"Ah, yes, how could I forget the time at our first ultrasound when the sonographer thought she might've heard two heartbeats, and you freaked out so much that you passed out and hit your head," Emma mused.

Of course, she would have to bring that day up. While it hadn't been his finest hour, his reaction was warranted. Noah was barely eight months old, and the thought of Irish twins was scary enough, least of all actual twins. When they'd swung by the ER to have his head checked, he'd begged the doctor on call—who also happened to be a personal friend—to give him a vasectomy that day.

Dr. Nadeen had talked him down from the ledge, and upon many discussions, Aidan and Emma had decided three was their sweet spot when it came to a family. When Caroline hit two, they decided it was time to start trying again, and in their true fertility fashion, Emma got pregnant the first month of trying. That fact just once again reiterated how they needed permanent birth control, or they would be looking like a true Irish Catholic family with a household full of kids.

After a knock at the door, a nurse appeared. "Our first opening is two weeks from Thursday, and then—"

"We'll take it," Aidan and Emma replied in unison.

CHAPTER TWO

Two Weeks Later

AFTER EYEING THE clock on his computer, Aidan began logging off his laptop. He then tossed it in his bag, so he could get some work done at home. Tomorrow was the big day—Vasectomy Thursday. He'd planned to take off Friday as well as having the weekend to recuperate.

He made a quick trip home to the burbs. When he pushed open the garage door into the kitchen, he was met with two excited kids and a woofing dog. "Hey guys!" he called. Getting home from work was one of his favorite times of day. There was nothing like experiencing Noah and Caroline's excitement at seeing him.

"Daddy!" they cried at the same time his four-year-old black Lab, Beau, barked again.

He swept both of his children into his arms before bestowing kisses on the tops of their heads. "Did you have a good day at school?"

The two of them attended a small preschool for a few hours a day. Although he knew it pained Emma to have them gone, it was good for them to be around other kids. "We made you 'Get Well' cards," Noah replied.

Aidan's brows furrowed. "You did?"

Noah nodded. When he glanced up at Emma, she was giggling. "Noah told his class you were having surgery. His teacher thought it was something serious from the way he was talking, so she had them all make you 'Get Well' cards."

"Fucking hell," Aidan muttered under his breath. When Noah's smile began to fade at his reaction, Aidan quickly plastered it back on. "That was so sweet of you and your friends to make me cards. But you don't have to worry because I'm just having a procedure, not a surgery."

"What's a perceeder?" Noah questioned.

Well, it's where a doctor is going to punch a hole in my balls and use a laser to burn off the ends of the tube that brings my swimmers in from my balls. "It's just something a doctor will do in his office, rather than Daddy having to go to the hospital and have a surgery."

"Oh, that's why we have perceeder shirts!" Noah replied.

It was then Aidan focused on the writing on their shirts. "Swim Team Survivor," he read aloud.

"Mommy has one for you!" Caroline squealed.

As if on cue, Emma unfurled a shirt she was holding in her hands. It read, 'Time to Retire the Swim Team.' On each side, there were two smiling white sperm. When Aidan cocked his brows at her, Emma laughed. "Come on, it's a good joke. Especially considering how you were a champion swimmer back in your day."

"What are the odds a picture of me modeling this shirt is going to end up on social media?"

Waggling her brows, Emma said, "Wait until you see the decorations and dinner!"

"You didn't."

"Oh, but I did."

It was at that moment Aidan truly lamented the fact Emma was such a gifted party planner. After Noah's birth when she had quit work, party planning had become her side hustle. Now it was a full business. While it worked out great for the kids' birthday parties, there were other times like now it was a real pisser.

Balloons filled the living room and kitchen. Messages of *Balls Voyage, 100% Juice, No Seeds,* and *Shooting Blanks* adorned the balloons. "Seriously?" he questioned to Emma over his shoulder.

She giggled. "Check out the cake."

With a groan, Aidan walked over to the kitchen table. Gazing down, he couldn't help snorting at the round cake. In large black letters were the words, *Snip, Snip, Hooray*! There were also puffy swimming sperm with x's over their eyes. A small gray stone sat on the top reading his birth date and then tomorrow's date. "This is too much," he mused.

"I thought you'd like it."

"You *are* too much," he added with a grin.

"Why, thank you."

"Do I dare ask what's for dinner?"

"Well, we have a vegetable tray for an appetizer." Emma motioned to the multicolored peppers and carrots that had a sign that read, *'Just the tip'* in front of it.

"You have way too much time on your hands," Aidan joked.

"Well, I kinda tapped out with the main course. It's just wieners with chips and baked beans."

"I'll take it." He pulled her to him. "Thanks for going to all this trouble."

A mischievous look twinkled in her green eyes. "Just wait until you see your other present."

"There's more?"

"While it should be a surprise, I'll give you a little tease." After glancing around to see where the kids were, she went over to the pantry and took out a bag. Reaching inside, she flashed him with a costume.

"You bought a Naughty Nurse costume?!"

She grinned. "Yes, I did."

"Damn, I think you just made my night."

"Trust me, it was no easy feat finding one. They don't really make maternity sex costumes."

"They should. Maybe I should lead the charge at my company to find a distributor," Aidan joked.

Emma playfully rolled her eyes. "Of course, you would think that."

They were interrupted by Noah and Caroline coming back into the kitchen. "Mommy, I'm hungry."

"Okay baby, we'll eat dinner."

Clapping his hands together, Aidan said, "Bring on the wieners!"

CHAPTER THREE

A FTER DINNER, AIDAN headed upstairs to the playroom with the kids while Emma double-checked Noah and Caroline's suitcases. Even though they were only going to be gone for two nights, Emma couldn't help the pang of sadness that entered her chest at the thought of their absence. At the same time, she and Aidan hadn't had a night on their own in a few months. Thinking of the night ahead, she couldn't help the shiver of anticipation that ran through her.

Once Emma was sure they had everything they needed, including their nighttime stuffies and blankets, she called to Aidan. "Ready!"

He came in from the playroom to pick up the suitcases. "Come on, guys. It's time to go to Pop's," he called over his shoulder.

"Yeah!!" Noah and Caroline cried as they came running across the hall.

Aidan's father's house was one of Noah and Caroline's favorite places to go. Emma smiled at the thoughts of the spoiling that lay ahead for them. Her father-in-law loved to do ice cream for breakfast and late bedtimes. Although she tried to discourage Patrick from the sugar overload, she tried remembering they were his problem while at his house, not hers.

Even though he was in his seventies, Patrick seemed to have boundless energy when it came to his grandchildren and great-grandchildren. Emma was thankful Patrick's girlfriend, Patty, would be staying over as well to help out.

When he started down the stairs, Aidan pointed a finger at her. "You. Stay here."

"Excuse me, caveman?" Emma demanded.

He flashed her a wicked grin. "I want you to stay here and get ready." He waggled his brows. "For tonight."

"All I have to do is slip on my costume." Cocking her head at him, she asked, "Are you trying to insinuate I need extra time to make myself desirable for you through epic ladyscaping and showering?"

Rolling his eyes, Aidan replied, "I couldn't care less if you're furry and stink."

With a laugh, Emma replied, "You're such a charmer."

He grinned. "Just get ready and then take it easy." Giving her a pointed look, he added, "You're going to need your energy."

"Whatever," she murmured. She then drew Noah and Caroline into her arms. "Give Mommy some bye-bye loving."

As her babies squeezed her tight, Emma kissed Noah's blond head and then kissed Caroline's auburn head. "You be good for Papa and Patty. I better not hear you were giving them attitude or throwing tantrums."

"Yes, Mommy," they promised.

When she still continued clinging to them, Aidan snorted. "Babe, they're just going across town. You're acting like they're leaving for the Foreign Legion."

"I can't help it," Emma replied before finally prying herself away. "I'll make sure to FaceTime you guys in the morning."

After another quick kissing session, Emma finally stepped back and let Aidan usher Noah and Caroline down the stairs. "Be careful!" she called.

"We will," they all chimed in.

✧ ✧ ✧

A QUICK SHOWER and ladyscape session later, Emma had barely gotten into her Naughty Nurse costume when she heard the sound of the garage door. She couldn't help laughing at the thought that Aidan must've thrown Noah and Caroline out before speeding away.

"I'm back," Aidan called.

Poking her head out of the bathroom, she joked, "Did you even turn the car off when you dropped them off?"

"Nope. Didn't even pull into the driveway either. Just rolled them out at the street," he teased back.

"You're terrible," she shouted.

His voice came from the bedroom. "Are you ready?"

"Yes. But I want you to close your eyes."

"Mmm, okay."

After a few seconds, she asked, "Ready?"

"Yessss," Aidan replied.

"Are your eyes closed?"

"Emma, get your fine ass out here!" Aidan growled.

She couldn't help giggling at his response. Throwing open the bathroom door, she stepped out into the bedroom. "Okay, open your eyes," she commanded.

Aidan's lids immediately flipped wide open. At the sight of her, he sucked in a breath. "Holy fucking shit, Em," he muttered.

His reaction sent warmth ricocheting from the top of her head down to her toes. With a grin, she did a slow spin around. "Do you like it?"

He slowly bobbed his head. When he didn't verbally respond, she asked, "Have I rendered you speechless?"

"Uh-huh," he grunted before licking his lips.

"Who would've thought throwing on a Naughty Nurse costume would have this much effect on you?" she teasingly said.

"It isn't the costume."

"Oh really? You haven't looked like you wanted to devour me in ages."

"There's never a time I don't want to devour you."

Warmth filled Emma's chest at his words. "I'm glad to hear that."

"Tonight, it's the costume." He motioned around her. "It's what the costume does to your body."

Her hands came to rest at her protruding bump. "There wasn't a lot I could do with this."

Aidan shook his head. "It accentuates every delicious curve and highlights your fabulous tits and ass."

She shivered at both his words and the way he continued to look at her. "You sure know how to make a gal with a mom bod feel appreciated."

His response was to close the space between them in two long strides. Wrapping his arms around her waist, he jerked her against him. His breath teased against her cheek as he whispered, "Your body is sexy as hell."

Although she hated herself for it, she couldn't fight the tears that pricked her eyes. "Thank you, babe," she whispered.

"Do these costumes come in different colors?"

"I don't know. Why?"

"Because I think you should have one in every style and color to give me sexual healing."

Emma laughed. "I'll see if I can arrange that."

Bolstered by his compliment, she leaned in and brought her lips to his, sliding her tongue into his mouth. His hands slid down from her waist to cup her buttocks. He hitched one of her legs over his hip, grinding his growing need into her.

No matter how many times Emma felt Aidan hard and eager against her, she couldn't help moaning at the exquisite feeling of him through her thin panties. As he moved against her, she wanted to feel more of him, his bare skin on hers. Even though they had the whole night, she was already desperate to have him inside of her.

"I need you naked," she murmured against his lips.

"Then take me," he replied.

Emma's fingers reached for the buttons on his dress shirt. After making quick work undoing them, she pulled his shirt apart before pushing it down his arms and to the floor. She then ran her hand down the center of his chest, over his washboard abs, and down to his belt buckle, causing Aidan to suck in a breath and his stomach muscles to clench.

She hastily unhooked the buckle and jerked the belt out of the loops. Before she tossed it to the ground, she jerked her arm back to give him a quick spank. Aidan's nostrils flared in response. "Is the Naughty Nurse going to punish me?"

"Maybe. For right now, she wants your cock too much to tease you."

His heated gaze burned into her, and she felt a warmth flood her cheeks and go down her neck. She then made quick work unbuttoning and then unzipping his fly. She leaned in against him, pressing her body flush to his as she reached into the back of his waistband to push his pants over his buttocks. Her hands momentarily stopped to cup both of his cheeks before grabbing the material. Keeping her eyes on his, she slid down his body in the same motion as his pants.

Cupping the backs of his legs, she pushed her way slowly back up. Her fingernails raked over his calves and thighs. Aidan never took his eyes off of hers. Once again, she found herself cupping his buttocks as she moved her fingers to the waistband of his underwear. She quickly pushed them down to the floor.

When she stood back up, Aidan crushed his lips to hers, plunging his tongue into her mouth. She wrapped her arms around his neck as he massaged her tongue with his. Aidan kissed a warm trail from her mouth over to her ear as his hand came up to cup her bodice. "My old friends," he teasingly murmured.

Emma giggled. "You're their biggest fan."

"How could I not be?" Jerking the cups of the costume down, he freed her breasts.

"They've seen better days after nursing two kids."

"Bullshit," Aidan murmured as he closed his lips over one of the nipples.

Emma sucked in a breath at the feel of his tongue swirling over delicate flesh. "I think after Liam, I'll get a reduction."

Aidan jerked away from her breast. "Over my dead body."

Once again, she laughed. "Why don't we argue about that another time?"

"Just promise me you won't go too small," he pleaded.

"I promise, you silly Breast Man."

With a laugh, Aidan said, "I can't help myself."

Emma moaned as Aidan began kneading her breasts. He then began alternating licking and sucking each one. Emma felt the heat rising between her legs and shifted on her feet, pressing her thighs together for relief. She couldn't fight the cry of pleasure that escaped her lips. Her fingers automatically went to his blond hair, tugging and grasping at the strands as the pleasure washed over her.

The ache between her thighs grew, and she knew if he touched her there, he would find she was drenched with need for him. As if he could read her mind, Aidan snaked a hand down her stomach. His fingers feathered across her belly teasingly, causing her hips to buck. He hesitated before finally dipping them between her legs.

Emma panted against his lips when his fingers worked against her sensitive flesh over the fabric. Her hips arched involuntarily against his hand as she rubbed herself against his fingertips. "Although I love the hell out of it, I think it's time we ditched the costume."

"Uh-huh," she muttered almost incoherently.

He chuckled as he made quick work of relieving her of her costume. Kneeling before her, Aidan's fingers delved between her legs, seeking out her swollen clit. The moment he stroked it, she cried out and gripped his shoulders tight. His thumb continued rubbing as his fingers slid into her wet folds. They swirled against her tight walls, working her into a frenzy of desire. She bit down on her lip to keep the ecstatic cries buried in her throat from escaping, but it became useless as he continued his assault on her core and brought her closer and closer to coming. She dug her nails into Aidan's back and thrust her pelvis hard against his hand.

Just before she went over the edge, Aidan rose off the floor. She fought the urge to protest. Aidan kept his hands tight on her waist to steady her as she tried to get her bearings. Gently, he nudged her toward the bed and then eased her down onto her back. Pushing up on her elbows, she scooted higher on the mattress. Aidan loomed over her, desire burning bright in his blue eyes. Emma shuddered under his gaze.

As his body covered hers, he pushed her legs wide apart. He then kissed a path from her neck, down through the valley of her breasts, and over her belly. When his head dipped between her legs, Emma's eyes pinched shut in ecstasy. As his fingers entered her again, his tongue swirled around her clit, sucking it into his mouth. Emma fisted the sheets in both hands. "Oh Aidan!" she screamed, and her hand immediately flew to cup her mouth.

"There's no one here, babe. Scream all you want."

He was right. She didn't have to temper her response out of fear of waking the kids. His fingers kept a rapid pace while he kept licking and sucking at her center. "Oh yes! Yes, Aidan…please," she gleefully shouted, twisting the sheets tighter in her hands. Her hips kept up a manic rhythm as he plunged his fingers and tongue in and out of her. Finally, it sent her over the edge, and she climaxed violently.

When she started coming back to herself, she realized one of her hands had abandoned the sheet and had twisted into Aidan's hair. "Was I too hard?" she sheepishly asked.

He shook his head. "I love it when you pull my hair."

"Mmm, I love it when you pull mine, too. Especially when I'm giving you head."

"Is that an invitation?"

"Mm-hmm."

"Man, you really know how to make my day, don't you?"

Emma laughed as she reached between them to grab his length. "I couldn't have you going under the knife without some oral attention."

Aidan groaned, and she realized it wasn't from her hand pumping him. "Did you really have to mention the procedure?"

"Come on, big boy. Let me take your mind off things."

Aidan gave a grunt of pleasure when her free hand went to his balls, massaging them gently.

After a few minutes, she pressed his legs further apart. With her hand gripping him, she licked a trail from his navel down to his base. She then swirled her tongue around him teasingly, causing Aidan to groan. "You're killing me."

Flashing a wicked look at him, she then sucked him deep inside her mouth. Her head bobbed up and down as he slid in and out of her mouth. "Fuck me," Aidan muttered.

"Fuck my mouth," she coyly replied.

His eyes bulged at her command, but he didn't have to be told twice. His hips began rising up and down, sending his dick deeper into her throat. His grunts of pleasure sent moisture between her legs.

When she started to feel like he was coming close, Aidan stilled the movements of his hips. "Don't want to waste it, babe," he replied when she glanced up at him.

"If you say so." With a grin, she added, "You've got a pretty good refractory period for an older guy."

"Older? Since when is thirty-five older?"

"You're mid-thirties, babe."

"You're not far behind," he countered.

Wagging her brows, she replied, "Why don't you punish me for calling you old?"

His mouth gaped open. "You really are bringing out all the stops tonight, aren't you?"

"Call it a mixture of your impending surgery, my pregnancy hormones, and being child-free."

"I'll take it." He flashed her a wolfish grin. "Just like I'm going to take you."

"Mmm, please."

"Get on your knees."

"Yes, sir."

After placing her palms on the mattress and widening her legs, Emma glanced back at Aidan over her shoulder. She didn't have a moment to prepare herself before he thrust inside of her, causing both of them to gasp with pleasure. He momentarily withdrew before plunging back deep inside her. As his hips smacked against her ass, Emma dipped her head and panted against the mattress. Aidan's fingers dug into her waist as he pulled her back against his thrusts.

When he slipped one of his hands between her legs, she let her cries of pleasure ring throughout the room. "Yes, please, Aidan!" she cried. His fingers swirled around her clit before rubbing it. She began building to another orgasm. When he pinched her clit with one hand and smacked her ass with the other, she went over the edge. Her fingers clung to the sheets as she rode out the orgasm.

As she started coming down, Aidan pulled out of her. He flopped down onto his back before pulling her on top of him. "Take me, babe," he ordered.

"I can barely move after that orgasm," she protested.

"Ride me."

Since she loved when he got demanding, Emma eased down onto Aidan's cock. He lay still, buried deep inside her, waiting for her to take the reins. Tentatively, she rocked against him until she slowly started speeding up the pace. Leaning back, she rested her palms on his thighs. She rode him hard and fast, grinding against him.

Aidan rose up into a sitting position. He took one of her swaying breasts in his mouth and sucked deeply while gripping her hips tight. He changed the rhythm to work her against him, pulling her almost off his cock and then slamming her back down on him. She felt him go deeper and deeper each time, and as much as she was enjoying the feeling, Aidan was grunting in pleasure against her chest.

Just when Emma thought she might come again, Aidan pushed her onto her back and brought her legs straight up against his chest so her feet rested at his shoulders. She whimpered when he rammed himself back inside her. He smirked down at her with satisfaction, and she knew she was in for it. As he pounded into her, his balls smacked against her ass. He groaned as the position took him deeper again. Her cries of pleasure seemed to fuel Aidan on as he thrust again and again. She felt the tension in his body and realized he was getting close. Suddenly, he spread her legs and brought them back to their original position; they were face to face and wrapped in each other's arms.

When Emma's last orgasm tightened her walls around Aidan's cock, he thrust one last time and then let himself go inside her. "Oh, fuck, Emma!" he cried before collapsing on top of her.

They lay entangled together, catching their breath. Turning his head on the pillow, Aidan gave her a satiated grin. "Damn, Em, I can't remember when it was that good."

Inwardly, she did a victory dance at his words. Outwardly, she didn't have the energy to do anything but smile back at him. "Me either."

He rolled over to kiss her tenderly on the forehead. "I love you."

"I love you, too."

Cocking his brows at her, he asked, "Will you love me even when I'm not producing swimmers?"

A laugh burst from her lips. "Of course, I'll still love you. Why would you even think that?"

"It's just the whole reason we got together was because of my swimmers."

Although she was completely depleted of energy, she scooted over to snuggle against him. "Aidan, I want you to know something very important."

"What?" he implored.

"You are more than your semen," she teased.

"You and that mouth," he grunted.

"I'm serious, babe. The swimmers have amply served their purpose. But you have many, many more years of serving your purpose to me both in and out of the bedroom."

With a chuckle, Aidan replied, "I'm glad to hear it."

"Enough worrying. We need to get your beauty rest before your surgery."

"Do you really think you're getting off this easy? This is my going-out-of-business sex night."

Emma snorted. "You are not going out of the sex business."

"For a few weeks," Aidan lamented.

"You'll survive. You have the six to eight weeks we've had to wait after we had Noah and Caroline."

"You assisted me orally then. The whole area will be closed for repairs."

Emma giggled. "Should we put some caution tape over your crotch?"

"Smart-ass," he muttered before rolling over on top of her.

"Aidan, you aren't really serious about more sex tonight, are you?"

At the wicked gleam in his eyes, she knew she was in for an exhausting but very, very good time.

EPILOGUE

"T HAT'S IT, BABE. Deep breaths," Aidan instructed. As he stared into Emma's face contorted with agony, he wished more than anything he could take some of the pain away. Seeing her handle contractions reaffirmed for him once again how women truly were the stronger sex. Silently he patted himself on the back for manning up and getting a vasectomy, so this would be the last time she would have to ever go through the pain of childbirth.

When the contraction had passed, the pain drained from Emma's face. "That was a rough one," she remarked.

With a grin, Aidan replied, "I'll take your word for it."

A mischievous look flashed in Emma's emerald eyes. "I could always knee you in the balls repeatedly to let you somewhat experience it."

"I think I'll pass," he replied with a wink.

Emma laughed. After gazing around the hospital room, she shook her head. "You know, after Noah and Caroline's arrivals, I can't believe how inconspicuous this time is for us," she mused.

"I'm sure Pesh will feel a little left out that his presence didn't have something to do with this delivery," Aidan mused." His mind immediately went back to Noah's early arrival and how he had been out of town on a business trip when Emma went into labor. With no available flights out of Charlotte, their friend, Alpesh "Pesh" Nadeen, had flown his private plane up to get Aidan. Miraculously, they had made it back in time for him to witness Noah's arrival into the world.

With Caroline's birth, Emma had been overdue and celebrating at Pesh and Aidan's niece, Megan's, engagement party when her water broke. It was lucky they were at a hotel in the city close to the hospital because Caroline arrived a mere two hours later.

As for Liam, he had decided a lazy Sunday afternoon was the perfect time to begin his arrival. Emma had been lying around the pool watching him with the kids in the water when the contractions began. After depositing Noah and Caroline with Megan and Pesh, they'd headed on to the hospital where they now found Emma hovering around three centimeters and waiting for the sweet spot to get an epidural.

Their attention was suddenly drawn to the doorway where a nurse hustled through. With a tight smile, she came over to the bed. "Can you try staying on your back during the next contraction?" she suggested.

"Um, sure," Emma replied, as she shifted.

Nodding, the nurse then went over to the monitors. Apprehension filled Aidan as he noticed her paying particular attention to the fetal heart monitor.

"Is something wrong?" Emma asked—her voice wavered slightly with fear.

"We've been monitoring you through several contractions, and your baby's heart rate has started dropping."

Aidan felt his own heart shudder to a stop. "What does that mean? Is he okay?"

"Your doctor is on the way to check the reading."

As Aidan read the fear in Emma's eyes, he squeezed her hand before pinning the nurse with a hard stare. "You didn't answer my question," he countered.

"It might be necessary to take your baby by C-section."

Emma gasped. "It's that serious?"

Before the nurse could answer, Dr. Middleton came through the door. Ease filled Aidan at the sight of the doctor who had delivered Noah. Instead of her usual warm expression, Dr. Middleton's face was streaked with worry. Nodding her head in a brief hello, she went straight to the fetal heart monitor. A tense silence hung heavy in the air.

When she finally turned around, she shook her head. "I don't like what I'm seeing. Some doctors prefer to take a wait and see approach but not me. I want to go in, and I want to go in immediately."

She then reached over to hit an alarm on the bed. As the sound assaulted Aidan's ears, another sound tore at his heart. A strangled sob erupted from Emma's lips. "Is there a chance we could lose him?"

"That's why we're going in now."

"What about an epidural?"

Dr. Middleton shook her head. "There isn't time. You'll need to be under anesthesia."

Now the tears streamed down Emma's cheeks. "I won't even get to be awake to see him born?"

"I'm sorry, Emma. The most important thing right now is getting Liam out safe and sound."

As the fetal monitor went off again, the room filled with medical personnel. Aidan was pushed to the side as someone shouted, "OR 6!"

Aidan watched fearfully as Emma was transferred from the bed to a gurney. The nurses then started pushing Emma out of the room. "Aidan!" Emma cried.

When he rushed forward to grab her hand, a nurse stopped him. "I'm sorry, Mr. Fitzgerald, but you'll have to stay here or in the surgical waiting room."

"What? I can't go in with her?"

She shook her head. "Not in an emergency situation like this. There isn't time to get you scrubbed in."

Aidan fought the rising panic in his chest. How could he possibly let Emma go through an emergency C-section alone? He needed to be there by her side, assuring her and keeping her sane. Biting down on his lip, he fought the urge to throw back his head and begin screaming madly.

But he couldn't fall apart now. He had to be strong for Emma. She needed all the strength he could give. Forcing a smile to his face, he kidded, "And here I was all excited to get to see you from the inside out."

Emma didn't respond to his joke. Instead, tears streaked down her cheeks. "If something should happen to me—"

Aidan wildly shook his head. "Don't talk like that. Nothing is going to happen to you or to Liam."

"If it does, I want you to promise you'll take good care of the kids."

He didn't have time to argue anymore with her, so he merely nodded. "Of course, I will. I love you, Em. You're my world. They're my world."

"I love you, too."

And then she and the team of nurses were gone. Unable to keep himself upright, he sank to his knees. There was only one person he could imagine calling at that moment. Fumbling in his pants pocket, he pulled out his phone.

After dialing the number, he cried, "Pop, I need you."

✧ ✧ ✧

FEELING SUBMERGED IN murky water, Emma fought to reach the surface. Even though her brain told her legs to kick and swim, they remained motionless. Her arms felt weighed down, and no matter how hard she tried, she couldn't lift them.

With her lungs burning in agony, she knew if she didn't reach the surface soon she was going to die. Fear sliced its way through her. At the thoughts of leaving Aidan and her children behind, an anguished cry bubbled from her lips.

But then a voice broke through the depths of the water. "Emma? Open your eyes, sweetheart."

At the realization of the voice, she fought harder to break the surface. Her eyelids fluttered like a hummingbird's wings. A groan of frustration escaped her lips just as light exploded all around her.

"Em? Look at me, Emma. I'm right here."

After staring momentarily at the bright light overhead, Emma realized it was a panel of fluorescent lights, not heavenly white light. It was then the memory of where she was came rushing at her so hard she shuddered. "Aidan!" she cried.

A warm hand took hers. "I'm here."

Slowly, she swiveled her head on the pillow. At the sight of her smiling husband, tears welled in her eyes. "I'm not..." She couldn't bring herself to say the word.

Aidan shook his head. "No. You're very much alive and in recovery."

Although she should've felt relief, another fear seized her. "Liam?"

"He came through just fine. They wanted him to stay in the NICU for observation."

"For how long?"

"Maybe twenty-four hours." Aidan wiped the tears from her cheeks. "He's beautiful, babe. Seven pounds, eight ounces, and a head full of blond hair."

Emma hiccupped a cry. "Just like his dad."

With a smile, Aidan said, "Actually, he looks a lot like Caroline did when she was born, so I think he'll be taking after his very beautiful mother."

"I can't wait to see him."

"Dr. Middleton said once you came out of recovery, we could wheel you up there."

It was then Emma realized how much differently she felt. While it didn't feel like a Buick had driven through her vagina, her abdomen definitely felt like something strange had occurred. At the thoughts of the surgery, she remembered those scary last minutes of consciousness. The surgical lights overhead, the flurry of activity from the surgical team, and then the mask being put over her nose and mouth.

"I was so scared," she admitted to Aidan.

"Me too. I even called Pop, I was so scared."

Emma smiled. "You did?"

Aidan nodded. "He's in the waiting room with the rest of the family."

"They're all here?"

"Not all of them. As soon as most of them heard what was happening, they hurried down here."

Tears once again filled Emma's eyes. "We're so blessed."

"Yes, we are." He bent down to bestow a tender kiss on her lips. When he pulled away, he smiled. "I think it's worth saying again how you're my hero for everything you've been through bringing our children into the world."

With a laugh, Emma replied, "I think this procedure certainly tops yours, don't you?"

Aidan chuckled. "Yes, it does. How fitting you would have to one up me."

"Well, you could always undergo the knife again to have it reversed," Emma suggested. She fought her laughter when Aidan's eyes bulged in horror.

"After everything you've just gone through, you'd want more kids?"

Unable to hold back any longer, Emma giggled. "I was just teasing you."

"Thank God." After a shudder rippled through him, he said, "I don't think I could go through it again. The fear of losing Liam and you broke me."

At the sincerity of his words, Emma reached for Aidan's hand. "I don't think I could go through it either." As a relieved breath whooshed out of Aidan, Emma added, "We could always adopt."

Throwing up his hands, Aidan countered, "Are you trying to kill me?"

Emma laughed. "No, babe. Teasing you makes me feel alive, and I'm so very thankful to be here and that our son is here safe and sound."

"As usual, that mouth of yours will be the death of me."

"Not until we're old and gray, babe."

With a smile, Aidan replied, "Damn straight."

✧　✧　✧

Thank you so much for reading my story *The Procedure*! You can read more of Aidan and Emma in *The Proposition*, which is free on all channels.

ORDER THE PROPOSITION NOW
www.katieashleybooks.com

Through Her Eyes

Kelly Elliott

PROLOGUE

Six months earlier

A VOICE SOFTLY cleared behind me as I glanced over my shoulder to see my best friend, Lucy, standing with an umbrella over her head.

The rain hadn't been in the forecast but started when the funeral had started, and a steady light rain had begun to fall. I hadn't been the least bit phased by it, though. I was already numb inside, surprised I could even feel the slight chill from getting wet.

"Kadie, are you about ready to go?" she asked. "You shouldn't be standing in the rain, sweetie."

I nodded, then turned back to look at the casket in front of me. "I'll be right there, Lucy."

My eyes focused back on the casket in front of me. In it was my husband of six years. He had died in a car accident on his way to Hawaii with his mistress. Of course, I hadn't known he had a mistress. As far as I had known, Jimmy was heading to meet with one of his clients. I had asked if I could go. Maybe a trip like that would be good for us since we had been growing distant. My desire to start a family wasn't what he wanted. As usual, he had said it would be best if I stayed home.

Now I knew why he never wanted me to go with him on trips. He took her instead. Together they lived the life I had thought I was signing up for. Jimmy had offered me the moon and stars when we were dating. He filled my head with all the things we could do together. Once we got married, though, everything changed. I kept my feet on the ground, making sure everything ran smoothly with our house and all the charity functions I was involved in, all the while attempting to grow my photography career that had been put on hold after getting married. And Jimmy, well, he soared above the clouds living out his dreams as an entertainment lawyer to some of today's hottest actors and musicians.

"Mrs. Roberts?"

The male voice caused me to spin around. A man stood before me dressed in a black suit and black tie. He was crazy insane handsome, and I knew who he was instantly. Gage Mason. One of the most famous musicians around. He sang pop, rock, and blues. He was also one of Jimmy's clients. His wet brown hair and sky-blue eyes made him look like an angel from above. A sudden chill ran through my body, and it wasn't from the rain or my damp clothes.

"Yes?"

He took a step closer, and I fought a strange urge to move toward him.

"I'm Gage Mason. Your husband is um he was…"

I smiled softly. "I know who you are, Mr. Mason."

He looked relieved. "I just wanted to say how sorry I am."

"Thank you."

Even I could hear the disdain in my voice. It wasn't a secret that my husband had died with his mistress in the car. Or that they had been having an affair for the last four years. It seems I was the only one in the dark.

Four. Years.

My husband had been sleeping with another woman for four years while I begged him to start a family, and he kept putting me off with one excuse after another.

Gage nodded and then looked around before focusing back on me. "Did you need a ride anywhere, or can I do anything? I mean, I'm not sure…"

His words trailed off.

I glanced over to Lucy in her car, then back to Gage. And suddenly, the craziest idea I'd ever had came to mind.

I knew Gage Mason had a reputation for being a lady's man. Even Jimmy had mentioned it a time or two. I'd lived the last few years acting like the dutiful wife. I'd given up so much, and I was tired. Damn. I was so tired.

"How about a drink, Mr. Mason? I honestly don't think I can stomach being around anyone talking praise about my cheating bastard of a husband."

His brows shot up before the corner of his mouth lifted into a slight smirk.

"Drinks it is."

I nodded. "Let me just go let my friend Lucy know you'll be giving me a ride."

He motioned for me to lead the way, then fell into step behind me.

Oh my gosh. What in the world am I doing?

I was leaving my husband's gravesite to have drinks with another man. Not only another man, but one I knew was younger and had a reputation for taking women to bed. What exactly was I hoping to get out of this?

One quick look back at Gage Mason, and I knew what I wanted.

Lucy got out of the car and looked between me and Gage, who gratefully gave us some privacy as he headed toward what I was guessing was his Mercedes-Benz sports car.

"I'm going to be heading out with…"

Glancing toward the black sports car, I stared at the man leaning against the car. Just patiently waiting in the misting rain for me.

"Gage Mason?" Lucy said in a whisper. "You're leaving with Gage Mason? Kadie, what if someone sees you get into his car?"

I looked back at her, then around at the empty graveyard. "Who? No one is here, Lucy. And I can't even think about going to the celebration of life. The last thing I want to hear is all of those people talking about him. I can't do it, or I'll say something. I know I will."

"Then I'll take you home, and we'll skip it. Why leave with an actor of all people? I mean, he's hot. Really hot, but this is so unlike you, Kadie."

If only I had the answer to Lucy's question. Why was I leaving with Gage? Maybe I knew the answer and was simply afraid to admit it.

"I think that's why I have to do it, Lucy. I want something for myself. And call me selfish for doing it on the day I buried my husband. But I'm tired of always doing the right thing. I've lived the last few years with a man who hardly even looked at me. I want…"

My voice faded away as Lucy's eyes widened.

"Oh my God. Are you planning on sleeping with him?"

I chewed on my lip and shrugged. "I mean, I won't say no if he suggests it."

Lucy's hand came up to her mouth in an attempt to either hold back a gasp or a giggle. I wasn't sure which.

Slowly shaking her head, Lucy glanced over to Gage, then back to me. "Kadie, just be careful. Sometimes the things we wish for aren't the things we need."

All I could do was nod, take her hand in mine and squeeze it.

"I'll be careful, and stop worrying. What is the worst that could happen?"

Looking back on that day, I'll never know what prompted me to get into Gage Mason's sports car that day. I'll never understand why I suggested we head to a hotel for drinks or why I asked him to take me up to a room. And I most certainly will never forget how alive I had felt that night. How Gage Mason, a man ten years younger than me, a playboy at best, made me feel the most alive I'd ever felt in my life.

And I'll never understand why I got up at five in the morning and left without saying a word to him.

CHAPTER ONE
Kadie

Present Day

"I THINK WE got them all!" I called out to Jen and Roby, the young couple whose engagement session I had just finished photographing.

"Kadie, I think this is some of your best work yet!" Lucy exclaimed as she started to put away the equipment we had hauled up to the waterfalls for the shoot.

Smiling, I peeked over to the happy couple who were still in an embrace with the water cascading down behind them from Sturtevant Falls.

"I think it is also. I feel like I've discovered who I am these last few months. I never really saw how much Jimmy was holding me back until I was free to do what I wanted."

Lucy glanced up at me. "He was holding you back from everything, and the change in you has been...crazy."

I laughed and put my lens back into my case and then let out a long exhale as I dropped my head back and let the warm sun hit my face.

"How are you feeling?" Lucy asked as she stood and took the bag from my hand. "Are you tired?"

"I feel fine."

"The hike wasn't too much for you? I mean, do you need to rest before we head back down?"

Laughing, I turned back to my best friend. "Lucy, I'm wonderful. I'm better than fine. This is the best I've felt in a long time."

She raised a single brow. "Really? You weren't saying that when you were throwing your insides up for almost five months."

I rolled my eyes. "Well, the morning sickness is long gone, and I feel amazing."

"You look amazing too!" Jen said as Roby helped her down off a large boulder. "I hope I'm that hot looking when I'm your age and six months pregnant."

Lucy covered her mouth to hide her laugh.

I blinked a few times as I stared at Jen. She was twenty-four and adorable to boot with her long brown hair which had been pulled up and put into an elaborate updo. Her doe brown eyes were soulful for a woman of such a young age.

When I had glanced at myself in the mirror this morning, hot wasn't a word I would use to describe myself. I had pulled up my honey-blonde hair into a ponytail. I had on leggings and a long-sleeve T-shirt that I had taken from my older brother, Nate. It was comfortable, and I could move around easily in it. The only thing I had going for me was the constant blush on my cheeks due to the pregnancy and my blue eyes. Okay, my body wasn't bad for a woman who was six months pregnant. Especially my boobs. They had never looked so good. But hot? No. I was thirty-five, single, and pregnant.

When the silence went on a bit too long, Jen blushed and said, "Wait, that came out all wrong. I meant to say…"

Holding up my hand, I said, "You're fine—no need to explain what you meant. You two are free to keep hiking and exploring, but Lucy and I will head on out. I'll start editing these and send them to you in the next few days."

"We had a blast, but we'll head back down with you guys," Jen said as she looked at her fiancé.

He jumped to attention without her saying a single word. "Yes, let me carry some of that, so you don't have to," Roby said as he took two of the bags from me.

"Honestly, Lucy and I can get it."

"Nope, we're helping! You've made this whole thing such a beautiful experience, and the least we can do is help you trek all this back down the trail," Jen stated.

Lucy winked at me, and I had to admit, the idea of them helping sounded amazing. Not that I didn't think I could do it. I worked out every day, ate great, and felt like a million dollars. But I was getting more and more tired as each day went by. I wasn't about to look a gift horse in the mouth.

The climb down was much easier, and once Lucy and I said our goodbyes to Jen and Roby, I climbed into my Toyota Highlander and started it up.

"Are you still in the mood to go to that charity dinner tonight?" Lucy asked.

I let out a groan. "I forgot about that. Lucy, I need to finish packing."

She crossed her arms over her chest. "I still don't understand why you need to move?"

I pulled out onto the road and tried not to let out a frustrated sigh. "We've been over this time and time again. I'm not raising a baby in Los Angeles, and there are too many memories here, and I want a fresh start. No, I *need* a fresh start."

"And you think Half Moon Bay is going to be better?"

"Yes, I do. The only reason I'm staying in California is because my parents are in San Francisco. Otherwise, I'd go to Oregon, maybe."

She remained silent for a few minutes before she turned and looked at me. "Kadie, you're not running because you think he'll find out, do you?"

I gripped the steering wheel tighter and took a quick look at my best friend. I could see the concern on her face, and I knew her heart was in the right place. What she didn't realize was I was far from running.

"Lucy, I love you like a sister, but you are so off base with this."

"Well, how am I supposed to know? You don't ever talk about him."

I sighed. "Because it was a one-night stand. Let's also not forget I got pregnant the night of my husband's funeral."

She waved that off. "I wouldn't even care about that."

"Well, other people might. Besides, I had Pete reach out to Gage's manager and tell him I was pregnant. I didn't want anything from him, but I did want him to know."

Lucy gasped. "What! You didn't tell me that. So Pete knows?"

Pete Hathaway was Jimmy's partner in the law firm. When I had approached him about Jimmy and his mistress, he had claimed not to know anything about it. I had wanted to believe him, but a part of me wasn't so sure. I could feel the stares of pity from the people in the office. Of course, if they hadn't known before Jimmy died, they certainly did after. Jimmy's mistress was a well-known actress who was also his client.

"I had to tell Pete. I had no way of getting in touch with Gage."

"When was this?"

I gave a half shrug. "Not long after I found out I was pregnant, and I was almost three months pregnant. Pete never heard anything back, so I'm assuming Gage Mason doesn't care about the baby."

Slight tightness in my chest caused me to draw in a deep breath. It wasn't that I wanted Gage in my life. Sure, we had one hell of a night together, and he made me feel things I had never felt before. Something I hadn't even felt with Jimmy. I was positive that was the reason I snuck out like a coward. I did, however, want my child to know their father. I'd have Pete try one more time in a month or so. I just needed Gage to realize I wasn't looking for anything, but I at least wanted our child to know their father. No matter how big or small of a part he wanted to play.

Lucy harrumphed. "He probably has a plethora of little ones running around—a guy that good looking and always out on tour. I mean, look at how easy it was for him to take you up to that hotel room and sleep with you. For fuck's sake, you're ten years older than him!"

"Gee, thanks for that reminder, Lucy."

She sighed. "That's not what I meant. It's just, why did he even approach you that day at the funeral?"

"I don't know."

It was her turn to let out a long breath.

I reached for her hand and squeezed it.

"I'm just worried about you, Kadie. You're going to be a single mom living in a new area, and you're just now getting your photography business growing here, and now you want to start all over somewhere else."

"I've done a good job of building it up the last few months, and I do not doubt that I can do it there as well. I've already talked to the event manager at the Ritz. I sent her over some of my work, and she will list me down as one of their preferred photographers. She loved my stuff. Besides, Jimmy did do right to make sure all of his ducks were in a row. I got a pretty good inheritance from him. Plus, Pete bought out Jimmy's partnership. And he was more than generous in the payout."

"He should be. I still think he knew about her and felt guilty, hence the large payout."

"None of it matters. The only thing that matters now is I'm starting my life over, and I'm more than ready." I placed my hand on my swollen belly. "Both of us are ready."

CHAPTER TWO

Gage

I DROPPED MY suitcase onto the floor and face-planted onto my bed. Nearly five months of being in Africa and parts of Europe on tour had left me exhausted.

A light knock on my bedroom door had me rolling over and letting out a groan. "Go away! I just got home."

The sounds of high heels clicking on the hardwood floor alerted me to who it was.

Oh, hell no. She can't even give me a fucking day.

Rachel.

My bitch of a sister and also my manager.

I threw my arm over my eyes as I said, "Rach, not now. Please."

"Gage, we need to talk, and it's…well, it's rather important. Now that you're back home, we can get it all settled."

"It can wait, Rach. I'm fucking exhausted from traveling for nearly sixteen hours."

"This can't wait; I'm sorry."

The bed moved, and I opened my eyes to see her sitting on the end. I quickly sat up when I saw the worry on her face.

"What's wrong?"

I knew it wouldn't be anything to do with our parents since I had hung up with my mother only fifteen minutes ago. I'd called to let them know I was back in California and had made it home. I lived in Malibu on the beach in a spectacular home. One that I was never hardly in.

"First, I need to know why you took off early to Africa."

No way I was telling my older sister I slept with Kadie the night of her husband's funeral. Not to mention said wife got up at the ass crack of dawn and slipped out of the hotel room we had gotten for our little tryst.

"I just needed to get away. It's hard to explain, Rach."

She narrowed her eyes. "Try me."

I stood and grabbed my suitcase, tossing it up on the bed. "I just needed to get out of town for a bit, and why do you care? That was months ago."

It had been me running like hell to get out of Dodge. I'd never felt the things I had felt with Kadie Roberts. The moment I saw her standing there in the rain at her husband's funeral, something about her struck me. I would typically never approach someone like I had Kadie, but a part of me needed to make sure she was okay. I couldn't explain it at the time, and I sure as hell couldn't explain it now. When she had turned and looked at me, my breath had caught in my throat. Even wet from the rain, she was the most beautiful woman I'd ever seen. Her blue eyes looked so defeated it broke my heart in two.

When she had mentioned getting drinks, I should have said no. But the idea of getting to know her more was something I couldn't resist. At first, I thought it was because she was older. Ten years older, to be exact. The thrill of being with an older woman alone had been a turn-on. But when she looked at me, standing there with the rain coming down at that gravesite, and the hurt and anger in her eyes screamed for release, something inside of me snapped. I had an overwhelming need to make her feel better. Rumors of her husband's cheating were all over the news. She was hurting and mad as hell. After two drinks, when she had suggested getting a hotel room, I had zero reservations about it. It had been the best night of my life if I had been honest with myself. So when I woke up to find her gone, it had gutted me.

Listen, I've had my share of one-night stands. But that night was different. Everything about it was different. The woman, the way we made love and didn't just fuck for the sake of fucking. The way I held her in my arms while she poured her heart and soul out to me, and I had done the same. All of it was different.

"Did it have to do with the fact that you slept with Kadie Roberts on the night of her husband Jimmy's funeral? You know Jimmy Roberts, the lawyer we've used since you broke out into this business. The man who had a hand in negotiating every single one of your contracts?"

Fuck. Fuck. Fuck.

"How did you find out? Did someone see us? Is Kadie okay?"

When I looked at her, she wore a smug expression. "I don't know if she is or if she isn't. The only thing I know is that Pete Hathaway, Jimmy's partner, reached out to let me know that Kadie Roberts was pregnant. With your child."

My legs felt like jelly, and I suddenly heard nothing but the pounding of my heart in my chest. I stared at my sister as I worked on swallowing the sudden lump in my throat.

"How...how does she know it's mine?" I asked. From the little I had learned about Kadie that night, sleeping with a virtual stranger was not something she did. Hell, she had remained a dutiful wife all those years while her husband was out living it up. And fucking more than just the actress he had on the side.

One of my sister's perfectly plucked brows rose slightly. "It seems she hadn't slept with her husband in months. Do you want to tell me how she ended up in a hotel room with you that night?"

I stared at my sister. "No, I don't."

She exhaled and cursed. "Gage, if this gets out, it's going to do some serious damage."

I let out a bitter laugh. "How exactly is it going to cause serious damage? And I would think if she was going to run to the media about it, she'd have already done it."

Rolling her eyes, she stood. "If this gets out, it won't look good that you got her knocked up on the night she buried her dead husband."

"Who was a cheating bastard, and she wasn't even in love with him anymore. People would probably applaud her."

She titled her head. "Did she tell you that she wasn't in love with him anymore?"

I swallowed hard. "She shared some things about her marriage that night, things I'm not going to repeat, and she told them to me in private."

Her hands went up in the air, then fell to her sides. "Gage, no one is going to care that her husband was a cheating bastard and she was unhappy. You slept with a married woman, an older married woman, and got her pregnant. Did you even say anything to her, or did you just get up and sneak out of the room before she woke up?"

I clenched my fists together to keep my anger at bay. "First off, it wasn't like she committed adultery, Rachel, so knock that shit off. Second, Kadie left; I woke up, and she was gone. I didn't reach out to her because, well, she made it clear she just wanted that one night. So that's what I gave her."

She laughed. "I beg to differ, little brother. You gave her a going-away gift. A baby."

"When did you find out this little bit of information?"

She looked away, drew in a breath, then faced me again. "Three months ago."

My heart dropped to my stomach. "Three months ago? And you didn't think this was something you should have told me sooner?"

With a shake of her head, she replied, "I tried calling you a few times, and you never answered. It wasn't something I was going to leave on a voicemail or put in an email."

"Why didn't you say it was important, for fuck's sake?"

She stared at me for a moment, then shook her head as if confused. "For starters, I didn't want your mind to be somewhere else. I needed you to focus on the tour, Gage. You've got a real shot of getting nominated for a Grammy and possibly entertainer of the year. This is one of the biggest tours you've done to date. The last thing I needed was for you to run back home to be by this woman's side and hold her hand because she stupidly got herself knocked up."

I opened my mouth, but nothing came out. Rachel went on.

"It's not like you're going to marry her. We can draw up an NDA so she can't go to anyone with this news, throw some money at her, and you can move on with your life."

I slowly shook my head. "This is why you're still single. You're coldhearted, Rach. The only thing you care about is money and who is standing in the way of you making more of it."

"What would you have done, Gage?"

"The right thing, Rachel. Reached out to her and helped her in whatever way I could. Be there. Goddamn it, Rach, if that is my baby, I have the right to be in their life. Every process of it."

A horrified look crossed her face. "The right thing? The. Right. Thing? Marriage? To a nobody who is ten years older than you? Your fans will tear her apart, Gage. They'll say she trapped you. She drugged you to sleep with her or something. You might get some bad press out of this, and we can spin it and most likely recover, but it could destroy her. Is that what you want?"

I laughed. "I'm sorry, Rachel, but have you ever met Kadie Roberts?"

She squared off her shoulders. "No, I haven't met her yet. I wanted to, but I figured you needed to speak with her first before I attempted to negotiate anything on your behalf."

There went my stomach again. "You won't do any such thing. This is between Kadie and me, and we'll work it out ourselves. And let me tell you, Kadie Roberts is a stunningly beautiful woman. Very beautiful, both inside and out. Any man would be an idiot to think otherwise. It doesn't matter that she is older than me, and I'm not saying I will marry her. I'm saying I'll do the right thing and be by her side. Help her with the pregnancy and after. Be part of the child's life. Mom and Dad would want that. I want that."

My sister slowly tilted her head as she regarded me for a beat too long.

"What?"

"Oh, my, God. You like her. That's why you ran, and you like this woman."

Yanking my suitcase open, I grabbed some clothes and tossed them onto the bed.

"I'm exhausted, Rachel. Just give me Kadie's number, and I'll take care of everything."

"I can't."

Turning to look at her, I asked, "What do you mean you can't?"

"She used Pete to contact me, and he didn't give me a number to reach her. When I found out you were on your way back, I called him, and he said Kadie had moved. When she didn't hear back from you, she assumed you didn't care about the baby and told Pete she would be leaving Los Angeles. He said she left a week ago."

A rush of heat swept over my body. "So let me get this straight. The woman who is carrying *my* child is gone and with no way of contacting her?"

"I didn't say that, Gage. Just contact Pete and find out where she moved to. I'm sure she left her information with him."

I slowly shook my head. "It's been a few months, Rachel. Why would she want to talk to me now when she thinks I blew her off?"

She gave a one-shoulder shrug. "Explain to her that you were on tour, and life didn't stop because you had sex with her."

My hand went through my hair. "This is so fucked up. Mom was right when she said I should have never allowed you to be my manager, and you had no right keeping this from me."

She spun around on her heels and glared at me. "I did what I thought was right. Besides, I told you I tried to call you when I first found out."

"And since then? Not a single fucking word has come out of you about this? Hell, Rachel, I've spoken to you on the phone a dozen times."

"I wasn't even sure if it was true, Gage, and I honestly thought it was a joke a first and that she was losing her mind with grief or something. Come on, Kadie Roberts isn't your normal type of woman you hook up with, and I will say it does say something about her character that she hasn't gone to the press with this."

I glared at my sister. "And she wouldn't because she isn't that way."

"And you know this after spending one night with her? I'd imagine you didn't talk much. How many hours were you even with her, Gage? Six? Seven? Maybe twelve?"

I pointed to my sister. "You're fired."

Her eyes went wide. "Excuse me?"

"You. Are. Fired. Get out of my house, Rachel. Now."

A cold expression appeared on my sister's face as she walked closer to me. "I'm going to forget you just said all of that. Let's not forget what I did to get you where you are today, Gage. I'm going to leave Pete's number right here. When you decide to call him, make sure he knows this is to stay under wraps. No press. No leaks. If it gets out, we'll take baby momma to court."

Never in my life did I want to harm my sister until that moment. "Get. Out. Now."

Flashing me a bright smile, Rachel turned and headed toward my bedroom door. "We'll talk when you've calmed down."

The moment the door shut, I picked up a vase and threw it. I stared at the water that was now in a pool on the floor in front of the door.

I stumbled back until my legs hit my bed. Dropping down, I scrubbed my hands down my face.

Holy shit. Kadie is pregnant with my baby.

Glancing back at the closed door, I slowly shook my head. "What in the hell is wrong with you, Rachel? Why would you keep this from me?"

I stood and walked over to where my sister had left Pete's card on my dresser. Picking it up, I stared at the phone number for what felt like an eternity, and I pulled out my phone and punched in the numbers.

"Pete Hathaway's office."

"Hi, um, this is um, Gage Mason. Is Mr. Hathaway available?"

"Please hold, Mr. Mason, and I'll check for you."

Soft music came over the phone as I waited. Pacing, I made my way over to the window and stared out at the Pacific Ocean. My house was on the beach with a killer view. Once upon a time, I had loved being here. Now it felt like I was in a cage, and it seemed to be the only place I found any peace.

"Gage Mason, this is Pete Hathaway. How are you?"

"I'm not sure. I just returned home from Europe and Asia, and I was on tour. My manager, who is also my sister, just informed me that Kadie Roberts is, well, that she's pregnant and the baby is mine."

There was a long pause before Pete spoke. "Let me get this right, and you *just* found out about the pregnancy?"

I cleared my throat. "Yes. My sister decided I wasn't the father and decided it would be best if I focused on the tour. Trust me; I'm not happy about it. I want you to know if I had known, I would have reached out to Kadie right away."

"I'm glad to hear that. By the way, Kadie has gone back to her maiden name. It's Kadie Barton now, and she moved a little over a week ago."

"Is there any way you can give me her contact info or give her mine? I can give you my direct cell phone number, and that way, she can decide if she even wants to talk to me. There is one thing, though, Pete."

"Go on."

"I will understand if Kadie is upset with me. I know I would be. I'm assuming she thinks I just blew her off. I do want to be a part of this child's life. To help Kadie in any way I can."

"I've got to say, Mr. Mason, not many men in your position would feel that way."

I frowned. "Well, I guess I'm not like most men, then."

There was a slight pause before Pete spoke. "Kadie left her information for you, in case you decided you wanted to be a part of the child's life. She isn't interested in money or anything such as a commitment in any way to either her or the baby, and she was simply trying to do the right thing by letting you know she was pregnant with your child."

My hand came to the back of my neck, and I rubbed at the sudden tension. I'd never met anyone like Kadie before, and most women I was with always wanted something from me. And if any of them had ended up pregnant, let's say they wouldn't be handling the situation at all like Kadie Ro—Kadie Barton was.

"I appreciate that. I honestly do."

"Should I send the information over to your manager or…"

"No!" I quickly said. "Please send it directly to me. As far as Rachel is concerned, nothing goes through her about this."

It was his turn to clear his throat. "Not even business-wise? We still are the law firm that handles things for you, Gage."

"Just anything to do with my personal life and Ms. Barton. None of that goes through my sister, and if she reaches out for information, do not give her any."

"I'll make a note of it. I have your email address here in your file."

After he confirmed my email, he said, "I'll get the information over to you as soon as we hang up."

The sound of typing on a computer caused me to pull my laptop out of my bag and open it. I set it on the bed and waited for it to boot up.

"Thank you, Pete. I'll be on the lookout for it."

"I'm not sure if you want a congratulations or not, so I'll simply wish you the best, Gage."

I closed my eyes and focused on calming my suddenly hammering heart. "Thank you. Appreciate the help, Pete."

"Any time, Gage. Any time."

After hitting End, I stared down at my computer until the ding of an email caused me to drop to my knees. I quickly opened the email from Pete and read it.

Kadie Barton
261 San Clemente Road
Half Moon Bay, CA
213-555-5555

I picked up my phone and looked up Ron's number. Hitting it, I stared at the information on the screen.

"What's up, dude? Are you back in town? How did the tour go?"

"Hey, um, yeah, I got back a few hours ago. Tour was good, exhausting, but sold-out shows, so I can't complain. Listen, I need a favor."

"Okay. Is everything alright? You sound serious."

"This is serious. And it has to stay between you and me."

I could just see Ron nodding his head as he replied, "Always. We've been best friends since first grade. Nothing is going to change that now."

Smiling, I turned and looked at the suitcase on my bed. I spun on my heels and headed to my closet.

"I need you to fly me up to Half Moon Bay."

"Yes! Dude, are we having some bro time?"

Laughing, I grabbed a duffle bag and quickly started to pack some things up.

"No. I need to go there so I can track down the woman who is carrying my baby."

In all the years I'd known Ron Reynolds, I had never experienced him at a loss for words. Of course, never in a million years would he imagine me dropping that kind of bomb on him either.

"Did I hear you right? Did you say…"

His voice trailed off.

"You heard me right. I'm going to be a dad."

"That's the secret, I'm guessing."

I took my shaving kit and bathroom bag out of my other suitcase and put them in the duffle.

"That is the secret. Are you able to leave in the next few hours? The faster I can get there, the better."

"Dude, I've got a million and one questions, but I'll wait for the ride up. I'm leaving now. Meet you at the airport."

I threw the bag over my shoulder, grabbed my keys, and headed out of my bedroom.

"See you soon."

Four hours later, I was standing outside the front door of Kadie's house. I was nervous as fuck, like I was on my first date, and worried she wouldn't want to go out with me.

It hadn't taken much to convince Ron to stay back at the hotel while I made my way to Kadie's house. The blonde out by the pool was the reason he had stayed behind.

I lifted my hand and rang the doorbell as I drew in a deep breath.

The front door opened, and for a moment, I forgot to breathe. Kadie stood before me in overalls. Her dark blonde hair was pulled up in a pony, and white paint was on the tip of her nose. She was the most adorable thing I'd ever laid eyes on.

My eyes drifted down to her swollen belly, then right back up to see her blue eyes staring at me in shock.

I did the only thing I could think of doing.

Stepping closer to her, I lifted my hand, pushed a stray hair behind her ear, and then leaned down and kissed her.

✦   ✦   ✦

Thank you so much for reading the sneak peek at Look for *Through Her Eyes* coming 2023. You can find more information on my books on my website. www.kellyelliottauthor.com

TRUCE

WILLOW ASTER

CHAPTER ONE
Alex

AT FIRST, I don't recognize her.

The last time I saw her, I'd been scaling down a castle with her clinging to me like a spider monkey, and then I made sure she was thrown in prison.

Princess Solvang of the Sea of Caninsula stands proudly at the end of the banquet hall in an elaborate gown, jewels sparkling in her elaborate braids and against her neck. I can tell the moment she sees me.

I smirk and stride toward her, not letting the inferno she's trying to send my way with her eyes affect me in the least. When I reach her, she nods slightly, her refusal to bow before me making me laugh, which only infuriates her more.

"Alex Forbrush," she says coolly.

I tilt my head. "That's *King* Forbrush to you."

Her cheeks darken to a rosier brown. I'm certain she'd love nothing more than to knee me in the balls, but she maintains her cool and says nothing.

"Congratulations on your pardon. I hope this means we can agree to a truce. King Shua and I have managed to get along quite well in the time since you and I last saw each other, so I trust that we can as well," I say.

"What my brother does with our kingdom is ultimately his choice, but I assure you that I have no interest in agreeing to a truce with you, *King* Forbrush." Her eyes rake down me in disgust, and my cock jumps to attention.

I grin. "I've heard you were able to work things out with my friend, Queen Delilah. If she can forgive you for attempting to take her life, I can certainly do the same."

She scoffs at me, and I don't know why it turns me on so much. Her full lips purse as she takes a step closer to me. "You know I was at a vulnerable time in my life when that happened and that I wouldn't have killed her. If you'd given me a chance to explain that to you, I could've avoided being miserable in that cell for all those months."

I take a step closer to her and lean toward her ear. "You have me to thank for the soft linens and a room to yourself in a place that was more like a hotel room than any jail cell I've ever seen. You're welcome for the massages you were given once a week." I chuckle and get a surge of satisfaction when I see goose bumps skate across her neck. "Let's not pretend you suffered any hardship, my dear princess."

She turns her head to face me, and our lips are a breath from touching. I almost close the distance between us.

"Oh, I suppose you think I should thank you for the time away from my brother when he needed me most? You'll excuse me for not feeling any amount of gratitude toward you. And I am not your dear *anything*. Certainly not your princess, just as you are not my king. Kindly step back."

I do, but I'm unable to stop smiling at her fire. With women falling all over themselves when they talk to me most of the time, it's rare that I meet someone who can rise to the occasion when I need to verbally spar. I lower my head and I can tell she doesn't want to return the gesture of respect, but she does anyway, a testament to her good manners.

I walk away and am immediately surrounded by friends I haven't seen since I became king. It wasn't that long ago that I bounced from one party to the next, one adventure to another. Dragging Solvang out of Delilah's quarters was just one adventure of many, but it has stayed with me longer than most. I think maybe because I know she spoke the truth tonight. She *was* at a vulnerable time after losing her father. The man she'd thought she'd be matched with—Jadon Safrin—was in love with Delilah. And there I came, jumping in without giving her a chance to explain herself and dragging her from extensive heights down a rope with her legs around my waist.

It's no surprise the woman is hostile.

Orinna latches on to me, her hands and arms like tentacles, as I try and fail to pry her off of me. I made the mistake of sleeping with her once when I was sixteen, never went back for seconds, having learned my lesson the first time, and she's never given up trying all these years.

King Shua walks by and stops to greet me.

"Excuse me, Orinna, I need my arm back, thank you," I say, attempting to get her hands off of me. "King Shua, wonderful to see you again. How are you?"

He grins at me, seeing through the situation at once, even though we're both surrounded by people. He smiles at Orinna, and she lowers her eyelashes. *Yes, keep working your magic,* I want to shout at Shua.

"Did you work things out with my sister?" he asks, his eyes full of humor. "I hope she didn't give you too hard a time." He leans in. "She actually admitted to me that the time away allowed her to rest more than she had in years." He pulls back and winks.

A surprised laugh bursts out of me, and I glance across the room to see Solvang watching us, her eyes narrowed in suspicion.

"She will murder you in your sleep if she ever finds out you told me that," I say, still laughing.

"Then I beg of you—keep it between us." He glances at Orinna. "And this fine beauty," he adds.

I want to reach out and hug him when Orinna's hand drops off of my chest and she turns slightly toward Shua. "Orinna, you must meet King Shua. We've become friends, if you can believe it," I tease, glancing at Shua again. "King Shua, my friend, Orinna. You should save a dance for one another later. The two of you would be well-matched on the dance floor."

"Is that right?" Shua says, taking her hand and kissing it.

And that settles it, she takes a step away from me and I pick my moment to escape. Shua looks as entranced by her as she is by him, so he's not doing me any favors. Maybe I've just been the witness of a match made in heaven.

When we're seated for dinner, I am placed next to Princess Solvang. Her brother is on the other side of her, and I hear her ask him to switch places so he can sit next to me.

"I planned this party just so you and King Alex could work out your differences," he says, his voice light.

My lips press together to keep from laughing. I knew Shua brought me here in hopes that his sister would soften toward me. If she finds out his true intention is to produce a love match between our two countries, I'm certain she would not be sitting here right now.

I don't intend on marrying her either, never mind that I'm entertaining her brother's farfetched idea that this could be beneficial in every way for both of us. But I did want to see her again. There was something about the way she held on to me, her eyes trusting me in that moment to keep her safe, that has stuck with me. And something about the way she looked so betrayed when I left her that I still haven't forgiven myself for, despite the things I said about it being a luxurious experience. Even despite her being guilty.

She was still locked in a room for an extended period of time, and I wouldn't wish that on anyone.

"The more I'm around Alex Forbrush, the more our differences are painfully obvious," she says, her voice cold.

Damn if my cock doesn't like that too, her icy looks and sharp tongue.

I grin and lift my champagne glass toward her. "To painful differences," I say. "May they be thrust into a tight hole and clenched like a vise as they shatter into a thousand convulsing pieces."

CHAPTER TWO
Solvang

"**W**HAT?" I WHISPER. My core clenches at his words as my mind plays it back, certain I must have misunderstood and that he couldn't have meant that as sexual as it sounded. "*What did you say?*"

"To painful differences," he repeats. "And having them relieved."

I clink his glass, unsure if we're having a language barrier or if he meant that exactly as I heard it. He speaks many languages fluently; I remember that about him. He'd spoken in the Caninsulan tongue as he'd whispered reassurances on our way down the castle, and it had helped ease my mind.

But he looks too pleased with himself, too cocky, and I'm positive he's getting his kicks out of aggravating me tonight. I ignore him as best I can while we eat, although he never stops trying to make conversation. Finally, when dessert is brought out and some begin dancing, my brother finding a blonde woman who stares at him like he's God's gift, I take a few bites of mine and turn to Alex.

He's just asked if I've had any good massages lately.

I roll my eyes exaggeratedly and take his champagne glass from him, setting it down on the table. His eyes widen and his pupils dilate as he leans in slightly, his tongue reaching out to wet his lips.

He is a ridiculously beautiful man. It is not fair that one person was bestowed such good looks. And unfortunately, Alex is aware of the gifts he's been given. The man is insufferable, and it is almost impossible to not stare at him and feel grateful that you're getting the chance to do so.

I would die a thousand deaths before those words would ever come out of my mouth, but it's the truth.

"If I allow you one dance, will you stop talking to me and we can forget this night ever happened?" I ask.

A tiny frown appears between his eyebrows and his full lips poke out in a tiny pout as he thinks it over.

"If we dance and I make you laugh, will you give me another dance?" he counteroffers.

"What game are you playing, Alex?"

"Does a man need an excuse to dance with a beautiful woman?"

"Oh, now I'm a beautiful woman." I shake my head. He's a piece of work, he really is.

"You've always been a beautiful woman, Solvang." His voice turns silky, my name on his lips like a caress and my eyes narrow on his once again. He laughs. "Have you always been so distrustful?"

"Only of silky-tongue conniving bastards who throw me in prison." I don't know why I sound so breathy, or why my heart is racing.

He pushes to his feet and offers me a hand. I look up to see Shua leaving the beautiful blonde when Garzon, his right-hand man, whispers something in his ear, and he hurries away from the table. Alex notices as well, but he escorts me to the dance floor.

I'm lost in the moment. Lost in the way he holds me possessively against his hard body. The way his lips graze my ear when he whispers so only I can hear, "How is it that you fit so perfectly against me?"

I wait to pull myself together, desperate to prove that he doesn't affect me. "It's not the first time you've held me against your body. Will you betray me once again?"

He pulls back to look at me, his desire impossible to miss. "Give me a chance to show you that I won't."

"I'm sorry to interrupt, but I need a moment with you both in my office," my brother says with an urgency, startling me from the moment.

Alex's hand finds the small of my back as he leads me off the dance floor, and we follow Shua down the hallway. We step into the elaborate red and gold office space and settle in the two leather seats across from his desk.

"Demarco Tamar has been spotted near the premises. I thought we were rid of him when I sent him away after his last stunt. I think the man's obsession with you is alarming." My brother's concern sends a shiver down my spine.

"Tamar? The son of the man who worked closely with your father?" Alex asks, and he looks between my brother and me.

"Yes. He has an obsession with Solvang that has become alarming. We found him hiding in her bedroom when she first returned home, and I had him sent away with a warning not to come near her again. He's made his desire to marry her known, but the feelings are not mutual. He's been building a small army of men in an attempt to challenge my leadership over this kingdom, his obsession with marrying my sister his main goal." Shua pushes to his feet and runs a hand down the back of his neck.

"So, he's threatened both your sister and your kingdom?"

"He's fixated on her. He's made her uncomfortable on more than one occasion."

I rub my hand down my arm seeking comfort and clear my throat. "He's always been jealous of Shua."

"Tell me how he's fixated on you?" Alex asks me.

"He wrote to me every day while I was locked up. He speaks like we've had a relationship and we haven't. His father worked for my father, and we grew up together, but we've never even been friends. The way he's watched me has always made me uncomfortable, and he talks of us ruling this kingdom together." I shiver, my underlying fear about Demarco deeper than I want to admit. The endless letters. Showing up everywhere I go. Almost like the man has eyes on me at all times. I've had our home searched for cameras numerous times because he seems to know my every move. Thankfully, Garzon found him in my room before I'd been allowed to step inside when I returned home after being locked up.

"I've warned him several times to stay away from her and I sent him to Niaps to work for Luka Catano in hopes that he would move on and could find peace again at some point. But clearly, that hasn't happened. Luka reached out to let me know he'd fled Niaps, and that he'd found him to be unstable. The thought of him having a group of supporters behind him is alarming. The Sea of Caninsula is vulnerable since my father's death, which is why my hopes to join kingdoms with you is so important. It would benefit us both."

Shua has spoken of his desire for me and Alex to marry. It would solve a lot of problems. My father raised me to put my kingdom first, but the thought of marrying a man who betrayed me once is not one that I can support. However, my fear of Demarco is stronger than my disdain for Alex Forbrush.

"I understand. But I will not marry a woman against her will." He shrugs and grins. "I'm not sure I'm the marrying kind anyway." I roll my eyes. I know what that means. Alex's reputation with women precedes him. "But what I *can* do is give you my word that I will protect her." Alex pushes to his feet. "You're coming with me."

I stare at his hand as he holds it out to me. "Coming with you where?"

"To Yuman. I will have my men take us to the plane. Tamar is here, and we won't wait for him to act on his threats," Alex says as I push to my feet and take his hand.

"He is. With a bigger army than I thought him capable of gathering. My men are preparing now to protect the castle but getting Solvang out of here is my priority." My brother looks at me apologetically.

"So, I'm just supposed to run and hide?"

"Please, don't be stubborn right now, Solvang. I don't know what he's capable of, and I don't know that I can protect you here," Shua admits.

I tug my hand away from Alex. "So, I'm a prisoner once again."

Shua and Alex share a look, but they don't deny it.

But this time I will not go quietly.

CHAPTER THREE

Alex

IF THERE IS an award for being a major pain in the ass, Solvang Otto would be the reigning champ. She puts up a fight when we hustle her out the door, and I board the plane carrying her over my shoulder when she refuses to get out of the car.

Although, I've never seen a woman sexier, nor desired anyone quite the way I do her. It's unexpected, as I rarely allow attraction to affect me much beyond a mutual night of unattached fucking. But this woman has definitely made an impression. I don't even mind the way her little fists punch at my back. The way she narrows her gaze and flips me the bird when I drop her on the seat beside mine and buckle her as she slaps at my hands. The blatant disrespect should piss me off when I'm trying to help the woman and follow her brother's—the king of the kingdom I'm currently a guest of—request, but instead, it turns me on.

She doesn't speak to me on the flight, and when we arrive in Yuman, she holds her hand up to let me know that she'll be walking off the plane herself.

"If you put me over your shoulder again, I will lock your balls in a grip so strong, you'll have no need of a vasectomy," she spits out. I back away, laughing, the desire to hold my balls strong. "You don't need to treat me like a child," she hisses, and I follow her toward the car, my cock jumping to attention at the way her hips sway from side to side as she huffs in front of me.

"Then stop behaving like one."

We don't speak on the car ride over, and I've called ahead to make sure we have extra security at the castle to protect her. Once we arrive, I guide her inside, as she slowly takes in the grand foyer.

"Are you locking me in a cell like a prisoner again?" she asks, her arms crossing over her chest.

Mrs. Huntinger greets us and lets me know that Solvang's room is ready. I nod but tell her that I will take Princess Otto to her quarters and excuse Mrs. Huntinger to go tend to the kitchen.

"Stop throwing a tantrum and understand that you are here because we want to keep you safe. You can leave your room anytime you'd like, but you will not leave the castle without informing me."

"Says who?" she shouts, disrespecting me in my own kingdom.

"Says the King of Yuman." I crowd her, her back hitting the wall as she looks up at me, and I can't tell if it's anger or desire I see in her gaze. Her chest rises and falls, and my hands fist at my side to keep from reaching for her. The silky skin of her neck beckoning me like it's the oxygen I seek. Her tongue swipes out to wet her lips, and I swear I nearly come undone.

"Forgive me, King." She oozes sarcasm, but it only makes me want her more. I'm not a desperate man. I can have just about any woman I desire. Unfortunately, I appear to desire the only woman who doesn't want me. "I'd like to go to my room now."

I back away and guide her up the stairs. Jenika is just leaving Solvang's guest suite as we arrive. "Everything is as you asked. There are fresh linens on the bed, and her closet has been stocked with clothing for her while she's here." She turns her attention to Solvang. "Would you like tea sent up to your room, Princess?"

She startles a bit at the kindness and her gaze softens. "That would be lovely. Thank you so much."

"I'm Jenika, and King Alex has asked that I am at your service for anything you need. We hope you'll be comfortable here."

"I appreciate it, Jenika. Thank you."

Jenika hurries down the hall and I follow Solvang inside the plush quarters. A white gown lies on her bed and I long to see what she looks like beneath the silky fabric.

I sit on the edge of the bed as she takes in the space. She turns to look at me, and her lips turn up in the corners the tiniest bit, just enough to let me know she's pleased, even if she won't admit it. I pat the bed beside me.

She surprises me by sitting next to me without argument, and I breathe her in. Jasmine flooding my senses. "Tell me about these letters from Demarco."

Her shoulders stiffen, something I noticed earlier when we spoke in her brother's chambers. She held back. She didn't want to worry Shua, but I need to know what we're dealing with.

"How do I know I can trust you?"

"Do you have a choice?" I ask, my hand moving closer to hers on the bed as it rests between us. My finger brushing against hers.

The pull is so strong that I don't think a thousand men could pull me from this room right now if they tried.

"I always have a choice."

"Solvang," I say, her name leaving my tongue harsher than I meant it to. "I want to keep you safe."

"Why?"

"I don't know, but I'm quite certain you feel the same pull that I do. I'm just man enough to admit it."

"You aren't the first man to be attracted to me, King Forbrush," she whispers, and I can feel her walls coming down as I move a bit closer to her. My leg touches hers, and I long to comfort her.

"I'm quite certain there isn't a man on the planet who could resist you. Now stop being stubborn and tell me about the letters."

"The letters started out saying that he missed me. Missed spending time with me, even though I've never spent any time with that man. But they grew more alarming as time went on. He wrote of how we'd be married once I was released from my sentence. How he'd seek revenge on you and my brother once we were reunited again. How we'd rule the Sea of Caninsula as man and wife. I never responded. But I need you to know that I never needed *saving*. I can protect myself."

So stoic. Fierce. I can feel her strength as I sit beside her.

"No doubt about it. But a man with an army behind him is not something you can fight alone."

She nods, and when I look up, I see the fear before she quickly looks away.

I reach for her chin, turning her to meet my gaze. We stare at each other for long, silent moments that have my heart pounding, something my heart just doesn't do. I move closer, my lips grazing hers. "Let me keep you safe, Princess Solvang."

Her breath tickling my skin has me moving even closer. Her lips part and allow me access. I kiss her slowly at first before my need for this woman takes control. She moans into my mouth, and I pull her onto my lap, my hands moving up her neck, feeling her pulse race as I take the kiss deeper.

Her fingers tangle in my hair, and she tips her head back, allowing me more access. When our tongues collide into each other, deepening the kiss, she gives my hair a hard tug, and for a moment, we lose ourselves in each other.

The sound of footsteps startles us both and Solvang jumps off my lap, almost falling as she moves to sit beside me. I reach for her shoulders and steady her as Jenika steps into the room, her cheeks rosy as she realizes she's interrupted us.

"I'm sorry." She bows. "I'll just leave this here."

"No." Solvang jumps to her feet. "I'd like your help changing into my night-gown. King Forbrush was just leaving."

I stare at her for a long moment, and she raises a brow, daring me to challenge her request. I make my way to the door as Jenika busies herself pouring tea before moving into the bathroom with Solvang's white nightgown.

"You could join me in my bedroom if you'd like?" I ask with a smirk that I can tell pisses her off. But getting a reaction from this woman is all I care about.

"That was a mistake," she whispers.

"Oh, Princess Solvang, nothing about that was a mistake. And now that I've tasted you, I'm afraid I only want more."

"What if I don't?" she says, tipping her chin up in challenge.

My hands grip her waist and I glance down to see her hard peaks poking through her dress. She wants me as badly as I want her. "Your body says differently."

"Goodnight, King Forbrush," she says, stepping back.

"It most definitely has been. Get some rest." I kiss her cheek before exiting the room.

I make my way downstairs where Harkin sits waiting for me in my office. He smirks as if he knows exactly what I've been up to. The man is my eyes and ears of the kingdom and he's always been my most loyal guard.

"Took you long enough." He raises a brow.

I make my way around my desk. "Find out everything you can about Demarco Tamar and double the security for Princess Solvang."

"Feeling protective, are we?" He smiles and I roll my eyes.

"I'm loyal to Shua."

"I think it's a bit more than that. Tell me I'm wrong."

But I can't. Because I am most definitely feeling protective of the gorgeous woman who will be staying in the room next to mine.

And I have no idea why.

CHAPTER FOUR

Solvang

THE CASTLE BUSTLES with people when I exit the bedroom. The clothes they've provided me are gorgeous, and Jenika informs me that King Forbrush ordered my room to be filled with all the finest clothing and bedding and fresh blooms. She gushes about what an amazing leader he is and how everyone that works at the castle adores him. I'm surprised to see such adoration amongst staff, as it's easy to envy the man you work for. But he doesn't run his kingdom with an iron fist. He's kind and honest and protects his people with the fiercest loyalty.

Her words, not mine.

When I make my way downstairs, he's waiting for me at the bottom of the staircase. His gaze finds mine, and I know in that moment, that I'd seek this man out in a crowded room and I'd find him every time. Alex Forbrush is correct. There is an unexplainable pull that I've felt since the moment I saw him again at the party. If I were to admit it to myself, I felt it when he carried me out of that building so long ago—I was just too ashamed and frightened by how far I'd been willing to go. It's always been there under the surface between us. I feel desired and wanted and now, surprisingly, I also feel safe in his presence.

I have been unable to think of anything other than the way his lips felt against mine last night. The way my body craved his touch.

His taste.

"Good morning, King Forbrush."

He reaches for my hand and purrs. "Ah, I see someone is cooperating this morning. Do I have the comfort of your room, my staff, or the feel of my mouth claiming yours last night to thank for this greeting?"

I feel a blush creep up my neck and along my cheeks, but I shrug. "I don't know what you're talking about. I barely remember."

He barks out a laugh, and I can't help but smile as he leads me into the dining room and pulls out my chair before taking the seat beside me. After Mrs. Huntinger and the staff serve our breakfast, he excuses them to go eat themselves. This is not common practice for a king. But nothing about Alex Forbrush is common.

"Tell me what it was like growing up in the Sea of Caninsula," he asks, surprising me with the question.

"Why?"

"Because, Princess Solvang. If I'm to entertain the thought of making you my queen someday, I'd like to know everything about the future mother of my children." He pops a strawberry in his mouth and winks, and I nearly lose my breath.

"Oh, please, you aren't the only one who isn't the marrying kind. You've suddenly decided you want to strengthen both kingdoms?" I press, needing to know he's joking.

"My kingdom is plenty strong. But that kiss last night could change my mind about a lot of things."

I bite down on my bottom lip and try to hide the smile that threatens to take over my face. We spend the next two hours talking about everything from our childhoods to our families to our kingdoms. I tell him how I enjoy painting and sculpting, and he shares that he is an avid horseback rider. We walk the grounds of his palace and I'm taken by the beauty that is Yuman.

We end in his stable where he introduces me to Holt, his favorite stallion that he rides daily. My hand glides over the gorgeous black hair of the horse, as Alex tracks my every move.

"I want to kiss you again, Princess," he whispers, as his hand finds my waist and he backs me up against the wall.

I want him, there's no denying it. In the short time I've been here, I've thought of little else.

But I barely know him. This man who's chosen to keep me safe. To protect me. To kiss me in a way I've never been kissed.

His mouth claims mine. Seeking and owning and claiming. My body melds into his as he kisses me into oblivion.

His hand finds my cheek when he pulls back, and someone clears their throat behind us. I peek over his shoulder to see the man that was with us last night on the plane, Harkin.

"I'm sorry, sir. King Shua would like to speak to you on the phone. He says it's urgent."

"Thank you. I'll be right there."

I glance at him, concerned, but he interlocks his fingers with mine and even that is both comforting and sends heat across my body.

"I'm sorry we were interrupted, but I need to speak to your brother."

I nod. "All right. I'd like to sit outside in the garden. I'm assuming that's allowed," I tease, raising a brow.

His brows cinch together, but he nods. "As long as you're okay with having guards around you at all times."

"Of course."

We walk out of the stable, and he motions for the two men standing outside the barn as we exit. "You are not to leave her. She'd like to sit in the garden. Give her space, but stay close."

"Yes, King Forbrush," they both say in unison.

He kisses my cheek. "I'll find you soon."

I sit out in the garden taking in the beautiful scenery. There are roses and gardenias and hydrangeas every which way I turn. I imagine what it would be like to paint out here. I glance up at what I believe must be Alex's bedroom balcony overlooking this gorgeous landscape, and for a moment I allow myself to daydream about him.

To feel those lips on mine any time I wish.

I close my eyes and allow the warmth of the sun to heat my skin, along with thoughts of him.

I get lost in the sound of the birds chirping around me. The bustle of the leaves that blow in the light breeze.

Fingers skim the back of my neck and I startle. It's not the warmth of Alex's touch that meets my skin. I freeze at the sound of his voice.

"I'm here, my darling. I told you I'd come."

I whip around to find Demarco standing behind me. The two guards watching me are nowhere in sight, and just one man that I don't recognize stands a few feet from us. He must be here with Demarco because he's not doing anything to help me.

"How did you get in here?" I ask, attempting to push to my feet, but his hand moves to my neck and tightens, holding me still.

"I will always come. You should know by now that I intend to make you mine, once and for all." He yanks me to my feet, and my eyes search the grounds as he tugs me along with him.

"Demarco, let me go." I fight to get free of his grip and he turns around, my body slamming against his as his mouth comes over mine. I bite down hard on his lip before stomping on his foot.

There is a ruckus in the distance, and everything blurs as I catch him off guard and break free of his grip, kneeing him in the balls. I hear shouting and gunshots, and Demarco screams out in pain as the ground beneath me disappears.

Everything goes dark.

CHAPTER FIVE

Alex

MY MEN HAVE seized the small army Demarco Tamar brought onto my grounds. Solvang's brother had phoned with word from Luka Catano that Tamar knew where I'd taken Solvang. Luka had learned that someone in Shua's inner circle had been working for Tamar all along, and once captured, the man had told of Tamar's plans to take Solvang back to the Sea of Caninsula, where he planned to assassinate the king.

I didn't do as Harkin asked of me. I refused to go to the saferoom and wait for word that she was safe. Demarco Tamar was here on my grounds. In my kingdom.

I knew what he wanted. But Princess Solvang is not his for the taking, and I'll do whatever it takes to keep her safe, just as I promised.

Gunfire broke out as I'd advised my men to do whatever necessary to keep her safe. And that's exactly what my men had done. Solvang kicked and fought Tamar as I ran toward the scene, and shots fired around her. I waved my hands shouting for them to cease firing, once Tamar was down. But he'd reached for her one last time as he fell to the ground, causing her to trip before I could get to her. Her head came down on the cement bench in the garden and I ran for her like my life depended on it.

Now, I shout for a medic as my men surround the area, making sure we're secure. I hold her in my arms as she lies limp and lifeless, knowing I've let her down and vowing I'll do whatever it takes to make it up to her. To keep her safe.

✧   ✧   ✧

TWO DAYS PASS, and I sit by Solvang's bedside waiting for her to wake up. Her brother and mother are staying at the castle, sitting beside me as we watch her sleep. The doctor shares that she's sustained a head injury and he hopes she'll wake soon, but there are no guarantees. My sister, Nadia, rushes over when she hears the despair in my voice over the phone and holds my hand in hers as we sit in silence.

Hoping.

Waiting.

Demarco Tamar is sitting in a prison cell in Yuman where I'll make damn sure he spends the rest of his days. He'd been shot in the leg twice, but I'd spared his life, not willing to risk any shots hitting Solvang.

"She's going to wake up," Shua says as he paces the room.

The next few hours grow more excruciating, and at my insistence, everyone leaves to have dinner. But I'm unable to leave her. She looks so vulnerable lying here in this bed, and I think about how strong she is, how I hope she'll fight to get better with that same fire she's always shown me.

The night sky comes, but the light of the moon allows me a glimpse of Solvang. Sleep takes me as my hand remains locked with her fingers.

"Alex," she whispers, and I'm certain I'm dreaming when she squeezes my hand. My eyes fly open.

"You're awake." I'm on my feet, my hands cupping her face and looking for any signs of distress.

"Where is Demarco?" she asks, and I don't miss the panic in her voice.

"He's rotting in a cell where he will stay for the rest of his miserable life. Are you all right? Let me get the doctor."

She reaches for my hand. "Thank you for having my back," she says.

"Are you kidding? You didn't need me." I grin. "But I'm not going anywhere." I lift her hand to my lips and kiss her fingers.

There's no fucking place in all the kingdoms I'd rather be.

CHAPTER SIX
Solvang

T HE LAST TWO weeks have moved by in a blur. My mother and brother have returned to the Sea of Caninsula, and I've remained here in Yuman, with a king waiting on me hand and foot. I'm ready to leave this room and start living again, but he continues to fuss over me.

"I'm fine. Dr. Garp has released me as his patient. You need to stop hovering and holding me captive," I tease, cupping the side of his face. He has not left my side since I woke up after the head injury.

"Yeah? You sure?"

"I'm positive. I'd like to go outside and sit in the sunshine."

"There's something I'd like to show you first." He helps me to my feet and leads me out the door and to his room next door.

"Ah, finally." I laugh because the man hasn't touched me as he's slept beside me every night, too afraid to do anything to hurt me aside from kissing me until I'm dizzy.

"I won't be holding back any longer, Princess. But that's not what I want to show you." He pushes the door open and it's the first time I've seen his suite. It's gorgeous and large and there is a turret to the right of his room. We pass the hall leading to what I assume is the master bathroom and continue in that direction.

My breath hitches in my throat as I take in the floor-to-ceiling windows in the circular space and the French doors that open to a large balcony overlooking the garden. Easels line the space, with paints and charcoals and colored pencils covering the tabletop.

"What is this?" I whisper.

"I've gotten attached to you," he says, his eyes crinkling as he smiles. "I want you to stay here with me in Yuman...for as long as you can stand me. And I'm kind of voting on that being forever."

I laugh. "What?" I tease. "What do two non-marrying types do when they like hanging out with each other?" I lean up and whisper in his ear, "People might get the wrong idea." When I back away, I lift one shoulder and he reaches out and pulls me flush against him.

"I think we might have to make our own rules when it comes to the two of us," he says. "Let people think whatever they want." He grins.

"What kind of rules did you have in mind?" I ask.

"Uh, well, for sure I want you to sleep beside me every night. And kiss me every morning. And if you could just live here with me for the rest of our days, you know...that sort of thing," he says, as I cover my mouth to keep from laughing out loud.

"You don't ask for much, do you?"

He shakes his head. "I'm a simple king really."

"So, I can remain the princess of my brother's kingdom and be what to you exactly?"

"Be my everything," he says.

My mouth falls open and I'm suddenly speechless.

"What do you say?" he asks.

"When you say *sleep* beside you every night..."

"You know sleep is the last thing I want, Princess," he purrs, and I tangle my fingers in his thick hair. I've never craved a man the way I crave him.

"Well, before we write any crazy rules, we should see how it goes when we *don't* sleep together…since you keep driving me mad with kisses and then stopping right as it gets exciting. Who knows? Maybe we're awful together—"

He laughs and leans down and kisses me hard before I can speak any more nonsense. He picks me up, wrapping my legs around his waist and carries me to his bed. He places me on the bed carefully and I lean up on my knees, slipping my dress over my head.

His pupils dilate as his eyes roam down my body. I unclasp my bra and toss it toward him. He catches it and grins, his thumbs reaching out and circling over my nipples.

"I've changed my mind," he says, leaning down and taking my nipple in his mouth. He looks up and my heart drops to my feet. "I've decided I *am* the marrying kind."

I laugh and it dies out when he slides my lacy panties to the side and teases me with his fingers, dipping in and out, his thumb circling my sweet spot and then pressing down as I squirm against him. "You just needed to see me naked? That was all it took?" I ask, breathless.

He kisses down my body, his mouth joining his fingers, and when his tongue starts working its magic, he looks up at me, his eyes full of promise.

And much later, when I've writhed all over this bed, chanting things like, "Okay, you *are* my king. You are…" I manage to get his pants off of him finally, and my eyes widen when I see his body for the first time. His broad shoulders, chiseled stomach with the enticing V, and the most glorious, thick, *long*—

"I've changed my mind too," I say, pulling him down on top of me.

He laughs at me, but neither of us are laughing when he slides a condom on and thrusts inside of me, taking his time for me to adjust to his size. When he is finally balls deep, he leans his forehead against mine, holding still for a moment while it's eyes-rolling-back-in-my-head good.

"We are most definitely not awful together," he whispers.

✧ ✧ ✧

Thanks so much for reading *Truce*!

You can read more in my *Kingdoms of Sin* series, starting with *Downfall*.
www.willowaster.com/store/downfall-kingdoms-of-sin-1

Wolf Ranch Legacy

Vanessa Vale & Renee Rose

WILLOW

WHERE IN THE hell was my husband?

I looked around the packed place to see where Rob stood at the bar ordering us drinks. Cody's Saloon was hopping. There was a live band rocking the cover tunes and crazy people riding the mechanical bull.

My friends surrounded me at the table, but I felt itchy with Rob clear across the room.

For some reason, I was feeling extremely territorial of him tonight. The she-wolf in me seemed to have an alpha streak lately. Especially this past week.

We came here often, so it wasn't the women who were ogling Rob—because he was hot and exuded alpha, even to humans—that made me extra sensitive. Tonight, everyone from Wolf Ranch was here to celebrate Colton's birthday. Rob's brother. We'd found a spot in the corner with enough room for all of us, including Becky and Clint, who left their sweet baby with Clint's parents for a few hours.

I couldn't focus on the conversations around me because two pretty girls stood beside Rob, chatting him up. One of them was blonde with a high ponytail and off-the-shoulder cropped sweater. The other, a brunette, wore painted-on jeans that left nothing to anyone's imagination.

Oh, hell no. Rob was mine. *All* mine.

I pushed back from the table and stalked over. I wasn't going to pee on Rob, but I was definitely going to mark my territory. "Excuse me, ladies." I wedged myself between my mate and the woman on his right, not even caring that my action pushed her backward.

Rob's lips twitched. "Well, hello there, angel. I'm still waiting on the drinks."

His voice was calm and even and carried over the loud music. I shivered at the deep rumble. Just him calling me *angel* did it for me.

"I see that." I narrowed my eyes at him. It was irrational, but my jealousy had me pissed off at both the ladies who'd been rubbing up against him.

Rob turned his head to take in the woman behind him. "Charlene, have you met my wife, Willow?"

Grr. Why was he still talking to this woman? And why did he know her name? I was seriously going to kill him.

The blonde looked at me. She might be friendly enough but it was hard to tell because I had on green goggles. The kind that made you want to throat punch any woman who comes near your man? Yeah, those. Good thing I wasn't armed.

"No, we haven't met." Charlene stuck out her hand. Her smile was genuine. "It's great to meet you. Rob and I went to high school together."

Okay, for starters, there was no *Rob and I*, sugar. Also—back the hell off. *He's mine.*

Of course, I said none of that because that would make me irrational and slightly insane, which I felt like I was becoming more and more so by the minute. Instead, I bared my teeth and attempted a smile, then immediately shifted my condemning gaze to Rob, who for some reason found all this amusing.

I loved it when he smiled, which wasn't often. He was alpha, and unlike his brothers, he was the serious one.

He leaned down, putting his nose close to my shoulder, and dragged in a deep inhale. It was a strange move for a human, but not for a wolf. He was drinking in my scent. "Your wolf is showing, angel," he murmured against the skin of my neck.

I shivered again and stifled a whimper. Instantly, I craved him.

He meant the color of my irises had changed. Before I met Rob, I'd had no idea I was half shifter. A she-wolf. I'd grown up in foster care, alone, then moved on to law enforcement and then a DEA agent. A case had led me to the area and to Rob. Now I was the female alpha of the Wolf Ranch pack. Rob's marked mate.

Right now, I was wondering why the hell I never marked *him*. Shouldn't females get to permanently embed their scent in their male as well? Maybe if these two women saw my mark on his neck, they might steer clear. But no. It wouldn't keep humans away.

Thankfully, Charlene took our intimate moment as a hint and moved along. "Good seeing you, Rob."

Hopefully she didn't notice anything strange about my eyes, but I was too riled up to care.

Cody came down the bar and set drinks in front of us. Rob scooped them up, but kept his eyes on me. "Come on, angel, I need to talk to you. Somewhere quiet."

As if that was possible in this place on a Saturday night.

"Yeah, I have a few things to say to you, too," I told him, but I was already mollified being near him, following his rock-hard sexy cowboy frame in the direction of... the storeroom? Where were we going?

His large body cut a swath through the crowd, ensuring I had a clear path to follow him.

He opened the storeroom door like he owned the place—that was an alpha wolf for you—and ushered me inside.

I took in the small space. Shelves full of liquor and cleaning supplies lined the walls. "What are we doing back here?" I asked.

"I thought you might need a reminder." Rob set our drinks down on a shelf beside a stack of paper towels.

I frowned. "Reminder of what?"

"Who I live for."

My breath caught as he picked me up by the waist and set me atop a stack of boxes. Suddenly, my anger morphed to a choked-up love. The kind that gripped you by the throat and makes your eyes water. God, what was wrong with me lately? I wasn't usually the emotional type. I prided myself on keeping a cool head in the toughest of situations, just like Rob. For some reason this past week my emotions were all over the place.

Rob pushed my knees wide, sliding his thumbs up the inseam of my jeans until he reached the apex, where he rubbed.

All the tension in me melted and heat instantly kindled in my core.

Rob leaned close and inhaled my scent along my neck again. "You smell so fucking delicious," he murmured. He nipped the place on my shoulder where he'd marked me and his fingers worked the button on my jeans.

I tilted my head back and whimpered.

"What... what are you doing?" My voice was husky with laughter and heat. Desperate need.

"Teaching you a lesson."

My nipples got hot and tingly, my tender breasts heavy. "What kind of lesson?"

"One where you learn you need something from me, I give it to you. You need a good hard fucking. Isn't that what you crave, angel? I can scent your need."

I tried to clamp my knees closed, desperate to alleviate the pulsing ache between them. Oh, I *needed.*

"Hmm?" He pulled me off the boxes and slid his thumbs into the waistband of my loosened jeans. "You need that jealousy fucked right out of you."

"What? How—"

"I know, angel. I see you. Know every emotion on your face."

He shoved my jeans down to my thighs, spun me around and gave my ass a slap.

The sting morphed into heat and I moaned. Arched my back.

I gave him a wild look over my shoulder. "Yes," I practically hissed. "You better make it good, Rob Wolf," I warned.

He grinned and was staring at my ass, probably at the hot-pink handprint he'd just made.

"Oh yeah?" He stroked his fingers between my legs and my already wet pussy gushed for him. "Have I been neglecting this pretty little pussy?"

No. He hadn't been. He'd spent a solid thirty minutes with his mouth between my legs just this morning, but apparently it still wasn't enough. I was the horny version of hangry. Horngry.

"Enough talking," I snapped. I needed him. Craved him. I didn't care we were in a storeroom. Or that anyone might walk in.

Rob chuckled and unzipped his jeans, freeing his erection. "I'll give it to you, angel. Don't worry. I have everything you need."

With a hand between my shoulder blades, he pushed my torso down over the boxes. I felt the head of his cock as he dragged it between my legs, parting my lower lips and teasing my entrance.

"Rob." I was so damn impatient as I wiggled my hips, thrust them back. Seriously. I didn't want foreplay. Rob had been right—I needed it hard and firm, and I needed it now.

Thankfully, he got the message. Gripping one of my hips, he shoved into me.

I shuddered with the satisfaction of it. "Yes!" I cried.

I didn't want slow and gentle. Not tonight. I needed to feel all of him in that possessive, claiming way of his. I needed him to claim me the way my wolf had wanted to claim him tonight out there at the bar.

He eased back and slammed in hard again and I moaned my satisfaction. "Like that, angel?"

"Mm-hmm."

"Harder?"

"Harder."

"Yes, ma'am." Rob slammed into me, lifting me up onto my toes with an upward thrust.

"Yes!" I gasped.

He gripped my hips and took short, faster strokes, bumping my ass with his loins, making both our jeans slide down our legs.

I didn't care. I was delirious with need now, starting to sense the shimmering edge of satisfaction. "More," I demanded.

"You don't have to beg, angel. I know what you need, and I'm going to give it to you."

And he did. His fingers tightened on my hips and he jackhammered into me at the perfect angle, hitting my G-spot and making the coil of pleasure crank tighter, ready to spring.

"Rob," I whimpered.

"That's it, Willow. Let me take care of you. I'm always gonna take care of you."

My inner thighs spasmed, my toes curled in my cowgirl boots. "Rob!" I cried. I wasn't worried about making too much noise—there was no way anyone would hear me over the thump of music and chatter of loud drunken voices beyond the door. "Please," I begged.

Rob reached around and pinched my clit and I went off with a scream of satisfaction. My internal muscles clamped around his cock, milking it for everything I was worth. He groaned out his release, shoving deep and wrapping a strong forearm around my waist.

I moaned as he stroked in and out slowly, drawing all the quakes, tremors, and aftershocks out of me. He kissed and nipped at my neck.

Even though it was amazing, I still felt like I needed more, that one orgasm wasn't enough. It hadn't taken the edge off. That was how I'd been lately. Just absolutely wanton.

"We should get back out there," I said, even though I wanted to stay right here with his cock buried in me. "Or Colton will think we ditched him."

"Colton's a big boy." Rob eased out and helped me pull my panties and jeans back up. I didn't care that I'd be sticky and damp. I felt marked in another way. "You want to ditch the party? I'm sensing you still need more."

I turned to face him, zipping my jeans. "Yes," I admitted. "God, hopefully that's just a warmup, right? We should at least make an appearance before we do this again."

Rob's normally stoic expression had gone soft. He brushed my red hair back from my face with the backs of his fingers. "You don't have to take care of the pack tonight, angel. Let me take care of you."

Aw, shoot. There were those tears again.

"I love you, Rob Wolf." I stood on my tiptoes to loop an arm behind his neck and claim his mouth. We'd just had sex, but this was the first kiss we'd shared.

He claimed mine right back, his tongue sliding between my lips, his hand capturing the back of my head. When we broke apart, he said, "Do you have something to tell me, angel?"

My brows went down. "No. Why?"

His lips twitched. "Do you feel different, Willow?"

It was as if he knew something I didn't. "What are you talking about?"

He held my gaze, his expression still soft with love. "You smell different, angel. You're horny as hell. As possessive as a male wolf."

I blinked at him, trying to put it together.

Oh my God. My eyes flew wide. "You don't think—"

His grin held more satisfaction than the Cheshire Cat's. "I don't think, I know."

I clapped a hand over my mouth as my vision went blurry.

"You're carrying my pup. I'm guessing a male, judging by your aggressive sexual and territorial behavior."

"Oh my God! *Rob!*"

He picked me straight up, holding my legs beneath my butt so I towered over him. "We're having a baby."

Tears escaped my eyes, making rapid tracks down my cheeks. "I can't believe it. I mean, I guess I'm late. I just didn't think about it. Wow."

Rob lowered me and cradled the side of my face with his large palm. "I'm so happy, Willow. You're going to be the most amazing mother."

I fell into him, dropping my head against his massive chest, overwhelmed by the most humbling form of joy. "You'll be the perfect dad," I sniffed.

He gripped my nape and kissed the top of my head. "Want to go home?"

"No." I shook my head, pulling back so I could see his face. "Let's go tell everyone."

He leaned down and brushed his lips over mine. "Whatever you want, angel. I'm here to take care of you."

✧ ✧ ✧

Don't miss Rob and Willow's full story! Read Feral and all the steamy, cowboy shifter-filled books in the Wolf Ranch series. READ FERAL NOW! vanessavaleauthor.com/v/wg

A Little Bit in Love With You

Willow Winters

CHAPTER ONE
Brianna

I FORGOT HOW hot it is back home. Pulling my tank top out at the center of my chest offers a cool bit of air to filter down, but the relief is lost on me. Until I see Asher and tell him exactly how I feel, there's not a damn thing that's going to ease this anxiousness inside of me.

Nearly slipping in a pothole I didn't see in the long gravel pave up to his parents' house, I let out a hiss of irritation. It's too darn hot for August in Beaufort, South Carolina. The coastal sea island is supposed to keep this place from hitting the high 90s, but there isn't a breeze to be found.

My white jean shorts are a bit too tight since I gained a little weight my first year of college. Freshman 10 and all that. I huff, feeling my cheeks redden in this heat as I turn the corner of the backroad surrounded by thin trees that don't offer any shade and the airplane hangar in the distance.

I haven't been back home for more than 48 hours and I'm already miserable. Although if Asher was answering his phone, if he would just talk to me, I know it would all be okay.

We didn't spend three years together to be off and on and constantly fighting because we're long-distance now.

I love him and he loves me. Letting out an exaggerated exhale and pulling my dark brown hair up into a makeshift ponytail, I pretend I'm stopping right in front of his house just to catch my breath and cool down before I pull back the flimsy screen door and knock on the old worn door to the farmhouse.

We've been together all through high school, heck half of my memories are from that airplane hangar that doubles as a mechanic garage on the lower level. My first sip of beer… even though I'm only eighteen. Our first kiss… our first, everything.

My throat closes up tight as I tighten the ponytail and wipe the beads of sweat from my forehead.

I'm sure I look a mess, but that's exactly how I feel, so… I suppose it'll have to do.

With one step, the gravel crunches under my feet, but then I halt.

The screaming from inside makes my already hammering heart go into high gear. Asher yells at his father in return. The two of them are going at it.

I take a hesitant step forward, unwilling to turn back and needing to know what the hell is going on. The two of them have had their issues butting heads, but the rage in their tones is something I've never heard before. He didn't tell me anything was going on.

I can't quite make out what they're saying, apart from the cuss words and his mother begging them to stop.

My body goes cold and begs me to stop as I near the wooden porch steps.

Swallowing thickly I pull my phone out from the back pocket of my shorts and check my messages.

He didn't respond to the series I sent him:

Hey, I'm sorry. Can we talk?
I miss you.
You know I love you right?
Please talk to me.

Emotions swarm me as something is thrown from inside, glass shatters and I instinctively step back, my mouth parted in both shock and fear.

Are you okay? I'm here.
What's going on?

My fingers fly across the keys and just as I hit send, Asher storms out, nearly ripping the screen door off as it bangs against the house.

He gets three large strides out the door before he sees me. His tanned skin and rough around the edges decorum fits his blue collar ways to a T. His hair is a bit messy on top, his piercing eyes hitting me with all the intensity in the world. First the anger and hurt, then the recognition and with it a touch of shame. Like he didn't want me to hear that and he's very aware that I did.

Only I'm not sure what the fight was about.

He slows his pace, turning to look back once, and then focusing his gaze on the porch floor before looking back up at me. He licks his lower lip and all I see is a wounded man. Worn blue jeans and a graphic dark blue tee complete the image.

"You okay?" I whisper. 'Cause really that's all that matters.

His parents don't come after him. It's far too quiet for far too long. He doesn't answer me, but emotions filter through his expression and every second that passes, it crushes me more and more.

"Want to get out of here?" I offer, feeling the heat at my back and knowing right now the only thing I need in life is to get that look off his face.

I can't even try to count the number of times Asher has held me while I cried. Fights with my friends, with my parents, losing my grandparents and so many other things throughout the years.

I've never once seen him cry and I'm not sure he's going to now, but I think if I wasn't standing right here, right now, he'd have gone up to the apartment in the hangar and... and I don't know.

"I wanted to talk, but we don't have to, we can go anywhere you want," I offer him when he doesn't respond.

All I want to do right now, as the porch creaks with his shifting weight, is love on him.

However he needs and never leave his side again.

CHAPTER TWO
Asher

"**Y**OU SHOULD COME with me," she pleads with me.

My hands fist at my side, a cold sweat lines my back although everything inside of me is too damn hot. Anger forces adrenaline to surge through me.

None of it is for her. Not an ounce of this is for my Bri. I hate that look in her eyes. That hurt and even sympathy she has for me right now. My face flames with embarrassment.

My throat's tight as I swallow and attempt to calm down. With a tension ringing throughout my body, I attempt to answer her without any of that shit back there being shown to her.

"What all did you hear?" I question.

Her head shakes, that ponytail sways and her gorgeous green eyes widen as she tells me she couldn't make out what we were saying, but she heard us arguing.

I love this girl more than anything, but I don't want to share this with her. I can't. I can't let her know what happened.

Heaving in a breath, I take a look behind her and I don't see her father's car.

"Did you walk?"

"Yeah," she whispers at the same time that there's a commotion behind me. Probably my dad pushing the sofa out of the way. A heat flows over my body and I move before either of them can come out here.

She can't see this.

"Come on," I pull her by her elbow as I walk past her. All I want is to get to my car and get the hell out of here. Her flip-flops catch in the gravel as she tries to keep up.

"Shit," she curses beneath her breath.

My sweet little Bri cursed. *Fuck.* I stop everything and turn to face her fully.

"You alright?" She's bent down, those little shorts creeping up as she grips her toe and hisses.

"Fine," she mutters, her expression scrunched and then she reaches up, grabbing my hand in hers. That right there. There's a shift, an immediate change.

I feel like breaking down though and I'm quick to turn back and head to the car. Focused on keeping my shit together.

I can't speak, I'm barely conscious of opening the car door for her. But I'm all too aware when I squeeze her hand and she squeezes back before letting go.

After I close the passenger door, I nearly stop before heading around to the driver's side. Just so I can deal with this shit before getting in. Just a moment.

I just need one fucking moment but it never comes.

Pushing through it all, I get into the driver's seat, turn the ignition of the Chevy and drive off. As the car is pulling away, I peek up into the rearview to see my father walking out onto the porch. Arms crossed and a beer bottle dangling from one hand.

I hate it here.

I hate him sometimes too.

"You okay?" Bri asks, her small hand landing on my thigh as I turn down the gravel road, my family home from view.

Words tumble at the back of my throat, all the thoughts that have been weighing me down compete to be heard. I don't know what to say. That's the God's honest truth. But I settle on one thing as I flick on the AC to high.

"I just want to leave sometimes." It's far too simple. But at least it's true.

"Where do you want to go?" The innocence and surprise isn't hiding in her question.

"I don't know." Truth is, I've never even let myself think of where. Because the moment I think of leaving, I know I can't. I barely passed high school. I put all my savings into the garage to start my own mechanic shop… and I can't leave my mom.

"I don't know, but right now I just need some space I think," I tell Bri honestly as I drive down the long road to get to town.

I could go to Robert's. I could stay there. He'd let me just like I've let him for years.

"Please don't say that," Bri whispers.

I have to take my eyes off the road to look at her. It's a quick glance but then I take another. I love Bri, I've always loved her, but she keeps at it with needing more from me than I can give her.

Hell, I have nothing. No way to come see her across the damn country and that's all she wants from me.

"I don't know what you want from me," I tell her. The last time she texted me, she gave me an ultimatum. Come up to see her or we're over. I almost tell her, as far as I knew we were done, but that vulnerable look keeps the thought locked in the back of my throat.

"I want you to come with me," she murmurs. Her hand shifts on my thigh and I think she's going to take it away, but she doesn't. She turns in her seat to face me, the leather of it groaning.

"Just come up north with me."

"And how am I supposed to do that? Really Bri? I don't even know if we're together anymore." I can't help it as my hand twists on the steering wheel. It just flies out of my mouth. "You change your mind every five fucking minutes."

"Don't cuss at me," she scolds and takes her hand back to cross her arms. Just like my father just did.

"Don't—" I start but bite my tongue. I'm frustrated and worked up. I know better.

"I'm sorry," I apologize and she doesn't react other than to soften slightly in her seat.

I glance up and see the sign for main street but I drive past it. I don't even know where we're going.

"I'm sorry too," she tells me after a moment. And her hand comes back, I'm quick to grab it and steer with my left.

"I need you right now," I don't know where it came from, but I'm guessing something in me had to tell her that truth too.

"I'm here. I'm right here."

CHAPTER THREE
Brianna

MY PARENTS WENT to the movies. I know they're doing a grocery run when they're done that. The back door to the patio slides open easily as Asher and I sneak in. The thought hits me for a moment that it's crazy for us to 'sneak in' at all. We're nineteen and there's no reason at all to not go right up to the front door and waltz in... except that this town likes to gossip. They make a big deal out of everything.

Whether or not Asher and I are going to last is a topic of conversation in the hair salon according to my grandmother. With the floor creaking as the back door closes softly, all I can think is, it's none of their damn business.

Asher's hand, hardened from years of working in the garage with his father, slips into mine. The lock clicks up into place at the same time that I peer up at him.

We've been together for years and I've never seen him look at me like this. With a hurt that can't be covered up by an asymmetric grin or a half-hearted, dry humored joke. The dark circles under his hazel eyes tell the story of him not sleeping well. We're only just learning what life and being adults really is, and it's so very apparent that it's taken a toll on Asher and I have no idea why.

Turning fully to face him, I ask again, "Can you tell me what happened?"

Instantly his gaze is ripped from mine and he tries to pull his hand away, angling his body toward the kitchen.

"Let's go upstairs," I'm quick to push the words out and grip his hand tighter, adding my second hand as well and giving him a gentle pull. "We can just lay down and if you don't want to talk, that's fine."

"Just lay down," he repeats my words with a hint of humor and a smile that doesn't reach his eyes. "Since when do we just lay down?" he jokes.

It awards him a playful smack to his chest and in return I get a rough chuckle and he squeezes my hand back. There's a shift, something more natural and more 'us' that happens with the small moment.

I cling to it and to him as we climb the stairs. Taking them slowly. Every step he gets closer, to the point that when we're at my bedroom door, his arm wraps around my waist like it's supposed to. Leaning back, I fall into him slightly, until the door is opened and I make my way into the bedroom, kicking off my flip-flops.

"Hasn't changed a bit," Asher comments. He's right. I've had the same off-white furniture since high school. The posters of the boy bands I love are still hung up, the stacks of fantasy novels haven't budged except the top one, my comfort read, and the matching off-white desk is still cluttered.

"Mom said they might paint it and if they do she's going to rearrange some things for me," I tell him easily.

"Your parents love you," Asher slips his hands into his jeans and looks around as if he hasn't been in this very room a thousand times before.

"Come on," I urge him. The bed groans as I climb in and crawl to the side pressed against the wall. It's not a large room, my older sister got the biggest room apart from my parents'.

"I don't know if that's the best idea, Bri," Asher confesses with a shrug and a spike of fear races through me.

Sitting up, I stare him down. "Just come lay with me," I request and when he hesitates, shifting his weight, I add, "please. Please just come lay down."

I nearly add that we don't have to talk but he asks me, "Do you even want to be with me or do you just feel sorry for me right now?"

Emotions swell in my throat. "How could you think that?"

"Don't be mad... for all I know you were coming over to formally break up with me."

"Firstly, I'm not mad and secondly—"

"You didn't answer me Bri."

Tears prick my eyes as my voice raises. "Answer what? Do I want to be with you?" I've never felt regret like I do now. "It's been hard not seeing you." My bottom lip wavers and I strengthen my voice, "but all I want every day is to see you. To be with you. To have you more in my life. Of course I love you and I want to be with you." Every sentence his expression softens. The resistance is all but gone when I'm finished. "Come here." I pat the bed and take in a deep steadying breath. "Please, just come here and lay down with me because I miss you and I love you and all I want is to make us right again."

"Can you stop giving me ultimatums?" he asks me and my head feels light and dizzy. "I know I don't come to see you like I promised I would but I need you to be with me if we're together. Really be with me and not sending texts at three a.m. that if I don't do x, y, or z we're done."

"I'm sorry." I raise both of my hands and all the reasons I've been upset with him this last year race to the forefront of my mind but I push them away. Summer break is almost here and then I'll be home and we can figure those things out. "I won't," I promise him. Right now I just need him to be okay and for us to be okay... and then everything will be okay, won't it?

Asher swallows thickly and that hurt from downstairs comes back. "You sure you still love me?" he asks and for a moment it looks like his eyes glass over but then that emotion vanishes.

"I love you, I'm in love with you and every way you can say it." I confess and ball up the floral navy comforter in my hand. "You?"

"I might be a little bit in love with you," he answers with a smirk and a grin spreads across my face as I grab the closest pillow and chuck it at him.

That's how he told me he loved me for the first time behind the bleachers in the gym. *I might be a little bit in love with you.* The pillow thuds as he catches it and he lets out a small genuine laugh that is rough and masculine as he smiles back at me. Before I can press him for more of a reassurance he says, "I'll always love you Bri. Even when you're mad at me and overthinking everything, I love you."

CHAPTER FOUR

Asher

FIRST I PULL the shirt over my shoulders and drop it to the floor, then I pull the covers back. I keep them up so Bri can get it inside with me. I know every little movement she'll make as she slips in. How her shoulders do a shimmy when she nestles down beside me and the contented little sigh that slips from her sweet lips as she rests her head on my shoulder and I lay my arm over the covers and over the curve of her hip when she's settled.

We've done this a hundred times before, and I'd take this every day for the rest of my life if I could. I love the moment when she's right here and everything's safe and still. There's not a worry in the world. Just me and her.

"Are you trying to sleep?" she questions and my heavy eyes open as I tilt my head to peer down at her. The comforter rustles as she lets the tips of her fingers skim over the rough stubble lining my jaw.

"I'm exhausted but no," I joke and tighten my grip on her. I worked all morning to finish the jobs that were due to be done by my father last night. "I only slept a few hours last night," I tell her and leave it at that. My father was screaming at me for taking over his job—I can't have peace in that house. Not if there's beer in it with my father's reddened face and clenched fists. There's never any peace anymore.

She's quiet for a moment, before she says hesitantly, "Was it because of my text?"

My throat tightens, I don't even want to think about her texting me that I needed to be a better boyfriend. I can't. I'm barely hanging on as it is.

"I promise you I'll do the best I can, Bri. You know that right?"

"I know." Her head falls to my shoulder and I know there's something she wants to ask. It's from the way her lips stay parted and how she glances up at me before down to my chest where her fingers play with the bit of hair there. I almost tell her I bought a ring. I almost ask her to marry me right here and now, but I don't have it on me and I don't want to propose like this. All I want to do is give her the security she's begging me for. I may not be able to fly out to see her every weekend, but I show her she's mine. I can show her I'm serious.

"You smell like you just got out of the shower," she changes the subject and I let out a huff of a laugh. "I love the way you smell," she murmurs and then kisses me on my throat. My cock stirs slightly from how tender and soft her touch is.

"Bri baby, don't..." I warn her.

"I'm not doing anything," she teases under the covers.

"I know that hip roll"

"Which one?" Her tone is tempting. "This one?" she mocks and a grin forms on my face before both of us laugh. She's just playing around and I pull her in closer, kissing her temple before she settles back down.

Everything about her is warmth and comfort. Before I can stop myself I tell her, "I missed you."

She doesn't hesitate and doesn't hide the agony of longing in her voice, "I miss you every day, Asher. Every single day you're not with me, I miss you."

She's quick to kiss me again and this time it's on the lips. It's short and isn't meant to tease me but she does.

I kiss her back if for no other reason than to soothe that bit of pain. But one kiss turns into another. Testing and tempting, her soft body never leaving mine. My cock's hard in an instant and when she kisses me again, I deepen it. Slipping my tongue along the seam of her lips until she parts them for me. The moment my tongue strokes against hers, she moans into my mouth, her thigh slipping around mine until she's straddling me under the covers, her forearms resting on either side of my head.

When I break the kiss, I look up at my gorgeous girlfriend. Her sun-kissed skin and the kindness in her green eyes. "I thought you said don't?" she questions teasingly.

With an asymmetric grin, I wrap my arm around her waist and flip her under me in a swift motion. A squeal leaves her as she grips onto my shoulders in surprise. The moment her back lands and she's under me, that smile hits her face.

The genuine one that I wish I could see every day. That thought forces me to take her lips back, mid laugh of hers and kiss her with everything I have. She moans again, this tortured sound of need that I fucking love.

Her legs are spread for me, her heels digging into my ass. As I rock myself against her, she writhes against me.

"Too many clothes," I scold her playfully as I pull back. The heat around us is more than working us up. I work her shorts off first, letting my fingers glide down her skin as I do. A beautiful blush hits her cheeks when I move my hand between her thighs, the thin lace that'll go next separating my palm from her pussy.

"Already wet for me?"

Her gaze rips from mine as her cheeks redden even further. Leaning up, I nip her neck and her entire body tenses with a wanton gasp. "Answer me, baby," I command.

"Yes." She whispers.

"Yes, what?" I look into her eyes and she stares back. There's a skip in my chest, one beat and then another that's harder and more needy. Like she can control the beat of my heart.

"I'm ready for you."

Knowing what this woman does to me makes me pause as I realize I can never lose her.

"Take your hair down," I tell her and she obeys. Then I help her with her own shirt and flick the snap of her bra undone. The moment her breasts are exposed, I tease her nipple, suckle it into my mouth. My tongue flicks against them as they peak and harden.

I take my time toying with her, but my girl is needy and so damn ready. She pushes against my jeans with her feet, as if they could be enough to rid me of them.

"Too many clothes," she mocks me with a lust-filled gaze as her chest rises and falls more heavily than before.

It's tense between us, the pull not letting me take my eyes off hers as I kick off my pants. I stroke myself once, a bead of precum already at the head of my dick. Slipping myself between her slick folds, I tease her clit as I kiss her.

The way she gasps with my lips right there is everything. It's all I want and need.

"Bri," I whisper her name as I line myself up.

Her questing look meets mine. "I love you."

With both of her hands splayed in my hair, she tells me she loves me and kisses me with every ounce of sincerity there is in this whole damn world.

Her lips press and mold to mine and I slam into her in one swift stroke, filling her and forcing her head to fall back from the sudden sensation.

She's tight as all hell. So I give her a moment to adjust. A mewl leaves her and I rock against her, not moving just yet and kissing down her neck. It doesn't take long for her body to remember mine and I pull out then thrust back inside of her in an easy rhythm, then harder and faster.

A cold sweat lines my skin as her nails gently scrape along my back. As I fuck her deeper and her small cries of pleasure fill the room, she tightens and spasms on my cock. Coming undone so easily for me.

I ride through her pleasure, kissing along her jaw and she clings to me. It's only when my thumb finds her clit again, that her piercing eyes find mine and she moans my name.

"Asher," my name on her lips is wrapped in a desperate need for love.

And fuck do I love her. We nearly say it at the same time and I take her again and again, not wanting this to end.

✧   ✧   ✧

I'VE LEARNED MY lesson before, so before I go down the hall to get what I need to clean her up, I slip my jeans on. She's still as can be on her bed, trying to keep the evidence of what we've done from getting onto the sheets.

I can't help but smirk as I stare down at her with that just fucked look. Her hair is a messy halo and her chest is still flushed.

Once all is taken care of, I get back under the covers to cuddle with her again, and it's not long before reality sets in.

"When are your parents going to be home?"

"You thinking of going back to the hangar?" she answers me with a question of her own.

"I don't know," I answer honestly. I don't want to go back home at all. "I know I don't want to be naked and in your bedroom when they do come home though."

"We could go downstairs and turn something on... would that—"

"I'd love that," I cut her off. We have time to go from cuddling on the sofa to sitting up right when her parents come home. We've done it a thousand times before.

As I gather her clothes for her, I can't stop thinking about what's going to happen when I do go back home. They'll both probably pretend it didn't happen. They won't talk about it and if they do, it'll be a promise that it won't happen again.

My expression shows my thoughts, because Bri looks back at me with nothing but concern. I'm far too late to hide it from her.

"Asher?" she questions and I just kiss her. A quick peck as I hand her the bundle of clothes for her to put back on. That doesn't satisfy her though.

"Are we going to be okay?" She's the only thing in my life that is okay at this moment. I can't lose her. I love her too fucking much and I need her more than she could ever know.

"Of course we are. I love you and you love me. That's all that really matters."

"You promise?"

"I promise you, Bri; I'm going to love you forever."

✧   ✧   ✧

Craving more of Bri and Asher's story? There's far more to it than this sexy little short. Have a look at A Little Bit Dirty...

I've got a thing for men who work with their hands.

I thought I learned my lesson years ago. But here I am, back in the small town I grew up in, staring down the man who broke my heart years ago.

ORDER A LITTLE BIT DIRTY HERE >
www.willowwinterswrites.com/online-shop/single-books/a-little-bit-dirty

Post-It Notes

Debra Anastasia

CHAPTER ONE

Taylor

I COULDN'T MAKE out the writing on the Post-it notes that were stuck to my ceiling in the dark. I could barely make out how many there were. The ceiling of the dorm was completely covered. Her handwriting had a manic scrawl to it.

The roommate from hell was lying on her bed less than ten feet from me, buck-ass naked. She did it just to make me uncomfortable.

It worked. I was uncomfortable. It was her goal and she succeeded.

I rolled over and faced the wall. This sucked. College sucked. Living with a complete weirdo really sucked.

Randomly assigned roommates was a horrible idea. At first, Roberta had seemed nice. She hadn't responded to the email I sent when we were assigned, but when I moved in, she was all smiles. Of course, I had my crew with me then as well. So all my football-playing friends, some of my bestie's brothers, were milling around in the common room. Her smiles were fake. Or for them.

For me? As soon as everyone hugged me goodbye, and Peaches fake sob cried, and then cried for real, that was the last I saw of Roberta's smile.

When I was unpacking my stuff into my closet, I tossed her some easy, small talk questions.

"So, where are you from?" I tucked my tank tops next to my underwear.

From behind me I heard what would most likely be described as a growl.

I waited for a few seconds before I turned. She was standing in front of her now open closet with her hands on her hips.

"Um. Hi." I had two tank tops in my hands.

Roberta's eyes were slits, like a shark, and her lips curled downward.

"Enjoying that closet?" She slid her gaze to my new one, and all the empty space inside. Well, all was a strong word. The closet was far from generous.

"I guess so?" I wasn't sure what the correct answer was. I looked past her into her closet that was jammed so full of stuff it looked like a shipping container.

"That was my closet." She pointed at the offending space with her pinkie.

I looked around, confused. Clearly, she was on her side. Her bed was on her side, she had a footlocker on her side. But it was cluttered. Like really cluttered. Like *she had brought far too much stuff for the size room she was assigned* kind of cluttered.

"Aren't we in a shared dorm room?" I held my tank tops out like they had the answers she needed.

She snatched them out of my hands. I looked at my empty ones and tucked them under my armpits.

"Oh, you're funny now? Now you're the funniest girl? You know, when you were moving in, I thought to myself, maybe she's sweet. She has a stuffed animal." She pointed my tank top at the teddy bear on my bed.

"But ever since I met you. I've got a bad feeling." She shifted her shoulders around like she was low-key practicing a TikTok dance.

"We met like an hour ago." I pulled my phone out of my back pocket. Okay, an hour and thirty-four minutes, but still.

"Yeah. Exactly." Roberta took my tank tops and crammed them in her closet. I was surprised it didn't burst from the added material.

Oh no. Roberta was an angry person. I was living with someone that didn't want me there at all. I had to reach out an olive branch. "Uh, if you need to put some of your stuff in the closet..."

I was careful not to call it mine.

Roberta's eyes got wide. "Yeah. Ya think?"

And that's how I wound up rolling all my dresses into my one suitcase and jamming it under my bed. Somehow, Roberta filled up two closets to the brim with her bullshit. And she was still mad.

But that was four weeks ago. Four horrible weeks ago. I found out from our suitemates that Roberta had lived in our dorm room by herself for a full year, she was technically a sophomore.

Oh and my suitemates? They steered clear of me. I was a marked woman. Roberta would make their lives hell if she caught them talking to me. That information was whispered to me when I was in the shower, so I didn't even get to know who had bent a little in the kindness-to-Taylor direction.

I was miserable. Even Teddi and Peaches, my two incredible friends, were worried. Now they were busy too. Peaches was in school in Michigan, hoping to become a veterinarian. Teddi was in school as well, staying with friends. She hadn't declared a major yet, but she was so driven I was sure it would happen soon.

I heard Roberta fart. A naked fart, with her whole ass out of her comforter. Then, there was a knock on our door.

I rolled over and Roberta stuck her tongue out at me, then spoke up, "Come in, babe."

Our door opened. Roberta had it rigged so it couldn't lock so that Peter could come in whenever he wanted.

It was Tuesday at 2:00 a.m.

He took off his shoes and his shirt as he stumbled in the door. "Smells like burning cigars in here. Ugh."

The smell hit me as soon as he said it.

Roberta pointed at me. "She farts all night. Get me the Post-it notes."

Peter put his hand on her dresser and came back with the bright yellow notes. In her accusatory scrawl, Roberta spoke while she wrote, "FARTS ALL NIGHT!" And then she slapped the note on the space next to her.

Peter leaned over to take off his socks and grabbed his ankles with his butt facing me. "I got you, babe. No worries." And then Peter farted in my direction.

And I snapped. I snapped, I snapped, I snapped. I had had enough. I was sick of her bullshit. Her blatant bullying and her naked ass crack.

I tossed my blanket aside. I grabbed my backpack. In it I tossed my essentials—the phone with the charger. My wallet was already in my backpack. I grabbed my teddy bear and keys and yanked the door open.

"Oh she's mad now. Look what we did, Peter. She's leaving."

I put my hand to my forehead. I couldn't knock on any doors because everyone here was afraid of Roberta. My resident assistant? Also afraid of Roberta. I had only one person in the city I could call at this time. On this night. He was a nuclear option. But I was about to blow.

I slammed the door on my way out. All my shit was still in that room, but screw it. I pulled out my phone and scrolled to the one name that sent my heart beating every time I saw it.

My bestie's older brother, Austin Burathon. I hit the button and the ringing started.

✧   ✧   ✧

FINE, I HAD a crush on him. Fine, I had a crush on him my entire life. Fine, I wasn't over it. Wasn't planning to get over it either. BUT, and that's a huge but, I was never going to step over the boundary beyond harmless flirting.

Which is why he was the nuclear option. Who is Austin? Austin was first and foremost, my best friend's older brother. And when you're really young, three years older can seem like a lifetime. I mean, when he started driving we were thirteen.

But he drove us a lot. He was good like that. Being Teddi's friend came with perks. Instead of parents picking us up from cheer practice, sometimes it was her piping-hot brother.

What was it about him? Girl, sit down. You don't even understand the amount of fuck-hot sexuality that poured off this man. It wasn't even fair. Just swoon and yum and exotic while also being the realest person you spoke to all day. He was a flirt. You could be a boy or girl. He'd flirt. It was so hot. And evolved. He was like a beautiful movie star in the midst of us normal people. He'd wear skirts sometimes. Nail polish other times. He was the first real human boy I ever saw wearing eyeliner and it sculpted how I viewed my dream guy. The confidence to put that on and just...be himself? Everyone wanted to know him. Be around him. And I was lucky enough to have that happen quite a bit.

He was super involved in his family's affairs. They seemed to be collecting teenagers lately. First it was Gaze, just a year younger than Austin who was a foster kid for the last few years of his teenhood. Then Ruffian showed up on the Burathons' doorstep, and like the superheroes they are, they just folded him into the family.

And he fell in deep love with my friend Teddi. Then he robbed our friend-enemy, Meg. It was a little complicated. But the good news was he was out of prison and Teddi was in love still.

I did a stint at community college, and now, finally, I was transferring my credits and in college in Loveville City. The same city as Austin.

I got a text message back from him:

Stay in your foyer, I'll be by in a few minutes.

So that's how I was in the vestibule of the dorms in my Wonder Woman pajama set waiting for my dream man.

I wasn't sure what car to look for when a figure walked up to the door and rapped his knuckles on it.

How did this feel so personal? Well, usually Teddi was involved, and now it was just us. Austin and I.

"Kitten. What's up, baby?" When I opened the door to let myself out, his arms were waiting.

I just shook my head slowly in his chest. He wrapped his hands around my back and my head.

"There, there. This city can be an ass buster. I'm sorry. Let's go back to my place." He put his arm around my shoulders. And even though I was scurrying out of my dorm room in the middle of the night, I still felt a thrill. People walking by would think we were together. Like together together.

"Wonder Woman's having a tough one?" He pulled out his phone and ordered us a car service. He took my backpack and slung it over his shoulder and we strolled to the nearest stoplight. I finally took a look at him. He gave me a soft smile. His eyeliner was smudged and I was pretty sure there was glitter in the crease of his eyelid. He threaded his fingers in mine. "We have to wait for like four minutes. Do you want to talk about it?"

I didn't have to as the window three stories up cranked open. "Run, bitch, run. I told you you couldn't hang."

Austin took one look and then glanced back at my face. "Oh. She's expanding it a little. Don't look now. That's her butt crack. Sweet Jesus. Her butt crack."

I wiped at my eyes with the back of my hand. "I know what her butt crack looks like better than I do my own. Literally, she is naked so much. It's so uncomfortable."

Austin pulled on my hand and I buried my face in his chest.

"Oh? You got a boyfriend now? Tell him how you can't put your shoes away and you steal phone chargers in your spare time!" Roberta's voice echoed off the surrounding buildings.

"She's charming." He turned his head to shout up, "Hey, crazy person, can you stop freaking yelling and put some clothes on?"

Roberta's voice was fired up now. "Oh really? Pretty boy? You want to come up here and say that to my boyfriend?"

"No, sweetheart, I don't do deliveries. But if he comes down here, I'll be happy to kick his ass." Austin pulled me in closer.

"Don't get in trouble because of me." I turned my head and saw a car approaching. Judging from the blinker, it was getting ready to stop near us. Most of the road was deserted. Even in a city, this late at night on a weekday was quieter. "Uber's here."

Austin turned me by my shoulders and opened the back door. "Hop in, angel cake. I just want to tell these two assholes something." He shut the door and hollered a few more things at Roberta and her boyfriend before coming around the side of the car to get in the backseat near me.

"I can't believe I hate those people so much. And I just met them." Austin gave a middle finger out the back window while telling the Uber driver his address.

"Thank you." Sitting with him now, I realized how tense I was in the dorm room. He was a bit of home and it made my emotions bubble up inside.

"Come here." He put his arm around me and pulled me in.

I rested my head on his chest. He smelled good. Like the outdoors and a muffin. He was cuddling me like he did his sister, Teddi, all the time. If I wasn't so freaking discombobulated and tired, I would have loved to take a selfie. And maybe get a shirt made with the picture on it.

I had issues. He was insane to be close to. My heart was beating so hard.

That he knew I just needed hugs—ugh. He was just so intuitive.

The Uber driver pulled over. Austin gave me a quick squeeze before opening the car door and throwing my bag over his shoulder in one swift movement. He held out a hand like I was royalty or dressed for the Oscars or something. I took it and held it still after thanking the driver.

He pulled out his phone and led me towards the front door. I watched as he tipped the driver on the app and swiped to his key for the building app without letting go of my hand.

Why was he so physical? I was eating it up. I was feeling so safe. Lord help me, this man was too much.

After the app granted us entry, Austin pulled me along to the elevator. The doors opened immediately.

"Why were you out on a Tuesday this early?" I was realizing he'd appeared so quickly—he had to have been close by, and not at this building.

"I was partying with friends. Tuesdays can be Saturdays if you know the right people." He winked at me.

My ovaries found a way to clap for joy inside me.

"Just a heads-up though. My roommate and I were fighting—although he was gone when I left earlier—he might be back. Just ignore him. I've paid all the rent for the last six months, so he gets no say in who comes and goes."

I nodded, feeling bad for interrupting. "I'm sorry if this is a rough time for me to be here for you."

"Baby, you're family. You need help—you get help. No other choices." The elevator dinged on the tenth floor and Austin reached out a hand to hold the door open. His rings clanked against the metal.

I was grateful to be given this out but part of my heart kicked rocks because if he and I were family, we weren't ever going to be kissing buddies.

Austin opened his front door with a code and stepped in, propping the door so I could walk in. His place was so freaking awesome. He had a very lucrative social media platform, and his apartment was the set for many of his videos and pictures. The furniture was all curves and block colors. Some sharp pieces with black and white were edged in. A wall had all different ring lights and filming equipment hanging on it like art. The whole place had a musky lavender scent that I associated with Austin.

"Have a seat. You need a drink? Hungry?" He set my bag next to me.

"I'm good." Was I feeling out of place? Was I feeling rescued? All of it.

Austin went to the fridge that was painted with a subtle pattern and filled up a glass with ice and water.

He came and sat down next to me, holding out the glass. I took it gratefully, tipping it back to quench my thirst.

"See, angel? I knew what you needed." Austin reached over and moved some of my hair away from my face. The edge of his finger skimming my temple.

Did he know what that touch did to people? I couldn't even imagine that the whole world wouldn't feel that tender contact in their soul and their naughty bits at the same damn time.

There was a gentle tone from the front door.

Austin mumbled, "Shit."

The door flung open before he could even explain. Stumbling in the entry was a tall guy, his face had tattoos scribbled all over it. When he snarled in our direction, I could see some of his teeth were capped in gold.

"That's how it is. Quick, right?" The door swung closed and slammed from the weight.

"Taylor, please ignore everything he's about to say." Austin moved my bag and slung his arm over my shoulder, holding his hands over my ears. It didn't matter, I could still hear perfectly.

"Oh, Taylor? She's hot. Fuck hot. I bet she's perfect for you. Into you." I was gathering this was the roommate from the earlier fight. The man looked me up and down. "Young for you though."

"She's my little sister's best friend. So maybe be a little respectful, asshole." Austin stood and held a hand in front of me—signaling for me to stay put, I was assuming.

"Oh, so picking up some trash from home, I see." The roommate stepped forward and squared up with Austin.

He was for sure wobbly, like his executive functions were off. Drugs. I bet he was on drugs.

Austin's eyes flared and his hand shot out. He had the man's jaw in his hand as he hissed, "Respect-ful."

I'd been around plenty of boys in fights in my day. Teddi and I had run with the football players and her brothers our whole life. But there was something different about the way this guy and Austin were threatening each other. It was almost...sexual.

Oh. Then I figured it out. They were roommates and possibly lovers. Hence the extra anger and tension.

The other guy gave Austin a harsh, hollow chuckle. "Oh. So you haven't been able to replace me after all, then. What did I tell you? My leftovers are tainted. You won't find anyone to love you."

I felt my eyes go wide. This guy was straight up gaslighting Austin. And this sure, headily awesome human that had so much confidence was knocked down a peg. I watched as the man's words hit Austin's soul.

I pushed up from the couch and strode over to Austin. He wasn't getting told that he was less than in front of me. I stepped between the two men, and Austin let go of the man and put his hands on my shoulders. Swimming in his eyes I saw embarrassment and concern.

I wrapped my arms around Austin and went to my toes. I did something I had been dreaming about all my life. I kissed Austin Burathon. I kissed him with how much I wanted him. I kissed him with how hot I found him. I made sure that my lips told him that I was awed by him, and his kindness and his bravery.

He kissed me back. Austin kissed me back with such skill that I literally swooned and he had to steady me. His lips tasted so good, his talent so sure. I was dying. I was dying right here and right now.

The only thing that snapped me out of it was a hard slam of a door.

I jolted back from the shock of the noise. I had been instantly transported to another world in Austin's kiss.

I covered my mouth as the realization of what I did hit me. Oh god. I kissed him? I kissed him!

He looked over my head in the direction of the door slam and then sent a sad smile in my direction. "I guess we're busy saving each other tonight, huh?"

"I'm sorry. I'm sorry I kissed you. It was the only thing I could think to do because I'm pretty sure that dude would not have been affected by a punch from me." I thumbed the indication over my shoulder. "And I had to do something. Fuck him. Wow. Fuck him so much."

Austin shook his head and held out his hand. I took it. "I've fucked him a lot, angel. It doesn't change who he is—I've tried."

"Who is he?" I followed Austin as he stopped to grab my backpack and I got my water glass.

"Him? That's Torin." Austin opened his bedroom door and I was treated to another magazine layout. The furniture was all low and minimal. The brick wall behind his bed towered to a high ceiling.

He set my bag on the top of the dresser.

"Endgame," I offered as the stories shared by Teddi flooded back to me. She never referred to Torin by his name—only Austin's complicated ex-boyfriend that everyone called Endgame. Because they were so much in love. Teddi didn't like Endgame at all. Felt he was a toxic hanger-on that didn't value Austin. But the last I'd heard of Endgame had to be in senior year of high school.

"Teddi told you." Austin sat on his bed.

I sat next to him. "She's not a fan."

"I know. My sister is opinionated. It is what it is." He flopped backwards on the bed and a sliver of his toned stomach peeked out from under his shirt. There was a hint of a tattoo there.

I flopped back as well, both of us staring at the ceiling. "Yeah. She hates the hell out of him. I hope I didn't make things more awkward by kissing you." The entire kiss replayed in my mind—a flashback of literal minutes, but I was grateful to have the memory nice and clear. I would revisit it for the rest of my life.

"Nah. The kiss was fire. Thank you for that. He and I were likely to get into a hate brawl anyway. It was a total mood diffuser." He turned his head to look at me and I kept my eyes firmly on the ceiling.

The last thing I wanted our kiss defined as was a mood diffuser.

He propped up on his elbow and turned his hips toward me. "So what are the implications of you walking out tonight? You had to be in a rough spot."

And like that, Austin switched the moment to be about fixing my problems and ignoring his own.

I let him move the conversation in that direction because I was still hurt that the kiss hadn't meant the world to him. The moon to him.

I sighed. "Roberta—the roommate—had a single dorm room before I came along. I guess it was luck of the draw or whatever. She really wanted it to stay that way." I turned to prop up on my elbow facing Austin. Lord, he was pretty. Sexy.

"And she decided to make your life miserable so she can have it back that way again." Austin correctly surmised.

"Yeah. And I like to imagine I'm tough—but when her boyfriend tries to fart at me in the middle of the night? Apparently I bounce the hell out." I ran a hand through my hair and watched as amusement hit Austin's face.

His unrestrained smile was lighter fluid on my heart. It started clodhopping around in my chest. I was the one that made him smile and I knew I was addicted to that whole feeling instantly.

"So can you find a new roommate?" He narrowed his eyes like he was trying to plan my future for me.

"It's difficult because I'm on two scholarships. And they are tied to my room and board. They are super picky about the awardees maintaining a proper decorum. Roberta knows this and has threatened to tell the whole college all the ways I'm evil. She has literal fistfuls of Post-it notes with my flaws wallpapering the dorm room."

"Oh, doll. I'm so sorry. Crap." He held out an arm and we hugged briefly, on our sides. "That's so rough. Fuck her so much."

"Yeah. She's really like all of my problems right now." I rubbed my thumb on his comforter.

"Listen, stay with me. What can they do if you just move out?" He tilted his head.

In every crush dream I had about Austin since I was old enough to fall in love, this conversation would happen over and over. "Really? That's a lot to ask."

"Nah. You and I can be boyfriend and girlfriend—which keeps me away from Endgame and him away from me, plus you can live here and not have that stress from Roberta and her revenge farts." Austin held out his hand for a shake. A special deal. A secret. I wanted to lick his hand, but instead, I shook it.

I was going to get to live with my dream man and pretend to be his girlfriend. I knew the long-term damage was going to be substantial to my heart—but there was no way in hell I was saying no to him.

"You've got a deal."

✧ ✧ ✧

Love Austin and Taylor? The good news is there are TWO full, gripping books already finished and ready for your beautiful imagination! Find more at DebraAnastasia.com.

CONSTELLATIONS

CATHERINE COWLES

EVERLY

"JASPER, JUNE," I called as I shook the feed bucket.

The two miniature horses ran towards me as fast as their little legs could carry them. Kelly, one of the sanctuary's volunteers, laughed as they skidded to a halt in front of us. "That will never stop being funny to me."

I grinned at her as I poured the feed into their trough. "These two are basically only motivated by food."

"Be honest, half of the terrible twosome is a menace to society."

I shook my head as I patted June's rump. "This one is as sweet as can be."

Kelly scratched behind the mini's ears. "I feel bad for her that she got lumped in with this terror."

"Aw, I don't know." I moved to Jasper to give him a rub. You could never tell how he was going to react. Sometimes you'd get a nuzzle, other times, a nip. And if it really wasn't your day, you could get a swift kick, too. "He's still finding his way."

The two horses had been all but abandoned, left to fend for themselves in a field. Thankfully, the property had a stream running through it, or they surely would've died. The fact that they hadn't had human interaction had manifested in the opposite of ways. June was starved for affection, always looking for a pat or a scratch. Jasper was skeptical of all things human, and I didn't blame him for it.

Kelly sent me a sidelong look. "You've got a lot more patience for him."

"I've just seen his sweet."

"Just promise me you aren't going to start letting the kids around him."

I chuckled. "No, we're not quite there yet."

Field trips had become the sanctuary's bread and butter. Schools from all over the country brought their students here at least once a year. I'd even started a program with our local elementary school where the fifth-grade classes came once a month as part of their science classes.

There was nothing more rewarding than watching the kids' faces light up as they interacted with the animals. I got to see their compassion stretch and grow, and I knew they would become better human beings because they'd spent time here.

My gaze traveled over the property like it often did, remembering all the pain that this land had once carried. And now, it was nothing but goodness and light. My eyes burned. That had been my one hope for returning to Wolf Gap, and my load was lighter for seeing that vision become a reality.

"Ev, are you okay?" Kelly asked, a hand coming to rest on my arm.

It seemed as if I'd cry at the drop of a hat these days. I waved a hand in front of my face. "I'm fine. Just getting a little weepy thinking about all the good this place does."

A smile spread across Kelly's face. "It really has. Not just for the animals but the community, too."

The sound of tires crunching gravel had us both looking up. A familiar SUV with a sheriff's star climbed the drive. My stomach flipped the same way it did every time Hayes made his way home. And I hoped that never changed. But this evening, there was a little extra flutter in my belly.

"Oh, crap. Wipe your eyes," Kelly said.

My gaze jumped to her. "What?"

"Wipe your eyes. The last thing I need is Hayes thinking I did something to make you cry. He's cool under pressure, but if he thinks someone hurt you…" She let out a low whistle.

I laughed. "He's not that bad."

She shook her head. "On that note, I'm gonna head out. Unless you need me for something else?"

I waved her off. "You're good to go. See you next week."

Kelly jogged towards the fence but called over her shoulder, "I'm bringing my niece on Saturday, so you'll see me sooner."

"Sounds good."

She ducked through the fence rails just as Hayes' SUV came to a stop, and he climbed out. "Hey, Hayes. Enjoy your night."

He gave her a wave and a perplexed look. "She's in a hurry."

I took a second to drink in my husband. I'd never get tired of calling him that, even in my mind. And I'd never get tired of looking at him, either. Broad shoulders and a tall form. The uniform he wore was tailored in a way that hinted at the muscle I knew lay beneath. But it was the eyes that got me. Every. Single. Time.

Those dark blue eyes that I could get lost in for hours. The eyes that shone whenever Hayes told me he loved me. The eyes that sparked and heated whenever he took me, whether that was slow and tender or demanding and just a bit rough. Those were the eyes I was going to look into every day for the rest of my life.

"Ev?" Hayes asked.

He'd hopped the fence and was striding towards me. "You okay?"

I laughed, and that made a smile stretch across his face. The smile I loved. "I'm just thinking about how hot you are."

Hayes' brow quirked. "Are you, now?"

I made an exaggerated show of fanning myself. "I just might be."

He hauled me into his arms, his head dropping as he did. "Love that you like looking at me."

I'd made a study of his body in all forms. Working around the sanctuary. When he was on duty. Relaxing after a long day. Running with Koda. In the shower. Okay, the last one might've been my favorite.

Hayes took my mouth in a long, slow kiss. His tongue stroked mine in a mixture of comfort and heat. When he pulled away, those dark blue eyes were sparking. "Missed you."

"I saw you this morning."

"Too long," he said, kissing me again.

His words and tender expression made my heart rattle in my chest. I took a deep breath. It was time. I'd thought about calling him at work today, telling him to steal away for lunch or an afternoon break. But I hadn't wanted him distracted when he went back on duty, and I knew with my news, he would've been.

"Hayes—"

My sentence was cut off as Hayes howled and let out a stream of curses that would've had his mom smacking him upside the head. He spun around and glared at Jasper. "That creature is the devil. A damn menace. It's a miracle he hasn't permanently maimed someone yet."

My eyes widened. "What happened?"

"He tried to take a chunk out of my ass." Hayes rubbed his backside gingerly.

I couldn't help it, I burst out laughing.

Hayes glared at me. "It's not nice to laugh at your injured husband. I could have internal injuries."

"I certainly hope not because I have plans for you later tonight."

Hayes huffed. "My butt cheek is gonna turn black and blue, the least you can do is tend to me in my injured state."

I grinned and shook my head. "Fair enough. Why don't I feed you first?"

I bent to pick up the feed bucket, and as I righted myself, the world went sideways. I reached out a hand as my vision tunneled, and Hayes had me in his arms in an instant.

"Whoa, what happened? Are you okay?"

I blinked a few times, trying to get my bearings. "Yeah, I think I just stood up too fast."

Hayes' brows drew together. "You eat enough today?"

I thought about how nauseous I'd felt for most of the day and made a face. "Maybe not."

Hayes huffed and lifted me into his arms.

I smacked his chest. "Hayes, I'm fine. I just got a little lightheaded."

"Not taking any chances."

He somehow managed to climb over the fence with me still in his arms and strode towards the house. As we approached, Koda let out a happy bark and nosed open the screen door with his snout. He ran towards us, jumping and setting free a series of yips as if this were the best game ever.

"Come on, boy," Hayes said. "Let me through."

He managed to open the screen door and carried me straight through to the kitchen, where he set me on a stool at the counter. He quickly moved to the fridge, grabbing juice and what looked like string cheese. A few seconds later, he pushed a glass into my hand. "Drink."

I arched a brow. "Please?"

He rolled his eyes. "Please drink this orange juice so that you don't pass out on me. I'm getting used to the idea of having you around."

I chuckled and took a testing sip of the juice. It tasted amazing. The orange flavor was so much stronger than it usually was. Before long, I'd downed the tall glass. When I set it down, Hayes was eyeing me carefully.

"You sure you're okay?"

My stomach flipped, but I nodded. "I'm sure. But, uh, there was something I wanted to talk to you about."

Worry creased Hayes' brow, and he moved in closer. "You're freaking me out a little here. You're sure you're okay? I can call Beckett and have him come take a look at you."

Beckett was the last person I wanted to examine me, even though Hayes' brother was an amazing doctor. It would be way too awkward.

"Ev?"

"I'm pregnant."

The words tumbled out of me as if they had a mind of their own. No finesse. No sweet sentiments.

My husband simply stared at me.

"Hayes?"

"You're pregnant?" The words were more breath than actual syllables.

"That's what the test says. I mean, we should have a doctor confirm. I know we'd talked about waiting a little longer until—"

He cut me off with a kiss, his mouth taking mine, but the contact was heart-achingly gentle. As if I were the most precious thing in existence. When he pulled back, his eyes were shining. "Pregnant."

"Does that mean this is good news?"

One of Hayes' hands went to my stomach, and the other slipped under my hair to squeeze my neck. "I can't imagine any better news than this." His thumb swept back and forth over my still-flat belly as if he could feel a swell there. "How?"

"I took those antibiotics the other month, and we were careful some of the time…"

"But not every time."

We shared a look and at the same time said, "The barn." Then dissolved into laughter.

Hayes moved in closer, his head pressing to mine. "Can I tell you something?"

"You know you can tell me anything."

"I've been ready. I think I wanted this from the moment I first kissed you."

I pulled back, studying his eyes. "Why didn't you say anything?"

His thumb continued its stroking motion across my stomach. "I didn't want to push you. I know this sanctuary is important to you, that you wanted it solid before we had kids. And I want you to have all your dreams."

My heart squeezed at Hayes' thoughtfulness. "I didn't want to pressure you. I know you've had so much to deal with at work, and you're stretched thin—"

"That changes today. I'll always have emergencies, but I'm offloading some of the admin work onto my lieutenants and other staff. I won't be missing diaper changes and dinners."

I wrapped my arms around him and pressed my face to his chest. The steady beat of his heart against my cheek was the sweetest music I'd ever heard. "You're going to be the best dad."

"You were made to be a mom."

My head lifted at that, and tears filled my eyes. "I want to give this little one everything I didn't have growing up. I want them to always know how loved they are, and I always want them to feel safe."

Hayes' jaw went hard. "Oh, they'll feel safe."

The corner of my mouth kicked up. "No armed guards for the baby."

"Maybe," he muttered.

My fingers twisted Hayes' shirt between my fingers. "I want to give this baby some of the good things from my childhood." He was quiet, just letting me get it out. "I want to teach them about all the wildlife around here—the plants you can eat, the ones that have medicinal properties. I want to teach them the constellations."

My voice cracked on that. My family hadn't been all good, my dad certainly hadn't been. But they weren't all bad, either.

Hayes pulled me into his arms. "We'll teach them. Your mom would be so proud of you."

A tear slid down my cheek. "You think?"

"I know. You have the kind of strength she always wished she had. But that kernel grew in you." Hayes brushed his mouth against mine. "You steal my breath,

Ev. Never met anyone who is more of a walking miracle than you. Can't imagine a better person for our kids to look up to."

The tears fell harder. "Kids, huh?"

A devilish grin stretched across Hayes' face. "You think I'm stopping at just one?"

He dipped and lifted me into his arms, taking off at a run.

"Hayes!" I shrieked. "I'm already pregnant. You can't knock me up again."

"Practice makes perfect, Ev."

Find more information about Catherine and her books at catherinecowles.com.

Dirty Crazy Bad

Siobhan Davis

NOTE FROM THE AUTHOR

This short story is the prequel to the full-length stand-alone dark bully college romance novel, *Dirty Crazy Bad*, coming summer of 2022. Readers who have read my *Sainthood-Boys of Lowell High* series will recognize Ashley, Jase, and Chad from the cameos they made in those books. You do not need to read *The Sainthood Series* to enjoy this short story or the impending full-length novel.

Content warning: Descriptive sex scenes. Profanity. Drug references. Cheating. Happy reading!

THE TEMPTRESS
Ashley

"I NEED YOUR pussy," Jase says, scraping his teeth along my earlobe as one hand slides between my thighs.

Chad snorts from his position next to me on the gray leather couch. My boyfriend doesn't glance at me or his best friend as he skillfully wields the game controller in his hand, giving *COD* his full attention.

"They'll be here soon," I remind Jase, stopping his upward trajectory underneath my short black dress.

"I don't need long," he counters, squeezing the inside of my thigh before removing his hand and yanking me to my feet.

Chad snorts again, this time looking up at us for a split second. "Make it a quickie. We need to present a united front. You only get one chance to make an impression on The Sainthood."

"I don't get why we need to impress them," Creed says before cursing under his breath as Chad outmaneuvers him on the screen.

"Remo is screwing us on price, and we can't let him get away with that shit." Jase slings his arm around my shoulders. "Now it's our turn to screw him over." He steers me toward the stairs which lead to the upper level of the pool house.

"Leave the business discussions to the big boys," Chad drawls, delivering the death blow to Creed and forcing him from the game.

"As long as our supply is guaranteed, I don't give a fuck who we get our shit from," Nix says, joining the conversation as he executes an expert move which results in Chad losing a precious life.

I don't protest as Jase ushers me up the stairs. Chad is ridiculously competitive, especially with his buddies from the football team. If he loses this game, he'll be grumpy as fuck and sulk for at least an hour.

Jase shoves me into the bedroom, slamming the door shut with his foot. "Get rid of your panties and get on all fours on the bed, Temptress," he commands, his pupils darkening with wicked intent as he locks the door.

Liquid warmth pools low in my belly and my nipples harden to sharp points, poking against the silky material of my dress, as I shimmy my lace panties down my legs and kick them away.

"Heels on," Jase instructs when I attempt to remove my stilettos.

My jaw slackens as he whips his shirt over his head and tosses it to the floor. My eyes unashamedly roam every inch of hard carved muscle on display. Jase's broad shoulders, toned chest, and chiseled abs are a work of art. No matter how often I'm naked with Jase and Chad, I still can't get over how fucking incredible their bodies are. All those hours spent in the gym, training, and out on the football field have paid off. My boys are easily the two hottest guys on the Lowell Academy team and I'm the envy of all the girls on the cheer squad.

He pops the button on his jeans, smirking as he advances with a predatory gait that has my ovaries quivering. "Tick-tock, Temptress. On the fucking bed, *now*." I don't let my guys boss me around anywhere or anytime—except when it comes to the bedroom, where I'm happy to relinquish to their control.

I never have any complaints.

Jase shoves his jeans down his legs as I turn around and crawl up onto the bed, getting into position. Adrenaline floods my veins as my skin prickles in excited anticipation. The bed dips as Jase moves up behind me, and butterflies swoop into my belly. Cold air blows across my overheated skin as he pushes my dress up to my waist, exposing me to him.

With rough hands, he shoves my thighs farther apart and arches my hips up. "Such a pretty pussy," he murmurs, his hot breath wafting over my sensitive flesh before his tongue darts out and he licks my slit from top to bottom. A primitive moan escapes from my mouth as he proceeds to devour me with his tongue while his thumbs part my pussy lips, granting him full access. "You taste so fucking good, babe. I wish I had time to feast," he adds, bringing his hand down on my ass in a succession of firm slaps.

I whimper, my pussy clenching and unclenching with need as I feel him move into position. The telltale rip of foil only heightens my arousal, and I'm dying to feel him inside me. "Hold tight, Temptress. I'm about to destroy your cunt."

Jase is so dirty, but I love it—and everything he does to me.

I scream as he thrusts into me, embedding his cock so deep I swear I feel him nudging my womb. Digging his hands into my hips, he holds on tight as he pulls back out, almost all the way, before ramming back in. He sets a punishing pace, slamming in and out of me, grunting and spewing a ton of expletives, as he fucks me hard. Clinging to the bed, I hold on for dear life as he ruts in and out of me, filling me full of emotions and sensations I'm easily becoming addicted to.

"Damn, Ash. You feel so fucking good," he says over a moan, as one hand moves around to the front of my body. "Come when I tell you to," he demands, his fingers brushing against my clit. Moving my hips, I push back against him, and we work in tandem, both of us chasing that heavenly high. "Goddamn, babe. I can't get enough," he hisses, rocking into me so hard I scream again. Pressure is building inside me, climbing higher and higher, and every inch of my skin feels like it's on fire as Jase fucks me into the bed. "Now, Temptress," he yells, pinching my clit as he pivots his hips and emits an animalistic roar when he comes.

My climax crashes into me in wave after wave of sheer bliss and I'm screaming and moaning as we rock against one another, grinding in slow thrusts until we're sated. We collapse on the bed in a tangle of limbs, and I hold his hands against my stomach as he spoons me from behind. "That was—" I can't finish my sentence, can't find the right words to describe it, as I turn around and face him.

Jase brushes strands of my long blonde hair back off my face. "Other-fucking-worldly," he replies, leaning in to kiss me. His kiss is surprisingly sweet and tender. The opposite of the savage way he just took me. I know Jason Stewart harbors hidden demons, and one day I hope he'll open up to me about them. Threading my fingers through his thick dark hair, I angle my head and deepen the kiss, drowning in the feel of his warm soft lips gliding against mine.

When we break apart, the look on his face is one of complete adoration. "I wish we got to do this all the time. Out in the open, with no sneaking around."

I sigh as a familiar weight settles on my chest. "I know, baby." My fingers trek lightly across his gorgeous face, exploring his high cheekbones, strong nose, full lips, and the thin layer of hair coating his chin and angular jawline as he watches me through piercing green eyes. "We'll find a way to get you out of the arrangement." I don't know how, but I'm determined.

He's *mine*. He'll never be hers. I *will* find a way to make it happen.

A pounding on the door ends all further conversation on the topic. "They're here. Get your shit together," Chad hollers, and we instantly scramble off the bed. Jase gets dressed while I fix my clothing and tidy up my hair and makeup.

Chad looks a little tense when we open the door. "Relax, hon." I stretch up on tiptoes and plant my lips on his. "It'll be cool. Harlow is cool."

"It's not Harlow I'm worried about," Chad says.

"Well, you should be. From what I hear, Lo has Saint and his crew wrapped around her finger," Jase supplies.

"I don't doubt it." I agree as we walk down the stairs. "Harlow Westbrook is a force to be reckoned with. We have always gotten along well. Let me deal with her and I bet everything else slots into place."

It's not like Chad to be tense or worried, but a lot has changed in his life the past three months and he's not himself. When we reach the ground floor, I take my boyfriend's hand and pull him over to a quiet spot in the corner. I clasp his face in my hands. "I know you have a lot riding on this. I know you want it to be the start of something, but you don't need to worry. This isn't on you alone. We've got this." Wrapping my arms around his neck, I press my body against his broader, more muscular form and slant my lips over his. My fingers toy with the ends of his dirty-blond hair as I coax him to relax.

Chad's tongue instantly prods the seam of my lips, and I open for him, unable to deny my boyfriend of two years anything, because I love him and I hate seeing him so on edge. Our tongues dance against one another as we kiss passionately, and I feel his muscles loosening up against me.

Chad breaks our lip-lock, resting his brow against mine. "I couldn't do any of this without you, Ash. You know that, right?"

I peer deep into his gorgeous blue eyes. "Ditto, babe. You're my rock." Easing my head back from his, I tease my fingers through the longish top strands of his hair. "It's going to be fine. I promise."

Chad takes my hand, lifting it to his mouth and kissing my knuckles as he nods.

"They're making their approach," Creed says from behind me, holding his cell in one hand. Chad straightens up.

"I've got this." I peck Chad's lips briefly. "Stay here and I'll bring them to you."

"Go get 'em, babe." He swats my ass as I move to walk away, and I'm smiling to myself as I exit the pool house, heading in the direction of the main house.

I wave at a few Lowell Academy students congregated outside around the enclosed pool. Overhead, people are smoking and drinking on the upper-level wraparound balcony. Inside, throngs of boys and girls from school occupy the lower level of the plush mansion I call home.

Friday night parties at my house have been the norm for the past couple of years, ever since I turned sixteen and my parents deemed me responsible to be left alone while they travel the globe for business. I see them one week a month, tops. Even when they are back in Lowell, they are rarely at the house.

I might as well be an orphan.

I wasn't lying when I said Chad was my rock.

Without him, and Jase—when he's able to come over—I would slowly go insane inside this rambling mansion all by myself.

"Where are they?" I murmur, coming up alongside Nix in the kitchen, subtly glancing around.

"They just arrived," he quietly replies, handing me a vodka cranberry.

"Thanks." I sip from it as I grab his elbow and reposition us so we have a good view of the entryway. My lips curve into a smile when I spot Harlow making out with Saint Lennox against the wall, while Theo, Galen, and Caz—the other three members who make up the Sainthood junior chapter leadership—lounge in front of the doorway, watching as they talk in quiet tones.

"Oh shit." Nix dribbles beer from his mouth as his eyes widen in alarm.

A groan builds at the base of my throat as I watch my so-called best friend, Julia, push her way through people to get to them. "Oh my God! Harlow Westbrook," she says in that high-pitched whiny voice that pierces my skull every time I have to listen to her.

Nix chuckles as Saint pins the full extent of a hella scary glare on Julia. Of course, the Manford heir is completely oblivious, like always, and she continues prattling away while blatantly eye-fucking him. Saint has a possessive hold on Harlow and he exudes hostility in potent waves I feel from this distance.

"Do you think it's all an act?" Nix asks, keeping his eyes peeled on Julia. I know Chad gave him orders to ensure this goes smoothly, and Nix won't let his captain down. "Or is she really that stupid?"

"Honestly, I'm not sure. If it's an act, it's a damn good one, but I don't under-stand how she could be that stupid with the DNA that flows in her veins." Her father is the owner of the world's largest media corporation and he's worth billions. He's a shrewd player, so I find it hard to believe one of his offspring could be that dumb. I have often wondered if Julia is playing a well-timed game.

We share a chuckle as Harlow firmly puts Julia in her place. Predictably, Julia doesn't take that well, stomping her foot and glowering as she calls out, "Jason!" Impatience bleeds into the air as she looks all around for her boyfriend. "Where the fuck are you, Jase?"

"Well, I know where he was ten minutes ago," I dryly reply, though she can't hear me. "Buried balls deep inside my cunt."

Nix cracks up laughing, lifting his bottle and chinking it against my glass. "Promise me I can be there the day she finds out you've been fucking her boyfriend for months. I cannot wait to see that go down."

I dig my elbow into his ribs. "Shut the fuck up!" I hiss, glancing around to ensure no one heard us. Only the jocks closest to Chad and Jase know about us, and that's the way I want to keep it. Not that I wouldn't love to rub Julia's face in it, but that would be akin to igniting a bomb under Jase's life, and he's the only one I care about in that scenario.

So, as much as I hate it, it needs to remain a secret for now.

THE SAINTHOOD
Ashley

I GLANCE BEHIND me, watching Jase and Chad deep in conversation with the Lennox cousins, discussing plans to restructure the drug supply chain at the Academy, replacing their current supplier Remo with The Sainthood. The Sainthood owns pretty much all of the territory by now, having moved into the area a few months ago. The guys are from Prestwick, where the notorious criminal organization was founded many years ago. Now, The Sainthood has chapters all over the country and it's rumored they have high-level contacts in government and the legal and justice systems. They are not to be messed with, so I hope Chad knows what he's getting himself into.

"They'll be fine," Lo says, dragging my attention away from the guys and back to her. She's sitting beside me on the couch in the pool house, and both of us are nursing vodkas. Theo Smith, the financial genius behind The Sainthood junior chapter, has his arm draped around Lo as he watches Caz battle Creed and Nix at *COD*. Caz has a reputation for being the muscle in their operation, but I think that does him an injustice. He's a smart guy with a fun sense of humor, and he's clearly smitten with Harlow, the way all four of the guys are.

"Don't you worry?" I ask, leaning back against the couch.

"Why borrow tomorrow's troubles?" She shrugs, looking like nothing fazes her. "I worry about what I have to face today, and I trust the guys. They know what they're doing."

"Chad has been through some stuff lately. He has a lot riding on this deal." It's more than that, but I don't want to say too much. I like Harlow. I always have, but we don't know one another all that well. That honestly puzzles me, and it's something I intend to rectify.

Lo got kicked out of the Academy over summer break because of the now infamous sex tape, so she no longer goes to my school, attending the public high school for senior year instead.

"It'll work out."

"Why were we never friends?" I ask.

Lo stares at me in contemplation for a moment. "I genuinely don't know. I could have used a friend like you at the Academy."

"Same, sister."

"We ran in different circles," she adds. "You have the cheer squad and Julia, and honestly, I couldn't spend two seconds in the company of those girls without my brain trying to climb out of my skull in protest."

I bark out a laugh. "You're not wrong, though not everyone on the cheer team is vacuous and vain. A couple of them I genuinely like."

"Give me your phone," she says, and I unlock it and hand it over. She punches her digits in, sends herself a text, and hands it back to me. "We can keep in contact now. Maybe hang out sometime."

"I'd like that, and I'm here if you ever need me. Even if it's just to vent, because dealing with all that testosterone on a daily basis can't be easy." I'm grinning as the words leave my mouth, because, come on, what woman wouldn't want that problem?

Theo angles his head, eyeing me with amusement. Long blond hair curtains his gorgeous face, and it's hard not to ogle him. But I try, because I would never objectify him or disrespect Harlow like that.

"You're not wrong, but the pros definitely outweigh the cons," she says, arching her head back and lifting her face to Theo. He leans down, pressing his lips to hers in an upside-down kiss, and I look away, affording them privacy. My eyes meet Caz's, and he grins, waggling his brows as he looks at Lo kissing Theo with a hint of longing. I have heard rumors that Caz is bi, and now I'm wondering if Theo is too and if something might be between them.

The guys end their meeting a couple of minutes later and return to us. Everything looks amicable and I breathe a sigh of relief. I invite them to stay, but they have plans of a personal nature, so they leave after saying their goodbyes.

✧ ✧ ✧

"I'M GLAD EVERYTHING went well," I say, looping my arms around Chad's neck from my perch on his lap. We relocated to the main house after Lo and The Sainthood left, and I'm enjoying the chill vibe now that the party is winding down. Jase has departed for the night, wanting to avoid spending time with Julia. She threw a hissy fit when she heard he left without telling her, leaving shortly after him, thank fuck.

"We still need to execute the plan, but I have a good feeling about it." Chad nuzzles his nose in my hair, inhaling deeply. "I tentatively suggested we could expand our arrangement in the fall when we're at Lowell University, and I definitely saw a spark of interest, though they played it cool."

"Take it one step at a time," I caution, as I have regularly in recent times.

Chad stiffens a little, and I reposition myself on his lap so I'm looking at his face. "I know you're worried about your mom, and college, and you need the money, but you need to be smart about this, baby. You don't want to risk attracting the attention of the authorities or picking up the kind of enemies who shoot first and ask questions later."

"I don't have the luxury of time," he replies in a clipped tone, before knocking back a mouthful of beer.

"But you do." I know I shouldn't broach this subject here, when there is an audience, but it needs to be emphasized again. "I got access to my inheritance when I turned eighteen and I can—"

"I'm not taking handouts from my girlfriend," he growls, his gorgeous face contorting in anger. "I'm sick of having this argument, Ash." His brow puckers as he glances over my shoulder. His lips pull into a thin line and flames dance in his eyes as he swiftly lifts me off his lap onto the couch and jumps up. "What the fuck is that asshole doing here?" he bellows, storming in the direction of the kitchen. I hop up and race after him, screeching to a halt in the middle of the kitchen when I spot him squaring up to an unfamiliar group of guys.

"You're not welcome here, Haynes," Chad says, shoving the tall muscular guy in the shoulders. The dude is flanked by three shorter, stockier guys, but they look no less scary.

Haynes tilts his head in my direction, staring me in the eyes. I'm sure I have never met the guy before, because there's no way I'd ever forget his imposing figure and stunning face. He's got a couple of inches in height on Chad which means he's pushing at least six-four. Ink crawls up the exposed tan skin on both arms, and creeps up one side of his neck. His nose, brow, and lip are pierced, and his jet-black hair is teased into a faux hawk with the sides cropped close to his head. Piercing sage-green eyes penetrate mine, though, upon closer inspection, I think his eyes are hazel. I see little flecks of gold in his irises. His arms are crossed against an impressive chest, his biceps straining under his shirt. Ripped dark jeans hug his toned legs, and he's definitely the full package.

I bet he has girls crawling all over him.

Guys like him usually do.

"Your girl begs to differ," he says, fixing me with a dark heated look. "She's drooling and panting like a dog in heat."

What the actual fuck? I glare at him, letting him know exactly what I think of his bullshit assessment.

He grabs his dick through his jeans, rubbing it suggestively as he stares at me, his lips curving into a condescending smile. His friends chuckle, watching me with blatant interest, raising all the tiny hairs on the back of my neck. I don't know who these guys are, but they are not the type you mess with. That said, no one comes into my house and insults me. A crowd is gathering around us now, so I know we're in control of the situation, whether the newcomers want to accept that truth or not. I hold eye contact with Haynes and feign nonchalance. "Dream on, deadbeat."

Chad places a protective hand on my lower back, but it's a subtle move, because he knows I can hold my own and I hate him treating me like a damsel in distress. "Leave. Now." Chad glowers at Haynes, and out of the corner of my eye, I spot Chad's free hand clenching at his side. His entire body is primed for a fight, and I need to defuse the situation before it descends into chaos.

"This is a Lowell Academy party," I say, stepping in front of Haynes and daring him to disrespect me. "Last I checked, none of you attend our school, so I'll politely ask you to leave."

The guys trade amused grins, and I'm gradually losing all semblance of patience.

Haynes lowers his face to mine, and it takes ginormous effort to hold my ground and not back down. "Or what, doll face?"

Reaching my arm back, I hold on to Chad's wrist, issuing a silent warning to not intervene. "Or I'll shoot you," I coolly reply. "I have an arsenal of firearms at my disposal." That's no lie. Dad collects guns and loves hunting. I have my choice of guns as well as my personal Glock. "I'd enjoy using you four as target practice."

"Damn, girl. Ditch the jock and take a ride on the wild side," the guy with reddish-brown hair says. "We know how to show a girl a good time."

I roll my eyes, but don't dignify him with a response. Angling my body, I point at the door. "Out. Now."

Tension bleeds into the air as Chad's remaining jock buddies line up alongside us, clenching their fists, flexing their biceps, and silently snarling. The outsiders don't look in any way threatened, and I reluctantly admire their attitude.

"We'll go." Haynes eyeballs me. "But I'll be back." He exchanges another sly smile with his friends, and prickles of apprehension tiptoe up my spine.

"Come back and I'll gut you like a fish," Chad says, cracking his knuckles.

"That's not a threat. It's a promise."

THE DIVORCE
Ashley

"YOU'RE SO TENSE, baby," I say, sitting naked on top of Chad as he lies on his stomach on my bed. Kneading the corded muscles of his shoulders and back, I massage him with some of the expensive oil I found in my mother's en suite bathroom. "Are you ready to talk about it yet?"

After Haynes and his goons left, I got rid of everyone else because I could see my boyfriend was wound tight.

"Nope." Chad slides sideways across my king bed and flips over onto his back. "I have something better than talking in mind." Grabbing my slicked-up hand, he brings it to his erection.

"I like the way you think," I tease, crawling in between his legs. If he thinks I'm letting what happened downstairs go, he's got another think coming. Sex should relax him and then I'll force him to talk.

Pushing his thighs apart, I lower my head and lave my tongue against his straining cock. Dragging my tongue up and down his shaft, I lick and softly suck on his velvety-smooth skin before blowing across his crown. Chad groans and his dick jerks as he lifts his hips, his body craving release. I swipe my thumb across the precum beading at the tip of his large dick and thrust it into my mouth, grinding my hips and moaning as I taste his salty sweetness on my tongue.

Chad growls and his eyes darken with lust as he grabs me by the neck and pulls my face down to his hard-on. "Suck. Now."

Lowering my mouth over his throbbing length, I keep my eyes focused on his face as I swallow as much of his hardness as I can. I go to town on him, sliding my lips up and down his length while loosening my throat and stretching my mouth so I don't gag on his girth. Chad fists handfuls of my hair and takes over, controlling the movement as I slide up and down, and he rocks into my mouth.

Without warning, he yanks me off his dick and throws me down on my back, shoving my legs up over his shoulders as he rolls a condom on. In one quick move, he plunges inside me, fucking me in rough thrusts while his fingers alternate between playing with my clit and caressing my tits.

Leaning down, he bites on my lower lip before his tongue darts out to ease the sting. He claims my mouth in feverish need, his tongue stroking mine as his cock drives in and out of my pussy. Maintaining a frenetic pace, he jostles me on the bed as I pivot my hips, matching my movements with his, and it isn't long before we both fall over the edge, moaning and screaming and clinging to one another.

Chad drops down beside me, his muscular arm snagging me around the waist as he pulls me into his body. I rest my head on his chest, listening to the steady beat of his heart as he brushes hair off my face. "You're my world, Ashley," he whispers before dotting kisses into my hair. "When everything else is changing, you're the one constant I can always rely on."

"Jase too," I remind him, rubbing my fingers through the thick scruff on his chin.

He nods, peering solemnly into my eyes. "Haynes is *her* son," he says as a muscle clenches in his jaw, and he doesn't need to explain further. "He knows who I am."

"Meaning he knows who I am," I add, and he nods.

"He came here on purpose. I saw the way he was looking at you. He's up to something, but whatever it is, it's not happening."

"It's not," I agree, pressing a slew of open-mouthed kisses underneath his jawline. "Whatever he's up to, we'll stop him."

✧   ✧   ✧

I STARTLE AT the sound of footsteps in the hallway, turning around with a spoonful of granola still in my mouth. The cleaning crew left thirty minutes ago, and I only ventured out of bed then. Chad left hours ago to attend the regular Saturday morning training session with his team, and I took advantage of the opportunity to sleep in late. I'm not expecting him back until tonight, because I know he'll want to check on his mom after football. The only other person who has a key is Jase, but he's at the training session too. Reaching into the top drawer of the island unit, I remove my Glock, unlock the safety, and pull back the chamber before pointing it at the open door which leads from the kitchen into the hallway.

"Jesus, Ashley," Mom says, slapping a hand over her chest and staring in horror at the gun in my hand as she appears in my line of vision. "Put that thing away." An extra set of footsteps echoes behind her and then my dad is there too.

"What are you doing here?" I inquire.

"We live here," my father says, brushing past Mom and striding toward me.

"Barely," I mumble under my breath as I set the Glock back in the drawer.

Dad pulls me into a bear hug. "Missed you."

Could have fooled me. I don't return the sentiment, because why lie? "What's going on?" I ask, shucking out of Dad's squeezing embrace.

"You get more beautiful every time I see you," Dad says. "You're the spitting image of your grandma."

I wouldn't know. She died when I was a baby, and it's not like Dad is around much to reminisce over old photos.

"Were you drinking?" Mom asks, her critical gaze roaming my messy hair, bloodshot eyes, and the sheen of sex that probably still coats my skin. I'm wearing Chad's shirt which hits mid-thigh, and little else. It wouldn't take a genius to figure out what I was up to last night.

"Yes." I don't see the point in lying. She frowns, opening her mouth to lecture me, no doubt, but I shut her down. "Don't attempt to parent me now, Pamela. I'm eighteen. You're too late."

"You're still living under our roof," she retorts, narrowing her eyes at me as she removes her expensive coat, draping it over the back of one of the stools.

She's dressed to the nines, like always. Her cool-blonde hair is tied up in an elegant chignon, and the tiny pearls embedded in a circle around the bun matches the string of pearls around her neck. A cream silk shirt is tucked into her form-fitting black pencil skirt, and her legs look slender and smooth with her feet fitted into a pair of killer high heels. I don't think I have ever seen my mom look anything but perfect. No wonder she looks horror-stricken at the state of me.

"Pamela. Don't." Dad fixes her with a warning look. "We didn't come here to lecture our daughter."

"Why are you here?" This is getting tiresome.

"We need to talk to you," he replies. "Why don't you grab a quick shower while we make some coffee."

I don't bother protesting, because I believe in the "pick your battles" mantra, and retreat to my room to make myself presentable. I feel more human, and less hungover, after I have showered and changed into designer skinny jeans, an off-the-shoulder pink cashmere sweater, and my silver ballet flats. I deliberated wearing something slutty or grungy just to annoy Mom, but I would rather they said what they came here to say and then left. I have plans with the guys tonight and the rents being here throws a wrench in the works.

"So, tell me," I say when we are all seated in the formal living room, nursing steaming cups of coffee. "What is so important you had to come home mid-weekend to tell me?"

Dad wets his lips, looking uncharacteristically nervous, and it sets me on high alert. I straighten up, looking from him to Mom. "There's no easy way to say this, pumpkin," Dad says, while Mom blurts, "We're getting a divorce."

I sit in stone silence for a few seconds before my brain reconnects. "What?" My gaze bounces between my parents as I attempt to process my shock.

"Don't look so surprised." Mom places her coffee cup on the end table. "It's not like we've ever had a normal marriage."

I blink profusely as I look at her. "What does that even mean?"

"It means, our marriage was arranged," Dad replies, drawing my attention to him. He rises, moving over to sit alongside me. He takes my hands in his. "You're old enough now that we thought you would've realized the truth."

"Which is what?" I ask, wondering if I have wandered into some alternate realm. Yes, I knew my parents didn't have this crazy mad love affair, that they are both married to their jobs, but they have done everything together for years. They run Dad's family business like it's an extension of their marriage, pouring more love and attention into it than their only child. I didn't think love mattered. It always seemed like teamwork was more important to them, and in that regard, they are on the same page, so this has come completely out of left field.

"We respect and love one another as individuals," Dad explains, his eyes pleading for understanding. "But we have never been in love with each other. We thought that was obvious."

"Maybe if you were here more than a few days a month, I might have noticed," I snap, extracting my hand from his. "But you are never here, so when exactly was I to come to this realization?"

"You're right." Dad claws a hand through his hair.

"It doesn't matter." Mom sits up straighter as she looks me directly in the eyes. "You're an adult now. You'll be off to college in a few months. You have your whole life ahead of you, so whether your parents divorce or not really doesn't matter."

Her cold, clinical assessment is so far off the mark it's almost funny. "You have no clue, Pamela. None." I stand, glaring at my mother with unconcealed loathing. "You don't have a single maternal bone in your body, so it isn't really a surprise you can't understand how much this impacts me. That you don't care speaks volumes."

She rises to her feet like butter wouldn't melt in her mouth. "Grow up, Ashley. Your father and I are divorcing but we are still your parents."

I harrumph, thrilled when I detect a subtle flinching motion in her jaw. "Your parenting skills are questionable in the extreme," I say, uncaring if I hurt them. "I practically raised myself."

"I'm sorry." Dad sounds sincere as he climbs to his feet. "We left you alone too much, but you were always so independent."

"Whatever you have to tell yourself to appease your conscience, Dad."

I move to walk away, but he takes my hand, stalling me. "I'd like the chance to make amends. I'm moving back full-time. We will have time to reconnect before you leave for college."

I don't know whether that's a good thing or not.

"I'm permanently relocating to Switzerland," Mom informs me, sliding the strap of her purse over her shoulder. "I will run the European operation while your father will handle the US one." She walks toward me. "I know this has come as a shock. I *am* sorry you have taken the news so hard. I wasn't expecting that." I see no hint of emotion on her face, and I wonder if she's capable of feeling anything. "I don't want to upset you further, Ashley, but you should know I'm getting remarried next week and I'm expecting a baby with Richard."

"Richard?" I croak, completely shell-shocked.

"Richard has been your mother's partner for ten years," Dad explains, and I stare at both of them like the strangers they are. "I know it's a lot to take in, and there is more you don't know, but I will fill you in on everything."

"What about you?" I ask, gulping over the messy ball of emotion clogging my throat. "Do you have a long-term partner?"

He shakes his head as Mom says, "Your father has always favored more casual attachments, though I believe that has changed recently." She glances at the Rolex strapped to her slender wrist. "I need to leave. My flight is due to take off soon." She gives me an awkward one-armed hug before stepping away. "You have my number, call me if you need anything, and you are welcome to visit any time."

"I'll talk to you Monday," Dad says, jerking his head at her as she walks toward the door. "Have a safe trip."

Eerie silence descends after she leaves and I'm grappling with my emotions, struggling to understand how I truly feel about the bombshells they've just dropped when the doorbell chimes.

I lift my head, and Dad grimaces. "They're early."

My eyes narrow to slits as I stare at him. "Who is?"

"Your mother is correct. None of my, uh, dalliances were ever serious, but I met someone recently and she's different. She's important."

"She's *here*?" Disbelief oozes from my tone. He nods, tapping out a message on his cell before he makes a move to walk away. "You can't be serious, Dad?! You have just dropped all this shit on me and now you expect me to what? Welcome your sidepiece with open arms? Pretend to play happy family? Act like you haven't just thrown me for a loop?"

"I'm sorry, Ashley. I really am. I didn't think it through."

I throw my hands in the air. "Ya think?"

"Look." He clasps my face. "I know this is a lot to ask, pumpkin. Can you just say hello to her and her son? You can leave then. I'll make excuses for you."

"Her son?" Dread creeps over me like a thundercloud and I have a super bad feeling about this.

"He's a senior, like you. He goes to Fenton High. This is his first time meeting me. I'm sure he'll be nervous too. I thought you might help each other adjust to the new situation."

Oh, hell to the no. "What new situation? What aren't you telling me, Dad?"

"It can wait," he says, exiting the room before I can force him to tell me.

I move to the window, staring at the unfamiliar SUV parked in front of our house. It's a brand-new Lexus and I'm wondering if it was a gift from my dad. Fenton isn't an affluent area. Anyone with wealth lives in Lowell, so I think it's a fair assumption to make. My dad is no fool, so it must be serious if he's already buying her a car.

A feminine laugh trickles in the open doorway from the hall and I turn around as Dad steps into the room with a stunning woman holding his hand. She's petite with curves in all the right places. She grips his arm tight as she stares up at him like he hung the stars in the night sky. She only just reaches Dad's chest, and they look kind of awkward together. Her womanly curves cling to the floaty maxi dress she's wearing with ballet flats, much like my own. Lustrous midnight-black hair falls in thick, soft waves down her back, and her smile is wide as she looks over at me. Her full mouth is painted a glossy nude color, but it doesn't look like she's wearing much makeup.

She's not who I thought my dad would fall for. It's almost like he went out of his way to find a woman the exact opposite of my mother. Not that I can blame him for that.

Her smile is genuine as she looks at me, and I warm to her instantly, which surprises me. Big green eyes framed by long black lashes blink quickly as she takes me in. "Your father said you were a beauty and I see now he wasn't exaggerating." She walks confidently toward me, pulling me into a gentle but warm embrace. "It's so wonderful to meet you, Ashley. Your father has told me all about you."

He's told me nothing about you. I think it, but I don't say it. I'm mad at Dad, but I would never be rude. This woman hasn't done anything to deserve my wrath, and if she's going to be a part of Dad's life, then I want to start off on the right footing. "It's lovely to meet you too."

Dad beams and I swear it's the first time in years I have seen him smile so broadly. His arm slides around the woman's shoulders as he shoots me a grateful look. "This is Hera."

"That's a beautiful name."

"Thank you. I'm of Greek descent." She glances over her shoulder. "Ares! Where are you?" Turning around, she rolls her eyes. "I'm sure I don't need to tell you about teenage boys."

"I'm not a boy," a gruff masculine voice says, and all the blood leaches from my face as Haynes strides into the room with an arrogant swagger.

You have got to be kidding me.

Dad frowns as he gives him the once-over, and I know what he's seeing. The hair. The ink. The piercings. The sheer size of him. The giant chip he's clearly carrying on his shoulder. Dad's frown deepens when Haynes, Ares, whatever his name is, blatantly runs his eyes up and down the length of me.

I barely manage to trap my snarl when he steps toward me, his eyes lingering on my chest as his tongue plays with the ring secured to his lower lip. "Told you I'd be back." He waggles his brows, smirking at me with ill-conceived arrogance.

"Wait, you two know each other?" Dad asks, looking and sounding perplexed.

"No," I say, the same time Ares says, "Yes."

"He showed up here last night, uninvited," I explain to Dad while maintaining eye contact with the douche.

"I *was* invited," he says, amusement dancing in his eyes. "I thought you'd give me a tour so I could pick which room would be mine."

Dad almost chokes on a breath, and my head spins in his direction. "What is he talking about?" This cannot be what he's insinuating. Please God, let him be bluffing.

"I didn't have a chance to talk with Ashley yet," Dad says, glancing at Hera and pleading with her for help.

"I'm sorry," Hera says. "We shouldn't have barged in here before your father had time to talk to you about it."

I tune out the rest of what she says, and whatever my father adds to it, as I glare at the gloating asshole in front of me. His obvious enjoyment irritates me to no end. I'm on high alert when he leans in, pressing his mouth to my ear. "Ares was the son of Zeus and Hera, and he was the God of War. My name literally means ruin." He pulls back a little, his eyes glittering with deathly promise as he threatens me, clearly getting off on this. "I revel in chaos and destruction and enjoy taking down spoiled little bitches who have had everything handed to them on a platter. Buckle up, doll face, because I can't wait to ruin you."

✧   ✧   ✧

Subscribe to my newsletter and be the first to hear when the full-length version of *Dirty Crazy Bad* is released. Go here or copy this link into your browser: http://eepurl.com/dl4l5v

GRAVITY

ALEATHA ROMIG

"Someday, after mastering the winds, the waves, the tides and gravity, we shall harness for God the energies of love, and then, for the second time in the history of the world, man will have discovered fire."

~ Pierre Teilhard de Chardin

CHAPTER ONE
Charli Demetri

STARING AT THE website, I marveled at the responses to Mom and Oren's wedding. After all these years, even more if I went back to before...before it all, my mother had finally agreed to marry. From the first time I saw her with Oren—or Oren with her—I knew there was more between them than she'd ever had before.

I couldn't blame my mother for being hesitant about marriage. After all, as a two-time widow from two loveless marriages, my mother was burnt. While I'd been much more fortunate in the love category, until Oren, a father's love was something I only remembered in childlike dreams. Despite my mother and father's relationship, I knew he loved me. He died when I was young and memories fade. Mother never shied from telling me stories of him reading bedtime stories, swimming in the pool, and picnics near the lake at Montague Manor.

Her second husband, the marriage that was arranged by my grandfather Charles Montague, was barely worth the breath it took to say his name—which I wouldn't. That brought me to Oren Demetri.

There was something about the man from the first time we met. The father of my boyfriend/contract owner—never mind, that was complicated too. The father of my sexy and loving husband, Oren was an enigma. His background was complicated, yet despite what Nox thought at the time, Oren was a man capable of immense love, whether for his first wife—Nox's mother—his son, daughter, daughter-in-law, grandchildren, or the woman who captured his heart at a time he believed himself incapable of love—my mother—Oren loved fiercely. Through the years, his capacity to heal and love became more evident.

Oren never rushed Mom. He didn't push her to take his last name. He saw her in a way that no other man had. Oren saw my mother for her beauty and talents, a woman beyond his means, and a gift to be treasured. If that meant that they would live and love until their dying day remaining unmarried, Oren was there for the ride, sitting beside Mom, and holding her hand.

Imagine our surprise after all these years when Mom called to tell Nox and me that she and Oren were going to marry. Her plan was for a small private ceremony at the manor. She wanted Nox, me, our children—Angelina, Dominic, and Janie—Silvia, and her husband to be present.

It took some convincing, but Nox and I won. We convinced our parents to let us throw them a wedding. We promised it wouldn't be too large or ostentatious. The world needed the opportunity to celebrate the union of two damaged souls who over the last decade made one another whole.

The venue was set. Woodland Cliffs Country Club in Monterey, California. Sitting on the coastline, it was a spectacular private country club. Working with their new director of services, Rae Watson, I hoped we'd planned a wedding and reception worthy of the two people who loved our family unconditionally.

Sitting in my office in our home in Rye, New York, I began to count the affirmative responses as my stunningly sexy husband entered. He'd aged since our first encounter, but like a fine French wine, time only made him bolder, stronger, and better.

"Have you seen Angi?" he asked.

Angelina Demetri, named after Nox's mother, was ten years old and a bundle of energy with a vocabulary that rivaled college students. She had both her parents' love of learning and an uncanny ability to get her way. Nox said she'd gotten that skill from his father. Now looking at the website, I believed Nox was right.

Oren Demetri finally got his way.

"She's next door at Lindsey's," I replied.

Nox took a deep breath. "I thought we said no playdates on school nights."

I grinned. "She had a very convincing argument."

My husband shook his head, his light blue eyes shining my way. "She's only ten. We're in so much trouble."

"Dominic and Janie are upstairs with Jane."

In only a few strides, Nox was at my side, peering over my shoulder. Sweeping away my long auburn hair, his firm lips came to my neck, sending goose bumps over my flesh and causing my nipples to tighten.

His deep voice sparked nerves, setting off explosions throughout my body. "Since the children are occupied, we should slip away for a bit and have our own playdate."

Turning, I met his gaze. "I love you. We can have a playdate later tonight. Look at this list."

Nox's focus went to the computer screen. "Look at that. The Rawlingses will be there."

"Just the two of them. We invited Nichol, Nathaniel, and Natalie." I paused and turned to Nox. "Did you know Nate is having a child?"

Nox laughed. "I didn't know that was possible."

"If it were, you'd be having our next one."

His blue eyes opened wide. "Next one?"

"No, I'm not pregnant. I just mean…it's your turn."

"Look at that list," he said, changing the subject. "Uncle Vincent and Aunt Bella will be there."

Uncle Vincent happened to be one of the top leaders in New York. No, he wasn't elected. He was part of the New York top crime families. That said, he and his wife were among the first to welcome Mom and me into the Costello family—Nox's mother's maiden name. Soon both Mom's and my last name would be Demetri. In the Costello way of thinking, we were family—family was family.

I shook my head. "If this wasn't a joyous occasion, I might be concerned about the testosterone we've gathered together. Sterling and Araneae Sparrow said yes. I sent invitations to his entire upper echelon."

"Surely someone has to stay in Chicago."

"You told me to include them. I remember meeting Lorna a long time ago at Tinsley Constantine's coming of age party. Anyway, all eight will be there. Mom adores Araneae. I think she's donated to and even visited the Sparrow Institute."

Nox took a deep breath. "Uncle Vincent and Sterling Sparrow."

"Oh, there's more. Today I heard from Emma Ramses, she and Everett will be there." Before Nox could make a sound, I added, "And you know Lorenzo Dellinger?" Another top man in New York's underworld. "He also said yes. His son, Dante, and a plus-one and granddaughter, Cecilia, and her husband, Greyson, are coming too."

Nox's neck straightened. "Is that wise, with the Ramseses?"

I shrugged. "Mom gave me the list."

"And Dad knows that half the mafia world will be at his wedding?"

"Did I mention Maxwell Tiller?"

"San Diego."

"Yep." I nodded. "He said with the wedding in California, he wouldn't miss it."

Nox shook his head. "New York, Chicago, New Orleans, San Diego. What kingpins are we missing?"

"To your earlier question, as to if your dad knows, I don't think he minds. He's lived in the thick of it." I remembered something. "Not to make this more uncomfortable, but remember when Mom worked with that FBI agent about the smuggling problem with Montague Tobacco?"

Nox's brow furrowed. "Don't tell me."

I nodded. "She wanted him to be invited. Agent Jacoby McAlister and his wife, Stella, said yes."

"Have you heard from Donovan Sherman?"

"Not yet. But Lena Montgomery said yes, no plus-one."

"Maybe we should have stuck with a small wedding at the manor."

Standing, I lifted my arms to Nox's shoulders. "It's a wedding. Mom and Oren should have their friends and family there."

"Maybe they should have made safer friends."

I laughed. "Too late."

Chapter Two

Araneae Sparrow

A S CLOUDS FLOATED beneath our plane, Lorna said, "Oh, I met Alexandria Demetri the night I met Reid. She was sweet and took me under her wing. Which was great. My date was rather non-attentive."

Mason laughed as he listened to his sister, his colorful arms showing below his short sleeves, and his hair tethered back behind his neck. "Good thing, or I would have scared off this guy." He nudged Reid.

"You could have tried." Reid scoffed. "You're not that scary."

At another time, living another life, being scary was Mason's thing. I supposed to an outsider, he still was. To us, like all the men, he was family.

Currently, the eight of us were flying on the Sparrow plane—yes, it's painted to look like a sparrow—on our way to Monterey, California. Following the sun, we were taking advantage of a small break and adult time. Arriving tonight, we had one day of relaxation before the big wedding on Saturday.

I turned to Madeline. "Do you think Ruby can handle all three children?"

"She adores them. They're planning a sleepover in the penthouse living room."

My husband's dark eyes opened wide as he turned toward Madeline.

"Oh," Madeline said with a grin, "Ruby's been planning. They're going to build tents, watch movies, eat popcorn and s'mores. A regular camping trip."

"As long as there's no plans for a campfire," Sterling said.

Reid joined the conversation. "They're secure. Garrett is on '2' monitoring everything, and the top floors are on lockdown."

"You know who else I met that night?" Lorna asked, sitting back against the leather seat, her bright red hair hanging down around her shoulders.

We all shook our heads.

"Claire Rawlings."

I couldn't help but smile. "She's a significant donor to the institute. So is Adelaide Montague. Oops, I guess that's about to be Demetri."

Lorna leaned forward. "Have you heard of *MY LIFE AS IT DIDN'T AP-PEAR*?"

"Oh, I read that," Laurel, Mason's wife, said. "It's out of print." Her blue eyes widened. "That's *this* Claire Rawlings?"

"Have you met Anthony?" Sterling asked. "I bet he paid a fortune to get that book removed from sale."

"Wait." I asked, "What's the book about?"

Lorna and Laurel looked at one another. It was Lorna who spoke. "You know what, forget it. I don't know if the contents were true, or some made-up story to hurt Anthony. It was released after something happened."

"What happened?"

Sterling lifted his hand. "I know what it's about, but fuck, is it real? Did that shit happen?" He shrugged and reached for my hand. "Sunshine, not everyone had a perfect courtship like us."

My eyes opened wide. "Perfect? Umm, was it the tricking me into coming to Chicago or kidnapping me to Canada that was perfect?"

Lorna nodded. "That's what I mean. If I didn't know you two and I heard that story, I'd assume the worst about Sparrow. The biography was a hatchet job on Claire's husband. Honestly, she was classy and kind. I didn't detect anything resembling what's in that book."

"Sometimes," Madeline said, "women are good at hiding it."

Patrick leaned over, giving his wife a kiss. "Sometimes, after all the shit that gets thrown our way, life works out."

Taking a sip of champagne, I sat back and sighed. "You still didn't tell me the contents, but from what you're saying, that biography reminds me of a psychological thriller I read."

"Me too," Madeline said.

"That was fiction." Thinking about Patrick's comment, I said, "I hope *life working out* is what this wedding is about. Adelaide has shared a few things. For lack of a better word, she has shit in her past, but when she talks about Oren, her face absolutely glows. It's not that they're that old, but they are older. This wedding proves that love knows no age and has no limits."

As we approached Monterey, the sky beyond the windows filled with vibrant shades of crimsons and lavenders. I reached for Sterling's hand. "I miss Goldie, but I like this getaway."

Sterling leaned toward me, bringing our noses close as his dark gaze dominated my vision. "I plan on taking advantage of a locked bedroom door."

Warmth filled my cheeks.

"Patrick said we all have suites at the Monterey Plaza with ocean views."

"And the rooms around us," Patrick added, "are filled with Sparrows who flew ahead."

"Oh, good," I said, sarcastically, "bodyguards."

"Not in our suite, sunshine." Sterling turned to the men. "I arranged some meetings."

"Tiller?" Mason asked.

Sterling nodded. "Also, Ramses. I haven't seen him since Madeline's tournament in New Orleans. He helped us out."

"What about Costello, from New York?" Patrick asked.

Sterling nodded. "Reid, did you secure a location? Oren doesn't need business at his wedding."

"Yes. The Sparrows on the ground have it covered."

I turned to Lorna, Laurel, and Madeline. "Pool time or shopping?" Before they answered, I turned to my husband. "Yes, we can have Sparrows with us. Heck, maybe Marsha would like to join us. I'm assuming she's already there."

Marsha was one of the top Sparrow bodyguards. Petite and slender, she was a dynamic force in an unassuming package.

"I'd feel better if she did," my husband replied.

"I was reading about all the boutiques," Lorna said.

"And the beaches are beautiful," Laurel added. "I was in this area a long time ago."

"The hotel has a nice pool," Madeline added.

"Then it's settled," I said with a grin, "shopping, beaches, and pool. And wine. After all, it's California."

CHAPTER THREE
Claire Rawlings

SETTLING IN OUR hotel suite, I went out onto the balcony. My husband stood at the railing, peering out at the Pacific Ocean or more specifically Monterey Bay. While Tony's dark hair had lightened with age, his penetrating gaze was as dark as the first night we met. He appeared lost in thought as I laid my hand on his back.

"What are you thinking?"

"This is gorgeous." He turned my way. "I prefer your island."

A smile curled my lips. "You like the island because we get it all to ourselves." I shrugged. "The island is special and warmer, but I agree"—I looked out at the sparkling surf—"this view is pretty. I wish the kids were here."

Releasing the railing, my husband reached for my waist. "They're all adults. When will they stop being *kids*?"

I lifted my chin, my gaze meeting his. "Never. They're our kids."

His finger and thumb held my chin in place. "Mrs. Rawlings, I'll never tire of your emerald stare. You're stunning. You'll be the most beautiful woman at the wedding."

A smile lifted my cheeks. "And you the most handsome."

Tony laughed. "I won't be the oldest, for once."

"I think that at Adelaide's and Oren's age, it's fantastic that they're making it official, after all this time. It's a true love story. Throw in the fact that their children married one another." I shook my head. "Life can be stranger than fiction." I turned back toward the sea, letting the breeze blow my hair and taking in the salty air.

A knock from the suite door caused us both to turn. "Are you expecting any-one?"

"Yes, my dear, our dinner. I thought sitting here, watching the sunset with my wife was better than a crowded restaurant."

"I like the way you think."

I waited as Tony went to the door. Soon he was back with a member of the hotel staff, pushing a linen-covered cart. "What are we having?" I asked.

"You'll see."

"Mrs. Rawlings." The young man nodded, before wiping the glass table, cleaning away the salt residue. Next, he placed two domed dishes on the table followed by settings of silverware and napkins. The last addition was a bottle of red wine. The young man showed the label to Tony who nodded. After unscrewing the cork, he poured a small amount into a glass and handed the glass toward Tony.

Shaking his head, Tony gestured toward me. "Let Mrs. Rawlings decide."

With a grin, I stepped forward, taking the glass by the stem and swirling the contents. The rich aroma filled my senses as I took a sip. "Cabernet, my favorite," I replied, handing the glass back to the young man. "Very good."

"Only the best, ma'am."

That was the way it was with Tony—only the best.

Soon we were alone, seated at the balcony table enjoying seared halibut, roast-ed red potatoes, sautéed green beans, and a side Asian salad. The sky above the surf faded from blue to shades of pink and red as the sun settled below the horizon. Stars glistened above the now darkened water as the waves continued to crash upon the shore.

Tony lifted his wineglass. "To the woman who completed my love story."

My glass met his with a clink. "My knight." I sighed, looking out at the dark-ened sky. "Do you have business tomorrow?" Tomorrow was Friday. The wedding was scheduled for Saturday.

"I'm retired, remember. Nichol is in London representing Rawlings Industries, and Nate is holding down the US side."

I smirked. "I'll ask again. Do you have business tomorrow?"

He nodded. "In the morning. Oren's guest list is too influential not to make some face-to-face contacts. After breakfast, I'm meeting with Donovan Sherman."

"I've heard you talk about him."

"He's young but has an impressive résumé. Lena Montgomery is joining us."

"Are they married?"

"No. Lena is a mutual friend. She has sharp business sense and made a killing in tech—the epitome of a startup success story. I think Rawlings could benefit from a relationship with both Donovan and Lena."

I nodded.

"My dear, what are your plans?"

I shrugged. "Monterey has more boutiques than Iowa."

"Enjoy."

"I'm sure I will. Lorna Murray messaged. We met years ago. She's a friend of Araneae Sparrow." I added the last phrase to spark Tony's memory.

"Sparrow...the institute. And Sterling Sparrow's wife."

I nodded. "That's her. Lorna asked me to meet her, Araneae, and their friends for coffee." I shrugged. "I never pass up coffee."

Tony's cheeks rose. "Most of the time, that's a good decision."

CHAPTER FOUR
Cecilia Ingalls

G REYSON'S TOUCH CAME beneath the blankets as light began to infiltrate the darkness, bringing dawn to a new day. I wiggled as his scratchy cheek came to my neck, and his deep voice sent chills over my flesh.

"I never thought I'd let you back in California," he said, his voice gravelly from sleep.

Rolling toward my husband, I grinned, taking in his protective blue gaze. "That threat is gone."

"That doesn't mean I'll let my guard down."

My eyes closed as Greyson's touch roamed. Sometime during the night, my nightgown had joined Greyson's boxer shorts on the floor. Pressing my breasts against his wide chest I felt wanton need twist within me. It wasn't need due to deprivation, but instead, due to my lust for the man holding me in his grasp.

Greyson's lips captured mine as he rolled us on the big bed. Soon, I was straddling his torso, our lips still attached, as our tongues tasted and twirled. Pushing up from his broad shoulders, I looked lovingly down at the man I'd found, the one who found me. "I think this is exactly where we were last night, before falling asleep."

His grin grew. "What can I say, princess? I love watching you move, as your tits grow heavy, and your pussy squeezes me."

Shaking my head with a smirk, I lifted myself until we were ready to become one. My eyes closed and lips opened as my body sheathed his erection. Arching my back, I relished the stretch within as my knees bent, slowly lowering my body.

"You're fucking amazing." Greyson's praises were ever present, as was his encouragement and love. We'd come together under the most unlikely of circumstances, and yet our devotion, after only a short clandestine relationship, was resilient. In what seemed like a lifetime ago, we'd found love, support, tenderness, and desire, only to have it ripped away.

That time in our history was why Greyson didn't want me in California. However, that incident was years ago, and now the San Diego kingpin was considered a friend, a friend to my grandfather, Lorenzo Dellinger—one of the top men in New York's crime families—and a friend to my husband, the man who took a job that changed our lives forever.

My fingers splayed on Greyson's wide shoulders as I flexed my knees, moving up and down. Our rhythm was steady as Greyson's grasp of my hips tightened. His lips opened, yet his blue eyes stayed focused on me, as the fever within us built.

Beyond the windows, the sky lightened as our hotel suite filled with sounds—primitive noises that echoed through this world for centuries. They were reverberations of pleasure and desire, repeated by both humans and beasts alike. Raw and relentless, the melody signaled the union of bodies and souls. My throat clenched and toes curled as my orgasm built.

Greyson rolled again, my head landing upon the pillow as my long dark hair fanned around my face. My view was spectacular. I found myself mesmerized as my husband's expression contorted and his thrusts came quicker.

Lifting my heels to his ass, I held tight to his neck as Greyson took over. The conductor of all things sexual and sensual, my husband had no hesitation in giving me the reins to lead our journey. At the same time, he was competent and in control, the one who could bring us both ecstasy and highs beyond my wildest dreams.

Perspiration coated our skin as our bodies slapped one against the other.

"Fuck," he growled.

Biting my lip, I succumbed to the release as my body imploded, nerve endings firing at record speed as we panted for air. Greyson's toned torso fell to mine, smashing my breasts, as his warm breath tickled my neck. Holding one another, our breathing settled as our heart rates found their normal cadence.

When Greyson lifted his face, his smile lit the room. "You'd think we'd get tired of that."

"Never," I said, pushing his blond hair away from his forehead. "Forever, that's what we vowed."

Breaking our union, Greyson rolled. Looking up at the ceiling, he said, "I promised your grandfather I'd accompany him on some meetings today."

Turning his way, I nodded. "Tiller?"

"And Costello."

"Why Costello?" I asked, my pulse quickening.

Vincent Costello and my grandfather were both kingpins in New York. They'd worked out their territories a long time ago. Life was—if not peaceful—non-violent. "They could meet in New York."

"In New York there are other eyes. Here they can talk without being seen."

I shook my head. "It seems an unlikely gathering." My grandfather had received a copy of the guest list. "Costello, Sparrow and his men, Tiller, and who knows who else is going to be here. They all have eyes. Everyone is watching."

Looking at my husband, I saw lines of worry around his eyes. "Greyson, are you worried about Grandfather? Darren's here. I know you want him looking after me, but if Grandfather needs him. Surely, Grandfather and Dante have their own protection."

Dante was my uncle and co-vice president of Dellinger Hotels. That didn't mean he didn't dabble in the darker side of our family business.

Greyson's gaze met mine. "Lorenzo's safe. There's protection, and I'd lay down my life for him."

My hand went to his chest. "I don't want that."

"Oh, Cici, I'd lay down my life for you, too."

My thoughts went to our children back in New York. "I don't want you to lay down your life. I need you. I don't care that I'm the vice president of Dellinger Hotels, I'm as equally proud of being your wife and a mother. I need you."

His hand came to my cheek, gently palming my warm skin. "Last night on the plane, Lorenzo confided in me about other guests attending the wedding."

"Is he worried?"

Greyson's nostrils flared as he sat up, moving his feet to the floor.

My gaze scanned the man I loved, as he stood, fully nude, with an erection that hadn't gone away. The defined muscles on his abdomen complemented his wide shoulders and trim waist. With powerful legs, he strode toward the bathroom.

"Greyson," I called.

He reached the bathroom door and turned my way, his blue eyes clouded with concern. "The Ramseses will be here." He closed the door.

Shit.

CHAPTER FIVE
Donovan Sherman

LENA MET ME in the lobby of the hotel. Her short auburn hair swung near her chin. As usual, her makeup and attire were on point. Lena and I had known one another for years—for decades. We'd both come from nothing and worked our way up through the world of high finance. Along that road, we made mistakes. We made more successes—both of us in our own right were accomplished players in this world.

I hadn't made the journey without help.

That was why we were here in Monterey, California. The man who kicked my ass, and then stuck around to point out my failures and successes was throwing a wedding—for his parents. Not really *his* parents. The wedding was for his father and his wife's mother. I wasn't as well versed on their relationship as I was on their individual stories.

Lennox's father was first-generation college and a hard worker who made a worldwide name for himself and his son. He also had some questionable ties to the underworld of New York. Nevertheless, Oren Demetri kept his nose clean and stayed away from legal trouble. In doing so, he built an empire, one that his son, Lennox, now controlled—mostly. Oren Demetri retired in the same way the man Lena and I were about to meet retired. In other words, they couldn't let go.

As for Adelaide Montague, she came from incredible family wealth. In Savannah, Georgia, her family made their fortune in tobacco. After the death of her second husband, with the help of Oren and their children, Adelaide took a more involved role in Montague Corporation. Under Ms. Montague's oversight, the company diversified—a wise thing to do in the day and age of healthy living.

"Are you ready?" I asked, as I laid my hand in the small of Lena's back.

There was nothing sexual between the two of us. Well, there had been, but it wasn't born of love, not the kind that makes your heart beat too fast or palms sweat. That inexplicable attraction was what my grandmother called red sin—a wives' tale she'd told when I was young. I didn't believe red sin existed, until I met the perfect woman—perfect for me. Nearly twenty years my junior, Julia McGrath was everything I desired and everything I didn't know I needed.

As it turned out, there was a lot more to our story—ex-lovers, siblings with a grudge, stock trading and buyouts, and an undeniable connection. Julia once called the happenings a 1980s soap opera. While my knowledge of those shows was limited, I believed she was onto something.

Our journey was complicated at best. The moral of the story was that my heart and soul belonged to Julia. Years of trust, friendship, and mutual admiration defined the woman at my side.

Lena leaned my way, her perfume tickling my senses. Her painted lips parted as she whispered, "Anthony *fucking* Rawlings."

My lips quirked into a grin.

I would like to say that at this stage in my success, I wasn't easily impressed. I could say that. I could also say that currently, I felt a bit like a child about to meet his idol.

In his seventies, Anthony Rawlings still dominated a boardroom, much to his children's chagrin. Anthony had passed the mantle to his two oldest children—

Nichol Rawlings and Nathaniel Rawlings. His youngest daughter was rarely mentioned in news articles regarding Rawlings Industries. It wasn't that she wasn't around. I didn't know her story.

My smile broke through. "I have a car waiting."

A few minutes later, Lena and I were in the back seat as the driver wove around the quaint streets of Monterey. The sun glistened as the streets came to life with patrons, residents, and tourists.

Lena lifted her chin. "I've always enjoyed the West Coast."

"Better than Chicago?"

She laughed. "At one time, I thought Chicago was hell itself."

"Did you hear that Sterling Sparrow, his wife, and his top men are here?"

Lena nodded. "Of course, I heard, Van. Nothing gets past me. I have no beef with Sparrow. Hell, I think he's done a better job than the ones before him. And I've met his wife. She has a great business mind, like someone else we know. How is Julia?"

That was such an open-ended question.

Julia was fucking perfection in every sense of the word. Intelligent while willing and wanting to learn. Beautiful to the core. Yes, that could have two meanings—her pussy was perfect—and she had a stunning soul. Caring and forgiving. Loving and understanding. The universe chose to present her to me on a frozen night, knowing if I'd met her twenty years earlier, I would have fucked it up.

"She's good," I said. "She'll be at the wedding tomorrow."

"Good. We can catch up."

My lips quirked. "Why don't I trust you?"

"You do. That's why we're here. Now tell me what to expect."

"Lennox arranged this meeting. It's more about coffee and networking. There isn't a deal simmering, but instead, the opportunity for the connection when there is."

"Should we be talking to his children?"

I smirked. "Those children are competent adults. They're younger than us, but older than Julia."

"Well…" Lena said with a shrug.

"Lennox is under the impression that Anthony still has the final word in Rawlings Industries. This connection will open doors with Nichol and Nathaniel."

"I met Nichol at a conference. She's sharp—knows her stuff. I've heard she can be cutthroat."

"In other words, you two hit it off."

Lena laughed. "Yes. I find women will support one another until they're given a reason not to. Speaking of women in high finance. Do you know Cecilia Ingalls?"

"Dellinger Hotels." I hadn't met her, but I was aware of the Dellinger name. Their hotels were worldwide.

"Yes. Her grandfather Lorenzo Dellinger is here for the wedding, as well as Cecilia and her husband, Greyson Ingalls."

I shook my head. "I give Lennox and Alexandria credit. They've assembled quite an eclectic group for this celebration. Did you bring a plus-one?"

Lena shook her head. "Too many potential possibilities to be saddled down with a man."

"I can't imagine you saddled, Lena. You're the one holding the reins."

The car came to a stop in front of a small café.

"Are you ready to meet Anthony fucking Rawlings?" I asked.

"Fuck yes."

CHAPTER SIX
Stella McAlister

"THIS IS AMAZING," I said, making a complete spin as I took in the hotel suite. I turned to Jacoby. "I can't believe we're here."

My husband's forehead furrowed. "Me either."

"Oh, come on. It's like spending a weekend in *Glamour Magazine*. The lifestyles of the rich and famous, and we're really here." I shook my head. "You have to admit, it's better than a compound in the Arctic Circle."

"True, but that isn't setting a high bar."

"I find it makes every obstacle in life conquerable. We survived that; we can do anything."

"Okay, let's see if this is really better." Jacoby opened the glass door to the balcony and stepped outside.

As the warm breeze blew my hair and dress, I grinned. "Yep, better."

The reason we'd been invited to this wedding, was because of Jacoby's work. An older woman involved in a smuggling case took a liking to him—I didn't blame her. There were many things to like about my husband. While it was highly unusual for an FBI agent to accept such an invitation, Jacoby received clearance.

His fingers blanched as he gripped the railing and stared out at Monterey Bay.

My hands went to his wide shoulders, squeezing and massaging his tight muscles.

His head rolled back and side to side. "That feels too good to tell you to stop."

After another minute, I let go and turned. With my back to the railing, I crossed my arms over my breasts. "You're stressed about being here. You didn't have to agree."

His nostrils flared as he took a deep breath and stood straight. "We haven't had a vacation in years. Ms. Montague offered to pay for the entire trip—a way to show her appreciation for how the bureau helped Montague Corporation."

"Relax. You cleared it with your superiors."

"It still feels wrong. Agents aren't supposed to accept gifts."

"Then we'll pay her back."

Jacoby reached for my hands and tipped his forehead to mine. "I'm working, Stella. The bureau paid for this."

I took a step back. "You're working?"

He nodded. "Don't look so concerned. We have today to sightsee and the wedding tomorrow. Sunday, we fly home. I'll never leave your side." He scoffed. "Unless that's what you want."

"I don't understand. Why is the bureau paying for"—I spun around—"this fancy of a hotel?"

"Because we're guests at the Montague-Demetri wedding. We'd stand out like sore thumbs if we were staying at a roadside motel." He feigned a grin. "I even have an expense account. Monterey and Carmel have famous boutiques. I say we buy you a new dress."

My stomach twisted. "I don't need a new dress."

"Montague-Demetri."

I grinned. "Okay, I probably need a new dress. What about you?"

"I have my suit. A suit is a suit. You, Stella, should shine like the beautiful beacon you are. I'm sorry you don't have a husband like the other women at this affair. You deserve the best of everything."

My palms framed Jacoby's cheeks. "I have the best. I have you."

"Then let's go hit the shops. Later we can walk on the beach and watch the sunset."

"I'd like that."

As Jacoby started to walk back into the room, I reached for his hand. "Is your work dangerous?"

"In general, or here?"

"I know in general," I said. "Here?"

He shook his head. "We're just guests. Adelaide Montague invited us herself."

"What about her offer to pay?"

"I respectfully declined while accepting the invitation."

"What's your job?"

Jacoby grinned. "To be the best damn husband I can."

My smile grew. "You can't tell me, can you?"

He shook his head.

"I'll have you know, I'm not just some wife, I'm an investigative journalist. Now you have me thinking. I'll figure this out."

"Don't try. Instead, let's enjoy our vacation. Sunday, we fly back to reality."

CHAPTER SEVEN

Lorna Murray

THE BAKERY IN Carmel was famous for its pastries. The line to get in the door was a good indication. "Are you sure you want to wait?" I asked the other ladies.

"Didn't you tell Claire that we'd meet her here?" Araneae asked.

"I did." My stomach twisted at the idea of Claire waiting in line. "Maybe I should have chosen somewhere with reservations."

Marsha's eyes were this way and that, checking out the crowd and the others on the street. Marsha wasn't our only line of defense, not because she needed backup, more because our husbands were protective—overprotective.

"Excuse me. Lorna Murray?" an older gentleman with white hair asked.

"Yes." My gaze went to Marsha.

The other women all quieted as they looked at the man asking my name.

He offered me his hand. "Hello, my name is Phil. Mrs. Rawlings is expecting you. She has a table in the courtyard. Please, follow me."

"I didn't know there was a courtyard," Laurel whispered as we followed Phil around the building. He opened a gate on a tall fence.

As we stepped within, I couldn't help gawking. The courtyard was beautiful with orange pavers and strung lights that illuminated the space at night. There were multiple round tables. Only one had a linen tablecloth. The petite dark-haired woman sitting at the table stood. "Lorna, Araneae. Welcome, everyone."

We all made our way to Claire Rawlings. Her mesmerizing green eyes rivaled my brother's and the ones I saw every day in the mirror. While I knew Claire was older, with her trim fit and welcoming smile, she hid it well.

After a quick hug and introductions, we all took our seats.

"Ladies," Phil said, "if you'll let me know what you'd like from the bakery, I'll be happy to pass along your orders."

I smiled at Claire. "Thank you. You saved us from waiting in that line out front."

"Good, more time for you to enjoy Monterey."

"Are you familiar with this area?"

"Oh, a long time ago, I lived north, in Palo Alto."

"I love the West Coast," Laurel said, "especially Northern California."

"It's beautiful," Claire said. "Araneae, tell me all the wonderful things you're doing at the Sparrow Institute." She lifted the edge of a beautiful scarf she had tied around her neck. "And I must admit, I'm addicted to Sinful Threads."

Araneae grinned. "I think that's one of this season's releases."

"It is."

Araneae turned to Laurel and Madeline. "Let me tell you more about Dr. Laurel Pierce and Madeline Kelly. Not only are they friends and great people, but Dr. Pierce works at the institute. She has a lab there, and in the future, I believe she'll have promising results to share."

"Oh, I'm intrigued."

"And this is Madeline. She's the institute's intake coordinator and oversees volunteers. The institute wouldn't make it a day without her." She smiled Marsha's way. "Marsha is a help in all things."

That wasn't exactly the whole story on Marsha. She took her job with Sparrow seriously. And we knew, without a doubt, we were safe on her watch.

A few workers from the bakery entered the courtyard carrying cups and plates.

Another woman came with a large platter of assorted pastries. "Ladies, we're honored to have you here." She gestured toward the platter. "If you run out of anything or want more, please let us know."

For the next hour, we sat, drank delicious coffee, and filled ourselves with phenomenal pastries. "This is definitely off diet," Claire said as she sipped her coffee.

"Whatever your diet is," Madeline said, "I want to know."

"Oh, you don't need a diet. You're beautiful."

Pink filled Madeline's cheeks.

The truth was that Madeline was beautiful inside and out. Life hadn't always gone her way. At one time, she'd been in the center of a Russian Bratva. Today she was seated with the wife of one of the top businessmen in the world and surrounded by friends.

I guess I could say the same for me—life hadn't always gone my way.

Born into poverty, life had thrown me curveballs.

I swung.

And with the help of the people I love and who love me, I hit a homerun.

"Will you join us at the boutiques?" Araneae asked Claire.

"I believe my husband's meeting will be done soon." Her emerald eyes shimmered. "It's not often I get him out of the house. I think there's a beach waiting for a stroll." She smiled. "I'll see you tomorrow at the wedding."

We all stood. Leaning in, I gave Claire a hug. "Thank you for this secluded area. Our husbands will be thrilled."

"I've learned that husbands worry because they love. Your husbands' concern is because they love you."

"If concern is the meter," I said, looking at my friends, "our husbands' love is off the charts."

After saying goodbye to Claire, with Marsha at our side, and more Sparrows in the shadows, the four of us walked the sidewalks of Monterey. Together we visited boutiques and purchased some must-haves, including gifts for the children back home.

CHAPTER EIGHT

Emma Ramses

STANDING IN FRONT of the full-length mirror, I secured the diamond drop earrings. My hair was up in an elaborate hairdo with curls dangling behind my head. The black satin Sinful Threads dress was alluring, yet modest enough for a formal wedding. My heart raced at the sight of the man behind me. Turning, I grinned.

Rett grinned, catching me gawking. "Mrs. Ramses. Do you approve of what you see?"

At the moment, my husband was fully nude, his body and hair damp from the shower. I undoubtedly approved. I was also a bit envious. That jealously didn't stem from his toned muscular body or long and thick appendage. While they were part of him, they were also mine for the taking. I didn't even mind his ability to dominate a room—I was rather partial to it.

My envy was that I'd spent an hour at the spa, two hours at the salon, and another hour getting into my long dress and tweaking my hair. Rett had been at another meeting this morning—I'd lost count of how many he'd had since arriving to California—and gotten back to the hotel in time to shower and dress.

It wasn't fair that he'd look incredibly sexy and dapper with twenty minutes' preparation.

My grin grew as my husband stalked toward me. His dark stare shone as he moved closer. In his gaze I had the sense of being prey. That's what I was, prey to the predator who had me in his sights. "I do. I approve."

"Are you ready for me?"

I smirked. "If you mess up my hair or this dress after all I've done to look presentable for this wedding, you're in trouble."

"I am?" he asked, his tenor lowering, causing my nipples to bead.

Ignoring my body's physical reaction, I nodded. "Yes."

Rett gently reached for my chin and brought his lips to mine. Heat radiated from his touch as my breath mingled with his. His cologne mixed with my perfume; his smooth, freshly shaved cheeks caressed my own. In only a few seconds, my resolve melted. That's what Rett did to me and had done since our first encounter.

Everett Ramses was the flame to my candle. His blaze left me melted much like a puddle of wax. Despite my declaration, my body continued its traitorous ways as my core twisted.

When Rett pulled away, he said, "Tell me more about this trouble I'm in."

"Yeah." I sighed. "You're lucky I can redo my lipstick."

"Emma, you're stunning." He took a step back, his laser focus moving over my body, sending heat to the skin hidden beneath the fabric. "Forget that. You're spectacular."

"Tonight, after the wedding."

Rett tilted his head.

"I'll be ready then."

My husband grinned. "Out of respect for your pampering, I accept that answer."

My lips came together and brow lengthened.

"Oh, Emma, if you want me to keep my hands off you, don't give me that defiant smirk. It makes me want you more."

"You have me, Rett. Do you know the Demetris well?"

Rett shrugged as he went to the dresser and found a pair of silk boxers. "I know the Costellos. They're Lennox's mother's family. The world is rather small—our world."

"Do the Costellos do what you do?"

"Yes, in New York."

"I thought the Dellingers ran New York."

"It's a big area."

Thinking about the wedding, I said, "I think it's fabulous that Oren and Adelaide are marrying at their age."

A smile came to his firm lips. "I think it's evidence that you can't fight love's attraction—gravity wins."

"Gravity?"

"Yes, it pulls you close, holds you in its orbit, and no matter how you try, you can't resist it."

Stepping into his tuxedo pants, Rett slipped a starched white shirt over his broad shoulders. "That's you, Emma."

"What is me?"

"Whether you're dressed up like tonight or naked on your knees, you're my queen, New Orleans' queen, and I'm hopelessly drawn to you."

His deep tenor and loving words had me in the same state—drawn to him.

With Rett wearing his tuxedo, he opened a long jewelry box. "I brought this for you."

My eyes opened wide. "It's your mother's ruby necklace."

He walked behind me and placed the heavy gems around my neck. Closing the clasp, he lowered his lips to my neck. "For my queen." Holding on to my waist and peering over my shoulder, he spoke to our reflection. "In case you have any other ideas, Mrs. Ramses, your dance card is full. All of your dances are taken."

I spun and looked up into his brown eyes. "Forever and always." My thoughts went back to dances we'd shared in our suite, the courtyard of our home, and in public, with eyes upon us. "There's no one's arms I'd rather be in."

Rett took a deep breath. "Before we go, I need to tell you something."

I sensed something in his voice. "Is something wrong?"

"There's no way to sugarcoat this. Your brother and his wife will be at the wedding."

CHAPTER NINE
Lennox Demetri

"**M**R. DEMETRI, EVERYTHING is set," Rae Watson said. "The guests are being directed to the Tertian Lounge. It's a lovely place, for our most special guests. There are hors d'oeuvres and we have a full bar with only premium labels. Our best staff is there to serve. When the wedding is ready to start, I'll direct everyone to the balcony."

The director of services was younger than Charli and I imagined by speaking to her over the phone, but her competence was clear. She had everything for the wedding under control.

"Thank you, Rae."

Before going upstairs to the lounge, I went back to the groom's dressing room. Turning the knob and pushing the door inward, I found my father and other family members including Dominic. My son was dapper in a tuxedo matching Dad's and mine.

"Is this conversation suitable for my son? Or should he stay with me to greet guests," I asked.

"I want to stay here, Dad. Uncle Vincent is telling stories about when Grandpa was young."

My gaze met my father's.

He lifted his hands. "PG, son. I promise."

My concern wasn't sexual inappropriateness. It was excessive violence that my son wasn't ready to learn. At this point in his young life, he didn't need to know about Vincent's world.

My uncle went to the highboy and poured a finger of bourbon. Handing the tumbler my direction, he said, "Lennox, a toast to your father."

There were powerful people assembling in the Tertian Lounge. One could argue there were powerful people in this room as well. Nodding, I took the glass. My cousin Luca lifted his tumbler, Vincent his, and finally Dad.

"Just a moment," Vincent said. Setting his glass down, he took another tumbler from the tray, opened the refrigerator, and removed a diet soda. He looked my way. When I nodded, my uncle smiled. After pouring some of the soda into the new glass, he handed it to Dominic. "You're a Costello. Your great-grandfather would be proud that you're here with your mother and father, supporting your grandparents."

Dominic's eyes opened wide, taking in his great-uncle, as he took the tumbler.

Vincent lifted his glass. "Oren, it takes a good man to find love twice in one lifetime. May God bless you and Adelaide and allow you many more years of happiness, surrounded by family."

Drinking the strong liquid, I wouldn't admit that hearing my uncle's toast made my vision blur.

It was the damn salt air.

When I was younger, I viewed the world through a narrow lens. Now I understood that my father loved my mother. Their story was happy and sad, but through it all, there was love. Losing her was a hardship on all of us—Silvia, Dad, and me.

As I aged, my view of the world broadened. I also found love for the second time in my life, and through the years, our family came together. Putting down the glass, I spread my arms. Hugging my father, I patted his back. "You and Adelaide deserve only the best."

"We have the best, son. We're blessed. I'm just damn happy I convinced that woman to finally take my name." He laughed. "Hardest negotiation of my life." He looked at Dominic. "Never give up, my boy. Never give up."

I took a deep breath. "I'm headed up to the Tertian Lounge, your guests are arriving."

"Let the festivities begin," Vincent said.

I made my way down the hallway toward the grand entrance.

"Lennox."

Turning, I saw an old friend. "Donovan."

There was a new quality evident in his smile. Donovan Sherman was always confident and was now successful, but through it all, there was something he lacked. In only a glance, I saw what was no longer missing—the woman at his side.

I bowed. "You must be Julia."

Dressed in a long golden dress, the young woman at Donovan's side was lovely. More than that, she radiated the qualities I'd seen in Donovan years ago—confidence and determination. From what I'd learned, her family was involved in pharmaceuticals. Together these two were a power couple in the making.

Julia offered me her hand. "It's nice to meet you, Lennox."

"I must introduce you to Charli."

Her head tilted.

"My wife. Sorry, Alexandria."

"I'd like that."

I patted Donovan's shoulder. "Damn wedding. I wanted more time to talk shop."

"We'll figure it out," he said. "Thank you for arranging the meeting with Anthony."

"Did it go well?"

"I'd say yes."

"Then it wasn't a wasted trip."

"Not wasted," Julia said, "we're about to attend a wedding."

"Speaking of which, follow me."

I held my breath as we approached the lounge. The din of conversation and background music filled my ears. To my delight, people were mingling, holding drinks, or standing by tall tables, eating and chatting.

No guns were drawn.

No confrontations were happening.

Beyond the wall of windows, the sun glistened on the sea all the way out to the horizon. On the balcony were rows of chairs decorated with white bows, blowing in the sea breeze.

"Lennox."

I turned to Anthony Rawlings. "Thank you for coming." I bowed to his wife, stunning in an emerald gown. "Mrs. Rawlings. Thank you for getting him to leave Iowa."

She grinned. "We wouldn't stay away. I'm sorry our children couldn't make it."

"Congratulations on the upcoming grandchild."

"Thank you."

I noticed a couple standing near the windows. Taking a breath, I excused myself and walked to them. "Agent McAlister."

The gentleman turned my way. "Tonight, it's Jacoby." He turned to the woman at his side. Beautiful in a long shiny gray dress. "This is my wife, Stella. Stella, this is Lennox Demetri."

She offered me her hand. "Mr. Demetri."

"Thank you for being here. Adelaide wanted you to come."

"That's why we're here," Jacoby said.

Across the room, I saw Everett Ramses. With his wife holding his arm, they were coming my way. After saying goodbye to the McAlisters, I met the Ramseses in the middle. "Thank you for coming." I bowed to the beautiful golden-haired woman wearing a black evening gown. "Mrs. Ramses."

"Emma, please. We're honored to be here."

The conversation grew louder as more people joined the room. The three in our group turned, seeing Sterling Sparrow and his wife, followed by his top men and their wives.

"Excuse us," Everett said, making his way to Sterling.

The smile on Sterling's face eased a bit of my concern.

I joined the two couples. "Do you two know one another?"

Sterling was the one to answer. "Mr. Ramses was an invaluable help to me a while back. I'll never forget your kindness."

Everett's gaze scanned the other members of the Sparrows. "Is she with you?"

Sterling nodded, before reaching for a woman's elbow.

With dark hair similar to Sterling's, she turned, her green eyes smiling. "Yes?"

"Madeline," Sterling said, "let me introduce you to Everett Ramses and our host, Lennox Demetri."

"Madeline," I said. "Welcome. You're married to Patrick Kelly."

She grinned. "I am. Thank you for having us." She turned to Everett. "New Orleans."

It wasn't a question, but Everett nodded.

"Thank you," she said.

Everett turned to his wife and back to Madeline. "Sometimes the road to happiness isn't straight."

"You're right," Madeline replied, "but it's worth the journey."

I caught sight of the newest arrivals.

Lorenzo Dellinger was the first of his party to enter. His granddaughter, Cecilia Ingalls, was next, holding the arm of her husband. I took a breath as the air shifted beside me. Though Everett's unease wasn't visible, it was present.

Before anything was said, Maxwell Tiller came forward, boisterously greeting the Dellingers.

"I should welcome our new guests," I said, excusing myself from the two kingpins and making my way to two others.

Only my father.

Shaking hands with Tiller, Dellinger, and both Ingallses, I welcomed them to the wedding.

Mrs. Ramses came up behind me, her expression noticeably tense. "Kyle."

"Emma." Mr. Ingalls smiled. "It's good to see you."

Everett was a step behind his wife.

Greyson's gaze went to Everett.

Before either one could address the another, Lorenzo Dellinger spoke. "Mrs. Ramses, how is your amazing mother?"

I turned to a tap on my shoulder.

"Mr. Demetri, it's time for the wedding to start."

CHAPTER TEN

Adelaide Montague Demetri

"**M**OMMA, YOU LOOK beautiful," Alexandria said, fussing with my hair. "Grandma," Angi said, looking up with her father's blue eyes. "Mom's right. You do."

Janie nodded, holding tight to her flower girl's basket.

I turned to Jane. "You're a guest. Go to your husband and be a guest."

Jane spread her arms, wrapping me in an embrace. When she pulled away, her big brown eyes glistened. "It's been quite a journey, Miss Adelaide." Her smile grew. "You being happy. Praise the Lord."

I grinned. "Jane, you beat me to the altar. Both of us happy. Miracles do happen."

"When you find a good man, you need to snatch him up."

"I found a good one."

"Yes, you sure did."

I turned again toward the mirror, taking in my cream-colored dress. It wasn't long, and I didn't have a veil. The satin material shimmered under the lights, and my pumps matched the dress. Alexandria's and Silvia's dresses were similar styles in a shade of light gray. I reached for Oren's daughter's cheek. "Thank you for being here, Silvia. He loves you and so do I."

Silvia smiled. "Oren is blessed to have found you." She looked around, her smile dimming. "This is the family she wanted."

The *she* Silvia was referring to was Angelina—her and Nox's mother. The reference to Angelina didn't make me sad. In a way, I believed we had her blessing, that she was smiling down on us and filled with joy as Lennox and Silvia found love and Lennox and Alexandria filled her home with children.

"I believe Angelina is smiling," I said.

"Me too."

Next, I reached for my daughter's cheek. "You're beautiful. You kept me going, Alexandria. Thank you. If it weren't for you, I wouldn't have made my way back to Oren."

"Momma, you're a force. With Oren, you've been able to soar. He loves you."

"I love him too. I think I have since we met. I was afraid to love back then. I was still afraid to love when he saved me. I had my own demons to slay. The greatest gifts Oren has given me are peace, safety, and comfort. He's my gravity. He keeps me steady, loving me without demands, listening and helping when I ask. I didn't know men like him existed."

"They do, Mom. I know two of them." She smiled. "Are you ready?"

I looked at Silvia and down at the girls. "Angi and Janie, are you ready for Grandpa and Grandma's wedding?"

"Yes," came loudly in unison.

Silvia reached for my hand. "Be happy."

Nodding. I sighed. "I guess we're ready."

When we opened the door, Rae was waiting for us in the hallway. "You're beautiful, Ms. Montague."

My cheeks rose. "I guess I'll need to get used to Demetri."

"It's not that hard," Alexandria joked.

By the time we reached the top floor, the lounge where the prewedding festivities were held was quiet. Through the tall windows, the chairs were filled with guests, and beyond, the afternoon sun sparkled like diamonds on the sea.

From our angle I recognized many of the guests.

Preston and Gwen, my brother and sister-in-law from my second husband were here, along with their son, Patrick, and his husband, Cy. Jane and her husband were seated toward the front, as were the Costellos. I also recognized the McAlisters, Ramseses, Sparrows, Rawlingses, Tiller, Ingallses, Dellingers, Montgomery, and Shermans...

"There are so many people," I whispered.

"They're all here because of you and Oren."

Rae led Janie to the doorway as the music began. I grinned as she walked as we'd practiced. One step—throw a petal. One step—throw a petal.

"Hurry up, Janie," Angi called.

"Shush," Alexandria scolded. "Your turn is coming." My daughter grinned. "Was I ever that demanding?"

"We won't talk about that right now."

Angi was next, followed by Silvia.

Alexandria kissed my cheek. "I love you, Momma. You've been strong because of you."

I watched as she passed through the doorway.

Finally, it was my turn.

Standing in the doorway, my focus went to the end of the aisle.

My heart was full as I took in my family, standing at the altar, waiting for me—Oren, Alexandria, Lennox and their children, and Silvia.

Never could I have imagined having what we shared today—family and friends who loved us and were willing to share in our special occasion with wishes for a bright future.

Dreams did come true.

At the altar, I handed Alexandria my bouquet. Oren reached for my hands. Staring into his blue gaze, I saw the man I'd met decades earlier. Time flashed as images through my memory. Every moment of joy was because of him and the loved ones standing with us.

When the officiant asked me to repeat after him, I did. "I, Adelaide, take you, Oren, to be my wedded husband, and I promise to always be your truest and best friend. I vow to support and respect you, to be patient and gracious toward you, to work together jointly with you as we strive to live and love. I promise to accept you fully and unconditionally and to share my life with you and our family from now until forever."

AND THEY LIVED HAPPILY EVER AFTER.

Sometimes all we need is gravity to help us realize that our dreams in those we love.

✧ ✧ ✧

Oren and Adelaide are married!

Thank you for joining them. In lieu of a gift, please tell others about this anthology. As peace was found with the coming together of my worlds, may peace come to Ukraine and the world we share. ~ Aleatha

Do you know the characters in this story? You can read the Demetris, Oren's story, the Rawlingses and more on Aleatha's website.
www.aleatharomig.com/books-by-aleatha

JUST ONE SPARK

CARLY PHILLIPS

Note: This stand-alone scene takes place nine months before Just One Dare.

DASH KINGSTON STEPPED off the stage at the last concert of The Original Kings U.S. Tour in Santa Clara, California. He was a long way from East Hampton, New York, and so ready to get home to his wife. The last few times they'd talked on the phone, Cassidy had sounded off, and when he'd asked her to join him for the last couple of shows, she said she'd been tied up at the production company where she worked. But Cassidy was never moody, and she micromanaged like a pro, so Dash was uneasy. Then again, she was supposed to be here for their final night on stage but the film she was working on was running long and she couldn't get away.

Sweat dripped from his hair and his t-shirt stuck to his body. The band followed him down the hall, heading into their dressing room. Surrounding them were their crew, who were pumped from the success of the six-month tour. They'd started in Europe and ended back home, on the West Coast. Normally post-show, they'd debrief and discuss what had gone right or wrong, but tonight, Jagger, the guitarist, Mac, the bassist, and Axel, the drummer, wanted nothing more than to head to the party they'd decided to throw in Mac's hotel suite.

"Dash, are you showing your face at the after-party tonight?" Mac asked, grabbing his things.

Dash had already gotten his shit together and was ready to leave. They needed to get out of the stadium before the bus was swarmed. "Hell, no. I want to shower and head out. I can't wait to get on the plane. Will any of you guys be on the flight?" Linc had sent the Kingston business plane for them, and Dash intended to be on it. He was more than ready to go.

"Hell, no. I've got pussy waiting," Jagger said, laughing.

Dash rolled his eyes. "Asshole," he muttered. "Everyone good to walk out now?"

After muttered affirmations and nods, Dash swung the door open and tipped his head at their security guard. The bulky man led them to the bus, pushing screaming fans out of the way. Once on board, Dash sat back in his seat, shutting out the joking and talk of getting laid. Because the only woman he wanted surrounding his dick was across the damned country.

Once he was back in his hotel suite, he locked the door and took a shower, then tried to FaceTime Cassidy to let her know he was leaving for the plane. But she didn't pick up, which, again, was unusual. She knew his schedule and always made it a point to be around after a concert.

His girl wasn't jealous and she trusted him. But she knew what he'd been like B.C. *Before Cass.*

She liked to talk to him before he turned in for the night. And he needed to see her face. A post-concert video chat usually led to some phone sex, which would hold him over until he had her in his arms again. It was way more than enough.

For years, he'd taken advantage of what the groupies offered—free pussy in whatever city or town the band played. He'd enjoyed it...until he hadn't. His brothers and sister had started to settle down and his own restlessness had kicked in.

The night he met Cassidy, a stalker who'd been terrorizing his sister-in-law—the famous actress, Sasha Keaton, now Kingston—had gone after Cassidy by mistake. Dash had looked into her dazed green eyes and his life had never been the same.

Not that he'd realized it immediately. They'd spent one night together and he'd panicked. The sex had been *that* good. Genius that he was, he'd bailed before she woke up. Then a near-baby scare with a woman he didn't remember had almost derailed his future. Still, even though he'd been an asshole, Cassidy had stepped up and helped save his reputation. He'd fallen for her in the process.

And now he couldn't wait to get home.

He packed up his clothes, grabbed the shit he'd spread out on the bathroom counter, and left his room. The same bodyguard who'd walked them into the hotel was waiting for him in the hall, just in case any determined fans had managed to breach their defenses. Dash made it to the bus without incident, and before long, he was at the private airport, greeting the pilot as he climbed on board.

"Jimmy, my man, ready to take me home?" he asked the fifty-year-old pilot he'd known for five years.

"Always, Dash."

Dash smiled. He'd drummed the "Mr. Kingston" out of Jimmy's mouth early on, though it reappeared every now and then. Unlike his more formal oldest sibling, Linc, Dash preferred the more casual approach.

"After takeoff, I'm going to the bedroom to crash," he told the pilot.

The other man nodded. "You might want to put your case in the room first. I know you like to keep your guitar with you." He pointed to the case in Dash's hand.

Dash laughed. "Thank you, Jim."

He walked through the plane and past the seats. Though they were comfortable, he couldn't wait to lie down. He opened the door to the small bedroom and came to a stop. His wife lay on top of the mattress wearing a barely there black lingerie camisole top. Triangular scraps of lace covered her breasts, pushing up two luscious mounds of flesh. Her long blond hair flowed over her shoulders and light gloss covered her pouty lips.

She leaned against the fabric headboard, one leg bent, another stretched out and slightly parted, giving him a view of the pussy he could spend hours devouring.

"Surprise!" she said with a wide smile.

"Holy fuck, Cass. What are you doing here?" He placed his guitar on the floor and kicked the door shut behind him.

"Can't a girl visit her husband after a very long couple of weeks?" she asked in a sultry voice.

He turned to the door.

"Dash! Where are you going?" she asked.

"To tell Jimmy there's no rush to take off." The urgency he'd felt had been to get to Cassidy. But she was here. Thank God.

She laughed. "Already taken care of. Don't you realize I planned this surprise?"

He turned back to her and walked to the bed, yanking at the back collar of his shirt and dumping the tee onto the floor. Feeling her eyes on him, his cock grew hard and thick. Not even undoing the button on his jeans released the pressure.

He pulled the jeans off his hips and legs and his dick sprung free. Then he kicked off his shoes, and shucked the jeans before diving onto the bed.

"You went commando," Cassidy said, laughing as he pulled her into his arms.

"Damn, I missed you." He sealed his mouth over hers and kissed her hard.

Their tongues slid against each other, tangling together, matching one another's breaths. He delved deep and thrust his tongue in and out, fucking her mouth the same way he intended to take her body.

Her fingers grasped his shoulders, her nails digging deep.

Slowing things down, he lifted his head and softened the kiss. "It's been too damned long."

"I know," she said through kiss-swollen lips. "That's why I'm here."

"Is that why you haven't sounded like yourself the last couple of days?" He studied her with concern, making sure nothing was wrong.

She nodded. "I'm not good at keeping secrets." She shrugged and gave him a sheepish grin. "At least none of your family blabbed. Good surprise, right?"

He grinned, his hand sliding down to cup her full breast. "The best. But I would have been home in six hours. You didn't need to make the round trip," he said, toying with her nipple, teasing it with his fingers.

She let out a soft groan. "I thought this would be more fun. Besides, I couldn't wait."

"I'm so fucking glad you didn't."

✧   ✧   ✧

CASSIDY LOOKED AT the man adored by women around the world and still marveled that he'd chosen her. Tours took him away—this was the second one the band had done since she and Dash had gotten together—but she trusted him. They'd worked hard to get to this point and she believed him when he told her he loved her. She believed in him.

He pushed down the straps of her cami and she shook her head. "Let me take it off." She lifted the silk from the bottom and drew it over her head, shaking out her hair when it caught in the garment.

He watched, his blue eyes growing dark as she revealed her breasts, then with a groan, he dipped his head and pulled her nipple into his mouth. He sucked and teased the tight bud, pausing to graze it with his teeth and sensation shot from her breast to her clit.

"Oh, God." He flicked his tongue back and forth, teasing her until she wasn't sure which part of her needed him more.

Her hips bucked and he placed his hand over her belly, holding her down. Then he released her nipple from between his lips with a pop and slid his hand between her thighs, rubbing her sex with his roughened finger.

"Dash, please. I need you inside me." Her hips jerked against the press of his palm.

He reached over her, opening the nightstand drawer and pulling out a condom. With all the Kingston men coupled up, Cassidy could imagine how much action went on in this bed. She shook that thought away—because eew!—just as Dash rose to his knees and rolled the condom over his straining erection.

"You're ready for me?" he asked, sliding his finger through her wet folds once more.

"Always." He braced his hands on either side of her head and nudged his cock into her.

She met his gaze and was lost in the sea of blue, the warmth in his expression, and the tight set of his jaw. He slid into her in one smooth glide, filling her completely.

"You're my world," he said, before pulling out and slamming back in, setting a demanding rhythm that let her know just how much he loved and needed her.

She felt every ridge, every inch as he took her hard and deep. Before long, she was digging her nails into his shoulders and crying out words she barely recognized. She bent her legs and arched her hips, needing more of him.

"Harder," she said, meeting him thrust for thrust.

Dash always gave her what she needed and he pounded into her. Soon she crested and soared, waves of pleasure crashing over her, pulling her under. Seconds later, he stiffened, his climax hitting him as he groaned, and called out her name.

He collapsed against her, his breathing rough in her ear. He didn't stay long, though, taking his weight off her and allowing her to pull in short breaths.

"Shit," he muttered.

"What's wrong?"

"Condom broke." He rose from the bed and walked over to the small bathroom.

She swallowed hard. They'd been together for a little over three years but she had issues with the pill, problems with an IUD, and instead of trying a shot, they'd just agreed to use condoms.

He returned to the bed with a washcloth and helped her clean up. He left it on the nightstand and turned to her. "Sorry, Cass."

She faced him and gathered her courage. "Is it bad that I'm not?"

He propped himself up beside her. "You're ready for kids?" He reached out and curled her hair around his finger, his calm demeanor telling her he wasn't upset either. She breathed a little more easily.

"I wouldn't have thought about it if this hadn't happened, but the tour is over and you're going to be around for a while. I know you and the guys were talking about pushing off the next one." She bit down on the inside of her cheek as she let the idea roll around her head. "I wouldn't mind a little mini-you running around." She eyed him warily.

His smile was all she needed. "I'd rather have a mini-you."

She placed her hand on his chest and laughed. "Does this mean we'll see what happens with this oops? Or are we going to try?" she asked, holding her breath. Because now that they'd talked about it, she wanted their child more than anything.

"I get to come inside you bare? Then we're trying for a baby." His eyes danced with amusement.

"Dash!"

He shook his head. "I shouldn't joke about it. I want a family with you more than anything," he said, rolling her over and sliding right back into her.

She moaned and captured his lips in a long kiss before pulling back. "Sounds like the perfect plan to me."

❖   ❖   ❖

Check out the entire Kingston Family including Dash and Cassidy's story in Just One Spark here.

www.carlyphillips.com/bookspage/kingston-family

Love You the Most

Carian Cole

Dear Reader,

Thank you so much for purchasing this anthology to help support the people of Ukraine.

My contribution to the anthology is a selection of bonus chapters for my book *Torn*. Although *Torn* was published in 2015, Toren and Kenzi have continued to be my readers' most beloved characters. Even if you haven't read *Torn*, you can still enjoy these bonus chapters, and I hope this glimpse into their love story intrigues you enough to read their original novel. These bonus chapters will also serve as the beginning of a full-length sequel for Tor and Kenzi, which will be published at a later date.

I'm sending you my heartfelt gratitude for supporting this project.

With love,
Carian Cole

CHAPTER ONE

Kenzi

My love,
Walk in the rain with me. Kiss me in the misty fog.
Let me hold you all night under the hush of the wind.
I'm waiting for you. Throwing pennies. making wishes.
I'm wishing only for you. Always for you.
Come back to me.
I'll fight for you. I'll fight for us.
Wish for me, too…and I'll make it come true.

✧   ✧   ✧

THE FRAYED PARCHMENT paper is soft in my fingers, perfectly worn and aged, and I'm very aware that he chose this texture of paper, this color of ink, with careful consideration. Because he knows how much it means to me. Because he knows me. Like no one else ever has or ever could.

I read his words over and over again; long after I have them memorized and they're burned into my heart and soul, yet I still hold the handwritten note and stare at the words until they blur. I can hear his voice saying them—deep, yet soft and sensual. *Raw.*

I like touching the paper that I know he held in his hands. The hands that had once held me. Caressed me. Ignited passion and desire in me so deep that I still can't forget.

And I don't ever want to.

The faint scent of his cologne drifts from the paper. Or maybe I've just wished for it so much that I've imagined it. Either way, it's comforting and stirs memories. *So many memories…*

Reading his words, all the feelings rush back like acid on a wound that won't heal. He's my other half, the one who makes my heart beat. The man who makes me feel every feeling that could possibly be felt—and then some. The man who held me and loved me through almost every moment of my life. I have no past without him, no future without him. Quite simply, he is my world. There's no way I will ever move on from a love like ours. We belong to each other. I've always known it, and I am utterly exhausted from fighting it, denying it, keeping myself from it, and hiding it—as I'm sure he must be too.

And now after the silence…he still loves me. He still believes in us, and his words assure me he's willing to take on the world for me. For us.

It's time for me to go back home to my love and to my heart. Time is precious, and I don't want to give any more up.

I lift the lid of the small antique wooden trunk on my desk and pull out a sheet of sky-blue paper and my favorite rose gold calligraphy pen.

Tor, my love…

My wishes have always been, and always will be, for you.

I'm coming home with a clear mind and a strong heart. We'll fight our battles together from now on.

I love you. I've loved you in so many different ways, and I want to continue to love you in all the beautiful ways we've yet to discover. I refuse to hide anymore. If there are some who cannot accept our age difference then that is their choice, but I will not let their thoughts keep me from being with you—the love of my life. All I ask is that we tread gently with my father, as his heart is just as precious to me as yours is. I know you feel the same.

I will call you as soon as I'm settled in my new place. I cannot wait to be in your arms, and I promise we will never be apart again.

I love you the most,
Kenzi

I fold the letter into an envelope, write Tor's address on it, and slip it into the mailbox on the corner. On my way back to the inn, I walk down the beach to the water's edge, and I toss in the penny that Tor sent with his note.

I wish for all the things that would heal our hearts and give us—and everyone we love—a happily ever after.

CHAPTER TWO
Kenzi

MY UPPER ARM stings and throbs as I leave the tattoo shop, but the pain was *so* worth it. Lukas did an amazing job—the design came out even better than I'd envisioned. For the past four hours I sat as still as I could, babbling his ear off in an attempt to distract myself from the burn of the needle while he worked his magic. Lukas—my dad's youngest cousin—is known as much for his kindness and patience as he is for his brilliant, ultrarealistic tattoo work. And now I understand why.

Lukas refused to let me pay him, even though I've been saving up for months. *"Consider it a belated birthday gift,"* he'd said with a smile before he disappeared behind the black velvet curtain that screened his work area.

"Don't worry about it. He never charges family," Rayne assured me from her post at the reception desk where she's effortlessly braiding a thin purple scarf into her long dark hair. She's my dad's sister, which also makes her my aunt. She's twenty-one years old, a little more than a year older than me.

Welcome to my strange, but very blessed, life.

I head toward the parking lot with my keys in one hand and my phone in the other, scanning the text messages I missed while getting my tattoo. My best friend, Chloe, has sent me a photo of her new bob cut—which looks adorable—and my dad has sent two messages asking how my tattoo appointment went.

I tap out a reply to my father and then *BAM*—I run straight into something solid in the middle of the sidewalk.

Or some*one*, to be more accurate.

My keys and phone hit the ground. I bend down to pick them up and my purse falls off my shoulder, spilling its contents because I never snap it closed. Three pens scatter. A rabbit-head Pez dispenser bounces to the side and coughs up a pink rectangle candy. A tube of glittery lip gloss rolls across the sidewalk until the tip of a large black leather boot stops it. The owner of said boot kneels in front of me and gathers up my belongings.

"Shit," he mutters. "Sorry. My bad. I wasn't paying attention."

His deep voice penetrates through flesh and bone and settles around my heart like a cat cozying up to a fire. A rush of warmth spreads through my chest. I peek through the curtain of my blonde hair, and my breath catches in the hollow of my throat.

"Neither was I," I whisper.

He visibly swallows. "Kenzi..."

"Tor." His name rides the breath I'd been holding. Much to my parents' dismay, it was my first word as a baby. I wonder how many times I've said his name since then. It must be thousands. Possibly millions. It's still my favorite word, my favorite name, my favorite everything.

He is my favorite everything.

Our eyes lock together, exchanging telepathic messages in a way we've been able to do for the past nineteen years. *I missed you so much. I love you. Am I dreaming? Don't ever leave me again.*

He stands and holds his hand out, pulling me up to my feet. With a racing heart, I shove my things into my purse and comb my hand through my hair as I take him in. How is it possible that he keeps getting more attractive with age? He looks absolutely deliciously sinful. His black T-shirt is tight across his arms and chest. The thin material does nothing to hide the fact that he's been working out hardcore again. His dark hair is shorter than it was the last time I saw him, but it still reaches the top of his broad shoulders.

"I had no idea you were in town already," he says. My body hums to life under the gaze of his soulful, hooded eyes that are now dark, serious, and slightly troubled. Butterflies awaken and stir in my stomach.

How can he be as familiar to me as my own reflection, but at the same time feel so breathtakingly new and exciting?

"I moved back here about a month ago. I'm living with Rayne." I point back to the tattoo shop. "That's why I'm here. She works for Lukas, and I had to drop something off for her." Lying isn't a habit of mine, but I don't want him to know about my tattoo yet.

He nods, still holding my gaze. "I was just heading there for my appointment."

I smile at the memories of trailing my lips and fingertips over all his tattoos while making love under the veil of his soft bed sheets. Tingles buzz in my thighs and shoot up my spine.

"I'm surprised you have any open skin left to ink," I tease.

"We're working on my legs now." He pauses and I catch the slight tick of movement above his cheek. It would go unnoticed by a stranger, but I know his jaw is clenching involuntarily with stress or worry—something that started when his father passed away many years ago. "How have you been?" he asks.

I can read Tor like a well-loved book. He's wondering why I didn't call him the moment I was back in town. I wanted to. It's been nothing short of torture to be just a few miles away from him and not go see him, wrap myself around him like a ribbon, and never let him go.

But I promised myself I would do this right. Or as right as I possibly could.

"I'm doing well," I say. "My calligraphy business is doing great. I'm designing a lot of hand-lettered tattoos, especially for Lukas's clients, and I'm selling a lot of those cookies I wrote to you about."

I've been proud of the success of my artwork and baking ventures, but I can't help comparing my little budding career to those of Toren's ex-girlfriends, which include a famous rock star, a nurse, and a bank loan manager. Will a thirty-four-year-old man think my steps into adulthood are glaringly immature?

As much as I believe in us, sometimes small waves of doubt creep in—making me wonder if our age difference might cause bumps down the road.

"The cookies with the writing?" he asks.

"Yeah. A lot of brides have been buying them. I write the bride and groom's names on them in icing, or the names of the bridal party. And I just started making all-natural cookies that have cute words on them for dogs."

"That's really cool. I'm proud of you, Angel."

My heart flutters and I want to forget all this awkward small talk. This isn't us, and this isn't how I wanted our reunion to go. My chest aches with the need to touch his face, to feel his lips on mine and his muscular arms around me. I want to be alone with him—at his house or by our favorite rocks near the river—and have a *real* conversation.

"Thank you." I take a deep breath and continue. "I was going to call you as soon as I got settled."

The tiny lines on his forehead furrow. "Why didn't you tell me you were coming home so soon?" His voice is low and tinged with a painful disbelief that just about cracks my heart in two. My waiting was never, ever, meant to hurt him. "Why were you waiting to call? What if I hadn't just run into you right now?"

Tears burn my eyes as I meet his, silently begging him to understand my need to come back home—to this town, to my friends and family, and to him—in a way that would do the least amount of damage.

"I wanted us to reconnect with me being on my own. Not living in my father's house. Even though he's doing his best to accept us, I couldn't have you coming over to see me in *his* house. Or make him watch me leave his house to go to yours and then come back again later that night, or the next day, with him knowing we're in love and being intimate. I don't want to rub our relationship in his face that way. His house is the place where you were my pseudo-uncle and I was your niece, and I think we need to stay away from those memories for a while, especially in front of him. I need us to start our relationship with me as an adult, living in my own place. I hope that makes sense."

Slowly, he takes in my explanation then nods. "Okay. I can accept that."

"I was definitely going to call you, Tor. Please don't think I wasn't. I just wanted us to start off right, and I wanted some time with my father too. I had to make sure he's really okay with all this. I couldn't live with myself if our being together destroys my relationship with him, or his with you. I just want to do everything right."

And that's the mountain I've been facing and trying my best to tackle: Is there any way to make falling in love with your father's lifelong best friend right for everyone involved?

He reaches for my hand and holds it tight in his. We stare at each other, taking careful breaths. It's the first time we've ever touched in public as a couple. I squeeze his hand and smile reassuringly.

This is right. We can do this.

"Can I take you to dinner?" he asks.

His question sends my heart into a spasm of frantic beats filled with long-suppressed hopes and wishes. "I'd love that. Just tell me when."

Tonight. Please say tonight. I can't wait another day or I might burst into a million tear-shaped pieces right here on the sidewalk.

Tor's boyish grin—my favorite—flashes across his full lips. "Is tonight too soon?"

A small laugh of relief and sheer happiness comes out of me. "Tonight is perfect." My brain is already mentally scanning my closet, trying to choose the perfect outfit.

"Can I pick you up?"

"Of course. Let me write down my new address for you. Me and Rayne are renting a studio apartment In a converted barn in Amherst," I explain as I dig through my purse for a pen and a scrap of paper. "I know this is awful, but I keep forgetting the address." My fingers tremble with excitement as I jot the address. "I've only been there for two weeks. I stayed with my dad for a few weeks before I moved in with Rayne and—"

His fingers brush against mine when he takes the paper from my hand. I want to grab onto them and pull him closer. "You don't have to explain, Kenzi," he says, staring at the note like it's a winning lottery ticket. "It's all okay."

I have so much I want to say, but for right now, there's just one thing I need to tell him.

"Tor," I say softly. "That message in a bottle you sent was amazing. It really made me see everything so clearly. I loved it. Every night before I go to sleep, I read it."

His chest rises and falls with a deep breath. "I was hoping you would."

"And I did make a wish that night. With the penny you sent." I close the space between us and take his hands in mine.

"You want to share it with me?" That subtle, sexy, teasing tone almost makes my knees buckle. He laces his long, rough fingers between mine and presses our palms together. His are warm and slightly calloused, just as I remember them. I've missed his touch so, so much.

"I wished for you. And us. And happiness."

He releases one of my hands to gently lift my chin. I stare up into the eyes of the man who has loved me, taken care of me, and been my very best friend without falter, since the day I was born.

Sharing such an unconditional, timeless love and connection with him is indescribable. To me, it is the very essence of a fairy tale.

"I can make all those wishes happen," he whispers, lowering his lips to mine. I cling to his arm as he kisses me long, deep, and tantalizingly slow, his hand cradling the side of my throat, holding me to him. As if I'd ever think of breaking our kiss after waiting all this time. His possessive touch steals my breath and sends ripples of excitement through my veins.

Tonight can't come fast enough.

"I still love you the most," I whisper to him between kisses. "I never stopped."

He leans his forehead against mine and lets out a contented sigh. I can almost feel the weight of worry from the past year lifting from him. "Neither did I, Angel. I never will."

CHAPTER THREE

Kenzi

I TURN THIS way then that way in front of my full-length bedroom mirror. The little black dress clings to all the right places, with a scalloped V-neck and a matching scalloped slit up one thigh. I'll wear a cropped, red leather jacket to cover my new tattoo until I'm ready to show him. I thought I'd have more time to prepare for our first date—to get my hair and nails done, maybe get a spray tan so I didn't look so pale against the black fabric. Five hours might seem like a long time, but it's really not when the date you've been daydreaming about for over a year is finally happening. After running into Tor earlier, I spent the next hour basically hyperventilating with nerves and excitement before I did a turbo cleanup of our apartment and jumped into the shower.

Rayne appears behind me in the mirror and nods her approval at my reflection. "You look gorgeous. You should've seen Tor when he walked into the tattoo parlor after he saw you, Kenz. The dude had the biggest smile I've ever seen on his face."

My insides dance. "You guys didn't tell him about my tattoo, right? I want it to be a surprise."

"Of course we didn't."

"Do I look okay?" I ask, chewing my lower lip. "I really wanted to look perfect for him. I wasn't expecting this to happen today." I glance back at the mirror. "I feel like my head is one big split end."

She places her hands on my shoulders and forces me to look at her. "Kenzi, you look amazing. He's going to lose his mind. Trust me, the last thing he cares about is your hair, which looks beautiful, by the way. He's already madly in love with you. You don't have to impress him with perfect hair and makeup."

That's easy for Rayne to say. She looks absolutely stunning just crawling out of bed in the morning.

And I don't ever want to stop trying to impress the man who holds my heart.

"But it's our first date," I say. "It's special."

"Exactly. It's special because you two can finally be together and go on a real date without worrying about my brother kicking Tor's ass again or locking you away somewhere."

"I know. I just want everything to be right. I'm afraid that instead of looking pretty, he's going to see me as a little kid playing dress up. I think the only time he's ever seen me in a dress was for my senior prom."

Ah, memories. My actual prom was a disaster. Later that night, after Tor took me back to his house because the guy I went to the prom with proved to be a total asshole and abandoned me, something changed. Me and Tor danced in his living room, our bodies barely touching but so close I could feel the heat of him. I didn't recognize it at the time, but there was innocent yet subtle banter that I now realize was actual flirting. Chemistry sizzled between us like butter in a skillet. He'll deny it, and I love him for it, but we almost kissed that night. I was only seventeen, but I'd wanted him to kiss me more than I'd ever wanted anything in my entire life.

I still feel that way.

Rayne shakes her head at me. "Stop it. He's going to look at you and see a beautiful woman because that's what you are. He wouldn't wait a damn year for you if he saw you as a child, Kenzi. He's way past that."

Smiling nervously, I say, "I hope so."

In the letters I wrote to Toren over the past year I felt so confident, mature, and brave. I'd stay up late at night with candles burning on my nightstand and pour my heart out to him—sharing all my wishes, dreams, and fantasies. I was delighted that he did the same. Now I just need to feel that same confidence off the page.

"I think he's here," Rayne announces as we move into the living room. "I just saw lights in the driveway."

My stomach pitches sideways as I pull on my jacket. "Am I supposed to feel so nervous?" I ask her. "I've known him my whole life, why do I feel like I'm going to faint just because I'm going to dinner with him?"

"It's totally normal! If you were feeling nothing right now I'd be worried about you. I'd worry that there's no real spark here and you guys just went through a weird phase last year. When I start dating someone, if I feel super sick and can't eat for days, then I know I got it bad for him."

I laugh. I've had no appetite since I moved back here. Every time I think about Tor I feel like a family of acrobatic chipmunks is living inside me. "That's a really strange way to gauge how much you like someone. You *do* know that, right?"

Just as she's about to reply, the doorbell rings. "Should I get that?" she offers. "Or do you want to?"

"I think I should."

She nods and grins. "Agreed."

When I open our front door, he's all but buried behind a bouquet of lavender and white tiger lilies.

"Hi," I manage to say around a huge smile.

"Woah," he replies.

My brows raise. "Woah?"

He shakes his head. Opens, closes, then opens his mouth again. "You look...*damn*..."

"See?" Rayne says from the couch, where she's pretending to leaf through a magazine. "I told you. You look amazing."

"Amazing is an understatement." He leans in to me and presses his lips to my cheek, right on the sensitive spot near my ear. "Fucking breathtaking is what you are," he whispers. The slight growl in his voice sends a warm shiver up my spine.

Still looking at me like he wants to devour me right there at the front door, he silently hands me the bouquet.

"Thank you. They're beautiful." I lift them to my nose and inhale their sweet scent.

"I thought they were too. Until you opened the door and totally redefined beautiful."

My cheeks flush with heat. He's always made me feel loved and adored, but feeling desired by him is indescribable.

"Maybe skip dinner and just go fuck," Rayne suggests playfully.

Would I veto that idea right now? *Nope.*

The interruption gives me a chance to really look at him. So *this* is what romantic-date-night Tor looks like: black dress pants, unscuffed black boots, a white button-down shirt, and a charcoal gray suit jacket. His long hair is silky and brushed back in a low, short ponytail. I don't think I've ever seen him out of old faded jeans or sweatpants. He looks fine as hell.

Leaning against the door frame, he flashes me his adorable, sexy smirk. "Like what you see, Angel?"

"You *can* enter the house, Tor," Rayne quips.

"I'm afraid if I get any closer to the bedroom we're not gonna make our dinner reservation," he shoots back, not breaking eye contact with me. A slow, hot-as-hell grin curves his lips. My God, I love it that he can openly flirt with me. Stolen glances and smiles across a room when we had to hide our feelings were sweet, but this...*this* is intoxicating to me.

Grabbing his hand, I tug him inside. "I *love* what I see," I tell him. "I love you in jeans, but this new look is yummy."

He snakes an arm around my waist and pulls me against him. "I'll give you yummy..." His low, deep voice is full of promise.

Laughing, and internally swooning, I reluctantly pull away. "I'm going to put these in water, then we can go."

"Just so you know, Tor," Rayne says as I find a vase in the small kitchen. "I've always been team Tor and Kenzi. I don't want you to think because he's my brother I took Asher's side. I know he was upset, but he never should've beat the hell out of you, even though I'm sure the two of you fighting was probably like a really hot wrestling match. All that muscle and tattoos and sweaty bodies. Yes, please." She licks her lips and I feel like I might throw up in my flowers.

"Thanks for the compliment. And the kinky, yet disturbing visual it was wrapped in," Tor says. "But it's all water under the bridge now. We're good. I would've done the same thing if I had a daughter."

"Did you just refer to your own brother, and my boyfriend, as hot?" I ask Rayne.

She shrugs. "It's just a factual observation. They're both hot."

Tor looks to me, stifling a laugh. "On that note, let's go."

"You two have fun," Rayne calls before I close the front door behind us. "I won't wait up!"

With his arm around me, he walks me down the stone path to his truck. The autumn night air is cool but not yet chilly. He opens the passenger door for me, but before I can climb in he grabs my waist and presses my back up against the side of the truck. Leaning his arm against the glass next to my cheek, he tilts his head, letting his gaze drift from my lips, down the length of my body, then back up to meet my eyes.

"My angel," he says hoarsely. "We've waited so long to catch up to each other." His lips capture mine, soft and lingering. "And you're more beautiful than I ever could've imagined."

I wind my arms around his neck and clasp my hands behind his head.

"This feels like a dream."

He gently caresses my cheek with the back of his hand. "No more dreams and wishes," he says. "From now on, everything between us is real."

My chest swells with overwhelming emotion. "I like that. A lot."

"You ready for our first date, then?"

Once upon a time, we had tea parties on my bedroom floor, drinking imaginary tea from flowery plastic cups. I made him hold my favorite stuffed bunny, and he fed me make-believe cookies. Tor lit up my world.

Love can start at any moment. It can change and grow into something beautiful and special. You'd be wrong if you thought it can't, or it doesn't.

It can, and it does.

The boy who drank invisible tea with me is now a man taking me on my very first romantic date.

I smile up at him as the memories fade back where they belong. "I've been waiting for this forever," I reply.

CHAPTER FOUR

Toren

H EADS TURN AS the maître d' leads us to our table at the back of the restaurant. When I made the reservation, I specifically requested one of the quiet tables that overlook the river because I heard the view was beautiful.

A year ago, I'd be worried people were judging us because I'm a thirty-four-year-old guy having dinner with a nineteen-year-old girl. Those worries are in the past. Truth is, they're looking at us because Kenzi has that classic, sultry Marilyn Monroe beauty that both men and women can't help but admire.

I look pretty damn good too.

It takes all my willpower to resist snarling at the men ignoring their wives and ogling Kenzi's legs as we cross the room. I keep my hand at the small of her back and pull her chair out for her when we reach our table.

"This is a huge step up from the happy meals you used to take me for," Kenzi teases as we open our menus.

Shaking my head, I flash her a crooked grin. "I'm laying down one rule." I lean forward and lower my voice. "Let's keep the trips down memory lane to a minimum. I love those memories, but I don't want to think about taking care of you when you were a little girl while I'm also thinking about you riding my face in about two hours."

Her glossy red lips part with anticipation. She blinks at me and silently nods. I love knowing I can make her panties wet with just a few words.

I lift my menu in front of my face but peek over it after a few seconds. "I'm not opposed to you calling me Uncle Tor when I'm making you come, though. Just sayin'."

She lets out a tiny gasp and her eyes widen to the size of saucers.

"I'm kidding," I say, reaching across the table to hold her hand. I can't stop touching her. "I'm not that twisted."

The toe of her high-heeled shoe drives into my shin. "That's not funny," she says, but her eyes are dancing with laughter.

We order food we can't pronounce. She dares me to steal a tiny seafood fork because she thinks it's adorable. It's now hidden in my jacket. We eat one-handed, each refusing to let go of the other's hand. We laugh and stare into each other's eyes, getting so lost in the moment we forget what we were even talking about. It doesn't matter because all I can see is her smile, all I can hear is her laugh, all I can feel is her hand in mine.

By the end of dinner, my chest aches and my face hurts. I've never laughed and smiled so much in my damned life. I've never felt so grateful to be alive and finally able to let myself love and be loved. My heart has never felt so safe.

I'm afraid to blink. I can't believe she's here. With me.

Mine.

This is all I've ever fucking wanted. *She* is all I've ever wanted and needed.

Smiling, she cocks her head to the side and looks at me with that look of pure adoration that I've been waiting a year to see again.

"What are you thinking about over there, Mr. Grace?" she asks softly.

"Spending forever with you."

She inhales, breathing in my words. I'm sure I can hear her heart beating from behind that little black dress she's rocking.

When she was in Maine, we wrote to each other about our future. The house we wanted. How many kids we wanted to have. The things we'd do together. How we'd celebrate holidays and anniversaries. I considered every word I wrote to her a silent vow as to the husband I would be.

I'd drop down on one knee right in the middle of this restaurant if I had a ring with me. But I don't.

There *is* a ring, though. A one-carat, heart-shaped diamond—clear as crystal, bright as day—set in rose gold with tiny canary diamonds glittering down the side of the band. For eleven months, it's been waiting for her in a plush velvet box.

I never had any doubt she'd come back to me.

I do, however, have doubts that Asher will give us his blessing, and I can't ask Kenzi to marry me without that. Last year, Asher—known for being the eternal peacemaker—found out about me and Kenzi and went into an unheard fit of rage. He came to my house in the middle of the night, pummeled my face into a bloody mess and broke three of my ribs. I know how important Asher's blessing is to Kenzi, and despite him beating the shit out of me and rearranging my face, it's important to me too.

"I have a surprise for you." Her voice is laced with a hint of shyness as she slowly slips her leather jacket off and turns her left shoulder toward me. I've kissed, touched, and memorized every inch of her body, so the tattoo on her upper arm immediately catches my eye. It takes a few seconds for my eyes to adjust in the dim light and make out exactly what it is. My breath stills when the image comes into focus. I recognize the detailed black-and-white portrait style as Lukas's work. It's an image of her favorite toy when she was little. Mopsy—a plush stuffed gray bunny I gave her on her fifth birthday. She never let it out of her sight. Until she lost it. But that's a story for another day. The bunny is sitting on the floor, long ears flopped to the sides of its face, leaning against a doorframe. The words "I love him the most" are engraved in the door, with a scribbled heart below. All of it has special meaning to us.

"You broke my rule, Angel," I say, my voice low and husky. "You plastered a memory right into your flesh."

"So did you," she reminds me. It's true. Last year I had her childhood drawing telling me she loves me tattooed right over my heart.

"Touché."

"Do you like it?" The quiver in her voice makes me want to pull her across the table and kiss her until I erase any doubt that I could *ever* not love every part of her. "I really wanted to show it to you when it was healed, but then we ran into each other earlier…"

"It's fuckin' perfect," I say. "I love it."

Her smile returns. "I get your rule…but I think it's okay to be reminded of our memories sometimes. Without them, we wouldn't be here."

I nod in agreement. "You're right, babe."

"Do you want dessert?" she asks.

"No." I want *her* for dessert. "Do you?"

She shakes her head. "I can't eat another bite." Her eyes twinkle. "Besides, don't I have a face to ride?"

My cock instantly hardens like a rock, and I can't get out of here fast enough. Signaling for the check, I bring her hand to my lips for a kiss. "You better text Rayne and tell her you won't be home tonight."

CHAPTER FIVE

Toren

SOME THINGS NEVER change, and I wouldn't want them to. I couldn't wait to get home and finally have Kenzi all to myself, and here I am watching my dog, Diogee, and my cat, Kitten, crawl all over her on the living room floor. Diogee is doing his howly *woo-woo*, excitedly licking her face, while the cat has climbed on her lap to do the happy-paw dance. Kenzi went from looking elegant and glamorous to sprawled on the carpet, covered with white and gray fur. But my girl is smiling and laughing, reveling in all the love, and my furkids are happy to have their other human back. That's all that matters.

"I missed them so much," she says with teary eyes. "I was afraid they'd forget about me."

"Not a chance." I don't tell her that after she left for Maine, I dug two of her hoodies out of my laundry basket from the last time she was here. I've kept them on the couch for the past year so the pets would still have her scent. I may have sniffed them sometimes too.

When did I get this weird?

Shrugging, I toss my keys onto the table by the front door and cross the room. Kneeling in front of her, I take her foot in my hand and slowly unbuckle the thin leather strap of her shoe. Her calf is long and toned from walks on the beach at her aunt's bed and breakfast. She watches me with an enticing smile as I do the same with her other foot. Under her gaze, I slowly run my hand over her knee and up her thigh. Her eyes fall closed as I slide under the hem of her dress to grip her outer thigh. The heat of her skin warms my palm. Inching farther up, I hook my finger under the strap of her lace thong and slip it down her leg.

"You won't be needing these," I tell her, spinning them round and round on my finger before shoving them into my pocket.

"You're so bad."

The pets have retreated to their usual sleeping spots, happy that they've properly mauled her and expelled a significant amount of fur to mark her as their own again.

Now it's my turn.

Scooping her up in my arms, I carry her to the bedroom and set her down at the edge of the bed. She watches me kick off my boots, then grabs the front of my shirt and pulls me to her. The glint of desire in her eyes makes my heart race.

Slowly, she unbuttons my shirt. Tormentingly slow, and she knows it drives me wild. Her nails are like red gems weaving through the stark white fabric of my shirt. I close my eyes, and in a breath, my shirt is gone and her lips are on my stomach, warm and wet, tracing the indentation of my abs. The muscles beneath twitch to life from her touch, wanting more. Her hands grip my waist as her tongue and teeth graze across my flesh. After a few moments, I fist her long hair and pull her head back. Letting out a small gasp, she stares up at me with hooded eyes, lips parted, wet and glistening. Red lipstick kisses trail across my stomach. I wish they could stay there permanently.

I bring my hand around from the back of her head to cradle her cheek.

"What are you supposed to be doing?" I ask, running my thumb across her smudged lips.

The corner of her mouth tilts up. "Riding your face."

I love when she talks dirty. It lights a fire in me like nothing else.

"Good girl."

I pull her up to her feet and kiss her hungrily. A moan vibrates in her throat when I slide my tongue into her mouth, sweeping over hers. The faint taste of mint is still on her breath from the candy she sucked on the way home from dinner.

Reaching between us, I finger the lace hem of her dress and lift it up, breaking our kiss just long enough to pull it over her head and toss it on the bed. I circle her waist with my hands and pull her against me to grind my hard cock between her thighs. She's bare against my pants, and I can feel her, wet and hot. Kissing her deeper, I move my hands to cup her ass, kneading my fingers into her firm flesh and driving my hips harder against her. She whimpers and digs her nails into my shoulders like tiny talons.

I pull back and drop my gaze from her eyes. The black silk bra holds her tits perfectly, and I can't resist sliding two fingers into the valley of her cleavage to unsnap the front closure. The fabric falls to her sides, and I bend down to kiss the curve of her breasts, dragging my tongue to her nipple. As I suck her into my mouth, she inhales a sharp breath, and winds her thigh tightly around my hip.

Holding on to her, I spin us around and fall back onto the bed, pulling her on top of me. Her hair tumbles into my face as she leans down on her arms to kiss me.

"Before you ask," she begins in a sexy, playful voice. "I will not call you Uncle Tor, or say giddyup."

Fuck, I love her. I love the confidence we've built together. We didn't let our time apart let us drift away from each other. We used it to get closer, and damn, it's fucking amazing.

Grinning, I slap her on the butt cheek. "Get your sweet ass up here."

She's the most beautiful, sexy thing I've ever seen as she kneels above me and straddles my face. Her body is long and toned, sculpted thighs and swelling hips curving into the perfect hourglass. Grabbing her waist, I pull her down on me, knowing I'll never, ever get enough of her. I could make love to her ten times a day every day for the rest of my life, and I'd still want more of her. I tease her with my breath first, lightly blowing on her, letting my mouth linger, barely touching her pink flesh. When she can't take anymore, she lowers herself onto my face, covering my mouth with her folds. I delve my tongue into the haven of her, finding her hot and silky wet. She gyrates her body into a slow, sensual dance above me, palming her full breasts, nipples hard and tilted up. My cock throbs, straining to break free of my clothes and plunge into her. It's been so long since I've been buried inside her.

But, I've never let my dick run my life, and tonight is no exception.

I run my hands up the length of her body to cup her breasts, and she covers my hands with hers, intertwining our fingers, caressing her body with me. Nothing could be fucking hotter. My heart and cock surge with a potent mix of love and desire.

My tongue explores her folds, lapping every ridge. She writhes against me, spreading her thighs wider and pivoting forward, directing me to her pulsing clit. Flicking the nub with my tongue, I run one hand down her back, over her ass, and reach around to slide two fingers into her.

"Tor..." she moans my name and rocks faster against my mouth and fingers. "I need to come...I can't wait."

I want to make her hold back—bring her down, then work her up again. I want to revel in hearing her beg for release, and then giving her everything she wants. I can't torture her by making her wait, though. Not on our first night back together. Not when her walls are clenching my tongue and fingers with need, and her thighs are quivering uncontrollably around my face. I have all night to devour her—to send her over the edge again and again until she slips into a euphoric slumber in my arms.

Sucking her clit between my lips, I roll my tongue against her and plunge my fingers faster and deeper into her. She rides me hard, crying out my name and grabbing the headboard for leverage. Her entire body trembles.

I drink her in, licking her through ripple after ripple of ecstasy, then flip her onto her back next to me. I move between her legs, and she wraps herself around me, pulling my mouth to hers.

"I want you inside me," she gasps, reaching between us to unzip my pants.

I grab her hand to stop her. "Nope," I say.

Her forehead furrows. I press my lips to the thin creases.

"What do you mean, nope?" she asks between ragged breaths.

"I decided we're not making love until we're engaged."

Her lips push up into a pout. "What? *You* decided?"

"Yeah. Once we have Asher's blessing, and my ring is on your finger, then that's it, you're mine, and I don't plan to let you out of this room for at least seventy-two hours."

"But...why do we have to wait? He knows we're together."

I touch her cheek, not sure how to explain that I just need it to be this way. With zero resistance or guilt hanging over my head. It's something I need for me— an entirely clear conscience to give every part of myself to her, and take every part of her.

"You know how you needed to do things a certain way when you came back home? I need this part to be my way. It's not that I don't want you, baby, because fuck I do. I just need it to be right in my head."

Nodding slowly, she stares up at me and threads her fingers through my hair, pushing it behind my ear.

"I love you, Tor," she says with such sincerity it makes my heart clench. "I understand. Thank you for being so patient with everything. And for all the letters and poems while I was gone. For taking care of me. For always being you." Her fingertips trail down my cheek. "For gently catching me as I fell in love with you."

I lean down and plant a kiss on the tip of her nose. "I love *you*, Angel. Thank you for always seeing the good in me."

"I'm going to break your rule for a second." Her lips curve into a grin. "I knew from the moment you held me as a baby that there is only good in you. I told you when I was five years old I was going to marry you someday. Somehow, I always knew you were my person."

Admitting to myself that I always felt that way, too, was hard. For a long time it made me feel sick.

Not anymore.

"I felt it, too, Kenz. You've always had my heart."

I could lean over and open my nightstand drawer right now. I could open that little velvet box, slip the ring on her finger, and ask her to be my wife. The moment is perfect.

But *fuck*...I can't. Not yet.

Sometimes doing things right can really fucking suck.

"Will you come outside with me?" I ask her instead.

It takes her a beat to switch gears. "Of course."

We climb out of bed and pull on hoodies and sweats. Barefoot, we walk out into the backyard. Diogee comes with us and trots around the perimeter of the fence, nose up, sniffing the crisp night air.

Taking Kenzi's hand, I lead her to the little pond in the far corner of the yard.

"Oh, Tor, it looks so magical with the fairy lights," she says, squeezing my hand. "I missed coming back here. How are the koi?'

"Still alive and swimming."

We had a lot of talks in this spot by the pond. Our first fights, too, when I was struggling like hell—pushing her away and deep in denial over my feelings for her.

She points to the jar of pennies wedged between the rocks. I haven't touched it since the last time we sat here together. It feels so long ago.

"Did you bring me out here to make wishes together?" she asks.

I sit on the wrought iron bench and pull her onto my lap. Her arms immediately wrap around my neck, and she leans her head against mine. "Not tonight." I turn my face toward hers and capture her lips with mine, kissing her softly. "Want to know why?"

She nods, running her fingers through my hair, sending tingles through my scalp.

"We don't need wishes anymore. We can make all our dreams come true together now."

Her breath catches. "We're really going to make it all happen? Me and you? You promise?"

"We are, Angel. You and me. No matter what. We're gonna get married, and have a baby, and I'm going to love you like crazy every day. I promise."

Tears glisten in her eyes under the moonlight. She holds my face in her hands and kisses me fervently.

"I can't wait," she whispers against my lips. "I love you so much."

I have one memory that I've never shared with her. When Kenzi was about two years old, I took her to the park to feed the ducks so Asher and Ember could have some alone time. Kenzi found a penny on the ground and immediately tried to put it in her mouth like little kids do. I stopped her just in time and told her to throw it in the water. She smiled, wound her arm up, and tossed the penny into the pond, clapping her hands after.

"Now make a wish," I said.

She screwed her little eyes shut tight for a few seconds, then opened them triumphantly.

"What'd you wish for? I asked her.

"Us!" she squealed. It was sweet, and purely innocent of course.

I laughed and said, "No, you gotta wish for something. Like a toy. Or a puppy."

She shook her head, pigtails flying. "Us!" she repeated.

After that, she'd ask me for a penny every time we were near water so we could make wishes. She never wished for *us* again. At least, not until we were much older.

And that's what started our little tradition of throwing pennies and making wishes.

Now, all these years later, I can't help believing that her very first wish really did come true.

✧   ✧   ✧

If you enjoyed this glimpse into Tor and Kenzi's love story, you can read *Torn*, a full-length book that tells their entire journey from friendship to falling in love.

Torn is available now! You can get it by going here >
www.cariancolewrites.com/all-torn-up-series

Movie Night

Roni Loren

Note: In this story, there are spoilers for Reality Bites *and* Pretty In Pink. *If you haven't seen those movies—why not?? ;)—but you've been warned.*

CHAPTER ONE

"THAT'S BECAUSE YOU don't get it," I say, hitting pause on *Reality Bites* and turning to face my roommate, ready to make my case. Somehow, we always end up in debates on movie night—the film major vs. the pre-law major—but this time I plan on winning.

Tasha sighs and twists her black hair into a sloppy bun on top of her head. "Oh, I get it. I get that it's a dumb love story plot device that just ends up with half the people who are watching disappointed with the outcome."

I'm already shaking my head.

"Hard disagree. Love triangles are..." I frown, trying to put my feelings into words. "First of all, you can save yourself from disappointment because there's usually an obvious choice as long as you're taking into account the movie's era. The winner of the love triangle is almost always the ideal hero or heroine of that generation."

"You're telling me Ethan Hawke's character in all his grungy toxic masculinity was the ideal of Gen X?" Tasha asks, looking wholly unconvinced. "Because *wow*, Gen X. If I'm Winona Ryder, Ben Stiller's character wins. Nice guy. Good job. *Earnest.* So you know he'd be like *eager* to please in bed. Yes, I'll take one of those."

I smirk. "No, it's gotta be Ethan. We talked about this in my film studies class. The nineties were about being authentic and not selling out to the man. Winona Ryder is not going to pick the corporate guy, not in 1994. Just like Molly Ringwald can't pick Duckie in *Pretty In Pink*. The eighties ideal was the rich, pretty yuppie guy. Andrew McCarthy had to be the guy. If it had been made in the 2000s, the nerd would've been the hero, but not in the eighties."

"See, you've just made my point. They always pick the wrong guy." She points a Twizzler at me. "This is why love triangles suck and you're wrong. Duckie forever. And Team Ben Stiller."

I laugh. "Oh, come on. Can't you see a little of the appeal? Love triangles are angsty and full of tension and I don't know, *sexy*. The woman has all the power."

"Power?" Tasha tips her head back against the couch, almost upending the bowl of popcorn in her lap, and groans before giving me her best closing argument expression. "Do not give me that bullshit, Alexis Wayne. This is not about female power. In love triangles, the guys are just in a dick-measuring contest and the woman is caught in the middle like some piece of property they want to claim."

I pull my legs onto the couch, wrapping my arms around them, and set my chin on my knees. I grin. "Is it bad if the thought of being fought over like that totally does it for me?"

Tasha snorts and sets aside the popcorn. "I swear. It's always the quiet ones. You looked so sweet and innocent when you showed up in our dorm room freshman year. Now look at you."

I smirk. "Yes, look at me. The twenty-one-year-old near-virgin spending Saturday night watching old movies with my best friend. I've really gone off the deep end."

She nods. "Yep. If you want to be in a love triangle, you definitely have fallen into the dangerous end of the pool. Just find one guy and go have some fun. Skip the drama part."

"That's what you don't get. It's not about the drama." I pause, trying to find the right words. "It's about the wanting. You don't think about it because guys trip over themselves trying to get a chance with you. You basically live *The Bachelorette.*"

"Well, I don't know if that's totally—"

"But no one has ever fought over me for anything," I say, dropping all pretense of academic film discussion and just laying it out there. "Not even my parents. It was like, meh, whoever you want to live with is fine. I was basically the blue couch."

Tasha gives me a patient look, that look that says *I'm still entertaining this conversation because I'm your best friend but I think you may have taken a hard left turn into crazy town.* "The blue couch. You're losing me, pumpkin."

"Yes, this non-offensive but totally bland couch we had that wasn't good enough for the living room but wasn't horrible enough to get rid of. When my parents were dividing up the stuff, neither cared who got the blue couch. They fought over the fancy toaster and who got to keep the bookshelves, but the blue couch could go anywhere and so could I."

Tasha's brown eyes soften. "I'm sure that's not true. They probably just figured you'd choose for yourself. You were a teenager by then."

"Yeah, I guess, but it would've been nice for them to at least…I don't know, *act* like they wanted me to live with them." I grimace. "God, how did we get here? Hello, therapy couch. Can we go back to grungy nineties Ethan Hawke?"

Tasha smiles sympathetically. "You're not a blue couch, Alex. Not to your parents and not to anyone else. And you don't need a love triangle to make things interesting or hot. You just need to get in bed with someone who is going to look at you and make you feel nothing like a blue couch." She cocks an eyebrow at me. "Lack of love triangles is not your problem. Your lack of a high-quality lay is. You've been with one groping high school idiot who basically blamed you for not being able to orgasm your first time. That shouldn't even count as losing your virginity. But since you haven't had great, real-life sex yet, you end up fantasizing about all these movie scenarios instead. In real life, it doesn't have to be movie-complicated to be fun. You just need a guy who knows how to identify a clitoris and cares enough to make sure you have as good a time as he does."

I snort. "Yes, sure, let me just hop on Tinder and find a clitoral expert for a quick hookup."

"Eww. Gross. No." She scrunches her nose and shakes her head. "You don't need to go to a stranger. Just ask one of the guys for a friendly lesson in quality boning. I bet Dominic would be game if you really need your broody-musician itch scratched. Or Preston if you're more into the athletic, future-CEO type. I saw him playing hoops without a shirt on the other day and…*girl.*"

Her words hang in the air as if suspended for a moment and then crash loudly in my ears.

"Hold up. You want me to ask *Dominic or Preston?*" My voice pitches louder at the ludicrous suggestion. "To sleep with me? Are you high? Did you dip into your mom's gummy bear stash again?"

She laughs. "I'm serious. They're our friends and neither are seeing anyone right now. Plus, you're amazing and they'd be damn lucky to get the privilege. I bet either would be more than happy to volunteer." Her smile turns devious. "You'd just have to decide, are you going for an eighties hero or nineties hero? Are you an Andrew McCarthy or an Ethan Hawke girl?"

I stare at her, my thoughts going in a direction they definitely shouldn't because this is a ridiculous thing to even consider. "Neither."

She gives me a droll look. "Because you hate happiness and don't want to have great sex?"

I do, actually, want to have great sex. At some point. The right situation just hasn't presented itself yet. The right *guy* has never presented himself. Anytime I've gotten close to taking that leap with someone since that awful night in high school, I've hit the brakes. "That's not the point."

"Okay. So, you don't think Dominic and Preston are hot?"

"Also, not the point."

"Ha." She points at me like she's just gotten the defendant to admit his crimes on the stand. "Which one have you already pictured naked?"

"What? Neither! They're our friends." I try to sound haughty and absolutely offended by this accusation.

"Oh my God. Liar. It's both, isn't it?" She clasps her hands together at her chest, her version of a victory dance. "I mean, I don't blame you. Nic and Pres aren't my type, but they're definitely not hard to look at."

I give in and roll my eyes. "Fine. I'm celibate, so I've pictured lots of guys naked. That's all I've got to work with. It doesn't mean anything."

Tasha laughs and pats my sock-covered foot. "Deprivation is bad for the soul. We need to fix this."

I sit up straighter, not liking her eager tone. "We for sure do not. I've got a good imagination and a working vibrator. I'm good."

She nods like she's responding to someone else and climbs off the couch, grabbing her phone from the side table as she does.

"What are you doing?" I ask. "We haven't finished the movie."

"I need to pee," she says and disappears into her room.

I let out a frustrated breath and stare at the frozen TV screen. Winona Ryder has just told Ethan Hawke that she was really going to be something by the age of twenty-three and he's telling her, *honey, all you have to be by age twenty-three is yourself.* I'm not twenty-three yet, but I'm not even sure who myself is at this point. I'm not even sure I've started to become her.

I'm stuck.

With my movies and my silly film-based fantasies.

A love-triangle fantasy? Tasha's right. What *is* wrong with me? It's like I'm craving dysfunction.

"Ugh." I reach for the bag of Twizzlers and promise myself that next week, I'm only watching blow-'em-up action movies. No more angst.

No more love triangles.

And definitely no more picturing my two closest guy friends naked.

CHAPTER TWO

I'M *DEFINITELY NOT picturing Dominic or Preston naked. Nope. Not at all.*
The four of us are hanging out on a patch of grass in the quad after class on

Friday like we always do. I haven't said much because my brain is liquefied after a particularly brutal math test. Why I still need to take math classes as a film studies major is one of life's great questions that I have yet to solve. Tasha is sipping on a cold-brew coffee like it's her life's blood and scrolling through her phone. Preston is lying on his back in the sun, eyes closed, light brown hair blowing in the breeze. He seems oblivious both to the activity around him and to the fact that I'm working really hard not to notice how his T-shirt clings to his baseball-player arms.

Dominic, on the other hand, is tracking me. His long, adept fingers are picking out a quiet tune on his guitar, but those dark brown eyes of his keep finding me. When I catch him watching me, his mouth quirks a little at the corner, like he's thinking about something particularly amusing. It's unnerving.

"What?" I finally say, setting the e-reader I was pretending to read aside.

Dominic lifts a dark brow. "What what?"

Preston cracks an eyelid open.

"Do I have something on my face?" I ask, touching my mouth and wondering if that chocolate muffin I grabbed from the cafeteria has left evidence.

"Irritation, mostly," Dominic answers, a pleased note in his voice. "Rough day?"

"Shit," Tasha says, breaking me from the eye contact with Dominic.

"What's wrong?" I ask.

She frowns at her phone. "I just got an email that the assignment I sent in this morning came through with an error in the file. I need to go print out a paper copy and bring it over to my professor or I'm going to get points off for being late."

"We can go to the library, print it there," I say, reaching for my bag.

Tasha looks my way and waves her cold brew at me. "No, it's fine. You stay. If you leave before I'm back, I'll just see you at home."

I shrug. "All right. Well, just let me know if you need any help."

She's already on her feet and grabbing her backpack. "Thanks."

I watch her walk off, and only after she's disappeared from sight, do I realize that I'm alone with Preston and Dominic. Normally, that wouldn't be an issue, but now Tasha has put *ideas* in my head and I can't not think about them.

I pick up my e-reader, determined to stop making this weird. The soft notes of Dominic's guitar fill the background again. I read the same line four times.

"How'd the math test go?" Preston asks, propping himself up on an elbow and shielding his blue eyes from the sun with his other hand.

"Like math," I answer. "We're still in a very fraught relationship."

"If you ever need help with it, let me know," he offers. "I'm a pretty good tutor."

I smile. "Thanks, I—"

"Oh, come on," Dominic says with a scoff, cutting in and looking at Preston. "That's your line, dude? Do better."

Line? I stiffen.

Preston sits up fully and flips him off. "Right, like aimlessly plucking at your guitar is not a total tool move. Why don't you do some brooding too? You know, make it really count."

My breath freezes in my chest, and I must make some distressed noise because they both look my way.

Reality dawns slowly. Painfully. My face is getting hot. "She told you."

Neither says a word. They don't have to. I can see it on their faces. That's why things have felt weird since we sat down. I wasn't just imagining it. They *know*.

"Oh my God." I toss my e-reader in my bag like it's on fire and move to get up, but a hand lands on my arm, stopping me.

"Hey," Dominic says, "hold up. Come on. Don't freak out."

"Not freaking out. I just need to go murder my roommate." And then dig a hole to crawl in and die of embarrassment. "And I'm going to make it painful."

"Well, now that you've told us your plan, if we don't stop you, then we're part of the crime," Preston says with a little smile. "Don't let us go to jail, Alex."

"I can't—"

"You can," Dominic says, releasing his hold on my arm. "It's not a big deal. Stay. Talk. Everything's fine."

I close my eyes. Breathe in. Breathe out. "What *exactly* did she tell you?"

Preston clears his throat. "Nothing embarrassing."

I open my eyes and give him a don't-fuck-with-me look. "The fact that you're saying that means she told you like the most embarrassing version possible."

Dominic sets his guitar aside and runs a hand through the dark, messy waves of his hair, looking slightly apologetic. "For what it's worth, we weren't supposed to *tell* you that she told us. She was just giving us information, and we could do with that what we wanted. Let things unfold naturally if the spirit moved any of us." He glances over at his roommate. "And apparently many spirits were moved by the thought of...well, you know, *you.*"

I blink.

Then another piece clicks into place. The way they were acting with each other...the verbal jabs.

"Oh my God, did she like tell you to *act out* some faux love-triangle thing? Because now I'm truly going to kill her." I'm grabbing for my bag again, unable to look at them. "And the fact that y'all would play along? You're assholes, too. I'm sure you both got a good laugh over your friend's silly movie fantasies."

I'm on my feet now, not sure where I'm going to go but needing to get the hell out of there, but before I can take two steps, Dominic is in front of me. He puts his hands on my shoulders, halting me. "Hey, hey, hey, hold up. I think there's some miscommunication here."

I'm staring past his left shoulder, refusing to look at him, fearing I'm going to cry from humiliation.

Preston steps up next to him, blocking out the view of the quad, leaving only the two of them in my vision. "Alex, he's right. I think we have wires crossed. All Tasha said was that you had a shitty experience in high school, which has made you a little gun-shy, and that you were thinking a hookup with a friend might be a safe, low-pressure situation to fix that. She mentioned that you hadn't ruled out one of us as a possibility. That's all we know."

I dare a glance his way. His expression is open, honest.

"He's right," Dominic says, "but now I feel like she left out the best part. What's this about a love-triangle fantasy?" There's a note of delight in his voice. "I need details. Possibly diagrams and pictures."

I shoot Dominic a look. "Don't even. If you're any kind of friend, you'll pretend anything I said in the last few minutes didn't happen."

"Hmm." Dominic frowns. "Unhearing things is not my best skill. I'm more of a ruminator, an extrapolator, a guy who's going to read all kinds of things into what you said and come up with his own conclusions unless you set me straight. In this love triangle, do we like physically fight for you while you watch or is it more like who can write the best love poem and woo you? Because—"

I automatically reach out and press my fingers over his mouth. "Shut. Up."

He smiles behind my fingers.

Preston is unusually quiet.

I sigh and lower my hand. "It's not about love. I obviously love both of you as friends. That's not what it's about. It's nothing. It's stupid. It was a silly conversation you have with your friend while watching old movies *that she is not supposed to repeat.*"

Dominic moves his hands from my shoulders and his expression turns serious. "Whatever it is, don't call it stupid or nothing. If something flips your switches and it's not hurting anyone, own it."

"But if you don't want to tell us, that's your business, too," Preston says. "Just know that on that first part, the looking-for-a-friend part…" He gives me this little half-smile that makes my stomach flip over. "You'd just have to ask, you know?"

"Either of us," Dominic adds. "The only thing you'd need to do is choose. You're going to get a yes either way."

The offer startles me. Because they're serious. There's no humor or teasing on their faces just…open interest. *Holy shit.* "I…uh…obviously this can't actually happen. I mean, it'd make the friendships weird and how would I pick and I really appreciate the offer, but y'all really don't have to—"

"Have to," Dominic says, dark brows lifted. "Have to? Like we're helping you do your taxes or study for a test? Alex, you do realize you'd be offering one of us like…a fantasy, right? *Oh man, I have to spend a night figuring out the best ways to get my hot friend Alex to come. Poor me.*"

Heat is creeping through my body, but I can't tell if it's embarrassment or something else much more dangerous.

"You don't think I've thought about what it'd be like with you?" Dominic continues and cocks his head toward Preston. "That he hasn't? We just couldn't ever cross that line. You've been off-limits since freshman year because of the friend edict."

My mind is whirling. "The friend edict?"

"You don't remember?" Preston asks. "Tasha declared it that first night when we ended up drunk together at that party. She caught me checking you out and said we all would only remain friends if everyone kept it in their pants."

"You agreed and then you vomited on my shoes," Dominic says with a smirk. "It was a magical night."

"I have zero recollection of this," I say, searching for the memory and coming up empty.

"The point is," Preston goes on, his voice calm but direct. "We love you, too. You're one of our best friends. And don't want to mess that up either, but we also—"

"Would take you to bed in a hot second," Dominic finishes. "And take *very* good care of you. At least I would. I don't know what Pres gets up to behind closed doors, but I can't imagine he'd be worse than some two-pump chump in high school."

"Fuck you," Preston says to Dominic with no ire behind it, then to me. "I promise you'd be in good hands."

Hands. Preston's hands. Or Dominic's. *On me.*

There's a knot in my throat the size of a softball. My two closest guy friends are standing in front of me, casually offering to fuck me. This is ludicrous.

I should laugh this off. I should tell them it was all a big joke. I should definitely not risk two of the most important friendships I have for one night with one of them.

But that's not what's making me hesitate.

The *wanting* is a living, pulsing ache inside me.

No, what's making me hesitate is that I don't know who to choose.

Dominic is the obvious choice if I'm looking for a little rebellion. He'd make me laugh and not take things too seriously, but he'd also get me blushing because he's got no shame. He'd be game for anything. I can imagine my hands gripped in that wavy dark hair, that raspy singer's voice of his whispering dirty things in my ear, those guitar-callused fingers touching me in my softest places, playing me like a song.

My thighs clench as a bolt of desire crashes through me.

But Preston.

Preston's never done anything in his life halfway. He gets the As. He got the starting first baseman position. He's got the highest batting average. He would never let me walk away from this without giving me every ounce of pleasure he knows how to give. On the surface, he may seem like the Boy Scout, but I've seen glimpses of another side of him. It's in his eyes right now. I get the feeling that in bed, he'd be intense and *utterly focused.* Plus, he's got shoulders that make me want to bite them.

"You could also tell us both no," Preston says when I'm quiet for too long. "If you've changed your mind. We won't bring it up again."

"I haven't changed my mind," I say without thinking.

Satisfaction flickers across both their faces. Dominic recovers first. "Excellent. So, I guess the only question now is...who do you want, Alex? There's a whole weekend in front of us. Who should clear his calendar?"

Panic is trying to edge in as I look between the two of them. *Dominic. Preston. Dominic. Preston.* I shake my head. "I don't know. I can't—you're both..."

"We're both what?" Preston asks, his voice edged with something that makes me shiver.

I inhale a deep breath, trying to find courage to just say what I'm thinking. "Irresistible and you both know it. I've thought...*things* about both of you."

Dominic smiles like he's just been given a huge piece of chocolate cake. "Things. The way you say it, that word has never sounded filthier." He leans closer like he's sharing a secret. "Alexis Wayne, I've thought lots of things about you too. I'm thinking a lot of things right now. I have a feeling Pres is as well. He's going to be real disappointed when you pick me instead of him."

Preston snorts derisively. "And you're going to be real disappointed when you listen better and realize what she really wants." His gaze meets mine, pinning me. "Because you already know your answer, you're just afraid to say it."

I bite my lip, my heart racing. It's like Preston is looking right through my skin and seeing inside me, pulling out my secret thoughts with deft fingertips.

He steps a little closer, holding the eye contact. "Go ahead, Alex. Say it. Who knows? Maybe you'll get it."

My throat is dry. My skin electric.

Dominic is watching me, a line between his brows, but then the realization dawns on his face. "Oh fuck."

"Yeah," Preston confirms. "Welcome, Nic. Glad you caught up." He reaches out and cups the back of my neck, his palm smooth and hot against my skin. He leans in and his lips brush my ear. "Say it, Alex. Tell us who you want."

I shiver and close my eyes. Every ounce of my good sense is telling me to keep my mouth shut, to take the safe route. But I always take the safe route. I'm the girl no one would make a movie about. I push the words out into the space between us. "Both. I want you both."

Preston breathes in my answer with a deep inhale, and when I open my eyes, there's heat flaring in his gaze. I glance over at Dominic, expecting him to balk.

But he shakes his head and laughs. "Well, here I was, thinking one of us was going to give *you* a first. But turns out, you're offering us one."

I smile, quivery with nerves but also comforted that these two are still the guys I know, my friends. Knowing that makes me brave. "And?"

Dominic takes a step closer and throws an arm over Preston's shoulders. "Al, have you ever seen us play basketball together?"

I'm not following where he's going with this but I nod. "Yeah. You nearly murder each other."

He gives me a sly smile. "Well, if we're that competitive with basketball, just imagine how we're going to be when the score is how many times we can make you come?"

My body ripples with awareness, invisible fingers of arousal brushing over my skin, making everything tighten.

Preston reaches into my bag and pulls out my phone. "Call Tasha. Tell her you're not coming home tonight. And then we'll grab some dinner because…I have a feeling we're gonna keep you up real late."

"And you're going to need the energy," Dominic adds. "We have our pride, you know. We're each going to have to give you the best we've got."

"Tonight?" I blurt. "Like tonight, tonight? Like *now?*"

"Yep, we're not dumb, Al," Dominic says, coming to my side and taking my hand, kissing my knuckles. "When a beautiful, smart woman offers you a threesome, you don't let her go home and overthink it. You bring her home and show her why it was a really, really brilliant idea."

My nerves are trying to take over, but I know they're right. They know me well. I will overthink the ever-loving hell out of this if I go home. Then will always wonder *what if I'd taken a chance.*

I'm tired of wondering, of fantasizing, of pondering *what if.* I'm tired of being on the sidelines. Maybe this will pale in comparison to my fantasies. Maybe it will make things awkward. Maybe I'll embarrass myself. *Maybe maybe maybe.* But if I don't go, there won't be any maybes. Only sureties. That the guy from high school won. That I'm scared to take a chance. That I'm still alone, left only with my movie fantasies.

No movies are made about that girl. The girl who hears the call to adventure and just says, *meh, I'm just going to go home to watch Netflix instead.* That movie would be dead boring.

I swallow down the welling panic and look to each of them. "Okay."

Preston takes my other hand and runs his thumb along my palm, sending a shiver of anticipation through me. "Okay."

It's time to take a starring role in my own life.

At least for one night.

CHAPTER THREE

E VERYTHING FEELS MOSTLY normal as we clean up after eating takeout at Preston and Dominic's apartment. We've hung out here together countless times, shared meals, watched movies, played games, gotten drunk, gotten silly. Tasha is usually with us and typically there would be alcohol of some sort, but other than that, it could be any other Friday night. I've almost convinced myself that our conversation earlier didn't happen—until I head for my normal spot on the couch.

Dominic catches my hand before I can get there. "Come 'ere, Al."

He guides me back to the fluffy arm chair he favors and pulls me down with him. I land on his lap, my blue sundress rucking up a little and the rough denim of his jeans brushing the backs of my thighs. Preston is watching us as he takes a seat on the couch, only an arm's length away from us.

Dominic cups my jaw, turning my face gently toward him. His brown eyes are flecked with green. I've never been close enough to notice the pattern before, but I find myself searching for every new thing about him. His thumb brushes my bottom lip. "Still good with this? You're trembling."

I hadn't noticed, but now I feel the subtle tremors moving through me.

"Sorry. I'm nervous as hell," I admit. "And maybe a little scared that I'm going to embarrass myself. It's been a long time. But yeah, still good."

His gaze is searching, a little flash of concern there. "I know it's personal, but can you tell us what this guy did in high school to put you off of sex? If it was…bad, we need to know what not to do. We don't want to do anything to scare you."

I wince inwardly, the memory of that night more mortifying than scary, but I'm touched that Dominic's taking this kind of care with me. "He didn't hurt me. Not physically at least. I just…couldn't orgasm. And he basically told me I was doing it wrong. That I was too uptight."

"He didn't know what he was doing and that was *your* fault?" Preston says from the couch, irritation in his voice. "You were a virgin. What the fuck is wrong with people?"

"I think he got all his sex tips from bad porn," I say. "I know now that he was an idiot. And even then, I knew I was capable of orgasm. I'd done it on my own. But at sixteen, when an older guy tells you you're basically failing at sex, part of you believes him. After that, it was just easier doing things on my own."

"Fuck that guy," Dominic says, his fist curling against the arm of the chair. "I hope he's spent the last few years with only his shitty porn to keep him company."

I lean down and press a quick kiss to his mouth, testing out my comfort level a little, but also just feeling a wave of affection for my friends. "Thank you."

His gaze dips briefly to my lips, and I think he's going to pull me back down for a real kiss, but he seems to reel himself in. "I'm glad you knew how to take care of things yourself, but does that mean you've never gotten off with someone else?"

Apprehension shimmers through me again. "No. Anytime things have gotten close to that point with someone, I tap the brakes. I think part of me still worries that I can't get there with someone else."

Dominic frowns. "I don't want you worrying about that with us. If for some reason we can't get you there or your nerves get in the way, it's fine. This isn't a test to pass. We're not math."

A tension I didn't know I was holding between my shoulders loosens, a knot unwinding. "Thanks."

"Plus, if you feel comfortable enough with us, we'd happily watch you get yourself off, see the expert in action," Dominic says, a wicked gleam in his eye. He traces his finger along the seam of my thighs, sending sparks of electricity along my skin, and slips his hand just barely under the hem of my dress. "In fact, if we're fulfilling fantasies tonight, can we add that one to *my* list?"

Preston groans. "Fucking hell. Why did we wait so long to do this? That friend edict was the stupidest decision ever."

I laugh and look over at him, but my laugh catches in my throat. His palm is pressed along the thick outline in his jeans. I can't stop looking at the way his hand is curved around himself. It's like seeing through a secret door I've never gotten to peek through before. My friend, turned on, over me.

"Well, if I was worried having Nic here might make this awkward or weird, I guess I can put that concern aside." Preston's mouth lifts at the corner. "Because I'm hard as fuck just thinking about his fingers moving higher."

Dominic shifts beneath me, turning me more toward Preston, and suddenly, I can feel all of Dominic, the steel of his erection pressing against my backside like a hot promise. My tongue curls against the back of my teeth. I still can't believe this is happening. His hand moves higher, and I brace a little, wanting him to continue, to cross the line, but also nervous. I keep my gaze on Preston, the way he's watching me holding my attention captive.

Dominic skims his fingers along my thighs, up and down, up and down, nudging my dress up higher with each pass. It takes everything I have not to squirm. He puts his chin on my shoulder, looking at Preston. His scruff tickles my neck. "You think she's wet for us, Pres?"

I shiver. *She.* Like I'm something to discuss. Like it's not up to me anymore what happens. Maybe I should be offended, but the little shift in pronoun feels like a gift. I don't have to be the director of this movie. I can just…trust them.

Preston is watching Dominic's fingers mark a path along my skin. He licks his lips. "I think you'd better check."

Dominic presses a kiss to the sensitive spot behind my ear and then slides my dress to my waist, exposing the simple pair of lavender cotton panties I put on this morning, never anticipating anyone would see them. I don't have to look down to know that the state of my arousal is more than obvious. But Dominic isn't going to leave anything to chance. His finger outlines the edge of my panties, teasing, making my pussy clench. My knees widen without conscious effort, and he tugs the swatch of thin cotton aside. Cool air kisses my skin, and Dominic's roughened fingertips glide over the slick center of me. I gasp.

"I'd say the answer is a resounding yes," Dominic says and then gently pinches my clit.

My back arches and I grip the arm of the chair. *God. How does that feel so good?*

He makes a hungry sound in the back of his throat. "So hot." He rubs small circles, grazing the most sensitive spot with each pass but not enough to get me where I suddenly desperately need to go. "You feel fucking perfect, Al."

I mutter something unintelligible, my hips rocking against his touch.

"Is that how you touch yourself?" Preston's low voice drifts into my ears, but I don't open my eyes.

"Or do you use toys?" Dominic asks. "Do you like something deep inside you when you come?"

They expect me to talk. This seems like a monumental expectation at the moment, but I take a breath and try to focus. "Sometimes just like this but sometimes a vibrator or a toy. Depends on if I'm in a hurry or not."

"Fucking hell. Now I'm picturing it." Hands are yanking my panties down and off. *Preston.* I can smell the beachy scent of his shampoo.

"We don't have any toys but, lucky you, we have an extra set of hands, extra mouth, extra cock," Dominic says. "Maybe we can help you out."

My heart is beating everywhere, and any threat of embarrassment about discussing how I get myself off dissipates like a ghost. I force my eyes open, not wanting to miss this, to hide.

When I look down, Dominic's tanned fingers are slick with my arousal and working my pussy with the adept skill he uses on his guitar. That would be enough to fill my fantasy coffers for a while, but now Preston has gotten to his knees in front of me. His hands are on my thighs, spreading me open for him. Before I can even brace for what's about to happen, he lowers his head and drags his tongue along my inner thigh and I whimper.

He smiles up at me like a villain, like I'm caught in his evil trap, like he knows some secret I don't.

He eases two fingers inside me, making my body clench around him, and then his head dips down again. His tongue hits me like sweet fire, like he's starved for my pussy and only full-out feasting will satisfy him. I almost leap off of Dominic's lap because it's all so much. Preston's fingers, his tongue, the feel of Dominic's cock still hard against my ass. I've never...not like this, not with anyone.

"Watch him, Al," Dominic whispers against my ear.

He holds me tight against him, keeping me in place, and I lower my gaze. I watch in rapt amazement as Preston's tongue burrows between Dominic's still stroking fingers to get at my clit. The view of both of them...

I can't. I can't. I can't. Not yet. Not when the night has just started, but I'm only a passenger on this train and it's careening off the tracks.

Preston looks up, watching me watch him, and sensation explodes through me. I cry out, my head falling back against Dominic's shoulder and my hips rocking against tongue and lips and two men's fingers. The pleasure rolls through me like a thunderclap, big and sudden and powerful.

I hold on tight. One arm thrown back, wrapped around Dominic's neck, the other hand gripped tight in Preston's hair. I'm afraid I'll melt into the floor if I let go.

They don't let me fall though. They let me ride out the pleasure until I'm gasping for breath, and then Preston is easing back, draping my dress over me again, and Dominic is murmuring soft, soothing words into my hair.

I turn and curl into Dominic, letting him hold me. I don't know if he's a cuddler, but he's just going to have to get over it if he isn't. I have no choice. My bones are now made of honey. He's just going to have to carry me everywhere from now on.

Dominic chuckles beneath me. "Honey bones, huh? I guess that means we did okay?"

"Did I say that out loud?" I ask, pressing my face into his shoulder.

He kisses the top of my head and then lifts me. "Come on, Honey Bones. We've got more plans for you now that we've established that you definitely don't have any problems coming—in fact, you're kind of easy, Al. I mean, you really should've made Pres work harder."

I huff and lift my head, prepared to be properly offended, but I find him grinning. I roll my eyes. "Shut up. It's been a while."

"It was ridiculously hot," he says. "Feeling you? Watching you ride Pres's tongue? I never get a view like that."

Preston is a step behind us and I catch his eye, feeling shy all of a sudden, but he smiles and gives me a little wink. "My view was better." He pats Dominic's shoulder. "And Nic was smart to send in the A-team first, you know, guarantee you get off and take the pressure off of him."

"Joke's on you, man," Dominic says. "I didn't want to go first and set up unrealistic expectations for Alex when you got your turn. You were the opening act. Headliner still to come."

Preston sniffs. "Keep telling yourself that."

The easy way they take jabs at each other chases away any weirdness that was threatening. I lay my head against Dominic's shoulder. "I don't know whose band is whose, but I'm definitely staying until the encore."

CHAPTER FOUR

DOMINIC CARRIES ME into his room, and Preston clicks on a lamp. I'm impressed to see the bed is made, a soft-looking flannel blanket tucked neatly over navy-blue sheets. There's a worn paperback on the side table and little bowl filled with colorful guitar pics. The only sign that this is a college guy's apartment is the basket of unfolded laundry in one corner.

He sets me down on the bed and they both stay standing, looking down at me with unreadable expressions.

I frown. "What's wrong?"

"I think I'm still processing the fact that you're here...on my bed," Dominic says. "That we get to do this. I think I'm half-expecting to wake up and realize I've just been having another filthy dream about my good friend Al."

I lean back on my hands. "Another, huh?"

He shrugs. "I'm a bad friend. No mental boundaries."

"And I'm trying to figure out what to do first," Preston says, stepping closer and going to his knees in front of me. He runs his hands along my thighs, holding my gaze. "I want to make this great for you, but I'm not going to sit here and pretend that I know how this is supposed to work. I've never done the threesome thing. I've never shared."

"Neither have I," Dominic says. "But I bet it's going to be fun figuring it out."

Their admissions are like sweet pieces of candy slipped onto my tongue. We're all figuring this out together. There is no expert. If we don't get it exactly right, so what?

I loop my arms around Preston's neck and touch my forehead to his. "How about we just focus on making each other feel good? If something isn't working, any of us can say stop at any time."

His hands move higher, squeezing my hips. "Sounds like a solid plan."

He leans in, hesitating for just a moment, and then he kisses me. When his lips touch mine, it's as if we've broken the seal on the night. What happened in the living room was just a test case, an experiment, a *will this work?*

But with this kiss, we're committing to the night. This is happening. Preston's tongue parts my lips and his hands go to my face, holding me there as I open to him. His kiss is slow and exploring, the taste of me still on his lips. He may not be totally confident on how to manage a threesome, but he definitely is a confident kisser. Any remaining nerves I had are melting like ice cream on a hot day. My hand goes to the hair at the nape of his neck and I grip tight, losing myself to the moment.

But this isn't just another kiss. We have an audience and soon another partner. The bed dips, and the heat of Dominic's body fills the space behind me. His thighs bracket mine and his chest presses against my back, his erection a seductive reminder nudging the base of my spine. The clean scent of his shampoo drifts over me as he kisses the spot behind my ear. "I want to see all of you."

He gets a grip on the hem of my dress and slowly drags it upward. Preston and I break our kiss only long enough for Dominic to sweep my dress over my head. He tosses it aside and, with deft fingers, unhooks my bra and gets rid of that, too.

The cool air of the bedroom drifts over me, making every part of my body hyperaware. Dominic's palms slide along my rib cage and then he cups my breasts from behind, the heat of his hands like a brand on my skin. He gently bites the curve of my neck. "Fucking gorgeous."

While Preston tugs at my bottom lip with his teeth, Dominic pinches my nipples just hard enough to make it count, and I moan into Preston's mouth. Pres pulls back and looks down, hunger flashing across his face. "Jesus Christ. Look at you."

I glance down, the view almost too much to process. Dominic's long fingers are stroking me, my nipples taut and sensitive. He plumps one of my breasts in his hand, an offering. Preston dips his head and takes one nipple into his mouth, sucking and grazing his teeth over it.

"Fuck," I gasp, the sensation surprisingly intense, like he's tugged on a wire that originates between my legs. He sucks a little harder, his eyes closing like he's never tasted anything better, and I'm lost to it. "Yes. That's...*God.*"

"Oh, I think we found something she likes," Dominic says, his voice a low rumble against me.

While Preston lavishes attention on one breast, Dominic licks his own fingers and then pinches and teases my other nipple, making everything slippery and oh so sensitive. Neither seem to be in any rush. I arch against their touch. I'm on the edge of coming again, which is unfathomable. They're not even touching me below the waist, but the pulse between my thighs is almost unbearable.

I squirm, unable to stay still, the need building and becoming urgent. I need...I don't know exactly but I need it.

"Please," I beg. *"Please.* I need you. Inside."

Preston breaks away abruptly, his breath ragged, and tucks his hand between my legs, burying his fingers inside me and stroking. I moan and tighten around him.

"Christ," he says. "You're so responsive, baby. I can't believe you've been deprived this long. We're going to take care of you. I promise."

I'm riding Preston's fingers, my need taking over any potential shame, but his words cut through the erotic fog. Affection for these two guys swells inside my chest.

"Damn straight we are," Dominic says, softening his stroke against my breast.

"You've been on a deprivation diet way too long. Now you get to gorge."

The pressure of Preston's fingers disappears. I open my eyes, ready to beg, but Preston is standing, looking at Dominic. "Condoms?"

"Top drawer," Dominic says. "Grab a few." While Preston goes to the side table, Dominic turns me and lays me out on the bed. He strokes my pussy, just enough to drive me wild but not enough to send me over. "You're gonna need us both, huh? Greedy girl. One cock isn't enough."

I wet my lips. "Why have one when I can have two?"

"Touché." He smiles that wicked smile of his and sits up to unbutton his shirt.

I'm mourning the loss of his hands on me, but when he throws his shirt aside, I'm distracted by the view—all that lean muscle dusted with a line of dark hair that disappears into his jeans. When he comes close again, I run my hand up his chest. "You're pretty."

He chuckles. "Back at ya, Honey Bones."

I tug at the button of his jeans. "I've shown you mine. When do I get to see yours? Fair's fair."

His dark hair has fallen into his eyes, but I don't miss the hint of smugness there. He knows he's nice to look at. "Yes, ma'am."

He stands by the side of the bed, unbuttoning his jeans, and glances over at Preston, who's taken a spot on the other side, a strip of condoms in his hand. "Guess this is the part where we prove we're really comfortable as roommates."

I look between the two of them. The thought had never occurred to me. That this might be uncomfortable for them and that I'm asking for too much. They still have to be roommates after this. "Hey, if this is too—"

"Stop," Preston says with a little shake of his head. "We're good. More than good. Watching him fuck you?" He tosses Dominic one of the condoms. "Not a fantasy I knew I had, but now I can't think of anything hotter. Except for when it's my turn for him to watch us."

I bite my lip, a full-body heat wave moving over me.

The sound of the condom packet draws my attention, and I turn to Dominic. His jeans and boxers are gone and his hand is wrapped around the hard length of his cock. He casually strokes himself, watching me.

I'm mesmerized by the sight of him. He's even sexier than I imagined in my fantasies, not just how he looks but the easy confidence that rolls off him. The gleam in his eye says *I'm going to ruin you for other guys and you're going to fucking love every second of it.* I want to crawl over to him and beg to explore him, to run my hands through the dark hair at the base of his cock, to feel the weight of him in my hands, taste the drops of fluid on the smooth head. My tongue runs along my bottom lip.

He doesn't miss it. He nods at me. "Say it, Al. Say what you want and you can have it."

I swallow hard. "Let me taste you."

He tosses the condom onto the bed and glances at Preston. "Keep her ready."

My belly tightens in anticipation as Dominic climbs onto the bed and then straddles my upper body. He braces a hand on the headboard, looming over me, his cock inches from my face. "This what you want?"

"Yes," I whisper. It's all I can manage.

"Lucky me." He eases closer, his hand around his cock, and rubs the tip over my lips. The velvety heat and salty tang of his skin makes me hum with pleasure.

I part my lips fully, wanting more. I want to suck him, make him feel good, but he shakes his head.

"You do that, Al, and you're going to do me in. When I come the first time, I'm gonna be deep inside you. You just get a taste for now."

The mild order in his voice sends a hot shiver through me. I like this game. *This is all you get. Make it count.* So, I use my tongue and lips, and he rocks his hips, hovering over me, letting me lick and kiss the length of his cock, nuzzle the tight weight of his balls, explore all those secret male places.

Dominic groans, cursing under his breath. "You're a goddamned menace. But I love that you love it. Does this make you wetter, Al? You like licking cock?"

Before I can answer, a hand slides along my pussy and a hot zip of pleasure moves through me. Preston's fingers dip inside me, and the slick sound the contact makes leaves nothing up for debate.

"She's fucking soaked," Preston confirms.

"Dirty girl," Dominic says, a playful note in his voice. He pulls his cock away, climbing off of me, and drops a quick kiss to my mouth before he's gone. My eyelids flutter open. Preston's fingers are working magic again and my muscles aren't fully cooperating, but I manage to prop myself up on my elbows to watch the two of them.

Dominic's hand joins Preston's as their fingers explore me, the sensations and visual making me groan. Preston has stripped down and those bitable arms are almost within my reach. Where Dominic is long and lean, Pres is all honed athlete. Broad shoulders, smooth muscular chest, and an ass that has me shifting my plans for biting to a new area.

He looks over at me and gives me a playful smile. "Ready to judge the contest?"

"What contest?"

"Who's going to make you come first. The longer you can hold out, the more fun you have." He stands up, exposing his full body to me, and I watch as he rolls a condom onto his thick erection. "Count to one hundred, Alex."

"What?" I ask.

But he just smiles and climbs onto the bed. Dominic stands, watching. Preston runs a hand along my thigh, and lifts my knee, opening my body to him. The head of his cock presses against me, the pressure delicious. He lowers his head and kisses me softly, no doubt tasting remnants of his roommate there. Then he whispers against my lips. "Count."

I have no idea why he's asking but I say, "One..."

Preston enters me with one smooth stroke, and my body protests briefly at the pressure. *Goddamn.* My toys aren't as big as he is, and the heat of him is a shock. I've forgotten how a real-live man feels. But then he tucks a hand between us and circles my clit with the tip of his finger as he thrusts again, and warm pleasure rolls in like the tide. He seats himself impossibly deep inside me and I tighten around him like a vise grip. He groans against my ear. "Fuck, you feel good. Maybe I'm going to lose right out of the gate."

"Maybe. *Two,*" I say, closing my eyes and running my hands along his back, his muscles flexing beneath my touch. *"Three."* I get to his ass and dig my nails in, urging him deeper and earning a sexy grunt from him. *"Four."*

Preston's breath quickens and his rhythm gets faster, deeper, almost angry. The shift in demeanor nearly undoes me. My normally cool and in-control friend is fucking like he's trying to permanently nail me to the bed, and I can't get enough. I know I'm leaving marks on his ass with my fingernails, but I can't stop myself from gripping him, from wanting him buried to the hilt, stretching me and fucking me senseless. I'm lost in the counting and feeling on the verge of orgasm again, but when I gasp out *one hundred,* he jerks back, grips the base of the condom, and pulls out.

"What's wrong?" I ask, protest in my voice.

He's breathing hard, his skin dewy with sweat. "You wanted to be shared, Alex. Sharing requires taking turns."

Understanding dawns and I watch in awed silence as Dominic replaces him above me.

"I could've come just watching you take him like that, but I'm glad that's not all I get to do." Dominic takes my hand and kisses the inside of my palm. "Get on your hands and knees, Honey Bones. I want full access to touch you. Pres, feel free to make use of her mouth. I have a feeling she'll like feeling full all over."

I roll over, my mind whirling but my excitement humming. They're going to pass me back and forth until I come. They want me to hold out, to make them work for it. Best. Game. Ever.

Preston gets onto the bed, condom discarded, and leans against the headboard, legs open, cock hard and fisted in his hand. I crawl over him, staying on my hands and knees, and Dominic runs his palms up the backs of my thighs, spreading me.

"Show him how good you are with your mouth, Al," Dominic says. "And I'll show you how good I am with mine."

Preston threads his fingers into my hair and guides me down. I take his cock into my mouth slowly, keeping my gaze on him, feeling oddly powerful. But then Dominic's thumbs rub along the edges of my pussy and spread me wide. When the flat of his tongue licks over me, I nearly choke on Preston's cock.

Preston moans, his grip in my hair tightening, and doesn't let me release him. "I'll count for you, baby. *One.*"

I close my eyes, rolling my tongue along Preston's cock, and Dominic begins to destroy me with his mouth. I've never been licked from behind and never with such dedicated intensity. Dominic's tongue is as agile as his guitar-playing fingers, and my body sings under his attention. Preston finds my breast with his free hand and strokes.

I'm on fire everywhere—and may end up as ashes—but it will be worth it. I whimper and moan and writhe. I can imagine what I look like, how desperate I must sound, but I don't care. Whatever they want to do to me, if it feels like this, they can do it. I'm theirs.

The numbers become background noise. When I hear one hundred, I'm bereft, expecting Dominic to pull away, to stop the intense pleasure of having them both, but he doesn't stop. Instead, he shifts and presses his tongue inside me.

I die a little.

Preston stops counting.

Time loses meaning.

But just when I don't think I can hold out anymore, Dominic pulls back. I cry out in protest, but then the sweet crinkle of a condom wrapper fills my ears. The scent of maleness surrounds me like a fog.

"Not good at taking turns," Dominic says, breathless.

"Screw turns. Fuck her, man," Preston says, his voice tight and urgent. "And do it well because her moaning around my dick? Jesus. I want to feel her come."

The pleasure in his voice fills me up and makes me want to give both of them everything I have.

"And, Alex," Preston says, warning in his voice. "You better pull away right now if you don't want me to shoot down your fucking throat because when you come, there's going to be no stopping me then."

I give him my gaze and circle my tongue around the head of his cock.

He groans and cups the side of my head. "You're perfect. I always knew you would be. I've wanted you for so goddamned long, Alex."

The words are a shock, but I let them move through me, settle in.

"You and me both," Dominic says as his hands slide along my hips and he positions himself behind me. "And I hope you don't think we're letting you walk away after this. Sorry, Honey Bones. Now that you've given us a chance, we have a lot more to prove to you. We're only just getting started."

We're only getting started. Maybe that should scare me. But it feels exactly right.

Dominic pushes against me and plunges slow and deep, filling me to the hilt and making me sigh around Preston's cock. We're joined. All of us.

The moment crystalizes and then the rhythm of our bodies takes over, like we were always meant to do this dance. Like we already knew the song and the steps. Dominic is as confident in his lovemaking as I expected. His hands stroke over my hips, my back, my pussy, knowing just where to touch. Preston is teasing my breasts, tugging my hair, bringing me to the edge. My tongue is working, my hips rocking, tilting to meet Dominic's thrusts. And he knows how to angle me just right, his cock dragging over a new perfect place I've never been able to find on my own, making a delicious sensation build deep in my muscles.

Preston groans and Dominic grunts, and I'm building to something that's too big.

A desperate noise builds in my throat as they both fill me. Over and over, like they can't get enough of me. I can't get enough of them. But my body is cresting, soaring to dangerous heights. I'm going to break apart, turn into shards of the girl formerly known as Alexis Wayne. *I can't I can't I can't.*

But then light bursts behind my eyelids, and I scream around Preston's cock. Waves of sensation smash into me, and I lose a sense of where I am. I'm tumbling, tumbling, *falling.* But they've got me. Dominic holds me in place, fucking me with urgency now, and hot jets of fluid fill my mouth as Preston loses it. I swallow on reflex, and Dominic shouts, holding my hips hard against him and finally falling into the abyss with us.

The sounds of our collective undoing bounce around us until we're all left in a heap of sweaty limbs and panting breaths on the bed.

I don't know how much time passes, but eventually, someone rolls me onto my back. I lie there, eyes closed, body spent. "I'm dead. Move along."

There's a soft chuckle.

"Most beautiful dead girl I've ever seen," Preston says.

I lie there as warm hands take care of me. There are damp cloths to clean me, a sip of water, then a soft blanket wrapped around me. I finally open my eyes when one of the guys lifts me up and sits me up against a pile of pillows. Preston and Dominic flank me on the bed, stretching out on either side of me.

Dominic puts his arm around me. "Welp, that's one effective way to ruin a friendship, Al."

Preston adds his arm, cuddling me between them. "Yep. That's done. Way to go."

"What?" I sit up straighter, looking between the two of them, a dart of panic surfacing. "What do you mean?"

Dominic lifts a brow. "Because after tonight, how are we not supposed to fall shit-faced in love with you?"

"It's inevitable," Preston agrees. "Better prepare yourself now, Alex. We'll probably be annoyingly persistent getting you to love us back."

I turn fully so I can face both of them, trying to see if they're fucking with me, but their expressions are smooth, like they're delivering obvious news.

"You're serious," I ask. "The two of you. And me?"

Preston shrugs. "Would you rather us fight for you? See who wins?"

I look between the two of them and a slow smile curves my lips. "I already know who wins."

❖ ❖ ❖

WHEN I COME home late the next day, Tasha is sitting on the couch watching the end of *Reality Bites*. She immediately hits pause and turns toward me, giving me a long look. She breaks into a triumphant grin. "Oh. My. God. I can see it on your face. You fucked one of them. My evil plan worked!"

I cross my arms. "You are definitely evil."

She claps excitedly. "I am so brilliant. And I'm dying. I need all the details—like all of them—but first I need to know the answer to the big question." She does a little mock drumroll on the arm of the couch. "Which one did you choose? Sexy Dominic and all his artistic brooding or Preston with his pretty-boy looks and hot body? Is my friend Alex an eighties girl or a nineties girl?"

I smile, grab the remote, and turn off the movie. "Neither. I'm a twenty-first-century girl. I get to have both."

❖ ❖ ❖

Thanks for reading! If you'd like more, sign up for my newsletter. It's low on promo, big on content, and you get **a free romance reading journal** when you sign up!

roniloren.com/free-reading-journal

OUR NEW FOREVER

CLAUDIA BURGOA

LEYLA

I REGRET STEPPING into a Target.

The place is too bright and too crowded. I still have a two-hour drive home, and it's getting late. I could wait and talk to Blaire, but I don't want to get everyone's hopes up. There's the pharmacy in Happy Springs, but everyone in Baker's Creek hovers around that town too.

My phone buzzes. It's Pierce looking for me. I snuck out first thing in the morning while he was still sleeping. It's not that I didn't want to talk to him, but there's so much going on inside my head that I don't want to worry him—or give him hope.

Not yet.

I slide my finger across the screen and check his text.

Pierce: Where are you?

Leyla: I'm still in Portland.

Pierce: Do you want me to send one of my brothers to pick you up?

Leyla: No, I just need to run a quick errand, and I'll head home.

Pierce: It's getting late.

Leyla: I'll drive safe. If you want, I can call you, and we can spend the two-hour drive chatting.

Pierce: I don't want you to be distracted.

Pierce: I texted Vance, he said he'll be happy to fly to Portland.

Leyla: Let me finish this errand, and I'll text you back.

Yes, I want him to come and pick me up. I'm tired, I need to piss, and I'm starving. If I could skip this errand, I would. This might look like a simple shopping trip, but it's not. No one in this city would know the difference of a random woman perusing the store's aisles or someone who's searching for an specific item. Unlike in Baker's Creek, where people follow my every move.

I drag the red-orange shopping cart and glance at the Starbucks. The smell of caffeine is inviting, and the idea of drinking a latte with three shots sounds really good with the amount of sleep I got the night before. I bite my lip, huffing.

Coffee, please…but I can't drink it. I've been caffeine-deprived since this morning. Maybe I'll drink two pots tomorrow, or…*what if?* That voice keeps saying the same thing over and over again.

I slip my gloves, hat, and scarf into my purse. Hopefully, I will get what I came for before I go home.

Before I go *there,* I do a lap around the store, beginning with the home decorations. Our new house is almost ready, and we're moving in a couple of weeks.

I've purchased all the furniture, but it's time to pick things that will make it a cozy home. This time, it's forever. Pierce and I understand what each other needs. A family, children, and our farm kids. We'll live in Baker's Creek and have a small house in Portland for those days when I have to visit the practice I'm about to open.

I pick out a few frames to hold our wedding pictures, which we haven't printed yet. Talk about procrastination. The only photographs lingering around our room are the ones we've taken of our baby, Carter. He's my little miracle, and maybe... I touch my belly but try not to hold on to any hope. At least not yet. I stop at the women's clothing section. I keep talking myself out of buying some of the winter clothing in clearance. My eyes linger on a maternity mannequin. I tug down my jacket, wondering if I'll ever buy clothes from that section.

Maybe I won't, and the only person I'm fooling is myself. How often have I tried to get pregnant in the past and...but that was then, and this is different, isn't it?

I keep stalling and decide to look through the toy section, trying to find something new for Carter or any of his cousins. It's not like they need them, but I love to see the excitement on their little faces when they get something new. It doesn't have to be big, just different from everything they have.

My next stop is the electronics section. Pierce could use a new set of earbuds, but I can't find his favorite brand.

Move, just do it, a voice inside my head says as a thrum of anxiety lies just under my skin.

And just because I like to torture myself, I end up in the infant section, in front of the baby clothes, running my fingertips against a pink onesie.

I donated all the clothes I bought a couple of years ago after adopting Carter. After all, I finally had the baby I had yearned for. We didn't need more.

But what if I can finally have a little girl?

Being in the infant section didn't make me feel trapped and forever unloved. The wounds are closed, and I know I'll be fine if it's negative.

I grip the shopping cart handle as I approach the feminine care aisle where a young couple stares at the condoms. They look overwhelmed at all the brands. I can't help but snort when I notice the irony of placing them right on top of the pregnancy tests.

They're broadcasting quality assurance.

"If you believe that our condoms fail, you can check with a foolproof pregnancy test," I mutter, taking a picture and saving it for later. Blaire, Grace, Hadley, and Sofia will get a kick out of it. But I won't show it to them until later. Much later.

After dumping three different brands of tests in the almost full shopping cart, I take another lap around the kitchenware and the bedding.

I spend about twenty minutes at the self-checkout kiosk. I only came to Target for a pregnancy test, and as usual, I ended up with a full cart, spending three hundred dollars. I'll never learn that this store can be dangerous.

Once I have all the bags in the truck, I go back inside Target and rush straight to the restroom, ripping the packaging open and pulling down my jeans. I'm an expert at peeing on a stick. Guilt constricts my chest. I should wait for Pierce, he'd want to know, and maybe—maybe—I'm falling into old patterns.

Instead of waiting for the test results, I shove the stick back in the box and text Pierce.

Leyla: *Pick me up, please.*

Pierce: *Are you okay?*

Leyla: Yes, I just need...you.

Pierce: I'll get Vance to fly me to you.

Leyla: I'll drive to the hangar.

Pierce: Just tell me that you're okay, please.

No, I'm not. I thought this was going to be easy, but...I'm afraid to see the same result. I had no idea I wanted another baby until last night when I realized that I hadn't had my period.

I blink back the tears.

Leyla: I'll be better when I see you.

Pierce: I'll be there. Remember that I love you.

I smile because this time I believe him, and whatever that test says doesn't matter, we have each other, and we have Carter.

PIERCE

I WISH I could ask Vance to fly faster. Leyla is in trouble. I can feel it in my bones. What happened?

My leg bounces up and down. She left the house too early in the morning, it felt as if she was avoiding me, but I didn't take it personally. We're past that behavior, aren't we? Fourteen months ago, we said I do, and this time we promised to stop selling the pretty version of our lives. We promised to love each other without restraints and with respect.

She's my entire universe and my home. I'd die if something happened to her. The thirty-minute ride toward Portland feels eternal and draining. I'm exhausted when my brother lands the helicopter.

"Should I wait here?" he asks as we climb down.

I nod when I spot the truck. "Yes, give us a few minutes."

The short distance between the helicopter and the truck feels like a mile stretch—like the hallway of *The Shining* where the creepy twins wait. I'm trying to keep myself calm, but it's almost impossible.

She wears a hat that hides her fiery red hair. She looks beautiful, as always, and so well relaxed, but she's not. I can feel it, the anxiety eating her insides.

Once I reach her, I take her into my arms and kiss her deeply, like it's the first time I possess those luscious lips or the last time I'll ever get to claim her. I take her breath away but infuse her lungs with all the love I have for her.

"Hey, Ley, are you okay?"

She nods. "I am now."

"What happened? Is the new clinic okay?"

"Yeah, I..." She pulls out a box from her coat.

"What is this?" I ask before I read the words: *Rapid Pregnancy Test. Results 5 days sooner.*

My thoughts stumble one on top of the other as I try to make sense of this box. This small blue cardboard that seems to be open and with a huge meaning behind it. Obviously, I know what it means, but were we trying to have a baby?

Not that I mind, I would love to have a house filled with little tikes to love and raise with my wife. "Why are you shaking like a leaf in the middle of a fall windstorm?"

She swallows hard. "I'm late. My period..." She stares at the ground.

"Okay?" I mumble the question cautiously.

"Maybe..."

I lift her chin. Our gazes meet, and I notice her lips are trembling.

"Why didn't you tell me earlier, love?"

"What if it's just another illusion? I tried for so long."

And I want to punch myself because I created this fear. "That's on me, and I'm sorry for that. I'm so fucking sorry."

"I know, which is why I called you because no matter what that says, I want us to find out together."

"If we open the box, will there be an answer?"

She nods and smiles shyly. "I bought a onesie."

"You did, huh?"

"It's pink."

"But it's okay if we have a boy, isn't it?"

She nods again. This time I notice her neck is more relaxed.

"I don't want to ruin whatever is happening, but we need to go," Vance calls out.

Leyla chuckles, relaxing and letting go of all the tension. I brush my lips against hers. "It's going to be okay. This time it's different. I love you. I love you in all the ways I should've from the beginning, but I didn't know how to do it then. You're not alone. We're a team, and I need you to remember that I'll go to the deepest parts of the ocean and the highest mountains for you."

She hugs me tightly before whispering, "Open it, please."

Leyla hands me a tissue. I use it to pull the stick out with a shaky hand. I shouldn't feel this nervous, but if there's something I want to give her, it's a baby. I know we have our miracle boy, but if we can have just one more...are we being greedy?

The digital screen reads, *pregnant.*

Pregnant.

Leyla burst into tears.

Many beautiful happy tears.

We did it.

"We're having a baby," she whispers.

I pick her up and twirl her around, then press her tightly to my chest.

"A baby," I mumble against her lips, kissing her hard.

We laugh and cry at the same time. The wounds continue healing, and the scars are there, like faint lines reminding us of our journey, giving us hope because even in the darkest days, we were able to find our way home and to each other.

LEYLA

Seven months later...

I WAKE UP around two in the morning in Pierce's arms, his hands resting on my protruded belly. We don't have a name for our peanut yet—we're going to wait until the baby's out to find out the gender. Carter is so excited to be a big brother. I rub my tummy as the baby kicks, and that's when Pierce kisses my forehead.

"Hey," I murmur.

"How are you feeling?" he asks, nuzzling my neck.

I close my eyes, taking a deep breath.

These have been some of the best months—probably years—of my life. I was just passing by Baker's Creek, getting ready to divorce Pierce Aldrige and start anew. I had no idea how that would look, but I never left. I ended up finding my husband's heart. It was buried underneath a miserable childhood and two cruel parents.

Now, well, we're part of a big family and we're creating our little family. I couldn't be happier.

"Happy and nervous," I say, as he hugs me as tightly as he can without upsetting the baby. "How about you?"

"I don't have a baby pressing on my bladder and making me go pee all the time, so I guess I'm in better shape than you."

Playfully, I poke him with my elbow. "You're not funny."

"I'm happy. I have everything I've ever wanted and a lot more."

I turn around, wrapping my arms around his neck. I kiss him hard, almost as if this is the first day of the rest of our lives. I don't know how many times I can fall in love with this man over and over again, but I do keep falling—forever.

✧ ✧ ✧

Thank you for reading Our New Forever.

You can read more about Leyla & Pierce, or begin your journey through the Baker's Creek Billionaire Brothers here >
claudiayburgoa.com/wp/the-bakers-billionaire-brothers

Playhouse

Amo Jones

I T HAPPENED IN a flash. This was the kind of stain that didn't wash off during the first cycle, or even third. It was ruined. I knew it, everyone else around me knew it, and most importantly, my body knew it.

Coffee. It stains like a bitch.

"Jesus Christ, Ivy!" Tamara carefully took the thermos cup out of my hands, side-stepping a passing pedestrian to toss it into the trash. Tamara and I had been best friends since high school. She went off to college to get her law degree, and I, well… I own a publishing company. When I say I own, I mean it was passed down to me from merely having the last name Lee. My father started the company from the ground up. As soon as my mother told him she was pregnant, he decided to take his bestselling author name to a whole new level and offer a platform for other authors to be seen and heard, without crossing difficult paths that typical houses have you cross. Black Widow Publishing was born three months after I was and right after my mother left us both for a sixty-year-old hippie guru who lived in a straw shack in the Bahamas. Needless to say, she and I aren't really on solid ground.

Pulling back my blouse, I can't help but laugh around the misfortune of my morning. This was just the tip, I knew it. I hadn't been fully penetrated by this shit show of a day that I knew was still brewing. "Luckily I have spare clothes in my office. And you called me conceited for having a work closet…"

"No." Tamara raised one perfectly manicured finger. "I didn't say that. I said you didn't need a walk-in for your work closet." She flicked her black bob over her shoulder and shrugged. "But I get it."

"Hmm…" I murmured, falling into step beside her as we both continued down the busy streets of Chicago. "I'd hate to hear what you think of the rest of my life."

Tamara hooked her arm in mine. My publishing house was a block away from her firm, so we spent every waking minute around each other. Some would say we were tight; others would say co-dependent. "What, like your private jet?"

I laughed into my coffee and stopped outside her firm. "You know, I still think you should go out on your own."

She rolled her eyes, pulling open the door and casting one last look at me over her shoulder. "I told you, I don't want your money!"

"Love you!" I called out to her just as the door closed. I had one last thing to do before I went back to the office, though I really didn't want to do it right now. Parker and I weren't at a good time in our marriage, well no, that was a lie. We haven't been in a good place ever, yet here I was. Organizing our yearly trip to Colter Hills, even though the thought of being in a town with the population of roughly ten thousand locals and a few more tourists, snowed into the edgy mountains that were as cold as Alaska, sounds like a fucking bad idea. But it was something we did. With Parker's best friend and his wife, and my best friends, it was always something I looked forward to because it reminded me why I fought so hard. It grounded me like no other, and with this marriage, I needed it. Marriage is like a rose garden, it either wilts or flourishes, but either way it's going to hurt because those thorns are not something you can outgrow.

After getting off the phone with the airline and organizing our flight out of here, I changed my mind and called my assistant.

She answered instantly. "Mrs. Lee, hello. Is everything okay? I made sure to add the pile of submissions onto your desk. I have to admit, there—"

"Thank you, Natasha. I'm just calling to say that I'm heading home for the day. Can you let Jacob know that I won't be in for the meeting with Hera Anne this afternoon but that I look forward to hearing all about it when he's done."

"Oh!" Natasha's tone perked up higher. Natasha was a sweet girl, but maybe too sweet. She was currently on an internship with BWP and I have it in her best interest to toughen her up a bit. Not a lot, just enough to survive the demands of the job. "Will do, have a lovely day, Mrs. Lee."

I hung up the phone with her and called my driver to pick me up on the corner of Sixth, with a bottle of cheap rosé. Money doesn't buy class, and class doesn't exist in the dictionary of Ivy Lee.

I closed the door to our home and dropped my handbag on top of the console table near the front door. Parker wasn't home yet and for that I was thankful. I moved through to our open-plan kitchen, flicking the lights on with me. It was a little after three p.m., but it was five o'clock somewhere. I told myself this as I opened my display cabinet and took down a goblet glass, pouring the contents of my rosé. Our house was nice. Parker would say conventional, I'd reply boring. Basic white interior paint with simple black and white artwork which hung effortlessly on every wall. No family portraits, nothing personal. After we got married, I couldn't be bothered decorating so I hired a designer to do it all for me. Nothing in this house had substance, but it was comfortable, and I was well aware how lucky I was to have the life I did. We had the best of everything, the ridiculous TV, the oversized couch, all the newest gadgets. For fuck's sake, our fridge talks to us, yet... everything is so cold. Empty. Like touching a human with no soul.

I flicked through my phone and hit FaceTime with Tamara. She answered straight away, her eyes bored on me. "Girl, some of us can't just knock off when we want!" She set her phone up and started typing on her keyboard.

"Why can't you come on the plane with us? I think you should."

She stopped typing and her bright eyes once again came to mine. "I told you, I have to wait for Sam to finish work. She wants to come too." Right. Sam, the new girlfriend. Still not sure how I feel about her but that was another subject.

"I'm bored." I looked out in front of myself at the leaden art piece that's staring down at me like I was a scolded child.

"Girl, go and pack your bag. You leave in the a.m. and you and I both know Colter Hills requires top fashion."

"True," I said, bringing a finger up in front of myself while taking a large gulp of wine. It left a taste on the back of my throat that gave away its cheap label. Most people hated that palate of cheap wine, I loved it. "But did you see there's some event happening there this week? There are going to be fucking kids taking up all of the good spots."

"It don't matter!" Tamara scolded me. "We're still going to have a good time. As long as Bill and Hannah don't start fighting an hour in again." Bill and Hannah, Parker's best friend. Meh. The presumptuous twit that she is, I need a fucking Xanax just to have a conversation with her.

"I'm going to pack. I'll call you tomorrow."

"You do that! And don't worry. Del is flying out after you so you will only have to tolerate a couple hours max." I didn't bother telling her that that was beside the point. Usually we all flew in the same jet but this year we're all coming in different fucking planes.

I hung up with her and sent a quick text to our other best friend Del, telling her that I'll see her tomorrow and that I'd make sure a driver was at the airport to pick her up. Del and I have been best friends for longer than Tamara and I have been, but I'm nowhere near as co-dependant on Del as I am with Tamara.

Leaving my phone on the sofa, I headed upstairs to the master bedroom and pulled out my Louis Vuitton suitcase, placing it onto my bed.

I needed this trip. *I needed to forget.*

He stared down at his phone, ignoring my question. This had become the norm between him and I, and I didn't know when the decline in our marriage started, but I'm guessing it was right after I said I do. *You know exactly when... and why.*

My phone was vibrating in my pocket, but I ignored it, because I wanted him to look me in the eyes and answer the question I'd been wanting him to answer for three fucking weeks.

"So what do you think?" I asked again, my Valentino shoe tapping against the floor of the private jet.

"What?" He asked from above his phone, without looking up at me.

"About me buying into Le Chat?" Le Chat was the business of my friend Del, who, instead of asking me for a loan, would rather allow me to buy half of the shares. I wanted to do this to help her, since Tamara wasn't in a position to do so yet.

"Why do you think this will be a good idea, Ivy? I fail to see the pros."

I blinked at him with the knowledge that he refused to pay me any attention. I was too expensive for him anyway... I knew it. "Well, would you like facts and numbers, or my ethical reasons as to why I am buying in?"

Parker finally stopped what he was doing and raised his eyes up at me from behind thick brows. "Well if you have already decided, why are you asking me?"

I hated when he said this. I hated this response. How do you tell someone that they make you feel like you need their permission to do anything? I once told him this. I told him that he made me feel like I needed to ask, and you wanna know what his response was?

"Well, it's not my fault you feel that way. You do whatever you want to do..." Alas, this was a constant cycle for him. He would imply that he had issues with things, and then circle it right back to me to make the decision. That way, he would never have to wear the guilt of being controlling.

That way, he would never be the victim.

"I'm not asking you, Parker. I'm curious to know why you are against it. There's a difference."

He sighed, placing his phone face down onto the chair beside him and gave me his full attention. Shocking blue eyes threatened me. The kind that are not kind. The kind that has been tainted by whatever dirty shit he has ever done. "Because you don't need to. How many billionaires do you know would willingly buy into a shitty restaurant? That's right. None." He leaned forward and I watched as his long fingers wrapped around the crystal tumbler.

My mouth opened to respond, before I closed it. I needed to choose my next words carefully, because although I ran a tight ship at work, he most definitely liked to think he was the skipper of my life.

Plot twist. He wasn't.

I cleared my throat, hopefully along with the foul words that I wanted to slap across his face, took a sip of whisky and allowed it to burn my throat before finally saying, "It's my money, Parker, and this isn't about making money. It's about helping a friend when a friend is in need." That took him aback, which I intended it to do.

"You wouldn't have this money if it wasn't for your parents, Ivy, don't try to make it out as if you're self-made." His words annoyed me more than I'm sure mine did to him. I swallowed my anger and plastered on a fake smile.

"Mm-hmm. Okay, Parker." There's a level below the one you reach I think when you're done with someone. That's where I was at with Parker, yet any time I told him I wanted to leave, he reminded me why I couldn't...

The plane landed smoothly, and as soon as I stepped down onto the tarmac, I was slapped in the face by a gust of cold wind that I'm sure would leave a trail of frost down my spine. Colter Hills was a prestigious community built right in the middle of four of the largest ski mountains and resorts known to man. You couldn't find a house here for less than five million, and the majority of the owners here were people like me, who owned holiday homes and came for the season. The social circles here would put the ones in New York to shame, and I was almost certain that every single person who lived here shat gold.

Me included.

I slid into the waiting Range Rover and grabbed my phone out of my puffer jacket, answering instantly when I saw Jacob's name flashing across the screen.

"Yes?" I put on a sweet smile, ignoring Parker's presence beside me. Any time he was near knots formed in my belly that I couldn't shake. Marrying him was the worst thing I ever did. How could I be so smart yet so dumb all at the same time.

"Just making sure you don't have too much fun without me there." His voice always brought a smile to my face. Jacob had been with me since the get-go. He was also the president of Black Widow Publishing and has been one of my oldest friends. His father and mine were best friends growing up, which meant Jacob was also mine.

"I still wish you could have come."

He sighed, but I knew it was forced. "What can I say, having babies is lame."

"Hey!" I laughed, shaking my head as the Range Rover pulled us out of the private airport. "Leave my niece alone."

"Bring her back something expensive."

"I will. Hey, how did the interview go yesterday? What's Hera like? I'm still thinking about her novel." Something tapped against my thigh and I looked up to a scowling Parker. It wasn't that he was unattractive. In fact, most people who met Parker always complimented his looks before anything else. Attractiveness doesn't mean anything when it's painted onto a douche. God. What the fuck is wrong with me. Maybe I'm getting—wait what's the date? No, I'm not due.

"She was friendly and personable. She ranted on about her muses for the next three books. I think she'll be a great author to sign, you know. She's got spunk too."

"Spunk is good, and she's a great writer."

Jacob agreed. "Alright, well I hope to see some scandal on Instagram. Oh my God, are you going to have a tea party with Mrs. Williams again? Fuck me, you need to FaceTime me if you do. And steal me some of her Magic Mushrooms."

"Jacob!" I scolded, hiding my laugh behind a smile.

"What! I'm a parent. I need it now more than ever."

I shook my head and hit end, my best friends were fucking weird.

"You know you could wait until the fucking snow melted off your hair before you started working." Parker looked out the window to ignore me.

"I was actually answering his call, which I always will. God," I exhaled, my anger simmering below the surface. "You know what, can we not ruin this trip?"

"Sure," he muttered, but started fiddling on his phone.

When you marry, be sure to check his closet before you say I do…

We pulled up to my holiday home after driving through the quaint town. The town is one of my favorite parts of this place. The small shops that line the main road, glittered with snow and LED lights. Fresh meat butcherers and fruit produce stores line the cobblestone pathways, with small convenience shops that have everything you'd ever need. No fast-food chains, all five-star restaurants and high tea bars. There was even an underground ice club in town, where they racked lines of cocaine across ice cubes the size of coffee tables. My retirement plan was definitely to live here and do absolutely nothing but snowboard. I'd joke to Jacob all the time that he could buy me out so I could retire. Apparently, no one had a spare billion dollars lying around to do that.

The house sitter I have who lived here while I was away stepped down the grand stairs that lead to the house, a smile on her face. She was in her early twenties and had an online business that meant she could live anywhere while working. She chose here, rightly so. She was a money-making weapon who discovered online trading at a very young age. She dropped out of school and made her own way. As soon as one of the rich assholes who own a property here decided to sell, Punk would be sweeping in to buy.

"Hey, Ivy!" She pulled me in for a hug and I stepped back to take her in.

"You look great, Punk!" Punk had bright pink hair, a diamond in her front tooth, and tattoos all over her body.

"Thank you! The house is ready. I'll leave you guys to it and retreat to the pool house." She hiked her thumb over her shoulder.

"Don't be silly. Have a drink with me first, I need it."

Her eyes darted between Parker and I, but I stepped into her line of vision. Punk and I don't have a friendship, per se, but women are smart. They smell toxicity on men from a mile away, it's just up to us whether we decide to ride them like a carousel or not.

"Please."

Her little mouth curved to a smile. She was a beautiful girl. She had big, blue eyes and flawless skin. Ah, to be that young again. "Okay. But just so you know, my boyfriend is flying in tonight. Is it okay that he stays, I mean I didn't even think to ask you." Again, to be young…

"Of course." I smiled at her widely as we made our way up the stairs and through the double doors. I stopped in the entry and took a deep breath. Fuck, I missed this place. There was something about being around snow that seemed to freeze all my nightmares. The cool air and hot tubs… the shredding. The mulled wine. *The blood, the screams, the death.*

"So," I said, forcefully removing my shoes and placing them near the front door while unzipping my jacket. "Tell me about this boyfriend." She started explaining her new man, but I was too busy looking around my home to listen. It was a ranch style home with wooden pillars out the front and full floor to ceiling glass windows to overlook the front driveway. There were twelve bedrooms, six bathrooms, a theatre, and access to the Northern Mountain which sat directly behind us and adjacent to the heated pool outside. This wasn't a home that I hired a decorator for, this home I did all myself. From the cozy man-sized fireplace to the large twin grand staircase, to the colorful art of Banksy hanging on the wall. I put my soul into this place and left nothing for the house in Chicago. I didn't know what that said about me as a person.

"So, what do you think?" Punk was flashing her phone at my face and I took it from her without looking.

"Sorry!" I fell onto one of the sofas in the family room that had an entire wall made of glass to look out to the pool and mountain in my backyard. I often rode that mountain when the others were full of tourists.

I was about to look down at her phone when the chef entered, stepping down the steps that adjoin this room to the dining and kitchen area.

"Mrs. Lee," I winced at the Mrs. title. "We have dinner cooking and would just like to double check that everyone eats meat?"

I smiled up at him. "Yes, thank you so much, Roger. We would love anything you make." His cheeks flushed red as he bowed his head and made his way back the way he came.

"He missed you," Punk said, flopping onto the sofa opposite mine. "I could tell. Every time I ran into him in town, he'd ask how you were."

"He is so sweet. I don't know what I'd do without him." Roger was one hell of a chef, and was always on high demand in Colter Hills. "I'm very lucky that he cooks for me when I'm back."

Punk raised an eyebrow. "So?"

"So?" I asked, just as she shot up from the chair and busied herself in the corner bar, pulling out a bottle of whisky. She snatched up two glasses and danced her way back to the sofa. "My man!" She pointed to her phone, but it had already turned dark and locked itself.

I placed it onto the table. Hopefully she won't know that I didn't look at his picture. "Hot. How'd you meet?"

Being in a failed marriage created good liars.

She waved her hand in front of herself. "Wait, you don't know who he is?"

"Punk, I'm old."

"So!" She chuckled, and it made her little pixie nose scrunch up in the middle. "You're not even old. You're thirty, that's not old."

I took a glass from her and pointed before taking a sip. "Ten years older than you."

Her face paled. "Jesus, when you put it like that."

I threw a pillow at her. "Hey!"

She laughed, resting into the corner chaise. "I'm just kidding. You know you look ridiculously young for your age, and also, you're fucking hot so... I don't think it matters."

"Anyway, what were you saying?"

"Ah," she clicked her fingers. "Astro Henley. He's like, the greatest snowboarder of our time and is also the son of the Jameson Henley."

"Ah, I know his daddy..." I joked, smirking behind the rim of my glass. I didn't know who the fuck she was talking about though. I don't live the kind of life that offered me the luxury of being able to watch TV. But I wasn't lying about knowing his father. Jameson Henley was one rich ass old man. He and I often battled in the Forbes list, but I shook him off last year by a few hundred million. I didn't know him personally, but everyone knew his hotels.

"How have you not heard of his son? Jesus, Ivy."

I hid a laugh behind my glass. She was clearly smitten with the boy, which was cute. I remembered how that felt—or did I? I couldn't remember the last time I genuinely liked anyone except for my friends. Parker didn't count. "Well, I can't wait to meet him. When does he get here?"

"Tonight!"

I listened to her chat about her boyfriend for another thirty minutes before we parted and I went off to find Parker. We needed to talk and I'd rather do it before our friends arrived and anyway, I was ready after two fingers of whisky.

The master bedroom was my favorite room of the house. No walls, just glass. Full three-sixty view of mountains, snow, and the pool. I loved it up here. I felt as though no one could touch me. Unfortunately, the one person who could was the person I shared a bed with.

He stood near the bathroom, which was completely open into the main bedroom. You could see the clawfoot marble tub, the twin rain showerheads, and the crystal chandelier that hung in the middle. Everything was open and in the center of the room since the walls were all glass. "What, Ivy. You want to have this talk again?"

I blinked, staring up at the man I prayed would leave. "Yes, Parker. I think it's time. Don't you?"

He walked toward me, and every step he took stole my breath. The closer he came, the more my skin crawled.

As soon as he was directly in front of me, his hand flew to my chin and he forced my eyes onto his, squeezing roughly. "You're a spoiled little cunt, Ivy. And anyway," he tightened his grip until I was sure my teeth would crack in my mouth while directing me down onto my knees in front of him. "You can't get rid of me, or have you forgotten?" His tongue rolled in his mouth and he spat on my face, slimy saliva stuck to my lashes. "I know where you buried the bodies." He shoved me down onto the carpet and left the room. I waited until the door closed before I rolled onto my back, swiping his saliva off my face. *You will not remember.* Truth was an ugly tool, but the mind was stronger. You could train it to forget even the ugliest of truths…

I pushed myself up from the ground and looked at the clock that flashed on my floating bedside table. Del would be here any minute and I looked a mess.

I emptied all my makeup onto the marble vanity, turning on the light around the mirror. My brown hair hung down to my waist in gentle waves and my eyes were the color of autumn with every palette of green lost inside. My skin was soft, yet always had a slight tan to it. Punk was right, I did look younger than my age. My body was tight from all the gym time, and Tamara would always go on about my best asset—aka—my ass. She once made me balance a glass of champagne on it, just to prove her point.

I quickly scrubbed my face, and then scrubbed it again with an exfoliator until it was red enough to sting when I touched it, before dropping some moisturizing oil onto my cheeks and massaging it in gently. I ran a brush through my hair and tied it into a bun, before slipping into some comfortable loungewear. White linen crop top and shorts with fuzzy Louis Vuitton slippers.

Collecting my glass of whisky, I made my way back down the hallway and stairs to meet with Del in the kitchen. The front door opened and I smiled up at it, finally happy to see my best friend when Punk's pink hair came into view as she directed a tall man inside, wearing a hoodie and jacket. She's laughing with him as she closes the front door.

They both paused when they noticed me, and I winked at Punk. "Hey, lovers."

The boy's hands came to the edge of his hoodie, and I watched as his long fingers wrapped around the edges before he pushed it back to rest around his neck. Tattoos curled up the front of his throat, outlining his jaw before tucking behind his ears. His shoulders straightened when he stood to his full height. My God, he was tall. He couldn't be as young as Punk. My eyes travelled up, and when they landed on his face, my knees buckled and I had to force myself upright.

Oh. My. God. I really wished I would have seen the image of him now, at least it would have prepared me for what I'm staring back at. His cheeks were high and sharp, his skin flawless with a natural blush from the frosted air outside, His lips were soft, yet full, and his eyelashes as thick and dark as the hair on his head. He stared back at me like he could see every single dirty and dark secret that I have buried, and I swear that he could. His eyes reminded me of snow, right before it melted back to water. So blue they were almost white. His hair was longer on the top, but shaved on the sides where more tattoos were carved into his skull above his ear. This kind of perfection should never exist.

He stepped forward, and I looked down to his tattooed hand before going back to his eyes. I wanted to just stare at him, but that would be creepy. Wouldn't it? Oh my God, he was probably way too young, but there was no way he could be. He looked to be in his late twenties at the very least.

"Nice to see you, Ivy…" My name wrapped around his tongue like it belonged there, and I cleared my throat, placing my hand in his.

"Nice to meet you."

He stared down at me, before the corner of his mouth turned into a sly smirk. There was something about him that just seemed off… Someone this perfect could only mean one thing; distraction, and when his tongue snuck out and dampened his bottom lip before he slid back and tucked Punk under his arm, I knew.

This man had secrets, and I'm pretty sure I was going to become one of them…

✧   ✧   ✧

Thank you for reading PLAYHOUSE! Want to read more from author Amo Jones? Visit her website here.

www.amojonesbooks.com

PUCKS, STICKS, AND A NEW BARN

TONI ALEO

I'm Sorry

Baylor

I 'VE BEEN MENTALLY and physically dreading this appointment.

The boys are with Mom and Dad—yes, I still find it weird that my dad married my husband's mom, but it's been a while now, so I need to just accept it and move on. Still, weird, but it's great because the boys love being with their grandparents. I guess I could have left them at the house alone. Dawson is old enough to keep an eye on Louis, but I feel as if maybe Jayden and I might need some time alone.

To accept.

To grieve.

I've watched my strong, resilient husband fight against his injuries. Though, when the dreadful and terrifying injury happened, I think I knew he'd never play again. It was such a freak fucking accident, one I am still very upset about. The Nashville Assassins, the team Jayden captains, were playing the Jets. He was positioned behind the goal, waiting for his team to set up with new players after a line change. He'd done it tons of times, no big deal, except one of the Jets' forwards felt he could pick off the puck.

The player rushed Jayden, much to his surprise, so Jayden went to defend, but the toe of his skate got caught in the back of the net. His leg stayed stuck, while his body went the other direction, snapping his knee. That wasn't the worst of it, though. When he fell, he fell right into the forward's knee, face first, shattering his nose, knocking out his front teeth, and receiving a concussion. To add insult to injury, the Jets scored while my husband lay on the ice, blood and teeth in his gloves.

It was traumatizing, to say the least.

Especially for the boys.

That was a little over fifteen months ago, and while his knee and nose have healed and he has new front teeth, he still can't kick the effects of the concussion. He's been having terrible migraines, and the prescriptions have been working, but I know doctors are fearful of another concussion. I was terrified when I found out this wasn't his first.

Instead, it was his sixth. Since childhood.

Don't get me wrong; concussions are a part of all sports. It happens. But even as a female hockey player, I've only had one, and I played with boys all my life. Broken bones—a lot of those—but thankfully, I didn't suffer the head injuries like Jayden has. It's all so frustrating and scary, especially since now they seem to have caught up with him.

The doctor looks over the scans of Jayden's last CT. I hold Jayden's hand in both of mine as he rubs his thumb along the inside of my left wrist. I gaze at his profile as he watches the doctor, visibly on pins and needles. He wants so badly to be released. He wants to be on the ice with his team. He goes to practice and even works out with the guys, but not being on the ice makes him feel as if he isn't on the team. I get it since I had to medically retire after just one year in the NHL. I shattered my knee during a game, and they told me I'd never play again. It took a long three years, but I proved them wrong. I didn't make it back to the NHL, but I did win a gold medal in the Olympics in women's hockey.

I still haven't decided whether that's better than a Stanley Cup.

But all that doesn't matter; I needed to focus on Jayden. I know I'm just scared, and that's why I'm lost in my thoughts. I want nothing more than for Jayden to be healthy and happy. He's been so hard on himself. Borderline depressed. When I noticed, I started encouraging him to go to therapy. He listened, and we stayed ahead of it. Together. Like we always have.

God, he is the love of my life.

I found him early in life, and just as I was on the day I met him while on vacation in Florida, I am still completely and utterly attracted to him. I'd played hockey with boys for as long as I could remember, but when I played against Jayden, I knew it was different. I wasn't playing to win; I was playing to impress him. I wanted him and knew he was my future. Now, with two kids and many years of marriage behind us, I've never been more in love with him than I am now.

His dark hair is longer these days, curling around his ears and neck. Both boys have longer hair and wanted their dad to match them. I'm not used to it. I'm used to the clean sides and trim top, but I have to admit, he's gorgeous either way. His eyes are still such a devastating green that capture my heart every time they lock on me. He's still so lean and strong. Even now, when I know he's scared out of his mind, he sits with such confidence.

My forever.

I tuck his hair behind his ear, and he meets my gaze, a tight smile on his lips. *It's okay*, I mouth. He nods. Though, I know he knows I know it's not. He lifts our hands and kisses the back of mine just as the doctor clears her throat.

She doesn't look at us, but our gazes are like razors as they cut to her.

Dr. Lothrop doesn't look happy, and I know she's about to ruin my husband's life. She is one of the top sports doctors in Nashville, Tennessee. She's on the younger side, but she graduated very early as a teen. Her glasses sit low on the end of her nose as she uses her pen to outline the front of Jayden's temporal lobe on the scan. I know what she's indicating because I've watched her do this many times.

"Mr. Sinclair, I'm sorry to have to say this, but there is still damage to your brain, which is why you continue to have the migraines and the balance issues." He grips my hands tightly in his. Her gaze moves from the screen to us. "I know this isn't the answer you want, but in my opinion, you should not continue your career as a hockey player. There is too much risk of doing more damage and causing more extensive injury to your brain."

She says more—hell, she doesn't stop talking for over fifteen minutes—but all I can do is watch Jayden. His breathing has sped up, his eyes are glassy, and his jaw is so damn taut. I know he is replaying the injury in his head, or maybe he's even thinking that everything he has ever known is gone. He comes from a hockey family. His eldest sister is the wife of a retired hockey player, and their daughter is engaged to an up-and-coming hockey player. His eldest brother plays for Tampa, and his youngest plays for Fort Lauderdale. Hockey is all Jayden knows, and I know he's scared. But he isn't alone.

I'm by his side, and I'll do everything to remind him he's more than just a hockey player.

He's everything to me.

When he looks up at me, I smile confidently and squeeze his hand. "It's okay. Everything is great. We're going to be great. Together."

His lips tip up at the sides. "I never thought you'd have to use my words against me."

My smile grows, remembering the moment he told me the same when I was riddled with injuries. "Hey, you were right, and I will be too."

He leans his head into mine, and our lips touch lightly. "Thank you, Bay."

I kiss him once more. "Always, Jay."

BULLSHIT

Jayden

I KNOW BAYLOR knew I was done when I got injured. She never said it, but I can read her like a book. She's so intuitive. And while she's been supportive and uplifting throughout this, I know she did it out of love, not because she believed I'd come back. I think I knew too, which is how I'm able to keep the tears at bay. In all honesty, I cried enough when everything first happened and the migraines started. I think that's when I grieved my career.

When I knew I wouldn't be my boys' hero anymore.

As we walk out of the clinic, with paperwork for my next appointment and a new treatment plan along with prescriptions, I FaceTime my brothers. I know they're both gearing up for a new season, and I don't expect them to answer. But they both knew I had this appointment. It's a blessing that I grew up with my best friends. Jude and Jace are my ride or dies, and not once did we consider I would be done. We all figured we'd retire at the same time and enjoy being old and crusty together.

I got old and crusty first.

When their faces come up, both of them radiating concern through the screen, my stomach drops. I don't want to tell them.

"So? What did she say?" Jude asks first.

"You good? You heading back?" Jace asks then. My niece Ashlyn sits in his lap, reading a book. She's a bookworm and fucking cute as a button. She wants to be an author, which makes sense since Avery is a songwriter and is creative as hell. Ashlyn leans her head on Jace's chest, side-eyeing the screen, and I smile.

"Hey, baby girl," I call to her.

She grins at me. She is the spitting image of our older sister, Lucy. "Hi, Uncle Jay. Hi, Uncle Jude."

Jude waves. "Hey, Ash."

"How's Aunt Claire? When's the baby coming?"

He smiles proudly. "She's doing great, and very soon. A couple weeks, I think. You excited to find out what it is?"

She nods. "I think it's a girl."

We all grin, Jude most of all. "Man, I hope so!"

Jace picks her up then and whispers something in her ear before getting up. "Sorry, what's up? I need to know."

I exhale heavily as the boys look back at me. Baylor holds my hand in support. "I'm done."

Jace shakes his head as Jude's shoulders fall. "Fuck, man. I'm sorry."

"Such bullshit," Jace says, and I nod.

"Yeah, I'm not okay. But I will be."

Jace nods. "Hey, this could be a good thing. Gives you time with the boys through the years they need you most. You could coach their teams, like how you used to do for Shea Adler when Angie was little."

I nod. I hadn't thought of that.

"No matter what, Jay, you're still the best hockey player ever. So, no worries. Now, you get to be a full-time dad and husband," Jude adds. "But it's still bullshit."

"Straight bullshit," Jace agrees. "But Jude is right. You'll go down in history as the youngest captain of the Assassins and the second-best defensemen after Shea Adler."

I love my brothers. I nod as I smile. "Thanks, guys."

"I love you, dude. I'm sorry," Jude says. "Y'all can come down here. Stay for a bit?"

Jace loves this idea. "Fuck yeah. We'll drive up and spend some time at Jude's mansion."

Baylor nods, popping her head in. "We would love that. Let's get home, tell the boys and Mom and Dad, and get our ducks in a row."

"Love you, Bay," Jude says. "You're a great wife."

She nods. "Love you too. Thank you."

"Love y'all," Jace says, and we share the sentiment before hanging up.

I look at Baylor, and she nods. "They're right, you know. You're already a great dad—just think how it's going to be now that you'll be around full time?"

I nod, unable to share in the excitement of that. Don't get me wrong. I love my kids and I love being a dad, but all I know is hockey. It's terrifying knowing my career is over, but I won't allow myself to fall into a hole about this. Everyone is right; I'm going to be great. It's what we Sinclairs do. I'll coach the kids or maybe play in a no-contact men's rec league. There are options. I have options. I'm still alive and walking.

I just have to keep reminding myself of that.

When we get home, I get out of the truck and look up at the home Baylor and I bought once we signed on with the Assassins. It's a very modern home, minimalist style, with big-ass windows and lots of wood planks everywhere. Our door doesn't just open. It slides, automatically. It's basically a house from *The Jetsons*. We love it. Especially since it's on a two-acre corner lot with no one around us. Makes for great pool parties because no one gets upset. Inside, we have six bedrooms. The top floor has three, and that is where our room and the kids' are. Downstairs is an office for Baylor and two guest rooms. We usually house a single hockey player when they first arrive to play for the Assassins, giving them a place to stay until they get on their feet, or when my brothers or my mom stay.

It's a great house that we've made a home.

I lock the truck door as we head inside. Baylor hasn't said much, probably allowing me to gather my thoughts and prepare to steer the conversation. We are able to read each other after all these years, which only proves I was right from the jump that she was the one for me. Man, she gave me a run for my money, but she was damn well worth the fight. I wrap my arm around her waist, bringing her in close as I kiss her jaw.

She leans into me, her eyes studying mine. "How you feeling?"

"I think I'm a little in shock about it all."

"Yeah," she agrees. "Maybe a vacation to see Jude and Jace and the kids before our kids start school again is a good idea. It'll be nice to get away."

"Maybe. I gotta tie up some loose ends, and I'll need to clean out my locker and shit."

She makes a face. "I feel like that can wait."

I shrug as I reach for the button to open the door. I know she probably thinks I want to rip the Band-Aid off as fast as I can, and I guess I do. It took her a month to clean out her locker when she had to retire. I can't do that; I can't wait that long. As much as I don't want to accept my career is over, I can't drag this out. It is what it is. I gotta keep moving.

Before I can push the button, though, Baylor stops me. "We are great, Jayden, but it's okay to mourn this."

"I think I already have been," I admit, meeting her gaze. "It's been fifteen months, Baylor. I've made progress, but not enough, not fast enough."

She visibly swallows. "I don't want you to hurt."

"It's hard to hurt when I'm loved so completely by such an incredible wife and sons," I remind her, kissing her nose. "I just gotta find my new thing."

Before she can stop me, I push the button, and the door slides open. As we enter, the first picture I see of is of Baylor and me, her holding her gold medal and me holding my silver at the last Winter Olympics, as we kiss happily with the kids standing in front of us. Man, what a ride that was. We had such a blast and made so many awesome memories. Especially since Jude and Jace competed as well, so the whole tribe was there. I swear, we had the loudest cheering section. We were considering going for the next set of Olympics, but I don't think Baylor wants to go without me. I hope she does if she's asked. I know we'll go with her, and I'm sure Jude and Jace will play too.

Hopefully soon, we'll go for our kids.

Speaking of our kids, Dawson comes around the corner first. At fourteen, the kid is massive. He's taller than me and builds muscle like Baylor. He is the spitting image of Baylor but with my darker features, while Louis is me made over. On cue, Louis shows up right behind his brother, growing like a damn weed. He's already at eye level with me, which is annoying. I don't know what the kids eat, but they're going to make some great defensemen one day.

Or great football players. They do both.

My mom and River, her husband and my father-in-law, bring up the rear, all of them awaiting the verdict.

Dawson meets my gaze, and his shoulders fall almost immediately. I don't know how, but he knows. He comes to me, hugging me tightly. And, mirroring his brother, Louis does the same. I hug my boys and fight back the tears.

"I'm retiring," I say, mostly to our parents, and within seconds, my mom's eyes start to fill with tears. I tap the boys' backs, and they both look up at me. "But it's fine. I'll be able to coach your teams and take you to school. I know for a fact that I won't miss any more art shows, Lou. And I'll even learn a bit about football and maybe coach that."

When I notice that Louis has started crying, I hold him closer as Dawson exhales hard. "I'm sorry, Dad. That sucks, but I'm glad you'll be home."

"Me too," I admit, hugging him tighter. "Also, we're going to go see Uncle Jude and Uncle Jace!"

The boys light up almost instantly. "Really?"

"Really. Probably leave tomorrow. I'll look at flights."

It's not much, but it's a welcome distraction from sending an email to Elli Adler about what the doctor said. She'll want to talk, and I'm nowhere near ready for that. How do you tell the woman who believed in you so greatly that you can't captain her team? I don't know, and I'm not sure I'm ready to figure it out.

"Can I help?" Louis asks, and Dawson nods.

"Me too, Dad."

"Sure. Let's go get on the computer."

Before I can get far, my mom wraps her arms around me, telling me she loves me before exclaiming, "We'll come too!"

But then River says, "I can't. I have those meetings, but I'll keep an eye on the houses."

"Meetings?" Baylor asks, and he nods.

"Yeah, with the university." Her brow perks, like she knows something we don't. "Reminds me, I need to talk to you."

I want to ask about what, but I know she'll tell me later. So, with my mom and my boys in tow, I go look for flights and call to work things out with Jace and Jude. The whole time, my family smothers me between them on the couch, but I'm thankful for it.

I'm pretty sure it's the only thing keeping me together.

FAMILY TIME
Baylor

I LOVE WHEN all the kids are together.

I also love and appreciate my in-laws. Jace and Avery drove up from Fort Lauderdale as soon as we got on the plane this morning. Even about to pop, Claire made sure the house was ready for visitors, and the fridge was stocked to the brim when we arrived. Dawson was quick to let us know. Kid is starving—all the time. Jude and Claire's house is massive, with eight bedrooms, nine baths, a pool house, *and* a guesthouse. On the beach. It's absolutely insane, but they both worked hard for this home. Now, they want to fill it with kids.

And they're on the way. Claire is standing in the ocean with Harrison between her legs, letting him kick the water. Her belly is huge, and it fills my heart with so much joy to see her pregnant. She has wanted to grow a baby so badly. Though you wouldn't know that Harrison didn't come from her belly. Well, except if you notice his skin has a darker tone and he has a mass of dark curls and dark eyes. I hope they have a lot of babies or adopt or whatever. As long as that grin stays on her face.

I watch as she sets him on her hip, checking her phone, and then mine sounds. I should have known. When we arrived, and Dawson and Louis started for the fridge, I offered her money. She wouldn't take any from me, so I Venmoed her. Now she's returned the Venmo. Again. We've been sending money back and forth for over four hours. It's downright pathetic, but we're both too hardheaded to stop at this point.

As I look around, I can't believe how big everyone is getting. Lucy and her family came too—I should have known they would; the Sinclairs are extremely close. I went from having just my dad to now being a part of a massive, suffocating, loving family. It's both a lot and everything I always wanted, all in one. Lucy's boys, Max and Ryder, have joined my boys and Avery and Jace's youngest, Jamieson, surfing and playing football in the water. Lucy and Benji's youngest, Charlotte, and Avery and Jace's eldest, Ashlyn, hunt for seashells with Autumn, Lucy, and Avery. The only kid missing is Angie, but she's off being engaged and helping people with their mental health.

We are all so proud of her.

I notice that Jace, Jude, Jayden, and Benji are drinking beer on the back porch. Well, Benji has a soda instead. I watch Jay for a moment, and I can see he's doing well. I don't think he's totally processed everything, but I know he needed this. His brothers have a way of calming him and helping him to see reason. Benji is always a joy to be around, and since he retired a while back with his own concussion issues, I know he is giving Jayden all the advice. It eases my concerns and worries, knowing Jayden has such great support. He told his teammates last night, and of course, they all wanted to come and be with him, but we were leaving for Florida. Shelli Adler-Brooks and Elli Adler, the owners of the Assassins, called this morning, and both were sad but loving. Not that I'd expect anything else—those Adlers are good people.

"Mom! Mom, look!"

I look out to see Dawson riding a wave, and it kills me how big he is getting. He's going to be graduating before I know it, and he's hoping to play at a college somewhere. Not sure which sport he'll commit to. He's got a damn good throwing arm, but also a wicked slap shot. Plus, he's huge. The future is uncertain, but I know he'll do something amazing and we'll be proud.

"Awesome, babe!"

He grins widely at me before falling, much to everyone's entertainment. I know I should probably join some part of my family instead of catching rays, but my mind is racing. I haven't had time to process what my dad told me before we left.

Team USA wants you for the Olympics this year, but that's not all. I'm leaving Bellevue, and I put your name in for the women's hockey team. They want you, Bay. You should take it.

Talk about information overload. Not only has my husband's career abruptly ended, but now mine could potentially take off again. I've focused so much time on charity work and my boys, I've never thought about picking up my career again after the last Olympics. While we did great and killed the competition, there are so many more talented women than me. I didn't expect to be asked again, and I sure as hell didn't expect to have a job opportunity appear out of nowhere. That's my dad, though. He has always had my back. Always pushed me to be better than I thought I was.

It's probably why I do the same for my boys.

I swallow hard as I glance back at Jayden. I don't know how to tell him. I don't want to possibly make him feel worse since I'll be returning to the ice full time and he's been forced to retire. I almost don't want to bring it up. Just let things happen. But I have my interview next week. He'll want to know where I'm going or where I've been, and I don't lie to my husband. I want to be honest, but I also don't want to hurt him.

When Lucy comes over, I grin up at her before she falls into a lounger beside me. Then Harrison is in her lap before Claire lowers herself into a chair.

"Why didn't y'all tell me pregnancy was this hard?"

We both laugh as I tickle Harrison's little double chin. He is a gorgeous baby. "It's worth it," I say, and Lucy agrees.

"Absolutely. But then they grow up and leave."

I turn my lips down as I look out at the kids. All so big. "How's Angie?"

Lucy beams. "So damn happy. She is working on an autism program right now, while still working hard with the players. Plus, she's head over heels for Owen, and he for her. They're adorable."

Claire grins. "They sure are gorgeous together."

"So gorgeous."

"I know. I love their faces. They've officially moved in together, which Benji is not a fan of, but I don't care. As long as she's happy. She went too long without being happy."

"Absolutely," Claire says. "That's what I had to tell Phillip. It's so funny, but I think he still doesn't like Jude. Insane since we've been together for, like, ever, but he still thinks of me as a baby."

"Oh, just wait. You'll do the same to Harrison and the new one. It's rough," Lucy says, laughing. "Angie may think she's an adult, but in my eyes, she's my little girl, running around fighting ninjas with my dildos."

That has all of us laughing hysterically. Kids do the darnedest things. Autumn walks up as we laugh, and I see that the girls have joined the boys in the ocean. I look up at my mother-in-law and see such bliss on her face.

"You needed this, huh, Mom?"

She reaches down, cupping my shoulder. "We all did," she says, looking back at Jayden. "Sometimes family can be a lot. But most of the time, family is what you need to heal."

I glance over to where she is watching Jayden laugh so hard. His eyes are watering, and his face is red. My heart explodes in my chest at the sight of him, and I'm so thankful for our family. When I look back to Autumn, I nod. "You're right."

She meets my gaze. "Did you tell him yet?"

"No."

She scolds me with her eyes. "You should. He won't be upset. He'll be proud." I swallow past the lump in my throat, and she cups my face. "I know he will."

I don't have the words for a response, and I'm thankful. Because if I had said something, I might have missed Jayden, Jude, and Jace racing into the water for the kids while Benji watches with a smirk on his face. His days of running are over after a nasty ankle injury that was a contributing factor to his retirement. The boys dunk one another, they play, and they splash with no cares in the world. We all watch them in awe because of how perfect it is.

Our laughter is loud, but our love for one another is louder.

And that'll never change.

GROWTH IS CHANGE

Jayden

I KNOW EVERYONE was upset to miss the birth of the newest member of the Sinclair clan, but I think Claire knew she had to get everyone out of the house before she went into labor. When we landed in Nashville, we got the picture of Claire, Jude, Harrison, and the brand-new addition, Hadley Reese Sinclair. Talk about the cutest little girl I've ever seen. I remember when Angie was born and how overwhelmed I was by her beauty, but seeing Hadley is different. She has the longest lashes and the cutest little nose. I adore her just from the photo. I think it's because I know how much my brother and Claire wanted her.

My mom? Well, she got off the plane and then got on the next flight out. It was funny as hell, and I tried to talk her out of it to give Jude and Claire some time to adjust, but she didn't hear a word I said. It was comical, to say the least.

I sit in my truck outside of the arena, looking at pictures. I'm buying time. I don't want to go in and clean out my locker. Baylor asked if I wanted her to come with me, but I said no. I needed to do this alone. She, of course, was agreeable and told me if I needed her, she'd come up. Even the boys wanted to come. I didn't want them to see this part.

While I really mourn the loss of my career.

I enjoyed the time with my family to the fullest. I love that they know I need them when I do. It sucks to see all the kids getting so big, but then it's fun because they're great kids. I know my mom enjoys being with all the kids more than being with us. She did her time with us; now it's time to spoil those grandkids. But Mom being Mom, she spoiled me too. With love.

Hockey is something great about you—it's not who you are. You are a fantastic dad, my love, a great husband, and the best son a mom could ask for. Don't forget that.

I love my mom. She told me that when I got up to get a glass of water in the middle of the night and she was up watching crime shows with Charlotte. She's right, and I know that, but still, it's hard to stomach when all I've ever known is hockey. I've learned a lot through this injury, though, and there is more to life than hockey. Family. My sport doesn't always love me back, but my family...they love me even when I don't love myself.

When a tap comes to the window of my truck, I look over to see Aiden Brooks. He grins at me as I roll down my window. "Hey, man."

I'm a little confused since no one is supposed to be here. Practice was over hours ago, but I smile anyway. "Hey, what're you doing?"

"Bringing Shelli some lunch. You going in?"

Shit, I guess I have to. "Yeah," I say, shutting off the truck and rolling up my window. I grab my bag that I brought to bring everything home in before I get out and lock the doors.

"Cleaning out your locker?" he asks as we head toward the back entrance of the arena.

"Yeah," I say, a little gloomier than I intended. "I've been putting it off."

"Understandable. We're going to miss you on the ice."

I nod. "Same." I walk through the door he opens for me. "How's Shelli doing? Baby should be here soon, right?"

He looks a bit nervous. "Yeah, next month. She's great. Hungry all the time, but so am I."

We share a laugh. "Yeah, toward the end is the worst. Baylor would get so hot sleeping next to me, she would kick me out of bed, but then come to the couch and sleep with me anyway. Pregnant women are insane."

Aiden laughs. "I hear that." He continues to walk with me toward the locker room, but I don't have time to ask why, given that the offices are in a completely different direction, because he says, "I saw your brother had his new baby.

Congratulations."

"Thanks. She's an adorable baby."

"She is. Kind of makes me want a girl."

I shake my head. "No way. They're expensive. Boys are where it's at."

We share a laugh, and I look at him, confused, as he holds the door to the locker room open for me.

"I thought you had—" Before I can finish, though, I see the whole locker room is full of my team. My brothers. I feel as if I've been hit square in the chest when everyone starts clapping and hollering my name. My best friend for like forever, Markus Reeves, comes over and hands me a beer. I'm in total shock as I take it. Everyone is here. Including past Assassins players, like Shea Adler, Tate Odder, Erik Titov, and even Benji. My heart aches in my chest as I catch my breath.

"What is going on?"

Aiden grins at me. "It's your send-off into retirement."

Markus holds up his beer then. "To one of the greatest captains this team has ever been blessed to have. We love you, man. And know, every time we hit that ice, we're hitting it in your honor."

I'm choked by emotion as everyone says my name before taking long pulls of their drinks. I do the same, completely overwhelmed, but then Shea Adler comes toward me with a huge shadow box in hand. He turns it around as he says, "We had this made for you."

Inside it are all my jerseys from my long career with the Assassins. Each is folded, displaying my name and number. All the special event jerseys and even the jersey I was wearing when I was injured. I can see the bloodstain. I hand my beer to Aiden and take the box from my captain. I meet Shea's gaze, his eyes full of such compassion and wisdom.

"It's a hard pill to swallow, that your career is over. But when you need the reminder, I want you to look at this, and instantly, you'll be reminded of one hell of a legacy," he says to me, mentally knocking me on my ass. "I knew I was leaving the team in good hands."

I swallow hard as everyone claps once more. Still holding Shea's gaze, I say, "Thank you. Honestly, some may say I am one of the great captains of this team, but I wouldn't be who I am if it weren't for you."

Shea reaches out and hugs me, and I hug him back. Before River stepped into the role of my father, Shea was the man I looked up to most. For him to say those things to me doesn't make losing my career easier, but it makes it sting a little less. For the rest of the afternoon, I eat and drink with my teammates. We laugh, we joke, and we razz one another.

It's the send-off I didn't know I needed.

One thing I didn't expect was to see River here. It's not until we're leaving, when he's helping me with all my stuff, that I finally have time to say, "Thanks for coming. It means a lot to me."

My father-in-law nods as he helps me load the truck with my gear, the shadow box, and other crap I had stuffed into my locker. I was excited when I found Dawson's old hockey stick from when he was little. "It just so happened I was signing my contract when I heard the party was going on."

I bring in my brows. "Huh?"

He grins widely at me. "You're looking at the new head coach of the Nashville Assassins."

Pride fills me within seconds. "No shit!" I exclaim, smacking him in the chest. "That's fucking awesome. Congratulations!"

He laughs as his grin grows. "Thank you. I really wanted this."

"I know! But hell, you couldn't come before I retired?"

"Right? I thought the same thing since you were one of my favorite players to coach besides Baylor."

Our laughter mingles as I grin at him. "You have to say that since I'm married to her."

He shrugs. "Maybe, but mostly 'cause I'm married to your mom."

We laugh some more. "You're going to do great, but who's taking over the Bullies?"

"Not sure, but I suggested you."

My eyes widen. "What?"

"I think you'd be a great coach, and it's your alma mater. They're gonna contact you tomorrow for an interview."

Wow, I feel like I have whiplash. So many emotions. I just blink at him. "Holy shit."

He grins. "I think it'll be good for you. And with Baylor being hired for the women's team, the athletic director thinks it'll be good to keep the hockey program a family affair."

Huh? I raise my brows in confusion. "What? Baylor was hired?"

My father-in-law presses his lips together as he reads my face. "What?"

"You said—"

"I gotta go," he says, cutting me off, and then he walks away.

Like he didn't drop a bomb on me.

What the hell just happened?

HERE WE GO

Baylor

I DON'T OPEN the email from the University of Bellevue since I know it contains my contract and my commitment letter for the job as head coach of the women's hockey team. I thought when I told them I'd have to take a leave of absence to go to the Olympics, they wouldn't offer me the job, but I was wrong. They wanted me even more, which is hard to ignore. Everyone loves to be wanted, and I'm excited. But I'm still worried about what Jayden will think or how it'll make him feel.

Today will be hard for him. The guys are having a little retirement party for him, and I know he didn't want that. I know he wanted to sulk in there, get his shit, and leave, but Shea Adler wanted more for him. Because of that, I can't sign or commit to Bellevue today. I need to wait for the right time to tell Jayden about all the changes that are coming our way.

I click the email from the USA team coach with my training schedule. We'll train individually at first, and when it's time to go to the Olympics, we'll practice as a team. Some local women are on the team, so we plan to train together with my dad. After I close my training email, I see a message from one of the coaches at the kids' private school. I open it, and it's a bunch of links for different football camps. I bring in my brows; I thought Dawson hadn't decided yet.

"Hey, Daw!" I holler.

"Yeah, Mom?"

"Come here." I hear him moving through the house, and then he enters my office. He's still in his PJs with his hair a hot mess, and his headset from his games is around his neck. "What're you doing?"

"About to play some *Call of Duty* with Max and Ryder."

"Cool," I say with a smile. "Hey, I got an email from Coach Daniel with some links to football camps and the schedule for training camp. Did you decide and not tell us?" I watch his whole demeanor change. He looks away, his hands locking behind his back. When he does that, he looks like a child instead of a massive, growing young man. "Dawson?"

He clears his throat. "I told him I might when I saw him last week."

"Okay? So, do you want me to sign you up for these?"

He shrugs, and I watch him for a second. "Can I do both? Uncle Jude said it would be too much and too big a strain on my body to do both hockey and football, but I think I can swing it."

"I'm sure you could. But not only does Jude have a point, it's also a higher risk of injury. You don't want to completely burn yourself out—plus, you have school too, my love. I'd rather you choose one."

He nods slowly, defeated.

"Which do you love more?" He shrugs once more, and I know he isn't ready to make the decision. "Okay, well, I have until next week for you to decide."

Dawson kicks the carpet of my office. "Would you be mad if I played football instead?"

I gawk at him, but before I can answer, Jayden says, "Absolutely not. We just want you to do what you love."

Dawson looks back at Jayden as I do, and I point to him. "What he said."

Jayden wraps his arms around Dawson's neck, holding him tight. "Whatever you decide to do, we support."

He hugs his dad back before saying, "Okay, I'm gonna think some more."

"Okay," I say sweetly, and Dawson removes himself from his dad before heading out of the room. I stand up and wrap Jayden in my arms. "How was it?"

His eyes are so full of love. "Great. I needed it."

I lean into him, kissing his nose. "I know."

He kisses my top lip and takes my hand. "Come see what they got me."

I already know what it is, but I follow him as if I don't. When we enter Jayden's and my hockey memorabilia room, I see that the shadow box came out better than I could have ever imagined. "Oh, it's gorgeous."

"I thought so too. I think I want to hang it here," he says, pointing to a spot beside our medals.

"Sounds good to me," I agree, bending down to take a better look. "I wish I had one of these. It's awesome, and I agree, it's gonna look great with our medals."

"I think so," he says, nodding. "Your dad was there, signing his contract."

I go still. Please don't tell me my dad told him. "Really?"

"So, you knew."

I look up at him. "Yeah. I knew before we went to Florida."

His eyes widen. "Wow."

"I didn't want to say anything because I didn't want to add insult to injury. I know you love how my dad coaches."

He nods slowly, eyeing me. "So why didn't you tell me you got hired at Bellevue for the head coach position?"

Thanks, Dad. I swallow hard. "I was offered the job, but I haven't accepted because I hadn't told you yet."

"How long have you known?"

"Since the night before Florida."

He shakes his head. "Bay. Come on."

I stand up then. "I didn't want to upset you. Your career ends, and mine picks up? Like, that's shitty. I wanted to wait until after you cleaned out your locker and you felt better before I told you everything—"

"Everything?" he asks, his eyes holding mine. "Is there more?"

I press my lips together. "I was offered a spot on Team USA."

His eyes widen, but not with surprise or shock, more like pride instead. "Baylor! That's incredible!" He wraps his arms around me, kissing me fully on the lips. "I'm so proud of you."

I hold him tight. "You're not mad or sad?"

He laughs. "Not at all. I'm proud. I mean, shit, baby. I've always been your biggest fan. Why would you think I would be jealous or even upset about your accomplishments?"

I hold his gaze. "I don't know. I just didn't want to come at you with all my good news when you have bad."

He gives me a dry look. "We're a team," he reminds me. "Your good news is my good news, as my bad is yours. And vice versa. I don't want you to hide your good fortune because of what's going on with me. In the end, we're winning—as a team."

I cup his face. "Are you sure?"

"Baby," he scolds as his eyes burn into mine. "Since the moment I met you, I've known you were always going to succeed and do things that would blow me away. Every day from that first time we kissed, I have known I would love you for the rest of my life. Just as you celebrate my wins, I celebrate yours. We're in this together, right?"

I nod, tears burning my eyes. "I just want you to be happy."

He grins at me, his lips almost pressing into mine. "As long as I have you, I'm happy."

We kiss then, my heart soaring and exploding in my chest. I have loved this man for as long as I can remember, and I am so lucky to still feel that unconditional love after all these years. As we kiss, I'm taken back to the first time I set eyes on him, when we played street hockey, and our first kiss. The times he skated beside me as my equal, unlike the other guys on the team, and how he always protected me. The day he asked me to marry him and our first kiss as husband and wife. When we had Dawson and watching Jayden become a dad. I think I fell in love with him all over again when I saw him hold our son. And then it happened again when we had Louis. It's as if I continue to fall for him, over and over again, through all the phases of our life. Today is no different.

I've fallen head over heels for him once more.

As we part, I lean my nose into his while he holds me closer, basically becoming one.

"I've got news," he says.

I meet his gaze as I wrap my arms around his neck.

"While your dad was telling me about his new coaching position and yours, he told me he put my name in for the coach of the men's team."

I feel the side of my mouth quirk up. "Did he?"

He nods, our noses rubbing against each other. "He did, and I called. They want me to come in tomorrow."

My lips turn up. "Are you going to take it if they offer it?"

His eyes sparkle as he holds my gaze. "I couldn't say no if I tried. I always want to be where you are."

I kiss his top lip, so excited.

"I want to do this together."

"As a team."

He nods. "The best team."

We kiss again, and I'm so overwhelmed with emotion. Together, we can do so much. We've already proven that, but no one is ready for what is about to come from us. We may not know what Dawson or Louis will choose to do, but no matter what, Team Sinclair will always succeed.

Because we have each other.

A New Barn for the Sinclairs

Dawson

I STAND BESIDE my dad, his arm around my neck and mine around his waist. My mom is beside him with Louis tucked up next to her as we smile for the camera. Bellevue wanted family shots of us for the announcement of my parents' new coaching positions. As a hockey family, we are all in skates on the ice, with Louis and me holding sticks. My mom is stunning, with her long blondish-brown hair in curls along her shoulders and wearing her teal Bellevue Bullies tee from when she was a student here. Dad has on one of his original logo shirts too, while Louis and I got new ones with the new Bullies logos.

It's funny how quickly everything changed.

I thought for sure my dad was done with hockey. I was really worried for him and thought he wouldn't bounce back. He loves hockey, as do I, but I saw him moving on and being a stay-at-home dad because he wouldn't know what else to do. I should have known better. Like my grandma said, we all knew he couldn't sit still for long. I'm not upset, though; I want this for him. He belongs on the ice, and it's gonna be cool watching him coach along with my mom. They're both so savvy when it comes to hockey and incredibly smart. Just as they've raised Louis and me to do big things, they're gonna teach a lot of other people's kids the same.

I'm excited for them.

The only problem is...now I feel even more pressure.

I've been playing hockey since I was able to put on skates. I'm pretty sure I skated before I walked. At least, that's the running joke my dad tells. I love hockey, I do, but there is something about throwing a football that does it for me. I mean, hockey and football are so different, but I love them both. I enjoy the rush of getting a ball out of my hands before getting sacked, but I also love slamming into guys on the ice and scoring a huge, game-winning goal. I love it all. But now that my parents are both coaching for Bellevue, I feel as if I have to play hockey. I have to make them proud in the sport they love, but I don't know if I love it like they do.

Thankfully, we're done taking pictures pretty quickly, but before we can leave the ice, my mom asks, "Who wants to play?"

Louis jumps in excitement. "I'm on Mom's team."

Dad and I laugh, and I say, "Oh, you're going down."

Mom snorts. "Bring it, but don't hit Dad. Especially not in his head."

Dad gives her a dry look that she laughs at before kissing him on the lips. Louis complains as they kiss, but I don't mind it. Most parents don't show their love for each other, but ours do. Not only to each other, but to us.

While I love to play with my parents, I also hate it because as soon as we start, it turns into one-on-one between them. Louis and I are basically just passers at this point because my parents are beyond competitive. The story is that's how they fell in love.

Playing hockey.

So how can I choose football with that shadow looming over me? It's my legacy— to play and succeed just like they have. Not many people can say their mom played in the NHL, but I can. My parents have also won Olympic hockey medals. The weight of all that is so damn heavy. Do I turn my back on my family tradition? Do I follow my heart? I don't know. But as I watch my dad lift my mom while she laughs after scoring on him, I do know they'll always love me. That should make the decision easier, but it doesn't. Instead of dwelling on that, though, I join in on the laughter with my family when we all fall to the ice.

As the ice melts against my skin, I look up into the rafters of the Bullies' arena, seeing my mom's and dad's numbers up there. A grin pulls at my lips as pride fills me completely. I want to be up there with my parents, I want to be a part of the Sinclair legacy, and I want to make them proud. When my dad smacks his hand playfully into my chest, I look over at him as he laughs, his face so happy and full of love.

"I can't wait for you to come here. I'll get to coach you."

I share his grin as my stomach churns, the unknown terrifying, but I can't let that bother me right now. Not when today is a good day in our new barn. It's full circle, really. My parents started here, and now they're back. This time, though, Louis and I are here for the ride, and I'm excited for the future. Even if I have no earthly idea what *my* future holds. No matter what, I know my parents and my brother will be by my side.

Because we're a team.

Team Sinclair.

✧   ✧   ✧

Wanna know how Jayden and Baylor got here? Read Clipped by Love now! Plus, all my books, including the Bellevue Bullies series where you'll meet this couple! tonialeo.com/books/clipped-by-love

Room Enough for Two

Sara Ney

PART ONE

Eva

I NEEDED THIS time off.

Not because I'm overly stressed or wanted a break from work, but because I've always believed taking time for myself and giving myself a vacation was healthy and necessary—which made this cottage by the lake perfect.

Waving off my ride from the airport, I set my suitcase by the front door. I punch in the code the owner had sent me earlier, cross checking the numbers before tapping them into the keypad.

Click. It magically opens.

Pushing through the door, I pull my bag through behind me, letting it fall to the ground—along with my sunhat—gaze cutting straight through to the lake out back.

I don't waste my time unpacking, nor do I give myself a tour of the place— that can come later when the sun begins to set. The last thing I want to do is waste daylight and squander the sight of the sun reflecting off the water; I want to watch the loons diving and the family of ducks swimming by as dogs woof in a far off distance, their barks echoing.

I find a wine glass in the cabinet and twist open a bottle of red wine, pouring myself a glass before grabbing a blanket from the couch, walking across the yard, and to the pier. The deck chair is comfortable. I simply gaze out in the distance, looking at all the houses, the restaurant clear across the lake, wondering if I can drive the little boat across and get myself some dinner.

Maybe they deliver?

I'm not sure how much time passes; I give a little bit of energy to think about work. All my patients that I'm gonna miss while I'm here—my precious babies. My job as a pediatric doctor is stressful, one that doesn't afford me much time off.

That's by choice, obviously.

It's not as if I have a family of my own. I'm not dating anyone either so that's off the table. The truth is, I have a lot of free time and choose to spend it at work. I mean, what else am I supposed to do?

I sip at the wine.

Red isn't my favorite but that's all this place had, and I'm not in the mood to leave in search of something different.

Cozy.

Content.

It's so quiet—I'm already in love with this place and I've been here all of twenty minutes, enamored with the solitude and the lull of the rippling water at the shoreline.

My eyes fall closed.

Ahhh. Nothing but—

"You there. Where should I put my bags?"

Startled, I crane my entire body around in my chair so I can see where the voice is coming from, a large man filling one whole side of the sliding glass doorframe.

Tall.

Dark.

Bearded.

Bald.

I recognize this guy.

Holy shit. What the hell is Rocko Martinez doing in my cottage, in the middle of nowhere? Better yet, how did he get in?

Wait. Maybe this is his place—maybe he owns it?

This guy is famous.

The spitting image of The Rock, he stands idly in the doorway, sipping on a glass of wine—my wine, it has to be the bottle I just opened and set on the counter.

"Your bags?" I tentatively call out from the deck chair, not sure if I should sit or stand or run for the hills screaming. "Can I help you?"

"Yes you can help me. I asked where I can put my bags." Rocko Martinez cocks his head. "Why is there a suitcase in the entry hall?"

"That's mine." I rise, setting down my magazine.

"Who are you? A reporter?"

He thinks I'm a reporter? How absurd. Lips pressing together, I rationalize that I may recognize this man but I do not *know* him; what if he's a killer or a murderer?

I still don't know what he's doing in *my* vacation cottage.

This isn't a hostel, this is my personal rental.

Singular.

Un cuarto. *My bedroom.*

Mine.

Rocko is huge. Larger than life, intimidating and *vastly* out of place.

One of these things is not like the other, one of these things just doesn't belong...

"No, I'm not a reporter." Far from it, actually. "I'm a doctor."

"Like—a physical therapist?" His face contorts as he steps outside. "I don't need any rehab, I haven't been injured since the Super Bowl."

"Um, no—I'm a pediatrician."

"A kid doctor?" He scratches his beard.

"Yes. A kid doctor."

"That makes no sense. Why would I need a pediatrician?"

Oh boy.

Clearing my throat, I tread carefully. "I'm not here for work. I'm here on vacation." Pause. "What are you doing here?"

"Hiding."

When he turns to go back inside, I have no choice but to follow, glad I did when I see him dragging his suitcase toward the one bedroom in this place.

My bedroom.

"Um, excuse me—that's my room. You can't go in there."

He pushes through the door and disappears. "This room is empty and I'm the one paying for it."

"No—I'm the one paying for it."

His head sticks back out. "'Scuse me?"

"I said I'm the one paying for it."

"Oh, I heard you just fine. I've been knocked in the head plenty but I've never lost my hearing." His chuckle is low and deep, sending a weird thrill through my girl parts.

Stop it, Eva.

"No offense, sir, but I don't know you. There seems to be a huge misunderstanding. This is my cottage, you'll have to leave."

"Why the hell should I leave?" He disappears again. "You're the one squatting."

"I reserved this place months ago. Months. This is my one weekend off in months."

He walks out of the bedroom and walks to the bathroom. "Not my problem."

"You can't just say it's not your problem—obviously this place has been rented to both of us, we both have a right to be here. But obviously we don't want to be here together."

His head pops out of the bathroom. "Why wouldn't you want to be here with me? I'm a big deal."

And modest, apparently.

"I do not know you, sir."

I hear him laughing. "Sir? That's cute."

"I'm going to message the property manager."

He snorts. "Have at it."

Still, I hear him organizing his things in the bathroom and wish I'd at least unpacked my bag to lay ownership to the space he's gone and peed all over.

Shit.

He's taking over!

"Fine, I will."

"Great. Let me know how that goes."

My heart races as I tap out a text message to the manager, letting her know about the mix up, asking her if there's another property nearby they can stick Mister Fancy Pants football player in because I've already connected with nature and this place is mine.

Ha.

I sit at the barstool at the counter and wait.

And wait.

And wait.

Rocko reenters the room, walking around the island counter to the galley of the kitchen. Unceremoniously, he yanks open the fridge and peers inside. "Good thing you're still packed. It'll make things easier when they come grab you."

"Who is *they*?"

The man waves his hand in the air, aimlessly. "I don't know. The car service or whatever. The next resort."

"I'm not staying in a resort. I came here to be alone, ergo: not with other guests."

"And I came here to escape. Hence, not with you." He squints into the fridge. "Why is this empty?"

"This is a rental, not a full-service hotel. You have to get your own groceries."

He glances over his shoulder at me. "Why haven't you gotten groceries?"

Oh my God. "I don't want to cook."

"So what are we going to eat? I need food." He shuts the fridge. "I don't know if you've noticed, but I'm a growing boy."

I'm confused. Is he more interested in getting us food or getting one of us gone?

"I'm still waiting for Vicki to message me back." I inform him. "So far, nothing." Though the message is showing as READ.

"Well, tell her to bring food. I could eat the ass out of a rotisserie chicken and a pot pie." He pauses, filling his wine glass again. "Oh, and some beef sticks and a gallon of OJ."

Gross. Beef sticks and OJ? That sounds hideously vomit inducing.

"The woman is not bringing us food. She's going to get one of us a place to stay." I give him a pointed look, looking my fill. He takes up the entire kitchen it seems, broad shoulders and broad chest.

Rocko is wearing a plaid flannel shirt that strains against his biceps, tucked into well-worn jeans. He's had the courtesy to remove his shoes, his socks are gray woolies.

"I'm settled in. Plus, I can't go driving around town, someone might see me."

Oh, that's right—he said he was hiding. "Who are you on the run from? The law?"

I get an eye roll. "No, smart-ass. I'm hiding from the paparazzi. I signed a new contract with a new team and my agent wants me out of the public eye when the deal is made public—which is," He checks the watch on his wrist. "About two hours ago."

He leans against the counter, drumming his fingers on the stone surface.

"I guess that makes sense."

"Fans sometimes take things to an extreme level." He is still drumming his fingers.

"Sure." Personally, I'm not a sports fan myself, but when I first started my residency I thought I wanted to do emergency medicine. So I've come into contact with a pro athlete or two. And where there is a professional athlete, there are photographers and fans—even at the hospital trying to catch a glimpse.

Ultimately, the ER was not for me, and I switched gears to a slower paced area of practice: children.

I love kids.

Would love a dozen (not literally) so every one of my little patients are precious to me. I treat other people's children like my own when they come through my office.

But.

Because of all the time I put into my job, occasionally, I have burnout and need a break.

"I assume the paps aren't out to get you?" Rocko deadpans, beginning a ransack of all the cabinets.

"You assume correctly. None of my patients are famous; none of them have ever been tailed to my office." I watch as he opens one cabinet after the next. "You're not going to find food."

He scoffs. "Don't be a quitter."

"You can't conjure up snacks just by—"

Rocko whips a bag of mini-Oreo cookies out of the last cabinet he opens.

"Wah-lah! See!" Without hesitating, he rips the bag open and jams a cookie into his mouth. "God is smiling on me." He holds the bag out in my direction. "Want one?"

"No thanks." I'm holding out for a real meal, complete with a baked potato and sour cream. Yum. Actual, bonafide, north woods grub.

"Has Vicki messaged you back yet? It would suck if you had to sleep on the couch tonight."

"It would suck if you had to sleep on the couch tonight, considering you're about two feet too tall to fit on it."

"Har har." In goes another Oreo. "I guess I could message my agent. He could figure this out."

"You wouldn't take the couch? To be a gentleman?"

"Do I look like a gentleman to you?"

No.

He looks like a lumberjack.

Or a biker. Or a carpenter. Or…

A fisherman. *A strong, strapping, burly fisherman that lives alone and has been on the high sea for weeks, hasn't seen a woman in as long, has kept himself hidden away from polite society,*

Oh Lord—I've been reading one too many romance novels at night before bed…

Stop staring at him, Eva.

It's not as if I can help it. The man is standing three feet from me, sucking up all the good oxygen, filling the room with his woodsy cologne, large hands holding that tiny bag of cookies.

I watch, transfixed, as he roots another one out of the bag.

"It's going to get dark soon, we should come up with a plan."

I swivel on the kitchen barstool, letting my feet hit the ground. "We don't need a plan. If Vicki doesn't get back to us I'm taking the bedroom and you're going to be on the couch. Easy."

"So you think just because you're a female you're entitled to the bedroom."

Yes. "No. I think just because I was here first I'm entitled to the bedroom."

"But your bag is still sitting in the hall." He sounds pious. "You didn't call dibs. *I* called dibs."

Dibs?

I throw my hands up. "I wasn't expecting company! Why should I have laid claim to a bedroom?"

"Ma'am, if I'd been on that pier and seen you coming through the door, the first thing I would have done is bolted for the bedroom."

That makes me laugh. "Okay, now you're full of shit. And my name is not ma'am—it's Eva."

"Eva." He repeats, watching me with dark, brown eyes. "Nice to meet you. I'm Robert."

Robert.

So Rocko must only be a nickname.

Interesting.

Robert puts his hand out for me to shake it and when I do, I swear I feel a bolt of something.

Energy.

Heat.

Sizzle.

Retreat, retreat!

I pull it back, making a show of checking my phone again. Low and behold, Vicki has messaged me back. Hallelujah!

Vicki: Hello Eva, I am so sorry to hear that there's been a mix up! Unfortunately, inventory in the area is low since it is still summer; I checked with a few other homeowners and have come up empty.

Vicki: There are also no hotels available within twenty miles, but I did find a room on Loon Lake, in the town of Bella Blue. Does that work for either of you?

I bite my lower lip. This is not the cozy, relaxing vacation I was planning or expecting and disappointment churns my stomach.

"Bad news?" Robert watches me intently.

"Um. Yes." I put the phone on the counter. "Unless we're willing to stay at a hotel a half hour north of here, we're stuck together. That is—one of us can head home."

"I flew here and had to rent a car. I live in Chicago."

Dang, that is a hike.

It only took me an hour and a half to get here.

Pittance compared to a plane ride.

Robert crunches up the bag and finds a trash can to toss it in. "I'm out of cookies—should we run to the grocery store?"

"I had my heart set on a baked potato with butter and sour cream."

"That's oddly specific." He rolls his eyes. "I think I can manage baking a potato."

"Sure, I guess I don't have to go to a restaurant for dinner." As I'd been planning to do when I thought I'd be *alone*.

Oddly enough I look forward to running errands with him as I grab my coat and slip on my sneakers, trailing behind him toward the sleek, black SUV parked out front.

How had I not heard it drive up?

As I buckle up, he punches in the address for town, taking a left when we exit the driveway, both of us fairly quiet while he drives.

"Is there a baseball cap anywhere in the back seat?"

I twist my body around and search for one. "Yeah. Here."

I hand it to him. "Do you honestly think this is going to prevent anyone from recognizing you?"

Is he serious? He's larger than life and walks as if he were twelve feet tall, of course people are going to recognize him. I doubt there's a single thing he could wear or do to disguise himself, short of wearing a bigfoot costume or something like that.

"No, but it'll make me feel less bald."

He swipes it out of my hand and grins.

His smile wipes the smile off of mine and my lower half does that strange tingling thing again.

Not good.

Not good at all.

I haven't dated anyone in a long time and for good reason; decent men are hard to find! I'm not about to fall for the first Neanderthal that makes my mouth water, especially not the guy who steals my bedroom.

Ha!

We silently make our way to the only grocery store in town, which is more of a convenience store slash gas station slash bait shop, there's only one other car in the parking lot.

We slip inside and begin walking up and down the aisles, filling our baskets with all sorts of treats—filling them as if we already plan on staying the entire weekend, together.

Robert has potatoes, butter, and sour cream already, and I find him at the dinky meat counter grabbing steak filets.

"Do you want a steak or would you like something else?"

"Sure, that sounds good."

I locate more wine and grab two bottles. Vegetables for steaming or for a salad. Salt. Dressing.

A French baguette.

Fruit for tomorrow along with some eggs, breakfast links and tomato—the perfect omelet ingredients. Oh—and a magazine once we're back at the counter, setting our things on the conveyor, the young man behind it casually giving Robert a once over.

"Um. Not to be rude but are you…Rocko Martinez?"

Robert hesitates a few seconds too long and I can tell he's warring with himself about whether or not to be honest with the man.

"Yes, sir." He holds his finger to his lips and lowers his voice. "But don't tell anyone I'm here."

"Holy shit." The kid stops scanning our groceries. "Can I…"

Can he…

What?

I wait for him to finish his sentence but it seems he has no words left inside of him, the sight of Rocko rendering him mute.

"Did you want a picture?"

"Could I?"

"Sure," Rocko laughs. "As long as I'm in it."

We all laugh at that, the kid hastily pulling his phone out of his apron pocket and coming around to the front of the counter so he can take a selfie with Robert, who has to hunch over so he fits in the frame.

The young kid stares at the photo before remembering he's at work and hasn't finished bagging up our things.

"Thanks man—so much!" He hits the total button. "That'll be, um—eighty nine seventy three. I'm sorry, the steaks are really expensive."

"Don't worry about the total dude. I just signed with the Mavericks."

Robert grabs all our bags with a wink, leaving the kid slack-jawed as we walk away.

PART TWO

Rocko

DINNER IS…
Fun.

Correction: Dinner with *Eva* is fun.

Obviously I wasn't expecting anyone to be in the house when I walked in earlier today—my agent assured me everything would be arranged before my arrival and those arrangements did not include a roommate.

This whole entire rental turned out in disaster, not to mention it was probably unnecessary. It wouldn't have killed me to stay holed up in my Chicago penthouse apartment for a few days until the paparazzi finally got bored of stalking me and moved onto other news.

So here I am with an uninvited occupant.

No food.

I messaged Elias when I'd gone into the bathroom to unpack my things—without telling Eva I'd been in contact—my agent most certainly could have rectified this entire situation.

But I hadn't.

Really.

Wanted him too.

Call me crazy but *Eva is adorable*. Beautiful, smart, and funny, the more time I spend in her company the more I want her to stay; or, at least—not kick me out on my ass.

We can absolutely both stay the weekend, though it's obvious there isn't enough room for two.

One bedroom.

One bathroom.

Two strangers.

Except she doesn't feel like a stranger anymore and she's a stranger I wouldn't mind crawling into bed with me later, if only to snuggle.

I watch her from across the kitchen table as she happily digs into her baked potato, the one I lied about knowing how to make and had to Google directions even though it's a goddamn potato.

Eva's dark hair is pulled up in a messy bun; messy but cute and definitely effortless, the hoodie she's got on somehow feels chic.

Women are always trying to impress me.

Or flirt. Or hit on me.

Eva has done none of those things.

Eva is a damn doctor.

What she does is way cooler than what I do and requires more skill. I throw a damn ball around, she saves lives.

Not just any lives—kids' lives.

While I cooked dinner, she showered, emerging from the bathroom in sweat-pants and the hoodie, bare feet and a sassy little grin to match.

Yeah—she's not going anywhere tonight, especially not in this weather.

The beautiful weather we had when we arrived is gone, in its place, a thunder-storm that's been flickering the lights most of the evening.

Outside, the shore station covers flaps in the wind.

Rain pelts the windows from all sides, and I turned the heat on and made sure there was enough dry wood near the fireplace to last us through the night.

She seems thrilled I've made her dinner, smiling with each forkful.

"Hasn't anyone cooked for you before?" I tease, cutting my filet with a knife. It's tender and grilled to perfection.

Obviously.

"You mean has a man cooked for me before?" She pushes a piece of potato around her plate before stabbing it with the fork. "No, can't say that one has. I think…" Eva hesitates. "I haven't found anyone that's put in the extra effort. Many men I've dated have been…" She makes a humming sound. "Too busy."

"Too busy to *try*?" What the fuck does that even mean?

She glances up and looks stunned by my question, but I genuinely have no idea what she's talking about. Who are these men that can't put in an effort when they're dating someone—especially a someone like Eva.

She's a catch.

I've barely spent an entire day with her and I already know she's an incredible woman—one worth more than a modicum of effort.

"Where do you find these idiots?"

She shrugs, loading her fork with more potato and a bit of steak for the perfect bite. "Mostly the internet, I guess. It's not like I'm out there at the bars meeting people, and I never get approached in public."

Are these idiots blind as well as dicked in the head?

"If I saw you in public, I'd totally hit on you."

Obviously.

I busy myself by cutting into my steak while she ponders my last comment, her face flushing with heat. Don't think it's the red wine we're drinking—still the same bottle as earlier, just a little left that we were each able to have one glass with our meal.

I'm not a big drinker, but when I'd come through the cottage door and seen it on the counter I thought, "Wow! What a nice gesture the hostess made! A glass of vino just for little old me? Lovely."

Little did I know it was Eva who'd opened the bottle and Eva who was out on the pier enjoying the peace and quiet.

I hadn't exactly invaded it.

After all, I was here to relax, too. Well—if you count hiding from the paparazzi as "relaxing," which I most certainly did not. It was more stressful, if anything. I couldn't even go into town today for groceries without worrying that the young kid behind the checkout counter was going to post my photo online with a geotag that led everyone straight to me.

Hell, before I know it, there could be some photographers renting boats at the marina, and I was going to wake up in the morning with pictures being taken of myself drinking coffee on the back deck.

Damn. Who knew signing with a new team would cause such a shitstorm.

I'm just a defensive lineman—not the quarterback.

Those are the dudes who typically cause a media frenzy.

Just a guy who grew up in Tennessee, I'm here for the love of the game, not the fame. Which is why I'm here in this cottage. I could have gone home to my mom and pops, but I want to avoid the photos and the questions for as long as I can, and they would have found me there.

After this weekend it's back to reality, spring training, press conferences *and the life* until the season starts.

I could kill my agent for doing this to me in the off-season.

Sullen, I stab at a mushroom and eat it with a hunk of meat, chewing as Eva watches me from across the table.

"Somehow, I doubt it." She says at last.

Eh?

"Doubt what?"

"That you'd hit on me if you saw me in public. I'm hardly your type."

"What makes you think you know what my type is?"

An unladylike snort leaves her nose. "Please. Don't you guys love that beach bottle blonde who aspires to stay at home and collect diamond jewelry."

"First of all, that's an unfair stereotype that my teammates wives and girlfriends probably wouldn't appreciate." She flushes even further. "Secondly, my last serious girlfriend was a mergers and acquisitions lawyer with three kids."

This gets Eva's attention. "Why did you break up?"

"I wanted to get married and she didn't."

"Why is getting married so important to you?"

"Don't know—I suppose it's not, actually. But at the time it's what I wanted. I wanted to know she was in it for the long haul and was the stability I needed in this fucked up world I lived in. I've rationalized that it was stupid giving up an amazing relationship because of my old fashioned values, but…at the time, that's how I felt. Do I regret it? One hundred percent."

"Where is she now?"

That makes me laugh. "Married with another baby."

Eva looks crestfallen on my behalf. "Well. Then it wasn't meant to be."

"Obviously."

Outside, rain pounds at the sliding glass door.

"I'll admit; this isn't how I thought I would be spending my first night here, but it is very cozy."

Same. "You know what we should do?"

"What?"

"Get our jammies on and binge-watch movies about people who get stranded in cottages and then get murdered."

"Let's not."

"Let's not get our jammies on?"

"Let's not watch murder mysteries that take place on lakes."

"Oh." Hmm. "Alright. What about we binge some romantic comedies and eat the popcorn we bought."

"That I'll consign."

"Sweet. When we finish eating, I'll clean up while you change, and then you can get the snacks ready while I change."

That makes Eva laugh. "Deal."

My chest puffs out having amused her.

Me.

I made her laugh.

A lady doctor.

A smart, beautiful woman who I would one million percent approach in the grocery store—what does she think I am, a shrinking violet? Has she met me?

Nothing intimidates me, unless you count snakes and parasailing—but that's only because I tried it once and was too heavy that the boat couldn't get me in the air no matter how hard that poor bastard of a boat captain tried.

After we're done with our meal, I clean up, as promised, cleaning the plates and stacking them neatly in the dishwasher, wiping down the table and countertop, and stashing our leftovers in the fridge.

It pleases me to see food inside when I open the door.

Eventually, Eva emerges from the bathroom and I laugh—she's wearing a pink, adult onesie and I'm not certain but I think it might have ears.

"What are you supposed to be? A rabbit?"

"I forgot I packed this as my pajamas, okay? I was worried I would be cold." Her paws flop across the hardwood floor. "I'm always cold."

"Well, you're adorable."

Sexy adorable.

"Your turn to use the bathroom, smart-ass."

"What?! What do you want me to say, Peter Rabbit, you're adorable!" I sigh loudly. "I wish I had one of those, but a gray one. A gray rabbit—I wonder if they make them in my size."

"Go away!" She laughs as she begins rummaging through the cabinets in search of a popcorn bowl, and who knows what else. "What will you want to drink?"

"Water is fin—no. On second thought, how 'bout that lemonade we bought?"

"Comin' right up."

I make quick work out of changing, cleaning myself up a bit, giving my beard a hasty trim, adding cologne for whatever godly reason.

I'm attracted to Eva, okay? Sue me if I want her to think I smell nice!

My pajamas aren't nearly as interesting or exciting as hers; just a basic tee-shirt with my team logo on it, and plaid flannel pants. I slide into leather slippers with a shearling liner.

The top of my bald head gleams back at me in the mirror with a wink and I scowl, but all of that is forgotten when I join Eva in the living room, logs already glowing in the fireplace.

Damn. She's a regular Boy Scout!

Impressed, I settle myself beside her and watch as she flips through channels, scrolling through movies on the apps, cursor resting on a winter romcom more suited for the holidays.

"How about this one? I know it's a Christmas movie but I've wanted to see it forever and I had planned on watching it this weekend?"

"Totally. Let's do it."

Whatever the woman wants, *the woman gets.*

And it turns out? Her selection in movies is decent; I'm not hating this goofy chick movie, not in the least. Plus, Eva and I are laughing at all the same spots, cringing in all the same spots, yelling at the television in all the same spots.

"Why doesn't she just tell her damn family to mind their own freaking business?" I shout, irritated. "Why would she bother bringing a date to every holiday? That's way too much work, she needs to tell her mom to piss off and stop nagging."

"Would you tell your mom to piss off?"

"Um, *no.* My mama would kill me."

"See? A grown man, afraid of his mama."

"I didn't say I was afraid of her!" But I am. My ma don't fuck around—she raised me. Doesn't take any shit, especially from me or my brothers.

Eva's brows go up in a *'yeah, I don't believe you,'* motion but instead of responding, she pops a handful of popcorn into her mouth, chases it with a mini chocolate cookie, and chomps away as she reverts her gaze back toward the TV.

Then, she adds.

"I think it's great that you respect your mother."

I nod. "Can't deny it."

She looks back toward me. "You look like you'd be more rough and tumble than you actually are."

My fingers go to my chin. "It's the bald head and beard. Really fucks me sometimes."

"I can see that." Her eyes seem to study me. "Wait. Did you *shave?*"

I feel my face flush. "A little."

"Ahh, you shaved for me!"

"I didn't shave for you. I shaved because it was itchy."

Lies.

"You're not so tough after all."

I never said I was. "Just a big softy I guess."

Her gaze softens. "I guess."

What's this look she's giving me? It's hard to decipher and she won't stop staring, though I'm not about to complain, the sexual tension I've been warding off all day suddenly rearing it's flirty way in.

Thing is, I'm not looking for any kind of hookup—not on a weekend retreat. I'm not that hard up, and I'm certainly able to keep my dick on its leash.

I'm a relationship kind of man, not a fling man.

The fire glows and crackles, making the room we're in warm and toasty, while the rain outside rattles the windows.

The lights flicker again.

"I have an idea." I muse out loud. "You know what we should do?"

Eva winces. "Why does the thought of you having an idea terrify me?"

"*What if...*" I say it slowly for dramatic flair. "We both sleep in the living room? It can be like we're camping."

She laughs. "You do *not* want to sleep on the floor." Her hand comes down on it like a hammer a few times. "It's hard as a rock!"

True, but, "Let's be real, I'm never going to fit in the bed that's in that room. I'm way too tall."

"I'll fit in it just fine."

"True."

"But...the idea of having a slumber party in the living room does sound fun."

"Doesn't it?" A fun, sexy slumber party with a woman dressed like a cartoon rabbit.

Eva glances around taking a mental assessment of the room. "We'll just remove all the cushions from the couch and lay on those. And you can grab all the blankets from the bed and closet."

"We could build tents in the morning and watch cartoons."

She stares at me, trying to decide if I'm being serious. Jokes on her because I am. Dead serious.

My roommate nods. "Okay, weirdo."

"We're doing it. Don't complain."

Matter resolved, we haul all the blankets into the living room from the bedroom and hall closet, pillows, too. Remove the coffee table and footstool, arrange our booty into makeshift bedrolls, my "mattress" longer than hers.

"This is hilarious," she tells me when we're settled, lying next to each other on the floor, the only thing glowing in the dark is the TV and fireplace, with the occasional lightning bolt in the distance.

"I feel like I'm eleven."

"Right?"

Eventually we both drift off. Eventually, sometime in the middle of the night, I feel a hand in mine and I rolled to the side, toward Eva, her quiet whisper waking me from my sleep.

"Robert, are you awake?"

"I am now. What's wrong?" I'm instantly alert, sitting up.

"Oh my God, the storm is so bad—it's freaking me out."

I hadn't noticed the thunder or the lightning because I'd been dead asleep; but now that I was awake, it was hard to miss that our small cottage was shaking from the storm. And chances were, if we've had any lights on, we'd have lost power and they'd have gone out.

"Are you scared?"

"Terrified. Sorry, I'm just...I hate storms. It woke me up and now I can't fall back to sleep."

Misery loves company, they always say, except I doubt Eva intentionally wanted to make me miserable. She just wanted the company or a hand to hold.

Tiny hand in my giant one, I give it a little squeeze.

"Can we like—ugh, I hate asking you this."

"Just say it."

I can practically hear her chewing on her bottom lip.

"Eva. Just say it."

She inhales a breath. "Can we move our beds closer together? So I can hide?"

My chuckle is drowned out by the loud thunder. "Sure."

Quickly, she rolls off her bed and pushes the couch cushions against mine, creating a double bed, pulling at the blankets and repositioning the entire setup before hopping back on it and beelining for my chest.

She buries her face and *I ain't even a little mad about it.*

Damn, it feels good to have someone beside me.

I lay stoically, still as a corpse, not wanting to move or freak her out, or come off the wrong way or—

"Dude, put your arm around me." Her muffled demand makes me laugh again.

I obey her order, moving my hand to her hip.

"Does this work?"

"Yeah, that's fine," she sighs. "Although I wouldn't push you out of bed for moving your hand to my back and giving me a massage. That will probably relax me."

"Um. It actually sounds like you're trying to extort a massage out of me by pretending to be afraid of a storm?"

"Potato, po-tah-toe."

My fingers are large and strong, kneading her back with only one hand but covering a massive amount of her shoulder.

"Oh God." She moans. "Oh yes. That feels amazing. You can push harder if you want."

Push harder?

What the fuck is she trying to do, *make* me hard?

"Mmm." She moans again. "*Right there.*"

I'm not interested in flings but I'm also not a monk; if she insists on dirty talk while I'm simply rubbing her shoulder and back, there's no way my dick isn't going to get hard.

I'm no saint.

Eva shifts, causing a commotion, throwing her blankets over mine, pulling here and there until we're both buried under the same set of blankets, her body pressed against mine, my arm around her shoulders, our pelvises touching.

That little minx...

Is she coming on to me? Or is she innocently just trying to get comfortable? Just trying to relax?

Don't be an idiot, Eva wouldn't be hitting on you. She's a successful, smart, gorgeous woman who isn't interested in dating a lummox of a football player, no matter how famous I am.

Robert Ramone Martinez, shame on you! Don't you dare be thinkin' this way! You are a handsome, strong man—any woman would be lucky to be with you! My mother's voice scolds from out of nowhere, causing me to scowl in the dark.

Jesus Christ, Mom, get out of my damn head! NOW IS NOT THE TIME.

"You smell so good." Eva's nose gives a whiff near my collarbone, the tip of it pressing against my skin.

I pull back, searching for her face in the dark, grateful for the bright burst of light shining into the room from the storm—I want to get a look at her.

"Um. Thanks?"

"You sound so suspicious," She laughs. "Can't I tell you that you smell good?"

"Of course you can, it's just I don't want…"

…you to make me hard.

"You don't want what?" She pushes, her hand moving from the cushions beneath her to my arm, fingers gently caressing my bicep.

Shit.

It's a meaningless motion but still sends a shiver skyrocketing down my spine, activating the one launch sequence I've been staving off most of the evening.

In about three seconds she's going to notice.

Three.

Two.

"Ohhh, now I get it!"

"You don't have to sound so happy about it."

She laughs, hand still moving up and down my arm, palm sliding under the sleeve of my tee-shirt.

"Well at least I know how you feel about me." She teases.

"Leave me alone," I tease back, unable to keep the flirtation out of my voice.

"I think you want the opposite of me leaving you alone."

"My dick is an asshole—he does what he wants, but my dick is not in charge."

She wiggles, sending another burst of lust coursing through my body. "I wouldn't be so sure about that."

"You're mean." My laugh timbers through the room, a harmony to the thunder. "Besides, we just met."

Eva pulls back and I instantly regret my words, not loving the small space between us. "So what are you saying?"

"I'm saying…" I don't know what I'm saying. "I…"

I suck at this, apparently. Making my intentions known, out of the dating game for a very long time. Years. A few of them, at least. Enough that I'm rusty and clumsy discussing it with a woman, not welcoming any kind of impending rejection.

"You know what would be nice?" she says at last, filling the silence, moving closer. Closer still.

I can feel her breath on my skin again, warm near my ear.

I gulp. "What would be nice?"

"If you found me when we got home and we went out. Like, on a date."

Whoa.

Eva has some massive lady balls, throwing it down like that.

Bigger balls than I have.

I've been acting like a goddamn pussy all night, sitting here filled with doubt like a teenage girl.

CHRIST.

Embarrassing.

"We are one-hundred-percent doing that." My brain does a mental fist pump to celebrate this win, excitement has me rolling over and bringing her along with me so she's sprawled out on top.

Life is good.

"So you want to? Actually go on a date?"

"Fuck yes. I wouldn't say it if I didn't mean it."

Her fingers play with the collar of my shirt. "Know how we should celebrate our first date?"

"The date we're going on next week?"

The date that will be photographed by the paparazzi, her face plastered all over the tabloids on every newsstand in America and gossiped about by sports broadcasters and bloggers alike? That date?

"We should bang."

Bang? What woman says that?

"Dang, Eva—I hit the jackpot with you."

Leaning forward, her lips kiss below my jawline. "God you are so sexy, Robert."

ROBERT.

So few people call me that.

Sounds unbelievably intimate on her lips.

The lips making their way toward my mouth.

Lips.

Tongue.

God, she's a good kisser...

Feels so good.

Everything about the kiss, and her, and this.

Her body moves above mine, and she sits, unzipping that stupid fucking pink rabbit onesie, sliding it down until she's practically naked, perfect breasts illuminated by the lightning.

Her hands slid under my tee-shirt; moving over my stomach and chest.

Eva purrs, I swear she does.

It's not long before we're naked; even sooner that she's beneath me, hair fanned out on the couch cushion bedding, and I can see her smile in the dark.

"I can't wait to take you out," I murmur, the length of me slowly dragging between her thighs. "Bet you look fucking sexy in a dress."

Her back arches. "I bet you look so handsome when you're all dressed up."

"I do," I mutter. "You tell me what to wear and I'll put it on."

"Would you wear matching outfits?"

Duh.

"I'm getting you a gray rabbit onesie."

My dick teases her wet pussy. "Talk dirty to me."

"I can't," she whines. "It's too hard."

"Goddamn right it is."

I slide in. Ease in slowly, so much larger than she is, afraid to break her even though I know she's formidable.

She's going to break me, I just know it.

Knew it from the second she looked at me and said, *"No, I'm not a reporter. I'm a doctor."* You idiot.

"Like—a physical therapist? I don't need any rehab, I haven't been injured since the Super Bowl."

"Um, no—I'm a pediatrician."

Eva nudges my shoulder, giving it a little push with the ball of her hand. "I want you on your back."

Bossy, this doctor of mine.

Her hair falls in waves, falling so I can't see her face but in the sexiest way. She rides me, hands on the couch behind us, bracing herself as she moves back and forth, back and forth, my hands cupping her tits.

Playing with them.

Licking, sucking.

Moaning.

Gasping until we both come. And when she's breathing softly against my chest and I'm stroking her back, we both sigh at the same time.

"This was the best trip ever."

She's going to break me, I just know it—but I'm fucking ready for it.

I've been waiting for it my whole life.

✧   ✧   ✧

Thank you for reading Room Enough for Two! Want more from author Sara Ney? Visit her website.

authorsaraney.com

SWEET TEMPTATION

A. ZAVARELLI & NATASHA KNIGHT

CHAPTER ONE
Judge

"**Y**OU HAVE GOT to be kidding me." Santiago sets his drink down and stalks to where his little sister has just entered the Baroque room at the IVI compound. Well, she's not so little anymore. Twenty-four today in fact. And from the way she looks like she's been poured into that dress, she wants to make sure everyone knows it.

A waiter pauses for me to take my scotch off his tray as I watch the scene unfold. I lean against the wall and sip, catching Mercedes's eye for all of a split second before Santiago takes her by the arm and walks her away from the entourage of young men who appeared out of nowhere the instant she set foot in the room. I can hear the two of them argue before they even stop a few feet from me.

"That is not the dress I approved," Santiago tells her, and I understand.

"I got a spot on that one and had to change at the last minute."

"A spot?"

She shrugs a shoulder and bites her lower lip, her gaze flitting to me over her brother's shoulder. I raise an eyebrow.

"I was having a snack. I didn't want all the champagne to go to my head."

"You were having a snack? Before your party where you chose all your favorite foods to be served? I wasn't born yesterday, little sister."

"The way you're talking to me, Santi, you'd think I planned it."

I can't help my chuckle at that.

"You're going to go home and change. Now."

Mercedes resists as he tries to drag her toward the exit. "It's my party! I'm not leaving—"

"You should have thought of that before pulling this stunt. Christ, Mercedes, I can see the outline of..." he trails off, looking away, gritting his jaw.

I approach. "Happy Birthday, Mercedes."

She looks up at me, panic in her eyes. A plea for help. "Thank you," she says and tries to tug free of her brother.

"Santiago," I say quietly to him. "You're drawing attention."

"It's her dress drawing the attention!"

"No." I gesture to his hand wrapped tightly around her arm.

"I'm twenty-four, Santi. I think I can choose what I wear to my own party."

"I thought you said it was a last-minute decision after you made a mess of your other dress."

Mercedes opens her mouth, closes it and turns perfectly winged dark eyes to me for help.

I look her over, see how her hair lies in thick, black waves across one shoulder as if to carry the eye to the swell of her breasts which are lifted and presented on a shelf of gathered crimson silk. Two diamond-studded straps hold the dress precariously in place. The silk hugs her tiny waist and curves around her hips to drop to the floor. A high slit shows off slender but well-toned thighs and five-inch heels.

"This is what I mean," Santiago says, giving me a look. "Even Judge can't seem to drag his gaze away."

I clear my throat. "You look beautiful, Mercedes," I say, aware how my heartrate has accelerated at my own lingering perusal.

She is your best friend's little sister. You have watched her grow up literally from birth. She is off limits.

"Thank you, Judge," she says coolly as Santiago releases her arm. She rubs it. "Maybe you can talk some sense into my brother. Remind him I'm an adult and isn't this party to secure me a husband anyway?"

As soon as she says it, something dark wakes inside me. Like a slumbering beast disturbed, lifting its heavy head, a low growl warning of its presence. Do they hear it, I wonder, before I can clear my throat to mask the sound?

"You won't secure a husband looking like that," Santiago says. "You'll give men the wrong impression."

"What's wrong with it? It was made by a Society approved designer. It's elegant and my color and made just for me so no one will be wearing the same dress. How embarrassing would that be?" She looks over Santiago's shoulder and I follow her gaze to her friends, a group of women whose names I don't know and don't care to know. "Vivien is going to be beside herself with jealousy," she says with a very satisfied grin and wave. She quickly looks back to her brother. "And besides, if some man gets the wrong idea, that's on him, not me. I can't be responsible for how men behave."

"Mercedes," Santiago groans.

"Come on, Santi," she says more sweetly. "Don't be mad. Please? It's my birthday."

"Judge?" Santiago turns to me, already softening to his sister.

"She is twenty-four and as intelligent as she is beautiful. She's also right. How the male population behaves is not her responsibility. Besides, I have no doubt it's the boys who will need rescuing should anything untoward transpire, not Mercedes."

Mercedes watches me and if I didn't know better, I'd think she was hanging on my every word. I make sure to break eye contact first. I don't want her to get the wrong idea.

"Thank you, Judge," she says then turns to her brother. "Santi?"

"Go. But I warn you, anything inappropriate, and you're going home. I don't care if it's your birthday party."

She smiles her most charming smile and gives her brother a hug and a peck on the cheek which have him stiffen awkwardly. Then she's off to her circle of friends who, even from here, I can see aren't true friends. I wonder if she's aware of this.

"She is more vulnerable than she lets on," Santiago says. "With all that's happened."

"I can see that."

He turns to me, gaze intent. "Can you?"

"She'll be fine, Santiago. I meant what I said. She can handle herself."

He smiles proudly, both of us shifting our gazes to his sister who has a group of about a dozen men surrounding her once again.

CHAPTER TWO

Mercedes

I FEEL HIS eyes on me as I move across the room to join my friends. Friends, being a loose term. Vivien, Dulce, and Giordana are more like frenemies. The Society approved women I'm allowed to spend time with because outwardly, we look like we belong together.

We're all upper echelon Society princesses. We come from money. We have influence. And we fill our days doing charitable work for the Society and pretending it satisfies us, while really, we're all just biding our time until we get married. Preferably to a Sovereign Son. In my case, I know Santi won't approve anything less.

The De La Rosa family name has taken too many blows already. It's up to me to represent my family dynasty in a way befitting of a Society daughter. My husband will need to be rich. Powerful. Influential, as well. And ultimately, he'll have control over my life and everything I do. An annoying little detail I try to forget as I sip from my first glass of champagne.

"God, he is delicious." Vivien practically groans into her glass as her eyes move over my shoulder. "He's totally checking me out right now."

I resist the urge to roll my eyes and break her heart by telling her Lawson Montgomery, aka Judge, aka my brother's domineering best friend, doesn't even know she exists. His eyes are on me. They're always on me. It's a secret game we like to play. He falls into his role of the protector, the man looking out for me, while I act like the spoiled little brat he expects me to be.

Maybe it's because I like his attention. Maybe it's because I've never felt the physical caress of a pair of eyes until I felt his on me. And yet, we act like we hate each other. As if we can hardly stand to be around one another for longer than a few minutes. Because if there's one thing I know from overhearing his conversations with Santi over the years, Judge has no intentions of marrying. Which means, as far as he's concerned, I'm off limits. He can't touch me without destroying my virtue. And I can't let him without a ring on my finger.

A deep sigh falls from my lips, souring my mood as Vivien continues to eye-fuck the man across the room.

"Get me an introduction." She looks at me, pleading.

"You've already had an introduction." My teeth clink against my glass, annoyance bubbling in my chest.

"Come on," she hisses. "Don't be a bitch. He wants to talk to me. I can tell."

I offer her a sweet smile. "Trust me. If he wanted to talk to you, he would. Judge doesn't play coy."

At this she stiffens, her eyes flashing with indignation. "That sounds a little like jealousy, Mercedes."

"Oh please." I set my empty glass on a passing waiter's tray. "You're the one that's obsessed with him. I've known him my entire life. If I wanted him, I would have him."

"Really?" Her lip curls into a sneer. "From what I hear, he's not so easy to catch. He's been known to spend time at the Cat House, but I've never seen him court a woman publicly."

Vivien's shot hits me where it's intended. I don't like being a jealous little monster, but sometimes, I can't help it. It isn't even rational. But the thought of Judge fucking random women at the Cat House crawls under my skin and eats at me.

It's about this time I decide two can play this game. I'll show Vivien and everyone else here tonight, including Judge, that I have plenty of willing suitors.

I grab a crab cake from one of the waiters and pop it into my mouth, scanning the crowd, looking for someone I can manipulate with an easy smile.

"Are you sure you should be eating that?" Vivien's appraising eyes move over me. "You might want to cut back."

"You think so?" I cut my eyes to her, my words laced with vinegar.

I've never been in better shape, and she knows it. This is her last desperate attempt to knock me off my game tonight.

"Just a suggestion." She shrugs a shoulder.

"Well, don't you worry about me, Vivien." I savor the last of my appetizer as my eyes laser in on a Sovereign Son. "I'll let you know if I have any problems finding a man to entertain me tonight."

CHAPTER THREE
Judge

I KNOW WHAT it took for Santiago to arrange this party for his sister. I know the effort it costs him to leave De La Rosa Manor. To have the eyes of The Society on him, speculating behind his back, wondering at the reclusive man he has become, a sort of phantom of the opera with his half-skull tattooed face and all his rage.

I pity the woman who will one day bear the brunt of his punishment. I know who she is. He's just waiting. Biding his time. Making his plans. It's coming, though. The reckoning of the Moreno family.

So, when Santiago tolerates as much as he is capable of tolerating and asks me to bring his sister home when she's ready, I agree, and he takes his leave.

I keep a close eye on her throughout the evening, noting her dance partners. Counting the glasses of champagne she drinks. Making sure she is served seltzer after her third. No one will notice the switch but her and the instant she takes a sip from her fourth glass, I have to subdue a chuckle when she almost spits it out in her friend Vivien's face.

She searches the room and catches my gaze.

I raise my drink to her.

She gives me a sneer. Subtly lifts her middle finger at me. She's charming like that.

The cake is rolled into the ballroom to much fanfare and I walk out to the courtyard to get some fresh air. It's a clear night, the sky like black velvet dotted with diamond stars. Pushing a hand into my pocket I stand in a corner and watch people drift in and out of the party, most of them having drank too much. When I'm finished with my drink, I set it aside and take the long way back to the Baroque room, checking the time on my watch. The party is almost over. I'm glad for it.

The corridor I walk down is dark, the rooms closed off for the night. The only people I pass are couples making out where they don't think they'll be seen. Don't they know there is always someone watching? Especially here.

I have almost reached the back entrance of the Baroque room when I see the door to the Red Room is ajar. The Red Room, named for its décor, is used for smaller cocktail parties. Everything from carpet to furnishings to the ceiling draped with silk is red. I place my hand on the doorknob to pull the door closed. But just before I do, I hear something. A woman's voice. A man's.

Hers I recognize. His is harder to place.

I open the door farther until I see the couple in the corner. He has his back to me and is blocking her view of me. I slip quietly inside and watch, that beast of earlier alert again, making that rattling sound inside my chest.

"You're so fucking beautiful. The most beautiful woman in that room," he says like an inexperienced buffoon as he leans down to kiss the curve of her shoulder. He stumbles on one foot, and I realize he's drunk.

I clear my throat and he startles, spinning as if a boy caught with his hand in the cookie jar. Which he is.

"Sir. Mr. Montgomery," he stutters.

I raise my eyebrows. He's maybe five years younger than me. A Sovereign Son. But an idiot all the same.

"David." I meet Mercedes's eyes. "Mercedes."

She leans her weight against the wall and folds her arms across her chest, annoyed.

"I was just giving Ms. De La Rosa her gift," David says.

"And what was the gift? A kiss?"

"Christ Judge," Mercedes interrupts. "It was a pair of earrings. He was helping me put them on."

"In the dark?"

David clears his throat. "Perhaps I should go."

"Perhaps you should."

Mercedes exhales as the boy takes his leave. I wait until he's gone to turn back to her. She pushes off the wall to walk away, but I step in front of her blocking her path.

She's tall, five-feet-ten-inches barefoot but even in her heels, the top of her head barely comes to my chin, and she has to crane her neck to drag her gaze up to mine.

"What?" she snaps.

"Did you enjoy that? Because you looked bored."

"How long were you watching?"

"Long enough to see the boy's attempt at seduction fail miserably."

Her cheeks flush. She's embarrassed. She shifts her gaze to the side, and I see the woman beneath the mask, the one even her brother knows is in there, buried deep.

"He was drunk in case you failed to notice."

"Lucky him since you cut off my drink."

"And it's a good thing I did. I convinced your brother to let you stay given the dress."

She sighs. "What happened to me not being responsible for how men react?"

"Oh, you're not, but you need to be smart and not put yourself into situations where you might get hurt."

"He wasn't going to hurt me."

"He was drunk."

"And I'm stone-cold sober."

"Even so, he can overpower you."

"He wasn't going to overpower me. You sound just like Santi."

"Besides, you're my responsibility tonight."

She rolls her eyes. "Excuse me, Judge. I'm going back to my party." She tries to sidestep me, but I set a hand against the wall to block her.

"Don't do that."

Her gaze moves slowly over my arm, to my chest, up to my face. I see the pulse at her throat jump in double time.

"Do what?"

"Roll your eyes at me."

She lowers her lashes, and I can't help my glance to the swell of her breasts. But when I look up, I realize she has caught me looking.

She licks her lips and I remind myself who she is.

"You need a man, little monster. Not a boy."

CHAPTER FOUR

Mercedes

HIS LOW SPOKEN words are still vibrating through my head when he helps me into the back of his Rolls Royce. Raul, his driver, shuts the door after Judge gets in beside me. He's at least a good foot away, but his presence seems to suck all the oxygen from the space. I can smell his cologne, the warm spicy scent unique to him. And almost against my will, my eyes drift to the pulsing beat in his neck. That gorgeous column of skin is masculine and alluring in a strange way. My fingers itch to touch it. To feel the warmth there, just to see if he's affected by me too.

"You're staring," Judge murmurs, his lip tipped in amusement.

"I was just trying to figure out if you're actually human," I remark dryly, tearing my gaze to the window.

"I imagine it must be difficult for you to comprehend," he says.

"What?" I turn back to him, arching a brow.

"When a man doesn't cow to you like all the others."

"Oh please. Isn't that what all Sovereign Sons think? You rule the world, after all."

"I'd rule you with a firm hand because that's what you need, Mercedes."

His words feel like a warning and a threat, and I can't help my audible swallow in response. I get the impression he's always trying to warn me away. And yet his words hold weight because he is to become my guardian should anything ever happen to my brother. He would be tasked with the responsibility of keeping me in line. I can't help wondering how exactly he would do it if he were ever given a chance. But my pride won't allow me to give him any indication that he affects me either way.

"Lucky for me you'll have to save that firm hand for the unfortunate souls who entertain you at the Cat House."

There's a lingering silence after the inappropriate words leave my lips where his eyes catch mine, and it feels like I'm catching fire. Heat blazes from the dark depths of his soul, and it penetrates me in a way that feels discomforting. Like he's unraveling me from the inside out, extracting all my secrets, my wants, my insecurities. Judge has a way of doing that. I suppose he makes for a terrifying presence for anyone who has to face him in the courtroom.

"Does that bother you?" His smooth voice slides over me like silk.

"Why would it bother me?" I answer with a cold laugh.

His gaze dips to my lips, and my heart slams against my chest. Then, to my horror, my own lips part, as if in invitation to something I don't understand. This thing between us feels different tonight. More dangerous. Like we're toeing the line we know we can't cross. We're flirting with danger, and if Santi were to find out Judge spoke to me this way, he'd probably try to chop off his hands. That knowledge hangs heavy between us, and yet it doesn't stop him from reaching out to touch my chin, tipping it up so I'm forced to endure his gaze that feels like a visceral penetration between my thighs.

Jesus.

He's never touched me this way before. Never. And the brush of his fingers, his skin on my skin, sends sparks shooting through me. My heartbeat is skittering in my chest, my breath coming weird and too fast. Judge sees it. He sees every goddamned thing. And he likes it. I can tell by the way his eyes flare and then melt into liquid flames.

For a brief moment, I'm wondering how far he'll take it. Would he kiss me? Would he... *do more?* And why do I feel like I want him to? God, this man is an arrogant asshole. I know this, but I seem to have forgotten it. Judge, however, hasn't, and that becomes obvious when he releases me, a cold expression returning to his ridiculously handsome face.

"I'm not the man you want to play games with," he clips out.

I sit back, forcing my armor into place. "Who said I was playing games with you?"

When he doesn't answer, I pull out my metaphorical knife, sliding it between his ribs in a way I hope stings.

"Don't worry, Judge. I understand it's common knowledge I'm in want of a husband, like any good Society daughter. I'll need to marry soon, and I have many fine prospects, but you don't fall anywhere on that list. So, there's no need to get yourself worked up that I've caught you in my sights."

The vein in his neck throbs, but his lip tilts even further as he returns the blow. "Is that what you told Jackson Van der Smit? I wonder, does that wound still burn? Considering he passed you up for his pretty new wife, I'm sure it must."

Despite my best efforts, I falter. I hate myself for it, but I do. And he sees it, that lingering vulnerability in my eyes I never show the world. It isn't about Jackson Van der Smit. I hold no love for him. But he humiliated me, and Judge knows it. He discarded me like yesterday's trash for a woman he barely knew. This after a public courtship everybody was certain would lead to a proposal. For Judge to bring that up makes me angry, but worse than that, it hurts. I hit him with an arrow, and he fired back with an atom bomb.

For once, I'm all out of insults. And I decide I'm tired of this verbal sparring with Judge. So, I turn away and watch the scenery fly by as an uncomfortable silence settles over us. I can feel his eyes on my face. His warmth still penetrates me somehow, even as space lingers between us. It sucks the breath from my lungs as something heavy sinks into my stomach. It's the unwelcome realization that this man gets to me. And I don't let anyone get to me.

The car pulls through the gates of De La Rosa Manor, and I'm grateful when we roll to a stop at the entrance. I've never wanted to scramble from a car faster, but before I can, Judge captures my wrist in his grasp, halting me.

"Mercedes."

I close my eyes, drag in a deep breath, and then turn to look at him. "Yes?"

His thumb skates over my pulse, his eyes softening in a way I rarely see from him. "He doesn't deserve you. He never did."

Those words feel like an apology, and for a second, I consider telling him it doesn't matter. Because Jackson doesn't matter, and he's not what I'm upset about. But that confession is too raw. Too vulnerable. So instead, I offer him one of my fake smiles and slip from his grasp.

"I know."

CHAPTER FIVE
Judge

THE IMAGE OF Mercedes with that boy doesn't bother me half as much as that of her face when I made the remark I made. It was childish. Tit for tat. She's younger than me. Inexperienced in every way. She may rule the boys who encircle her, pay homage to her, but I am no boy. I know better. But when her comment cut me, I struck back.

"Pull over," I tell Raul the following morning as we navigate rush hour traffic toward the compound where I have a meeting with Councilor Hildebrand.

He pulls to the side of the road, neither of us caring when the driver of the car he cuts off honks his horn and waves his middle finger at us.

"I'll be a few minutes," I tell him and climb out of the car. The idea sparked the moment I saw the jeweler, but it feels older. Like something I've wanted to do for a long time and perhaps now, given the excuse of her birthday, it may not be seen as inappropriate.

I walk half-way down the block to the shop where I am buzzed in by the woman who usually serves me when I place an order from the exclusive shop.

"Mr. Montgomery, I wasn't expecting you," she looks concerned. "Have I missed an appointment?" She hurries behind the counter to open the heavy, leather-bound ledger.

"No, Anna. I have no appointment and you didn't miss anything." I usually call ahead and leave the choosing of the gift in Anna's capable hands. So, I can understand her surprise at seeing me. "This is a spur of the moment stop."

She closes the book and tilts her head. "That's not like you, but let me know how I can help," she says as I begin to peruse the glass shelves displaying their one-of-a-kind jewelry, creations that range from simple elegance to over-the-top pieces fit for royalty.

"Earrings," I say. Because the boy had given her earrings. "I am looking for earrings."

Truth is that her comment about the Cat House got to me. I don't know why. It wasn't untrue. I do make use of the services offered at the establishment, a perk of being a member of The Society. Beautiful courtesans always ready to serve you a drink, make conversation, or satisfy any other need. And I know my decision not to marry is something often gossiped about by Society women. I am the right age to marry. I come from good stock. The Montgomery name is synonymous with wealth and power. And yet I have no desire to take a wife or procreate and I won't be bothered with the acceptable rituals of The Society. I don't court. I don't even casually date. What I do, though, is provide a juicy topic for conversation. And that is what Mercedes has heard. It is mostly true, I'm certain. The only thing is that I am bothered by *her* knowing this. Even if she heard it mentioned by her brother in passing. Although I'm sure given the women who form her little clique the matter has been discussed to death.

"Mr. Montgomery?"

I turn to find Anna watching me. I realize she was speaking and I haven't heard a word.

"I'm sorry, Anna. I was distracted."

"I understand. I wanted to show you this. It's a new piece." I walk to where she sets a satin cushion on the counter and pulls away the velvet covering to reveal a pair of earrings like none I've ever seen.

They are lovely.

"Thirty-two individual diamonds suspended as if in air," she starts, letting me know the carats and the 18K gold setting. "Some of the diamonds are polished, some not. Elegant but not overstated. One-of-a-kind, of course."

I take one of the earrings, lay it in the palm of my hand. Two rows of diamonds alternating in white polished and green and pink rough diamonds. The gold will compliment her olive skin, the diamonds as unique as she.

"They're perfect," I say. "I'd like to take them with me now. Put them on my account please."

She smiles happily because I am certain she can close shop before it has officially opened for the day, or perhaps the month, given what I am sure the earrings cost.

"As you wish. Would you like me to wrap them?"

"Yes, please."

"A lucky lady," she says, eyeing me curiously.

I smile but give nothing away. A few minutes later, I leave the shop and return to the Rolls Royce where Raul is still waiting.

"Thank you, Raul," I say as he drives to the IVI compound. I send a quick text to Hildebrand letting him know I will be a few minutes late because this morning is the lady's breakfast. Mercedes organized it to benefit underprivileged children of the community as part of her birthday celebration. A fitting thing for someone of her standing to do.

The morning is crisp and bright, and the courtyard is busy with staff setting elegant tables beneath the tents they must have erected just hours ago because they weren't here last night.

"Is Ms. De La Rosa here?" I ask one of the staff.

"Yes, sir, she's inside. Just through there." She points through the double French doors, and I see the outline of her profile as she discusses the menu with the chef.

My phone pings with a text. I ignore it because I'm certain it's Hildebrand letting me know he's displeased with the delay and cross the courtyard to enter through the open doors. I clear my throat, stopping a few feet from them.

Mercedes looks up and does a double take because I'm sure she's not expecting to see me. She's wearing a custom-made pantsuit today with a cream silk blouse. It is cut to fit her perfectly and shows her to an advantage although differently than last night.

"We're good," she tells the chef, dismissing him, and brushes her fingers over her hair which has been tightly twisted into a chignon at the nape of her neck. She is all business today.

"Judge," she says, barely looking at me. I hear in her tone that she is still upset. "The Tribunal building is that way." She points toward it.

"I am aware of where the Tribunal building is," I say with a smile. "I came to see you."

"Me?" She raises her eyebrows in surprise. "Why would you need to see me?"

A waiter interrupts us, asking Mercedes a question she answers. I wait until he's gone to continue.

"Perhaps you have a moment?"

"I'm busy, Judge." She turns to walk away but I catch her arm. She stops, looks down at where I'm holding her. I don't let go. I'm not sure she won't slip away.

"I was unfair," I say when she shifts her gaze up.

"You're fine. I need to go." She tugs.

"And in the midst of things I forgot to give you your birthday present." I take the small box out of the inside pocket of my jacket.

Her eyes fall to it. I'm sure she recognizes the jeweler. I release her and she clears her throat, meets my gaze.

"I'm using the office there," she says, pointing to a closed door behind me.

I gesture for her to go ahead. When she passes me, I inhale the subtle scent of her perfume. It's one that is made especially for her that I have somehow come to memorize. She turns her head just a little and I catch the IVI tattoo on the back of her neck. The empty space above it where one day a man will etch his mark.

That beast of last night stirs. I tell it to quiet and reach around her to open the door then follow her into the small office reserved for use for events such as these.

I close the door and turn to her. She is lovely. Makeup fitting the more serious business of the day although no less sensual. But that's Mercedes. Stripped to bare skin she will be at her most sensual, I am certain.

She looks expectantly at me. Eyes the gift in my hand.

"Happy birthday," I say, holding it out to her.

She takes my gift and pulls the ribbon. I watch her face as she unwraps and opens the box. As her gaze falls on the diamond earrings, and she gasps.

"These are…" she looks up at me, mouth open.

"If you don't like them—"

"No, I love them. They're beautiful. Just… I'm sure they're very expensive."

"Only the best for you. It's what you're used to, isn't it?"

"Is that a cut? Because I believe you and I grew up in similar circumstances."

"It's not a cut." I step toward her, reaching out to take off the diamond studs she's wearing. Probably the gift from the idiot boy. "I don't always bring my sword and nor should you, little monster. At least not with me."

She stands very still, her breath a tremble as I remove the earrings she's wearing and set them on the desk. Her cheeks flush when I meet her eyes before taking one of the set I gave her and slip it into place, repeating with the other. I brush my thumb over her cheek. I don't know why. And then I stand back to look.

"Beautiful," I say. "The earrings pale in comparison."

She blushes fully, lowering her gaze, an almost shy smile on her lips. I watch her in this rare moment. She is herself. She is vulnerable. Uncertain.

Inexperienced, I remind myself. In every way.

And not for you.

The beast that slumbers inside me, lazily opening one eye, awakens fully now. Because it wants. It desires what it cannot have.

When I step closer, she turns her face up to mine. Her lips part and her pupils dilate. She sets the tips of her fingers against my chest and the touch of them burns. Her fingers trail toward the pulse she was staring at last night.

She brings her face closer, and I hear her inhale. But when her fingertips brush the exposed skin of my neck, I step back. I clear my throat, seeing how her nipples have pebbled against her silk blouse. And I am fully aware of my own arousal at being so close to her.

How thin the ice I have just skated onto is. How dangerous for us both.

"You should go," I tell her, my voice hoarse.

A sudden cold seems to ice the room. It takes Mercedes a moment to recover, to slide her mask back in place. She stands up to her full height, steps toward me. "Don't tell me you're human after all, Judge. Cowed by a mere woman." Her fingertips dance low across my abdomen and I capture her wrist.

"Careful, little monster. You play a dangerous game."

"I'm not afraid of you."

"Perhaps you should be."

"Like you said last night, it's the boys who will need rescuing from me."

I take her other wrist and walk her backward until her back is against the wall and I tower over her. I grin, letting the beast out for a moment, just for a taste, to catch her scent. I brush my cheek close to hers and feel her shudder. She tilts her head back, baring her throat, offering it to me.

Would she give herself so freely if she knew me?

It doesn't matter, I remind myself. I cannot have her. Not now. Not ever.

"That is correct. But you make one mistake." She shudders at my whispered words. "I am no boy, Mercedes. I am a man."

✧   ✧   ✧

We hope you enjoyed this prelude of Judge and Mercedes's story! You can learn more about The Society *here*.

natasha-knight.com/book-series/the-society-trilogy

THE MATCH

NATALIE WRYE

MIA

"**Y**OU'RE FIRING ME? But I—I just walked in the door two seconds ago."

More like one second ago. But Jerry doesn't seem to give a damn.

I'm sure my restaurant manager doesn't give a damn about many things—unless they have nipples on them, but today, that normally smarmy smile of his is almost sad, his thin lips pressed in a soft frown that lets me know it's exactly as I feared.

I'm being canned. And I don't even know what I've done.

Okay, scratch that. I don't know what I've done lately.

I shift on my black kitten heels in the doorway of the noisy restaurant kitchen, my chest starting to squeeze as I run down a list of the mistakes I've made since I started this waitressing job.

And the list ain't short.

"It's not that I'm firing you, Mia. Because I'm not." He glances at my chest. "With your set of...skills, I'm definitely not. It's just that...we can't have you spilling hot coffee on customers. Especially customers whose business we like to keep." He lowers his voice. "Now, I didn't tell you this: But this guy—the customer you pissed off? He knows the owner. So it wasn't me." He raises his sweaty hands, taking a step back, his brown eyes muted under the dull fluorescent light streaming just two feet away.

Having successfully dodged the blame, he smiles again, and a disgusted shiver crawls down my spine as I wring my waitress apron in my hands.

"So that's it, then? I'm not being fired. But I'm obviously in trouble. So, what is it? What's my situation? Am I still serving customers? Or should I pass that nice lady at table seven without her afternoon coffee?"

Jerry shrugs. "Just think of it as a warning. A strong warning. One more of those, and I think Scotty the owner might have another girl auditioning for your wait spot next week..."

"Probably one with even bigger breasts," I mutter, glancing over towards the restaurant's main floor. I plaster on a smile, raising my chin. "You got it, Jer. Won't happen again."

His gaze flickers to my chest again. "Oh I'm sure it won't. I believe in you, Mia. I know you wouldn't do anything to jeopardize this job."

Like hell, I wouldn't.

But I bypass him anyway, slipping into the kitchen, my hands tying my apron around my waist.

I try not to let my fingers shake.

It's been four months that I've been working at Sopra. Four months of making the biggest tips I've ever seen.

Working at one of Seattle's most famous, four-star restaurants has its perks, least of all the customers.

And though I wasn't winning any awards for World's Greatest Waitress, I had managed not to kill anyone or seriously injure them.

Sure, I'd splashed a little orange juice on a few suits and dropped a few muffins more than once. But serving wasn't rocket science.

But today, it might as well be as I pick up Table Seven's order, trying to keep my brain focused on making it through the day—just one day without any mishaps—as Jerry's words spin like a record in my mind.

I've just slipped the plate on Seven's table when someone waltzes in step beside me, their footfalls echoing softly over the understated dark marble floor as they whisper near my ear.

I almost jump back.

"Sooo?" Christina hisses inches from my eardrum. "What do you think? You like the new job?"

I keep walking. "Well, I struggle not to coat my customers with one drink or another every time I serve and I'm struggling not to get fired. But so far, so good." I tilt my head, blinking my eyes. "Luckily, I've got a calming crystal in my purse. Which I think is keeping me from eating my own shoe in embarrassment."

Christina nudges me, following me closer to the kitchen, her brown bob swinging in my direction. "You and your crazy crystals. And no, I'm not talking about this job. I'm talking about the 'other' one. The one I got you last week? How was that?"

"The one last week was with a private investigations firm. And I have less than zero interest in what they're asking me to do."

"What? It's extra money. Money for that magazine competition of yours. And it's photography! It's what you've always wanted to do."

"Yeah, Teen." I spin by the bar, keeping my voice low. "Photography. You know... Art. Actual photos. Not snapping away at philandering husbands caught with their pants down."

My closest colleague rolls her eyes. "Beggars can't be choosers."

"And fifty-year-olds with erectile dysfunction shouldn't be cheaters. But here we are."

I grab for another tray from the oak bar, my hands struggling to balance it, and Teen luckily leaves it alone, letting me walk away.

I'm already too amped up to walk straight in my kitten heels. And her bringing up last week's embarrassing job interview isn't helping me stay mishap-free...

But the bright side is: I'm only two thousand dollars away from my goal.

So far, Table Seven made it without wearing her favorite Americano. But the rest of my customers remain to be seen.

And I won't even think about the one customer who ratted me out. I already have a good idea of who it is.

And as I load my plate with dishes for Table Twelve, I try not to think about him. About his infuriatingly smug face. His chiseled jaw. Or even those stupid, blue, stunning eyes.

I hit the main floor of the warm, cozy Italian restaurant, counting my steps, praying I don't fall.

Luckily, I make it.

"Here you go," I say to the two businesswomen sipping their Seattle martinis. "The chef's favorite. Buon Appetito."

Only about two more million of those to serve and I can count this day as a success. Another day to put money towards the photography competition hovering over me like a money cloud for months.

Three hours pass and not a drop spilled.

As the cool northwestern day falls into a colder evening, I glance out the front glass wall of the building, counting down the minutes until the end of my shift.

Only two orders left and then I'm out of here.

With the clock striking six o'clock, I head back to the kitchen in a daze, grabbing the next table's order.

I'm just about to slide it over to the table that ordered it when a strong pair of hands come into sight, whisking the glass of dark whiskey right off my tray.

I look up to find a random customer grabbing the drink.

But not just any customer.

It's him. Asshole of the month.

He passes by me in a blink, slinking into the corner booth. His eyes on his phone, he barely notices me. But when I stand there, gaping at him from where he sits, he raises a pair of cool blue eyes, assessing me, his gaze guarded.

Under Sopra's dim gold recessed lighting, his golden-brown hair gleams, the blue-white screen of his cell phone screen making the perfect strands shine.

The device buzzes several times in his hands, signs of incoming texts, and he dismisses me just as coolly as he grabbed the glass from my tray.

"Can I help you with something?"

His gaze stuck on his phone, he pads his thumbs over the small screen in his hand, and I have to struggle not to breathe out fire, I'm so mad.

Instead, I even manage to grit out a few words. Yay me.

"Uh, yeah, I think you can," I respond, at last. "Mind handing me that stolen drink back?"

"I'm sorry?" He doesn't glance up.

"Yeah, the drink. The one in your hand? You mind putting your lips on something that belongs to someone else?"

That gets his attention.

"Unfortunately, this glass has an owner. And she's right over there." I reach over, snatching the thick-plated glass from his hand before I can stop myself. Tension holds my body rigid, brittle enough to break in half. "Maybe you should wait for your waitress to return to your table with your order."

He frowns. "That's not my drink?"

"Well, I do think that me saying so about five times confirms that fact, so yes…that's correct. That was not your drink. You should talk to your waitress."

"I don't have a waitress. Not yet, at least. I ordered a whiskey at the bar, and they promised they'd bring it right over."

I shrug. "Well, I'm not the 'they' they promised. Good luck with that."

I try to turn away. But his voice stops me, the words as smooth as silk.

"A shame," he says, his head tilting back to the phone. "How much would it take for a man to get a drink around here?"

"Our prices are on the menu. I'm sure you can find out there."

"I mean for that drink. The one I almost put my lips on." He smiles at his phone, but I know it's meant for me. And no, it doesn't make me feel funny things happen in my pants.

I stand very still, trying to convince myself of that fact.

And Mr. Perfect keeps talking, not missing a beat—as if he's practiced this.

"I'll pay double the price on the menu, if you sit it back down. No questions asked."

"See, that's the problem." I sway on my feet, gazing at his downturned face, the tray in my hands growing heavy. "If I give you this drink, then the woman who ordered it might have to wait another twenty minutes for another one. As you can see, the bar's kinda full."

"Three times the price," he says, still typing. And I don't even know how he manages it, his attention's so focused.

"This isn't an auction. You don't have to keep jacking up the price."

"Four times."

"I really don't think you need to—"

"Five times the cost." He finally gazes upwards. "And I'll buy you one, too, whiskey police. You look like you could use it."

And I'm not the only one who could. The guy seems busier than a one-man circus show, his typing never stopping, his fingers constantly moving.

He's like a machine this guy. Completely cold. Totally calculating.

And I don't know why it intrigues me. Why his total nonchalance and dogged focus drive something in me that wants to take a peek behind his perfect curtain.

I decide to give it a try. "Look, you seem like a guy who's used to getting what he wants. So, I'll make it easy for you…" I straighten my shoulders. "This drink does not belong to you. And neither do I. Like I said, I'm not your waitress. Now…I'm sure your actual waiter or waitress will be happy to serve your needs whenever they come. But as for me? I'm already spoken for. Have a nice night. And while you're at it, try not to steal any more drinks. The managers really frown on that kind of thing. And so do the cops, I hear. Good luck with your whiskey."

And with that, I spin away, feeling triumphant, like I won some unspoken contest.

Like I've rightfully pissed him off.

A little payback never felt so good.

That is, until in all my spinning and walking off, I twirl my tray right into a customer standing a few feet away.

The glass goes flying, whiskey spilling everywhere. It sloshes and splashes with a final drenching…right onto the suit of Scott Macpherson—known to everyone in this restaurant as the Big Boss.

The one who writes all the checks.

The owner of Sopra…and, subsequently, of my ass.

And within seconds, after staring in horror at his wet face, I think I know what exactly is going to happen to that ass tonight…

So much for avoiding mishaps.

I swallow thickly, my job and the magazine competition I'd been hoping for flashing before my eyes.

DEREK

SHE WAS RIGHT. It's been a long time since I've heard "no."

And her "no" might be the sexiest one I've gotten in some time.

I might be distracted. But I'm not blind.

I like to think of myself as a master of multitasking, and even in my efforts to secure a whiskey, respond to my assistant's texts, answer a thousand emails, and finish off this after-hours meeting, I don't neglect to notice that my waitress is goddamned stunning.

One first look is all I need. But the last look confirms what I suspected from the instant I crossed her path...

She doesn't really like me. She wouldn't be the first person in Seattle.

And sexy or not, I'm just about to let her go, let her leave with that sassy attitude and the whiskey I wanted so bad when she collides with some stuffy-shirted dickhead in a polo—some prick that acts like wetting his collared shirt is a cardinal sin.

I watch from where I sit as he wipes rivulets of dark liquor from his face, his bald head gleaming under the gold light.

"Jesus fucking Christ," he curses out loud, drawing attention. "You think you could watch where you're going?"

"I am so sorry, Scotty—um, Mr. Macpherson," the formerly slick-tongued waitress stutters. "I could get you a towel—"

"No, leave it. You've done enough already."

But she's already turning, whipping into another waitress. And down waitress number two goes.

Her tray goes flying in the air, sending more liquid splashing all over the place, and if I weren't supposed to be in the middle of the most important meeting of my life right now, I'd laugh.

Instead, I tuck my phone away to avoid the spray, standing to my feet, when I notice that my unwanted waitress is wearing some mystery orange sauce on her uniformed blouse from the small melee.

I try to hide the smile that hits my face.

"Well, at least it's your color," I mutter, taking in the mess.

The brunette glances at me, horror imprinted on her face, not seconds before the man in the polo turns to her, his face turning an unnatural shade of red, his neck strained.

"Could you be any worse at your fucking job?"

He approaches her, still dripping wet.

God fucking help me, I don't know what gets into me. Because instead of calling Simon Disrick and rescheduling our meeting location and getting the hell out of Dodge, I step suddenly into the balding man's path, hands up, my body blocking his path to the cute little server that was just making my life a living hell.

And somehow it feels natural as hell to me.

My fingertips nearly touch his damp chest, I'm so close. I can smell the cigarette smoke on his breath.

"Look, she said she was sorry, guy. Let her get you a towel and someone'll get you another drink. Preferably one you don't have to wear on your shirt. How's about that?"

He goes to say more but a slew of waitstaff come to his aid, whisking him away. And stuck between a wet spot and an angry waitress, I turn to the latter, eyebrows raised at the look of dismay on her face.

She says nothing, quiet for the first time all night. And I break the silence.

"You do have a helluva way of making friends around here, don't you?"

She shoots me a look, that stubborn gaze of hers wilting by a fraction, and without another word, she takes off towards the back of the restaurant, in what I'm sure is the direction of the restrooms.

And I feel like a fucking tool.

I could go after her.

Sure, I could do that. Or I could sit back in my booth, shoot a text to Mr.

Disrick and close this acquisitions deal before the stroke of nine.

Securing his publishing house would be the much-needed cherry on my shit-sundae of a year, and I know if I act now, I can clinch the deal, grab a shot of whiskey or two, and crank my Alice in Chains playlist to ear-splitting levels all the way home.

Yeah, I could do that.

Or I could go after that crazy waitress.

And from the looks of the puddle on the floor, I already know what the better choice is.

But for the first time today, reason doesn't win out. My feet do.

And they drag my unreasonable ass in the direction of the retreating waitress, who, as guessed, hightails it in the women's restroom, the door closing behind her with a dull thwack.

I stand on the other side of the heavy wood, lost for where to even begin. I clear my throat.

"I—uh... Look, that joke was tasteless. I shouldn't have said anything."

Nothing but silence on her end. I keep going.

"Look, don't listen to that walking, talking penis out there, alright? You're not a bad waitress. A mean one, maybe. But not bad. You didn't deserve that."

I wait but still nothing.

Seems like the version of the waitress I first met—the whiskey police—is still here after all.

I run a knuckle along the door. "That offer on the drink still stands, by the way."

I'm just turning away. I have places to be. Places that don't include the inside of a ladies' room. But just as I'm turning to make my escape, the door slides open.

"Really?"

I'm doing my best to rein in the need that's suddenly clogging my throat. She's standing there in the doorway, her thumb and pointer finger holding the door, the rest of her arm red and stained, some of the sauce having found its way onto her skin.

She's still sizing me up. I try not to glare when I can feel my eyebrows rise at their own willing.

"What I mean is, do or don't you want to take that drink?"

Like some kind of idiot, I smile—fully aware that it's probably not something she'd appreciate. I mean, I was clear in those flirty jokes, but now I'm just making things worse and belittling her.

But before I can continue with the gloating, the door slides open some more and I'm face to face with the waitress I wish I could forget, the same dark, curly hair peeking out around the edge of the door.

She's got her hair swept to the side, the end curled under, making it appear shorter, framing her pretty face.

A good look on her.

"I'm sorry," she starts. "For before. For whatever I did back there. I—I don't know why I just did that. It...it wasn't right."

What do I say to that?

Instead of looking in her eyes, I focus on her lips, her knuckles.

"Hey, no worries," I say. "It was my fault, too. I should've stepped in sooner. And I do apologize. I had it coming. Forgot who I was dealing with."

She stares at me, eyes wide. "Oh."

"That's my asshole way of saying that you're tough." I snort. "'Tough' is a good thing. It means you can handle yourself and that's an admirable trait to have in Seattle." I pause. "You're not from here, are you?"

Out of nowhere, she raises an eyebrow at me. "No. I'm not."

"So…what are you doing here?"

"I… That's a rather personal question."

"Well, you didn't answer the other one, so I'm asking you again."

She pauses, her heels hitting the ground softly. She glances at her shoes before looking up at me and clearing her throat.

A knot that was dwelling in my stomach unwinds slightly.

"Okay"—my waitress lifts her chin suddenly—"to answer your first question: I think I do want that drink. And to answer the other unspoken question in the air right now: Yes, I haven't stopped thinking that you are still in fact a jerk."

I smirk. "That's good to know."

She blinks hard. And then: "I'm Mia."

"So it would seem. So, what'll it be?"

"I'm not letting you buy me a drink."

"I thought you said I could buy you a drink."

She scoffs lightly. "I said I'll have a drink with you. I never said you could buy it. I'm not letting a customer spend money after I spilled drinks on him tonight."

"At least they weren't my drinks."

"Still, I'm not letting you buy me a drink."

"Fine. How about a dick shooter?"

"What—" she sputters, momentarily taken aback. "What in the world is a 'dick shooter'?"

I laugh. "A mix of Jack, Jameson, and two types of whiskey. It barely classifies as a drink. It's more engine oil than anything else. I'll mix up a pour for you."

The waitress tries and fails to stifle a smile.

"And don't do that."

"What?" she asks, biting her lip, a move I now know I'm not immune to.

"That thing you're doing with your lip. That says more about you in this moment than whatever words you could possibly say to me. Your lip is saying 'I'm rethinking that drink' and that is cheating. So stop it. And stop saying 'what' after everything I say."

She reaches up and touches her lip lightly, a perplexed look in her eyes. She rests her hand on her chest.

"Fine," she says. "You can buy me a drink. But whatever you're thinking, a 'dick shooter' is not appropriate."

"Fine. Cock shooter."

"I'm not drinking that." She huffs, her nose in the air.

"Are you always this difficult?" I ask, my lips in a tight line.

She holds her hands up. "Never."

"Fine. A plus-one shot."

"Less gallant than the cock shooter, right?"

"Something like that. It's a classy drink."

She twists her lips, a lopsided expression. "It's still rude."

"I never claimed to be anything else…Mia. And to extend this rude kick I'm on, let me just tell you this: If that guy out there was your boss, then you're way too good a waitress to be dealing with that," I say, gesturing to the door. "This place needs people like you. Not the other way around, remember that. Keep that in mind…and you just might make it in Seattle after all."

I hold out my hand, making sure it's not just some reflex thing, my eyes on her as I slowly extend my palm.

"But in case you don't make it here—in this restaurant or Seattle at large, at least you can say you've made at least one friend out of a customer…albeit one thieving, whiskey-guzzling one."

Slowly, she takes my offered hand.

"Is that what you're doing here? Making a friend?" she asks, and I look in her eyes, somewhere between skepticism and blankness. And then, I catch a hint of a smile.

"What I'm doing here," I answer, softly, running the pad of my thumb across her knuckles, even as I realize that I'm blowing Mr. Disrick off, "is making a really big fucking mistake. And I usually don't make those. It's refreshing."

"Ah, I see we have that in common today."

"Yeah?"

She nods once.

I pull my arm back slowly, and wait for her to take the bait. Wait for her to tell me no again, wait for her to change her mind.

But she doesn't.

Instead, she looks at me for a long, hard moment, her eyes moving from my eyes to my lips before she brushes past me to walk out the restroom door. I follow, every bit of reason I thought I'd brought here tonight vanishing over the past few minutes as I realize that, despite being on the cusp of securing a new publishing deal and a so-called "brand-new life," this is the first time I've been excited about anything in—I don't even know.

Years?

I step out of the door, following her through the restaurant, through the kitchen to the back door, where she throws her coat on, shrugging her shoulders as she puts it on. I wait until she's buttoned her coat and looks up at me.

I'm nervous.

I can't figure out what I should say. What I want to say, how I should set up the next step, what is the right thing to do.

All I know is that I want her.

No matter the cost.

I want this Mia, someone who just cursed me out over whiskey, who looks like she's got the cojones to jaw a guy three tables over and then compete in the Miss America beauty pageant in one night.

An oil-stained waitress just passing through town and a guy like me, who hasn't had a relationship in—when did I have a relationship last?

"So, are you always dressed like you're heading to an important business meeting?" she asks, looking up at me, tilting her head.

I don't hesitate. "Yes. I was born in a suit. This is my natural-born state."

"Hmph. Funny. Because this seems to be mine," she says, gesturing downwards.

I look over at her, my eyes on her stained shirt, low heels, and pressed skirt.

"I have to say"—she talks as she walks—"or a guy who looks like he's never had his khakis wrinkle, you certainly know how to be charming."

"One"—I lift a finger—"I don't wear khakis. Two, I'm not charming. Just saying what's on my mind. It's a gift."

"Packaged in with your many, many lines."

"That a good thing or a bad thing?"

She blinks. Takes a deep breath. "I don't know. Maybe. Definitely. I haven't decided yet."

"Noted."

I gaze out at the evening rain just starting to fall into the streets, the lights of downtown shimmering to the west and my hotel being just to the east, the car I've rented for the night just a few blocks down, parked outside the hotel's front door.

With a glance at the city before us, I almost start to tell Mia that she changed my usual mode of operation tonight.

My playing field has been rocked by a woman I don't know.

A woman who doesn't particularly like me.

My thoughts never stray from her, from the meeting of the eyes, from the regret in her voice, from the way her lips curled when she told me her name.

Sounds crazy. Maybe it is.

But I don't have time to figure that out.

Because I just have time enough to catch a whiff of her skin, grin a little too hard, and walk out the back door with her.

✧   ✧   ✧

There's more twists, quips and sexual tension to come.

Don't forget to join the Wrye on the Rocks VIP list and claim your very own free and exclusive Billionaire Romance right now (full of all the sexy turns, heat and surprises you can handle)...
http://bit.ly/NatalieVIPlist

The Offering

Shantel Tessier

WARNING

The Offering is set in the Lord's world. Please remember this dark romance is a work of fiction. Nothing about this is to be taken seriously, and I do NOT condone any situations or actions that take place between these characters.

AUTHOR'S NOTE:
The Offering may contain triggers for some.
Trigger Warnings include:
graphic violence and drug/alcohol use.

If you have any questions, feel free to email me, and one of my assistants or I will get back to you.
shanteltessierassistant@gmail.com

PROLOGUE
L.O.R.D.

A LORD TAKES his oath seriously. Only blood will solidify their commitment to serve those who demand their complete devotion.

*He is a **Leader**, believes in **Order**, knows when to **Rule**, and is a **Deity**.*

A Lord must be initiated in order to become a member but can be removed at any time for any reason. If he makes it past the three trials of initiation, he will forever know power and wealth. But not all Lords are built the same. Some are stronger, smarter, hungrier than others.

*They are challenged just to see how far their **loyalty** will go.*

*They are pushed to their limits in order to prove their **devotion**.*

*They are willing to show their **commitment**.*

Nothing except their life will suffice.

Limits will be tested, and morals forgotten.

A Lord can be a judge, jury, and executioner. He holds power that is unmatched by anyone, other than his brother.

If they manage to complete all trials of initiation, he will be granted a reward—a chosen one. She is his gift for his servitude.

CHAPTER ONE
Adalyn

I SIT QUIETLY on the expensive leather couch in the middle of a massive living room. I've never been in a house this size before. It's what someone like me would consider a mansion. The room smells of leather and wood. Bookshelves fifteen shelves high on either side of the oversized fireplace and mantel. The shelves are full of old books. But from what I can see where I sit, they're not in English.

This is my first time here, but I know the man who lives here. Or kid, per se. His mother is dying of cancer—leukemia. And I feel sorry for him. I know what it feels like to lose a parent. But that was a long time ago. And my life has changed since then...

"Here we are," the boy who goes by Snake says as he enters the living room and interrupts my thoughts. He's my age, a senior in high school this year. I wish I was still in school. My brother, Jake, didn't think my education was important. Like I said, things have changed.

He smiles as he holds up a bag in his right hand.

"About time," my brother growls from the brown leather recliner to my right. His tone implies he's irritated, but you wouldn't know it by his posture. He sits back, his arms resting on the armrests. His legs are stretched out and crossed at the ankles. He wears a black T-shirt with a pair of worn-out jeans. His dark-brown hair hangs low on his forehead—he hasn't had it cut in weeks. And he tops off his I-don't-care look with a pair of black shades that cover his eyes. Even though it's after midnight and we're in a house.

"This better be good shit!" the man who sits to the left of me on the couch says, sitting up.

My brother's best friend.

He's also my boyfriend.

I tense when he places his hand on my knee, digging his rough fingers into my skin. He notices and turns to face me, his dark-brown eyes softening as his search mine. "Okay, baby?" he asks.

I swallow nervously and nod my head quickly. Leaning into him, I whisper, "I'm ready to go." I don't like this. And he knows it. They both know it. They just don't care.

He doesn't respond but loosens his grip only to tighten it again. His silent command to *shut the fuck up*. We'll leave when he's ready.

Snake kneels before the coffee table, facing us, and laughs. "Well, they don't call me the King for nothing." My brother snorts as the kid dumps the contents onto the table.

Cocaine.

I've seen it enough that the sight of it alone makes me want to vomit. Drugs make people do things they wouldn't normally do. Bad things. I've seen it firsthand with my brother and boyfriend.

Snake takes a razor blade and starts separating the powder into lines. He pauses and looks up. His eyes crash with mine, and my breath gets caught in my throat at the way he smiles when his dark-blue eyes move from mine down to my chest. "How much are you gonna want, sweetheart?"

Trevor's hand tightens on my thigh, and I bite my inner lip to keep from showing any emotion. "She gets none," he snaps at Snake.

I'm not allowed to do drugs, which is fine by me. I have no desire to try any of it.

The guy smiles wider. "What's wrong, baby?" he asks, looking back at me. "Everything is better when you're fucked up." Snake licks his lips, and this time, his eyes fall between my legs. "Especially fucking."

I go to cross them, but Trevor's hand gripping my thigh keeps it pinned down to the leather couch. I can feel my body break out in goose bumps in fear as sweat beads on my forehead.

I've had plenty of sex while Trevor has been high, and it wasn't better. He's rougher when he takes me while on drugs. He doesn't care if I like it, or if it gets me off. All he cares about is what he feels. And usually he's so fucked up that he can't even get himself off.

Snake chuckles as he looks back down to his task at hand.

Trevor's hand leaves my knee and slides into my hair, pulling my head to face him. He likes to do that—control me. He gives silent commands that I don't dare disobey. We've been together three years, and I've only tried to fight him once. I lost that battle.

His hand tightens in my hair as he pulls my head back, and I hiss in a breath at the pain from him pulling my hair. He licks his lips, and his nostrils flare while his eyes trace my lips. They part as I start to suck in ragged breaths. He leans in, pressing his lips to mine, and kisses me. His tongue enters my mouth with the same dominating and demanding roughness he always gives.

When he pulls away, my lips are wet and bruised. What should have been a show of affection was more a show of dominance. He's telling Snake that I'm his and to quit staring. That's one thing about Trevor—he would never share me because he likes having me to himself.

He lets go of me as he sits back, and I lick my lips, his familiar taste still lingering.

No one says a thing, but my brother pulls himself up from the recliner and makes his way to kneel beside Snake. He pulls out his wallet and rolls up a hundred-dollar bill. Without saying a word, he places the tip on the table and runs it along the white line, sucking it up into his nose like a vacuum.

My stomach twists at the sight of him throwing his head back and sniffing a few more times. I wish the drugs would just kill him. But I'm not that lucky.

Trevor pats my leg, a silent order to stay put, and I sink back into the seat, crossing my legs and folding my arms around myself as he too makes his way down to the floor to take his turn.

"Where did you get this stuff at?" my brother asks as he rubs his nose with the back of his hand.

"My brother," Snake answers.

Trevor pauses with the rolled-up hundred-dollar bill in midair. "Will he be joining us?" The way he asks tells me they were not expecting anyone else to show.

Snake waves off his concern. "He's in jail. It's just us tonight."

He could give me three guesses to why he's in jail, but I'd only need one.

I tune them out as my stomach rumbles. I'm starving. We were on our way to get something to eat when my brother got the call from Snake to come over and get fucked up. My brother could literally be on fire, and drugs would trump putting the flames out.

They talk amongst themselves about their dirty little secrets—drugs. And I look around the living room some more.

There are pictures everywhere in here. Some smaller ones sit on the bookshelves, and a few larger ones hang on the wall. There's one above the mantel of a boy. Well, I'd guess he's a man. It looks like a senior picture but I'm not sure what year. He kneels on a football field in his jersey. He has dark hair and dark-gray eyes. He must be the older brother.

"So what do you like?"

I blink a few times, pulling my eyes away from the picture to Snake, who still kneels in front of the coffee table. "What?" Did he say something?

"I said what do you like?" he asks again. "I can look to see if I have some Molly—"

"She doesn't do drugs." Trevor interrupts him.

He frowns and turns his attention to Trevor. "That's no fun." He looks back up at me and tilts his head to the side as if he can't understand why I choose to stay clean rather than a fucked-up mess.

"That's how I like it," Trevor snaps.

And the boy smiles as his eyes meet mine again. "Do you allow him to make all your decisions?"

I avert my eyes down to my arms wrapped around my legs. I don't want to be in the middle of a pissing contest. Those never end well. I know.

"Babe?"

My head snaps up to see Trevor now standing in front of the couch staring down at me with his hand stretched out to me. "Come on," he commands.

I undo my arms and uncross my legs before taking his hand. "Are we leaving?" I ask, hoping he says yes. Maybe Snake pissed him off enough that he's ready to go.

He doesn't answer. Instead, he jerks me away from the couch and out of the living room. He pulls me down a long hallway and then he takes a left at the end. Opening a door, he shoves me into a room and then shuts it behind me.

"What are we doing in here?" I ask, turning in a circle. This room isn't as fancy as the living room we were sitting in. It doesn't have any expensive artifacts or that expensive leather smell. It smells like a teenage boy's room. Of sweat and aftershave.

I'm shoved forward but manage to stay standing when two arms wrap around my shoulders from behind. "What…?"

"Shh," Trevor whispers into my ear. And my heart picks up, knowing why he brought me in here.

He wants to fuck.

"Trevor," I whimper. *I just wanna go home.*

"This is his room." He growls. "I didn't like the way he looked at what is mine." His hands cup my breasts over my shirt. "I'm gonna fuck you in here, so when he goes to bed later, he can smell you and know that I did that. Not him."

"No…"

He spins me around and wraps his hand around my throat. He shoves me backward until my knees hit the side of the bed. "No?" he asks, arching a light brow.

I swallow the lump in my throat. He owns me. No isn't an option when you're owned. I can't think of anything to say, so instead, I reach down and grab the hem of my shirt. He lets go of my neck so I can lift my shirt over my head.

He smiles before ripping it from my hands and throwing it behind him. Then he's going for my shorts. They're unbuttoned and unzipped lying by my shirt in no time. I bow my head and lower my eyes to the floor. I can't look at him when he's like this. When his eyes are lost to the drugs that he allows to take over. I reach behind my back and undo my bra and then slip out of my shorts.

I watch him kick off his shoes and then I hear the sound of his zipper followed by him removing his shirt.

He places his hands on my hips and my body trembles from his cold hands. "You're trembling, baby," he whispers in my ear. His already hard cock presses against my belly.

My heart pounds and my breaths come quicker and quicker as I wonder how he is gonna take me. He likes it rough. He likes to bring pain. That's what gets him off. He says that's what men like him need. My brother is the same way. I'm just a doll they like to torture when they want to play.

Trevor pulls back and lifts his right hand, placing it on the back of my neck. He guides me over to the bed where he pushes me down and then crawls on top of me. He spreads my legs, and they shake as he positions himself between them.

He runs his fingers along my pussy and sighs when he feels I'm dry. I wish I was wet. I wish I liked the way he spoke to me and treated me, but I don't. I despise him. But the only other person I have to protect me happens to be his best friend. And my brother always takes Trevor's side over mine.

He gets my attention when he spits in his hand and then rubs it over my pussy before sliding into me. I refrain from cringing. I hate when he does that. It makes me want to puke.

He pushes into me as his body lowers down onto mine. "Fuck," he hisses as he pulls back and pushes forward again. "Yes," he says. "That's what I need. You. Baby. My girl."

I never got the chance to choose to be his girl. Circumstances out of my control put me in his life. He took that opportunity and ran with it, and here we are, two years later.

Forget that he's twenty-two and I'm eighteen. I used to fight him, but I got tired of losing. Giving in is easier. More bearable.

He leans over and rolls us to where he's on his back and I'm hovering above him. Even on top, I don't have any control. He reaches up to wrap his right hand around my throat and tightens his grip. My body shudders from the lack of oxygen. He takes that to mean I'm turned on.

Tears start to sting my eyes. My hands hit at his chest as I try to beg him to stop, to let go of my neck because I can't breathe.

He closes his eyes, his hips bucking while he fucks me.

I slap at his face, and he opens his eyes, smiling up at me. "Fight me, baby. Fight me all you want. You won't win."

His sadistic smile is replaced by dots, and my face pounds from lack of oxygen.

A faint male's voice booms through the room followed by a *bang* outside the door has him stopping. "What the fuck?" he growls, letting go of my neck, and shoves me off him. I hit the wall before falling to the bed that is pushed up against it. Not at all surprised by his strength.

I'm coughing, rubbing my throat as my vision starts to return. "What...?"

Another banging sound interrupts me this time.

"Get dressed!" Trevor snaps, already grabbing his jeans off the floor.

"What's going on?" I ask, still trying to catch my breath from our activities.

"Just get fucking dressed!" he demands, buttoning his jeans.

I scramble off the bed and grab my shirt, bra, underwear, along with my shorts. Trevor never overreacts. He stays calm and collected in almost all situations.

Unless…unless they involve my brother. He's the reason we are at this house in the first place.

I'm holding my clothes in my hands when Trevor reaches the door. But before he can open it, the door swings open, almost hitting him in the face.

My brother enters the room. "Jake?" I squeak. Trying to cover myself, I jump back onto the bed and use the sheets to hide my body under. "What the hell are you doing?" I ask, heart pounding.

"Time to go," Jake orders us.

My gaze falls to his right hand, and I see a gun in his grip, resting against his thigh. My eyes instantly start to water. "What did you do, Jake?" I ask thickly. "Where did you get that?"

His blue eyes meet mine, and I hate how cold they look. How such a pretty color can be so ugly at times. They look me over and then to my boyfriend. "Fuck time is over! It's time to leave," he snaps. "I'll meet you out back with the car."

I shake as he slams the door shut and Trevor turns to face me. "Fuck!" he roars, his hands yanking on his dirty-blond hair.

"Trevor?" I ask roughly, my heart pounding and palms sweaty. I wish this was a very bad dream, but I know I'm wide-awake. I'm only eighteen, and my life hasn't changed. Same game just different players. But my brother has never shot someone before. That I know of.

Trevor runs over to me and jerks me off the bed. My legs get tangled in the sheets I'm holding tightly to my body, and I crash to the floor with a whimper. He yanks me off the floor. Without saying a word, he places my underwear and bra in his jeans pockets and then slides my shirt over my head. It's backward, but I'm too numb to do it myself. Then his hand is on my chest, pushing me to sit on the side of the bed as he slides my legs into my shorts, before pulling them up. He grabs his phone off the floor and mine as well, and then he's dragging me through the hall of the now silent house.

I don't dare say a word as he navigates us through this mansion. We come back into the living room, and I see red footprints on the dark wood floor. I place my hand over my mouth when I realize it's blood.

I slam into the back of Trevor as he comes to a stop before a glass door that I know leads to the back patio. He turns to face me. "Don't look," he orders with hard eyes.

Mine widen. "At what?" My voice shakes, and he looks at me as if I'm the one who needs to pull their shit together.

He doesn't answer but opens the back door and pulls me onto the patio, and I gasp when I see Snake lying in a pool of his own blood on the lounge chair. "Oh my God!" I say, feeling my chest tighten. "Did Jake do that?" I ask, already knowing the answer. One bullet went through his neck and another through his chest. His eyes are open and his mouth slack. The smell of copper hits me, and a wave of nausea almost knocks me off my feet.

"Get in!"

I pull my eyes away from the kid to see we are running to a car parked in the back driveway. It's a little two-door car that looks more expensive than some houses. And it's fire-engine red.

It's not ours, but my brother is sitting in the driver's seat with the passenger window rolled down. He lifts a bottle of Jack to his lips and swallows as he watches us run toward him.

"No!" I say, bringing us both to a stop, catching Trevor off guard.

"Adalyn, get in the fucking car!" my brother yells, now annoyed with me.

I shake my head and yank my hand from Trevor's grasp. He's been drinking and doing drugs. When my brother is like this, I try to stay as far away from him as possible. I don't wanna be in a metal box with him. "We have to call the cops…"

"Trevor, get her ass in this car now!" he roars, revving the engine.

Trevor steps toward me, and I turn to run from him, but his arm wraps around me from behind, and he yanks me off my feet. "Stop!" I yell, kicking my legs out as my arms fight to pry myself free. "Let…go…of…me!" I yell as loud as I can while digging my nails into his arms. *God, he's so strong.*

"Shut her up, for Christ's sake before someone hears her!" my brother orders.

I go to open my mouth to scream again, but Trevor's free hand clamps over my mouth to silence me.

My brother leans over to open the passenger door, and Trevor shoves me into it. I cry out when I hit my head on the doorframe and then I'm falling into the back seat. Before I can get myself up, Trevor falls into the passenger seat and shuts the door. The window rolls up as my brother hits the gas.

I'm trapped! I don't do well when trapped.

I sit up and lean between them, pretty much sitting sideways on the narrow center console, facing my brother and start to hit him. "What the fuck is wrong with you?" I scream as tears run down my face for the man who we left back there. That he can so easily take a life and not give a damn. He's so fucked up. We're all so fucked up!

"Get her off me!" he snaps at Trevor as he tries to dodge my hits.

"I'm trying," Trevor growls as he tries to grab my arms, but I have the advantage. My position between them in this small car doesn't give them much room to move their larger bodies. And my brother can't let go of the steering wheel if he wants to keep from crashing into the back of the house.

"You killed him!" I continue to scream. "You fucking killed him for nothing!"

He slams on the brakes; the sudden stop making me slide forward on the center console, my side hitting the gear shift. He lets go of the steering wheel and grabs me by the hair, slamming the side of my face into the dash. Pain shoots through my face and head. I try to cry out, but my breath is momentarily taken away.

My vision blurs, his hand still in my hair and then he shoves me into the back seat. My body twists as I once again fall into the small back. Making my way up to sit in the seat, my shaky hands come up to my bleeding face. My skin is on fire where it's split open. And I can feel every beat of my heart in the cut as blood gushes from the open wound.

I can't see him through my tears, but I can tell by the sound of his voice that he has turned to face me. "You wanna be next?" he snaps.

I cower back, remembering who I'm dealing with—a fucking psychopath. "Do you?" he shouts and I flinch.

"Nnnnoooo," I say through a sob.

"Then sit back there and shut the fuck up!" he shouts.

I slink into the seat behind him and touch my bloody face. I flinch and decide to wipe my tears away as he puts the car back in gear.

He sucks in a breath and then hisses, "Stupid bitch." I know I got a couple of good hits on his face. He's probably bleeding.

I close my eyes and take a few calming breaths because all you can hear in the car are my cries. And I know he'll tell me to shut up again in a matter of seconds. Opening my eyes, I rub the tears from them even though they continue to fall. My eyes land on Trevor. He is looking at me over his left shoulder from the passenger seat with narrowed eyes and a tight jaw. And I know it's not toward my brother for smashing my face into the dash of this car. Trevor's angry with me for making him do it.

"Put your seat belt on," he orders and then turns to face forward, dismissing me as if he really fucking cares if I have the safety of a seat belt tonight while my brother pulls out of the long driveway and onto the street.

CHAPTER TWO
Adalyn

Six Years Later

I SIT IN the smoky club. The bass from the pounding music vibrates the floors and couch I'm on. A small glass of water is held in my hand. It's our Saturday night routine. We go out, the guys get fucked up, and then we go back to our house for an after-party that lasts late into Sunday. They love it. This is how they reel in new clients. You name it, they sell it.

Drugs.
Guns.
Women.

That's what keeps repeat customers. Give them some drugs and then a naked ass to snort them off and *there you go!* They'll always come back. That is until they die from their nasty little habit. Or their wife finds out and sends their ass to rehab. Both have happened.

It's sickening, really, how these women so willingly spread their legs for a little cut. And I do mean little. My brother is stingy.

The man sitting to the right of me sits back in his seat and places his left arm over my shoulders. He pulls me into his side, and I take a sip of my water as he leans in to whisper into my ear. "You okay?"

I look over at him. He hasn't changed much since the day I met him—eight years ago. "Yeah," I answer and realize he probably can't hear me over the music, so I nod and give him a big smile.

He frowns, knowing it's fake. Trevor knows me all too well. Just like my brother. They can read like a book, and I hate it.

My brother stands from the other black leather couch and leans over, slapping Trevor on the knee. He looks away from me to stare up at my brother. "Let's go. He's here," he says, nodding to the little red rope that blocks off our private section.

"I'll be right there," Trevor tells him, and my brother turns and starts to walk away as Trevor turns back to face me. He slides his right hand into my hair and leans across my chest, placing his lips by my ear. "Stay here," he orders, and then with a kiss to my cheek, he stands and follows my brother to go do whatever the hell they plan on doing. I never ask questions. They can't get information from you if you don't know anything. Just one of the many things I've learned the hard way.

✧　✧　✧

AN HOUR LATER, I'm still sitting in the same spot they left me. I don't dare move. Not in a place like this. Our private section is the only one in the entire club. It sits up on a platform in the far corner of the club so we can see out over it. The guys had them put it in just for them. So they can see who exits and enters. That way, if a client tries to skip out without paying, they can catch them and beat their asses.

My brother and Trevor bought everything in our area. They haven't ever told me, but I know they have something on the owner of this club. Even my brother gets a percentage of what the bar sells. That should tell you enough.

"Would you like a drink, dear?" the server asks as she looks down at me.

She's older, maybe in her late forties. I feel sorry for her that she works in this type of establishment. I wonder if she ever had a dream or a career. Then I remind myself that I'm no better off than her. I'm twenty-four and never graduated high school, let alone attended college. Not everyone has a rainbow life while attending private school and then an Ivy League college.

"I'm fine. Thanks."

She smiles down at me. "Let me know if you change your mind." Then she turns around and walks out.

I look down at my watch and blow out a long breath when I see it's almost two o'clock in the morning. I'm not allowed to bring my phone to the club with us. Jake had originally made the rule, and when I tried to convince him differently, Trevor agreed with him. Those two stick together like fucking glue. My life would be so much easier if they were gay and in love with one another. Then maybe I wouldn't have to fuck one and pretend to love the other. It's exhausting at best.

Another hour goes by, and I'm pretty fucking pissed off. They've never left me here this long. The bar is closing before my eyes. The music has shut off, and the lights just came on.

Releasing a sigh, I stand from my place on the couch, my ass numb from sitting for so long, and pick up my clutch.

I walk past the red rope and down the three stairs to the corner of the dance floor and look around. The drunks are stumbling out the exit up front, and I let out a huff. Walking over to the bar, the bartender looks up at me. "Hello, Adalyn. What can I do for you?"

"Phone," I bark, holding my hand out. I'm not in the mood for small talk. He takes the phone off the wall and hands it to me. I give him the number as I place it to my ear. One ring and then it goes to voicemail. "Fucking bastard," I hiss at my brother.

I give him a new number and it rings twice and then goes to voicemail. "Fuck!" I know they just expect me to sit here for however long until they decide to come and get me.

"Are you looking for your brother?" he asks me, placing the phone back on the wall.

"Yep," I say clipped.

"They're out back in the alleyway..."

I start making my way to the back exit immediately and shove the door open. And sure enough, there they are.

I start to walk to them, but stop when my brother speaks. "Where is it?" he demands.

There are two guys down on their knees with a man I don't know standing in front of them next to Trevor. The mystery man stands tall, his hands behind his back, shoulders back and his legs wide. My brother stands behind the two kneeling, pacing while looking down at his feet.

The man standing with his hands behind his back is dressed in dark jeans and a black T-shirt. And a chill runs up my spine because he looks the evilest. And that means a lot when being compared to my brother and Trevor. He doesn't have to show his face for you to know you should fear him. His tall and strong stance makes him look like the devil himself.

"Please. I'll get it by tomorrow," one of the men begs as he kneels on his knees.

"You said that yesterday," my brother says calmly, still pacing. "I'm done with waiting. You're done." He then looks up at the guy standing with his hands behind his back. "Prickett?" he asks.

The guy on his knees jumps to his feet as if he's about to bolt. Trevor grabs him, wrapping his arms around the man's upper chest and holding him in place while *Prickett* snaps his neck.

He's dead!

I wish I could say I'm shocked, but that's not possible anymore.

My brother who is still pacing comes to a stop and looks down at him as well. "Is he...?"

"Yes." The guy named Prickett confirms it for him as if he already didn't know.

"How about you? Do you have an excuse as well?" Jake asks, coming to stand behind the other guy who remains kneeling.

He shakes his head, not saying a word. He doesn't look up. Nothing. He knows his friend is dead, and he's next.

"Well then. Let's get this done," Jake says, clapping his hands excitedly, and I grind my teeth at how cold he can be.

"Are you going to run?" Prickett asks. He comes to stand in front of the man. They have him caged in. "Like your friend?"

"No." His voice is broken, and my heart breaks for them. "Just do it," he says as he takes in a deep breath. His back rises and falls as he lifts his head to look at Prickett. The man closes his eyes, and without another word, Prickett removes a gun from the back of his jeans. Before I can even blink, he points it at the man and shoots.

There's a flash, but not much noise comes from the gun before the man hits the ground. Blood pours from his head onto the ground as he lies next to the other guy.

Trevor bends down to pick up the guy who the mystery man killed first while my brother grabs the one just shot as I stare at the new guy. He must feel eyes on him because he looks up from them, and his eyes land right on mine. I expect him to lift his gun and shoot me too. For all he knows, I'm just some random woman who watched him commit two murders. But instead, he looks at me as if he knows me. His gaze travels down to my heels and then back up to my eyes. And he smirks.

I turn around and walk back through the exit. The only person in the silent club is the owner who stands behind the bar, counting out his register and getting my brother's cut.

He waves up at me, and I ignore him. Making my way back up to our section, I sit down as if I've been here all night.

✧ ✧ ✧

Prickett

"GOOD JOB," TREVOR says reaching out to clap my shoulder as I load the last body in the trunk.

"Anytime."

"I told you he was worth the money," Jake tells him.

Trevor seems skeptical about my work, but nods after a second.

"We're having a party tonight at our house. Join us," Jake offers.

I'm about to say I can't when he adds, "I'd like to talk business. See just how good you really are."

I smile because he already knows how good I am, but I'll play along. "Come inside for a moment. Get a drink," he says, giving me no room to argue.

We walk away from the car where the bodies are stashed and into the back exit. Everyone long gone from the club. Jake walks right over to the bar and picks up a manila envelope that I know has a wad of cash in it. His share of this place. I know just about everything there is to know about this man. I've done my research. No one would walk into his life blind. Well, the ones who have are dead.

"Ready to go, babe?"

I hear Trevor ask from behind me, and I turn to look at the woman I spotted earlier outside walking down a set of stairs from their private section with a pissed-off look on her face.

"What's wrong?" he asks her, and Jake looks up to watch them.

"What's wrong is that I've been sitting here for over three hours," she snaps at him.

"We had business to handle," Jake informs her with an arch of his brow, daring her to snap at him as well.

She turns her head to shoot daggers at him. "Next week, my ass is staying at home," she says and then heads off toward the exit.

"No, you're not!" Jake yells at her just as she slams the front door shut. "Get back here!" he shouts, but she's already gone.

"Let her go," Trevor says with a wave of his hand.

Jake looks at him. "You baby her too much."

"And you treat her like shit." He shrugs, and I have a hard time seeing him treat her any better than Jake. "I wouldn't be surprised if she someday stabs you in your sleep."

Jake throws his head back laughing. "Yeah, like she would have the balls to do that." He turns around and grabs the tequila bottle off the shelf and then two shot glasses. "We'll see you back at home." He dismisses Trevor.

Once he walks out of the front door, the smile drops off Jake's face. "Fucker," he mutters, then looks at me. "Sure you can handle that?" he asks, nodding to the now closed door.

I smirk. "Of course." I'm a Lord. This is what I was raised to do—take care of problems.

He picks up the manila envelope and slides it to me, nodding once.

"What's this for?" I ask. He's already paid me.

"Consider it a bonus," he says with a sinister smile. "You'll deserve it. Trust me."

✧   ✧   ✧

Want to know where the Lords started? Read ***The Ritual: A Dark College Romance*** here. Grab your copy now!
shanteltessier.com

COPYRIGHT

CPSIA information can be obtained
at www.ICGtesting.com
Printed in the USA
LVHW080133070522
718085LV00037B/1150